MW01406857

IMMORTALS OF NEW ORLEANS Box Set

(Books 1-4)

Kade's Dark Embrace
Luca's Magic Embrace
Tristan's Lyceum Wolves
Logan's Acadian Wolves

Kym Grosso

MT Carvin Publishing, LLC
West Chester, Pennsylvania

Edited by Julie Roberts
Formatting by Polgarus Studio
Cover design by Cora Graphics
Photographer: Golden Czermak
Cover Model: Caylan Hughes

DISCLAIMER
This book is a work of fiction. The names, characters, locations and events portrayed in this book are a work of fiction or are used fictitiously. Any similarity to actual events, locales, or real persons, living or dead, is coincidental and not intended by the author.

NOTICE
This is an adult erotic paranormal romance book with love scenes and mature situations. It is only intended for adult readers over the age of 18.

KADE'S DARK EMBRACE

Immortals of New Orleans, Book 1

Kym Grosso

Acknowledgments

I am very thankful to those who helped me create this book:

~My husband, for encouraging me to write and supporting me in everything I do.

~Julie Roberts, for proofreading and editing.

~My beta readers, Barb & Sandra, for volunteering to read my first novel and provide me with valuable feedback.

~Cora Graphics, for designing Kade's sexy cover.

~Romance Novel Covers/Jimmy Thomas, for shooting the custom image for Kade's new cover.

~Polgarus Studio, for formatting Kade's Dark Embrace.

~Gayle Latreille, my admin, who is one of my biggest supporters and helps to run my street team. I'm so thankful for all of your help!

~My awesome street team, for helping spread the word about the Immortals of New Orleans series. I appreciate your support more than you could know! You guys rock!

Chapter One

The sultry, summer night bustled with mortals seeking entertainment in the heart of the city. Listening to the sounds in the distance, Kade recognized a familiar jazz song being played by street performers. After the long flight to Philadelphia, he needed to stretch and gather his thoughts. Unable to resist the lure of the waterfront, he leaned against the cool railing, watching the lights of the boats passing by and flickering in the rushing water. Sensing great evil on the horizon, he breathed deeply, letting the sight of the water soothe him.

His cell phone buzzed; glancing at the text, he swore. A dead body had been found near the airport. *Goddammit.* He was too late. Kade waved to the waiting limo driver, gesturing that he needed to leave. Pivoting, he noticed an attractive woman sitting alone at the end of the dock, far away from the crowd. She appeared confident yet alone, as she sat in the darkness, her long blonde hair shimmering in the moonlight. *What the hell is a woman doing down on the docks alone this time at night?*

Glancing at the enchanting stranger, Kade struggled to push sex from his thoughts. It had been far too long since he'd felt the touch of a woman. Aroused by the possibility of an encounter with her, he swore once again. *Not now.* He needed to concentrate on the real reason he was here in the city. Tristan, an old friend and Alpha of the regional wolf pack, had called him in New Orleans nearly a week before, requesting his assistance. He had planned on seeing Tristan later that night at his club; there he'd find a donor willing to play. Right now, this woman was just a lovely, human distraction. One who was naive to be sitting alone in the dark by the waterfront. Yet he could not seem to tear his eyes off of her. The thought crossed his mind that maybe he should just have a sip of her sweet, young blood before work. Her delicious scent registered in his brain, and his fangs began to elongate.

Over the centuries, he'd been with plenty of women, but none held his heart. As for his thirst, there were many willing women who offered themselves to vampires these days. What was it about this alluring stranger that he found so intriguing? Perhaps it was the chase? Like a fox spotting a rabbit in the woods, he could not resist the temptation of the hunt. Slowly approaching her, he admired her long curly blonde hair, wishing he could run his fingers through it. She was of average height, around five-four, if he had to guess, with a strong, athletic build. As she stretched her toned arms up over her head, he admired her full breasts which strained against her tight white t-shirt. Her black spandex miniskirt accentuated her lithe tanned legs. He watched with curiosity as she glanced at her watch and folded her arms impatiently. *Is she waiting for someone? A date?*

She lifted her gaze, scanning the docks. Kade darted into the shadows and attempted to cloak his presence, yet she stared straight at him. *Bloody hell. Can she see me? Interesting…is she supernatural as well?* His cell phone went off again, reminding him that he needed to get to the site. With a parting glance, he memorized her face, hoping he'd see her again. Silently he returned to the car, reluctant to leave the woman, but anxious to wrap up this case and mete out justice to the murderer.

Down by the river, Sydney waited for her friend. God, it was a beautiful night in the city. She always enjoyed coming down to the waterfront. She worked such long hours; she rarely had evenings available for pleasure. She loved her job as a cop, busting criminals in one of the toughest cities in America. Even on a good day, working in Philly could be rough, but she enjoyed the city's history and rich culture. Tonight, though, instead of cracking heads, she'd made plans to meet a girlfriend. All work and no play made Syd a dull girl, and she was looking forward to playing hard tonight. She needed a stiff drink and good conversation. *Where the hell is Ada?* That girl was always late. They had reservations at Vincent's at nine, and she didn't intend to miss out on dinner. She hoped like hell Adalee hadn't got called back into the office.

A cold breeze came off the water, sending a chill up her spine. She truly wished it was the sudden rush of air that put her on alert, but she'd been around the block long enough to recognize danger when she felt it. Inspecting her surroundings, she spotted an innocent pair of lovers strolling past the tall ships. Still, she felt eyes on her. In the distance, Sydney spotted a large, very male silhouette in the shadows. *Criminal? No, someone else, something else, a supernatural?* Human or otherwise, someone was out there. It wasn't that she was naive about supernaturals, it was just that she generally didn't arrest them. *Damn. I so don't need this tonight.*

Reaching up under her skirt, Sydney checked the silver knife holstered to her thigh; it was secure. She nonchalantly slid her hand into her purse, unlocking the safety on her trusty Sig Sauer. Then she casually pulled out and applied her favorite pink lip gloss and pretended not to see him. Her body tensed ready to spring into action. She smiled and tossed it back into her bag. *A girl has always got to look her best when she kills.* She glanced away for a second to the couple on the dock, who remained infatuated with each other. Within a split second, her eyes darted back to the shadow in the night. He was gone. *Where the hell did he just go?*

As the sounds of the jazz band filled the air, she willed herself to relax.

Maybe he was a lost tourist? Whatever, he was gone, just another predator in the city. The music in the distance reminded her of the last time she was in New Orleans. Damn if she didn't love everything about that town, from its delicious beignets to its unique architecture. Sydney shook her head, disappointed that she didn't have a vacation planned this summer. *Shit, I am so stuck in Philly,* she thought as she took note of another wasted loser being cuffed by the local beat. Okay, sure, there were drunks in New Orleans, but this was Philly. Inebriated fools here wouldn't think twice about booing Santa. They got in more trouble than a dog with an Easter basket, and like the dog, they usually ended up either sick or dead. Ah yes, another lovely eve in the big city.

"What now? I'm supposed to be having fun tonight," she snapped as her cell phone went off. *The Freaks Come Out at Night* blared from her purse. She could tell from the ring tone that Tony, her partner, was calling.

"Hey, Tone, what's up?"

"Gotta floater out of the Delaware down near the airport. Captain said it looks messy, and I was kinda hoping you could join me for the party."

"Okay, but you owe me. I'm at Penn's Landing right now waiting for Ada. Guess our girls' night isn't happening."

"Uh, Syd…One more tiny detail…"

"Seriously?"

"P-CAP is meeting us there."

"Hell no, I don't feel like dealing with their shit tonight." P-CAP: Paranormal City Alternative Police. Sydney wasn't a fan of working paranormal cases. For the most part, she stuck to the cut and dry, run-of-the-mill human murders. She didn't have to work with supes, nor did she want to. She wasn't exactly prejudiced without reason. Two years before, when working a supposedly simple hit and run, an unknown were-bitch had shifted into tiger mode and killed two cops. It turned out the perp was related to the hit and run driver, and the tiger had thought she could fix the problem by killing the humans. Too bad for her, Sydney always carried a silver knife. Sure, she came out with a few scratches, and almost died in the I.C.U., but Sydney came out of the skirmish alive. The tiger didn't.

Sydney sighed. "Okay, Tony, but I swear if there are any kitty cats workin' this case I'll be taking them directly to the vet to be fixed and declawed. I'm not dealing with shifters tonight."

"Yeah, yeah, one close call with a pussy cat and now you're allergic to all of P-CAP?" he jokingly asked.

"It's all fun and games until their claws come out, and the next thing you know the knives are flying. Good thing I've been practicing my aim. See you in ten." Okay, so it was probably more like twenty, given the city traffic on a Friday night, but at least she was going. She was annoyed that her one night off was screwed thanks to a floater. It was probably just another fool who had thought it would be a great idea to take a swim in the Delaware on a muggy August night.

By the time Sydney showed up on the scene, there must have been at least ten black and whites, not to mention the crowd of spectators who had decided to show up to see if they could catch a glimpse of a dead body. *What the hell is wrong with people?* She knew damn well the answer to that question was 'everything'. It wasn't as if she hated the general population, but she tended to see the worst in people, human or not: drug users, rapists, murderers, and perhaps the worst of the bunch, child abusers and pedophiles. The sick bastards never ceased to amaze her. She shuddered, thinking about what might be waiting for her beyond the yellow tape tonight.

Walking down the gravel sidewalk, she ended up in trampled, soggy weeds that formed a makeshift path. The scene teemed with CSI and fellow officers. She felt a chill in her bones and swiveled her head around, searching for its source. It was ninety degrees outside. Something was off, really off. Unable to find an immediate cause, she continued to make her way to the body. She tried to remain steady on her feet as she gently eased down the slope of the slippery grass.

"Sydney! Over here!" she heard Tony call.

As she approached the body, the smell hit her first.

"Oh God, what the fuck is that smell? Dead body mixed with algae? Shit, that is just terrible," she complained.

"Nice mouth, Syd. Soon you're going to have to carry that cuss jar around with you in the car," Tony teased.

"Yeah, well, fucking sue me. I've given up on the damn cuss jar. I'll just write your favorite charity a check. That should cover me for the year." She winked.

"Okay then, I'll be waiting on it. Yeah, I know the smell is pretty bad, huh? I guess I failed to mention that the gal who discovered the body passed out from it. Buck up, Syd. I'll buy you roses afterward," he chuckled.

Tony thought he was so damn funny. He was a tough cop, born and raised in South Philly. Six-three, Italian goodness wrapped in a hot, witty package, he had no difficulty getting dates. He had dark olive skin and cropped raven hair. Muscular, he looked like he could bench press a bus. To top it off, he knew the city like the back of his hand, and there was no one Sydney would rather trust to have at her back.

She loved him…as well as she could love anyone. He was a good friend. Sometimes she thought of him as a very good friend and was often tempted to turn things into a 'more than friends' arrangement, but she had worked hard to get where she was in the department. Sydney would be damned if she gave in to her primal urges to screw her partner and then end up an office joke as the 'cop who liked to be on top'. Still, she couldn't help but admire his physique, which reminded her that she needed to get out tonight and find someone to play with. A meaningless quickie would give her the release she desired, one she very much needed to prevent her from breaking her own 'no-dating-on-the-job' rule.

Thoughts of sex were pushed to the back of her mind as the body came into view. It was that of a young woman. Her skin was nearly translucent after being in the water for so long. She was dressed in a long white gown, which shimmered in the harsh lights. She resembled the porcelain dolls Sydney's mother used to collect, beautiful to look at but no touching allowed. Yes, this girl looked innocent, fragile. How old could she have been? Maybe twenty-one?

Sydney blew out a breath. "What a fucking sicko. What the hell? What is that stuff on her eyes, her face?"

As she leaned in for a closer look, Tony tapped notes into his cell phone. "I know, Syd. We definitely have a demented one on this case. It's almost as if the perp wanted her to look a certain way, cared about her appearance…well, except for the whole 'sew her eyelids shut and dress her up like a doll' shit…and of course, we still need to find the cause of death. The coroner is on her way. Take a look at her face."

The girl's eyelids were sewn shut in the shape of an 'X', and she still had what looked like makeup on her face. She'd been in the water for at least a day or two. Maybe it was something else besides makeup? Tattooing? Sydney had a friend who tattooed eye makeup on women so they looked fresh as a daisy, day or night, no muss, no fuss. Well, except there was plenty of muss here. The waterlogged loose skin looked like you could pull it right off the girl, as if it were a translucent glove. Sydney might be a cop, but the unusual way murderers killed their victims never ceased to disgust her.

"Tony, her skin looks so pale. Paler than what I would expect from your average floater. It's almost as if…" Sydney's skin pricked in awareness. It was like the feeling she'd had on the docks. The guy who'd been watching her earlier, had he freaking followed her? What the hell?

"It almost looks as if her blood was drained from her body, and indeed, it was. Allow me to introduce myself. I am Kade Issacson from P-CAP, and I am now officially in charge of this case. You're welcome to stay on and assist." Kade stepped into the spotlights, dominating her space and finishing her words. He spoke confidently, concealing his excitement. He could not believe the woman at the docks was here at his scene. What was she? Her sweet scent called to him, arousing all his senses. He struggled to remain professional, determined to find out who she was, while controlling the situation.

Sydney tsked. She could not believe the sheer audacity of this guy. As she spun on her heels to address him, her eyes locked on the source of her chills. The heat began to rise to her face as she realized this guy was a serious supernatural being…dangerous. Added to that, he was drop dead gorgeous. She could barely bring words to her lips to argue with him. Desire pooled in her belly. She quickly focused her thoughts back on the body, letting her anger rise to the surface.

"Name's Willows, Detective Sydney Willows." She was infuriated that P-CAP thought they could come in here and boss the little human woman around. *Nice try.* "Seriously? You guys finally decide to show up and you're all like, 'It's our case now.' Well, here's a newsflash. This girl's a human. According to the regs, 'human vic, human cops'. So you can move along, friend, or watch. Whatever you're into. Just stay out of my way." Damn if she was going to let some hot, supernatural guy tell her what to do at her scene.

Kade smiled. "Ms. Willows, while you are indeed correct that the vic is human, she was murdered in a very supernatural way. Therefore, according to the regs, this is officially a P-CAP case that requires your mandatory cooperation," he lied.

Sydney rolled her eyes and blew out a breath. *Well good and fuck.* She was having a fine evening up until now, day off and all. And now this. She had no idea what the hell he even was. "Mister?" she spat out.

"Please, call me Kade." He spoke with just the slightest hint of a British accent.

"Kade, our police department would *love* to cooperate with P-CAP just as soon as we get the coroner's exam completed," she said, her voice dripping with sarcasm.

"That would be lovely, Ms. Willows. Now, may I please continue with my work?" he asked.

"Yes," she curtly replied, moving out of his way so he could get past her. Sydney could not believe her day. She reasoned that maybe she could work with Kade, as long as he didn't bite her, or claw her or bespell her, or whatever other supernatural shit he did. Even if she didn't know what his deal was, she was convinced that he was capable of doing things that she would not like. She crossed her arms, irritated with the entire night. She knew one thing for sure; working closely with Kade was going to add exponentially to her overall sexual frustration.

She glanced over at him as he conversed with Tony. Kade's sexy frame towered over her. He was well over six-five, with dark blond hair that reached his collar. The strikingly handsome, hard planes of his face accentuated his piercing, ice-blue eyes. Sydney could tell he was athletic and muscular, and wished she could see what was hidden beneath his navy linen sport jacket. He defied her notions of how she imagined most supernaturals dressed; she would have expected him to be clad in black leather and chains. Instead, he struck her as classic, masterly, sensual. Sydney smiled to herself, thinking that Kade looked like he had just stepped out of a freaking Ralph Lauren ad. His cream linen pants hung loosely on his tapered hips, revealing just a glimpse of what supernatural 'assets' he had under them. *Shit, Sydney, are you really looking at the man's crotch at a crime scene? You so need to get laid.*

As she looked up, he caught her eyes and smiled. *Oh, God...please don't let him have seen me looking there.* She quickly glanced at Tony, who chuckled.

"Hey, Syd, whatcha lookin' at? There really is a lot to observe at the scene, huh?"

"Shut it, Tony. Need I remind you that I was supposed to be off tonight?" she retorted.

"Off or getting off?" he quipped.

"Ha, ha. Tony. You boys keep talking. I'm actually going to work. I'll be with Ada, finding out what she's got." Her face flushed red in embarrassment. Sydney was eager to put some space between herself and Kade. She needed to get her hormones under control and concentrate. Why cover the body with tattoos? Why all the presentation? Obviously the perp must get off on some kind of ritual during the actual killing. Some killers liked to take their time, play with the victim.

The coroner made her way down the hill toward the body. Dr. Adalee Billings had been on the job as long as Sydney could remember. With not many women on the force, Adalee was the closest female friend Sydney had. She was a beautiful, African-American woman with dark cocoa skin. At five-eight, she could have easily been mistaken for a model. Her ebony shoulder-length hair was usually pulled back in a scrub hat. But because she was supposed to be out having dinner with Sydney tonight, her hair was fashionably coiffed into a French twist. Quick-witted and insanely intelligent, Adalee could go toe-to-toe with any person in the department, so the men just didn't mess with her. Sydney loved having a smart girlfriend on the force, given she usually worked in a sea of men.

As Adalee leaned in to examine the body and set down her evidence kit, Sydney sidled up next to her, anxious to get her first impressions. The scent of the body was overwhelming. Death, animal or human; it was a smell that permeated the lining of your nostrils and could get into your clothing. Damn if she hadn't just dry cleaned this blouse.

"So, what ya got, Ada?" Sydney inquired.

"Hard to tell without being in the lab, but the tattooing is interesting. Maybe some kind of ritual? Magical protection?" Adalee stared narrowly at the girl's face and hands.

"Yeah, I was thinking ritual. The perp took his time on the girl; the dress, the makeup. Sick fuck. What makes you think magical protection?" Sydney asked.

"Early tattooing was thought to have mystical protection, to be a talisman of sorts worn on the skin. We'll take pictures of the tats and get them to research. Damn, if this city isn't getting freaky tonight. Is P-CAP down here? Honestly, Syd, my take is that this might be their case, but if you want us to run the body, I'm on it."

"Yes and yes. P-CAP may end up taking on the case, but all the same, I'd like you to run the body first. So if you could put a rush on it, I would appreciate it. This could be a human copycat playing with magic, trying to make it look paranormal, or it could be something that needs to go over to the wild side." She glanced toward Kade. "And if that happens, they can have it. Personally, I wouldn't mind turning it over to what's-his-name…Kade over there, so I can get him out of my hair."

Adalee looked at Kade and smiled.

"You mean that whole lot of sexy goodness over there talking to Tony? I would love to work with him, or just work him, period. Whatever, you send him down to the lab, and I'll be happy to review the results in detail with him. I bet he'd give a girl some sugar."

"Yeah sure, if you'd like a bite with your sugar, I'm sure he'd be happy to oblige you. Not sure if he's got fangs or claws, but something's going on there."

"Girl, you sound like you doth protest a little too much. Why not just look at it as a perk of the job? Lord knows there aren't many. Or maybe that hot partner of yours could spice up your coffee?" She laughed.

"Yeah, you're right about that. There's a whole lot of sweetness there, but tasting his candy wouldn't be good for my career. Ada, I just need to get out and satisfy my needs with someone safe. Unfortunately, that's gonna have to wait. Can you tell that I'm a little distracted tonight?"

"Well, girl, you have about five hours to satisfy your needs, and then you need to get your ass down to the lab. I'll bag her up, start the autopsy, snap the pics, and get the trace out. Now, look at this thread." Adalee held up a tiny, brown, stringy substance in her tweezers. "Maybe something unusual about that, too? Could be regular sewing thread, or something else?"

"Okay, run it. We gotta move quickly. This girl was tortured, and I have a feeling she isn't going to be the perp's last play toy. It's like the killer enjoyed this…took his time. He's sharing his work with us. Wanting us to see what he did to this girl. God, it makes me sick."

"I know. We've got a predator here. Not sure if there's anything to the tats or the thread, but I'll start right away." Adalee shook her head in disgust. "Now why don't you get back to your night off? Well, at least for a few hours until I gather some evidence. Kade over there looks awful lonely. He certainly looks like he could take care of all your needs."

"No way, Ada...not him. I'm outta here for now. See ya down at the lab." She gave Adalee a wave and turned to leave, determined to get at least a few hours to herself. As Sydney readied herself to go, she felt eyes on her back. She glanced at Kade, to find him staring at her. She nodded and turned around quickly so he wouldn't think she was interested in him.

Something about him bothered her despite the supernatural, hotter-than-hell vibe he had going on. He had told her he worked with P-CAP, but his story didn't jive with her instincts. Sydney read people well, and there was something about him that said he wasn't a cop. Or even a supernatural cop. He looked like he belonged at a country club. Maybe he was a lawyer, or a businessman? Taking in one last glance, she memorized his clothing and shoes. The suit wasn't right. So not the inexpensive cop wear she was used to seeing at the station. Boss? Calvali? And the shoes, he was wearing Salvatore Ferragamo. Something wasn't adding up. He looked too perfect to be working a detective beat, even for someone not human.

She hurried to catch up with Tony, who was heading towards his car. "There's something not right about him," she said, glancing back toward Kade. "I want to see his credentials."

"Already checked them. He's good. And the boss says he's got full access to the scene," Tony confirmed.

Sydney wondered what kind of supernatural he was. *Wolf?* No, he didn't strike her as the rugged, outdoorsy type. Kade was refined, sleek, and uber-sexy. Primal and dangerous. *Vampire?* Yes, she'd bet he was a vampire. Damn curiosity was getting the best of her as she surreptitiously hoped she'd see him again. Kade might be keeping a few secrets, and Sydney was going to find out exactly what he was up to...as soon as she engaged in a few secrets of her own.

Chapter Two

Sydney wasn't looking for love; her current career didn't afford her that luxury. When she wasn't working, she was still thinking about work, but that wasn't the only thing that kept her from getting seriously involved with someone. She was acutely aware of the very real danger she faced every day on the streets. In her profession, the odds were higher than average that she might not go home after a shift. Why bother with a husband and family when they would need to live with the constant worry that she could be killed on the job? Given that she was only twenty-eight, she didn't feel the need to have kids at the moment. She loved kids, but she didn't want them to grow up motherless because something had happened to her. Maybe someday, when she moved into management and found someone she loved completely, she'd consider having kids, but not now.

As she walked into Eden, the pounding music and glaring lights hit her hard. The smell of cigarette smoke and sweat from the dancers permeated the room. There was a faint hint of bleach; the place was clean even if the activities were down and dirty. Eden was an upscale club that catered to singles and couples who were looking to watch or be watched, serving both humans and supernaturals.

The multicolored lights bounced off the mirrored ceilings. The bluish walls appeared to move as the lights danced. A large, wall-sized water fountain ran along the entire length of the club opposite from the bar. If you stood next to it, you could faintly hear the hiss of the water and feel the spray on your face. Behind the bar, a fifteen-foot yellow boa constrictor named Eve, slithered behind the glass of a vivarium. Inside, Eve moved about the large space, wrapping herself around a tree. In the club, a large, winding staircase led upstairs to the private rooms where clients could go to talk, or engage in sexual activities in private or public, depending on what they wanted.

Sydney knew that she could comfortably lose herself in here for a few hours before going back to death; death always waited for her. It was patient, but never kind. Quickly scanning the room, she darted into the ladies' room. She changed into her tiger-striped, spandex minidress with matching fuck-me heels; she was ready to hunt. Her tanned skin shone beneath the plunging cowl neckline exposing her ample cleavage. A black lacy thong was all she wore under the dress. She shoved her clothes into her tote bag and the custom locker Eden provided its guests. Pulling her hair free of the ponytail holder, she let her blonde curls slide down her back. With a quick spritz of hair spray, she was ready. Sydney had officially transformed from cop to chick, and looked every bit the bait she intended herself to be.

"Hey, Tristan. Perrier with lemon, please." She waved to the bartender.

"No champagne? What's up, mon chaton?" Tristan shouted over to Sydney. He liked calling her 'my kitty'. Tonight the nickname fit, given that she appeared to be a cat on the prowl.

"No alcohol for me tonight, mon loup. I've only got a few hours for dancing and fun. Then I'm outta here." She certainly had every intention of making him her wolf. She took the glass from Tristan, sipped the effervescent water and then made her way into the crowd.

Sydney could feel people watching her as she danced, swaying her hips as she felt the music. There was a reason she came to Eden; music, sex, all of it for the taking, confidential without judgment. It was everything she needed this very moment. As she danced on the floor, she slowly opened her eyes to see Tristan coming straight at her. She yearned to release her sexuality, to relax, to forget, and he could take her there.

Sydney's Alpha wolf was sex on a stick. His rugged, earthy, dominating presence commanded attention when he walked into the room. He was good-looking but not exactly handsome. With captivating amber eyes and wavy platinum-blonde hair, he looked as if he could have been a California surfer. And even though his tan skin gave off a radiant glow, his hard eyes served as a warning to others that he, indeed, was a predator. Tonight he was dressed in light blue jeans and a white linen shirt that he wore untucked. Casual, but not messy, serious, but cool. He entertained the guests with his adventure stories, and was able to deflect the interest of ladies in a way that made them still feel special.

As Sydney danced, she felt strong hands clasp her waist. She leaned into his embrace, recognizing the feel of the muscular chest up against her back. She loved the woodsy, clean scent of Tristan, and felt his arousal as they moved to the music.

"Hey, Syd." Tristan pulled her around so he could see her face.

"Yes," she whispered, glancing from his chest into his intense, golden eyes.

"Tell me, how do you want it, mon chaton?" He gave her a wicked smile.

"Tris, I don't have a lot of time." She shivered at the thought of him taking her quickly. He was dominating, pushing her to tell him her fantasy.

"No games tonight. How do you want it?" he pressed.

"Fast, hard, private," she teased.

"Let's finish our dance, shall we? Your wolf has everything you need."

Sydney smiled and let the arousal overcome her, feeling the warmth grow in her womb. She wanted this…no, she *needed* this tonight. Both the stress of the grisly murder, and then Kade showing up at her scene trying to run the show, had put her on edge. She wanted to forget, and Tristan could give that to her. He understood her the way no one else did, a lover who didn't judge her. She laid her head back on his chest, enjoying the warmth of his arms.

The crime scene disturbed Kade. Killing and violence was part of his world, but the torture of an innocent was unacceptable. As the leader of vampires in New Orleans, he suspected that he knew who had committed the crime, but he would have to investigate further to be sure. Kade had convinced the head of P-CAP to let him on the scene, because he did not trust the local authorities to handle the case. It wasn't his job to investigate the murders like a detective, but being the leader he was, he planned to find the rogue and mete out justice.

He worked out of a brownstone graciously loaned to him by Tristan, the local Alpha. They were good friends from times long ago. Tristan was the one who had phoned him to tell him there was talk of a possible rogue vampire in his region who was practicing black magic. There were rumors of rituals, but nothing solid to go on. Finally, the evil had shown itself, and Kade had jetted out of NOLA on his private plane as soon as he got the go ahead from his inside source at P-CAP. As much as he wanted to leave it up to P-CAP to find the perpetrator, he felt compelled to come to Philadelphia, suspecting the magic was being drawn from his territory.

What he hadn't expected was the confrontation with the spirited Miss Willows. What an interesting, sexy distraction she was. She smelled of lilies, and he could practically taste her sweetness in the air. *What would it be like to taste her?* He had to stifle his arousal in front of her. Had she been a paranormal creature, he wouldn't have lied to her. Given that she was human, however, it had been necessary to do so for her own protection. Despite what she may have thought, guns were no match for dark magic or vampires.

But damn, if he didn't enjoy a little sparring with the blonde detective. She was altogether alluring with a sharp mind to match. The scent of her arousal at the scene had driven him wild with desire. He craved her. He admonished himself for his lustful thoughts, knowing he wasn't there to get involved with women. Kade figured he was a little agitated from all the stress of flying up to Philadelphia in such a hurry. He needed blood, maybe sex, not necessarily in that order. What this vampire didn't need were complications.

"Luca, let's swing by Tristan's place. I could use some refreshment. I told him I would fill him in on what I've learned." He signaled to his second.

Luca barked out an order to the limo driver and turned to Kade.

"We'll be there in ten minutes. Do you wish for me to find a private room… procure a donor?"

"Yes. Thanks," Kade replied as he stared out the window, his thirst gnawing at him. He was growing irritable; he needed blood soon.

On the dance floor, Tristan grabbed the nape of Sydney's neck and pushed his long fingers through her hair. She leaned back, giving him full access to her throat and chest. The wolf in him howled at her submission, and the man in him was left breathless at the sight of her smooth skin and the rise of her breasts. He continued to pull her head back, and kissed her throat near her ear. Looking down, he could see the rosy edge of her hardened nipples. She wasn't wearing a bra. God, this woman was killing him.

"Tristan, please…" Sydney gasped as Tristan slid a hand up her belly and cupped her breast. She moaned in response.

He leaned and whispered in her ear, "Like that, mon chaton, do you? Come on now, tell me what you want."

"Tristan, you and me upstairs…now. I am done playing." Sydney had had enough with the games. She could barely speak as she licked her lips. Dancing and pulling him close, she ground against his hard arousal.

"Ah fuck," Tristan grunted, noticing that Kade had just walked into the bar. "Sorry, Sydney, but an old friend just came into the club. You have no idea how I hate interrupting our fun, but I have to talk with him…important business. It'll only take a few minutes, though. Do you want to go up to my room and wait for me? I'll meet you upstairs in ten minutes." He was irritated with the interruption, but this was important.

As Sydney contemplated her answer, she felt a chill similar to the one she'd felt down at the docks. The hair on the back of her neck stood up. *He's here.* Rapidly scanning the room, she saw Kade sitting at the bar staring at her. She wasn't imagining things. Kade was actually in the bar, and for some reason he didn't look happy. What in the hell was he doing at Tristan's club? Did he follow her from the crime scene?

Unable to control her curiosity, Sydney took off across the dance floor toward Kade. She glanced back to Tristan whose face told her that he'd suspected her intention. Irritated that the vampire had followed her, she struggled to control her anger.

"What the fuck are you doing here? Are you following me?"

"Miss me, did you?"

"Perhaps we need to get a few things straight if we're going to work together." Her heart began to race in his presence, and she suspected it wasn't caused by fear. As her eyes caught his, she was drawn to him. Her arousal flared and she found herself even angrier that her traitorous body was responding to his presence.

Before Kade had a chance to answer, Tristan held out his arms to his friend.

"Hey, Kade! Welcome! I've missed you, brother."

The men exchanged hugs and then both stared back at Sydney, as if waiting for her reaction. He wasn't sure how, but so far this didn't look good. Immediately, Tristan recognized that Sydney had switched into work mode, and that meant things could get ugly.

Confusion swept over Sydney as she watched the two sexy men hug and talk as if they were good friends. *Tristan and Kade know each other? Friends? Shit. Seriously? Can my night get any worse?* She had been trying so hard to relax, trying not to think about the murder or how Kade had completely thrown her at the scene and tried to steal her case, or how he turned her on beyond belief. Now here he was, watching her while she danced and practically had sex on the dance floor. *Just freaking great.* Worse, he was looking at her seductively, noticing her clothing…or lack thereof. She guessed her air of professionalism was shot to hell. Whatever, he wasn't supposed to be here anyway, screwing up her entire night.

As she was about to bolt, Tristan grabbed her possessively around the waist, and turned to Kade. "So, you two know each other? Care to share?" he asked.

Sydney wanted to shove Tristan's hand away, but she didn't want Kade to suspect she desired him. The thought crossed her mind to let Kade think she belonged to Tristan. What would it hurt? Tristan knew the truth. Didn't he? He was holding her as tight as a dog held onto his bone, so she decided to go along with the charade.

"Yes, we do." Sydney sighed. She shot Kade an annoyed look. "As much as I despise discussing work while I'm at play, and I was so about to get into some play, Kade and I met today on a case. Would you like to enlighten me as to how you know Kade?"

Tristan smiled, knowing she wasn't telling him everything.

"Well, Kade and I go way back, good friends from the bayou."

She raised an eyebrow. "Bayou? Really? Okay then, well, you two have fun, talk about old times and all. Sorry, Tris, can't wait around tonight. Gotta get back to work. Until next time, mon loup." She placed a chaste kiss to Tristan's lips as Kade watched with jealous eyes. Narrowing her eyes at Kade she quipped, "And you, mister P-CAP, not sure if or when I'll see you again, but later."

Kade reached out to grasp Sydney's hand at the same time Tristan released her waist. He gazed intensely into her eyes and spoke firmly. "Yes, my dearest Sydney, when we meet again, and we will meet again, it will be a pleasure. I promise."

Sydney stared at him for a moment, almost unable to break their gaze. Unsettled by her reaction to him, she thought it must be some strange kind of a paranormal, chemical reaction. His smooth voice wrapped around her like silk, and she imagined how it'd sound while he embraced her in his arms. The disturbing thought jolted her back into the moment, and she tore her palm from his grasp. She had to get out of there before she lost control. Taking a deep breath, Sydney turned on her heels and walked away, not looking back.

She practically ran to the ladies' room, her mind racing with confusion. She'd wanted to have sex with Tristan when she'd first arrived. Leaving, the only man she could think of was Kade. As she began to change her clothes, questions spun in her head. *How well does Tristan know Kade? What the hell is happening to me? I know that Kade is lying, but he's freaking hot. Down, girl, get a grip.* Short on answers, she decided to get back to the lab as soon as possible. Since sex was out, work was officially back on the schedule.

Tristan laughed out loud, shaking his head. He wasn't exactly sure what was going on with Sydney, but he loved watching her dress down another guy, even if it was a friend. Sydney was a great girl, but she did get her feathers easily ruffled when her 'needs' weren't met.

As much as he hated being interrupted, he knew exactly why Kade was here, and he didn't want to wait to get the details. He also wasn't ready to share information with Sydney. That was why he'd told her to go upstairs. But the stubborn woman didn't ever listen. He expected nothing less from Sydney though; she was a detective, after all. But he still didn't want her involved in the paranormal business that he needed to discuss with Kade. Sure, Sydney was a tough as nails cop, but she was still human, and he was determined to protect her from whatever evil had just set up shop in his city.

"So, what's the deal?" Tristan inquired. "I'm glad I called you. I knew that shit was going to go down soon. Just glad you were here and could go to the scene."

"Definitely black magic, but it was a vampire; the girl was drained. I'm not sure of the ritual, but if I had to guess, I'd say someone is trying to build power. I'll be encouraging P-CAP to recommend full takeover of the case in the morning once the coroner has run an autopsy," Kade disclosed.

"I want you to know that I'm very appreciative of your offer to come and help." Tristan's face hardened. "It's bad news that a rogue vamp is targeting women. I want to assure my pack that P-CAP and the vampire community are taking care of it. Even though the vamp went after a human this time, the next victim could be a wolf. I can't have it."

"Tris, I'll take care of this asshole. I'm sure it's a vampire, but there may be more than one person involved. Whoever is responsible will be dealt with. You can trust me on that."

Tristan blew out a breath, and sat next to Kade. He spun his stool around to face the dance floor.

"So, what else is up? Seems you have been a busy boy since you've been in town. Getting in trouble already, huh?" he joked.

"Who, me? I can't possibly know what you're talking about," Kade said.

"Yes, you. What the hell's up with you and Sydney? You know, the hot woman I was about to have sex with until you arrived and so kindly interrupted us. My girl was really pissed at you. You haven't even been in town twenty-four hours. What did you do to her?"

"First of all, I did nothing to her. I simply informed her that she was not leading the case, and I think you'd agree with me on that point. She may be a cop, but she's human. I might let her consult after the coroner is finished, but she will not lead this case. And secondly, from what I can tell, my friend Miss Willows is not *yours*. You may have thought you were getting sex, but it didn't take much to interrupt you. She flew off like a little bird. So she must be just a friend, and I've been around long enough to know that she certainly does not belong to you." Kade was dead serious as he challenged Tristan. The tension was palpable, thanks to the words that had just left his lips. *What the fuck is getting into me that I would challenge a friend, let alone an Alpha, for a human woman on foreign territory?*

"My brother. You challenge me in my own club?" Tristan raised an eyebrow and reached over to put his hand on Kade's shoulder, asserting his dominance while diffusing a potential argument. "I realize you've had a long day of travel, so I'll overlook the way you just expressed yourself. As for Sydney…let's just say that she is, shall we say, a close friend, a very close friend. A friend who occasionally shares and experiences her most intimate desires with me. However, as you so eloquently just pointed out, she remains uncommitted. And while I would love for her to figure out why she builds emotional walls around herself, I am a businessman, not a psychologist. Most days, Sydney is a bad, ass-kicking, ask-questions-later cop, but she does walk on the wild side here in my club. I may join her or even watch her at times. But make no mistake about it; even though we are not committed, Sydney is under my protection and the protection of my pack. She will not be hurt if I have anything to say about it. And from where I'm sitting as Alpha, I have everything to say about it." He sighed heavily and paused for a second to judge Kade's reaction and then continued, "Kade, you and I have known each other for a long time, so I can tell by the look in your eyes that something is stirring in you. You want her. I can't tell you not to pursue her, but I am warning you; do not hurt her, emotionally or otherwise, and if at all possible keep her away from this killer."

"She'll be safe," Kade promised, refusing to address the rest of Tristan's observations.

He blew out a breath, frustrated with his attraction toward the blonde. He shouldn't give a shit what the wolf did with the cop, but he did care. He tried to shuck that pang of jealousy that stuck in his gut. What was he thinking? Frustrated with himself and his feelings toward the human woman, he struggled to focus on why he was even here in Philadelphia. He was supposed to find a killer and then get back to business in New Orleans, nothing more, nothing less. He needed to put Miss Willows out of his mind if he was going to get anything done.

"Are you going to offer a vampire a drink or what?" Kade asked with a smile. "I just need some blood. I'm not looking for extras tonight."

"You just traveled a long way. We have plenty of anonymous donors available tonight. If you want to grab the first private room on the right, I'll send up a few donors for you and Luca. Is it just the two of you tonight?" Since when did his friend not want extra, as in extra-sexual activities? Tristan was growing tired of trying to figure out what was going on in Kade's head.

"Yeah, just Luca and me tonight. Thanks, Tris. I appreciate your hospitality. It's been a long day." Kade nodded to Luca. "Let's go, Luca."

Tristan notified his manager to send two donors upstairs immediately. Now that weres and vampires were out in the open, there were plenty of humans who were willing to come to the club. Either they were interested in sex and the orgasmic bite of the vampires, or they just enjoyed the bite sans the sex.

Management kept a list of volunteer donors as they entered the club, and they were given a buzzer that was worn around their neck or clipped onto their clothing. If it buzzed, the donor would approach the hostess and be directed to a private room. Everything was consensual and safe. Vampires who wanted a donor were vetted out so Eden could ensure the safety of its guests. Draining until death was strictly forbidden. Tristan could not afford for there to be mistakes, so security monitored the rooms to make sure there were no issues upstairs, and donors could opt out at any time.

While vampires were sexual in nature, not all vampires were looking for sex when they ate. Many who came into the club were committed to another person and were only looking for fresh blood. Vampires did not need to feed every day, nor did they require large amounts of blood to sustain their strength. There were humans who sought excitement, who were looking for the vampire experience any day of the week. Eden capitalized on the synergistic relationship between donors and vampires. Instead of going for just a coffee, humans could get a coffee and a bite.

Orgasm and coffee to go…what more could one ask for?

As Kade relaxed on the sofa, he let his thoughts drift to Sydney. While he'd initially felt angry seeing her on the dance floor with another man, he could not deny his arousal as he'd watched Tristan touch her breasts, wishing it was he who was touching her. His cock had been rock hard when Sydney had approached him earlier. He'd tried to hide his arousal by acting pissed. Maybe Sydney hadn't noticed, but he was quite sure that Tristan had.

An attractive, bleached-blonde twenty-something, walked into the room and knelt down next to Kade. She lifted her eyes.

"No extras tonight, sir? I promise to make it good for you," she purred as she rubbed her hand across his thigh and over his hard bulge.

On another night, he would have sucked and fucked blondie high and hard, but not tonight. He was growing tired of meaningless sex with his food. Kade sighed.

"No thanks. Just a drink and then I'm out of here." It had been a long day. Yes, he did want extras, but he wanted them with a certain fiery detective. This donor would quench his thirst for blood, but would do nothing for the erection pressing against his zipper.

Looking disappointed, she laid her bare arm against his chest. He could smell her young aromatic blood. He put his fingers around the woman's wrist and held it to his nose. She moaned in delight when he licked the inside of her arm. His fangs elongated and he bit into her soft, pale flesh. He closed his eyes as he drank the essence of the strange woman. Kade fantasized that he was biting Sydney, pretending she was the woman before him writhing in ecstasy on the floor. When he was sated, he licked the wounds so they healed, then he strained to stand up. Shit. He was harder than ever. *Why am I so attracted to that damn woman?*

He glanced over to Luca who had just finished fucking his donor up against the wall. As Luca released the girl, his eyes met Kade's. Luca raised a questioning eyebrow at his boss, clearly wondering what was up with him, but Kade just silently watched. They were out of town, and it was customary for them to blow off some steam. Drinking blood and having sex were acceptable within the vampire community, especially when neither of them was committed.

Luca was Kade's right hand man in charge of security operations in New Orleans. Although raised in Australia, Luca had returned to his father's British homeland as an adult, and had subsequently found himself in New Orleans fighting in the War of 1812, where he was severely wounded during battle. Kade found Luca dying in a field and offered him the choice to be turned into a vampire. Once Luca agreed, Kade drained him of his blood to the point of death, and then he fed Luca his own lifeblood.

After the transformation, Luca had sworn allegiance to Kade. He worked for Kade, but they were also best friends, comrades in life. He was loyal and forever grateful to his savior. When they traveled, they often fed and fucked, casually enjoying the women donors.

"Hey, I'm almost done here," Luca said. "You okay?"

"Yeah, I'm fine. Finish up. I'm eager to get back to the brownstone. I have some calls to make. I'll meet you downstairs." Kade had to get the fuck out of there. The club smelled of blood, sex, and sweat, but none of it was Sydney's. He had to see her soon and find out exactly what the little detective had found out at the autopsy.

Chapter Three

After Sydney left the club, she drove directly to the station. She was used to working night shift, so even though it was midnight, she had plenty of time to get organized before she met with Adalee to get the initial findings from the autopsy. She was lost in thought when Tony slammed a wrapped cheesesteak on the desk. "Hey, Syd, thought you could use some food."

"Oh, you do know exactly what a girl wants." Sydney licked her lips and ripped the wrapping away. She bit into the sandwich, letting the onions fall down her chin. "Thanks so, so much! Mmm….messy, but soooo good."

Tony shook his head, laughing. She looked like she was coming, not that he knew about that. He would love to have her just once, but he knew that was a line that he probably should not cross. Ever since he'd met Sydney Willows, he'd fought the urge to kiss her senseless and slam his cock into her, but he was pretty sure she didn't date guys that often, and he was one hundred percent sure she didn't date fellow cops. No use thinking about what he couldn't have. Dragging his thoughts back to the case, he pulled out the file on the girl.

"Glad you like the sandwich, Syd, but you gotta eat quickly. Billings called an hour ago. She said she's ready for us to review her initial findings and is expecting us in thirty minutes. Eat up. I gotta stop in and see the captain, then I'll wait for you over by the elevator, so we can go down together."

"Sounds good to me. And Tony…thanks for the steak sandwich. You're a lifesaver. Not sure what I would do without you." Sydney was miffed after the incident at the club and couldn't stop thinking about Kade. She was about to get her freak on with Tristan when that damn vampire came in and interrupted things. If he was a detective, she was the Queen of England. There was no way on Earth that guy was a rank-and-file detective. He was lying to her, and he was cocky. And shit, he was hotter than hell. *Fuck. I have to get my shit together, get the vamp off the case, get some sleep, and then solve this murder.* It was turning into the longest night she'd had in weeks.

After inhaling her food, she and Tony rode the elevator in silence, ready to get some clues from the coroner. As the doors opened on the basement floor, Sydney and Tony walked down the long, gray corridor that led to the morgue. The overhead lights flickered, providing a dim path to their destination. She had walked this hallway more times than she cared to count, but every time she did, the gray walls reminded her that she was there to face death. No amount of fresh paint could make it seem like just another hallway in the building.

She pushed ahead of Tony through the black double doors that led into the autopsy room. The smell of death hit her as the air wafted into her nose. It was something she never got used to, but it reminded her of why she became a cop. Someone's life had been stolen. The girl was dead, and she would catch the bastard who did it.

"Hey there, Ada. So, what ya got?" Glancing around for a mask and gloves, she leaned over the body, inspecting the girl's wrists.

"It's a damn shame. This city is filled with some sick fucking bastards, but this one…he just…well, come see." Adalee looked up through her plastic mask. She gestured down to the girl's torso.

"She was tortured." Sydney peered over the now naked body. The translucent skin seemed to float over the young woman's muscles. Her body was littered with small cuts and marks, but none appeared to be deep. Sydney gritted her teeth and took a deep breath.

"That would be a yes." Adalee took samples from the body as she spoke. "Not sure what made all the cuts, but it looks like she was whipped with something. Also cut with a small knife of some sort. And these," she pointed to the girl's wrists, "Looks like she was bound with rope. I found some fibers embedded in her skin, still waiting on trace. As for the cause of death, we're looking at exsanguination. How she lost the blood? Not sure yet, but there's no blood left in this poor girl's body."

"So we have a tortured girl who is drained of all her blood? Sounds like a vampire, which would mean we have to turn this case over to P-CAP. But there are no bite marks on her, so that means it could still be ours. What's the deal with the tattoos on her body, on her face?" Tony scribbled a few notes and glanced at Sydney.

"Well, it looks like he not only tattooed her face, but also something here." Adalee pointed to the girl's breasts. "This poor girl suffered before she died. I'm estimating that she's been dead for a day or so but the water sped up decomp."

Sydney pointed to the tattoo on the girl's breast. "The tat…it looks like a sun, but the face, it's strange. It's possible she got the tattoos on her own."

"Maybe, hard to tell with the decomp. There's something going on here that makes my skin crawl. What if the tats are ritualistic?" Tony suggested.

Sydney was about to comment when she felt him around her. Kade. *What the hell is going on? It's him, and how do I know it's him?* She spun around to find Kade's ice-blue eyes staring at her.

"Very observant. The tattoo is the sun god Huitzilopochtli. He symbolizes a belief in the afterlife. Could be a ritual, or could be nothing." Kade took note of the body and started walking toward them.

Sydney looked over at Adalee, seeking her input, but she shrugged in response. "So, I take it you've been down here already?"

"Indeed."

"Then you know that this is our case, not yours."

Kade smiled at her, turning her insides to jelly. Everything in her past had told her to stay away from vampires, yet there was something about the way he spoke to her. She needed to establish her dominance before he took over not just her case but her resolve not to date vampires.

"It was great meeting you, Detective Issacson, or whoever you really are, but we've got this." She cleared her throat, attempting to compose herself. "We have a lot of work to do. Really, you can go now."

"Well as much as I would like to make you happy, and trust me, Miss Willows, I would, I have already talked to your superior, and it looks like you and I will be working together from now on. As you well know, when there is even the slightest chance of paranormal activity on a case, P-CAP has a right to request a co-investigation. I requested. Your department agreed."

Sydney's face reddened. She took a deep breath and exhaled.

"Okay then. But this is my city and my ass on the line. I expect honesty from the people I work with, and they expect the same from me. I'm telling you right now that I'm not putting up with your P-CAP secret shit. If you know something, you share it, and vice versa." She wasn't going to bring up the fact that he was lying to her, or question him about how he really knew Tristan.

"By all means, detective. Now, how about we get out of here and walk through the case? For the record, I know there are no bite marks, but I still suspect the perp is a vampire. We certainly prefer to bite our donors to satisfy our nutritional needs and our sexual appetites, but there are other ways to drain a body to get the blood. I intend to ask my vampire contacts to see if there has been any strange activity in town."

Sexual appetite? Sydney's face grew hot, and she cursed her reddening cheeks. She thought for a moment about what it would be like to have Kade's lips on her neck, his teeth grazing her tanned skin, biting her, drinking as he thrust into her. She felt warmth pooling downward, desire flowing through her blood. She shook her head, trying to think of something else, wanting to shake the lust she was feeling.

"Well, we better get going." Sydney forced herself to look away from Kade and glanced back to the girl on the table, a cold reminder of the task at hand. She caught sight of a pile of photos on Adalee's desk. Snatching one off the top, she sighed. "Well, you may know some vampires, but I've also got some sources in this city. I think we ought to take a trip to a tat shop I know. If this girl got work done here in the city, we'll find out who did it. And maybe even get an ID on her."

"I'll let you know as soon as I find anything else," Adalee commented, snapping off her gloves.

"Sounds good. Thanks for the update."

Sydney started to walk out the door. As she brushed by Kade, a chill ran up her arm. There was something about this man, this vampire. She didn't know why he was making her so crazy but she'd have to get it together if she was going to work with him.

Kade smiled to himself, smelling her arousal. She might not like him but she lusted for him. He would take that for now. In the meantime, he would play nice so she didn't end up staking him first.

Chapter Four

Sydney drove her convertible down South Street, enjoying the feel of the warm wind on her face. Owning a new car wasn't an option, but she'd splurged on the used Mercedes. It gave her the feel of luxury without the worry of how she'd replace it were it to be vandalized or stolen. By the time she arrived at the tattoo parlor she felt slightly more relaxed than she had in the morgue. The captain had put Tony on another murder case just as they left. Her new partner, Kade, would be with her. She didn't trust him, but the captain was crystal clear that she was to work with him on the Death Doll case…that was what the press was calling it.

Sydney had grown frustrated with the political games involved with her job. She was a good cop, but not exactly the most tactful person. Diplomacy wasn't her strength. Despite her reservations, she had come to terms with the fact she'd be working with Kade to solve the case. Once it was all over, he'd go back to New Orleans to bite necks and suck blood, or whatever else vampires did with their time.

On her way out of the station, she'd told Kade she'd meet him at Pink's Ink Tattoo shop. As she waited outside the storefront, a black limo pulled up and beeped at her. *Kade. A limo? Detective, my fucking ass.* A door opened and a large, good-looking man with long, dark hair got out of the car. She recognized him as the man who had been with Kade at Tristan's club.

He walked around the car and opened the door. Kade exited with grace, as if he was going to a movie premiere. He was almost beautiful, if one could use that word to describe a man, but there was no mistaking the predator he was. Dangerous, no one would mess with this guy…even on the cold streets of Philly. Sydney caught her breath, noticing how handsome he was in khaki pants and a blue linen shirt with rolled up sleeves that accentuated his broad, muscled chest. He smiled at her as he caught up with his vamp friend.

"Hope you weren't waiting long. Sydney, meet Luca. Luca, this is Sydney."

As Sydney extended her hand to Luca, he gently took it and kissed the top. She was captivated by his green eyes that seemed to draw her in. With an Aussie accent, Luca whispered, "Nice to meet you, Sydney. So, it is you who has Kade out of sorts." He let her hand go and chuckled to himself.

"I'm sorry, but I'm just not used to the hand kissing." Sydney laughed as Luca released her hand. "In my business, I usually have guys either running away from me as I'm trying to cuff 'em or trying to grab my ass. I know I should appreciate the chivalry, but it took me by surprise. Nice to meet you,

Luca, you coming in with us?"

"Luca, you stay out here and keep watch. Let's go, Sydney." Kade shot a look over to his friend and stepped between them.

For the first time since he'd met her, Kade saw Sydney smile. He felt a stir of jealousy knowing it was Luca who'd brought it to her lips…so soft and full. He couldn't help but wonder how it would feel to have those lips on his cock. Her scent was like breathing in the aroma of a fine wine, delicious. He wanted a taste. He couldn't wait much longer. Damn, he almost forgot why the hell he was even here. What was it about her that seemed to distract him from any rational thought?

Kade held the door for Sydney. She'd walked past him, pretending not to notice that he had effectively blocked Luca from touching her any further. The shop was filled with teenagers and young adults whose eyes were fixed upon the pictures on the wall. They were searching for the perfect artwork, discussing where they'd paint it on the canvas of their young bodies. Holding up her badge, Sydney pushed through the patrons as if she was parting the Red Sea. It was crowded, so Kade was forced to stand up behind her, against her. She could feel the hardness of his chest on her back as they stood waiting at the counter. The contact between them distracted her, but there was no room for him to move back. Attempting to concentrate, Sydney scanned the room looking for her source. Her eyes lit up when she located her.

"Pinky! Hey Pinky! Over here," she yelled over the rumble of voices.

Pinky was the owner of Pink's Ink. She was a petite girl whose black, cropped pixie hair had just a wisp of hot pink flowing through her bangs. Her bright pink halter-top showed off her back, which was adorned with two large butterfly wings in various shades of pink and indigo. Pinky was well known as one who ran her shop with an iron fist in a velvet glove, and lived up to her reputation as she turned around to yell at a potential customer who was peeling a drawing off the wall.

"Get the hell off the art or get the hell out! Hey, girl, what ya doin' down here? Finally come to let me put on that tat we talked about? And who is mister tall, dark and lickable behind you? Yummy." When she turned to face Sydney, her large voluptuous breasts almost spilled out of the tiny top, which complemented her short black latex skirt. She turned up a corner of her mouth and ran her tongue across her lips, eyeing the large hunk of man standing behind Sydney.

While Sydney was used to Pinky and her flair for the English language, she could not help but feel slightly embarrassed. She could feel the hard heat of Kade up against her back and found it difficult to speak. For a second, she found herself wishing they were alone, naked, Kade thrusting up into her and…*Get back in the game, girl! Focus!*

"Hey Pink, this is Kade. Listen, I need a favor." Sydney coughed, trying to act nonchalant. She held out the photo of the girl's sun tattoo. "Before you ask, don't. It's a case I'm working." She looked over her shoulder at Kade. "Ugh, a case *we* are working. All you need to do is ID this tat, okay? Is there anything about it that looks familiar? Do you recognize the artist's work? Maybe a customer who got a tat like this recently?"

Pinky stared at the photo and turned white. She peered over her shoulder to make sure no one was listening. "This…the lines, points and turns…it looks like the work of a guy who used to work in here. I fired him six months ago. I caught him wanking off in the alley. Just no. Seriously, who can't keep it in their pants at work?"

"So, what did he say when you eighty-sixed him?" Sydney glanced at Kade and quickly focused her attention back on Pinky.

"Well, that's the thing. He just looked up at me and kind of just…well, he just kept going, ya know? He finished. I told him that if I ever saw him near here again, I was calling the cops."

"And you never thought to mention this to me over drinks?"

"Come on. You know how it is. This city is filled with sickos. No offense, Syd, but I can't call the cops every time some asshole is out there waxing the bishop. I know it isn't pretty but look around here. Cops got murders to solve. They don't have time to arrest assholes who worship their dicks."

"Point taken. So what's his name? You got an address?"

Pinky began flipping through a candy-red, glittered address box on the counter, and pulled out a dingy index card.

"His name was Jennings, Drew Jennings. This address might be old, but here you are…it's on the card. Looks like he was staying in North Philly…a few blocks off Broad Street. Syd, I know you're a cop, but watch your ass. You and I both know it isn't the greatest area."

"Thanks. Okay, we're out of here." Sydney turned to Kade, brushing her thigh against his. "We can take my car. Your limo's going to look a tad out of place up there, and I'd like to try not to get shot at before we even get out of the car."

"Listen, Sydney, if we do this, we do it my way," Kade stated decisively. "I get this is your city, but I will not allow you to put yourself in danger. I see that you are strong, but you're not strong enough to go against a vampire."

"You may be a bad-ass vamp and all, but I know what I'm doing, this is my job. I am going. There will be no more discussion. If you need to enlighten me about the various ways you folks suck the lifeblood out of others, I'll be happy to listen on the way up Broad Street. But let's get this straight; it's not my first time at the rodeo. I have studied supernaturals and even sparred a few times with a werewolf. I know how to kill a vampire as well as I know how to kill a human, so let's go. We're taking my car. If Luca wants to follow in the limo, that's his funeral, but I'm outta here." She stood with her hands on her hips, tilting her head in defiance. All thoughts of how sexy he was rushed out of her mind and were quickly replaced by anger. *Does he see me as some kind of damsel in distress? I'm a cop; what doesn't he get about that?*

"You don't seem to understand what I told you down in the morgue. I lead this case, and you bloody well do not. You will go with me, because I allow it to be so. Do not make the mistake of thinking otherwise, Ms. Willows." Kade shot her a look of irritation.

"Yeah, yeah, vampire. Keep talking but I'm the one who got us this address, and I'm the one driving. So sit your butt down in the car and let's go." She jumped in the car and started it, watching as he silently sat down next to her, looking as if he was about to explode. Working this case with him was going to be a lot of fun, just a laugh riot, she thought. She rolled her eyes and started off toward north Philly.

Chapter Five

As the wind whipped Sydney's hair forward, she pushed it behind her ears. She loved her car, especially when she drove along the open highway. Philly was finally starting to quiet down. Aside from a few transients sleeping on the sidewalk, and the police, not many people were on the streets.

She glanced at Kade, who stared at her. She couldn't help wondering what he thought of this place. She knew that vampires could be very old, and suspected Kade was an elder of some kind. Aside from his arrogant presence, he seemed well-spoken, well-traveled, and knowledgeable. She could only imagine how many things he knew about women; how to please them, make them scream. She wanted him to make her scream, but she knew getting involved with him would not be a good idea. But no matter how hard she tried, Sydney couldn't deny her attraction to him. He was dangerous, hot, and sexy. And he would probably shatter her heart in a thousand pieces if she let him get close.

And then there was the little fact about his lying. Kade was not a run-of-the mill detective. He was not telling the truth, and she damn well knew it. They were about to go into a fucked-up situation that could get her ass killed, and she had a right to know what the hell was going on with him. *Enough of the games.*

"So, what's your deal? I can tell by your pretty shoes and overall style that you are *so* not a P-CAP detective. We're about to go into some shit, and I want to know what the hell's really going on," she yelled over the rush of wind,

"Ah, you're quick, Detective Willows," Kade replied. "You are correct that I'm not a detective, but I am in a position of authority in my world. So for the sake of argument, let's just say that I'm a third party who is very interested in seeing this case come to an end expediently. As you know, Tristan is a close friend, and we have mutual interests. He requested my assistance, and I'm here to put a rest to this situation."

"Okay, so you're telling me I'm about to go into a potentially deadly situation with an amateur?" *Just fucking great.*

"My dearest Sydney. I may be many things, but an amateur is not one of them. I have lived many centuries, fought many wars. I will protect you with my life," Kade replied. "You must know that while I respect your desire to apprehend the perpetrators of this girl's death, I have every reason to believe a vampire is responsible, and I will bring him to justice. That is all you need to know for now; this is the truth."

Truth? Yeah right, mister sexy vampire. Whatever. Sydney shook her head, unsure of what to believe. Maybe he was telling the truth, maybe not. At this point, she had already made the decision to find Jennings.

As they neared the location, she noticed the street was deserted. Several of the row homes lining the block had been boarded up and covered in graffiti. Sydney pulled her car into a parking space, which was not hard to find. She took a deep breath and cased the street. "See the house over there with the boarded up windows and red door? That's it. Here's the deal. I'm going to go around the front. How about you hit the back…keep the exit covered."

"There is no way you're going into that house alone."

"We need an element of surprise. I'll go in the front and you can come in from behind, scope out the house while I distract him. As you keep saying, I'm a human, so Jennings will perhaps think I'm alone. He'll be surprised as long as he only sees me, not you."

Kade raised a questioning eyebrow at Sydney. "What if Jennings doesn't answer? What if a vampire answers? What then?"

"You vampires have some kind of preternatural senses, right? I promise I'll yell for you if I get even a hint that something's wrong. And then you can take him by surprise."

"Do you have weapons? Human or vampire, you need to be ready to defend yourself." Kade looked at the house and then back to Sydney.

"I'm good. I've got silver in this gun here, so at the very least, I can slow a vamp down." Sydney quickly checked her ankle holster where she kept her secondary Sig Sauer. Before she left the station, she'd loaded it with wooden bullets in case she needed it for vamps. Her primary Sig Sauer in her shoulder holster was loaded with silver. If you shot a human or were with a silver bullet, the perp was going down either way. She also kept a silver knife in a secret compartment in her sleeve and another one in the tip of her right boot.

"Look at me, Sydney." Kade reached for the door handle. Pinning her with a hard stare, his eyes narrowed and his mouth tightened. "If you sense anything off, call for me immediately. I'll go around back and sneak in quietly so he doesn't hear me, and search the back of the house while you distract him. I still don't like this, but we'll do it your way. If there is a vampire, stay out of the way and let me handle it. Do you understand?"

Sydney nodded. "Let's roll."

Before she had a chance to open the car door, Kade was gone. *Damn vamp speed.* She shook it off and approached the front door and knocked once.

"Police. We're just here to talk." Met with silence, she lifted the rusted metal knocker and slammed it down several times. "Police! Open up!"

Sydney sucked a breath and kicked the door open, with her gun drawn and pointed. *Fuck me. Here we go.* The house looked empty, but she knew that things weren't always as they seemed. As she entered the building, the smell of urine and vomit hit her. *What the fuck?*

"Who's there?" she yelled into the darkness. "This is the police, just here to ask questions. Come out with your hands up and we'll talk. Let's do this nice."

While Sydney heard nothing, she sensed she wasn't alone. She reached into her vest and pulled out her flashlight, flicking it on. She steadied her gun and proceeded into the darkness. As her eyes adjusted to the lack of light, she noticed movement across the room. A shadow lurked in the distance. Slowly she crept across the floor. When she approached the area where she'd seen it originate, she shone the light on the floor; blood. Adrenaline rushed through her veins as she attempted to see who was in the room. A small creaking drew her attention. But as she swiveled to locate it, a rush of pain seized her upper back. Sydney fell hard against the wooden planks, struggling to breathe as her face hit the bloodstained floor.

"What are you doing here? You're desecrating the ritual area, bitch! He'll like you, though. Yes, he'll enjoy hearing you scream as he whips your flesh."

Sydney pushed onto her side and caught sight of a dirty, apparently human, man. He was holding a fourteen-inch wooden baton, which she recognized as a martial arts tonfa. The man was overweight and bald, and could not be more than five-eight, she estimated. His eyes were empty and cold as he poised to strike her again with the weapon. Sydney took a breath, gritted her teeth, and turned all the way over so she was sitting on her bottom. Facing him straight on, she scooted backward into the corner, using her hands and feet. She wanted to stand up and run, but her muscles spasmed, bringing tears to her eyes. She scanned the room, looking for her gun that was lying lost in the darkness. She considered her options, aware that she had another gun. A surprise. *Just keep him talking.*

"Jennings, is it?" He loomed above her, refusing to reply. "Yeah, okay, don't bother answering. Listen, I'm not going to hurt you. I just need to sit up."

"You're going to suffer more than you ever thought possible. I don't even care why you're here. Let's just call it a fortunate circumstance. I will give you to my master. He'll be happy with my gift. He'll take everything from you while you bleed," He laughed.

"Jennings, I hurt my ankle." She feigned injury, wrapping both her hands around her leg until she was able to finger the grip of the pistol. *Almost there.* "I think I might have broken it in the fall. It hurts so badly."

"Listen, this will go easier if you just put out your hands." He pulled out a roll of duct tape from his jacket. "If you can't do it, I have no problem bashing your head in until you give up the fight. What's it gonna be?"

Sydney's pulse raced as her assailant leaned forward to grab her. As she drew the Sig Sauer and fired, a blur jetted across her vision. She coughed as dust scattered throughout the air. As the cloud settled, Sydney could make out a dead body slumped against the wall. A scream tore from her lips, realizing the blur had been Kade.

"Sydney, look at me. Are you okay? Are you hurt? Let me see." Kade rushed to Sydney's side and carefully lowered her arm, taking the gun from her hand. While he had been out back staking a rogue vamp, he'd heard a loud noise, and immediately regretted his decision to allow her to go in alone. He should have been with her. Whoever was behind this would easily be able to kill humans, and he knew it.

Flying into the room, Kade had grabbed Jennings by the shoulders and thrust him hard against the brick wall. In an instant, Sydney had fired off a round, the shot landing in Jennings' chest. Kade heard his last heartbeat. And even though he was disappointed that he hadn't had a chance to interrogate him, Sydney was okay. Bleeding yes, but she was alive.

"Don't touch me. It's just a little blood. I'll be fine," Sydney protested, shaking. She stared at her bloodied hands, red streaks dripping down her fingertips. Furiously, she rubbed them onto her pants as if she was afraid he'd be enticed by the scent of it. "Please, let's just call this into the station so they can scrub the site for trace."

"You're hurt, love. Please let me help you." Sensing she was in shock, he moved slowly toward her as if approaching an injured animal. This time instead of recoiling, she fell into his arms, allowing him to comfort her. "Just because I can smell your blood, that does not mean I am going to bite you. You're safe with me. Let's get you home."

As he took her into his embrace, the sweet lily fragrance in her hair filled his senses. Kade was angry with himself for leaving her side. She was his responsibility. He wanted to take her to her home and tie her to the bed so she would stay the hell away from the vampire who was killing these girls. He didn't care that she was a cop. She was human nonetheless.

"I'll be okay. I just need to rest a minute. I'm fine. I'll probably have a huge bruise on my back though." She winced as she tried to move in his arms. Forcing herself to relax, Sydney let her head fall onto Kade's shoulder. For a moment she let herself enjoy the hardness of his chest and the spicy scent of his skin. She knew she should push him off and walk away, but what could it hurt to pretend someone cared?

Without letting Sydney slip from his arms, Kade managed to pull out his cell phone with one hand and place a call. "Luca, call the station and give them the address. Yeah, Jennings is dead. They need to scrub it. I want you here with them. You get anything, call me, got it? Okay. Bye."

Kade's conversation jarred her from her brief respite, reminding her that she was on this case. Sydney pulled away from Kade, breaking their embrace.

"Let's check the rest of the building and make sure no one else is here. Jennings got me with the baton before I ever made it upstairs. Did you find anyone out back?" Her cool demeanor returned, as she resurrected her emotional walls.

"I had myself a dance with a rogue vamp in the yard." Kade noticed the change in her demeanor and played along, respecting her independence. He might not like that she put herself in danger, but that was part of her job. And he needed to try to worry a little less about his detective. Soon he would stake the offending vampire and catch his jet back to NOLA. As much as he wanted Sydney, he knew the reality of the situation. He would have to let her go. "They must have seen us coming. If you want to check the rest of the place, let's do it together this time."

Thirty minutes later, Kade and Sydney had searched every square inch of the row home. Soon after backup arrived and with no clues to be found, Sydney did something she had never let any man do; she let him drive her baby, her convertible. She'd been hesitant about turning over the keys, but she was nursing a major headache and the lump on her upper back was throbbing. The bleeding on her hands had stopped, but she was pretty sure she was going to be black and blue.

As they pulled up to her building, Kade carefully parked the car. He got out, handed her the keys, and opened her car door. Sydney groaned as she shoved herself up onto her feet.

"Thanks for driving. You sure you don't want to take my car back to the station? I can have Tony pick me up later."

"I'm quite all right. No need to inconvenience you."

"Um…you wanna come up for coffee?" She felt stupid even asking. Did a freakin' vampire even drink coffee?

"You tempt me with your offer. While I do enjoy a spot of tea, I am afraid that my tastes require more than you are willing to give," Kade said, his voice cold. He didn't want to tell Sydney yet, but there were rumors back home that someone was working black magic to gain power, but at the moment it was just talk. There was always some asshole looking for more supernatural power. Once you were a vampire, there was no democracy. You reported to the head vampire in the area; comply or die. Most accepted their new life, some didn't. Luca would have a full update on possible suspects for him when he arrived. "I have to make some calls."

"You've got my cell number. If I don't hear from you, I'll be in touch tomorrow afternoon and we can plan the next steps. It's been a hell of a night, and I need to get a shower."

"Sydney."

"Yes?"

Kade reached for her hand, turned her palm upward, and kissed it.

"I will call you with any news. Please do the same. Please forgive me…ah, my car is here." The limo pulled up to the curb.

As Sydney entered the code for the building, Kade caught her stealing a glance back at him. In that moment, he considered his attraction to her. But almost as soon as the thought came, he shoved it to the back of his mind. Any distraction whatsoever could cause him to make deadly mistakes. And Miss Sydney Willows, while beautiful, was a distraction he could not afford.

Chapter Six

After taking three Advil, Sydney showered and dressed in her favorite red sundress that accentuated the swell of her tan breasts. Unfortunately, it also showed off her upper back that had started to turn bluish. She didn't bother to dry her hair; her blonde locks looked wild and curly. It was late at night, no use blowing it out.

She had considered going to bed. It was nearly two in the morning; she knew she should get into her pajamas, read a book and get some rest, but accustomed to working nights, she was wide awake and her nerves were on fire. Nearly dying can do that to a girl, but it wasn't what was making her jumpy. It was Kade. She wanted, she needed, needed something, someone, him. But she wasn't going to have *him.* Like a wanton slut, she'd asked him to come in with her 'for coffee' a.k.a. 'sex', and he seemed uninterested. She had thought there was a sexual tension there, but maybe she was wrong. He had lied about being a detective. He seemed to have plenty of other secrets. *What else is he lying about? Maybe he has a girlfriend. Or worse, maybe he's married.*

Sydney longed to forget her lustful thoughts of Kade. She didn't believe in love at first sight anyway; lust maybe, but lust could be controlled…or redirected. Determined to get him out of her system, Sydney decided Tristan was just what she needed. She knew he cared about her, desired her. He'd always been there for her, the one stable man in her life besides Tony. Life was too short to sit around moping. After her attack, she didn't want to be alone tonight, and Tristan would help her forget.

As Sydney strolled through Eden's doors, she spied Tristan leaning against the bar, talking to a redhead who was flirting with him and flipping her hair. Setting her sights on him, she strode across the dance floor, ignoring the stares from all the other men. They meant nothing to her; this was a club, a place to come and be noticed. Dancing, drinking, sweat, blood, sex, it was all here, and she was going to sate herself until she felt better. Stepping in front of Tristan, she flashed a badge at the girl.

"Get lost. I've got business here," she ordered. Her face held no smile. Her competition promptly rushed away, not wanting to be involved with the police.

As she'd expected, Tristan was not going to be bossed in his own house. He instantly grabbed her arms, dominating the situation. He pulled her flush against his firm body.

"What gives, Syd? My girl looks a little tense. You need something tonight?" he whispered in her ear, his cheek brushing against hers.

"I need you," she responded.

She quivered in his arms, his erection pressing into her belly. There would be no stopping him tonight. It had been weeks since they'd been together. Even though there was no commitment between them, tonight she was his. She allowed him to take control, leading her up the stairs.

Tristan led her into his private office. Soundproofed and secure, its royal-blue walls were decorated with modern art. A cherry desk sat center, complete with matching chairs. He flicked a switch and flames flared to life in a gas fireplace.

Sydney stood still, unable to make the first move. Even though she'd felt an instant attraction to Kade, she told herself that he was nothing more than a mysterious stranger, one who was uninterested in pursuing a relationship. She needed to be with someone who cared about her; she needed Tristan. He'd always been there for her, and she for him.

"Tristan, I…." she stammered.

"Shh…you don't need to say anything. I missed you." He brushed the back of his hand across her cheek, and she leaned into him and kissed his hand.

"Tris, this case. It was a rough night. I just need to relax. I just need you."

Tristan raised an eyebrow at her. "You sure, baby? You seem, I don't know, a little different tonight. Distracted. You okay?"

"I'm fine, Tris, really. I got hurt earlier tonight out with Kade, but I'm okay." Sydney didn't want to tell Tristan that she'd asked Kade to come up to her apartment or how she'd almost got killed tonight. She was reluctant to tell him the truth, but knew that he'd discover her bruises.

"Dammit, Syd. What happened? Let me see you." He pulled her closer to the fireplace and circled around her, inspecting her skin. When he caught sight of her back, he sucked a breath and ground his back teeth. "You're hurt. Mon chaton, did you go to the doctor? Where was Kade when this happened?"

"I'm okay," she whispered, a tear escaping her eye.

Tristan leaned over and kissed her gently on the shoulder, rubbing her neck. Sydney moaned in response, relaxing into his touch. Allowing him better access to her throat, she submitted to his wolf's need to dominate. Usually, she had to be in control. But here, she could let down her walls…only with Tristan. He knew what she wanted in life, sexually. She would never let him fully into her heart. Wolves never mated with humans. Long ago, they'd both accepted that this would have to be good enough. But within Tristan's arms, she would purge the thoughts of Kade from her mind. She'd get her release, go home, sleep and be back on the job tomorrow with a smile on her face.

A sigh escaped her lips as Tristan slid his fingers over her skin, pushing down the strings of her sundress. The fabric fell to her feet, her bared back exposed to him. He reached around her belly and cupped her breasts. His hands were full as he took her nipples between his forefinger and thumb and squeezed. She moaned again as heat rushed to her sex. Tristan gently turned her around and pressed his lips to hers.

"Tristan," she gasped, "I need you now."

"I've got you," he replied.

Reaching down, he cupped her ass. With his other hand, he grazed over her breast and stomach, sliding his fingers underneath her silk thong. His entire hand covered her mound, his fingers exploring her folds, gently building a rhythm.

"More, Tristan. In me. Please." She rocked into his hand.

He loved it when she begged. His wolf was aching to fuck her but he wanted to make her come first. He knew how to please a woman, especially his Syd.

"That's it, mon chaton. Feel me."

"Don't stop," she pleaded as she dug her fingers into his shoulders as if she was holding on for dear life.

Tristan slowly inserted a finger inside her, circling her clit with his thumb. As she trembled, he knew she wouldn't last long. Intent on pushing her over the edge, he slowly added another finger, increasing the pace.

"That's it, baby. Just let go."

Her chest heaved for breath. Trembling, she came by his hand. Clutching his shoulders, she rested against his chest.

Tristan eased up his hold, and Sydney knelt down in front of him. She wanted to taste him, make him feel good too. Tristan groaned as she reached up and grabbed the outside of his pants, cupping his groin. She quickly unbuttoned his jeans and let his erect length jut out. She grabbed the base of his sex, slowly stroking him, and looked up into his eyes. Taking him into her mouth, she pleasured him until he came.

After his release, they fell gently to the floor, relaxing on the rug in front of the fire. Even as she lay in Tristan's embrace, her thoughts drifted to Kade. She wished she could understand why she wanted him so badly. He was both good looking and charming, but she'd just met him. It was as if the sexual tension between them escalated exponentially every time they exchanged a glance. She closed her eyes and prayed that whatever she felt for Kade would go away when he left town. Kade hadn't wanted her when she offered, so why shouldn't she enjoy a little fun with Tristan? Despite her rationalization, knowing she'd done nothing wrong, she felt a twinge of guilt, having made love to Tristan.

"What's going on in that pretty little head of yours?" Tristan asked, as if reading her thoughts. "Listen, I know something's got you upset."

"What are you talking about? I'm fine," she denied.

"Come on, Syd. I can feel it. Remember, Alpha magic and all? I know you're just off today…even if you did just blow my mind." He laughed. "You're so alone all the time. It's not good for you. Maybe you should think about being here more often…with me. I can protect you. And before you get all riled up, I get that you are a super cop and all, but face it, you're a little beat up tonight…albeit a beautiful shade of blue. You need someone to care for you. You know you mean a lot to me. I don't want you getting hurt while you're working this case. Why don't you think of spending the rest of the night here with me? No pressure. Just spend the night and we'll see how it goes tomorrow."

"Tristan, I really appreciate the offer. But nothing's wrong," she lied. Sydney kissed him gently, rose off the floor, and started to get dressed. "I just have a lot on my mind. I swear I'll be fine."

"Okay, but I'm here for you if you need me. And Kade will protect you too. He and I have been friends for a long time. He's a tough son of a bitch and has sworn to me that he'll protect you with his life, if needed."

"Don't worry. I'll be okay, Kade or no Kade." Sydney sighed. Kade was her problem. "Thanks for everything tonight. I really gotta get going. You were exactly what I needed."

Tristan quickly shrugged on his clothes, and opened the door. Sydney kissed him as she brushed by him. As they walked down the winding stairway, the pounding music reminded her she was in a club, not someone's house. Halfway down, she felt his presence and looked across the crowded dance floor. *Again? Really?* She could not get away from that damn vampire. Sydney looked over to Tristan and saw him wave at Kade. She glanced back to Kade and found him glaring at her. *He knew.*

Sydney momentarily wondered how the two men had become friends, given their different personalities. Even though she'd been intent on going home and getting a good night's rest, seeing Kade ignited the flame of desire in her that had only slightly dimmed during her little tryst with Tristan. She'd known it would be temporary but she'd been hoping to at least get through five minutes without thinking about Kade. *Damn.*

As she descended the rest of the stairs, she fought the guilt that rose in her throat. She silently told herself that she had nothing to be ashamed of, she was single after all. She had no ties to anyone. Sydney turned to Tristan, whispering goodbye and placing a kiss to his cheek. She kept her gaze toward the door, attempting to ignore Kade as she pushed through the dance floor.

Kade spotted her on the stairs with Tristan. He fought the instinct to run up the stairs and rip into his friend. What the fuck was he thinking? He held no claims to Sydney yet and could not challenge his friend here in his territory. In fact, a few hours ago he'd refused her invitation. He damn well knew she wanted more than coffee the instant she offered. But he'd chosen to meet Luca instead, so he could continue working the case without her.

After Luca picked him up, Kade's deepest suspicion was confirmed. He'd found a Voodoo bracelet with a vampire's scent on it. A vampire who Kade knew well. There was no denying her scent; this vampire had come for him, and was somehow using the humans, perhaps a mage, to assist her. He did not intend to tell Sydney about Luca's findings tonight. She was mortal and too vulnerable. Kade planned to oust his determined detective from the case, keeping her safe and off the radar.

As his eyes met hers, he could not deny the intense feelings that were growing inside of him. He almost lost it, watching her kiss his friend. As she attempted to reach the door, her scent grew stronger and he could smell Tristan as well. The thought that she'd been intimate with the wolf bore a hole in his belly. Jealousy flared as he rushed over to stop her from leaving. Certain he'd made a mistake earlier, refusing to come up to her apartment, he grew intent on letting her know in no uncertain terms to whom she would belong someday. She was his. He wasn't sure how or when, but she would belong to him.

In an instant, Kade slipped behind her. He softly placed his hands on her shoulders, frowning at the now deep black and blue marks on her upper back.

"And what do you think you are doing out here? Your bruises…you must be in pain."

"I've been through worse," Sydney said, her voice calm as if she were all business. She turned to face him, pushing out from under his hands. "Did you talk to Luca? What did he say?"

"A dance, love? Indulge me." He slid a hand around her waist and drew her into him, sniffing her neck. "I can see you have been busy."

"One dance," Sydney agreed. Slowly, she reached up and put her hands around his neck, leaning her face against his chest. "Just tell me….did Luca find anything we can use?"

"He found a bracelet. It is a Voodoo bracelet, possibly charmed. I have contacts in New Orleans I will consult."

"Ada called me. She's running the hair. By tomorrow, we should have something else to go on. I'll meet you at the station tomorrow night around six."

Kade felt her stiffen in his arms, as if she was struggling to fight what he knew was happening between them. He held her closer, refusing to let her go just yet as they continued to slow dance. "I know you're a cop, but this danger…you cannot fight it. You must trust me when I say that there are evil, supernatural forces that await us…you will need me to keep you safe." He leaned in and kissed the top of her head.

"Evil is a reality of this city. This is what I do."

Kade stopped dancing. He reached over and cupped her face gently with both his hands, his eyes pinned on hers.

"We will do this together, love, but know that it will be done my way. I will keep you safe, and after this evil is extinguished, you will be mine and no one else's."

Sydney felt the blood rush to her face. She wasn't sure whether to yell at him or fuck him right there in the middle of the dance floor. Somehow she knew his words were true…she would be his.

Determined not to let him see that he had just gotten to her, she pulled away, turned and looked back at him over her shoulder, and smiled. "Kade, love, you should know here and now that I belong to no one but myself."

With that, she walked out the door. She knew it wasn't true. Something about him drew her in and threatened to change her entire life. He made her want to belong to him. She wanted to love someone and have him love her back…she wanted Kade.

Chapter Seven

After sleeping a good ten hours, Sydney got dressed. She sped off to grab a latte at her favorite coffee shop then stopped by the sporting goods and craft stores to pick up a few things for the kids at the children's center where she volunteered. She loved seeing their faces as she brought in her weekly presents. New markers meant more pictures, more happy faces, and more creativity. Sydney knew how great it felt to create: inspiring, fulfilling, accomplished. These kids felt it too. Their creations were evidence they had a future, not one on the streets, but a future perhaps in art school or college. These kids had a dream to get out from under the poverty and violence of the streets, and Sydney was determined to help them.

Even though she had a busy life, mostly filled with work, the truth was that she had only a few trusted friends and no family to speak of. Her mother had been tragically killed by a drunk driver several years ago, and the grief from her death had brought Sydney to her knees. She just wasn't the same after losing her mom and neither was her dad. Sydney's father fell into a deep depression, moved to Arizona and died a few years later.

Death was a merciless teacher. It taught Sydney to steel her emotions, build a wall big enough so she would not have to feel the grief. Having her mom die only confirmed her decision that she would not get married, because she couldn't stand the heartbreak of losing someone else. She'd had several boyfriends over the years, even a few she thought she could have loved, but she never really could commit to any of them, because of her job. In addition, she had watched the men she worked with get married and then divorced more times than she cared to. The hours and the stress of the job did not make a marriage easy. In her mind, it didn't make you available enough to be a good parent either. It was easier deciding to be happy with the life she did have: a good job, a few good friends, a boyfriend here or there who was willing to just be a boyfriend and nothing more.

Although Sydney loved kids, she'd convinced herself that she would never have any of her own. So she devoted much of her spare time and money to a local after-school center. Every week she would spend a few hours at the center, talking with the kids, playing games, and doing crafts. She wasn't the only one who was alone; these kids needed her. The fact was that many of the city's kids were raising themselves. Their parents never made it to the PTO meetings or teacher conferences. Whether they were too busy working or missing entirely, it didn't matter. The result was the same; kids alone on the street after school. The center gave them something constructive to do. Through play, they learned.

Sydney knew she was lucky to have been raised by loving parents in a middle class home where chocolate chip cookies and encouragement were plentiful. She might not ever have kids of her own, but she had the knowhow to help other kids. She knew how to teach a group of girls to bake a cake, do their algebra homework, learn about science, sing a song, or paint a picture. Her mom had been an artist so creativity was valued in her house. Sydney wanted these kids to have every experience she'd been allowed to have, even if at the end of the day the cold streets awaited them. They deserved to know about the wonderful activities that could fill their young lives instead of gang banging, prostitution, and drugs. Despite the bitter poverty, the center helped girls and boys to grow up educated, strong, and empowered.

Sydney knew she wasn't a saint, but she still gave as much of herself as she could. At the end of the day, the kids filled her soul with hope and love, two things that she very much needed.

After spending a few hours with the kids, Sydney hurried back to the station, to Kade. It was still light outside. She wondered where he was sleeping. Did he even sleep? Did he go out during the day? She knew much more about werewolves, both the good and the bad, than she knew about vampires. She got the fact they drank blood, but other than that, she tried not to hang out with them to find out the details of their habits. She did have a sense of self-preservation.

As she buckled up, her cell phone buzzed with a text from the station. *Shit.* Another dead girl had been found. She hated the evil that lurked within humans and paranormals. Why did they kill? Power, hate, passion, mental illness? There were many reasons, none of them good. Sydney didn't even care anymore. She was growing tired of the death. Sure, she would try to understand motive to the extent that it would help her find the perpetrators and lock them away forever, but aside from self-defense, there was never a justified murder.

The dead girl had been found in Olde City at Elfreth's Alley. America's founding fathers had come together in this very place, creating documents that would give birth to a country. Benjamin Franklin had once walked these streets. Its cobblestone alley was lined with renovated row homes that proudly displayed the preserved eighteenth century, working class homes that remained. The country's past, and sadly, now the present lay across the stones, marring the historic site.

Sydney ducked under the crime scene tape and approached the body. She knew she should have called Kade, but she figured someone on his team would let him know. After last night, she was afraid of her body's response to him. Eventually she would have to see him, she knew, to hear his voice, and breathe in his delicious masculine scent. He would be pissed that she hadn't waited for him. But Sydney figured she'd take action and apologize later.

She leaned in to get a better look at the body, another "Death Doll." The girl was a brunette this time, but had the same almost pure white, porcelain skin. She was not damaged by water like the other victim had been. Instead, it looked as if she had been gently laid on the street only hours ago. She appeared as if she were simply sleeping. She was as young as the other girl, in her twenties, but was dressed differently this time, in a long evergreen velvet dress, sans shoes. Again, her eyelids had been sewn shut with thread. Someone had taken care to put makeup on her face. She looked like a collectible doll you would buy on home shopping television. The scoop neckline dress was fitted tightly around the front of her body. Sydney snapped on a latex glove and reached over to lift the neckline slightly.

The tattoo was small enough that it adorned the top of the girl's breast. It looked almost like a cross, but with a round, large protuberance on the head.

"Jennings is dead, so either he did this before he died or there's someone new doing the tattoos, and what is this? It isn't exactly a cross. I know I've seen this somewhere." Sydney stood up straight and spoke aloud to herself. She shook her head at the needless loss of life.

"It's an Ankh. Ancient Egyptian symbol of eternal life."

Sydney spun around, startled by the velvet caress of Kade's voice. But his tone was not warm. No, he was angry with her, presumably for not calling him. *Great, here we go.*

"Forget something, Sydney? You know, I'm not above punishing you for your blatant disregard of my orders."

After Sydney had left the club the previous night, Kade talked to Tristan about what Luca had found; a ribbon with *her* scent on it. *She* was back, *Simone*. Kade had first met Simone in New Orleans in 1822. He found her beaten and starving in an alley. Newly turned, she was a lost fledgling. Not wanting to watch her kill or be killed, he took her under his wing and taught her how to feed on humans without killing them. Along with several other young vampires, including Luca, Simone lived with him in his safe compound that he had created within the city. Despite the apparent abuse she had suffered over the years, she came to trust Kade.

Simone had told him that a man named John Palmer had sent for her from England and brought her to Jamaica. She was given as a gift to his new wife, Annie Palmer. She worked as an indentured servant, a handmaiden. It was in Jamaica where she had learned Voodoo from Annie, who was a dangerous and abusive mistress known as the White Witch. Annie regularly tortured Simone and the other workers and slaves on the plantation. Simone had been beaten or whipped nearly every day she'd been there. Nothing ever made the mistress happy except when she practiced her dark arts. During these sessions, Simone was expected to assist the mistress, but she was not happy to merely assist. She kept her eyes lowered but secretly copied Annie's notes and memorized whatever spells Annie cast.

One night during one of the many extravagant parties they held on the plantation, a guest had expressed interest in Simone and Annie had offered her handmaiden as a gift to him to use as he wished. Simone reluctantly took the stranger's hand out of fear of a whipping. The stranger had led her out into the fields, where he raped and turned her.

She was not aware that she had left Jamaica until she awoke in a dirty hotel room in New Orleans. Her new master sat on a chair next to her and explained she'd been turned into a vampire; she'd be his new slave. While she shook in bed, trying to come to terms with what he was saying, the door burst open, and a man shot a wooden arrow into his chest. The vampire disintegrated on the spot. Assuming Simone was an innocent human, the killer said nothing as he turned and left the building. Simone scrambled out onto the street, but realized she was weak. She had stumbled into the muck and had lain helpless until Kade found her.

During the next few years, Simone had adjusted to life in New Orleans and transformed into a beautiful woman. Her pale skin highlighted her lush, ebony hair. It wasn't long before Kade and Simone became intimate. He wasn't in love with her, but he'd been lonely and she was available. He couldn't risk being involved with a human during those times, so another vampire offered him the companionship he needed. What Kade hadn't realized was that Simone never gave up practicing Voodoo and had started secretly practicing the dark arts when he was out of town. She knew Annie's secrets and wanted the power she knew could be hers. It wasn't until a werewolf, named Tristan, approached him and told him about his missing sister, that Kade found out Simone had evil intentions. Tristan had come for Kade's help, and an agreement. Tristan would offer peace with the local wolves. In exchange, Kade would get his sister back from Simone.

Kade was horrified to find Simone in the barn that day. She had captured at least ten girls, including Tristan's sister, and was holding them hostage. The girls were barely alive, cuffed with silver, beaten and naked, hanging on the walls. Infuriated, he commanded Simone to him and shoved her to her knees. While he initially wanted to kill Simone for her crimes, she begged for her life. Granting her mercy, Kade banished her forever from the United States. Forced to leave, Simone went with only a ticket for passage overseas and the clothes on her back. He destroyed her ritualistic objects, her spell books, and all that remained was a burned field where the barn used to stand.

He had nearly forgotten about Simone until Luca told him he had scented her at the Jennings' scene. If Simone was involved, he knew she would kill Sydney without a second thought. If she was able to capture and torture strong werewolves, like Tristan's sister, she could easily kill a human. He didn't know what he could do to convince Sydney of the danger that she faced. He knew he couldn't stop her from continuing the investigation, but damn if she was going to go out on the streets without him. He had to be serious with her and make her understand that she had to obey his orders in order to work with him. He needed to tell her about Simone.

Sydney tensed at Kade's remark that he'd punish her. She'd never seen him this angry. Yet his outrage only served to put her on the defensive.

"Newsflash, vampire, I'm not your daughter, nor are you my boss. So, let me make myself clear. I don't take orders from you. We may be partners for now, but this is my city. I apologize for not calling you, but I figured you'd be…I don't know…sleeping or whatever it is that vampires do during the day. I figured your office would call you." She knew she was wrong, but that was the best apology she could cough up at the moment. She was not going to let some guy tell her what to do. There was a murderer killing women on the street. They'd catch the guy and then, next year, it would be a different perp out killing people; that was life in the big city. She was here to catch bad guys, and was not a little girl playing cops and robbers. "How about we just move on? You're here now, so let's get to work."

Kade stared down at her and moved closer. God, he was sexy, but dangerous. Sydney could see his muscles bulging out of his tight black t-shirt. For a minute, she thought about what it would feel like to slip her hands under his shirt and skim her fingertips along the hard ridges of his stomach.

"Sydney, love, I know you know these streets like the back of your hand, but we need to learn to trust each other. There are things you don't know about. I promise I will tell you everything when we get time, but right now, I need you to give me a little trust. Do not go on calls by yourself. It isn't good practice anyway, and you know it. Even though we are technically sharing this case, I could easily get you pulled off it if you don't listen to me. There is a vampire involved in these killings, and possibly another creature with supernatural abilities. I don't want to push you off the case, but I will if you don't start cooperating, and that means that I lead the investigation, not you. Most importantly, you go nowhere alone, am I clear?"

"Crystal," Sydney responded, refusing to look him in the eye.

Sydney focused on the body. Arguing with Kade wasn't going to solve the case. *What other similarities are there to the first girl?* She pulled another glove on and reached for the girl's wrist. The dress had long sleeves that fell past her fingers. Sydney gently pulled up the material to see if the girl had marks on her. Sure enough, she had bruises on her wrists, indicating that she'd been bound and then perhaps cut loose after she died. Sydney scanned the site for evidence of cuffs or ropes, anything that may have been discarded in the rush to dump the body.

"Check out her wrists. She was bound, too…just like the other vic. We need to scour every inch of this alley to see if anything else was dumped with the body. Killers are careful, but these guys always make mistakes. We just need to find them."

As she turned around, Sydney saw the coroner's van pull up. She waved to Adalee, who walked toward her with kit in tow. "Hey Syd, another vic, I see?"

"Yeah, I can't be sure but it looks like she's been drained. The site looks clean, no blood or urine around the body."

Adalee blew out a breath while she stared down at the dead girl. She glanced at Kade, who was coming over to see her, and then back again at Sydney.

"So listen, trace came in on the wrist fibers from girl one. Get this, looks like the hair was human, also hemp mixed in. So, whatever rope or binding this is, it's got human hair in it."

"Do we know who the hair belonged to?" Sydney asked.

"No. But I can tell you that it doesn't match the vic's." Adalee bent down and started working on the body, but kept talking. "And there was something else. We found residue on the body, some kind of oil. Trace came back showing mostly lemongrass. A few other small things, but it definitely was some kind of lemon oil. This case keeps getting weirder and weirder."

"Lemongrass? Maybe it was just some kind of skin cream or lotion? We don't know it has anything to do with the perp."

"Well, all I can tell you is that it was only on her forehead, nowhere else on the body." Adalee spoke to Sydney as she pulled out the body thermometer. "The only time I've seen that kind of thing is in the church.

You know, like Catholics do with the healing masses."

"What is it, Kade? You're awfully quiet over there." Sydney waited for Kade to weigh in on Adalee's assessment.

"I told you, Sydney. There are forces here that you are not used to fighting." Kade knelt down to inspect the girl's face. With a gloved hand, he reached over and carefully pushed a stray hair off her face. He sighed. "Lemongrass oil. Voodoo, Hoodoo. These are all practices which use oil and herbs. Sometimes practitioners create a hybrid of Voodoo, Hoodoo, witchcraft, and black magic. Not all are pure of heart. Some seek power or money, even love."

"Seems like a sick way to find love." Sydney shook her head. "Honestly, Kade, this just sounds like a bunch of mumbo jumbo to me, but I've seen people kill for all kinds of reasons…even for a pair of damn sneakers."

"In Hoodoo, there is a substance called Van Van oil." Kade stood up, his face tightened. "Lemongrass is used to make it. I will need to contact my sources to find out the purposes of the oil, but I assure you the folks who use these tools are serious in their desires. The perp may be anointing the victims."

"Even if they aren't purposefully placing the oil there, there could have been some kind of cross contamination. I agree that we need more information on why someone uses the oil in the first place. It could help with determining a motive. What about the hemp and human hair? Why the hell go through all the trouble of making a rope with human hair when you can just go to Home Depot and get a synthetic rope?"

"Human hair and hemp have uses in witchcraft. My guess is some kind of cord magic, possibly intended to make death more painful. My understanding is that cord magic is not usually used as an actual rope to tie someone. I have heard of it being placed under a victim's bed, or such. The witch or mage could have used it as part of a ritual while they were binding the girl."

Witches? Mages? Vampires? Sydney suddenly felt like a fish out of water. This was exactly why she hated to deal with the supernatural. She was not part of that world. But a killer was a killer no matter how they did it or who they were. She had learned long ago that evil was not exclusively a supernatural phenomenon. Sydney contemplated turning the entire case over to Kade. She'd be done and could resume fighting normal, everyday human crime. But already the faces of these poor girls were ingrained in her mind, and she felt a duty to find their killers so they could be at peace. Besides, Sydney was too far into this case to simply turn it over to Kade. What she wouldn't admit was that she was too far into Kade to let him go.

"Ada, Kade, I don't see any tattoos on this girl's face. The other vic had them. You think maybe Jennings didn't get a chance to finish his work on her?"

"Maybe Jennings did the tattoo on her breast? And did the other tattoos post mortem? He could have been a human slave to whomever is killing these girls, but he wasn't the mage, and there definitely is magic here. I can feel it…there are remnants of it all around. But even though there are signs of magic, I am certain a vampire is behind these killings."

"Kade, Sydney…what the hell is this?" Both Kade and Sydney snapped their heads around to see what Adalee was talking about. They both knelt down and watched Adalee cradle the girl's chin in her left hand, while with her right she took out a long pair of tweezers. "There is something in here. Syd, flashlight please."

Sydney grabbed her flashlight, flipped it on and shined the light down the girl's throat. Kade reached around to lift the girl's head and helped to keep the mouth open so Adalee could work. Slowly she reached in and pulled the tweezers back out. "It looks like maybe a small scroll or a piece of paper?"

Kade held out his gloved hand and took it from her. The object was a red paper, folded into a five-sided star, a pentagram. He carefully unfolded it.

"Looks like someone's been practicing witchy origami. There's writing on it. Let me see." Sydney leaned in close to Kade, attempting to get a better view of the object. As her shoulder brushed his chest, the heat of his body enveloped her. Her nipples tightened in response. She needed to get this case finished soon before she lost her mind from lust. *Hello? Crime scene. Dead body.* Sydney pulled her thoughts back into focus and read the note.

Written in black ink, there were only four words. '*You will be mine*'. As she leaned toward the note, she smelled the faintest hint of cinnamon. She turned her head, her eyes locked on Kade's.

"You will be mine? What kind of note is that? Kade, do you smell that?" She knew he had super vamp senses. She wasn't sure if it was her imagination.

"Cinnamon? Yes, I smell it. It's a common ingredient in witchcraft, probably infused into the ink." Kade tried to keep a poker face as Sydney read the words. *Simone.* He had banished her from the country and from his bed. He would never be hers no matter whom she killed. Kade's protective nature urged him to take Sydney right then and there and lock her up to protect her from this evil woman. He knew that he had to tell Sydney. He needed to find a way to share with her what was happening so he could get her off the case without completely pissing her off. If he could get her alone, he could tell her everything. "I have to consult with a few people about what we found. I have a witch on retainer back home. Let's get the scene cleaned and then we can go back to my place and make some calls, together."

"All right, let's get the scene wrapped up," she agreed. "The faster we get this done, the sooner we can call this witch of yours."

Kade felt an enormous relief as she acquiesced. She was finally beginning to trust him, and they were starting to work as a team. He was acutely aware of the intense sexual connection growing between them, one that he wanted to explore as soon as he knew she was safe from Simone. Sydney was turning him inside out, and he suspected she was destined to be his, and not just for a night. Kade wanted to make love to her until she screamed his name in ecstasy. He wanted her to know that with every cell of her being, she was his.

For now, he needed to keep his feelings hidden. It was hard enough keeping his hands off of her every time he saw her, let alone torturing himself with thoughts of what would happen in the future. If Simone was indeed after him, she would see Sydney as competition to be eliminated. He would not let her be harmed, even if that meant taking her off the case. Better she hate him than end up dead.

Several hours passed before everyone had left the scene. Sydney continued inspecting the area as Kade called Luca. She carefully paced the perimeter of the alley, hoping she'd find something the killer left. A cold breeze swept across her neck, causing her to shiver. She looked back at Kade, who seemed unfazed, as if he hadn't felt it. She didn't think they were expecting rain tonight, but it was common to get thunderstorms in the summer.

As she moved further away from Kade, she heard laughing. A conversation? She couldn't be certain, but it sounded like a woman's voice. Sydney waved over to Kade, getting his attention and pointed down the small covered tunnel that ran between two of the row homes.

Sydney covered her nose as the stench of trickling, stagnant water hit her. The odor was overpowering; urine, rotted food, feces. Struggling to see where she was walking in the darkness, she dug in her vest to find her flashlight. Her fingers touched its metal casing and flipped the switch. A woman's laughter cackled in the distance. As if she was frozen, Sydney watched in awe as a small orb of light appeared about twenty feet away from her, floating in the air like a tuft of feathers. It flashed, instantly replaced by an apparition.

A ghostly woman with a beautiful face and long flowing black hair hovered in the cramped, dank alley. Sydney could hardly believe what she was seeing. While the woman seemed to have the outline of a body, there were no feet, only a long, red dress that stopped a foot off the ground. The woman began to laugh maniacally as she glared at Sydney. The laugh died into deadly silence as the woman's lips straightened into a tight line.

Sydney had dealt with enough women to know that this one was aggressive; there was no mistaking a bitch on wheels. Ghost or no ghost, she had no intention of letting any woman frighten her off the street. Sydney quickly reached for her gun. She had no idea what killed ghosts but she wasn't going down without a fight.

"Kade! Could use a little help down here!"

"He! Is! Mine!" the ghost shrieked.

In a flash, the spectral woman flew toward Sydney, and she fired off a round. Dodging the apparition, she fell into the gritty, wet alleyway and everything went black. She fumbled for her broken flashlight, her heart racing. She felt Kade pick her up off the ground and promptly wrapped her arms around his neck, allowing him to carry her out of the tunnel.

"I'm good. Really, you can put me down. I just fell, that's all. She's gone," she said, aware that she was enjoying him picking her up a little too much. She blew out a breath as Kade gently let go of her legs, placed her upright and pulled out of the embrace.

"Sydney, are you sure you're okay? I heard you scream for me. And then I heard a shot. What happened down there? I sensed no one. No humans. No supernaturals. Wait, who do you mean, *she*?"

"Yeah, I'm fine." *Really? A floating ghost woman and my vampire sees nothing?* Doubt crept into her mind. "I have to tell you…it's going to sound crazy. I heard voices, a woman. She was laughing. In the tunnel, there was just this small light and then it turned into this ghost She was beautiful, with long black hair, and then she seemed like she wanted to attack me. That's when I called for you…and then she screamed, 'He is mine,' and rushed me, and that's when I got off a shot. Do bullets even kill ghosts? All I know is she missed me and then I fell down. And shit!" Sydney looked down at her clothes. She was covered in slimy, malodorous water. "Look at me! Ewwww. This is so gross…I gotta get home and take a shower. What the hell was that thing back there, anyway?"

"Wait, Sydney. Let me see you and make sure you are okay," Kade said, checking her for injuries. There was no blood and she appeared uninjured as she claimed.

"I'm fine. Really, I just fell when that…that 'woman' flew at me. I'm telling you, Kade, I didn't really believe in ghosts before tonight. But that was no person. I don't know what the hell it was." Sydney shook her head in frustration.

While Sydney may have been surprised by her spectral experience, Kade was shocked at her description. It was Simone. But how had she transported herself as an apparition? Magic? Someone or something was helping her. He had to get Sydney home and away from this place.

On the ride back to Kade's brownstone, they told Luca what had happened in the alley. Kade knew that though he didn't mention Simone by name, Luca would know from Sydney's description exactly who had visited them in the alley.

"I want you to locate Ilsbeth," Kade told Luca. Ilsbeth was a local witch from the French Quarter. She was cagey at times and not always easy to deal with, but she and Kade had been allies for several years. He could not claim they were close friends, but she could be trusted.

"You got it. I'll call her on my way over to Eden. I was planning to go there to feed and see Tristan. Do you want me to update him on today's events?"

"Thank you, yes. Please let him know what happened, but do tell him up in his private office. We cannot afford to be overheard. Tell Tristan that Sydney and I will be at the brownstone for the rest of the night."

Sydney shot him a look of surprise, but didn't voice her concern. *I'm going to be there all night? Working the case? Or working Kade?* They did need to go over the details and work through the facts of the case. She suspected Kade wasn't being completely honest with her. She hadn't pressed him back at the crime scene, but she would damn sure find out after she got a shower and some food.

When they arrived, the garage door opened to let the limo in under the house. As they entered Kade's home, Sydney took in the sight of the mahogany walled rooms. Its décor was both rich and masculine, suiting Kade.

"Nice place. I love the woodwork. Dark, but beautiful," she commented.

"Thanks. It's a rental that belongs to Tristan. As much as I like visiting, I have no plans on living here. As soon as the case is over, I need to get back to New Orleans."

Sydney wasn't sure why she felt sick hearing him say that he was going to leave. She'd known he wasn't going to stay here forever. A small part of her had hoped that maybe he'd visit longer if he found something, or someone important enough. His statement spurred her to build up that emotional wall she'd learned to do to protect her heart. She didn't want to have feelings for him, but she was having a hard time denying her emerging desire for the mysterious vampire. She needed to get back to business…talk about the case, in an attempt to shift her focus.

"Kade, can you show me to the bathroom? I've got to clean up."

"Yes, sorry. This way." Kade would love to show her his shower…with her naked and him thrusting into her against the tiled walls, he thought. Silently they walked up the stairway and down a long hallway. He opened a door and gestured for her to enter. "Here you go. I can have your clothes laundered while we work. Just put them in the laundry chute. I will call for the maid to take care of them. There are towels inside the closet, and there is a black robe hanging on the back of the door that you can wear until your clothes are finished being cleaned. Just come down when you are done. I'll have some Chinese food delivered while you're bathing."

As they stood alone in the quiet hallway, Kade's eyes fell to her lips. He took her hand in his, trailing his thumb over her palm. His gaze moved to meet hers, and he fought the urge to kiss her.

"Sydney…" he began.

"I just want you to know that I was glad you were there today," she interrupted, her voice trembling. "Um…I mean…I know I wasn't hurt, but it felt good to have someone at my back. I don't know what the hell that thing was tonight in the alley, but I'd be lying if I said it didn't shake me up a little. So anyway, thanks."

Before Kade had a chance to respond, she tugged her hand out of his, entered the bathroom and quickly shut the door.

Sydney leaned against the back of the bathroom door and sighed. She had almost kissed him. What was she doing? *Get your head out of your ass. He just told you that he's not staying. He's leaving and going back to New Orleans.* Frustrated, she reached over and turned on the hot water, stripped out of her rank clothes and tossed them down the chute. A maid was going to *launder* her clothes? *Must be nice,* she thought. She stepped underneath the hot spray of the water and let the tension run down the drain.

As she washed her hair with shampoo, she noticed that it smelled of strawberries. *A vampire with strawberry shampoo?* She smiled, thinking of Kade. As she washed her body with soap, she let her hands run over her breasts. What would it feel like to have Kade's strong hands massage her breasts? To have him suck her nipples? Sydney closed her eyes and moaned, letting her hand wander down over her bare, waxed mound. She slipped a finger into her folds, finding her core. Gently circling her most sensitive area, she imagined that it was Kade touching her. She groaned as the tingle built in her womb, shaking as she came. Sydney let her forehead rest against the dark blue tile, afraid to face him.

Kade nearly died when he heard Sydney moan and smelled her arousal. He wanted to charge up the stairs, break down the door and fuck her senseless. Didn't she know that vampires had enhanced senses? Or maybe she knew exactly what she was doing? As he listened to her pleasuring herself upstairs, he couldn't hold back. He sat back in the large leather chair and unzipped his pants, pulling out his rock-hard cock. Was she thinking of him as she touched herself? He stroked his shaft, faster and faster. He could not believe he was doing this in the den, but shit, she made a man lose his mind. Another moan from upstairs. He could sense she was close. He glided his palm up and down his length, bringing himself closer to climax. She was coming. He was coming. Kade cursed as his seed went flying onto his pants.

"Ah…fuck. What a fucking mess. What are you doing?" *What am I doing? Great, now I'm talking aloud to myself, just fucking great.* He was going to need to see a therapist after this little incident. He grabbed a wad of tissues, jumped up, and stomped up the stairs to his bedroom. He needed to get changed before she saw him.

Kade jumped in the shower, washed, and quickly dressed in a pair of worn jeans and a black cotton t-shirt. He heard her in the shower. If he hurried, he could get downstairs first. He was just about down the flight of stairs when the doorbell rang; the Chinese food. He quickly paid the driver and set off to get things ready in the kitchen.

Sydney padded into the kitchen wearing just his robe, and sat at the granite counter bar. Relaxed from her shower, she smiled at him.

"So, Kade, not to be rude or anything, but vampires and Chinese food? What gives? Thought you guys only had blood on the menu. Unless you got that delivered too?"

Kade laughed. "Ah, you do have quite a bit to learn about us, and I would love to be the one to teach you." He winked at her, causing her to blush. "Vampires do need blood to survive, but we only need to feed a couple of times a week. We can eat food, and it tastes great, but it will not keep us alive; only blood does that. My favorite food is Peking duck, but I also got Szechuan shrimp, dumplings, moo shu chicken, and garlic broccoli. I wasn't sure what you liked."

"So, are we having company?" Sydney laughed.

Kade shook his head, no.

"Well, it smells wonderful. I'm so hungry. And just so you know, I love everything you ordered…it's as if you knew what I'd like."

"You are very welcome. And I do believe I know what you would like," he teased, desire in his eyes.

Looking down into her shrimp, she tried to hide her embarrassment. He knew she wanted him. Then it occurred to her that he might have known what she was doing in the shower. *Shit.* She was hoping that he wouldn't hear or smell anything, with the shower going and that delicious strawberry shampoo. Guess she was wrong.

"So, you like it spicy? I must confess that I love it that way as well. I just can't seem to get mine hot enough."

Oh yeah, she loved it hot all right. Sydney gazed into his sexy blue eyes and smiled. She would have loved to have had some pithy response but her mouth was full of duck and she enjoyed his play on words.

After they finished, Kade poured her a glass of brandy. He lit a fire, and they sat on twin leather recliners that faced the fireplace. "So, what's the deal with the note?" Sydney wanted to sit back and relax, but knew it was time to get down to business. The man had secrets, and she was going to find out what the hell was going on. "I know you're keeping something from me. We're partners. It's time to talk." She stared at the crackling fire, hoping it would make it easier for him to tell her if she wasn't looking at him.

"You know, we live a very long time. There is a specific vampire I suspect is involved in these murders. Luca found her scent at the Jennings' scene. I wasn't sure, but today, after the note, the apparition you saw…it's her."

Sydney knew she wasn't going to like whatever he had to say. But she needed the truth.

"Whatever this is, whoever this is, you can tell me. Evil is evil. Supernatural or human, all races can be touched by it."

Kade was aware that she was trying to make him feel better, but there was nothing that could do that when it came to Simone and what she had done to those girls. He stood, getting closer to the fireplace, with his back to Sydney.

"Simone, Simone Barret. She was turned in the 1800s. I found her on the streets and took her in. I was lonely, we…we were lovers."

Sydney cringed. Okay, so this was it. She pulled her knees up to her chest and kept still. What had she thought? That he was a virgin? Of course not. The man had lovers. He was a hot, sexy vampire. Logic told her that he'd probably had hundreds of lovers over the years. So why did she feel jealous all of a sudden?

"I have not had as many lovers as you would think." Kade turned around and gazed directly into Sydney's eyes as if he could read her thoughts. "Sure, I am a vampire, and it is no secret that we often have sex during feeding, but that is all it is, sex. Lovers have been few, a person to share my home and life with…but there has been no one I have ever been in love with. Simone, she was vulnerable and I…I was lonely. We helped each other. She had been trained in magic, Voodoo, and she betrayed me. When I found out she had captured and tortured several young women, I banished her. I should have killed her on the spot, but times were different back then. I thought if I banished her, that would be punishment enough, but it appears that I was wrong."

Sydney could not believe what she was hearing. He had a lover, an evil lover, who killed and tortured girls and now was coming back to kill more girls? *What the hell?* She wanted to get up and leave right then, but decided to hear him out. She knew that things were not always how they seemed. She stood up and walked over to Kade.

"So, what? Are you in love with her? Why is she here? To get you back?

Why kill the girls? She's in this city?" She heard her voice getting louder and louder; so much for staying calm.

"I am over two hundred years old. You must understand that while I loved her, I am not nor was I ever *in love* with her; there is a difference. Why is she back? Revenge, I suspect. I banished her and maybe even broke her heart, if she had one. But if you could have seen what she did to those girls…I should have killed her." Kade blew out a breath. "And why here? My guess is Tristan."

"Tristan?"

"Yes, Tristan's sister, Katarina, was one of the tortured girls. He came to me seeking my help. He knew it was Simone who took the girls. He offered pack protection in exchange for finding his sister. It was how we met and later became friends. But Simone, she knew it was Tristan who told me. She may have come here seeking to stir up trouble in his territory. She would have known I would come to his aid eventually. What she didn't count on was that Tristan would be smart enough to recognize right away that a vampire was stirring up problems in his community, even before the first death occurred. He contacted me right away."

Sydney's thoughts were spinning. Simone was here in Philadelphia? How did she know where they were? Why did she come as a ghost?

"Okay, so lover girl has an ax to grind. She comes up here instead of New Orleans to get at Tristan? And to get back at you? Not buying that. I get that she's mad at Tristan for ratting her out to you. But she isn't from this area. You said she left the country. And what the hell is with the ghost? Why not just show up in person?"

"My best guess is that she is not here physically. She may have a mage or witch helping her. Possibly vampire or human minions, maybe both. Jennings belonged to her, there could be others."

"Nice trick, huh?" There was a reason Sydney didn't get involved with the supernatural, and this was it: human slaves, witchcraft, Voodoo. She felt she had heard enough for tonight. As much as she wanted to be with Kade, she had an overwhelming need to get home.

Kade approached Sydney, taking her hands in his. "Sydney, I have given this some thought, and I believe Simone is somewhere in New Orleans. Somehow…maybe through magic…she is projecting herself here. I need to go search for her there. I know you want to work this case, but things are going to get more dangerous. I need to keep you safe. I am going to talk with Tristan and leave tomorrow night."

She had felt the electric desire running up her arms and throughout her body, but at his words, she snatched her hands away from him. Who the hell was he to tell her that she had to get off the case? And he was leaving?

"Listen, Kade, if you want to jump a plane back to the bayou, be my guest, but I'm not getting off this case just because you think there could be danger. Danger is part of my job; I'm a big girl. A girl who happens to own a lot of guns and knows how to use them. There is no way I am just giving up this case while you go off chasing an old girlfriend, *so* not happening." She paused and glanced away. She couldn't just stand around and let innocent women be killed in her city, she had to help find the perpetrator. "Listen, I appreciate you telling me everything. I need to think on this…get some sleep. Ada may have run more trace, and I want to get down to the station tomorrow to talk it through with her. Where are my clothes?"

"Upstairs bathroom," he said, gesturing to the stairs. "I asked Sara to put your clean clothes in there when she finished with them."

"Thanks." Sydney set her glass on the table, avoiding eye contact as she went upstairs to get dressed. As she worked through the details of what Kade had told her, it wasn't making sense. She found it hard to believe this was as simple as a lover scorned. Why all the drama with the girls? The ritual? The tattoos? Something wasn't right. Maybe Simone did want revenge, but there was something else. Sydney wasn't sure what the missing puzzle piece was, but she certainly wasn't going to let Kade push her off the case.

Kade refrained from chasing after Sydney despite his desire to do so. Knowing that she was so close to his bedroom made him crazy. He wanted to kiss her full lips, taste her and make her his. Although doing so at this point would only draw attention to her, and that was not something he would do. She was already in enough danger. Tomorrow he would request that she be taken off the case. She'd be angry with him, but at least she'd be safe.

He had to get back to New Orleans and find Simone. He planned on questioning Ilsbeth to find out what Simone might be trying to accomplish with the oils and the girls. She was up to something, and he was going to find out what it was. This time she would not go unpunished.

While he was gone, he'd ask Tristan to keep an eye on Sydney, even though he hated that she might go to Tristan for more than friendship. It was killing him to know that Sydney and Tristan had been sexually involved, so asking the Alpha was not something he wanted to do, but he needed to try to keep her safe and he could trust Tristan to do that.

They rode in silence on the way back to Sydney's condo. She stared out the window, willing herself not to look at Kade. She struggled with her emotions, still aroused by their earlier encounter. Even though she knew it was irrational, a twinge of jealousy ate at her, as she thought about Simone. As the limo pulled up to her building, doubt crept into Sydney's mind. She sat still, unsure about leaving Kade. Her hesitation gave Kade the opportunity to move closer to her. She reached for the door handle, and Kade placed his hand on hers.

"Sydney love, after I take care of Simone, I will be back for you. We have unfinished business."

"Kade…I…" Her words trailed off as Kade pressed his lips to hers. Sydney kissed him back, slowly allowing him access. Kade reached around and held her by the nape of her neck, deepening the kiss. It was passionate, yet tender. Sydney knew she had to go. She shouldn't let herself get distracted by a man, but he tasted so good, and she wanted him here and now, inside her. She wanted more, but he was leaving. Coming to her senses, she reluctantly retreated from him, averting her gaze to the floor.

"Um…yeah…goodnight, Kade." Her hands shook as she pushed open the door. Flustered as she was, she still had enough wits about her to get up and out of the car on two feet. *Just keep on walking, girl.*

Chapter Eight

Sydney woke to the sounds of the city: beeping horns, trucks, yelling, and laughter. It didn't bother her, though; she was used to the constant buzz of urban, background noise. The cacophony meant Sydney was alive, and so was the city. Like the swashing hum of the ocean, it was soothing to her ears.

It was late afternoon when she heard her door buzzer go off. She doubted it would be Kade. While he had told her that he was old enough to go outside during the day, it weakened him. And besides, why would he come by her condo when he was returning to New Orleans? She wondered if he was packing and when he was leaving. She kept thinking of the kiss: hot, passionate, erotic. She'd fantasized about melting into his arms, making love to him right there in the back of the limo. It had taken every bit of self-control to pull away and go home without him. She had to force herself to remember she was irritated with him because he wanted her off the case, and that he was about to go chasing after a psycho ex.

She felt frustrated, wishing she could order him to stay, but then that was part of what attracted her to him. He was strong, authoritative, domineering. She laughed. What was wrong with her? She swore she would not pine over a guy, especially some bossy vamp. She had plenty of men on her dance card. *Whatever, Syd. Get over it. He's leaving anyway.*

Checking her security camera, she saw a man in a uniform holding what appeared to be a vase. He held up a name tag, indicating he was from Belle's Petals, a local flower shop. She clicked on the security panel, answering the call.

"Hello. Can I help you?"

"Yeah, I'm looking for Condo 225 B. Miss Willows."

"Okay, come on up," she said, buzzing him in.

There was a knock at the door. Sydney peered through the safety hole in her door and all she could see was red.

"Delivery for Miss Sydney Willows," he announced.

Sydney slowly opened the door, gasping at the sight. There were more roses than she had ever seen in her life.

"Oh my God, they're beautiful! Here, put them on the dining room table," she instructed.

As soon as she ushered the deliveryman into the hallway and locked her door, she ran over to inspect her gift. She was astonished at the five dozen long-stemmed red roses tastefully arranged in an enormous Tiffany crystal vase. She leaned into the flowers to sniff one of the buds, which smelled heavenly. Attached to a plastic holder was a small, red envelope. There was a single name written in calligraphy on it; *'Sydney'*. She gingerly opened the envelope, not wanting to accidentally tear the card. She pulled out the card and read it. 'Dearest Sydney, Your kiss is still on my mind. Be good while I'm gone love. I will return soon so we can finish what we started. Yours, Kade.'

Her first thought was that he'd mentioned the kiss. The hot, steamy kiss. He had not forgotten that. But 'be good'? Did the man seriously think a bunch of flowers, albeit an incredibly gorgeous and very expensive bunch of flowers, was going to convince her to leave the case willingly? She knew he wanted her safe, but it was her job to solve cases. She laughed at the irony. He infuriated her and aroused her all at once, and no matter how hard she'd tried, she couldn't stop thinking about him.

Sydney glanced at the time on her cell phone. Damn, it was almost six o'clock and she was late. Sydney had promised Adalee earlier in the day that she'd meet her at the station. She considered what Kade had told her about the danger they faced. She padded down the hallway to her guest bedroom. In the far corner, an antique cedar trunk sat against the wall. She flipped open the top, pulling out several blankets. Reaching inside, she retrieved two metallic cases. She laid them on the carpet and unzipped one.

Tristan had given her these as a birthday gift, having known that she loved weapons of all kinds. A dozen silver knives of different sizes lay sparkling, encased in foam liners. Sydney grinned as she ran her fingers across the flat side of the sharp blades. "Thank you, Tris. The gift that keeps on giving."

She moved to the second case, which held a small crossbow with a strap that could be slung over the shoulder, several wooden darts, and five large, wooden stakes. Sydney was well trained in how to use weapons to kill both humans and supernaturals, but she'd never imagined using them before now. Usually her Sig Sauer was more than enough to bring down a human, but whoever was killing these girls clearly was not in that category.

Sydney gathered the weapons she intended to use and put them next to her jeans and t-shirt. She planned to arm up before going on duty tonight. She tested the feel of the stake in her hand as she walked toward the bathroom, slashing it through the air. She would have no problem turning a vamp into ash, if needed. She shoved the stake in the pocket of her robe, hung it up on a hook, and went to turn the shower on. It was getting late, and she wanted to get going.

Sydney reveled in the hot spray of the shower. Feeling relaxed, she yearned to stay a little bit longer, but didn't have the time. As she shut off the water, she heard a hiss coming from outside her door. Grabbing a towel, she haphazardly dried herself, and threw on her robe. Someone was in the living room.

Did Kade stop by before leaving? No, Kade would never break into my condo. Who's here and how the fuck did they get in? Thinking quickly, she reached into the vanity cabinet, where she kept a spare gun for emergencies, and peeked out the door. Nothing. Maybe she was just being paranoid. She looked both ways down the hallway and saw no one. Quietly, she tiptoed down the hallway into the living room. Before she had a chance to look around the room, something rammed into her, sending her and her gun flying across the room.

She lost her bearings for a second, stunned from the hit. As pain tore through her body, it brought her back to focus, making her remember where she was. *What the hell was that?*

A huge man stood across the room. He had to be at least three hundred pounds, and was bald with a scar across his face.

"Hey, chica, you think you can kill me with that gun of yours? I got news for you, we vamps don't die easily. My Mistress is not pleased with you. She doesn't like that you have been sniffing around her mate."

Kade?

"Yes, that's right. My Mistress says you are a distraction, but maybe I will have you for myself before I kill you. You like big men? Oh yeah. I might break you in half, but man, it will be sweet." Did this sick vampire think he was going to rape her? Good fucking luck with that. Too bad, she had other plans for her attacker. *Keep him talking.*

"You always take orders from a girl?" She scrambled to cover herself, keeping her eyes on him as she used her peripheral vision to search for the gun.

"I only obey my Mistress. And you…you have angered the Mistress." He stalked toward her. "She wants you taken care of, but I didn't expect it was going to be so much fun. Your blood smells so sweet. I'm gonna have a nice little taste. How 'bout we play a game before you die?"

Sydney slowly scooted backward on her buttocks and hands, inching toward the kitchen. *Where's the damn gun?* She spied it over near the refrigerator. Then she remembered the stake in her pocket, but in order to use it, she would need him close to her. She pretended to move toward the gun, hoping he would think she was going for it.

"You are a bad little girl, aren't you? You think you gonna reach that gun? Stupid concha. You really think you can run from me? Maybe I will fuck you so hard that you can't walk before I drain you. I am gonna make you bleed. Oh yeah…you'll scream for me. I love to hear a girl scream," he snarled.

Sydney would die before she let him rape her. There was no way in hell he was taking her down without a blazing fight. She'd let him keep thinking she wanted the gun. She wasn't stupid. Sydney knew the gun might slow him down, but it wouldn't kill him. No, he'd just be even more pissed. She needed to use the stake; that was the only thing that would kill him. She just needed to get him closer so she could drive the stake into his heart. Closer without getting herself killed in the process.

"You want me, huh? How about you bring it. And while you're at it, I got a little message for that bitch of a Mistress who has you leashed." With those words, she fake-lunged for the gun, hoping to draw him to her.

In a flash, he flew across the room and grabbed her by the throat with one hand; he smashed her head several times against the refrigerator, jamming her up against the wall, leaving her feet dangling off the floor.

"I'm goin' to enjoy this. Nice and slow," he grunted, the spray of his saliva hitting her face. He weakened his grip around her neck and reached for his groin.

As he fumbled to unbutton his pants, Sydney quickly kneed him in the *cojones*, she'd remembered that much from Spanish.

"Puta." He slammed her head hard against the wall.

Sydney saw stars, her eyes teared as the pain sliced through her skull. Using every last bit of strength, she yanked the stake out of her pocket. Choking, she prepared to strike.

"Tell your Mistress," she spat, "tell that bitch that I said I'll see her in hell!" Sydney drove the stake up into his heart, and he instantly disintegrated into a pile of ash. Her body crashed to the floor as she lost consciousness.

Kade had argued with Luca on the way over to Sydney's. He knew his friend hated disagreeing with him, never wanting to appear disrespectful or insubordinate. Luca had always been respectful of Kade, having owed him his very life ten times over. But Kade knew Luca would never forget they'd discovered the girls in the barn. If Simone was back in the country, they both knew there was no time to stop and play kissy face with the nice detective. It wasn't as if he didn't understand Luca's point, but he wanted to say goodbye in person, alone.

When they pulled up to Sydney's condo, Kade insisted Luca stay in the limo. He went to push the buzzer, but no one answered. He rang Sydney's cell phone, but no one answered. *Where is she?* As someone opened the door to leave the building, Kade slid into the condo complex unnoticed. When he approached the door and knocked, it swung wide open. Tearing into her condo, he yelled for her and searched her apartment.

"Sydney! Where are you? Sydney!"

His heart sank as he entered the kitchen. Sydney was sprawled on the floor, wearing only a robe, which was spread wide open exposing her naked body. Next to her was a pile of ash. *Vampire.* Blood, he could smell blood,

Sydney's blood. He could hear her heartbeat. She was alive. He knelt down and gently lifted her head, speaking to her softly.

"Sydney, love, can you hear me? Damn it to hell," he cursed when she didn't respond. Gently kissing her on the forehead, he thanked God she was still breathing. "It's going to be okay. I'm here now. I'll take care of you."

Needing to see where and how badly she was injured, he turned her head slightly to inspect her wound. A tiny cut bled from the back of her skull. Later she'd have a goose egg and a bad headache, but she'd be okay. Kade held a handkerchief to her wound. He shook his head, suspecting that Simone had sent a vampire to Philadelphia. And his girl had staked him well and dead. But if one vampire was here, more could be on their way. Kade needed the protection of his home and security team to keep her safe.

He had to get her out of here. Kade reached for his cell and texted Luca. They needed to collect Sydney, take her to the jet and get to New Orleans, now. Luca ran into the apartment, quickly finding Kade on the kitchen floor next to Sydney. Kade had forgotten her nudity. Glancing up to Luca then back to Sydney's naked body, he pulled her robe shut and covered her. She was his only.

"Grab a blanket and pillow from her bedroom and let's go. I'll carry her down," Kade told him.

Luca promptly did as he was asked. Within minutes, they'd all made it safely to the car and were on their way to the airport.

With Sydney in his arms, Kade gently brushed the hair away from her face, twirling a blond curl with his finger. He was overwhelmed with guilt. He'd known damn well what Simone was capable of, and he had left Sydney alone anyway. Kade's heart squeezed as he studied her face. She looked peaceful as she slept, vulnerable. He tucked the blanket around her neck, ensuring her warmth. Nothing would happen to her now that she was with him. She'd be spitting tacks when she woke up to find she was in New Orleans, but from now on, she wasn't getting to call the shots. Those days were over, and she would just need to deal with it. There was no way she was leaving him. She was his, and he would protect her with his life.

Chapter Nine

Sydney woke in a warm, soft bed that smelled of lilac. She stirred, her eyes fluttering as she was blinded by the light. She had a killer headache, and brought her hand to her head. *Where am I?* She wondered if she was dreaming. *Need Advil, now.* If she could only get out of bed and look for her pills, she'd be good. Sydney placed her palms flat against the bed and slowly pushed up. She felt soft but strong hands easing her back down into the bed as she heard Kade's smooth voice.

"Easy there, everything's okay. Just lie down, and I'll get you some water. You in pain, love?"

"Kade? Where am I?" Sydney was starting to panic as memories flashed into her head. She looked around, struggling to get her bearings. "Oh my God. A vampire. My condo."

"I know, but you're safe now…"

"Am I…in a plane? How the hell did I get in a plane? Where are we going?" She had traveled enough to recognize the hum of the engines.

Kade smiled. It didn't take her very long to try to control the situation. That was his girl. "Yes, we're in my plane, and we're on our way to my home in New Orleans. But you're safe now. The vampire who attacked you…not so much. You took care of him back there. He's dead."

Kade resisted asking details about her attack. He didn't want her to talk if she wasn't ready, but it was hard to ignore the fingerprint bruise marks that were starting to appear around her neck. She had been strangled.

"You have a small cut on the back of your head, but it's stopped bleeding. I iced it, but I can get you some more. Here, take these for your headache." He handed her pills and a bottle of water and sat down next to her. "Sydney, about what happened at the condo…I'm sorry."

"Considering that I can barely open my eyes, I'll forgive the fact that I'm in a plane heading to New Orleans. Couldn't you just take me to a hospital or something?" She was just too tired to fight, but when she regained her strength, Kade had some explaining to do. On the one hand, she would prefer to work the case in Philly, on the off chance more dead girls showed up. On the other hand, if Kade was going after Simone, she wanted to be there. Payback was a bitch, and after her little encounter with the sumo wrestler vamp, she was so up for it.

Sydney was starting to remember pieces of what had happened back in her home. It wasn't her first fight, but she'd be lying if she said it hadn't shaken her up a bit. She wasn't used to battling against vampires, or any other supernaturals, but she was a fighter and that was what counted. She lay her head back, closed her eyes, and took a deep breath. She glanced up at Kade.

"I was in the shower and heard a noise. He slammed me to the floor, before I had a chance to see who was in my condo. I always keep a spare gun hidden in the bathroom, and a few other places, you know, just in case. A girl can't be too careful. Anyway, the gun went flying into the kitchen. Before my shower, I'd been going through my weapons, and I was fooling around with a stake and shoved it in the pocket of my robe. But the gun I had in the bathroom…it didn't have silver bullets or anything, so I knew it wouldn't do much good. I played like I was going for the gun."

Sydney shook her head. She suddenly remembered the vampire saying something about Kade being his Mistress's mate. *Is Kade married? He said they were lovers, but did he marry her?* "He said Simone sent him to deal with me since, apparently, I was messing with her *mate*." She looked to Kade, hoping for a response. *He must be good at poker,* she thought, because he remained expressionless.

"He thought he could play a little before killing me. I don't even know how he got in…broke into my apartment." Her voice trailed off. She stared at the water bottle, unable to look at him when she said the words. "He…he was going to rape me. I staked him instead." She fought back tears, knowing how close she'd come to being violated, killed. Kade was about to interrupt, but she held up her hand, preventing him from speaking. "Kade, please. Don't say anything. You warned me. I'm a big girl who makes her own decisions. Rape, violence, it's not new to me. Every day this happens…just not to me."

Kade didn't want to show emotion, lest he freak the hell out right in front of Sydney. He was so furious that another vampire had dared to lay a hand on her that he wanted to break something. But he resisted, aware that any further violence would only demonstrate to Sydney what monsters vampires were. Now was not the time. What she needed was comfort. He needed to calm her, soothe her. He decided to save the anger, to harness it for when he obliterated his enemy. Simone, and whoever else was helping her, would pay dearly for hurting Sydney. As incensed as he was, he needed to help her heal, physically and emotionally.

He moved to lie down beside her, and held her in his arms, cradling her against his chest. Instead of fighting him, Sydney laid her head across his chest and allowed him to hold her, to care for her.

"Kade, I'm sorry. You need to know that this is who I am. I'm a fighter. And what just happened…I just can't forget it. I plan on finding this bitch and taking her out. The dead girls, and now this. I have a feeling that it'll only continue. Killers like Simone, they don't usually stop. They hone their craft, believing they're smarter than the cops, but we usually get them. She'll make a mistake, something…I sure as hell hope we get some clues about where she is down in New Orleans."

Kade kissed the top of her head. His heart swelled at his brave warrior's words. She'd just been attacked, and here she was ready to get back in the fight. He knew that telling her 'no' would be useless. He would put a security detail on her once they got home. *Home? His home. Their home.* He would protect her, so this never happened again. No matter how tough she thought she was, a vampire could easily kill her. She had gotten lucky back in the condo. She wasn't even trained to fight with vampires; a few stakes didn't make a human safe.

As he held her, Kade felt Sydney start to doze off to sleep and he considered how right it felt to have her in his arms. He heard a knock at the cabin door.

"Come in," he said. Kade continued to lie motionless in the bed with Sydney, unwilling to disturb her. He wasn't ready to let her go yet.

Luca stepped into the bedroom and raised an eyebrow at him. Kade knew his friend was wary of the woman he'd brought into their lives. Luca didn't trust humans, believing they were weak, easily broken.

"Kade, we're landing in about thirty minutes. How's the detective?"

"She'll be fine tomorrow. Right now, she needs rest. I will make sure she sleeps so she heals. Is security in place for when we land?"

"Yes, it's all in place. Etienne and Xavier are meeting us at the airport to help with the transfer. Dominique is at the compound securing things."

"Thanks, tell Dom that I'll need her help with Sydney when we get there. Make sure they all know she is arriving. Also, make sure they understand that she is under my protection and must not be touched. Am I clear?" Kade knew the other vampires might feel tempted with a new human on site. While they often had human donors and staff work at the compound, he did not want anyone to think she was available for their needs. She was his.

"Yes, it will all be ready. Do you need help with Miss Willows?"

"No thanks, I've got her. Just make sure Etienne and Xavier are ready to go. I don't want to waste time at the airport. Simone could have minions anywhere at this point. We need to get to a safe location. Any word from Ilsbeth?"

"Yes, she's been in seclusion with her coven. I summoned her to the compound, and she's expected to arrive tomorrow."

"Thanks. We'll need her assistance locating Simone. We also need to get details on what kind of magic is being used…why the girls were killed in the manner they were. Something is off."

As Luca left, Kade pulled the blanket up over Sydney's shoulders. He sighed, relieved that they'd soon be back in New Orleans. He could feel his power increasing, thrumming throughout his body as they got closer to the city. He breathed in the scent of the fragile woman who lay against his chest. He swore that no one was going to hurt Sydney again and live to talk about it.

Chapter Ten

Sydney woke in the middle of the night, finding herself naked in a strange bed. *Nice. This is turning out to be a fine damn week.* Not that she generally had a problem with nudity, but it was a little disconcerting to know someone had undressed her somewhere between thirty thousand feet and here…wherever 'here' was. She guessed she was at Kade's house…well, she sure as hell hoped that was where she was. She scanned her surroundings, surprised by the feminine décor. The violet bedroom was decorated with cream, shabby-chic furniture. If she hadn't known better, she would have thought she was in a Vermont bed and breakfast.

"Hey, Sunshine, 'bout time you woke up. My ass is getting sore sitting here playing nursemaid."

Sydney caught sight of a beautiful, tall, red-haired woman sitting in a large white leather chair.

"Nursemaid? Really? Okay, number one, I'm fine." Sydney winced as she sat up in bed, covering her chest with the sheet. She felt like shit, but she wasn't about to let 'Ginger' think that. The stranger's unearthly beauty and pale skin led her to surmise that her companion was a vampire. *Show no fear.* "Number two, where's Kade?"

"Yeah, okay. Well, Kade says you are not fine. And with Simone looking for your pretty little ass, I would be a little more grateful for a personal guard." The woman walked across the room, opened a large wardrobe, and held up a dress, giving Sydney a cold smile. "I guessed your size and brought over some clothes. Your purse is in the bathroom. Luca brought it…thought you might need it. Shoes are in the closet. As for Kade, he should be here soon. So you might as well know that you really don't look so great. Might want to go take a shower." She put the dress back into the wardrobe and opened another door. "Bathroom's here. Robe and slippers are in there too. Just like the freakin' Hilton, huh? So, guess that's about it. As soon as Kade gets here, I'm done. Xavier will be on next."

Sydney had had just about enough of the welcome speech. She felt as though she was in a bad horror movie.

"Thanks for the tour. But for the record, while it's true that Simone sent someone to attack me, I don't need a guard. You can ask the last vamp…oh, that's right, you can't, because he's now a pile of ash." Sydney sat up straighter, trying to appear as if she wasn't in pain. "I'm not planning on staying here long, but I appreciate the clothes."

The strange woman zipped across the room and was face to face with Sydney within seconds.

"Sydney, darling, I work for Kade, not you. If he says you need a guard, you get one. If you have a problem with that, take it up with Kade. I follow orders…that's how this goes. And if you like living, human, you should accept it." And with that, she strode out of the room and slammed the door.

Sydney shrugged, irritated with the encounter and left wondering what the stranger's relationship to Kade was. Her priorities at the moment were getting showered and fed. After that, she was leaving. There was no way in hell she was spending her days living in a house full of vampires. She recalled the compassionate way Kade had tenderly held her on the plane. There was no denying the desire he'd awakened inside her, but she wanted no part of his world. Living in his home wasn't an option. She reasoned that she could get a room at the Hotel Monteleone and work with Kade from there. She was willing to continue her partnership with him until they found Simone, or another dead girl showed up in Philly.

Sydney's thoughts moved to the case. There was so much to do. She needed to call into her office, let them know what happened. Panicked, she remembered that she had no weapons with her. *Where is my gun?* She walked over to the wardrobe and retrieved her purse, thankful that Kade's brooding friend had thought to bring it. Well, at least something had gone right; wallet, cell and charger were there, but no gun. Her weapons, that she'd so carefully prepared, were back in her condo. She felt naked, and it had nothing to do with her nudity. She clicked through her contacts and pressed the call button for Tristan. He picked up.

"Tristan! Thank God."

"Hey, Sydney. You okay? Kade called me and told me about the vampire. Listen, Syd…I need to talk to you." There was a period of silence as if he was seeking the right words. "Kade said that he told you everything about Simone. I know I should have told you, but I was just hoping that it wasn't her."

"Don't worry about it. I know you guys have a connection to her. But Tristan, this is just another killer. We'll get her."

"But, that's just it. You don't know what she's capable of…what she did. Aw hell. I just don't want to see you hurt. Before you even say it, I know it's your job to protect people, but there are forces that could easily kill you. You're human. She got my sister, and she was a strong wolf. If you could have seen what she did to those girls…you just need to be extra careful on this case." He sounded exasperated. "Look, I'm coming down there. My brother, Marcel, is the Alpha in the region, and before you say anything, which I know you will, don't argue. It's not negotiable."

"Okay, Tristan. I get it. Simone - evil vampire. Me - weak human." She rolled her eyes. *Men.* "I won't argue…well, not now anyway. But I need a favor. I need you to stop by my place and bring my weapons. You know, the special gifts you gave me a few years ago. I also need my guns. I left them in the condo. I might need them down here."

"Okay Syd. I'll bring the weapons, but please just stay with Kade until I get down there. You'll be safe with him at his compound. We can talk about next steps when I arrive."

"Okay, Tris, call me when you get down here. Thanks for bringing my stuff."

As she hung up, she sighed, resigned to the fact that it was going to be even more difficult working with both Kade and Tristan. Both men, the Alpha and vampire, thought they could boss her around. It was their nature to dominate, but it wouldn't deter her from her task. It might be a challenge to navigate around their domineering ways, but she was determined to catch the killer.

After taking a shower, Sydney gingerly brushed out her hair, still feeling the goose egg on the back of her head. At least the headache was gone. She dressed in a pair of black leggings and pink workout top, both of which clung to her figure, revealing a hint of cleavage. Her stomach growled. She recalled eating dinner with Kade, but she wondered what nourishment, if any, they kept in their own homes. She cringed, thinking about what they really ate: people. She wasn't stupid. She knew that human donors, both women and men, served themselves up on platters at Eden, but Sydney had never witnessed a 'feeding'. And in a house full of vampires, she didn't plan on offering herself. *Just play it cool, get your weapons, and you'll get a hotel room in the French Quarter. You'll be fine.*

Deciding not to wait for Kade, she ventured out in search of food. A hand gently blocked her way as she took her first step out of her room. She looked up to see a good-looking, African American man smiling down at her. He must have been at least six-five, lean and strong. He was dressed in casual black sweatpants and a white sleeveless, spandex shirt that showed every hard line of the muscles in his arms. He was statuesque and reminded her of a Greek god.

"Where do you think you're going without me, cher?" He grinned knowingly.

Sydney smiled back. She didn't know this man, but her gut told her that he had good intentions. "I take it that you're Xavier? Hi there, I'm Sydney Willows, Detective Sydney Willows. Nice to meet you."

"Ah, so very nice to meet you." He reached for her hand and kissed the top of it. "Yes, I'm Xavier. I've been assigned to accompany you during your stay at the Issacson Estate. I'm a good friend of Kade's, and we do intend to keep you safe." He let go of her hand.

Okay, here we go again with the chivalrous hand kissing; so polite, so deadly. Sydney sensed he was a nice guy, so she decided just to go with the flow, no use fighting with the hunky, vampire guard. She would save her energy and deal with Kade once she found him. "Xavier, I really need something to eat." She laughed a little. "You know, like human food. Also, I really need to talk with Kade."

"This is N'awlins, girl. You kidding? We've got plenty of food." He laughed as if she was crazy. "Come on, you must be famished after your ordeal. We heard all about it, tough girl you are."

They made their way to the kitchen table where an older woman served bread, eggs and andouille. Sydney was pleasantly surprised that they had a human cook in the house. As she ate her meal, enjoying her hot, chicory coffee, she wondered exactly how many people lived here. She talked with Xavier and learned that the mansion was located in the Garden District. She was pleased to learn that she was in a place where she could easily get to the French Quarter without needing directions. On one of her previous trips to the city, she had stayed in a lavish bed and breakfast in the area and knew exactly where she was.

Xavier told her how he'd come to know Kade in the year of 1868. His father was of Acadian descent and married his mother, who was an African American freed slave. He grew up in Lafayette Parish on the bayou, learning to fish and trap as his forefathers had done. Around his twenty-eighth birthday, he was attacked by the Southern Cross KKK and left to die in a field. As he struggled for his last breath, Kade had found and turned him. Soon after, he'd come to live with Kade, Luca and the others. He was a loyal friend to Kade and currently worked for him as a technology specialist.

After she finished eating, Sydney explored the lower level of the home, discovering a large sunroom, which was filled with orchids, lilies, and various other flowers. Someone had designed this room as if it were an indoor garden. Moonlight poured into it through glass walls, and she found herself resting in a large, overstuffed chair. Xavier had told her she could wait there for Kade and that he would be nearby if she needed his assistance. Even though she thought there were other vampires living in this home, the house was curiously quiet. All she heard was the rhythmic serenade of the cicadas.

A familiar tingle danced up her spine, and Sydney quickly turned her head, aware of his presence. *Kade.* She blinked, and as if by magic, he stood in front of her. Seeing him again, her stomach filled with butterflies. Her breath caught as he reached for her, taking her hands in his, bringing her to her feet. Face to face, mere inches apart, this was the first time she would really get to talk to him since he held her in the bed on the plane…since *the kiss*. She wanted to be mad at him for bringing her down here, yet her body reacted as he placed a chaste kiss to her lips. Aroused, her nipples hardened in anticipation of his touch. She wanted more, but it was clear he wasn't about to give it to her yet. Kade sighed, and sat down on the ottoman. Sydney followed, resting back down into her chair. He placed his hands on her knees.

"Sydney, love, so sorry to have left you alone for the past hour. I have much business to catch up on since I've been to Philadelphia. Please forgive me." He appeared relaxed, as if his home was the one place they'd be safe.

"Thanks again for getting me out of the condo," she began, her voice soft. Sydney found it impossible to keep from touching him as she reached for his hands. "As much as I love New Orleans, this was not how I expected to return. I…I don't think it's a good idea that I stay here in your home. It makes me really nervous…all these vampires roaming around your house. Besides, I know this city. I'd be okay on my own in a hotel. I don't know it as well as I know Philly, but I can get around, and we can still work together. I talked to Tristan this morning and…"

Kade removed his hands from hers, stood, and walked across the room. He turned to her, astonished that she'd said she was leaving. Unbelievable. This woman had been in his home for less than twenty-four hours and was thinking about leaving already. And damn it all, she'd talked to Tristan about it. Sure, Tristan was a good friend, but he would not have her going to another man for protection, no fucking way. It was time he set her straight.

"Sydney, I'm not sure what you talked to Tristan about, but while you are in my city, in my home, you will abide by my rules. We will catch Simone together, but you will do this my way. I am completely serious. And before you open that lovely mouth of yours, I will not have any arguments about it. I've already called your captain and given him my assessment of what happened back at your condo. There is agreement between P-CAP and your department that you are here on a consultation basis only. That means no leaving this house without my knowledge and protection from me or someone from my security team. On the case, I tell you what to do and when to do it. I will not have you getting yourself killed while you are here."

Kade blew out a breath, steaming with anger and arousal. *That lovely little mouth*; he wanted to kiss it, to make love to it, to feel himself surrounded by her lips. But she wouldn't listen to reason, and he'd had enough of this 'I am a cop' nonsense. Simone would hang her from her wrists and skin her alive…he'd seen her do it before. They could work the case together, but

Kade refused to let Sydney go it alone anymore.

"How dare you go and talk to my captain without my knowledge!" she yelled, jumping to her feet. She began to pace. "You don't get to tell me when to leave this house! I'm not waiting around while you go off and do business, or whatever you do. I'm the detective. You are…you are…I don't even know what the hell you are. I sure as shit know that you aren't a freakin' detective!"

Kade frowned. She was the most stubborn woman on the face of the earth. She was hot, sexy, beautiful, and damn hardheaded.

"I run this city, love. All of the supernatural activity in this town, including any P-CAP investigations, only happen with my approval and permission. That is all you need to know about my business. I am the law in New Orleans." He moved toward her, closing the distance. "So unless you'd like to be tied to a bed, and believe me, I would love to have you tied to mine, you had better follow my rules."

"Okay. Fine. No going out on investigations without you, but I'm not staying in a house full of vampires. This just isn't practical or safe. I'm not going to end up a happy meal because someone got the munchies. And I'm not going to waste my time sitting around here while you do business. Where you go, I go. We work this case, get the bad guy, and I go home. Seriously, I can't stay forever, so I want to make the most of my time."

Finally, capitulation.

"Sydney, I want you to know that I admire your independence and tenacity. I just want to keep you safe. I want all my people safe." Kade didn't want her to know how deeply he was starting to care about her. He was pissed as hell knowing that she'd called Tristan instead of talking to him first. Hell, he wasn't sure he even liked that he was so captivated by her. After all, he'd been alone for a few centuries now. He didn't lack for female attention, and he had enough to keep him busy in life without complications. And Sydney was a huge complication. Yet he could not deny that he was very much connected to her and she to him. He gave a small smile as she backed away from him, making her way back into her chair. It was as if he could almost see the wheels spinning in her head.

Sydney pulled her legs up underneath her, glancing up toward her dominant but ever so sexy vampire, feeling conflicted about her situation. *Tied to his bed? Duly noted and under consideration.* She hated that she was starting to care about him, hoping that he'd kiss her again. He acted like he cared about her, like he wanted her, but she questioned his motivation. Was he making her stay here, because he was some kind of a control freak? After all, he didn't just want to keep her safe…no, he'd said that he wanted to keep everyone safe. And he hadn't kissed her either. It upset her to think about how disappointed she'd be if he really was just trying to manipulate her. It wasn't as if she hadn't accepted long ago that she would spend her life alone. That was how she wanted it. Sydney averted her gaze, attempting once again to pull up her emotional wall, nice and high.

"Don't worry about stroking my ego, Kade. I get it, you are the protector, and I am the consultant. No problem. So what's next? Where do *we* find Simone?"

As she was about to make a suggestion, Luca entered the room. "Kade." He nodded and turned to Sydney. "Sydney. I've got a lead on Simone. There's been rumblings that she was seen collecting donors downtown at Sangre Dulce."

"Sangre Dulce?" Sydney asked.

"Sangre Dulce is a local club specializing in…how would you say?" Luca looked over to Kade, clearly hoping for some assistance. Finding none, he continued. "It is a fetish club. S&M. Caters to the supernaturals and humans alike. If Simone was looking for someone to torture, she could easily find a submissive there who would go off with her. I talked to Miguel, the owner, and he said a bartender reported that a woman who looked like Simone was in the club well over a month ago. We cannot be certain it was her, but we could ask around. And Kade, if we do go to Sangre Dulce, I would advise against taking the human."

Sydney wanted to smack Luca. Why did he always have to be such a condescending ass? "Hello? Luca? That human is right here. I already established with Kade that we're going together."

"Kade, she serves no purpose on this trip," Luca commented, stone-faced. "Simone will have spies, and they will see her. And others…vampires…they'll view her as available. She is not marked, nor claimed, nor does she work for us. They will recognize her as an outsider. It's not wise to bring her. I must insist that you reconsider."

"Luca, your concern is taken under advisement. Effective immediately, Miss Sydney Willows is my employee." Sydney shot him a look of surprise. "I'm pleased to introduce my new Director of Security. She's in charge of my Philadelphia operations and arrived yesterday to learn from you about security operations in New Orleans. She is known to accompany me to events. After introductions to Miguel, no one will touch her."

"But how will she fit in? They'll sense she does not belong. It'll be bad enough that we have no business that would even call us there."

"What if we were there for some kind of inspection? If it's true that Kade approves all activities in this town, could we tell Miguel we were there because of a complaint? Cops do it all the time for other businesses when we suspect criminal activity. Or, we could just say I was there to see New Orleans. Lord knows there are plenty of freaky things going on in this city. What's a little S&M in this town? Seriously you two…have you ever been to Bourbon Street on Halloween? Everyone lets their freak flag fly."

Kade burst out laughing. A hearty, sexy laugh that made Sydney want to let her freak flag fly right there, right then, on the floor with him.

"You bring up a good point. But going in under the guise of an inspection will only put people off. You must understand that the people who frequent this club, go there for privacy. Any complaints would be handled directly by Miguel. We don't want people on the defensive. But if we go in as mere patrons? A date even? Now that would work, and I am more than willing to get freaky with you." Kade smiled at Luca who he could tell had resigned himself to the fact that they were taking the human. He knew that Luca felt indifferent towards her, having learned long ago that humans simply could not be trusted. They both knew that Simone was dangerous. If she went after Sydney, it would put them all at risk. He didn't like the fact that Voodoo and magic were involved either. They needed Ilsbeth.

"Kade, I need to get out tomorrow. And before you say no, which I know is coming, I need clothes and shoes. This has got to be believable. I need to look like the kind of girl who is looking for a little adventure, if you know what I mean. These sweats aren't going to cut it."

"Okay, you'll go shopping in the morning," he began. Kade knew she was correct, but she could not go alone. Unfortunately, he had a few meetings that he must attend. "But you go with someone. I will send Xavier with you. Even though vampires have weakened powers during daylight, Simone could be out looking for you, or have human minions spying about."

"I'll need a few weapons too: stakes, crossbow. Tristan is bringing my gear, but he may not be down before we leave tomorrow night."

"They will not allow weapons into the club. For your shopping trip tomorrow, Luca will give you a gun with silver bullets and a few stakes that you can easily stash in your purse." Kade approached her and sat on the ottoman. "Tomorrow night, we'll need to give you a few *special accessories* before we leave…undetectable weapons that you can wear into the club. You should be safe with us, but should you have any issues, you'll have the protection you need."

After Luca had left them alone, Kade's eyes met Sydney's. She'd gone silent, yet had adjusted her legs so that they were inches from his. For several seconds, they gazed upon each other. His hand touched her knee. When she didn't protest, his palm glided up her thigh until he'd captured her hand. Standing, he brought her up to him, so that they stood close, his hand on her waist.

"Sydney, I know you're mad that I called your boss. But if you want to stay on the case, we need to do this my way. I'm sorry I have to put so many restrictions in place. We'll go downtown tomorrow night and get more information about Simone's whereabouts. I promise that this will be over soon."

Sydney's body came alive as she felt the strength of his hands on her. She didn't want to forgive him so quickly for bossing her around, but my God, she yearned for his touch. Although she'd questioned what he'd done, she found herself justifying it. Deep down, she believed that he'd meant what he'd said; he'd keep her safe too. For so long, she'd had no one, but for now, it felt like she had him. Her body responded to his as she allowed the palms of her hands to lie flat on his chest. She wanted to know what it would be like to be flesh to flesh with him, tasting him.

He leaned into her and held her tight against his chest. She breathed in his clean masculine scent, allowing herself to imagine what it would be like to have him inside her. A rush of heat caused her sex to ache. He looked down at her wantonly, searching her eyes for permission.

"Kade, this thing between us…I don't know what to think…" She didn't get a chance to finish her thoughts.

"Don't think, Sydney, just feel." Kade brought his mouth to hers and she opened for him, allowing him to sweep his tongue into, over and around hers. He was demanding, passionate.

Kade was tired of waiting. He wanted this human woman so badly, and he was finding it difficult to make excuses for why he shouldn't just take her. Sydney moaned and kept pace with him as she ran her fingers through his hair, possessively pulling his head down to meet hers.

Refusing her the control she sought, Kade slowly pushed her back up against the wall and held her hands above her head with one of his. With the other, he pushed up her shirt, feeling the soft skin of her belly, and then slid his hand up, slowly cupping her breast. Shoving up her bra, he freed her breast from its confines. Kade's breath quickened, overwhelmed with excitement that he'd finally touched her silky peaks. He tore his mouth away from hers, lowered his head to her ripe flesh and licked her rosy tip.

Sydney shivered and groaned under his touch, submitting to his need to dominate. She wanted to be dominated by him; he was so strong, intoxicating.

"Kade, yes, please," Sydney begged, unable to keep silent in the throes of their passion.

Kade sucked the nipple harder until Sydney felt a twinge of pain, then pleasure. She couldn't believe she was letting him do this to her, but she felt helpless to stop him. The desire she felt overrode any sense of logic she had. He pushed up the other side of her bra and gave her other hardened peak equal attention. As he released her hands, she held onto his shoulders for dear life as he made love to her breasts.

"I want you so much, Kade," she confessed. "Please, don't stop."

The sound of clicking heels on the floor broke her concentration. Dazed and swollen-lipped, she opened her eyes to see the redheaded vampire watching her and Kade. *Voyeur much?* Refusing to be intimidated,

Sydney glared at her. Interrupted by the intrusion, Kade slowly lowered Sydney's shirt.

"Dominique, you must learn to knock," he growled. Irritated, he blew out a breath. "This is my home, not the office. And as you can see, I am quite busy. What do you want?"

"Kade darling, I just came by to see how things were going with your lovely human."

"As you can see, she is quite well. Now it's getting late, anything else?"

"Yes, Ilsbeth contacted Luca. He asked me to tell you. She's coming in to see you tomorrow night before we go to the club. She's nervous about coming here, so Luca and I will go to her coven, secure her and bring her in safely. We should be here around seven. I would like to discuss the details, if you have time."

Sydney felt oddly out of place during this discussion. Instead of getting pushed out of the conversation, she decided to remove herself. She was tired again anyway and needed a break from the vampires who seemed to be crawling everywhere in this house.

"Kade, uh, I think I am going to head upstairs. I wanna give Ada a call." She placed a kiss to his cheek and pulled away from him.

"Okay, love. Oh and Sydney, remember our discussion earlier. No running off without me," he warned.

Sydney smiled without necessarily agreeing and began to leave. As she passed Dominique, she purposefully avoided eye contact. She wasn't sure what kind of relationship Kade had with her, but that woman irritated Sydney. Dominique had made it apparent that she wasn't going to go out of her way to make Sydney comfortable. If anything, Sydney suspected that she'd interrupted them on purpose. As she rounded the corner, she caught Kade's warm smile. Unconsciously, she brought her fingers to her lips, his kiss still seared on them. She closed her eyes briefly, leaving the room. Sydney wasn't sure how she and Kade would ever have a relationship. It seemed impossible. Yet, with the sweet taste of him fresh in her mind, she could feel her heart melting.

Chapter Eleven

Sydney locked the door to her bedroom and began searching for her phone. Logically, she knew a locked door was not enough to keep a vampire out of her room, but it gave her a small comfort knowing she wouldn't make it easy for them. Even though no one had tried to bite her yet, strange vampires milling about the house made her a little nervous. Finally locating her cell in her purse, she dialed Adalee at the lab. Sydney wanted to get the latest autopsy results and hoped they'd get an additional clue to help stop the killings.

"Hi ya, Sydney girl," Adalee said cheerfully as she picked up on the other end.

"Hey, Ada, sorry I didn't make it into the station last night."

"Yes, I heard all about it. And are you just gonna act like you aren't down in New Orleans with that fine piece of vampire who you've been working with? I mean really…do tell. I heard from the captain that you're down there with him. And what did he call it? Oh yeah, consulting? Is that what they call it these days? I'd like a consulting job in a romantic city with a hot hunk of vampire goodness." Sydney could hear Adalee laughing hard on the other end of the line.

"Very funny. But seriously, I nearly got killed back in my condo, and Kade brought me down here to…ugh…help him. I'm the detective on this case. So yeah, I am consulting, that's it."

"Whatever you say, Syd. You just keep telling yourself that, okay?" Adalee chuckled. "Now listen, I'm glad you finally called in. Got some new information on the second girl. Same cause of death, exsanguination. Again, no marks indicating fangs. No sexual assault either. This girl was tortured though. Looks like someone was using her for a pincushion, and I'm not talking tiny push pins either." There was a pregnant pause before she continued. "Syd, I've never seen anything like this. I can't be sure what made these holes, but I'm guessing right now maybe knitting needles or possibly large surgical needles. There are two holes in the chest region, two in the stomach, and one behind the ear. It looks like these were inflicted antemortem."

"The girl was alive during it. Anything else?"

"Yeah, we found traces of lemongrass oil again on the head and also on the wrists. Also, there were traces of human hair and hemp embedded in her wrists. Syd, I'm not sure what's going on down there but the person who's doing this…it's downright disturbing." Adalee sounded disgusted.

"I know, Ada. Isn't this some shit? Kade thinks he knows who's doing this. We're following a lead tomorrow night, so hopefully that will yield some good results. In the meantime, text or call me with any updates. Thanks."

"You take care, Syd. Talk to you soon. And hope you enjoy your…um…consulting gig," Adalee teased.

Sydney considered getting some more sleep after the call, but then she thought she'd better go tell Kade about what Adalee had discovered. Why the hell did the killer use needles on the girl? It had to be related to Voodoo. Was Simone making some kind of human Voodoo doll? Sydney didn't know the least bit about Voodoo dolls except for the fact they sold the little trinkets in the tourist shops. She knew a little bit about the background of Marie Laveau, the renowned Voodoo priestess of New Orleans. Sydney and a friend had once taken a walking "Voodoo tour" on one of her many vacations to the Big Easy, and they'd toured a Voodoo museum, even visited the mausoleum where Marie Laveau was buried. But aside from the legends, she was no expert on the subject and suspected Kade would have answers.

Leaving her room and quietly descending the large, spiral staircase, Sydney heard familiar voices in the great room. As she entered, Kade, Luca, Xavier, Etienne, and Dominique were sitting around discussing the witch. *No time like the present to interrupt the family fun.* She thought about being serious, all vampire-like, but then decided that flippant was more her style.

"Hey guys. Forget to invite the human to the party?" They all looked up at her at once as if she had three heads. Maybe serious would have been the best approach, grumpy vampires.

"Okay, guess the party is over. I have some news, if you're interested." Not waiting for an invitation, Sydney deliberately sat next to Luca, knowing it would irritate him. He seemed to have a stick up his ass, and she was about to dislodge it. "Hey, Luca, how's it shaking? What, no big hello for me?" She smiled up at him, knowing he was itching to remove her from his side.

Kade grinned in response to her antics.

"Sydney love, please refrain from poking the bear." Both Xavier and Dominique laughed.

Okay, things were loosening up a bit…at least with a couple of these vamps. Sydney decided to keep pushing.

"Let's play a game, Luca. You show me yours, I'll show you mine."

As Luca lifted one corner of his mouth, suppressing a grin, Sydney sensed that his hard exterior was showing a few cracks.

"I guess as long as Kade doesn't mind, I have no problem showing you mine," he replied, eyeing his friend.

"As if half this town hasn't seen it," Dominique snorted.

"We were just discussing Ilsbeth. It appears that instead of Luca and

Dominique escorting her tomorrow night, she will be arriving within the hour with her own escort. Ilsbeth said she has important information for us, and feels it is a bit of an emergency. I would like you to meet her so you can review the evidence that was found on the two victims. She should be here soon," Kade told her. He gave her a smile. "And Sydney…"

"Yes?"

"Just so we're clear we understand each other. In my home, should you decide to share, you will only be showing *yours* to me."

Sydney's cheeks heated, and she resisted bringing her hands to her face. Kade's words were not lost on her. *Possessive? Jealous? Maybe I've misread what he said? Definitely not.* She had almost made love to him earlier in the sunroom, and he knew damn well that she wanted to show him…well, everything. But he'd had no problem dismissing her upstairs in lieu of Dominique and business.

"Kade, you had the opportunity a few hours ago to see all of mine, and if you recall, you chose business," she said, referring to Dominque. "Luca on the other hand, needs some loosening up."

Sydney patted Luca's thigh and stood up. She considered pretending like she was going to remove her clothes just to tease him a bit more, but thought better of it. Kade did not look amused. She glanced at Luca to find him actually smiling at her.

"Okay, here it is." With one hand on her hip, she rubbed her forehead with the other hand, pushing a stray hair out of her face. "Ada said the last vic had the same hemp and human hair fibers and same lemongrass oil on her. This time, there were no whip marks on the body. But what is really sick is that someone was playing human Voodoo doll with this girl. She had five holes in her. Ada thinks they were made with knitting or surgical needles. To be honest, they are not really sure yet what made the holes. And to top off the shit sandwich, all the needles were inserted antemortem."

As Sydney observed their expressions, she could tell the vampires appeared to know something she didn't. Before she got a chance to ask and insist that they get a Voodoo expert in on the case, the doorbell rang. The witch was here.

As Ilsbeth entered the room, the air lightened; it was almost dizzying. Sydney was surprised by the witch's nearly ethereal arrival, her escort trailing behind. Ilsbeth's long, platinum hair flowed well below her waist, accentuating her petite figure. She was dressed in a purple velvet blouse that was complemented by a fitted, black leather jacket and pants. Ilsbeth took Kade's hand as they headed toward the dining room. She seated herself at the head of the table, as if she'd been there before, gesturing to Sydney to sit beside her.

Not sure about witch etiquette, Sydney followed Ilsbeth's nonverbal cue and sat down next to her. She couldn't help but admire the woman's deep violet eyes. Sydney was not sure what she'd thought a witch would look like, but she certainly wasn't expecting this. Maybe a green nose and a broomstick? No, but she was expecting someone a little scarier looking, certainly older. But Ilsbeth was anything but scary, or old. She looked barely twenty-one years old, with an angelic face.

Once everyone was seated at the table, Ilsbeth spoke a protection prayer. Sydney guessed it was your basic, 'keep evil spirits out of this house' prayer, from what she could tell. Hell, she wasn't even sure she believed in witchcraft mojo, but in order to catch the killer, she would give angel girl the benefit of the doubt. Sydney was getting anxious, but could tell that the witch was running the show. All the vampires at the table stayed silent as they listened to Ilsbeth finish her prayer.

Sydney nearly jumped out of her seat as Ilsbeth's eyes flew open and all the candles on the table and along the shelves in the room flared to life. *Okay, nice trick.* She glanced at Sydney and then to Kade.

"My dearest friends, there is a great evil in our city. She may have initially come for you, Kade, but now she is here for all of us. I felt it a week ago when I was working. It was a rumbling at first, but now there is a constant state of unease. The wind of evil has blown throughout our streets. Something bad is coming for all of us…something that wants to take over this city. I will help if I can, Kade, but I must know why this evil woman is here for you."

Kade recounted the story of Simone to Ilsbeth, including her banishment and the recent killings in Philadelphia. Sydney filled in the missing pieces with regards to the oil, the rope fibers, and needle marks. Ilsbeth listened carefully before speaking with great seriousness.

"If all that you told me is true, there must be someone helping Simone, a witch or mage perhaps, or possibly a Voodoo priestess. Simone may have some of this knowledge, but a practitioner would need supplies to help to carry out these killings and spells. It is possible that Simone is experimenting…using a living girl as a Voodoo doll. She seeks the assistance of evil spirits to help her with her goals." Ilsbeth stared deep into Kade's eyes. "Kade, Simone may have started off with a simple goal of revenge, but the darkness of her practices points to a monumental goal, perhaps to have power…power over all the supernaturals in the city. If her experiment showed any promise the first time, she'll kill again until she takes over this town."

"Thank you for your insight, Ilsbeth. As always, you bring profound knowledge and perspective to the problems we face. Tomorrow night, we are going to follow a lead on Simone. Do you have any recommendations about how to proceed with regards to the witchcraft? More importantly, do you know anyone in the witch community who would want to help her? Someone must know. It is hard to keep secrets within covens."

"You are correct in your assumptions. I plan to scour the books, seeing who made the purchases necessary to create the oil and rope. These ingredients are widely available online, but any self-respecting witch or mage from New Orleans would buy them in our shop. We certify the authenticity of ingredients for all our products and supplies, which includes Van Van oil as well as hemp and hair. And if a vampire attempted purchasing these supplies at any stores in the city, I am confident someone would remember. That would not go unnoticed."

"Thanks, Ilsbeth," Sydney interjected. "Look back a year or two in your records, just to be safe. We aren't sure how long she's been in the city. If you send us the list of possible suspects, Kade and I can check it out from there. We really appreciate your help on this. If you saw what was done to those girls…well, we've got to stop it." While she didn't understand witchcraft, Sydney had to admit that she felt glad the witch was helping them. It was possible Ilsbeth could lead them to tangible clues so they could nab the killer.

Ilsbeth nodded. "I will contact you if I find anything. Like I said, I have been with my coven the past week. I will need to go back to the shop for the records. My escort, Zin, has been with me. He is my cousin, a practicing warlock, but most importantly, he's trained in security. I will be going everywhere with him. We cannot be too careful. I must go, but I will be in touch."

After everyone had said their goodbyes, Sydney quietly retreated to her room. She wanted to give in to her desire to be with Kade, but she was on business and had to get up early. Being around him was beginning to cloud her judgment. If she could only get some sleep and shopping therapy, she'd be good…okay, maybe not good, but she'd be ready to go out tomorrow night. They needed to catch a break on this case.

Chapter Twelve

Dressing up to fit into a vampire fetish club was a bitch. Sydney spent the better part of the morning shopping for clothes that would say, 'I roll with kinky vampires'. She hoped she'd fit in. She knew better than anyone that people had a tendency to clam up around cops, and the supernatural crowd was even more tight-lipped when it came to revealing secrets. They had their own code of honor and laws.

Xavier had accompanied her on her shopping expedition to help her choose just the right outfit. She wasn't above letting Kade pay for everything; after all he was the one who had dragged her ass down here to New Orleans. Xavier had promised not to reveal the details of her 'costume' to Kade. Oh yeah, baby, she wanted this one to shock him. They all needed a good laugh, she supposed; a human girl dressing like some kind of sex-crazed dominatrix. She was planning on cracking the whip all right.

She finally managed to get the damn, thigh-high, fishnet stockings attached. Garters were not as easy to put on as they looked. She had to admit, glancing at herself in the mirror, that she looked smokin' hot. She would have preferred to look dangerous, but tonight she was playing a part; sexy, wanton, open to handcuffs, whips and paddles.

She had chosen a tight black fishnet camisette with garters, and a black leather miniskirt. The fishnet cami was tightly woven and see-through, so it showed off her pert, rosy nipples underneath. She topped the outfit off with a sexy pair of Christian Louboutin, black leather over-the-knee boots that were adorned with silver zippers that ran all the way up from the back of her ankle to the back of her thigh. Xavier had given her slim, silver stakes that fitted into the boots nicely. No one would feel them even if they patted her down. She also concealed a small silver knife and chain in her right boot that she could easily pull out if necessary.

Sydney conceded that she could not do much about her long blonde hair. There was no way she was dyeing her hair black, or any other freaky color just for one night. She tried on a few wigs, but they were too hot, so she stopped by a local salon and had them tightly curl her long locks. Her perfectly spiraled, golden curls flowed over her shoulders.

Sydney fingered the mask she'd purchased in Jackson Square. Its swirling diamond rhinestones added an enigmatic flair to her sexy, fetish look. She held the delicate black metal to her face and fastened the ribbon behind her hair. With one last glance in the mirror, she left her room, wishing she was home going to a Halloween party instead, but this was her life. There was no room for games or mistakes tonight. She would play the part and do everything she could to glean information about where Simone was and who else was helping her. She knew from experience that seedy bars were good places to get intel, as long as you had sources who were either afraid of you or trusted you; either worked. Unfortunately, in this town, she had neither.

Kade gaped at Sydney as she descended the staircase. *Holy mother of God. What is she wearing?* His cock jerked to attention and his eyes widened as he struggled to remain composed in front of his fellow vampires. In all his life, he had never wanted one woman so badly. He immediately noticed how her tight, hard peaks pressed against the fishnet weave. He could not believe she would freaking wear a see-through top to a vampire club. What was she thinking? Every supernatural in the place would want her. *Let them try*, he laughed to himself. She belonged to him and no other.

"So, who wants a spanking?" she asked seductively. Despite her bravado, her face flushed, aware that she was half naked in front of a group of free-loving vampires. "Mistress Sydney is here to make your fantasy come true."

Everyone started laughing, except Kade. He strode across the room, possessively grabbing Sydney's waist. Pulling her flush against him, he captured her mouth. It was a hard, dominating kiss, one that let everyone know she was his. His tongue forced its way into her mouth, and Sydney opened for him. She kissed him back, letting him know that she would not simply be taken. No, she would take as well. Her hands snaked up his back, feeling the soft leather of his jacket. She breathed in his masculine scent, feeling controlled in his arms, seeking all of him.

Dominique coughed loudly from across the room.

"Okay, you two, ya want to get a room and fuck, or go catch bad guys? Come on!"

Interrupted, Sydney and Kade broke their heated connection.

"Uh…yeah, that would be 'go catch bad guys'," Sydney responded, dazed from Kade's kiss.

Sydney glanced away from Kade to Dominique. She wore a dark purple bustier with matching leather pencil skirt and calf-high, patent-leather lace-front boots.

"Nice leather. And those boots…We need to go shoe shopping together someday, seriously," she suggested, attempting to bond with the vampire.

Dominique smiled at the compliment. "Okay, girl, so we actually do have something in common. I'll take a rain check. It may be nice to have another woman around all this testosterone."

"Listen up everyone," Kade ordered. All eyes fell on him. "Before we go in, Luca will be clearing the site. Sydney, you will enter with the second group. I will approach Miguel and introduce you as my director of Philadelphia security. Luca and Sydney, stay close in the club. You are supposed to be working together. The rest of you work the club and try to find out anything about Simone's whereabouts, or accomplices. The witch who is helping her may also frequent the club. Stay on your toes, and try to fit in. It cannot look like we are there investigating, or people won't talk. Luca, please run down the security situation."

"We've got two limos. Xavier, Dominique and I will take the first one. We'll go in and case things out before we give you the all clear. We need to make sure Simone is not in the club. If she is, Kade will enter. *You*," he said, pointing to Sydney, "will stay in the car. Under no circumstances are you to enter the club if Simone is in there. I am serious, Sydney. What happened with the vampire in Philly is child's play compared to what Simone could do to you." Sydney rolled her eyes.

"Once the go ahead is given, we can all enter the club. Spread out. Like Kade said, we are not there to investigate, so it can't look that way. Play, feed, gather information. Kade will give the signal when it is time to go. Kade and Sydney will leave first."

Kade put his hand around Sydney's waist, clutching her to his side.

"Okay, everyone, let's roll. Sydney love, stay close to Luca or me. Remember, while you carry my scent at the moment, other vampires will most definitely try to lure you."

Sydney shot Kade a defiant look, growing annoyed with his rules. Kade might be the boss of his vampires, but he was not the boss of her. She would play nice so long as she was on the case, but no man, not even a sexy as hell vampire, was going to run her life.

Chapter Thirteen

After Luca had given the all clear, Kade entered Sangre Dulce with Etienne and Sydney flanking him. A tall, thin man with jet-black hair and a goatee rushed up to greet them. He almost looked like a pirate with the black leather pants and white ruffled linen open-chested shirt he wore.

"Sir, I am honored to have you here. We have a special VIP table set up for you and your guests, which provides a wonderful view of the dance floor as well as the public play area," he explained.

Sydney struggled to keep her mouth shut. *Public play area? What the hell?*

Miguel was soon joined by a naked petite woman with long bright red hair, which was braided down her back. The woman wore a small chain around her neck that Sydney assumed was some kind of a collar. Sydney didn't know much about fetishes, but assumed this pixie of a woman was a submissive. Miguel placed his hand on the woman's back, gently pushing her toward Kade.

"Sir, this is Rhea. She will serve you and your party tonight, in any way you wish. She is human and has agreed to be a donor. Rhea can procure additional donors, submissives or Doms for your party, should you need these services. And of course, she will be your waitress for the evening. She is new to Sangre Dulce, but as you will experience, she was born to serve others. She is quite the little obedient sub. I am certain you will enjoy her."

Studying Sydney, he extended his hand. She reluctantly allowed him to take it, cringing as he kissed it. Before letting her go, he turned her arm over and smelled her inner wrist. Sydney snatched her hand away from him, shooting Kade a pointed look.

Miguel didn't seem to notice.

"Sir, what a lovely human you have brought to my club tonight. Shall we expect a public performance from her? I would most enjoy seeing her tan skin turn pink." He licked his lips and smiled, displaying his fangs to Sydney.

Showing very little emotion, Kade approached Miguel in an authoritative manner. "Miguel, this is Miss Willows. She is director of my security operations in the Philadelphia area. She is being mentored by Luca." Kade's eyes narrowed. "Miss Willows is in my employ, and is not to be touched or seen by anyone but me." He paused and winked at Sydney. "That is, unless I grant permission for her to be touched."

Sydney fought for self-control as blood rushed to her face. She was pretty sure Kade was teasing her. Wasn't he? Oh my God. She *so* needed to get this case over with so she could get back to her less than exciting life in

Philadelphia. What the hell was wrong with these freaky vampires? She took a deep breath in an effort to gain her composure before she said anything she'd regret. She tried to remind herself she was just playing a part…here on a case.

"So sorry, sir, it is just that she is so very beautiful and so very human. She smells lovely." Miguel bowed his head. "Please forgive me."

"No harm done. Rhea, please show my guests to our table. I have business that I need to discuss with Miguel."

Sydney was about to lose it. What was Kade doing? He was not just sending her off with some naked waitress? Etienne gestured for Sydney to follow Rhea. She reluctantly followed the submissive up onto a raised platform area to a large table, where she agreed, the view was great. They'd be able to see pretty much everything that was going on in the club, except for the private rooms. She took a seat and Etienne sat down next to her. He looked at the wine menu and ordered.

"Please bring us three bottles of Salon Le Mesnil, 1997. We are expecting additional guests." Rhea bowed her head and scuttled off.

Sydney straightened in her chair, trying to appear as if she regularly frequented kinky, BDSM, vampire clubs. Trying not to look surprised, she noticed several dominatrix-type women at a table across from them. They were drinking and laughing while naked men with collars knelt at their feet. The dance floor appeared to be rhythmically moving as one. Waves of bodies in various forms of dress - from fully clothed to no clothing at all, danced.

Observing what they referred to as the public play area, she saw a large naked bald man who was tied to a bench. He writhed in pleasure and pain as an older woman dressed in red leather spanked him relentlessly with a pink paddle. Sydney shook her head. To each his own, she supposed. Not that she was totally opposed to spanking, or being tied up every now and then, but tied to a bench in the middle of a dance club? Guess it took a lot to get that guy's adrenaline going.

Dominique, Luca, and Xavier approached the table and sat down to discuss the next steps. Kade was the last to arrive, and he sat next to Sydney.

"So, curious thing, our friend Miguel said the bartender who reported Simone's appearance, quit. He's gone. So we've got no one specific to question. Sydney, what are your impressions?"

"I say we question the submissives first." Sydney scanned the room, focusing on Rhea who was all the way across the club waiting for drinks at the bar. "I know we can't act like we're investigating, but we could ask around to see who they've played with. Maybe some prefer women Doms and would remember her. It's likely that if Simone was here she could easily have shopped for a victim. We should also question the Doms and find out if there are any new ones on the scene who match her description. We need to do it in a subtle way, so they don't suspect we're investigating. I have to say, as kinky as this place is, it only looks like maybe fifty percent of the people in here are regulars. Is it possible that some of them are tourists?" Sydney took note of the several patrons who appeared out of place. A casually dressed couple sat at a table, nervously playing with their drink straws.

"Yes, I'm sure some are, but there are also regulars," Kade agreed. "We'll need to spread out. Etienne and Xavier, start with questioning the submissives. Go ask Miguel to line them up and pretend you are looking for a sub. Be discreet. Do not make it seem as though we are conducting an investigation. Dominique, take on Rhea. Something seems off with her. Miguel said she just started, yet he assigned his least experienced server to our important party? It doesn't make sense."

As the other vampires left the table, Kade, Luca and Sydney moved together so they could more easily talk.

"I don't like this thing with the bartender going missing. If Simone found out that he told someone she was here, why wouldn't she take out Miguel too? She expected to have this reported, so why kill him?" Sydney asked.

"Good question, indeed." Kade took notice of Miguel, whose gaze lingered too long on Sydney. "Right now, I want you and Luca to go dance. You are supposed to be close. I don't want anyone questioning our intentions. I will join you in a few minutes then we will retire to the private rooms to investigate."

"As you wish…Sydney?" Luca stood and gestured for her to take his hand.

Sydney knew she wasn't Luca's favorite person, but he was polite, she'd give him that. She stood, glancing from Kade to Luca, finally going to him. He led her onto the dance floor and as she went, Sydney's eyes never left Kade's. She'd stopped counting how many times a day she wanted Kade to make love to her. She had never felt so connected to one man in her life, but she couldn't admit to herself that this might be a real opportunity for a long-lasting relationship.

Luca took Sydney in his arms, pushing his thigh between her knees. Sydney felt his strength against her, his muscular, lethal body brushing hers. She leaned into him and put one arm around his neck, swaying to the music. As Luca pressed his hips to hers, Sydney's eyes flashed open, surprised to feel his hardness against her belly.

"So, Luca, is that a stake in your pocket or are you just happy to see me?" she joked.

"Sydney darling, let's just say that you are starting to grow on me, and that outfit of yours is delectable. I may be a vampire, but I'm not dead."

Luca grabbed the back of her head, pulling it toward his and whispered in her ear. "Even though you belong to Kade, it doesn't stop me from appreciating you…all of you."

Horny vampires, geez. Sydney had been somewhat unnerved at his sudden sexuality on display for all to see in the club. She kept trying to remember that she was there playing a part. They were supposed to be acting, and it was easy to do. She was attracted to Luca as well, as most women would be. He was ruggedly handsome, but not a pretty boy. Despite his forward comments, she felt, oddly, as though she could trust him. But she also wondered what Kade's reaction would be to having another man's hands all over her. But he'd told her to be with him. *Look like you are close to Luca.*

Just as she was beginning to relax, Luca spun her around straight into Kade's arms. Her breath caught as his lips met hers. She expected Luca to leave, but instead he sandwiched her in the middle, grazing his erection against Sydney's ass, reaching his arms around her waist. His hands slowly inched up under Sydney's breasts as Kade kissed her passionately.

Sydney's senses were overwhelmed. *What the fuck is going on?* She was letting two vampires monopolize her body, loving every minute of it. Kissing Kade took her away into a headspace that she rarely went, one of pure pleasure. Yet it scared her that she was letting him see her raw, so exposed. And worst of all, she felt the tingle all over her body, leaving her wishing the situation could be permanent.

Kade tore his lips from hers, leaving her breathless. He grasped the nape of her neck and leaned in to speak sensually in her ear.

"You are stunning tonight. Indeed, I am going to find it hard to let you go after this dance." He pressed his lips to the lobe of her ear. "You seem to like playing with two men. Enjoying our dance with Luca, aren't you, love? But remember this, Sydney, I don't share, and at the end of tonight, you will be mine." *Mine?* He could not believe he'd used the word but at the same time, he could not deny the all-consuming need to claim Sydney as his. He had every intention of making love to her over and over again, and was looking forward to hearing her scream his name in ecstasy.

As the song ended, Sydney was relieved to put some space between her and the boys. She ached between her legs, extraordinarily aroused from their dance. She longed for Kade's strong arms and wished he'd take her out of the club. He'd told her that she would be his tonight. She found herself wanting to let him take control and make love to her until dawn. She was conflicted, knowing that she was an independent woman, yet she could not deny wanting to belong to him.

As Sydney tried to regain her composure, she watched Luca leave the dance floor. Deciding to take control of the situation, she reached over and laced her fingers with Kade's.

"Come on, let's go check out the private rooms. My take is that some of the rooms may not be that private. Maybe everyone in our group is back there with the subs and Doms. We could help, or at least look for suspicious activity and clues to where Simone is. Even though this place is screaming 'erotic experience', I just have a feeling that sex isn't the only thing happening in this club. If Simone has spies here, they'll be watching for us…and may slip up by looking just a little too long."

"Let's make our rounds and see who's interested in our visit." Kade led them off the floor toward the back of the club.

Sydney braced herself for whatever kinky sights they'd see along the way. She wasn't a prude, but she wasn't used to seeing so many naked people prancing around in collars and leather. As they approached the back, they pushed through a red metallic beaded fringed curtain door. A sensual, hard, driving pulse of music spread throughout the hallway, which was dimly lit with black light.

A crowd gathered at the entrance of one of the rooms where a couple was performing. As Sydney pushed her way to the front, Kade settled behind, letting his hands fall protectively around her waist. A tall, lithe, gothic-looking woman stood spread-eagle with her hands secured by leather cuffs to an upright, wooden contraption that looked like an X. Although the woman was blindfolded and bound, she appeared to quiver in euphoria as her male partner teased her bottom with a blue leather whip.

The crowd silently watched as the woman begged her partner for release. It appeared that she had somehow earned her reward, because her partner unzipped his pants and entered the woman from behind. He was thrusting over and over into the bound woman while she screamed. Sydney could not believe she was watching such an intimate act with Kade and was growing embarrassed by her own arousal. Yet she knew this was why people came here…to arouse and be aroused. Concerned by her reaction, Sydney pushed back slightly in order to turn away. Kade's arms tightened, holding her still against him, forcing her to watch. She could feel his rock-hard cock pressed into her back, and knew he wanted her to see this.

Kade chose to make Sydney watch the lovers in the room, so she could experience a taste of his world. He was not a frequent visitor to this club by any means, but this kind of activity was not uncommon in the supernatural world. It was a harsh reality, albeit arousing. If Sydney was going to be with him, she needed to be aware of the dangers and temptations that lurked in his city. He could smell her arousal as she watched the strangers make love. His rock-hard cock strained against his leather pants, begging to take her in the same manner. He could not resist the opportunity to tease his normally self-composed detective. He leaned his mouth down to her ear, making sure she heard his every word.

"Do you like this, Sydney? Would you like me to tie you up and take you from behind? I promise not to be gentle with you, detective." He smiled, knowing he'd ruffled her feathers. "Now don't lie to me…I smell your desire."

Damn vampire senses. Sydney was mortified and had had enough of this crazy sex show. She pulled herself out of his strong grip, knowing he'd chosen to let go of her. It was time to get back to business. There wasn't anything suspicious going on in that area. Just a couple having sex, and a dozen horny people watching. What had she gotten herself into on this case?

As they walked further down the dark hall, Miguel appeared out of nowhere, calling for Kade.

"Sir, I thought it might be a good idea for you to speak with Gia, a back bartender who works here. I remembered that she was friends with Freddy…you know the guy who quit? Maybe she has information about Simone's whereabouts? Please forgive me. I should have thought of this earlier."

"Sydney, come with me. We can talk to her together."

"No, you go. I'm fine. I want to find Dominique and perhaps, *play* with Rhea." Sydney did not intend to play, but she did want to question the waitress. She also didn't trust Miguel. She wanted him to think she was only here for fun, not to investigate.

"But as my director of security, you may find my questioning of interest. Please come with me." Kade's lips tightened, anticipating her refusal.

"But you said we're here to have a little fun, not work. I promise I'll catch up with you later. As you know, I like to play with the girls. Dominique should be back here somewhere. When you're finished, come find me. We can play later," she purred, rubbing her hands up and down his chest.

"As you wish, my love. But know this, we will play later," he said in warning, blowing out a breath. "I can sense both Xavier and Etienne back here, so give them a shout should you run into any issues, okay?"

"I promise. I'll be fine," she assured Kade as she pressed her lips to his cheek.

"Be careful," he whispered.

She winked at Kade as he and Miguel headed toward the light at the end of the hallway. Something about Miguel made her skin crawl. He wasn't lying, but he wasn't exactly telling the whole truth. She wanted Kade to go find out what the bartender knew. They could not leave any stones unturned, and so far this evening was a bust. Besides kinky sex, there didn't seem to be anything dangerous going on at the club.

She sobered at the thought of what had happened to those girls in Philadelphia, renewing her purpose. She considered that Dominique had been gone with Rhea a little too long. She'd like the opportunity to interview her as well. Sydney scanned the hallways, trying to decide which way to go next. *How the hell am I going to find them in this labyrinth?* Putting one foot in front of the other seemed the only way, so she continued walking and glancing in rooms that were open to public viewing. Nothing seemed amiss. She could see a blue light coming out of one of the rooms at the far end of the hallway on the right. It was so dark in this area she really hoped there weren't any bugs or mice back here, or she'd freak out.

Caution told Sydney she might want to check her weapons, so she reached down into her boots, making sure the silver stake, knife and chain were still there. As she looked up again toward the end of the hallway, someone slammed her hard against the wall. She could barely see the outline of a bearded man who smelled of stale cigarettes and whiskey. He firmly held her to the wall with a stubby hand on each of her bare arms. She struggled but was unable to dislodge him.

"Hey, missy, what ya doing back here all by yourself in the dark? Your blood," he leaned in to sniff her neck, "oh yes. It smells so good. What kind of a master would let his human run around back here unprotected? You need a real master to get you in line. How I'd love to spank that pretty ass of yours and drown in your sweet blood. Come on now, this is going to be fun."

Sydney recoiled from the putrid smell emanating from the vampire. She could see the fine points of his teeth glinting off the black light. Should she play innocent? Or pretend she belonged to him? But then again, Sydney was Sydney. She did not do damsel in distress well. *Fuck that. This foul-assed vampire is so going down.*

"Listen, pal. I'm giving you fair warning, get your fucking hands off me or you're going to regret it, last chance." She stared at him defiantly, planning her next move.

The vampire cackled in response, undeterred.

"Feisty one, aren't you? It's going to be a pleasure whipping you into submission."

He barely got his last word out when Sydney kicked him in the balls. Yep, no matter how supernatural you were, testicles were always vulnerable. Tried and true, Sydney loved how that worked. The vampire let go of her to clutch himself, and she whipped out the silver knife from her boot and held it to his throat.

"Sorry, pal. I must admit this has been fun…whipping your ass into submission and all…it's been a laugh riot. Now down to the floor, on your stomach, hands up over your head, or you're going to eat silver. And in case you feel like trying again, you best remember that I have a few vampire friends of my own back here, not to mention the silver stakes in my boot that I'm just itching to try out."

The vampire stretched out his hands and Sydney wrapped a thin silver chain around his wrists, effectively immobilizing him for the night.

"Now listen here, be a good little vampire and I'll let Miguel know you're waiting to be freed. I know you vamps have your own laws, so I'll let Kade know what you did to me, and he can decide what to do with your ass."

As she strode further down the hallway, Sydney stopped in her tracks on hearing the cry of a woman's voice coming from one of the rooms. It was familiar and in pain. Although several people might be in pain in a place like this, the hair on her arms stood straight up as she heard the woman scream again. *Dominique.* Sydney started running down the hallway, screaming Dominique's name. She turned left, then right until she found a closed metal door. Shit, it was locked and wouldn't open. She wished that she had some of those vampire super-strength skills about now. She shoved against the door, and then tried kicking it, but it wouldn't budge. *How am I going to get this open?*

Sydney pulled out the thin silver stake and her knife. Slowly manipulating them, she picked the lock and the door clicked open. As Sydney burst through into the room, she found Dominique handcuffed, lying on a large padded table. Sydney rushed over to help her. "Dominique, what happened? I thought vampires could easily break cuffs. Where's the key?"

"Sydney, please." Tears streaked down her face through a black blindfold. "Silver. The handcuffs…it's burning, please help me."

"It's going to be okay, Dominique. Just take a few deep breaths. I don't see the key anywhere, but I have a knife. Just hang in there."

Sydney finally picked the lock and broke the last handcuff off of Dominique, horrified by the oozing and third degree burns they left on her skin. Dominique was too weak to get off the table. Sydney cut off a piece of her skirt and began to dry Dominique's face.

"Thank you. I thought no one would find me back here. That little bitch Rhea did this to me. I was questioning her about Simone when she said her master wanted to play with me. I let her blindfold me, thinking it was a game and I could earn her trust enough so she'd talk. But when she cuffed me in silver, I fell onto the table." Dominique slowly sat up inspecting her burned wrists and ankles and then fell back onto the table, unable to stand, woozy from the silver. "Damn, now that's gonna leave a mark. Listen, Sydney, I need one of the guys to bring me a donor. I can feel them coming now. But I can't get up yet. I need blood."

"You'll be okay, Dominique. Just lie back until they get here. Are you sure Rhea was the only one here with you? Did she bring someone else into the room?" Sydney asked, determined to find out what had happened. A noise caught her attention and she observed an opened back door that led out to an alley. As much as she wanted to go investigate, she was not about to leave Dominique alone.

"I'm not sure if someone else was here." Dominique shook her head in confusion. "Usually we can sense such things, but the silver, it doesn't just burn like a motherfucker; it weakens all of our abilities. I was screaming at Rhea, but there could have been someone else. The fact is that Rhea is a human, possibly a witch cloaking her talent, but most definitely human. So she could have been thralled into doing this to me, but the vampire or mage would have needed to be close. But I didn't feel anyone when I entered the room with her."

The conversation with Gia, the bartender, garnered no tangible leads except the last known address of the staff member who had reported seeing Simone. Kade was getting frustrated. Simone was somewhere in this city and had been at this very club. They needed to find her before she killed another girl. After getting the address, Miguel stalled Kade at the bar and seemed to talk endlessly about nothing. Kade thanked him for his help and started to make his way through the crowd back to Sydney. By the time he reached the dance floor near the entrance to the back, he sensed something was wrong. He sped down the darkened hallway to find a male vampire attempting to escape silver chains. He could feel something was wrong with Dominique, but halted as he smelled Sydney on the dirty predator.

"Where is Sydney?" Kade growled.

The vampire strained to get a look at Kade. "Who? You mean that human bitch who chained me? Get me out of these. You really need to teach your slave girl better manners. I will be honored to watch you beat her. She needs to learn a lesson. Look what she did to me!"

Kade, furious beyond words, reached down with one hand and grabbed the vampire by his throat, bashing his head into the wall. "You touched her? You insolent fledgling. She's mine. You're going to pay for your misguided actions!"

"What, that human girl? You are kidding, right? You can find pussy anywhere you like in this city and you would seek to punish me for being who I am? A vampire?" he sneered at Kade.

With restrained emotion, Kade slammed him again, holding him up so far against the wall that his feet no longer touched the floor.

"No, I will punish you for being an animal who doesn't know his place in our society. You will never touch her or any other woman ever again. Your time on Earth has officially come to an end." In a swift move, Kade pulled a small thin wooden stake from his back pocket that telescoped like an antenna and snapped into place. With precision, he jammed the stake into the heart of the vampire. The hallway filled with ash as Kade ran forward in search of Sydney.

Kade rushed into the room followed by Luca and Xavier. Spinning Sydney around, he hugged her tightly.

"Sydney love, I leave you for ten minutes and you manage to find trouble? Are you okay? He didn't hurt you, did he?"

"Who, stubby vamp boy in the hallway?" Backing out of his embrace, Sydney laughed it off. "He may have left a bruise on my oh-so-delicate skin, but as you probably noticed, he won't be messing with me anymore. Don't worry about me....Dominique's the one who needs help. She said she needs a donor, and as much as I would love to help her I'm kind of attached to my blood."

Sydney and Dominique explained what had happened with Rhea. While a vampire could have been responsible for Rhea's actions, Kade suspected that Rhea was a witch who was working with Simone.

"Luca, Xavier, go sweep the alley. She's probably gone, but we should check anyway."

Sydney was strangely touched as she watched Kade hold Dominique's hand. He felt something for this female vampire, but she wasn't sure what it was. Love? Responsibility? She questioned herself, wondering if she should be jealous, but she wasn't. No, what she felt was admiration for Kade, a leader taking care of his own, comforting Dominique as a father would a daughter.

Soon Etienne entered the room with a donor in tow. He was a ready and willing strapping young man, nearly twenty years of age. He appeared to be strong enough to feed her. Kade waved him over and held the man's wrist up to Dominique's mouth as she bit into him and sucked greedily.

As Sydney glanced away, she grew concerned that she should give them privacy. Such an intimate act, yet no one seemed to mind her presence. At that moment, she wondered what it would be like if Kade bit her, drank from her. Would it hurt? Would it bring pleasure? The word on the street was that women found it incredibly pleasurable, often orgasmic, but she wasn't just any woman. And Kade certainly wasn't just any vampire. Did he yearn to bite her? Would he try to bite her if they made love? As she contemplated the scenario, Sydney realized her thoughts were more than curiosity. No, she wanted Kade to bite her. As she stared at Dominique, latched to the donor's wrist, she glanced up to find Kade watching her, not smiling, but giving her a sultry, all-knowing look as if he knew what she was thinking. Sydney demurely averted her eyes; it was all too much.

When Dominique had healed and was strong enough to leave, their small group walked back through the dim hallway. Sydney stopped dead in the corridor as she kicked a pile of ash up into the air. Where was the chained vampire?

"Hey guys? Uh...did anyone see a vampire here? Silvered by the wrists? Smelly guy?" Without speaking another word, it clicked with Sydney that the vampire had not escaped. He was dead. She'd been kicking his ashes around with her boot. Yuck.

She looked down again at the floor and then up to Kade. He was dangerous; primal, unyielding. Sydney's breath hitched as he snaked his hand around her waist, holding her tight to his side.

"No one touches what is mine."

Sydney didn't flinch as she processed his words. He had killed the other vampire for attacking her. The police weren't called. No one even batted an eyelash that the guy was gone. Vampire justice. She shuddered at the power Kade held in this town and he drew her to him like a moth to a flame. She straightened her back and held her head high. If she was bothered or surprised by what he did to the vampire, she would not let him see it. Sydney gladly allowed Kade to usher her out of the club and into the limo. It had been a hell of a night, and she could not get out of there fast enough.

Chapter Fourteen

"Kade, what's going on?" Sydney asked as Kade shut the car door behind them. Only one limo had returned to the compound and Luca stayed in the car. "Where is everyone? I thought they lived here with you."

"No, love, they do not. While it is true that Luca lives on the compound, he doesn't live in the main house. His home is located next door, but is within the borders of the compound for safety." Kade trailed behind Sydney, appreciating her fine assets. Tonight she would be his. He smiled at the thought.

"Never a dull moment around here," she quipped, entering the foyer. Sydney unzipped her boots, took them off and started up the steps. "Just when you think you're shacking up with a bunch of vampires, you find out that there is really only one vampire. Lucky me."

Kade rushed toward Sydney, pinning her against the railing. His hands on her waist, he placed his forehead to hers. Their lips were mere inches apart.

"Sydney, there is only one vampire for you, and there is only one human for me, *you*. You are an incredibly courageous woman, fighting that vampire and saving Dominique. You never cease to amaze me, but you do worry me." He sniffed her neck. "I cannot bear the smell of that derelict on your sweet skin. We should both wash away the filthiness of the evening and rest ourselves for tomorrow night. A hot shower should relax your muscles nicely. Go on up. I'm going to get us something to drink, and then I will be up to massage your neck in a few minutes." Kade released Sydney, turned, and walked away into the kitchen. Wanting to kiss her, he'd make her wait until she craved his touch, begging for mercy.

For once in her life, Sydney was speechless. Her body was humming with excitement, she wanted, no needed, Kade to make love to her, but he hadn't. Where was her trusty vibrator when she needed it? What a crazy night, and now this. She sighed. Kade was right about one thing, she needed to relax, and apart from him or her battery-operated friend, a shower was the second best option. She was disgusted by her experience with the vampire; she could still smell the odors of cigarette smoke, sex, blood, and sweat from the club clinging to her clothes and hair.

As Sydney undressed and walked into the guest bathroom, she admired her surroundings. A bathroom like this would take up half her condo. The huge granite shower had several nozzles that sprayed overhead as well as sideways. Jumping into the spray, she shut the glass doors. The hot water rushed over her hair and body. Sydney closed her eyes, willing her mind and muscles to relax.

Her eyes flew open when she heard the bathroom door click open and shut. *Kade.* He was in here with her? Her heartbeat sped up knowing that he was near. She leaned further into the pulsing rain, anticipating his touch. Her body awakened, tingling with the knowledge he'd come for her.

With her face to the wall, she sighed as Kade came up behind her, his erection brushing against her back. As his hands worked their way into her hair, she smiled. He gently scrubbed her hair with shampoo, letting the bubbles sluice down her body. She let him tease her, drawing out the tension.

Holy fuck. Sydney could barely take it. The man finally had her naked, and he was driving her crazy with need by simply washing her hair. She laid her hands flat against the granite tiles and rolled her head back to give him better access. She couldn't stop herself from moaning out loud as she felt his hands rubbing the soapy bubbles across her shoulders and down around her waist. She hungered for his touch, feeling his strong hands slide over her wet, shivering skin.

"Kade, please. We've waited so long. I just…I can't wait anymore."

"Sydney," he whispered. "Goddess, you're so soft. Do you remember when I told you that you would be mine tonight? I meant it. Are you ready?"

His cock stood to attention at the sight of her shapely ass. Unable to abstain any longer, Kade glided his palms up across her belly, pulling her toward him until his hard length rested firmly above her bottom. His hands roamed over her soft breasts, gently caressing them and rolling her nipples between his thumb and forefinger. He moaned in pleasure at the feel of her soft body against his.

"Yes. I'm more than ready," Sydney replied.

"I have waited centuries for the right woman, and you are most definitely the one." He breathed in deeply, trying to resist burying himself in her right there.

"Please, Kade, please," she begged.

Kade massaged her breast with one hand, letting his other hand drop down between her legs. She opened her thighs, allowing him better access. Sydney screamed his name as he reached into her slick center, exploring every inch of her warmth. He circled her clit and then plunged a thick finger deep inside her. She rested her forehead against the cool tile, panting with desire.

"That's it, Sydney, feel me in you. Let it go. You are a beautiful, amazing woman, my woman." The one? In the heat of the moment, she wanted to believe that what he was saying was true, but she couldn't think clearly when her senses were so delightfully assaulted. As Kade pinched her nipples, blood rushed to her clitoris. She ached to be touched. She wanted him inside her, now.

As Kade added a second finger inside of her, she cried out loud. A crescendo of pleasure built up in her that was about to come crashing down. Kade coaxed her on, encouraging her to reach her climax.

"Yes, love. Come for me. That's it."

His fingers stimulated her sensitive nerves inside, and she couldn't hold back any longer. Sydney's orgasm crashed over her in waves as she trembled at Kade's hand. She thought she would collapse in the shower except for the fact that he turned her in his arms and held onto her tightly.

Reaching over, Kade turned the water off. Sydney protested.

"No Kade, don't leave. Please, make love to me now."

"I have every intention of doing just that, but I want our first time to be special. I plan to take my time with you slowly savoring every part of you. Come here…with me." He wrapped a warm, fluffy towel around her. After drying their bodies, he took her hand in his and led her into the bedroom.

Sydney's heart squeezed as she noticed at least two dozen lit candles scattered all over her room. The bedspread had been turned down, and there were rose petals on the sheets. Her vampire was a romantic. No one had ever done anything like this for her.

"Kade…it's beautiful," she gasped.

Smiling back at her, Kade wrapped his hands around her waist, drawing her into him so her breasts crushed against his hard chest.

"I am glad you like it. Now I intend to show how special you are to me, every last inch of you," he said suggestively.

They both stood naked at the foot of the bed. With reckless abandon, Kade speared his fingers through Sydney's hair, grasping her locks in his hands, and he kissed her. Not a soft kiss, but a hard, demanding, possessive kiss. Sydney welcomed his tongue, tasting him, lost in his dark embrace.

Kade yearned for this woman like no other. He planned to claim her tonight, but knew she was the one claiming his heart. They fell upon the bed together, their arms entangled, reaching, touching. Struggling for dominance, Kade pinned Sydney on her back. He dipped his head down, his mouth seeking her rosy tips. He finally found what he was looking for, laving her peaks and gently biting down. Sydney moaned and arched her back at the erotic pleasure and twinge of pain.

Reaching up, Kade caressed her breasts with his hands as he slowly kissed his way down her stomach. Sydney writhed on the bed in anticipation. She felt a kiss to her hip, a kiss to her thigh, a kiss below her belly button. He slowly spread her legs, feasting upon the sight of her waxed, bare beauty. He ran a hand down her mound and felt her shiver underneath his touch. He planned to tease her again and pleasure her beyond her wildest dreams. Lowering his head, he kissed along the crease of her legs. Not being able to resist any longer, his tongue ran up and down her lips. He pressed his mouth into the core of her, sucking her tender nub.

Sydney splayed her arms to each side of the bed and grasped the sheets in a tight hold. Her reaction to his mouth on her delicate skin was so intense she thought she would fly off the bed. Colors danced in her head as Kade licked and suckled her sex. Sydney began to beg him again as her body filled with overpowering sensations.

"Oh my God. That feels so good. I…I…please."

Kade slowly plunged a finger, then two into her pussy while continuing to lick her, concentrating on her soft bundle of nerves. He slipped in and out of her as he drank her luscious essence, bringing her closer and closer to release. He loved hearing her beg and longed to reward her. He gently curved his fingers inside, stroking her thin line of sensitive fibers. As he stroked her, he flattened his tongue, pressing down hard, then sucking, tantalizing her over the cliff of arousal.

Sydney convulsed in orgasm as she felt his fingers stroke her while he continued to kiss her sex. Wave after wave of orgasm descended upon her as she screamed Kade's name over and over. She curled over to her side for a minute, feeling as if every nerve of her skin was on fire. She was exhausted but ready to take Kade inside her. She needed him, in her arms, making love to her.

"That was incredible…oh my God."

Kade stalked above her like a hungry panther. She reached up, sliding her palms over his hard, lean muscles. She hungered to lick every bulge of his ripped abs. As he rested on his arms above her, they gazed into each other's eyes. Kade's focus fell to her lips, and he kissed her gently, their tongues dancing with each other. Loving. Caring.

"Sydney, you are exquisite…I look forward to tasting you over and over through eternity."

"Please, make love to me. I can't stand it…I ache for you."

"Are you sure, love? After tonight, there is no going back."

Sydney quietly nodded.

Kade grasped her wrists with one hand, pushed her arms up over her head, and pressed his lips to hers in a passionate kiss. Confident that she was ready for him, he thrust his cock into her core in one primal stroke. Pumping slowly in and out of her, he reveled in how wonderful her tight, warm sheath felt around him. He wanted so badly to make it last but was struggling to hold his orgasm at bay. Sydney was finally his. The resplendent woman beneath him provoked an appetite that he hadn't known existed. For all of his physical strength, she simply had no idea how much power she wielded over his heart.

Sydney stretched to accommodate Kade's ample size. Allowing him to hold her arms above her made it possible for her to give in to her most carnal desire to submit to him. She arched her hips up into him, her clitoris grazing his nest of curls. Shuddering in pleasure with every stroke, Sydney wrapped her legs around his waist, pulling him closer.

Kade slowed his pace, his eyes locked on hers.

"Kade, need more. Please, God, don't stop."

"Things will never be the same for either one of us after tonight," Kade growled, his fangs elongating. He licked the curve of her neck, losing himself in the lusciousness of her warm skin. There was no going back. He couldn't hold on any longer. "You. Are. Mine." He pulled back his hips and drove into her hard as he bit into the soft flesh of her neck.

Sydney's sweet blood filled his mouth as he continued to pump voraciously into her body, spilling his seed deep within her. Releasing her hands, he rolled onto his back pulling her to him, embracing her closely. Kade closed his eyes, overwhelmed by his response to her. Not just her body and blood, but her mind as well. Without a doubt, he knew this woman was the one, and he had just claimed her. Forever.

Chapter Fifteen

Sydney awakened to the sounds of birds chirping outside. Kade lay unnervingly still next to her. She reached over and stroked the hard lines of his chest, reminiscing about their lovemaking. He'd insisted that she was his, and Sydney struggled to understand what that meant to a modern woman like her. *How many women belong to him?* She knew he'd been around for a very long time, but he'd told her that he'd only loved a few women.

Sydney's heart constricted at the thought that there could be anyone else in his life. Then she knew in an instant that meant she was in trouble. *Shit. I'm falling for him. No, no, and hell no.* This couldn't be happening, yet it was. No one in her entire life had made her feel the way she had last night: wicked, euphoric, loved. That was it…loved. Did he love her? Was that what he meant when he kept saying she belonged to him? Eventually they would need to talk about what this all meant.

How was she supposed to have a relationship with a vampire? First, there were location issues. She lived in Philadelphia, he lived in New Orleans. She had a job, commitments. Second, he would totally outlive her. She'd be an old woman, and he'd still be looking like he stepped off the cover of GQ. Third…third? Why was she even running through these scenarios? She wasn't even sure he was serious about her. For all she knew, being 'his' meant he thought she was one of many women. *A harem? A bloody vampire harem. Stop worrying, Syd!*

Needing to clear her head, she tiptoed away from the bed into the bathroom, convinced that a nice, hot shower would make everything okay. An ache grew in her chest as she stepped under the hot spray. *Nice job, Sydney. You're falling in love with a vampire. A hot, sexy, romantic vampire.* Shaking her head in disbelief, she quickly washed her hair, soaped her skin, rinsed, hopped out of the shower, and dried herself.

When she opened the door to the bedroom, disappointment washed across her face. The bed was sadly empty. Where had Kade gone? Feeling a sense of loss, she dressed, avoiding looking at the bed where they'd made love. Hearing a familiar buzzing, she frantically searched for her cell phone. *Why can't I be more organized?* Finding it in a pile of clothes, she answered the call. "Hey." It was all she could manage amid her confusing thoughts.

"Hey to you too," Tristan replied. "I got down early this morning. I'm staying at my brother's condo on Royal Street. How about you grab a taxi and meet me for beignets?"

"Now, that's what the doctor ordered. You've got my weapons?" Sydney felt as if she was suffocating in the guest room. A little time away from vampires would be good for her.

"Sure thing. I packed them up in a backpack so no one will notice. It's about four o'clock now. Can you get down here in about forty-five minutes?" he asked.

"Yes, sounds great. Meet you there. Thanks Tris!" Sydney sighed, clicking off her cell. She and Kade would have to talk later, but for now, it was back to reality. She desperately wanted her weapons, especially after last night's incident with the vampire in the hallway.

Sydney slid on a flirty, purple sundress and adjusted the thin straps that supported her C cupped breasts. She slipped on a sexy black lace thong on the off chance she'd get surprised by Kade later. Thank goodness she'd been able to find a pair of comfortable sandals on her shopping trip the other day. Comfort was a must for running around in the city. Glancing in the mirror, she pulled her long, blonde hair into a ponytail and added pink shimmer lip gloss. She almost left the room without grabbing her silver knife. With nowhere to conceal it on her body, she quickly slid it into her purse on her way out of her room.

Walking through the house, she noticed it was quiet, too quiet. Nothing but silence filled the great room. Where did Kade get off to now? She steeled her emotions, afraid that he might not be serious about her. What man leaves a woman's bed while she's in the shower, wet, naked? Sydney peeked down the long hallway past the kitchen and heard Kade's voice coming from one of the rooms. Even though the door was cracked open, she didn't want to intrude on his business. But then again, why the hell not? He did leave her bedroom after the most fabulous night of making love, ever.

Brimming with confidence, Sydney swung the door open and leaned against the doorjamb. With a hand on her hip, she watched Kade intently as he leaned back in a black leather chair, his feet propped on an antique, cherry desk. *Nice desk,* she thought…a picture formed in her mind of her bent over it, with Kade taking her from behind. She gave him a wicked smile. He grinned, blew her a kiss, but kept on conversing about Issacson's company investments while she stood there waiting for him to get off the phone. God, that man was sexy as hell…but infuriating. *He's not hanging up for me, really?* Sydney gave him an innocent wave, turned on her heels, and trudged back toward the kitchen. She decided that since he was busy, then the man was getting a note.

She quickly scrawled a message, letting him know she was going to meet Tristan and that she'd be back in a couple of hours. Convinced that Kade wasn't getting off the phone any time soon, she taped it to the inside of the front door. Patience wasn't her strong suit, but at least she'd let him know where she was going. Sydney loved New Orleans and was hoping she'd get a chance to window shop for antiques on Royal Street on her way back. She really wanted to go over and check out the address they got last night, but she knew that the other vampires wouldn't be at full strength until sunset. And after last night, she hadn't planned on going to the address by herself without backup.

Deciding against a taxi on a warm summer day, Sydney opted for a ride on the St. Charles Streetcar from the Garden District to the French Quarter and then grabbed the Canal Streetcar over to the Riverfront Streetcar to meet Tristan. She loved taking in the sights of the city, while riding on the train. Within a half hour, she arrived at her stop and hustled down the riverfront steps to Café du Monde.

Tristan was already seated at a corner table under the open-air canopy with a large platter of beignets sprinkled with powder sugar and a café au lait awaiting her. Sneaking up behind him, she wrapped her hands around his neck and planted a chaste kiss to his cheek.

"Hey, mon loup, you want some company?" she teased seductively.

"You really are looking to get me killed down here in New Orleans, aren't you, Syd?" Tristan laughed.

"What are you talking about? Can't I give a wolf a little love? I missed you. You don't know what it's like being surrounded by vampires twenty-four-seven. You have to come back with me to Kade's. We have an address we're checking out as soon as the sun goes down."

Tristan handed her a mug, sliding the plate of beignets in front of her. "First things first, you really don't get how a little wolf lovin' could get me killed, do you, mon chaton?" he asked. "Look, Kade and I go way back, we're close. And let me tell you that in all the years that I've known him, he has never expressed his desire to claim a woman. I can smell him on you. Remember? Super-wolf sniffer? And as hard as you tried to hide it with makeup, I can see that he marked you. You may not know it, sweet Syd, but you are his." He grinned, bringing his cup to his lips.

Sydney nearly spilled her coffee, slamming it down on the table. "Marked? Claimed? What the hell is that supposed to mean, Tristan? Claimed like luggage? I'm sick as shit of all this supernatural lingo, and rules! Rules that don't even apply to me, by the way, as everyone down here keeps reminding me that I'm human, which I pretty much take to mean 'less'." She picked up another beignet, fully intending to shove it into her mouth. "You know what; don't even explain it to me. I'm sorry I asked. As much as I love the Big Easy, I am so ready to get back to Philly where I'm appreciated for my kick-ass human qualities." She bit into the beignet, and powder sugar sprayed over her plate.

Tristan laughed out loud. Poor Sydney just had no idea what was going on with her and Kade. And Kade didn't seem to be doing a very good job communicating it. He had a tiger by its tail, one that had sharp teeth and bit. This was going to be fun to watch.

"Listen Syd, I didn't come all the way down here to get you riled up. Look what your Alpha brought you…a pretty pink backpack with all kinds of fun toys." He held up the bag and smiled.

"Now, that's what I'm talking about. Thanks." She took out her cell and glanced down at the time. "As much as I'd like to soak up the sounds of the city, we'd better start making our way back to Kade's. The sun will be down in an hour or so, and I don't want to waste time finding this bastard."

Tristan stood and left money on the table.

"Okay, let's roll," Tristan suggested. As he went to leave, he caught sight of her weaving her way through the maze of tables, smiling as if she hadn't a care in the world. *Oh yeah, this is going to be fun all right.*

Kade finished talking with his overseas contacts and sighed. As much as he'd wanted to hang up the phone and go make love to Sydney again, he needed to take care of Issacson's investments. Issacson Securities was a firm he'd built over the years, one that catered to supernaturals. He'd been neglecting business while in Philadelphia, so completing the call was a necessity. Kade was a man who honored his commitments and his clients trusted him with their finances.

Just as he was about to go look for Sydney, Luca entered his office. Waving a piece of paper in the air, he seated himself in the chair across from Kade's desk.

"So, did you hear from the witch?"

Kade nodded. "Yes, and interesting news, the address she gave me matches the one we got from the bartender last night. A mage by the name of Asgear bought Vin Vin oil around six months ago…fits our time frame. So maybe we'll get lucky tonight and find Simone. When is everyone coming over here? We should prep Sydney and the others."

"Yeah, about your girl." Luca smirked knowingly. "Do you happen to know where she is?"

"She is here in the house. I just saw her a few minutes ago standing at my door. Why do you ask?" Kade's lips tightened.

"Well, you might be interested to know that she took off to meet Tristan in the French Quarter, alone." He threw the note across Kade's desk. "You must have been on your conference call a little longer than you thought."

Kade read the note, feeling blood rushing to his face.

"Damn, stubborn woman. I specifically told her not to go out alone. She does not follow instructions," he muttered.

"Or simply does not wish to and ignores them on purpose. She's with Tristan, though. Surely he will protect her?" Luca could not resist stirring the pot.

"She is mine," Kade barked.

"I see," Luca said quietly. "I must inquire, Kade, does she understand how you feel? Does she know that she has been claimed, or what that means? That she is yours? She is only human after all."

"Hell, I don't know. You know me better than anyone. I've had many women over the centuries, but only a handful of actual lovers, women I cared about. But this human woman, she…she makes me crazy. Crazy with lust, crazy frustrated, infuriated at times. She won't obey orders, putting herself in danger left and right. Worse, danger is part of her job, so she acts like it is perfectly normal. And as insane as she makes me, I cannot resist her. There has been no one like her, ever." He rubbed his brow with one hand and stretched his neck from side to side. "I must talk with her when she returns. This nonsense has got to stop. And if she has been with Tristan…" He could not even go there. He loved Tristan, but would rip out his heart if he touched her today. He knew they had a past relationship, but he had informed Tristan of his intentions with Sydney, which Tristan had agreed to honor.

"Listen, I'm sure she'll return safely." Luca rose and patted Kade's shoulder. "It's daytime, and Tristan will escort her back here. Even I must admit that Sydney is a very capable woman. You know that I'm generally opposed to getting humans involved in vampire business; their weakness puts us all in danger. But the woman has staked two vampires so far and rescued Dominique, so I have to give her that. I'm still not crazy about having a human working the case with us, but she is proving her worth.

"As for Tristan, you are friends." Luca crossed the room to the doorway, knowing he needed distance for what he was about to say to Kade. "He will honor your intentions with Sydney…as will I."

Kade listened, already aware of what Luca was thinking.

"Last night, on the dance floor, dancing with Sydney, with you and her. It was intimate. I have not danced with a woman in a very long time. She is…" He lowered his eyes in submission. "She is very desirable, but Tristan and I are your friends. Even if Sydney doesn't yet understand the extent of your feelings, we have a pretty good idea. None of us will pursue her, knowing she is yours. Well, not unless you invite me in on the fun again," he joked, trying to diffuse the tension. Kade knew Luca had been aroused the previous night. But he'd controlled the situation, had given Luca permission. He'd felt no jealousy, as he danced erotically with them both. It wasn't as if he and Luca hadn't shared women in the past. But there would be no sharing Sydney. Dancing was one thing, making love was another. Kade was falling in love with her. Sydney was his, and he needed to make her understand they could have a future together.

Sydney pushed through the front door feeling refreshed. Kade stood waiting in the foyer, his arms crossed, aiming a menacing glare at her and Tristan.

"Look, man, I told her you'd be pissed for not telling you where she was going. And before you vamp out on me, no, I did not touch her." Tristan retreated a few steps and held his hands up in surrender. "So, looks like you guys have a lot to talk about. I'm gonna get something to eat."

Kade shot his friend a look of irritation as Tristan waved, making his way toward the kitchen.

"Listen, Kade, I'm not sure why you're boring holes into me, but I just went out for beignets and I needed to get my weapons and…" Sydney began.

Kade tore across the room, possessively grasping her arms and pulling her into him closely. Her bag dropped to her feet. They were so very close, chest to chest, face to face, forehead to forehead. He would never hurt a single hair on her head, but she needed to understand the seriousness of running around in this city alone. Most importantly, she needed to understand that she belonged to him for the rest of time.

"Sydney, love, what don't you understand about my directions? I told you not to go out alone. Outside this house, Simone can get to you, any time, any place. You scared the life out of me," he growled.

"You said that I was expected to consult on this case, not pursue leads on my own, and follow your directions…all of which I've been doing. Furthermore, you do not get to tell me what to do in my spare time," she said, pointing a finger at his chest. Showing no remorse, Sydney defiantly wrenched out of his arms. "I would have been more than happy to tell you where I was going today had you actually stuck around in my bed this afternoon to find out, or if you had taken the time to talk to me when I came looking for you. You did neither of those two things, so I left you a note. Which by the way, I believe was a perfectly acceptable alternative considering how you treated me."

This woman was trying to make him insane. Her full, lush lips beckoned to him, as did her engorged tips straining against her tight, purple sundress. She needed to be taught a lesson all right, but his cock grew in instant arousal, with a very different activity in mind.

"You, me, now. My office." He pointed down the hallway and took her by her hand. He was not having this conversation out in the middle of the house where Tristan and Luca could hear every last word, not to mention the others who would soon be here.

Sydney winced as Kade slammed the office door shut, plowing his fingers through his hair. He paced the room, finally positioning himself directly in front of her chair, and her eyes drifted to his groin. *I did not just look there. Okay, I did.* Averting her eyes to his desk, which also brought dirty thoughts to mind, she huffed.

"I didn't deliberately set out to make you angry, but you've got to look at this from my perspective. It's not my first time in New Orleans. You were busy; I left a note and went directly to meet Tristan. I was perfectly safe."

"Sydney, first, let's get something clear, until Simone is caught, you cannot go out on your own. We found a mage suspect who happens to reside at the same address the bartender gave us. Said mage would not be limited during the daylight hours. So even though you thought you may have been safe, you could have been bespelled at any time."

"Okay, point taken," Sydney conceded. *Spells? Witches? Mage?* The last thing she needed was for someone to put a whammy on her while she was looking to get her beignet on. "I promise. No going out alone, but in my defense, I did leave a note. So, it wasn't as if I just went missing." She'd known he'd be angry but hadn't expected the intensity of his reaction. The cop in her told her to be mad at him, but his pure masculine strength reverberated throughout the room, making her grow wet with desire.

"No going anywhere without me," he repeated. Like a predator, he deliberately locked in on his prey, closing her knees together as he straddled her legs, dominating her personal space.

Sydney nodded in agreement. As he towered above her, she could feel the heat of him upon her. Blood rushed to her face as she became swollen below with need. The man was so sexy, delicious, and all hers.

"Last night was electrifying," he continued, twirling a strand of her hair. "Making love to you…I have never felt for a woman what I feel for you. You must understand that we are halfway bonded to each other. When I bit you…" He trailed his finger along the mark on her neck. She shivered in anticipation, wanting more. "When I bit you, I claimed you as my own, my woman. I am falling for you, Miss Willows, and I don't intend to let you go…not after this case is over…not ever."

Sydney's heart ached, finally hearing him say that he wanted to be with her. She gazed up into his piercing eyes and felt as if he could see into her very soul.

"Kade, I'm falling for you too. I…I don't know what this all means, but I want to explore this with you…our feelings, our relationship. I can't believe I'm even saying this, but us…last night…it was amazing. You overwhelm me. I want you so much I can't think straight."

Sydney craved him; his kiss, the taste of him. Reaching up his hard, muscular thighs, she let the palms of her hands roam toward his growing arousal. Ripping his belt off within seconds, she unzipped his pants, releasing his straining masculinity.

"Yes," he groaned as she took him into her hands.

"I have to taste you now, can't wait." Stroking his throbbing shaft, she licked the underside of him, laving it from root to tip. Drawing out the pleasure, she pressed the crown between her lips.

"Sydney, you're killing me." Kade's head lolled back.

That was exactly what she was planning…to bring him to his knees. Pumping his stiff, wet shaft in her hand, she gradually slid his thick hardness all the way into her warm, parted mouth. She pumped him in and out, sucking and relishing every hard inch of him, while sweeping her tongue along his length. Reaching under his rigidity, she caressed his tightened balls, tenderly rolling them in her hand.

"Sydney, stop, please, I want to make love to you…which I won't be able to do if you keep that up." Kade sucked a sharp breath, unable to endure the sweet torture of her moist, warm mouth.

Seductively, Sydney released him from her mouth pulling his pants down and off in the process. It was her turn to dominate, to take the initiative. God, she loved this man. She thirsted to enjoy his magnificent body. Standing up, she switched places with him, and pressed him down into the soft leather loveseat.

"I want to enjoy every inch of you, Mister Issacson, every hard inch," she purred. Climbing over him and yanking her dress up, she pulled off her thong and balanced her knees on either side of his thighs, hovering over his narrow hips, but not yet touching him. Kade clasped his strong hands around Sydney's waist, allowing her to direct the play.

The deep aching heat between her legs threatened to hasten her approach, but she wanted this to last. Desperately needing to taste Kade's skin, she slowly unbuttoned his shirt and threw it aside.

Kade reached under her dress to touch her, only to find the bare, silky skin of her soft flesh. "Aw…love…you're so very, very wicked. A naughty girl, my naughty girl. Truly, I cannot take waiting. Come here."

Placing his hand behind her neck, he pulled her toward him and fiercely kissed her. He captured her soft lips, his tongue finding hers. Sydney gave in to his intoxicating kiss, running her fingers through his hair. His fingertips dug into the smooth skin of her ass and massaged her toned muscles.

Allowing her hand to roam below, she rubbed his straining cock against her slick, wet crease, readying him for her. A burst of ecstasy shook her body as she guided him into her slowly, one incredible inch at a time. Slowly she sank all the way down on him, enveloping his entire length, joining their bodies as one.

"Yes! Kade, oh my God. You're so hard, so big. Please, oh yes!"

She arched her back, moving up and down in a rhythmic motion that stimulated her most tender nub. Sensing her increasing arousal, Kade reached a hand up and slid down the straps of her dress, freeing her full, heavy breasts. Leaning forward, he captured a nipple in his mouth, sucking and biting its tortured peak. Sydney moaned again, opened her heavy-lidded eyes and watched as he mastered her body.

The sight of him pushed her over the crest. She began forcefully riding him, both of them rocking to her rhythm. Sydney felt dizzy as her body started to shake intensely. He bit her softly on her breast, pushing her into an explosive climax. She cried out his name as she shuddered, riding out the last wave of her orgasm.

Kade reluctantly separated from her, dominantly lifting her from his lap. He glanced to the desk and raised an eyebrow at her.

"Desk. Now," he ordered.

"Yes," she breathed.

Kade gently bent her over it, placing her hands flat onto its surface. She grew hot as the cheek of her face settled on the cold leather desktop. He lifted her dress to expose the creamy flesh of her backside.

"You ready for me, love?"

"Please. I need you now. Inside me. Make love to me," she pleaded, her breath quickening as she anticipated his entrance.

Flattening his hands on her buttocks, Kade plunged inside of her core, filling her with his hardness. Her warm, moist sheath massaged his cock as he pumped in and out of her. He knew he wouldn't last long. Letting a hand slide up her back, he wrapped the long hair of her ponytail in his fist, tugging her back into him. She screamed his name in rapture, the pain and pleasure of the moment almost too much to bear.

Their bodies moved together as one. As he drove himself deep inside her, she pushed back on his shaft. Both Kade and Sydney fought for breath as they approached climax, moving in response to one another. Kade let go of her hair to tightly hold her by the waist, thrusting harder and harder. Knowing they were both close, he leaned over, pressing his chest to her back.

"I love you. Forever, you are mine," he whispered in her ear.

With those words, he slammed into her one last time while biting down on the back of her neck, releasing her divine blood into his mouth.

The slice of his teeth drove her into an uncontrollable orgasm. Pulsating waves of pleasure resounded throughout every square inch of her skin. Her contracting sex convulsed around Kade's cock, and he groaned loudly, erupting inside of her.

Sydney didn't resist as Kade slipped out of her, pulling her into his arms. He kissed the top of her head, and Sydney contemplated what he'd just told her. *I love you.* She could hardly believe that within days of meeting Kade, she'd fallen so hard for him. A vampire. Surreal as it was, she couldn't deny what was in her heart.

"Kade?" she whispered.

"Yes, love?"

"I'm not sure how it happened, or what kind of a future we can have…but," she began.

"Yes?"

"I love you, too." Sydney buried her face into his chest, surprised at the words that had spilled from her lips.

Sydney's heart raced as Kade lifted her chin and gazed into her eyes. He smiled in response, and she knew in that moment what he'd said was true, she'd forever be his.

Chapter Sixteen

Delightfully sore after making love with Kade in his office, Sydney sighed, reflecting on their night together. Her chest blossomed with the love she felt for this man. She couldn't believe she'd told him she loved him. She wasn't sure how it was going to work with her living in Philadelphia, but she decided not to dwell on the details.

Nothing was going to put a crimp in her day, except for Simone. Damn Voodoo, vampire bitch. Sydney sobered with the thought that they were about to go bust a mage, one who could very well put their lives in danger with dark magic. The address traced back to a large, abandoned building in the Warehouse District. Going in at night would give them a greater advantage, since the vampires would have the full use of their powers. Sydney, on the other hand, knew she'd be at risk, given her many human frailties, like not being able to see in the dark. Luca had provided her with a pair of state-of-the-art, night goggles so she could see better, but she still lacked the speed and power of the vampires.

After securing her hair in a neat French braid, Sydney pulled on a pair of black leather pants. The rugged fabric clung tightly to her finely toned figure. It might be a tad hot wearing leather on a warm, summer night in New Orleans, but her skin needed protection, given the abandoned building they planned on searching. She yanked a black cotton long-sleeved t-shirt over her head, but not before hiding a miniature curved sheathed Kerambit knife in a hidden compartment of her sports bra. Strapping on the bullet and stab proof Kevlar vest, she was almost ready to go. The clothing wasn't very comfortable. Sydney added a lightweight concealer jacket, which sported several hidden pockets and compartments where she could stash her ammunition: stakes, darts and silver chains. She strapped on both waist and leg holsters, loaded them up and paced the room, satisfied with the weight of her trusty Sigs. Before lacing up her military boots, she shoved a small, sheathed push dagger next to her ankle. The arrow-pointed knife was small, but effective in hand-to-hand combat.

Lastly, she pulled her pistol crossbow out of her backpack, checked and counted the wooden darts. Confident everything was in order, she strapped it across her chest, and it slung behind her back. Lifting the night goggles off the bed, she sucked in a breath, letting courage run through her veins. It was time to go kick some mage ass, and hopefully get one step closer to capturing Simone.

Entering the great room, Sydney steadied herself, taking in the sight of the vampires towering above her. They were also dressed in black combat outfits, ready to fight. In the doorway, she was surprised to see a large black wolf with amber eyes staring at her. She was tempted to ask if someone brought their dog, but thought better of it, realizing it was Tristan. Sydney didn't think he'd appreciate the dog joke, so she just nodded at him, not sure of what to say to his wolf. He yelped in response, and padded over to her side, rubbing against her leg.

When Kade entered the room, his presence dominated the space, and the air shifted. The wolf retreated away from Sydney, sensing Kade advancing directly over to her. Her body tingled in response to the sight of him. Dressed in black leather, he approached her. Looking dangerous and formidable, he was an animal in pursuit; hot, menacing, enticing. Sydney's pulse raced as if she and Kade were the only two people in the room.

He leaned toward her and captured her soft lips. Releasing her, he whispered in her ear, "You are ravishing in all that leather, love. It makes me want to take you upstairs and show you how very much I appreciate your outfit." He kissed her once again, asserting his claim on his woman.

"Seriously, you guys?" Dominique snorted. She flicked her long red nails which had been filed into fine points. "Enough with the lovey-dovey crap. It's time to go kill some bad guys. I'm looking forward to finding that little bitch who silvered me to the table and drinking her dry."

"Hey Dominique, how are the wrists? Your nails look great, love the color." Sydney smirked at the sight of a badass vampire girl worried about how her nails looked when she was about to go into combat.

"Thanks, Syd. Wrists are great. Amazing what a little blood can do." She laughed and held out her hands, showing off her polished talons. "The color's Sanguine Red. Want to make sure I look my best when I tear open Rhea…if that's even her real name."

"Okay, then. Good plan." Sydney raised an eyebrow at her, grinning. She didn't ever want to be on Dominique's bad side. "Can't say that I blame you after what she did to you yesterday. Hopefully we'll find her there tonight."

Kade moved to the center of the group, commanding attention.

"So, here's the deal. We are going downtown to the Warehouse District. Even though the building is abandoned, the area is active with humans, so keep a low profile. That means no killing within sight of others. Keep it in house." His lips tightened. "All we know so far is that Asgear is the mage who purchased the Van Van oil. So it is a good possibility that he is the one who is helping Simone. Asgear may be harboring dark magic, so no going it alone…stay together. Watch your step for traps. We'll be partnering up…Luca and I will go in first, then Xavier and Sydney. Dominique and Etienne, you bring up the rear. Tristan will be monitoring the outside, making sure we don't get any surprises while we're in there. If possible, we need the mage alive so we can get Simone's location. Got it?"

A sea of nods erupted, and Luca coughed. "We need to take two vans so we have enough room for all of us when we bring Asgear back to the compound. As for Simone's fledglings, my advice is to stake them and put them out of their misery. They'll be unable to give us any information because of their blood tie to Simone. That's about it. Everyone stay safe tonight."

"Let's go," Kade ordered. As the sober group filed out the door and into the vans, Kade prayed they'd all be coming back tonight.

The abandoned building was located on the outskirts of the Warehouse District. Sprinkled with restaurants, galleries and bars, the 'SoHo of the South' bustled with people on summer nights. Luckily, the address was located a little off the beaten trail, far enough away from most activities, reducing the risk of human interference. From the outside, the two-story, large brick building appeared desolate, with indecipherable graffiti painted on the walls. Sydney noticed all the front windows had been boarded over, some with new plywood and some with old. Perhaps a recent tenant had made the repairs?

As they circled the block, Kade pointed to the front doors, double steel with small square windows that had been spray painted over in black. There was another single door lower down, which looked like it could possibly lead to a basement. Driving around to the back of the building, they parked the vans. Kade, Luca and the others silently exited, seeking an entrance. Sydney guessed the vampires might have been telepathically communicating, as they appeared well synchronized, quickly locating and shimmying open the rusted locks on the rotting, wooden warehouse door.

A rush of stale air choked Sydney's lungs as the door swung open. Many of these old buildings had been abandoned in the late 1800s, outliving their usefulness as factories or mills. But this building stank of stale blood, decaying bodies, urine, and garbage, smells she was all too familiar with, working the city streets of Philadelphia. She may not have been a vampire, but she was certain recent activity had happened in this place. A chill ran up her spine as she remembered the vampire who'd attacked her in her home. Were there more just like him waiting here for them?

Total darkness descended upon them as they entered the dark hallway. Sydney flipped on her night vision goggles, and swung her pistol crossbow to her chest. Looking behind her, she saw Dominique and Etienne moving in stealthy silence. A confining, steep staircase led to a gray steel state-of-the-art security door. Pivoting around to face the group, Kade silently signaled his intent to breach the door. Muscular vampires would have no difficulty breaking it down. Bracing himself for impact, Kade raised his fingers. One. Two. Three.

Sydney crouched as dust and debris flew ubiquitously throughout the stairwell. Coughing up dust, she charged after Kade. At least twenty vampires flew at the doorway, fangs drooling and snapping at Kade and Luca. Immediately, a fight ensued in the spacious area. Sydney backed against a wall and systematically began picking off vamps with wooden darts to the heart. She was a good shot and ashes flew as they disintegrated on the spot.

"Remind me to stay on your good side, woman. You're damn good with the darts," Luca commented, sidling up next to Sydney against the wall. "Kade and I are heading toward the basement. Etienne and Xavier are taking the second floor. Now! Cover me!"

Luca dashed across the room with unnatural speed, catching up with Kade who was already at the basement door. Sydney took aim at a vampire lunging after him. Pop! The hit to the leg slowed him down, but Luca was struggling to shake him off. She didn't want to come off the wall just yet, but two more vamps were descending on Luca and Kade. *Where the fuck are they all coming from?*

Hoping she'd be fast enough, Sydney sprinted across the room, nearing Luca. In a last minute decision, she leaped onto the vamp's back and shoved a silver stake deep into its heart. Luca struggled to his feet. Grabbing Sydney's arm, he pulled her up with him. Sydney shook off the ash and backed against the doorjamb next to Luca.

"Going old school?" Luca asked with a small grin. "I appreciate the save, but don't get reckless. Kade will whip both our asses if something happens to you. Looks like he's already headed downstairs. Let's go with him. Stay close. I go first," he ordered.

Kade was already three quarters of the way down the stairs when Luca and Sydney started after him. The air hung heavy, an audible hum resonated from the basement walls, yet no apparent source could be seen. Illuminated in candlelight, a thin wiry man, who wore a glowing crimson robe, sat perched upon a stone pedestal. *Asgear.*

Kade attempted to maneuver toward him, but slammed against an invisible barricade. *Dark magic.* Asgear released a wicked laugh.

"Foolish vampire. Did you really think it would be that easy to capture me? My Mistress has anticipated your every move thus far. And while I've had great fun playing with you, the time grows near. She will ascend. You will be no more."

"Your Mistress, Simone, was banished over a hundred years ago. She has no right to be here and will soon be exterminated as punishment for her crimes. Give it up, Asgear. Tell me where she is. I will be fair meting out your sentence," Kade demanded.

"You're an arrogant vampire." Asgear ascended from the pedestal, floating across the room toward Kade, his feet never touching the floor. "You know nothing of the strength of my magic. I've been honing my craft for decades. Now, my power is growing exponentially every day as does hers. Soon, you'll be begging on your knees in agony as she drains the blood of your whore!" His eyes shot daggers at Sydney.

Luca and Kade pounded their fists against the barrier seeking a weak point, but it was unyielding. Attempting to kick at the invisible blockage, Sydney unexpectedly penetrated it, falling to her knees. Her hands scraped the concrete floor and began to bleed. Asgear laughed maniacally, amused by how easily the spider had caught the fly.

"Ah, Sydney. Welcome to my inner sanctum. We have such plans for you. You will serve a greater purpose. We have almost perfected the ritual."

"You must be out of your fucking mind if you think I will be part of any plans you have. I'm gonna bring you down. There are a few girls back in Philly who have a message for you and that bitch you call a Mistress. Now, do you want to come willingly or are we going to do this the hard way? You should know that I'm more than pissed, and could care less which way it goes," she spat at him. Sydney aimed her dart at Asgear, guessing a few holes would loosen his lips.

"Tsk. Tsk. Must you be so vulgar? You're less than nothing, a simple harlot, one who will serve nicely in our next Voodoo ritual. The Mistress seeks revenge for taking her husband. She's going to consume your spirit as you writhe in pain. Oh yes…your life force will add to her power quite nicely. The spirits will reward her greatly for the ritual. Now, come to me, Sydney, the portal awaits…we will take hedonistic pleasure at the palace of Voodoo. The spirits will bless us!"

Asgear's demented, Sydney thought. *A portal? Hedonistic pleasure? What the hell is he talking about? Fuck that.* She had no plans of going anywhere with this psychopath, let alone to some pleasure playground for dead people. She caught a glimpse of Luca and Kade, who were still pummeling against an invisible enemy. Sydney drew her pistol crossbow and fired twice, score. The darts tore through Asgear's leg and shoulder. He tumbled to the ground, spitting obscenities at her. She went to approach him, but he rose off the floor wickedly grinning at her, unharmed.

"Did you really think a few darts would hurt me? You stupid, stupid little whore! I am done playing. This game is over!" He lifted his hands into the air, mumbling chants that Sydney couldn't understand.

A rush of confusion washed over her as she began to feel dizzy. What was he saying? More importantly, how the hell did he get back up? Sydney started to waver as she desperately tried to retreat to Kade, but the pull of the air whirled around her, immobilizing her limbs. *Shit. This can't be good.* She flailed her arms and legs, struggling against the air current, but it was of no use. The air spun around and around, stinging her face.

"Kade! Help me! I can't move! Please!" Screaming into nothingness, Sydney hoped Kade could hear her. She stole one last look at him before she faded into blackness.

Kade and Luca choked on the stale dust as they rushed to Sydney, but it was too late. She was gone.

"Shit!" Kade yelled, outraged. "She's gone. She's fucking gone. My God. Asgear took her. They must have transported through a portal of some kind. We've got to find her."

They quickly searched the basement, but found nothing.

"There is no trace of her or Asgear," Luca said. "Where would he take her?"

"Let's just think. He was babbling about Simone, her plans." Kade plowed his fingers through his hair, frustrated. "Voodoo. Simone wants to use her as a doll. Something about using her spirit. But what she really wants is me. And power. She won't be satisfied by killing Sydney. No, she wants more. Asgear and Simone both want more. They want control over all the supernatural beings in New Orleans." He started to pace, trying to think where Asgear could have taken Sydney. "But where? This city is a hotbed of supernatural activity. They could summon spirits literally anywhere."

"She wants us to find her, Kade, so she can get to you." Luca blew out a breath, as Tristan, Etienne, Xavier and Dominique joined them in the basement. "Asgear, he said, 'palace of Voodoo'. A Voodoo museum? Maybe he meant the field where you burnt down the barn where Simone tortured the girls?"

"The cemetery, St. Louis cemetery." With ferocious intensity, Kade's eyes met Luca's. "Marie Laveau. Her mausoleum. It is the one place in New Orleans where even humans go to give sacrifices in the name of Voodoo. They could be anywhere on the grounds. Don't ask me how she's using the sacred cemetery to garner evil spirits, but that is where she's going. I just know it."

Chapter Seventeen

Sydney moaned in pain, realizing her hands were shackled in rusted metal cuffs linked to a two-foot chain above her head. Her body, sans clothes, slumped against a cold steel wall. A surge of panic rushed through her veins as she struggled to remember what had happened. *Asgear. Portal. Where the hell am I?* She stretched her legs, thankful that she still had on her underwear. Unable to reach down to her torso, Sydney jostled, hoping to feel the Kerambit knife still hidden in her bra. *Hello, baby, still there.* Relieved she still had a weapon, she took a deep breath, but nearly gagged on the stench of urine and vomit that permeated the air.

As her eyes adjusted to the pitch-black room, she sensed she wasn't alone. Hearing a moan, she called out into the darkness.

"Hey, is there someone in here with me? Who's there?"

"Over here," a weak, feminine voice answered. "I'm Samantha."

"Samantha?"

"Please don't hurt me," she begged.

"Willows. Detective Sydney Willows. I'm with the police. Listen, it's okay. I won't hurt you. How long have you been here? Are you injured?"

"I've been here a few days. Lost count after being beaten. I think I can walk, but I'm bruised. The cuts are healing. It's hard to see," she whimpered.

"You remember how you got here?"

"I was taken. My friends and I went to Sangre Dulce for fun. I'm not even from New Orleans. I was at a computer conference. It was my first time at that kind of club. We were just dancing. Then I met him. James…he seemed so nice. He bought me a drink. I don't remember anything else except for being here…him beating me. Oh my God. I'm going to die in here."

Sydney heard her crying. "Listen, Samantha, this is not your fault. There're some sick people out there who do bad things. I'm going to get us out of here. If they take me, just stay calm, okay? I promise I'll come back for you." She sighed, knowing things were about to get worse before they got better, and she didn't want to lie to the young woman. "I'll be honest, I'm not sure how this is going to go down, but my colleagues are coming for me. I'm sure of it." *I sure as hell hope they come soon.* "I need your help though, okay? Who else is here? Who have you seen since you've been here?"

"James. He brings me crackers…water. I tried to hit him the first day, tried to escape. Then he beat me. I haven't seen anyone else. But I think there might be a woman. I think I've heard her voice. I don't know, though. I haven't seen anyone else. I feel like I'm going crazy…maybe dreaming it. Even though I hear her voice, I've only seen James."

"Good girl, Samantha. Listen, this is how I'm going to play this. When James comes for me, I'm going willingly. I don't want him using me as an excuse to hurt you. You stay quiet, okay? Just let him take me, got it?" Sydney had to keep the girl alive.

"Please don't leave me here. I've got to get out of here. He's going to kill me. You promise you'll come back for me?"

Sydney didn't want to freak the girl out, but she figured she'd better warn her that there were *others*, other supernaturals who were coming for her. "I promise. Now listen, I have some friends who are vampires. They won't hurt you, and there's a very large, black wolf. They are friends. You'll be safe. If they come for you…if I don't make it back, you go with them, okay? They're the good guys."

"All right," Samantha sniffled in the darkness. "Oh my God. Shhh. I hear him. The keys. You hear the keys? It's him. He's coming."

Silence fell over the small closet-like prison cell as the girls awaited their captor. Feigning sleep, Sydney lolled her head back against the wall and closed her eyes. The sound of clanging of keys was followed by a creaking door. *Asgear.*

"Wakey, wakey, little whore," he called.

Sydney shivered as his clammy hands clamped onto her skin. He briefly freed her from her shackles but her hopes of freedom were crushed as she heard the unmistakable click of handcuffs closing around her wrists. She stumbled as he jerked her up onto her bare feet.

"The Mistress is pleased with my success. You're going to make a fine offering. Your smooth skin…ahhhhh." He ran a wet finger over the swell of her breasts. She recoiled from his touch. "Now, now, little whore. You will not get away from me so easily. Consider yourself lucky that I cannot take your body for my own carnal pleasures before giving you to my Mistress. So greedy she is…she wants you all to herself."

Sydney resisted telling him to go fuck himself as he continued to run his palms over her belly. She needed to conserve her energy, to get him to release her from her bindings.

"Go," Asgear ordered, propelling her forward into the bright hallway. "No funny business. I'd hate to have to bruise that pretty skin of yours before Mistress has her way with you."

Shuffling ahead, Sydney squinted as her eyes adjusted to the light. The cold linoleum floor appeared oddly clean. She'd take small favors at this point, given her lack of shoes. The hallway was only about twenty feet long, which initially led her to believe the space was small. A frigidness chilled Sydney's nearly naked body. *What was this place? A basement?*

A small vestibule led into a large, cathedral-like room made entirely of smooth, grayish limestone. Large silk scarves in various shades of blacks, purples and greens draped the walls. A shiver of terror tingled up Sydney's neck as Asgear dragged her across the chilled stone floor. Sydney spied a long, planked table with ropes attached to its legs and an enormous white chalk pentagram drawn underneath it. *Hemp and human hair rope?* At the front of the room stood an altar of some sort. Black and green candles burned brightly, illuminating a modest wooden box covered in black cloth, a golden chalice, and a long, silver sword.

"Oh great Mistress!" Asgear grinned widely, as if he was high as a kite. With grandeur, he spoke into the open space. "Our offering has arrived. She will serve us nicely so that the spirits of the dead will grant us their powers."

"Delusional much?" Sydney said, unable to resist. Eyeing the table, she refused to let him sacrifice her without a fight. She held onto the thought that Kade would find her. She just needed more time. "Asgear, even if you do manage to conjure up some evil spirit, do you really think that bitch mistress of yours plans to share the power with you…little mage that you are? Get real! So not happening."

She attempted to yank her arm free from his firm grip, but he dug his fingers into her skin. Angered by her actions, he spun Sydney around by her shoulders and backhanded her across her face. She fell to the floor as blood sprayed out of her mouth.

"Now look what you made me do, little whore!" he screamed violently.

Sydney spat at him as he reeled her up and thrust her onto her back upon the splintered wood table. She struggled unsuccessfully as he uncuffed her wrists one at a time and bound each hand to the legs of the table. She flung a leg toward him as he went to bind her ankle. She landed a blow to his nose, his bone crunching upon impact. Sydney tugged her wrists, trying to free herself, but he rapidly recovered.

"Be still!" he yelled and landed a slap to her face.

Sydney refused to give up, wildly kicking her legs, hoping to make contact again. Within seconds, her eye began to swell, blurring her vision. Asgear continued his task. He wound the rope around her ankles, fully securing her to the table until she was laid out spread eagle.

"Wait until my Mistress sees what you made me do!" He glared at her in disgust. "Your skin is marred. She won't be pleased at all."

Sydney continued to writhe on the table, struggling to liberate her hands from the cutting rope. Twisting to the side, her adrenaline spiked as she spied several of Simone's vampires entering and assembling in a circle at the perimeter of the room. *Shit, shit, shit. Freaking bloodsuckers.*

Asgear knelt in front of the altar and started rhythmically chanting. The din of the crowd quieted and Sydney turned her head toward the antechamber. Her heart raced as a pale, thin, tall woman entered and approached the altar. *Simone.* Her flowing, alabaster silk skirt grazed the floor as a train of fabric streamed three feet behind her. A matching silk bustier bolstered her small, ashen breasts. Simone's long raven tresses were pulled and parted down the middle flat on her head with a full, massive ponytail of tight ringlet curls, a late eighteenth century hairstyle. Sydney cringed at the overwhelming scent of gardenia perfume as Simone floated past her.

"Hey you!" Sydney screamed at Simone. Blood trickled from her eye and mouth. "That's right, I'm talking to you…you lily white, vampire bitch."

Simone glided over to the altar, scanning her worthy sacrifice.

"Silence, human! So, it is you who attempted to steal my husband. You are nothing more than a mere dollymop…a whore for his liking. You are nothing. I shall take my vengeance tonight and the torture will be sweet. The spirits will infuse me with gifts, supremacy. This city will return to its greatness under my rule."

"Fuck you! This isn't the eighteenth century, and Kade is not your husband. He doesn't love you. You are an evil, sick bitch who will regret the day you ever met me."

"I said SILENCE! It is time for the offering. I sentence this human to death in the name of Satan and all the spirits who wish to grant me their gifts. She is guilty of crimes against me, the high priestess vampire." She waved her hand, and the candlelight flickered as a cold breeze blew throughout the room. The circling vampires hissed at Sydney, their fangs dripping saliva.

Sydney tried to speak, tried to move, but she was completely paralyzed except for her breathing. Her eyes peered wide open, feeling the chill across her flesh. *This is not good.*

Through her peripheral vision, she could see Simone preparing some kind of concoction at the altar. Asgear spread oil on Sydney's forehead, chest, and abdomen while he continued his chanting. He pivoted, cupping the golden chalice with both hands, and hovered it above Sydney's head. Panic began to set in as Simone laid the cold, flat surface of a silver sword against Sydney's belly, dragging the sword crosswise. Blood pooled on Sydney's skin as Simone drew an X on the soft flesh.

"Your blood is my blood. Your life force is my life force. You give it to me freely as a punishment for your crimes. We shall drink your essence in preparation for the sacrifice." Simone spoke in a monotone, as the room fell into total silence. "Now, whore. I want to hear you scream!" She sliced deeply into the underside of Sydney's forearm, cutting so far through the tendons that the blood flowed freely. Crimson liquid rapidly filled the chalice to the brim. Asgear watched in exhilaration as Simone licked

Sydney's arm, sealing the wound.

Released momentarily from paralysis, Sydney cried out in pain, yet refused to give in to tears as her arm was slit open. She fought the vomit that rose in her throat as she watched Simone's acid tongue lick over her bloodied skin. Asgear began offering the chalice to the vampires to drink as some kind of a preparatory, bloody communion. One by one, they drank of her blood, passing the chalice to the next vampire.

Fear washed over Sydney as she spied the tool she suspected was used on the second murder victim. Simone inspected the twelve-inch-long needle, holding it to the candlelight. She raised the instrument into the air, and both Simone and Asgear began to chant in tongues. Vampires swayed in a trance to the nonsensical vocalizations. A strong hum started to vibrate the room and the wooden table shook.

In the middle of the chaos, Sydney felt him. *Kade.* She wasn't sure how she knew, but she did. He was here for her. *I love him.* It was her last coherent thought before Simone shrieked and slammed the full hilt of the needle down into Sydney's torso, penetrating her belly clear down into the table.

Chapter Eighteen

"What in the hell just happened?" Tristan questioned his friends accusingly. "Goddammit! You were supposed to keep her safe! I should have gone with you instead of guarding the perimeter!" Tristan felt guilty, knowing he too had planned this failed operation with Kade and Luca. Although she wasn't wolf, he considered her under his protection since the day he'd met her. Former lover, good friend, Sydney was his one link to the human world that he trusted with his life. Now, because of their miscalculations, she might be dead. Tristan howled loudly, frustrated with their defeat and the potential loss of his friend.

"You're right. Luca and I lost her, but we cannot focus on failure right now. We need to plan on how we are going to kill Simone and extract Sydney safely. You know our girl is not going to go down without a fight. She is strong." Kade deliberately called her, 'our girl', trying to get the group focused on the task that needed to be done. They needed to find her quickly and kill Simone. Sydney was no one's but his and everyone knew it, but he was a leader and could not let them dwell on their defeat. No, he needed to get Sydney back safely into his arms. He had not lived through centuries only to lose his chance with her, his one true love. "Tristan, take Luca's cell phone and call your brother, Marcel. Let him know the situation has escalated, and that we need his pack's assistance with backup."

As they arrived at the cemetery, Kade stiffened, sensing Sydney's presence.

"I feel her. She's here."

"Kade, please forgive my question, but I sense no human or paranormal presence in the area. Are you certain she is here?" Etienne asked.

"Yes. Do you forget? I have claimed her. I'm certain that she is here. Quickly, search the grounds. Stay in pairs," Kade ordered.

A high-pitched howl emanated across the darkness; Tristan. Weaving through the tenebrous labyrinth of crypts, Kade and the others converged on a nondescript tomb that no one would give a second glance to, compared to its ornamental counterparts. *Sydney*. Like Tristan, Kade could smell the sweet scent of her blood everywhere in the vicinity, as well the repugnant odors of Asgear and Simone.

"She's here, but Asgear and Simone are also present. We must move with caution. Simone will be expecting us," Kade warned. He'd need to rely on his friend to distract them so he could get to Sydney. "Tristan, you go in first and disable Asgear. We cannot be certain if he will conjure a thaumaturgical barrier like the one we experienced back in the warehouse, so make sure to cover the whole area. If Simone is in there, then it is likely that all vampires can pass. We won't know for sure until we get in."

Tristan transformed back into his naked male form, extending his claws, planning to pry open the stone door. A chorus of wolves howled in the distance.

"Ah, Marcel and the pack are here. They will come in behind us, and kill any of Simone's vampires who try to escape."

"Now, let's see what is in this tomb." Tristan ran his claws up and down the hard, smooth stone, loosening it. "Open up for papa."

"Back off, Tristan," Kade commanded. *Wolves always think they are so damn smart.* "Watch and learn, wolf." He smiled, unfolding his Smith & Wesson tactical knife. "Sometimes a vampire is well suited going old school, now is one of those times."

Plunging the edge of the knife far into the dusty stone seam, he jerked it upward, disengaging the primitive lock mechanism. The heavy mason door creaked open as it revealed a limestone staircase. The tunnel was illuminated by candles that sat on small wall shelves. Transforming back into his wolf, Tristan padded down the steps tilting his head back up toward Kade, awaiting his orders at the door at the bottom of the stairs.

A blood-curdling scream resonated throughout Kade's mind. Sydney's scream, Sydney's blood. He kicked the door open, letting Tristan run first into the madness. The wolf narrowly escaped being clawed by several vampires converging toward him. Slipping between their legs, he targeted Asgear who was holding a chalice above Sydney, who appeared to be strapped to a table. Razor-sharp teeth shredded Asgear's right shoulder and arm as Tristan pinned him to the cold floor. The wolf held him down, allowing Kade and the others to enter the chamber in order to get to Simone.

Scarlet body fluid sprayed the walls as Kade, Luca, and the other vampires tore into Simone's fanged puppets. Kade caught sight of Sydney, who was bound and bleeding. Enraged, he slashed through a sea of vampires, advancing toward her.

"You will die!" he spat at Simone, who ran at Tristan with a knife.

As Kade reached Sydney, he sliced at the rope, freeing one of her wrists. She lay bleeding on the table, her life's essence spilling out onto the floor with the thin spear lodged inside her gut.

"Sydney, I'm here. Just hang on…stay with me. I've got to get this out of you. Please don't leave me," Kade begged. He gently kissed her cool, pale lips and clutched the needle. Realizing it was jammed into the wooden table, Kade wrenched it out in one quick stroke, hoping to minimize the pain. "I'm so sorry, love."

Sydney arched in agony, screaming uncontrollably as the pain slammed into her once again. Her eyes flew open, and she stared up at the cold, gray vaulted stone ceiling above her.

Kade licked the small hole, sealing her wound. It wouldn't stop the internal bleeding, but it might buy her time. Knowing he would need to give her blood for a full healing, he sought her permission.

"You're going to be okay, but love…" He paused. He shook his head. This was all wrong, but she needed his blood to heal. "You're bleeding internally. I can give you my blood, but you must understand you will be bound to me forever. I will not do it without your agreement. I love you as much as life itself. You have no idea how much I wanted to give of myself to you, but not like this."

"Do it," she whimpered. Sydney's eyes fluttered as tears spilled over her cheeks. "I love you, Kade. I want to live."

"Are you sure?"

"Yes, but Kade?"

"Yes, love?"

"That woman of yours from the 1800s? She's a real bitch." She cracked a small smile. "Now, I just need to sit up. The rope…cut the rope."

As Kade pulled out his knife to free her, a vampire smacked him clear across the room.

"No! No! No! This is not going down this way! Get me off this fucking table!" Sydney screamed in frustration. Remembering her knife hidden away in her bra, she felt around with her hand. *Thank you, baby Jesus. Still there.* Blood sprayed her face as she cut the rope and released herself from the table. Wolves and vampires bit and slashed each other as she gently eased herself onto the floor.

She looked over to see Dominique tearing the heart out of one of the vampires and silently cheered her on. Both Etienne and Xavier were also fighting, slashing through the crowd of vampires with wooden stakes. Ash started to cloud the room as one by one they staked their foes.

Sydney was shocked to see Simone fighting Tristan against the far wall. She sliced his wolf with a knife as he bit tightly into her other arm. Sydney struggled to locate Asgear. *Where is he?* Tilting her head upward, she spied the gleaming face of a sword on the altar. Pain shot throughout her entire body as she stretched her arm up to reach it. Blindly fingering the altar, her hand clasped around the hilt of the sword. She slowly lowered her arm, clutching the cool blade flat against her chest.

Kade honed his eyes on Sydney's, seeing she'd gotten free. He needed to get her out of the melee, but there seemed to be no end to the vampires who were attacking from all sides. Tristan was yelping in agony; several small knives stuck out of his bloody fur. Luca, Dominique, and the others were engaged in battle as well.

"Your little whore is going to die tonight, vampire. You cannot stop us." Blindsiding Kade, Asgear struck him in the head with the heavy metal chalice.

"You are the one who will die tonight. Even your magic wanes in the light of war." Kade shifted and delivered a side kick to Asgear's thorax, pounding him into the floor.

"She tried to fight me. I think she likes it rough." Asgear crawled toward Kade, trying to push himself upright. "She bled nicely when I beat her. When you die, I'm goin' to take her for my own. She'll serve me on her knees!"

Kade had had enough of Asgear's venomous words. He stood erect over the mage and kicked his face hard. Once, twice. Blood spritzed out of Asgear's mouth as he rolled onto his back.

"This is not the end, vampire!" Asgear hissed.

"Wrong again. This is the end of the road." Kade smirked at him. "Rot in hell!"

Kade pinned him to the floor, cracking his neck and wrenching his head off its spine. He bared his fangs, shredding Asgear's throat until there was not a single drop of blood left in the mage.

Sydney couldn't see Kade, but heard him arguing with Asgear. She grabbed the edge of the table, pulled upward and steadied herself on her feet. As Tristan came into sight, she screamed. Simone repeatedly stabbed the wolf.

"Hey bitch! Over here! Leave the wolf alone! It's me you want," she baited.

"You! You! You distracted me from my purpose!" Simone turned from Tristan, all her focus on Sydney. She tore across the room, grabbing Sydney's throat with one hand. "All my hard work. The girls' deaths …it was all for him. I was practicing. My power was growing. And you had to stick your nose into my business…ruin my ritual!" She spat at Sydney's face. "I will make him watch as I drain every last drop of your whorish blood. I will rule this city! Nothing will stop me! Nothing!"

Sydney choked and struggled to breathe under the pressure of Simone's strong, bony fingers. Her eyes darted to Kade, who stealthily approached Simone.

"Let her go, Simone. She is a mere human. This animosity is between you and me."

Simone's eyes darted to Kade, but she didn't release her prey from her deathly grip. Sydney felt herself starting to lose consciousness. Even as both her arms fell to her sides, she fought to hold on to the sword.

"I do not love you, Simone. I never did." Stepping a hair closer to Simone, Kade refused to relent. "You'll never rule this town. You're finished."

"You do love me." Simone threw Sydney to the floor, and rushed over to him. "I'm here now. I am your queen. My power, I will share it with you. We shall rule together." She laid a pale hand upon his chest. "This is our time. You are mine."

Reaching for the table's edge, Sydney quietly pulled herself up so she was standing once again. Her abdomen throbbed, and she felt dizzy with pain. *Never give up.* The sword hummed underneath the warmth of her grip. She quietly approached Simone. *Time for the bitch to go.* With a final thrust of strength, Sydney whirled the heavy sword above her head. As the sword hissed, it sliced through the blood-tinted air and Simone's fine, pallid neck. Simone's dismembered head went flying across the room as blood and ash sprayed Kade's face. A clank of the sword on the ground was followed by silence in the room, as Simone's spell was broken.

Sydney fainted and her head cracked loudly against the ebon floor, blood covering her golden braid. Kade fell on his knees screaming her name. Biting into his wrist, he pressed it to her still lips hoping she would swallow the precious fluid.

"Sydney! You cannot bloody well leave me!" He laid her head in his lap, smoothing her hair across her head. Sydney's swollen lips began suctioning against his wrist. "I love you so much. Please, drink. That's it, love. Don't give up."

Kade kissed her forehead, knowing she would survive. He delicately lifted her frail body into his arms, carefully cradling her head against his chest. As he ascended the stairs, a healing breeze grazed his face. He sighed in relief, finally exiting Simone's diabolical stone creation. He called to Dominique to beckon Ilsbeth. Whatever demonic forces held the walls from the water table, they needed to be dismantled. The tomb and its rooms needed to be destroyed and blessed so that nothing remained of the malignant force within.

Luca approached him, carrying a small, unconscious woman with long, red hair. Kade immediately recognized the woman as Rhea.

"Where did you find her?" he asked.

"She was cuffed to a wall. The room was barbaric." Luca took a deep breath. "She's been recently beaten. Bloody whip marks all over her body, black eye…the works. She said her name is Samantha. Kade, something strange is going on here…it was as if she had no recollection of the club or the night she silvered Dominique. When we released her cuffs, she fainted. Exhaustion maybe?"

"Take her to my compound," Kade told him. He glanced to Sydney in his arms, concerned with getting her home as soon as possible. "Clean up the girl, make sure she's healing, and lock her in the downstairs security room until I get a chance to read her thoughts. It is possible that she was under Simone's thrall, or that Asgear bespelled her, but we need to make sure she holds no culpability before we return her to her home. And whatever you do, don't let Dominique see her yet. She is looking for payback, and will ask questions later. Now go."

Luca sped off across the cemetery, human in tow. Kade scanned the area and found Etienne kneeling on the ground, holding a naked Tristan, who drank at his wrist.

"How's Tristan?"

"Simone stabbed the hell out of him. He'll survive, but we need to get him back to the compound before his brother comes sniffing about. He will be pissed beyond belief. Marcel means well, but Tristan needs more vampire blood if he is going to make it." Etienne winced as Tristan continued suckling his wrist.

Kade caught sight of Dominique and Xavier exiting the tomb, and yelled over to them. "Let's get moving. Xavier, help Etienne with Tristan. Get him out of here now. Dominique, I need you to wait for Ilsbeth to get here. She needs to clean up this mess. You know what to do."

Kade was tired and angry. How could this have gone so very wrong? Sydney had been beaten, stabbed. He should never have let her leave Philadelphia. She was human, a strong human, yes, but still very human at that. She could have died tonight. His heart ached knowing she might need several days to recover from this ordeal. And then, would she still want to be with a vampire? The blood, the violence, the danger?

He trudged back to the van, his mind swirling with doubt. The only thing he knew for certain was that she was his. He was fooling himself to think he would let her go without a fight. He kissed her forehead as she slept peacefully in his arms. He prayed his beautiful, fighting warrior woman would be okay and that she would forgive him for involving her in this mess.

Chapter Nineteen

Sydney slowly opened her eyes to a candlelit room. *Kade's room?* Peering up, she noticed the intricate carving of the dark stained mahogany on the ceiling of the four poster, Tutor bed. Luxurious black velvet curtains were tied to the elaborately patterned posts, held back by red silk tiebacks with tassels. *Nice bed, Kade.* She smiled and turned her head toward the center of the bed where Kade slept soundly on his side with his hand possessively touching her stomach.

She moved to get out of bed when Kade pulled her into his arms and rested her head against his chest.

"Now exactly where do you think you are going, love?" He pressed his lips to her hair. "How are you feeling?"

"I don't know. It's weird. All that's happened...but I feel energized...as if I hadn't been beaten and stabbed to a wooden table by some crazy vampire bitch." Sydney vividly remembered her last vision before blacking out...blood spraying profusely as Simone's head flew off her shoulders clear across the room. She shuddered, thinking about the torture she'd endured, but felt strangely rejuvenated. "Seriously, though, I feel great; no bruises, no soreness. I take it you gave me your blood? Pretty potent stuff, huh? Hey, do I need to worry about turning into a vampire?" she teased. She nuzzled into his chest, taking a deep breath of his masculine scent.

"No, you are not a vampire. You would have to essentially lose every last drop of blood and then have me replace it with mine. But, Sydney...we are bonded now. You have taken my blood. I wanted it to be special, but it is done." Kade sighed.

"I know you asked me before you gave me your blood, and I really do appreciate that, given we exchanged bodily fluids and all, but what do you exactly mean by bonded?" Sydney questioned.

"You are mine. I am yours. When we made love before, I bit you. Your blood runs through my veins. And now, my blood has been introduced into your human body. We are formally bonded for eternity. I will always know where you are and be able to sense you. As our bond becomes stronger, you and I will be able to speak telepathically like I can with some of the others. And as long as you continue to take my blood, you will not age. We are linked." He lifted her chin to look into her eyes. "I want you to stay with me, Sydney. Here with me in New Orleans. You belong to me now."

A rush of emotion flooded Sydney's mind. She felt as though she could deal with being linked to Kade. She'd never loved anyone the way she loved him. He made her feel womanly, empowered, and erotic all at once. He'd fought with his life to save her, never giving up on her. He was everything to her. After so many years of frivolous sex and meaningless relationships, Kade filled her soul, captivating both her mind and body. She wanted to submit to him. To give herself over to him, becoming one heart with his. But seeds of doubt grew in the pit of her stomach. He hadn't said he wanted to marry her. He said he wanted her to move in with him.

And for eternity? What about her job? She'd worked so hard over the years to make it through the ranks to where she was in her division, and now he expected her to give up everything on a whim and move down here? And what about the children's center? How could she just leave the kids and give up all the work she'd done at the center? And her condo…was she just supposed to abandon it? As much as Sydney wanted to think with her heart, her mind was jolting her back into reality.

"Kade, you know I love you, but I have commitments back at home and my job and…."

"Yes, but you'll stay here with me." He softly pressed his lips to hers, stifling any rejection she might give him. "All the things you mention are minor details…we will work it out. Now come…come to me. Let me show you how much I love you."

"Kade…"

"Sydney," he interrupted, capturing her lips once again. Kade slid his hand across the healed, smooth skin of her stomach until he found what he sought, gently cupping her breast. He deliberately chose to be gentle with her, acutely aware of the trauma she'd been through in the past week. Although her physical wounds had healed overnight, it would be a long time before either of them forgot the evil they'd faced and defeated. As he kissed her, he reveled in her strength and beauty. This woman, his woman, she was everything in life; his warrior mate, his friend, his lover.

Sydney squirmed under him, impatiently awaiting his next touch. Her skin tingled with anticipation, knowing he was capable of providing her immeasurable pleasure. She let her hands explore the hard smoothness of his chest. Ripping her mouth from his, she licked her tongue across the hollow of his neck and bit down on the flesh of his shoulder.

"My girl likes to bite?" He growled in ecstasy.

She laughed in response, gliding her tongue down his muscled flesh, licking and sucking his nipple.

Releasing one of her breasts, Kade allowed his hand to delve into the slick, wet heat of her sex. Sydney sucked in a startled breath as she felt a finger slip deep into her pussy. She bucked into the rhythmic intrusion, needing more.

"Oh God, that feels so good."

Responding to her erotic desire, Kade pumped another finger into her while circling her clitoris. With quickening gasps, Sydney arched toward his hand as she spiraled hopelessly into orgasm, shattering in a million pleasurable pieces. Screaming Kade's name repeatedly, Sydney curled into him, quivering in his arms.

"You're the most incredible, fascinating woman I have known in all my years; so responsive, so soft. I love you so much." Kade gently rolled her onto her back, straddled her and held her arms down with his strong hands. "Look at me. Watch me love you."

Dipping his head, he captured a rosy, hardened tip in his mouth, gently taking it between his teeth. She moaned as he alternately bit and laved her hard peaks, driving her mad with need.

"I can't take it anymore. Please. I need you…in me now."

Kade smiled and kissed the pink point one more time before settling himself at her entrance.

"I want you to see the pleasure you bring me. I want to look into your soul as we join as one."

Kade shifted the weight of his body, supporting his hands on the bed, and Sydney opened her thighs wide, inviting him into her. Frantic with desire, she lifted her hips up to Kade, moving to accept him. He groaned in blinding delight as he slid his rock-hard cock into her warmth. He moved slowly, letting her stretch to accommodate him. Sydney gazed into the depths of Kade's eyes, acknowledging the love in every thrust.

"I love you," she whispered.

He smiled as he continued to plunge in and out of her, increasing the pace, building the sexual tension. The slick heat of her center massaged his manhood as he leaned in to kiss her swollen lips.

Sensing the nearness of her climax, Sydney lightly circled her hips into him, stimulating her most tender flesh. She was quickly losing control.

"Kade, yes, Kade, I'm coming. Don't stop. Yes, please."

"That's it, love. Come for me. You're beautiful," he told her as she climaxed.

At his direction, the crescendo rose to the edge of ecstasy.

"Fuck yes. Oh my God. I'm coming! I'm coming! Yes! Yes!" Sydney rocked frantically against him as her orgasm slammed into her.

As her hot channel convulsed, making it impossible for him to hold back, Kade sank his fangs into the soft flesh of her neck. Thrusting deeply into her one last time, he exploded inside her as pulsating waves of pleasure washed over him. *Mine.*

Kade fell back into the bed off of Sydney, rolling her with him so she lay upon his chest once again. He would never let her go. She would stay here and build a future with him. He knew she was worried about her job, but he would get her one here if that's what she wanted. He'd spare no expense making sure she had everything she needed to stay.

Sydney fought back the tears, overwhelmed by the emotions from making love. God, she loved him. He was everything she could ever want in a man; masculine, honorable, sexy, and intelligent. She'd never met a man like him before in her life and was pretty sure she'd never meet another. Kade made her feel loved, desired, wanted. Hell, he made her *feel,* period. It had been years since she'd dated anyone for more than a month, let alone someone who made her consider moving hundreds of miles away to live with him.

But give up her entire life for a man she met less than a week ago? Could she really just move all her stuff down here, not knowing if they had a real commitment? It was true that she had bonded with him, but as a human, she still wasn't exactly sure of the implications. As much as she was tempted to tell him 'yes' right away, she had responsibilities waiting for her at home; her job, the center, friends, a life. Okay, so she didn't have that many friends or family, but still, it was her life.

Her chest tightened as she wondered if what they had was real. She knew that working long hours with a partner often caused simple emotions to escalate. With Kade it had gone so much further; she'd fallen deeply and utterly in love with him, a vampire. There was no going back. If she left New Orleans, hoping for a long distance relationship, it would crush her. She reasoned that she needed time to think about how she could make it work. She'd been held up in this dark, fantasy world for days. She knew life and death situations had a way of skewing one's perspective. If she could just get some fresh air…maybe a Philly cheesesteak…get back to the office, she'd be able to make hard decisions with a clear head. The thought of leaving him, even for a few days, caused her heart to break.

"Kade," she whispered, "I need to take a shower."

"Okay, love. You sure you don't want me to join you?"

"I would love you to, but I really think I just need to take a nice, relaxing bath. You know…decompress after the past few days."

"As much as I would like to wait for you, I really should get downstairs to help Luca. The woman in the cell…she needs to be questioned."

"Samantha?" Sydney asked.

"I'm not sure what her real name is, but we need to find out before we release her."

"I was in that cell with her. Now granted, I couldn't read her facial expressions, but her story rang true with me. I didn't even recognize her as Rhea. I mean, how will you know the truth?"

"It shouldn't be hard. I'll try to scan her mind. See if she shows any signs of deception. I called Ilsbeth over here to see if she's been bespelled. It is possible Asgear put a spell on her that could enable her to lie so well even she would think she's telling the truth."

"But he's dead," she countered.

"True. But Jane Doe down there may still harbor dark magic. If Ilsbeth senses any residue, she will take her to the coven to be cleared of spells and blessed. We cannot be too careful, considering Asgear may have schooled others in his dark ways."

"Others?" Sydney shivered at the possibility that Asgear had spawned other mages.

"I sense your fear, Sydney. I would tell you not to worry, but you and I both know the truth of the situation. All I can say is that supernaturals sometimes are not all that different from humans. Evil has no boundaries. And you and I…we both seek justice, albeit in very different worlds."

"Yes. Crime is everywhere, that's for sure." *There is crime waiting for me back in Philadelphia.* "I hope Samantha is okay. She deserves a lot better than what happened to her. Please, Kade…just go easy on her."

"I'll try, but we have to be safe. I promise that if she's innocent, she'll get her life back."

"Thank you," she replied, convinced he'd treat the girl with compassion. Not wanting to end their time thinking of leaving, she kissed Kade, savoring his warmth once more. She knew what she had to do. She also knew he'd be really pissed, more like infuriated, but she needed to clear her head. Not looking back, tears pricked at her eyes as she scurried off to the shower.

Chapter Twenty

Luca shot Kade a look of desperation as he entered the safe room in the basement. The girl was crying again. Shit, no man liked crying. Kade felt a pang of guilt for essentially saving the girl from Simone, only to imprison her yet again, in his home. Granted, the room was a large, comfortable guest room with its own private bathroom. It didn't scream 'prison cell'. No, if anything, it looked like a luxurious room at the Four Seasons. Regardless, the girl was scared and confused. She crouched on the bed with her knees pulled up against her chest, glaring at him as he went to sit in an overstuffed guest chair. He needed to get control over the situation, but fast. Taking a deep breath, he readied himself for the interrogation.

"Samantha, my name's Kade. Now listen, we are not here to hurt you. I'm sorry that we needed to keep you here with us, but we need to make sure it is safe to let you return home. The people who took you were an evil pair of criminals who apparently used you to further their exploits. You may not be aware, but you attacked a very good friend of mine a few nights ago at Sangre Dulce. Do you have any recollection of this activity?"

"No. I…I don't know what you're talking about," the girl sniffled. "Where is Sydney? She said she'd come for me."

"Sydney is recovering." Kade glanced at Luca, who passed Kade a snapshot of Rhea standing naked serving drinks at the club. He flipped over the photo, not yet wanting to shock the girl. "I need to ask you some questions, Samantha. The faster we do this, the faster you get out of here."

"Do you remember being at Sangre Dulce?"

"Yes, I told Sydney. I'm so stupid. It was my first time. I went there with friends. I don't even live here in New Orleans. I was at a computer conference. My friends and I went there, you know, just to have fun…see what it was like. There was this guy…James…he seemed so nice. I remember having a drink with him. Then…all I remember after that is being in that cell…he beat me…I couldn't get out. I told Sydney," she sobbed, tears spilling down her face.

Not detecting deception in her words, Kade needed her to understand what had happened, and unfortunately what was about to happen. She wasn't going home.

"Okay, listen, Samantha. Here's the thing. James, the man you mentioned, was a powerful mage. His real name was Asgear, and he practiced dark magic. I'm very sorry to tell you that you were bespelled by him. I have someone who can help you, but I've got to be honest with you. You need to know what happened. I have a photo here." He held it up to her. "This is you in Sangre Dulce serving drinks and engaging in various other duties." He coughed, not knowing how to tell her. "Miguel, the owner, introduced you to us as a submissive. You know what that is, right?"

"Yes." Nodding her head, Samantha whimpered. "Oh dear God. No, no, I would never do that. I just went there with friends for fun. Oh my God. How did this happen to me? What did I do?"

"That night, you took one of my friends. You silvered her to a table. Now, before you get too upset, it's entirely possible Asgear did most of the silvering. You see, my friend was blindfolded. At any rate, you helped this man. So we need to make sure whatever he did to you is lifted and cleansed, so you don't do it again."

"What do you mean? I promise I won't ever do anything like that again. Am I going home now? I need to get home. My family, my job." She wiped the tears from her eyes.

"I would love to send you home, Samantha, but like I said, we need to make sure you are free of the dark magic. A friend of mine," he hesitated, "a friend of mine and Sydney's, she is a witch, a good witch. Her name is Ilsbeth. She is coming here and taking you to her coven. Now, I am not sure how long it will take, but I promise you that you will return to your home…soon enough."

Samantha put her face into her hands, crying softly. Lifting her chin, she wiped her tears.

"I'm sorry. I want you to know that I am normally a very strong person, but this past week…I feel quite shattered right now. But I will be fine. I just need to get home."

Luca glided across the room, put a hand on her shoulder and gave her a tissue. This frail human stirred something in his cold, dark heart. Over the centuries, he'd seen many a human cry. It was the hard reality of life. But this fragile woman with long, fiery red hair ignited a small, caring flame inside of him.

"Samantha, it'll be okay." He ran a hand over her soft hair and patted her shoulder, attempting to provide comfort. "Ilsbeth is a strong and kind witch. If you have been given magic, she will cleanse you. All will be well again."

Kade raised an eyebrow at Luca, wondering what was going on with his old friend. Luca didn't do comfort, or sympathy, or humans. There was a long list of all kinds of things Luca did not do. Kade wondered if some kind of magic was rubbing off on his second. *Where the fuck is Ilsbeth?*

A loud knock at the door jolted Luca away from Samantha. Kade shook his head in confusion at his friend's actions.

"Enter," he ordered. A blinding glow shone through the doorway as Ilsbeth opened the door. "Please come in, Ilsbeth." Kade gestured for her to sit in a guest chair, but Ilsbeth wandered over to sit next to Samantha on the bed. "Ilsbeth, this is Samantha. She has no recollection of her actions in the club the night she silvered Dominique. I sense no deception, but we need to be sure she is safe to be around others…and herself."

"Samantha, I am Ilsbeth." She ran her lithe, pale fingers across Samantha's cheek. "You understand you have been in contact with a great evil, yes?"

Samantha nodded silently.

"This evil, it made you do things, things against your will, things you do not recollect?"

She nodded again.

"Do I have your permission to read you…your aura? Do you come to me willingly?" Ilsbeth asked in a soft, lilting voice.

"Yes, I am so sorry. Please help me," she begged.

The air thickened as Ilsbeth closed her eyes and raised her hands, palms up above the crown of Samantha's head. She hummed a cyclical melody as she lowered her hands around the girl. Opening her eyes, she blew out a breath.

"This young woman, dark magic tints the edges of her aura." A somber look crossed her face as she locked her vision on Kade. "She must come with me to the coven where my sisters and I can purge the darkness and cleanse her soul." She was holding back.

Kade knew there was something else. What was it? He'd promised this girl she could return home. "Ilsbeth, thank you for your reading. As always, I am appreciative of your magical insight. Yet, I sense there is something else."

"It is the magic." In disgust, she shook her head. "It has been infused."

"Meaning?" he questioned.

"The magic has been infused. We can cleanse her aura and remove the darkness, but the magic, it will stay. In short, Samantha is now a witch. She will need to stay with the coven, learn the craft, grow into the light." She regarded Samantha. "Do you understand, dear girl? You are now a witch."

"I am a witch?" she asked, saying the words back to Ilsbeth as if it would get easier if she spoke them aloud. "I have to be honest with you. I'm not sure what that really means, but I will try. I want this evil out of my body now. I promise to do whatever you say…just please help me get on with my life."

"It will be okay, Samantha. I will help you," Ilsbeth reassured her. She hugged her, knowing this would be an uphill battle. It was not an easy life being a witch, let alone being turned into one so late in life. Being thrown into the supernatural world after spending your entire life as human was difficult to comprehend.

Samantha pulled out of Ilsbeth's arms and looked up to Kade. "Sir, one thing before I leave. Please…I want to see Sydney. I owe her my life. I just want to thank her."

"Go get Sydney." Kade motioned to Luca. "I know she'll want to see the girl before she leaves."

Luca nodded and left the room, giving Samantha one last glance.

"Thank you again, Ilsbeth. We do seem to make good allies, don't we?" Kade hoped to lighten the mood before Sydney arrived. She had been through enough this past week, and didn't need to come into a room full of serious faces.

"Ah yes, that we do. The coven is in your debt for eradicating Simone and Asgear. If we hear of any other activity related to Asgear, I'll make sure to contact you immediately."

Within minutes, Luca returned to the room sans Sydney. He gave Kade a hard stare, needing to speak to him in private. He glanced to Samantha, who stared back at him with wide eyes.

"I'm sorry, darlin', but Sydney isn't available to come down to see you at this time," Luca explained in a gentle tone. "She promised that she'll visit you at the coven as soon as possible. Now, if you don't mind, a vampire situation has come up that Kade and I need to attend to. Etienne will see you up to the foyer, and then I will escort you back to Ilsbeth's."

Upon hearing Luca's words, Kade sent out mental feelers to locate Sydney within the house. When he was unable to detect her presence, his jaw tightened in anger.

"Where is she?" he demanded.

"Kade, please, you must understand, no one saw her go, and there's been no evidence of foul play. It appears she just left. The maid saw her jump in a cab about an hour ago. Maybe she went downtown to get beignets again?" Luca sighed.

No, Goddammit. Kade knew that she wasn't shopping or sightseeing. His woman was running, running from her feelings, running from him. Sydney Willows could run, but she could not hide. He would find her any place on the face of the Earth. What exactly did the woman not get about them being bonded?

"That woman is going to be the death of me. Seriously, Luca. I ask her to stay here and move in with me and she takes off? What the hell? Get Tristan on the damn phone, and then call the airport and gas up the jet. We, my friend, are going to Philadelphia tonight. She is mine, and it is damn well time she starts to understand precisely what that means."

Chapter Twenty-One

Sydney felt sick as soon as she got in the cab. She kept telling herself she just needed time to think, time to figure out how she could have a relationship with a vampire, one who lived a thousand miles away. She'd call Kade as soon as she got to Philadelphia, tell him that she loved him, and that she just needed space. If she called him before she got on the plane, she would fold and return to him. If she just had some time to make a decision without Kade tempting her with his sex-on-a-stick gorgeous body and demanding presence, then she'd know she was making the right choice. She couldn't trust herself to think clearly around him. Her libido had officially taken over in New Orleans. She had lost the capability to make intelligent decisions with her brain when she was thinking with her wanton, aching loins.

Sydney had to call Tristan before boarding the plane. There was no way she was staying in her condo after the attempted rape. She needed to repaint and decorate it anyhow, since the place had been trashed.

"Tristan," she began as Tristan picked up the phone. "It's Sydney. Listen, I need to talk. Um…I mean I need a favor."

"Syd, uh…what's going on?" Tristan responded, suspicion in his voice. "Why do I hear airplanes? Where's Kade?"

"Please, Tristan, just hear me out." Sydney sighed heavily. *Damn Alpha wolf.* She couldn't keep secrets from him on a good day. "Okay, here it is. I ran out of Kade's house, hopped a cab to the airport, and I'm about to board a flight to Philly." She silently cringed, guessing what Tristan's response would be.

"Sydney dearest, excuse me for saying so, but are you fucking crazy? Kade is going to go ballistic when he discovers you just left without telling him. Hell, even if you told him, he'd freak out. You do get that he claimed you? And then there is the whole completing of the blood bond, not to mention he keeps telling everyone that you are freakin' his! My God, woman, have you lost your ever-lovin' mind?"

"Thanks for the lecture, Dad. And yeah, I know he's going to be mad. I understand everything… yadda, yadda, yadda…blood bond. I love him too, more than life itself. But I need some time to think. I need to get back to my job, the kids. Things are too intense down here. I need to make sure that I'm making the right decisions."

"What is there to think about? No, forget it. You human women are irrational…unreasonable…whatever. I just want you to know that when this all goes down, I reserve the right to tell you, 'I told ya so'. Now what do you need?" When push came to shove, Tristan would always be there for her. She was part of his pack…wolf or no wolf.

"My condo. The vampire. You know what happened." She didn't want to even say the words. "I need some time to get the place back together. I'm going to sell it…especially given the fact I might, and that is a big might, move to New Orleans. So, can I stay at your place for a while?"

"Mon chaton, you're truly trying to get me killed, aren't you?" He laughed. "Since I do not have a death wish, I will politely refuse to let you stay at my house, but I have several rental properties. I've got one that'll work. It's an empty, furnished apartment and most importantly, it's in a safe part of town, okay? You're welcome to stay there. When are you getting in? Do you need a ride from the airport?"

"Thanks, Tris. You're a lifesaver. And no, I don't need a ride. Tony's picking me up and taking me to the Hilton. If you could get the keys and address to the station by tomorrow, I'd be forever grateful."

"Yeah, you better be, girl. Kade's goin' to be supremely pissed when he finds out you're gone. I love you like family, but I'm not going to lie when he comes a-knockin'. And he will, just warning you."

"Fair enough." Sydney slumped in her chair, knowing he was right. Too late now. She already took off…might as well see this thing through. "Hey…I just wanted to say thanks for saving my ass the other night."

"And what a fine ass you have. You know that I should be the one thanking you. If that vamp bitch had stabbed me one more time, it could have been the last howl for the wolf. You were pretty badass with that sword. Listen, call me when you get settled, okay? I'm worried about you."

"I will," she promised.

"Can I give you a bit of advice? You know, from a wise, old Alpha?"

She laughed softly. "Sure, Tris."

"You think too much. Open your heart to him, Syd. You deserve love. You get me? Stop thinking, start living," he told her. "You take care. Safe travels."

She hung up the phone. Tristan's words resonated throughout her very being. *You deserve love.* She loved Kade with every cell of her body. And he loved her. Maybe Tristan was right. Maybe she did think too much. As she boarded the plane, tears welled in her eyes. *A mistake.* She shouldn't have left Kade's house. Taking a deep breath, she held the emotion back. She just needed time to get her life in order, and if she still felt like she did today, then she'd return to Kade, the love of her life.

Chapter Twenty-Two

Tony glanced over at Sydney, who silently stared out the window, looking a million miles away. Something seemed off with his partner.

"I'm glad you're back. The cases are piling up, and it sure will be good to have you back here." Sydney continued gazing out the window, oblivious to his words. "Hello? Sydney Willows? What's up, Syd? You seem really out of it. Are you sure you're ready to come back to work?"

"Sorry," Sydney sighed. "I just…was thinking, that's all…about work. Yeah well, I want to finish up the paperwork on the Death Doll case, even if it officially belongs to P-CAP. Just want to clean it up a little, tie up loose ends."

She rubbed her eyes. *What next?* She was supposed to be clearing her head, but thoughts of Kade consumed her.

"I think I'm gonna take a few days off after that. My condo is a mess, so I've got to get it cleaned up. I'm going to sell it…maybe. I don't know. Anyway, I'll spend tonight at the hotel and then go over and get my stuff in the morning…pack a bag. My friend Tristan is letting me stay for a while in one of his rental properties."

Tony rolled his eyes. He knew she wasn't telling him everything, but they'd been partners long enough that he knew when to push her and when to just let it go. He could tell she was on edge, that she'd been crying recently. Pulling the car into the hotel entrance, he put it in park.

"Syd," he paused. "You and I. We've been partners a long time. I know something's going on, and if you don't want to talk about it, that's okay. But I'm just a phone call away. If you need me, just call and I'll come running. You sure you don't want to stay in my guest room? I feel kind of bad just dropping you off at a hotel." He placed his hand on her shoulder, trying to comfort her.

Sydney put her hand on the car door handle ready to bolt. She turned to him. "I'm okay. I promise… I just need some time to myself. A lot went down in New Orleans. Now, get going. I'll see you at the station tomorrow afternoon. Thanks."

Sydney reached over and quickly hugged him. Releasing her partner, she popped the car door open and headed into the hotel.

Sydney felt even worse the next day. She was in misery knowing she'd left

Kade. What had she been thinking? She would have given anything to wake up in his arms this morning. Instead, she awoke to strange voices talking though the paper-thin walls and an air conditioner on the fritz. She checked her cell phone for the hundredth time hoping Kade would call or text her. Nothing.

Dammit to hell. She'd left New Orleans in order to think clearly, but all she could think about was Kade. She almost took a cab back to the airport, but reason won out, and she landed back at her condo. She breathed in deeply as she laid a hand against her door. Memories of the attempted rape flooded her thoughts, but she let a small smile grow, knowing that she'd won out in the end. She was the one still alive and kicking, and that asshole vampire was nothing more than ash. Her thoughts drifted back to Kade, thinking of how he saved her butt…waking up on a jet? *What kind of a world does that guy live in?* Certainly not the gritty, very real, paycheck earning world she lived in.

She gave the door a shove, and it squeaked open. Thank God, Luca and Kade had thought to lock the place when they left. Not that she had too many valuables, but one couldn't be too careful in the city. Scanning the room, she felt nauseated, taking sight of the dried blood. She dreaded straightening up the mess. The station had offered to pick up crime scene cleaning expenses since the incident had occurred while she was working a case. Not having the emotional strength to pick up even one broken vase, she decided right then and there that she'd hire a service to do it.

Ignoring the overthrown furniture, and bits of glass, Sydney strode down the hallway into the guest room, hauling out the largest travel bag she owned. She emptied her drawers, underwear, sweatpants, and t-shirts spilling into her luggage. *Nothing like summing my life up in a suitcase.* Instead of folding up clothes that were hanging in her closet, she grabbed them by the hangers and threw them onto the bed. Scooping up several pairs of shoes, she dumped them haphazardly into a duffel bag.

Rifling through her guest room chest, she gathered up any weapons Tristan had left and stowed them with her clothes…including her guns. Sydney's skin pricked with discomfort being in this condo. *Goddamn vampires.* If she hadn't insisted on working this case, nothing would have happened, and she could have gone about life not knowing all the evils that existed in the supernatural world. But she also wouldn't have known love…desire…ecstasy…Kade.

She gathered a few treasured pictures of her family and friends, and looked around once again to see if there was anything else she wanted to take with her. Deciding that she'd packed enough, she collected her possessions and left her apartment. After making her way down to her car, she carefully laid her hanging clothes flat in the tiny trunk of her convertible and squeezed the large suitcase into the passenger seat. Tight fit, but it would have to work. Silently saying goodbye to her home of seven years, she took off toward the station.

The parking lot buzzed with activity as she parked her car. She checked twice to make sure it was locked, before she padded into the station. Waving hello to her fellow officers, she slumped into her chair and flipped on her laptop. Her plan was to bury herself in her work for the next few hours. She wanted to forget New Orleans for a little while; to forget evil vampires and mages, and most of all, to forget the ache that was burning a hole through her gut from missing Kade.

Hours later, after a mountain of paperwork, she sighed in exhaustion. She was startled as Tony slammed a cheesesteak down on her desk.

"Hey. What's up? Thought you could use one of these. Now, I know they don't have these babies down in the Big Easy." He grinned.

"Oh. My. God." Her mouth watered as the scent of fried onions and cheese teased her nostrils. She couldn't wait to tear into it. "Thank you, Tony."

"Yeah, I have been called a god by certain women. And funny you say so…women do usually like my ten inch…just not a steak sandwich." He busted out laughing.

Sydney punched him in the arm. "Real nice, Tone. You're a smooth talker, you." She bit down into the sandwich, letting the grease, soft bread and steak entice her senses. "Okay, Tony. Did I ever tell you how much I love you?" she grinned, wiping her mouth.

"Yeah baby. I know you want it." He smiled, seeing that she was starting to get back to normal. "Hey, if I knew all you needed was a steak sandwich, I would have fed you last night." He straightened in his chair, a serious expression washed over his face. "Seriously, Syd. You need something, I'm here. There's no going it alone. We all get pummeled down by this job every now and then. You and I both know it. I don't know all what happened down there in New Orleans, but this is just a bump in the road. You're tough. It'll be all right."

Sydney avoided the heavy conversation by nodding and stuffing her mouth full of steak and pickles. She wished lifting her spirits was as easy as eating a sandwich…although the cheesesteak was pretty damn good.

"Delivery!" The station secretary dropped a small Fed Ex envelope on her desk. *Kade?* She ripped open the package only to find a key and a small, engraved card. *Tristan. The key and address to the rental property.* Shoving away the rising disappointment, she fingered the black shiny key, which was attached to a copper Liberty Bell key chain. Only in Philly, she grinned to herself.

What was she thinking…that Kade would call her? Text her? Send her a card? She was the one who had up and left without saying goodbye…after making love, at that. Waves of guilt flooded her mind. Why did she do that to him? He said he loved her, wanted her to stay. Why wasn't that enough for her? But he didn't seem to really understand that she had responsibilities. She did recall him saying that they'd work out the details, but she'd been so freaking impatient as usual. She didn't even try to talk to him. No, she just panicked, overwhelmed by emotions, and ran back to Philly. *Shit.* She needed to call him tonight and set things right. In the past twenty-four hours, she may not have cleared her mind entirely, but she knew one thing to be true, Kade was hers. She loved him. With each passing hour, her heart cried out for him as she yearned to be in his arms.

Rubbing the key, she shut down her laptop, deciding she couldn't wait one more hour to call him. Once she got to her new place, she'd sit down, call him, apologize for leaving, and possibly beg for his forgiveness–okay, only if necessary–and figure out a way to make this work. Maybe she could get a job at the NOLA PD. Myriad thoughts and solutions swirled in her head. Before she lost her nerve, she needed to get out of the station and make the call.

Tapping Tony on the shoulder, not wanting to interrupt his phone call, she mouthed the words "thank you" and waved goodbye. Jumping into her convertible, she pulled the top down, cranked up the radio, and set the GPS to the address on the card. Her heart sang in joy knowing that it wouldn't be long before she heard the loving tone of Kade's voice again.

Chapter Twenty-Three

Sydney gasped at the sight of the newly built, Penn's Landing riverfront condo building. *Swanky*. She could not believe Tristan would let her live in this place rent-free for a week or so, let alone the couple of months she'd initially planned on. She had a feeling she'd never want to leave, considering the incredible view of the river and city. Why wasn't Tristan living in this fabulous location? She knew he dabbled in real estate, but had no idea that he owned a place down on the waterfront. She double checked the address before pulling her car into the valet parking.

"Excuse me, Miss," A bellman approached her car and leaned forward, "but do you need assistance with your luggage?"

Sydney coughed, trying desperately to compose herself, hoping she was in the right place. "Uh…yes. I have some clothing in the trunk, a few bags. My friend, Tristan Livingston, is letting me stay in his condo for a while."

"Of course, Miss. We've been expecting you. I'll take your keys, park your car, and bring your things to you shortly." Smiling, he opened her car door, gesturing for her to get out.

She gave him the keys, confidently striding toward the door where another bellman awaited her.

"Hello…I'm Sydney Willows. I…."

"Greetings, Miss Willows. My name is Bernard. Welcome to Riverfront Estates. As Fred indicated, we've been expecting you. Please follow me, and I will escort you home."

Home? Sydney obediently followed Bernard, having no idea where she was going. It dawned on her that Tristan had failed to provide her with the condo number. She didn't want to appear as if she didn't belong, so she trusted that she'd figure it out from Bernard eventually. Standing in the elevator, Sydney noticed the numbers went up to forty floors. Nervously playing with the key, she tried to remember which button Bernard had pushed. The elevator was moving, but no numbers were illuminated.

As the elevator settled and the doors slid open, she saw a small foyer that led to a lone set of double doors.

"Your condo, Miss. Do you need me to open the door, or show you about? Your bags will be up in just a little bit via the service elevator."

"No thank you. Please, just leave my things in the hallway here. Seeing as this is the only condo on this floor, my things should be okay for a little while. I have a phone call to make, and it's important that I'm not interrupted. Thanks again." She stepped into the vestibule and reached into her purse.

"Thank you, but please, no tips. This is your home now." He waved as the elevator doors silently closed.

Finally alone, she blew out a deep breath. My God, this place was unbelievable. She could hardly wait to see the view of the river. Not knowing what floor she was on, she sensed she was up fairly high. She steadied the key, slid it into the lock and quickly opened the deadbolt. *Secure door, very nice.*

As Sydney clasped her palm around the door handle, she felt it. A warm, tingly sensation ran up her spine. *Kade. What is he doing here?* After everything she'd been through in the past week, she trusted her instincts enough to know that Kade was behind this door. Taking a deep breath, she tried desperately to gather her thoughts. *What can I say to him? Take it easy Sydney…apologize…just pretend he's on the end of the phone like you were planning.* But he wasn't on the phone in New Orleans. No, he was truly here in Philadelphia. In Tristan's condo. *Shit. Shit. Shit. Breathe, Sydney, breathe.* Feeling as if she could use an oxygen mask, she sucked in a deep breath, turned the handle and pushed the door open.

Across the great room, she spied Kade, who gazed at the river, the muscular frame of his silhouette darkly carved against the incandescent moonlight. Sydney's soul wrenched, begging her to go to him so she could lose herself in his embrace, but he was a dark, lethal predator who she'd wounded. She didn't have the courage to seek what she needed from him. No, she would approach him cautiously, thoughtfully. She needed to make things right with him.

"Kade, I'm sorry." Although he said nothing in response, as if he hadn't heard her, she knew he had. He would make her come to him, and she'd willingly go.

Sydney cautiously approached, walking into an open space. Moonlight shone through the sun lights of the cathedral ceiling, illuminating the entire room. As she passed the kitchen, the black, pearly granite countertops and stainless steel appliances sparkled. She crept slowly toward Kade, noticing the condo was completely void of furniture, save for patio furniture on the enormous, outdoor terrace. A stray thought passed through her mind as she wondered why Tristan would send her to an unfurnished property, a minor issue compared to the menacing, aggravated vampire standing in front of her.

Sydney's heels clicked softly on the hardwood floors. She extended her fingertips, letting them graze the hard planes of his back. Attraction did not begin to describe the intense desire that grew in her belly.

"Kade, please. What are you doing here?"

Kade silently waited as she came to him, sensing his prey ever closer. He could smell her desire. He fought the urge to ravage her right there on the floor, burying himself within her hot depths. But he needed to teach this stubborn, sexy woman a lesson she would not soon forget. She had run from him, not willing to discuss her emotions, her fears, or their life together. Not acceptable. No, she needed to learn that without a doubt they belonged together…forever. And that he loved her more than life itself, and was willing to do anything to keep her in his life. Not looking back at her, he took a deep breath, steeling himself for the conversation that would change his life.

"Ah, Sydney love, I am here…because this home is my home…our home." He pivoted around, pulling her toward him, settling her body so that she also faced the river. Grasping her hands, he rested them on the cool terrace railing. The view of the river was magnificent. Lights twinkled from the boats and the bridge spanning the rushing water.

"Your home?" Sydney asked, her voice shaken. "Wait…what do you mean, our home? This is Tristan's condo. He gave me a key. He's letting me stay here. Did Tristan tell you I was here?"

Snaking his hand around her waist, he pulled her into him so that their sides pressed against each other. At his demanding touch, he felt Sydney straighten, quivering as if electricity had run through her body. Every sensual cell in her body stood wide awake, ready to engage with him.

"Precisely what I meant." Smiling at her response, Kade continued. "This is our home. I bought this property last night after you so very cleverly left New Orleans." He turned her body so it was flush with his, hip to hip, their lips mere inches apart. She did not attempt to move away from him, allowing Kade to hold her tightly in his warm, muscular arms. His blue eyes pierced down into her soul as his lips tightened somberly. "You see, Sydney, you did not seem to quite understand what I meant when I said you are mine. I thought we established things in my office that fine day, but it appears you need another lesson."

"Kade, I…I…I," she stammered, her words caught in her throat.

"Don't say a word, not one word." He lifted a finger to her lips, silencing her excuses. "It's my turn to talk, your turn to listen. I want to be clear…*so* very clear…that you never misunderstand me again. You are mine, I am yours. We are bonded. I love you, Sydney, not just this minute, not just today, not just this year, I love you forever. This means the next time you get upset or confused, you do not run out on me. Never again will you do that, understand? We, us…we work on things together from here on out. You lean on me. You share with me. We are one together, no longer on our own. Together and always we shall figure out this world."

Kade smiled, twirling a strand of her hair with his finger.

"Now, before you say anything or even attempt to protest, I am going to tell you how this is going to work. Since you left me in New Orleans, instead of working together on answers to how we would make our relationship work, I took it upon myself to figure it out for us."

"But Kade," Sydney began, still trying to capture control over the situation. Something she was failing at miserably at the moment.

Kade jerked her closer into his body, grinding the hardness of his maleness into her belly. He leaned in close, almost touching her lips with his.

"Shhh. You really have trouble listening, don't you, woman?"

A small giggle escaped Sydney's lips, releasing a nervous energy.

Dominating her space, he parted her legs with his thigh. As her feminine scent called to him, he resisted the urge to take her right there and fuck her senseless. But he needed her to accept their future as it would be before he went any further.

"First, your career. I would never ask you to give up your job. You've worked hard to get where you are, and I'll support you in whatever you decide. That being said, I will not let you rush foolishly into supernatural cases again…at least not without me. I took the liberty of speaking with the powers that be, and your police department has graciously agreed to lend you to my security forces as a consultant whenever I see fit. Therefore, you can work here in Philadelphia for months at a time, should you choose to do so, and then we can go back to New Orleans and work down there for however long we need to remain. Your city is close to New York, and I frequently have business there, so this location is advantageous for me as well. We will live in both locations."

Sydney was about to interrupt, but she chewed her lip instead. Sensing her imminent interruption attempt, Kade raised an eyebrow at her, challenging her to disobey his earlier request to let him finish speaking.

"Secondly, you shall drink a scant amount of my blood…just often enough so that you do not age or become ill. In doing so, we can be together throughout eternity. I am quite sure that I'll be doing enough worrying about your safety due to the nature of your job. I certainly don't need to worry about you getting sick from human diseases. Likewise, I'll drink from you whenever possible, as I want no other woman for my sustenance. I am quite sure that you would agree to this point, given you would not want me with another woman, especially given the erotic, intimate nature of feeding."

Kade stopped speaking for a minute, drinking in the silence of the night. The crux of his argument rested solely upon point number three. He sighed, hoping he would say all the right words so she finally understood how very much she meant to him.

"Third, and most importantly, I love you, Miss Willows. When I asked you to move in with me and stay in New Orleans…let's just say, I do not take commitment lightly. I told you before that there have been few women in my long lifetime who I have considered a lover, but there has been no woman that I have ever considered a soul mate. Or a wife…until now." Kade pressed his forehead to Sydney's. He desired so deeply to make love with her, but he wanted her head clear of the throes of sexual passion so she never doubted his intentions…or her answer.

Tears ran down her face as he withdrew a small, blue and white box from his pocket. "You, Sydney…you came into my life unexpectedly. You are a stubborn woman, infuriating at times. A woman filled with a heart of courage so large…well, what can I say? Even though you feel fear, you continue to fight in the name of justice, giving everything you have…willing to give your life to save others. Blood, sweat, tears. Then there is the soft side of you…my woman…my lover: caring, sexy, beautiful. I am simply enchanted by you. More importantly, I love you. I want to be with you forever. I want you to be my wife. Marry me, Sydney."

Kade opened the small box, offering his gift to his bride-to-be. An enormous, princess-cut diamond sparkled in the moonlight.

"Yes, I would be honored to become your wife," Sydney cried.

As Kade slipped the ring on her finger, a tear ran down her face. Feeling guilty for how she'd run out on him, she pulled out of his embrace, but did not release his hands. "Kade, I'm so sorry I left without telling you. I was just so overwhelmed. You have to understand. I never thought I could love someone, let alone as much as I love you. I was scared. Worried about my job and the children's center. So when you asked me to move…I just panicked. It was wrong, and I am really, really sorry for hurting you. Please forgive me?" she purred.

"Ah my lovely future wife, I'll certainly forgive you but perhaps I should punish you first," he teased. "A spanking perhaps?"

"I guess I would agree to a consensual spanking every now and then." She winked. "But you know it goes both ways!"

"Both ways? I'm not sure I can agree to those terms. Let's say that some things aren't up for negotiation. Now come to me, my sweet fiancée. I plan to make love to you in every room of this penthouse."

No longer able to control his lust, Kade leaned forward and pressed his lips to Sydney's. Their tongues danced in delirium, finally sealing their future. He speared his fingers through Sydney's soft, blonde hair, pulling her head into his. She tasted like sweet honey on a fine summer day. His lover…soon to be his wife.

Sydney moaned in delight, breaking away from his lips for a second.

"Um, Kade, considering we have no furniture in our home yet," she glanced over to the oversized, outdoor day bed, "maybe we should start right here on our wonderful balcony." She grabbed his hand, led him over to the soft bedding and pushed him backward so he lay on his back at her mercy. "Kade, I plan to make it up to you and then some…over and over again for the rest of our lives." She straightened above him, seductively stripping off her clothes until she was completely naked in the moonlight.

"Love…oh…you are such a naughty woman." Kade groaned and massaged his rock-hard cock through his jeans. "The way your skin shines in the moonlight, I cannot resist you for one minute longer. Come here," he demanded.

Sydney moved over him, straddling his legs. Kneeling, she slowly leaned over, gently kissing him, her soft hair falling onto his face and shoulders. Without warning, she rose, resting her hands on his shoulders, rubbing her plump, ripe breasts into his face. He moaned as he cupped and suckled her soft peaks, teasing them until they hardened in pain.

"Yes, Kade. Oh my God. Yes…I want to taste you. Now," she begged.

Slithering down his body, she made quick work of his pants, freeing his straining manhood. Taking him into her mouth, she greedily sucked his shaft, moaning in pleasure as she tasted his salty essence. Sydney grazed her teeth along his hardness, teasing him, hoping to make him beg. Finally, her vampire cracked, his breath began to quicken into pants.

"I…I need to be inside you. Hurry…I want to come inside you. Please," he pleaded.

Sydney smiled. Her big, bad vampire's begging was music to her ears. She crawled up him slowly and lowered herself onto him until her sex settled fully onto his cock. Sydney's receptive body welcomed him, her hands clutching his shoulders for support.

"Yes, baby. That's it. You feel so good inside of me," she said, staring deep into his blue eyes. "I've never loved another man like I love you. You're everything to me."

Connecting on a higher level, Kade and Sydney slowly rocked together as one in total harmony, allowing their arousal to consume them both. Pressing her hips into his, she gradually increased the pace, her climax building as he stimulated her most sensitive area. Kade moved his hands, grasping her by the waist, supporting her while she seated herself upright onto him, taking every inch of his throbbing hardness. Throwing her head back, she moaned in pleasure, undulating against him with reckless abandon.

"Oh yes, Kade. I love you! Please…I'm coming," she cried out as her explosive orgasm washed over her. She splintered in glorious rapture, writhing above him.

In a swift move, never leaving her body, Kade brought her to him so they faced each other on their sides. He swung his leg possessively over hers, linking them together. In a delirious frenzy, Kade and Sydney passionately kissed while he thrust up into her again and again. Sydney surrendered to his rhythm, losing herself in his rich, intoxicating scent. She loved this man with all her heart. Kade slowed his movement within her warm sheath, reluctantly pulling his lips from hers. He pressed his forehead to hers once again, gazing into her eyes.

"You're everything to me. My future, my love, my wife. I love you."

Sydney bared her throat freely, offering her blood to him in anticipation of his erotic bite. Her gift of submission sparked a primal instinct deep within him. He growled possessively and powerfully thrust into her, and pierced her soft flesh with his fangs. Sydney excitedly drove her fingers through Kade's hair pressing his mouth into her neck. She screamed in sheer bliss as her release shattered simultaneously with his. He sated his thirst, losing control as he spilled his seed deep into her.

They lay still within each other's arms, embracing, not wanting the moment to end. Sydney was elated knowing that not only had he forgiven her for leaving, but he was totally committed to her in every way. She never thought in a million years she'd be the kind of woman who could fall in love so completely, but she had. And now, she would never let her vampire go.

"Mmmm….that was awesome. You're amazing, do you know that?"

Kade chuckled softly. "Ah…my love, it is you who are amazing. I am not sure how I ever survived all these centuries without you."

"Kade," Sydney smiled, realizing they'd just made love on the balcony, "as much as I love being naked in your arms outside on the terrace, the sun will be rising soon. People could see us out here. Where are we going to sleep?"

"Funny thing, since I was short on time," Kade laughed, "I only purchased the bare necessities for our penthouse. In doing so, I realized that most furniture is highly overrated. However, a bed, my love, is most definitely a necessity when it comes to you and me. And since I planned on making love to you all night and well into tomorrow, I purchased two beds: an outdoor bed, so we could make love under the stars, and a bed for the master bedroom. If you're ready, we can test that one out now. Shall we adjourn for the evening?"

"I would love that," Sydney agreed. She kissed him once again. Feeling light as a feather, she let Kade lift her up into his arms and carry her into their new home.

Epilogue

Sydney woke feeling optimistic, looking forward to her future with Kade. She gazed up at the stark white ceiling, dreaming of how she would decorate their new home. The open penthouse was quite a contrast to the historic, Garden District mansion in New Orleans. She wondered how Kade would adjust to the cold hard streets of Philadelphia, but guessed he could more than hold his own. She looked forward to living in both cities, in both of their homes.

She laughed to herself, thinking about how much she actually liked belonging to Kade, and having Kade belong to her. She moved to lay her head on his smooth chest, his vampire heartbeat resounding in her ear.

Letting her thoughts drift back to New Orleans, she wondered how Samantha was doing. She'd left the mansion before she had a chance to visit with the girl, and in the fray of taking off back to Philadelphia, she'd forgotten to ask Kade how she was.

Kade glanced to Sydney, having been awake for over an hour. Without a doubt, he knew that he was the only person Sydney had ever really loved, would ever love. Ecstatic that she had accepted his proposal, he looked forward to their life together. She was the woman of his dreams. Kade hugged her closer into his embrace and kissed the top of her head.

"What are you thinking about so hard this morning? I may not be able to read your thoughts clearly yet, but I certainly can sense you thinking…very loudly. Is something wrong?"

"Just wondering about Samantha, that's all. It's hard to believe that girl in the cell with me was the same girl we met in Sangre Dulce. Samantha seemed so innocent and scared, but not in a submissive kind of way. She was a fighter, no doubt about it."

"Don't worry." Kade sighed. "I promise Ilsbeth will take care of her. Your instincts are correct, though. She's not the person who was in that club. Not of her own accord, anyway. Ilsbeth detected dark magic on the girl's aura. Even though the coven can eliminate the darkness, the magic is infused within her. She is forever a witch." He shook his head, feeling frustrated about how he'd left things with Luca. "There is something else that bothered me, though. Before you left, Luca seemed off. I don't know if the dark magic emanating off of Samantha was affecting him or what, but he actually seemed…I don't know…caring?"

"Caring?"

"Yes. He seemed caring toward the young woman."

"What's wrong with that, Kade? I mean, Samantha has been through a lot. Asgear...did you see what he did to her? Anyone would show feelings after seeing what happened to her."

"I know. It's not caring that is a problem per se. It's just that...I've known Luca for nearly two centuries. Other than Tristan, he is my best friend. He has many good qualities. He's loyal, respectful, honest, a valiant warrior, but caring about the feelings of a crying, human woman? That is not something he does. Usually, he wouldn't care in the slightest. No way. That isn't his style. Honestly, I've never seen him in love with a woman in all our time together. Sex with a woman, yes, but never love. When we were with Samantha, he actually comforted her. It was strange...for him anyway. I don't know. It's probably nothing."

Sydney turned her naked body beneath the sheets, pressing her soft flesh against his chest. He leaned down, kissing her warm lips, parting them with his tongue. Growing hot with need, she reached down to explore the evidence of his arousal. They both jolted when Kade's cell phone rang loudly.

"Damn phone. I'll get it later. Don't stop."

"You sure?" She smiled. "Maybe you should just answer it this one time and then turn off the ringer so we can make love in peace."

Kade reluctantly pulled out of her arms and reached down to the floor, scavenging through his clothes. He glanced at the cell. *Ilsbeth?* Why was she calling? He shouldn't be hearing from her so quickly. Answering, he sensed that something was terribly wrong. They'd been attacked on the way to the coven. Ilsbeth and the girl had made it back safely, but Luca was missing.

LUCA'S MAGIC EMBRACE

Immortals of New Orleans, Book 2

Kym Grosso

Acknowledgments

I am very thankful to those who helped me create this book:

~My husband, for encouraging me to write, editing my articles and supporting me in everything I do. Also for listening to me read the love scenes out loud to him, which he thinks are the best parts of the book. Ooh la la. Keith definitely provides me with ideas on how to make them even better.

~ Tyler and Madison, for being so patient with me, while I spend time working on the book. You are the best kids ever!

~Mom & Dad, for giving me a loving family and guiding me along my way. Dad is my biggest supporter and I am so grateful. My brother Kevyn, who is the very best sibling a sister, could have.

~Julie Roberts, editor, who spent hours reading, editing and proofreading Luca's Magic Embrace. I really could not have done this without you!

~My beta readers, Sandra and Diantha, for volunteering to read novel and provide me with valuable and honest feedback.

~Carrie Spencer, CheekyCovers, who helped me to create a sexy novel cover and my new website.

Chapter One

Naked. Bound. Luca strained his wrists and ankles upward, seeking a release from the silver cuffs and chains that burned his flesh deeper with every movement. The sound of sizzling skin echoed in the room with the slightest movement. Luca lay imprisoned flat on a stone altar, his battered body racked with pain. His arms were spread to each side, the chains on his wrists wound around the hard pedestal legs. His feet were tightly bound together, effectively immobilizing him.

Where the fuck am I? Scanning his surroundings, Luca realized he was in an abandoned building, a Catholic church. He could see the Stations of the Cross painted on the faded, chipped walls. Streams of light shone through a broken, stained glass window. The church smelled of mold, urine and blood. His blood. Used surgical syringes littered the floor. A rubber band was loosely tied to his arm. Because there were no marks on his arm, he reasoned he must have healed himself. *Shit. Someone had been syphoning his blood.*

The last thing he remembered, he had been escorting the witches to their coven. An attack, a blinding silver spray flashed in his mind. Luca couldn't remember how long he'd been unconscious. *Weak, so weak.* It took everything he had to wriggle his arms. The silver burned and drained his energy as uncontrollable thirst enveloped his thoughts.

He screamed into the desolate cathedral, hoping someone would hear him. "Help me!" No answer. His eyes burned with fury, knowing it was unlikely help would come. How long had he been shackled without blood? Would his captors return to torture him? In his diminished state, he was surprised that they hadn't staked him. Why was he still alive and not dead? Crying out in agony, he was again met with silence. It was useless.

Lying on the altar in his stink and dried blood, he felt like an animal. Glancing around the dilapidated structure, he could not assess a feasible means of escape. He closed his eyes and concentrated, praying he could establish a connection with his maker, Kade. Kade would not rest knowing something had happened to him, his best friend and confidant. Luca prayed to the goddess that he could link with him soon. Feeling his life slip away like air leaking from a balloon, there wasn't much time left. If he wasn't rescued soon, he'd die.

Kade's eyes flashed open, sensing Luca's consciousness. *He's alive.*

Sydney stirred in Kade's arms and placed a kiss on his bare chest. She felt him tense beneath her; something was amiss. "Kade, what's wrong?"

"It's Luca. He's alive. I can sense him. I need to concentrate and see if we can make contact."

"Oh my God, Kade. Where is he?" she asked excitedly. Luca had been missing for over a week. Attempts to find him had been fruitless.

"Shhhh, love. Just give me a minute to focus on him. Lay still." Kade closed his eyes, letting his mind wander. Settling his thoughts on Luca, he mentally reached out across New Orleans. Since Luca had disappeared, Kade had been unable to establish contact with his progeny.

While in Philadelphia with Sydney, Ilsbeth, a local ally and powerful witch, had contacted him with the news that they'd been attacked while returning to the coven. Both Ilsbeth and newly transformed witch Samantha, had made it safely home; Luca, however, had been taken. Kade, the leader of New Orleans vampires, and his fiancée, Sydney, a police detective, had searched the area of the attack for days on end and had turned up no clues to his abduction. Immediately after the fight ensued, the coven had been set to lock down, so none of the witches could describe Luca's abductors or provide assistance in finding him. Kade had tried numerous times to reach out to Luca psychically. Throughout time, they'd always shared a connection. But since the attack, only a silent hum remained of Luca's existence. Kade could not sense Luca's death, but neither could he sense Luca's location. It was as if he'd dropped off the face of the Earth.

Kade surmised that the lack of communication meant one of two things: either Luca was incapacitated to the point of death, perhaps silvered, or he had purposefully left the area, refusing to contact Kade. Luca had been a loyal friend since Kade had turned him at the start of the nineteenth century, so Kade knew for a fact that Luca would not take off without notice. Because of this, the former conclusion concerned him greatly. If Luca was hurt, it would be nearly impossible to find him.

As Kade meditated on Luca, a flicker of vibration resonated back to him, alerting him again to Luca's presence. It felt as if Luca was far from the Garden District but still within the city limits. *Luca, can you hear me? Where are you?*

Drifting into unconsciousness, Luca perceived the sensation that Kade was there with him. He wasn't sure if he was hallucinating or dying, but he moved his lips, trying to speak into the darkness. No matter how he strained to talk, no more words could be spoken aloud; he was too weak. His thoughts raced. *Please let this be real. Help me. An abandoned church. Mold. I can't…I can't last much longer.*

Kade swore, "Goddammit. I felt him, but he's lost to me again. He must be unconscious or badly hurt. I heard something…something about an abandoned church. And mold. But shit, that could be just about anywhere down here. The only thing is that I can feel he's within the city limits; not in our district, but he's not far." He raked his fingers through his hair in frustration. "Shit. I should've sent someone else with him to escort the witches so soon after that clusterfuck with Simone and Asgear. This could be related to them, or maybe someone's trying to get to me," he speculated.

Sydney scrambled out of bed, pulling on a pair of faded jeans and a t-shirt. "Don't blame yourself. This is not your fault. We don't know that this is related to Asgear or Simone. We'll get him back," she said determinedly. "Where could the church be? There were hundreds of abandoned buildings after Katrina. But there has been lots of cleanup. Where could there still be a church? Lower ninth ward?"

"No, he feels closer. We need to get the car and go for a drive." Kade quickly got dressed, pulling on a pair of black denim pants and a black polo shirt. He pushed his feet into his leather boots and began to pace, anxiously wanting to resume the search. "This isn't good, Sydney. If he hasn't fed, he could be dangerous. I'm just warning you in case we find him. He'll need human blood immediately. You'll have to do what I say, no questions, okay? It feels like he's almost gone…not yet dead to us, though."

Sydney wanted to comfort Kade. A lot of shit had gone down over the past few weeks; she was determined to help find Luca. Kade felt helpless not being able to locate Luca and blamed himself for not anticipating the attack. She wasn't sure how to make him feel better except by comforting him in the one way she knew how. Wrapping her arms around Kade's neck, she kissed him lightly, letting him know she was there for him. "Kade, I will do whatever you need me to do. I promise we'll find Luca. I love you."

"But Sydney…"He wasn't convinced. In the nearly two hundred years since he'd turned Luca, they'd never gone without speaking for so long. Kade felt Luca dying; they needed to work fast.

"But nothing. I mean it. I would do anything for you. No exceptions. You felt Luca. Maybe it was just a slight sense, but he's here somewhere. Now, let's go get him."

Kade zipped through the streets of the Garden District, driving feverishly towards the French Quarter. "It's getting stronger. He's not far away."

"Is he in the French Quarter?" Sydney asked.

"No, a little farther. Maybe Foubourg Marigny?" Kade guessed.

"Hmmm…along the water? Well, that would explain the odor Luca described," she replied.

"Sydney, we don't know who took him or if there will be danger where we're headed. Please. For the love of God, let me go in first. We can't take any chances." He knew Sydney had a tendency to act first and think later.

"Really? Are we doing this again? I have my guns with me. And do I need to remind you that you are the one who's weakened during the day, not me? How about this…we go in together, I stay behind you." She smiled coyly at Kade, knowing he could not refuse her during the daytime. She swore to him that she'd do what he said but that didn't mean she couldn't hold her own.

"All right. But no heroics and as promised, you do as I ask. We go in, get Luca, put him in the back of the SUV and get the hell out of there. Luca will most likely need emergency attention. Étienne, Dominique and Xavier are procuring donors to feed him when we return."

Sydney cringed at the term 'donors'. She knew there were plenty of humans out there who would willingly donate their blood in exchange for the pleasurable bite of a vampire. Given that most humans climaxed during the experience, she couldn't understand how someone would let a strange vamp bite them, regardless of the high it guaranteed. She sighed. "I promise I'll behave myself. Let me know if you sense any vampires or witches, though. I hate surprises."

Kade reached across the seat and ran the back of his hand across Sydney's cheek. He loved her so much. She was brave and beautiful. And she'd agreed to be his wife.

Sydney felt chills run throughout her body straight to her womb. God, how she loved that man. She didn't want to worry him, and after the mess with Asgear and Simone, she'd learned her lesson. Vampires were seriously dangerous creatures, and she worried about how Luca would react to the smell of a human after being injured. Luca was formidable on a good day, let alone when he was hurt.

As they approached the riverfront neighborhood, Kade slowed the car. "There!" he shouted, pointing over to a church.

Sydney noticed the heavy broken padlocks lying on the concrete sidewalk. "Looks like someone has been goin' to church. The locks have been broken," she observed.

The enormous stone building must have been beautiful in its heyday. Three large arches adorned the front of the building, giving way to large, wooden double doors. Ornately carved gargoyles perched along the top of the structure guarded its entrance, providing a gothic warning to evil ne'er-do-wells. Remnants of stained glass mosaic windows accentuated the church in broken shades of indigo and evergreen.

Kade parked the car but left it running. "Sydney, you stay behind me. Remember what I told you. It's possible that Luca hasn't eaten in days. If he's injured, he won't be himself."

"What do you mean? Luca's always just so pleasant and friendly with us humans. Warm and fuzzy comes to mind," Sydney joked sarcastically, knowing that Luca wasn't crazy about humans. She made a face.

Kade frowned. "It's more than not winning the mister congeniality contest. I expect that he'll want to see you, but not because he necessarily wants to have a chat. It's more than possible that the man hasn't eaten since he was taken. You're food. Need I explain more?" He shook his head, knowing his friend would not be in good shape. "You can follow me in and assist me if…and this is a big if, I need help. Otherwise, just stay back. I will get Luca. Please Sydney. I need you to obey me on this."

Sydney nodded. She'd been in more than a few scuffles with vampires lately and did not want to become Luca's dinner. She was as tough as they came, but she knew with certainty that Luca would not be the cool and collected vampire she knew. People were warned never to touch injured wild animals, because they might attack due to fear or pain, and you could get injured in the process of trying to help. A starved and injured Luca could be like a large and dangerous lion. And a lion tamer she was not. As much as she wanted to help, she needed to be cautious. *The road to hell is paved with good intentions and all that business.* She decided to follow Kade's directions to the letter.

Kade exited the car. The warm summer breeze blew against his face; his nostrils flared, concentrating on finding Luca inside the church. "I can smell him. Something's wrong."

Sydney placed a comforting hand on his shoulder. "Kade, he'll be okay. Luca is tough. Come on…let's go. I promise to stay back." She reached for her Sig Sauger and clicked the safety off.

With a great shove against the decrepit, weather-worn doors, Kade stumbled into the open vestibule. Rank, moldy air choked their lungs and dust danced throughout light beams, pulsating through the cracked stained glass windows. Sensing no one but Luca, Kade cautiously proceeded into the antechamber. Glancing back at Sydney, he held up his hand to her, reminding her to stay behind. She nodded in agreement as Kade entered the church.

With preternatural velocity, Kade rushed to the stone altar and hissed at the sight of Luca chained to the slab. "Sydney, come quickly. He's silvered. I need you now."

Sydney sprinted up the aisle, aghast at seeing Luca's handsome face now crusted over with dried blood. His once muscular body looked emaciated, with burns oozing from the silver chains. "Oh my God. What did they do to him? Luca…we're here. We've got you." She reached over and began unraveling the heavy chains from his limbs. Sydney expected Luca to wince but he remained unnervingly still, unresponsive to the pain. The chains clanged onto the floor, dispersing the dirty needles and dried leaves that had blown in through the broken windows. "Kade. Look at all the needles.

What the hell? Why would they do this?"

Kade showed no emotion while circling the altar, scanning the mess around them. He waited patiently for Sydney to remove all the silver. "Fucking assholes. They probably took blood from Luca to be sold on the black market." Anger surged as he kicked the needles aside, silently vowing revenge on the perpetrators.

Since the vampires had become known to the public, both pharmaceutical companies and entrepreneurs had been looking to capitalize on the immortality of vampires. Try as they might, no progress had been made towards perpetual life without incurring that nasty little side effect of becoming a vampire. While plenty of vampires were willing to sell their blood for profit, it didn't stop the gangs from kidnapping and draining vamps to sell their blood on the black market at a discounted price.

Kade lovingly swept his hand across his old friend's face, trying to clear the dried blood off of him. "Luca," he whispered. "You are safe now. We've got you."

Luca and Kade had been friends for over two centuries, meeting during the early eighteen hundreds. While Luca had been born in Britain, he had been raised in Australia. He'd come over to America during the War of 1812. When he'd been badly injured and lay dying on the battlefield, Kade had turned him. He was indebted to Kade; they were partners, best friends.

Kade was infuriated; whoever had done this would pay dearly. "Sydney, you drive. I'm going to lie in the back of the SUV and feed him. Don't get near us. When he wakes, he could be dangerous." Kade frowned. "Look at what they did to him. He's starved."

"Will he be okay?" Sydney didn't know that much about vampire medicine except that they had healing properties in their blood. Said properties were most effective on humans and werewolves but held minimum benefit for other vampires. She knew he needed a mortal donor.

"Yes, he'll heal, but we've got to get him human blood. Call Dominique and tell her to bring the donors into the house and get them ready now. She knows what to do." Kade gingerly slid his hand underneath Luca's head and knees, bringing him close to his body. Swiftly, he lifted him and carried him out of the church.

"Put the back seat down," he ordered.

Sydney clicked the release on the seats, pushing them until they were flat. Kade laid Luca in the trunk and climbed into the back. With his hands underneath Luca's arms, he gently pulled him all the way into the car. Thank God they'd brought the Escalade. It would be a tight fit with two large males lying in the back, but they'd fit.

Kade sighed as he leaned up onto his side, and reached over to Luca's mouth. Placing one hand on Luca's chin and cupping his cheeks with the other hand, he slowly opened Luca's cracked lips.

Sydney started the engine and stole a glimpse of Kade biting into his wrist. No matter how many times she'd witnessed a vampire feeding someone or feeding from someone, she was always fascinated by the intimacy of the act. It felt almost intrusive to watch them together. Anxious to get home, she pulled her eyes back to the road and drove.

Kade cradled Luca's head as he pressed his wrist downward. The crimson droplets trickled down the sides of Luca's face; he wasn't swallowing. Kade reached with his mind, willing Luca to drink. *Please Goddess, let me through to him. Drink Luca, drink.*

Luca jerked in Kade's arms as a single drop of the life-giving blood was absorbed into his body. Yet he didn't wake. He could not move. Immobilized within his friend's arms, Luca's consciousness awakened. *Safe. Kade. Friend.* He tried to move, but couldn't manage more than a swallow.

"That's it, Luca. Drink," Kade ordered. Relief flooded his mind; he'd been worried about Luca's ability to recover. While vampires only needed to drink a few pints every couple of days, they needed to feed regularly. Going without feeding could send them into a frenzy, which could cause them to lose control and kill a human. Going several days without feeding could cause their demise.

Pulling into Kade's compound, Sydney saw Dominique waiting impatiently near the mansion's entrance. Dominique, another vampire, was a longtime loyal employee and friend of Kade's. Sydney described her as a badass fashionista. She and Dominique had initially clashed when they'd first met over a month ago. Since then, they'd forged a friendship based on mutual respect and a love of leather.

Parking the car, Sydney ran around the SUV and slowly pulled open the hatch. She understood that Luca could be dangerous, so she moved slowly with no sudden movements. Yet looking at his frail, battered torso, she couldn't fathom what harm he could do in his weakened state. While typically well-composed, her breath caught in her throat at the sight of him. She could not resist the need to provide both Luca and Kade with comfort. As she reached to touch Luca, his eyes flew open; he strained to break free of Kade's hold. *Human blood.*

"Don't touch him! Get away now, Sydney!" Kade hissed at her.

Sydney jumped back, startled at the bloodlust in Luca's eyes. He was dangerous. Hungry. She thought she must look like water in the desert to him. Heeding Kade's order, she ran inside to see what she could do to help.

Dominique intervened, helping Kade to restrain Luca. "Fuck, what the hell happened to him?" Dominique questioned.

"He was silvered, starved. Possibly tortured. Not sure what all they did yet. But I know they got his blood. There were needles all over the damn place," he spat out. So many years had passed since he'd been turned. At times, he was astonished by how little progress humanity had achieved. Evil, hate and torture still beat strong within the hearts of so many. *How could they have done this to him?*

He sighed wearily. "Sydney's blood is making him crazy. We need to get him inside. Where are Xavier and Étienne? Do we have donors?" Kade held tight onto Luca while trying to move him slowly out of the SUV. Luca was still in no condition to walk and he'd be damned if he'd chance letting him loose.

"They're on their way. I have a room prepared upstairs. I can help carry him," she said, looking around to make sure Sydney was gone. Like Kade, she could not trust Luca not to attack her. They had human donors waiting upstairs, and they would monitor the feeding closely so Luca didn't end up draining them.

"Where's Sydney?" Kade asked.

Dominique looked around. "It seems your woman had enough sense to make herself scarce when he looked at her like she was lobster dinner. Don't worry, she'll be fine. It isn't her first time at the vamp rodeo."

"I know. It's just that she's not used to seeing Luca like this. Neither am I." He shook his head. Seeing Luca in such an animalistic state would serve as a reminder to Sydney that she was marrying into this lifestyle. He needed to find her and make sure that she was all right.

Kade easily lifted Luca, with his arms under Luca's neck and the crook under his knees. Luca's eyes were wide open, yet he wasn't speaking. Kade wasn't sure if Luca understood what was happening as he took him upstairs to the guest bedroom. Dominique motioned Kade into the bathroom, where she had a bath filled with warm water. "Kade, over here. The warm water will help get his body temp back up."

Kade placed Luca's emaciated naked body into the warm, soapy water. "Shit," he said as water sloshed over the sides of the tub and all over the floor. Without even taking the time to undress, Kade carefully climbed into the tub and lay next to Luca so he could hold him still while he fed. Deeply concerned about Luca's state, he waved over at Dominique. "Where's the donor? We need him now!" he commanded.

She pointed at a shirtless, twenty-something male who was waiting in the bedroom. "You, over here, on your knees by the tub."

"Yes ma'am," said the donor as he willingly and quickly complied with her demand, and held out his arm. Donors were easy to come by these days. They signed up at blood clubs, hoping to experience a sexual encounter with a vampire. At the very least, they hoped to be chosen for a bite, knowing the orgasmic properties that could be granted by the vampire.

Issacson Securities, Kade's company, had contracted with Sanguine Services to procure donors when needed. Dominique had called in advance to procure a couple of strong males who would be able to provide enough blood for Luca. She just hoped the blood would be enough to bring Luca back from his atrophied state. She had never seen a vampire so far gone and wasn't convinced they could save him. But she didn't want to cause Kade further worry, so she kept her reservations to herself.

Dominique gently took the donor's wrist and flashed him a quick smile. "Hey there, what's your name?" she asked.

"Milo," he obediently replied.

"Okay, listen, Milo. This person here; he's a good friend of mine. His name is Luca. He hasn't eaten in days, so this might be a little rough at first but I promise you will be safe." She hoped he would, anyway.

Kade tried reaching out mentally to Sydney to tell her to stay away. Their telepathic connection was in its infancy, but short of yelling for her, he needed to send some kind of warning to stay away from Luca. Sensing she was in the house but not near, he breathed a sigh of relief. It was time to get started. He nodded at Dominique to begin.

Dominique brought Milo's wrist to her finely-painted, coral-colored lips. Her tongue darted out, licking his sensitive inner wrist. She resisted the urge to play with her food, knowing that Luca needed blood as soon as possible. Expeditiously, her razor-sharp fangs pierced his flesh; he moaned aloud, sexually excited by her bite.

Leaning over to Luca's lips, with the donor's wrist in her mouth, she seamlessly transferred Milo's bleeding wrist from her mouth to Luca's. Another loud groan of excitement resounded along the granite-tiled walls as Luca began to voraciously feed.

Kade had his arms locked around Luca's upper body, preventing him from making any violent attack on the donor. "That's it my friend. Drink. You'll be fine, and we'll find out who did this to you," he said, looking directly into Luca's eyes. He could tell Luca was starting to become fully conscious, but he still couldn't tell if Luca's cognition was stable. Their mental connection was still severed.

A loud groan emanated from Milo, indicating sexual release. Dominique had already readied the second donor as Kade pulled Milo away from Luca. They were very careful to ensure that Luca did not kill the donors. Luca latched onto the second donor and was starting to regain color, warmth. Despite being close to getting enough blood, something wasn't right with Luca.

Kade released Luca as he pushed the second donor away. Luca again closed his eyes as his physique appeared to regenerate before their eyes. Kade climbed out of the tub and grabbed a towel as Xavier and Étienne entered the bathroom. "Nice of you to join us. Please attend to the donors and make sure they get safely home," he said as he rubbed his hair vigorously with the towel, annoyed that they'd just arrived at the mansion.

"Sorry we're late, Kade. Downtown traffic is a bitch this time of night,"

Étienne explained. "He's looking well, no?"

"Looks can be deceiving. Something's not right. Our mental connection's shut down. He isn't verbally responding either. But he's had quite enough vampire and human blood to bring him back physically." Kade was worried about Luca.

Xavier leaned down and touched Luca's head. "Mon ami, what happened to you?" Xavier tried reaching for him mentally and also failed to contact him. "I see what you mean. Do you know what's going on? He's here but not here."

"Not sure. Perhaps he needs time to rest. For now, let's get moving, people. Get the donors out of here." He looked over at Dominique. She had a single, blood-red tear running down her beautiful face.

"Dominique, look at me," he ordered. She complied, meeting his eyes. "Luca will heal. Finish bathing him, and get him to bed. Watch over him until I return. I'm going to call a doctor, and I need to find Sydney. She may be able to help him…"

"But how, Kade? Look at him…he's not responding to us," she cried.

"Trust me. I've been around a very long time. I know what needs to be done, even if I'm not happy about it."

Sydney could not stop thinking about what had just happened outside of the car. Luca and Sydney had had a rough start. Because she was human, which equated to weak and vulnerable in his eyes, he hadn't been happy about her working with them on the Voodoo murder case. But they had forged a deep friendship during battle. Sydney was a hardened detective from Philadelphia, so she'd seen most of the worst the world could dish out. But it didn't stop the pain in her heart from seeing a friend injured. Nor did it stop the surprise she felt seeing the look in his eyes. She could feel the pull of him mentally, wanting to feed from her.

She was confused about how this could be possible. Sydney had been regularly drinking small amounts of Kade's blood since they'd got engaged. Blood sharing was an incredibly intimate and sexual experience. As a result of their bonding, she was starting to be able to feel a mental connection to Kade. Right now, she could sense single words or feelings from him, but he told her that soon she'd be able to send messages back and forth. She had thought that connection would only be with Kade.

However, today at the car, Luca's eyes had bored into her soul, calling to her to help him. It was if she could hear him speaking to her. Frightened, she obediently ran into the house at Kade's command. She wasn't afraid of Luca attacking her. No, she was afraid of the message she sensed from him. He needed her blood.

Chapter Two

Dr. Sweeney, Kade's personal physician, had assessed Luca's health. Even though he'd received human blood, there was the possibility he might not return to who he had been. The doctor estimated he'd gone without blood for at least seven days, which would have been long enough to easily kill a younger vampire. She said there was a chance he would recover fully after several feedings, but they might have to wait over a month before they knew for sure. Devastated by the news, Kade went to search for comfort in Sydney.

Sydney was hunched over, with her face in her hands, sitting in the master bedroom when Kade found her. He would never get used to the feel of his heart squeezing in his chest when he was around her. Detective Sydney Willows was his woman, his fiancée: strong, sexy, loving. She was all he would ever need in this life, but would he risk her to save his friend?

"Sydney, love. You okay? What's wrong?" he questioned, kneeling before her.

Sydney silently shook her head.

"You cannot hide from me. We need to talk about what happened back in the car…Luca," he whispered. Kade removed and discarded his wet shirt and pants. He then knelt before Sydney and slid his hands up her calves. He would never get enough of her, feeling the strength of his woman's body.

Sydney snapped her head upward to gaze into Kade's eyes; her mane of long, curly blonde locks spilled over her shoulders. A chill of sexual excitement shot into Sydney's body, but she tried to quell the feelings in the wake of what had just happened to Luca. "How is he?" she asked, knowing Kade would remain stoic in the face of crisis. That was just the kind of man he was: authoritative, confident and courageous. He'd be strong for Luca, for Sydney.

"Dr. Sweeney came over and checked him out. She says he'll most likely recover. But it could be a month before we know for sure. But you know Luca; he's strong. He's fine…physically," he answered.

She cupped his face in her hands and leaned into him for a brief kiss. She needed Kade's warmth, to bring him comfort.

"What do you mean, baby? Did he tell you what happened, who did this to him?" She realized she had shifted into detective mode. Stopping herself, she changed her approach. "Kade…in the car…he…" *How could she tell Kade?*

"What happened in the car, love, was that Luca smelled your blood and was simply ravenous for human blood; he was starved. He wouldn't have hurt you. I'd swear my life on it. But he may still need you..." *How could he ask Sydney for her help?*

Sydney got up out of the chair, raked her fingers through her long hair and began to pace. She was confused, scared. She was afraid for herself and how Kade might react. "Kade, something happened in the car. Luca. I don't know how to explain it. Our mental connection. Somehow, Luca...when he looked at me. He needs me." She stood still, waiting for Kade to respond.

Kade loved her so much. He hated having to tell her what might help Luca heal. But somehow, Luca had communicated with her instead of him. Rushing over to embrace Sydney, Kade let himself briefly enjoy the feel of her soft breasts against his bare chest, the smell of her strawberry-scented hair. Pulling back, he kissed her, a soft loving kiss. "Sydney, I don't know how he communicated with you. Maybe the blood connection. He is mine...of my making. Please don't be afraid."

Sydney held her chin high, feigning courage. "Me? Afraid? Seriously?" Then she giggled nervously, knowing that she was very much afraid. But she didn't want Kade to have to worry about her in addition to Luca. It was too much.

He smiled, letting her save face. "My brave detective, I know you're as tough as they come. And I love you for it. But we need to be honest with each other. This is serious, understand?"

"Okay. I'm a little afraid," she whispered.

"He needs you. More specifically, he needs you to feed him. Your blood...it's special. You have my vampiric blood in you, and your own very special, sweet mortal essence." Kade was confident in their relationship. He loved her unconditionally, and she him. Yet he wanted Sydney to feel safe. Sure, she knew the dangers and realities of his world, but she was still a novice. He knew that she was just starting to become comfortable around the other vampires.

"Yes," she quietly responded, unsure where he was going with his explanation.

"You know how it is when I bite you, correct?" He needed to make sure she was clear about what could happen and had no regrets. "Sydney, if you do this, I will be there with you. You'll be safe. But I want to be clear, it very well could be...well, you know, sexual in nature. You know how it is..." his words trailed off.

Before he met Sydney, Kade and Luca had often shared women. He had even shared a brief dance with Sydney and Luca, at Sangre Dulce, a local bondage club, where they'd been investigating a crime. But he'd had no intentions of sharing Sydney with Luca, ever. It hadn't been an option...until now.

Kade watched Sydney as she pulled away from him and resumed pacing.

He could see her thoughts spinning in her head. She'd been attracted to Luca that night in the club but that didn't mean she'd wanted anything further to happen. Added to the fact that she wasn't a big fan of vampires; would she agree to let another man bite her?

Kade blew out a breath. He hated to rush her, but he felt as though they were running out of time. "Sydney, you don't have to do this if you don't want to. But if you do agree, I want to be crystal clear that I am not asking you to have sex with Luca. You should be aware by now that I have grown quite possessive of you." He smiled and approached her, seeking her touch. "But you need to know that Luca may, indeed, touch you, and you, in return, may feel the need to touch him. And I don't want you feeling guilty or uncomfortable with it. It is our nature."

Sydney closed the gap between them and wrapped her arms around Kade's neck. "I love you, Kade. I love you so much it hurts sometimes. I would do anything for you, or to save Luca. And I want you to know that I'm not afraid, because I know you will protect me. I'm nothing but secure in our relationship. I know you and I are meant to be. So if I do this for him, whatever sexual feelings bubble up during this…this feeding…it's just a feeling that happens. Like that night in the club…" She blushed, remembering how she had felt, sandwiched between both Luca and Kade's hard, sexy maleness.

Kade nodded knowingly, "Yes, I remember." He knew his reserved detective had been inordinately aroused by dancing with two men.

"It was overwhelming that night…dancing so intimately with both you and Luca. I never thought I would enjoy my little walk on the kinky side, but I did. But I also know that I love you…You and you alone. So I don't plan on making love to Luca when we do this…no matter how good he bites," she joked.

Kade tightened his hold around Sydney's waist. "As if I would let you make love to another man, love. You are mine," he growled. Kade captured Sydney's lips, his tongue swept over hers, drinking in her sweet nectar. She was the most amazing, sexy woman. He wanted to make love to her right then, right there, but Luca was waiting. He reluctantly drew back from their kiss. "Okay, this is how it's going to happen. I will be directing this show, understand?"

Sydney nodded in agreement, eagerly anticipating helping Luca.

Kade and Sydney stood at the entrance to Luca's room watching Dominique busy herself. She was placing the dirty towels in a laundry bin and straightening the sheets on the bed as if they somehow affected Luca. Sydney knew that Dominique was simply struggling to keep her mind off of the fact that Luca was unresponsive. Despite her typical flippant comments and hard exterior, Dominique cared deeply for Luca.

Luca was resting quietly in the bed with only a white cotton sheet covering his legs and groin. His broad, muscled chest, now restored, quietly rose and fell as he slept peacefully. His dark, shoulder-length hair was tousled across the white pillow case. He looked peaceful, rested and healthy. Yet they all knew he wasn't.

Kade, still shirtless, wore loose-fitted, faded blue jeans; he wanted to be comfortable when they did this. Sydney had nervously changed into a casual, spaghetti-strapped, black sundress that could easily be mistaken for a nightgown, deciding that she needed to be in comfortable clothing. She wasn't exactly sure of the logistics but since Luca was still in bed, she figured she would at least be on a chair or kneeling beside the bed.

She was about to ask a question when Kade interrupted her thoughts. "Dominique, leave us. We'll watch him," he ordered.

Understanding his meaning, Dominique quickly left the room and shut the door.

"Sydney, you ready?" he asked.

"Yes. Where do you want me?" she responded.

"Remember Sydney, I am in charge here. Luca will not be dangerous. You are safe with us. But you must listen to me, no questions. I am in control," he said matter of factly.

Sydney had to admit that was one of the things she loved about Kade. He was one hundred percent alpha male. He gave orders, didn't take them. And Sydney always felt safe giving him control sexually. She was under a lot of pressure most days to lead teams and investigations. Sexually, she desired to submit to him occasionally. It wasn't in her nature to submit, but Goddess, this man brought out things in her personality she never even knew existed.

"Sydney?" His voice brought her thoughts back to Luca.

"Sorry. Yes, I'm ready." She listened intently for her instructions.

Kade grabbed her hand and kissed her palm. "Luca's resting, so we need to get his senses awakened enough to feed…to bite you. The best place to let him bite you would be your neck." He traced his fingers around the side of her face, down her neck. "Come."

Sydney felt her body shake in anticipation of what would happen. She trusted Kade, but damn, she was nervous. *What the fuck was I thinking, telling Kade I'd let Luca feed from me?* But she'd promised to help Luca. For both their sakes, they needed him back.

"Lay on your side, next to Luca. I will be right here behind you, love," he directed. "Get in." He patted the bed.

Sydney got into bed; her breasts struggled to stay in her dress as she pressed up next to Luca's arm. "Is this okay?"

"Move closer, Sydney. Put your arm across his chest. Press closely up against him without getting on top of him. He will sense you. Concentrate. Reach out mentally for him. He's there." Kade spooned Sydney and put his strong arms protectively around her waist. "There you go, love. That's it…I feel him. He knows we're here. Why we are here. Don't struggle, Sydney. Just let yourself go. Don't worry about losing control, okay? Remember that I'm here. You'll be fine."

In Luca's mind, he could hear her calling him. *Sydney.* But how could that be? Then Luca heard another voice. *Kade.* He struggled to listen. He knew he was at Kade's home but he couldn't talk, move. What was happening to him? The scent of strawberries teased his nose. Soft, warm hands on his chest. Female hands. *Samantha?*

No, not Samantha, Sydney. He sensed Kade, too. The scent of Sydney's sweet blood called to him. Not just human blood. No, mortal blood infused with the blood of his maker. He needed it to survive. The desire to live was strong.

Tendrils of awareness fingered throughout his body awakening his senses. *Feed.* The command coming from Kade was strong. Yet, it didn't make sense that he would share Sydney. No, he wouldn't do that to his friend. Sydney belonged to Kade. *Feed.* Luca started shaking his head; his eyes opened. "No," he pleaded. His first words since the attack.

Feed. This time from Sydney. He could hear her speaking to him telepathically. She was offering herself to him. No, that couldn't be. He couldn't understand why this was happening. Confused, he looked down to see her stroking his chest, cuddled up next to him, staring into his eyes.

"Yes, Luca. It's me, Sydney. We know what you need. It's okay. Kade and I are both here." She reached up and caressed his face, placing her finger on his lips.

"Luca, feed. Listen to Sydney. Her blood's special. She offers her blood to you freely as do I. Now feed," Kade ordered again. He knew Luca would resist, but he'd force him if necessary. Sydney's blood would restore him.

Luca's fangs descended on hearing Kade's command. He rolled over onto his side, to gaze into Sydney's eyes, wanting to be assured of her permission. Luca glanced at Kade who nodded. *Feed.*

Luca had always found Sydney incredibly sexy but never wanted to infringe on his friend's woman. Yet, here she was in bed with him, offering herself to him. He slid his hand around her waist, feeling the back of Kade's hand holding her gently in place. Luca whispered to Sydney, "Thank you." With those words, he let his lips fall onto hers, kissing her softly, pressing his chest to hers.

He pulled his head back slightly. "I promise to be gentle, Sydney."

She gasped as she felt the slice of Luca's fangs at her throat. "Kade…" It was all she could manage as moisture flooded her core. She ached for release as Luca held her closer still, draining her blood. Sydney felt strangely at peace having two strong male bodies surround her in such an intimate way. *Kade. Luca.* She embraced his bite, realizing she'd lost control.

Luca moaned as her nourishing blood swept into his throat. A magical mixture of human blood infused with his maker's awoke his consciousness. Memories of the past two weeks flashed before his eyes. The killing of Simone and Asgear. Touching Samantha's soft hair, comforting her in Kade's basement. Traveling to the coven. An attack. Silvered. Drained of blood. Tormented. Malnourished. Dying. A rushing vortex of energy propelled throughout his entire being as he voraciously drank her gift to him, her blood. Exhilaration rose within Luca as his emotional connections regenerated.

Kade watched intently as Luca suckled Sydney's neck, careful to make sure Luca kept himself under control. He disliked the thought of sharing her with any man, but he was desperate to save Luca. Watching his friend feed from his fiancée, he sensed Sydney's growing arousal from the bite. Luca's dark kiss could send her into erotic bliss or agony, depending on his intentions. He cared for her, so of course, Luca tried to make it pleasurable. Sensing Sydney's desire, Kade reluctantly grew aroused as well. Lost in the moment, Kade pushed up Sydney's dress, and slid his hands along her flat stomach to cup her bare breasts. He found himself grinding his hardness into her ass, and yearned to make love to her while Luca drank.

"Oh, yes, Kade. Please, I need…" Sydney found herself begging, writhing between Kade's aching erection at her back and Luca's bare hardness on her belly. She needed something but couldn't articulate her thoughts. She struggled for control in an effort to relieve the ache.

"Sydney, love. You're safe. Remember who's in control. I'll take care of you," he reminded her. Kade unzipped his jeans and made short work of undressing himself. Pulling Sydney's thong aside, his fingers slipped into her wet folds and found her most sensitive area. He began to rub her clitoris firmly but gently in circles.

"Yes, Kade," she cried out as he touched her. She knew in her mind that she shouldn't be doing this with two men, but she also understood that vampires were sexual at their core. At the very essence of their nature, they were capable of inflicting extraordinary pleasure or pain. Under the best of circumstances, they could restrain their need to climax and simply feed. Depleted of all nourishment, Luca had suffered tremendously; he wasn't capable of holding back. They needed to restore him by tending to his every physical and emotional need.

Kade understood that she'd feel conflicted. She was still very much human, not accustomed to the ways of vampires. "That's right, Sydney. Don't fight how you feel, just go with it," he coaxed. "Take Luca in your hand. It's okay."

Sensing Luca had drunk enough of Sydney's blood, Kade directed him to stop feeding. She'd be too weak if he didn't stop now. "Luca, release Sydney. Enough."

Luca did as told, licking over the holes in her neck. He hissed as Sydney reached to stroke his velvety steel hardness. His forehead fell against her shoulder as she cared for him. Luca caressed her breast with one hand as Kade paid attention to the other one.

Sydney was completely overwhelmed. It was so wrong, but so right. She'd never done anything like this in her life. She wanted to save Luca but how had she gotten herself into something like this? Worse, she admitted to herself that she didn't want to stop. She just needed release. "Kade!" she screamed as he entered her from behind in one thrust. She felt full with him, yet needing more.

"Sydney, so tight, warm. I won't last like this," he whispered into her ear. Kade began pumping in and out of her moist heat. He felt so connected to both Sydney and Luca in this single moment. The love of his life. His best friend. Kade felt Luca speak to him; *"Thank you, friend."*

Sydney couldn't keep her orgasm at bay much longer. She was grabbing the back of Luca's head, pulling him into her shoulder while taking Kade into her from behind and stroking Luca. *Too much. Can't hold on.*

Hearing her urgency, Kade reached around with his thumb to press her sensitive nub. "That's it love. Come for me. So good. Let go."

At his words, Sydney began to convulse against Luca and Kade, riding the waves of her climax. Kade slid one last long stroke into Sydney, holding her tightly against him and releasing his seed deep within her.

As Luca came along with them, a single thought escaped his lips as he cried, "Samantha!"

Kade quickly slipped out of Sydney and turned her around to him to hold her. He looked her directly in the eyes, realizing the gravity of what they'd just done. He was concerned about how she'd feel now that it was over.

"I love you so very much…more than life itself." He feathered her closed eyes with kisses. "This thing between us, here, will never happen again. But make no mistake, we helped Luca come back to us, and I will be forever grateful for what you did today."

"No regrets, okay. We helped him, didn't we? Is he okay?" she asked quietly. *Yeah, we helped him all right.* She rolled her eyes thinking about what they had just done. She hoped Luca was healed after all that.

"Yes, love, he's healed," Kade replied.

Sydney felt embarrassed, but didn't want to show it. She wanted to leave and give them space. She sat up, turned around and looked at the two very naked vampires lying in bed. "Okay, so who's hungry? I get that you vamps only need blood, but a girl like me has got to get some real food," she joked, desperately needing the levity.

Kade and Luca looked at each other and laughed. Kade made a move to sit up, and Luca reached out to put a hand on his arm. "Kade. Sydney. I don't know what to say, so I will just say 'thank you'. Thank you for rescuing me. Thank you for this, now. I am not sure what to say. After I had the donor blood today, I still couldn't function. It was like I was there but not there. I know you both took a risk feeding me," he looked around at the sheets. "And a risk knowing it might turn out to be a little more than just feeding." He smiled knowingly.

Luca felt refreshed but angry as he recalled every detail of his attack and capture. Remembering the look on Samantha's face as they'd attacked, he needed to know she was safe. From the minute he'd met Samantha, he'd felt protective of her.

"Listen, I know I have been out of it, but what of Samantha? I blacked out right before her and Ilsbeth…" Luca questioned.

"Ummm…she must be on your mind, huh, Luca?" Sydney grinned, interrupting his train of thought. "I know you aren't crazy about us human women, but perhaps this one has gotten under your skin? You did call her name instead of mine. I'm crushed," she teased and hopped off the bed towards the door, knowing that Luca had feelings toward Samantha. She smiled, thinking that her friend could actually be attracted to a mortal. *Could it be that Luca was actually growing a heart?*

Kade got up out of bed, leaving Luca leaning against the headrest. He watched Sydney leave the room, pulled on his jeans and turned to his friend. A serious expression washed across his face. "Luca, let's be clear. You are my best friend. But know that I will not be sharing Sydney with you in the future. What we did today…" He looked to the bed and then met Luca's eyes. "We did it to heal you, to bring you back. And while I am grateful you appear well, you need to stay out of trouble. I am not sure I could do this again."

Luca smiled. It was unusual for him do to so, given his serious nature. "Understood, Kade. Sydney is beautiful, indeed. But I have always known she was yours and yours alone. It was very hard for me to accept her blood knowing she belonged to you. Thank you again for finding me. Healing me." Luca stood up. Realizing he was naked, he wrapped the sheet around his waist. "I need to know though. Are Samantha and Ilsbeth safe?"

"Yes, it was Ilsbeth who called me to tell me you'd been attacked. Since your absence, she's called me a few times to let me know that Samantha was cleansed and continuing her training. She's at the coven still."

"Kade." He paused, thinking through the events of his kidnapping. "Whoever did this to me weren't after me. I mean, they could have killed me, but they didn't. Whoever attacked us knew better than to kill me lest you would rain hell down upon them in this city. They knew who I was and left me alive. It wasn't me they wanted. No, they were after the witches."

"Perhaps," Kade pondered. Was Asgear working with someone else besides Simone? "I don't know, Luca. Why would they want Samantha? She doesn't know what she is. Ilsbeth holds a lot of power, but I can't imagine who would be foolish enough to try and capture her at her home. Besides the magical wards she's set, she could literally transport herself away from the captor."

"Kade, there's something about Samantha. I don't know..." Luca was troubled. Something wasn't right. Why hadn't they killed him? "Talk to Sydney. Get her take on what happened. I plan to rest today while the sun is up, but tonight I'm going to the coven to see Ilsbeth and the girl."

"Luca, my friend. You refer to Samantha as a girl, yet you cannot deny she is a woman. Perhaps there is another reason why you feel compelled to see her?" Kade asked.

"A human? No way, Kade. You know I'm not into mortal women. Give me a break. I was just drained and starved for over a fucking week. I'm pissed as hell and there's got to be a goddamn good reason why this happened. Who the hell even knew I was transporting the witches? Who else knew about Asgear and Simone's plans to take over the city? What if there's more to Samantha than we really know? Ilsbeth should know by now what the hell kind of magic the girl has. Is it even real? Over a week has passed and I need to know what the hell is going on over there. Something isn't right with what happened." Luca was steaming mad.

Luca sighed, *Samantha*. Remembering the first time he'd met her, he wondered why she dominated his thoughts. Something about the human woman stirred his emotions, yet he could not fathom why he would care. The pixie-sized, fair-skinned beauty had barely been holding onto reality the last time he'd seen her. After she'd been bespelled by the evil mage, Asgear, who'd turned her into a submissive and beaten her to a pulp as a prisoner, she learned that the magic had infused itself into her very being. She was now a witch. Yet, she was technically still very much a mere mortal who knew nothing about witchcraft.

The last time he saw her she'd been in 'protection' at Kade's estate. *Protection*. Hell, who was he kidding? After they'd rescued her from her shackled existence, they imprisoned her once again, albeit in a gilded cage. Tainted by the evil, infused by magic, she could not return home. Instead, Ilsbeth, a close confidant of Kade's and a well-respected witch, insisted Samantha go with her to the coven to be cleansed and learn her new path in life.

The very first time he'd met Samantha, she was working at Sangre Dulce. He and Kade were working a case that night. As she had stood naked before them, serving drinks to his group of vampires, Luca was instantly attracted to the submissive, red-haired beauty. Samantha, who'd been introduced to him under the false name of Rhea, had offered herself for 'play'. Luca had turned her down. He'd been there to work the case, find clues to a killer, not fuck. And then there was the undeniable fact that she was human. Not his first choice for playing. Humans were good for feeding, but way too emotional and breakable. No, when it came to sex, he preferred a supernatural with no attachments. As for love, it simply was not an option.

The next time he'd seen Samantha, she'd been bruised and battered, a shell of the woman he'd met at the club. He wondered how such a fragile woman had survived life locked in that desolate, filthy prison cell. When he'd broken the locked metal cuffs off her naked body, Luca had cursed the monster that had injured her. Later at Kade's house, his heart had constricted as he'd watched her come to terms with what had happened to her. With no memory of the club or her actions, she had learned of her fate as a witch.

She was shocked on discovering that she'd never return to her work, her friends, her life. Vulnerable and shaken, she'd agreed to go with Ilsbeth to the coven…as if she'd been given a choice. Her soul was tainted; Kade would have never let her return without cleansing her soul.

Luca stared at himself in the bathroom mirror; the hard planes of his muscles looked as if he'd just returned from the gym. There was no indication that he had been on the brink of death. Luca touched his hardened abs, slick from sweat. He reveled in being vampire, in being indestructible. *Almost.* True, he was pure alpha male, perhaps even tougher than Kade, yet not as old. And despite being vampire, his time on Earth had almost ended. He didn't have time to dwell on how he'd almost died. Rather, he contemplated why he was attacked. *Why the fuck am I still here? Who wanted Samantha?*

His thoughts raced as he stepped into the shower. He needed to see Samantha just one more time. This time, no crying…just talking. She would be calm. She'd had a week to adjust. Perhaps not much time for a human but it would be better than the last time when she couldn't stop 'leaking'. Humans, such weak creatures. Luca had no time or patience for their outbursts. The only human he'd tolerated was Sydney, and clearly that was due to Kade's influence. She had proven her warrior abilities, fought alongside him, earned his respect.

One human woman in his life was enough. He decided that he would go to the coven, investigate what had happened and sate his curiosity. He'd question the little lovely human and find out who exactly was behind the kidnapping attempt.

As he rinsed the soap from his body, his cock jerked at the thought of seeing her again. *Shit.* He admonished himself for the thought. Yet as he stroked his hardness, he could not circumvent the vision of her. *Samantha.*

Chapter Three

Samantha pushed open the cabin door, thankful to be back in Pennsylvania. She tried thinking of something else, anything else but what had happened to her in New Orleans. She felt dirty. Violated. A loss of identity.

She should have listened to those who'd told her not to go to New Orleans. Her family had warned her that the city was dangerous. Ignoring their concerns, she'd gone anyway. At the time, going to the computer conference had seemed like a great way to go on a 'working vacation'. After a day of lectures and workshops, her co-workers had talked her into going to a local bdsm club in New Orleans. She had heard that supernaturals supposedly went there. Samantha had expected maybe to meet a vampire or a werewolf. She'd thought they'd dance, maybe get to watch some interesting scenes and have some fun. That was all it was supposed to be. A night of fun.

Now her life was destroyed. No friends who she could talk to about what happened. No job. No life. No Samantha. The man she'd met at the club, James, had turned out to be a mage. His real name was Asgear. She vaguely remembered the beating he'd given her after she dared to escape his lair. A beating that she could barely remember was something she could get over. She'd trained in karate when she was younger and had earned and given her fair share of fighting bruises.

No, this was far worse. Memories locked away, stolen. She couldn't remember anything of what had happened or what she'd done. Being taken to a vampire's mansion, Kade Issacson had shown her the disgusting evidence of her violation. Naked. Submissive. She'd been under the control of Asgear and had done his bidding. Her body was used. Her mind was taken over as well, but the memories refused to surface. Despite being told she'd been bespelled and seeing the photographic proof, she could not accept that what she'd done was real.

Was she raped? Did she willingly have sex with others? Did she hurt anyone? She had no recollection. They told her that she may have hurt a female vampire. But that wasn't her. It was a nightmare; one she could only escape by running.

Witch. She despised the word. While Ilsbeth had been nothing but kind to her, she refused to believe she was a witch. She didn't want to be a witch. This was not happening. She would take the medical leave she'd requested from work and take a long rest in the mountains, and then try to get her life back. Maybe remember what had happened. Maybe not. Regardless, she was determined to heal.

No one was guaranteed an easy life, she knew that. You worked hard, and reaped what you sowed. Working in a sea of men in her technology company hadn't been a walk in the park when she'd first started. A female programmer worked twice as hard and long to prove herself worthy. And she'd done just that, earning her rank as one of the very best engineers. The phrase, 'giving up', wasn't in her vocabulary. She preferred to fight the good fight in the face of adversity. Samantha steeled herself; she resolved that nothing would break her spirit.

The cabin she rented in the mountains was a welcome reprieve from the intense training sessions she'd experienced over the past week. The weather was lovely, as was the foliage. Towards the end of August, evenings were beginning to cool off, beckoning fall to approach. After being in the humid, hot air of New Orleans, Samantha welcomed the change in temperature.

Samantha opened the sliding glass door to check for firewood. The rental agency had assured her that the cabin was fully stocked, which meant she could have a fire on a cold night. Drinking in the tranquil setting, she sat on the Adirondack chair and breathed in the fresh, mountain air. She stared out at the large lake situated on the property. Aside from the small clearing leading to the lake, the house was surrounded by woods. Samantha was pleased the property was isolated, as had been promised.

Alone at last. No vampires. No werewolves. And no freakin' witches. While Ilsbeth was friendly, she'd not received such a warm welcome from all the others. They'd glared at her, resenting her newfound gift. Most witches were born with magic, not accidentally infused with it. To the other witches, she was an unnatural freak who was tainted not blessed.

Ilsbeth had sat with Samantha and gently cleansed the evil then explained how Samantha could draw power from within. Out of respect for Ilsbeth, she did try. Unsuccessfully. Night after night, she sat in the calming room, meditating and chanting, yet nothing stirred.

Fed up with the insulting comments from the other witches, and her lack of apparent powers, Samantha resolved to get her old life back. She was very grateful to Kade, Luca, Sydney and Ilsbeth for rescuing her. She didn't want to seem unappreciative, but she'd had enough of the mystical side of life. She yearned for normalcy. It was like a hardened nightmare from which she could not awake. Finally, yes, finally, she was feeling like her old self, relaxing into the forested wilderness.

Samantha reached across the table and lit a small citronella candle. She laughed to herself; the only bloodsuckers out here were the damn mosquitos. *No way are you getting me tonight.* The crickets and cicadas sang her a soothing lullaby. Convinced she was finally finding peace in her rustic sanctuary, Samantha let out a breath, closed her eyes and fell asleep, breathing in the crisp air.

"She what?" Luca could hardly believe it as he stood before the always ethereal Ilsbeth. "She left? Where the hell did she go?"

Ilsbeth's golden hair shone in the candlelight that illuminated the coven's foyer. While well over a hundred years old, she looked like she was in her twenties. But there was no mistaking the power that flowed within the beautiful witch. She was like a graceful swan; gorgeous and generally calm, but would kill in an instant if provoked.

"Luca," she spoke in an unemotional even-toned voice. "Please come in and have some tea."

Ilsbeth motioned him into the parlor. The room was comfortably airy, almost spa-like, decorated in hues of tan and blue. A large, four-foot tall pillar candle stood in front of the fireplace; its flame appeared to dance to the new age music softly playing in the background.

Luca strode into the room and turned to face Ilsbeth. He was enraged that the coven had misplaced Samantha. "Over a week ago I brought her here to remain in your charge. Did you fail to see or understand the seriousness of my attack? She's in danger."

"Luca, please sit." She gestured for him to have a seat. Power rolled off of her, filling the room with a gentle, soothing hum.

Luca reluctantly sat on a large, linen covered chair. Ilsbeth elegantly walked across the room and sat on the matching sofa across from him.

"Luca, I understand your concern, but you must consider two factors. While the attack could have been intended for Samantha, it could equally have been meant for you or me. As you are aware, I'm not without my fair share of enemies, nor are you." Ilsbeth closed her eyes, took a deep cleansing breath and then opened them again. "Second and perhaps most importantly, I cannot keep Samantha against her will. After purifying her, I was required by the Goddess to let her go her own way. She asked to leave, knowing the dangers, and I had no choice but to let her go."

Luca could have cared less about what the Goddess wanted. "They could have killed me, Ilsbeth. Yet they did not. No, they wanted her. She's special. There's something…something I cannot put my finger on." Luca raked his fingers through his raven hair. He wore it loose tonight and it fell into his eyes.

"I don't disagree, Luca. She is, indeed, special. Goddess knows we don't see a human turned witch very often. It is extremely rare. But she should have had more powers. The magic should've shown itself by now. Magic is drawn to its witch, knowing where to go, wanting to be utilized. But she couldn't concentrate; there was simply nothing. She was frustrated with her progress. Now it may have been caused by stress. You know, even though her physical injuries have subsided, she's quite vulnerable emotionally.

What that awful man did to her…" Ilsbeth gritted her teeth in anger, her eyes lit with fire. She quickly composed herself; her face transformed back into its normally placid expression.

"And you should also be aware that she doesn't fully accept her gift yet. She does not wish to be magical. I'm sorry we couldn't do more for her, but she's a grown woman. She knows she can return anytime. Perhaps her leaving the state will keep her from danger," Ilsbeth speculated.

Luca's thoughts raced. Was it possible that she'd be safe away from New Orleans? It was true that she'd be away from the heart of magic, after all. But then he remembered that Asgear was able to extend his reach to Philadelphia. He might not have physically been there, but he was able to funnel his magic to others in the area, making them do things, awful things. No, she needed to come back to the safety of the coven where the magical wards would protect her. She'd be safe with her sisters. Ilsbeth was the most powerful witch on the East Coast. Not even a mouse could get in her courtyard without her permission. Luca knew in that moment that he needed to bring her home.

"I will go get her, explain the danger. She cannot refuse me. Where did she go, Ilsbeth?" he asked authoritatively. While Ilsbeth was powerful, Luca was older, and emanated his own energy. He could not believe the sheer idiocy of the coven rules. It made no sense that because a person didn't want to be there, they could simply walk out the door with no regard for safety. And the coven would wave goodbye and let her do what she wanted, because the Goddess said so. *Fuck coven rules.* He would go get her and bring her back. End of story.

Ilsbeth slowly rose off the sofa. She'd acquiesce to Luca this once. He appeared to care about the human, her sister witch. *Interesting,* she thought to herself. Everyone who knew Luca would be quite surprised to know he cared about a mortal woman.

"Fine, Luca. We shall do as you wish. But know this; I will not keep her here against her will. Should she refuse to stay at the coven, she's in your charge," she explained. Ilsbeth would not go against the Goddess's rules.

"But of course. However this will not be an issue. She will want to return once I speak with her."

"What makes you say that, Luca? She was quite adamant on her departure that she would not be returning to New Orleans. She is quite traumatized, you know," she said softly.

"Does she remember what happened?" Luca inquired, remembering how Samantha could not stop crying at Kade's that night, dark bruises on her face. He'd wanted to kill the son of a bitch who'd hurt her, but Kade had taken care of it. Unfortunately he couldn't fix the emotional damage left in Asgear's aftermath. The best he could do that night was listen and comfort her by placing his hand on her shoulder.

"No, I do not believe so. Anything she shared with me is her story to tell."

"Understandable. No matter. She must return to the safety of the coven," Luca said without emotion. He walked over to the front door and grabbed the handle.

Ilsbeth followed and put her hand on his. Luca turned to face her. "Luca, be gentle with the girl. She's young and scared. Not a very good combination." She removed her hand, went over to her desk and began to write down the address Samantha had given her.

"Ilsbeth, I may not be fond of human women but I can certainly handle getting one on a plane back to New Orleans. I don't know who tried to attack her but I'll be damned if I'm goin' to just sit by and watch her get kidnapped again. Or worse, die. No," he said shaking his head. "It's settled. I'll go and get her. In the meantime, Kade and Sydney can look for clues as to what in the hell is going on down here, who abducted me."

"Okay, Luca. Please call me if you need my assistance. I can work spells from a distance. Also, call me if she shows any signs of magic." She handed him a business card with an address written on the back of it. "She's in Pennsylvania. In the mountains. May the Goddess be with you on your journey."

Taking the card from her hand he walked into the warm, humid air, breathed deeply and turned back again to Ilsbeth. "Thank you, Ilsbeth. Be well."

Luca had an address. *Samantha.* He would go to her now. He'd take the jet and be there within hours. For a split second he wondered if there was something more about this mere mortal that he was drawn to. Dismissing the thought, he slid his cell phone on and called Tristan. He was the person physically located closest to where she was.

"Tristan here," he answered gruffly.

"Tristan, it's me, Luca."

"Mon ami, so good to hear your voice. Kade told me you got yourself trussed up like a silver chained turkey," he joked. Leave it to a wolf to lighten the mood about his attack.

"Yeah, it was quite the ordeal, to say the least. But I'm back. Sydney and Kade saved my life," he said nonchalantly. He did not wish to discuss the feeding with Tristan, knowing how intimate they were. "Unfortunately, this isn't a social call. I'm in need of your assistance, Alpha." Luca deliberately used his title as a sign of respect.

"Just ask, Luca. What is it?"

"It's Samantha. She ran away from the coven. Apparently things didn't go so well with her training so she split," he stated, unhappy that she'd left.

"Ah…the little witch you rescued. How is it she got away from Ilsbeth?"

"Long story short but essentially, she left of her own accord so Ilsbeth had to let her go. She escaped to your neck of the woods. Pocono Mountains. Do you think you could go find and guard her…as wolf until I get there?" Luca asked. "I don't want her to suspect that I'm coming for her lest she'll probably run again. She may not take kindly to another supernatural like you coming after her either. After all she's been through, it may be best to just blend into nature and watch her from afar. Guard her and don't let her leave."

"No problem. I was looking to take a little run anyway. This just gives me something to look forward to. As I recall, she's a pretty young thing. Hot body and a fiery mane you could run your fingers through," Tristan teased, sensing Luca had a personal interest in finding her. He loved Luca but couldn't resist teasing him, given that he was always so serious.

Luca growled. "Alpha, do not touch her. She's been through enough." What the hell was he doing telling an Alpha what to do in his own territory? Luca forced himself to relax, unclench his fist and gain his composure. "I apologize, Tristan. I didn't mean to tell you what to do. It's just that she's vulnerable right now. Ilsbeth said she couldn't find her magic. She's afraid. She needs our help."

"No worries, Luca. I'm on it. I know you've also been through a lot lately. Text me the address, and I'll meet you there. I'll try to keep it wolf, but if she spots me, I won't tell her you're coming."

"Thank you, Tristan. See you later tonight. " Luca ended the call. He'd go up tonight and be back by tomorrow. Then he'd help Kade and Sydney find whoever had kidnapped him, and rip their throats out.

Chapter Four

Visions of blood dripping from her mouth clouded her thoughts. She was chained, beaten and naked in a concrete cell that reeked of urine and feces. Yanking her wrists forward, blinding pain racked her body; the unyielding cuffs bit into her skin. Screaming at the top of her lungs; no one came. Cold and alone, she sat in the dark and waited for death, praying her torment would come to an end soon.

The only memory she'd had was a recurring nightmare. Samantha woke in a cold sweat, terrorized, like she had every night since she'd been rescued. Realizing that she was outside at the cabin, she jumped up out of the chair. *Goddammit. I fell asleep outside.*

"Great. I'll probably have a thousand bites all over me," she said aloud to herself. Samantha started rubbing her arms and legs, checking her skin for bumps. "Hmm….candle must've worked."

As she turned to blow out the citronella candle, she heard a branch break. She froze and looked out into the darkness. *Eyes.* She breathed slowly, willing herself to relax. She was only a few feet from the house; she could make it inside. But instead of moving inside the house, she stepped forward out of curiosity. Maybe there was an animal in the woods. *A deer?* Eyes flashed again, and she stifled the urge to scream. Reaching behind her, her fingers blindly fumbled for the door handle. She felt something…a switch.

"I will not be afraid," she whispered to herself. No, she'd had enough of being scared. And she was sick and tired of feeling as though she was a field mouse waiting for the hawk to strike. She was a grown woman and could handle whatever was in the woods. She was in the mountains after all. *There is nothing to fear.*

She blew out a breath and flipped the switch. Light flooded the edges of the forest, and she spotted what she thought was a dog. *A dog? What the hell?* Samantha loved dogs, but there was something strange about the very large mongrel standing between the trees. The dog's eyes glowed a deep amber, and its fur was midnight-black. *It almost looks like a…wolf?*

No, that couldn't be. There hadn't been a report of a wolf in Pennsylvania for over twenty years. Bears, yes. Coyote, yes. Wolf, no. So logically, it must be a dog, she told herself. Maybe it was a breed that looked like a wolf - an Alaskan Malamute or a Czechoslovakian Wolfdog? She steeled her nerves; a dog she could handle.

Samantha slowly moved forward, walking down the stairs. If the dog was lost, he might have a collar and tag. She held out her hand, palm up and spoke to him in a high voice as if she was speaking to a baby. "Hey doggy? Whatcha doin' out here in my woods all by yourself? Are you lost, baby?" The dog calmly sat staring at her as if he understood what she was saying.

She approached carefully, sensing the animal was uninjured and not aggressive. "Come here, boy. It's okay. Are you hungry?" She blew little kisses towards him as if he was a ten pound Shih Tzu. "Come on, now. Don't be afraid."

She stilled as the large dog stalked towards her. Why the hell couldn't she have just gone inside the freakin' cabin? *Okay, I can do this.* Samantha lowered herself toward the ground so she appeared smaller to the animal. Once again, she offered her hand to it.

The dog loped over to Samantha and lay in front of her. She reached forward, letting him sniff her hand, and then proceeded to rub his head and ears. "That's a good boy. Oh yes, who's a good dog? You're a good dog." She praised him as she caressed his soft fur.

"Now how did you get in the woods, doggy? I've got some food in the house. Are you hungry?" Samantha asked. The dog tilted his head and yipped.

"Okay, then. Let's go inside. Come on. Maybe there's rope inside to make you a leash. I'll help find your owner…" As she turned to try to lead him into the house, she glanced back. *Where is the dog?*

"Hey doggy, where'd ya go?" Samantha called. Out of the darkness, a gorgeous, very naked male walked out of the trees. "What the hell?" Samantha screamed and ran as fast as she could towards the cabin.

Large hands grabbed her arms, holding her frozen. *Oh God, not again. This cannot be happening to me.*

"Settle down, petite sorcière. It's okay. You're safe with me." Tristan had expected that the little witch would not react warmly to his arrival. Her fear permeated his senses. He needed to calm her without revealing that Luca had sent him. He was hoping that he could have gone unspotted. *Damn that branch.* Once she saw him, he couldn't resist walking up to her. Getting a good rub down was a benefit of pretending he was a dog, but there was no way he was letting her leash him. Shifting to human was his next best plan.

"I'm Tristan. Ilsbeth sent me," he assured her.

Samantha exhaled a deep breath, relaxing into his hold. "Ilsbeth? Why?" She looked up to study his face and then her eyes roamed down to his groin and back up again. Her face flushed. "Oh my God. You. You're naked. You're a…a wolf," she whispered, hardly believing the words she spoke.

"Yes on both counts. Now unless you plan on stripping down with me, it's hardly fair that I stay naked for your pleasure. Let's go inside, and we can talk." He winked and opened the sliding glass door, gesturing for her to go in.

Stunned by his flirtatious nature, Samantha walked inside. She struggled to understand why Ilsbeth would send a wolf to her in Pennsylvania. "Tristan, please, I don't understand. Why would Ilsbeth send you here? I'm perfectly safe. Is she okay?"

Tristan made himself at home, grabbing a throw blanket off the couch and wrapping it around his waist. Samantha could not help but stare; his tanned, six-pack abs looked like she could bounce a quarter off of them. He was well over six feet tall, and ruggedly handsome. He looked like a California surfer with his platinum blonde hair brushing his shoulders.

And while she found him attractive, she felt a dull ache in her chest. The knowledge of what she may or may not have done at Sangre Dulce ate at her. She doubted she'd be attracted to anyone in a sexual way for a very long time.

Tristan sat down on the large Italian-leather sofa. He felt sorry for the girl. She had no idea what kind of danger she was in or that she was going back to New Orleans tomorrow. And worst of all, she didn't know Luca was on his way. He thought that he should at least attempt to soften her up for Luca. Perhaps he should plant a few seeds that would make the soon-to-be happenings a little more palatable.

"Petite sorcière, I am Alpha of this area, so I know everything that happens here. And everyone who comes into my territory does what I say. Do you follow me? I want to explain a few things to you…explain why Ilsbeth sent me. Now sit," he ordered as he patted the loveseat adjacent to him.

As if she had a damn choice in the matter. She walked over and sat rigidly in the chair. She glared at him, her pensive lips sealed in a tight line.

"Now that's better, mon cher. Please understand a few important things. First of all, know that you are safe with me. I won't let anyone have at you. And the reason I am assuring you of your safety brings me to my second point. There is no other way to put this; you are still very much in danger. We have reason to believe that they were after you." Tristan could see Samantha's face blanch with fright. He reached over and put his hand on her knee.

"Look at me, Samantha," he commanded.

She silently complied.

"Remember what I said first. I will protect you."

"But…" she interrupted.

"Samantha, I was there that day when we rescued you from Asgear. I know what they did to you. Now, I don't know you very well but if you are tough enough to survive what was done to you, you can survive this. You're not alone."

She wanted to believe him but the images of Asgear beating her bloody flashed through her mind. She could not survive again. She glanced over at the front door and fought the urge to run away. He said he'd protect her. She took a deep breath, willing herself to relax long enough to hear him out. She needed to know why they thought she was still in danger.

"I need to know. Who's after me? I mean, Asgear is dead. What could anyone possibly want from me? They say I'm a witch but apparently I can't do that either. If you've spoken to Ilsbeth then you know that I've felt nothing, done nothing…magically. If I really do have magic in me, I'm a sorry excuse for a witch. Honestly, I just want out of this nightmare. That's why I came here. I need to get away from all that craziness." She put her face in her hands, sighed and fought back a sob; she refused to cry one more tear over what Asgear had done to her.

Tristan took her hands in his, sending waves of calming power over her. "I don't know who took Luca or why they wanted you. But Kade and Sydney are working on it right now. In the meantime, I'll keep you safe. In the morning….well, we'll cross that bridge tomorrow. Now, how about I get you something to drink. A brandy?"

Samantha silently regarded Tristan, feeling numbness wash over her body.

"Okay, you don't need to say anything. Just sit. I'll be back." Tristan rose and strode across the room, quickly finding a bottle of whiskey in one of the cabinets. *Close enough.* At least they had something to drink. From across the room, he could hear her heart racing, probably from both fear and anger. Fuck, if he had told her she was going back to New Orleans tomorrow, she'd probably pass out. No, he'd leave that little doozy for Luca.

After Tristan handed Samantha a glass, she took a long, strong pull of the golden liquid. Immediately, she had a coughing fit, raising her hands to signal she was all right. Composing herself, she regarded the Alpha sitting in front of her. "Little rough, huh, Tristan? You know what, wolf? I have no intention of being a victim again. No fucking way. If one of Asgear's flunkies is coming after me, they aren't taking me alive again," she resolved.

"Now that's the spirit, ma petite sorcière," Tristan replied.

"Petite sorcière?" Samantha questioned.

"Ah yes. Little witch. That is who you are now. Whether you feel your power or not, it's there. I can literally smell the magic emanating off your skin."

"Yeah well, maybe all that is true, but I couldn't create one little spark when I was at the coven. Couldn't even light a candle. Some witch I am. I'll tell you this for nothing, I am way better at computers than all this mumbo jumbo that supposedly lurks within me. You know, I was good at something, really good at it. Now, I'm afraid I can't even go back to that," she huffed.

"When this is all over, Samantha, you can start anew. There are lots of supernaturals in the area. I can help you find a computer job in the Philadelphia area with folks who understand…who know who you are and what you are." He smiled, taking another swig of the whiskey.

Samantha's head was spinning. *He thought she should go work for supernaturals? Get real. So not happening, Alpha wolf.* She rolled her eyes, and threw back her head, resting it on the sofa.

"Thanks for the offer. But that isn't happening any time soon. I took a leave of absence from my job, so I could get my head together. Heal. And that is exactly what I plan to do. Then I'm going back to my boring, so not magical life. And I can't wait." She placed her empty glass on the end table. She continued talking, determined not to let fear overcome her. "Listen, since there's nothing I can really do at this point if someone breaks in, I'm taking your word that you'll protect me. So here's the plan. I'm going to go over to the kitchen, find a big knife and take it to bed with me. I'm overwhelmed, angry and generally unhappy right now." She gestured to the sofa. "The sofa is all yours, Alpha. Talk to you in the morning."

With those words, she strode into the kitchen, selected the biggest sharpest chef knife she could find and walked down the hall towards her bedroom. Sure, she was afraid. But she was not about to get kidnapped again without a knockdown, drag-out fight. She undressed, throwing on a comfortable cami, and climbed into the freshly lined bed. Reaching over, she placed the knife carefully under her pillow, in easy reach if she needed it, and closed her eyes, praying the nightmares wouldn't come.

A loud knock resounded throughout the cabin's wooden interior. Tristan strode over to the door, throw still around his hips, and opened it. From outside, Luca glared at Tristan, noticing he was wearing next to nothing.

"What?" Tristan asked. He shrugged his shoulders, walked back over to the couch and stretched out, putting his feet up on the coffee table.

Luca followed after him, shutting the door. "What? Really, wolf? I asked you to watch her, not give her a male review."

Tristan laughed. "Hey man, I can't help it if the ladies like to see my goods. Besides, I'm a wolf. Can't exactly carry clothes with me."

Luca sat down and let out a huge sigh. "Okay, just tell me now. Where is she? And why aren't you furry?"

"She was asleep outside on the porch. So I watched and waited. When she woke up, she heard something and flipped on the floodlights. Don't worry, though. She's handled the wolf fairly well. And I can't lie, Luca, the woman gives a good rub," he joked. He jerked his head towards the hallway. "Samantha's sleeping."

"Well, I do appreciate you coming up here to guard her. Tomorrow, we'll return to New Orleans. The jet is ready to go." Luca would be relieved once they were back home.

Tristan smiled and shook his head. "Yeah, about that. You know, you might want to wait a few days before taking her back. Maybe give her a day or two. Get to know her more, earn her trust."

"What the hell, Tristan? Are you kidding me?"

"No, mon ami. I'm dead serious. Just listen. The girl's been through a lot. I talked to her tonight, made her understand how she's still in danger. But you've got to ease her into going back. She doesn't even know you're alive."

"Not happening. We're going back tomorrow. She'll have to deal with it. Look, I'm not a therapist or a babysitter. Do I feel a slight sense of responsibility for the witch? Yes, but only because Kade initially put her into my charge." Luca knew that there might be another reason for why he felt he needed to keep the girl safe, but he wasn't going to share.

Tristan's face tightened and his eyes narrowed. His friend did not seem to hear what he was saying. "Luca. Try to remember what happened to her and what that might've been like for her. I know it's been a long time for you, but try to remember what it's like to be human. The girl was drugged, bespelled, beaten, possibly raped, and to top off her shit sandwich, she can barely remember anything but lying naked in a prison cell. Oh, and let us not forget her being told she's a witch, one who can't seem to conjure up a clue, and whose entire life as she knows it is about to come to an end. Can't you see? It's too damn much," Tristan pleaded.

Luca rubbed his eyes, thinking through Tristan's argument. He didn't want to stay here. This was supposed to be a simple trip. Fly up to Philadelphia, get witch, return to New Orleans. Easy peasy. Not. But Luca could not deny the empathy he felt for the little witch who tugged at his heartstrings. Aside from dragging her kicking and screaming back to the jet, it would be easier if he could get her to agree to go home with him. If that failed, kicking and screaming was always an option.

"Okay. I'll talk to her and stay here for one day…tops. She'll be waking soon, and I should have all day to talk reason into the human." He hated when Tristan was right, but knew he needed to go easy on her. "On our way back, I'll stop at your club to feed. If I stay around her more than a day, I'm pretty sure I would be tempted to taste her. And that's the very last thing I need or she needs. I very much doubt she'd willingly donate her blood." He shook his head as he imagined asking her to let him bite her. She'd probably freak the hell out and try to escape yet again. No, he'd wait to feed at Tristan's club to keep things nice and smooth. Complications were something he was trying very hard to avoid.

"Yeah, I don't think it would go over too well if you asked her to be your donor. Awkward." Tristan laughed. He stood and removed the blanket, unaffected by his nudity, and walked over to the back door.

Luca averted his eyes in an effort not to look at him. It was a good thing the naked wolf was leaving. The thought that Tristan had displayed his generously endowed body to Samantha flew in his head and caused his stomach to clench in anger. Did he just feel jealous? No, that couldn't be possible. He quickly stifled his emotion, not wanting Tristan to sense his feelings.

"Remember Luca, go easy on the female. She'll come round. See you in a day or so." As Tristan shut the sliding glass door, he appeared to seamlessly change into his black wolf, and loped out of sight.

Chapter Five

Luca paced the room. How was he going to stay here for even a day with the witch? Would she remember him? Would she fear him? Would she fight him? As self-composed as Luca normally was, being here in the cabin, knowing she was in the other room, spurred his curiosity. What did she wear to sleep? Was she cold? Scared? *I should go check on her.* He could hear her soft breathing from a distance. He knew she was just fine. But he wanted to see her again, not later, but now. What would it hurt to just take a peek at her?

Walking down the hallway, he knew what he was about to do wasn't right. He felt like some kind of a pervert, looking in on a woman that he barely knew. Yet he felt compelled to keep going. Once at her door, he laid his palm against it and took a deep breath. Looking at his watch, he confirmed that at five am, she'd still be asleep and not likely to wake. *I really am going to do this.* Slowly he turned the handle, and pushed open the door.

Luca struggled to control his instinct to reach over and touch the lovely woman sprawled out on the bed. Immediately he was filled with desire; his breath caught as he stood frozen, watching her sleep. Samantha lay on her back, her skin exposed from pushing the covers off her body. Dressed only in a white cotton camisole and pink boyshorts, her pert breasts peeked out of the flimsy material. Her long, wavy strawberry hair fanned across her pillow; she almost appeared to smile in her sleep. She was even more beautiful than he'd remembered.

Back at Kade's mansion, after he'd rescued her, she'd appeared quite frail; her thin body marred by bruises and scratches. Her hair was straight and dyed neon red. He'd wondered at the time if that was the real color of her hair. She'd looked like a victim fighting to regain some semblance of normalcy, dignity. No, lying here before him this night was a healthy, resplendent woman who was enticing, alluring and very much human.

His last thought jerked him back to reality. *Human.* No, he would never fall for any woman, let alone a human. Feed from them, try not to screw them and never, ever fall in love with them. It was simply not an option, no matter how much the rise of cock told him that he should do otherwise. He refused to acknowledge that he had any feelings whatsoever for the mortal lying on the bed in front of him. Yet his body reacted as if he should take her right there. *What the hell is wrong with me?*

Luca rolled his eyes and softly sighed. What was he going to do? He wasn't here to fuck her; he was here to bring her back to the coven. Yet he felt the need to be near her, to protect her. He needed to be close to her, tonight.

Spying a brown leather lounge chair in the corner of the room, he walked over, sat down and put his feet up on the ottoman. He decided that he wasn't going to leave her unattended. He could just as easily guard her from the living room. Staying with her here was merely an excuse for him to fill his senses with her; he drank in the sight of her with his eyes, smelled her perfumed skin. He prayed whatever he was feeling would go away.

He hadn't had sex in a long time; well, not for a few weeks anyway. What had happened with Kade and Sydney earlier couldn't exactly be called sex. He'd felt out of control with them. He still couldn't believe Kade had let him feed from Sydney, let alone kiss her, touch her. She was a beautiful woman and a seriously toughened warrior, one whom he respected immensely, but she was not his. Nor did he want her. Sydney had been a means to health, no more, no less. And he was grateful to both of them for bringing him back from the brink.

Samantha shifted on the bed, turning away from him. He inwardly groaned as he admired her perfectly shaped ass; she was killing him. Adjusting himself, he tried to relieve some of the strain of his erection. *Repeat to self, 'Samantha is human'.* Luca was happy that he planned on stopping at Tristan's club on the way back to the airport. He'd pick a donor who'd satisfy his appetite for blood and sex. If he got it out of his system, he'd be able to control himself around Samantha. He relaxed slightly, knowing he'd devised a plan to get the devilish little witch out of his system.

Naked. Pounding music. Slapped across the face. Blinding pain. A pool of blood on a cold stone floor. Samantha gasped for air, jolting herself upright in bed. Another nightmare. She threw herself backward, focusing on the cedar ceiling beams. She was safe. Away from New Orleans and away from vampires. She closed her eyes, practicing the deep breathing she'd learned from Ilsbeth. Tense shoulders, breathe deeply, release breath, shoulders relax. By the time she got to her toes, her heartbeat had slowed, and she considered going back to sleep. Her thoughts began to race once again as she remembered the nightmare. She'd been naked in a nightclub and later had been imprisoned in a cell. *What did I do in New Orleans? I want my life back.*

Thinking she'd go for a run and take a nap later, she decided to get up. Then she remembered that Tristan would be sitting in her living room. Why couldn't they all just leave her alone? Why did they think someone was after her? The attack could have been meant for Ilsbeth, not her. She decided that no matter what Tristan had to say, she wasn't going to agree to return to New Orleans with him. She'd taken a leave of absence from her job so she could get herself together and return to work and her life. And that was what she was going to do.

As she sat up, her heart caught in her chest. A large male sat in the darkened corner of her bedroom. For a minute she relaxed, believing Tristan had come into her room, but then she noticed his hair wasn't blonde. No, not Tristan. Someone was here for her already. Her heart beat wildly as the adrenaline pumped. She would not go without a fight.

Silently, she reached under her pillow and curled her hands around the hilt of the knife she'd taken to bed with her for protection. The man wasn't moving, his feet propped up on the ottoman. In the darkness of dawn, she couldn't see his face. Samantha didn't want to be a victim. No, this time she'd be the aggressor. She couldn't survive being taken hostage again. She'd kill before being taken again. She dragged her legs across the bed in one smooth motion and leapt at the stranger with the knife.

Luca had heard Samantha gasp, watching her sit straight up out of a dead sleep. He'd wanted to go to her, to calm her. But as she lay back again, he heard her heart slow. So he decided to watch and protect. He could not risk touching her while she was barely dressed and in bed. After his arousal earlier in the night, he didn't trust himself to merely comfort her. Her sweet scent called to him like no other human's blood ever had before, yet he swore to not get involved with the witch.

As soon as he lay his head back on the chair, confident she was going back to sleep, he sensed movement. Samantha had spied him and was coming at him with a sharp knife. He grabbed both her wrists and pulled her towards him, so she straddled him. Gently, he applied pressure to her thumb and was relieved that she dropped the knife without incident. Smelling her fear, he sought to assure her of her safety. "Samantha, it's me, Luca."

"Luca…you're alive!" she exclaimed. Samantha was overcome with relief. That day at the coven, she was convinced she'd never see him again. Seeing him brought forth a rush of emotions. He'd been so caring and gentle with her at Kade's house and then had fought valiantly to save her and Ilsbeth when they were attacked.

Wide eyed and shaking, Samantha extended her fingertips and placed them on Luca's cheeks. She couldn't believe he was with her in the cabin and alive. As Samantha adjusted to the dim light, she was captivated by Luca's piercing dark green eyes. His jet-black, shoulder-length hair hung loosely around his handsome, chiseled face. Feeling his strong jawline tense in her small hands, the stubble prickled her fingers.

Luca froze as Samantha reached to touch him. Her hands burned his skin, and he felt as if he was on fire as desire built deep within him. As soon as her skin touched his, he instantly released her wrists, freeing her. Why was he having this visceral reaction to her? He'd hoped she'd jump away from him, and was regretting his action of pulling her onto him. His hands nearly crushed the arms of the chair as he held on for dear life. Blood rushed towards his groin. He breathed deeply, trying to control the rise of his erection. *Christ, I have got to get back to New Orleans.*

"What are you doing here, Luca?" Samantha asked. Instead of releasing him, she moved closer and pressed her forehead to his.

With her lips inches from his, he sucked in a breath and struggled to answer. "Samantha, I've come for you. You aren't safe. I've come to take you home."

Samantha searched his eyes for truth in his statement. Sensing he was entirely serious, she leaned closer still, feathered his lips with a small kiss, then stood up and walked away. She turned to look at him as she entered the bathroom. "Luca, as much as I appreciate everything you've done for me, there is no way in hell I'm goin' back to New Orleans." With that, she shut the bathroom door.

Stunned from her kiss, Luca threw his head back in frustration. He placed two fingers on his lips; how was he going to get her back to New Orleans without fucking her senseless? He cursed his erection and adjusted himself yet again as he pushed out of the chair and walked out of the room. He didn't want to be there when Samantha was finished in the bathroom. His so-called 'protecting' her from her bedroom had officially ended. He could not trust himself. He'd wait for her in the safety of the living room and talk to her there.

Samantha laid the back of her head against the bathroom door and sighed. After being beaten and imprisoned, she thought she'd never think about sex again. Yet seeing Luca right now, she'd kissed him and was most definitely thinking of sex. Maybe she was attracted to him because he'd rescued her from the mage and then again from the attack. Maybe she had some kind of hero complex? No, it was something else. He'd been kind to her on the night at the mansion and later at the coven, had valiantly fought their attackers. It was as if there was some small part of Luca that understood what she'd been through. She could tell he cared by his words and his touch. And even now, instead of waking her and dragging her out of the cabin, which she knew he was capable of doing, he silently waited, protecting her. It was obvious to her that he'd been watching her sleep, waiting for her to agree to go willingly.

Looking deep into his eyes, she'd sensed sadness, hesitation, but also lust. From the second she'd touched his face, she'd felt the chemistry and soon after, she'd felt him grow physically hard beneath her. But then he said he really just wanted her to return to New Orleans, and she just could not do that. She understood from Tristan that she was in danger, but she wanted time to figure out another way to escape it. Any way to do that would satisfy her, as long as she didn't have to return to New Orleans.

Samantha huffed and stared at herself in the mirror as she brushed her teeth. She wondered if her nightmare would ever end. For a split second, she contemplated sneaking out of the cabin but knew her effort would be a futile attempt at freedom. She'd learned that vampires could sense the tiniest sound or scent. Even if she somehow managed to get out of the house without Luca hearing her, he'd soon realize her scent was gone and would just follow her.

Samantha pulled on a pair of black spandex yoga pants, and topped it off with a royal-blue tank top. As she looked at herself in the mirror once again, she decided to stay and deal with Luca. She refused to run. Contrary to whatever he thought, he wasn't the boss of her. She'd calmly explain that she was staying in Pennsylvania and convince him to leave her alone.

Luca was staring at the lake when Samantha walked into the living room. He sensed her enter but chose not to look at her; what he needed to say would be better said if he wasn't distracted.

"Samantha, we need to have a serious talk. Perhaps when I told you we needed to return to New Orleans, you thought it was a request. However, I assure you it's not. Quite the opposite, in fact." Luca turned to face her; his face hardened. "It's simply a matter of fact. We'll leave tomorrow morning to return to New Orleans. You can come willingly or not, but you'll be returning with me."

Samantha's eyes flashed angrily at him as she grabbed an apple out of a bag on the counter. "What the hell is that supposed to mean, Luca? How exactly do you intend to get me on a plane if I don't go *willingly*? Are you going to kidnap me just like Asgear did? Bespell me?" As she continued to rant, she paced back and forth in the kitchen.

"Oh, I know what you vampires do. What do they call it? Enthrall me? No way, Luca, no one is going to mess with my mind. I thought you were different from the others." She stood and hung her head in despair. She was barely getting her thoughts back in order and now he was threatening her too. He was just like the rest of them.

Samantha's words cut to his core. Maybe he didn't care for humans, but he was not as cold-hearted as she'd just described. Why couldn't she be reasonable and see the danger? Regardless, he felt he owed her the truth.

"I am vampire, Samantha. Nothing more, nothing less. I won't lie to you. If given the choice between leaving you here unprotected or bringing you back to safety, I will enthrall you to get you back on that plane. I'm sorry if you're angry with me, but this is how it must be. When the danger has passed, you can return to this area and Tristan will help you get settled, living as a supernatural." Luca felt bad about having to be so strict with her, but he needed to keep her from danger.

He approached her slowly and placed a finger under her chin, tilting her face upward. His eyes met hers. "Trust me, Samantha. It will work out for the best. Please, just come back to New Orleans, willingly, until we figure out who attacked you. I promise to make this as pleasant as possible. I don't want to enthrall you. I just need you to be safe."

A tear fell from Samantha's eye as she looked up at Luca. "Okay, Luca. I'll go. But I don't want to go back to the coven. Maybe no one told you, but I can't do anything remotely witchy. The witches don't even like me there, and frankly, I don't want to be there. Ilsbeth is fine but I'm just not comfortable staying with the coven. Can I return to Kade and Sydney's? Maybe I could stay with them until we get this figured out?"

Luca did not think it was a good idea for her to return to Kade's house with Dominique milling about the place. When Samantha had been bespelled, she'd silvered Dominique to a table in Sangre Dulce. Dominique could have cared less that Samantha had no control, and she wanted very much to tear into her throat and drain her dry for what she'd done to her. She was incredulous that Kade had saved her and taken her to the coven. If Dominique saw Samantha, it was likely blood would be shed.

"No, there's no way you can *safely* stay at the mansion with Kade and Sydney. As much as Sydney would love to have another human visit, Dominique is at their place way too often, and she's looking for payback. She probably won't kill you, since Kade has made it clear you're off limits, but I'm afraid I couldn't trust her not to at least attack you," Luca continued, knowing he was going to regret his next words. "You're welcome at my home, however. I live next door to Kade within his compound. There's plenty of room, and I have a spare bedroom."

Samantha nodded in relief. "Thank you, Luca." She toyed with the apple in her hands and broke eye contact. "You have to realize that things are so out of control for me. I just need to have a few things I can control, like where I live." She rolled her eyes. "I can't believe this is happening to me. You know, I haven't even told my family. My mom and dad live outside of Baltimore, and I haven't even gone to see them since I got back. I just called my sister, Jess, to tell her I was the unfortunate victim of a 'mugging' per the story Sydney set up with the police and my employer. I told her to tell mom and dad I was staying in New Orleans on a consulting job and would call them when I got a chance. I'm lying to her…I'm lying to everyone. What am I supposed to tell them?"

She walked away from Luca, looking around the floor for her shoes. "Luca, you don't need to say anything. I know you didn't cause this to happen. I'm just frustrated. I need to think."

Luca couldn't resist her any longer. She reminded him of a wounded puppy, albeit a very sexy one. He confidently strode over towards Samantha and put his arms around her, raking his hands through her hair as he brought her face against his chest. Settling his lips into her mane of hair, he kissed the top of her head. He wrapped his other hand around the small of her waist as he spoke gently to her. "Samantha darlin', it's goin' to be all right. We'll find who's responsible for this attack and you'll get your life back. I promise you."

Surprised by Luca's tender embrace, Samantha hugged him back, enjoying the feel of the sinewy muscles of his back. Somehow within his arms, she knew she could trust him. He made her want to feel again: desire, lust, love. But he was vampire. Strong and lethal. At six foot five, he could easily overpower her and drag her to New Orleans, bend her to his will. But instead, he was comforting her in the best way he knew how…with words, with an embrace.

The growing desire within her chest frightened her. How could she be so attracted to Luca? She inwardly laughed, knowing that it was not so hard to be physically attracted to him. He was ruggedly gorgeous but not a pretty boy. No, nothing boy-like about him; he was pure virile male. Samantha could feel his tight abdomen against her own and longed to see the hard planes of his chest without clothing hindering her view. Whilst he was muscular, he was also lean, with a spectacularly athletic build.

Reluctantly, she stepped out of his arms, and sat on the ottoman, struggling to understand what was happening to her when she was around him. She blushed as she scrambled to put on her running shoes.

"Thank you, Luca. Um…for comforting me," she stammered, trying to tie her shoes as quickly as possible.

"And where do you think you're going? It seemed just a minute ago that we'd come to an understanding," he said, raising a questioning eyebrow at her.

"Going for a walk around the lake," she replied as she walked back to the sliding glass door leading to the back deck. "Our deal is that we leave tomorrow. So for today, I'm going to do my best to relax. You're welcome to come with me. If not, you could stay here or meet me down at the pier when I'm done. I promise to yell should I see any bears," she teased.

"I'll watch you from the deck. I don't sense any supernaturals in the area right now, so you'll be okay. But stick close to the lake and I'll meet you down at the pier in ten minutes. I just have to make a few calls. I want to let Kade and Sydney know when we'll be arriving. I have to call Tristan too."

"Okay, meet you down there." Samantha bit into her apple, walked outside, closed the door and headed down the path towards the lake.

Watching Samantha like a hawk, Luca took a deep breath, grabbed his cell and called Kade. He explained to him that he'd be back down tomorrow and purposefully left out the part about Samantha staying with him. He couldn't believe that he'd offered to let her stay with him, but at the same time, he secretly wanted to spend more time with his little witch.

After calling Tristan to let him know they'd be stopping by his place early in the morning, he opened the door and headed towards the water. He didn't relish having to stop at Eden, Tristan's club, but he needed to feed and Tristan had promised to keep a blood donor waiting for him. He wasn't about to feed on Samantha; she'd been through far too much trauma over the past weeks. His fangs elongated at the thought of tasting her sweet, magical blood. *Goddammit. I have to keep it together.* He retracted his razor sharp teeth, not wanting to risk Samantha seeing them.

As he got halfway down the path, he watched her stretch on the dock. He halted, admiring her firm ass as she bent forward to grab her right calf. His cock jerked to attention as he fantasized about ripping off her clothes and taking her from behind on her hands and knees right out in the open on the wooden pier. No one would see, he surmised, looking around at the isolated woods. Shaking himself from his thoughts, he sighed. He could not get involved with this human. He knew how fragile they were, how easily they could die. Luca refused to let that happen again.

Just as he thought he'd regained control of himself, his mouth dropped wide open. With her back facing Luca, Samantha crossed her arms in front of her and removed her flimsy, stretchy tank top. *Jesus, what was she doing?* He continued to watch in awe as she kicked off her sneakers, hooked her thumbs on the waist of her pants and stripped them off until she was standing on the end of the dock stark naked. She reached a hand up into her ponytail and freed her fiery mane; the soft tendrils scattered over her creamy pale shoulders, teasing the small of her back. The perfectly-formed globes of her buttocks called to him; his erection pressed tightly against his zipper.

Luca could not believe she'd stripped nude in front of him and every small creature in the woods. He couldn't help but smile as she launched herself off the dock in a perfect dive. Did she know he was watching her? How could she not have known? He'd told her he'd keep an eye on her at the lake. Little temptress, what was she doing?

With preternatural speed, he arrived at the dock just as her hands breached the shimmering dark-blue water. Samantha bobbed up to the surface and spun to face him. He could hardly believe the reckless abandon she demonstrated, given that she'd been held up in a strange coven less than a week ago. She was resilient, young and full of energy, representing a zest for life that he'd long forgotten.

Samantha smiled as she waved to him to join her in the deep abyss. She called out to him, "Come in, Luca! The water's great!" She laughed and dove again; her white bottom peeked out for a second before submerging yet again.

"Darlin', I've got no suit. Besides, vampires don't swim." He wanted desperately to go in after her, but knew it would lead to so much more than a morning swim.

"You've got your birthday suit. Please, you're not gonna make a girl swim alone, are ya?" she purred.

"Is it cold?" He was starting to waver in his firm decision to stay on shore.

"Naw, it's plenty warm. It's late August, had plenty of time to heat up. Come on!" she begged.

"You a good swimmer?" Luca asked.

"Yes. Why're you asking?" she replied.

"Because I'm coming in to get you!" Losing all control, Luca quickly pulled off his white t-shirt and began to undress.

As he unzipped his pants, Samantha screamed playfully and started to swim away. Stripped naked, Samantha admired his rippling abs out the side of her eyes. She knew he'd be coming for her.

Breaching the water, Luca cursed. "Damn, it's cold. You lied to me, woman. You'd better swim fast because I'm goin' to catch you!"

Luca dove under the water once again, determined to catch up with the very slippery, naked woman who'd enticed him to jump into a cold mountain lake in the middle of the day. It had been at least a hundred years since he'd indulged in such a childish activity, but he simply could not resist her. While vampires could be exposed to sunlight, he was weakened to the state of a human during the day. Breaking the surface, he searched for her and spied feet splashing several yards from him. He dove once again, knowing he'd soon catch his prey.

Samantha gasped for air after racing away from Luca. She spun in a circle, treading water as she looked for a trace of him. The smooth lake gave no clues as to where he was. She knew he was somewhere. Somewhere close. Looking towards the cabin, she screamed loudly as hands came around her waist.

Luca pulled her close to him and began to tickle her mercilessly. "Ah, little witch, you lied to me. The water is nearly freezing. And since I can't spank you in the water, this is your punishment." He continued to tickle her as she laughed hysterically, thrashing in the water.

"I'm sorry," she pleaded. "Uncle! Uncle!"

Luca stopped tickling her but didn't let her go. Instead he let his hands move from her waist to just under her breasts, encircling her ribcage. Samantha relaxed back onto him, letting her head fall back onto his shoulder as they both floated on their backs in the peaceful reserve.

"I'm happy you joined me. I love it up here in the woods. It's so peaceful." Samantha wrapped her arms around his, fully aware of where his arms supported her. As they moved as one in the water, she could feel the hardness of him brushing her bottom. Yet she wasn't afraid. She was aroused and excited that he'd joined her in such a very human activity.

"I'm happy you convinced me to swim with you," Luca responded. "I haven't done this in such a long time. I'd forgotten how wonderful it is to skinny dip."

"How old are you, Luca?"

"Very old, indeed, my dear Samantha. I was turned in the eighteen hundreds. So I'm well over two hundred years old....give or take a few years."

"Do you miss being human?" Samantha asked.

"No, darlin'. Being human is so ordinary. And now that you're a witch, you've joined our little club of supernaturals. I sense your fear. But I promise you that you'll be all right. In fact, you'll probably love it once you find your magic." Luca squeezed her tightly and kissed her shoulder.

"Ah, and there's the rub my friend. I have no magic. Nothing. Ilsbeth seems to think there's something about me, but I can't do a thing. Believe me, I've tried. Nothing happens," Samantha huffed.

"It will come, Samantha. I can smell the magic on you, and it's as sweet as honey. It's there. Maybe it hasn't shown itself yet, but it will."

"You sound so confident, Luca. I wish I could be like you. But I feel so defeated. Seriously, Luca. I've been kidnapped, forced into working at a sex club, beaten and then told I was a witch. I've had to take a leave of absence from my real life. I can't tell anyone human what's really happened to me. And now, on top of everything, you think I'm in danger, and I have to return to that God forsaken city where it all started. I just want to lie back in this lake and forget everything," she confided.

"Do you remember what you told me that night we were at Kade's?" Luca asked.

"Yes. No. I don't know. I said a lot of things. I was crying. I was upset. What do you mean? What did I say?" Samantha laughed a little, knowing how confused she sounded.

"You said you were a strong person. And while I don't know you very well, I believe that's true," he continued. "Since you've been here at the cabin, you've stared down a wolf, talked with an Alpha and held a knife to a vampire. You're either crazy or strong, and I can tell you that I know it's the latter. You'll survive what's to come. You can do this, Samantha."

"Luca, where have you been my whole life?" she joked. She smiled, realizing there was something about him that made her feel better. "Maybe you're right. Maybe I can do this, but I can't do it alone. You make me feel like I'll get through this as long as I'm with you." She'd never known such encouragement in her entire existence, and here was a man who had faith in her even when she didn't have it in herself.

Luca's heart beat against his chest at her words. He knew he shouldn't fall for a human, but she was chipping away at whatever resolve he had left to stay away. Unable to resist her any longer, he kissed the side of her neck and slowly trailed his lips behind her ear. She moaned in arousal as he slid his hands up to caress her breasts. He wanted to take her there in the lake.

"Luca," she whispered as he kissed and touched her. "Yes."

With her words, he turned her around to face him, pressing his lips to hers. Their tongues swept together as they passionately kissed. Samantha wrapped her legs around Luca's waist, aroused by the feel of his rock-hard cock bobbing up against the crease of her ass. She fingered his long hair and kissed up his cheeks as he licked her neck.

"Luca, please," she panted. God, she wanted him. She wanted to forget everything in that moment but him.

"Samantha." Luca wanted to stop, to tell her that they shouldn't continue. She was so vulnerable after what had happened. As much as he wanted her, he didn't want to take advantage either. And then there was his vow not to get involved with humans. But she tasted sweet as peaches on a warm summer day. So soft and slippery in his hands. "Mmmm…you're so beautiful," he murmured, unable to stop kissing her. He needed to have all of her.

As he was about to suggest they go inside the cabin, Luca tensed. He immediately released Samantha to stop and sniff the air. *Smoke.* He growled, baring his fangs.

"Luca, what's wrong?" Samantha asked, frightened.

"Swim Samantha," he ordered. "The cabin. It's on fire."

Luca and Samantha immediately swam toward the dock. Luca reached it first and effortlessly leapt up onto the wooden surface. Extending a hand, he pulled Samantha out and they both dressed within minutes. Luca held Samantha's hand as they ran towards the black smoke billowing from the cabin. Orange streaks of fire danced towards the trees as they stood helplessly by and watched the inferno.

"Luca, who would do this?" Samantha gasped.

"I told you that you were in danger. Looks like whoever attacked us in New Orleans has just found you in Pennsylvania." He released Samantha's hand and began to search around the edge of the house for evidence. "Stay back from the flames. I just need to check. I might be able to scent whoever did this."

Samantha stood silently for a moment, looking at the blackened embers; the flames licked toward the sky. Part of the exterior walls remained even though the front of the building was completely gone. Luca walked over to the entrance while Samantha relegated herself to the perimeter of the woods.

Looking down toward the walkway, Luca's anger rose as he read words scrawled on the slate. "*Where is the Hematilly Periapt?*" Luca frowned. What the hell was that supposed to mean? He knelt down with his cell phone and snapped a picture. Then he ran his fingers over the clotted, blood-red substance; he held it to his nose and sniffed. Bat's blood. What the fuck was someone doing with bat's blood out here in the middle of the mountains? It was a common ingredient used in witchcraft, usually made with indigo dye, cinnamon, myrrh, and a few other benign ingredients. But the sanguine ink was genuine blood from the veins of a freshly slit bat's throat; it was used for revenge. Someone had intended to burn them to a crisp in that cabin; fitting retribution for a witch.

What is the Hematilly Periapt? An amulet, he pondered. Ilsbeth had said nothing to him about her owning it. Could Samantha have such an object? Did she know what it was? And if existed, what did it do? Who would want something so badly they'd be willing to kill for it in broad daylight? Deciding not to tell Samantha about the writing, he smeared the fluid across the sole of his shoe, blurring the words. He wiped his finger on his jeans, looked up into the flames and sighed. They needed to get out of there.

Samantha's eyes pricked with tears as she watched her rental cabin burn. She looked up to the surrounding trees, which had begun to catch fire. Anger burned deep within her soul. She'd had enough of the evil and destruction. Luca was right about one thing; she was strong, and she would find a way through this. Not only that; in that moment, she resolved to be part of the solution and not idly stand by while life happened to her. She remembered what Ilsbeth had told her about how she had magic within her but she was the only one who could call it to be. It was her decision, her power.

Closing her eyes, Samantha reached out her hands, palms up toward the heavens and focused on her need to put the fire out. She called to the elements as if they were servants; instinctually, she knew that they were within her control. She felt the tingle in her fingertips as her eyes flew open. The clouds had already drawn close, and lightning flashed in the distance. "Rain, come," she commanded.

Nothing happened, and she looked up again as if readying to scold an insolent child. Anger surging, she encouraged the tendrils of magic to dance over her skin until she was within a mystic trance. Unconsciously, she chanted over and over as the words came to her from within, "Aqua Dei tui eu nunc. Aqua Dei tui eu nunc. Aqua Dei tui eu nunc!" She shook with power as the water began to fall from the sky.

Luca stood back as a bright aura surrounded Samantha. Although he'd known her magic existed, she had doubted its existence. As streams of light pushed from her palms, he knew she'd found it. He blessed the rain as it poured down in droves, putting the fire out within minutes. When it was clear all the embers were drowned, he called out to Samantha, "It's done

Samantha. You can let go, darlin'. You did it."

Samantha barely registered Luca's words as the power within her died. She slumped over, holding herself up by propping her hands on her knees. It felt as if she'd run a marathon. Colors danced in the whites of her eyes as she fell into blackness.

"You did it!" Luca exclaimed. "You put out the fire." As he turned to smile at her, he panicked; she'd collapsed into the muddy mixture of dirt and ash. He rushed over, fell to his knees and gently cradled her in his arms. "It's okay, you did it. Come on now, wake up, Samantha." He kissed her head and pulled away, realizing they needed to get out of there. He traced his fingers from her temple down around her chin.

Her eyes fluttered, "What?"

"You scared me. You're okay now, let's get going." He stood up with her cradled in his arms. She pressed her face into his chest, afraid to look at the cabin.

He walked with her over to his SUV, opened the door and carefully sat her in the front seat.

"Stay here, Samantha," he told her. "I need to get my keys. Is there anything you need out of this rubble?" Luca knew full well there wasn't much left worth salvaging. But after all she'd been through, he would've tried to save anything important to her.

She silently shook her head no and stared out the car's front windshield, not wanting to face what had happened. Denial could be quite a peaceful state if she only embraced it; alas, she could not tear her eyes from the debris. A dazed veil fell over her face as she silently contemplated the fire, her magic. It was as if her inner light dimmed as the cold splash of reality dowsed her. She was still in danger, and if she'd had a doubt before, her magic, while unpredictable, was intact. It was a wicked blow to the fragile sense of balance she'd worked hard to build over the past week.

Samantha, still in shock from creating the rain, shook her head silently. She hadn't brought anything of importance with her to the cabin. She hadn't had a chance to replace all her credit cards since New Orleans. The only thing she'd replaced was her smartphone, which had all her financial information on it via the apps. And luckily, she'd worn it on her walk so she could listen to music.

Luca trod into what was left of the home, watching carefully where he stepped. The crunch of the charred wood beneath his feet resounded in Samantha's ears as she watched the smoke-filled sky dissipate from gray to blue. The smell of burnt wood engrained itself in the surrounding woods and grass; there was no direction either of them could turn where they could not detect the evidence of what had happened.

Luca came out of the house with nothing more than a single set of keys. "Got the keys!" he grumbled. He quickly strode over to her, got in the car and started it. "Let's go. You're in shock and we've got to get out of here before whoever did this comes back. It's odd. I can't smell a vampire or a wolf, no magic either." *Smells undeniably human.* He didn't want to tell Samantha that wolves, shifters, vampires and those of the magic persuasion could all use human minions to do their dirty work. "Samantha, this may not be the best time to discuss this, but your magic back there…the rain. Do you wanna talk about it?"

"No. Yes. I mean, not right now. I don't even know what I did, those words I spoke. I just was so upset about the cabin. Something just happened in me. Let's just drop it, Luca. I'll call Ilsbeth when we get to New Orleans. I'm just so upset right now that someone would burn down the cabin." Samantha just wanted to crawl into a hole. Some good her so-called magic was. She didn't really even know what she'd done to bring the rain. She needed to talk to Ilsbeth about what had happened, but right now she wanted to hide, sleep and forget. She hadn't asked for this life, and felt a great sense of loss; she'd never be normal again.

Looking over at Samantha, Luca realized how small and fragile she appeared curled into the seat, leaning her forehead against the passenger side window. He wondered what thoughts swirled behind her pale blue eyes; she looked a million miles away, silently considering what had happened perhaps. Luca swore silently for indulging himself with her in the lake. He'd been foolish to allow himself the pleasure of holding her soft pliant body: kissing her swollen pink lips: tasting her sweet honey-like essence. *What was I thinking? I've been thinking with my dick.* God, he needed to get it together. She was defenseless, innocent to his ways. No matter how much he wanted to make love to her, he couldn't allow himself to do it. He could not allow himself to kiss her again. Even though she was technically a witch, he wasn't sure if she'd ever accept her circumstances. And what of her life expectancy? Would she do what she needed to do to become immortal?

He knew that Kade had resolved that issue with Sydney, giving her his blood to keep her youthful and healthy. But Sydney was a toughened cop who'd fought side by side with him and Kade. She'd faced death time and time again. And while he'd initially hated that Kade had let a human go after Asgear, Sydney had proved her worth. Kade was determined to marry Sydney, and Luca respected their special connection, knowing Sydney could hold her own in the supernatural world.

But Samantha? No, she was like most humans. She was delectably, wonderfully normal: a computer analyst, for Christ's sake. Her only experience with supernaturals was being bespelled, possibly raped, beaten and now being turned into a witch. And now she could add 'passionately kissed by a vampire' to her done list. He reckoned that she could find a much better mate than him. He rolled his eyes even thinking of the word:

mate. In over two hundred years, he had never even considered marrying, mating, bonding or any other supernatural or human word that meant commitment. Never again.

Raised in Australia, Luca had known that loving someone brought nothing but heartache. In the late seventeen hundreds, his father, Jonathon Macquarie, a marine, had taken his family to the colony of New South Wales so that he could work on the development of the penal colonies being set up by the British. It was a rough life for the soldiers and their families as well as the prisoners; life in a strange new world was not kind, and often inhumane. During the summer of his twenty-fifth birthday, he'd found comfort in the arms of a lovely woman, Eliza Hutchinson. She was the abandoned daughter of a prisoner who'd been brought to the island ten years earlier, caught pickpocketing on the streets of London.

When he'd turned eighteen, Luca's father had secured a guard position for him. A few years into the position, he was stationed to guard the factory where Eliza's mother had worked. One day, he'd caught Eliza sneaking in food for her mother, but hadn't had the heart to turn her into the authorities. Instead, he'd courted her every chance he got at her farm stand in the market, where she sold fresh honey and wool.

Using his influence within the marines, he'd worked hard to secure a 'ticket of leave' for her mother, ensuring her freedom as long as she stayed out of trouble. Within months, Luca and Eliza fell very much in love, and she agreed to marry him. Then one night on their way home from dinner, a drunken group of soldiers had cornered them in an alley. They'd taunted Luca and Eliza, as they expressed interest in sexually assaulting her. While Luca was a trained guard, he was outnumbered five to one. In a brutal fight, he'd lost consciousness as a bottle smashed upon the back of his head.

Luca had woken in his parents' home to find that Eliza had been raped and killed. His legs had been broken and his skull fractured, but somehow he'd survived the attack. During the months he'd spent under his mother's care, convalescing, Luca was despondent, determined to leave Australia. He'd grown up in the brutal colony watching soldiers punish convicts. Sometimes they were beaten, humiliated or hanged for the smallest infraction. He'd planned to leave someday with Eliza and take them back to London where they'd escape the constant stress associated with forging the path to civilization in the settlement. After her murder, he'd had nothing: no love, no desire to live, and no faith in humanity.

As soon as he could walk again, he'd spent his savings on a passage back to Mother England. Upon arrival Luca immediately 'took the King's shilling', and enlisted as a soldier for the War of 1812. Because of his experience as a guard and his father's service in the marines, he entered as an officer.

Hopeless and wrathful, Luca had wanted to kill and looked forward to each battle, seeing the face of Eliza's murderers in every opponent. There would never be enough blood shed to satisfy his need for vengeance against a faceless nameless enemy who'd never seen the shore of Australia. But it hadn't mattered to Luca. He'd heard that Eliza's true murderers had been hanged. However it would never be enough to quench his rage and the burning loss he'd experienced. Battle after battle, he'd fought with the utmost intensity, earning the respect of his fellow officers. One fateful night, however, it was his blood that had been shed.

On January 8, 1815, Luca had pushed out with his unit into the darkness of night as the fog clouded his vision. As chaos erupted in the field along the Mississippi, Luca had fallen to the ground in a barrage of musket fire, as had many other officers of the British army.

The next day, as he was saying his last prayers, a stranger had happened upon him. Sensing his impending death, Kade had offered him immortality in exchange for his loyalty. Luca, no stranger to adventure, had accepted his proposal and thus began his life as vampire.

Luca shook his thoughts free of his troubled past. Eliza was merely a distant memory, albeit an everlasting reminder of how fragile mortality was. Since turning vampire, he'd pledged his loyalty and friendship to Kade. Over the years, they'd done almost everything together including fighting, feeding and fucking. Yes, they'd shared quite a few women over the years, but those days were over now that Kade was getting married. And while Luca was glad of Kade's new-found happiness, he had no plans to follow in his friend's footsteps.

No, he'd been perfectly content over the past two hundred years with his non-committed sexual escapades. The closest he'd ever come to commitment was with women he'd considered to be 'friends with benefits', long before the saying was popular. He was devastatingly handsome, so finding women who'd throw a night of passion his way was never an issue. If they acted as though they were in love, he could just enthrall them to think otherwise.

As vampire, he was as physically strong as anyone could be, yet emotionally he'd never be strong. The death of Eliza had brought him to his knees, and he'd never forgive or forget what humans could do. Nor would he forget how it felt to have his heart ripped from his chest, to lose someone he loved with all his heart. He'd rather stake himself than go through the pain of loving and losing a mate again.

Whatever he was feeling for Samantha needed to be squelched. The seed that had been planted inside his heart had to be crushed and the best way he knew to do that was to find another woman who could sate his needs for blood and sex. Perhaps then, he'd lose interest in the red-headed witch seated next to him.

Chapter Six

Samantha startled as she woke; driving rain and booming thunder seemed to shake the large SUV as it sped down Broad Street. She looked over to Luca, who was distracted by the city traffic. How long had she been sleeping? If they were in center city, it must've been for hours, she thought. Sitting up and combing her hand through her dried frizzy curls, she tried to get a bearing on where she was. "Hey, Luca, where are we? South Philadelphia?" She'd answered her own question.

"Uh huh, we're goin' to Tristan's club, Eden. It's only three in the afternoon, so we should be able to get showered and have something to eat before leaving. The plane is cleared to take off at nine tonight, so we have a few hours to wait. I was hoping to leave earlier but they had to make some minor repairs to the jet," he replied, glancing towards her. "You okay?"

"Yeah, I'm okay. You?"

She licked her lips, and Luca tried not to notice. He grew hard with arousal, dreaming that her soft pink lips were wrapped around a particular part of him. He shifted in his seat. Damn, even after nearly dying in a fire, the woman looked sexy.

"I'm vampire. As soon as I get a little blood, I'll be more than fine," Luca grumbled.

Samantha wondered what was making him so irritable, and assumed he was hungry. She had honestly never given a thought that he might need food or that she was considered a part of his food chain. Samantha pushed the thought to the back of her mind, knowing that regardless of her qualification as a meal, he'd never hurt her. And she needed his help to find whoever was after her so she could get her life back in order.

"I'm hungry too. And I smell like a fine combination of smoke and lake water." She crinkled her nose in disgust.

As they pulled into a driveway, she noticed they had driven into a subterranean garage. After going down two levels, Luca pulled the car into a large parking spot next to a set of elevators.

"This is it. Let's go," he ordered as he turned off the car and got out. "Listen, this is a club for paranormals and humans. It's pretty much a meat market in there." He didn't want to sugarcoat the situation. He also didn't want her getting hit on or going off with strangers. "So when you go with me into the open part of the club, stay close to me. Or stay with Tristan. You never know who might be around. Not to mention someone just tried to turn us into French fries."

"Yum. Fries," she joked. She couldn't stop thinking of food. She'd only eaten an apple all day. "I really am hungry." She smiled up at him, hoping she could sway his foul mood.

Seeing her smile at him melted his anger, and he lifted the corners of his mouth in a wry smile. "Okay, hungry girl. Let's see if we can go get cleaned up and find you something to eat."

He flipped up a security pad located near the doors and punched in a code. The elevator opened, and he placed a hand on the small of her back, guiding her into a small, mahogany-lined lift. Samantha felt a flip in her stomach and couldn't decide if it was from going up so quickly or from Luca's touch on her back. Following the commotion over the scorched cabin, she'd forgotten the desire she'd felt while kissing Luca in the lake. She blushed, thinking of how he'd tasted her mouth and caressed her breasts. She grew aroused at the thought of taking it further, touching his naked body once again, feeling him inside of her. She tried shaking the thought, knowing this wasn't a good time to resume what they'd been doing. They hadn't even spoken about what had happened between them, and she wasn't sure if it was such a good idea to talk about it here, at Tristan's.

Luca's eyes flashed red and then back to green, sensing her thoughts. Scenting her arousal was hard to ignore in the tiny, private elevator. He balled his fists and then stretched his hands, as he caught a glimpse of her hard nipples poking through her exercise top. He considered kissing her against the wall but was prevented by the ding of the doors opening.

"Finally," he muttered and strode across the room, hoping that putting some distance between them would help temper his rock hard erection that was begging to be set free.

"Where are we?" Samantha asked as she walked into a royal-blue room furnished with a large cherry desk and a black leather sofa. Very rich and masculine, she thought to herself as she admired a spectacular bronze wolf sculpture on the fireplace mantle. It was delicately balanced on a black marble base. Samantha recalled Tristan in his wolf form, black fur with amber eyes.

Luca walked over to a large wooden door and opened it. Pointing across the room, he addressed Samantha. "We're in Tristan's private office. Listen, there's a shower over there across the room. Go ahead and shower, and I'll send someone up with a fresh change of clothes once I talk to Tristan. After you're done getting dressed, come downstairs. Just follow the long hallway out towards the staircase, and you'll be downstairs."

"What about you? Where are you going to shower?" Samantha was hoping for a repeat performance of today. She'd love to see the strength of him that she'd only felt in the slippery cool water.

"There's a men's locker room downstairs. I'll shower there. See you at the bar." He waved and shut the door. Luca took a deep breath and blew it out. For a long minute, he'd been ready to take her in the elevator and now she was asking about the shower. She was fucking killing him. *Shit. Looks like I'll be having a cold shower.*

Samantha watched Luca leave with a puzzled look on her face. She knew what she'd felt in the lake had been real chemistry. But now Luca seemed like he couldn't get away from her fast enough. She knew she shouldn't trust a vampire, but she felt safe with Luca. Lying back in his arms in the lake felt like the first time she'd relaxed for weeks. He was so strong yet gentle. They'd talked like old friends but felt like new lovers. She'd never experienced such a passionate kiss in her life. Sure she'd had a few lovers, but no one that had evoked such a fiery, passionate reaction in her. And certainly no man had kissed her with such fury, naked beneath azure waters.

Samantha poked her head into the bathroom and found it surprisingly clean for a bachelor's. She looked on the shelf and saw herbal shampoo but hoped for a razor and if she got lucky, a toothbrush. She pulled open the vanity drawer: condoms, a single toothbrush, straight edged razor and deodorant. This bathroom definitely belonged to a man, she mused. Opening the second drawer, she found a stash of disposable pink razors and new toothbrushes. A ladies' man's bathroom, she corrected herself silently and laughed.

After taking the most delightful shower in a strange bathroom, Samantha dried herself with a clean towel. She heard a door open, and butterflies danced in her stomach. Luca had returned. She checked her face and rushed out with the towel wrapped around her.

"Hello there." A stunning, tall female held up clothing with a smile. "It's okay, Samantha. I'm Kat, Tristan's sister. Tris said you could use some clothes, so here I am," she chirped.

Samantha walked over to her, extending her hand. "Hi Kat, I'm Samantha. I really appreciate you bringing me something to wear." She was disappointed Luca hadn't returned for her but hid her feelings from the stranger.

Kat shook her hand and placed the clothes on the desk. "I brought you a choice: yoga pants or sundress. Tris said you were a petite little thing, and he's right. I co-own a shop a few blocks over, Hair and Heels. We're a beauty salon and spa but also sell clothes and accessories. I'm pretty sure both will fit. So what do ya think?" She put her hands on her hips, waiting for a response. Kat played with the red sundress, holding it up to herself by the spaghetti straps.

Kat was naturally beautiful; an exotic woman with long auburn hair and deep brown eyes. Even though Tristan had platinum blonde hair, he and Kat had the same intense eyes and straight nose. Samantha wouldn't have known they were siblings if she hadn't been told, but now saw a slight resemblance.

"Since I've been in yoga pants all day, I guess the sundress will work. But I don't have any shoes except sneakers," Samantha answered.

"No problem. I've got some flip-flops in my bag," she added, smiling.

"Thanks so much. I really appreciate you taking time out of your day to help us." Samantha used the word 'us' as if she and Luca were a couple, even though a more accurate description would have been traveling companions, or friends due to circumstances.

"Like I said, not a problem at all. A friend of Tristan's is a friend of mine. We take care of each other. Especially us girls," she winked.

Oddly, Samantha felt at ease with the lovely woman and wondered if she was a wolf like Tristan. She smiled at Kat. "Well, thanks again." She waited on her to leave.

"Come on now, Samantha. Don't be shy. Lord knows, us wolves aren't. I'm staying; at least until I make sure the dress fits you. I've gotta get back to the shop soon, but I've got time for a bit of a chat," she said, plopping herself in the overstuffed leather sofa.

Samantha never thought of herself as shy, but she didn't know the woman in front of her from Adam. But she really didn't have much choice, given that Kat wasn't moving. Deciding to go with the flow, she stripped off her towel and pulled the cotton sundress over her head. Looking down and feeling around to make sure it wasn't too tight she smiled over at Kat. "It's lovely," Samantha declared, running her hands down her sides. "Thanks again."

"No problem." Kat came over and stood in front of Samantha, admiring the smooth fabric and the fit of the dress. "Looks great on you. That plastic bag over there has the flip-flops in it and a pair of undies. Good thing the dress has a shelf built into it 'cause I don't sell bras. Well, I better get going."

Samantha waved as Kat opened the door. "Thanks again, Kat. I actually live in Philly too. Maybe when I get back, I'll look you up," she offered.

Kat just smiled and waved back as she shut the door.

Samantha walked back into the bathroom and began to comb out her wet hair. Thinking about her conversation with Kat, Samantha felt quite relieved to have a normal conversation with a human-looking woman…even if she really was a wolf. She smiled to herself wondering if all wolves were as friendly as Tristan and Kat. Taking one last glance at herself in the mirror, Samantha felt satisfied with her attractive new dress. Clean and clothed, she was refreshed and ready to go downstairs; she wanted to find Luca and get something to eat.

Shaved and showered, Luca walked into the main club room and sat at the bar. From behind it, Tristan faced the wall and reaching up, grabbed a bottle of Martell Cognac off the top shelf and two glasses, and set them on the brass bar.

"So, long day, huh?" Tristan asked. He poured two fingers into each snifter. Even though it was four in the afternoon, happy hour started early in Eden on a Friday night. Patrons were already starting to pour through the front entrance, but no one had come to the far end of the bar yet.

"Yeah, you could say that. Someone torched the cabin and left our witch a little message. Something about a periapt." Luca took a long draw of his drink. "It was written in bat's blood. Real bat's blood. But I didn't scent any supernaturals so it must have been a puppet. Haven't told Samantha yet."

"A periapt, huh? Could be for anything, but what does this one do and why would someone want it so badly and why would Samantha have it?" Tristan mused.

"And those, my friend, are all very good questions I've asked myself. Perhaps Ilsbeth can help us. I don't know. To be honest, I really just need to feed right now and maybe fuck. This whole situation's wearing on me, and I need to blow off some steam, before I get onto that plane and head down to New Orleans." He tapped nervously on the edge of his glass.

"Yeah, about that…" Tristan hesitated and looked up at his sister. She bounded down the stairs toward them, silently signaling to Tristan to be quiet, obviously wanting to surprise Luca.

Luca spied a female refection in Tristan's eyes. Immediately recognizing her scent, he spun on his bar seat and held out his arms. "Kat!"

Kat jumped into his arms as he spun her about as if she weighed nothing. "Luca, baby!" she cooed. "I'm so glad to see you. I can't believe you're here. I've only got maybe twenty minutes 'til my next appointment, but I've been looking to go down to visit ya. "

Things were about to get interesting. Luca and Kat had met years ago when Kade's ex-lover had kidnapped and tortured her in the mid-eighteen hundreds. Luca had been there that day to rescue her and bring her back to Tristan. As the years passed, Luca and Kat had had their fair share of romantic moments, but it was always free and easy; neither of them was looking for commitment.

As they hugged tightly, Kat kissed him on the cheek, and pulled away, leaving her arm around his waist.

"You knew she was here?" Luca questioned Tristan.

"Yes I did. And you know, if you're going to New Orleans tonight, I've been thinking maybe you could take Kat with you," Tristan suggested.

Luca looked at Kat and then back to Tristan. "What's up?"

Kat looked at her shoes, not wanting to recount what was happening.

Tristan's eyes narrowed. "Kat, here, has an unwanted suitor. And it's none other than Jax Chandler, the Alpha from New York. Now, he's been told that he can't have her, but he's not one to take no for an answer. I don't want anything happening to her."

"What? Are you afraid he'll kidnap her?" Luca asked.

"Well, that I'm not sure of, but I think if she takes a little trip down to see our brother Marcel, it'll help to bolster my verdict on this. I don't want him thinking he can get stupid and try and take her." Tristan hopped over the bar and put his arm around his sister. "Kat wants Marcel to call the pack out on this, and I agree. So what say you? Can you take her with you?"

"Certainly. But she can't stay with me. She'll have to stay with Kade or Marcel." There was no way he was going to let two females stay at his house. He had a feeling that Samantha wouldn't take too kindly to having him let a former lover stay with them. Nor did he want the two women ganging up on him. No, she'd have to stay with Kade or go to her brother's.

"Thanks Luca!" Kat kissed him again; this time on the lips.

"Okay, it's settled then. Now let's see what I can do about a donor. I'll go check the list," Tristan announced.

Eden's maître d' kept a donor list at the front desk of willing human and shifter donors who wished to experience the orgasmic bite of a vampire, sex, or both. They wore beepers around their necks that buzzed should they be called to 'volunteer'. There were private rooms upstairs for these activities that accommodated pairs and groups. The rooms were video monitored for the safety of guests to make sure all activities were consensual and safe. It was against the law to kill during a feeding, and Eden's state-of-the-art security system kept things legal.

Kat stopped Tristan from leaving and looked over to Luca. "Luca, I'll feed you," she offered.

"You sure? I thought you had an appointment. And you need to get your stuff together. We've got to leave soon," Luca said.

"I'll call the shop and give Sherri my client. They're expecting me to leave soon anyway. Now they'll just have to rearrange the schedule a little more quickly. Call it a perk of being an owner. And I don't need anything else but my purse and cell phone, which I have. As soon as I get to Marcel's, I plan to go wolf for a while. Any clothes I need, he'll provide from the pack," Kat answered without hesitation.

"Tristan, you mind? This isn't our first time, but she's still your sister." Luca was old-fashioned in many ways and felt it necessary to get her older brother's permission.

Tristan trusted Luca with his life and his sister's. Luca and Kat had been tight ever since Luca rescued her, and while he hadn't exactly talked about sex with his sister, he was pretty sure that they'd been together several times over the years.

"No problem. Go have fun, kids. Don't do anything I wouldn't do," he quipped.

Luca grabbed Kat by the hand and started up the stairs toward the private rooms.

As they walked down the hallway, looking for an open feeding room, Kat grabbed Luca's arm tighter and giggled, hoping she'd have at least an hour to make love with him before they had to take off. It had been years since they'd been together, and she was looking forward to reminiscing.

Luca, thirsting for blood, could feel his fangs pushing through his gums. Kat's blood, heady, woodsy and potent, would surely sate his thirst. As he went to turn the handle to one of the feeding rooms, he froze. *Samantha.* She stared straight at him down the long, dimly lit hallway. There he stood arm in arm with another woman after he'd kissed her only hours earlier. The instant he locked eyes with Samantha, he registered the pain he was causing her.

Samantha stopped dead in her tracks, observing Kat hold Luca's arms as if they were long-lost lovers. Rationally, she knew that he needed to eat and that he'd use a donor. She hadn't offered her own blood to Luca. After everything she'd been through, she just couldn't bring herself to do that. She honestly thought that she understood what it meant for him to feed off of someone else, but there in the hall, seeing another woman wrapped around his waist, she felt jealous. Her anger flared.

She felt like a fool for kissing him, for believing that they could have possibly had a connection. At the cabin, he'd kissed her passionately. He'd acted like he was ready to make love to her. It must have all been a ruse to get her to go with him back to New Orleans, she thought. Obviously he hadn't felt the same toward her if he was letting Kat put her hands all over him. She felt sick to her stomach at the thought of him kissing that woman, holding her in his arms. But what could she do? He did need to eat. And a display of jealousy would be akin to showing weakness. She would not let herself be a victim again. Biting her lip, she steeled herself and began to walk toward them.

Luca watched her contemplate what was happening. He felt a strange, unfamiliar feeling in the pit of his gut. *Guilt.* No, he refused to acknowledge it. Just as Samantha came within twenty feet of him, he acknowledged her presence with a nod, opened the door, pulled Kat inside and slammed it shut.

Luca growled in hunger as he caged Kat against the door. In anger, he pressed his lips to hers, pushing his tongue deep within her mouth. Sensing his predatory nature in full force, Kat submitted, keeping her arms down and against the door, and kissed him back. Luca knew immediately something was off as soon as he kissed her. That damn witch had cursed him; he was sure of it. He had kissed Kat many times in the past, but now the only picture in his mind was Samantha. Luca bared his fangs, threw his head back and roared.

Kat reached up slowly, pulled off her t-shirt and bared her neck to him. She wasn't sure what was wrong with Luca but it wasn't the first time she'd seen him upset. She could tell that she probably wouldn't be having sex with him like she'd been anticipating, but understood that Luca had something on his mind.

"You're sure, Kat?" Luca asked. No matter how many times he fed, he always asked his donor. He wanted to make sure he wasn't taking someone against their will, no matter what their original intentions.

"Yes, Luca. Take me," Kat whispered.

A split second later, his fangs sank deep into her neck. As he drank, he tried to block Samantha, but couldn't stop thinking of her.

Kat pressed her flattened palms against Luca's chest. Then her fingers clasped his shirt tightly as she felt an orgasm rip through her. She reached down to feel Luca's hardness and had him in her grip, when he pushed her hand away and released her.

His eyes remained red as he fell down onto the sofa. "Fuck!" he yelled.

"Luca, what's wrong?" Kat panted. She was still riding hard from the explosive release. She knelt before him.

Luca laid back with his head resting on a pillow and his feet up on the armrest. "I can't, Kat. And I don't want to talk about it, okay. Just don't ask." He closed his eyes, wiping her blood from the corner of his mouth.

"Luca, it's fine. You know I want to, um, finish, but if you're not into it today, that's okay. Your bite is quite satisfying," she teased and put her hand over his chest. "Whatever it is, we can talk about it later, when and if you're ready."

With a pat, she jumped up and put on her shirt. "Luca, since I have the time, I'm gonna run over to the shop and just check in before I leave. I'll be back in forty-five minutes. I promise it won't take long." Kat leaned over and kissed her friend's forehead.

Luca barely saw her walk out the door, but heard it slam shut. He opened his eyes, which had returned to green, and stared up at the stark white ceiling. He'd gone centuries feeling nothing, and it had served him well. Now he was good and fucked. Guilt. He was sure he felt guilt about being with Kat. And why? Because he'd had a kiss and tickle with Samantha in the lake? No, he'd known there was something there between them ever since the first time he'd stroked Samantha's hair in Kade's basement. And now that he'd kissed her, he couldn't forget the taste of her sweet, soft mouth and the feel of her breasts in his hands.

"Shit! Shit! Shit!" he said aloud to himself. Feelings. Very human-like feelings could threaten his entire existence. Yet he knew in his heart that he was done for. It didn't matter what his mind said or the logic it possessed; his heart spoke and knew what it wanted. He had to have the witch.

From across the room, Tristan could tell that Samantha had been crying. Her face was reddened from her attempts to dry her eyes. He wasn't sure what was wrong, but pain washed over her aura. He knew that she'd been through a lot of trauma over the past few weeks, but she'd seemed relatively calm during their encounter at the cabin. Perhaps she was having a meltdown after watching the cabin burn? Or maybe she was just hungry? He knew he got cranky when he didn't eat.

Deciding not to leave her to any of the sharks looking for a hot date, the Alpha strode over and pulled her into an embrace. "Come on, ma petite sorcière, whatever it is, it'll all work out. What'd I tell you up at the cabin? Go to New Orleans for a little while and then come back. I'll help you get settled back here at home." He rubbed his hand over her hair. She was quite petite indeed, maybe five-three, he thought to himself. The top of her head barely reached his neck.

"Thanks, Tristan. I know it may not seem like it to you, but I'm a relatively strong person in spite of the fact that my life has turned into a living hell, and I have no control over what's happening." She spoke into his chest, pulling herself closer to him.

Samantha knew Luca had come here to feed, but couldn't believe it when she saw him with Kat. They clearly were well acquainted with each other, and she knew damn well that vampires often had sex when they ate. She suspected more than feeding was going on tonight in 'those rooms'. She couldn't believe that after what they'd shared this morning, kissing and touching each other in such an intimate way, he'd take another woman to bed as if it was nothing. But then again, she didn't really know Luca or any of the supernaturals that well. She was attracted to Luca, lusted after him, but all those feelings did not amount to a hill of beans when it came to men. Conflicted, she silently sighed. Even though they hadn't known each other very long, Luca seemed honorable. He certainly didn't seem like the kind of man that would touch a woman's breasts and kiss her and then fuck a different woman less than six hours later.

Sensing her tumultuous thoughts, Tristan rubbed his hands over the top of her head and then slowly moved them down her back, sending out waves of calming reassurance into her skin. Given the temperamental nature of wolves, Tristan was well-trained in using his powers to both excite and pacify supernaturals and humans alike. He could feel her muscles relax as they began to slow dance on the floor. She held onto him tightly as if she needed security, a lifeline to hold onto.

"Tristan, I'm okay, really. Thanks. You…you're a really good Alpha." She giggled and looked up at him. "I can't believe I just said that. Okay, I admit that I really don't know what an Alpha does and you're the only Alpha I know, but you're a good person. I would really like it if we could be friends when I come back." She honestly had never met someone as grounded and down to earth as Tristan before; he was a caring leader.

"That sounds like a fine plan. Tell you what…I'll teach you all about wolves when you get back…everything you want to know, baby," he flirted and spun her around quickly as the music changed into a sultry R&B song.

Samantha laughed out loud and threw her head back and then rested her forehead against his chest. "I just bet you would, Tristan." He was incredibly handsome and charming and seemed to know all the right words to make everything seem all right.

A stranger's hand on her shoulder and a loud growl jolted her back to reality.

Tristan's face hardened as he pulled her tighter against him.

"Stand down, Luca, my friend. Remember where you are," Tristan said calmly with an even-toned voice.

She looked up to see Luca, his eyes a fiery red. What was wrong with him?

"Did you eat yet, Samantha? We don't have much time before we have to leave for the airport," Luca asked, irritated that she'd found comfort so easily in another man's arms.

She reluctantly pulled away from Tristan, yet still kept one hand on his forearm. "No, I haven't eaten." She spoke in a businesslike manner as if she'd just met him.

Tristan looped his arm through hers and began walking them towards the bar. "Ah, see here, Samantha. Dinner is ready now. I wasn't sure what you liked, but I figured most girls like a steak dinner, salad. And who can say no to chocolate cake?" He pointed to a place setting at the bar.

"Thanks, Tristan. It looks delicious. I'm starving." She kissed Tristan on the cheek and sat down, but not before shooting Luca an icy look that could have frozen water on a hot summer day.

"Luca, over here," Tristan commanded, pointing to the end of the bar.

As they both sat down, Tristan glared at Luca. "What in the fuck is wrong with you? Don't you get that she's been traumatized? I know you don't care for humans, but you've got to give this witch a break. I thought you'd be in a better mood after being with Kat."

"I like a particular human a little too much these days. That's the problem," he mumbled. He caught a glimpse of Samantha, who was voraciously eating her steak and totally ignoring him. Then he looked over at Tristan, who was smiling like the cat who ate the mouse.

"I see," he laughed. "Luca, if I hadn't seen it with my own eyes, I wouldn't believe it."

Luca shook his head silently.

The look on Luca's face made Tristan laugh even harder. "Oh my God. Wait…wait until Kade finds out!" He extended his hand and put it on Luca's shoulder. "You're jealous. And you know what that means, my friend? Oh yeah, that's right my man, you're developing feelings. That icy excuse for a heart beating in your chest is starting to melt."

"No, no, no," Luca protested.

"Yes, yes, yes. Let the Alpha guess what happened. Hmmm. Let's see. You went upstairs with my lovely sister expecting to get your rocks off and your fang on, and you couldn't do it. Luca Macquarie cannot fuck and feed, because he's falling for a little red-headed witch. I never thought I'd see the day."

Luca shoved his hand away, disgusted by the truth of the situation. "Fuck you, Tris." He gave him a small smile. "Okay, so maybe you're right. Maybe I'm in deep and not sure what to do. It's not like I have experience with this…with relationships. Hell, most of my relationships consist of 'hey, do you want to have sex? You wanna bite? Okay, done and done'. Now I'm turned on my head. I don't even know what to say, to do. And she's pissed at me. I've been around long enough to know when a woman's jealous. I am so fucked."

"Perhaps you are. For a while, anyway." Tristan grinned broadly. "Don't worry, you'll figure it out, Luca. You're an honorable, decent man. Always have been, always will be. But I can't say I envy you your plane ride back to New Orleans with Kat and Samantha. That's gonna give a new definition to turbulence."

Luca shook his head again, looked at Samantha, and then to Tristan. "Yes, I'll have my hands full on the way back. So, how about you give us a ride to the airport once she's done eating? I'm ready to face this head on. What other choice do I have?" He shrugged.

"Not much. It'll work out, mon ami. I'll call the driver and ask him to get the limo ready," Tristan said.

"Hey Tris."

"Yeah," Tristan answered, standing up, wanting to go check on Kat.

"Thanks buddy. Sorry about going all vamp on the dance floor. I'm out of sorts. And I appreciate the chat. Besides Kade, you've always been there for me. I'll never forget it," Luca said.

"Back at ya. Now, let me go round up my favorite sister. I wanna make sure all of your women are accounted for so you can have a good time for the next few hours." Tristan laughed and punched Luca's arm.

Yeah, it's going to be a laugh riot, Luca thought to himself. As he looked back at Samantha, she glared at him then quickly looked away. He could see the hurt and passion in her eyes and was determined more than ever to go to her. But as he started over to explain things to her, Tristan walked in with Kat.

All four of them looked at each other, and Samantha rolled her eyes, shoving a piece of chocolate cake into her mouth. It was going to be a damn fine flight home to New Orleans, indeed, Luca brooded.

Chapter Seven

Flying in luxury was not all it was cracked up to be, Samantha thought, as she stared out the small porthole window. The plane was beautifully decorated, with plush tan leather seats, mahogany tray tops and undertones. In her life, she'd never known such decadence; she was used to being crammed like a sardine into a coach. But she knew that it wasn't the plane that was the problem.

Learning that Kat was coming on their trip and that she'd be trapped in a tin can for three hours with the two of them made her want to spit tacks. The four-seat luxury jet was not nearly big enough for her to breathe, let alone survive an entire trip with Luca and Kat. Perhaps if she just settled in against the window and tried to sleep the entire flight, she would not have to look at or talk to either one of them. On the way into the plane, Samantha chose to sit away from them in a cabin chair nearest to the front of the plane, essentially separating herself. Luca and Kat sat side by side in their individual bucket seats with only the aisle between them.

In the elevator on the way down to the limo, Luca had informed her that Kat was coming with them; Samantha had silently nodded and pulled a mask of indifference over her face. Whatever had happened at the lake was clearly an insignificant bleep in Luca's social calendar. She wondered if Kat was Luca's girlfriend and perhaps she was the other woman. Did Kat know Luca had kissed her mere hours before making love to her? God, she felt so stupid for ever opening herself up to him.

After nearly an hour of total silence, Kat wondered what the hell was up with Luca. He hadn't said a word since leaving the club and wasn't acting his normal self. And while she didn't know Samantha, she felt an icy coolness wash over her as if she'd killed her cat. The last time she'd seen her in Tristan's office, it had seemed like they were on their way to a friendship. Not able to take one more minute of the tension, she broke the dead air.

"Luca, are you feeling all right?" She reached over and put her hand on his arm.

Luca flinched at her touch, but Kat held firm. "I never thought I'd see the day when a vampire was jumpy. Too much coffee, dear?" she teased.

Hearing the term of endearment, Samantha's eyes flashed up and held Luca's gaze. Her tight-lined mouth and intense stare told Luca all he needed to know about what Samantha thought of Kat.

Pulling his arm away from Kat, Luca unbuckled his seatbelt and stood up. "I'm fine. Just have a lot on my mind. I'm going back to the office to make a few calls. I want to make sure Marcel is ready for you and that Kade and Sydney are aware of our ETA," he responded. He made his way toward the back of the plane and shut the office door.

Kat looked over at Samantha, who gazed out the window into the darkness of night. "Okay, I know witches don't have night vision, so what could possibly be so interesting out there? You've been boring a hole into the window ever since we left."

"Huh? Yeah, well, it's better than staring at you all. I feel caged up in this tiny excuse for a plane," Samantha replied tersely. She hadn't meant to sound so rude, but she was losing patience with the situation.

"You can put your claws back in, kitty-cat. What's everyone's problem around here, anyway?" Kat was taken off guard by Samantha's snarky attitude.

"Sorry, Kat. I just need to get this over with and done. I guess I'm just nervous," she lied. "So, what's with you and Luca? I was supposed to stay in his guest room when we get there, but I can go to the coven if that'd make you all more comfortable." She silently cursed herself for asking, but she couldn't take not knowing what was going on between the two of them. Were they lovers? Engaged?

"No need, I'm going to my brother's house. Marcel. He's the Alpha in New Orleans. I…I've been having a bit of guy trouble lately," she continued, looking out the window and then back to Samantha. "There's this Alpha in New York. He wants me as his mate. Tristan and I have both told him it's so not happening, but wolves don't always play fair. I'm worried he might try to take me. So, I figured I'd go see my other brother, and have him talk with my persistent suitor. Two brothers are better than one. Plus, I'll get to go wolf for a while down there, run with the pack in the bayou. I miss it."

Samantha studied Kat's face, confused by why she needed to escape to New Orleans and why Luca wouldn't just help her if they were together. It didn't make sense.

"But what about Luca? Why can't you just tell the New York Alpha you're with him?" she asked.

"Samantha, I'm not sure what you think you saw at Eden, but Luca and I are not mated, nor will we ever be. We're just very good friends who enjoy a good roll in the hay every now and then. Don't get me wrong, the man is yummy, but I should not have to lie about my relationship in order to rebuff an overly assertive Alpha who doesn't know the meaning of respect." Kat was starting to put two and two together. Samantha's cold demeanor; Luca's distant emotions combined with his lack of desire upstairs at Eden; his evident angst. Luca and Samantha were involved. It was all starting to make sense.

Samantha's eyes pricked with tears hearing Kat practically admit they'd had sex. She wanted to tear off her seatbelt and parachute out of the plane, so she could be anywhere but near the two of them. She managed to get control and took a deep swallow.

"It's none of my business, Kat. I'm glad you could get a ride with Luca so you'd be safe on your way to your brother's." Samantha tried to sound gracious, but in reality, she wanted to vomit. Part of her liked Kat, which made it all the worse knowing her and Luca had slept together.

"Hey, Samantha. I just…" Kat searched for the right words. "I just want you to know that Luca and I did not have sex today. I mean, I did come, but that was all. Oh God, that didn't come out right. Geez. Okay, it's like this. The man has got to eat. And I offered. And sure, I was hoping to get my freak on with him a little. I am single, after all. I mean, I had no idea you were together or anything. If I'd known, I would have never…"

"We are not together," Samantha spat out.

"Whatever you say, but I want you to know the truth. Luca, he didn't. We didn't. He just fed. Sure, I came but that's just a side effect of his bite. I'm sorry," Kat apologized. She came over to where Samantha was sitting and sat crosslegged in front of her on the floor. She placed her hands on Samantha's knees.

"Samantha, Tristan told me all about you, ya know. I thought we could be friends, because I know what it's like…what happened to you. Well, a very long time ago, it happened to me too. God, it seems hard to talk about even now." She rubbed her eyes and raked her fingers through her hair. "Simone. She took me too. And others. Tristan went to Kade for help. He and Luca found me. Luca dragged me out of that hell hole and brought me back to Marcel. We share a special bond because of that, he and I. And now, you and I. All I'm saying is that it gets better over time."

Samantha felt like a jerk for being so jealous and mean-spirited towards her. Maybe not Luca, because he damn well knew how she'd felt at the cabin.

"Kat," Samantha put her hands out to Kat's. "Thanks. No one else could possibly know what it's been like for me, and it helps to know there's someone else on God's green earth who understands what happened to me. It's been difficult." She blew out a breath and continued. "As for Luca, I wasn't lying. We really aren't together. We just shared a moment, and I thought it meant more than it did. But I appreciate you telling me what's going on with you two. As much as it pains me to admit it, I felt…I felt upset." It was the best Samantha could do at the moment.

"Hey, don't worry 'bout it. Whatever's goin' on with Luca, I suspect it wasn't 'just a moment' as you put it. I mean, he seems wound tighter than a two dollar watch. And for that man to turn down sex with moi," she laughed, "he'd have to either be a damn fool or starting to fall for someone else. And I'm guessin' the latter, girl."

Samantha smiled, feeling like a weight had been lifted off her. She might not know where she really stood with Luca, but it felt good to bond with another woman.

"Thanks, Kat. The only thing I'm sure of right now is that I've got to stay safe and help find whoever wants me dead. Piece of cake, right?" she joked, just as Luca came through the door.

He raised a questioning eyebrow at Kat as she buckled herself back into her seat. "Everything okay here?" he asked.

"Fine," both women answered at once. They both laughed and looked out the window.

The air in the plane felt lighter, but he wasn't sure what'd just transpired between the two very special supernatural ladies. He'd been on the earth for over two hundred years and still couldn't say he understood women. He did understand enough, though, to know he'd be having a very long conversation with Samantha when they got home.

Kat hugged Samantha tightly, before getting into the waiting limo. They had exchanged email and phone numbers so they could stay in touch. Luca waited until Samantha was done before embracing Kat. He was worried about the situation with the New York Alpha, but knew she'd be safe with Marcel.

"Listen, Kat. Call me if you need anything. I talked to Marcel, and he's going to help straighten out this mess." He kissed the top of her forehead. "Now, get going little wolf. Make sure those gators don't get your tail in the bayou," he teased as she ducked into the limo and shut the door.

Samantha and Luca got into the back of the other limo, and she purposefully put space between them by sitting on the side which faced the trunk. She was still irritated with him and questioned his intentions, but at the same time, she couldn't help noticing how great he looked tonight in his loose fit blue jeans and black t-shirt. His biceps were exquisitely carved, and she noticed he had a black tribal tattoo on the right one. She remembered the strength of his arms holding her up in the water, and wondered what it would be like if he bit her. Would she offer herself?

Her thoughts were broken when Luca shifted and sat beside her. She felt his jeans brush her bare leg, and struggled to act nonchalant.

"What are you doing?" she asked.

"What does it look like I'm doing? I'm sitting next to you," he smiled at her.

She shot him a look of annoyance. Moving closer to the window, she tried not to let her bare leg touch him again.

"So little witch, I think you and I need to have a bit of a talk," he said.

"Don't call me that," she insisted.

"You are testy, aren't you?" He took a deep breath. She wasn't going to make this easy. "I'm sorry for what happened at Eden."

"For what?" she feigned ignorance.

"Let's not play games," he countered.

"Games? Games? I don't know what you are even talking about, Luca." Samantha's normally soft voice was growing louder and louder.

"Yes, games. I know you're mad at me, and I know why. I just want to talk about it, so we can…"

"So we can what, Luca? What? I mean, this morning at the cabin we kissed; that was all. You don't owe me any explanations. Besides, Kat told me everything," she interrupted.

"Did she now?" he chuckled. *Women.* "I told you when I went to Eden I needed to feed. I prefer to have live donors. You see, when vampires feed…" He stopped himself from explaining any further as she looked straight at him and held up her hand to him.

"Just stop. I don't want to know," she stated.

"Okay, well here's the bottom line. Kat and I are friends who've known each other a very long time. I'm not going to lie to you, Samantha. In the past, we've been lovers, but we have never been a couple. And today, I just…I just needed to feed. And as much as I would love to taste your sweet blood, and believe me, I would, Kat was there."

"And you were going to make love to her?" Samantha asked.

"Yes," Luca answered quietly and truthfully. "But Samantha, I didn't." He reached over to run his fingers along the side of her face, and she brushed his hand away.

"But you wanted her?" Samantha challenged.

"No, Samantha, that's the thing. I wanted you," he whispered. He moved back to sit across from her as the car pulled into the driveway. Samantha's eyes widened in disbelief, and he wasn't sure what else he should say in the few minutes they'd have in the car. He decided to wait until they got settled before continuing the conversation.

Samantha didn't know how to respond. She was confused. Why would he take Kat instead of her if he did indeed want her like he said? She tried to think of how she would have reacted if Luca had asked her to let him feed from her. Would she have said yes or have gone running in the other direction? As much as she liked him, she couldn't honestly say that she would have said yes. She felt so raw from her abduction that she just wasn't sure she could trust someone to bite her, to risk putting herself in danger, to risk pain.

As they pulled into the Issacson compound, she gaped at the huge southern Victorian mansion. She didn't remember leaving there, but could still remember the luxurious prison cell accommodations located in the lower level of the home. She couldn't help but wonder what the rest of the place looked like.

The car circled around the front of the mansion and took a small, almost hidden road that was lined with breathtaking, majestic live oak trees. The private road went on for about one hundred feet until they reached a secondary Greek revival styled mansion, which was equally impressive, with its white columned entrance greeting its guests.

As the limo stopped, Luca got out of the car and offered his hand to Samantha. She stepped out of the car, and silently followed him to his home. At the front door, he flipped open a security panel, typed in a code and placed his face and palm into the box. Within seconds, the lock clicked open.

Samantha was impressed. "Biometric facial recognition, iris security and palm identification?"

Luca smiled. She was sexy and smart. "Yeah, well, you can't be too careful. Unlike Kade, I don't have any security personnel working in my home. What you can't see is the instantaneous DNA detection in the palm identifier. Look." He pointed to a black panel with a neon green outline of a hand on it. "It's hard to see, but there's a microscopic needle that extends into the thumb of the user. Facial recognition is great, and while this software is essentially hack-proof, there's still a small percentage of failure."

"Yeah, I read hackers have been trying to demonstrate failure. Even though it's a small percentage, I could see how if you were to invest in such a system you'd want redundancy," she commented.

As they walked into the foyer, Samantha was amazed to see Luca's finely decorated home, adorned with antiques and paintings. "Wow, Luca, your home is beautiful. It looks like a museum in here," she gasped.

"Thanks. I don't use the upper levels, though. It's pretty much for show. If I entertain, I use this first floor area for guests. But I don't live up here. Come on, follow me." Luca walked down a short hallway, punched another security code into the wall, and a door with an antiqued face opened. "This is it. Ladies first." He held out his hand to usher her down.

Motion detector lights illuminated the circular oak staircase which deposited them into a great room, which appeared more as Samantha had expected Luca's style to be; an ultra-modern bachelor's dream: sleek with minimal décor. A single chrome wall ran the length of the area; it was decorated with black and white still-life photos. The other three whitewashed brick walls complemented the cherry hardwood floors. A large overstuffed black leather sectional sofa directly faced a ninety-inch flat screen TV. Across from the living area, a half-moon, black granite bar swept around a small kitchen area. Royal-blue, spiral-shaped lights hung down from the ceiling from fine silver chains; the delicate illumination danced and reflected across the chrome walls.

His home screamed masculinity, refinement, and wealth. Yet as he tossed his phone on the bar, and pulled open the refrigerator, he seemed casual, relaxed and very much at home.

"So, this is where I spend most of my time. You can stay upstairs in the guest room, but I'd prefer it if you stay down here with me. I don't sleep much, so you can stay in the master bedroom, and I'll take the couch." He pulled out two bottles of water and set them on the counter.

Samantha ran her hand across the bar and sat down on one of the black and chrome stools. "Are you sure, Luca? It's bad enough that I agreed to stay with you. I feel badly putting you out of your bed." Luca. Bed. As she said the two words in a sentence she realized she'd much rather be saying a different sentence with those two words. *Luca, take me to bed.* She blushed, grabbed the water, opened it and drank it slowly, while looking up at Luca.

He could sense what she was thinking, and he needed to take this opportunity to set things straight with her. She was in his home now; his domain. He had control, and she was his. He walked around the bar, put his hands on her shoulders and began to rub her neck. Inhaling her feminine scent, he instantly hardened.

"What I said in the car, I meant. It's important we're clear." He continued massaging her as she released a tiny moan of pleasure.

"Today at the lake, I did not forget what had happened between us. How could I forget? But you must understand. For over two hundred years, there has been no one for me. Lovers, yes. But human lovers have been few and far between. I don't do relationships. And now, there is you." He shook his head, but she couldn't see because she held her head downward as he caressed her muscles. "Today at Eden when I saw you in the hallway, I felt guilty. I know that isn't what a woman wants to hear, but I could not ask you to let me feed from you. And I know Kat, and well…she was there. And if I'm being honest, I was trying to forget you."

Samantha slowly raised her head but just stared forward, afraid to look at him. "Why forget me?"

Luca stilled his hands and his breath hitched. He slowly swiveled her stool around so she was facing him. She instinctively reached out and placed her hands on his hips, but kept her head down.

"Because, my dear Samantha," he cupped her face, tilting her head upward to meet his gaze. "I want you more than I've ever wanted any woman in my life, and it scares the living hell out of me."

Luca took Samantha's hands, gently lifting her onto her feet. Reaching around the nape of her neck, he ran his fingers into her hair and pulled her towards him. Luca kissed her slowly, hungrily, wanting to savor her intoxicating essence. She was everything he remembered from the lake and more. So soft and pliant; he couldn't wait to sink himself deep within her.

A thousand butterflies danced in Samantha's tummy in anticipation of making love to Luca. She opened her lips as his mouth engulfed hers. He wanted to be with *her*. No, there would be no other women, just her. She'd decided in that moment to give herself to him, body, soul and blood.

Their tongues intertwined with one another as the kiss deepened, and Samantha rose on her toes, pressing herself tightly against his muscular torso. She could feel the hardness of his arousal against her belly and the growing ache between her legs.

Swiftly, Luca picked Samantha up, one arm behind her back and one under her knees. For a brief second, they stopped their kiss to gaze into each other's eyes. Samantha saw the fire burn within his eyes as they quickly flashed from green to red. This was who she wanted: her vampire. She reached up, cupped his cheek and let her pointer finger slide down into his mouth. He roared in erotic lust as his fangs elongated, and she stroked one of them.

"Samantha, are you sure?" he asked in a breathy, rugged tone. He was close to losing control, finally giving into his desire for his witch.

"Take me, Luca. Now," she softly demanded.

Luca carried her down the long hallway and kicked open the door to his bedroom. Candles along the shelving flickered into life at Luca's command. Samantha caught her breath at the sight of Luca's dominating presence. He was primal; pure unadulterated male. She grew wet awaiting his touch, the feel of him deep inside her sex.

He placed her feet on the floor and stood close to her, barely touching her, then brushed his face against the side of hers, smelling her hair. Luca's cock twitched at her feminine scent. He was turned on seeing her in an overwhelming state of arousal, her cheeks flushed, her breath quickened. She was ravishing. Never breaking eye contact with Samantha, he glided his palms down her shoulders, the sides of her arms, her hips, to the edge of her dress. He grabbed the hem of her sundress and deftly pulled it upward until she stood before him all but naked; she wore only a pair of black lace panties.

Samantha went to cover her breasts, but he grabbed her wrists and placed them back to her sides. "No. Leave your hands to your sides," Luca ordered. "Let me look at you. So very, very beautiful, you are. I was a fool to ever believe I could stop thinking of you."

Even though Samantha had gone skinny-dipping earlier, she felt oddly exposed standing perfectly nude in front of Luca while he was still dressed. Yet his request drove her mad with need, and she complied. Samantha moaned softly as Luca dropped to his knees and grabbed her ass, pulling her smooth taut stomach to his face.

Luca thought he'd died and gone to heaven. The smell of her silky soft skin against his face drove him wild. He wanted to taste every last inch of her. He could tell she was ready for him. Kissing her belly, his tongue celebrated the feel of her body against it as he made love to it. He'd tried so hard not to want what he shouldn't have. But now that he'd resigned himself to his feelings, he would take what she so freely offered.

"Stay very still, darlin'," he whispered. He ran his hands up her calves to her thighs and hooked his finger around the top of the lace. He teased her by running his pointer finger back and forth along the rim of her panties, barely brushing the top of her curls.

"Ah, Luca," she sighed. She went to wiggle away but Luca held her hips firm in his hands.

"Hmmm…you're so delightful, Samantha. I can smell your desire, you know. I can hardly wait to be deep inside you, but first…I must taste you. " Luca removed his hands from the sides of her panties and placed them behind her knees. Slowly he kissed the top of her belly, along the line of lace. Sliding his hands up the back of her thighs, his fingers slipped underneath the flimsy fabric until each hand was full with a curve of her ass. His thumbs hooked around her hips, jerking her towards him as his tongue teased an inch under the elastic in the front.

"Please, Luca," she pleaded. "You're driving me crazy. I need you, please touch me."

Grabbing the sides of her panties, he slowly eased them down and off her legs until she stood completely naked to him.

"I want you so much. I need to know you want this as much as I do. I won't be able to stop once I taste you." With his forehead pressed to her stomach, Luca waited for her approval. He wanted to make love with her, to taste her blood, to possess her.

"Yes, Luca, take all of me." Samantha's heart pounded against her chest as her adrenaline spiked. She felt a rush of excitement. She knew there was no going back, and she didn't want to. Her human life was over as she knew it, and Luca was her future. She'd known it from the minute he'd held her at the cabin. She waited in silence for Luca to respond.

He responded by softly kissing along the crease of her legs, as he gently sat her on the bed. Then he spread her legs open until he was comfortably caged between her knees. He quickly lost control as he teased her outer lips open with his tongue.

Samantha moaned loudly at his sweet invasion. Her hands fisted into his long raven hair as he kissed her sex mercilessly.

Luca flicked over her clit with the tip of his tongue, and heard Samantha release a small scream. She tasted delicious, so sweet and wet for him. Running his fingers into her soft red curls, he parted her so he could kiss her deeply. His tongue darted into her core as he brushed the pad of his thumb over her sensitive nub.

Samantha felt her blood rushing as Luca tormented her with oral finesse. She threw her head back in delight. "Yes, Luca. That feels so good.

Please don't stop," she begged.

Luca inserted a finger, then two, pumping into her as he licked her sensitive petal. He was careful not to nick her with his fangs, not yet. As she began to quiver in his arms, he could feel she was close.

Samantha began to shake as her arousal built. She bucked her hips up to him as he took her over the cliff of pleasure. She thought she saw stars dance as her orgasm tore through her. "Oh God, Luca. Yes!" she screamed.

Luca sucked on her clit as Samantha shook above him. Releasing her for merely a second, he licked over the smooth skin of her inner thigh, and bit into her. As the blood trickled into his throat, he groaned in delight at the taste of her. He wanted more of her magic-laced liquid, but restrained himself, licking the wounds shut.

In a silent haze, Luca stood up, while Samantha lifted her heavy-lidded eyes to meet his. Without speaking a word, she unbuckled his pants, never looking away. He pulled off his shirt, and Samantha grew aroused once again, admiring his rock-hard abs. His chest was smooth and muscular, his shoulders broad. He watched her with great intensity as she unzipped his pants. His cock sprung forward into her small soft hands.

Luca hissed as Samantha jerked him toward her slightly so she could lick the tip of him. His head rolled back when she cupped his testicles and began to run her tongue up and down his shaft.

Samantha hadn't given oral sex to very many men. But the instant she saw Luca's virile masculinity, she craved the taste of him. She deliberately glided her tongue along the sinewy length of him, and could detect a slight pulse as she swirled her lips over his tip. She held him firm with one hand as she parted her lips, seductively taking him into her mouth.

They held each other's gaze as she gently sucked him, back and forth, pumping him in and out; her warm soft lips firmly viced on his straining sex. This witch surely was performing a spell on him because he felt helpless in her hands. He growled as he struggled not to come.

"Darlin', you've gotta stop. Please. I want to be inside you." He put his hands on her shoulders, trying to cease the intense sensation. "Now." He gritted his teeth, resisting the urge to come.

As she released him, he pulled her to her feet, and they spilled into the bed together. She eased backwards on her hands and feet, feeling like a lion's prey, yet smiling, as if she was thoroughly enjoying the chase.

Luca stalked over to her on his hands and knees, until she was caged against the bed. He felt a primitive need to claim her, so she'd never know another man. With a hungry urgency, he leaned over and captured her lips.

Samantha deliriously explored his mouth, lost in his animalistic kiss. She wanted him so badly, feeling as if he were her first. And she knew in that moment, that there would be no other for her. Captivated by his raw power, she submitted to the overwhelming pleasure she felt within his snare.

Breathing heavily, he tore his lips from hers, yet again silently seeking her acceptance. She nodded, unable to speak, and he lowered his head to suckle the rosy tip of her breast. Samantha screamed in ecstasy as he bit gently and teased the shimmering bud.

Unable to submit to the glorious torture any longer, she found her voice. "Please Luca, I need you in me."

Reluctantly releasing her breast, Luca gazed into Samantha's eyes, and he slowly sheathed himself inside her. Samantha's eyes widened as she gasped. He halted his entrance to give her time to adjust to his substantial size. She started to rock up into him, letting him know she was ready for him. Luca groaned as he joined his body to hers fully.

"Aw, yes. You feel so warm and wet. You're amazing." He sucked her lip, until she opened for him. They kissed in rhythm as he began to pump in and out of her.

Samantha had never felt so womanly in all her life. No man had ever made her come before, and Luca's finely-tuned movements started to build yet another climax in her womb. He knew exactly how to brush his pelvis against her clit, teasing her senses, mounting her arousal and waning it back again.

Luca kissed up and down the alabaster skin of her neck, feathering kisses behind her ear down to her breast. He dipped his head down and suckled a sensitive peak. Holding himself up with one hand, he caressed the other aching bud. Samantha moaned with pleasure as he pinched the taut nub between his fingers. She responded in turn by wrapping her legs around his waist, driving him deeper into her tight moist heat.

Completely enveloped by her, Luca felt on the precipice of his own release. He began to hasten his movement, thrusting himself in and out of her softness.

Samantha couldn't hold herself back any longer as he slammed into her hard. She screamed against his throat as the climax rippled throughout her body. The pulsating sensation was so intense she shook against him.

Luca felt her tighten around him, massaging his hardness. Surrendering to the exquisite pleasure, he exploded within her. He felt as if he'd been hit by a lightning bolt, realizing his orgasm was like nothing he'd ever experienced in all his two hundred years. He wished it was her magic making him feel this extraordinary pleasure but knew it was his heart; she was taking it, and there was nothing he could do to stop himself from falling.

Chapter Eight

Luca opened his eyes and glanced down at the beautiful woman in his arms. After making love the previous night, they had both fallen into a deep sleep. It was a rare indulgence for Luca to sleep with a female. He listened to her heartbeat and felt the rise of her belly with her every breath. Samantha had somehow touched his heart, and he couldn't even say in that moment that he regretted giving it to her. After two hundred years of a self-imposed moratorium on love, he couldn't resist Samantha. She was vulnerable, yet intelligent and strong. She was a survivor, and Luca admired her spirit and resolve.

Thinking of Eliza, he knew she would want him to move on and be happy. It had been such a long time. And while he truly did love Eliza, it was a young man's love that had attracted him to her. He wondered how he would have felt after years of marriage to her if they hadn't been attacked. Yet it had been a different time then. Women were very proper, and he'd been quite the respectable lad. The truth was that he'd never known Eliza in a biblical sense. They'd only kissed, which had been appropriate for that time period.

As he lay spooning Samantha, he pulled her closer to him. Luca might not have wanted a human lover, but now that he'd made love with her, he was certain he'd never let her go. Deep inside her last night, he'd fought the urge to claim Samantha. If he'd bitten her during climax, they would begin to bond. But he wasn't sure how Samantha felt about him. Did she want to live with him? He was vampire, and she'd barely adjusted to the fact that she was a witch. She was adamant about returning to her life in Pennsylvania.

He found himself dreaming of her, what it would be like to have her live with him; turning the mansion into a home instead of a showcase of expensive antiques and paintings. Could they have children? The idea of Samantha having his children excited him, as he regretted never having had any before he was turned. While most vampires were sterile to humans, he'd heard rumors from the witches that they could be impregnated. One night while attending a coven party with Ilsbeth, he'd been told that because of a witch's magical blood, they, in only very special circumstances, could accept the infertile vampire sperm into their body and infuse it with their life-force, creating the perfect conditions for fertilization. He made a mental note to check with Ilsbeth to see if this was simply an urban legend, or a real possibility.

While Luca stroked Samantha's delicate hand, her eyes started to flutter.

She didn't want to wake up from the wonderful fantasy she'd experienced last night. Encased in Luca's well-built arms, she felt safe, happy and loved. *Loved?* The minute the thought popped into her mind, she tried to push it away. No, vampires like Luca don't do love. He'd already told her that he didn't get involved with mortals, let alone fall in love with them. Yet she couldn't shake the thought. Luca was such a caring and sensual lover, like no other man she'd ever been with. She'd only been with a handful of lovers over the years, but none had ever made her come. Most men just quickly came, and then asked her if it was good for her. But Luca was different; he knew exactly what he was doing and played her body like a virtuoso played a Stradivarius. She tingled, thinking about the mad earth-shattering orgasm she'd experienced under his hand. He was a master.

Growing aroused, Samantha pushed her bottom backwards, feeling the hardness of him. She began to rock back and forth, brushing against his erection.

Luca squeezed Samantha as she began to grind against him. "Good morning, my little witch," he said, kissing the top of her head. "This is the finest way I've woken up in a long time. But are you sure you're ready for me?"

"Ummm….yes Luca. I can't seem to get enough of you," she purred as she increased the pressure.

Luca reached both hands around her and cupped her breasts, gently caressing her pink flesh. "I can't seem to keep my hands off of you, either. I need to have you, be in you." He kissed the back of her neck, sending chills down her arms. Luca's straining shaft eased into her warm heat in one hard thrust from behind.

"Ah, yes, Luca!" Samantha screamed.

"My God, you feel so good. I won't last long this morning. You're so tight. Hmmm." Luca massaged her breast in one hand while he reached into her warm, wet folds. He began to rock in and out of her, slow and steady while he feathered his fingertips over her clitoris.

Luca's fangs elongated; there'd be nothing more satisfying than drinking her sweet blood while climaxing inside her. But if he did that, the bonding would begin. He fought the urge, retracting his fangs, and kissed along the back of her neck instead.

"Please Luca," Samantha begged. "I need to…I have to…" her breathless words trailed off.

He knew what she needed, and he needed it too. Losing control, Luca increased his pace and felt them going off the cliff of pleasure into a simultaneous release. Samantha yelled out Luca's name as they both rode out the incredible final moment of ecstasy.

Luca just held Samantha, not wanting to let her go. "Samantha, you're so intoxicating, darlin'. I…I just want you to know that I'm glad you came down here with me." He wanted to tell her how he felt, but registered the oddest sensation of fear, a rare feeling indeed for a two hundred year old vampire. What if she wanted to leave and go back to Pennsylvania? He'd never see her again; he knew a long distance relationship would never work.

"I didn't want to come down here, but I can't say that I'm upset right now. What we shared Luca....it was incredible. Thank you," she whispered.

He could feel Samantha's breathing slow; she was falling asleep again. Easing himself from the bed, he went to take a shower. He needed to get the upper hand of his emotions before he lost control to the seductive female in his bed.

Samantha woke alone, experiencing an odd sense of loss that he'd left her. She looked around the spacious room, noticing the sleek, modern furnishings. His black, king-sized platform bed stood alone save for a long matching bureau and armoire. It was a sharp contrast to the antique furnishings upstairs, and she found herself wondering if he'd decorated both. While he seemed to consider this subterranean domicile his primary home, he clearly must have had a hand in the magnificent interior décor on the first floor. Perhaps this suited Luca's dynamic personality. On the one hand he was stoic, refined and dominating, yet he'd showed her that he could be caring, erotic and loving.

At the cabin, he didn't mince words when he gave her no choice in returning, even threatening to enthrall her, and then last night, he seemed to open up about what had happened at Eden, when he could have simply ignored how she felt. He'd made love to her with primal fury, yet he'd made sure she was in agreement about moving forward at every turn. He'd showed a gentleness and tenderness she hadn't experienced from any man in her life, ever.

Softly padding across the wooden floor, Samantha felt her stomach grumble. Vampires might not need actual food, but she needed to eat something soon. She also realized how sore she was from all the lovemaking with Luca. She sighed and smiled, thinking of how she'd lost all sense of responsibility with him. He was a gloriously irresistible male.

Pushing open the bathroom door, she was impressed by the oversized charcoal, soapstone shower lined with beveled glass blocks. A shelved wall held black, neatly folded, clean towels. Two gray pedestal sinks stood in front of a single, wall-sized square mirror. Masculine and luxurious, she thought. She reached over to the shower head and turned on the water. After waiting a few minutes, she stepped into the hot steamy spray, enjoying the beat of the droplets on her back.

She startled, hearing a door open, but settled when she saw the outline of her sexy vampire through the glass. Luca poked his face into the shower, taking a long drink of her bare creamy white skin. Smiling back, she wished he'd join her.

As if reading her mind, he grinned. "Hello darlin', as much as I'd like to join you, if I do I'm afraid we won't get any work done today. It's nearly three in the afternoon, and we've got an appointment with Ilsbeth at six. We'll start with her, and then go from there. While you were asleep, Sydney stopped over and brought you a goody bag. Clothes, toothbrushes, good stuff like that. Anyway, she and Kade haven't found any leads, but they're on call if we need them. We have some things to discuss with Ilsbeth, including having a little chat about that rain making trick you did at the cabin." He winked at her, sending a thrill up her spine.

"Okay, sounds good. I'm anxious to get this over with," she said, using both her hands to apply the conditioner through her long mane. As she leaned back into the spray, her firm breasts pushed out toward Luca, beckoning him into the shower.

Luca raked his fingers through his hair. "You're killing me. You know, I'm finding it hard to resist you, let alone wet and naked."

She shot him a wry grin. "Then why don't you join me?" She turned her face into the drizzle, wiggling her behind at him.

Luca adjusted himself as he blew out a breath. They'd never get anything done, making love all day. "Later, temptress. I've got brunch out here for you, courtesy of Sydney. Now come on and hurry up. We've got work to do."

Samantha squeaked as she felt a firm spank on her butt cheek. She laughed and complied, turning off the water. She was hungry, and Luca was right. They needed to do research and get information out of Ilsbeth. She was tired of being a victim. Whoever was doing this had sorely underestimated her ability to fight back.

Eating a wonderful array of fresh fruit, beignets and bacon, Samantha listened to Luca tell her about the writing at the cabin.

"Hematilly Periapt? What's that?" she asked.

"A periapt is an amulet. They're usually made by someone of magic, like a witch, warlock or mage. So for example, if it was blessed with white magic, it would be used for something good, like protection. But I'm guessing that it has been created by someone using black magic, and has a nefarious purpose like hexing or perhaps a curse. To be honest, I've got no idea what it does or why someone would want it. But it must be pretty important to someone, given they followed you to Pennsylvania and burned down a building to try to get it."

"But why would anyone think I have it? I mean, I don't remember much of what happened to me, but I can tell you that I don't have it. This is the first I've heard of it. I swear. I don't even know what it looks like or what it does."

"I'm not sure. But this has got to do with Asgear. He probably has something to do with this, or should I say, had something to do with it."

"Can't we just search his house? What about that warehouse Sydney told me about?"

"No. Kade and Sydney searched all his properties after the crypt was destroyed. He owned the warehouse in the business district, which has since been demolished, thanks to Kade. They also ran a search to see if he owned any other properties and came up empty. Now he may have owned or rented other properties under an alias, but so far there's no evidence of their existence. The periapt could literally be anywhere in or out of this city," Luca speculated.

"Well, I can't just sit around doing nothing until we go see Ilsbeth. If this thing is real, maybe there's something about it online. I know that the witches were in the process of converting some of their books over to digital versions, in case of flood or fire. Of course, I wasn't allowed access to anything when I was at the coven, but I heard them talking about it."

"We can ask Ilsbeth to let us see the books when we go there tonight," Luca suggested.

"No offense, Luca, but the witches aren't going to let a vampire look at their books. The one thing I learned in my week there is that they are very secretive. And since I didn't agree to join their sisterhood, I wasn't allowed in the library either. We can ask Ilsbeth, but I know she'll say no. Don't get me wrong, she can be very kind. But she also can be a tough as nails bitch. She does not bend rules, period. Besides, I think we should try a backdoor approach at the same time we're playing nice."

"What do you mean, backdoor?" He smiled at her, knowing she had something up her sleeve.

"Well, if they are putting all the books into a database, then we just take a peek," she proposed. "You know, hack in and look at the files and then sneak out. I can do this, Luca."

"Very impressive, tell me more."

"I'm considered a 'white hat' hacker. That means I purposefully spend time trying to hack into systems to expose their weaknesses, so that I can help clients and our company. There are some folks out there who are considered 'black hat' hackers. They do the same thing, but they're not doing it to help anyone. They might be stealing or just trying to cause trouble. There are other titles in the hacking world too, like 'grey hats' who break in and then offer to fix systems for a fee. Regardless, I've had to learn all kinds of hacking techniques when I'm testing. The only caveat is that hacking isn't always as quick as they make it seem in the movies. If I can't find a gaping hole in their system, I may need to try a few other tactics that might take longer," she explained.

Prior to her abduction, Samantha had worked as a high level computer engineer for a large government contractor and was known to be one of the best 'white hat' hackers in her division; she regularly attempted to hack their own computer systems as part of quality assurance. If the *Hematilly Periapt* existed and its information had been recorded digitally, she could find it.

A business call interrupted them, and Luca took it in his office, leaving Samantha to work. Borrowing Luca's laptop, she ran a search on 'Hematilly Periapt', suspecting that initial searches would turn up nothing. She had a hunch that this item was only known in supernatural circles and wouldn't show up on poser sites. People who knew about the amulet were not wannabe witches or vampires. And whoever was threatening her and looking for this item knew that it held seriously potent power; they'd been willing to kill for it.

Samantha knew the coven had a huge physical library that she hadn't been given access to yet. Ilsbeth had told her that she'd be given the key once she'd completed her training and had sworn allegiance to the coven. Rowan, a young but powerful witch who worked as the librarian, had befriended Samantha. Although she was kind during Samantha's training, she had gone out of her way to tell Samantha to stay away from the mystical athenaeum. At the time, Samantha hadn't thought twice to ask about the room, why she couldn't go in there or what kinds of archives were stored within. She just knew that she wasn't allowed to go in the library, and that there would be serious consequences for breaking coven rules. But now she wanted very badly to see what was hidden behind those doors.

The one thing that Rowan had let slip during tea one day was that the witches had started moving information to online storage, as it could be safely backed up. Critical data could be kept safe from all kinds of natural disasters and recovered easily. If for some reason their wards failed to protect the coven house, a fire could take out their library within minutes.

Contemplating where to search next, Samantha typed in the name of the coven, *Cercle de lumière Vieux Carre*, and waited. A single site popped up in her Google search and she clicked. A blank screen flashed onto her computer with two blank spots for identification and password. Knowing she wouldn't have the identification, she'd need to obtain another witch's security information, or find a weakness in their system. Samantha switched windows, and logged into her home server, so she'd be able to pull over the software she needed to hack in.

Within minutes, she ran a vulnerability scanner on the coven's site. She was hoping easy in, but it didn't show any cracks. *Damn.* "I'll find your secrets," she muttered to herself. "It may take a while, but I'll get in."

Picking up her cell phone, she moved forward with a typical 'black hat' hacker approach and called the hosting system administrator's number that she'd been able to search out. Unfortunately for Samantha, they'd been well trained and had not given up the security information despite her name-dropping and helpful attitude. She had to give them credit for not falling for her tactics.

Being one never to give up, she decided to resort to her most reliable but time-consuming method for breaking into computer systems. She accessed both Rowan and Ilsbeth's email addresses and sent them an email letting them know about the cabin burning and that she was looking forward to seeing them tonight. The email looked innocuous enough, but in reality she'd attached a worm to it. When opened, the worm would infiltrate their systems and attach a key-logging application with a Trojan horse to keep it hidden. The second Ilsbeth or Rowan accessed the online site, their keystrokes would be recorded and sent via messaging to Samantha's iPhone. They'd never be any the wiser, and eventually Samantha would get the passwords.

She felt a little badly for taking advantage of their kindness, but she knew they'd never simply agree to give her access. It had been made clear that unless she was a fully-fledged member, she would not get access, online or otherwise. Knowing that having information on the *Hematilly Periapt* was a matter of life or death justified the hacking, in Samantha's mind. She would ask Ilsbeth in person tonight again for access, and if granted, she'd remove the software. But until that happened, she'd wait for the passwords to pop up on her hack.

Samantha shut the laptop and decided to go upstairs to look around Luca's mini-museum. It was almost five in the afternoon, and they needed to leave soon. She peeked into Luca's office and told him she was going upstairs to look around. He was on the phone, clearly listening, but yet he gave her the okay sign when she told him where she'd be.

Her breath caught as she entered the great room on the main floor. The tan walls were offset by the cream wainscoting; the entire first floor was richly decorated with both paintings and sculptures. Samantha resisted the temptation to run her fingers across the floral upholstery of a lovely French empire settee. Its mahogany arms were rolled and adorned with acanthus leaf carvings. She'd never seen anything so beautiful or intricately designed.

Samantha's eye caught a spectacular oil painting which had been set in a sophisticated gold leaf frame. She studied the landscape, admiring the way the artist appeared to capture the sun's rays.

"You like?" Luca came up behind her. Samantha jumped, but calmed under the touch of his fingers on her shoulders. "Paysage vers Canes-sur-Mer by Renoir. Lovely, isn't it?"

"Stunning. I can't believe you have all this stuff. No wonder you have such a serious security system. It's like the Smithsonian in here."

Luca chuckled. "All memories. Keepsakes. But I see nothing here as beautiful as you." He released her shoulders to move over to the baby grand piano. He'd been accumulating all the art pieces for well over a century. Kade had suggested he needed a hobby, so he'd started collecting, piece by piece. "Some pieces are souvenirs. Others I just wanted for my collection. Kade said I needed to find something constructive to do with my time, immortal as I am, so I started antiquing. I live in New Orleans after all," he joked.

"That you do," Samantha said in amazement as she walked over to look at a marbled bust of a woman that sat on the hearth of the old fireplace. "She's beautiful." She touched the cheek of the marble and then quickly withdrew her hand, fearing she'd break something. "She must be a very important lady to command the attention of the room."

Luca frowned. "She was…she was my fiancée, Eliza."

Samantha's stomach dropped. He'd been engaged. She had never thought that Luca might have been married. She silently admonished herself for being jealous of a dead woman. "Your fiancée? I'm sorry. I assume she's passed."

"Yes, it was a very long time ago. She was killed before I had the chance to marry her…before I was vampire. I had an Italian artist create this in her memory. Such a long time ago but the memories remain." Looking out the windows to the gardens, he didn't want to say any more about Eliza to Samantha. It didn't seem the right time to tell her all the sordid details of how she met her demise. He felt he'd told Samantha enough of the truth for now. If and when they grew closer, he'd share the story with her.

Samantha resisted pressing him for details, realizing Luca didn't want to talk about it. She knew what it was like to experience loss, and understood that there were times in life when you just needed to let things go. When he was ready to talk about it, he would tell her. She was about to tell him not to worry about telling her the details, when a tall gorgeous woman burst into the great room, looking pissed as hell. It took all of two seconds before Samantha realized the angry female was a vampire.

Glaring at Samantha, the woman bared her fangs and hissed. "You little bitch! I knew you survived Asgear, but I heard you'd left. What the fuck is she doing here, Luca?" she demanded to know. "No, don't even tell me because I don't care. I told you I'd get her back for what she did to me and now it's game on."

The livid female vampire raced across the room with preternatural speed, knocking the wind out of Samantha as she grabbed her around the throat and held her against the wall. Samantha's eyes bulged as she watched Luca snatch the other vampire with one hand and throw her across the room. He growled as Samantha held up a hand to him indicating she was okay.

"Dominique!" he yelled. He strode across the room, where the woman shot daggers at him, looking like she was ready for round two. "Enough! It's over. You will apologize now. And if you ever touch her again, I'll stake you myself."

The woman vampire acquiesced and quickly stood up, holding both her hands up in surrender. "Me? Apologize? Luca, how can you take her side? You know what she did! How could you?" she pleaded.

"She is mine," Luca declared. "And you will not touch her. You will treat her with respect. She doesn't even remember what happened to her. Samantha," he glanced over to her and back. "This is Dominique. Unfortunately, when you were bespelled, you silvered her. And while she did suffer that night, she is no worse for wear as you can see. She most definitely does hold grudges but she will be respectful in your presence. Isn't that correct, Dominique?"

"Goddamn you Luca. I can smell you all over her. Yes, I will try not to kill your plaything," Dominique spat through her teeth with a sickening sweet smile that promised retribution. She hated having to follow Luca's order but would do it for him. He was her superior.

"Now that we're done with introductions, I believe you'd best get back to Kade's to continue working. Dominique is the Director of Public Relations for Issacson Industries. We have a downtown office, but she spends a lot of time here if Kade is working from home. She also helps me with security when needed." Luca came to stand next to Samantha and put his arm around her shoulder; he wanted it to be clear to Dominique that Samantha was his. "We're going over to see Ilsbeth. I'll contact you later if I need your assistance. Goodbye, Dominique."

Dominique shot Samantha an icy scowl and nodded at Luca. "Goodbye, Luca. I hope you know what you're getting into with this one," she huffed. As Dominique walked out the door, she slammed it in defiance.

"Are you okay?" he asked, checking Samantha's neck for injuries.

"I'm fine, just a bit shaken up is all."

"Dominique can be a bit of a handful, but she's very loyal. I promise that she won't hurt you now that I've talked with her."

"I sure as hell hope so. That was one pissed off vampire bitch." Samantha rubbed her neck. "I don't even remember her, but I certainly will now."

"I'm really sorry about her. She'll get over it, though. I meant what I said to her, and she knows it," he assured Samantha.

"Thanks, Luca. I appreciate you saving me. She's kinda scary," she admitted.

Luca couldn't resist pulling Samantha against his hard chest. He caressed her back and neck. Her shiny red hair now smelled of peaches, and he smiled, remembering how responsive she'd been the night before. She'd nearly killed him when she took him into her mouth. Growing aroused, he knew it wasn't the time to start something he couldn't finish. They needed to go soon and get some answers. He reluctantly released Samantha, putting some needed distance between them.

"Darlin', as much as I'd like to play museum curator and show you all my fun toys, we'd better get going over to the coven. I'm barely holding onto control. If we don't leave within the next five minutes, I might be tempted to have my way with you yet again," he teased.

"And I might like that very much," she countered. She blushed, thinking about how they'd made love the night before. She'd never met a man who could make her climax during intercourse, let alone make her feel as if she'd gone directly to heaven. It was as if he intimately knew every square inch of her body so well that he could send her into a blinding rapture with just his lips.

Luca could tell Samantha was silently reminiscing about how incredible last night had been for them both. The mind blowing sex wasn't something he'd soon forget. He couldn't remember ever having been with someone who was so vibrant and loving. Envisioning her beneath him, writhing in pleasure, he groaned, willing his erection to subside. He needed to think about something else besides making love to Samantha.

"So did you have any luck getting into the database?" he asked, grabbing his keys off of a hallway desk.

"Yeah, about that. I tried breaking into the coven database, while you were on the phone. It was pretty tight, so I have to take a more indirect approach. I sent both Rowan and Ilsbeth emails that have a hidden key stroking tracking worm attached. I'll be alerted once they go online and then we can nab the password. It might take a little while but the method is tried and true." Samantha was confident they'd have the passwords within the day. Ilsbeth might not go online that often, but she was sure that Rowan would do so, since she actively worked in the library.

"Smart and beautiful." Luca hugged her and brushed a light kiss on her lips. "We'd better go now, before I decide to take you back downstairs and ravish you senseless." Luca wished he was joking but knew she was quickly becoming an irresistible vice.

Chapter Nine

Samantha and Luca sat in the parlor waiting on Ilsbeth. Feeling her hands tingle, Samantha wondered if maybe she was feeling her magic. The only other time she'd felt a similar feeling was at the cabin. In an effort to dull the sensation, she closed her eyes, breathed in a deep breath, held it for five seconds and then blew it out. She reasoned that she might know shit about magic but she was pretty good at meditation. Relaxation seeped through her veins as she repeated the exercise.

It was not that she hated the idea of the existence of a witch's coven; she just hated what it personally represented. It was where she'd been sent to be cleansed of the dirt that had tainted her very soul. Whatever Asgear had done to her was beyond human reason, possibly demonic. She shuddered, wondering what could have happened if the evil had been allowed to grow within her. Would she have stolen? Murdered? Learned and utilized black magic for her own gain?

The thought of deliberately hurting someone made her sick; it all seemed unbelievable. Even after she'd left the coven to return to Pennsylvania, she'd felt normal, perfectly human. But she couldn't deny the surge of electricity and power that she had called when pushed into a fit of rage. Seeing the cabin ablaze had given birth to an uncontrollable reaction.

"Luca. Samantha. So glad to see you safely made it back to New Orleans." The lilt of Ilsbeth's voice jilted Samantha back into reality. Ilsbeth sat in a chair across from Luca and Samantha, who sat side by side on the sofa. Noticing their closeness, Ilsbeth quietly smiled. "Samantha, you are welcome to move back into the coven and continue your training," she offered.

"No thank you," Samantha refused kindly. "I…I'm staying with Luca." She looked to him for comfort and then returned her gaze to Ilsbeth. "We came because we need your help with a few things. The first is my magic. I did something in Pennsylvania that I think you should know about. The cabin I was staying at. Well, someone set it on fire. I was so angry and scared, and before I knew what was happening, something called to me within, like my skin was crawling. I felt out of control, like electricity was bolting through my body. I felt this need…to call rain. And it worked. It rained and put out the fire. I guess I just wanted you to know…" Samantha's voice trailed off as she stared at Ilsbeth. *God, I sound crazy. Although I'd take crazy over 'witch' right now.*

Laughing out loud, Ilsbeth stood and began to pace the length of the room. "This is wonderful, Samantha! Don't you see? Of course you don't.

How would you know?" She quickly returned to her seat and held Samantha's hands. "It sounds as if you are an elemental witch, my dear. The elements: fire, water, earth and wind. They will come to you when needed and when called. You may not have good control right now, but with practice, you will be quite powerful someday. Please consider returning to the coven. It will be great fun to teach you."

"Thank you for the offer, Ilsbeth. But right now, I need to stay with Luca. He's keeping me safe. Nothing has happened since with my magic. I'll let you know if something else does. I guess that I'm just…I'm just not ready for this. Maybe someday." She sounded unsure, but after all, she didn't seem to get a choice about when or how the magic came. She didn't want Luca to send her back to Ilsbeth. "I promise to think it over, but right now we've got a more pressing problem. Whoever is after me wants something called a *Hematilly Periapt*. Do you have any idea what it is, or why someone would want it?" she asked.

Ilsbeth's face hardened; her lips pressed together in a fine line. An icy sheet fell across her face. "Now listen here, I am not sure who told you about that, but the *Hematilly Periapt* is not to be trifled with. It's a very powerful amulet, and it belongs in the care of a coven. No one currently knows its location and thankfully, it is probably lost or destroyed. Whoever is asking for it is nothing but trouble. Now, I suggest you forget about it."

Samantha hesitated then pressed forward. "Ilsbeth, I'm sorry if this line of questioning bothers you. But someone could have killed us and they wanted that amulet. And for some ungodly reason, they think I have it. So please forgive us, but I have to ask about it. Could you tell us, you know, if you had to take a wild guess, who might have it or where you think we should start looking for it?"

"Samantha, maybe I am not making myself clear. There are certain things that are not up for discussion. You are welcome to train with us, to be accepted within the sisterhood. By doing so, there are many secrets that will become known to you. Until that time, I am sorry, there is nothing I can do to help you," Ilsbeth replied coldly. She stood as if expecting them to leave. "Is there anything else I can help you with? I'm very busy."

"Would it be all right if I went up to my old room? I think I may have left some notes there, and I really would like to collect them. I wanted to keep a journal of my transformation," Samantha asked. It couldn't hurt to look around to see if perhaps she'd left any clues during her time at the coven. Samantha barely remembered the first few days she'd spent there, but there was a small chance she'd left a note about the amulet. It was a long shot, but grasping at straws was about the only thing she could do, now that Ilsbeth had clammed up about the *Hematilly Periapt*.

"Please, feel free to search your room. However, I believe the sisters have cleaned the area of any belongings you may have left behind. I'm serious, Samantha. No more talk of the periapt. Sometimes just talking about something can affect our universe," she warned.

Samantha nodded and hurried up the stairs.

Luca stood to walk Ilsbeth to the foyer. "Ilsbeth, I do have one more question, which may seem quite odd. Definitely off topic."

"Yes, what is it, Luca?

"It's rumored that it's possible for witches to bear the child of a vampire. Is this true?" He knew Ilsbeth would put the puzzle pieces together and surmise what he was thinking. At the same time, he needed to know if it was possible for him to father a child.

Ilsbeth's face softened, and she smiled slightly. She put her hand on Luca's forearm. "Yes, it's true, Luca. It is uncommon but has occurred a number of times over the centuries…very rare, though. I certainly would not plan a future based upon it. Witches bear children to humans and witches…sometimes shifters. It is the natural course of our kind. Luca, I'm not sure what you're thinking, but please be cautious in how you proceed in your relationship with Samantha. I can see how she trusts you. I must counsel you to be honest with her before you decide to claim her. She's getting stronger, but she's still fragile," she advised.

"She may have once been fragile, but she is not as delicate as you would think. In fact, she's quite a bright and capable woman," Luca acknowledged.

"Luca, today you are full of surprises. I never thought I'd see the day when you would come to care for a human woman, albeit a witch. Very interesting indeed," Ilsbeth smiled slyly. "Take care, Luca. Please keep her safe." Shaking her head in disbelief, she turned and walked behind the shimmering curtain that blocked the view of visitors from seeing further into the coven's home.

Luca considered Ilsbeth's insights. Yes, Samantha was emotionally delicate. But that was only because of the unwanted circumstances that had been thrust upon her; she'd suffered a loss of control. Luca reasoned that any human would have crumbled, given the same situation. Samantha could have chosen to give up, but instead, she'd fought with him to get her life back, to find out who was after her. Luca knew that Samantha was substantially stronger than he'd initially judged. She'd proven herself resilient and resourceful at each step of the journey; she was more determined than ever to find the *Hematilly Periapt* and get her life in order.

Upstairs, Samantha feverishly searched her guest room for evidence of an amulet or some kind of clue. When she'd spent time at the coven, she'd written herself little notes every day, hoping that one would spark her lost memory. She was certain that she had left a few in the room when she left for Pennsylvania. Yet, scouring the room, she could barely find a speck of dust in the cleaned out desk, let alone any of her memos. No wonder

Ilsbeth had allowed her to search her room; everything she'd written had been thrown in the trash.

Samantha walked down the circular, cedar-lined hallway. As she approached the library, Rowan, the librarian, sat working at her desk, guarding the entrance. She sat in front of the ornately-carved wooden doors, working on her laptop, appearing not to notice Samantha. Rowan's long, frizzy black hair cascaded over her petite figure. She was oddly attractive, dressing as if she was a college student, in a mini-skirt with a sharply pressed white oxford shirt. While she looked as if she was only in her twenties, Samantha knew that she was nearly fifty years old.

Casually approaching the witch, Samantha cleared her throat. "Hi Rowan, long time no see."

"Ah you're back, Sam. Are you moving back into your old room?" she inquired.

"Uh…no, well not yet. Right now, I'm staying with a friend," Samantha responded. "I was just looking for my notes in my old room, but I guess they were thrown out. I really need to get going but I thought I'd stop by and say hi on the way out. I'm not sure when I'll be back. Do you have my cell number? Maybe we could go out for coffee sometime," she suggested.

"Yeah, sure." Rowan cautiously eyed Samantha, wondering why she was roaming around the coven hallways unescorted. She made a mental note to discuss this incident with Ilsbeth. Samantha was nice, but she wasn't a sister. They couldn't afford that kind of security lapse. Rowan got up from her desk and stood protectively in front of the library doors, guarding its entrance.

Typing numbers into their cell phones, Rowan and Samantha politely exchanged numbers. Samantha wanted to ask Rowan to let her into the library, but knew it would never happen. She might be friendly, but she was nothing short of ruthless when it came to protecting coven secrets. Explaining that she had a friend waiting, Samantha quickly ran down the coven steps and into Luca's waiting arms. On an intellectual level, Samantha knew the coven was supposed to feel like home, but on an emotional level, it felt like a prison and she couldn't wait to leave.

Luca turned the ignition and tried to figure out how he'd pitch his next idea to Samantha. They had come up with practically nothing at the coven. It was clear that Ilsbeth didn't want them to have the amulet or speak of it, but besides that, they didn't have much more information than before they came. If the object scared Ilsbeth, that was not a good sign.

Luca wondered what the amulet did that caused Ilsbeth to insist they stop looking for it. He knew one fact for certain; it was important enough that someone would murder in order to get it. It was possible that Asgear had had the amulet and then that Samantha had stolen it at some point. Perhaps she'd hidden it? Samantha's memory had failed her so far, and Luca wasn't sure he wanted her to remember the rest of the gory details of her abduction. Overnight, Samantha had appeared to grow stronger, and he didn't want to risk a relapse.

The problem, Luca surmised, was that there weren't many places he was aware of that they could even search. The only two locations she'd been at for certain were the mausoleum in St. Louis cemetery and Sangre Dulce, where Samantha had been bespelled into posing as a waitress and submissive. The mausoleum was out of the question, because it had been destroyed. Dominique and Ilsbeth had taken care of that.

As for Sangre Dulce, Luca was concerned about taking her back to the club. If they went back, there was a risk she could be traumatized all over again. When she'd been in Kade's basement during her initial interrogation, she'd nearly fainted after being shown pictures of herself nude, serving drinks. She only had a vague memory of having a drink with a man, James, who was really Asgear. No other memories existed for her.

Shifting in his seat, he drove towards home and sighed. "So listen, Samantha," he began. "Since Ilsbeth was a bust, we don't have many options. I have a plan, but I'm not sure you're going to like it." He didn't bother looking over at Samantha to gauge her reaction, and kept his eyes fixed on the road.

"Well, let's just say, I'm open to suggestions. There was nothing in my old room. In fact, they'd cleaned the place out. And until Ilsbeth or Rowan try to log into the coven site, we can't hack into their server. So, whatever's on your mind has got to be better than the whole lot of nothin' we've got now." She shrugged and glanced over at him.

"Okay, if you're open to it, here goes. I'm thinking it's a real possibility that Asgear stole or found this amulet. Maybe he knew what it did, maybe he didn't. I'm also thinking that maybe you took it and hid it before or during being bespelled. Just because he bespelled you, it doesn't mean you liked him. He could have told you what it did, and you inherently knew he wouldn't put it to good use. Now, how someone else knows you were with him or that you might have had it, is a true mystery." Luca steeled himself before telling Samantha that they were returning to her living hell. "I think that we need to go back to Sangre Dulce to take a look around, maybe talk to the other waitresses, look for clues. We know you were there."

Samantha silently contemplated his proposal. She loathed the idea of returning to that club. It had forever fucked up her life: one decision to go out with friends, one decision to have a drink with a stranger. Going back could bring back her memory or not. She wasn't even sure she wanted to remember. She could literally pick up with her life and move on, not having to worry about the frightening lost memories. Yet if she went back to the club, she might possibly find evidence to lead them to the amulet. Whoever was looking for that damn thing would not leave her in peace until they got it. There was a real possibility that she had done exactly what Luca had postulated. She would never know until she tried.

"Yes. Let's do it," she agreed.

"You sure?" he asked.

"Yes. Until we find this amulet, I'll never get my life back. I need this, Luca. I need normalcy. Maybe supernaturals are used to living in a state of constant stress and chaos, but I'm not. I want my boring, Starbucks drinking, nine to five working life back. It wasn't much but there's one thing I've realized; when you lose everything…your job, your home, your identity, the only person who can put the pieces back together again is you. I've got to do this." She caught Luca's eyes and put her hand on his thigh.

He reached down and covered her small hand with his. Slowly rubbing the inside of her palm with his calloused thumb, he realized how protective he'd become of her. She was so beautiful and brave, willing to return to Sangre Dulce. She wasn't a weak human lying down in defeat. No, she was a fighter. A quick glance at her smiling up at him melted his heart. *What was she doing to him?*

He hadn't even known her very long but felt a deep connection to Samantha that he didn't think he'd ever be able to break. His thoughts drifted to Ilsbeth's words; it was rare, but they could conceive. *A baby.* Silently admonishing himself for even thinking about it, he blew out a breath. What the hell was happening to him? Luca didn't do humans or love and here he was thinking about babies? While growing aroused at her touch, he was more concerned about the tightness he felt in his chest. *I'm falling for this little witch.*

"What are you thinking about? You okay?" Samantha broke his train of thought.

"Just planning our next move," he lied. "When we go to Sangre Dulce, I'll be by your side the entire time. You're not the person you were when you were Rhea. Rhea was mere illusion, someone you were forced to be. We'll go in, do our business and get out," he promised.

"You know, when I saw those pictures, at Kade's, I was just shocked that I could have been made to parade around naked like that in some kind of a magic stupor. I felt like a fool. And then there's that whole submissive thing. I mean, it's not like I'm not open to fantasizing in the bedroom, but what I did wasn't exactly private." She rolled her eyes and shook her head in embarrassment.

"You have nothing to be ashamed of, Samantha. Seriously. Number one, you were not in control of yourself. Asgear forced you against your will. And number two; even if you were a submissive, it's nothing to be embarrassed about. A lot of people experiment with fantasies. It can be fun." He winked at her, trying to lighten the mood.

"I, uh, I don't know, Luca," she hesitated for a moment before continuing. "It's just that I really haven't ever been so intimate with anyone…until you. What we did last night, it was amazing. It's not that I haven't, you know, had sex. God, this is embarrassing. Okay, I'm just going to say it. There's been no other man who made me, you know, come like that." She giggled a little. "Oh my God, I can't believe I'm telling you this." She raked her fingers through her hair, twisting the ends nervously.

"Well darlin', I'm glad to hear it. And if I have my way, I'll be the last man who makes you come 'like that' as you put it," he smiled at her, turning into his driveway.

"Look at what you do to me, woman." He moved her hand from his thigh onto the hard evidence of his arousal. "We're never going to get anything done," he sighed. "Seriously, as much as I'd like to take you inside and make love again, we need to get over to Sangre Dulce," He groaned due to his uncomfortable state of arousal. "When we get home, I'll call Sydney and see if she can bring over something suitable for you to wear to the club. I also think we should bring Étienne and Xavier for backup. I'm not expecting trouble, but after what happened the last time we were there…Let's just say that I'm not risking anything happening to you."

As Luca pulled his car up to his home and turned off the engine, Samantha jumped out. As he approached her, Samantha wrapped her hands around Luca's waist, pressing her face into his chest and hugging him tightly.

"Thank you, Luca. Thank you for talking me into coming back here to get my life together. Thank you for helping me. I don't know what I would've done without you."

"Well, I did threaten to enthrall you to get you home, so I guess that counts as talking you into it," he joked, and kissed her head.

She playfully pushed his chest with the palm of her hand. "I'm here, aren't I?"

"Yes. Yes, you are. And I couldn't be happier that you're with me." He gathered her into his arms for a brief embrace and then released her. If he started kissing her, they'd never get to the club. He was two seconds from tearing off her clothes as it was.

"Come on now. Let's get dressed." He lightly smacked her bottom as she quickly walked up to the porch. Adjusting himself, he fantasized about how delicious it would be to spank her pink while taking her from behind. He couldn't seem to stop thinking of Samantha and all the delightfully naughty things he wanted to do to her.

Knowing they had work to do, Luca decided it was safer to stay upstairs rather than follow Samantha down to his bedroom. He could barely keep his hands off of her for two seconds. She was driving him mad. It wasn't as if he could stay in a cold shower forever. He needed to get himself together, which was not going to be easy, considering they were about to go to a sex club. He sighed, resigning himself to the fact that he was going to remain uncomfortably hard for the next several hours. It was going to be a long night.

Samantha tugged at her short dress as they walked toward Sangre Dulce. Sydney had come over to Luca's to help her get dressed. After vehemently refusing to wear a little, very little, see-through number, she'd settled on a royal blue spandex mini-dress with a draped skirt that was gathered at her waist by rhinestones. One-shouldered, it exposed her creamy, pale skin; her golden red hair was straightened and tied back in a ponytail. Samantha enjoyed the black patent leather platform heels she'd borrowed. They made her feel more confident and tall, despite only adding a few inches to her five foot three stature.

She knew that the club catered to both humans and supernaturals; that was partly what had enticed her to go there in the first place. They'd all thought it would be fun to maybe see someone being bitten or spanked. Samantha didn't recall either. Still, with the knowledge that there could be vampires there, she nervously stroked her neck as if to protect it. Sydney had given her a silver chain in case of an emergency, which she kept stowed in her small clutch bag. She'd tried to get her to take a stake, but Samantha trusted Luca to keep her safe. She reasoned that not knowing exactly how to stake a vampire could be more dangerous for her, if she tried using the weapon without practice.

Luca put his arm around Samantha's waist and possessively pulled her against him. He planned to make it clear from the minute he stepped out of the car that she was his. He could practically feel her smooth skin through the barely-there, stretchy material that was her dress. He'd nearly had a heart attack when she came out of the bedroom tonight. With her hair swept up, he admired the fine lines of her neck; how he'd love to pierce her and taste her honeyed blood again. The spandex dress showed off every last curve of her luscious body without revealing a hint of cleavage. Samantha was simply stunning.

As they walked through the door, the pounding techno beat blared. Samantha slowly practiced her deep breathing, trying not to let Luca notice. She had said she wanted to do this, and she was determined to see it through. Samantha put on a mask of coolness as she observed naked girls serving drinks to customers. Straining to observe over a sea of bodies, it appeared a Domme and her sub were gearing up to engage in a public scene. A tall, lithe woman, dressed head to toe in spandex, led a good looking, muscular man around the room on a leash and proceeded to cuff his wrists to a Saint Andrew's cross.

Watching the preparation, Samantha lost her concentration on her deep breathing. Inexplicably drawn to what was happening to the sub, her heart began to race. Was this what she'd done? She couldn't help but notice that the man didn't struggle. He willingly followed his mistress and held his arms out to her, his jutting excitement conspicuously revealed to the audience. Samantha wasn't quite sure whether she was aroused by the sight of the virile stranger or disgusted, knowing it could have been her, a memory better forgotten. Conflicted, she could not tear her eyes from the unfolding exhibition. A cry of delight roared through the room as the Domme alternated between stroking him mercilessly and cracking the flat end of a riding crop against his reddening bottom.

Luca put his hand on Samantha's elbow, jarring her from anxiety. He could tell from the fascinated look on her face that she'd never seen anything like she'd just witnessed. On the one hand, he cursed Asgear for fucking with her memory. Yet it was probably best she didn't remember whatever had happened in the club.

Studying her face, he could see she was mesmerized by the intense sexual display. He observed her warring emotions. Was she excited by it? Perhaps. But her eyes told him she was also uneasy, anxious. She was worrying about things she couldn't remember nor control. He needed to get her refocused on their purpose, so they could get out of there.

Luca guided her around a semi-circular bar and signaled the bartender. They were addressed promptly; two bottles of water were placed on the bar. Samantha had made it clear that she wasn't drinking anything that didn't come in a sealed container. After what had happened last time, she wasn't taking any chances. Luca nodded at her and pointed to a small area that had been cordoned off by ultra-modern chrome leaf screens. It was partially open to allow the wait staff to enter and leave, but had no door.

"Over there. I'll stand right outside the entrance while you search the area. Are you ready to do this?" he asked.

"Born ready," she feigned confidence.

"Okay, let's do it quickly."

Several nude waitresses were leaving the break area as they approached the opening. Samantha winked at Luca and entered. The room was the size of a small walk-in closet, and she guessed that no more than four people could fit in there at a time. *One way to keep the waitresses working.* Plastic orange chairs lined one wall with a mini-fridge and plastic cups on the other side. Folded purple towels and blankets were piled high in a corner. Quickly she rummaged through the linens and refrigerator, but couldn't find anything.

Disappointed, she exited the room, and Luca caught the crook of her arm.

"Nothing, I found nothing," she commented tersely.

"Come dance with me," he whispered into her ear.

Nina Simone's *I Put a Spell on You* began to play as Luca pulled her out onto the dance floor. She felt herself melt into his body as he put a hand to the small of her back and held his other hand to her throat, slowly brushing his fingers down the hollow of her neck. Without words, he pressed his lips to hers, tasting her, deepening the kiss as she reached her hands around his neck.

Within seconds, she'd lost control, digging her hands into his hair. Desire pooled below, as she began grinding against his hardness. She wanted to make love to him there, not caring who was watching.

Grudgingly, Luca began to withdraw. Closing his eyes, he pressed his forehead down to hers. "Ah Samantha, I want you so much. But we can't do this here. We've gotta go back to the room where Dominique was silvered. Check it out." He was breathing hard, struggling to compose himself. A year ago, he'd have had no problem having sex in a club like Sangre Dulce. He wasn't in the lifestyle but liked to play lightly every now and then. When a vampire had lived as long as he had, he or she was always looking for something on the edge to spice up life. But now was not the time to get carried away; he'd only brought her out to the floor to talk with her briefly before they went to the private rooms.

"Back there." He nodded towards an entrance covered in red-beaded fringe. "We'll walk back together. Hold my hand and stay close. Sometimes people gather at the rooms to watch; we'll just walk around them."

"Any chance I can use the ladies' room before we go? Somebody has me all hot and bothered," she teased.

"Yes, come on, let's go. I want to get home as soon as possible so I can finish what we've started on the dance floor." It was more of a promise than a joke.

Léopold watched the mortal girl dance with Luca, cursing their pleasure. They were supposed to be finding him the *Hematilly Periapt*; instead, they were mauling each other like oversexed teenagers. He was sure Asgear had given it her, and she would lead him to it, even if he had to grab her by her long red hair and drag her through the streets of New Orleans himself.

Anger raced through his veins; he was incensed with their cavalier attitude. Obviously, she needed a reminder of her task. He'd thought the fire would have been enough to frighten her into this much-needed search. He required the amulet…now.

Luca spied Étienne and Xavier sitting at the bar, and casually nodded. He planned on introducing Samantha to them another time, letting them remain in the background. He watched as she took off down a long open hallway to the rest room. It was dimly lit with black lights and tea-light candles that sat in ceramic luminaires. As he turned back, Étienne and Xavier had crossed the room to meet him. He wanted to quickly brief them on the plan. They'd stay twenty feet behind them and watch for an ambush.

Samantha patted her face down with a paper towel and prided herself for holding it together. Not remembering a damn thing helped, she mused. But she didn't regret spending time with Luca. She found herself wanting to stay in New Orleans with him. She wasn't sure if he really meant it when he said that he didn't want to let her go. The more time she spent with him, the more she said goodbye to her old life.

Exiting the ladies room, dark smoke filled the hallway. Before she had the opportunity to register the cause, she found herself shoved against the wall. A large hand covered her mouth, while the attacker's body flattened against hers, effectively caging and immobilizing her. Unable to speak or move, her eyes widened at the stranger.

"Do not make a sound. I am going to release your mouth. If you scream, I will take you out of here. If you're quiet, I'll let you go. If you understand, nod your head," Léopold instructed.

Samantha did what he said, quietly pursing her lips together. She wanted to scream, but wasn't convinced he would not hurt her. There was something otherworldly about him. His hardened raven eyes seemed to pierce right through her, pinning her in place, like a dried butterfly stuck to a display board. She could see the slightest hint of candlelight glinting off the sharp edges of his fangs. *Vampire.*

"Maybe I haven't been clear, Samantha," he began.

"How do you know my name?" she interrupted.

"Do you know the meaning of quiet, witch? Do you? All you need to know is that I need the *Hematilly Periapt*, and you are going to find it for me. Now no more fooling around with the vampire. Find. It. Now!"

"But…but I don't know where it is. I don't even know what it is. Please just leave me alone," she pleaded.

"Listen to me, little girl. Asgear gave it to you. I don't give a shit what you have to do, but you will find it." He released her and shook his head. She was the only one who could find it. "Now go to your vampire," he ordered.

"But how will I find you if I get it?" she asked. She felt braver. He hadn't hurt her. There was something about him; she couldn't put her finger on it. He was powerful. Lethal. Yet he hadn't attempted to kill her or even bite her.

"Don't worry your pretty little head, Samantha. I will find you, so you'd better keep looking," he threatened.

Samantha looked up the hallway, and could see Luca's back to her. Readying herself to scream, she glanced back at the stranger, and he was gone. Vanished. She ran up the hallway, and embraced Luca tightly. "Luca, Luca. He was here. "

Luca growled. "Who was here? Who touched you?" An uncontrollable rage filled him at the thought of another man's hands on Samantha. Luca signaled over to Étienne and Xavier, who sensed something was wrong. They immediately came over to find out what had just happened.

"Are you hurt? Look at me. Tell me everything." Luca wanted to know every detail. This bastard had almost burned them to death, and now he was here in the club. How the hell did he get past him?

Without giving Samantha a chance to answer, he barked out orders to Étienne and Xavier. "Go down the hallway, and search for the man. Scent her first."

"Where did he touch you Samantha?" Luca asked through gritted teeth.

"He put his hand over my mouth, and pinned me to the wall, but he didn't hurt me. He wants the periapt. I told him I didn't have it, but he thinks Asgear gave it to me. He's a large vampire; I could see his teeth. At least as tall as you, Luca, so maybe six-five. Black eyes. I don't remember much else; it was dark," she quietly finished.

Xavier and Étienne leaned in, sniffing her dress. Samantha rolled her eyes upward, trying not to notice two strange vampires that she hadn't even been formally introduced to, within inches of her breasts. She huffed as they backed off and went down the hallway.

"We should go home," Luca suggested. "This is too dangerous."

"Excuse my French, Luca, but no fucking way." She had come this far and was not leaving without at least checking that room. "I'm telling you, he is not going to leave me alone until he gets that damn periapt. I've had enough of this shit tonight. Vampires looking for amulets I don't have and then disappearing into thin air. Seriously? Enough." She shook her head in disbelief. "Let's go to the room and then we'll leave. Please Luca," she begged.

Xavier and Étienne were back within minutes. "There are no vampires down there that match his scent. He's gone," Étienne said.

"Listen up. We're going down to the last room on the right, the one that Dominique was silvered in. Étienne, you go ahead of us. X, you bring up the rear. No stopping for shows or looking around. We're going to move fast and then get outta here. Understood?" he asked.

They all nodded and one by one passed through the red-beaded curtain, making their way to the room. Samantha held onto Luca for dear life, hearing screams of pleasure and pain as they crept down the darkened hallways. Finally, when they reached the room, they found it occupied by two very naked humans. The man had the woman bent over a spanking bench and was entering her from behind.

Samantha's mouth gaped open at the sight, while Luca strode in and interrupted them. He bared his fangs and roared. "Out!"

The people froze mid-coitus, the blond woman's mascara-streaked face staring at them defiantly. Luca knelt down to the man, who appeared not to have heard his order, and glowered. "I said get out. Now move! Move! Move! Move!" he yelled.

The couple scrambled around for their clothes. Upon seeing Étienne and Xavier's exposed fangs, they stopped looking for clothes and ran out the door. Samantha grinned. *Vampires are scary when they're angry.*

Luca slammed the door behind him, scanning the room. "This room's all we've got, so let's tear it up. There's got to be something here. Xavier, check all the floor panels. Étienne, you check the walls and light fixtures. Samantha, you've got the sofa. I'll take the equipment," he instructed.

They spread out and started searching. Samantha was more than grossed out by the plastic-covered sofa. She shuddered to think who and what people had done on it. "Gloves," she called out, finding a box of surgical gloves on a small table in the corner that also housed towels, sanitizing wipes and a bowl of flavored condoms. Snapping on the latex life-savers, she began to rip the cushions off and delved into the cracks, looking for a clue.

Xavier inspected the heavily worn, oak floor planks. While the floor appeared well used, it presented as if it was in good condition. Aside from a few squeaks, he couldn't find any loose boards.

Étienne scrutinized each brick in the wall, running his fingers along the grout. Not one stone was wavered. Save a few high hat lights, there was no other illumination in the room. Each one was tightly mounted and left no room for an opening.

Having already examined the Saint Andrew's cross and spanking bench, Luca moved on to the massage table. On first glance, the padding looked clean and uncracked. Running his fingers underneath, he felt only smooth particle board until he came upon a section that was worn. Losing patience, Luca flipped the table upside down, exposing its warped underside. He noticed that one of the corners did not seem to evenly match the rest of the seams; it was slightly raised. Digging his fingers into the juncture where the particle board met the padding, he tugged until it popped. *What the hell?*

Someone had put chewing gum inside the backing as makeshift glue. It had hardened into nothing more than a small tacky spud, yet it had held tight.

Luca peeled back the panel until he spied a flattened cocktail napkin. He carefully removed it and called the others over. "Got something. A napkin. Looks like there's writing on it, but it doesn't make sense. Samantha, take a look." Luca surmised it was not a foreign language, and sincerely hoped it wasn't nonsense. It simply read, "*NIJE QN QSMGIOT.*"

Samantha gently took the tissue paper into her hands and unfolded it. Her eyes widened in surprise, unexpectedly realizing she'd written it. "Oh my God, Luca. I wrote this; it's my handwriting. I know what this is; it's a code. A code to conceal a message. Knowing me, I probably created a cipher. My co-workers and I sometimes play encryption games with them. You know, create codes and see who can break it. I wouldn't have used something easy, though."

"Can you break it?" he asked.

"Probably, but I need to think about how I created it, and I can't think in here." She fingered the napkin and held it to her chest as if it was made of gold. This clue could give her back her life. Excitement coursed through her body; she could feel the tendrils of magic stirring under her skin.

"Let's go everyone, we've gotta get out of here," Luca ordered. "The back door. It leads to an outside alley. Although it looks like someone decided to lock it up good, since the last time we were here. Stand back while I break it." Luca went over to the door, the same one Samantha had used to leave after she'd silvered Dominique. Obviously management wasn't crazy about people using it as an exit, so they'd put a chain and lock on it. Whoever thought a chain would stop a supernatural was a dumbass, Luca thought. He knew a simple steel chain wouldn't keep vampires from breaking it, so why bother? Luca wrapped the steel chain around his fists, grunting as he broke it apart. He kicked the door open, and they all took off down the alleyway.

Samantha started to analyze the code as soon as they got into the car. She couldn't wait to get home to crack it. On the precipice of solving the mystery, she smiled to herself. Inwardly, she celebrated the fact that despite all Asgear's efforts to control her mind, some small part of her couldn't be controlled. The code was evidence that she probably had stolen the periapt, and had taken great care to hide it from him. Yet despite her small victory, its clandestine location had drawn a very powerful and dangerous vampire into her circle. She prayed she'd find it before he found her again.

Chapter Ten

After taking a hot shower, Samantha checked her cell phone for the hundredth time. Neither Rowan nor Ilsbeth had attempted to log into the database. She was still feeling exhilarated from finding the code. Wrapping herself warmly in Luca's robe, she held it to her nose and inhaled his masculine scent. Samantha shook her head, knowing that Luca was stealing her heart. She could feel herself falling for him, and wasn't sure how or if she wanted to stop it. All she knew for certain was that she was going to find it very difficult to go back to Pennsylvania without him after they found the amulet.

She sighed in defeat, conceding that her heart might break into a million pieces if she didn't have him in her life. Even though they'd only just made love, she felt as if she'd known him forever. She wasn't one to just have sex with any guy. But on a whim, she had given in to her most carnal desire and let him make love to her. In the aftermath, she couldn't shake the feeling that he was the one for her. She wished it wasn't true. He probably had a thousand women on speed dial who'd come willingly running to service him…to be his donor or whatever else he needed. *How could she leave her heart open to a vampire?* The answer didn't matter, because it was already done. Samantha contemplated whether or not she should move to New Orleans. As the thought popped into her head, she laughed to herself. Just a day ago, she'd been kicking and screaming to stay away from that city. But now there was Luca. And Luca was in New Orleans.

As she walked out into the kitchen, he was putting out sandwiches on the large granite bar. There was something heartwarming about seeing a large, sexy man preparing food for her.

"Hi there, the sandwiches look great," she said.

"Hey, beautiful. Thought you might be hungry. I had Kade's cook bring over something to eat, so you'd have strength to work. And to play with me," he joked, pushing a plate towards her. "But work before play. So first, let's take a look at the code while you eat, shall we?"

She took a healthy bite of turkey, and looked at the code: "*NIJE QN QSMGIOT*" What did it mean?

"So here's the thing. When I do my ciphers, I usually use something called a date shift cipher. That way, I can stack the ciphers when I'm trying to make it really hard to decode. Also, all I have to do is change the dates and it will change the codes. I wrote a program that can run through figuring out a date cipher, so that's not the problem. The real challenge is finding out what date I used."

"I've heard of date ciphers. It's going to make this tough to crack without the date," Luca commented. When he'd joined the war, they'd often put their messages into codes; if captured by the enemy, they were indecipherable without the key date.

"Yes, you're right. So what code would I have used?" she spoke aloud to herself.

"A birthday?" Luca suggested.

"No, too easy. I did this all the time at the office. Sometimes I would use someone else's birthday, but given that I don't know anyone down here, I don't think I would have done that. A family member's birthday would, again, be too easy. Sometimes I'd pick dates of important events. Things that only I would know," she explained.

"Your graduation date, perhaps?" Luca realized in that moment that he didn't know that much about her past; something he fully intended to investigate once they'd found the amulet.

"Maybe. I have used my high school graduation date in the past. Can you get me your laptop? I want to pull over my date cipher program from my home server, and try it." Samantha was starting to worry that she wouldn't be able to find the date. It literally could be any date, past, present or future.

Luca booted up the laptop and set it in front of her. He watched as she typed away; she chewed her lip, concentrating on what she was doing. He loved seeing her in his home, wrapped up in his black velour robe. She pushed the reddish curls of her freshly washed hair behind her ears as she waited for the program to open.

"Okay, read me the code," she instructed and typed it into the space designated for it. "I'm going to try my high school graduation date, which was June 23, 1999. So what happens is that the computer will take all this information and work backwards to see if we come up with something that makes sense based on the code and date variables. In a date shift cipher, the date is generated sequentially without the slashes over and over. The letters of the alphabet are assigned to each number. So then you take your message, and the code assigns a letter based upon how many spaces you need to shift," she explained.

"Can you give me a quick example before it runs?" It had been a long time since he'd deciphered a code on the battlefield and wanted to make sure he correctly understood.

"Sure. So my graduation date would be written like this." She wrote down the number sequence, six, two, three, nine, and nine and continued, "So I would write the numbers over and over again until I had a little more than the alphabet. Like this." She drew out the numbers until they were all the way over. "Then I would add the alphabet underneath, like this. So if I was looking to code the word, "sex" for example, I would go to the *S* which tells me to move over spaces. So the S turns into a *B*, the *E* turns into an *N* and the *X* turns into a *G*. So the code would be BNG. But still, you'd need to know the date I used in order to crack the code. But again, if you'd been given the secret code, BNG, you would need to know the date in order to solve the code."

6	2	3	9	9	6	2	3	9	9	6	2	3	9	9	6	2	3	9	9	6	2	3	9	9	6	2	3	9	9	6	2	3	9	9	6	2	3
A	B	C	D	E	F	G	H	I	J	K	L	M	N	O	P	Q	R	S	T	U	V	W	X	Y	Z	A	B	C	D	E	F	G	H	I	J	K	L

BNG

Luca laughed. "You're brilliant! Perhaps in need of some lovin', but brilliant," he teased. He came around the bar and sat next to her to watch what happened online.

She smiled over at him but turned serious again as she watched the progress of the program. Within seconds, it finished bringing up the message. It made no sense, which meant the date was incorrect.

"Shit. That's not it. You know what they say? Garbage in, garbage out. We need the right date," she huffed.

Samantha closed her eyes and put her hands to her forehead trying to rack her brain for the correct date. Luca rubbed her neck while she concentrated. *Think. Think. What date would I have used? I was in a hurry. In danger. Scared.* It occurred to her that maybe she'd used the day she was taken by Asgear. It would have been fresh in her mind, something she'd want to remember. She reached back into her mind to search for the date but couldn't seem to do it without a visual calendar in front of her.

Opening her eyes, she pulled up her calendar on the screen. "August. I was taken in August. August 11, 2012." She flipped back to the cipher program and typed in eight, one, one, one, two and pushed enter.

Luca and Samantha watched patiently as the program worked backwards through the sequence to find out the code. Within seconds, the screen came up with a message: *MAID OF ORLEANS*.

"Maid of Orleans? What's that?" Samantha asked.

"Maid of Orleans," Luca said thoughtfully. "The Maid of Orleans is a statue of Joan of Arc. It was given to the city by France in the seventies. I'm not sure what we'll find there but we've got our next lead. You did it, Samantha!"

Samantha was overwhelmed with relief that Luca knew what the message meant. She was one step closer to freedom. "Where's the statue? Why would I have been there?"

Luca went over to the refrigerator and pulled out a bottle of champagne. He talked as he uncorked it and poured it into flutes. "The statue's in the French Quarter over near the French Market on Decatur. It's not far from Sangre Dulce. Maybe wherever Asgear took you first, he had to walk you past it to get to the club. I'm not sure, but perhaps somehow you got away long enough to hide it. It might have taken only a few minutes to feign an escape, plant another clue or the amulet and then agree to go to the club."

"Joan of Arc, huh? Kind of ironic, isn't it?" Samantha commented.

"Ah yes, Joan of Arc. She was accused of witchcraft, and yet a very real witch chooses her as the place to drop the next clue." He grinned wryly, handing her a glass.

"Let's not forget she was burned at the stake," Samantha reminded him. "I'd like to avoid that if at all possible."

"Well, let's just take a few minutes to celebrate. It's getting really late, and I for one am growing tired of this chase. You see, I'd much rather be chasing you." Luca set down his glass and came up behind Samantha, putting his hands on her shoulders. As he massaged her neck, she let out a loud groan.

"Ah, Luca, that feels so good. I'm not used to walking around in heels like that all night. Or being in that kind of club. Seeing some of those people do what they were doing; it made me feel…I felt…" Her words trailed off; she wasn't sure whether or not she wanted to talk about it.

"Tell me Samantha. How did it make you feel to be in the club again?" Luca questioned her. He was worried she'd have a flashback or panic at the club, but nothing had happened. She was one cool cucumber. But he knew that beneath the surface, thoughts lingered. Fear? Anger? Arousal?

"I…I felt…I don't know. I was scared to be in the club at first. But nothing happened. I didn't remember anything. And then there was the whole meeting with 'mister freaky vampire'. He was really scary at first. But it was strange. He was very angry, but controlled. By the time he was finished telling me to get the amulet, it was as if I knew he wouldn't hurt me. I know it sounds crazy. I can't explain it. And then seeing the submissives parade around naked as if it was nothing. And the sex. I guess it was okay." Samantha sounded unsure of her own thoughts. She'd witnessed and experienced so many strange and new things.

Luca put his fingers around her pallid neck, tracing his fingertips from her hollow to the back of her shoulder blades. He wouldn't let her off so easily. He wanted to know what she really desired.

"Did the domination scene excite you, darlin'? I saw you watching," Luca whispered into her ear. She shuddered, feeling his warm breath against her.

"Luca, did you go to that club often? Is that something you like? Do you do those things? Do you do what that woman was doing to that man?" she asked.

"Answering a question with a question? No. Quid pro quo. You first," he answered.

"Fine," she sighed. "I found it erotic. I don't think it's something that

I'd do every day, but I wouldn't mind playing at home with someone I trusted. But there is no way I'd do that in public like they were doing. I don't mean to sound judgmental, it's just that it's not me. When I saw them, naked, and her touching him so intimately, I was aroused, but also upset. I kept picturing me in that club. I can't believe that I did that, served drinks that way. I guess it's not too bad, not at this point, considering I can't remember. It's like you're telling me I did it. I see a picture in my head, but it doesn't seem at all real to me. Then, later tonight, dancing with you on the floor; that was real. Okay, enough about me. Now your turn. Dish." She got up, walked around the stool to stand next to him and put her arms around his waist.

Luca looked down at his beautiful woman. He was falling for her. He planned on telling her about the bonding, about everything. But tonight? Gazing into her eyes, he knew it was right. She was his and he knew in his heart he'd never let her go.

"Samantha, I'll be honest. I don't ever want to lie to you. You know I've lived hundreds of years, and yes, I've had sex with many women. But I haven't loved anyone since Eliza. I really want to tell you about her sometime, but tonight all you need to know is that there's no one in my life right now except you. As for the club…well, yes, I've been there a few times over the past couple of years with friends. I've played in the rooms, sometimes dominated women who were looking for fun with a supernatural. But it's not something I do all the time or feel compelled to do. Until you came along, I was just passing the time. I work for Kade, collect antiques, travel and that's about it."

"And do you want to do that to me? Do you want to tie *me* up?" she said, flirtatiously rubbing her breasts against his chest. Samantha hugged Luca, and he embraced her back, holding her tightly in his arms.

"Perhaps. Are you interested in playing with me, little witch?" His sultry voice washed over her.

"Um, yeah, that might be fun. Playing with you, experimenting with you actually excites me a lot. Is that wrong?" she giggled.

"No, it certainly is not. I'd love to play with you in all ways possible. But Samantha," he continued, "before we make love again, I need to talk with you about something. You know, there's a connection between us."

She nodded.

"Well, you need to know that I want more than just a casual affair. I want to be inside you, tasting you, bonding with you. I want you to be mine."

Samantha didn't really understand what he meant by bonding with her, but she knew for certain that she wanted him to make love to her. Her heart pounded against her ribcage, hearing him say that he wanted her. She'd been unsure about how he felt. Every minute she spent with him made her never want to leave. Her prior life and job in Pennsylvania were becoming a distant memory as he was becoming her future. She admitted silently to herself that she wasn't sure of the consequences of what he was asking. She only knew that she wanted him: to make love to him, to be with him, to be his.

Samantha looked up at Luca who was patiently awaiting her answer. With great anticipation, he heard a single word from her soft lips. "Yes."

Intense green eyes locked on Samantha's as he leaned in to kiss her. Her heart raced, anticipating his kiss, his every touch. With trembling lips she opened to him as he fiercely captured her mouth. His tongue danced with hers, tasting her magical spirit.

"Yes," was the only word he heard in response to his proposal; Luca lost control. Passionately and provocatively, he took her with a hungry urgency. It wasn't sweet. His mouth claimed hers, savagely taking what was his. The intoxicating nectar of Samantha only made him kiss her more deeply. He wanted her in a way that he'd never wanted any woman. Determined to possess every part of her body and mind in the moment, he would claim her tonight. She'd be his forever.

Luca tore his lips from hers. "Bedroom. Now," he commanded. Leading her by her small soft hand, he stopped her before they got to his bed.

"I will have you tonight, Samantha. After tonight, you'll never forget that you are mine. And I will be yours."

Samantha silently nodded in response. She was ready to commit to this man, this vampire. Luca was everything she'd ever wanted in a male: strong, loving, trustworthy, and passionate. She knew in her heart that giving herself over to him was all she desired now and for her future.

Luca unraveled the belt on her robe, slid his fingers underneath the soft fabric and slowly pushed it off Samantha, letting his hands glide from the smooth skin of her shoulders to her hands. As the robe pooled at her feet, he gently took her hands in his. She stood bare before his eyes. "You're enticing, Samantha. I cannot seem to get enough of you. So the question is, do you want to play with me tonight? Be honest with me, darlin', because I plan to take you to places we've never been before."

Samantha felt womanly, exposed to Luca. She trusted him completely as he released her hands and placed his on her waist. "Luca, please, hurry. I can't seem to keep my hands off of you."

"Well, I guess we'll have to do something about that," he smiled knowingly. "Turn around, face the wall. Don't move unless I tell you. It's time for some fun."

Without question, she complied and waved her bottom at him, shooting him a sultry look that said, 'come and get me'.

Luca loved how responsive she was under his direction. He didn't ever bring women into his home, and certainly engaging in a little light bdsm was something he rarely did anymore. Yet he'd wanted to do this to her since the minute she'd danced with him in the club. Luca slid his hands slowly up the sides of her waist, under her arms, pushing them upward and placing the palms of her hands against the wall. With the same precision, he glided his hands back down her arms, waist, until finally, he reached her bottom.

"Samantha, you are everything I've ever wanted in a woman; beautiful, smart." She let out a small moan; he rubbed his hard aching bulge against her. He wanted to fuck her right now, but he wouldn't dare. No, he planned to make her beg for mercy as he slowly brought her to orgasm over and over.

Though he was still fully clothed, she could feel his magnificent erection against her bum. She wanted him in her now; she grew wet from the intense ache between her legs. "Please, Luca."

His hands slid from her ass around to lie just beneath her sensitive bosom. She moved slightly to urge him to cup her breasts. He smiled, smelling the overwhelming scent of her desire, but he wanted to draw out the anticipation, tease her with delight. "No, no, no, darlin'. Not tonight. You don't get to decide when or how the pleasure happens. You wanted to play, so play we shall," he whispered into her ear. Goosebumps ran over her skin in response to his hot breath. "Tonight is about wanting what you can't have until I give it to you. It's about me savoring every stroke of your flesh. The ultimate pleasure, tasting you while you come, screaming my name. Now, do you want me to touch your lovely breasts? Tell me, Samantha."

"Yes. Please Luca, please touch them. I need..." Struggling to keep her hands pressed to the wall, she threw her head back in sexual frustration and sighed.

"Since you asked so very nicely." Luca glided his hands over her sweetly curved flesh, while rocking his aching shaft against her behind. "So firm. Just right. And your perfect little nipples; they demand my attention too. You want me to pinch them?"

Samantha was lost in the sensation. He was driving her mad with need. She could feel her throbbing tips growing hard, but she was helpless to relieve the ache. She managed a strained response. "Yes, oh yes."

"Such a good pet." He tweaked her hardened pink tips and released them, then repeated it several times until he heard her moan. "This? Is this what you want?" Luca slowly brushed the pads of his forefingers across the straining peaks.

"Mmmm...more, Luca. Please," she begged.

As much as Luca delighted in the sweet torture, he needed more too. He took each pink tip between his thumb and forefingers, and pinched even harder.

Samantha screamed in a heightened mixture of pleasure and pain. She rocked her hips back into Luca's incredibly sexy and very hard male frame. She longed to touch the muscles that she knew rippled down his arms, flat stomach and strong legs.

"Like a little pain with your pleasure? Interesting." Luca couldn't resist kissing along her neck behind both of her ears. "How about a few spanks for my beautiful woman? Tell me, Samantha, is that something you want?"

"I don't know. I've never…" She was embarrassed to admit that she was excited about the idea of his firm hand on her cheeks so close to her core.

Luca shook his head, sensing her desire. So his little witch wanted a spanking? He smiled. Without giving her warning, he stood to her side, letting his left hand slide down into her hot, moist folds, and then, in an alternating, successive order, he delivered four sharp slaps to the sides of her ass. He rubbed the inflamed, creamy skin with one hand as he inserted a finger inside her with the other.

"Ah, Luca, yes!" Samantha spoke between ragged gasps. "I know I shouldn't want this but I do. Oh my God, please," she was begging.

Luca felt the surge of wetness flow between her legs as she responded to his hands. He wanted to give her everything she needed but was finding it difficult to contain his own arousal. He'd like nothing more than to sheathe himself within her and fuck her senseless. Deciding to proceed with her pleasure, he inserted two fingers and began pumping them in and out, resting his chin on her shoulder as he whispered into her ear. He loved watching her lose control, giving into her darkest fantasies.

"Aw darlin', you're so nice and wet for me. I'm going to fuck you so good and hard." Panting in pleasure, she snapped her head toward him; her eyes locked with his. "That's right Samantha; I said I'm going to fuck you. You like when I talk dirty to you, don't you? And you liked it when I spanked your ass too. Do you want more, Samantha? Come now, tell me."

She sucked in a startled breath when she felt his thumb brush her clit. "Yes," she said through gritted teeth.

He smiled at her, gazing deep into her eyes. "Get ready to let go, Samantha. I'm going to spank you while I finger your sweet pussy. Do you understand?" Her mouth opened, not sure what to say to his crass words. She'd never been one to say anything during sex, let alone something dirty. But his words were more of an instruction than a random thought. She was aware that he knew the words made her grow even more ready.

"Yes, please," was all she managed to say before she felt four more spanks to her ass and Luca's thumb pressing hard into her sensitive nub. She heard herself screaming as she plunged over the crest. In a molten sensation of release, she shuddered; her fists balled against the walls.

Releasing her, Luca spun her around and erotically kissed her, fisting his hands into the back of her hair. She reached for the hem of his t-shirt and pulled it up over his head; they separated for only seconds as the shirt flew across the room, and then recaptured each other's lips in a desperate act of passion. Samantha ran her fingers up the muscled planes of his back. They each fought for breath: tasting, sucking, wanting.

Luca grabbed her wrists and pulled out of the kiss. With a burning look into Samantha's ice-blue eyes, he regained enough control to direct their play.

"Samantha, on your knees. Take me into your mouth," he quietly commanded.

Seductively, she smiled, and obeyed. Gracefully, she knelt, but not before brushing her rosy peaks against his chest, teasing him. She couldn't wait to taste him, and she planned on tantalizing him like he'd done to her. Thinking this was going to be oh-so-sweet, she provocatively sat back on her heels, pushing out her breasts. Slowly, she unbuckled his belt, and pulled it out of the loops, tossing it aside. After unbuttoning the button, Samantha took her time lowering the zipper. He wanted to draw things out for her, so she planned on taking her time, making him beg in turn. In a quick pull, she removed his boxers and pants until he stood gloriously naked in front of her. Like some Greek god, he stood motionless above her as she admired his steely contours.

Reaching behind him, Samantha languidly glided her hands up his thigh and abs until her hands rested just above his erection. With her lips mere inches from his cock, she darted her tongue out, running it over its smooth wet tip. He tasted wonderfully salty and masculine; she needed more. Unable to hold back, Samantha licked up and down his throbbing shaft, taking his tight sac into her hand. Her other hand reached around so she could dig her fingers into his hard muscular ass.

In a single motion, she parted her lips, relaxed her throat and took him all the way into her mouth. Sucking him, she retracted her lips, releasing his ridged manhood. Grabbing onto the base of him, she slowly repeated pumping him in and out of her warm lips.

Luca rocked himself into her mouth in rhythm with her demand. He hissed in ecstasy, realizing that she knew exactly what she was doing, paying him back for what he'd done to her. Did she comprehend how much power she had over him? He didn't care in the moment; pleasure was all he could feel.

His swollen flesh couldn't take much more without him exploding in her mouth; no, it was much too soon for that. After one more sweet kiss of his shaft, he receded, pulling Samantha onto her feet.

"I need you now, Samantha. I have to be in you. On the bed," he ordered.

Samantha sashayed over to the bed, and fell backwards, giggling. "Come and get me, vampire." She wasn't going to make this easy for him.

Picking up the sash of his robe, he played with the tie, eyeing her from across the room. "Hmm….sassy witch, huh? Perhaps you need to be reminded who's directing the show tonight, darlin'."

Her eyes widened when she saw him fingering the velour belt. Her heart began to race in excitement and her sex grew damp in anticipation.

Luca confidently strode across the room, drinking in the sight of his beautiful red-haired woman, splayed out spread-eagled on his bed. Leaning down, he methodically began to tie a loop around one of her wrists. After securing the knot, he weaved the belt through the slats of the head board and secured her other wrist until her arms were nicely tied above her head.

"Luca," she protested against the bindings.

"Tonight, your pleasure is mine, Samantha. If you really want to get out, your safe word is "cabin"; otherwise, we continue to play. Now what you might not know is that I could hear your heartbeat race as soon as you saw the belt. And since I don't smell fear, I know it's because you are aroused. Am I correct?"

Damn vampire senses. She smiled at him. "Yes, so what are you going to do to me?" She wiggled her hips around on the bed a little, hoping to tempt him into her.

"This." He trailed a finger down her arm, down her side. Goosebumps broke out over her body; she started to beg. "Please, Luca. It's not fair."

He laughed. "This isn't about fair, Samantha. It's about control. Dominance. And your submission." With those words, he left the room, leaving her tied to the bed.

She wondered what he was doing in the other room, hearing a banging noise, and struggled to see what he held in his hand when he returned, literally within seconds.

"No peeking, Samantha. In fact, I think it would be best to remove another one of your senses, don't you agree?"

She simply smiled at him, wondering what he was going to do, and eagerly awaiting his rapturous torment.

Luca straddled Samantha on the bed. He loved seeing her bound, awaiting his pleasure, desiring to make everything special. He smiled down at her, and held up a black scarf. Placing a slow, passionate kiss to her lips, he fastened the scarf over her eyes.

"Luca," Samantha whispered. She felt on fire with want. This man was pushing her to do something she'd never done, and she loved every second of it.

Samantha squealed in surprise as Luca ran an ice cube around her rose-colored areola. The cold sensation was immediately replaced by the warmth of his lips; he sucked the tiny pink bud until it hardened and ached. He gave her other nipple the same attention and she felt herself floating in the absence of her sight. The lips, tongue and teeth on her aching tips sent a jolt of need to her clit, and she found herself writhing, trying to get him to touch her below.

Within minutes, his lips abandoned her breasts. Moaning in delight, she felt his glorious hands caress her delectable pink mounds, while working his way downward to her abdomen with the cool wetness. The icy surface glided for seconds only to be replaced by his warm lips. Her hips rocked up into him; she wanted his frosty heat on her sex, in her.

Moving his hands to the side of her waist, Luca held the almost melted ice cube in his teeth, and slid over and through her wet folds. He could feel her quiver underneath his lips. With nothing left to hold, Luca darted his cool tongue into the crease of her sex, letting it graze over her clit. She writhed under his kiss, but he held her firmly by her hips.

"Luca, I can't take it anymore. It feels so good," she cried.

He didn't answer as he continued to lick and suckle her sex relentlessly. As two fingers entered her without warning, she moaned loudly, bucking her hips into his mouth. He curled his digits upward and stroked the long sensitive spot within her. "Aw darlin', your pussy is so wet and sweet for me." She barely registered him talking dirty, overwhelmed with her impending orgasm.

Luca could feel her squeeze his fingers. She was so close. "Come for me, Samantha, let go," he demanded, sucking hard on her ripe pink nub. He lapped at her sweet cream, so grateful to have her with him.

Samantha saw fireworks as she shattered into a million pieces. It was the most spectacular release she'd ever experienced in her entire life. She screamed Luca's name over and over again, shaking as he untied the scarf over her eyes.

She was panting, trying to catch her breath. She struggled to speak. "Luca. Amazing. Oh my God."

Not giving her any time to recover, Luca roughly grabbed her legs from behind her knees jerking her bottom toward him. Resting her ankles on his shoulders and holding the back of her thighs, his eyes flashed red as he plunged his rock hard cock into her glistening sex.

He grunted in ecstasy; her warm heat tightly fisted around his swollen flesh. She was absolute paradise, accepting all of him into her heat. They locked eyes as he continued to possess every inch of her, pounding into her in a fierce furor.

Samantha tilted her hips upward, craving him deeper still. His eyes burned deep into her soul. In that moment, she knew. She loved Luca. She forced herself to remain silent, afraid she'd cry out the words.

Luca shook her thoughts, as he stopped to release her wrists, catching her attention again. "Samantha, my magnificent, enticing sorceress, from this night forward, we will be together. When I taste of you tonight you will be mine. I will be yours. Do you understand? I need to have your permission. There is no going back."

"Yes, I'm yours," she agreed. "Make love to me, Luca."

He quickly flipped her onto her stomach; sliding his hand under her tummy, he pulled her up so she was on her hands and knees. Reaching his strong hands up her back, he glided them down her spine. With one hand on her waist, his fingers slid down over her bottom. Pressing a finger inside her sex, he teased the wetness up along her puckered rosebud. He felt her tense slightly, but then she rocked back toward him.

"It's okay, pet, relax for me. I want to explore every inch of your lovely body. Have you ever been touched here?" he asked as he ran his fingers over her.

"No," she gasped softly. She enjoyed the feel of his fingers on her anus. A rush of excitement surged through her, knowing what he might do. "But I want to try…with you."

"I'd like to take you with my cock someday, but not today, darlin'. I'm afraid that's something we'd need to ease into. I'll let you think on the sensation of my fingers there for now. Let me know how it feels."

"Um, it feels good. I know I shouldn't like it, but I do," she gasped as he continued to touch her in the place she'd never been touched before, slowly working a finger in her rosebud as his velvety steel shaft pressed into her warm center. Slowly, he eased into her. He didn't want to hurt her. Because of his larger size, he wanted to take his time, and make sure she enjoyed this.

"You're so wet and tight. You feel so good. Ah, Goddess. I need to claim you as my own and I'm afraid I can no longer wait." Within moments, Luca had fully joined his body with hers; she enveloped all of him. As they began to move together, Luca moaned. "Yes, that's it. We fit so well together."

Driven by desire, Samantha pressed her bottom back onto him. She impatiently rocked back and forth, desperately urging him into her sex. "It feels so good, Luca, so full, please don't stop. I need you harder," she demanded.

A primal instinct took Luca over as he began to thrust up into her to meet her need. Keeping one hand on her bottom, he moved the other hand around to rub her soft pink flesh. She was so very close, and he was taking her there again. Over and over, he slammed into her as she begged for more.

"Yes, Luca, I'm coming, Luca, don't stop!" she screamed.

Luca felt the beginning of her spasm around his throbbing shaft. His fangs elongated, and he reached up and fisted his hand into her hair, exposing the creamy skin of her fine neck. In a final glorious moment, Luca thrust one last time against her while sinking his sharp fangs into her sweet silken flesh; he drank her essence, pulsating deep within her.

Samantha was seized by a rush of sensation so intense she could barely breathe. As she came down off the pinnacle of her orgasm, white hot pin-pricks sliced into her shoulder; she shuddered uncontrollably as another strong release claimed her again. Luca held her tight until they both fell over in exhaustion into the sheets.

Perfectly spent, the sated couple fell back into bed. Luca cradled Samantha in his arms, resting her head on his chest. His breathing slowed as he pushed the hair from her face.

"Samantha," he needed to tell her.

"Hmmm," she sleepily responded. She tipped her chin upward to meet his eyes.

"I love you." He smiled down at *his* woman. Luca could not believe that after two hundred years he was, without a doubt, in love with a woman. No longer would he live his life alone, searching for purpose. She was the one; the one he would spend the rest of his days on earth with; the one who he planned to marry; the one who he wanted a family with. *Samantha.*

"Luca," she gasped and then beamed. "I love you too. I never thought. I mean, I've been so caught up in getting my life straightened out, getting everything back to how it was before and now…"

"Now?" he raised a questioning eyebrow at her.

"Now, I don't want it. I only want you."

Samantha kissed his smooth chest as he kissed the top of her head, embracing her in his arms. Luca's heart swelled; he never wanted this moment to end. Watching Samantha drift off to sleep, he was more determined than ever to get the amulet and kill the vampire who was threatening her, whichever came first. He could feel her blood sweep through his entire body. The bond had begun.

Chapter Eleven

The aroma of coffee wafted under her nose. Samantha's eyes fluttered open; a broad smile spread across her face, seeing Luca holding a cup of coffee. He was already dressed; a casual black t-shirt teased the contours of his chest and his blue jeans hugged his tapered hips. She noticed he was wearing gray alligator boots that suited his personality: sleek and lethal.

"Come on, sleepy head. Time to eat and catch bad guys. It's one o'clock in the afternoon. We've got to get goin'."

She sat up, pulling the sheet up over her breasts, and he handed her the cup of café au lait. He'd placed a beautifully decorated breakfast tray in the middle of the bed.

"Mmmm…this is wonderful. You make this?" she asked.

"Oui Mademoiselle. I've been livin' down here in New Orleans long enough to make a fine cup of chicory and steamed milk. I did not, however, make this delicious spread of eggs and bacon. Kade's cook brought this over; Mandy makes a great southern breakfast," He grabbed a piece of bacon off the plate and bit into it.

"Looks great. Hey, what are you doing stealing my bacon!" she joked as she picked up a piece for herself. "You know, I was wondering. What's the deal with vampires and food anyway? I mean, I've seen you eat food but I know you need blood." She lightly ran her fingers over the small bumps on her shoulder, remembering how he'd bitten her the night before, and then picked up her fork.

"Well, I can eat small amounts of food, but there's no nutrition in it. It's just like a comfort kind of thing, reminds us of our human life. But we don't need it. And some vampires no longer eat human food at all." He smiled slightly. "But they most assuredly do eat humans. The fact is that we need human blood to survive, but not every day and not a lot of it. At least a half cup or so every two to three days keeps us in fightin' shape. If we don't get it, we wither, die. For example, after they attacked us at the coven, the thugs starved me. I was silvered, so I couldn't move, couldn't communicate."

Luca's face hardened, remembering what had happened to him and what Kade and Sydney had done to save him. He hesitated. Luca did not relish telling Samantha the details of his recovery but didn't want secrets between them.

"Listen Samantha, speaking of the attack, I don't want there to be any secrets between us. I know we've just met over the past weeks, but you should know that when that happened - when I was attacked - I didn't recover right away. Kade and Dominique gave me human blood, a donor, but it wasn't enough." Luca turned his head away.

Samantha put her hand on his arm. "Hey, it's okay. I know what it's like to have something happen that you can't explain. You don't need to tell me. What's important is that you're here now."

"No, it's not that. It's just Sydney. Kade." He shouldn't feel guilty. Yet that was exactly how he felt. "Sorry, I'm just not sure how to explain this but Sydney's blood is special. It's because she's human, but not entirely anymore. She's bonded with Kade."

"Like you did with me?" She blushed, recalling their wild lovemaking the night before.

"Well, yes and no. You and I, last night, the bond began. When we made love and I bit you at the same time as we climaxed, it started the bond. So, soon I'll be able to sense where you are, maybe sense your thoughts, but not entirely be able to read them. But we are not fully bonded. That only happens when I give you my blood when we're making love. When that happens, it changes the human slightly. So Sydney, for example, will live as long as Kade. She'll be immune to illness et cetera, but will not become vampire."

"Okay," Samantha was happily eating the last of her eggs, listening intently.

"Okay." Luca laughed at her casual attitude. She was so brave and open to the unknown, quite unpredictably so at times. "What I'm saying is that Sydney's blood is special, more powerful. So when no other human blood would revive me, Kade let me feed from Sydney." Silence blanketed the room.

Samantha thought on it for a minute before commenting. Remembering how it had felt when Luca bit her and what Kat had told her happened at Eden, she was starting to put together what he was trying to tell her. Her stomach clenched in a pang of jealousy. What exactly was he trying to tell her? "So when you say feed, do you mean 'I drank her blood' or do you mean 'I drank and had sex with Sydney'?"

Yes, she was definitely putting it all together.

Luca took her hand in his, craving contact with his lover. "Yes and no. We were all together in Kade's house, his guest bedroom. If you're asking if I had intercourse with Sydney, then no, I did not. But if you're asking if I fed and it was an erotic experience? Yes. I'm not sure how to put this tactfully." He chose his words carefully. "I experienced a release during the process. But it was once, and if they hadn't done it, I could have died. The blood of people like Sydney, the bonded humans, it is rare. I'm sure Kade could have found someone else besides Sydney but it would have taken more time than I had. And besides, they are my friends."

Samantha pondered his words. She wondered exactly what the three of them had done if it wasn't intercourse, but it sounded like they engaged in some kind of a ménage; they all came. Samantha knew he needed the blood but still, what had he done with Sydney?

"Seriously? A release?" She laughed indignantly. "You mean you came? With both of them there?"

"I really don't want to get into the details of the entire session but let's just say it wasn't intercourse and it wasn't oral sex. But yes, the gist of what you are saying is correct. I fed from Sydney. I touched her, and she me. I came." Luca prayed she wouldn't freak out and take off running again. It wasn't as if he'd exactly had a choice in the matter. He would have died without Sydney's blood and was lacking any kind of control during their healing encounter.

"Is this experience something you intend to repeat with them? I mean, I may be experienced sexually, but I'm not that open. I have firm limits, Luca. And sharing is one of them. I won't share you with other women if we are going to be in a relationship. Not an option, Luca." She felt sick thinking that he might have to drink the blood of other women.

"No, no, no. Samantha. I would never ask that of you. It isn't something I wanted. I just needed to be honest with you about how I healed, what happened. There can't be secrets between us, especially when we will be with Kade and Sydney. Believe me, what happened with them, it will never happen again. And you should know that I don't share either. Never," he said through gritted teeth. He'd kill the next man who laid a finger on his woman. "I want you. I love you. And if you will agree, I want to fully bond with you."

Relieved, Samantha jumped up out of bed naked and straddled the clothed Luca. He leaned his head against the back of the headboard, enjoying the view of his beautiful woman, resting his hands on her hips.

"Luca, I love you." It felt strange saying those words yet Samantha couldn't help but tell him how she felt. "Whatever you had to do to stay alive, I get it. But, I'm grateful Kade and Sydney saved you. Okay, I'm not crazy about the three of you in bed, but what's done is done, and today, you're here in bed with me. My vampire."

"My witch." Luca waited patiently as Samantha pressed her lips to his. Their tongues danced, gently tasting and exploring. Samantha began to grind into his hardness, eager to make love with him again.

Luca broke the kiss and threw his head back again. "You are tempting something fierce, darlin', but we've got to go find ourselves an amulet. We can't stay in bed all day."

"Ugh. Hate that you are right." Samantha pouted. "Okay, I'm getting in the shower but you owe me later." She winked at him as she bounced off the bed and padded into the bathroom.

Luca smiled to himself, thinking that the woman was going to be the death of him, and what a sweet death it would be.

After getting dressed in jean shorts and a pink tank top, Samantha walked into the kitchen with a spring in her step. Her cell phone buzzed while she was lacing up her sneakers. She glanced at the message. "Luca! Someone accessed the coven's database. I'm goin' into your laptop," she yelled up the stairs.

Luca ran down the steps, and sat next to Samantha as she opened up her program. She typed furiously.

"Ilsbeth went in this morning. Yes! Gotcha." She brought up the coven's website and quickly entered Ilsbeth's ID and password, pressed enter and waited. "Okay, baby. Here we go. We're in! Now let's see how we can search. Looks like they have things categorized. We've got witchcraft by country. We've got witchcraft by modern types, Wicca, Stregheria…yadda, yadda, yadda. Okay, I see spell casting, ingredients, necromancy. Ew…so not ever doing that. Here's book of shadows, demonology, ceremonial magick, scrying, shamanism. Come on, there's got to be something here." She kept scrolling down, hoping there'd be a category for the *Hematilly Periapt*. "Come to mama! Yes. Talismans. It's an amulet. Does that sound right?" she questioned Luca.

"Yes, that should be it. A talisman usually guards against evil, but considering we've got no idea what it does, let's give it a try."

"There must be thousands of these things, but I'll give it to the sisters, they have each one detailed: what it's made of, purpose, who created it, how to make one. Looks like some of these are blank. They must still be in the process of creating this database. Oh my God, Luca. Here it is, the *Hematilly Periapt*. I can't read this. Is this Latin? What is this?" The description was written in a foreign language:

A potens pythonissam, Maria Voltaire, in septimodecimo saeculo ad certate pestilentia de lamia. Et facta periapt Hematite ex Graeco sanguinem. In actu periapt est proxime duo digitis per unum inch in figura lacrima gutta. Ita dominus periapt oportet esse in magica persuasione potest etiam actiones lamia voluerint. In ordine ad pythonissam ad eu in periapt, requirit gutta intentum lamia. Semel occurrit, in lamia erit sub veneficas imperium vsque mortem. Eam scriptor current location est ignotum.

Luca read the description and translated. "It's Latin. So basically it says that the periapt was created by a powerful witch. Her name was Maria Voltaire. She made it in the seventeenth century to combat vampires, presumably during the great mass hysteria over vampires during that time. Anyway, it says that the periapt is made of the mineral hematite. The word, hematite is derived from the Greek word for blood. Then it describes it; it says the actual periapt is approximately two inches by one inch, in the shape of a tear drop. The owner of such a periapt must be a witch, warlock or mage. Here we go, here's the crux of it. The periapt can control the actions of any vampire. But in order for the witch to activate the stone, it requires a drop of blood from the intended vampire and then the vampire shall be under the witch's control as long as the witch keeps it on her person. It lists its current location as unknown." Running through the scenarios in his head, Luca's eyes narrowed in anger.

"Goddammit, now we know why the hell everyone seems to want it. Imagine if a witch got the amulet and the blood of a vampire. Like my blood, for example. Fuck." He slammed his fist down on the counter, remembering what Kade and Sydney had told him about the needles all over the church where they'd found him. Perhaps someone had taken his blood for a different reason than they thought.

"What's wrong?" Samantha watched Luca pace, visibly agitated.

"What's wrong is that when we were attacked and I was taken, there were needles all over the floor. It's a fairly good guess that someone has my blood. If the same person who took my blood gets the periapt, they could control me, according to what we just read," he said, piqued.

"Okay, maybe it's true, maybe it isn't. We'll get it back. We'll destroy it," Samantha promised. Hoped.

"What I can't figure out is why another vampire would want it? How does he even know about it? According to this notation, only a witch can use it." He dragged his fingers through his hair.

"I don't know, Luca. But we'll get to it first and then we'll get rid of it. If we can't destroy it, we'll take it out into the sea, and dispose of it there. We can do this." She didn't want to admit it to Luca but she was scared too. She prayed that she'd left a clue to its whereabouts.

"Well, thank God you took it from Asgear. And now that we know what it does, we know why someone wants it. We'd better get going to find out what's at the Maid of Orleans. I sure as hell hope this leads us to the amulet. We also now need to find out who took my blood." Luca would be damned before he let anyone control his actions. He knew better than anyone that he was a lethal killing machine when he needed to be. And so did the vampire who was trying to get the periapt. Maybe that vampire was working with a witch? He couldn't focus on the myriad scenarios right now. The only thing that was important was locating the *Hematilly Periapt,* and he hoped the Maid of Orleans would be his savior.

Chapter Twelve

The afternoon sunlight glinted off the shiny golden metal. There stood Joan of Arc with her armor and steed in Orleans. Proudly displayed atop a large stone base, she sat surrounded by landscaping and pavement. Tourists busily shopped on both sides of the wedged streets, oblivious to her history or potential.

"Well, I'm not sure what I was doing over here. It's a couple of blocks from the club. I don't think I could've escaped to this statue on my way there. Maybe I came here on my way out of the club?" Samantha estimated.

"Maybe you did. And maybe Asgear lived around here and that's why you came this way. Maybe you stopped here first before you planted the clue at the club? There's a lot of vegetation in and around the statue. I brought some tools with me. They're in the back seat. I'll grab the clippers and hand shovel just in case we need them. Sydney knows we're coming here today, so the NOLA PD are expecting folks to be digging around it." Luca got out of the SUV, opened the trunk and picked up his toolbox.

Samantha was out of the car and across the street ahead of him. She should have worn jeans, not shorts, she thought to herself. Bushes and bugs. Just great. Stepping into the brush, she began to look for something, anything that would lead them to the location of the periapt.

"I wouldn't have had a lot of time. Whatever I did, it had to be fast. Asgear would've seen me run over here across the street. It's gotta be in or around the brush, maybe over near the cannons." She broke through the branches, searching around near the ornamental artillery that sat in the shrubbery.

Instead of jumping directly into the brush, Luca examined it for evidence of damage such as broken branches or torn off leaves. As he rounded the statue to the front, he noticed the landscaping was not grown as high in one of the corners. Reaching down over the embankment, he pulled off a leaf that had been slightly ripped. Looking up, he silently thanked the saint. With caution, he climbed up into the bushes. Something was off with the ground near the concrete barrier which held the landscaping. Luca stomped his foot down on the dirt. *Hollow?*

"Samantha, over here." Luca knelt down and began pushing aside dirt and rocks until he saw black. He rapped his knuckles on the hard surface. Metal. "Now, what's this? It could be a sewer lid, but I don't know. It looks more like a door of some kind."

Samantha trudged over, reaching the spot Luca was clearing. Something small bounced off her feet, catching her eyes. She knelt down and picked it up. A rock? No, the dark metal covered in dirt was perfectly round.

"Hey Luca, look at this." Rubbing the object, she examined her prize. "What is it? It almost looks like a golf ball." She placed it into Luca's dusty hands.

"It feels smooth, but look at its color; it seems to be made out of pewter." Brushing off the crusted earth, he held it up to the sunlight. "There's an inscription. Something I've never seen before. Maybe an ancient language? Possibly Sanskrit. Now what does this do? That's the question." He rolled the small globe in his hands and pocketed it. He shrugged, continuing to clear the ground. "Well, whatever it does, I have a feeling we're about to find out soon. Ah, what do we have here?"

Luca returned to his original task, fully exposing the black metal trapdoor that had been hidden underneath the boscage. Slipping his fingers around a small loop handle, he pulled up. Dust and dank air bellowed upward. He coughed.

Samantha carefully leaned over, taking a peek at the dingy cavity. She was full of questions, nervously anticipating that they would need to descend into it. "What the hell? There's a ladder on the side here. Where does this go? Hey wait, New Orleans doesn't have tunnels, does it? Don't they have a high water table? Even the cemeteries are built above ground because of it." As she was talking through the feasibility of the tunnel, she remembered the underground prison Asgear had created. "Magic? Maybe he used magic to keep the water out, but how's it possible it's still here?"

"Not sure. It hasn't rained at all over the past two weeks. Anyhow, no use worrying about how it got here. Here's a flashlight. You ready to go in?" he raised an eyebrow at her; a corner of his mouth lifted in a slight grin. He dug out a stake and a few other items from his tool bag and pocketed them.

"As ready as I'll ever be. But I swear, I'm going to freak out if I see any giant city rats in there. I hear y'all got rats the size of cats down here." She shivered at the thought of running into one of the furry little beasts.

"Darlin', now you know you'll be safe with me. Besides," he joked, "the nutria lives out in the bayou. Come on now, I'll go down first."

Samantha followed Luca down the metal ladder into the tunnel, cursing the day she'd decided to go to a computer conference in the big easy. *Shit. Revolting tunnel. Excrement and other unknown foul smells. Rats. Possible Spiders. Roaches. Ew. Who cares about a vampire trying to kill me for an amulet when I could be eaten by some kind of creepy crawling critter?*

Halfway down the ladder, she heard a splash. Samantha flicked on her flashlight and saw Luca step into a few inches of brown, unidentified liquid. She froze.

"Luca, I don't know if I can do this. What's in that water?"

"Not sure, but you can do this. Come on, I'll carry you. Get on my back," he ordered.

"Are you sure?" she asked, still not moving.

"Yes. We need to go find this damn amulet. Both our lives are on the line. Come on, I'm ready for you."

Samantha released her hands from the rung and put her arms around Luca's neck. Once she had a firm grip, she held tight and wrapped her legs around his waist. The walls of the tunnel looked relatively modern, yet she knew Asgear had probably held it with magic. And now that the magic was atrophied, the walls were leaking. She prayed they would hold, uncertain of their safety. Within one hundred feet, the tunnel abruptly turned left, and they began a long journey into the darkness. The flashlight illuminated barely far enough for Samantha to see where they were going. She assumed Luca had night vision, because he appeared to have no problem walking even when the light flickered.

Samantha glanced over her shoulder; nothing but blackness. Fear blanketed her as she heard a noise behind her. "What's that?" she whispered.

"It's okay. It's just a tiny creature. He won't hurt you. You'll be all right. We probably don't have much further to go," he cajoled.

She rolled her eyes. What was it about men that they didn't mind little beasts with tails? After walking for over fifteen minutes, they finally came upon another metal ladder leading upward.

"A ladder," Luca observed. He sidled up next to it so that Samantha could reach it. "Looks like this is the end of the road. Okay, we're going up. Can you get on? Here, let me get you closer to it so you don't fall."

"Got it, thanks." Samantha easily grasped the metal rungs, and caught a lower one with her feet. She held tight, knowing what lay below her.

"Okay, let me pass. I'll go up first. Looks like there's a different kind of hatch on this one. Look down and protect your eyes. I'm goin' to force it upward. Don't come up until I say it's safe, okay?"

Samantha nodded, curled her head into her shoulder and put a hand over her face. A rush of sunlight and dust beamed onto them both as Luca easily removed the circular cover. He began his ascent and peered over the rim.

A large, spacious courtyard awaited him. Climbing up onto the patio, he scanned his surroundings. Sensing no humans or supernaturals, he called down to Samantha. "You can come on up. All's safe. We're in a courtyard. Well-kept from what I can see."

A decorative three-tiered fountain stood in the center of the courtyard. It was surrounded by several potted impatiens, hibiscus, palm and banana trees. The old red brick patio contrasted with the white clay pottery.

"This is beautiful," Samantha commented. "I love the fountain. Do you think Asgear lived here?"

"Not sure. He could have rented the property. But still, if it belongs to him, then he did it under an assumed name. There's nothing on the records of him owning or staying anywhere else but the warehouse." Luca was not deceived by the immaculately cared for garden. He felt something was off. "Samantha, be careful. Stay close. We'll sweep the courtyard, but I'm guessing that whatever we're looking for isn't out here in the open. Unfortunately, I think we'll find what we seek through that door over there." He pointed to the robin's-egg-blue door that led into the home.

After a thorough but unsuccessful exploration, Luca and Samantha readied themselves to enter the house. As they stood outside, a feeling of consternation swept over Samantha. She stared up at the home, and examined the exterior for any signs of overt destruction. On appearance alone, it held a warm façade, welcoming to all. Looking beyond the surface, a menacing sense of foreboding rained down from above. She might not have been psychic, but she clearly perceived the trickling damnation emanating from this structure. Every cell in her body told her to stay outside.

Anything could be in that house. A trap? A latent spell? It was true that Asgear was dead. But Samantha knew for certain that magic didn't always die with its creator. Magic was a living energy which waxed, waned and only sometimes died. It carried with it the good and evil for which it was intended. She knew it was waiting. What 'it' was remained to be seen. She steeled her nerves, determined to conquer her fear.

Luca guardedly turned the knob and entered. "It's unlocked."

A tidy kitchen located in the back of the home was decorated in red and black tiles with a fifties style chrome and white Formica kitchen set. *Quiet. Cold.* A long, narrow hallway led to the front entrance. As they explored the small home, Samantha couldn't help noticing the lack of furnishing or décor. The hallway led to a small living space which only contained a flat screen TV and a recliner that looked as if it had seen better days. The threadbare tan fabric was frayed, and spots of foam peeked through the tears. Stark white walls gave way to cream roller shades. Yet there was no other evidence of someone living in the home: no remains of food, dishes, glasses or newspapers.

"Whoever lived here sure was a minimalist," Samantha conjectured as she followed Luca upstairs.

"Yeah, that's an understatement. It's got fewer furnishings than a cheap motel. Hate to ask you this, Samantha, but are you sure you don't remember being here? Asgear must have kept you here at some point for you to have left these clues." Luca rounded another chalky-walled hallway.

"I don't remember being here at all. But this doesn't seem right. It doesn't feel right. It's like there's a maleficent presence that's ingrained into every pore of this house. And there are no bedrooms up here, except that one. Look." She pointed to a single brown wooden door. "It's the only one up here? How can that be? This is so strange. I get that this place is small but you'd think there was more than one room."

"Perhaps someone remodeled to combine the rooms?" The oak door was locked with a large nickel padlock. "It's locked, but not for long. Stand back, Samantha. Let's see what's behind door number one," he joked.

"What?"

"Monty Hall. Let's Make a Deal?" He shot her a sly grin. "Okay, here we go."

Samantha stood with her back against the wall, nervously watching Luca. She prayed the periapt was inside this room. She felt anxious, as though she was watching someone open a prank can of mints, waiting for the giant plastic snake to pop out at them.

Luca pulled a thin metal paper clip out of his jeans pocket. He straightened it then bent it back and forth until it snapped into two pieces. Shaping each piece into an "L", they could be used as a pick and tension wrench. He held them up and smiled. "Always prepared. If it were night, I'd just break the damn lock but the sun has me too weak to do it by hand. Here we go."

"By weak, do you mean human? Good thing you are quite the boy scout," she joked.

Luca grasped the lock with both hands, inserted and applied pressure with the wrench and picked at it until he heard it pop. Jerking the lock off in a single movement, he grabbed the antiqued glass knob and turned, pushing the door wide open. He felt around for a light switch but found none. He flicked on his flashlight and shone it into the darkened space. Settling a comforting hand on Samantha's shoulder, he tried to ease her fear. "It's okay. Nothing living is in here."

Samantha was curious to see what was inside. She pressed up against Luca's back, peering in from behind him. A large, darkened, rectangular room stood before them. Its walls and ceilings were draped in a black velvety fabric. The wooden planks had been painted a lacquered cardinal red. Elaborate candle wall sconces adorned the far wall; burnt candle wax splattered the floor. On the other side of the room, a metal ring was attached to the seam along the wall and the ceiling. Attached to the ring were long steel chains and two metal cuffs. Evidence of a kept captive were scattered across the floor; clothing, a plate, glass, remains of stale bread. On the farthest wall, opposite the entrance, an ornately carved circular wall hanging glowed in the distance.

"What the fuck?" Luca's words trailed off on seeing the entire room, realizing it had been used to shackle and hold a prisoner. *Samantha.*

Samantha turned on her flashlight and ran to the pile of clothing near the chains. "Oh my God, Luca. My clothes. These are mine."

It started to settle in that she had been here. Stripped of her clothes. Enslaved. She didn't want to cry but tears pricked her eyes. Even though she couldn't remember what had happened, she knew he'd done something to her. Gathering the filthy dress into her hands, she fell to her knees and began to sob.

"I was here," she whispered through small cries. "Oh my God. What did he do to me? Why?"

Luca ran over to her. Kneeling down next to Samantha, he put his arm around her, running his hand up and down her arm. "It's okay, he can't hurt you anymore. He's dead. It's just an empty room with memories that are best forgotten. You're safe with me. You'll be all right. Come on, now. Let it go." He took the dress from her hands, and placed it back on the shiny red floor. Pulling Samantha to her feet, Luca lovingly embraced her. "You're okay, now. Remember why we're here?" He kissed the top of her head.

Rubbing the tears from her eyes, Samantha released Luca. "I'm sorry. It's just so hard not remembering. It feels like a dream. A nightmare. Seeing my clothes just makes it real. I hope that son of a bitch rots in hell," she said, regaining her composure. "Okay, I'm fine. Let's do this."

"Over here," he said, pointing to the large circle. "It's carved with ancient markings. And look here in the center. A divot." He ran his fingers into the concave groove.

"Yes, a divot that looks like it might be the exact spot for our little golf ball. Do you have it?"

"Here, hold my flashlight. Shine it over there." He took the rounded pewter ball and held it up to the hanging. "Well, it looks like it might fit but I'm not sure how it would stay in there. It's not deep enough to put the entire ball into."

Yet as Luca placed the ball up into the indentation, there was an audible click. Samantha and Luca stepped back as the ball unfolded; eight pieces of metal pierced out from its internal structure, holding it securely against the carving. As if grabbing onto spider legs, Luca reached up and rotated the orb. A slight whoosh of air escaped as the wooden hanging hinged open, revealing the satin interior of a vault.

Samantha started to jump up and down in excitement, as she caught sight of a smooth, scarlet stone encased within the small repository. The *Hematilly Periapt.* It didn't look nearly as spectacular as she'd expected. A single, brick-red teardrop-shaped rock hung from brown sisal twine. It was exactly as described, yet nothing appeared magical to the eye. Unassuming, yet people were willing to kill for it.

Luca held the highly coveted gem up by its cord, regarding the amulet. "So this little baby is what's causing us all the trouble? I'm relieved to have it, especially knowing there's some freak out there with my blood," he exclaimed. "Would you like to do the honors?"

Samantha gladly took the periapt into her hands; she had no intentions of letting it go. Rubbing it between her fingers, she dreamt of the day she'd be free again.

"Luca, about your blood. We can't risk giving this away to the vampire. What if he decides to give it to a witch? It's too dangerous. No, we can't give this away," she insisted.

Luca raked his fingers through his hair, contemplating their dilemma. "I agree. The vampire who seeks it must be put to death. After that, we will destroy it so that no one can ever get their hands on this heinous object. But know this, Samantha, if it comes down between saving me or saving you, then the vampire gets the amulet. We have to keep it safe. Kade and Sydney can help us." He began sending them a text to explain what had transpired. "I'll send for a car and then we can decide how to proceed from there. The vampire said he'd find you, and believe me, I'll be waiting for him."

Just as Luca went to open the front door, Samantha saw a face peering through the rear kitchen window. "Luca, there's a woman out there." Samantha pointed and started walking toward the back door, inexplicably drawn outside. Intellectually she knew she shouldn't go by herself, but her legs kept walking one in front of another until she found herself at the back door.

"Samantha, no!" Luca yelled.

But Samantha didn't stop. She wanted to listen to Luca, she really did. But something pulled her. Samantha's body hummed with magic, high on power. The magic was beckoning her to keep going. She was drawn to the stranger like a piece of iron being pulled to a magnet. *Compelled.*

Samantha caught a glimpse of straggly black hair in the rain; Rowan stood waiting on the patio, her arms outstretched. What was she doing here at Asgear's home? Could she have followed her and Luca? How would she have known? Samantha couldn't understand what was happening; it didn't make sense. As Luca repeatedly called to her, she struggled to obey him and failed. No, this wasn't right. She shouldn't go. But the compulsion was too strong. She tried to fight, desperately attempting to shun the entrapment. Failing, she stumbled out into the courtyard, standing mere yards from the raven-haired witch.

Rowan laughed wildly, watching the novice try to fight her command. She knew that Samantha probably had no idea how to stop the compulsion. She almost felt sorry for her, but no, that ungrateful idiot had refused Ilsbeth's training. She was blessed with magic but had abjured both her ability and the graces of the coven. If Samantha had continued to train with Ilsbeth, she would have easily been able to deflect Rowan's will. Instead, she helplessly submitted, like the incompetent she'd always be. No pity for her; Samantha deserved to be overpowered because of her insolence. Rowan was disgusted with the level of disrespect Samantha had shown to her and her sisters by refusing to learn the craft.

She would have given anything to watch Asgear cringe as his puppet floundered. Asgear had always been so pompous in the magical circles, bragging about his new spells and artifacts. In a bar one night, she had learned from another witch that the wily mage was bragging that he had discovered the *Hematilly Periapt* as part of his grand plan to take over New Orleans. Now that he was dead, Rowan would have the last laugh.

After the stir with Samantha returning to the coven and searching her room, Rowan had grown suspicious. When Ilsbeth had told her that Samantha was looking for the periapt, she was thankful for the fortuitous conversation. It was then she knew for sure that she could successfully acquire it. The novice either knew the location of the artifact or with the help of Luca, would surely locate it. All she had to do was wait and watch; she already had the blood of a vampire.

She enjoyed watching Samantha stumble about, not quite sure why her body wouldn't listen to her brain. Enough of the fun. It was time to get down to business and take the amulet for herself.

"Ah, Samantha. You've found the periapt, I see. The rumors were true; it was here in New Orleans. You see, I've been wasting time searching, planning just the right location spell, and now you've helped me find it," she snickered.

"Rowan, what are you talking about? I need this. There's a vampire who's after me. I've got to give this to him," she explained.

Luca walked up behind her slowly, not wanting to make any fast movements lest Rowan might harm Samantha. He held the stake he'd brought firm in his hand.

"I just bet he does want it," she said sarcastically. "I bet all the vampires would like the amulet. Like Luca? Now, now, don't be shy, Luca. I see you back there. Don't make any fast moves, vampire."

She directed her attention back to Samantha. "You see, my friend, we all have powers. Ilsbeth told me you're an elemental witch, albeit a weak one. Do you want to see my power? No, really, I know you'll enjoy the show. You see, I'm a telekinetic witch, which means I can do this." She held out her arms and raised one palm face up toward Luca and Samantha, immobilizing them with very little effort. She laughed before continuing. "Now, let me help you with the amulet." Rowan's eyes flashed silver. "Dare me in periapt nunc, pythonissam!"

Samantha fought her own muscles as she felt her hand opening against her will. "No!" Samantha cried as the amulet flew across the courtyard, landing at Rowan's feet.

Rowan scooped it up in her hand, and pulled a small vial out of her pocket. "Now, the real fun begins. You know what's in here, don't you?" she asked, wickedly smiling.

Samantha shook her head. "No, please don't do this."

Luca continued his futile attempt at breaking Rowan's spell; he still couldn't move further than an inch. He needed to talk reason into the witch. "Rowan, Ilsbeth will ban you forever for your actions. You will lose all you have. Your coven. Your life. Now, give us the amulet. You can have it once we are done," Luca promised.

"Ha!" Rowan cackled. "Right, like you would simply give it back to me. Since you don't want to guess what's in the vial, should I tell you or keep it a surprise?" She laughed and waved her hand. "Okay, okay, I'll give you a hint. Remember lying in a church chained up? It was such a shame for them to mar your beautiful God-like body with silver, but it simply had to be done."

"My blood," Luca said with a growl.

"Handsome and smart. You vampires are so quick and strong. Very hard to capture, you know. Unless you happen to know when one is coming to your house, it is very difficult, indeed. But when you know one is visiting, well, it turns out it's not very hard at all…just need a little silver." Unscrewing the top of the vial, Rowan poured a drop of the blood onto the already sanguine stone. "So simple, really. It's done. Do you feel it? Come on now, Luca, do you know what this means? You are now my slave, vampire. As long as you are in my presence and I have the periapt, you are mine."

"I'll never be yours, witch. I feel nothing," he insisted.

"Really?" she grinned evilly, itching to play with her new toy. "Let's try it out, shall we? Luca, slave of Rowan, vampire born of Kade, kill Samantha!"

Luca reeled as the command drilled through his brain. The stake fell from his hands as he gripped the sides of his head. Never in his life had he been compelled to do what another told him, yet the desire to wrap his hands around Samantha's neck grew deep within his belly. He roared and shoved her to the ground. Samantha struggled against him, kicking wildly, trying to escape.

"Luca, no," she pleaded. "Don't listen to her!"

Luca fought his own hands as his fingers crept around Samantha's neck. He tried to fight, reeling his hands back. An excruciating convulsion racked through his body in response to his disobedience. He heard Rowan's laughter in the distance.

"Ah, what's that you feel, Luca? That's right; it's slicing agony, isn't it?

Get used to it my dear bloodsucker. You no longer have free will. Surely you will fight me, but I will break you over time. Keep ignoring my command, vampire, and you will suffer endlessly. You might even die. What a pity that would be, after all my hard work. Just do it. Kill her."

At Rowan's directions, his fingers wandered up to her neck and squeezed. Samantha pounded Luca's chest with her hands, trying to dislodge him as his hands crept around her throat once more. She could tell from his eyes that he was trying to fight the order, greatly suffering for his refusal to hurt her. But still, his fingers gripped tighter and tighter.

"Grab the stake. It's right there, on the ground. Kill me, Samantha. Don't let her do this," Luca grunted.

Samantha shook her head; the stake was within inches of her reach. "No! I won't. I can't," she protested as she heard a loud whoosh from behind. She lost sight of Luca, as the vise around her throat unlocked. Samantha heaved and sucked in air over and over in an attempt to catch her breath. Pushing up onto the palms of her hands, she sat up and ran her hands through her hair, dizzy from the loss of oxygen.

As she lifted her head, she gazed into the piercing black eyes of the vampire she'd met at Sangre Dulce. He'd rescued her from Luca's grip. For a split second, he caught her gaze, fangs bared. He had Luca in a headlock, threatening to break his neck. Luca struggled against him, unwilling to give into defeat.

Samantha screamed at the vampire to release Luca. "Don't hurt him! Please! I'll give you whatever you want. I promise," she begged. Samantha stumbled as she tried to stand. Pointing at Rowan, she tried to get the attention of the stranger. "Over there! Rowan, that witch right there. She has the periapt. He's under her control."

Luca growled at the other vampire. The clamp on his trachea loosened for a split second, allowing him to maneuver out of the stranglehold. The two magnificent vampires began to roll on the ground, wrestling for control over one another.

Rowan laughed maniacally, "Oh how I love to see the gladiators fight. It's a fine match. But alas, we must be going. Luca, are you ready to come with your new mistress? You really do need better training. I asked you to kill this insignificant excuse for a witch, and here you are playing games with a vampire. Ah, I must admit I am looking forward to making you my slave in every way possible. Oh yes, I plan to discipline you long and hard, night after night," she mused, staring down at Samantha.

"No!" Samantha screamed and lunged for her. Samantha shoved Rowan to the ground, but the witch was strong. She grabbed Samantha by the hair, pulling her downward, refusing to relinquish the amulet.

"You should have worked on your powers, little girl. Maybe if you had, you'd be like me. But, no, you wasted Ilsbeth's lessons. So tell you what, since I'm feeling generous, I'm about to teach you a little trick in transporting." Rowan held her by the hair and slapped Samantha across the face. "Pay attention!"

"Fuck you!" Samantha yelled and hit her back. "Give me the amulet!" She kicked at Rowan as they fought, but she couldn't pin her to the ground.

"Enough!" Rowan waved her hand, sending out a wave of magic; Samantha's body flew across the courtyard and slammed against a brick wall. Rendered unconscious, Samantha drifted into blackness.

Rowan waited for her vampire. After all the work she'd done, she had no intention of leaving without him. Chanting a spell, she opened a swirling gray portal. She turned to the vampires, who'd stopped fighting momentarily to observe the vortex.

"Come Luca, you're mine. You will come with me now," she ordered.

In confusion, Luca started to go for Samantha. He wanted to stay with Samantha and protect her. But as he did, searing pain ripped through his body; he knew he was being forced to go with Rowan. Thrown into an agonizing paroxysm, he doubled over, unable to stand. The periapt was the only key to his survival. If he could get the periapt and destroy it, then his binding to Rowan would be broken.

He looked over to the large vampire with whom he'd been fighting. Luca could tell the vampire was many years older than him, a great warrior. Luca was one of the strongest vampires in the world, yet this vampire was not overcome. More importantly, the vampire had saved Samantha from certain death that would have come at his own hands. He sensed this vampire didn't want him or her dead, but knew he also desired the periapt. *Could he be trying to destroy it too?* He had to make a decision, go with Rowan willingly and destroy the amulet or stay and try to fight against the compulsion.

He tried once again to go to Samantha, and he was blinded afresh as the fiery torture rippled throughout his bones. Falling on his hands and knees, he backed away, and the pain subsided. Through blurry vision, he glared at the devil who'd done this to him.

Rowan crooked a finger at him, giving him no choice. Stumbling toward her, he attempted an attack. With but a flick of her wrist, she threw him into the churning aperture. A rush of energy flooded his senses. Swept inward, he landed with a thud onto a rock-hard concrete floor. Luca hissed as a silver net blanketed his body. The smell of his own burnt flesh drifted into his nose as he prayed for mercy.

Chapter Thirteen

Samantha dreamt she was floating on a cloud, smiling at a rainbow. As she weaved her fingers into its beams, her eyes fluttered open, and she realized she'd been asleep. *Where am I? Where's Luca?* In a surge of panic, she shot upright. Scanning the room, she didn't recognize her surroundings; an achromatic theme teased her eyes. The room was bright white, with cream crown moldings. The white four-poster bed was covered in a white eyelet duvet with matching bed pillows. A large white dresser and mirror and overstuffed chair were offset by the dark cherry hardwood floor. Despite being devoid of color, the room was tastefully decorated.

Draped in silence, she sat up with her legs crossed. She sighed, relieved that she was still dressed. Her shoes, however, were on the floor next to the bed. Considering she wasn't naked or locked up, she surmised that whoever had taken her wasn't considering hurting her…yet.

Remembering Luca's attack, she carefully touched her neck, grateful she hadn't died. It was slightly bruised but didn't hurt too much. She started to panic again, wondering what had happened to Luca, when she looked up to see the intimidating vampire who'd been stalking her leaning against the door jamb. Coolly, he approached her. Her eyes widened as she systematically ran through feasible escape scenarios.

"Hello, Samantha. I am Léopold Devereoux," he said, with a French accent.

"You!" Samantha backed up against the bed, bending her knees to her chest, wrapping her hands around them. Her heart beat frantically. She looked for a getaway but saw none.

Léopold gracefully glided toward her and sat on the large lounge chair. "Do not be afraid, mon agneau. I will not hurt you," he assured her.

She studied the larger than life vampire who'd threatened her at the club. Remembering the feel of his body against hers, she knew that he had to be at least as tall as Luca. In the darkness of Sangre Dulce, she had barely been able to make out his features, but she'd never forget his midnight-black eyes. Now in the light, she noticed how striking he was. The hard contours of his masculine face accentuated his square jawline. Dark brown, wavy hair was styled into a modern shark fin. Even though his presence exuded power, he looked young, mid-thirties. Sexy. Deadly. Samantha wondered if every vampire had an underpinning of sensuality that kept every woman wondering if he'd bite her. While he was undeniably attractive, she felt nothing but fear toward the vampire standing before her. She realized she was staring, and averting her gaze, she looked away toward the wall.

Sensing her fear, Léopold attempted to soothe the pretty little witch. He didn't mean to scare her, but he needed the amulet. She was nothing more than a means to an end. Looking at her pale skin and full lips, he understood Luca's attraction to the mortal.

"Now, I know you don't trust me. Given my severe actions, I suppose you have reason. But mademoiselle, my intentions this evening are honorable."

"Honorable? You burned down my cabin!" she spat at him. "You could have killed us!"

"Oh yes, well, that was merely a diversion to get you to focus on the task at hand. You see, it was rumored that Asgear had the periapt. After his indiscretion with Kade Issacson's human woman, I searched his properties, or should I say what was left of his properties, but never found it. But I did, however, find you." He smiled wryly. "Convinced of its existence, I simply gave you the encouragement you needed to find it for me. Which you did, quite resourcefully, by the way."

Samantha glared at him in contempt and disbelief. "You risked my life and Luca's for that godforsaken amulet, and now what? Rowan has it. And Luca? Where is he?" she cried. Tears welled in her eyes.

"I'm afraid that is a bit of a problem. Rowan is a devious witch, and she knows exactly why I was so persistent in my search for the *Hematilly Periapt*. She is fully aware that she can control vampires. And now, to my dismay, she has Luca. She'll also have any other vampire whose blood she steals as well. The amulet is very dangerous to our kind. She must be found." He took a deep breath and blew it out. "I called Kade this evening, and he has been detained for several hours, something or other to do with the wolves. We agreed it would be best for me to take Étienne, Xavier and you to extricate Luca from Rowan."

"Me? What could I possibly do? You saw what she did to me." Samantha was embarrassed by what had happened. Rowan had called her and she had come like a dog. She hadn't called on her powers; instead she'd frozen.

Léopold stood, approached the bed and sat next to Samantha. "You are a mere babe in the woods, dear Samantha. But you do have your power. I saw you in the mountains the day you extinguished the fire. You need to concentrate this time. I will need your help to save Luca and acquire the amulet. Of course, Rowan will be expecting us. She very much wants to keep it, so that she can keep Luca. Do you want her to keep Luca?" he taunted.

"No," she whispered, putting her head in her hands. She rubbed her face and met his gaze with pleading eyes. "I can't lose him. We are bonded. What I mean to say is that we started it. He is mine. I am his." The reality of the situation was sinking in, and Samantha hated that Rowan had taken him.

"I would call that a no. And so what you must understand is that he is no longer yours. He doesn't even belong to himself. She is making him a slave as we speak, in every sense of the word. He will not be able to fight her. What she tells him to do, he will do. As long as the amulet exists, she is his."

"No, that can't be. He would never be with someone else. When she told him to attack me, he was fighting it," she protested.

"But it will kill him to continue to fight it…eventually he will give in. In another few days, he will be nothing more than a shell of a man," he calmly explained.

"What are we supposed to do? We don't even know where she is. Ilsbeth…we should call her to help us," she suggested.

"No. That's not going to happen. Any other witch may also be tempted to take it. The periapt is something the witches want in their possession. It must be destroyed."

"So why bring me?" she challenged.

"Because you love him. And only a witch can destroy the *Hematilly Periapt*. He needs you. Hell, I need you," he admitted.

For just a second, Samantha thought she saw a flicker of emotion in his eyes and then just as quickly it was gone.

Léopold continued speaking. "So here's what's going to happen. You're going to get yourself together and meet us downstairs. Étienne and Xavier are coming over to my flat and then we shall go to Rowan's. She bought a home, which she cleverly deeded in a different name, but I am certain she's there nonetheless. She'd never risk taking him to the coven, because if she did, she knows that Ilsbeth would immediately call Kade. To the best of our knowledge, Ilsbeth is not aware of what Rowan's done, but we are not involving her, either. No, this will be done with the four of us. Kade should be here in the morning, should we need to dispose of the witch."

"Dispose? What the hell is that supposed to mean?"

"It means that she will die, Samantha. Kade's the leader in this region and it's fitting that he metes out justice should she survive the night." Léopold walked across the room and opened the door to leave. "And Samantha, you should be aware that Rowan may have created others."

"Others?" she asked wearily.

"Yes, others. Other slaves, vampires. Possibly shifters. We cannot be sure what she has done."

"Who are you anyway? Why would Kade let you rescue Luca?" She couldn't fathom why this stranger cared what happened to Luca.

"I am Kade's maker," he stated with resounding authority. "Now let's not waste time. We have a vampire to save and an amulet to destroy. I need you ready, mentally prepared for what we are about to face. You must be focused. Draw on your power. Remember how it felt at the cabin. Bring whatever elements you need, but help us get Luca." Léopold shut the door behind him, praying that Luca's woman understood what they faced.

Samantha wasn't happy to be in Léopold's home. How could Kade leave her with him? She barely trusted Kade and now she was supposed to trust his maker? She put her face into her hands in grief. Luca was gone, and it was all her fault. If she could have resisted Rowan, she'd never have lost the amulet. If she'd listened to Ilsbeth and tried harder to learn her craft, she would've been able to fight back. Instead, she'd been nothing more than a marionette being played by a master puppeteer.

Wiping the tears away, she attempted to collect her emotions. She may've been useless to Luca in the courtyard, but she'd be damned if she'd give up on him. She couldn't let Rowan wear him down to nothing. Resolving to fight until her last breath, she pushed off the bed. She wasn't a quitter; she was a survivor.

Samantha knew in her heart that she loved Luca with every cell of her being. She wasn't sure that she could trust Léopold, but he'd told her Xavier and Étienne were coming with them. Luca trusted those vampires who'd been at the club. If he could trust them, she would try as well. It was all she had to go on.

Pushing open the bathroom door, Samantha went about her business and then caught a glimpse of herself in the mirror. Her long red mane frizzed out of the rubber band; her face was marred by dirt and a large thin scratch over her right eyebrow remained as evidence of her brawl with Rowan. "Shit," she said to herself, deciding she looked like a hot mess.

She ran the water hot and wet a washcloth. After gently cleaning the wound, she rubbed the cloth up and down her arms, in an attempt to freshen herself up. Wetting her fingers with water, she finger combed her hair, braided a single braid down her back and secured it with the band. Satisfied that she was ready to face Léopold, she walked out of the bathroom and into her bedroom. Her delicate fingers closed around the brass doorknob. She took a deep cleansing breath; it was time to get Luca back.

Barely conscious, Luca writhed against the burning silver cuffs. Through blurry eyes, he took stock of the sparsely decorated environment. The spacious area held only a single tattered sofa and a dusty area rug, which partially covered the oak planked floor. Intricate antiqued crown moldings around the upper perimeter clued him that it might once have been used as a ballroom. However, not a window revealed his location, as they'd been boarded over.

Footsteps alerted him to the svelte figure watching him from the doorway. Her inky curly tresses spilled over nearly white skin. As his eyes came into focus, he could see she was wearing a scarlet satin corset and matching lace panties; a translucent full-length robe trimmed with feathers, deliberately showed off her assets. Her cherry-red lips began to move as she slithered toward him. A flash of metal in her hands caught his eyes; scissors.

"Luca, darling. So nice that you are finally awake." She knelt beside him, running her long fingers up his chest. Pulling tightly on his shirt with one hand, she began to cut the material until his chest lay naked to her. She ripped the fabric aside until Luca felt the cool hardwood floor against his skin.

"Rowan," Luca hissed. "You've gone mad. You can't keep me here."

"Ah, that's where you're wrong, my vampire." She raked her fingernails down his chest until she felt the button on the top of his jeans. She unbuttoned his pants and unzipped him. "I can and will keep you here. You're my shiny new toy. I do love unwrapping presents."

She smiled wickedly and held the edge of the cold blades flat against his lips. "Keep quiet now, my pet. I'm going to enjoy every minute of this."

Luca jerked his head away in disgust. Rowan laughed as she trailed the scissors down his chest and slid the blade under his jeans, letting it rest against his groin.

"Don't worry, darling. I have no intention of damaging the goods. I have plans for you." She cupped his balls roughly then began to cut his jeans away. Within minutes, she had removed all the denim. Luca lay splayed on the hardwood floor naked save only for his boxers.

"Rowan, don't do this. Ilsbeth will find you. She's the most powerful witch in New Orleans. You're part of her sisterhood."

"Ha! Ilsbeth," she mocked. "All these years, you and Kade have been coming to the coven for her advice, her help. Using her like a whore. She makes me sick the way she panders to all you vampires. She'll never find me anyway. Of course you don't know since you've been out of it, but I'll let you in on a little secret." She straddled him, caging him with her arms placed to either side of his head. Seductively, she leaned over, rubbing her breasts against his chest. Lapping her tongue along the line of his neck, she whispered in his ear, "We're not in New Orleans."

"Are you mad? You know damn well that Ilsbeth can still find you."

"So you think. But you need to accept that I have grown quite powerful too. Even if she managed to locate me by scrying, I've set up wards especially for Ilsbeth."

"I am going to rip your fucking throat out and drain you dry, witch. Release me now and I'd consider showing you mercy," Luca growled, baring his fangs.

"Now, now, Luca dear. You've got to come to terms with what's happened to you. It will be much easier for us all if you simply submit to me. I am your mistress now. And I can do whatever I want with your mind and this fine body of yours." Rowan dug her fingernails into his shoulders and began to grind her pelvis against Luca's.

Luca thrashed against his bindings and tried to buck her off of him. "Bitch, it will be a cold day in hell before you'll ever be with me. You disgust me, you bloody cow. Get off me!"

"Come now, do be a good boy. You are forgetting that I have the periapt. I can make you do anything now, whether you want it or not." She fingered a silver necklace and held up the amulet; a key dangled next to it. Moving her body upward, she pressed the apex of her legs against the cheek of his face as she unlocked the handcuffs above his head.

"You will lie still on this floor, Luca. You will not stand. If you do, you will feel blinding pain. You see, you have no choice but to obey me." Rowan patted his face and got up to attend to his ankle cuffs.

Freed from his bonds, Luca stretched but was weakened from the silver. His arms felt like lead as he pulled them over his chest. Yet the burns from the silver were already beginning to heal. Luca could sense his power returning as the bindings on his feet were released. Remembering the pain in the courtyard, he decided to lie still and formulate an escape plan. If he could somehow get the amulet off her neck, he should be released from its will.

Rowan rubbed Luca's ankles, amazed at how quickly he healed. She congratulated herself for choosing such a fine vampire as her slave. She'd have him in her bed and for her warrior, she decided. Admiring his lean, muscled body, she glided her hands up his legs.

"Ah, you are an exquisite specimen. I can't wait to nuzzle my plaything." Her finger tips slipped into his boxers.

Luca heard a commotion in the hallway. Rowan froze. Five scraggly wolves tramped into the room. An enormous, menacing, auburn wolf growled at the others. Whimpering, the four lesser wolves cowered and scampered out of the room. The gray-eyed wolf approached Luca, sniffing his hair and chest. A piercing howl emanated throughout the room as it transformed into a naked, crouching man.

Rowan jolted upward and scurried off of Luca. Coming up behind the man, she placed her bony fingers on his shoulders. "Sköll, please forgive me, I was just amusing myself with my lovely prize while you were out. He's very pleasing, don't you think?"

Sköll stretched upward and hoisted Rowan into his burly arms. His fully bearded lips crushed Rowan's; a gruff hand fondled her breast. Wrenching away from her for a minute, he regarded Luca.

"You've done well, Rowan. He'll help us greatly in our cause."

"Your woman isn't very faithful, wolf. She was about to touch my dangly bits; sometimes only a vampire can satisfy a woman," Luca goaded. He was slowly gaining strength but continued to bide his time on the floor.

Sköll padded up to Luca and knelt beside him, grabbing his face with grubby strong fingers. "Brave you are, for a man whose balls are owned by a witch. You, my friend, will do as I say. The witch and I are business partners, nothing more. If she wants to fuck you when we're done, she's welcome to your sorry ass. Hell, I may join her." Sköll roamed his hands over Luca's chest, admiring the slave. "But first, you will go to war."

Disgusted by the wolf's touch, Luca batted his hand away. "War?"

"Marcel will pay for refusing my brother his bitch. Now, I'm gonna take his pack. And you will help me."

"Kat? What in hell makes you think I'll do that? Besides, you'll never win. Marcel knows this land blind. There's no way an outside pack could take over."

"I have an insider who's going to help me, vamp. As far as fighting for me, with this amulet," he fingered her silver chain, "you'll have no choice. Rowan here, is going to train you real good to obey her. By the time she's done you'll be as compliant as a little lamb. Not only will you fight for me, you'll lick my balls if she tells you to." Sköll clutched Luca's cheeks in his hands and forced his closed lips against Luca's. Laughing out loud, he walked across the room to Rowan.

Luca bared his fangs at the wolf, disgusted by the thought. "Fucking never, wolf. I will never help you or that bitch."

He watched as Sköll took Rowan in a rough embrace. She writhed and purred against him like a cat in heat, then ripped off her clothes, decidedly aroused by the wolf. Falling to the floor, growling and mewling, they began to have sex. Luca watched in abhorrence and planned his attack.

Sufficiently engrossed in their coupling, Rowan and Sköll had inadvertently exposed their vulnerability. Luca patiently waited for the perfect moment. He needed to rip the amulet from Rowan's neck. She needed it on her person to control him. If he could get the amulet away from Rowan, even for a second, he could escape.

Chapter Fourteen

When Samantha entered the foyer, she immediately recognized the extraordinarily good-looking vampire, Xavier. She felt relieved to see him, even though she'd only met him once in the dimly lit club. Sculpted, mocha-skinned muscles bulged from his black spandex tank top. Black jeans hugged every firm curve of his glutes; he looked like a Greek God.

He smiled at her as if he'd been expecting her. Extending his hand, he bowed. "Xavier Daigre, at your service, ma cher." He took her hand in his, brushing his lips across it. "I understand mon ami, Luca, was taken earlier today."

"I'm Samantha," she replied, noting his old world charm. "I know we didn't get a chance to talk at the club, but Luca mentioned you and Étienne. As for your question, yes, Rowan, from Ilsbeth's coven, took both Luca and the *Hematilly Periapt.* It's an amulet of sorts. It controls vampires but only someone of magic can use it and also only if they have the blood of the vampire they wish to control." She lowered her head and shook it. "It's my fault that she has him. I should've resisted her. She took it from me. Then she took Luca. You should have seen him."

Xavier placed a firm hand on her shoulder. "We will find him, Samantha."

Étienne walked in to see Xavier with his hands on the petite human woman who Luca cherished. Although he wouldn't admit it to them, they'd both known Luca had been entranced by the witch as they'd watched him dance with her at Sangre Dulce.

"Hello Samantha," Étienne nodded. "I'm Étienne. We met at the club but weren't formally introduced. Léopold told us what happened. Xavier is correct. Luca is very old and strong."

Samantha looked to Étienne who she sensed was a younger vampire. His dark-blonde hair was tied at his neck. Like Xavier, he was attractive and well-built. Wearing black jeans and a white polo shirt, he was casually cool and looked like he could have been in a GAP commercial. Samantha looked around to see if Léopold was nearby before whispering to them both. "What about him? Léopold. Can he be trusted?"

Xavier and Étienne passed a silent look between them. Xavier spoke first. "We are loyal to Kade. He sent us here because there is very serious trouble with Marcel's pack that he must attend to. All I can tell you is that Kade would never have left Luca in such a predicament if he didn't trust Léopold. Luca is his best friend and confidant. Kade explained Léopold's role and said he's more than capable of helping Luca. Being that Léopold is

Kade's maker, he is much more powerful and can help us retrieve our friend."

Étienne nodded in agreement. "It's true, Samantha. Léopold knows of the *Hematilly Periapt.* And he'll be much stronger when we need the power of another vampire, but in the end, it's you who is needed to destroy it."

"But how?"

"When the time comes, I shall help you, Samantha." Léopold strolled into the room. "Consider it on a 'need to know' basis." A corner of his mouth lifted in a slight smile.

He was so smug, she thought. Dressed head to toe in black leather, he shook hands with Étienne and Xavier and began to discuss their plan on what vehicle and route they'd take to the location. Samantha tried to concentrate on his words but soon found herself lost in his aura. Léopold emanated authority and command; energy had reverberated throughout the room on his arrival. Samantha's own magic started to hum in response, and she rubbed her arms up and down in an effort to ease the sensation. She was not only unsure of her magic, she was afraid. What if she accidently lit the place on fire?

Léopold stopped speaking to observe the small woman. She'd gone quiet, acutely aware of his vitality. He strode over to her and placed a calming hand on Samantha's shoulder. "You're okay, mon agneau. Breathe. Take deep breaths. You sense me, no?"

"I…I'm sorry. It's just your power. My skin. I feel like I'm on fire. I'm new to my own abilities. For a minute there, I thought I might set something ablaze. It's like I can't contain it once the magic surfaces."

"Save it for Rowan. You're going to need every last bit of energy you've got. Okay, now?"

She nodded. Something about the vampire excited her nerves, but his hand calmed her. She hated being out of control and was anxious to get Luca back. She'd never been a violent person but knew in that moment, she could kill. Rowan was destroying her life. Luca was her future, and she was ready to unleash her fury to save them all.

They'd been riding in the car for an hour. Marshes, fields and bayou sprinkled the landscape along the way. At night, she couldn't see much, but sensed they were in the country. "Léopold, how much further do we have to go? How do you know they'll be there?" she asked.

"Rowan's place is near Houma; we're almost there. She's got nowhere else to go. She inherited the antebellum several years ago, according to the records. What she plans to do with Luca is the big mystery, however. Ilsbeth and the other witches would have had the assistance of the vampires if they'd needed it. But then again, power is quite the aphrodisiac," he surmised.

Aggravated and confused, Samantha rested her head against the window, staring out into the darkness. She didn't care about why Rowan wanted the periapt; she only wanted Luca. Her stomach knotted as the SUV's tires turned into a narrow driveway lined with Spanish moss-covered elm trees. An eerie feeling blanketed Samantha's entire body. Quiet fog weighed onto the graveled road; the headlights pushed through the pale mist.

Léopold, in the front passenger seat, directed Xavier to park out of sight of the house. The thrum of the engine cut to silence. Samantha took a deep breath, knowing their battle was about to begin.

"Xavier, Étienne. Take the back of the house. Samantha. We're going to enter the front door together. Now listen up, everyone. We can't be sure who or what Rowan's got in there. She could have wards. It's even possible that she could have another vampire besides Luca. Not likely, but possible." He caught Samantha's eyes. "Samantha, I'll try to take Rowan, but as she demonstrated, her gift of telekinesis is strong. If she spots me, she can shake me off with a hand. You need to go after her with your gift in kind. Call on the elements. Show no mercy, for she will not show it to you. Understand?"

"Yes," she lied. Samantha nervously bit her lip. She wasn't sure if she could take out Rowan, but she'd die trying.

As they got out of the car, a humid breeze blew hard against them. Lightning flashed in the distance. Within seconds, thunder roared and Samantha reacted by wrapping an arm around Léopold's. She barely knew the lethal vampire, yet here she was holding onto him for dear life. She rolled her eyes silently in embarrassment but she held firm. *Better the devil you know.*

Léopold smelled Samantha's trepidation. He'd gone to war many times over his lifetime, accepting that battles seldom came without loss. But one thing he'd never done was knowingly go into a situation attached to a fragile mortal woman. If he'd had any other choice, he would have left her at home. But he knew damn well that he needed her to dispose of the amulet, for only a witch could demolish the diabolical object.

If Luca didn't survive the attack, he'd pursue the beautiful girl, he thought to himself. He knew he shouldn't think such things while on the brink of combat. He blamed it on the adrenaline coursing through his veins. Every sense was heightened, including his need for sex. He enjoyed the feel of her body tight against his and wondered what it would be like to bring her to climax.

Before climbing the staircase, Léopold shoved Samantha behind a tree. Her back pressed tight against the bark, the evidence of his arousal grazing her belly.

"What are you doing?" she whispered loudly, quite annoyed by his state.

"Patience, my dear Samantha. I'm listening." He smiled ruefully, aware of his surroundings.

"Do you hear anything?" She tried to ignore the fact that a large, sexy vampire had her pinned to an elm tree, not to mention the inappropriate hardness in his pants.

"Lovemaking." A broad smile broke across his handsome face. He leaned down to smell her hair.

"Excuse me?" It was obvious the man had sex on his mind. But Samantha couldn't for the life of her fathom how he could talk about it when they were about to go on the offensive.

"Lovemaking. Sex. That is what I hear. Someone is getting it on, as Al Green would say. A perfect time for a party, don't you think?"

Samantha's stomach lurched. She'd die if Rowan made Luca do something sexual against his will. She'd seen firsthand the power the amulet had had over Luca back in the courtyard.

"Don't worry, my sweet. We're about to go in now. You ready?" he asked.

"As ready as I'll ever be. Let's do this," she replied.

Stepping out from behind the tree, Samantha took in the sight of Rowan's home. The once magnificent antebellum stood dilapidated before them. The gabled roof peaked with an uneven slope and paint peeled from majestic Grecian pillars. Fig ivy had nearly taken over the sides of the home and was creeping onto the porch.

Léopold placed a silencing finger to his lips and pointed at the stairs. Slowly they climbed up toward the door. Aside from the cicadas singing, she could only hear her own heartbeat in the darkness. She trusted that Léopold was correct about the sex; yet as they approached the door, she heard nothing.

Silently, Léopold traced a finger down her cheek, seeking her attention. It was time. He held up a finger. On the count of three, he'd enter. One. Two. Three.

Chapter Fifteen

Luca watched as Sköll lifted Rowan to position her over the sofa. The sight of Rowan's pale ass in the air pointing toward him repulsed Luca. Sköll growled and looked over at Luca to make sure he was watching as he roughly entered her from behind. She screamed in delight and soon Sköll lost himself in his actions, ignoring his unwilling audience.

Luca breathed deeply as he steeled himself for attack. *Remove the amulet*; the words reverberated through his head. It was his only chance of breaking the spell. Lunging forward, burning agony tore through Luca's spine. He had disobeyed Rowan's command to lie still on the floor. His blatant insubordination was met with blinding torment. A thousand invisible knives pierced his skin; his head screamed for alleviation. Sucking in a breath, Luca charged onward into swift propulsion.

Immersed in passion, Sköll barely registered the danger before Luca sank his fangs into his shoulder. Energizing shifter blood rushed into Luca's mouth as he held Sköll in place. Plowing his hand madly toward Rowan's neck, his fingers felt for the periapt and slipped under the silver chain. A pop sounded as it snapped.

Luca saw the crimson amulet rattle across the floor. Instantly, the ghostly knives receded. Twisting herself round to look up at Sköll's attacker, Rowan met Luca's eyes with a clear understanding that the spell was shattered. Refusing to retract his fangs, he bit deeper into Sköll. Raging, the shifter jerked Luca upward, wildly attempting to dislodge his attacker. Sköll began to transform into a wolf, successfully bucking Luca onto the ground. Within seconds, the man turned wolf, and Luca renewed his assault, giving the beast little time to assume an offensive position. In the midst of the struggle, a loud crash sounded, distracting Luca. The vampire from the courtyard had erupted through the barricade, and his beautiful Samantha rushed directly into the skirmish.

Running through the foyer, Samantha chased Léopold as he shouldered his way through a double set of locked wooden doors. In the melee, she could have sworn she heard dogs growling, but didn't turn around to investigate the noise. Samantha froze upon entering. Rowan, nude, was scrambling around on her hands and knees. Luca, barely dressed, held the throat of a red wolf. Its jaws snapped at Luca's neck as they fought for dominance. Léopold, baring his fangs, turned toward her and roared. She ducked as he flew over her head. Crouching down, she peeked to see him wrestling two brown wolves. The crisp pattering of feet could be heard from the hallway; more wolves approached.

Spying the periapt in the corner, Samantha tore across the room. Out of the corner of her eye, she caught a glimpse of Xavier tearing the fur from a gray wolf. Blood sprayed across the room. Focusing on the amulet, Rowan and Samantha raced to get to it first. Rowan, deciding to use her magic, stilled and blasted Samantha, effectively smashing the back of her skull against the wall. Samantha gritted her teeth, staving off the pain. Touching the back of her head, blood trickled onto her fingertips.

Rowan grabbed the amulet and sneered in victory. "Stupid Samantha, did you really think you could come in here and take what's mine?"

Samantha stumbled to her feet. Instead of feeling lightheaded, strength and loathing rushed through the whole of her body. Samantha closed her eyes, concentrating on the element she wished to call. She'd had enough of death, fighting, torture. It was time for it all to end and she'd be the one to end it. The room started to slightly vibrate at first. The vampires and wolves barely noticed the buzz as they bit and tussled. Within seconds the house came into a full tremble. Dust cascaded from above as the ceiling threatened to collapse. Floor boards creaked and snapped as the foundations began to heave and rock. As the room began to shake violently, the vampires and werewolves steadied themselves against the barrage of tremors.

Rowan attempted to telekinetically bombard Samantha with magic, but was thwarted by her reflective palm. Rowan looked around as the planks beneath her feet began to split open and crack. Screaming out for help, she collapsed into the crawl space. Holding onto the sides of the flooring, her upper torso supported her weight. Rowan's face turned stark white in fear, unsure of how Samantha was causing the quakes.

Samantha's eyes flew open as she called upon the elements. "Care dea aperuerit mihi thesaurum terrae. Hoc malum pythonissam in sinu. Quia non est de hoc mundo. Adhaerere. Tolle eam nunc!" *Open the Earth.*

Rowan screamed Sköll's name as the earth began to cleave open at Samantha's command. Luca bit deeply into Sköll's shoulder, rendering him immobile. Helplessly he watched as his lover, Rowan, flailed her arms, shrieking as she plunged helplessly into the crevice.

Samantha walked over to the gaping chasm, and knelt down to Rowan.

"Save me, sister," Rowan pleaded. "I swear to you. I will share it with you. Please, grab my hand."

Samantha considered her plea but knew in her heart, that evil was speaking. "Dear sister," she chided. "You are no sister of mine. Back to the earth you go. May the Goddess grant you peace." Peeling open Rowan's fingers, Samantha took the periapt and shoved it into her pocket.

Rowan cursed her. "You little bitch. This will never be over. There are others who will want the periapt. They know of its existence. They will find you! This will not end!"

"That's where you're wrong, Rowan. This! Ends! Now!" Samantha yelled.

A seism rocked the entire house as the fissure grew wider and deeper. Samantha closed her eyes and called once again on the elements. "Lorem benedictionem, dea. Accipere, Rowan, soror Ilsbeth, in calore et munda eius eius malum."

Rowan clawed at the crumbling dirt in an effort to save herself as Samantha's words took effect. A loud shriek emanated from Rowan as she plummeted deep into the fiery core of the earth.

Samantha breathed deeply, willing the brown terra together again. Within seconds, the gaping crevice consolidated, leaving nothing but disturbed dirt in its place. As exhaustion racked Samantha's mind and body, she crumbled to the floor, and sobbed.

As the shaking subsided, Sköll sliced into Luca's arm. Not lethally, but it was enough to make Luca release his hold. Sköll transformed into his human form and scurried toward Samantha. "What have you done, witch? I needed Rowan. Now that you have taken her, I will take you." He wrapped his arm around Samantha's neck.

Xavier, Étienne and Léopold stood still, acknowledging her capture. They had killed all the wolves except one or two who'd retreated out to the woods. Luca stalked cautiously toward Sköll.

"Don't hurt her. You need me for your war. Take me," he ordered.

"Now you want to come willingly? Hmmm….this one smells good," Sköll growled and licked the back of Samantha's neck. She hung like a ragdoll helpless in his grip. "Ah, she'll do nicely. A fertile witch who can serve all my needs. And she's got the periapt." He reached around with his free hand to grope her breast and smirked. "Go now, and she'll live. I'll find another vampire to do my work."

"Get off her. She's mine, wolf," Luca snarled; his bared fangs dripped with the blood of his enemy. He was going to kill the wolf for touching his woman. But he resisted the urge to attack, knowing that Sköll could easily snap her neck. Cornered, Sköll was running out of options, and that made him particularly deadly and unpredictable. Luca was certain he'd kill Samantha just to make his point.

Samantha felt dazed as the wolf held his arm tightly around her, crushing her trachea. She barely felt his grubby hand touching her. All of the energy she'd exhausted on Rowan had left her weak. She peered up at Luca through teary eyes. Sucking in a quick breath, she tried to speak but couldn't.

"Wolf, you're making a mistake. I'm warning you, let her go or you die within minutes. Your choice," Luca growled at him. There was no way he was taking Samantha alive.

Sköll laughed violently and flashed his canines.

Samantha trembled under his touch and sought a means of escape. Closing her eyes, she intensified her thoughts, praying that she had enough energy to call an element. Unable to speak, she silently chanted to herself, "Adducam ignis ad manus… Adducam ignis ad manus… Adducam ignis ad manus…" *Bring fire to my hands.*

At first she simply felt a tingling. Soon, the smell of burnt flesh and hair wafted into her nostrils. Sköll hollered as the searing heat scorched his arm. Reacting to the scalding pain, he threw Samantha aside. Red handprints were branded into his bubbling flesh.

"What the fuck did you do?" he screamed at her.

Léopold rushed to gather Samantha from the floor as Luca charged Sköll. Wrapping his hands around the wolf's throat, Luca tore his fangs into Sköll's shoulder, tearing and spitting the raw flesh onto the ground. In a struggle for dominance, the two men lurched onto the floor. Sköll pinned Luca down, and landed a punch to his face. From the corner of his eye, Luca saw Xavier and Étienne rushing to help him. He held up his hand to them. "Back off. He's mine."

The pain of the strike only served to fuel Luca's anger. Adrenaline surged. Reaching up with both hands, he wrapped his fingers around Sköll's neck, digging his thumbs into his windpipe. Sköll coughed and faltered as his oxygen was depleted. Luca wrapped his legs around the man's waist and flipped him over. He straddled Sköll's chest. Sköll clasped his hands around Luca's wrists, but could not shake him off. For a second, he thought Luca was releasing his hold. Luca quickly grabbed the back of Sköll's head and palmed his chin. In a fluid, accelerated motion, Luca shoved upward and down, twisting Sköll's neck until he heard a loud pop. Bereft of life, death bled out of Sköll's eyes. Discarding his prey, Luca roared in domination, wild with fury. Rising, he scanned the room for Samantha.

Like a ferocious animal, Luca searched for his mate; he was dangerous, primal. Léopold carefully watched Luca approach him. Restraining Samantha had been the only way that he could keep her from attempting to enter the fray, in what would have been a treacherous and unnecessary effort to stop Sköll from killing Luca. Luca hadn't needed help; this kill was his and his alone. Cautiously, Léopold released Samantha's arms, facing his palms upward toward Luca, gesturing that he had not hurt her. Léopold was unsure if the already enraged Luca understood that he was friend, not foe, and did not want to agitate him further.

As Samantha broke free, she ran into Luca's arms. "Luca," she cried.

Possessively taking her into his embrace, he cupped her face, and pressed a punishing kiss to her lips. She was his woman. "Samantha mine," he said, his lips against hers.

"Yes, I'm yours. It's okay now," she said softly, reassuring him.

"It's over." Luca wasn't quite sure if he was trying to convince

Samantha or himself. He only cared that she was safe.

"Luca, oh my God. Are you okay?" she reluctantly pulled away, inspecting his face and body, noting the bruises and cuts that were already beginning to heal.

He laughed, wincing slightly as she touched a gash on his face. "Am I okay? I'm better than okay now that I've got you in my arms."

"But he bit you," she protested, continuing to inspect his body.

"Don't worry darlin'. I've had my rabies shots. Now come on, let's get the hell out of here."

"Not so fast, Luca. We must discuss the periapt." Léopold stepped up to introduce himself. "Mon ami, I'm Léopold. Léopold Devereoux. I am Kade's maker and you are descended from my blood."

Luca was shocked. Kade had never spoken of his maker, and Luca had never asked. He was loyal to Kade only. Despite Léopold's claims, he did not fully trust the vampire.

"You kept Samantha safe?"

"Oui."

"Pardon me if I sound ungrateful, but why the hell would you bring her here? And where the hell is Kade?" Luca asked.

"Ah, there is trouble with the wolves. Kade entrusted me with your safety while he provided them with assistance. I don't know the details, but I suspect these dead wolves here have something to do with the problem." He perused the room, counting six dead men. "There were others who escaped. They planned to use you?" He raised a questioning eyebrow at Luca.

"Yes, they're going after Marcel's pack. But why would you bring Samantha? She located the amulet. Wasn't that enough for you?" he demanded.

"We need her. The *Hematilly Periapt* must be destroyed and only a witch can do it. In addition, we needed her help in subduing Rowan. As you can see, she was more than capable."

Luca recalled Samantha's display. Her command of the elements was extraordinary. "You were amazing, my little witch." He kissed her again, hugging her against his bare chest.

"Hmmm…." was all Samantha could manage. She was exhausted from the ordeal; her legs felt weak.

"We must destroy the periapt now," Léopold informed him. "We can't risk it getting into the wrong hands. The wolf was correct about one thing. Others may know of its existence. The temptation will be too great for any witch who toys with black magic. To have a vampire as a slave is quite the coup. He could be used in war, to harm others, for all sorts of purposes. Do you have the amulet, Samantha?"

Samantha twisted around in Luca's arms enough so that she faced

Léopold. Luca's strong arms remained secure around her belly. She leaned into him. "Yes, I've got it here." She dug into her pocket and held up the teardrop-shaped rock. Eyeing the amulet, she affirmed her commitment to its destruction. "So, how do we destroy this thing?"

Chapter Sixteen

Back at Léopold's townhome, Samantha waited in his study for the vampires to join her. She ran her fingers over the volumes of antiqued books on the bookshelves that ran top to bottom on the wall around the entire perimeter of the room. He had quite the library, all alphabetically categorized. She wondered what it would be like to live so long. Would you miss those humans who died when your own youth stood still? Would you try a thousand different hobbies to keep boredom at bay? Her thoughts drifted to Luca and how he'd lived for centuries. *Centuries. What must that be like?*

Watching Luca kill Sköll had reminded her that Luca was more than a man. Vampire. He was immortal. In contrast, she was very much mortal. If she honed her witchcraft, she could extend her life considerably. But she considered what Luca had told her about Sydney. If she fully bonded with Luca, then she'd live as long as he did.

She knew deep in her heart that she loved him, but the human part of her still wanted normal everyday things: a home, a family, children. She and Luca hadn't discussed the future. Would Luca want children? Could she even have children with a vampire? After what had happened today, she reasoned that perhaps she had no right to bring children into the paranormal world where evil lurked and waited for weakness. All she'd known of the supernatural world was chaos and violence.

She herself had killed tonight. Rowan was dead by her hand. Samantha had never gone hunting before, let alone killed a person. She wasn't sure what she felt yet. Realistically, she'd been given no choice. Rowan would have killed her in a minute, given the chance. But still, she felt pangs of guilt knowing she'd taken a life. Conflicted, she threw herself into an overstuffed, brown leather couch; well worn, the soft grain caressed her skin. She closed her eyes, praying for forgiveness and also thanked her lucky stars that her magic had saved her and Luca from certain death.

Sighing aloud, she grew irritated and impatient. The only thing she wanted was to go home, take a shower and sleep. *Home?* She laughed. Samantha truly had begun to think of Luca's home as her own. She wondered if she should start making plans to return to Philadelphia. Tristan had promised he'd help her get a new job within the paranormal community. Should she try to start a fresh life so far from Luca?

Maybe Luca would ask her to stay. She certainly wasn't crazy about managing a long distance relationship. He'd told her he loved her. But declaring love wasn't the same as a commitment. It wasn't asking someone to move to where they lived, nor was it asking them to move in with you. It was a feeling. People threw around the word 'love' all the time, only to choke when it came to marriage. She knew plenty of friends who thought they were in love only to end up being dumped a week later. Then she knew some of her guy friends who, despicably so, used the 'love' word to get a woman in bed. People weren't always the way they seemed.

But deep in her heart, she knew Luca was honorable. He wasn't a user or the type of man who needed to trick women into bed. No, a man like that could have his choice of women at the snap of his fingers. She resolved to discuss her future plans with Luca at another time, considering they still had work to do.

Samantha pulled the amulet out of her pocket and rolled it between her fingers. Impatiently humming to herself, relief hit her as Luca opened the door. Showered, he was wearing sweatpants and a snug t-shirt that Léopold had lent him. She smiled up at him, admiring his fine physique. Almost all of his wounds were healed.

"Samantha," he said as he reached for her hands. He pulled her into his arms, waiting on Léopold to begin.

"Will this take long? I really want to go home," she said wearily.

"It should be quick, but we'll need to take a quick trip to dispose of it. Léopold will explain."

Léopold entered the room, commanding their attention. He walked around to his desk, opened a drawer and retrieved a black velvet pouch. He'd brought a marble cutting board from the kitchen and laid it on his desk pad. Looking up at Samantha, he explained what needed to be done.

"Samantha, as I've told you, only a witch can crush this particular amulet to mere particles. While it is essentially a mineral at its core, it's enchanted. You must be the one to destroy it, to dispel its magic. Once it is done, you and Luca will scatter the dust so that it can never be reconstituted, understood?"

"Yes, but how are we going to break it up? A hammer?" she quipped.

Léopold smiled, "You, my dear, are much stronger than any man made tool. This amulet is of the earth. And to the earth it shall return. You must manipulate it, break it down with your mind. After your demonstration earlier, this should be child's play."

"I'll try. But I don't know if I can do it. I mean, it seems to just kind of fire off when I get upset. I don't have much control, yet," she explained.

"You must try. Now," Léopold ordered.

The tension in the room became palpable. Xavier and Étienne entered and remained behind Luca and Samantha, who stood in front of Léopold's desk. Léopold watched with great intensity as Samantha placed the amulet on the marble platter. Closing her eyes, she tried to concentrate but felt no magic hum. Thoughts of the amulet before her formulated in her mind's eye, yet nothing stirred.

Sensing no magic, Léopold silently warned Luca with his eyes. He intended to agitate the witch into destruction. Luca had known this might have to happen, but still hated seeing Samantha brought to her knees.

"Samantha, we must try a different approach. Close your eyes, and hear only my voice," Léopold ordered. His accented voice was smooth as silk yet iron willed. "Picture the amulet. And Rowan. She took Luca. She took your vampire. She silvered him. Stripped him. She ran her fingers up his legs, felt his chest, felt his body in her own hands."

Her eyes snapped to attention, glaring at Léopold. *Why the hell was he saying all these awful things?*

"Close your eyes! Concentrate. You must destroy this object," he demanded. "That's right Samantha, she touched your mate. How does that make you feel? Are you angry enough yet? Think of what she did to Luca. She burned him. Used him. Think of what she did to you. She wrecked your life, laughing while you searched for the amulet. Think of Sköll. He helped Rowan. He was going to break your neck…he felt your breasts in front of your vampire. I sense your anger, Samantha, now focus it. Focus it into your magic."

Samantha let Léopold's words feed the angry beast within. He'd done nothing but repeat the truth. Rowan had silvered Luca, had touched him intimately, something that was hers. Sköll had groped her. She could still smell his foul breath against her neck. And for what? For an amulet that made slaves. A diabolic object that was utilized to propagate evil, wars. No, that damnable amulet must be annihilated so that no one could ever use it again. Fire built within Samantha's belly. The object began to glow into a red bright ball. She held her hands over the amulet, letting the magic flow as the destructive words spilled from her lips; "Natus ex inferno, cineri moriemini. Frangere ut revertatur in pulverem terrae." Willing the periapt to dust, it burst into flames and soon all that remained was a pile of ash.

Samantha opened her eyes and smiled. The vampires in the room all stared at her in amazement and fear. "What? Tell me it's gone. I felt it. It's gone, isn't it?" she asked innocently.

They burst into laughter at her words. Luca hugged her; she truly had no idea of the sheer magnitude of her abilities. Nor did she realize how frightening she could be when working her magic.

Léopold brushed the ashes into the bag and handed it to Luca. "Now go. The remains of the stone shall return to the earth as it should be. Xavier, Étienne. I shall see you again someday, perhaps." He nodded, curtly dismissing the two. "Luca, Samantha, it has been a pleasure meeting you albeit under the most unfortunate circumstances."

Taking Samantha's hand in his, Léopold drew her to him. Luca tensed, distrustful of the older vampire. Léopold met Luca's fiery eyes and proceeded cautiously. With a smile, he turned to Samantha and looked deep into her blue eyes. "My dear witch, while I'm certain you are glad to have Luca home, I admit there was the smallest part of me who wished he would not return. For I would have kept you as my own."

Gently, he leaned in and kissed her forehead. "I am sure your blood is as sweet as you are beautiful, but alas, it is Luca to whom you belong. Again, I do apologize for burning the cabin. Sometimes we all need a small incentive to do our best work."

His sexy voice warmed her although she stiffened at his confession. This man, smoothly and coolly, had just admitted he wanted her in front of Luca. Samantha wasn't sure what to think of Léopold. He was sensual and alluring, but powerful. Intimidating. Protective. And oddly caring. Giving into her desire to say goodbye to him, she briefly hugged Léopold and then quickly returned to Luca's embrace.

"Léopold, thank you for helping me save Luca. I do forgive you for the cabin. But next time you need my help, please just ask," she joked.

Luca and Samantha exchanged looks as they walked out of the office. As she went to steal a last look at Léopold, Samantha glanced over her shoulder to see only an empty office. Once again, he'd vanished.

Chapter Seventeen

The waves splashed against the side of the boat as the sun crested the horizon. Turquoise waters sparkled in the morning sun, while dolphins danced in a celebration of life. Samantha sighed in relief, knowing she was finally safe. She was looking forward to a new, hopefully calm, life. She silently reminisced about how much her life had changed. Once she'd spent hours in a cubicle, her only excitement driven by catching errors and breaking codes with co-workers.

It wasn't just that she felt different; she was different. She could no longer deny the magic within her. No longer a desk jockey, she needed to find a new calling. Or perhaps the calling had found her. A newfound witch, she resolved to do something positive with her powers. While she longed to have better control, she knew that would come with practice. She wanted to train with Ilsbeth but knew for certain that she wouldn't live in the coven.

She could not deny what she was any more than she could deny Luca was vampire. It was time to face the music. Either she'd have to accept Tristan's offer or move to New Orleans. Given that she didn't know the witches in Philadelphia, and she had a perfectly good mentor ready and willing here in New Orleans, in that moment, she decided to stay and learn her craft. She hoped that Luca would ask her to stay with him at his home, but wasn't going to pressure him.

No matter what he'd said about bonding and love, she knew men didn't always mean what they said in the heat of the moment. Since they'd left Léopold's, Luca had seemed distant, quiet. Samantha was utterly exhausted and didn't press him to talk. Now wasn't the time.

She glanced over at the deck clock, and realized they'd been on the boat for at least seven hours. Léopold's captain sailed the vessel down the Mississippi to the open Gulf of Mexico. Within minutes of boarding, she'd passed out in bed as soon as her head hit the pillow. After taking a hot shower, she made her way up to the back deck. The boat slowly bobbed and swayed to the rhythm of the ocean; she surmised they'd anchored. Peering out to sea, she wondered where Luca had gone.

When she'd woken to a cold bed, she'd missed the warmth of him. She hoped he wasn't having second thoughts about their relationship. She wasn't the clingy type, but was somewhat insecure about where they stood.

Love. Samantha had thought she'd known love before Luca. But she realized now that it had only been a shadow of love. Maybe infatuation? Maybe just her need to be close to a man? Regardless, Luca had shown her time and time again, through his actions, what real love was. He'd shown her what a real man was.

He'd cared enough to fly across the country and find her, to save her from her own foolishness. He'd let go of his inhibitions to earn her trust, swimming with her in the lake and sharing his past. He'd showed her the bliss of tender lovemaking and then pushed her limits to explore her sexuality. He'd fearlessly opened up to her emotionally and declared his love. He'd helped her discover what the amulet was and had fought with his life to protect her. And even though she'd seen him ferociously attack the wolf and kill, she didn't fear him. Respect for his courageous act swelled in her heart. Captured and tortured twice over the past weeks, the man seemed indestructible and had an unbreakable spirit.

Reaching in the pocket of her robe, she fingered the small sack Léopold had given her. The older vampire was somewhat of an enigma. Dominant and sexual, she felt drawn to him. Deadly as he was, she trusted him like an older brother. She knew he wanted her, but he didn't take what wasn't his. Nor was he the type to take women against their will. Given his dark and mysterious good looks, she knew someone like Léopold could have any woman, and had probably already had hundreds of lovers over the years. Even though he'd made attempts to put her at ease, she also knew he could be cold and calculating, remembering how he'd burned the cabin to get her to do his bidding. Encouragement, he'd called it. She smiled. Only in the paranormal world would someone call torching a cabin an 'incentive'. After watching Rowan bring Luca to his knees, she was certain Léopold had done what was necessary to protect his kind.

She looked down at the satchel with anticipation. Samantha couldn't wait to dump the dreaded contents, so she could finally be free. Looking around the spacious wooden deck, she hoped Luca would return soon. She wanted to tell him about her decision to stay. Butterflies danced in her stomach. She prayed he felt the same way about her as she felt about him. In the heat of passion, he'd said he loved her, but she longed to hear him say it again. She wanted a life with Luca and could not imagine loving anyone else. She was his.

Luca briefly spoke to the captain, explaining how they'd make a brief stop and then return to New Orleans. As much as he'd like to take a Caribbean cruise with Samantha, trouble was brewing with the wolves. Earlier, he'd slipped out of Samantha's arms to go call Kade. Both Kade and Sydney were at the pack house strategizing with Marcel. Apparently, Jax Chandler, the New York Alpha, had not taken kindly to Marcel's message refusing him access to Kat. Although it may have been typical in some packs for an

Alpha to pick a mate of his choice, Tristan and Marcel, both unmated, refused to take a mate who wasn't in agreement. Once mated, wolves could seldom separate without physical repercussions. The brothers fiercely protected their sister. Although she had a wild side, she was deeply loyal to their packs.

Ever since Luca had rescued Kat, he'd kept tabs on her over the years; 'friends with benefits,' but friends nonetheless. He was concerned for her safety, knowing how independent she could be. She often went missing for periods of time only for them to find out later she'd been on holiday with friends somewhere on the other side of the world. She lived life to the fullest, but now someone wanted her to be his. Someone, an Alpha, like Jax, who wouldn't take no for an answer.

He regretted that the wolves at Rowan's mansion had escaped them. Interrogation would have yielded critical information about their true purpose in causing a war. Sköll had insinuated that he was there because of Kat, but it could have been a ruse. He wasn't even certain Sköll knew Jax or was in his pack. He could have been lying to protect another wolf.

His thoughts turned to Samantha as he dug into the ice box and located a bottle of champagne. She was a feisty little witch, and actually a little scary now that he'd seen her powers. Petite and fair, she'd stolen his heart. He rolled his eyes in disbelief and laughed to himself. All these years he'd been so insistent that he'd never fall in love again, let alone with a human. When he reflected on his young love for Eliza, he realized that he'd never been in love with someone as deeply as he loved Samantha.

Fearless when faced with the unknown, she stood her ground. And she was smart as a whip, amazing him with her knowledge of cryptic code breaking and how she reveled in the challenge. Samantha had never backed down to Léopold either. When he was captured, she'd risked her life with the ancient vampire just so she could find Luca. Strong-willed. Beautiful. Intelligent. *His.*

Luca's thoughts drifted to their lovemaking and how passionately she had embraced the experience. He loved watching her climax, letting go of her inhibitions. He grew long and firm thinking of how she'd taken him into her mouth, teasing him endlessly. She trusted him, a vampire, to take her to places she'd never gone before. Remembering the sight of her tied to his bed sweetly moaning and writhing in pleasure, he smiled. Lascivious and loving, she brought him to a new level of felicity that he'd never known in his long life. He couldn't imagine what life would be like without her. It wasn't just the bonding. It was everything about her. He loved her more than life itself. He wanted her here, building a life together. Forever.

A broad smile broke across Samantha's face as she felt Luca's strong arms encircle her waist and a kiss to her ear. She turned in his arms to face him and smiled. God, she loved this man. The sight of the gorgeous male took her breath away. Shirtless, he wore white cotton drawstring pajama pants and padded around barefoot. He was confident and comfortable no matter his surroundings. Over her shoulder, she noticed the champagne and glasses he'd set on the glass end table.

"Hmmm…champagne? So early in the morning?"

"Yes, darlin'. This is New Orleans," he drawled. "Think of it like mimosas without the orange juice."

"Well, when you put it that way, how can a girl refuse?" She gave him a flirty smile.

"That's what I'm counting on. But before we toast, let's get rid of the remains, shall we?" he suggested. "Would you care to do the honors?"

"Nothing would make me happier." She carefully opened the packet, and turned it upside down. Red, gray and black ashes floated downward, falling gently into the sea.

When the pouch was fully emptied, Luca raised a knowing eyebrow at her and held up a lighter. "Just to be on the safe side."

"Just to be on the safe side," she agreed as she watched him light the bag on fire.

Tossing the lighter aside, he pinched the end of the sack and held it up to the air to burn. Devoured by flames, he cast it into the waves.

"I can't tell you how relieved I am to see that thing gone," she sighed.

"You and me both," he concurred. "Now for something really important, a toast and a proposition."

"A toast sounds wonderful. But a proposition? Sounds cryptic, but then again, I do love a good mystery."

"Ah, but you are good with puzzles. First, the toast." He held his flute to hers. "To finding more than just an amulet. To finding you, Samantha…the love of my life."

"And to finding you. To us," she countered.

Clinking glasses and then taking a sip, Luca took her slender hand in his and led her over to the open-air deck bed. He pulled her onto his lap and held her.

Samantha's cheek rested on his bare chest. The masculine scent of him piqued her desire. She wanted to make love to him again over and over. Sensing he wanted to talk, she resisted the urge to slide her hands down into his pants. Instead she caressed his chest and played innocently with his flat nipple.

"You are making me lose my train of thought, you naughty girl," he groaned at her touch. His arousal grew, but first, they needed to talk.

"Samantha, look at me." He placed a finger under her chin, tilting her head toward his.

"Yes," she said lazily.

"I told you about Eliza. She was my first love…long before I was turned. I was only a young man when I met her. When we were attacked that night and she died, I was devastated, just filled with rage. I swore never to love again. And for all these years, it's been fairly easy to do. In truth, I never met anyone who could make me feel. Sure, lust is something that comes and goes like the wind. But finding someone, someone like you; it is rare." He absentmindedly rubbed her palm with his thumb.

"What I'm trying to say is that I want you here with me. Not just now, but forever. I know this must seem sudden, but I can tell you that I am certain of my feelings for you. I want you as my wife. I want a family. I want a real home, not just a museum full of antiquities. Please. Stay here with me," he whispered as his words trailed off.

Samantha regarded him for a minute, stunned by his proposal. Her heart bloomed at the prospect of spending her life with Luca. She placed her hand on his cheek and looked into his eyes. "Yes, I'd love to stay with you. I know we haven't known each other very long, but over the past few weeks we've been through more than most people have been through in a lifetime. And now, I can't imagine my life without you. I don't think I ever really knew what love was until I met you. And I never knew what it meant to have a man love me back. There is only you. I am yours."

Luca gathered her red locks in his fingers and drew her soft, pink lips to his. He gently kissed her, slowly, deliberately. Savoring the sweetness of her mouth, his tongue found hers. She opened willingly, intoxicated as he sought to send her into ecstasy.

Samantha's blood raced in anticipation of his touch. She wanted all of him now, and couldn't hold back the urge to strip him naked and take what was hers. Sensually releasing his lips, she rose off his lap and straddled his legs. Leisurely, she untied the belt to her robe. As the panels revealed her skin, she seductively peeled the fabric down her shoulders and let it pool at her feet. Standing bare before him, she smiled as he tried to reach for her hips.

Luca marveled at the way her ivory skin glowed. She was a magnificent creature. The blonde highlights in her curls reflected off the sunlight and flowed over the soft, ripe swell of her breasts.

Flipping her hair aside, she exposed her pebbled pink tips. Flush with arousal, she held his hands firmly to her hips, teasing him, driving him mad with desire.

"Luca, I'm in control this morning," she purred. "Will you let me take care of you?"

"Darlin', you'd better do something soon. You know, I can't resist you for one minute longer," he said, hanging onto a thread of control. His rock hard erection was straining to be released.

"As you wish." Samantha agilely dropped to her knees, letting her fingernails graze his chest all the way to the fine trail of hair that led into his pants. Gripping the sides of his pajamas, she yanked hard until she tore the pants down off his body. Animalistic, she planned to take him in every way she could. She wanted to possess him, to be possessed.

Luca's breath startled as his cock sprang free. Samantha was rough, wanton. He'd never seen her so aggressive and loved every minute of it. He extended his arms backward, laying his palms flat to support his weight. Completely nude to her, he patiently waited as he watched her graze a path with her nails to the apex between his legs.

Excited by the sight of his exquisite musculature, Samantha grew wet, yearning to have him inside of her. Meeting his eyes, she leaned forward and attentively licked the tip of his firm flesh. She delighted in the spicy taste of him. He hissed in delight as she swirled her tongue around it, lavishing the head with long, wet brushes. Wrapping her fingers around him, she parted her lips and devoured the full length of his aroused manhood.

Luca thought he'd explode; her warm moist tongue caused his shaft to bob in eagerness. Unable to restrain himself any longer, Luca sat up and plowed his hands through her hair.

She mercilessly plunged him in and out of her hot mouth. She felt him grow close to climax and backed off. Still stroking his hard male heat, she lifted him up with one hand as she felt for his scrotum. Opening widely she sucked him into her mouth rolling them one at a time, licking and teasing.

Luca moaned out loud at the intrusion. The vixen was going to make him insane. "Aw fuck, that feels so good. Please," he begged for release.

Hearing his plea, she grinned and once again began to suckle his hot swollen flesh. Slightly twisting her grip, she built the sensation within him. He was so very close and bucked his hips upward into her warm sweetness. In and out, her head rose and fell, sucking him harder and harder.

"Samantha, I'm gonna come." He didn't want to release in her mouth without her permission.

Ignoring his pleas, she held onto him tight and increased her pace. "Mmmm, come for me." She resumed her assault, sucking him deeply.

Luca groaned as he lost control, stiffening as he exploded into her.

Greedily, she took all of him, milking his essence until he collapsed backward onto the bed. Licking her swollen lips, she stalked over him. Her naked body straddled his belly.

"Samantha," he panted. "You'll be the death of me, woman. My God. That was unbelievable." She quietly smiled down on him as he caught his breath.

"Tired, vampire?" she challenged.

"Not on your life, witch. It's my turn to feast!" With preternatural speed, he flipped Samantha on her back.

She giggled uncontrollably. "Not fair! Not fair!" she feigned a protest.

Luca captured a rosy taut nipple in his mouth and sucked it. "Mmmm….it's more than fair. You taste delicious. I love your breasts, so soft and so very ready to be plucked." He pinched a firm peak while laving the other with his tongue. "I plan to kiss and worship every inch of your lovely body."

"Um…Yes. That feels so good. I love you so much. I've never felt like this in my entire life. No one has ever…" Her words trailed off as she felt his lips kiss down her stomach. Her sex ached in need, awaiting his mouth on her core. She yearned to feel him on her, in her.

As he dipped into her sex with his tongue, she lost track of all thoughts. Biting down on her lip, she resisted the urge to scream, knowing the captain was somewhere on the boat. Not one for public sex, she almost forgot they weren't entirely alone. Yet she was too far gone to stop now.

As he parted her folds with his fingers, she sucked in a breath. Tendrils of magic wisped over her naked body; he swept around her most sensitive point. She pushed her hips up into his mouth, seeking what she needed. But he continued to tease her, licking, tasting but not directly licking her clit. She felt like she was almost there…almost. But she needed more. "Please," she begged.

Luca laughed a little as she wove her fingers into his hair, attempting to guide him to where she wanted. He planned to make love to her slowly. Her honeyed essence tasted so delicious on his lips. Feeling her quiver, he knew how close she was to going over the edge. Sensing this, Luca halted and began to leisurely kiss her pink mound. He wanted to bring her up to the precipice and back down, over and over until she was ripe with need. Teasing and tantalizing.

"Luca, please, don't stop. I need…I need…" She couldn't finish, feeling as if she was riding a roller coaster of passion, up and down.

"Mmmm….what do you need? Do you know how delectable you are? I could stay here all day," he joked as he began to create a crescendo of sensation once again.

She smiled, realizing he was purposefully driving her crazy. "Luca, please…please lick me," she pleaded.

"You mean here?" He playfully sampled her clitoris and started to build speed and pressure with his tongue.

"Yes, there. Oh my God!" She realized she was starting to scream. *Oh well. Fuck the captain.* She gave up on worrying about being seen or heard.

"Or do you mean here?" Luca inserted a thick, long finger into the heat of her sex, quickly followed by two. He pumped in and out of her core, sweeping his broad flat tongue over and over her clit.

"Yes!" She screamed again. Samantha was starting to shake. She fought for breath; her head rolled backwards as her body tightened like a spring.

"Or did you mean here?" Luca put his soft, firm lips around her swollen pink bead, sucking. At the same time, he stimulated the stretch of skin inside her by slightly crooking his fingers upward toward him. He loved hearing her scream in pleasure, loved making her feel good. It was music to his ears. Unrelenting, he kept up the torturous delightful invasion, bringing her into a rapturous state of frenzy.

"I'm coming! Yes! Luca! Luca!" The crest of an incredible climax broke over her. Samantha felt as if she was floating out of her body as a zenith of pleasure rocked throughout every cell of her being. She grabbed tightly on his hair, holding him to her. Quaking under his touch, she gasped for breath.

Relishing the sweet taste of Samantha and the sound of her climax, Luca was hardened in arousal. He climbed over her, resting his forearms next to her head. The tip of his erection pressed against her wet entrance. Belly to belly, he reveled in the feel of their flesh as one. He smiled down on her as she slowly opened her eyes.

Every inch of her skin was hypersensitive after the amazing orgasm Luca had given her. Feeling his weight above her, she gazed at him through heavy-lidded eyes, and smiled back. "Did you enjoy teasing me? Because I sure enjoyed it. That was unreal."

She couldn't get over how incredible he made her feel. She'd gone years never being able to come during intercourse, yet this man knew exactly what to do to make her body sing. It was as if he'd known her forever.

"I love you, Samantha," he affirmed. "You have no idea what you do to me."

"I love hearing you tell me that. I love you. I want to be your wife, to be with you, forever. I guess I just want to keep saying it and hearing it to make sure this is real."

"Oh, this is real, all right. So is this." Luca dipped his head and passionately kissed her. Their tongues danced together as he drove his velvety steel shaft into her hot center. Samantha was slick with need and ready to take all of him as he sheathed himself in a single, smooth stroke.

Luca stopped kissing Samantha so he could look into her eyes as he possessed her. She was so responsive to his every move, and he could not seem to get enough of her. Unhurriedly, he rocked in and out of her, enjoying her tight heat. Rolling over onto his back, he brought her with him so she was on top.

"That's it, baby. Ride me, good and slow," he directed. He placed his hands on her waist, letting her set the pace.

Samantha hadn't been on top very often, but it was something she had yearned to do. Writhing on Luca, she closed her eyes and let the sensation take over her body. Arching her hips, her breath hitched as her clit brushed against his pubic bone. She pressed down to meet his every primal thrust stimulating her sensitive nub.

Luca was lost in her rhythm. His heart beat for this woman. She was resplendent and sensual, so open to discovery. He took his time, provocatively surging into her again and again. Luca splayed his hands across Samantha's ass: massaging her, guiding her. The sight of her perky breasts mere inches from his face teased him. His tongue darted out to capture one. She accommodated his silent request, leaning toward him so that he could suckle her tightly beaded point. Taking it between his teeth, he bit down slightly, then sucked it once more.

Samantha moaned in blissful pain; his bite tingled down to her aching sex. She could feel the rise of her orgasm evolving. So close, but she needed more of him. As if he could read her thoughts, his fingertips approached the crevice of her bottom. The feel of his hands on her so close to her ass, where she'd learned to experiment, thrilled her. She couldn't explain her urge; it felt like a driving primal pulse within her. Encouraging him, she pushed herself further into his hands.

Luca sensed that she craved the touch of him inside her. Reaching around her mound, he glided his forefinger over her wet folds. Lubricating his hand, he moved around her back again. Softly, he feathered his moist digit around her rosebud. He felt her shudder under his touch, yet she pushed back again, seeking more.

"Is this what you need?" He continued to circle her bottom.

She shook her head, not wanting to voice her desire.

"Come on, Samantha. Let go. It's okay to let go. Tell me and I'll give you want you need."

"Inside me. Please," she panted. As the pace and tension increased, her heart raced. She wanted it, needed it.

"Yes, so nice. I love how you open for me," he whispered. Slowly and gently he slid a digit into her untouched need. Feeling her clench, he guided her. "That's it baby, let me in. Relax, feel me and push back a little. Ah yeah, you're taking me." He felt his finger slip all the way into her tight hole. Her core began to quiver and clench down around his cock. She was going over the edge.

A thrilling awareness ripped through Samantha upon Luca's dark invasion. She felt deliciously full. As soon as she'd felt his finger enter her from behind in conjunction with his engorged masculinity, a mind-shattering orgasm slammed into her. Rocking feverishly, she thrashed above him, riding the glorious climax. He was thrusting up into her hard; the sound of flesh meeting flesh rang through her ears. Her senses had never felt so abundantly bombarded. She screamed Luca's name wildly as she came. "Yes, Luca, fuck me, please," she cried.

Luca thrust up into her over and over, possessing her, taking her. Hearing his name, he reveled in how easily she submitted to the throes of passion. As soon as he'd filled her, she fisted his swollen shaft in a tingly hold, pulsating around him.

Seeking to bond with her further, he extended a claw, slicing his own wrist. He held the beaded blood to her pink lips, and she instinctively captured it, sucking greedily. Shocking her into another climax, his powerful blood filled her mouth. She came fast and hard and took him with her. Losing every last shred of control, Luca jarred and spilled his hot seed deep within her.

Lying still beneath Samantha, Luca's body celebrated the simultaneous wild release they'd experienced. Their bodies mingled as one as they drifted into a relaxed state of euphoria. Samantha rolled off Luca onto her back. He wrapped an arm around her, pulling her close to him. She lazily draped her leg over his and placed a palm on his chest. An awareness of calm settled between them. Having sated both their physical and emotional selves, they silently touched and luxuriated in their newly blossomed love.

Samantha immediately felt Luca's blood whirr through her veins. She loved everything about Luca and realized that after weeks of turmoil, she simply was at peace. She loved him more than she'd ever thought was possible. He'd helped her transform from mere mortal to witch and soon she was to be his wife.

Tracing a finger on his chest, she looked up to meet his eyes. "I want you to know that in this moment, I've never been happier in my entire life. These past few weeks have been life-changing for me. I felt horrible about what happened, not knowing. I was scared about being a witch…actually I hated being turned into a witch. And maybe my gifts still do scare me a little bit," she admitted. "But I don't care if I never remember what happened to me. I am who I am now. There's nothing but the future ahead of us, and I can't wait to marry you, to start our life."

He kissed the top of her head. "Me too. It's strange. I've been living for hundreds of years, but ever since I met you, I've realized that I haven't really been living. Or loving. Don't laugh, but I feel kind of reborn, so to speak. I need you in my home, my bed. You're already in my heart."

Samantha and Luca lay naked in each other's arms for over an hour on the deck, talking and planning for their future together. A lazy ride back up the muddy Mississippi eventually brought them back to their port. The sounds of street players ripping jazz tunes along the waterfront welcomed them home.

Chapter Eighteen

Two weeks had passed since Luca had asked Samantha to marry him. As if she was living in a dream, they had fallen into a comfortable rhythm. Samantha spent her days planning and training with Ilsbeth. She'd nearly forgotten the chaos of her tribulations with Asgear and the amulet. The stray wolves that had escaped had never been found. Pack troubles temporarily calmed, Kade and Sydney had returned to their mansion.

Having them as neighbors was great company for Samantha. She didn't know anyone else in New Orleans yet, except Luca's friends and Ilsbeth. She'd grown closer to Sydney, happy there was another human woman around to talk to on occasion. Sydney and she had lunched a few times, discussing wedding plans. Sydney and Kade planned to elope since Sydney had no family, while she and Luca were still deciding what to do.

She'd called her sister, Jess, and told her about the engagement. Jess was thrilled and making plans to visit within the month. She also filled her in on how she'd become a witch, and explained Luca's vampirism. Her older sister seemed to take it in her stride, wishing she'd been the one who'd been turned into a witch. Jess had always been a bit more adventurous than her. Samantha felt like she'd had all the adventure she'd ever wanted and then some. Passionate sex with Luca was all the excitement she needed to keep her blissfully content.

Samantha hadn't told her parents about her vampire lover or her newly-acquired magic. Her parents could be quite reserved and she thought it best to tell them in person. Ringing her mother, she simply told her that she'd fallen in love with a wonderful man, they were engaged and she was moving to New Orleans. Happy for Samantha, they'd congratulated her and told her they were anxious to meet him. She laughed when she hung up the phone, thinking about how that get together would go. *Hi Mom and Dad. Meet Luca, my fiancé. He's a vampire. And oh by the way, I'm a witch now. Yeah, I've given up computers and can make fire with my hands.*

She hadn't really given up computers. Kade had offered her a job working in Issacson Securities in the technology division. She agreed to do it part time, given her new responsibilities and training at the coven. Xavier, Chief Information Officer and fellow geek, would be her new boss. They got along really well, and she was looking forward to starting her new career once she moved. Having already given notice at her old job, she arranged for movers to pack and bring her belongings to her new home.

Her home. Luca's home. Their home. At first, she'd thought it would be strange moving into his lovely Garden District mansion, already furnished.

But Luca insisted they redesign the interior together. He desperately wanted, not just a menagerie of precious collectibles, but a warm loving space. A home they'd built together with love.

Sometimes Samantha was amazed at her gentle giant. There was no doubt that Luca could be a dominant, impressive man, especially in the bedroom. Yet time and time again, he'd shown Samantha his tender heart, caring for her like no other man had ever done. She loved him back with every ounce of her being.

That morning, she'd made plans for a dinner party with Luca's close friends and a few of her sisters from the coven, to celebrate their engagement. Samantha had even coaxed a reluctant Dominique into coming over, promising she'd find a willing human donor who'd be interested in taking care of her specific nutritional needs. Acquiescing to Luca's demand for peace, Dominique had agreed to call a truce, especially after hearing of their engagement and that they'd be co-workers. Samantha apologized for what she'd done to her even though she still had no memories of silvering her.

Even though Luca insisted she hire a caterer for the event, Samantha planned on making a few of the dishes herself. She'd always loved to cook, but had never had the time or anyone to cook for when she was single. She knew vampires didn't eat much, but planned on donating any leftover food to a local shelter immediately afterwards. Her aunt had given her the recipe for homemade bread, so she was busy kneading the dough when Luca walked up behind her and kissed her neck.

"Hey there, home early today?" she asked, enjoying the feel of his chest against her back.

"Yeah. Now that I've gotten things under control again at the office, I can work from home like I usually do. Besides, I thought I'd see if you needed any help today," he offered. "I can't tell you how delightfully strange it is to see a hot woman in my kitchen rolling dough in her hands. Once upon a time, I thought I'd be alone forever. Now here I am, wishing I was that dough."

"You're sweet. Let me wash my hands, and I'll see what I can do. I'd much rather be running my hands over your body than playing with bread." She winked. "Besides, there's not much I really have to do to get ready."

"I'm gonna go downstairs, take a shower and wait for you. Don't want to interrupt you, or I won't get to taste that secret recipe you've been hiding. Did I ever tell you how much I love hot buns?"

His double entendre wasn't lost on her. "Well I have some hot ones with your name on them. Just give me a minute, and I'll be down to join you," she promised.

Luca turned to look at her and noticed her cheeks were dreadfully pale. "Hey, you okay? You look as white as a ghost. I wish you'd let the caterers do everything. Come rest with me before the party," he pleaded.

"I promise I'm fine. I'm just a little tired from all our non-stop, mind-blowing sex. Now go on. Shoo. I'll be down soon. I promise."

Reluctantly, Luca went downstairs, but something was bothering him about the way she looked. She hadn't seemed tired but then again, he'd been gone all morning. Maybe she'd been out in the garden earlier and the late summer heat had gotten to her.

Samantha watched him go downstairs. The truth was that she hadn't been feeling well, but her optimistic spirit kept her going. She was so excited about the party that she wasn't about to let a little lightheadedness ruin it. A few times during the morning she'd needed to sit down from the dizziness. Normally not one to feel faint, she chalked it up to the intense sessions she'd been having with Ilsbeth.

Every day, Samantha spent several hours training and testing her powers. She'd learned how to better control her call on the elements, no longer afraid that she'd mistakenly set fire to something. Instead of spouting in tongues with little understanding, she had started studying Latin and other foreign languages used in the spells. Ilsbeth had given her the responsibility of shoring up the coven's digital library and website after she'd been able to breach its security. Reorganizing the database gave Samantha the opportunity to sift through and learn everything important to being a sister within the coven. She'd committed to learning the craft and actually found herself having fun every time she mastered a new skill.

Patting the dough one last time with oil, she covered the bowl to give it time to rise. After washing her hands, she dried them and decided to join Luca. Maybe he was right. Maybe she just needed a nap before the party.

Halfway down the stairs, her vision started to blur slightly as a wave of nausea rolled over her. Grabbing the railing, she steadied herself. A few more steps and she reasoned that she could make it over to the sofa. By the time she reached the landing, she could no longer stand. A tunnel of black enclosed her as she fell to the ground.

Luca took a hot leisurely shower, hoping Samantha would take it easy. He knew she was looking forward to celebrating their engagement, as was he. But he was worried she'd been overdoing it with all her training at the coven and then insisting that she had to cook at least one dish for the party. He would have been happy with just champagne, but had given in to her desire to create a more human-like affair that would allow her to meet his friends. It was also an opportunity to do something wonderfully normal, given all the nasty supernatural events that had preceded tonight's festivities.

But Luca worried that Samantha's usually fair skin looked a lighter shade of pale. Despite her best attempts to hide it from him, he could sense she was suffering from malaise. It didn't make sense. He was very careful with their blood exchanges, ensuring that he never drank too much from her and that she'd always drank his in return. Energizing and virile, his blood should have had her blushing pink with vitality.

Deciding to surprise her he lit the candles in their room, turned on soft music and lay naked on the bed, awaiting her presence. Fifteen minutes went by before he lost all patience. Annoyed, his worry rose yet again. *Stubborn woman, must still be cooking when she doesn't need to do that. What she needs to do is rest.*

Sliding on a robe, he exited the bedroom and spotted Samantha lying still on the floor. He felt a surge of an emotion he'd long forgotten, terror. Had she fallen down the stairs? Was she alive? He breathed a sigh of relief after hearing her normal heartbeat. Rushing to her side, he scooped her up into his arms. "Samantha, darlin'. Come on baby. Please wake up," he begged.

Slowly Samantha's eyes fluttered open. "Ummm….what happened? How'd I get here?"

"Dear Goddess, I'm so glad you're awake. What happened? Are you in pain? I'm calling a doctor." He knew doctors existed who served supernaturals. Kade had called for one who'd checked him out after he'd been kidnapped. He reached for his phone and frantically flipped through his contacts list looking for the number.

"No, Luca. I don't need a doctor. Please just call Ilsbeth; she can look at my aura. I think it must be the magic. Something's wrong. I've been using a lot of energy when I've been training. I told you it was exhausting. I just need to close my eyes and rest," she insisted.

There was no way in hell he was letting a witch diagnose his wife-to-be. Sure, he'd call her, but he was also calling the doctor. "Okay, stay here. I'm going to go get your robe, a glass of water and make the call. Don't move," he ordered.

After calling both the doctor and Ilsbeth, he phoned Sydney and Kade to ask them to come over. They waited outside his front door for the doctor to arrive. Within thirty minutes, Kade escorted the doctor downstairs. Luca was surprised to see how young the woman doctor was, given that he had no recollection of her from when he'd been ill.

She extended her hand. "Good day, I'm Dr. Sweeney. Do you think we could move the patient into the bedroom so I could take a closer look at her?"

"Certainly." Luca gently cradled a sleeping Samantha in his arms and carried her into the bedroom. He laid her on the bed and pulled a sheet up over her.

Ilsbeth poked her head into the bedroom, having come in late. "May I stay, Luca?" she asked quietly.

Luca shot her a look of irritation, blaming her 'training' for Samantha's health issues. "Come in, but let the doctor work," he growled.

Luca and Ilsbeth watched patiently as the doctor took blood and pulled out her small lab kit. "Exactly how long has she been dizzy?" the doctor asked.

"This is the first time she's passed out. She never even told me she felt sick. I noticed she was pale upstairs, and I insisted she rest. Right before you got here, she said she'd been exhausted from her training with Ilsbeth," he sneered. "Did you have to work her so hard?"

"Magic would never do this, Luca. If anything, she should be getting stronger, healthier. She's been taking your blood. I can see it in the brightness of her aura. In fact, her aura is the healthiest I've ever seen it. Quite extraordinary, really. It's almost iridescent. It's almost as if she's…" Ilsbeth shook her head, not wanting to speak without the doctor's consent. It was not her place to tell Luca what she suspected. Deciding to leave the room, she left him and the doctor to work alone.

Samantha slowly woke up, hearing voices in the room, and was surprised to find herself a specimen under several pairs of peering eyes. "What's going on?" she said with a hint of annoyance. "Oh my God. Did you call a doctor? I told you that I'm fine. I just need rest. You took blood?" She looked down at the band aid on her arm. Irritated with the unnecessary attention, she pushed with her hands and sat straight up in bed, much to Luca's dismay.

Dr. Sweeney sat on the edge of the bed and held Samantha's hand. "How are you feeling? Can you please follow my finger with your eyes?" she requested, shining a light into her pupils. Flipping off the light, the doctor glanced down at the blood results. While most doctors sent out for results, Dr. Sweeney carried a basic lab kit with her, since most of her clients were supernatural in nature. She ran a full lab out of her office.

"I'm fine. I can't believe Luca called you. I'm afraid my fiancé overreacted. Really, I'm just a little lightheaded. This is so embarrassing," Samantha said, trying to convince everyone she was fine.

"Well, it's good to know you plan on getting married," Dr. Sweeney commented nonchalantly and began to efficiently pack away her supplies.

"What the hell's that supposed to mean?" Luca was pissed. The doctor was supposed to be diagnosing Samantha and she was talking about marriage? He had a mind to call Ilsbeth back into the room.

"What I should say is congratulations, you're pregnant." She smiled ruefully and walked over to the door. "Now of course, this is quite a special event. It is rare that a vampire can breed, but I'm certain that as a witch, you knew it was a possibility."

Samantha couldn't have been more shocked if the doctor had told her she was going to the moon. It couldn't be. No, Sydney had said vampires don't have babies; they'd discussed it at length during one of their lunch dates. She wanted children but that didn't mean it could actually happen. And while Luca said that he also wanted children, she'd assumed he meant they'd adopt, not literally create one of their own.

Luca was sure his heart had stopped beating. A baby. He couldn't believe it. He'd queried Ilsbeth weeks ago, but hadn't given a thought to birth control, considering how seldom it happened. He couldn't help the broad, proud smile that broke across his face. He jumped into bed with Samantha, needing to be closer to the mother of his child.

As the shock wore off, Samantha held a protective hand to her belly. "A baby?" she whispered, and beamed at Luca.

"A baby," he repeated. "My precious Samantha, we're going to have a child. I love you so much." Luca embraced her on the bed, not caring that Kade, Sydney and Ilsbeth had come into the room. Despite having spectators, Samantha and Luca kissed each other gently.

"A girl to be exact," Ilsbeth noted. "Babies who are born of vampires and witches are girls. And your little girl will bring her own special magic into this world. She will be quite exceptional, of that I am certain."

"Well, of course she will be. Just like her mother. Beautiful and magical!" Luca could not stop smiling. *A baby. A family. A home.*

Sydney and Kade wrapped their arms around each other, happy for Luca and Samantha. It was unbelievable how this little witch had transformed Luca. Once cold and serious, he now was truly enjoying life, exuberant about the future.

"Okay, everyone, as much as I enjoy sharing this phenomenal news, I really need a bit of privacy. It's time to get ready for the party," Samantha stated as if she hadn't just fainted.

"No, no, no," Luca asserted.

"Doctor?" Samantha looked up at her with puppy eyes hoping she'd get the correct response.

"You're okay for the party, but you are to remain seated for the rest of this evening. Also, you should expect to be taking daily naps from now on. Don't wait until you feel dizzy to lie down. As soon as you are tired, rest. While the fatigue and nausea are perfectly normal, you need to go easy. Usually women don't faint but it can happen, as you just found out. As far as your training, no more than one hour per day. In another month, you'll be feeling much better. Luckily for you, your pregnancy will be only six months. One of the benefits of being supernatural," she quipped. "Okay now, I expect to see you in my office next week, Samantha. Luca's got my number."

After thanking everyone for their assistance, Luca and Samantha lay quietly in bed. She cuddled into him, resting her cheek on his broad chest. They were both thrilled to be having a baby together; neither thought it could really be happening. Unassumingly, Luca took her hands in his.

"Samantha."

"Yes, daddy-to-be?"

"I was going to wait for tonight, to surprise you. But now, this news. I'm so happy. I never thought. Damn, I sound incoherent. Okay, just close your eyes."

She closed her eyes and added, "I'm not sure if I can take any more surprises today."

"I think you'll like this one." Slipping an engagement ring on her finger, he smiled down at her. "Since I'm not so good with words right now, I'll simply say, 'I love you.'".

Samantha opened her eyes and glanced at the stunning ring he'd given her. "I love it! Thank you, it's beautiful."

His head dipped down as he captured her lips. Deliberately seeking her sweetness, he swept his tongue over hers. They kissed lightly, unable to stop smiling; altogether exhilarated from learning they were expecting.

Samantha laughed. "You know, this is crazy, don't you? A month ago, I was down here for a conference, and now I'm a witch who's getting married to a vampire. And we're having a baby who's going to be a witch."

Luca laughed. "How are we gonna explain this one to your parents?"

"Guess we'd better get married soon, huh?"

"The sooner the better. I can't wait to hear her little feet running around this house," he said excitedly.

"Hey, speaking of running, is Kat going to make it tonight? I invited her you know, but she hasn't called me back. I left a message on her cell phone. I sure hope everything's okay. And Tristan, it's a shame he couldn't be here tonight either. Told me had some sort of pack thing going on."

"I'm sure Kat is fine and we'll celebrate with Tristan when he comes down here again next month. No worries, my little witch. Tonight is for celebration, and I want to spend every minute showing off my new fiancée and sharing our good news."

Luca held Samantha as she drifted off to sleep. He did wonder why Kat hadn't replied to their invitation, but he didn't want Samantha to have concerns tonight over the wolves. In the morning, he'd phone Tristan to tell him about the baby and make sure he and Kat were all right. Regardless of wolf problems, he now had a family to care for; it was not his responsibility to monitor pack concerns. As requested, they had flown Kat down to New Orleans. He knew both Tristan and Marcel would have her back. As far as Luca knew, their pack was still actively patrolling the area in search of the two escaped wolves. He guessed they would have made their way back to New York by now anyway.

Kissing Samantha's soft hair, he gingerly touched her belly, knowing his daughter was growing inside. Peace. In all his life, he'd never felt it. Today, lying here with his mate, Luca had finally found it within her magic embrace.

Epilogue

Tristan burned down the open highway on his Harley. Aside from going wolf, there was nothing like the freedom of tearing it up on his steel horse. Returning from a week of running his wolves had brought a much needed peaceful vibe to both him and his pack. After helping out with the mess down in New Orleans with Kade and Sydney and trying to keep Kat out of trouble, his own wolves needed his attention.

He smiled, considering the she-wolves who had vied for his attention over the holiday. Preferring to keep jealousy and discourse to a minimum during their run in the wild, he'd rebuffed their advances. Sure, he'd danced with a few and flirted shamelessly, in his usual style, but he'd decidedly stayed celibate. Tristan wanted to keep his head clear and focused, and women certainly had a way of blurring the lines. At the very least, they took up a lot of his time, and time was a commodity when it came to pack activities. Instead of self-indulging, he'd given of himself, concentrating on the needs of all the wolves.

It was no secret that the pack elders yearned for him to mate, but Tristan knew it wasn't going to happen anytime soon. Leading the pack was an earned honor that he enjoyed doing alone. After all, he was by no means lonely; the ladies were drawn to him like bees to honey. Everyone knew that the Alpha happily played the field as long as no commitment was required.

Tristan had made up his mind a long time ago, that he wasn't willing to settle for any woman just for the sake of mating. Yes, there'd been women he liked a lot over the years, but no one female was a true mate to his wolf. The only serious relationship Tristan had had in recent years was his friendship with Sydney. While she was well and truly an Alpha female, she was human, not wolf. So while they'd made love on occasion, and he'd even asked her to move in with him, he knew she wasn't his mate.

He admitted to himself that watching his good friends find love struck a chord in his heart. Kade and Luca were at peace and truly seemed happy. At times, it made him wonder if perhaps he was missing out on something in life. Regardless, it wasn't as if he had even a hope of finding his true mate within his own pack. While many of the she-wolves appeared quite lovely on the outside, he knew that most only wanted him for his Alpha status. And the human women he'd met were mostly interested in his bank account.

Despite the pressures to create a breeding pair for the pack, which would greatly increase the number of cubs born to all wolves in the pack,

Tristan had no intention of giving into an arranged mating. No, he'd grown up seeing many an Alpha pair irrevocably tied through a forced mating, hating each other, yet shackled together for eternity for the sake of their wolves. Even though the archaic custom was still practiced in a few regions, Tristan and his brothers had long ago begun the tide of change from old world to modern pack laws. As a result, all of the Livingston brothers lived unmated, but were contentedly and successfully leading their packs. Adhering to the law of the natural selection of mates, they frowned upon imposing an artificial Alpha mating. The new tradition bred strength and happiness into his pack members. Tristan felt strongly about the law; he would not be forced into a pairing nor would he force others in his pack to submit to it either.

The shit storm that New York Alpha, Jax Chandler, had caused was brought about by his perverse belief that a male Alpha could simply pick his wolf as his mate, indifferent to her agreement. Tristan had always felt strongly that not only would his woman submit to him of her own volition, she'd also choose him as a mate. So when Jax decided he wanted Kat for his mate, there was no way Tristan was letting that asshole simply take his baby sister. From what Marcel had relayed to him, things had settled with Jax. Marcel had spoken to him over the phone, explaining clearly that Kat was in no way interested in becoming his mate. Jax was understandably irritated by her brush off but told Marcel that he'd back off if that's what she wanted.

However, Tristan didn't trust that Jax would give Kat up without at least a face-to-face meeting. It seemed too easy that with one call from Marcel, Jax would give up his claim. After Marcel had told him that Luca had been attacked and had killed Sköll, who claimed to be a New York wolf, how could he trust that Jax would back down? It had been reported that at least seven wolves had been killed outright, and two were missing. Over the past two weeks no one had spotted them, despite large sweeps of Marcel's territory. Despite Jax's insistence that Sköll and his wolves were not from his pack, Tristan and Marcel weren't convinced either way.

When he got home, Tristan planned to call Kat to tell her to stay down in New Orleans for a few more days, to take some more time off before returning to Philadelphia. It had only been a few weeks since Luca's attack and Tristan wanted to make sure things were nice and calm at home before she returned. Being down in New Orleans would make it harder for Jax to abduct her if he didn't keep his promise. By the time Tristan reached the city, the Sunday traffic had died down. Taking the direct route into town, he figured he'd stop off at Eden. While away, he'd left his longtime manager and friend, Zach, in charge of running the club. After a quick inspection to make sure there were no problems, he'd go home and call Luca to congratulate him. *Damn bastard was getting married, too. His friends were dropping like flies.*

He smiled, thinking of the petite sorcière that had captured Luca's heart. Now, she was a lesson in perseverance, he'd thought to himself. She'd been through hell and back and now was making great gains as an elemental witch. Before he'd left on his pack run, Luca had called, and spoke about her like she literally walked on water. Tristan had teased him about being whipped, but he honestly was happy for his old friend.

Rounding the corner, Tristan's tires came to a screeching halt as he pulled into the parking lot. Police cars and fire trucks flashed their angry lights as spectators watched the melee. Tristan jumped off his bike, and ran up to the front entrance. Grey smoke billowed upward as the firefighters put out the last of the flames. Zach held up his hands, begging Tristan to step back.

"What the fuck is going on here?" Tristan demanded.

"I had to run an errand. I was only gone for thirty minutes, man. I swear."

"I don't give a shit if you had to leave. I am only going to ask you one more time, what the hell happened to my club?"

"Police say someone broke in and set off a Molotov cocktail in the main room near the long bar."

"Security cameras?"

"Not sure, 'cause they won't let me in. I've been trying to tell them about the cameras. I don't know the extent of the damage yet. And Eve, she's still in there."

Eve was a fifteen foot yellow boa constrictor, who was on display behind the bar. She wasn't exactly cuddly but Tristan had raised her from a baby. He needed to get in the building to see if she was alive.

"Fuck!" Tristan raged. Someone had deliberately set fire to Eden; not enough to burn the whole building down, but enough to send a message. Sensing that the trouble with the New York Alpha was far from over, he pulled out his cell and called Marcel. His suspicions were confirmed; Kat was on the run from a couple of rogue wolves. Her car had been carjacked and they'd killed her driver. She'd managed to make it into the marshlands and had led them on a chase, narrowly escaping capture. Marcel was on his way to pick her up and was setting a trap for her attackers. Tristan cursed Jax Chandler as he ended the call.

Ignoring Zach's pleas to stay out of the building, he charged forward. As much as he wanted to interrogate Zach about witnesses or what else the police had said happened, he knew that he could find the kind of evidence that only a wolf could identify. A hair. A nail. Body fluid. A scent. The perpetrators might have left an identifier behind. This had just become personal, and he vowed to go on the offensive.

Firemen and policemen shouted at him as he tore into the building.

Tristan trod carefully as he entered the main room, near the dance floor. The entire area was charred; a fine black soot covered every surface in the room. A barrage of chemicals from the extinguishers along with kerosene permeated the scene. Normally, the club would have been thoroughly bleached in the morning hours; there shouldn't have been any odors remaining except the jarring whiff of Clorox.

Foam and water made walking slippery, but he was thankful it was now clear of smoke. Approaching Eve's vivarium, he noticed someone had broken the glass. She was missing. Maybe one of the firefighters or policemen broke the glass and took her? It was also possible that the perpetrators had done it and that she'd escaped on her own. Tristan walked behind the bar inspecting the area for evidence of his snake, but saw no trails in the soot or foam. Someone had carried her.

Sniffing the air, Tristan lifted a board that had fallen off the wall. Underneath it was a small pool of blood; he dipped a few fingers into it and held it to his nose. *Female blood.* The scent was heady, but he couldn't place it as a shifter, witch or vampire. Yet it wasn't exactly human either. If she wasn't a wolf, then that meant Jax might not be involved in this stunt. With no other identifiable scent besides Zach's, she was most definitely a person of interest. He'd tear up the city to find the woman who'd torched his bar.

Tristan wiped the blood on his jeans and scanned the room, surveying the vast damage. He predicted they'd need to tear the entire structure down and rebuild. Releasing a sigh, he resolved to find the arsonist and put an end to Jax's nonsense, especially given the ambush on his sister. The two events had to be connected.

Leaving the bar, Tristan heard screaming mere seconds before he registered the sickening sound of creaking. As if appearing in slow motion, flecks of ash floated gracefully from above. Tristan only had time to look up before the charred ceiling came crashing down upon him, crushing him into the rubble.

TRISTAN'S LYCEUM WOLVES

Immortals of New Orleans, Book 3

Kym Grosso

Acknowledgments

I am very thankful to everyone who helped me create this book:

~My husband, for encouraging me to write, editing my articles and supporting me in everything I do.

~My children, for being so patient with me, while I spend time working on the book. You are the best kids ever!

~Julie Roberts, editor, who spent hours reading, editing and proofreading Tristan's Lyceum Wolves. I really could not have done this without you!

~Carrie Spencer, CheekyCovers, who helped me to create Tristan's sexy cover.

~My beta readers, Stephanie, Liz, Nadine, Katrina, Elizabeth and Sharon, for volunteering to beta read the novel and provide me with valuable feedback.

~My street team, for helping spread the word about the Immortals of New Orleans series

Chapter One

Tristan smoothed the sleeves of his tux and straightened his tie. His platinum locks had turned a darker shade of blonde after the accident. Yearning for the warmth of the sun, there'd be plenty of time to run wolf later. Right now, he had other plans; tearing the city apart brick by brick in order to find the asshole who'd torched his club.

A mixture of anger and excitement simmered like a raging fire underneath the cool exterior of his Alpha façade. Not only had he survived the building's collapse, he'd orchestrated the unthinkable, a new club opening within a week. Tonight, he'd publicly demonstrate his steel resolve to the hundreds of patrons eagerly anticipating the grand opening. His team of warriors, trusted comrades, would seek retaliation for the destruction of his property and attack on his sister, Katrina. Whoever had sought to attack his family was in for a day of reckoning, as he was already strategizing in preparation for the battle.

The heavy pounding of a techno beat reverberated throughout his private office, reminding him that he needed to go upstairs to greet his guests. The new club was on the penthouse level, fifty stories into the troposphere. Customers, subjected to heavy security on the ground level, took express elevators that emerged to a spectacular indoor twenty foot, cascading waterfall which flowed into a limestone-encompassed Koi pond. Stunning crystal chandeliers and spectacular black marble floors presented an understated sense of elegance.

The main club, encased in floor to ceiling glass, gave way to a breathtaking, three hundred and sixty degree, panoramic view of Philadelphia. A large spiral mahogany staircase led to a magnificent rooftop deck, which opened to the warm September breeze. Landscaping adorned with tiny white lights, presented patrons with a romantic ambiance in contrast to the pounding club scene below.

Private luxury rooms, located below the main floor, allowed vampires and supernaturals alike, the privacy they sought for feeding and sexual escapades. State of the art video feeds fed into a central security station. Every corner and crevice of the club, including bathrooms, was meticulously monitored for suspicious activity by a team of experts.

Tristan hadn't had to rebuild the club; his real estate investments were both lucrative and substantial, but the club was popular with supernaturals and humans alike. While wolves and witches were welcome, it was the vampires who enjoyed the greatest benefit; easily finding willing donors to satiate their thirst without relying on bottled blood. Humans, on the other hand, often sought to indulge in an orgasmic feeding experience or simply enjoyed walking on the wild side, delighting in the paranormal conversation and sexual ambiance. It was a synergistic relationship, one that he intended to continue to cultivate.

A new beginning, Tristan thought, as he curled his hand around the cold brass doorknob. This was his city, his territory. Outsiders were already painfully aware of his presence, as he'd placed a moratorium on any new wolves from entering his territory. If found trespassing, they'd be killed without a blink of an eye. There were times when Tristan overtly exerted his dominance, reminding all those around him exactly why he was Lyceum Wolves' Alpha. And so it began. Letting his power flow out toward his wolves, alerting them to his presence, he advanced toward the partygoers. After a brief appearance at the opening gala, he'd meet with his advisors, then retribution would commence.

As the private elevator door opened, Tristan smiled confidently at his guests. Urbane and handsome, he nonchalantly strode into the room, commanding the attention of every male and female. He waved to Logan, his beta, who was chatting up a sultry redhead at the bar. Spotting Marcel, his brother, the New Orleans' Alpha, he crossed the dance floor. Tristan embraced his older brother in a sturdy hug, enough to hurt most men.

"Hey, why didn't you come up to the office?" Tristan questioned.

"What can I say, Bro? There are some mighty fine women down here who required my undivided attention. Nice job with the new club by the way." Marcel looked casually around the club. Calvin, his beta, sat at the bar, carefully observing the interaction.

"Always the ladies' man," Tristan joked. "Sorry, but tonight is all about business. When I finish my speech, we're meeting in the conference room. Logan and the others are aware of the schedule." He patted his brother on the back.

"Sounds good. See you in a few. Good luck," Marcel added, knowing his younger brother fully enjoyed the attention of speaking in front of a crowd.

Tristan smiled back at his brother as he made his way through the crowd toward the stage. The sea of patrons on the dance floor parted as he made his way toward the microphone, uber-aware the good looking Alpha was in close proximity to their gyrating bodies. Women strained to catch a glimpse of the sexy Alpha, demurely curtsying while showing off their cleavage. Males bowed their heads in respect, clearing a wide breadth for the lethal wolf.

The striking Alpha was the picture of exemplary health and strength;

not a scratch or scrape gave a hint that a building had collapsed on him less than a week ago. As he strode through the crowd, he silently acknowledged pack members. His dominant aura permeated the room. The band stopped playing. All talking ceased. Suave and cocksure, he grabbed a glass of champagne off a tray held by a passing waiter, and walked up onto the stage, commanding the attention of the entire room.

"Welcome to Noir, mes amis!" Tristan cheerfully announced to his guests as he took the microphone. "I am pleased to have all of you here tonight to celebrate the grand opening of Philadelphia's premier nightclub." A cool smile broke across his face as he raised a hand to quell the surge of applause. "Yes, yes, I know. It is quite impressive. I'd like to thank Logan for assisting me in this spectacular accomplishment. Please be sure to check out the magnificent views of the skyline from our rooftop bar."

He raised his glass to the crowd in celebration. "Once again, thank you for coming tonight. Vive les loups Lyceum!"

A loud cheer erupted as Tristan exited the spotlight, determined to meet with his pack leaders. While he felt a splinter of satisfaction with the expedient and successful opening, revenge consumed his thoughts. He'd let his patrons celebrate, while he strategized his plan of action. Shaking hands as he made his way through the crowd, Tristan eyed Logan and nodded. The band started up again, firing off a sultry rock song. Undulating bodies filled the dance floor, writhing and grinding to the music.

This is why he was Alpha. The blazing fire had barely made a dent in his daily existence. He had easily rebuilt in the face of the fools who'd attacked his territory. The cool vibe of his new club exemplified just as much about him as it did about what was coming; a day of reckoning. Whoever had decided to torch his property had knowingly declared war on his pack. It was time to get to business, find the enemy and obliterate the threat. No one attacked Lyceum Wolves and survived.

Tristan approached the private entrance behind the bar, and pressed his hand into the biometric security pad. Greeted with a ping and a green light, he typed the code and the door slid open. He marched down the mahogany-lined hallway. Logan and Marcel brought up the rear, making sure that no one followed as the door closed. As he turned the corner, a svelte blonde, well-dressed in a camel-colored suede suit, leaned against the wall admiring her long manicured nails. Mira.

"Ah, ma chère. You look beautiful this evening." Tristan slowed his approach, admiring her long legs. Mira Conners, alpha female of the pack, attracted every wolf on the East Coast. She and Tristan had made love on more than one occasion, but they couldn't seem to make it work as a couple. They were more than 'friends with benefits' but less than lovers. Mira was the first female to teach him that sex didn't equate with love. But his relationship with her also taught him about friendship and respect. A century of being together had a way of weeding out those you could trust from those you couldn't.

Tristan caged her legs and set his hands upon her hips. "Nice leather."

"Nice tux." She smiled, fully appreciating how delicious he looked dressed up for this evening's event.

"Listen Mira, we got work to do. I can't afford to get distracted, and you have a way of doing that to me," he whispered into her hair.

Without looking, he yelled over his shoulder. "Marcel. Logan. We'll meet you in two minutes. Make sure everyone's here."

Marcel and Logan looked at each other, before stealing a glance at Mira, avoiding Tristan's gaze. She'd been part of the pack since they were kids, and had been the strongest female they'd ever known. Both her physical and intellectual acumen set her far above other female pack members. Like Marcel and Tristan, she was destined to be Alpha.

Abandoned at birth, Mira had been raised by the Lyceum Wolves' Alpha. Both the Lyceum Wolves' Alpha and Tristan's father had been the best of friends, so they'd decidedly forged a strong alliance with their children. From a young age, she'd summered in New Orleans, running with her boys: Marcel, Tristan and Logan. Tristan's parents, the Louisiana Alpha and his mate, had welcomed the addition of the little female wolf to their home and pack. Tristan's mother had always wanted a daughter, so in a way, Mira had filled those shoes, at least for a few months each year.

Summer after summer, they ran the bayou and raised hell. As Marcel grew older, he had become focused on learning the role of the Alpha, determined to take over for his father. In his absence, Tristan, Mira and Logan had strengthened their friendship, spending their days fishing in the swamp and warm summer nights making love in the fields. There had been a time when the three wolves had been inseparable lovers. In retrospect, Mira honestly wasn't sure who she'd loved first, Tristan or Logan, but in the end, neither man had become her mate.

After attending graduate school, Tristan had come to Mira's side after her father died. Determined to protect her, he'd fought to be the Alpha of Lyceum Wolves. In his newfound position of authority, Tristan had taken her under his wing, ensuring she continued her college education. Once she'd graduated from Wharton Business School, she'd smoothly slid into Tristan's life as his executive assistant. She was the perfect fit for his real estate holdings corporation. Sharp dressed and tongued, she wielded great power in the boardroom and the pack house. Mira was in a league of her own among the females of the pack. And while she'd occasionally made love to both Tristan and Logan, they all knew it would not result in a mating pair for the pack. Still, she fit nicely into Tristan's life as his confidant and friend.

Tristan liked to play the field but Mira could still make him hard with just a look. As she laid her fingers on his cheek, he let out a small sigh. She bowed her head, her eyes not meeting his. "Alpha, your new club is amazing. Sorry I'm late. Good news is that I wrapped up the Rapkus deal but got stuck in rush hour traffic."

Tristan placed a finger under her chin, catching her gaze. "Great work, Mira. I'm glad you made it to this meeting. I know you usually work the business end of things, but I need you on hand to ensure the security of all ongoing deals. Something tells me this attack wasn't the last, and I'm about to go on the offensive."

Mira reached her hand up to cup Tristan's hand and rubbed her cheek into his fingers, seeking his touch. He responded by holding her hips still, bringing her body flush against his. His warm breath teased her throat; she moaned as he licked her flesh.

"Please," she begged.

Tristan laughed, knowing full well they didn't have time to make love. "No time, ma chère. But look what you do to me," he teased, groaning as he pulled away from her. Painfully aroused, his manhood pressed against his zipper. Damn, it had been a long time since he'd been with a woman.

"Later tonight, perhaps? Or do you have a date this evening?" he asked with a lopsided grin, knowing damn well that she had several wolves vying for her attention. She could have whoever she wanted any day of the week. Yet they both knew it didn't matter. She was his first, no matter what plans she'd made.

"Maybe," she hedged with a small teasing smile. "But I could reschedule for my Alpha. Seriously, Tristan, you know that you and Logan have ruined me for any other wolf. I mean, really? How will I ever find a mate who'll satisfy me the way you do?"

"Ah, come now, Mir. You know that when you meet your mate, no one will compare. That's just the way it is. Sadly, you'll forget us like yesterday's news…no matter what mad skills I have in bed." He shot her a seductive grin, like a spider drawing her into his web.

While Tristan was truly an incredible lover and she was a desirable female, they both knew that once she found her mate, she'd leave him in the wind. When a wolf found his mate and initiated the final bond, no sexual rival existed. Sure, a wolf could consensually decide with his mate to play with another during the full moon activities, but the wolf pair would make decisions as one party. All decisions would be in the best interest of both wolves. And their love would bond them only to each other.

But until they each found mates, they were all happily single and available. While the threesome didn't make love regularly, their strong friendship could easily turn into hot sex on the right night, waxing and waning like the moon. Given the kinky things they'd done to each other, Tristan knew it would be difficult for her to find another male who'd match the intensity of their trio.

Tristan held her gaze and reached for her again, sliding his fingers along the curve of her jaw, down the side of her neck until the back of his hand brushed over the swell of her breasts.

"But until you find your mate, you'll just have to compare them all to me…Someday, though, I'll have to give you up for good. You'll leave Logan and me to go have a house full of pups. We'll be hopelessly heartbroken." He feigned sadness.

"And what about you, Tris? Sydney's married now; it's time to get serious about finding your mate. The elders believe it is your time," she countered with raised eyebrows.

Narrowing his eyes on Mira, he released her and raked his fingers through his shaggy blonde hair. "Please don't start. I'm single for a reason and you know it. Besides *I* run Lyceum Wolves, not the elders. I appreciate their input, but we do not need a breeding pair to run things," he grumbled, irritated that she'd brought up the topic of his mating, which was so not happening any time soon.

"Okay, okay. God, I'm sorry I even brought it up." She smoothed her hair and stood a bit straighter, but still lowered her eyes in submission, sensing his agitation.

"I'm serious, Mir. I really do hope you find a mate soon, but I'm good. In fact, I'm perfect…single…the way I like it. Really," he emphasized with a grunt as if that would convince her to give up the subject. Granted, he knew she'd been waiting over a hundred years to find a mate. But that didn't mean he wanted any part of being tied down to one woman. *No thank you.*

"Come on, let's go. The boys should be ready for us."

Tristan had bristled at her questioning, knowing full well that he was not ready to settle down. Sure, he had asked Sydney Willows to move in with him over a month ago, but he did so knowing that they were not mates. Sydney had been his steady 'friend with benefits' for over a year. But now that she was married to his friend, Kade, he had no excuse not to play the field. Besides Mira and Sydney, Tristan didn't date nearly as much as was rumored. When he was younger, he'd sowed his oats as much as the next wolf, but he'd refined his tastes in recent years and was quite happy with his selective but dynamic sex life.

As they walked toward the door, he deliberately said nothing, letting the cooling sound of silence speak volumes. They entered the soundproofed meeting room without speaking another word. He'd had top of line conference facilities installed in the new club, including LCD projectors and wall to wall plasma screens. An oval cherry table with tan leather seating for twenty took center stage.

Tristan strode to the head of the table, where Marcel and Logan were already seated to his left and right. Three distinguished pack members, who Tristan held in high regard, also sat in attendance. Willow Marrow, the oldest living elder, had seen a lifetime of pack wars. When Tristan had fought to win Alpha, she'd been grateful, because he ensured her safety and status. Her brothers, also elders, Gavin and Shayne, flanked their sister.

Gavin's son Declan sat to his right, and was considered a senior wolf, strong and competent. Tristan could sense Declan had been itching to challenge him, yet he'd always been loyal to the pack. There was a good chance Tristan would need to call upon Declan in the coming weeks, and he wanted him on board with his strategy. As a leader, sometimes it was better to coax an opponent into becoming a friend, rather than cause fractures within the pack.

Tristan silently nodded at Mira to shut the door; she entered the security code to lock down the room and then gracefully sat down next to Logan and looked to the Alpha to begin. Tristan closed his eyes slowly and blew out a cleansing breath, aware that his power rolled off him, commanding the attention of his pack. His eyes flew open; the others felt his tension and waited anxiously for him to begin.

"Okay, people, listen up. As you all are aware, someone decided to wage war with Lyceum Wolves by attacking my club last week. Now that Noir is up and running and we've had a chance to investigate, it's time to go on the offensive. However, before we talk about how this is going to go down, let's review what we know so everyone's on the same page."

Heads nodded toward Tristan in acknowledgment but no one spoke; they all knew better than to interrupt the Alpha. While Tristan presented a cool and charismatic appearance, he was also reserved and lethal, like a Samurai sword waiting to be drawn from its sheath. Picking up the remote, he confidently circled the table. Punching a button, the large plasma screen flicked to life. Through the grainy video of a room in flames, a small, cloaked figure dashed across the room toward the aquarium behind the bar.

"Most of the video was damaged in the fire, but we were able to get this footage. Notice the one person we've got here. We're not sure, but we think it's a human woman. I smelled the blood before the collapse, and the one thing I could tell is that she's not a shifter or vampire. I couldn't tell at the time why all the blood was concentrated behind the bar, but as you can see here in this clip, she breaks the glass to get to Eve."

Eve was a large yellow boa constrictor, who'd been a centerpiece behind the bar. Tristan had raised her as a baby and had built an incredibly elaborate terrarium for her, including lights and trees. Yet, when he'd gone into the fiery building to save her, the snake was missing.

"There's only a few seconds left on this clip, and as you can see, she appears to cut her arm. She wraps it in a bar towel and proceeds to grab Eve. I find it damn interesting that someone would go through the effort to torch the place, and then take the time to save an animal, a snake at that. But this is what we've got. The only prints I saw when I went in were bloodied footprints, presumably hers, since they were small. There was no evidence of anyone else in the place, but then again, it was burning pretty good. I could barely breathe in there let alone detect the scent of a wolf or vamp. Magic is also still on the table as a possibility."

Tristan flicked the screen off, walked back around and sat down. He felt a silent vibration on the table, picked up his cell phone and read the message: *'D. on premises. Waiting for you in Luvox Suite'.* Tristan impatiently tapped his fingers on the table on learning that the vampire was present in the building.

Looking over to Marcel, he directed him to speak to his wolves. "Marcel is going to update you on the stray wolves that attacked Kat. Not sure how they tie into this situation yet, but I know they are a piece of the puzzle. Marcel?"

Marcel nodded and scanned the faces at the table. He was not their Alpha, but commanded the respect of Tristan's pack. "The day of the fire, Kat's car was attacked and her driver, Paul, a young member of our pack, was killed. Kat managed to draw two wolves into an area where we could trap them but both of them committed suicide before capture. I'll tell you that I've never seen anything like it. Cyanide tablets. That tells me they were fiercely loyal and didn't want to risk our interrogations. Unfortunately, the bodies had no identifiable markings. We did find the car; it'd been stolen. New York plates. And that's all we've got."

Marcel pinched the bridge of his nose and blew out a deep breath. He continued, "Now I've talked to Chandler by phone. He continues to deny any involvement. As much as I want to believe the guy, we can't be sure. I mean, he didn't give up wanting Kat for his mate until both Tris and I confronted him. So he's not one to take no for an answer. He may be pissed and looking for retribution. He could have sent those wolves to kidnap Kat and force a mating. Now, on the other hand, if it isn't him, it could be that there's someone trying to stage a coup within his pack. You can be damn sure that if he's clean, he's pickin' apart his pack lookin' for traitors."

Jax Chandler was the New York Alpha. Dangerous and cunning, he'd spent the last couple of months trying to convince Tristan's sister to mate with him.

Tristan stood again, interrupting his brother. "So for now, Kat is safely tucked away in New Orleans. Marcel's leaving tonight to keep a close eye on her and his pack. As for Lyceum, we are locking down. This new building has several empty apartments with state-of-the-art security. All pack members are welcomed and encouraged to stay here when in the city, or remain at the pack house up state. To date, no one's claimed responsibility for the fire, but that doesn't mean this is over. Logan?"

Logan, calm and stoic, raised his gaze to meet his Alpha's. He was Tristan's best friend and confidant. As beta wolf, he took second in command, and often shared responsibilities with his Alpha in both work and play. Logan had idolized Tristan when growing up, knowing his power first hand. Until recently, he'd helped run Eden, but now he vowed to stay close to Tristan, guarding him with his life. Over the past century, Logan had become accustomed to the visions that plagued his sleep; good or bad, he usually only shared them with Tristan. Today, he'd been asked for the first time to talk with a group.

Tristan strode over to Logan and put his hand upon his shoulder, giving him assurance of his protection. He wouldn't push Logan too far, realizing that he preferred to keep his visions private. But this time, Tristan needed him to tell the others what he'd seen.

"I've seen a dead wolf. A male. I felt he was ours. He definitely wasn't one of the wolves down in New Orleans. My visions," he looked up to Tristan, then back to the others. "My visions, they aren't always clear. But this, what happened to the club, what happened to Kat, it's only the beginning. All members of the pack need to be on alert for out-of-territory wolves. In the past, we've been relatively lax about wolves entering and leaving our territory. No more. Tristan's put out an advisory to all other Alphas. Anyone who comes into our territory as a non-pack member must seek the Alpha's permission or else there will be consequences."

Consequences. Mira and the others knew what that meant. Death. Tristan wouldn't hesitate to kill another wolf after the recent attacks. Nor would Marcel.

"In addition, there is no traveling outside our territory until after this issue is resolved," Logan explained; his serious expression cast a dark cloud over the room. No one was used to Logan speaking about his visions, and they now knew death was coming for one of their own.

"That means all wolves need to be brought up to date on this mandate. Willow, you're in charge of pack communications, so as soon as the meeting's over, get on it," Tristan ordered. "The visions. It's possible things can change, but our wolves are indulged, used to freedoms. It has not always been peaceful, and unfortunately, such is the way of territorial disputes. I expect everyone here to read and digest the security dossiers that Logan's put together in front of you. Any questions, see Logan."

Tristan looked over to Mira. "Mira, from here on out all deals through my corporation will need to be approved by Logan. In addition, I expect you to run in-depth background checks on all prospective clients, whether we're buying or selling properties."

She nodded in agreement. "Yes, Alpha."

"As for me, I'm setting up a face to face with Chandler to be held off territory in a neutral location. This meeting will be held within the next few days. Even though the location is neutral, that doesn't mean there won't be a confrontation. If I sense he is responsible, I will take action. You must all be prepared," Tristan pointed out with a calm demeanor. He heard Mira let out a barely audible gasp. They all knew it could mean his death if he didn't win.

Without encouraging their fear, he continued speaking. "Also, Léopold Devereoux is here in Noir, tonight. For those of you who don't know him, he's my friend Kade's maker. I'm not sure what he's got, but Kade said he's bringing me intel on the arsonist. So I expect I'll have more info within the next thirty minutes."

Tristan raised an eyebrow, surveying his wolves, and then looked down to check the time on his cell. "Any questions? Now's the time to ask them."

Declan was the first to speak up, yet again trying to assert his dominance over the other wolves. "Why are we bringing a vamp into pack matters? Wolf battles need to be fought by wolves."

Tristan smiled coolly at Declan, eyeing him until he lowered his gaze. "Ah, jeune loup. *'There is at least one thing worse than fighting with allies – And that is to fight without them'*".

A flummoxed Declan stared back at him. "What?"

"Churchill," Tristan quickly responded. "You will learn with experience that allies are allies, no matter the species. Wars are won based on both strength and information. It is foolish to cut off areas that bring you either. Any other brilliant questions?" He was losing his patience, knowing that Devereoux was on the premises. There was no time to waste. Whatever information the vampire had, it was important enough that he was visiting the club.

Léopold Devereoux was not only ancient and powerful, well over a thousand years old, but he was quite elusive. Tristan had been surprised when Kade called him to let him to know to expect a visit. He was even more surprised that Léopold was coming to see him and not Kade. Whatever the vampire had to say must be damn important for him to travel to Philadelphia, and Tristan wasn't waiting a minute more to hear it.

With no other questions, Tristan stood. Mira hurriedly entered the security code, unlocking the door.

"Well, then. Carry on with your orders. Anything out of the ordinary, contact Logan or me immediately. Meeting adjourned. Be safe, my Lyceum Wolves." With those words, Tristan strode out of the conference room with Logan close behind. Mira watched as her men walked away, knowing danger awaited them all.

Tristan knocked once. A response, "Come in", registered, before he proceeded to open the suite door. Entering, he heard the faint sound of a zipper being zipped as a man adjusted his pants, dressing in front of a long mirror. The debonair vampire turned to face Tristan, a smile on his face, quite comfortable with the intrusion. Léopold Devereoux, Kade's maker, looked as if he was in his late twenties, with short dark hair spiked into a shark's fin. Lethal and quick-witted, he casually and smoothly proceeded to button his tailored shirt. Admiring a naked blonde and brunette, who both slept contently on the bed adjacent to the long leather sofa, he licked over his fangs in delight. A moan escaped one of the women as she turned to spoon the other and found the warm breast she sought.

"Lovely, aren't they?" Léopold asked nonchalantly with a slight French accent. "Your club Noir… c'est magnifique. Exquisite blood and even better sex."

"Monsieur Devereoux?" Tristan questioned, confirming his assumption that the man before him was indeed Kade's maker.

"Oui."

"Monsieur Livingston?"

"Oui."

"Please call me Léopold," he insisted, checking his appearance once more.

"I'm pleased you've had a chance to enjoy Noir's amenities but we need to speak privately." Tristan eyed the nude women, smiling at Léopold. As much as he enjoyed viewing the opposite sex without clothing, business came first.

"Ah oui." Léopold snapped his fingers loudly and the women on the bed began to stir. "Up now, my lovelies. Time to go. Next time in Philadelphia and all that good stuff. Now off you go." He handed each of them a white fluffy spa robe, complementary from Noir. Each woman grabbed their clothing and shoes off the floor, sheepishly giggling as they left the room.

Tristan proceeded to sit in an overstuffed leather chaise, and propped his feet up on the ottoman. He gestured for Léopold to join him.

"Let me say that I am appreciative of any assistance you can provide with regards to finding the arsonists."

"Nasty business, no? Kade informed me of your troubles, cowardly, indeed. Not that I mind revenge or war, when justified," Léopold commented flatly.

"I can assure you that I do plan on revenge. And when I do, I'll look straight into their soul when their life leaves this earth."

Léopold let out a hearty laugh. "A man of my own heart. No wonder you and Kade are friends. Well then, I'd say you'll enjoy this little tidbit of information I have for you."

"I imagine I will." Tristan grinned, tasting the justice he was readying to mete out.

"Let's get to it then. You know Alexandra? My fille. My daughter. She runs our Philadelphia operations."

Tristan silently nodded with an utterly emotionless expression. Did he know Alexandra? Who didn't? She ran her vampire operations with a silk-covered, well-manicured, iron fist. Animalistic came to mind when he thought of how she lusted after anything with a cock, and provided little mercy for her enemies. Tristan considered her neither friend nor foe but generally avoided contact.

While it was true that he allowed her and her vampires to patronize his club, he'd had to refuse her sexual advances on more than one occasion and didn't relish the thought of having to interact with the black-hearted mistress. Alexandra was interested in one thing and one thing only; Alpha blood. Alpha blood equated to power. As far as Tristan was concerned, it'd be a cold day in hell before he ever fucked her, let alone let her drink from him. He silently prayed that whatever Léopold said next didn't involve quid quo pro.

As well as Tristan tried to hide his disdain for Alexandra, Léopold began to chuckle to himself. "Alpha, you need not conceal your feelings about her. I am not fond of the little witch, myself. But for now, she leads. And it just so happens that she's found a toy which you'd like very much."

Tristan raised an eyebrow. "A toy, you say?"

"Oui, a toy. If you know my fille; she sees most things or people as either food or toys. In some cases, they are one and the same."

"So let's say she does indeed have what I'd like to call a 'person of interest'. Why hasn't she come to me herself? Why send you?"

"Well, first of all, she very much likes her toy at the moment. And secondly, she'd want something in exchange for her troubles. However, when I heard you were looking for this 'person of interest', and I found out about her toy, I decided to force her to hand it over to you. You see, unlike Alexandra, I am very fond of Kade, and unlike most parents, I do play favorites. Sometimes she needs to be spanked a little to stay in line, no?" Léopold stated plainly as he fastened his cufflinks.

"Monsieur, I do appreciate your, shall we call it, intervention."

"You can go do a pick up tonight. She's expecting you. I can't promise your 'person of interest' won't be unharmed. I can, however, say that said person will be alive."

"You sure about that?" Tristan didn't mean to question the vampire but he knew Alexandra was nothing short of ruthless.

"Trust is a delicate thing, Alpha. You don't know me well, so I shall let this pass. But know that my children do not cross me. For if they do, well, let's just say that the immortal are not truly immortal. Death can come to us all given the right circumstance," Léopold responded indifferently as he stood and put on his suit jacket.

Tristan knew his words to be true. Stake or remove a vampire's heart or decapitate them, and a vampire would indeed die. Werewolves were nearly immortal and could suffer great injury, yet they could be killed by evisceration or broken neck. On that somber thought, Tristan stood up and faced the ancient vampire eye to eye.

"I want you to know that Lyceum Wolves is appreciative of your willingness to help. It will not be forgotten. If I can be of assistance to you in the future, do not hesitate to call on me." He extended his hand.

"Alpha, you've been there for Kade many a time, no? I am only returning a favor. And I must say that after visiting your club, I see why it is so important to our upper echelon vampires. Willing donors for blood and pleasure combined with a decadent atmosphere is quite the attraction in the City of Brotherly Love. C'est une excellente." Léopold reached for Tristan and returned his offer with a solid handshake. As Tristan opened the door, Léopold briefly raised his hand in a salute, before gathering his things to leave.

Logan gave Tristan a small grin. He'd stood watch outside, overhearing the entire conversation. "He's quite the vamp, huh?" Logan commented. "Hard to believe Alexandra's his daughter, although I will say they're both as deadly as a rattlesnake in a pit."

"That is true, my friend." Tristan put a hand on Logan's shoulder, not fancying a visit to Alexandra. Nevertheless, he couldn't contain his excitement over the possibility that the arsonist could be in his custody within the hour.

Chapter Two

Kalli slowly opened her eyes, entrenched in a hazy nightmare. Kidnapped and bled out, she could barely move her limbs, let alone try to sit up in bed. Two days ago, she'd left the hospital only to be attacked from behind by vampires. They'd knocked her out and brought her here, wherever here was. At first they'd chained her to the bed, but now her own body's weakness shackled her. For two nights, she'd been visited by a diabolical bloodsucking mistress. The demon sucked her blood only to spit it out; something about poison, she remembered her screeching.

Kalli wasn't naïve to supernaturals, far from it. She knew how evil they all were, and this nasty detour only proved her point. But Kalli was a survivor. She'd survived her so-called family; she'd survive this too. The effects of her pills were starting to wear off, as she could feel the beast within calling, begging to fight. She supposed she needed the extra strength it could bring her, but her brain refused to allow the animal to surface. She was human now, at least on the outside.

Looking around the opulent room, she craned her neck, struggling to identify where they'd brought her. If she didn't know any better she'd have thought she was in a luxurious hotel. But the thousand-thread-count Egyptian cotton sheets could not mask her hideous isolation; her deafening screams while tortured beyond reason. Still no one came to her rescue. Someone would have surely heard as she strained against the blood red talons that held her down while razor sharp fangs pierced her skin.

She spied a bottle of water and saltines on the nightstand. Had they been feeding her? Keeping her as some kind of blood bag? She didn't remember eating, but she couldn't deny she needed water. With great effort and a moan, she reached for the bottle and opened it. She felt almost human as the cool liquid slid down her sore throat. *Almost human.* That was the key, she thought to herself. For now, she thanked God that she was human enough to fool them. Repulsed by her blood, they hadn't discovered her secret. She could sense the bitch's confusion as her medicated blood hit her tongue. Damn straight, it didn't taste good. Yet the greedy bloodsucker kept going, probably to make her weak on purpose. She might have succeeded in draining her, but Kalli was a fighter.

Letting the beast take control was seemingly her only option for escape. She hadn't seen or heard anyone in the hallway. She reasoned from the short car ride, that she was still in the city. If she could just get out of this house, people wouldn't be far; refuge was within her grasp. But her medicine suppressed the beast. She wanted it that way. Being human was far underrated, yet in this situation she could not deny that being supernatural would give her the strength to at least walk, find help, and hide.

Seeing no other choice, Kalli closed her eyes and breathed deeply, searching for the one within who could save her from the torment that would surely seek her out again. Determined to find deliverance from the incubus, she let the power of the beast fill her veins.

Tristan pulled his SUV up to Alexandra's four-story, Victorian brownstone. While she preferred her ostentatious mansion in the suburbs, he knew for certain she'd be waiting for him in the city. Alexandra's narcissistic tendencies would drive her to make an appearance at the exclusive opening of his club. Anyone who was anyone was there tonight; she considered herself *the* one. It probably was killing her to have to wait for him to retrieve 'the toy', as Léopold called it.

Tristan conceded that she had her place in the supernatural world. Vampires needed a leader, and she kept hers on a tight leash, preventing them from wreaking havoc in the city or his club. For the past fifty years of her rule, vampire on human crime had been minimal. If someone was killed, it was with her knowledge and approval. Tristan respected her leadership toward shifters; she generally respected their existence. She never questioned Tristan's punishments on her own vampires if they got out of hand at his club, and they'd been able to amicably work out any disagreements.

But the one thing Alexandra coveted the most, she could not have; Tristan's blood. He'd refused her his vein many a time. The denial only fueled her desire, convinced she could seduce him given the right circumstances. But he knew that no matter how beautiful or alluring she was, he'd never give in to her wishes. She only wanted his blood to increase her power, and as far as he was concerned, she already had too much, paired with little restraint.

Tristan looked over to Logan who'd been deep in thought on the ride over to Alexandra's. Since the attack, Logan had had more visions and Tristan was certain that he wasn't sharing all he'd seen. He didn't press him, understanding that it was both a gift and burden to sense the future.

"Hey, man. You ready to do this?" Tristan asked, shutting off the car.

"Yeah, sorry. Just thinking," Logan grumbled.

"You okay, Logan? I know seeing that death wasn't easy. I'm not sure what's going on here, but it's not my first time to the rodeo. Things will be okay," Tristan assured Logan, hoping he would snap out of it.

Logan knew that whatever was in that house, more like whoever was in that house, would change things forever between him and Tristan. He couldn't get a feel for whether that change would be good or bad, blanketing him with uncertainty. But now was not the time to tell Tristan what he'd seen. Not only would the Alpha be pissed, he'd fight fate every step of the way. It had the potential to throw Tristan off his equilibrium during this time of battle; he couldn't risk divulging his speculation without being sure. Logan had decided, with heavy heart, to cautiously watch and wait before telling him.

Blowing out a breath and unbuckling his seatbelt, he placed a hand on his Alpha's shoulder. "I'm okay. Now let's do this thing. Not sure about you but I'm ready for a little action, myself."

"Okay, here's the game plan. We're in and out. You know Alexandra. She's goin' to want to keep me there, going all Playboy bunny slash Martha Stewart on me. Sex or food, she knows what I like." Tristan grinned; she knew him well enough to know his favorite things. "A man has his weaknesses."

Logan shook his head disapprovingly.

"Hey, at the end of the day, I'm a man. Who doesn't like a little cookie with their milk? Seriously though, we're in and out. No cups of tea. No bonbons. We get the package and get out. This is too serious to waste time."

"I'm with you."

"One more thing. The package may be damaged. Léopold promised it'd be alive, but knowing Alexandra and the fact that he referred to it as her toy, well, let's just say we may have to carry it out."

"As long as we can do an interrogation at some point, it'll be okay," Logan commented.

"Okay, you ready? Let's do it," Tristan ordered, getting out of the car.

Logan followed him up the cobblestone walkway. The extravagant brownstone had been fully restored and probably looked better than it had during the eighteen hundreds. Gas lights illuminated the heavy wooden, intricately carved door. Tristan knocked hard on the stained oak, knowing full well she was aware of his arrival. Survival instincts would alert her to the powerhouse standing outside her home; she'd be waiting for him.

A well-toned young man dressed in a turquoise harlequin vest and black tights opened the door and greeted them with a blithe smile. "The mistress awaits," he announced, ushering them into a spacious, octagonal foyer. Stained glass windows and dark mahogany moldings set against cream textured wallpaper with red swirls created an antiqued illusion for guests. Dark hardwood floors accentuated the expensive oriental area rugs.

Tristan and Logan watched the odd-looking man walk into a larger parlor where he lounged on a long, velvet sofa. He closed his eyes, ignoring them. Through an archway, they saw Alexandra gracefully navigate her way around a baby grand piano. Dressed in a red satin corset that pushed up her already firm breasts, she smiled coldly, baring her perfectly white teeth. A tight, black leather pencil skirt hugged every inch of her bottom, leaving little room to walk in a typical stride. Her jet black hair had been swept into an intricate updo that drew attention to her creamy pale skin. She looked every bit the enchanting, but dangerous sanguisuge. And while her beautiful looks most certainly drew men like bees to honey, Tristan knew all too well that her sting was deadly.

"Tristan, darling," she crooned, extending her arms for a hug. "Come now, I won't bite."

"Ah chère, but you do," he teased.

Tristan grabbed her bony hand in his and quickly blew air kisses to each of her cheeks. It was more a gesture of peace as opposed to genuine happiness to see her. He knew she'd appreciate the thought.

"And Logan, so glad you could join us as well," she smirked, feigning geniality, never taking her gaze off of Tristan. Her irritation with Tristan's second was hardly a secret, since she wanted to be alone with the Alpha. Logan would only serve as a barrier in her quest for blood.

Logan ignored her comment, scanning the room for others. He didn't give a shit if she was happy or not. There was no way in hell that he'd let his Alpha walk into that hornet's nest alone.

"Please, Tristan, come have a drink. Cognac perhaps? And I'd be remiss not to mention how sexy you look in that tuxedo. Sorry I missed your opening. As you know I'd been planning to be there right on time, but…"

"Stop. Alexandra. You know why I'm here, and I don't have time for nonsense. Give it to me now," Tristan commanded, not moving from the foyer.

Alexandra ran her palms up and down the lapels of his jacket. "You mean my mouse?" she purred. "Léopold really is no fun. I was having such a good time playing with her."

"Her?" Tristan raised an eyebrow.

"Please, don't pretend you didn't know. Surely Léopold must have told you."

"No, and frankly I don't care whether it's a man or woman. Whoever torched my club knowingly started a pack war. That being said, I'm interested in how you procured her. How do you know she was there?"

Alexandra admired her long nails, preparing to boast about her extraordinary hunting skills. "My strong Alpha, you do know just how important your little club is to me and my vampires. While you may not appreciate my interest in your venture, you know that I've always wanted you."

Tristan rolled his eyes. "Yes, tell me something I don't know."

"My vampires. They do treasure being able to go to the club for a bite to eat and to seek carnal pleasure. They watch. They protect what they value."

"You have surveillance on my club?" Tristan could hardly believe she'd go so far as to stalk him, but at this point, he just wanted answers.

"Please, darling, don't make it sound so crass. They weren't spying on you," she countered defensively. "They were merely making their rounds, making sure our ranks were behaving. They are my eyes and ears. As their leader, I'm acutely aware of their activities. One must keep vampires in line."

"Yeah right," Logan grunted under his breath. He didn't trust a single word that came out of those finely painted lips.

"Did you have to bring him?" Alexandra asked Tristan, quite annoyed that Logan was allowed to speak in her presence.

Tristan shot him a pleading look as if to ask him to curb his anger. He knew Logan didn't do diplomacy, whereas the Alpha was trying to get as much information as possible about what had happened. The last thing he needed was war with the vampires, as he might need their help with whoever had attacked the pack.

"Please go on," Tristan encouraged.

Alexandra huffed, smoothing her hair. "The day of the fire they were merely doing rounds of the city. All they saw was her leaving with that dreadful snake of yours in tow. Honestly, I don't know why you even kept that vile reptile." She rolled her black eyes in disgust. "But I digress. Long story short, we tailed her then snapped her up a few days later in a parking garage."

"What else did your workers see that night? Did they actually see her set the fire? Was she with anyone?"

"No, they did not see her set the fire, nor did they see anyone else. Please, Tristan. As if I would lie to you." She batted her heavily mascaraed eyelashes at him. "Now that I've already told you what they knew, can we please go into the parlor and sit like civilized people? I'd love to hear all the details about your new club," she pleaded, and turned to walk away.

"What do you mean by 'knew'? I want to talk to the vampires who saw her that day and the ones who captured her," he demanded. "They might be able to tell me something you overlooked."

She stopped in her tracks, slowly turning around with a cold sneer plastered across her face. "I'm afraid that's not possible, as they are no longer with us. The vampires who saw her and took her were one and the same. Unfortunately for them, they did not understand the meaning of 'do not touch' and tried to play with my new toy." *Vampire justice was swift and merciless.*

"Okay then. Since we are about to do a transport, I need to know if the woman's supernatural," Tristan inquired. He stoically waited for answers that did not come, while Logan began to pace.

"From what I can tell, she is not of a supernatural origin, now please, let's just go sit down and…"

"Alexandra, I don't have all day. If you have no further information, then we've got to get going. Where is she? Oh and she'd better be alive," Tristan snapped. He was growing impatient.

"Mouse? Don't worry, I didn't *kill* her," she scoffed. "I merely *played* with my toy. But if you are in such a hurry, I'll ask James to bring her down to you. Honestly, I'll be glad to be rid of the nasty little thing. I'll tell you this, my dear Alpha, the twit may not be supernatural, but I'm not convinced she's entirely human, either. Never in all my years has a human tasted so foul."

Kalli heard voices. Her beast had risen for mere seconds only to cower inward. Even though her medicine was starting to wear off, it wasn't enough to allow a transformation. After opening herself to what lay within, she'd hoped she'd have more energy. She was grateful that she could at least walk, which was more than she could have managed earlier. Slowly, she turned the door handle, sensing there were no guards. As she peeked around the corner, she spied the staircase.

She hesitated and looked down at her bare feet. What the hell had they done with her shoes? And even though they'd left her in her jeans, they'd torn her sleeveless turtleneck, exposing her bra. Out of modesty, she tried gathering the material together, softly gliding her fingers over the welts on her neck in the process. It was September, so she wouldn't freeze. Kalli made a split second decision; she needed to leave. It was either flee or die. A coward she wasn't.

She quietly padded down the long hallway, cringing at every little creak her feet made on the old hardwood floor. A shiver ran down her spine when she heard the demon female voice she'd come to know the past few days. Startled at the sound of a man's voice raised in anger, she jumped. Had she brought more vampires here? Were they here for her? She had to get out quickly. She'd die if she lost any more blood.

As she intrepidly descended the stairs, she found they led into a kitchen. Kalli caught sight of a backdoor only twenty feet away; freedom was so close she could taste it. A few steps more and she could reach the handle. She didn't see or hear anyone and darted for the door.

Pain seared through her body as a pair of large hands wrapped around the loose tendrils of her hair, yanking her backward toward the floor. Choked in fear, she gasped for air as vomit rose in her throat. A gut-wrenching scream tore from her lungs as the man dragged her flailing body along the stained wooden planks. Although fraught with confusion and despair, she took note of his perplexing attire; a clown? No, it was another monster, a vampire. His fangs bared, he silently continued to pull her toward the voices. Thrashing about, she grabbed onto his hands, trying to free herself from his iron grip. A flash of the vampire who'd bitten her and two strange men crossed her vision. *Saviors?*

"Please! Help me! They're going to kill me!" she cried out, begging for rescue. Tears streamed down her cheeks as she tried kicking her abductor in an attempt to escape the bloodthirsty, fanged savages who'd been holding her hostage.

Breaking his silence, the harlequin man stopped and straddled her. "Silence! The mistress wants her mouse quiet!" She recoiled as he raised the back of his hand to hit her.

As Tristan heard the screams, he caught a glimpse of the evil smile blooming across Alexandra's face. Growling, he rushed the vampire who sat atop the young woman, shoving him so hard that he flew across the room and smashed into a wall. Tristan cradled the woman's head in his lap, while Logan blocked Alexandra.

Tristan looked down at the battered woman, who looked emaciated and bloodied. Dark raven curls covered her face. Gently, he pushed the strands of hair aside. She whimpered and cringed in fear, balling herself into a fetal position. At first sight, Tristan found it hard to believe that such a vulnerable creature could be involved with starting a pack war.

"Logan, coat!" Tristan barked. He would have given her his own but he refused to let go of the woman for fear that she'd run. Obediently, Logan removed his tuxedo jacket and placed it over her quivering body, never taking his eyes off of Alexandra.

Even though one of his best friends was a vampire, Tristan was irate as he saw the puncture marks all over her skin. *Animals.* She might be a suspect in the fire, but he didn't condone torture. He scooped her small body up in his arms, and stood.

Without another word to Alexandra, Logan opened the door for Tristan, protectively shielding him. He slammed the door as they left, pissed at the vampire. Rage rolled off his Alpha, nearly making him tremble. If it hadn't been for the abused woman lying on the floor needing aid, he was fairly sure Tristan would have killed Alexandra. And he would have gladly helped.

Chapter Three

"That went well," Logan quipped from the driver's seat. He'd settled Tristan and the stranger into the back seat; she was tightly curled on her side, lying in his lap. Her eyes were still closed and she was breathing in soft, rapid pants.

"What a clusterfuck," Tristan responded. "I swear to God, I'd like to kill that bitch. Look at what she's done to this girl."

"Tris, hate to point out the obvious. But number one, Alexandra has been and will always be a bloodsucking monstrosity. And number two, the girl, as you put it, could have been involved with starting the fire. She could be involved with the wolves who killed Paul. So if it makes you feel any better, that woman back there may not be all that innocent."

"Goddamn Alexandra. It's not her place to do this," he snarled angrily, waving his hand over Kalli. "This…this is torture. And it will never, ever be condoned by me or anyone in my pack, understood?"

Logan solemnly considered his words, knowing that this woman was about to change everything, regardless of her culpability in any crime.

"Just playing devil's advocate. You know I'd like nothing more than to take that vamp's head. And I'd smile doing it," Logan affirmed. "So…how's the girl? She doesn't look too good."

"Still breathing at least, but she's going to need to be cleaned up." Mentally and physically, Tristan thought to himself. His wolf stirred, intrigued by the human nestled in his lap. He absentmindedly stroked a finger across her scratched forehead. She was beautiful, even with the bruise that was starting to form above her left eye. *How did she get mixed up in this nastiness?*

Kalli first became aware that she was no longer in the house when she felt the movement of the car beneath her. The scent of two different males roused her wolf. *God, she needed her pills; she was losing control.* She thought she must be dreaming. She could feel the dominant male calling to her. He'd come for her wolf, and she wouldn't be denied. Kalli clutched his jacket, pulling it up to her face, breathing in pure maleness. She needed more. Seeking comfort, she turned her nose into the soft material couched underneath her head, snuggling against the warmth. *Where am I?*

Tristan shifted uncomfortably in his seat as the female turned towards him, settling her head well into his crotch. He took a deep breath, praying Logan wouldn't look back and see what was happening. Not that he usually minded a woman with her lips on his zipper, but this was all wrong. Regardless of what he knew should not happen, his cock, apparently having a mind of its own, jerked in response to the pressure. There was no denying the warm sensation of her breath on his groin; her nose pressed against him. He tried to back into the seat, slightly moving her to relieve the pressure. Of all the things he'd expected on the car ride back to his condo, this wasn't one of them.

A gentle push on her shoulders roused her senses. Forcing her eyes to open, her vision came into focus, and she was shocked to see a belt buckle. *What the hell?* As she turned her head, golden eyes locked on hers. He was the most gorgeous man she'd ever seen, but it was the sheer amount of energy that took her breath away. *Authority. Domination. Alpha.* Even though it had been years since she'd been around an Alpha wolf, there was no denying the infinite potency emitting from this man. Her wolf sang for it, while her mind panicked.

Kalli started to shake uncontrollably as her wolf fought to emerge. *Oh God, this cannot be happening. I need my medicine.*

"Please," she begged, gasping for air.

"Calm down, now. You're safe," he assured her. She'd thankfully moved away from his zipper, but now was starting to climb up toward his face.

Kalli writhed in his lap, trying to fight the change. She found herself clawing at his shirt, placing her forehead against his chest. Her wolf wanted at this strange man, and she couldn't let that happen.

"Please. I need…I need my pills. The hospital. I'm sick," she lied. But Kalli considered changing a worse fate than being ill. She was content living her life as a human in hiding. She couldn't risk having others finding out she was still alive.

"The hospital? Sorry, ma chère. We'll tend to you when we arrive at the club." If they took her to the hospital, it was likely she'd try to escape. She was a bit scraped up and very much needed food. He'd have his healers tend to her once they got home.

"No, you don't understand. The University Veterinary Hospital. Garage, third floor. My pills are in the car," she cried, digging her fingernails into his chest.

Tristan remembered Alexandra saying something about how she tasted "foul". Perhaps it was whatever medication she'd been taking. Was she really sick? He needed her alive if he was going to get information out of her. Erring on the side of caution, he decided a quick detour couldn't hurt. Perhaps they could get her identification or other information from her car.

"Logan, drive over to UVH. We can check out the car while we're there. It'll only take a minute," Tristan called over to him. She stopped rubbing herself against his chest, and dropped back into his lap again. *Here we go again.*

"Got it, boss. What kind of car are we looking for?" he asked.

"Black. Black convertible. BMW," she replied, her voice starting to calm. Out of exhaustion she laid back onto Tristan. Thank God he'd agreed to take her to the car. She'd get her pills and regain control. Again she pulled the black fabric to her body, pressing it over her mouth in an effort to hide her face. Tired, hungry and weak, she knew there was no way she'd escape an Alpha wolf. But if she took her antidote, she'd get well and bide her time until she could escape him. Kalli wasn't sure why he'd saved her or what he wanted, but there was something about him. He wasn't hurting her; it appeared that he needed her for some reason. For what, she had no idea.

As Logan pulled into the garage, he glanced back at the girl who was still wrapped round his Alpha. Seeing her face, he knew for certain she was the one from his dreams. *Poor Tristan.* He silently groaned, knowing Tristan would have his hide once he found out the truth about the girl, and worse, found out that he'd seen it. But he wasn't sure how it all fit together with the fire or the death of the driver in New Orleans. Sure, the girl looked innocent, but he knew better than to trust a woman based on looks.

Logan navigated up to the third level, slowing as he approached what he assumed to be the car. All four tires had been slashed, presumably in an attempt to prevent her from getting away during her abduction.

"This it?" Logan asked, knowing it was more of a confirmation of what he already knew.

Kalli reached forward with both arms until she found the door. Slowly she rose, sliding up until her fingertips reached the lip of the car window. She moaned, unable to go any further.

"Hold on there. Let me help you." Tristan carefully slid his hands underneath her torso; one hand supported her just above her waist and another under the swell of her breasts.

She peered over the window's horizon to see her little convertible. Breathing a sigh of relief, a rush of hope washed over her. The silly car had been the one extravagance she'd allowed herself after she left. The hospital, where it was parked, was her home; it was everything to her. But would she ever get her life back now that an Alpha had her in his grip?

"My pills are in the center console," she cried, as a single tear rolled down her cheek. "Let me down. I won't run." She let her body go limp and fell onto her back, staring blindly up at the leather ceiling.

Tristan heard a resigned acceptance in her voice. It was better this way. Guilty or not, she had stepped into his world, and one simply didn't walk away after becoming a person of interest in a territorial war. He looked down into her sky blue eyes, realizing she'd disconnected from him. She needed time before he'd be able to get all the answers he needed.

Logan got out of the car, fully prepared to break open a window. Looking to get lucky, he tried the car handle but both doors were locked. Circling the car, he noticed a pair of shoes thrown against the concrete wall.

He squatted to inspect them, and guessed that they belonged to their girl. As he stood, he noticed metal glinting underneath the front rear tire. A silver keychain, shaped as a dove. He picked it up and looked at the writing, 'Libre Volonté'. *Free will? From what or whom was she fleeing?* Clicking the key, the car locks clicked open.

"Look at that," he commented, smiling over at Tristan who was watching him. "I'm good."

Tristan rolled down the window. "Yes you are. Now move your ass, Logan. There's something not right with this girl. Did you find her pills?"

Logan held up a brown tube and shook it. "Got it." He rummaged through the car a few minutes more, before he got out and shut the door.

"Took you long enough," Tristan commented as Logan handed him the bottle of pills. "Water?" he asked, hoping for the impossible.

"Sorry, man. I've got nothin'. Can't she just chew it?"

"Guess that's how it's going to have to be. Come on, ma chère. We've got your pills." Tristan opened the unmarked bottle, and he wondered what kind of medication it was. Even though he wasn't human and didn't use their pharmacies, he knew for certain that most pharmaceuticals were labeled. It seemed strange, but she obviously needed the pills.

"Please, just one," she whispered, her eyes locking on his.

Tristan took out a white chalky tablet and placed it on her tongue. She closed her eyes in relief while her lips sealed around his finger. The sweet bitterness burned her throat. *Thank you, God.* Her wolf whined in grief as she was pushed to the back of Kalli's psyche, jailed yet again.

A small sigh escaped as he pulled his wet digit out of her mouth. Goddammit. The woman was scratched and sick, possibly his enemy, and he was thinking of a damn blow job. Shit, he needed to get back to the condo, and fuck something, even if it was his own hand. The pressure of helping Kade, then the fire, his sister; it was getting to be too much. Something had to give.

"What's happening, Tris?" Logan asked, wondering if it had worked.

Tristan didn't want to tell him what was happening, because what he was feeling was inappropriate, to say the least. "She's falling asleep. Whatever was in those pills seemed to calm her. Let's get back to the condo. Call Julie. Tell her to meet us up in my condo. She can heal and watch over this woman. Then call Mira and have her meet us at your place."

Thirty minutes later they pulled up in front of Livingston One. The brand new skyscraper, home to Noir, offices and several luxury condominiums set aside for pack members only, gleamed with reflective black glass. Tristan had already owned the property prior to the fire; call it serendipity, but construction had just finished. With Noir taking the top five floors of the building, Tristan's penthouse rested safely underneath it, with Logan's under his.

As the car pulled up to the entrance, Logan handed the keys to the valet. "Hey Ryan, take care of my girl, here." He patted his car.

"Will do, sir," Ryan, a young wolf, assured him.

"Tristan's in the back. Hold it a second while I get Toby," Logan instructed. He whistled over to Toby, who jogged over, giving him a smile.

Both Toby and Ryan had been adopted into the pack by Tristan after they'd been abandoned as teens. He'd been putting them through college, and both kids worked for him, valeting cars.

"Toby, hold the door for me. Tristan's in the back with a guest," Logan said casually, wondering what else he should call her. Guest hardly seemed appropriate, but prisoner didn't suit the situation either. He shrugged; either way she was going upstairs. They'd have her name soon enough.

"Yes sir," Toby obediently responded.

Toby opened the car door, and held it wide open, and Logan leaned in to help Tristan. But Tristan held up his hand, gesturing for him to step back. *It's starting already*, Logan thought to himself.

"I've got her," Tristan told him as he effortlessly exited the car cradling Kalli against his chest as if he were holding a baby. "Thanks. Hey, how's school going? Keeping your grades up?" he asked in a parental tone.

"School's going well. My chem class is tough but I'm studying hard," Toby beamed.

"Good to hear. Just make sure you keep your mind on your grades and keep the distractions to a minimum. I've heard you two are turning into quite the ladies' men," Tristan teased, looking over at Ryan through the glass, who'd been playing with the radio, but glanced up in time to catch what his Alpha'd been telling Toby. He smiled and gave Tristan a thumbs-up through the glass.

Tristan nodded toward and smiled at him, acknowledging his response.

"Yes sir," Toby laughed, shutting the car door. He and Ryan had had a great summer, parking cars and meeting the sexy women who frequented the club. They weren't hurting for dates.

"Ready to go, Alpha?" Logan asked, rescuing Tristan from further conversation. "I'll run interference."

Tristan looked down at the tranquil woman who slept in his arms. "Yes, let's go."

They took the private elevator up to Tristan's penthouse, avoiding prying eyes. As the doors opened, Tristan immediately started toward the guest room.

"Did you get ahold of Julie?" he asked Logan, without looking at him.

"Yeah, she's on her way up. I'll wait for her here and let her in," Logan told him, knowing she'd have to be let in. Even though the private elevator opened directly into the foyer, only he and Tristan had the code to take it. All other guests arrived separately.

Julie was a nurse practitioner and all-round pack healer. While wolves healed fairly quickly on their own, given a full shift, it wasn't always possible to engage in a transformation. Younger wolves didn't transform until after puberty, and often got into scraps. Julie was also a midwife and attended most, if not all births, depending on what the mother wanted. She practiced both traditional and alternative medicine, catering to supernaturals. On occasion, she'd treat a witch or vampire, if it was a friend, but they generally didn't need aid.

Tristan nudged the guest room door open with an elbow, careful not to hit Kalli's head. She'd need to be cleaned up and fed before they settled her under the covers, so he decided to lay her atop of the comforter. Gently placing her down, he slid his hands out from underneath her warm body.

He sat on the edge of the queen-sized bed and sighed, watching her chest rise and fall under Logan's tux. His wolf had been gnawing at him the entire car ride home; he begged to smell her, nuzzle her, lick her. And shit if Tristan didn't want the same thing. He couldn't understand why he was having these feelings toward a mortal woman he'd just met, one who could be involved in the fire. Still, staring down at her sweet face, he wanted to touch her.

Julie and Logan watched as the Alpha ran his fingers through the woman's hair. *Shit, here we go*, Logan thought. He coughed, drawing Tristan out of his trance.

"Hi, Alpha. Sorry to interrupt," Julie apologized. She walked over and looked at the girl in his bed, shaking her head. "Now, I know you missed me, big guy, but there are easier ways to get me in your bedroom." She winked at him, trying to lighten up the atmosphere.

"Ah, Jules, thanks for coming," Tristan greeted her, reaching over to squeeze her arm, welcoming her to his home. "This, here, is a very important person of interest." He looked down at Kalli, and continued. "She's been roughed up and fed on by vampires. But I need her well enough to question. You should know that we think she's sick."

"Did she tell you that? What happened?"

"No, but during the car ride, she started freaking out, screaming for her pills. We managed to get them out of her car and gave her one. Alexandra claimed there was a strange taste to her blood. I don't know."

"So she's been with Alexandra? How long?" Julie asked in a professional manner, yet she was well aware that the girl had probably been tortured by the bloodsucker.

"Yeah. About two days."

"Can I see the pills you gave her?"

Tristan reached into his inside jacket pocket, pulled out the small bottle and dropped it into her hand. "Here, this is it. Logan grabbed her purse. I'll see if he found anything else."

Julie pushed down and screwed open the safety cap, and shook a few tablets into her hand. "Hmmm. Bottle's not marked and neither are these pills. Could be some kind of generic."

"Not sure, but she seemed damn anxious to take one. Almost like she was having some kind of a panic attack. As soon as she took it, she calmed right down. She's been sleeping for a good thirty minutes now. But I really need to talk to her."

"Okay, well why don't you go take a break and I'll get her cleaned up. Try to feed her something. Here, let me get my bag," She walked back into the hallway, where she'd left her medical kit. Picking it up, she caught Logan's eyes. She smiled and mouthed: "It will be all right." She could tell he was worried about Tristan.

"Okay you two, leave me be. I've got some work to do," she ordered.

Tristan stood, rubbing his hand over his face. Before he walked away, he turned again to Julie. "One more thing. She might be a runner. I'm going to have Simeon stand guard at the elevators. Unless she can sprout wings and fly out from forty stories, she won't get far. But we don't know if she's dangerous, so be cautious, okay. Text me when you think she's ready to talk. I'm gonna go downstairs for a while to Logan's."

"No problem. Will do, Alpha." Julie knew Simeon wouldn't let the girl out of the condo. He was one of the strongest wolves she knew. If anything happened, she'd call on him right away.

"Thanks."

"Thanks, Jules," Logan added.

Clapping a hand on Tristan's shoulder, he walked down the hallway toward the elevators, relieved to get away from the girl for a while. Logan sensed Tristan's frustration about not getting immediate answers, but even more overwhelming was his Alpha's attraction to a stranger they'd just met. Unable to stop fate, he'd be damned if he didn't fight tooth and nail to protect Tristan from being hurt. Despite his visions, he still wasn't sure whether her nature was good or bad. Regardless, he was certain that the woman they'd just saved was about to rock Tristan's world.

Chapter Four

Tristan fell back onto the soft leather sofa and sighed. "Well, that was fucking fun."

"Yeah, I hear ya. I was two seconds away from staking that vamp bitch tonight. Seriously Tristan, I don't have your diplomacy skills," Logan quipped. He went over to the bar and poured them each a sizable glass of whiskey.

"I know. If she didn't keep the vampires in this city on such a tight leash, she'd be dead. And I'd be the first one lined up to kill her," he declared flatly. And after tonight he meant it. *How did someone torture a human like that and feel nothing?* He just could not relate. It was as if the vamp was completely devoid of compassion. The only feelings she had were about her own needs.

"Not only is she narcissistic, she's a true sadist. Not that I haven't seen it before with other vamps, but damn, she's nasty." Logan fell alongside his friend, shaking his head and handing Tristan a tumbler.

Tristan took a large draw of the amber liquid, savoring the flavor as it danced over his tongue. "Thanks, brother. I swear I feel like I'm ready to punch something. I need to shift. Run. Something. I love the city, but it would be nice to just go wolf right now."

"I hear ya." Logan needed to run too, blow off steam.

"Have you got the purse?" Tristan asked. He needed to know more about the mysterious woman lying upstairs in his bed.

"Yeah, it's over by the door. Not much in it. Standard girl stuff. There was identification. Name's Kalli Williams. Twenty-nine years old. City address. Nothing really out of the ordinary for a human."

"Any more strange pills?"

"Nope, nothin'. Listen, I know you're frustrated, but the girl will wake up soon and we'll get answers." Logan wasn't really sure that what he was saying was true, but he was always the optimist.

"Will we? I gotta tell ya that I'm not convinced that girl laying upstairs in my bed has anything to do with the fire. What do we really know? She's guilty of taking a freakin' snake? And while I'd like to know where the hell she took Eve, not even the vamps saw anyone go into Eden. I'm telling you, Logan, something else is about to happen. I know you saw it in your vision, but I can feel it and it's not good. The meeting with Jax can't come soon enough. I've got to know if he's in on this." Tristan raked his fingers through his hair.

"Well, friend, nothin's happening for at least a couple of hours so we might as well just chill…maybe with Mira," Logan suggested, slyly raising an eyebrow at Tristan.

A grin broke across Tristan's face, knowing exactly what Logan was thinking, and it didn't exactly involve relaxing. But after sporting a hard on for the last half hour in the car, he couldn't deny that he needed to get laid as much as Logan did.

Soft knocking at the door got their attention. "Come in, Mir," Logan yelled, unwilling to get up to answer the door.

Mira walked in with a clipboard in her hands, tapping it with a pen. Tristan and Logan watched as she slammed the door and started pacing, immersed in thought.

Without looking up, she began speaking. "Hi guys, just wanted to bring you an update. Talked to Willow, and about fifty percent of the pack will be moved in with her by the end of the weekend. Most of the others are going up to the mountains. You may need to talk to Zed and Nile; both want to stay in the city at their own places. I don't know what's up. They told Willow it was work related, but I'd bet you it has to do with a woman. Probably human." She rolled her eyes and kept talking. "Um, let's see. What else did I need to tell you? Oh yeah, I ran through the list of all potential clients. Most are screened and clear. I have one or two that still need clearance."

She stopped in her tracks and looked over to the men, who were staring at her with wide grins on their faces, enjoying an adult beverage. "What? Am I boring you? Or is it that you've started without me?" she joked. She'd freed her long blonde hair from the confines of its clip.

"More like stopping," Logan responded.

"Thanks for the update. I'm glad to see you have it under control," Tristan replied, complimenting her work. She was nothing if not a type A person who could teach a course on responsibility. Her driven personality was quite congruent with her Alpha status within the pack.

"Want a drink?" Logan asked, toasting his glass up in the air.

"No thanks, I'm good."

"Yes you are," Tristan teased. He patted the cushion in between Logan and him. "Come, Mir. Sit with us. Relax a bit. It's been a long night."

Mira took off her suit jacket and kicked off her pumps. Obediently, she listened, and squeezed herself between the two strong men.

"Now, you don't think you're going to get away with sitting like that, do you? Come here." Tristan set his glass down on the coffee table, and then reached to swing her around so that the back of her head rested in his lap. Logan pulled her legs up onto him and began to rub her.

"I love it when you don't wear stockings," Logan remarked.

Tristan smoothed her hair out of her face and rubbed her head with one of his hands, resting the other below her breasts.

"Oh my God, okay, I think I died and went to heaven. What did I do to deserve this?" Mira moaned.

Tristan wanted release and Mira could give it to him. His wolf had been clawing at him; there was something about that human woman upstairs. Rarely did Tristan feel confused about his emotions. One of the benefits of being Alpha was the serenity of knowing what to do in almost every situation. He was a born leader: decisive, authoritative. Having the ability to quickly assess the state of affairs and determine the correct course of action, he didn't vacillate. He and his wolf were always in sync.

Yet ever since he'd taken Kalli into his arms, his wolf wanted what he shouldn't have. Not that Tristan's cock disagreed, but his head told him otherwise. You couldn't trust a woman based on looks alone. He didn't even know her. Perhaps Sydney marrying had affected him more than he thought. Or maybe it was that he simply hadn't had a break since the battle he'd helped Kade fight. He'd been dealing with Jax Chandler's relentless pursuit of his sister. Then the fire and club rebuild.

As he stroked Mira's hair, he reasoned that sometimes things just didn't make sense. What he did have was a red-blooded female in his arms, and his beta, both of whom would ease any tension he'd been feeling over the past month. Instead of worrying about the suspect, he needed to ease his own sexual needs.

"Logan, isn't Mir looking lovely today?" Tristan massaged her shoulders. She closed her eyes and moaned.

"Yes she is, Tris. You know, it's been a long time since we played. The three of us…together. I've missed this," Logan said as his fingers glided along the inside of her calves. He watched Mira's lips fall open as he teased up toward her thigh. Her hips began to wiggle slightly, calling him toward her center.

Tristan looked over to Logan and met his eyes. "I've missed it too. Now look at how beautiful she is, Logan. I bet she's nice and wet for you. Yeah, that's it," he encouraged as Logan pushed a hand under her skirt, still only barely touching her thighs. "Mir, tell him what you want."

"Please, Logan. Touch me," she whispered, reaching for Tristan's chest.

Tristan found the side opening to her skirt and unzipped it. Then Logan tugged the skirt off until all that remained were her panties. Tristan began to unbutton each pearl of her blouse. Before long, her breasts were bared save only her bronze-colored silk bra. He rubbed his hands all over her chest and tummy, teasing her without touching her breasts directly.

Mira sucked a breath as the cool air hit her skin. She stared into Tristan's eyes, intent on making love to both of her men.

Logan gradually slid his forefinger into the flimsy material, only enough to tease her.

"Logan. Tristan, please," she begged.

Tristan's cock hardened as she pleaded. Burying himself into her sweet heat could take the edge off of his day. God, she was so responsive, even after all these years. No, she wasn't his mate. But she was loyal, sexy and available. What else did he need? His wolf roared in protest, and Tristan pushed him aside. The rational thing to do would be to make love to this ready and willing woman in his lap. He'd done it many times before, so why was the wolf upset? Ignoring his beast within, he extended a claw, and cut her bra free, exposing her creamy flesh. Her nipples peaked in response and she gasped at the act.

"Touch me," she demanded.

Tristan, happy to oblige, grazed his fingertips over a nipple.

"More," she cried.

"Logan, I think our little she-wolf is getting impatient. Shall we help her?"

"Ah yes," Logan groaned as he slipped his fingers down into her slick folds. "She's so warm and wet. Aw baby." He withdrew his hand for a second, only to tear the panties off her body.

She moaned in protest. "Don't worry, we'll take care of you, Mir," Tristan assured her, cupping her warm breast in his hand. Shit, Logan was turning him on by the way he touched her. Sometimes Tristan wondered if he could ever give up having threesomes with his beta. Sharing sexual experiences with his best friend completed everything he needed. He and Logan never had sex alone with each other nor were they in love, but he loved him and wanted to share everything with him.

Logan circled her nub slowly with his forefinger. She pushed her hips upward seeking more pressure, but he wouldn't give it to her yet. No, he wanted to draw it out, make the tension and pleasure last.

Mira reached for Tristan's belt, frantically trying to free him. She desperately wanted him in her mouth, seeking out his steely length through the fabric of his trousers.

"Fuck," he hissed at her intrusion and cuffed her right wrist.

She moaned again in protest.

"Not yet, ma chère. Don't move, just feel. Concentrate on what Logan's doing to you."

"I need more," Logan grunted as he moved onto his knees, putting her legs over his shoulders. "I can't wait to taste you."

She reached for her breast and squeezed it, but Tristan took that hand as well and pulled her arms over her head, gripping her wrists firmly.

"No, no, no," he scolded. "No touching yourself, either. Hmm, we might have to spank her lovely little ass tonight. She's not listening." Tristan knew just the thought of it would push her over the edge; she loved being smacked on the bottom while he made love to her from behind.

"Stop teasing me. I can't take it. Oh my God!" she screamed, as Logan trailed the tip of his tongue between her inner lips.

Tristan reached down with his other hand and pushed her apart, allowing Logan better access. Mira raised her hips upward, seeking relief. The pressure of her orgasm was built. She was almost ready to come, but she needed just a little more.

"She tastes so good," Logan groaned as he pressed his fingers deep inside her. Mira began to shake; she was falling over. Logan's lips took her sweet pearl, sucking gently as he pumped into her. She screamed in pleasure as she flew apart into orgasm.

Aroused and ready, the spell broke for Tristan as his cell phone buzzed in his pocket. Releasing Mira's wrists, he immediately reached for his phone to read the text, *'She's awake'*. Tristan's thoughts slammed back to the woman upstairs in his bed.

"Sorry guys, party's over…well, at least for me. But please keep having fun, okay?" Tristan kissed Mira's head as she smiled up at him, sated for the moment. He gently moved away, straightened his clothes and walked toward the door.

"You need me?" Logan prayed he didn't.

"No, I've got this. I'll call ya later."

Logan scooped Mira up into his arms as if she weighed nothing. "Okay then…I guess your loss is my gain," he declared, smiling as he carried Mira away to his bedroom. He knew better than to ask twice.

"Bye, Tris!" Mira waved giggling as she disappeared into the hallway.

Tristan's mind raced; he couldn't wait to interrogate the suspect. There was something about the whole situation that didn't make sense. And Kalli was the key to getting the answer.

Chapter Five

Warm water pulsed around her body as the fragrant smell of lilacs danced in her mind. She felt warm and safe. Then images of Alexandra flashed. Blood. Vampires. An Alpha. Screaming, her eyes flew open, scanning her surroundings. Panic coursed throughout every cell in her body in a flight or fight response.

"Hey, you're safe. You're okay," a comforting female voice advised her. She looked over to see a young woman with long brown hair kneeling at her side by the tub. A tub? Her heart raced, realizing she was stark naked in a bath full of steaming bubbles and jets pulsating around her bruised flesh.

The woman regarded the tub as if she knew what Kalli was thinking. "It's just a warm bath to get you cleaned up, hun. Nothing happened. I'm a nurse. Really, see?" She leaned over and pulled a stethoscope out of her black bag.

Kalli said nothing as she surveyed her surroundings. She was in a large whirlpool Jacuzzi; warm heat lamps shone overhead. The bathroom felt dark and rich with its umber painted walls and fawn-stained crown molding. The flicker of a single candle danced across the black speckled granite countertop of a chestnut vanity. Although she could think of worse places to find one's self, waking up in strange places was really getting old.

She struggled to find her voice, aware that her throat was raw from screaming. "Where am I?"

"You are at the home of Mr. Tristan Livingston, Alpha of Lyceum Wolves," Julie answered cheerfully. "You're safe, but a bit scratched up from your run-in with that dreadful vampire. Don't worry, though. Your vitals are good. We just need to get you some rest and something to eat. You should be good in a few days."

"A few days? I really need to get home and…" her voice trailed off as Julie held up a hand, silencing her.

"Hun, I know you've had a rough time of it and all, and I'm not going to judge, but the Alpha wants to talk to you." She went about her business, readying up a warm towel. Throwing it over her shoulder, she bent down and slid her hand behind Kalli's back and under her arm.

"Come on now, I want to see if you can stand. Lean on me, and I'll wrap this towel around you. That's it."

Kalli let her weight fall back on the strange woman as she tried to stand. The Alpha wanted to talk to her? Oh God. She knew she shouldn't have gone in to get that snake. He was going to ask about the fire and what she'd seen. She didn't want to be involved. She could not let *them* find out she was alive.

Finding her legs, she pushed upright until she was standing. She sighed as the warmth of the towel engulfed her.

"That's it. Look at you, standing all on your own. God, Alexandra's such a viper. I can't believe she did this to you. Can you step out of the tub? Just hold onto me as you move, okay?"

"Alexandra?" Kalli did as instructed as if in a daze. She let Julie dry her, trying to focus on staying stable on her feet. Weakness was not something she was used to feeling and she disliked having to rely on someone to help her, but at this point, she had no choice.

"Yeah, you know, the bloodsucker who drained you?"

"I...I didn't get her name. I shouldn't have gone out to the parking garage alone. I should have..." Kalli's soft voice trailed off as a small tear ran down her cheek. She should have known that someone would have seen her at the club. Embarrassment washed over her, knowing that she had let this happen. But there was another emotion that racked her mind. Anger? Yes, she was mad all right. But most of all, at the moment, she felt violated. Was there no place on this earth she could be safe from the violence?

"Hey there, I know what you're thinking. Just stop it right now. The vamps. They can even get to us wolves, you know. A human woman is just no match for them. There's nothing you did to cause this to happen to you," Julie told her. A somber expression flashed across her face.

If you only knew, Kalli thought silently.

"Now, come on, let's get you dressed and in bed."

"I don't have anything to wear," Kalli began to say and stopped when she saw Julie hold up a large man's t-shirt with a black wolf insignia on it that read: 'Harley-Davidson'.

"This will do. Wait 'til the Alpha finds out I was digging around in his skivvies," she joked. "Ah, the thrill of it all."

Kalli had a hard time trying not to smile back at the lovely nurse. She gratefully allowed Julie to pull the shirt over her head. It was better than being dirty and infinitely better than being covered in her own blood and body odor.

"Now, for the pièce de résistance." Julie held up a black pair of man's boxer briefs. "You'll probably swim in these, but I found a new package in his room, and well, it's better than no undies. I'll leave it up to you."

"Thanks, I'll, um. I'll take them. They'll be okay until they stretch out." Then they'd probably fall right off of her, but there was no way in hell she planned on staying in a wolf's den with no underwear. She had to figure out a way to escape the hell she'd gotten herself into. Glancing over to the door, she considered making a break for it. Dizziness racked her brain as she started to wobble.

Julie grabbed onto Kalli's arms as she wavered, almost falling onto the floor. She eased her into a sitting position and rubbed her back. "Okay, I'd say that's enough exercise for today. Just take a second and breathe. That's it. You're sitting well. Better now?" Kalli nodded as Julie ran a towel over Kalli's long raven hair. After patting it dry, she dropped the towel on the floor, pulled out a comb and began to tease out the knots.

"Oh and hun, don't even think about leavin' this room right now. Yes, I saw you eyeing the door," she said, continuing her work.

Busted, Kalli groaned inwardly. Who was she kidding? She was barely well enough to stand, let alone walk.

Julie finished up and set the comb on the nightstand. "I probably failed to mention that you are on the forty-fifth floor of a city skyscraper, so there's just one exit out of here and my friend, Simeon, is keeping watch on that one. Besides, I'm telling you that you're safe, okay? Nothin' is gonna happen to you up here. I promise. And besides, you're in no condition to leave, anyway."

A skyscraper? Shit. There was no way she was getting out of here. Kalli liked a nice view of the city as much as the next person, but was terrified of heights. Resigned to the fact that she'd have to face the Alpha, she let Julie tuck her into the feather-soft bed.

"Let's see, so, soup is next on the agenda. I sent for some plain broth and crackers. It should be here about now. So is there anything else I can get you?"

"No, thanks for helping me," Kalli managed, wringing her hands nervously.

"No worries. You just rest, and I'll be right back."

Kalli let her head fall on the pillow and stared up at the intricate light fixture, which was made out of tiny royal blue, glass butterflies. The pretty winged creatures exquisitely complemented the shades of brown and tan of her warm and inviting gilded cage. She breathed deeply and blew out a breath, relaxing into the bed. Unable to deny how serene amenities helped to calm her nerves, she curled into her comforter, willing herself to heal. Closing her eyes, her thoughts drifted to the Alpha who'd rescued her.

In her mind's eye, she remembered how the handsome stranger had saved her from the vampire dressed in the ridiculous harlequin vest. A tall, muscular man with dark blonde hair, he looked like a sexy James Bond in the tuxedo. Struggling to picture his face, his piercing amber eyes came into focus. Like yellow-orange supernovas, they'd been striking and memorable. Did his eyes change when he went wolf? What color was his fur? His power rolled off him like a tidal wave in the car. Authoritative and deadly, an Alpha who took what he wanted.

Kalli thought back to her days in the pack she'd escaped; her stomach tightened. She'd been hybrid. Her mother, a human, had died when Kalli was only fourteen, leaving her to survive on her own within the brutal pack. Three years later, her father, a mean son-of-a-bitch, had fought to be Alpha and lost. The reigning Alpha had sent for her soon after, attacked her and explained how she'd be servicing his men for the rest of her life. Tired of the never ending violence, she'd made a decision to leave.

She knew that even though she was considered lower than omega because of her human genes, they'd never let her leave their ranks. They'd use her up and spit her out. Death was the only way out of the pack, an option she'd have willingly chosen, if necessary. So one late summer's afternoon, she'd taken her father's fishing boat out into the Atlantic off the coast of South Carolina, and jumped off into the cold dark water. Of course, her body was never found, but the small vessel was recovered two days later. The weather had forecast a small squall, so no one had questioned her disappearance; just another soul lost to the sea. With nothing but a backpack and some cash she'd saved over the years, she took off to New York City.

Upon arrival, she'd picked up a waitressing job and saved her money. It was easier than she'd thought it would be to find someone to change her name. With a few Benjamins, Kalli Anastas became Kalli Williams. Afterward, she'd continued working to put herself through college. By her sophomore year, however, she could no longer prevent the wolf from emerging. As a teen she'd starved herself, preventing the shift. But once on her own, she'd gained weight, and shifting into wolf became inevitable. For weeks she'd suffered nightmares, always with the animal scratching to come out and have its due. She'd remembered the tales the other pack girls had told, describing the symptoms of their first time. That was how she looked at it; an illness to be cured. Kalli knew it would come on the full moon, and there was nothing she could do to stop it.

Scared and alone, she'd managed to get out of the city and into the mountains in preparation. She'd rented an isolated cabin in the Catskills, and waited. The excruciating pain of the shift took her by surprise even though she'd known it was coming. After running and killing throughout the night, she'd woken up naked, curled into a hole of a rotted-out tree. Covered in blood and dirt, she'd cried hysterically, believing she was cursed for life. For years she'd repeated the ghastly process, month after month, until she became a doctor and discovered 'the cure'.

After graduation, she'd earned an assistantship, which paid for her grad school. The residency opportunity in Philadelphia had led to a permanent position at UVH. She was able to practice, utilizing state of the art medicine, while continuing to blend into society. And it was there she'd found salvation from the beast.

In reality, her drug didn't cure her of her wolf. But it kept her at bay, caged and unable to shift. Relentlessly, Kalli had worked; she'd rarely eaten or slept, determined to develop a drug to stop the transformation. On the twenty-second trial, it had worked; Canis Lupis Inhibitor (CLI) kept her from shifting, even on a full moon. Side effects, aside from preventing shifting, included chills and aches, but they only occurred if she missed a daily dose. Enhanced hearing and smell were slightly suppressed but not entirely gone. The discovery allowed Kalli to go months without shifting, and she reveled in finally being human. Best of all, no wolf or vampire could detect her wolf, as far as she could tell, anyway. Of course a simple blood test would reveal her true nature, but other than that, she appeared wholly human.

After she began taking CLI, she kept refining the drug, seeking other useful purposes for it. She experimented, theorizing the drug could help aggressive animals in the canis genus to reduce anxiety. Since they were not supernatural, she envisioned a one dose treatment that would positively affect their emotions. She hadn't come too far with that side of her research, but initial projections looked promising. Still, she kept all of her work under lock and key in an effort to hide her identity.

Truth be told, Kalli avoided purposeful contact with supernaturals. She'd only done one full-fledged test of the formula to see if she could or could not be detected as wolf. By all accounts, the exercise had been a success, yet that one experiment had proved to be her most critical mistake. Last month, she and a co-worker had gone to Eden. Well aware that it was run by a wolf and frequented by vampires, her curiosity had got the better of her.

Kalli had danced all night, hoping her pheromones would attract a vampire or wolf. Yet every man who approached was human. She'd even approached female wolves and vampires, engaging them in casual conversation, and not one had identified her as wolf. Rather, she was called out as a human by more than one supernatural. She'd left the club in triumph, celebrating the success of her drug.

But in her efforts to do research, she'd also noticed the fifteen foot yellow boa slithering around behind the bar. A spectacular and healthy specimen; it was like having a private viewing at a reptile exhibit at the zoo. While she didn't specialize in reptiles, she held an appreciation for a species that had survived through the ages.

The vivarium, extraordinarily large, with its heated rocks, trees and flowing water, was an excellent example of how a large snake could be kept safely in captivity. Personally, she did not advocate anyone owning or raising a wild animal, but boa constrictors were routinely sold these days in pet stores. It was refreshing to see how a pet owner would go to such great lengths to care for it, as opposed to what many careless owners did when the snake got too large; releasing it into the wild to fend for itself where it could procreate or die. Florida had a serious issue with the large serpents these days.

So that fateful day, she'd known that she had to save the snake. It had been her lunch break, and she'd been out taking a walk, clearing her head. As she rounded the corner, she smelled smoke and watched as two wolves ran out of the building. They were in human form, but she could tell that they'd been about to shift, noticing the claws extending on their hands. She'd ducked into an alley, waiting for them to pass. Wondering where the fire department was, she'd waited. But then when no one came, she ran into the club on instinct, to make sure everyone was out of the building. Noticing no one, she smashed the glass enclosure and pulled out the slithering animal. Unfortunately in the process, she'd cut her hand. But she'd still managed to carry the poor animal out of the building. As the fire engines raced toward the inferno, she'd made a rash decision to take the snake back to UVH to have it evaluated.

When she'd later pondered over the fact that the snake belonged to a supernatural, she'd decided to have a nurse call Eden and leave a message for the manager. But before she'd had a chance to issue the order, she'd been attacked in the parking lot. She wasn't supposed to have been working that day; having been called in for an emergency consult, she'd rushed into the hospital with only her ID and keys, locking her purse in her car.

After she'd finished, she'd returned to her car. Instantly, her skin had pricked in awareness as she saw two strange men approach her. Trying to run had proved futile, as they'd snatched her up with preternatural speed. Vehemently protesting, she'd kneed the first of her attackers in the groin. And even though he'd released her, the other vamp had quickly grabbed her by the shoulders, slamming her head against the concrete. By the time she'd woken with a splitting headache, Alexandra was at her neck.

As the history of what had happened to her racked her brain, she felt sick. Opening her eyes, unable to rest, she wished she was like one of the butterflies so beautifully reproduced in the lamp above, able to fly away from her troubles. At least she was clean, in a warm bed and about to be fed, she reasoned. She'd been upgraded from the house of horrors and was no longer a blood bag.

Closing her eyes, she flipped onto her side, hoping this new position would help her find the rest she desperately needed. As her body started to drift toward dreams, she heard the rustling of fabric. Frightened, she sealed her eyelids tight, feigning sleep.

"Hello, Kalli," a deep sexy voice said, startling her. Her heart began beating quickly. She didn't want to answer him. *Please go away*, she silently prayed.

Tristan had talked to Julie in the kitchen as she was preparing soup. She'd sternly warned him not to upset Kalli, updating him on her condition. She was afraid the little bird would try to fly, and was confident that if she tried, Kalli would fall flat on her face.

But Tristan was anxious to see the intriguing woman who had found herself in Alexandra's nest. He needed to see her face, smell her skin, touch her. Rolling his eyes, he cursed himself. His wolf had to be influencing his thinking. Struggling not to go to her, he took off his jacket, unbuttoned his sleeves and fell back into a large velvet lounge chair that sat diagonal to the bed. Her enticing hair sprawled over the white bed linens, begging to be touched. When he listened to her heartbeat, he knew she was awake.

"Kalli," he repeated, louder this time. "I know you're awake. Come on, now, ma chère. Let's have a chat, shall we?" His voice had a barely detectible southern Cajun accent to it.

Kalli gritted her teeth. She hated that wolves had such good hearing. Her heartbeat gave her away. Running her hand through her untamed locks, she pushed the unruly hair aside and turned over in bed. She pushed up so that she was laying more at a forty-five degree angle, not quite sitting, but clearly aware of his command. Averting her gaze, she played with her hands, hoping they could do this quickly. Determined to get the upper hand of the situation, she struggled to raise her eyes and direct the conversation.

"Dr. Williams. My name is Dr. Williams," she corrected, trying to separate herself from the wolf ranking that she knew all too well made her opinions less than important. She was human now, she reminded herself. She purposefully shielded herself in her title, embracing the professional decorum that always managed to seal off unwanted feelings.

"What?" Tristan asked, surprised at her pretentious tone. *Was she for real?*

"I said my name is Dr. Williams." She nervously forced herself to sit a little taller, but her breath caught as she made eye contact with the charismatic Alpha. He was ruggedly handsome, with those striking amber eyes she remembered. Except now, she felt as if he was seeing straight through to her soul. His slicked-back dark blonde hair framed his tanned face; a sexy five o'clock shadow broke the surface of his skin. A sensuous smile revealed perfectly white teeth. Why was he smiling? *Better to bite you with my dear.*

Her stomach dropped in anticipation. What was happening to her? Involuntarily, her nipples strained against the fabric of the shirt as her body recognized the incredibly virile male addressing her. Her wolf howled, begging to run to and jump on him. She took a deep cleansing breath, trying to force her body to relax. This could not be happening. *I am human now.*

Tristan laughed. So this was how she was going to play it. He could sense her arousal and damn if it didn't make him want to actually enjoy this little interrogation. Her heart was beating like a hummingbird, yet she played it cool. He licked his lips, and raised an eyebrow, shooting her a wolfish grin.

"Okay, Doc. Personally I think we'd both be a little more comfortable if we'd go informal, but by all means, suit yourself. I'm Tristan Livingston, Alpha of Lyceum Wolves. Welcome to my home."

Chapter Six

Kalli immediately lowered her head, gazing downward. "Thank you, Alpha," she said softly, taken aback by his commanding presence. Within seconds of doing so, she became conscious that she'd reverted to pack protocol. Confused by her own behavior, she quickly looked up, adjusting her posture. How could this have happened? She'd been away from wolves for nearly seven years, yet the man before her sent her reeling. His smooth voice registered deep within her as if she'd known him long ago. But he wasn't the Alpha from her childhood.

His manner was cool and dignified with a hint of humor that could be seen in his smile that reached his eyes. Instead of physically attacking her, he'd sent a healer to her side. He'd rescued her from the vampire, and ensured she was clean, warm and fed. Yet she knew deep down not to be fooled by his kind exterior. A dominant wolf lurked inside him; remarkable good looks and a compelling personality were only one side of the man before her.

She glanced down, noticing the gooseflesh on her arms. What was he doing to her? Bunching the silky sheet, she pulled it up over her pebbled breasts and held it under her chin.

"I, um, I really appreciate you saving me from the vampires. I didn't think I'd survive," she stammered, struggling to sound coherent.

Tristan considered her initial response, 'Thank you, Alpha'. It wasn't so much what she said but how she said it. Her submissive positioning came so naturally that he would have sworn she was wolf. Knowing that she was human was a paradox, given the gesture. The only explanation could be that she'd spent a lot of time with wolves. And then just as quickly, as if a light switch had been clicked, she easily transposed back into an underlying confident tone of voice.

He could detect her internal struggle as to how to appropriately interact with him. Watching her defensively bring the cotton material to her chest told him she knew she was teetering on the edge of arousal, fighting to gain control of her own body. While he was very much used to young adult wolves displaying erratic behavior in the presence of their Alpha, going from servile to aggressive, he could not reconcile why she, a human, would display a conflicting demeanor.

Her paled olive skin tone had not regained its healthy color as yet, but her beautiful blue eyes were bright with excitement as she studied him. She smelled of clean soap and lilacs, which pleased his wolf. Shiny raven curls spilled down over the sheets, teasing her elbows. The sight of her drove

Tristan to imagine how he'd like to run his fingers through her hair, bury his face into it, wrap his fist around the tendrils while he slammed into her from behind. His breath caught, and he quickly looked away, averting his gaze while attempting to hide his feral thoughts. *What was he thinking?* He was here to get information about the fire, not to figure out how he could get into her pants. But the more time he spent near her, the more he wanted her.

He needed to get control, and fast. Taking a deep breath, he attempted to get the conversation moving in the right direction. "Well, I too, am quite happy that you are alive. Alexandra can be quite deadly." He ground his teeth just thinking of what she'd done to Kalli. "But we were lucky. Jules said you'll recover quickly."

"Yes, thank you again for your kindness," she replied formally.

"Would you like to tell me why you think the vampires took you?" He was toying with her a bit, but he found people were more likely to talk when the discussion wasn't centered on the real topic.

"Well, I really don't know. You see, I'm a veterinarian at UVH. I got called in for an emergency consult. When I got back to the car, there were two men…waiting for me. I don't know why. I tried to fight, got in a few hits, but I couldn't get away," she explained through the tears that ran down her cheeks. Determined to stuff every horrible thing that had ever happened to her deep inside where she could compartmentalize the hurt, she swore she would not cry about this. Wiping the eyes with the back of her hands, she raised her gaze to Tristan's. *Please let me go home. I can't do this.* Silently she willed it to be, but knew it wouldn't happen.

"You're a vet?" Tristan asked, intrigued by her profession. Initially when she'd said she was a doctor, he thought she healed humans.

"Yes, I work in the ER."

"Interesting. So you wouldn't happen to treat reptiles at UVH?"

Her eyes widened. "Reptiles? Um, well, yes, I am more of a generalist, but I do treat reptiles now and then." Her heart began to race. The boa. *Please don't let it be his…please don't let it be his…please don't let it be his.*

He smiled, pinning her with his mesmerizing eyes. He could hear her pulse rate increase, smell her fear. Leaning forward, he placed his forearms on his knees and tilted his head.

"So you wouldn't happen to treat snakes on a regular basis, then? You know, like a fifteen foot yellow boa constrictor, for example?"

Like a dam bursting, she couldn't hold it in any longer, and the words began to spill forth. She wasn't sure whether to beg for forgiveness or simply tell her story. And before she knew it, she'd done both.

"Please Alpha; you must know that I was going to have my nurse call the owners of that club. I swear to you. I am *so* sorry. At first I wasn't sure who to call, and then I decided to have her call Eden and leave a message.

But then I forgot. I've been so busy. And then I got kidnapped, but you know that part. And oh, I guess I should have started with this first, but yes, I do treat snakes, and she's very healthy despite the smoke inhalation. A beautiful specimen, really. I promise that I will have her returned to you as soon as possible."

Shaking his head, he held up the palm of his hand to silence her. Resisting the urge to go to her and hold her in his arms, he opted to pace over to the end of her bed. Grabbing the end of the sleigh bed as tight as a vise with his two hands, a serious look washed over his face.

"Look, Dr. Williams, I am not sure why you took the snake but I need to know everything, and I mean everything, about the day of the fire. Did you set the fire?"

Oh my God. He thought she set the fire. She cringed. If she told him about the wolves she had seen that day, he might ask her to identify them. If she identified them, it might somehow get back to her pack that she was alive. Or worse, they'd come after her and kill her. What a damn fine mess. She should have just kept walking that warm September day, but it wasn't in her nature to stand by and do nothing. She was a doctor. A healer. And a fighter; she was no coward. She didn't think twice about running into a burning building to make sure others made it to safety.

"Kalli," Tristan said firmly, shaking her from her thoughts. He let go of the bed and circled around, stalking her like the wolf that he was.

"I was there the day of the fire," she began quietly. Determined to keep her dignity, she stiffened, and stared at him. "There was smoke. Two men exited the building. No one was there. No sirens. Nothing. I had to go in, because I knew that animal was in there. I mean, I did call in before I entered, you know. But no one answered. And then I saw the snake. What was I supposed to do? Let it die? I couldn't. So I ran in behind the bar and broke the glass, cutting myself in the process. But I managed to get her. I got the snake and left."

He sensed honesty in her words and mannerisms but had to know the extent of her involvement. "Did you set the fire?"

"God no," she gasped. "How could you think I'd do that?" It dawned on her that he didn't know her, not to mention that she'd admitted taking the snake.

He moved closer and sat on the edge of the bed, mere inches from her feet. "Tell me about the men. Can you describe them? Were they human?" His voice was like steel, every bit the cold tone she remembered from her pack days.

"Yes, but…"

"Yes, you can describe them, or yes they were human?" He interrupted.

She swallowed her fear, refusing to be intimidated by a wolf again. "Yes, I can describe them. But no, they were not human. They were wolf," she said in the most even voice she could muster.

"Describe them," he ordered.

"Oh God, please don't make me do this. It was just a fire. A building. No one was hurt. If I tell you, I know what will happen. You might find the wolves and begin some kind of a territory war, but I'll end up dead. You and I both know they will find me," she countered. Kalli inwardly shuddered, realizing how frankly she'd just told the Alpha to basically fuck off; also she'd revealed to him yet again her inner knowledge of pack society.

"Look, Dr. Williams, as a courtesy, I will overlook your insolence given that you are not wolf, but let me be perfectly clear. You will describe the men you saw. And pack business is none of your concern. Now tell me why you think these men were wolf," he demanded.

"Fine, Alpha," she drawled out the word, hoping he'd feel the anger in her words. "First off, I told you that I am a vet, which means I also understand human physiology. So unless a new trait for humans is to sprout claws, they were wolves." She refused to tell him that even though she didn't know their names, she recognized the two men as pack members from her old pack. But even if she couldn't name names, Tristan would know that she was in danger.

"Secondly, if they were vampires, they'd be moving more like a flash rather than running." She could feel emotion bubbling up like a fountain she couldn't control. As grateful as she was to him for rescuing her, she was also scared of him questioning her like he was.

Tristan could see she was on the edge of bolting out the door, before she even knew what she was thinking. He decided to press on; he had to get answers.

"Did you know the men?"

"No, I did not know them," she lied. She pulled her legs up to her chest and put her arms around them protectively. What if she was wrong about this Alpha? What if he was prone to violence like all the others she'd known? She needed to escape.

"Are you sure you didn't know them? Did you speak with them? Did you see them set the fire? Did they see you leave?" Tristan relentlessly fired questions at her, testing her honesty. Everything she'd said rang true, but it felt like there was something she wasn't telling him.

"I told you that I didn't know them. And no, I didn't speak with them or see them set the fire. I told you, I saw them leave and then I saw smoke. There was no one else around. I don't know anything else!" she yelled, her eyes darting to the exit. What was that last question he'd asked her? *Did the wolves see her leave?* The realization that the wolves could have identified her felt like a punch to her gut. She'd worked so hard to build her life as a human. A life that she treasured.

"Oh my God, I've got to get out of here. I've got to get back to my life. My job. Please let me go," she begged, as she threw her legs out of the bed onto the floor. After being held captive by Alexandra, she couldn't take any more of his inquest. Her stomach rolled at the thought of being forced back into her old pack. She refused to let that happen. In a foolish attempt to run, nausea and vertigo overcame her; she was pulled toward the floor as if she had an anchor around her waist.

Tristan cursed, realizing that he'd gone too far. His desire for the truth had pushed Kalli into hysterics. *Goddammit.* He should have assured her of his protection. After surviving being a human pincushion over the past forty-eight hours, no human would have been this strong. He could tell she'd been thinking of running, but couldn't believe she'd actually tried. Not only was she sick, she should have known there'd be no way she'd be faster than him. What sane person ran from an Alpha wolf? *What was she thinking?* She was thinking he was a total dick, and she was right, he thought to himself.

As she fell, he effortlessly caught her before she hit the carpet. Holding her in his arms, he backed onto the bed and sat, just staring at her. *Who are you, Kalli Williams?* There was something about her fiery spirit that called to him; something he couldn't quite identify. Her sweet warm body fit so nicely into his arms, and he suspected that cuddling her in his bed would feel nothing short of heavenly. He shouldn't be thinking about her this way given her condition, but damn, his wolf didn't care. It was so wrong. Brushing back the hair from her forehead, he watched as her soft pink, very kissable lips parted.

"Tristan," she whispered.

He stiffened, hearing his name on her lips like a lover's breathy call. "Kalli, you're okay, I've got you," he assured her.

"Doctor," she replied softly with a small smile on her lips.

He laughed. Fainting and unable to stand, she was joking with him.

"My fault," she croaked with a weak voice. "I shouldn't have tried to stand. What was I thinking?"

"You were thinking that I was giving you the Spanish Inquisition, and like any good prisoner, you tried to run. Granted, I've never seen someone in your condition try to outrun me, but you get points for trying," he added, hoping to make her smile.

"I'm scared," Kalli admitted. Her head had finally stopped spinning.

"Please don't fret, chèr t'bébé. No one can get to you here. It's safe." He sighed, pissed that he had purposely pushed her to the edge. "I'm sorry for all the questions, but I have to know what happened. It's not just the fire. I can't go into it all right now, but please know, that I had to ask. And I'll need your help finding them. But right now, you need rest. Come, get in bed. Please stay, I promise not to hurt you."

She wriggled away from him as he stood to place her gently back in the bed. In the process her shirt rode upward, scrunching up near her breasts. Her taut stomach exposed to the cool air, she glanced down to see her bare skin and caught Tristan's eyes as they roamed slowly down to her underwear. He raised an eyebrow at the discovery and smiled coyly.

"What? Julie said they belonged to you but were new. Would you rather have me wear no panties at all?" she quipped, tugging the shirt down. Flirting with the Alpha? She was playing with fire.

"Now that you ask, the thought did occur to me," he replied, not missing a beat. "Clothes are highly overrated, you know. But I might not get much work done if I knew you were sleeping nude in my guest room, not to mention that we've only just met. But don't you worry, we'll have plenty of time to get better acquainted tomorrow," he promised.

Kalli smiled, and closed her eyes, pretending he had not just said what she thought she'd heard. *Naked? With Tristan? Together.* She breathed in a deep breath and released it, trying to tamp down her arousal. Within minutes, a wall of exhaustion crashed into her, ushering her into a much-needed sleep. Her last thoughts were that she'd worry about her feelings for the sexy wolf tomorrow. Right now, she had to heal.

Tristan felt all the blood in his body rush to his cock at her mention of wearing nothing. And seeing her sweet body in his shirt and underwear…Jesus, was she trying to kill him right there? He would have to make sure Julie got her proper clothes to wear.

He pulled up the covers to her neck, willing his erection to subside. If he couldn't see what was under the fluffy mound of covers, he reasoned, he could get it together. Damn, he was losing it. Maybe he should send her down to stay with Logan? Staying in his condo, she would most certainly cloud his judgment when he needed to be at the top of his game. He was confident that his beta would guard her with his life and make sure no one got to her. But he knew his beta as well as he knew himself, and couldn't stomach the idea of Kalli naked in Logan's bed, at least not without him.

Tristan reached for her hand and slowly rubbed circles into the small of her palm. There was something about her that seemed extraordinarily supernatural. Bringing her satiny wrist up to his nose, he inhaled her delightfully feminine scent, detecting only human blood. He wasn't sure what to make of it, but as long as she was in his home and bed, he planned to fully explore the attraction.

Julie poked her head around the corner in time to see Tristan making his way down the long hallway. She quickly got back to work, annoyed that he'd gone so far with his investigation. Their voices had carried well into the kitchen during the heat of their argument. She'd been tempted to intervene, but knew better than to interfere with Alpha business.

Padding into the room, Tristan eyed Julie standing next to the stove, pouring the broth into Tupperware containers.

"She sleeping?" Julie asked, already aware of the answer. He'd been down in her room for well over an hour, sitting in total silence, watching Kalli sleep, and she found it curious that he was taking such an interest in the injured human woman.

"You didn't bring the soup," he commented.

"You were busy," she curtly replied.

"What gives, Jules? Just say it."

"I guess it shouldn't surprise me that you don't take direction well, Alpha. Although I guess you're more used to giving directions than taking them," she huffed. "I could hear the ruckus all the way in here. No disrespect intended, but I did say not to upset her, didn't I?"

"Yeah well, it's not easy being king," he remarked with a smart-assed inflection, grabbing a bowl of soup. He sat down at the counter and began eating while she finished working.

"Sorry, I don't mean to be so hard on you. I know you've gotta do what you've gotta do. It's just that seeing her like that….all those scrapes and bruises and bite marks. My God, she was a mess. I suppose I'm going a little mother hen on you. I'm not used to having to deal with such violence. You are good to us, here."

"No worries. We worked it out. She's a tough one, you know. Believe me; she'll be right as rain, soon. My spidey sense tells me so," he joked.

"All right then, I'm going to leave you some crackers and ginger ale to put next to her bed in case she wakes up in the middle of the night starving. I was able to get a little bit of the electrolyte fluid into her before she woke up all the way. I have to say that it's unusual for a human not to be dehydrated. I guess she must have been really, really healthy before this happened to her. It's almost as if…well, never mind."

Tristan stopped eating and stared over at Julie, who looked deep in thought. "What is it?"

"Oh, I'm just being crazy. I was just going to say that it's almost as if she had the constitution of a wolf. Silly, huh?"

"Yeah, silly." Tristan bit into a cracker, considering her assessment. Silly? Or right on target? He felt it too. Something about that woman wasn't exactly human, but then again, she wasn't at all supernatural.

Julie gathered up her purse and gave Tristan a quick hug and kiss on the cheek. "Okay, hun, well, call me if you need anything. I'll stop by tomorrow to check on our girl. Maybe bring up some clothes for her, too. Get some rest, okay? Love ya!" she chirped as she entered the elevator and the doors slid shut.

Tristan reveled in the quietness surrounding him. He needed to think about his next steps, his strategy. He planned to bring in a sketch artist, so they could put a face to the arsonists. The meeting with Jax Chandler was in another two days, and he needed to get his shit together before it all went down. Throwing his bowl in the sink, he went to take a hot shower. He needed to think, without his libido interfering. It was as if he'd just been given a few more pieces of a jigsaw puzzle for which he didn't have the picture. But he was cunning, and that's what he did best, work with the impossible to make the possible happen. He was Alpha.

Chapter Seven

Crimson droplets splashed her face. She tried smearing them off with her hand but they kept coming down harder until she was drenched in the sticky sanguine spray. She felt heavy, her clothes sodden with blood. Then she heard it; the voice. Whipping her head toward the ear-piercing scream, she winced, covering her ears. Then she saw it; the vampire, the fangs.

In a flash of a dream, she was shackled by iron cuffs to a wooden cross, teeth snapping in the distance. She squeezed her eyes shut, willing it to go away. But the creature wanted all of her: her flesh, her blood, her mind. Metal cut into her wet wrists; she was almost loose. A little more and they'd fly open. Escape was imminent. Her eyes snapped open; she only caught a glimpse of the razor sharp fangs before they sliced into her neck, tearing the tender skin to shreds.

Kalli screamed bloody murder, jolting upright in bed, throwing the covers aside. Sweat misted over her entire body. Clammy, she shivered from the cool air conditioning that stung her skin. She surveyed her surroundings; the quiet hum of a noise cancellation fan rested on her nightstand. Used to the urban sounds of the city, she reached over and flipped off the switch. Noticing the food and drink that had been set out next to it, she grabbed a few crackers and some ginger ale, sighing in relief at how good it felt to put sustenance back into her body.

After using the bathroom, she sat back in bed, still so very tired from the blood loss. She hoped by morning she'd feel stronger, be able to leave. Uncomfortable, she yanked at the collar of her t-shirt, finding it dampened. She couldn't sleep in the wet shirt, so she pulled it up over her head and turned to hang it on the corner of the headboard. Reacting to the cold, her nipples hardened instantly and goosebumps broke out all over her skin. As she twisted back around to grab the blanket, she saw the shiny eyes of a wolf standing in her doorway.

Deep in sleep, Tristan had heard the bloodcurdling scream emanate from down the hallway. *Kalli.* Immediately he shifted to wolf, readying for a fight. As he raced toward her room, he sensed that no one else was in his home. He poked his head into her room, careful not to scare her, and saw her consuming the snacks he'd left her. Thank God she was all right. She must have been dreaming.

He quickly fell back into the shadows, and stole off to check the rest of his condo. It would have been nearly impossible for someone to have gotten into his home without him knowing. Guards blocked the only elevators up to his home twenty-four by seven, and once inside, one needed a security code to ascend and then a separate code to open the door into the home. Both the private and public elevators had different combinations. The stairwell was the only other way in, and he'd installed a double set of steel security doors, again with sequencing codes and biometric security scans. He couldn't be too careful, sensing a war was upon them.

One more check of Kalli, and he swore he'd go back to bed. His brain and body needed rest, so he'd be one hundred percent in the coming days. Coming up to the guest room, he padded slowly and quietly, trying not to alarm her. She hadn't seen his wolf yet. Being that she was human and a veterinarian, she might not take too kindly to seeing a wild animal on the loose.

Within minutes, he returned to her and came upon the most fascinating and spectacular sight he'd ever seen in all his long life. *Kalli.* In the dim light, he observed intently as she grasped the hem of her shirt, exposing her creamy white breasts to the midnight light of the moon. Her perfect peaks protested the brisk temperature in response. As she moved to hang up her shirt, her hair swept over the tightened, pink areolae, hiding then revealing them, teasing him as he watched.

He knew he should leave, but was undeniably captivated by her beauty and the mere sight of her skin. She reached for the blanket, and froze. He was tempted to leave but instead he found himself slowly stalking her bed, as he had earlier in the evening as a man. Surprisingly, she sat still, letting him view her bare and defenseless.

Kalli knew it was him. *Tristan.* My God, he was magnificent. Lush black fur with the same amber eyes that had enthralled her earlier, he was the most stunning wolf she'd ever seen. She glanced down at her skin, well aware of her nudity, and realized that she wanted him to see her. Her wolf wanted it too, but unfortunately, she was well caged and could only admire how strong and dominant he truly was from afar.

Slowly she reached for the covers, and laid her head back on the pillow, never losing eye contact with her wolf. "Tristan," she whispered and curled onto her side facing him. "Come lie next to me. I'm not afraid. You can stay how you are. Please come sleep and protect me," she asked in a soft voice. There was no denying that she wanted the man, but tonight in the darkness, she felt safe with the wolf.

Tristan's heart jumped at her words. Even if she were unsure of wanting him as her Alpha, she wanted his protection and accepted his wolf. He found it extraordinary that she was capable of knowing it was him and that she spoke to him, cognizant that he understood her as if he was man. He went to her, curling into her side.

Kalli laid motionless, wrapped in soft fabric, oddly relieved he'd come to her. Within minutes, she could feel his warmth radiating through the covers. She relaxed, certain he would not shift. The last time she had slept next to a wolf, she'd been a young girl, nuzzling with her friends as the adults ran without them. But as an adult, she'd feared both the males and females, well aware of the brutality they could inflict. But at the moment, she felt a sense of tranquility and closeness that she'd never experienced as a woman.

No words were spoken. And while she knew he'd seen her naked, there was nothing sexual about the experience. It was a demonstration of trust. He revealed himself to her, and she revealed herself to him. It may have appeared as a physical exchange to an outsider, but she recognized the importance of the interaction; a significant milestone that created a bond between them. With deliberation, she reached over and placed her hand upon him, silently thanking him for saving her.

Tristan eased into her touch, trying to ignore the message his wolf was sending him. But he couldn't deny that he hadn't felt such intimacy with a woman for as long as he could remember.

Chapter Eight

Light streaked through the window, waking Kalli. Although it had only been a day since she'd been rescued, she already felt better. She knew it was her lupine genes which supported the advanced healing. The pills stifled the shift and lessened other traits, but they could not completely change her underlying cellular structure. If someone tested her blood, it would present positive for wolf.

Stirring in bed, she became acutely aware of heat emanating under her hand. Slowly opening her eyes, she quietly gasped, recognizing the feel of skin. Warm, tanned, manly skin. Skin that belonged to one very naked, very muscular, Tristan Livingston. Without moving, she allowed herself the indulgence of taking in an eyeful of the powerful Alpha while he lightly snored. Riveted, she couldn't take her eyes off his face; he was incredibly handsome. A straight nose, masculine jawline with smooth lips. She imagined he was very skilled with those lovely lips and shivered thinking about the things he could do to her with them.

Given that he was perfectly nude, lying atop her bed, she thanked goodness her own body was underneath the covers. She wasn't sure whether to be happy or upset that he'd fallen asleep on his stomach, but she couldn't help appreciating the hard contours of his body, from his well-corded back to his firmly sculptured ass to his strong thighs and calves. Dear Lord, the man was sheer perfection. Michelangelo's David paled in comparison.

She'd somehow fallen asleep with her hand on his shoulder and now let her fingers voluntarily wander down the length of his back. Curious, she couldn't resist, indulging in the experience of touching such an amazing male. Gently, she pushed into a sitting position as she continued to slide her hand over the cheek of his bottom and onto his thigh. Squeezing her legs together, she forced herself to concentrate as her arousal peaked. No internal conflict plagued her as the impulse to touch him took over her thoughts. Neither wolf nor human, she simply was a female who very much wanted the desirable male in her bed.

Tristan flinched slightly, awakened by the touch of her hand on his back and the sweet smell of her excitement. Shifting back after she'd fallen deep into REM sleep, he had to force himself to calm down. He could have sworn he'd been hard all night. This morning, he feigned sleep, knowing that if he opened his eyes, she'd go tearing off his bed like a scared alley cat. But when she skimmed over his butt with her fingers, he swore his steel shaft threatened to catapult him off the bed.

The subtle flinch alerted her that he could be waking up, and she didn't want to be in bed with him when it happened. So she snatched his shirt off the bed. Now dry, she slid it over her head and slipped into the bathroom to freshen up. After brushing her teeth and hair, she tugged again at the too large underwear that clearly had stretched out and no longer wished to stay on her hips. Losing the battle, she let them fall to the floor and decided to go without, resigning herself to a pantyless morning. Because his extra-large shirt fell down over her thighs, she felt relatively covered. Ready to face her Alpha, she cracked open the door.

She wasn't sure where Tristan had gone when she exited the bathroom, but she was hungry and wasn't waiting for him. Within a few minutes, she quickly found the kitchen and the ever-important coffee machine. She turned it on, popped in the coffee pod and started opening cabinets looking for mugs. Setting two cups on the counter, she opened the door to the refrigerator and pulled out creamer then continued looking through the clutter for the eggs. She felt ravenous, and needed protein. "Come on, where are you, little eggies? Tristan has to have eggs. Everyone has eggs," she mumbled, talking to herself.

"Tristan does," he told her with a grin, surprised to find Kalli rummaging around in search of food. Despite taking a cold shower, he was instantly hard again at the sight of her lovely bare ass which peeked at him from underneath his shirt. He wanted nothing more in that moment than to take her from behind and slide deep into her warm heat. The temptation was great, but he restrained his desires.

Kalli jumped at his voice, quickly turning around. "Hi, um, I was just going to make us something to eat," she said nervously.

"By all means," he agreed confidently, walking by her wearing only a towel around his hips. His erection tented the fabric, and he made no attempt to conceal it.

It was nearly impossible to ignore both the charisma and raw sexuality Tristan exuded. Slowly, Kalli's eyes roamed up and down his lean torso, astonished at the audaciousness he exhibited while wearing practically nothing. His hair, dampened from the shower, fell shaggy over his eyes. Hardened abs rippled down toward his low slung towel. Struggling for the words that never came, she couldn't help her natural reaction, which was to look him over one last time. Embarrassed, she just knew that he knew that she'd just looked at his groin area, which appeared to be growing. *Oh God.* She rubbed her hand over her eyes and smiled to herself. *What was it about this man? Get it together, Kalli. Say something.*

"Um, okay then, so the eggs." She opened the refrigerator, careful to hold on to the shirt so it didn't ride up again.

"Like what you see?" he asked seductively as he set a coffee mug next to her hand, proceeding to wait for the next cup to fill.

"What did you just say?" Shocked, she grabbed the egg carton and quickly stood up, banging her head. She turned around holding the package in one hand, rubbing the sore spot on her head with the other.

He set his eyes on hers, taking the eggs and putting them on the ledge. She backed into the counter as he caged her, pushing her body flush against his. "I said…Do. You. Like. What. You. See?" he whispered into her ear, accentuating every word.

She sucked a breath as a million pithy responses filled her head. But the hard bulge pressed against her body and her dangerously hard nipples made it impossible for her to speak coherently.

"Um." God, she felt like a complete idiot. Eight years of college and all she had was 'um'?

"I'll take that as a yes," he replied playfully, kissing her ear softly. He reached over to grab his coffee cup, which made him press against her even harder.

She sucked a breath at the welcome intrusion. There was a part of her that thought he might kiss her. Immobilized against his hard torso, he had her exactly where he wanted her, or rather, where she wanted to be.

Instead of kissing her, however, he wrapped his fingers around the clay handle and walked away with a broad smile across his face, without saying another word. He proceeded to sit down at the island, and switched on his i-Pad, checking his email as he pretended to ignore her. When Kalli turned around again to make the eggs, he let his eyes drift to her soft supple cheeks that strained to stay covered by his shirt. The hem teased higher as she bent over slightly to turn on the stove. Damn, this woman was killing him.

Tristan could not remember the last time he'd slept naked with a woman. Sure he'd fucked many, but not truly just slept with one. He'd stayed wolf as long as he could, treasuring her trust, teaching her that he wouldn't hurt her. But now that she was healing and walking around his home like she belonged here, he felt the pressure in his chest along with the ache between his legs.

They'd forged a bond last night, and he didn't want to rush forward and scare her off. At the same time, he knew she was withholding information. Something small, perhaps, but it was there. Bringing his full attention back to his tablet, he tapped out a quick email to Logan asking him to run a full security clearance on one "Kalli Williams". He wasn't a fool. The woman may have been a brilliant vet, but he found it coincidental that she just happened to be at the fire.

She could have gone any direction that day when she decided to take her break, but she'd passed his club. Why not just call right away after she'd rescued the snake? And then there was her hesitation to tell him about the wolves and what they looked like. He understood that she was in serious danger, but she had to have known the minute she saw them that they could find her based on scent alone. She said she didn't know them personally but her eyes held a terrifying trepidation, a foreboding of sorts, as if she knew exactly what they were capable of doing to her.

And then there was the odd way about her mannerisms, which suggested she'd spent time around a pack. He could tell that she was aware of protocol from the way she'd bowed her head submissively to him when she'd first caught a glance of him in the bedroom. Sure, she'd snapped out of the spell, dragging her eyes to his, but it had been forced. It was as if she was trying to hide the fact that she'd been around an Alpha in the past. Her 'tell' gave her away. She'd acted on instinct when she'd averted her gaze. But the confident posture she'd then adopted had been rehearsed. Like an actor playing the role of a prizefighter, it might have been believable to most audiences, but not to a champion. Others might not notice, but he knew. It was the little things that always gave people away, no matter how much they believed the lie.

Kalli breathed deeply while making the omelets, never turning around, afraid that he'd see right through her soul. Read her mind. She didn't want to lie to him, but she'd just met the man. The intimacy they had shared the previous night spoke volumes to the type of man he was but she wasn't ready to trust him with her secret. He'd never understand what it was like being a hybrid in pack, not even omega; she'd been the lowest of the low.

He was a beautiful, strong Alpha, who'd most likely been like that since birth. How could he possibly fathom the terrifying childhood she'd experienced? He might be able to empathize, but he was neither hybrid nor female, both of which were insubstantial, undesirable and often, irrelevant within pack life. Alpha females were utilized to mate and breed, but even that life wouldn't have been hers. She wasn't Alpha; she wasn't even full wolf; she was seen as nothing more than a tainted half-breed.

As such, the Alpha would have sent her to work for the pack in whatever capacity the others deemed necessary. Come the full moon, when the wolves were most sexually active, they had planned on pimping her out like a prostitute to any lower ranking males who hadn't earned the right to breed. And if by chance she'd become pregnant, it was made clear they'd abort the child, by force if necessary. No one wanted her to propagate the human genes within the pack. From puberty, the Alpha had made sure she learned pack protocol. He had no intention of letting her leave, but wanted her groomed for her new 'role' when she turned of age. Her life had already been a living hell growing up, and she refused to accept the brutal, misogynistic future he'd planned. Running was the only way, and she could trust no one but herself.

Yet Tristan seemed so different than the others she'd known. There was no mistaking his dominant spirit, but he'd saved her, asking for nothing in return but information about that night. She needed time to think, time to assess whether or not she could implicitly trust him with not just her secret, but her life.

"Hey, here you go. Hope you like lots of cheese," she said, placing a plate in front of him.

He raised his eyes from his work. "Thanks. It's been a long time since I've had someone make me breakfast." He started eating, only to be stunned by her next comment.

"I find that hard to believe. You're Alpha. Bet you have lots of women lined up to serve you." The words were out of her mouth before she could take them back. *Oh my God. What the hell did I just say?*

"What makes you say that? Have you spent a lot of time around an Alpha before? Do you have personal knowledge about how Alphas behave and who cooks their meals?" he countered, wanting to know exactly where she'd learned about packs.

She nearly choked on her eggs.

"Sorry, I shouldn't have said that. I'm just so nervous. You know, open mouth, insert foot." Glossing over her faux pas, unwilling to answer him, she forcefully swallowed her food and pressed onto her next agenda item. "So, Tristan, I really need to get back to work today," she stated flatly, changing the subject. She knew he was too keen not to notice, but she wasn't about to start discussing her knowledge of wolves.

"Yeah, about that. No." Nice try, he thought to himself. She may not want to talk about how she knew what she did, but damn if he was letting her out of his sight. "Great eggs by the way."

Did he just tell me no? "But I have to go. I've been missing for days. How am I supposed to explain this to my boss? I have patients; they need me."

"Again, that would be a no. You will not be returning to work until my pack business is resolved. I have a sketch artist coming over this morning. You can work with him, and we'll see what we get."

Frustrated, Kalli accidentally slammed her coffee mug on the counter a little too forcefully, spilling coffee. "Did you hear what I said? I have patients. A job. I don't want to get fired."

"Oh I heard you, but you need to remember who you are talking to, Doctor." He used her professional title hoping it would alert her that he meant nothing but business when it came to the topic of her returning to work. He stood, towering over her petite frame.

"But I need…" she stammered, immediately feeling small in his shadow. She was tempted to cower in his presence, but stiffened her spine and raised her chin at him. Thankfully, he moved around her to put his plate in the sink.

"But nothing. You're in danger. You're not returning until this is over. End of story. After we've done the sketches, we'll take you over to the hospital, so you can wrap up whatever you need for your 'leave of absence'. You can talk to your boss and explain that you need a medical leave due to the attack in the garage. I'll make a call over to Tony at PPD, and report it for you, if the hospital hasn't reported you missing already. If they give you any trouble, I'll put in a call to the president of UVH. I donate enough money to that place that they can go without you for a few weeks."

Kalli stood in awe that he had already worked it all out in his mind. She knew he was right. Where would she go? Her apartment? The vampires had easily found her at her work; it would be even easier to attack her at home. If the wolves decided to come for her, there would be nothing she could do to stop them. She reached up to her neck, feeling the freshly healed scars, and shivered. What if the spawn of the devil, Alexandra, came for her again? She conceded that she needed Tristan's help. And as much as she didn't want to admit it, he needed hers as well.

"You're right. I'll stay," she acquiesced. Going over to the sink, she began washing dishes in defeat. She tried to think of what she was going to tell her boss.

"Did I just hear you say I was right?" He laughed in triumph. She really had no choice. It almost was comical that she actually thought she did. He'd overlook her insolence, considering she wasn't in his pack. But in truth, he simply didn't want to argue with her. With the ladies, he'd much rather be a lover than a fighter.

"Yes I did. And I'm quite sure that you hear it all the time." He was Alpha. Deciding not to give him any more ammunition, she tried another request. "But I need to go by my apartment and get some things. Are you sure it's okay that I stay here with you? I could go to a hotel if you…"

"No," he interrupted coming up against her from behind. "You'll stay with me…in my home…in my bed. I am not letting you go, Dr. Williams." His firm tone left no room for misunderstanding. Standing close enough to her, he could feel the warmth of her skin. He wanted to rip off his towel, bend her over the sink, and slam his cock into her sweet pussy until she screamed his name over and over. But he wouldn't even consider talking her into it. No, when they made love, she would willingly submit to him, begging him for release. He wasn't sure why it was so important to him that she behave like pack; she was human, after all. Maybe it was his wolf warning him, but he just couldn't have her any other way. Until then, he'd tease and seduce her every second she was with him.

She wasn't sure if it was his commanding tone that set her on edge. Or perhaps it was the knowledge that his bare arousal lay directly underneath the towel around his waist, but Kalli's entire body hummed in excitement when he grazed the back of her shirt with his strong body. There was no imagining the sexual tension; it threatened to set the room ablaze. Tristan was incredibly magnetic, and she felt like a box of paperclips that was about to explode; she'd be stuck to him all over. She'd spent so many years hiding her true identity, never getting close to anyone. The men at work had asked her on dates, but she'd conveniently thrown up her "professional morals" speech. She couldn't let anyone into her bed, let alone her heart. But Tristan was larger than life in every way. Overnight, she'd become unraveled, and it was all because of him.

The alluring Alpha threatened to break down her carefully, hermetically sealed, stronger than steel emotional walls. The heat was just too much. And like any metal, given a high enough temperature, it would melt. She tried to concentrate. How was she going to collect herself? Needing to cool down, she looked for an escape. Setting the last clean dish in the rack, she turned off the water and slipped away past him.

Even as she squeezed by him, she knew it was because he'd let her go. She was practically shaking with arousal by the time she reached the corner to the hallway. She swore silently at the dampness between her legs. Tristan eyed her from the kitchen with a sly grin on his face. He knew. There was nothing she would get past him, except for maybe the secret that lay in her pill bottle.

"Ma lapin, I thought you were done running last night. You faced the wolf. Welcomed him." He stalked toward her then stopped and placed his hand on the end of the island.

Kalli's eyes caught his. Looking relaxed and confident, he was deliciously cool, like an ice cream cone on a warm summer day. Ready to be licked all over. She parted her lips, unconsciously moistening them in response. She knew that if he hadn't smelled her wet arousal that he'd surely seen her nipples, which pressed through the thin fabric of his shirt.

"Last night." She stopped midsentence as the memory flashed. Bared to him physically, emotionally. Welcoming him into her bed. He'd proved that he was trustworthy, revealing himself to her. Maybe it was time she gave him more of herself, as much as she was capable of, anyway. It might not be enough for him, but it was all she had.

He slowly moved toward her, sensing her internal struggle; the scent of her flooding his olfactory system, the sound of her quickening heartbeat assaulting his ears. But his little rabbit wasn't afraid; she was sexually excited, wanting him, even if she couldn't yet act on her feelings.

"Tristan," she began as he came nearer. "Last night, I needed you. I guess I didn't really know how much," she confessed. "Your wolf was…he was…you were magnificent, so beautiful. But you need to know that I've never…I've never done anything like that before. It was so intimate. I'm…I'm trying to make this work. You saved me," she whispered, hoping he could understand what she was trying to tell him. Intimacy had always seemed formidable for Kalli, if not unattainable….until last night. She shook her head in disappointment over her lack of articulation.

Her admission floored him. He'd felt it too, but he didn't understand how hard it was for her to talk about how she felt until now. Granted, he barely knew her, but he wanted to know her. He wanted to know every single thing about her, inside and out.

It was all too much, her arousal, her words. He couldn't hold back. In two strides, he had her backed against the wall. The wolf had the rabbit cornered yet again, except this time, she wasn't running. This time, she looked up at him with sad dreamy eyes. Her mouth parted slightly and he struck.

Raking his fingers into her hair, he pulled her mouth to his, sucking, tasting. Kalli felt relieved when he made the first move, kissing her, allowing her to finally act on her passion. As he pushed his tongue into her mouth, she teased hers into his, reveling in the power of his kiss. She moaned, but refused to release him as her hands wrapped around his neck.

Tristan was drowning in her sweet mouth. Needing more, he reached under her knee, grinding his body into hers. His towel came undone, and his flesh met hers.

Kalli felt his rock-hard cock press against her bare belly as his towel fell and her shirt bunched up around her breasts. Lost in his embrace, her lips broke free of his for a mere second, enough time for her to moan his name: "Tristan."

"Kalli," he groaned in response, finding her mouth yet again. He planned to thoroughly kiss her until she knew what he wanted from her; everything.

She slid a hand down his strong chest, fingering each ab and then reached down to cup his firm ass. At her touch, he shoved her harder against the wall, letting his own hands wander until he found her soft breast. He pinched a pointed nipple, making her cry out in pleasure, and then bent his knees so that the tip of his shaft ran up and over her mound. As much as he'd like to fuck her up against the wall, and he was about a minute from doing so, he wanted her in his bed with her neck bared to him in submission. The first time he took her, it had to be. She needed to give all of herself to him, no secrets.

A ding from his private elevator alerted him that Logan was about to come into his home. He tore himself away from her lips, peppering her neck with small kisses. "Kalli," he panted, trying to get her attention.

She was lost in ecstasy when she heard him call her name. Breathlessly, she dropped her leg as he released it from the crook of his arm. She instinctively pulled down the rim of the shirt which had been pushed clear up to her neck. She sighed, "Tristan."

They each had an arm wrapped around each other, reluctant to let go. Gazing into each other's eyes, registering the fireworks between them, a voice jarred them out of their erotic trance.

"Doesn't take you long, Alpha," Logan remarked. He wasn't trying to be disrespectful, but was naturally skeptical about Dr. Williams. He'd seen her in his dreams, but still, he was unsure of her intentions.

Tristan growled. "Enough, Logan. Living room, now. Leave us," he ordered over his shoulder, shielding Kalli from his beta's view and never taking his eyes off hers. "The sketch artist will be here soon, as will Julie with some clothes. Why don't you go relax in your room?"

Snapping out of it, Kalli realized what had almost just happened. It terrified her; making love to the Alpha, he'd tear her apart. But like a moth to a flame, she couldn't resist.

"Yeah, okay," was all she managed to say, slipping from his arms. She scurried down the hallway toward her room, needing to collect herself.

"Oh, and Kalli," he called.

She stopped dead in her tracks but didn't turn around. "Yes."

"This isn't over, not by a long shot. We'll finish this later. I promise."

Kalli didn't respond, choosing to flee to the safety of her room. What was she going to say anyway? She had practically thrown herself at him in the hallway. And she knew as Alpha, he could have whatever he wanted, at least that is how it worked in the pack. But she wasn't pack.

Chapter Nine

Tristan adjourned to his room and got dressed before talking to Logan, who was sitting on the couch reading the news on his tablet.

"Hey," he greeted him as he went into his kitchen to get another cup of joe. The open layout of his condo was such that the kitchen, living room and family rooms were essentially one large, shared space. "Coffee?"

"No thanks," Logan replied, not looking up.

"So, did you get my email? Give me the rundown."

"Yeah, I'm running her clearances right now. Should have some info by this afternoon. Tony's sending someone over to do the sketches within the hour. Meeting with Chandler is set up; two days from now. Neutral territory. Jersey. It's all been arranged. And don't forget the mayor's charity ball is tomorrow night."

"Anything else?" Tristan walked over and stared out the sliding glass doors.

Logan set his tablet down on the coffee table and looked up. "Uh, yeah. Are we going to talk about what I just walked in on?"

"What's to talk about?"

"Really? Okay, maybe the fact that we don't know her story yet. Or that you just met her yesterday. Come on, Tris; tell me that you didn't sleep with her." Logan had to ask, considering the strong scent of arousal that had hit him when the elevator doors opened.

"Seriously, bro?" Tristan shrugged. "Okay, let's go there. I questioned her, and yes, she's concealing something. But I can also sense that she's not dangerous nor did she set the fire. And no, I didn't sleep with her. Well, technically, I did sleep with her, but if you are asking if we had sex, then no." He wouldn't lie to Logan, but Tristan knew it was just a matter of time before he'd make love to her. And he planned on doing it all night long.

"Good to be the Alpha, huh?" Logan joked.

"Yeah, something like that. What about it?"

"So let me get this straight. You, my friend, just slept with her last night as in lying in a bed, eyes closed, no hanky panky?"

"It wasn't planned. Kind of just happened. I went wolf," he admitted.

Logan raised an eyebrow at Tristan. "Okay."

"She had a nightmare. She needed me. Come on, stop looking at me like that," he replied with a small smile. He held his hands up in protest. "Look, I'm nothing if not a gentleman."

"Yeah, okay, but do me a favor. Don't jump in any deeper until we find out what's going on with her. I know she's important to you, but..." his voice trailed off. He was tempted to tell Tristan about the visions, but they were unclear. If he told him that he'd seen her, there was no telling how he'd react.

"I got this. She's fine, really. And speaking of Kalli, we need to take her to the hospital today to tie up loose ends. I don't want her out of my sight. She saw two wolves leave the club on the day of the fire. They could have seen her go in or have seen her leave with the snake. And I still can't trust Alexandra to keep her fangs away from her. She was out of control yesterday. I'm sending a text to Kade so he can get a message to Devereoux. He needs to put the smack down on her, so she doesn't decide to try to snatch Kalli again. The look on her face yesterday when we walked out…she's one mean bitch."

"You can say that again." Logan shook his head. "I think that we should keep her out of Noir, too. I know she'll be pissed but she crossed the line."

"Agreed. But let's put that one back on Devereoux. He made her, and he needs to deal with his own. I can't have her going off when I'm in the middle of a territory war."

"So, is there anything else that I need to know about Kalli?" Logan asked, just as she walked into the room wearing Tristan's robe.

Tristan sucked a breath seeing her freshly showered, and hardened at the thought that she was completely naked underneath the black cotton terrycloth. He jumped to his feet, taking her hand, pulling her to his side. "Aw, chére. Sorry about the clothes. Listen, Julie will be up in a minute with something for you to wear. I promise."

Kalli felt shy, barely dressed. She awkwardly tried to stand behind Tristan in an effort not to look at Logan. Another wolf. Fear swept through her.

Tristan immediately noticed Kalli's apprehension and tried to reassure her. "Kalli, it's okay. This is Logan, my beta. Do you remember him from yesterday?"

Her wide eyes met Logan's, and she quickly averted her gaze. "I do remember seeing two men," she responded fearfully.

Concerned she was displaying the submissive behavior of a wolf and that he'd recognize her as something other than human, she forced herself to meet his eyes and extended her hand. "Hi, my name is Dr. Williams, but please call me Kalli. I can't thank you enough for coming to my rescue yesterday." There, she'd done it. Inwardly she congratulated herself for acting so completely normal….human.

Logan shook her hand, watching her curiously. It was as if she'd switched from submissive to dominant within seconds. He looked over to Tristan, shooting him a knowing look and then back to Kalli. *What the hell was that?* He'd ask him later what was going on with her. Tristan had to have noticed it. Subtle, but the Alpha missed nothing.

"Hey, no problem. Just sorry you had the unfortunate experience of meeting Alexandra. I'd call her evil but that would be an understatement," he told her.

"I will give her this; the mistress of Satan is true to her nature. Not that all vampires are bad people, but they definitely skate the line of morality. Alexandra is a predator and doesn't care who knows it. I have a feeling, though, that will get her staked. She's gotten worse over the past ten years," Tristan commented.

"Without a doubt," Logan agreed.

True to her nature. Kalli considered how she'd avoided her nature. Self-preservation had a tendency to drive one to do desperate things.

"Kalli is a veterinarian," Tristan explained. "Which explains why she was at UVH. She rescued Eve."

"Well, that's a good thing. I'm not a huge fan of snakes, but the old gal has grown on me. Where is she?" Logan asked.

"She's at the hospital. I have her in the observation area now. Such a beautiful snake, very calm, likes being held. She's thriving." Her eyes lit up as she talked about her patient. Anyone could see how passionate she was about her work. "If you want to send someone to get her, I'll sign the release papers when I go in today. I know I'm going to have to take a leave until this mess is figured out, but there were a few severely dehydrated puppies that someone had left abandoned in a dumpster. I want to see how they're doing. They might be ready to go to the shelter by now. I really don't know how people can just abandon animals, abuse them. People can be cruel," she remarked, thinking how humans could be every bit as evil as Alexandra. "I know my patients will be fine with the staff but I have to know how they're doing…peace of mind and all. I know you're not supposed to get attached, but sometimes, I just can't help it."

"That reminds me." Logan walked over to the elevator and picked something up off the floor. "Here's your purse. We got it out of your car. I'm afraid someone cut your tires. We'll call in a tow for you and get it fixed up, don't worry. Tristan here, tells me you'll be spending time with us for a while, so sounds like you won't need it."

"Thanks, and um, thanks for my pills," she coughed, remembering her desperation in the car. Rifling through her purse, she looked up. "You didn't happen to find my work ID by any chance?" The sequence of events was blurry, but then she recalled taking her ID and keys with her and leaving everything else in the car.

Before Logan had a chance to speak, she answered her own question. "It must have fallen off when they took me. I left my stuff in the car. Just took my keys."

"Hey, I know you've been through a lot, but I want you to know that we appreciate your help," Logan offered.

"Well, to be honest, I'm still in considerable danger. Those wolves I saw could be after me…if they weren't before, they will be once I do these sketches. And there's the vampire; I know she didn't give me up out of the goodness of her cold dark heart. Not happy about it, but I've got to lay low for a bit…if I want to live that is. And I do kind of like living. Pretty fond of it, actually," she joked half-heartedly.

"Alive works for me, too. Seriously, though, we'll keep you safe here. It'll be all right," Logan encouraged with a small smile.

Even though she'd initially been afraid of Logan, she soon found it was easy to talk to him. It didn't hurt that he was good-looking either. Like Tristan, he was at least six four, well-built and charming, she thought to herself. His dark brown hair fell past his shoulders, but even with long hair, he somehow looked quite the all American guy.

Logan studied the fine doctor, cognizant of her easygoing personality. He could see why Tristan found her attractive, with her innocent face and baby blue eyes. And that hair; the black curls were beginning to dry in shiny spirals, cascading over her shoulders. She seemed so vulnerable but at the same time, she exhibited strong tendencies. It was just yesterday she'd been passed out in the car, bitten and bloody. And today, although still bruised, she was conversing with them both as if she'd been around supernaturals her whole life.

Tristan watched his beta cautiously from across the room, as if he could hear Logan's thoughts. Was he flirting with her? His wolf growled; *mine.* Oh hell no, Tristan thought. He was not claiming this woman as his own. He hadn't even had sex with her. One night of sleeping with her, and his wolf was ready to take her? A human? Why did the wolf want her so? It was insane, yet the human side of him felt a sharp pain deep in his stomach as he watched Kalli flash Logan a smile. *What was that?* As Logan reached to put a comforting hand on her shoulder, Tristan heard himself growl.

Both Logan and Kalli stilled at the menacing warning. They both knew what it meant without hearing a single word spoken. Logan stared over at Tristan, surprised at the territorial admonition.

Tristan raked his hand through his hair, realizing what he'd just done. Like a common dog protecting his bone, he'd just snarled at them. *Fuck.* He couldn't believe that he was even capable of such an intense reaction. Yet there was no denying the confusing emotions swirling inside his chest. Relieved to hear the elevator ringing, he silently strode over and punched in the security code.

Julie's eyes darted from the Alpha to his beta and back again. She wasn't sure what she'd just walked in on, but the tension seemed thick. Regardless, she had a job to do.

"Good morning, peeps!" she chirped, walking in with a large tote bag. "Kalli! You're up. Oh my, I didn't expect you to be walking around today.

Are you sure you're all right? Did these he-men drag you out here for another interrogation? Um, I mean questioning," she corrected, shooting both Tristan and Logan a questioning look.

"No, they're fine. Um, I'm fine, thanks," Kalli responded, purposefully moving away from Logan.

"Well, let's get down into your room. I want to check your vitals. Brought you clothes too, which I'm quite sure you'll appreciate. You're already at a disadvantage around these two. And being naked won't help you. Maybe them, but definitely not you," she said with a wink to Tristan. Looping her arm around Kalli's, she led her down the hallway.

"What. The. Fuck?" Logan snapped, once the girls were out of earshot. He'd heard Tristan growl a million times, but rarely was it directed at him and never over a woman. Spending his life protecting the guy kind of earned him that privilege, to talk to him the way he just had. Logan was the only person in the world that when push came to shove, Tristan would allow to call him to the carpet.

"It's nothing," Tristan protested.

"Denial must be a great place to be, Tris. Seriously? Over her?" he pressed.

"All right. I'm sorry I, uh…growled. Let it go. End of discussion," Tristan replied, aware that he'd momentarily lost control.

"Yeah, okay," Logan agreed looking down at his phone, reading a text. "Hey, the artist is here. Mira's bringing him up."

Logan needed that clearance report on Kalli stat. He prayed it came back clear. She was alluring, no doubt, both physically and intellectually. But his sole purpose was to defend his Alpha and pack; something said he couldn't trust her. Not yet. He planned to stick close to her until he had something on her, and even closer to Tristan. Clearly irritated with his territorial nature over Kalli, Tristan had shut down. Logan backed off, knowing he needed space to get it together.

The Alpha was being sucked into the vortex of the mystery woman, and he suspected he knew the cause. Logan wished he could spare him from it; but like all things in life, it was the natural cycle of things. Fate was a coldhearted bitch. It didn't make sense to him how the Goddess would bring a human to mate his Alpha. Perhaps she wasn't the one. His visions weren't clear, but being around Kalli, seeing her face, her mannerisms, he felt more and more certain she'd been the one in his dreams.

Chapter Ten

Tristan took a deep breath, centering himself. He had to remain in control; so many people depended on him. He couldn't wait to get the sketches done. Not only would he share them with Marcel and Chandler, he planned to send the drawings over to Tony. They might help on his end. Tony Bianchi, Sydney's former partner, still worked homicide in the city police department. Since the fire had been ruled as arson, Tony wasn't working the case, but he was the only one Tristan trusted on the force.

P-CAP, the Paranormal City Alternative Police, was aware of the fire, but since no supernaturals were murdered, they wouldn't take the case. Tristan didn't want them involved anyway; given that Alexandra had vamps entrenched in their organization. The previous month, when a serial killer had been stalking young women, Kade had assigned himself to P-CAP in an effort to expedite the case. At the end of the day, pack business would be handled from within; he would mete out justice, not leave it up to the police.

But Tony could put out a city-wide bulletin on the suspects, or perhaps get a name on them prior to his meeting with Chandler. It was a long shot that Jax would even know the wolves who'd set the fire. And even if he did know them, Tristan wasn't certain that he'd cooperate. Working all angles was prudent given the lack of information.

Logan tapped in the code, allowing the ever-polished-looking Mira to saunter into the room. She wore a smart pink plaid dress suit with black pumps, her hair pulled neatly into a French twist. He smiled to himself, thinking how she could go from looking like a business barracuda one minute to a purring kitten the next. And had she ever purred for him last night.

A disheveled man, carrying messenger bags, followed her, stumbling into Logan.

"Logan. Tristan. This is Mr. Mathers. He will be doing the sketch. And before you ask, yes, I checked his badge," she stated, walking over to Tristan first, giving him a quick peck on the cheek.

"Please, sit," Tristan requested, gesturing to a guest chair in the living room. "Do you need anything to work?"

"Ah, no. Just the witness. I'm going to do the sketches. Afterward, I can send them to whoever you wish," he explained. Pulling out an oversized tablet and stylus, he situated his equipment. "It may be easier for me to work at the dining room table. Do you mind?"

"No, not at all. Mir, can you get him set up? I'm gonna go get Kalli,"

Tristan told her.

Kalli exited the bathroom, dressed in hip-hugging jeans and a tight yellow cotton short-sleeved t-shirt. Brushing her hair aside, she gratefully accepted a pair of beige ballet flats from Julie and slipped them onto her feet.

"Thanks again. I promise to get this stuff back to you once I get my clothes from my apartment. It feels good to finally have some clothes on again. I almost feel normal," she declared, smiling.

"No problem. I have to say that I'm pretty amazed at how quickly you're healing. You sure you're not feeling any more dizziness?" Julie asked, intrigued by how quickly she had recovered from her blood loss.

"I'd be lying if I said I wasn't a little tired, but no dizziness. I must have a strong heart," she suggested, knowing it was her wolf genes that helped her heal so quickly.

"Well before ya go, do you want to talk about these?" Julie held up the tiny bottle that held her pills.

"Um, well, they're just something I take to help keep me on an even keel. Helps control muscle spasms. It's kind of experimental; something I've been working on," she lied somewhat.

She hated deceiving Julie; the woman had been so nice to her. She'd always heard that if you had to lie that you should do it by sprinkling the fib into a story that was mostly truth. *Muscle spasms?* Well, technically that is what happened when she shifted. And being undetectable as wolf definitely was good for her mental state. As long as no one knew her true identity, she had been able to relax. Her old pack couldn't find her.

Kalli slipped the container into her purse, and rummaged around for her makeup. Finding a small tube, she pulled it out and slid the light pink gloss over her lips. As she dropped it back into her bag, she noticed Tristan by the door, watching her with the same heat he'd shown when they kissed. She smiled over at him, hoping that she'd be able to trust him soon with her secret. She felt guilty not telling him everything. He deserved to know the truth, but should she put her life into his hands?

"Can I take a break?" Kalli asked, after the first sketch was finished.

"Well, I really suggest we keep going. I need to get back to the station," Mr. Mathers replied, clearly annoyed that she wanted to stop working.

"Well, okay then, but it might be more productive if I just take a small break to refresh myself," she persisted.

Her face began to flush as she approved the first drawing. It brought back the reality of her situation. She was not going home or back to work. No, she'd decided to stay with strange wolves, when she had spent the past ten years trying to stay away from them.

Looking at the drawing of the wolf over and over again was enough to send her into a full-blown panic attack. Seeing his face reminded her that she'd been living on borrowed time. If they found her, they'd drag her kicking and screaming back to South Carolina. And if they decided not to kill her on sight, she'd be subjected to monthly rapes by the men who weren't worthy of breeding. *Oh God. I can't go back.* At the thought, her chest tightened; it felt as if she had an elephant sitting on top of her, making it difficult to breathe. *Air, I need air.* Her throat began to constrict. She put her head into the palms of her hands.

Tristan was talking to Logan and Mira about the latest acquisition when he heard Kalli gasping. Alarmed, he ran to her, pulling her into his arms.

"What did you do to her?" he yelled at the artist, who was tapping away on his tablet.

"Me? Well, nothing. I mean, she wanted a break, but it works better if we just keep going while the details are fresh," he explained nervously.

"Idiot," Tristan mumbled under his breath. He stroked Kalli's face with his hands, in an effort to get her to breathe normally again. "Time for a break. Come on, baby, it's okay. Breathe. That's it. Just feel me."

Tristan led her over to the sofa and lifted her onto his lap. He sent calming waves to her, hoping that his powers could be felt by a human. She cuddled into his warmth, trying to concentrate on his words. Hearing his breaths and strong heartbeat, she focused on matching her own to his as if they were one.

Logan and Mira both gaped, taken aback by the scene, as Tristan took the human to his breast. He acted so protective of her, as if he was mated. Yet he didn't know it. They both felt slightly voyeuristic but couldn't help but be drawn to the sight before them. Mira was more than astonished, she was irritated. *How could this happen? She was human.*

"I'm okay," Kalli reassured Tristan, lifting her head up and pressing a palm to his chest. "Oh my God. I'm so embarrassed. Really it was just a tiny panic attack. I'm fine."

"Don't be embarrassed. You've been through a lot in the past seventy-two hours. You're overcoming blood loss. He was a jerk. You asked, and he didn't listen. No worries, chére." Tristan felt as if his heart had been ripped out of his chest seeing Kalli so stressed over these pictures. He fully understood what they represented, but her face was as pale as if she'd seen a ghost.

Realizing that everyone was staring at them, Kalli attempted to get away from Tristan. She couldn't afford to show weakness in front of his wolves; they'd eat her alive.

"Hey, where're you going? You sure you're okay?" he asked, refusing to let her up. He held her tight, not caring what anyone thought.

"Thanks, I'm fine. You're right. It must be the blood loss. I think I'm okay now. I'll use the bathroom and be right back," she told him, hoping he'd let it go.

"Okay." Tristan released her, watching as she tore down the hallway. It may have been panic, but he could sense the sheer terror coursing through her body. She was afraid of something. Perhaps the wolves she'd been sketching scared her. But he got the distinct feeling she was not telling him the truth. It was just a matter of time before he found out what the hell was going on with her. Giving Logan a look, he gestured for him to come over to the sofa.

Logan complied. "What's up, boss?"

"How's the clearance going? Anything yet?' he asked impatiently.

"Not really. All we got so far is criminal records, which didn't tell us much. No arrests. Not even so much as a parking ticket. Pays her bills on time. Been on staff at UVH for two years. Still diggin'. Should have more information this afternoon."

"I want to know as soon as you hear from our guy. And I mean as soon as you hear it. No delays," he directed. "She's hiding something, and I damn well want to know what it is."

Mira overheard their conversation from across the room and came over to see what was happening. Tristan's intimate display with the human woman troubled her on a visceral level. What the hell did he see in her? Mira wasn't usually a jealous woman. He'd fucked lots of women over the years. He'd even been serious, holding long-standing booty calls with detective Sydney Willows. He'd even asked her to move in with him, but she had the good sense to turn him down.

But this woman had insinuated herself into his life in less than twenty-four hours. The only way that could ever happen would be if he met his mate. Mate? No fucking way. No Alpha had ever mated with a human. Besides, she would have known if he'd found a mate. Logan would know. The entire damn pack would know. They'd all feel it. And knowing Tristan, he'd be broadcasting it over a satellite. There was something about this human woman that was all wrong, and she was determined to find out what it was. In the meantime, she planned to make her life a living hell, even if Tristan had decided she was staying with him.

"Hey, what's up?" she asked innocently.

"Nothin'. Just talkin' to Logan about running a security clearance on Dr. Williams," he explained.

"Doctor, huh? Looks like she's the one who needs to take a pill if you ask me. And while we're all sharing, why the hell were you chasing her all over?"

Logan rolled his eyes, hoping Mira would know when to stop.

"I don't know what you're talking about," Tristan grinned, trying to get her to lay off the subject. "I'm just givin' her a little sweet Alpha love medicine. You should know all about that, Mir."

A chuckle came from Logan. The man had mad lines. He could talk the pants off a nun.

"Yeah, well, you'd better watch yourself, Tris. She's human. Not to mention that you barely know her," she warned.

"Thanks for your concern, chére, but I assure you that your Alpha can take care of himself."

"But you can't seriously be thinking of letting her stay here," she interjected, raising her voice.

"Already done. She's staying with me, in my home and will not stay with anyone else," he remarked, looking at Logan, remembering the incident earlier in the day.

"But…"

He interrupted her before she could get another word in. She was overstepping her boundaries. Pinning her with his eyes, he forced her to drop her gaze in submission. "Drop it, Mira. Seriously, not another word. She's in my care. She's mine."

He understood the implications of claiming her, the instant the word 'mine' left his lips. Looking at Logan and Mira's faces he knew they interpreted it as much more than the context in which it was meant. As Alpha, all wolves were his. They were all his responsibility. Just because she was human, well, it shouldn't make a difference. She needed his protection, and he needed her, for information only, of course. Sure, she was incredibly alluring and gave him an aching erection just about every time he talked to her, but it was just attraction, pure and simple. He'd have to be dead not to want to have sex with her.

As Mira and Logan gave each other quizzical looks, he narrowed his eyes on them. "What?"

"Nothing," they both said at the same time.

Finishing up the description of the second wolf, Kalli waited for the artist to work his magic. She sat patiently, anticipating that he'd ask for her to confirm the sketch. The tall blonde had been shooting daggers at her ever since she'd returned from her room. Kalli stole glances over at Tristan and Logan working on the other side of the room and noticed the woman never left Tristan's side.

Her business attire and laptop suggested she worked for Tristan in a formal capacity, but her intimate gestures toward both men indicated more than a professional relationship. *Friends?* No, her occasional touch to Tristan's face implied more. *Lovers?* For some reason the thought of him having other lovers gave her a slight twinge in her stomach. She silently admonished herself for the feeling. She'd only known him for a day. So what if she was lusting after him like a bitch in heat? He wasn't hers.

The phenomenon of physical attraction was undeniably compelling given the right chemistry between the right people. It could hardly be controlled. And then there was the very hard to ignore fact that Tristan was an Alpha who appeared to have made an art form of seduction, with the ability to turn on and off his intoxicating charm with the blink of an eye. Any woman who even looked his way would be hopelessly lost. She didn't stand a chance.

She damn well knew that he probably had a stable of women, supernatural and human, ready and willing to warm his bed. What kind of idiot would get involved with an Alpha when she, herself, was pretending to be human and was on the run from her own pack? *A fool.*

But she could not deny that she wanted him sexually, and not in a nice hand-holding, missionary position kind of way. Visions of her gripping the headboard while he slammed into her hard, fisting her long hair in his hands was more in order. And she, screaming as the pleasure bordering on pain sent her plummeting into orgasm…oh yes, that was how she wanted him. Fast and hard. Biting and scratching. Animalistic.

Regardless, she couldn't let these temporary lust-driven feelings cloud her judgment. She didn't do jealousy. Perhaps what did bother her, though, was that this woman who didn't even know her did not like her. Kalli didn't understand why but then again, it didn't really matter. And if she was reading things correctly, there was the possibility she'd also have to spend time with her over the next few days.

Not that she wasn't used to dealing with cantankerous and even cruel pet owners from time to time; she'd become an expert at pulling down her professional aura, speaking to them in a dominant but calm voice. Articulately eviscerating pet owners who were abusive was an unfortunate reality of life in the city. She wasn't the type to take shit from anyone when it came to protecting her animals. She reasoned that she could take care of the uptight blonde; it might not be pretty, but she wasn't here to do pretty. She needed to stay alive and help Tristan find the wolves who'd killed that man in Louisiana and set his club ablaze.

Once this ordeal was over, she planned to go back to her life's mission of healing animals and teaching others how to help them. She'd return to hiding as a wolf in human clothing. Maybe finally date a human who didn't mind a brainiac who worked long hours and was covered in pet hair when she got home. A hot kiss, one that brought her to her knees, with a spectacularly gorgeous Alpha wasn't going to change that very real outcome. She glanced over at him again, hoping he wouldn't see her looking yet again. *God, he is delicious. I could lick him up….*

"How does this look?" the artist asked, jarring her from her carnal thoughts.

"Um, yeah, that uh, that looks good," she stammered. "We done?"

"Yeah, just saving them and then I'll email them over to Tristan, Logan and Tony," he murmured, continuing to work.

"Okay, thanks." Tired from working, Kalli stood, unconsciously stretching her arms over her head like a cat who'd just awoken from a long nap.

Tristan stopped talking, noticing she was finished. His dick snapped to attention as she began stretching in front of everyone, her hard nipples pressing through her t-shirt. Was she aroused? Cold? He needed her close, thanking the Goddess that the artist wasn't watching her. He'd have a heart attack at the delectable sight.

A low growl emanated from him as he strode across the room and wrapped his hands around her waist. He didn't want anyone else seeing the lovely sight he'd just witnessed. Oh, he wanted to see her nipples hard, all right, but he didn't need other males seeing them, especially in his own home. Before he knew it, he hugged her, running his hands down her back where they rested right above her rear. Taking in a long draw of her scent, he moaned, and then released her, realizing they had an audience. He caught a glimpse of Logan's wide grin. Mira's mouth was drawn in a tight disapproving line.

"All done?" he asked Kalli and looked down to the artist who was putting away his tablet.

"Yeah," she said, surprised he'd just hugged her out of the blue. She wasn't sure what to make of it, but it felt so good to be in his arms.

"Mr. Livingston, I've sent the files to your email address. Tony should have them by now. Pleasure working for you."

"Thanks, I appreciate your work. And remember, you are to keep this in confidence. That means you are to tell no one, got it? Not even your mama," he ordered.

Apprehensively, the artist shook Tristan's hand. "Yes sir."

"Logan, please see Mr. Mathers out, would ya?"

The artist hurried over to the elevator, looking like he couldn't wait to leave. Sympathetic, Kalli understood what it was like to be intimidated by supernaturals. Even if the poor man didn't spend a lot of time with them, he'd be aware of the danger. They exuded a natural intimidating aura, and most humans had the good sense to be wary. An elk didn't need to know to be afraid of a pack of wolves skulking toward him. He instinctively knew to run.

"Come on over here. I want you to meet someone before we leave for the hospital," Tristan insisted, dragging her by the hand over to meet ice woman.

"Mira, I'd like you to meet…"

"Dr. Kalli Williams," Kalli interrupted, donning her professional mannerism. She extended her hand to her as she would a patient, looking her directly in the eyes. "Since you are friends with Tristan, please call me Kalli."

Mira shook the human's hand, astonished that she was so bold. Any wolf would have recognized her as an Alpha female and lowered their eyes. *Humans.* They grated on her last nerve. "Charmed I'm sure," she uttered briskly, darting her eyes to Tristan's.

Kalli quickly removed her hand. She didn't have time for pissing contests. And if there was going to be one, her opponent was going to drown trying.

"Yes. Okay, well, nice to meet you, Mira," she replied, not knowing what else to say to her. She wasn't sure what came over her but before she knew it she'd turned her back on Mira. Closing the distance, she pressed her body to Tristan, not quite touching, her breasts mere inches from him. Resting a hand possessively on his waist, the other touched a palm to his chest. The electrically charged tension hung in the air between them.

"I have to go freshen up. Then can we swing by the hospital? I've got to get in there before they fire me."

"Sounds good. I'm going to review the sketches real quick with Logan to see if anything about them seems remotely familiar. We'll get them out to the rest of the pack so they can be on the lookout, too. You go ahead. Take your time," he suggested, not moving an inch.

"Thanks." Kalli took a deep breath, removing her hands from him, but letting her breast brush him slightly as she turned.

Before Mira had a chance to say another word, Kalli spoke. "Nice to meet you." With confidence, she flipped her hair aside and walked away to go get ready.

"Humans," Mira sniffed. "God, Tristan, it's probably a good thing she's not wolf. I might have to take her down a peg or two."

Logan came up from behind her, wrapping his hands around Mira's waist, snuggling into her shoulder. "Mir, what's wrong, baby? Didn't we have fun last night? I've never seen you so prickly. Tris, our girl got up on the wrong side of the bed. You see what happens when you leave us in the middle of our play?"

Tristan tried to focus on Mira's reaction to Kalli, but was having a hard time, given the ache he felt below. The mere touch of Kalli drove him mad. He needed to take her soon, get her out of his system so he could think straight.

"What?" he asked, not having listened to the question. Ignoring it, he looked back to Logan and Mira. "Listen, Mir, I don't know what's gotten into you but you need to be nice to Kalli. She's already skittish around wolves."

"I was perfectly nice," she protested, gathering her up her things. "If you'd stop drooling for five seconds, you might notice that she was the one who was disrespectful."

"Seriously? Because she didn't avert her eyes? She's human. You need to get used to it. And she also holds a position of authority. In case you didn't hear it right the first time, she's a doctor. I get the feeling that she doesn't mince words. Despite what happened to her, she's no shrinking violet. She's tough. It's in her nature," he told her.

Humiliated, Mira rolled her eyes. "Human nature. Don't forget that, Tris," she countered, cupping his face briefly. She turned, giving Logan a brief kiss on the cheek, before entering the elevator.

Tristan considered what had just transpired. Consciously or not, Kalli had physically blocked Mira from touching him, possessively rubbing her hands all over his torso, thereby asserting her role in his life. And she happened to put on the display in front of his beta, who also took notice. Mira's feathers had been justifiably ruffled. He understood why, but it didn't change what had just happened. However vulnerable Kalli had appeared yesterday, there was no mistaking the lurking dominance within her.

Chapter Eleven

Kalli sat across from Dr. Marcus Cramer, who wasn't at all happy with her request for leave.

"Dr. Williams," he began. "We really can't have our doctors taking leave willy nilly. I understand you had an incident in the garage a few days ago, but you look fine to me."

"Dr. Cramer," she addressed him using his professional name, thinking that two could play that game. "You don't seem to understand. I really don't have a choice. I'm requesting a personal leave, effective immediately, which under my contract, I am entitled to do. And while I really do want your approval, I will escalate if necessary."

She didn't want to burn any bridges but she also wasn't about to let the jerk push her around. She reasoned he was trying to strong-arm her, because he knew that it was just a matter of time before she was completely in charge of her own department. She supposed he felt she needed to pay her dues before moving upward within the administration. But then again, the man just seemed to be a generally disagreeable person, regardless of who he spoke to, staff and patients alike.

"I feel that as a courtesy you should tell me why you are taking the leave. Is it medical? Are you pregnant?" he challenged, raising his voice.

"What?" she nearly shouted back at him, incredulous that he'd even ask such a personal question. "That is none of your damn business. I need to take a personal leave. I am under no contractual obligation to explain the reasons."

Tristan had heard quite enough. Kalli's boss did not just ask her if she was pregnant. *What the hell? Was that even legal?* Even though he hadn't wanted to leave her side, she'd insisted that he and Logan wait for her in the hallway while she explained the circumstances of her absence to her supervisor. Of course that didn't stop him from listening to the entire conversation, given his enhanced senses.

Logan raised his eyebrows at his Alpha and took a deep breath, realizing that the shit was about to hit the fan. Truthfully, Kalli's administrator seemed like a total dickhead and was about to get what was coming to him. He smiled, thinking to himself that this was going to be fun to watch.

Tristan launched out of his seat and stomped across the waiting room. To the dismay of a very concerned receptionist, Tristan opened the door to her boss's office like a wild tornado. Dr. Cramer literally jumped in his seat at the sound of his door hitting the wall. As it bounced back, he looked up to see a large, very irritated male glaring down at him.

"What are you doing in here? Who are you? Get out of here right now, before I call security," he demanded.

Tristan growled, hands fisted at his side. He restrained the beast within, which was ready to rip out the good doctor's throat.

Kalli shot to her feet, ready to pull him away. "Tristan, it's all right."

He shot her a look, warning her. "Sit, Kalli."

She found herself complying without argument. Nervously watching him, she tried to stifle the seed of excitement growing in her belly. His dominance called to her inner wolf.

"Dr. Cramer, allow me to introduce myself." Tristan leaned forward, putting his palms onto the desk.

"I'm calling security right now," the doctor tried interrupting.

Tristan grabbed the receiver from his hand and forcefully ripped the phone out of its outlet. Flecks of dry wall splattered all over the floor.

"So glad to have your attention. As I was saying, my name is Tristan Livingston." He deliberately emphasized his last name.

"Livingston? As in the Livingston Equine Rehabilitation Center?" The doctor's face paled. Mouth agape, he sat silently stunned.

"Yes, that Livingston. Now this is what's about to happen. You're going to apologize to Dr. Williams for your atrocious behavior. And if I ever hear you speak like that to her ever again, you'll be looking for more than a new job. Are we clear?"

"Yes, yes sir. I'm terribly sorry, sir. Mr. Livingston, please know that we very much appreciate your donations and contribution to our fine institution. We wouldn't be able to function without donors such as you."

Tristan rounded the desk in two seconds, grabbing the man by the scruff of his collar, lifting him out of the chair. "Apology. Now."

"Yes, yes, I'm so sorry Dr. Williams. Don't worry about a thing. Dr. Kepler can take over your caseload, and everything will be in order when you return." He actually looked like he was about to cry.

Kalli's eyes widened at the display of her Alpha's protection. *Her Alpha.* Her wolf wanted to roll over and bare her throat.

"Glad that's settled. Thanks so much for your understanding, Dr. Cramer. We'll be leaving now," Tristan snapped at him, taking Kalli's hand and gently helping her to her feet.

As they walked down the hallway, Kalli said nothing. She wasn't so much upset about what Tristan had done as she was about her reaction to it. To say she was aroused was an understatement. She swore silently as she felt the dampness in her panties.

"Tristan, I have to grab a few things from my office. Right here." She pointed to an open area, with several cubicles. "Um, I'm in here…over in the corner. Oh hi, Lindsey." She waved to a young woman whose cube was directly across from her office door.

"Hi, Dr. Kalli. Where ya been?" Lindsay, a pretty young graduate student shuffled papers behind her desk. Her long blond hair, streaked with bright red highlights, fell into her face.

Kalli had befriended Lindsey when she'd started interning over a year ago. She taught her how to help with research projects, and also the basics of day to day animal care. Kalli admired Lindsey's determination and strong work ethic. Her compassionate attitude toward the animals had her convinced Lindsey would make a fine veterinarian someday.

"Hey, just wanted you to know that I'm going to be on leave for a few weeks. If you need something, call my cell. Also, expect a call today or tomorrow for a pickup on the yellow boa. I signed the release."

"Okay, Doc. Is there anything I can do while you're gone? I can work on compiling the statistical data for you on MAO36, but I'd need access. Is your laptop here?" she asked cheerfully.

"No, all research will go on hold until I get back. I don't want anyone messing with my data. You know how it is," Kalli called through the opening of her door. She was shoving a few files into a bag, looking through her stuff to see if there was anything she really needed to take with her. She was hoping to be back in the office within a couple of weeks, but she wasn't entirely sure when things would be back to normal. Looking over at Tristan and Logan who both seemed to be studying her overflowing bookshelf, she was pretty sure things would never be the same for her again.

"I scent wolves. Stay back," Logan directed, as he pushed open the door to Kalli's apartment. Kalli had insisted on getting a few things to wear, since she was going to stay at Tristan's. But as soon as they entered the building, the smell was so strong that even Kalli had recognized its deathly scent: wolf.

"Hey Tris, maybe you ought to take Kalli back down to the car," he suggested, eyeing the disheveled mess they'd made.

"No," she cried, pushing past Tristan. "Goddamn fucking wolves." She could not believe they'd torn her apartment apart.

"Don't hold back, Kal," Tristan joked, slightly amused at her temper. Good, she needed to get mad, pissed even. This fight wasn't going to be easy.

"Why the hell did they have to do this? I mean, if they wanted me, they could have just opened the door, had a looksee and left. Why tear everything up?" she huffed.

The sofa was torn apart, knifed. Her bookshelf had been dumped. All the kitchen cabinets had been opened; the dishes and canned goods were strewn all over the counters and floors. She sighed, looking around at the mess. Sitting on a kitchen table chair, she put her head in her hands, while Tristan and Logan poked around in the bedroom and guest room.

She couldn't believe her world was coming unhinged. Why had they made this mess? It was as if they'd been looking for something. Something important. In a split second, Kalli's heart began to race in panic as the reason for the mess became altogether apparent. *No way. No one knew. They couldn't know.* All her research had been secret. She'd told no one. No one even ever saw her take the pills. Sure, in the beginning stages of her research, she'd taken her laptop to work. She printed only a few things off, but always on her private printer and always making sure there were no copies, shredding any remaining trash.

Since the actual development of CLI, she'd stopped carrying her laptop completely. After memorizing the composition and deleting all the data off her computer, she'd stored all the information on a flash drive which she kept hidden. But if someone knew….if they knew of CLI's existence or even suspected it was possible to devise a like drug, it'd be disastrous. It wasn't as if she hadn't gone through the scenarios during its creation: its possible use by the unscrupulous as a punishment by preventing a wolf from shifting, or worse, deriving the compound into a weapon. In the wrong hands, wolves everywhere would be vulnerable.

But she couldn't be sure that's what had happened. At this point, she had to assume that the wolves most definitely had seen her leaving the fire, and knew where she worked and lived. They could have just been on a power trip, trashing her apartment to scare her. There was only one way to find out if they knew. The only other supply of pills besides what she had left at Tristan's was her emergency supply, which she also hid. And she had to look for it now without alerting Tristan and Logan.

She jumped, startling as Tristan laid his hand on her shoulder. "Kalli, the bedrooms are a mess. I'm really sorry. Do you want Logan and I to help you get a bag together?" he asked softly. No matter how tough she was, this intrusion was bound to shake her.

Standing up, she pulled away from him. The impending lie felt like a lump in her throat. If the pills or thumb drive were missing, then she had to come clean. There was just no other choice.

"Can I just have a minute alone in my room?" she asked.

"You sure?"

"Yeah. I can do this. I have to do this."

"Hey Logan," Tristan called.

"Yeah, what's up?" Logan answered, walking back into the kitchen.

"She's going back to get her things. Alone."

"I just need some privacy. A minute to think." She gave them both a small smile, which didn't reach her eyes.

"Hey Doc. I'm real sorry about this. Assholes," Logan remarked, taking in the mess all over the kitchen. Cracked eggshells and dried yolk stuck like glue to every surface.

"Yeah, I won't lie. It feels like such a violation. Strangers going through my house, tearing it up. Really, really sucks. But you know, this stuff," she gestured to her torn books, cracked pieces of china and knickknacks. "It's all just…well, it's all just stuff. As opposed to animals or people, it can all be replaced."

Logan set a comforting hand on her shoulder. At the same time, he shot Tristan a nod, careful not to overstep his boundaries. Logan loved his Alpha. He knew things were changing. He'd dreamed of Tristan's mate. But unlike his Alpha, he'd had time to mentally prepare. However, he never imagined the sense of protectiveness he'd feel toward her. Confusion swept over him as he tried to resolve why. Considering she was human, not pack, it didn't make sense to him that he felt so compelled to shield her from danger, hurt. He'd first noticed it at the hospital. While he always enjoyed watching his boss dominate, hearing Tristan attack her nasty boss had given him unusual delight. He'd known that if his Alpha hadn't intervened, he would have been the one to do it.

Tristan studied him, tamping down his unreasonable possessiveness regarding Kalli. It continued to aggravate him that he cared at all. He kept coming back to the fact that he'd just met her. On top of that, it wasn't as if he didn't ever share women with Logan, so why was this any different? Logan was more than just a friend, given how many times they'd been intimate. They never were intimate with each other sexually during their trysts, but they did touch each other, share a caress; perhaps even direct each other's play with the lucky woman. Whether it was Logan's girlfriend or Tristan's, it was always understood that neither man was with their mate. Therefore, jealousy never reared its ugly head. There were no limits.

But with Kalli, he'd felt the need to possess her, mind and body. And if he ever shared, he knew it would be on his terms only. No one would touch her without his permission, and she'd only be touched the way he commanded. It could be no other way. Tristan grew irritated as his territorial feelings grew stronger every hour he was around her. It felt uncomfortable to think about a woman in this manner, yet it seemed as natural as being born.

As Kalli caught a glimpse of Tristan observing her interaction, she pulled away from Logan's touch. She was appreciative that he cared, but guilt ate her. She had to tell them about her formula. Dreading it, she'd have to confess sooner rather than later if the flash drive or pills were missing.

"Guess I'd better get my stuff," she commented as she resigned herself to her task. Looking terribly defeated, she walked out of the kitchen. When

Kalli reached her room, she locked the door. She knew that either wolf could easily break it down if they really wanted to, but they didn't seem the type who'd go bursting in on a lady in a locked bedroom.

She ran into the master bathroom, trying to avoid the shards of glass scattered all over the room. They'd smashed the mirrored closet doors as well as the sink mirror. Opening up the vanity drawers, she searched for the small pill boxes where she kept the spares. One by one, she came up empty. Her stomach lurched at the thought. *They'd stolen the CLI.* Thinking she might vomit, she bent over at the sink and took deep breaths, willing the bile back into her stomach.

She prayed silently that they hadn't taken the thumb drive. Without the data, they probably wouldn't be able to replicate it. Even if they analyzed the chemical composition, its creation was a complicated process. And said process and all the underlying details were on that drive.

Opening the bottom of the vanity, she looked for her cosmetic bag, the one she used to hold her makeup. Cleaning supplies had been spilled inside the cabinet and the boxes of tissues had puffed up, smelling like pine and bleach. What she didn't find was the drive. Bending her knees, she squatted, scanning the entire floor. Behind the toilet, her little pink bag peeked at her. She leaned over and scooped it up; even though it was open, most of the contents were still in it. Eyeshadow. Eyeliner. Foundation. Blush. Lipstick.

"Thank God," she breathed. Her pink lipstick was still there. Gently screwing off the top, it popped open, revealing its secret compartment. The drive was safely nestled inside. She'd bought the little diversion safe on an online spy shop. Given a choice of soda cans, shaving cream and books, she'd decided on the lipstick. It was small enough that she could easily transport it, but easily concealed, especially among a collection of lipstick tubes.

Pressing it into her pocket, she exited the bathroom and went to her closet to pack a bag. After collecting some casual clothes, underwear and shoes, she unlocked the door. Luckily, she had a small bag she kept for traveling which was already stocked with toothbrush, baby powder, razor and other convenience items. With a sigh, she took once last glance at the mess that used to be her room and shut the door.

They rode in silence on the way back to Tristan's condo. Tristan and Logan had both heard the lock click as she went to retrieve her things. Why did she feel the need to lock a door unless she was doing something in secret? Something she didn't want them to know about? She hadn't changed her clothes and was barely gone for ten minutes. What was she hiding? A nagging pull at Tristan's gut reminded him that she hadn't been entirely truthful. The feeling of distrust was confirmed when she refused to look him in the eyes after they left the building. It also didn't help that he could not stop wondering about the way the wolves had torn apart her place. Sure, they could have done it out of spite, but more likely they'd been searching for something. And if that was true, then Kalli was involved up to her eyeballs in trouble.

As the elevator ascended, Tristan decided he needed a break from her. He was angry she wasn't telling him everything. If he stayed with her, he was either going to force her to tell him what the hell was going on or take her up against the wall again. While both were feasible options, neither seemed like the right thing to do. He needed space. Time to think and get his head together. Tristan really didn't want to leave her alone with another man, but even he had his limits.

When they got to his floor, he addressed Logan, ignoring Kalli completely. "I need you to stay here with Kalli for a few hours, okay? I'm goin' up to my office to do some work and then may go for a ride or hit the gym. If you need me, text me."

"No problem. Take your time," Logan replied, sensing the tension. His Alpha looked like he was about to snap. And Kalli was running a close second.

Kalli said nothing as the elevator doors closed. She dropped her bag at the door, walked into the living room and fell back into an overstuffed lounge chair that faced the long wall of ceiling to floor windows. Throwing her head back, she put her hands over her eyes and blew out a big breath. She needed to tell them about CLI.

"Hey Doc. What's going on? Wanna talk about it? I'm a good listener," Logan offered, sitting on the sofa perpendicular from her.

Removing her hands, she stared out the windows. "I've gotta talk to Tristan about what happened today."

"What happened with your boss or what happened to your apartment?"

"They were looking for something," she stated flatly.

"Yeah, I assumed as much. Pretty sure Tristan already suspects that too."

"They took something." She bent over, placing her forearms on her knees and pinching the bridge of her nose with her fingers.

"You wanna tell me what it was?" he asked, biting his upper lip. He wished she'd just spill it.

"Yes. No. Okay, yes, but I have to tell Tristan first." She sighed in frustration. "Tell me, Logan, did you ever have to tell somebody something? Something that was a really big secret? But by telling the secret, you'd be putting your own life at risk?"

He silently regarded her, well aware her life was already on the line. She was a smart woman and had to know how much danger she was in; she had agreed to stay with Tristan after all. What the hell did she know that would put her in even more danger? Whatever it was, he could tell it wasn't going to be good.

"Here's the thing, Kalli. In Lyceum Wolves, we're pack. Lies don't fly too well here. And yes, I've kept things to myself on occasion." He didn't want to mention his visions to her yet. "But I can't say it put my life in danger. If my life were in danger, my pack would be behind me, so I wouldn't keep the secret."

"How well do you know Tristan?"

"Like a brother. Hell, I know him as well as I know myself."

"So what's he really like?"

"He's badass," he boasted smiling. "Has more confidence than I've ever seen in a wolf, but it's well deserved. He's extraordinarily powerful, both physically and mentally. Fierce in battle and loyal as the day is long. And here's something you'd do well to remember; at the end of the day, he's fair. I'd even go as far as to say that he's caring."

"You love him, don't you?" she blurted out.

"Well now, aren't you the inquisitive one? Come on, Doc. Of course I love him. I'm his second. We're best friends and do almost everything together. It's our way," he revealed thoughtfully.

"Wolves?" she questioned.

"Yeah. I mean, sure, there're fights within the pack every now and then, but we live to support each other. It's how it's meant to be. The communal love and devotion, it's in our nature and whatnot. Kind of hard to explain to someone who's human, but I'm sure you feel it a little. Right?" He wanted to tell her she was Tristan's mate, but it wasn't his place. They needed to find their way to each other via their own journey.

"Yeah, but what about the brutality? You know, the forced breedings and matings? The fights for dominance? That's not so loving," she remarked directly, remembering her life in South Carolina.

"Hold on there, Doc. That's old school shit and I can assure you that it doesn't happen around here. Now, it could be part of the reason we're about to have a territory war, who knows? I can tell you that Tristan and Marcel don't schlep out our females like prostitutes. They make their own decisions about mating when they're damn ready. As for the violence, put a group of human men together and you'll see what happens isn't too much different than around here. But I'll guarantee you won't see any 'brutality' as you so delicately put it." Logan narrowed his eyes on Kalli. Where the hell was she coming up with these things? Sure, brutality was common long ago, but things had changed, in most packs anyway.

"I'm sorry, Logan. I didn't mean to insult you or the pack. I…I just have a different experience is all. I spent some time around wolves before…not here…it wasn't pleasant," she admitted.

"No offense taken. Doc, I like you. I'd like for you to stick around a little and not just because you have to. Can I give you a bit of advice?"

She rolled her eyes and smiled. "Yeah, sure. Why not? I sure as hell could use some."

"Whatever is going on with you, we'll deal with it, okay? But you've got to tell Tristan. Like soon. I'm gonna be honest with you. Your life is already in danger. So whatever little nugget you've got stowed up your sleeve, it's not going to put you more at risk. But by not showing all the cards, you could very well be putting others in danger. I know you're not pack, but you should consider joining our team so to speak," he said with a grin. "And hey, it's a pretty good team. The only requirement for membership is honesty. Other than that there's all kinds of great benefits; not only do you get the protection of a tough Alpha wolf, you get his beta. It's a twofer. Also, there are lots of great friends here, runs in the wilderness, although you might need a horse for that," he joked.

Kalli laughed softly. "I'll talk to him tonight."

He cocked his head to the side, as if not quite believing her.

"I swear," she promised, standing. "Okay, I think I'm going to go take a long hot shower and try to relax before he gets back. Thanks. I really appreciate the talk."

As he watched her walk down the hallway, Logan found himself wanting Kalli to be Tristan's mate. She was intelligent, beautiful and full of life. The more time he spent with her the more it confirmed his visions. But he worried about her reasons for lying, sensing something very, very bad had happened to her. If he had to guess, he'd say she'd been abused. Something drove her fear of wolves, yet she exhibited a knowledge of wolves that could only be learned by spending a lot of time with a pack. The subtle way she lowered her gaze around Tristan told him she'd been with an Alpha.

But up until just now, she wouldn't readily admit she'd been around a pack. Why? Was she afraid of the 'brutality' she'd referred to in their conversation? Had a wolf done something horrible to her or her family? Now that he thought of it, she hadn't mentioned her family. Her entire being was wrapped up in her work. None of it made sense. But he prayed she'd come clean soon. She was wrapped tight. And Tristan. Shit. He'd been coming unglued since the minute he'd met her. Things were getting out of hand. The pack, including Kalli, needed to be strong if they were going to prevail.

A text came across the screen of his phone, slamming him back into reality. As he read the words, he shook his head. Knowing that Tristan was receiving the information at the same time, he took a deep breath and blew it out. Things were about to get real serious but quickly, and Kalli had better get ready to provide his Alpha with the truth as soon as he got home.

Tristan slammed down the weights. The text from Logan's investigator was the last damn straw. No past on a Dr. Kalli Williams since college. Everyone who was a real person had a past; good or bad, exciting or boring, rough or easy, it existed. On the contrary, people who didn't leave a paper trail of their past, were hiding something, possibly using another person's identity. They were liars. He'd like to pretend it wasn't a significant finding, but he just couldn't.

There was no doubt that the beautiful woman he knew, the one who'd gone to school for eight years in New York, who'd been working at UVH, was Dr. Williams. But before that, there was nothing. No birth certificate. No driver's license. Not a high school diploma. And then poof, one day Kalli Williams is a freshman at NYU. It was if she materialized out of the freakin' air.

Goddammit. Kalli was driving him crazy. He wanted to scream at her. Make her tell him the truth. At the same time, he wanted to fuck her senseless. The situation was maddening. What the hell was she lying about and why the hell wouldn't she tell him? Her apartment was totally trashed, and she was as cool as a cucumber. 'Things can be replaced' his ass. Who says that anyway? She'd had to leave her job. Her shit was destroyed. You'd need a fucking jackhammer to get the eggshells off the cabinets. Hell, the entire apartment would need to be gutted.

And what was her reaction? She calmly went to her bedroom and packed a bag. Seriously? Oh, and she'd locked the door while doing it. The million dollar question was why and what was she doing in there? When she'd returned, she'd refused to look him in the eye. Like a cat on a hot tin roof, she'd scampered out of the building. During the torturous car ride home, she'd said nothing, pensively staring out the window.

He was so damn mad that he could have thrown the hundred pound barbell through the window. Instead, he grabbed his towel, wiped it across his face and headed toward the locker-room. Fuck. He needed to get laid. Blow off some steam. He knew Mira would be down for anything he asked for sexually; she'd do whatever he wanted. If not Mira, others were willing and ready to service him. With a text, there was nothing he couldn't have. A one on one. Threesomes. The women were plenty. Wolves, humans and even vamps, as longs as they didn't bite, there'd been a time when he'd have been up for it. The women were available and willing twenty-four seven. And he was an equal opportunity lover…used to be, anyway.

Therein lay the rub; he wasn't that person anymore. For the past couple of years, he'd quietly made love to Sydney on the side; sometimes indulging with Logan and Mira. Was it a release? Yes. But was it fulfilling? Was his wolf at peace? Unequivocally no. But what was he supposed to do? Go in search of a mate? So not happening. He was happy with the freedom of knowing he could do what he wanted, when he wanted, and wasn't about to give that up. He wouldn't submit to a forced pairing, something that was done in the old days. It'd never feel natural. He'd be trapped like a zoo animal, never again allowed to run in the wild.

But meeting the good Doc had flipped his world upside down, and he wasn't sure it was in a good way. Within twenty-four hours, he'd gone from cool and confident to hot and horny, unable to think straight. He wanted to strip her, flip her and fuck her and not necessarily in that order. But then there was that damn thing that was stopping him, his conscience. How could he make love with her, knowing she was lying to him? He was pretty sure that she wasn't even *Kalli Williams*. Not that he needed to know the name of every woman he'd been with but when he had the Doc, he was going to make love to her hard and long. And he'd be damned if he'd do it not being able to call her by her real name when he sank deep inside her.

That settled it. There was no other option; he had to find out what she'd been keeping secret. No matter what it took, he needed to find out, deal with it and then get it together, so he could concentrate on finding the asshole who'd burnt down the club. And at this point, it wasn't just about the club. One of Marcel's wolves was dead, and they had no idea if it was even related. Kat was in hiding. There were too many loose ends. Unanswered questions and lies in the air.

Stomping into the bathroom, he flipped on a spigot. Tristan tried to shake off the feeling of foreboding that blanketed him as the hot spray of the shower danced on his skin. He planned to go back to his apartment and interrogate Kalli. He didn't want to hurt her but the responsibility of the pack settled on his shoulders. The truth was coming, and he'd see it realized.

Chapter Twelve

As Tristan strode through the elevator, ready to tear into her, demanding an explanation, he stopped short. *Candlelight? Garlic? Tomatoes? Shit. What did she do? And where the hell was Logan?* The anger he'd spent the last three hours building was melted away within seconds as it dawned on him that she'd cooked him dinner. No one, aside from his mother, had cooked him dinner. Sure, many a woman had tried, but he'd always managed to avoid the experience, knowing full well what it represented: commitment, love, marriage. His jaw fell open as he walked toward the heavenly scent. *No way.* He rubbed his hand across his face in disbelief.

Shock would be the best word Tristan could use to describe the surreal situation he'd walked into. Fully anticipating questioning her until she spilled the truth, he found his mind going haywire, like he'd stuck his finger in an electrical socket. Logically, he knew he should tell her they needed to talk now, force the argument to happen. But the food…the wine…and where did all the candles come from? He owned candles? And what was she dressed in? Boy shorts and a camisole, covered with an apron? What kind of woman cooked in underwear? He smiled, shaking his head at the sheer absurdity of the situation.

Kalli was bent over his stove languidly stirring a boiling pot. And yet again, the globes of her creamy ass beamed at him as the back of her apron rode up her back. The length of him immediately reacted at the sight of her. Of all the things he'd expected tonight, this was the very last thing he'd envisioned.

"Kalli?" He muttered, at a loss for words. "Where's Logan?"

"Hi there. He left just a minute ago; said he knew you were in the building," she explained, continuing to stir the pasta.

Tristan growled softly to himself, irritated that Logan had left her alone. He'd talk to him later.

"So, I hope you don't mind but I thought I'd cook us dinner tonight. Kind of like a thank you for saving my ass from Alexandra. Nothing fancy."

"Yeah, okay," he responded, walking toward her as if he was caught in a magnetic ray.

Kalli stopped stirring for a minute to look at Tristan. She'd been thinking all afternoon about how to tell him everything about her past, the formula and most importantly, the *stolen* CLI. She was terrified of the kind of violence she'd grown up with, never knowing when her old Alpha would strike. Even if Tristan managed to control his anger, she considered the possibility that she'd lose his protection, that he would toss her out to the wolves…literally.

As her gaze fell upon him, she instinctually lowered her eyes, letting them roam down his chest to his feet and up again. She sighed and briefly closed her eyes, as her belly pooled with desire. Tristan looked incredibly sexy in his tight white t-shirt and loose jeans. She looked to his feet, which were clad in black military boots. In his left hand he carried a black motorcycle helmet, and she wondered what kind of bike he rode. Rolling her eyes in an effort to gain her own composure, she reasoned she didn't care what kind of bike he had. She'd ride him, um, ride with him, any day of the week. She could feel her panties dampen at the thought. Clenching her thighs together, she prayed he wouldn't know how wet she was from just looking at him. *Get it together, Kalli.* He's going to know that instead of this wonderful dinner, you'd rather eat him right here, right now, she thought embarrassedly. He's Alpha. He'll know.

Kalli decided changing the subject was in order and looked back to the stove. She struggled to get her composure. "So yeah, I was going a little stir crazy being cooped up in here. Um, I mean not that your home isn't beautiful. It's really nice, warm and open feeling. I've never actually been to a penthouse before….you know, the kind where the elevator door just opens up into the apartment," she rambled.

She knew things were about to come to a head and figured that maybe if she tried opening up a little about herself, just crack that steel door on her past, just a tiny bit, maybe he'd soften.

"I actually like to cook, but I'm all by myself, so I don't ever really get to it. My mom," her voice became softer at the memory, "she was Greek. She was a wonderful cook. Made all kinds of great stuff. She was really amazing. I wish I'd paid attention."

"Where is she? Your mom?" Tristan asked, treading carefully, realizing that this was an in to his line of questioning.

"She's dead. She died when I was only fourteen. It was really hard losing her. Dad's gone too. Died when I was seventeen. I've got no family, well, blood related anyway."

She stopped stirring the pasta and turned to grab the romaine lettuce that'd been drying on a paper towel. "I really work a lot. And I co-run a no-kill shelter, so whenever I get the time, I'm there. I consider the animals my family. I need them as much as they need me. I'd really love to have my own pets someday, but I spend too many crazy hours away from my apartment. And my apartment isn't that great for animals anyway. It's small, doesn't have a yard, you know. Well, I guess I could do a cat, but it's not fair to the animal if I'm not there."

"Do you like horses?" Tristan sidled up to her, watching her chop the lettuce and toss it into a bowl. He wanted to discuss her parents, but he could tell she'd been on the verge of tears when she'd mentioned her mother dying. He figured if she started talking about her life, she'd continue to share with him what happened.

"Oh yeah, I love them. Of course, I never had any growing up, but I did do an equine rotation. By the way, I didn't say anything at the time, but I'm really impressed that you funded the rehab center. It's a terrific facility; helps so many horses. We should go there sometime and tour it. It's funny, I know all about it, but because it's so far outside the city, I just never get there." Kalli stopped talking after suggesting plans for the future…a future with Tristan in it.

Tristan smiled, catching her slip. Before there was any kind of a future for them, he needed facts. He could tell she was trying, but he needed more. He needed honesty.

"Yeah, sure, we could go to the center. We could ride, too, if you want. Hit the trails," he suggested.

"Really? We can ride? Oh my gosh, that would be so great. I did get to do it a few times when I was in school, but never for long, and I wasn't with a friend," she exclaimed excitedly.

Tristan smiled broadly this time, gazing into her wide eyes. She was like a child who'd been told she could go to an amusement park. It was almost as if she'd missed out on a lot in life and was getting an opportunity to live, experience. His heart squeezed at the tragic thought.

"Sure thing," he replied, picking up the salad she'd created. He walked over to the table and set it down.

"Um, so, I also thought we could talk after dinner. I, uh, I have some things I need to tell you. But let's eat first, okay?" she croaked. She was not looking forward to the conversation.

"Yeah, sounds great," Tristan struggled to reply, deciding that it could wait thirty minutes so they could eat dinner. He could see that she was getting ready to tell him, and he preferred for her to submit on her own and tell him without a quarrel. But if it was the last thing he did today, he would have verity from her within the hour.

Somehow, they'd made it through dinner without choking or ripping each other's clothes off. Both of which seemed possible considering the incendiary tension that threatened to combust the room. After everything was cleaned up, the time of reckoning had arrived. There were no more dishes to wash or food to put away. It was just Tristan and Kalli and the truth waiting to be told.

Tristan walked over to the sliding glass doors, sensing her hesitation. She'd cleaned the countertop and stove from top to bottom, procrastinating in order to avoid the inevitable. He was done waiting. As he was about to call her over, she nervously played with her hair then untied the apron, revealing a hot pink cami and black boy shorts. All the blood rushed to his cock, responding to the sight of the second skin material. Jesus, she was killing him. He prayed their talk would go quickly so he could peel her out of her barely-there excuse for clothing.

He pointed his finger at her and then crooked it, indicating it was time. He knew it. She knew it. He could hear her heartbeat quicken as she closed the space between them. Her breath hitched as she met Tristan's eyes. His finger beckoned her to join him. Her legs were moving before she thought she'd said yes. By the time she was within a few feet, he slid open the door.

"Come, Kalli. Let's talk," he instructed. He held out his hand gesturing for her to go outside.

"I…I can't go out there," she stuttered. "I'm not even dressed. Well not really." She was petrified of heights. The entire time she'd stayed with him she'd avoided the windows as much as possible. The view was lovely but her stomach dropped as soon as she got within a foot of the glass.

"Yes you will, Kalli. Truth. Now. Why don't you want to go?"

A test?

She looked down to her feet and then met his eyes yet again. She crossed her arms protectively across her chest. "Okay, fine. I hate heights. Satisfied? Let's just stay in here…please," she begged.

"No, Kalli. We're going outside. It's a beautiful night. Very few people get to see the city like this, alone on a Penthouse balcony. Call it my gift to you."

"Gift? I don't understand how…"

"As long as you live in my home, my building, I am your Alpha. You accepted this when you accepted my protection. The wolves, I protect them too. Guide them when necessary. From the youngest pup to the eldest grandwolf, I have their best interests in mind in everything I do. This is your gift. Teaching you to trust your Alpha. Now come to me, Kalli," he demanded with a smooth sexy voice.

It seemed as if there was nothing she'd consider denying him as she reached for his hand.

"That's it, chére. Come with me," he encouraged as he led her outside. He chuckled as she looped her arm within his, clutching him tightly.

She tried concentrating on her breathing in an effort to calm the fear that threatened to take over her sense of reason. As her bare feet touched the warm terracotta tiles, she closed her eyes.

"See how nice it is? There's nothing better than a warm September night." He looked down at Kalli to see that her eyes were completely shut tight.

"Cheating are we?" he laughed. "Okay, brave girl. Close your eyes all you want, for now. But I've got something I want to show you, and you will open your eyes," he stated confidently.

As he led her over to the wrought iron fence, he smiled. "All right, come on, turn around for me."

Extricating his arm from her deathly grip, he gently took her by the waist and slowly turned her toward the skyline. He peeked at her and saw she still wasn't looking. She was a stubborn little thing, he thought to himself. What fun it was going to be breaking her of that habit. He planned on teaching her a lesson she'd not soon forget.

Placing his hands on her shoulders, he rubbed them gently. A small moan escaped her lips. "That's it baby, relax. I want you to enjoy my gift." With a final caress, he let his hands roam down her bare arms, never losing contact with her skin. When he reached her hands, he pulled them over to the fence and placed her palms on the cool iron bars. He proceeded to wrap each of her fingers around the metal until she fully grasped it.

Sliding his hands around her waist, he pressed his body against her until the hard bulge of his erection was nestled into the crease of her bottom. She released a small gasp at his delightful intrusion.

"Okay, Kalli. It's time. You can do this. Your Alpha is with you. And you're safe. I won't let anything happen to you. You must trust me. Ready? One, two, three. Open your eyes. Now," he demanded.

By the time her eyes flew open, she was so aroused she'd forgotten where she even was. With Tristan holding her waist, and her hands clasped to the bars, she let her fear go and gasped at the incredible sight. The city vista danced with lights to an orchestra of urban music. It was magnificent, like nothing she'd never experienced.

"Tristan, oh my God. It's beautiful. Thank you," she breathed, aware that she truly had been given a gift, one that she'd never have experienced if it weren't for Tristan and the trust she put in him.

"What do you see Kalli?" he asked.

"Lights, buildings, shadows…" she wasn't sure of what he meant.

"Yes, all that is true. But let me tell you what I see. I see my city, my wolves. I see my responsibility. And whether my wolves are up the mountains or in the city, they know they can trust me to lead them and protect them. And you Kalli, you can trust me too."

"Yes, I know," she moaned again. She trusted him. But part of her was done talking; she simply wanted this man. "I have to tell you. Tristan…my apartment. They took something. Something really important."

"What, chére? What did they take?"

"Pills. My medicine. But I'm afraid… I need…I need…" She took one of her hands off the iron and reached behind her to touch his thigh.

Something in Tristan snapped. He knew he should keep up with her confession, but the feel of her warm hand on his thigh, mere inches from his hard arousal, flared his desire. His fingers slid under her stretchy cotton cami, until his hands were full with her soft breasts. He gently pinched her nipples, enjoying the feel of her tender, excited flesh.

Kalli released a loud breath at Tristan's touch. The sweet sting sent a rush of desire to her core. Needing more, she wriggled backward, relishing the feel of his cock on her ass.

"Yes, please," she begged.

"Ma chérie, what do you need? Tell me," he whispered into her ear. As the word, 'chérie' left his lips, he briefly took note of what he'd called her. It was a term he'd reserved only for a girlfriend. Intellectually, he knew that she wasn't, but his body disagreed.

"Please. Please touch me. I want you."

She was begging for him to take her. At her admission, Tristan groaned. He swore his dick was going to tear through his zipper as it pulsed in exhilaration. He promised himself he wouldn't make love to her without knowing everything, but that didn't mean he couldn't get a small taste. While sprinkling small kisses behind her ear, he slipped his hand into her panties. Stroking his forefinger into her slick folds, he ground into her from behind. Damn, he felt as if was going to come in his pants like a teenager.

"Fuck Kalli, you are so wet for me," he grunted. He slowly brushed her clit back and forth, loving the feel of her smooth skin.

"Tristan, yes," she cried. The touch on her bundle of nerves sent chills through her body; she could feel the precipice of her orgasm within reach. She didn't want to come so quickly but she could no longer control her own body. He was powerful and sexual and Alpha. And she wanted all of him.

He was teasing her, circling her nub then backing off. Reaching down further, he finally plunged two long fingers into her hot sheath, thumbing her clit. "Ah, that's it, baby. Take my hand. You are so damn tight."

She was panting hard. The city lights flashed in the sky, horns beeped. As soon as he penetrated her, Kalli's body exploded as the wave of a release crashed over her. She shook in orgasm, while he supported her body with his arm, clutched her waist.

"Tristan, yes!" She screamed, unable and unwilling to restrain her emotion.

"Ma chérie, you're so beautiful when you come," he crooned as he spun her around to face him.

Without giving her a chance to recover, Tristan quickly kissed her. It was a hard, forceful kiss that let Kalli know that he was her Alpha. She responded in kind by hugging her arms around his neck and jumped to wrap her legs around his waist, while he supported her butt. Their lips sucked and bit, tongues dancing with each other. Kalli had officially lost control. Her wolf cried, begging to be released. This man was hers; she'd give up anything to be with him, even being human.

"Tristan." A male voice called from inside.

"Ignore it," Tristan growled as Kalli bared her neck to him. His wolf howled at the submission. He gently bit at her throat, alternately licking and kissing it.

"Tristan!" Logan yelled again. He stopped still, watching Tristan and Kalli on the balcony. *Was she submitting to him?* He wished he didn't have to interrupt the intimate and very erotic sight of his Alpha at her neck, but he had no choice.

"Tristan," he repeated softly as he approached them. He knew Tristan was far gone and his wolf would consider attacking him, given the interference.

"Go away, Logan. Not now," Tristan ordered without turning around.

"Tristan, it's Toby and Ryan. Something's happened. We've got to go now."

Chapter Thirteen

Tristan had hauled ass on his bike, knowing city traffic could be a bitch by car. In the rush, he'd forgotten his helmet, but took off anyway. He asked Logan to drive Kalli, so they'd be there shortly. But he couldn't wait; nothing mattered, but the kids. He barreled into the Intensive Care Unit, seeking out a nurse.

"Ryan Pendleton. Toby Smith. Where are they?" Tristan more demanded than asked.

A young nurse peered up at him, while still typing into the computer. "I'll be with you in one second," she replied. After a few more key strokes, she looked up at him expectantly. "And you are?"

"Their father," Tristan bit out angrily. Toby and Ryan should not be in the hospital. Wolves rarely ended up in a human hospital, given their extraordinary healing powers. Generally, most injuries could be healed with a shift. And in other cases, they paid witches who could help with healing spells.

The nurse eyed him over and came around the desk. "Come with me, please," she instructed. "Their mother is already here."

Tristan assumed she meant Julie, who he'd been advised was already at the hospital. As they walked down the hallway, he caught sight of Detective Tony Bianchi, talking with doctors and nurses. *What was he doing here?*

The nurse pointed on the left. "Here we are."

"Ma'am, what's his condition?" Tristan asked quietly. He could see through the long rectangular window, Ryan appeared unconscious.

"The doctor has explained his condition to your wife, um, their mother," she corrected. "He came in with multiple gunshots. One in the leg. Another to his shoulder. The hits weren't in vital areas, but he lost a considerable amount of blood. So we're keeping an eye on him here for a while before transferring him down to Med-Surg."

"And Toby?"

"Sir, I'm terribly sorry," she said looking to her watch. "I'll send the doctor down to speak with you as soon as she's done with the detective. You go on in now....only two people at a time, okay? The doctor will be right with you, I promise."

A surge of grief hit Tristan upon hearing her words. He'd been around long enough to know that the nurse was avoiding telling him that Toby was dead. As he pushed his power outward in search of the boy, there was nothing. His jaw tightened in anger. He wanted to force the nurse to tell him more, but through the glass, he could see Julie crying. She needed him.

And so did Ryan. Goddammit, why hadn't the boys just shifted?

Julie looked up through puffy eyes, tears still evident on her face. She rushed into his arms. "Alpha, thank God you're here. The boys. Ryan, he's better. But Toby. Oh God, Toby," she cried. "They killed him. He's dead."

Hearing the actual words of Toby's death felt like someone had shot him; his gut burned in grief. It wasn't possible. How could he be dead? Both boys were like sons to him. He and Logan had unofficially adopted them when they were just pups, late teenagers really. They'd lost their parents in a territorial fight, and Tristan found them wandering the city streets. He took them into his pack, gave them shelter and food, sent them to school. The other mothers in the pack helped raised them. Pack was like that. It was everyone's responsibility to help raise pups. A parent was never left short of support.

Tristan held Julie, hysterically crying in his arms. He stared at Ryan, praying to the Goddess that it wasn't true. It didn't make sense. Gunshots could seriously damage a wolf, but a shift would surely heal most wounds. It could take several shifts before they were truly back to normal functioning, but most wolves survived.

Filled with rage and sorrow, Tristan stoically shoved his emotions away. He'd deal with it later. Right now, his pack needed their Alpha. The calm in the storm, he'd guide them out of the pain.

"Julie, what happened to Toby? Have you talked with Ryan?" he inquired.

Wiping her tears, Julie sat down again next to Ryan and held his hand. "Toby was shot, multiple times. But I think they may have used a knife," she cried; her voice wavered. "The doctor wouldn't let me see him. Whatever it was, it was awful."

Tristan moved to the other side of the bed, sat in a chair and took Ryan's hand. He stopped and sniffed Ryan's wrist.

"Did you smell it?" he questioned her with a firm voice.

"I know, Alpha. He smells…he smells…"

"Human." Tristan finished her words as she nodded in confirmation. "What the hell happened? We both know he's wolf."

"He took something," Julie replied. "Before you ask, I don't know what it was. He was awake for like a minute and said they'd been at a college party all afternoon. He and Toby took something…a drug."

"This doesn't make any sense. I know my boys; they don't take drugs."

"I know. But what else could it be? Something had to do this to him."

Tristan shook his head in confusion. None of it seemed real. Sensing Logan, he worried they would make it down to the room, given the rules. But then again, a little rule breaking was the least of their problems. Before he had a chance to ask Julie to go get Logan, both Logan and Kalli came into the room.

"Sorry we're late. Traffic was a killer as usual. Had to sneak in here 'cause they said only two people were allowed, so I arranged for a distraction. What is going on with…" Logan's words ended abruptly as he noticed it too. He rushed toward the bed and sniffed. "What's wrong with Ryan? What did they give him? He smells…" Perplexed, Logan ran a hand over Ryan's forehead in concern.

"Human. I know. We smell it too. Julie said he may have taken something," Tristan added.

"Where's Toby?"

"He didn't make it. He's gone."

Logan stumbled toward a chair in shock. "No, no, no."

Julie ran over to Logan and hugged him as they both wept openly.

Anxiety seized Kalli as she came to terms with what must have happened. There was no way in hell someone went from wolf to human without intervention; without CLI. Someone had taken her pills, and that same someone had given them to Tristan's wolves. Someone took the CLI, and used it as a weapon just like she'd imagined in her worst nightmares. Her heart sank in guilt and anger. Like it or not, she had to confess.

"CLI. Canis Lupine Inhibitor," Kalli whispered. "It's why he smells human."

Stunned, Tristan turned to Kalli. *Did she just say she knew why Ryan scented human?* How did she know this? Missing pills. On the balcony. She'd said that they took something from her apartment. His vision tunneled onto her, and for a few seconds, he felt as if he was seeing things through a kaleidoscope. Kalli was involved in Toby's murder?

Before he realized what was happening, he'd sprung out of his seat, growling. Logan jumped in between them, holding up his hands. "Calm down, Tris. Just let her explain," he pleaded.

"You knew about this?" Tristan accused Logan.

"No, I don't know anything. But we need her help. She might be able to help him or at the very least, tell us what the hell is going on."

"By all fucking means, Dr. Williams, which probably isn't even your real name, explain away. I mean, one of our young wolves is dead. And Ryan, here, is apparently human. For once, I'd like the damn truth," Tristan yelled at her.

Both Julie and Logan cringed slightly upon hearing his voice raised. Tristan was consistently calm, even during the most tense discussions or negotiations. But Toby's death had sent him completely off the edge; he was boiling over in anger.

Kalli, unable to deal with the situation on a personal level, reverted back into her professional persona. The only way she could deal with violence or death was to compartmentalize the information, otherwise she'd simply break down in tears, especially knowing it was her formula that had caused this. She straightened her spine, readying to face the Alpha.

"I tried to tell you earlier, Tristan. You know I did. But we…we ended up, you know what happened," Kalli insisted. "Can I look at Ryan? I mean, I need to see him to be sure."

Tristan nodded furiously and gestured for her to move toward the bed. He was pissed at her, and he was pissed at himself for fooling around on the damn balcony. He should have pressed for all of the truth but instead, he was weak. He darted his eyes to Kalli, watching her grab a stethoscope off the wall. She inserted the ear tips and began pulling open Ryan's hospital gown.

"I'm sorry Tristan. So sorry I didn't tell you everything but I was scared. And now," She looked down to Ryan. "Well, you wanted the truth? Here it is…the sad horrible truth. I told you that my parents died, but what I didn't tell you was that I was pack. That's right. My son of a bitch father was wolf, and my mother was human. And I was a lowly hybrid. Cross that. I was a lowly hybrid, who managed to survive abuse day after day. I was the hybrid that the great, almighty Alpha planned to utilize as concubine for the wolves who weren't allowed to breed. I hated that pack and everyone in it. So I ran far and wide. Changed my identity. But it wasn't enough. I needed to be human. Nothing else would do. They'd find me. Excuse me a minute."

Kalli stopped to listen to Ryan's heart. Then she picked up his wrist to listen to his pulse. Tristan and Logan stared at her in disbelief as she continued her confession. "I've been working on the formula ever since I was in grad school, but it wasn't until two years ago that I perfected it. No more shifting during full moons, waking up alone naked in the woods. No more fear of being discovered and dragged back to that hellhole. For once in my life, I could just live quietly with my work and my animals."

Kalli pushed the hair out of her face, and walked over to the other side of the bed. Her voice started to waver as tears brimmed her eyes. "And if I hadn't gone for a walk that day, saved your damn snake, I'd still be living that way. But that wasn't in the cards. The wolves I saw, they're from my old pack; I recognized the faces. As for the pills, someone, I don't know who, knows about my research. It's what they were looking for. They took my spare pills, and it's without a doubt what is running through this boy. But after looking at him, it appears that they didn't give him a full dose. Maybe they slipped it in his drink and he didn't drink it all?"

Kalli pulled the ophthalmoscope off the wall, lifted Ryan's eyelids and examined him. "I'd say, from my experience of taking CLI, he should be able to shift in another two to four hours. It's wearing off already. Whoever gave this to them knew what it was supposed to do. They probably were testing it, wanted to see if he could shift when injured, because that is exactly what this drug does, prevents shifting." Kalli sighed, looking to the exit.

She'd had enough: enough lies, enough violence, enough of pack. But at least it was out in the open; they all knew. And even though she was terrified the wolves from her old pack would find her, the worst thing was how Tristan was looking at her; she couldn't bear it. She feared that he'd never forgive her. Even though she hadn't intentionally set out to hurt him or anyone in his pack, her creation had killed that boy. Sure, it kept her hidden from others who'd see her dead, but now someone out there was using it to kill wolves.

Feeling as if she was going to be sick, she made toward the door. She had to go. She didn't belong here with Tristan or his wolves. After everything she'd told him, she wouldn't be surprised if he loathed her.

Tristan balled his fists at his sides, reeling from her confession. She was a fucking wolf and hadn't told him. He wanted to hate her, yet his wolf wouldn't allow it. But his human side was enraged. He watched in astonishment as she tried to leave the room, without even discussing it. *So not happening, Doctor.*

"And where the hell do you think you're going, Kalli? Is that even your real name?" he sneered.

"I told you that I had to change my identity. I had no choice. They'd find me. But just so you know, Kalli is my real name. Williams isn't, but I'm still the same person inside. And for all intents and purposes, Dr. Williams is who I am," she countered, stifling a sob.

"It's one thing to lie to me, but don't lie to yourself. You aren't human, no matter how much you want it or how many of these pills you take," he spat at her. "I can't talk to you right now. Fine, you want to go; then just go. Get out of my sight. I can't even look at you. Logan, take her to your condo. Move her things."

"I'll just go to a hotel…"

"The hell you will. Listen to me, Doctor, like it or not, I may need you to find the sons of bitches who did this…the fire…Toby's murder," he choked out, trying not to scream. "You're not safe. If anything, you're in even more danger. They know where you live; where you work…I will not lose you." Tristan shook with passion, well aware that he still wanted her badly. Conflicted, he needed space. As much as he hated the idea of her staying with another man, he knew he could trust Logan with his life.

As she realized that Tristan no longer wanted her, Kalli's heart felt like it was breaking into a million pieces. Filled with shame and disappointment, she deserved it, she thought. But, still, how could he send her off to live with another wolf? Logically, she shouldn't have been surprised given how she was raised, and the way the males treated the females. It was just that with Tristan, he seemed so progressive, kind…loving, even. Feeling downcast, she silently accepted that she'd have to move. Why bother arguing? He needed her to help him find the killers. She needed his protection. So she had to stay with Logan. Who else would she stay with anyway?

Raking her fingers through her long hair, she looked at Logan. "I've gotta get out of here. I'll be in the waiting room. Come get me when you're ready." Casting Tristan a sorrowful look, she walked out of the room, fairly certain that he and Logan wouldn't try to stop her. It would cause a scene and she was pretty sure they didn't want that.

Tristan considered going after her, but the doctor entered the room at the same time. Concerned that they already had too many people in the room, he looked to Julie to leave. With a nod, she understood, and left.

The doctor looked to be about forty years old with short, thick curly hair, wearing a traditional white coat with her name embroidered on it. Regarding the two males, she extended a hand to Tristan. "Hello, I'm Dr. Shay. The nurse said she'd filled you in on Ryan's injuries. He's a lucky kid," she commented, looking down at her patient. "Almost bled out, but we got to him before he hit hypovolemic shock, so he's going to make it. Both shots were fairly clean, in and out, but apparently he sat in the alley for quite a bit before someone found him. So we're going to keep him here for a few more hours just as a precaution, then he'll be transferred down to the fourth floor. Once he's released, he'll have to come back for follow-up to have the stitches removed. My biggest concern right now is the risk of wound infection. Even though we cleaned it out, bacterial infections still occur. Do you have any questions?"

"Yes, it is my understanding that anything we discuss needs to be kept in confidence, is this correct?" Tristan asked, already knowing the answer.

"Yes, that's right," she replied.

"I'm going to tell you something, and I don't want you to repeat it, not even to the nurse. Nor do I want it entered into his record," Tristan explained. "I'm not sure how much experience you have with supernaturals, but I'm Tristan Livingston, Alpha of Lyceum Wolves. And this boy, he's mine."

The doctor flushed at the revelation. "Why yes, of course I'm aware that there's others. Those who aren't human. But sir….well, there's no way he's wolf. I just operated on him, so I think I'd know if he weren't human. No, this can't be," she protested.

"Well, Doc. Sometimes things aren't always as they appear." He shot a look at Logan who knew he meant Kalli. "And when that happens, it truly is a bitter pill to swallow. Let's just say that I've come into knowledge that Ryan, here, was exposed to something very dangerous that thwarted both his shifting and his natural healing abilities. Both of which would have prevented him from visiting your fine establishment. We think he's going to shift in a few hours, and we'd like to stay with him until he does.

Afterwards, we're going to walk out the front door."

"Well, I don't know. But I guess if he shifts, then I can't really oppose his release, but I'll need to examine him first," she insisted.

"Thank you for your cooperation. But there's one more thing. That dangerous thing Ryan was exposed to…I need you to keep a tight lid on it until we find out who gave it to him. Tony…Detective Bianchi. We're going to have to meet with him too. He'll back up what I'm telling you. We're looking at a murder."

The doctor nodded solemnly. "Yes, I just spoke with the detective, but as I told him, I didn't see the other boy. He was found dead on the scene. The paramedics said he'd been shot and stabbed quite badly. I'm very sorry for your loss."

"Thank you," Tristan said quietly. The meeting with Jax Chandler couldn't come soon enough. When he found the wolves Kalli had helped to sketch, they'd die a slow death at his hand.

The doctor exited the room, leaving Tristan and Logan. No words could describe the loss of Toby. All that was left to do was to wait until Ryan shifted so they could find out what had happened. How did he even get the drug? He knew Ryan and Toby partied hard, but nothing that most college students didn't do. They never took drugs; he'd scent in a minute if they'd tried. No, someone gave this to them without them knowing, perhaps as Kalli had suggested in a drink or maybe even food.

The vigil was broken as Ryan stirred in his bed. Slowly opening his eyes, he licked his dry lips.

Logan rushed to hold his hand, while Tristan stood on the other side of the bed. He rubbed his hand over Ryan's matted hair, and leaned in to talk to him.

"Take it easy, Ryan. You're safe. We're all here with you," Tristan comforted him.

Tears filled Ryan's eyes. "Toby…he didn't make it," he whispered, weeping silently. "We couldn't shift."

"We know, Ry, we know. Trust me, we'll grieve. And we'll avenge his death. I promise you. But right now, I need to know what happened. Who drugged you?"

"We were at a party. Nothing big. A girl. Lindsey. She asked us if we wanted to take something. You know us, we said no. I swear it," Ryan asserted. His eyes locked on Tristan's. "We stayed for another beer, and left to go home. We walked. We always walk. Two men. Wolves. They had a gun and backed us into an alley. We knew we could've taken them, Tristan. But then we couldn't shift. We tried to run, but our wolves wouldn't come. I hid in a dumpster after I got hit, but Toby…" his voice trailed off as he looked away and closed his eyes.

"You listen to me, Ryan. This wasn't your fault. Someone drugged you.

There's no way you could have known. You need to rest now. Kalli said you'd be able to shift in a few hours. Afterward, we'll get out of here. See…Julie's here. Logan's here. We're all here for you. And when we get home, you know you'll be pawing off the pack mothers; they're never going to let you out of their sight. We'll make it through this."

Lindsay? Wasn't that the name of the girl from Kalli's office? He planned asking Tony to send someone over to UVH to find her. Tristan stood and turned toward the door in an attempt to hide the pain that threatened to rip him in half. Listening to Ryan recount what had happened through guilt-tinged tears killed him. It shouldn't be this way for them. They were only kids, yet someone deliberately went after his pups. Killed Toby. One thing was certain, blood was about to rain down in his city and it would be Lyceum Wolves who shed it this time. There'd be nothing sweet about this revenge, but it would happen.

"Logan, keep an eye on Ryan. I've gotta find Tony," Tristan grunted. He needed to tell him everything he knew about what had happened. There was no way in hell he'd let P-CAP take over the investigation. For all they knew, a human had been shot and killed. But on the off chance they decided to become involved, he'd call Léopold and seek his assistance. As much as he despised Alexandra, he knew he could count on her as an ally.

As he rounded the corner, he caught sight of Tony engaged in an intimate conversation with Kalli. *What the hell?* She nodded her head in agreement to whatever he'd just said to her. Her baby blue eyes, rimmed in red from crying, were focused on the detective.

Without a doubt, Detective Tony Bianchi, Sydney's former homicide partner, was one of the best cops in the city. Tenacious but good natured, the good-looking Italian detective never left a clue unturned. But Tristan could tell by the looks of him, that tonight he'd seen Toby's body. His dark, olive-skinned face appeared to be drawn and his cropped raven hair was no longer carefully coiffed. Like a bloodhound knowing where to find his bone buried deep in the yard, Tony was busy digging for his next lead.

Tristan ground his teeth as Tony put a comforting hand on Kalli's shoulder. She began to cry once again, and he could see that she was hurting too. Tristan wanted to be the man holding her, telling her everything would be all right. Deep down, he also knew that part of the reason she was coming unglued was because of him. Instead of mauling her on the balcony like a sex-starved maniac, he should have let her finish telling him the truth. He'd told her she could trust him, but the minute she'd confessed, he'd laid into her and ordered her to stay with another man. He felt like an asshole, but he could only deal with so many things at once. Coughing loudly, Tristan cautiously approached them.

Kalli scowled at Tristan before turning her back. She couldn't look at him without hysterically crying, and she hated being *that* woman. The woman who was so weak, she'd put all her trust and feelings into a man and now couldn't control her own emotion. She hated being a woman who a man would use sexually and then toss to one of his friends. She hated that she was the woman who'd created the drug that had eventually got Toby killed. Kalli refused to let him see how badly she hurt inside. If he didn't want her, she had to at least salvage what was left of her dignity.

"Kalli," Tristan offered, unsure of what to say to her. He wasn't ready to apologize but at the same time, he needed her. He needed her comfort as much as she needed his.

"I'm getting coffee," she snapped, unable to take another tongue-lashing. She'd spent the last hour telling the detective everything she knew about her past, the people who she worked with, every detail about CLI and how it worked and the names of every wolf she could recall. She didn't know the full names of the wolves she'd helped the artist sketch. She guessed the one was Sato and the other Morris, but wasn't sure. She could, however, remember the name of her old Alpha, Gerald. She'd even told him about everything that had happened to her including the fire, the kidnapping, and her rescue. She'd described in detail what she'd been doing at Tristan's, which involved a brief mention of what had happened on the balcony. Of course she left out the play by play, but she wanted to make sure he understood how she lamented her decision to trust Tristan enough.

Oddly, the detective empathized with her decision, given her past history of abuse. He said he'd too often seen battered women and children and could understand the deep-seeded fear that had been planted in her psyche long ago. Simply telling her to share information that could expose her to her abusers again was not enough to get her to open up about her past. She found it ironic that the one person who seemed to understand her plight was human.

Seeing Tristan as he rounded the corner, she fought back her first instinct which was to run into his arms. Despite his angry words, she didn't want to give up on their budding relationship, which definitely was well rooted into the 'it's complicated' category. At the same time, her healthy sense of self-preservation overrode the need to pursue a man who clearly didn't want her, no matter how incredible he was.

Tony nodded at Tristan. The pain rolled off him like an overflowing river. Even though Tony wasn't wolf, he swore he could feel it. He'd known Tristan for a long time, having been introduced to him by Sydney. Tony regarded him with admiration, as a leader who cared about his wolves and what happened in his city.

"Sorry for your loss, Alpha."

"Thanks Tony. You talk to Kalli?" Tristan inquired, already knowing he had. He just wasn't sure of the extent of their conversation.

"Yeah, she filled me in on everything. It's amazing given all the trauma she's been through," Tony remarked.

"Yeah, I guess she mentioned that Alexandra took her."

"Yeah, she mentioned that, but when I say trauma, I guess I'm referring to the abuse she suffered growing up. She's terrified, but she comes off so composed."

"Detached?" Tristan countered.

"In a sense. If you'd been beat down, told you were going to be tortured for the rest of your natural life, you'd build some walls too. We're talking about survival. Anyway, from her childhood to Ryan's examination, I feel confident that she's told me everything. You, uh, might want to go easy on her." Tony gave Tristan a concerned look.

Tristan inwardly cringed. Just how much had she told him? About what happened between them on the balcony? How he'd yelled at her? How he'd sent her to stay at Logan's?

"Anyway, it's a good thing she's still under your protection. She's sure gonna need it. I understand she was staying with you but now she's staying with Logan?" Tony questioned him, reading between the lines.

Yes, it appeared that she had, indeed, told him everything. Damn.

"Yeah, she's stayin' with Logan tonight." He tried to sound indifferent, but the words tasted like poison as he spoke them aloud. "My entire pack has moved into the new building except for a few wolves. Some have moved to the mountains."

"All right then. Well, I've got some names of males from her old pack. I'll run them tonight. A bulletin was issued of the sketches you sent me. The priority will be upped now that we're looking at murder. Anything else you want to tell me?" He gave him a small smile. "You know, while bearing in mind that I'm an officer of the law."

"Ryan mentioned that he was at a party with a girl named, Lindsay. Could be a coincidence, but Kalli's got an assistant by the same name. She works over at UVH, and she's a college student. Can you check her out?"

"Sure, I mean, we don't know how they even knew she had the CLI. Best guess is that someone at the hospital found out about her research. It's possible the wolves went there looking for Kalli and somehow got mixed up with this, Lindsay. If Lindsay knew about the drug's existence, she could have spilled."

"Yeah, I don't know. It's a long shot but I agree, someone at the hospital must have found out about her research. According to Kalli, she doesn't have much of a social life outside of the hospital and her shelter."

"Anything else?"

"Tomorrow night is the mayor's ball. The following evening we have a summit with Jax Chandler, the New York Alpha. Hoping that it'll be a fruitful meeting. Other than that, there's nothing more I can tell you…officer of the law and all that."

A silent understanding settled between the two men. Tristan was lethal when crossed, as were most supernaturals. Whatever their brand of justice, Tony didn't want to know the details. It wasn't his place to judge their ways; his purpose was to find a murderer. And if Tristan just happened to find the guy before he did, well, then that was all the better in his book.

"Listen, man, we'll do our best to find these sons of bitches. I've made Toby's autopsy a priority. The coroner will start tomorrow morning. I'll be honest, I'm not sure what else she'll find, but the killers may have left a trace. Unofficially, exsanguination from gunshot and stab wounds is listed as COD," Tony speculated.

"I'd like to get his body as soon as possible. Can you text me when he's done? We'll be taking him home. The burial needs to occur as soon as possible," Tristan told him quietly. Home referenced to their mountain compound. While it wasn't often they were forced to bury one of their own, Lyceum Wolves adhered to their own funeral rituals.

"Sure. It'll probably be a couple of days before they'll release the body. Again, I'm real sorry about your wolf. I understand he was in college." Tony extended a hand to Tristan in condolence.

Tristan nodded sadly, shaking his hand. He didn't want to reveal the explosive rage that begged for deliverance. Its time would come, though. Vengeance was coming, and he planned to ride it hard, until every last wolf involved in Toby's death was nothing more than fur and bones.

Chapter Fourteen

After finally getting Ryan settled in Julie's condo, it was nearly three in the morning. Even though shifting had healed Ryan's wounds, it did little to help the emotional scars that cut deep. Instead of having Ryan return to the small apartment he'd set up for the boys, Julie and he agreed that he should stay with her. Despite the fact that she had two younger sisters, it seemed the extra female attention would go a long way toward aiding his recovery.

Tristan had slept in until eleven in the morning; tossing and turning as he tried to resolve his feelings for Kalli and the fact he'd sent her away to spend the night at Logan's. As he sat at the dining room table, drinking coffee and doing work, he couldn't help but notice the emptiness around him. Within a day of her being in his home, he'd grown unusually accustomed to having her around. He smiled, thinking that it didn't hurt that she had a penchant for walking around in her underwear.

Of course, now that he knew her true nature, it didn't surprise him as much. It wasn't as if wolves were exactly known for their modesty. Even if that medicine suppressed her shifting, it couldn't erase the telltale signs that she was wolf. It also now made perfect sense why his wolf wanted her so badly. It was as if he'd been looking at an image, thinking he saw only a woman. But if one looked closer, the wolf was revealed, exposing the optical illusion. Aware of the mirage, he could now see both the woman and the wolf; never again would he be fooled by the trick of the eye.

He tried focusing on his email, noticing that Mira had sent him three different dossiers on potential real estate acquisitions. Tristan considered getting Logan's input before moving forward with the deals. In reality, he knew he could've made the decision himself, but part of him was just looking for an excuse to see Kalli. Unable to resist, he picked up his cell and tapped Logan's number.

"Logan here."

Tristan could barely hear him through the static-filled connection. What did he say? And did he just hear dogs barking? What the hell?

"It's me. Can you hear me?" he asked, sounding like a television commercial.

"Send you a text," was the last thing he heard before the call dropped.

His cell buzzed, alerting him to the text from Logan. 'At animal shelter with Kalli. Bad cell service.'

Where the hell were they? An animal shelter? Goddammit. Did no one listen? He'd specifically instructed everyone to stay home except for essential activities. And Logan was with Kalli at a shelter? Shit. They'd been alone less than twelve hours and already they'd started doing things together? It rubbed him raw thinking about Kalli, sleeping in Logan's bed. He wondered if Logan went to her like he had that first night. Had she bared her beautiful breasts to him? Thoughts of his beta and Kalli nearly drove him mad.

He tapped out an angry response: 'Where r u? Address?'

Tristan had to see her, unsure what he'd say. He was still angry about her lying. But he felt horrible not being around her. The conundrum was killing him. Facing it head on was the only option. Grabbing his helmet, he took off out of his condo, heading down to get his Harley.

From the parking lot, he could hear the barking and mewling. The large industrial warehouse had been converted to a good-sized animal shelter. As he walked into the brightly colored lobby, he noticed the wall behind the receptionist's desk was stenciled in neon paw prints. There was something childlike and fun about the atmosphere. He noted a pile of balls in a basket, with a sign instructing dogs and their would-be owners to 'Take one and play'.

An older woman with grey hair swept up into a bun, manned the desk. "Why hello there! Adopting?" she asked expectantly.

"Not at this time, I'm afraid. I'm here to see Dr. Williams. My friend Logan's here with her," he managed. In awe of the lobby, he couldn't remember ever seeing such an upbeat animal shelter. It was a far cry from the city pound. He knew Kalli co-owned it and wondered if the grandmotherly woman in front of him was her partner.

"Ah yes, we've been expecting you, Mr. Livingston. I'm Sadie. Dr. Kalli and Logan are just around the corner." She unlocked a door and ushered him into the corridor. A large Malamute barked a few times while jumping up to lick his hand. A half wall kept Fido inside of an enormous indoor running and play arena, complete with blue and green playground equipment. Tristan guessed that at least twenty dogs were running and playing, while a young man kept watch, occasionally throwing a ball to them.

As Tristan gave the burly pup a rub on the head, Sadie laughed. "Oh don't mind him; he's just a big baby. We'll find him a forever home one of these days. Come on now, Ace, leave Mr. Livingston be. Go on," she instructed. "Just this way." She pointed to a glass-encased conference room, which looked as if it also functioned as an office. Colorful paintings depicting grass and flowers on the bottom half of the glass, obstructed his view.

"Tris, over here," Logan called, coming out of a room to the left. Cats of all different kinds were silk screened onto the door.

"Hey."

"Mr. Logan," Sadie crooned. "I have a feeling you'll be leaving here with a kitten yet."

He shrugged, giving her a warm smile. "As soon as I get permission from my landlord."

"Okay, then. Well, I'll leave you two. Gotta get back to the front desk." Sadie shuffled down the hallway.

Tristan began to laugh. "Seriously bro? A kitty?"

"Yeah, why not? Can't a wolf get some love?"

"Sure, I'll rush right out and get you that 'Real wolves love cats' t-shirt you've always wanted," he joked.

"So?" Logan asked without stating the real question.

"What?" Tristan replied indignantly.

"Why'd you rush down here, Tris?"

"I missed you." He grinned.

"Yeah, right. You here to see her?"

"Maybe," Tristan admitted, looking over to the dogs.

"You know I respect you. You're my Alpha. We grew up together. We've hunted together. Hell, you know where this is going. Listen, about Kalli…"

"Don't, Logan," Tristan warned.

"Don't what? Tell you to go easy, because I'm going to. Damn, we're all torn up about Toby. But sending her out to me last night. That was cold, man." Logan looked over to the glass, wondering if Kalli could hear them.

"I know. But I needed to get her away from me. You don't get it, Logan. She's driving me crazy. One minute she's submitting to me on the balcony and the next thing I know, she's involved in creating this hideous drug. I was so freakin' pissed. I can't see straight when I'm around her. And now that I know she's wolf…fuck, what am I supposed to do?" Tristan rubbed his eyes with his fist. The more he talked about her, the more agitated he became.

Logan walked over to a sofa that sat next to the office and fell down onto it. He let the back of his head rest on the pillows, staring up at the ceiling.

"Let me tell you what happened last night when I, that's right *I,* took Kalli to *my* home….in *my* bed." He lowered his chin, eyeing Tristan again.

"I can't know, Logan. Don't tell me. What part of 'I can't think straight when it comes to her' don't you understand?" He held up his palms as if that would stop Logan's words from assaulting him.

"I'll tell you what happened. Nothing. Not a goddamned thing. She cried halfway home. Then I had the pleasure of watching her collect her things from your house like someone had kicked her in the stomach. Then, like the jerk I was for listening to you, I showed her into my guest room. And for the next thirty minutes, I heard her crying until she finally fell asleep."

Tristan fisted his hands and turned his back on Logan. As if he didn't feel enough like shit, Logan was forcing him to come to terms with what he'd done.

"Why are you telling me this? I'm the one who told you to take her. I knew there'd be consequences to my order," he bit out.

"This morning," Logan groaned, holding his hand to his heart as if reliving a great memory. "Aw man, do you know how beautiful she is when she wakes up? Prancing around in her underwear as if she's alone? She's totally unaware of what she does to a wolf."

Tristan grunted. Oh he knew how beautiful she was, all right.

"So when she asked me to bring her here, what was I going to do? Her eyes were all puffy, but thank the Goddess she'd stopped crying. She needed to see her animals, so how could I not oblige? It could've had something to do with those pink shorts barely covering her…well, you get the picture. Did I mention that she cooks in her underwear? She says they're pajamas, but they hug her in all the right places." Logan smiled as if he was the cat who ate the canary.

"Enough, Logan. I get the picture. You damn well know that as Alpha, there are times when I'm forced to make difficult decisions. And some decisions that aren't always popular, but that's what leadership is about. I need to think of what's best for the pack. I need to get my head on straight. Toby's dead because of her drug. Her lies," he reminded Logan.

"No, Toby's dead because some asshole out there is attacking our pack. And it's not her. Did she lie? Yes. But I've never known you to be anything but fair and compassionate with your wolves. She needs that part of you, Tris."

Tristan just shook his head. He loved Logan like a brother, but only an Alpha understood the weight of responsibility he carried. He couldn't afford the distraction. He needed her to help catch the perpetrators, nothing more, nothing less.

"Come here," Logan told him, almost instantly recognizing his insubordinate tone.

Tristan cast him a cautionary glare.

"My Alpha," Logan asked, respectfully lowering his eyes. "Tell me that this person, this abused she-wolf, this one right here is a danger. Look at her and tell me that she's a danger to your sanity, to the pack."

Tristan walked over and peered over the painted grass to view Kalli lying upon a carpet, covered in puppies. On her tummy, she was holding one up to her face, whispering endearments while blowing kisses at the furry baby. Two of the little pups were asleep, curled up with their heads on her feet. Wrestling over a rope toy, two others rolled as one in a ball.

Tristan sighed at the sight; his heart flooded with warmth. "She'd make a wonderful mother," he blurted out. As soon as the words left his lips, he cringed. *What the hell?*

Logan coughed, choking at the statement. "Shocked you noticed, let alone just said that out loud, but yes, yes she would."

Kalli could feel his presence without even looking up. She'd skipped her dose of CLI this morning, feeling as if she'd vomit at the sight of it. It was the reason that boy was dead. Being around Tristan was confusing her; thoughts of running wolf flitted around in her mind. She wanted so badly to hate him, to never speak to him after he'd sent her away. But her heart and wolf begged to be back in his arms.

"Hi," she said nonchalantly, not looking up at him as the door opened. She feared she'd start crying again.

"Hey." Goddess, she looked resplendent, puppies and all, but he held himself back.

"Do you want a puppy?"

"Um, uh, I don't think I have the time right now to take one on…" he stammered. Big Alpha male to bumbling teenager within thirty seconds, he thought to himself. This is exactly what she did to him and why he'd needed some space.

"No, I mean, do you want to hold a puppy?" She asked as if she was extending an olive branch. And in many respects she was. This time she'd give him a gift.

"Um, yeah, sure. Where do you want me?" Looking down at her firm bottom, he knew where he wanted to be.

She sat up, sliding her legs from under the warm puppy heads. Reaching over, she gently put a puppy into his big hands.

"His name is Lowell. Don't tell the others but he's my favorite," she whispered as if they could understand her.

"Little wolf?" Tristan smiled, cuddling his black and white pelt. The way she talked to them he was tempted to believe maybe they really did understand her.

She gave him a tiny shrug. "They make me feel better. I know technically they need me. But I need them. They're like children. These guys," She picked up a white one and kissed its furry head. "Their mommy got hit by a car. She didn't make it. So I've been raising them, since they were three weeks old. They're mutts. Beautiful, sweet mutts."

"Kalli, I'm sorry," he apologized softly as he nuzzled the pup. She was right; they did make him feel better, he thought. Or maybe it was the relief he felt, apologizing for his outburst.

Kalli stilled at his words. "It's okay. I was fine at Logan's." She looked away, willing herself not to cry. "I talked to that detective last night and told him everything. I plan on sticking around to help you find who did this to Toby. I won't try to leave…not that I'd be safe anywhere else."

"Thanks. I appreciate it. Tomorrow we've got a big meeting with the New York Alpha. I'll need you to be there."

"Okay," she quietly agreed. The very last thing in the world she wanted to do was be in the company of yet another Alpha. It was as if her self-imposed wolf drought had caught up with her and now she was facing a tsunami of them.

"The other thing is that we need to start working on an antidote to CLI. Regardless of whether we get the wolves who did this, the fact remains that they have some of your pills."

Kalli thought about it for a minute before rushing to speak. "I've got my research still, so I can certainly start on devising an antidote. I'll need a laptop and eventually lab equipment. I've gotta tell you, though, it could take a while to make it. Weeks at best but probably more like a month."

"Whatever it takes. I can get you the things you need. What else?"

"The thing is that there were only around thirty pills in the container that they stole. And honestly, the actual process for creating CLI is pretty complicated. So even though they'll probably break down the chemical composition fairly quickly, it'll be more difficult to duplicate the process with an end product that is the same. The point is that we've got a little bit of time, before they can make more and distribute it. But you should also know that once they figure it out, it's only a matter of time before someone decides to make it into a more functional weapon, like putting it into a bullet or dart for example. It could be honed to effectively thwart shifting if someone really tried," she reasoned.

"Good to know. Well, not really 'good to know', but that gives us all the more incentive to find these guys quickly." Tristan shuddered at the thought of how CLI could be used as a tactical weapon. Not only could wolves use it against each other, it could be used by humans and vamps against wolves as well.

"One last item. Tonight there's a charity function I need you to go to. The mayor's having a gala to raise money for the libraries. Aside from having committed to it months ago, I want whoever's responsible to see you out in public with the pack. It could help draw them out of the shadows." Tristan surveyed the flash of fear that flared in her eyes then left as quickly as it came. His little wolf had grown adept at hiding her emotions. He made a mental note that he'd need to help her with that. She wasn't doing him or herself any favors hiding her feelings.

Her stomach roiled at the thought of going out in public, but she owed him, owed the Lyceum Wolves. And she couldn't help but notice that he didn't say, 'out with him'. He specifically said, 'out with the pack'. Aware of the difference and ripe with anxiety, she reluctantly nodded.

Tristan put the pup down on the floor, picked up the rope toy and waved it in his face. Immediately, the puppy clamped down on the fibers, refusing to let go. Giving the rope a tiny shake, the puppy copied Tristan's motions. Before he knew it, the puppy was growling and shaking it hard, refusing to give up his prize.

"Look at your Lowell, Doc. He's really something," Tristan laughed. "What a tough boy you are," he sang in his best dog voice, making soft growling noises. He smiled broadly, feeling proud the puppy held on so well.

"He likes you," she acknowledged, grinning at the way Lowell ferociously challenged Tristan. There was something about watching the most lethal Alpha on the East Coast play gently with the tiny whelp.

Tristan's face fell into a soft wolfish grin, pinning Kalli with his gaze. "He's an Alpha, Kalli. Look at him holding on tight. He's claiming it, unwilling to share with another wolf. I don't let others take what's mine either."

"Is that right, huh? Takes one to know one? Perhaps that's why I love him so much," she flirted.

"Yes, he definitely isn't sharing. He knows what's his." Tristan continued to maintain eye contact, giving her a sultry smile.

Kalli's breath caught, feeling as if he was looking into her soul. Embarrassed, she lowered her head into a puppy once more. Was he insinuating that she was his? Last night, he'd been so angry, justifiably, but still, he'd sent her to stay with his beta. Maybe she'd misread his intention, but he'd surely pawned her off to his friend. And it wasn't as if Logan was chopped liver. With his thick brown hair, chiseled jawline and lean, muscled body, she was sure the girls flocked to him in droves. But while she found Logan attractive, she wasn't necessarily attracted to him.

With Tristan, however, he lit every nerve she had on end, filling her with desire just about every time she saw him. Even though he was fully clothed, dressed in denim and a black t-shirt, she struggled to resist the urge to devour him on the spot. She reasoned she could skip her meals and lick him head to toe. Shaking her head, she flushed at the thought. Her wolf must be putting these ideas into her mind. But still, she'd have to be six feet under not to want to at least kiss each one of his abs that she'd felt last night. It was as if she'd only had an appetizer, and she was still starving for the whole meal. It wasn't as if they were doing anything remotely sexual; just sitting on the floor, petting dogs. Yet the insane chemistry managed to infiltrate every single one of her carefully constructed emotional shields she'd built last night in Logan's guest room.

She realized, in that second, that there was more to what was going on between them. Not only did she want his apology and forgiveness, she wanted every part of him. The impending feelings threatened to tear her heart in shreds if he didn't return them. But the reality of the situation was that in a single act of not telling him the truth, she'd destroyed the fragile sense of trust they'd erected since they'd met. Sitting on the floor, she could feel it mending, albeit not fixed, but there was an air of openness that hadn't existed before. No more secrets. No more lies. Emotionally, she was bare. He could either make her his or walk away.

Tristan refused to release her from his gaze, watching the conflicting emotions on her face. He could tell she was struggling to hide her arousal, and he loved that even after everything they'd been through the night before, she couldn't conceal her reaction to him. But she'd lied, and well, he'd acted like a complete jerk by sending her to Logan as if she were nothing more than a female to be used by males. Something he knew would cut her to her core, given her past experiences in a pack.

He regretted the action, but was unsure how to proceed. Well fueled in anger the previous night, he'd asked Mira to accompany him to the gala. He justified it by telling himself that he needed Mira with him to field business questions. But as he sat next to Kalli in a room full of puppies, he was second guessing taking Mira. As he contemplated his predicament, his phone alarm went off, reminding him of an important meeting, one he couldn't miss.

"Kalli, I…I'm sorry, I have to go. Got a call to Japan in thirty minutes, and I need to get back to the office," he explained. "I meant what I said. I'm sorry about how I reacted last night. I'm torn up over what's happened to Toby, and it just got out of hand."

"I'm sorry for not telling you the truth sooner. If I had told you, maybe the boys wouldn't have gotten hurt," she responded in a barely audible whisper. As much as she tried to push the pain down, she found herself starting to cry again. A tear ran down her already reddened cheeks; her mouth parted as her tongue darted out to lick her upper lip.

"Chérie, look at me." Tristan cupped her face with one hand and wiped her tear with his thumb. He resisted letting his thumb slide in between her warm pink lips so she could suck his finger. Who was he kidding? He wanted her to suck more than his finger….just the thought of those plump lips, wrapping themselves around the hard length of him sent blood rushing down to his groin. He tried shaking off the dirty images running through his mind. *Don't be a selfish prick, Tris. Get it together.* He had to look away and take a deep breath before continuing. He tried to focus on his words and not the very naughty things he wanted to do to her.

"What happened is not your fault. As for you and I, we'll see, okay? I'm still kind of processing what happened, and I need to be on the top of my game in the next few days. Listen, I'll see you tonight."

Kalli swore he was going to kiss her as he ran his calloused thumb near her mouth. But instead of a kiss, he gently hugged her and stood to leave.

After he left, his words reverberated in her head: 'As for you and I, we'll see, okay?' What was that supposed to mean? They'd almost made love yesterday, and now they were at 'we'll see'. She smiled sadly, wondering if everything she'd been feeling was real or if it was all in her imagination. It sure as hell felt real, but his lack of intention made her wonder if she needed to protect her heart. Emotionally exposed, she could not have felt more vulnerable.

Although playing with puppies blanketed her with love and happiness, a hot shower really helped to relax Kalli's thoughts. It was if she let the stress wash down the drain while resolving to put on her big girl panties. She reasoned that no matter how much her hormones drove her crazy with lust, it'd be in her best interest to let her brain do the talking in the future. Allowing her heart to dictate how she handled the next few weeks in and around an Alpha would only lead to heartache. She was a well-educated, compassionate doctor, and it was about time she started acting like it. Forlorn lovesick teenager wasn't at all working for her. Either Tristan would forgive her and own up to his feelings or he wouldn't. In the meantime, it was time to buck up and get her act together. As the hot spray hit her face, she decided that it was time to snap out of it. Whether she liked it or not, she was stuck living with Logan, while trying to help catch killers.

Exiting the bathroom in nothing more than a towel, she gasped in surprise to find Logan waiting for her. Fixing his hair in the mirror, he turned and gave her a huge smile. She couldn't help but blush as she admired how gorgeous he looked in his tuxedo. While she wasn't generally modest, she felt extraordinarily underdressed, given she was naked under her tiny towel.

Logan looked her up and down. No harm done looking, he reasoned. Tristan was a damn fool for sending her away, and he might as well be the one to reap the rewards. He grew hard watching her nervously pull at her towel that barely covered her breasts. If she turned around, he was pretty sure that he'd be given another show of her firm little cheeks. Her long black wavy hair tumbled down her back in wet curls. Wide-eyed, she started laughing as he spun in a circle, showing off his fancy duds like a model.

"Nice tux, Logan. You're looking good," she commented. "But you do know as much as I love coming out of my bathroom to find a hot man waiting for me, this seems a little awkward." She smiled and went about drying her hair with a towel, wondering what Tristan would think if he came in here this very minute and found her nearly naked with his beta sitting on her bed. He'd probably go ballistic. And he'd deserve it, the still angry part of her thought.

"Hot, huh? Wait until you see my slick dance moves, girl. Fred Astaire, baby," he joked.

"Didn't you tell me that Julie was bringing me something to wear to this Godforsaken ball?" she asked, changing the subject. One could only hope that she'd forgotten and then Kalli would have a valid excuse to bail.

"Ah yes, well, there is something special that was delivered. Not by Julie, though," he affirmed with a wry grin.

She gave him an inquisitive look, wondering what it was and who had picked out the outfit. Walking over to the closet door, she saw an elegant deep red satin gown. Matching pumps sat on the floor.

"This is…it's exquisite. Really, I've never worn anything like this in my life," she exclaimed, admiring it up against her in the mirror.

"Come on now, don't you docs do these shindigs all the time?"

She rolled her eyes at him. "Uh, no way. I'm strictly a working class girl. Did you do this, Logan?"

"No ma'am. It seems you've got yourself a secret admirer. But I've been sworn to secrecy so don't bother asking," he teased with a wink. "And as much as I've enjoyed looking at your fine body in that little towel of yours, we've gotta go soon or we'll be late." He stood and walked over to the doorway.

Kalli approached him, and on her tiptoes, kissed him on the cheek.

Logan put his hand to his face as if he'd been lovingly branded. "What's that for? Not that I mind even one little bit."

"For being such a great person to me after everything that went down last night; for taking me down to the shelter today; for letting me stay here. Lots of things," she bubbled happily, guessing that Tristan had bought her the amazing dress. She returned it to the closet and went back to the dresser to brush out her hair.

"You're welcome, Kalli. You know, you're important to this pack, and to Tristan. Far more important than you even know," he said cryptically.

Kalli smiled, unsure of how to respond. Whatever he was referring to was a mystery to her.

"Not so sure about that, but I swear I'll do my best to help," she promised.

He turned to leave her, and looked over his shoulder. "Oh, and Doc. Don't forget to look in the box there on the dresser. There's something special there that will look great on you."

He wanted to tell her that Tristan had brought everything over for her, but it wasn't his place to do it. All in good time, he thought, but hoped that he'd tell her soon. It could prove to be a long, miserable evening if Tristan didn't address his feelings for her before they left. As Logan walked down the hallway, he prayed things would go smoothly.

Chapter Fifteen

The limo ride over to the Four Seasons had been nothing short of a nightmare. From the minute Tristan picked up Mira, she'd been peppering him with questions about Kalli and their relationship. In addition to the nonstop interrogation, she seemed overly affectionate, which only meant one thing: trouble.

It didn't help that he couldn't stop thinking about Kalli, since he'd left the shelter. His anger had dissipated after reflecting on her reasons why she'd been afraid to tell him. It wasn't as if he didn't know how tough things used to be in wolf packs. Forced matings and brutality used to be commonplace, but progressively, most packs had given up old practices. Both he and Marcel had consciously led their packs with authority and fairness, refusing to live barbaric existences. Burning with rage, he wished he could have prevented the abuse Kalli had suffered at the hands of wolves. It was no wonder she'd been afraid of him and Logan.

Intrigued, he'd found his attraction to her only grew deeper after talking with her at the shelter. Even though she was vulnerable, she still wanted to help him. Yes, she needed his protection. But she could have gone to the police and asked for protection. He was certain Tony would have given her sanctuary. And he returned the favor by sending her to Logan, as if they hadn't shared intimate moments. He saw the hurt in her eyes, knew she'd been crying because of him, yet aside from apologizing, things felt unresolved. He felt empty, as if he hadn't said what he needed to say. Treating the request for her attendance at the gala like a business transaction, he'd neglected to mention that he was taking Mira, something he normally wouldn't give a second thought to doing. But his connection to Kalli pulled strongly at his heart.

On the way home, he decided he needed to try to fix the mess he'd made of things. Even though cancelling with Mira wasn't an option, he'd be damned if he didn't straighten things out with Kalli during the gala. After his conference call, he'd visited with Ryan, happy to see that he was taking advantage of the female attention he'd been receiving at Julie's. Thankfully, he seemed a little better emotionally and was even asking about getting back to work. While he was there, he consulted with Julie about the best place to procure female attire for the gala. At some point during his spree, he considered that he must have gone mad, to be shopping for a woman. And perhaps he had. He wasn't usually the type to shop for himself, let alone someone else. In an effort to make amends, he sought to do something special for Kalli; to make it up to her even if his words hadn't soothed her hurt feelings. If he was truthful with himself, he'd just admit that he wanted every man in the room tonight to know she was his, that she was wearing something that he'd given her.

The cynical part of him, who had invited Mira out of anger, claimed the purchases were nothing more than business expenses. Kalli was a means to an end. A decoy. A lure. Whoever was targeting him was keeping tabs on his pack, so he'd give them something to think about. They had the pills, but they didn't have the research. He wanted them to know that he knew what they knew and was coming for them. A public show of confidence, in the wake of the death of one of his wolves, spoke of his strong constitution and power in this city. His wolves were not sheep, awaiting slaughter. They were wolves, out in the open, strong with their pack and ready to strike for the kill.

While it was true that he did want her at the gala for all those reasons, the primary reason was that he was fascinated with her. Secrets out of the way, he craved her touch, her kiss. Tonight she'd be his in every sense of the imagination.

"Tristan, do be a dear, and pour me a Grey Goose. This traffic is horrendous tonight," Mira commented, jolting him from his thoughts. They'd come to a screeching halt in the evening gridlock.

Tristan poured and then handed her the tumbler. This was going to be a helluva night, he thought. The only saving grace would be seeing Kalli in the incredible dress he'd procured.

"Thanks." She slowly sipped the warm liquor, wondering how long she'd actually have to work. "So anything I need to know about tonight? Parker and Mainer will both be there. Both have passed clearances, so I'm going to work them tonight, try to get a feel for whether or not they'll consider selling their waterfront properties." She rubbed a hand on Tristan's thigh, coming precariously close to his crotch.

Tristan gently grabbed her wrist and placed it back into her lap. "Not tonight, Mir," he warned. "And yes, I'd appreciate it if you'd chat up the mayor as well to see if there are any big deals or new players in town. He likes you and seems to have loose lips when in your company. Gotta keep an eye on the competition."

"No problem, but you owe me a dance," she flirted.

"We'll see," he hedged.

She pursed her lips, and rolled her eyes. "Seriously, Tristan? What's going on? This night should be fun. And by fun, I mean we eat, drink, dance and then leave here and dance some more, like naked in the bedroom. You, me, maybe Logan, although he's got his hands full with the human."

He glared at her.

"Oh sorry, excuse me, hybrid, whatever that means. Come on, even you have to admit that if it looks like a duck, walks like a duck, quacks like a duck…well, you get the picture," she sniffed.

"She's wolf. She just doesn't know it yet," he informed her.

"Yeah right, good luck with that."

"I don't need luck, chére. I'm Alpha, and she's all mine," he drawled.

Mira sat perfectly still, tensing every muscle in her body. "Are you fucking kidding me? Did you just say what I thought you said?"

"Watch your language, Mir. Geez," he sighed. "I'm not going to repeat what I just said, because it won't make a difference to you. You need to accept this, because eventually she will be part of Lyceum Wolves. I know you're not crazy about it when I date other women, but jealously is so not becoming."

Tristan expected that Mira would freak out when she found out he was going to bring Kalli into the pack. It wasn't as if he planned to ask Kalli right away to join, because he didn't want to scare her off. The more he considered the situation, the more he embraced the idea of keeping the lovely doctor in both his bed and his life. He wasn't sure how it would work out or if they'd last, but without a doubt, she belonged in his pack, with him. Last night, he'd been so close to making love to her on his balcony. Even though he swore he needed the truth from her, he couldn't be sure that if Logan hadn't interrupted them that he wouldn't have taken her anyway.

The electrifying connection between them was unyielding. And his wolf wanted her like he'd wanted no other. It scared Tristan, because deep down he knew the animal within would never be satisfied until he had her screaming his name, submitting to him in pleasure again and again. It conjured up all kinds of thoughts. Goddess almighty, he'd told Logan today that she'd make a good mother, and when he'd said that, he wasn't just thinking of anyone's kids. He was thinking of his own. He shook his head, laughing inwardly. Logan must have thought he'd lost his damn mind. He tried to stifle the longing, attempting to negate how deep his feelings ran.

Mira shifted in her seat, aware that he was thinking yet again of that stupid woman. Clearly he had a screw loose, she thought. "I cannot believe you'd even consider seriously letting that mongrel into our pack. After everything that's happened? Ugh. You're leading with your dick not your head," she accused.

Tristan straightened in his seat, putting distance between himself and Mira. It was true they were friends, but there was a limit to how much nonsense he'd endure, even from her.

"Mira," he growled loudly. "Knock it off. Kalli belongs with me. Do not antagonize her or me this evening. Am I clear? If you insult me again, there will be consequences." He was done discussing his love life with her. If she didn't get where he was coming from, then that was too bad, because frankly it didn't matter. As Alpha, he would do what he wanted. She needed to move on and get over it.

Mira hadn't been happy about Sydney either, but she'd survived it. But this was different; Kalli was wolf. The idea of another female wolf replacing her in his bed, let alone his heart, was driving her abhorrence. He knew it would come to a head, but tonight was not the time. She'd better curb her nasty tone, or she'd be punished. He wasn't beyond admonishing her publicly just to prove the point.

"Look, here we are. Thank the Goddess we can get out of this car," he breathed in relief.

To say Kalli had been disappointed when she found out that Tristan wasn't accompanying her to the gala would have been an understatement. The fact that he was taking Mira with him only compounded the situation, curtailing any lofty dreams she'd held about pursuing their relationship any further. If someone had taken a fire hose and sprayed her down, her hopes couldn't have gotten anymore dampened. The second Logan told her, she considered stomping back into her room, tearing off the dress and jumping into bed under the covers. But regardless of her previous lie, she was generally a woman of her word. She'd told him she'd go so she'd do it, even if she spat tacks the entire time.

As she and Logan advanced into the grand ballroom, the lull of conversation was accented by the orchestra playing Bolero. Arm in arm, they glided into the sea of attendees, joining the upper echelon of Philadelphia society. There were so many people, drinking, dancing and conversing, Kalli failed to see the purpose of their attendance. No one would even notice her.

Logan's chest puffed out slightly, honored at having such a beautiful date. When she had come into the living room earlier in the night, he'd nearly fallen onto the floor. She looked gorgeous in her form-fitting, sleeveless satin gown. The deep red fabric hugged her entire body from her breasts to her calves; a sash tied into a bow accentuated her small waist before falling into a long train. Her upswept curly raven hair gracefully displayed the lovely diamond stud earrings he'd delivered for Tristan.

Kalli had been beaming, right up until the moment he'd explained that Tristan wasn't coming with them. At the news he was going with Mira, her mood flattened. No tears marred her perfectly applied makeup, yet her tightly drawn lips and hurt eyes revealed her swirling emotions. Logan wished Tristan had just broken his date with Mira, given his extraordinary shopping spree during the afternoon. While she was showering, Tristan had slid into her room unnoticed, bringing her dress and shoes. He had given

Logan the earrings, telling him to make sure she wore them, and then made him swear not to tell her. Logan had tried talking him into taking Kalli, but Tristan insisted that he and Mira had business to attend to during the gala.

After essentially calling him out as an ass, Tristan had torn out of his apartment. Logan had been on the receiving end of Mira's tantrums, so he understood why Tristan didn't want to break the date. Mira would have been fit to be tied if Tristan had dumped her at the last minute. Tristan also persevered with his main excuse for not taking Kalli, which was that he was unable to concentrate on business around her. While that may have been entirely true, Logan was finding it hard to concentrate as well. Tristan knew damn well that he needed to make things right with Kalli. A few puppy hugs were hardly enough to mend fences.

In Logan's opinion, they needed to either talk or fuck. Whichever would do just fine as long as they'd get it over with so things could progress. Logan had silently congratulated himself when he'd heard she was part wolf. His visions made complete sense now. Still, Tristan needed to learn of his mate on his own timeline. As much as it killed him, Logan refused to interfere.

Logan glanced over to Kalli as they made their way through the crowd. The opulent ballroom was overwhelming and magnificent at the same time. He could tell that Kalli felt as if she was balanced upon a ball and could come crashing down any second.

"You're okay," Logan reassured her, patting her arm.

"Thanks. I just didn't know what to expect. Do you all go to these things often?"

"Every now and then. Tristan donates a lot of money, and the parties serve a business purpose. Lots of current and prospective clients to talk to. That's probably what he's doing now."

"Yeah, right. Business, I'm sure," she commented sarcastically.

"He really is working, Kal. But I have a feeling he won't quite be himself until he sees you. Come this way." He steered her toward the bar where he ordered two glasses of champagne.

Securely leaning against the heavy mahogany counter, Kalli turned to people watch. Her breath caught at the sight of Alexandra coming straight toward her. She grabbed Logan's arm, squeezing so tightly she'd thought she'd nearly drawn blood. *What was she doing here?* Tristan hadn't warned her. Like a missile approaching a submarine, it was too difficult to maneuver out of the line of fire. Too late, she thought, steeling her nerves.

"Ah mouse, I see you've landed the beta. Well done, I'm sure," she sneered.

Fear and hate washed over Kalli's face; a bright red flush rose to her cheeks. Alexandra's jibe was the last straw that broke the camel's back, sending Kalli spiraling into an unavoidable outburst. Having still not taken the CLI, her wolf lunged. A low growl emanated from within her, one she didn't even want to restrain. Her beast wanted out as the rage spilled forth at the vampire.

"Back. Off. Bitch," Kalli spat at her loudly enough so her voice was audible to the surrounding guests. "That's right, look around to see who's looking. You'll notice I don't give a damn who sees or hears me, given that this is the first and probably last time I'm invited to one of these things. I'm telling you right now, stay away from me or that silver carving knife over there in the roast beef will be the last thing you see before I slice your throat."

Alexandra gasped, astonished at Kalli's eruption. Logan watched with curiosity, surprised at how effectively she'd put the socially conscious Alexandra in her place. Embarrassing her at a public function was nearly a fate worse than death to Alexandra, who loved more than anything to be a 'who's who' in Philadelphia.

"Ah, I see the mouse grows her fangs. Hanging out with the wolves is doing that to you, I suppose." She rolled her eyes in disgust. "Very well, no need to get all riled. Just thought it polite to say hello, but I can see you're not ready to make nice. Ta-ta!" she sang, seething in retreat. Waving to the mayor, she turned and crossed the room as if the ugly incident had never occurred.

Tristan froze at the sound of a growl. *What the hell?* This was a mixed function, humans and supes. There was no growling at charity galas. Which one of his wolves was causing a ruckus? Quickly scanning the room, he searched for the owner of the snarl. Within seconds, he caught sight of Kalli laying into Alexandra. Whatever she said must have caused the bloodsucker to flee.

Stunned by her beauty, he could barely breathe. Goddess, the woman was spectacular. The fiery red gown clung to her in all the right places, and he noticed a small smile grow on her angelic face, presumably pleased that she had castigated Alexandra. He needed to get to her, hold her. As he rushed across the room, Mira stopped him with a hand to his arm. She gestured toward an elusive client standing to her left.

Logan laughed, seeing Kalli triumph over the demon spawn who ran the vampires. "Hey girl, I hate to point it out, but man you laid her out…and that growl. What was that?"

"Dance with me, Logan," Kalli declared, needing to move.

"Your wish is my command."

They crossed the floor, and Logan swept her into his arms. As amazing as Logan looked, she yearned for Tristan. She could feel he was close. As the music grew louder in her ears, she swayed along to the classical beats, hyper-aware of his presence. Leaning her head on Logan's shoulder, she finally spied Tristan near the buffet, surrounded by Mira and a short bald man.

His eyes caught hers, and her heart started to race. She wasn't sure whether it was his pensive expression or aggressive stance, but she could clearly sense he was agitated. Logan spun her, and she lost his eyes only momentarily, then caught them once again. His predatory gaze electrified the room, sending goose bumps over her skin. As he stalked toward them, her breathing hitched. Like a rabbit alert to the wolf, she froze save for the mindless dance steps she made while blindly following Logan. As Tristan came upon them, she forced herself to face him directly. Larger than life, Tristan was sophistication etched in dripping sexuality. His dominance was apparent to every man, woman and supernatural in the room; there'd be no denying him.

Even Logan stopped dancing to respect his Alpha. Lowering his eyes in submission, he bowed slightly. "Thank you for the dance," he whispered, releasing her.

Before she had a chance to say a word, Tristan wrapped a hand around her waist, pulling her tightly to him so they pressed together. She could feel his barely restrained erection nudging her belly. Suppressing a moan, she felt herself grow wet. She clenched her thighs hoping to hide her arousal; every supernatural within fifty feet would know of her excitement.

"Don't," Tristan ordered.

"Don't what?" she managed to ask.

"Don't try to hide it. Your delicious scent."

"But they'll know I …" Kalli's words trailed off as she lost her train of thought. God, he felt incredible.

"I want them to know. I want them all to know you're mine."

"But I thought…I mean you came with her." Her eyes darted to Mira.

"Business only, nothing more. Still, I'm very sorry I didn't bring you with me. Clearly I was an idiot to leave you alone with my beta. Every man in this room is looking at you, Kalli."

"No," she denied, shaking her head.

"Yes. And they should. Because you're magnificent. Everything about you from that alluring dress I bought you to your sexy growl. My Goddess, do you know what you do to me? Feel it," he whispered, grinding his groin against her.

"Tristan," she breathed. She was on the verge of orgasm from just dancing with the man. She couldn't imagine what would happen if they made love.

"Did you enjoy dancing with Logan?

"What? Logan?"

"Yes, Logan. Did you enjoy having your sweet body pressed to his?"

"Oh God, Tristan."

"It's all right, Kalli. Did you find it arousing? Tell me the truth."

"Another test?" she sighed.

"Truth?"

"Okay yes, but he's not…he's not you. No one I've ever met in my life is like you," she admitted.

"Ah, see how easy it is to tell the truth, ma chérie? Perhaps you'd like to explore two men at once?" he teased with a sexy smile as if he'd thoroughly enjoy it.

She blushed, not denying it.

"Someday we'll explore that little kink of yours, but tonight you are mine. In fact, I think you'll be mine for quite a long time."

"Confident, huh, wolf?"

"Would you ever expect anything less?"

He spun her around, continuing to brush against her. Tightening the grip around her waist, he ran his palm up her arm to her neck, until he reached her face. Caressing her cheek, he ran his thumb across her lower lip. "I want you so much, Kalli. I'm so sorry for everything. I shouldn't have sent you to Logan's. I was angry, but damn, I need you."

She groaned and threw her head back, publicly baring her neck to him. Submission, truth, she'd give it to him all right. But what he needed to learn was that he was hers as well, and after tonight she had no intention of letting him go.

Chapter Sixteen

The sight of her submission plunged Tristan over the edge. "We're leaving. Now," he urged, leaving no room for disagreement. Gathering her into his arms, he ushered her off the dance floor while Logan smirked at the sight and Mira glared. Within seconds, they'd reached the perimeter of the room. Tristan shoved open a door which led to a bridal lounge, and pulled Kalli inside, hastily locking the door. Tristan couldn't wait; he needed her now.

Without words, he captured her lips in an all-encompassing kiss. Kalli wrapped her arms around his neck, feverishly sweeping her tongue into his mouth, as he did hers. Starved, the passionate kiss only further ignited their arousal.

"Dress. Off now," Tristan ordered through their lips.

"Um. Yes. Zipper. Side," she agreed breathlessly.

Reaching downward, he deftly unzipped the dress until it pooled onto the floor.

"Aw chérie, you're so gorgeous." His lips quickly moved to suck and bite at her neck.

"Yes," she cried, as she threw her head back against the wall, lost in the feel of his mouth all over her skin. She panted wildly, anticipating where he'd touch her next.

"Baby, I can't wait. I need to be in you," he grunted. Goddess, she was so exquisite that he didn't know what to touch first. As his lips moved to her pink areola, he sucked hard, while massaging the smooth skin of her bottom. Moving his fingers around to the rim of her thong, he gripped it, ripping it from her body. Palming her torso, he slid his hand down her belly until his fingers brushed over her mound. Stroking up and down, he slipped his middle finger into her soft lips, finding her center of pleasure. Unrelenting, he pressed his thick digit into her hot sheath, and then followed it with two. He wanted to go slow, but lost in the moment, he pressed in and out, bringing her close to release.

"Oh my God, Tristan, please, it feels so good," she cried. "Fuck me, please."

Unable to wait any longer, he unzipped his pants, releasing his rock hard shaft. He stroked himself, while continuing to work magic with his fingers. "I can't wait, baby. You ready?"

"Yes!" she screamed in frustration as she felt him leave her warmth. He spun her around so she was facing the wall. She was so close to coming, feeling as if she'd come apart any second.

Tristan cuffed her wrists in one hand, flattened her palms against the door and spread her legs with his other hand, bending her over slightly, so he could see into her.

"Ah Kalli, you're so wet. So ready," he panted, sliding his finger over the crack of her bottom until he found her wetness. "I want to be gentle, but I need you fast. You're so…" Before he'd finished his sentence, he'd thrust himself all the way into her tight channel.

"Yes! That's it! Oh God!" Kalli screamed. She didn't care if every last person in the ballroom heard her.

"Fuck, Kalli, your pussy is so tight. So very, very tight. Are you okay, chérie?" As badly as he wanted to take her, Tristan was not a selfish lover.

Kalli could swear she felt herself stretch; the pain subsided within seconds, and she needed more. "Please, don't stop. I need…I need…" She was thrashing her head. She was so close, but she needed him to move.

Tristan began pumping in and out of her, slowly at first, building the rhythm. Soon he was pounding against her, his balls slapping against her ass. He reached around to caress her breast, but could sense she was on the edge of coming. Damn, he really wanted their first time to last longer, but the intensity more than made up for the time. With his thumb and forefinger, he pinched her nipple.

"Yes, more," she demanded. Reaching behind her, she grabbed a fistful of his hair.

Encouraged by her roughness, Tristan reached round with his other hand to touch her. Finding his prize, he brushed her clit, lightly at first, and then he increased the pressure.

Kalli felt as if she was out of her own body. She relished the feel of his cock slamming into her. Her body was on fire; his hands were everywhere. But when he increased the pressure on her sensitive nub, she splintered into delirium as an orgasmic wave washed over her. Shaking in release, Kalli shouted his name so loud she swore the people in the next building would hear her.

Tristan saw stars as her pussy tightened around him. He came hard, erupting inside her. He heard her calling his name, but it was as if he was sucked into a vortex of pleasure from which there was no escape. Pulsing into her, he resisted the urge to bite her smooth neck. Goddess, but he wanted to mark her. Make her his, not just now but forever. His wolf howled in ecstasy, begging to mate her. Tristan tried to ignore it. It couldn't be. It wasn't true. It couldn't be. Shoving the agonizing need aside, he resisted the impulse.

"Kalli, baby, are you okay?" He'd wanted to be gentle their first time but seeing her on the dance floor drove him into a wanton frenzy, craving her more than air. He hoped he hadn't scared her by their amazing yet animalistic tryst.

"God yes. That was amazing. Please take me home…so we can go again," she added, giggling, her forehead pressed against the door.

Tristan laughed a low sexy laugh. "My little wolf, you want more, huh?"

"I'm not all wolf," she reminded him. She didn't want to spoil the mood, but she was acutely aware of how others would view her hybrid status.

"You're mine. I don't care what you are," he assured, pulling out of her. He returned himself and zipped, then turned her around, anxious to see her flushed expression, the one he'd put there. "That's what's important, you know."

He lovingly cupped her face; he could see right through her anxieties. What he'd told her was true. He didn't care whether she was hybrid; he just wanted her to be true to her nature. He wanted her to feel safe, protected and loved enough to revel in her own skin.

"You're beautiful after you make love," he commented absently. His chest constricted at the thought of ever losing her.

She blushed, still engrossed in the afterglow of the moment. As her skin cooled, she was reminded that she was nude. "You're quite dashing yourself there, but this is hardly fair. You're completely dressed and me…well." She laughed and gestured to her naked body. Donning her gown, she quickly zipped it. Giving up on her now mussed updo, she pulled out the pins and sexily shook out her curls, combing her fingers through her hair.

"Wonder how fast that limo can go?" He teased. "I'm thinking that I can't wait to get you in bed so we can 'go again' as you put it".

She shot him a look, feigning shock.

"Hey, you're the one who suggested it. And this wolf aims to please," he winked.

"Well then, if you are asking, I bet it can go really, really fast," she purred, leaning in to kiss his cheek.

"Let's go home, ma chérie," Tristan suggested, hugging her to his heart. His home was now her home, and he realized that he didn't want it any other way.

After sneaking out the back entrance, Tristan held Kalli nearly the entire ride home. She'd fallen asleep in the car after their intense lovemaking, and he found it fascinating how enjoyable it was to simply watch her at rest. When the limo arrived at Livingston One, he easily cradled her in his arms, lifting her out of the car and walking into his private elevator. By the time they reached their floor, her eyes fluttered as she awoke. Smiling, she ran her hand down his cheek along his jawline.

"We're home? Oh my, now this is service," she teased with a yawn.

"I like the sound of that," Tristan replied, growing accustomed to the space in his heart she'd taken.

"What?"

"The sound of your voice calling my condo home. And don't tell Logan I said that. He'll call me soft."

"My Alpha, there is nothing soft about you," Kalli flirted, running the palm of her hand down his abs.

"You're insatiable, and I do like it." He softly kissed her warm lips, gently, in stark contrast to their kiss in the hotel.

Slowly separating from their embrace, they held each other's hands, both in awe of the emerging connection. The attraction wasn't just physical, as perhaps Tristan had hoped; it was more than that. Both Kalli and Tristan stood in the foyer, unable to articulate the visceral gravitation drawing them together. Cognizant of the overwhelming emotion brewing, Tristan broke contact and waved for Kalli to follow him down the hallway.

"Come with me," he grinned, gesturing her toward the guest room she'd previously occupied. "I've had your things moved back in while we were at the gala. Of course, I'd much rather have you in my bed from now on."

Kalli could hardly believe that he'd done this while they'd been away. The man was a force of nature.

"Confident, much? How did you know I'd want to come back?" she teased.

"Confident is my middle name, baby. And of course you'd come back. What girl can resist my southern charm?" he drawled.

"Charm? Is that what you call what happened on that dance floor, huh?" She raised an eyebrow at him.

"What happened between us…" He instantly came up behind her, running the palms of his hands up her belly to rest just under her breasts until he heard her release a small gasp. "That, my little wolf, is raw sexual energy between a man and a woman. It's unstoppable, you know. A crime to even try. And there's more where that came from. Much, much more."

Kalli felt her head fall backwards onto his shoulder. His sexy voice, laced with pure seduction, sent her reeling. But before she could completely set herself at ease, he stepped back toward the door. Damn, the man was unsettling. Yet again, he had her so excited she felt as if she was walking a high wire.

"Go ahead and freshen up. I'm gonna go get a bottle of wine. Meet you in my room." He wagged his eyebrows at her.

Kalli released a deep breath that she wasn't even aware she'd been holding. She was beginning to realize what it meant to be Alpha. It was as if he could do almost anything. He was so sure of himself and everything he did. Yet instead of being overtly overbearing, Tristan's flair for humor sparkled through the dominance. And like a cat drawn to a Christmas tree, she simply couldn't resist playing with the ornaments.

After going to the bathroom and brushing her hair, she removed her shoes with a groan.

"Sore? Why don't you let me kiss it all better?" Tristan leaned on the doorjamb.

Kalli nearly fell off the bed in surprise. He was fast and stealthy. *Sneaky wolf.*

"I think I might need to put a bell on you," she teased as she struggled to stand up without looking terribly clumsy. It was the best she could hope for; graceful was no longer an option.

"Sorry chérie, wolves don't do bells. 'Fraid you'll have to use those wolf senses that the Goddess gave you, but we'll discuss that later. Come with me. I've got something for you."

The master bedroom wasn't exactly how Kalli had imagined it would be. In contrast to his uber-masculine, sometimes bad boy image, his bedroom was warm and inviting. Blonde bamboo flooring contrasting with Tuscan tanned walls, contributed to the sensation of a wide open space, conjuring thoughts of running through a moonlit, golden wheat field. A king sized, antiqued mahogany four poster bed with white linens commanded attention; intricate carvings adorned its long pillars. Fire danced in the gas fireplace, apparently appreciative of the soft zydeco music filtering throughout the room.

"Wow. This is just…it's beautiful. Like it belongs in Homes and Gardens beautiful."

"Thanks. Luckily since it was a new building, I was able to customize everything to my liking before we moved in."

"You designed this?"

"Why yes. There's more to me than my smooth dance skills, you know." He winked.

"Hmmm…dance skills, huh? Is that what public seduction at a charity event is called these days?"

"Baby, you ain't seen nothin' yet. Come," he directed.

As they entered the master bath, Kalli let out a sigh of amazement. Another gas fireplace blazed to life with the flick of a switch. It gave light to the spectacular bathroom. Floor to ceiling windows exposed the night sky, which enhanced the subtle lighting. The oversized Jacuzzi nestled in the corner, awaiting them.

Tristan walked over and started the water. Sprinkling in soft lavender flakes, he continued preparing the space by lighting large pillar candles which surrounded the tub.

Kalli stood speechless. She'd never known a man like him in her entire life. "Alpha, you are something else," she managed, having lost all ability to articulate her astonishment.

"Well of course I am, chérie," he joked as he proceeded to pour two glasses of wine and set them on a restored trunk that served as a table. "You expect less?"

"I've just never…never…well no one has ever done this kind of thing for me," she croaked, unable to finish. Struggling to conceal the bubbling emotion surging in her throat, she wiped away a single tear.

Tristan regarded her. So strong and beautiful, yet she was incredibly fragile. The knowledge that someone had once abused her enraged him. It was no wonder that she tried so hard to swallow her feelings. He couldn't imagine that she'd never had someone treat her with kindness, the sort of kindness that was done out of a person's heart, unconditionally, without anything expected in return.

"Come over here, Kalli," he ordered in a soft voice.

She complied, still taking in her surroundings.

"You're way overdressed, do you know that?"

"As are you," she countered.

"Well, then," Giving her a closed grin, he silently indicated his intent. He reached over to her side, finding the hidden zipper he'd made himself familiar with earlier in the evening, and pulled downward. As her dress dropped to her ankles, she reached for his collar.

Stark naked, she slowly pulled at the silken fabric of his tie, taking care to unknot it, and then tossed it on the floor. She gave him a sizzling smile as she unbuttoned each tiny shirt button. His cufflinks clanked to the floor just before she removed his jacket and shirt. The man looked like a Greek god, she thought as she placed butterfly kisses on his bared abs.

Keeping her spine perfectly straight while maintaining his eye contact, she knelt to the floor, unbuckling and unzipping. His erection sprang forth as his trousers fell to the floor. Without touching his newly exposed skin, she continued undressing him, removing his shoes and socks.

Tristan tensed in arousal, watching Kalli slink down his body, slowly stripping him. Her warm breath teased his rigid thick cock. But he was mostly fascinated by the clouds of passion that lurked within her eyes. While most people didn't dare look him directly in the eyes, she did so with reckless abandon, challenging him to come to her.

As much as he wanted her warm lips wrapped around the length of him, he first needed her to feel loved. After the rough way he'd taken her earlier, in an alcove of a ballroom, nonetheless there was nothing he desired more at the moment than to simply care for her.

"Come, Kalli," he breathed, ignoring his pulsing need. Content with her compliance, he led her to the steaming water, and shut off the spigot.

Kalli allowed him to help her into the bath. She'd been so close to swallowing him whole, while kneeling before him. The scent of his masculinity enticed her, driving her craving to lick every inch of his body. But at his words, she acquiesced, allowing him to lead her into the heavenly vessel that awaited them. He always seemed to know what was best. *Was he ever wrong?* The question spun through her head as she relaxed, submerging into the sublime paradise. It was just what she needed, and he knew it. She found herself staring at him, wondering how he knew just about everything.

He quickly followed her into the bubbles, but lounged into the opposite side. As if sensing her impending protest at the lack of contact, he tugged on her feet, as his feet rested on either side of her hips.

Kalli gasped, slipping deeper into the tub.

"Give me those pretty feet." He began to inspect her perfectly pedicured, metallic blue painted toes. "You think too much."

"What?" she muttered.

"I can see you thinking, chérie. Whatever it is, you just need to accept it." He smiled knowingly. Rubbing her insoles, he was rewarded with a grateful moan. "You ladies with those high heels. As much as I enjoyed taking you from behind with you wearing nothing but stilettos, and damn you were hot by the way, I wouldn't last five minutes in those torture chambers."

Kalli laughed. "Hmm…somehow I think you'd manage it. After the past couple of days, I'm wondering what exactly you can't do?"

"I'll be happy to teach you my tricks."

"I just bet you would. Something tells me that I'd enjoy your lessons." She brushed one foot over his thigh playfully.

"The secret is taking advantage of all life gives you," he mused.

"Work hard. Play even harder?"

"Something like that. But it's more. Take you, for instance. I've thought long and hard about why you took those pills. But it's deprived you of your nature."

She quietly listened.

"Tell me about South Carolina, Kalli."

"I told you most of it. You know how it is in a pack. You're not just raised by your parents. My mom, she'd somehow managed to live in that hellhole. My Dad was verbally abusive from as far back as I can remember, but Mom was the one who protected me. When she died…I was alone. The Alpha, Gerald, he was nothing more than a bully. And by the time I was sixteen, my body was starting to look less like a child's. So I guess that was his cue to send for me one night. Of course, I went, because who says no to the Alpha?" Kalli quieted, as if she was reliving the horrifying experience.

"Did he rape you?"

"No, thankfully. He grabbed for me, ripped my shirt off, tried to maul me…but I fought him. I managed to grab one of those old-fashioned phones he had sitting on his desk; smacked him in the head with it. Of course, that earned me a good backhand. And that's when he informed me of my 'role' in the pack. Guess he didn't want me tainting his precious bloodlines. A few days later, I took off for New York City. Hid out. Got through college. You know the rest." She absentmindedly ran her hands up and down the tops of his calves.

Tristan forced every muscle in his body to relax as he listened to her recount what had happened to her. Strung out in anger, he tried to focus on her and not his own feelings.

"You know, I've been alive for a long time, watching the way most packs have progressed. These days we welcome hybrids, outlaw forced pairings and matings, et cetera. I can't take away the pain, but I'll promise you this," Tristan said, a serious expression washing over his face. "If this Gerald is still alive, he won't be for long."

As Kalli listened, she didn't bother telling him no. She wanted Gerald dead; the wolf in her screamed for his throat.

"When did you first shift?" He changed the line of questioning while still staying on the topic he wanted to learn about the most; her past.

"Not until my sophomore year in college."

"How'd you manage that?" Most wolves had shifted by their early teen years.

Kalli bit her lip, embarrassed to tell him what she'd done to thwart it. "I starved myself."

"What?" Tristan asked incredulously.

"I know, it's awful. I ate barely enough to sustain myself. But if I'd let myself change while in the pack, you know I'd have been raped within a full moon. Whatever… it worked. Of course as soon as I left, I started eating normally again. Still, it took a couple of years for my system to recover. And then one day, I just couldn't stop her."

"And?"

"And I found a safe, isolated place for me to shift in upstate New York. I'd shift alone," she admitted, knowing he'd ask her if she wasn't forthcoming. "But when I started taking the CLI about two years ago, it was the first time in my life that I could really stop hiding. Well, I guess I was still hiding, but it was in plain sight. People could sniff me all they wanted, and for all intents and purposes, I was human. No wolf to be found."

"Well now you can stop hiding. I mean it, Kalli; I won't let anything happen to you. You can stop taking the pills," he stated flatly.

"I don't know about that, Tristan."

"You need to learn to trust me. Do we need another lesson?"

"I think your lessons could be addicting," she smiled. "Seriously, I know you're there for me. It's just that, my wolf, she scares me. Well maybe not her exactly as much as the actual shifting. I've only shifted by myself…alone. Believe me when I tell you that it has unequivocally sucked, for lack of a better term."

"Maybe you just need a good teacher."

"A strong virile Alpha, perhaps?"

"Yes, someone who'd love nothing more than to see an enchanting she-wolf in the forest. With that raven hair of yours, I can't wait to see your coloring."

"I need to think about it," she hedged.

"Better think fast, chérie. After the summit tomorrow, we're heading up the mountains for the next week or so. Full moon is coming in a few days. I reckon if you don't take any more of those pills, you might be able to shift. It may take a little more time for you to be able to shift on demand though. It's not nice to mess with Mother Nature." Tristan leaned forward, letting his hands roam up to tease her inner thighs. His fingers magically massaged her. Nearing the apex of her legs, he trailed back toward her feet, purposely teasing her need.

Kalli sank further down into the tub, actively seeking his hands. "Ah…" she sighed in frustration, trying to concentrate on what he'd been saying. "Mother Nature, huh? Is that right?"

"The Alpha is always right," he joked, leaning back again.

Unable to take a second more of his teasing, Kalli sat straight up. Her hair fell forward as her tiny hardened tips poked through the long wet curls. She leaned over, crawling toward him on her hands and knees, until she was face to face with Tristan, mere inches from his lips. Her knees straddled his as she leaned over to kiss the hollow of his neck. Seeking to break his restraint, she continued her assault, pressing her lips everywhere but on his. As she brushed a kiss over his eyelid, she felt his hands on her waist pulling her toward him. She leaned into his ear. "I need you in me…now," she whispered.

Unacquainted with being prey, Tristan distinctly got the feeling she was about to make him hers. He struggled to lie still, letting her take the lead. Yet as her slippery flesh rubbed his, he just about snapped. "Kalli," he groaned. "You're killin' me." Seeking out her brazenly exposed breasts, he captured a taut rosy peak in his mouth. Feasting on her like a starving man, he switched to the other side, alternating his affections.

Kalli reached between his legs, closing her hand around his swollen shaft. Aching with need, she could feel her own sheath contracting in anticipation of him. Fisting his sex up and down, she rubbed the tip of him through her throbbing folds.

"Fuck, yeah." Tristan pushed his hips upward as she cuffed his sex with her fingers.

Slipping the head of his shaft slowly through her lips, he pressed at her pulsating core. She stilled a moment to catch his gaze before fully impaling herself on his cock.

"Tristan!" Kalli sucked a sharp breath as the walls of her sex expanded to accommodate him. Holding onto the sides of the tub, her head fell backwards in ecstasy.

"Yes, baby!" Tristan hissed. "Ride me. Ride me, hard." Pumping up into her, he held her waist. Goddess, she was so fucking perfect. Watching her rise up and down, milking him, he thought he'd pass out.

Pressing down to meet his every thrust, Kalli writhed against him while digging her fingertips into his shoulders. She could feel her clit rub against his pelvis, hurling her toward orgasm. As he let go of her waist, she felt his hand reach around to her bottom. She sucked a breath at the sweet sensation of his fingertips descending down the crease of her ass. His unexpected touch only served to fuel her as she increased the pace of the rhythm.

Tristan grunted as his hard muscled flesh penetrated her tight depths. As her hot core clamped down on him, he fought back his release. From the sound of her panting, he knew she was on the edge, readying to come. Brushing his forefinger against her bottom, he circled the tight flesh, envisioning taking her there someday.

"Oh God, please, yes, do it," she encouraged at the feel of him.

"Oh yeah, let me in, Kalli. Take all of me, amour." While teasing her rosebud from behind, he leaned toward her breast. Taking a wet, shimmering bud into his mouth, he gently tugged at her tight nipple with his teeth.

Overwhelming sensations seized her body, catapulting her into an orgasm like she'd never known. Water sloshed out and over the side of the tub as she convulsed in pleasure, screaming his name.

"Goddess, yeah!" Tristan roared, as the hottest, longest climax of his life ripped through him. As his seed pumped deep within her womb, he fought the urge to mark her. He knew in that moment that he'd eventually have to give in to the internal struggle to claim her as his own; his mate. It was hard for him to fathom, but his wolf demanded it.

Recovering from her release, Kalli gently lifted off him, and laid back into his arms. Her heart raced as she contemplated the scenarios of how things would play out in the long-term. Like no other man or wolf she'd experienced, Tristan swept her up in a tornado of lust and emotion. She wished that was all she felt for the man holding onto her tightly. The more he told her she was his, the more she was starting to believe him. Scared of her own feelings which grew deeper by the hour, she found all that she could do in that moment was to hold him back. She reasoned that if things continued, she might never let him go.

Chapter Seventeen

Making love in the morning was exceedingly satisfying, Tristan thought to himself. It had been the first time he'd spent the night at his own home with a woman, and he certainly could get used to having Kalli live with him. Watching her make breakfast, this time only in the apron, proved to be yet another perk. Determined to get started on an antidote, Kalli asked to use his laptop, and he'd set her up in his office to do her research. While she worked, Tristan chose to conduct his business outside, having to follow-up with the clients from last night's gala. Sitting on his balcony, he relaxed; catching some sun felt good. Winter would be coming soon, and the cool breeze wouldn't feel quite as delightful.

The only thing troubling him was the bittersweet need he'd felt to mark her after making love. The gnawing urge threatened to grow into a compulsion, and he wasn't sure how to contain it. He'd been so content all these years as a lone wolf. The need to mate was simply a myth as far as he was concerned. How one wolf could give up his freedom to commit to an eternal lifetime with another was beyond comprehension. Until last night, he'd only heard stories about the unnatural craving that afflicted both the man and wolf.

He prayed it wasn't happening; denial was such a pleasant place until his wolf clawed his way back into his psyche, demanding to be fed. Unlike the man, the wolf cared not of a human male's desire for freedom. He had all the freedom he ever needed within the sanctuary of the pack. The mate completed his being, needing her like a fish needed water to survive. There was no deep thought about whether or not he should claim her; rather, he accepted the mating as easily as he accepted his need to feed.

Tristan contemplated how he really felt. At one time, he'd asked Sydney to move in with him, made love to her whenever possible. But he hadn't ever considered marking her; claiming her or mating her. The thought never even entered his head, no matter how good the sex was. Yet with Kalli, not only had he thought about it, he'd actively restrained himself from biting her; marking her as his for all others to see. He feared the need was growing stronger, and was unsure of how many more times he could make love to her without doing it. Logically, there was no solution to the enigma except to acknowledge that perhaps he'd found his mate. He reasoned the best he could do was hold on tight for the ride, because he knew for certain that he wasn't getting off the train.

As his thoughts drifted to business, he couldn't curb how jacked up he was in anticipation of tonight's summit. If Jax Chandler was in any way responsible for Paul or Toby's death, he was primed and ready to kill. Revenge was not something Tristan took lightly. People had families. Death always brought consequences to both the executioner and the prisoner. Unfortunately as Alpha, he'd been forced to mete out justice more times than he'd like to count, but that was the burden and responsibility of his position. The scars on his bloodstained soul spoke of the heavy price an Alpha paid in return for the safety of his pack.

Tristan heard the sliding doors open and caught a glimpse of Logan making himself a cup of coffee. He could have sworn he heard laughing before Logan poked his nose around the glass doors.

"Hey George, how's it goin'?"

"What?"

"George Hamilton, you know. Tan man. I'd ask you to put some clothes on but that's like asking a shark to become a vegetarian," he joked, noticing Tristan was sprawled out on the lounger wearing nothing but his boxers.

"The boys have to breathe. Besides, when you've got it and whatnot," he laughed. "Goddess, isn't this weather great? I love September."

"Glad to see you're in a good mood today considering we're about to go kick some ass tonight."

"All part of the job my dear Watson. And I must say that it's about fucking time." Tristan adjusted his sunglasses. "Everyone ready to roll?"

"Yeah, Simeon and Declan are coming with us. They're good to go. Kalli, coming with?"

"Oh yeah. She's ready as she's gonna be. It is what it is. You stick close to her, okay?"

"Why I'd love to, Alpha," he said drawing it out as if he was really going to enjoy it.

"Yeah, don't get used to it, smart ass."

"So, are we going to talk about it?" Logan asked with a broad knowing smile.

"Talk about what? I may be Alpha, but I'm no mind reader." Oh, but he knew exactly what Logan was asking.

"You. Her. Dance floor. Oh and the distinct sounds of screaming that only come with hot sex. Nothin' like the sound of 'Fuck me' reverberating throughout the Four Seasons. Classic, bro." Logan slapped Tristan on the shoulder, busting at the seams laughing.

"What about it?" Tristan replied with a coy smile.

"You're done, man. Not that I blame you. Kalli is one sweet wolf. Ah, I love when I'm right," Logan declared.

"About what?"

"Oh, nothing. Sometimes it's best to let nature take its course. But you'd know all about that, wouldn't you, Alpha?" Logan chuckled, falling back into the chair.

Tristan scowled. Damn Logan and his visions. Tristan didn't want to even know what images had been flashing through his beta's dreams. It was nothing but trouble. Business was a different story, but his love life was off limits. Deciding not to encourage Logan, he ignored his comment. An Alpha knew when to hold 'em and when to fold 'em; therefore he kept his mouth shut.

On the ride over to the summit, Kalli kept quiet as she listened to Tristan and Logan run through different scenarios. Each and every one of them had dressed in all black with sturdy boots, in case there was debris in the meeting place. Due to the high probability of both shifting and violence, the facility chosen was selected for its privacy, not comfort. They'd agreed on an abandoned building in an isolated area of Camden for the summit. Considered neutral territory, the New Jersey Alpha had granted them permission to use the facilities, given the recent death of the Lyceum wolf.

The limo pulled up to the dilapidated building, and they poured out onto the street. Simeon, a muscular wolf, who rivaled any World Wrestling champion, led the pack, alert for any sign of an ambush. Simeon nodded, signaling an all clear to Tristan and Logan. Surrounding Kalli, they proceeded toward the two story, red bricked building. Once a neighborhood firehouse, the windows had all been boarded over; graffiti was scrawled across the whitewashed plywood.

The deafening silence reminded Kalli of the desolation she'd felt during her childhood. But tonight, there was a good chance that the disconcerting reticence would be sliced with the screams of death before dawn. Kalli swore she smelled the sickly odor of wolves from her old pack, yet the five men who stood at the long wooden table were unfamiliar. As they approached the table, the strangers rose.

"Alpha." Tristan nodded in respect toward the tall attractive wolf who held court in the center of the table. Exuding power, his strong facial features accentuated his Nordic complexion; cropped blonde hair gave way to piercing pale blue eyes. When he took notice of Kalli, she instinctively bowed her head in deference, and held tight to Logan's arm.

"Alpha, I'm pleased to meet with you tonight," he replied coolly.

"Shall we sit?" Tristan suggested, preferring to take them off guard by feigning a relaxed positioning. Yet his body was coiled tight; like an asp he was ready to strike. His wolf paced, eagerly awaiting battle.

"Certainly. This is my beta, Gilles." Kalli could have sworn they were twins, but kept her thoughts to herself. The last thing she planned on doing was talking at this meeting. The only reason she'd agreed to come was to identify wolves, if presented with the opportunity.

"And you know Logan. This, here, is Dr. Williams. She's here in the capacity of witness. You should also be aware that she's mine and under my protection."

"I see," Jax commented, looking Kalli over. She swore she could feel him undressing her even though she was buttoned up tighter than the queen's girdle. Opting for a simple nod, she swallowed, continuing to clutch poor Logan's arm, hoping she wasn't cutting off his circulation.

"As much as I'm enjoying the elegant accommodations, let's get to business. A little over a week ago, two wolves set fire to my club, Eden. The same wolves are suspected in the murder of a young wolf that occurred two nights ago. Sketches of the suspects have been provided to you via Logan. I'd be remiss not to mention that circumstances and specifics that led to a lupine death are confidential at this point as there is an ongoing police investigation. While P-CAP has presumably been notified of the murder, I believe we'd agree that as wolves we prefer to abide to our own rules," Tristan paused as Jax silently acknowledged his words with a small grin.

"In addition, as you may have been notified by Marcel, another young wolf was killed in New Orleans nearly two weeks ago. New York plates were found on the stolen car. I understand that he's forwarded the sketches of the dead wolves who drove the car, but to date, no Alpha has claimed responsibility. I am formally requesting your assistance in the apprehension of the suspects in both murders. With all due respect, and this is in no way an accusation, I need confirmation from you that your pack is not involved in either of these matters."

A deeply serious expression fell across Jax's face, and he addressed Tristan. "Alpha, please accept my sincere condolences on behalf of me and my entire pack. I take no offence to your need for confirmation, and I am pleased to inform you that I have not condoned nor have I ordered an attack on either the Lyceum Wolves or Marcel's pack. However, after viewing your sketch and careful distribution of the picture, I have brought you a gift. Call it a peace offering after the misunderstanding we had regarding your sister, if you will."

Tristan stared intently at Jax. He could feel his wolf readying to shift having smelled blood. The energy in the room thrummed with tension; he was aware he'd have his prize.

"Bring it out!" Jax barked, never taking his eyes off of Tristan.

A bright red wooden door with peeling paint flew open, and a stubby, dirty man wrapped in heavy silver chains was thrust into the open space by a burly, unyielding thug holding a gun.

Kalli eyes flashed to the weapon. She guessed silver bullets came with the shiny gun; ones meant to kill wolves. *Breathe deeply. Breathe deeply.* She swore by how quickly her heart was racing that she'd need a healthy dose of oxygen by the time she got out of there…if she got out alive. But as soon as the man was shoved into the spotlight, she gasped. *Sato. South Carolina Wallace Pack.* Relief momentarily swept through her until she realized that number one, the other wolf wasn't in attendance, and two, punishment would be served.

Easily identifying the man as one of the wolves from the sketches, Tristan turned to Kalli. "Do you know this man, Dr. Williams?" he asked formally.

"Yes, Alpha," she croaked, shrinking into Logan. It was as if she was a young girl again, cowering. She felt Sato's eyes bore into her and looked away. "I…ugh..I think his name is Sato. I'm not one hundred percent on the last name. But without a doubt, this man was at the fire, and he's part of the South Carolina Wallace Pack."

"You fucking bitch!" he screeched at her. Even chained, he was formidable. Baiting Kalli, he continued to yell. "You're nothing but a traitorous hybrid whore! Gerald's still waitin' for you, missy. Oh yeah, you owe him. He'll have ya on your back in no time spreading those filthy legs and…"

Before he had a chance to finish, Tristan slammed him into silence against a wall, crushing his larynx with the brunt of his forearm.

Kalli fought for air, attempting to quell both her burgeoning anger and fear. She glanced across the table and caught a glimpse of Jax smiling as if he was enjoying watching Tristan's attack. As if sensing that Kalli was about to lose it, Logan pulled her close to his side, putting a protective arm around her, and placed his finger to his lips, signaling her to remain silent.

"You killed my wolf; my son," Tristan roared, unrelentingly maintaining his hold.

An evil smirk broke across the man's face. "Not so tough now, Alpha, are ya? That kid was your weakness. We gutted him good."

A loud crack resounded throughout the room as Tristan smashed the wolf's head against the wall, leaving a dent in the sheet rock.

"Where's the other wolf?" Tristan spat at him.

"Like I'd tell ya. But don't worry, he's still out there. In fact, he'll probably find you first….he torched your club good after we got thrown out. And your bitch, Gerald is looking for her. You can kill me but this won't be the end for any of you," he sneered, spitting saliva into the air with each spoken word.

Tristan's steely eyes settled on the killer. In a cold, low voice, he deliberately and slowly delivered the death sentence, each word laced with intent. "Tonight you're goin' to die just like Toby. And like him, you will run for your life. As confusion and despair threaten to overtake your senses, dread will engulf your entire being. You will beg the Goddess for your despicable worthless life as I watch the life drain from your eyes. You've got a thirty second lead, but know this; within the next five minutes, your life will end."

Tristan released him, ripping the chains off of the man as easily as if he was pulling apart string cheese. The acrid odor of burning flesh from the silver burning Tristan's hands hung in the air. Like a caged animal, the man took off running, clothes flying in the process as he prepared to shift.

Kalli held her breath, trying not to hyperventilate at the sight. Witnessing Tristan's furor first hand jolted through her like electricity. She'd never seen an Alpha so fierce and primal; a purely spectacular male. Hating Sato and everything he represented, she felt no sympathy for the killer. Her only regret was that she wouldn't be able to witness his death.

Tristan ripped off his leather jacket, t-shirt and jeans within seconds. As soon as the air hit his naked skin, he instantly shifted into his beast. Turning his head just once to glance at Kalli, he howled and ran out into the darkness.

Stealthily, the black wolf weaved in and out of the shadows, scenting his prey. He crouched low to the ground, hearing a whine in the distance. Sprinting at full speed, he took off toward the enemy, who was attempting to hide in a nearby shed. Images of Toby flashed through his mind, surging the rage; the need for revenge. The thirst for blood danced on his tongue.

As he rounded the corner, the grey matted wolf darted into a deserted house, and Tristan closed in pursuit. Inwardly, he laughed, knowing the wolf had essentially trapped himself with his own irons. Hunching down, he quietly padded into the blackened entranceway. He could smell the blood of the wolf in the room; he must have cut himself in the street.

A rat squeaked in the corner, momentarily distracting Tristan. He growled menacingly toward the rodent, and it scurried off. Still smelling Sato's scent, he launched himself up the stairs, which led into a parlor of sorts. The waiting enemy snarled, beckoning Tristan to attack quickly, increasing the chance he'd make a mistake. But Tristan wouldn't make this quick. Sato had shown Toby no mercy, chasing him down, eviscerating him slowly. So he'd planned do the same to Sato, inflicting the exact pure terror Toby must have felt. Circling Sato, Tristan bared his teeth, approaching and then receding and back again. He snapped at him, tearing off a chunk of Sato's fur; blood sprayed the floor. *Is that how you made Toby feel? The pain of the bullets tearing through his skin. The scent of his own blood filling his nostrils as he tried to shift.*

Sato whined in pain, but refused to retreat. The large grey wolf advanced with great speed, jumping at Tristan's head. Teeth sliced through his ear as blood and fur flew into the air. Refusing to yelp, Tristan let the pain ignite his rage. He quickly flipped himself around, until his teeth were firmly rooted in Sato's pelt. The harder the other wolf tried to shake him off the harder Tristan held on, not killing him…yet. Sato twisted and turned until he finally fell to his back, baring his belly submissively. As Tristan went to release his hold, Sato gnashed his teeth in one last attempt to maul the Alpha. Anticipating his strike, Tristan struck, sinking his teeth into the soft tissue under the chin. Blood flooded his mouth as he shredded the wiry fur and flesh. Slowly he tore it apart, bit by bit, until his prey stopped moving. Releasing the wolf, Tristan circled around the body, until it transformed into the remains of a shell that used to be Sato. Throat torn out, the sanguine cord of the spine laid on the dusty floor, providing evidence of the kill.

Tristan howled in mourning for the wolf spirit; there was always a consequence for taking a life. As Alpha, the heavy scar on his soul settled. Responsibilities and vengeance to the pack ran deep. In his actions and thoughts, he felt he'd brought Toby a step closer to peace. Others would pay as well, but for tonight, he'd avenged for his pack.

Tristan strode into the warehouse, naked and bloody, fresh from the kill. Kalli screamed his name, struggling to break free of Logan's hold. Stifling her cries, the silence seemed to mirror Tristan's tenebrous disposition. Although he'd been gone for less than fifteen minutes, his somber expression spoke of war. Deftly pulling on his t-shirt and jeans, he slipped on his shoes and approached the table.

"I am in gratitude for your gift, Alpha. Clearly, this is just the beginning. One battle. You should be advised that after today's news, we'll be going after the Wallace Pack. Please contact me directly should you receive any more information on the other wolf," Tristan stated emotionlessly. His normally warm amber eyes appeared darker, tinged in sadness.

"You are very welcome," Jax remarked. Standing up from the table, he extended his hand. As Tristan shook it, Jax caught sight of his wariness. "Alpha, it had to be done. If there's one thing I know, it is the weight we both share. Good luck to you going after the others."

Tristan nodded in understanding. Taking Kalli from Logan, he hugged her tightly. "Let's go. Our business is finished here."

Before leaving, Tristan turned to Simeon. "Body's in the third house on the left. After we get home, grab a couple of the boys and ship it to South Carolina."

"Got it boss." Simeon knew the drill without Tristan saying any more. It was a message to the Wallace Pack wolves, and he'd be happy to help him deliver it.

Chapter Eighteen

The macabre vibe continued well after they'd left the warehouse. Rather than a slew of consolatory comments, a muted contemplation blanketed the car. On the way over the bridge to Philadelphia, Tristan received a call from Tony informing him that the body of Lindsay, Kalli's assistant, had been found in the UVH parking lot earlier in the evening. She'd been found stuffed under her car, throat slit. The cowardly act had been caught on tape, and one of the sketches matched the suspect; the second wolf, Morris.

Tony said they believed that both wolves had visited the hospital in search of Kalli, while she'd been held by Alexandra. During that visit, an exchange of information had taken place between Lindsay and the suspects. An intensive computer search showed evidence that Lindsay had been responsible for hacking into several computers at the hospital, including Kalli's. A large lump sum of money had been recently deposited in Lindsay's account, suggesting she'd sold Kalli out, and possibly others. Tony said it was too early to tell at this point. They weren't exactly sure of the motive for her killing, but reasoned that perhaps the wolves wanted to tie up loose ends after Toby's murder.

The news of Lindsay's slaying and betrayal angered Kalli. But she held the emotion in tightly, refusing to shed a tear or waste her thoughts on the foolish girl who'd helped kill Toby. The incident only served as a further incentive to help Tristan track down the other wolf. Seeing Tristan's display of power earlier left no doubt he'd be caught.

When they finally reached Livingston One, they were greeted by both Julie and Mira, who both offered assistance. Logan quietly confided what happened at the summit with both women, while Tristan and Kalli retreated to his condo. Normally jovial and confident, Tristan seemed distant and uncharacteristically reserved. Like Tristan, Kalli knew that things were far from over, especially since they suspected that the CLI was in Gerald's hands.

"I've gotta take a shower," he muttered, walking toward the master bedroom. "You wanna join me?"

"Sure, um, I've just got to stop by my room a sec, okay?"

"Okay, meet you in there."

She nodded, wishing she could take his hurt away. He needed comfort tonight, and she swore she'd do everything in her power to help him. The killing appeared to come at a great cost to him, or perhaps he was mourning Toby. Observing Tristan in the element of battle had been both exhilarating and exhausting. She couldn't even imagine what it had done to him, but she'd go to him, care for him, and make him whole again. But Kalli knew there was a critical singular task she had to complete before she could give herself to him fully; one which would allow her to start her life anew.

Going into her bathroom, she stared at herself in the mirror. Taking a deep breath, she peeled off the black clothing she'd donned for the summit. But even once her clothes were gone, the morose film of violence still clung to her skin. She needed to shake off this evening's events as much as anyone, but she couldn't stop thinking about Tristan, the man and the wolf. Reveling in his animalistic display of dominance, she could no longer deny her true self.

Stark naked, she wrapped her fingers around the tan bottle on the countertop, which contained the CLI. Remorse for Toby's death still remained, but pride for surviving all those years without detection surged through her veins. There was no use in regretting what her childhood could or should have been. There was only now. And without a doubt, Tristan and Lyceum Wolves commanded her future. In her mind's eye her alter ego awakened, enthusiastically prancing in anticipation. Unscrewing the white top, she took one last look at the pills before flushing all of them down the toilet.

Instead of going to his room, Tristan had decided to turn around and head toward the kitchen. He'd torn off his clothes, removed his shoes, and threw them into a black plastic bag. Texting housekeeping, they arrived within seconds to take it to the incinerator for disposal. The scent of the dead wasn't something one could wash out of clothing. Snatching a bottle of cognac and a couple of glasses, he retired to his private sanctuary.

Tristan let the hot spray sting his skin as his consciousness drifted to Kalli. Mulling it over all day, he'd struggled to comprehend the urge to claim her. Yet deep down, he knew exactly why. Although Logan's earlier cryptic comments had irritated the hell out of him, he realized at some point later in the afternoon that his beta knew for certain what he'd been renouncing. But his stubborn attitude could no longer deny fate. Never truly understanding what it was like for other mated wolves, the calling of his mate was a song he craved like no other.

Accepting and acting on this newfound realization were two entirely different things. Kalli hadn't even accepted her own wolf, so he wasn't about to slam her with this new information any time soon. Reflecting on the summit, he prayed he hadn't frightened the hell out of her. But like he'd told her, there was no hiding one's true nature. And his was lethal.

He placed his forehead against the cool tile as the calming scent of Kalli wafted into the room. Out of his peripheral vision, he could see her white robe drop to the floor, giving way to her silky olive skin. Through the beveled glass blocks, he watched the black curls spill down her back as she removed the band and pins, which had bound her hair.

In the reflection of the mirror, Kalli's breath caught as she noticed his sexy silhouette; like a powerful animal, he stretched his arms upward, leaning against the shower wall. Slipping around the enclosure in search of Tristan, she admired the sight of his bronzed dripping wet skin. The muscled planes of his back gave way to the solid curve of his buttocks and long powerful legs. Jets of water sprayed from each wall, and by the time she reached him, warm drops poured down her lithe but curvy body.

Within inches of his body, she placed her hands on his shoulders tracing her fingers upward until she reached hold of his rock-hard biceps. Giving them a gentle caress, her hands trailed down the hard muscles of his back. She heard him hiss; his head lolled backward in contentment. Her hands explored his trim waist until her arms were wrapped all the way around him. Pressing forward to embrace him, her swollen bosom crushed against the expanse of his back and her legs straddled his. Spreading her fingers, she touched his wonderfully broad chest down to the rippled abs beneath his warm bare skin.

"You okay?" she asked lovingly, closing her eyes while the cheek of her face pressed softly against his back.

"Chérie, there is no place I'd rather be right now," he mumbled. "Goddess, you feel so good. So perfect." He moved to turn around to face her, but she stilled his movement.

"Shhhh…My Alpha, let me take care of you tonight," she whispered, reaching for the soap. "Relax, baby."

Lathering the bubbly cleanser into her small hands, she sluiced slippery liquid over his clavicles, massaging his neck until he released a small moan. Her hands continued their assault, rubbing the globes of his bottom and down his crease. Brushing his thighs, she gently turned him until he faced her.

He stood silently watching her, enjoying the feel of her smooth palms on his skin. She rinsed her hands to fill them with cleanly scented shampoo. Reaching up into his hair, her pebbled pink tips grazed his chest. He sighed in aching need at the feel of them, but allowed her to thoroughly wash his blood-matted hair. Squeezing out the excess lather, she gently tilted his head back into the spray.

Again, she resumed washing him with suds. Moving from under his arms to his biceps, she carefully attended to him all the way down to his fingers. Kalli's breath caught at the sight of his tanned, sculptured chest. He opened his eyes to catch her gaze as she cleaned him all the way down to his belly. Keeping eye contact, she let her fingers deliberately trace the muscularly cut v that led to his groin. Whisking her palms downward, she spread his legs, stroking the juncture of his thighs. A ragged gasp escaped his lips as she cupped his velvety sac; his head fell backwards to rest on the tile, delighting in the sensation. Wrapping her other hand around his straining erection, she pumped him up and down, smoothing her thumb over the plump head.

Tristan had never in his life been so open and vulnerable to a woman, letting her roam free on his body. From the first touch of her fingers to his shoulders to the graze of her nails on his chest, he tensed in excitement, letting her work her magic. She'd asked him to relax, but the agonizing arousal coursed through his body like he'd touched a live wire. It took every bit of self-restraint to not rush to make love to her. Rather, he willingly submitted to the sweet pain of her titillating stimulation, anticipating her next touch. As if she was performing a purification ritual, he felt the dark cloud in his soul lift.

As he peered into the depths of her eyes, the intense affection he felt for Kalli teased his lips. He wanted to tell her how much she meant to him. More than lust, he was falling fast without a parachute. He bit his lip in resistance, thwarting the words that threatened to expose his heart. A jolt ran through his body as her tiny hands massaged his hot swollen flesh.

"Kalli," he cried out in pleasure before she released him. Lovingly, she turned his body once more, rinsing him clean. He gave into her direction, again his eyes meeting hers.

As if performing a sensual rumba, she refused to release him from her trance. Smiling, she gracefully knelt before him, combing her fingernails down the front of his thighs. Tristan sucked a blissful breath. The sight of his beautifully bared female on her knees, parting her lips, sent blood pulsating into his already hard cock. Incredibly stunning, her drenched hair clung to her skin. Puckered nipples brushed across his thighs, as she leaned forward. Darting her tongue outward, she licked the underside of his engorged shaft. He could have sworn he'd died and gone to heaven as her warm lips encased him.

Kalli relished his taste as she sucked him deeply. Releasing his sex from her mouth, she fisted his swollen staff while she laved his testicles, rolling them over her tongue. Once again she took his rigid flesh into her mouth, slowly swallowing all of him. Digging her fingers into the cheeks of his ass, she pulled him toward her until he began to pump himself in and out of her lips. She moaned, as the excitement of tasting him incited her own passion; her core ached with need, begging to be touched.

As the intoxication of her actions spread throughout his body, Tristan struggled to speak. "Mon amour…please." He grasped her hair. "I can't stop. I'm going to come."

His words only inflamed her arousal, taking him faster and deeper.

Refusing to let go, she grasped his bottom, encouraging him to thrust harder, edging him closer to his impeding orgasm.

No longer able to resist as her lips tightened around his throbbing hardness, he screamed her name, gasping for breath, "Kalli!"

His cry of deliverance resounded as he abandoned himself to his erotic release. Groaning as she took all of him, he poured himself into her, her unrelenting lips and tongue mercilessly milking him dry. He reached for her, pulling her up into his embrace, the warm water of the shower caressing their intermingled bodies.

Kalli's chest felt tight, so swollen with emotion, she couldn't look at him without revealing her feelings. Resisting the temptation to fall in love with him was going to be difficult, she thought. Everything about him from the way he playfully conversed to his resplendent black wolf captivated her. Her Alpha, the magnificent man within her arms, was hers.

Chapter Nineteen

"Anastas," Kalli confided.

"Hmm," Tristan replied, lazily drawing circles on the inside of her palm while they lay entwined in his bed. After turning off the shower, Kalli had insisted on drying every square inch of him with a warmed, fluffy towel. Within minutes, they both fell comfortably into Tristan's large inviting bed.

"Anastas. Kalli Anastas. That's my real name."

"Anastas," he repeated, the word rolling off his smooth tongue in a Greek accent. "It suits you. Thank you for trusting me with it. See, my lessons are working."

"Yes, professor, indeed they are, although I'm afraid I may require many more lengthy, hands-on demonstrations." She brought his hand up to her lips for a brief kiss.

Tristan chuckled.

"And I have something else to share with you," Kalli continued.

"Do share."

She quieted, pushing up onto her forearms and tummy so she could look at him directly. "The pills. They're gone."

"Gone?"

"Gone as in I flushed them gone. Gone as in I'm returning to my nature as a wise Alpha encouraged me to do." She grinned, remembering their previous discussion.

Tristan pulled her up into his arms and kissed her slowly and gently. "Mon amour, I was hoping…but you had to make the decision on your own. And now there's nothing stopping us."

"Stopping us from what?" She eyed him inquisitively.

"It's just that I'm looking forward to sharing that part of myself with you. I want to run and hunt and…" He let his words trail off on purpose, unsure of how much of his feelings he should disclose.

"And?" She left the question hanging, yet it went unanswered.

He simply smiled at her, somewhat stalling, somewhat just lost in her altogether.

"Mr. Livingston," she challenged. "Trust goes both ways. Do you need me to teach you a lesson?"

"I'm sure you would, chérie. The scary part is that I might like it."

"Come on Tristan. Spill it," she whined, in an attempt to rush the conversation, dying to know what he wanted to do with her.

"First let me ask you something." He stilled in preparation for her response. "Tonight at the meeting. What were your impressions? Truth."

"At first, I was terrified. It was suffocating in there. My whole life I've lived in fear of wolves. And then, there I am at a summit of all things, with two seriously lethal Alpha males." She rolled her eyes.

"Lethal?"

"Damn straight lethal. And then seeing Sato, I was torn between cowering and attempting to kill him myself. The thing is that I know that there is this part of me, a very big part, that abhors violence, but I wanted Sato dead. Not only did I want him dead, I was exhilarated by your power, your strength. I wanted to watch while you took him down." She let out a deep breath. "Oh God. It sounds awful, doesn't it?"

"No. Vengeance is bittersweet. No doubt he had it coming after what he'd done to you, even if it was indirectly. And he'd killed Toby. The man lacked remorse. He'd do it again," Tristan concluded thoughtfully.

"So, now that you know all my secrets, what gives? What else do you want to do with me? Besides having your wicked way with me?" She laughed.

He cupped her cheeks in his hands, letting his thumb brush her lips. "Kalli, I…I've been alone for such a long time. But now. Meeting you. My wolf. Fuck, I'm incredibly inarticulate tonight," he huffed in frustration.

Kalli giggled and cuddled closer, lying her back down on his chest again. Maybe it would be easier for him if he didn't look at her while saying whatever it was he needed to tell her?

"Okay, here it is. I've never in my adult life lived with a woman. Came close with Sydney, but she wasn't my mate. And I never felt this urge…this urge to claim her…Mira neither. I've never felt that craving…that need to mark someone. To claim them."

"What are you saying?"

"I can't resist any longer…this need. I don't know how to explain it. At first I blamed it on my wolf. It is, but it isn't. You and I…there's something serious between us. I mean the sex is amazing but it's not just that. I've got to have you…have you as in 'you are mine'. And not like 'mine' meaning part of the pack either. It's more. So much more than that." He blew out a deep breath, fearing he was fucking up the entire conversation.

"It's okay, Tristan. I know. I feel strongly about you too." *I'm falling in love with you.* "I wish I could play coy and pretend I don't feel it, but I just can't. I want this…what's happening between us. And my wolf, well, she's been at me since the minute you put me in your lap in your car," she admitted softly.

"I want to claim you, Kalli. Mark you. Do you understand what I'm saying?" Done with hedging the issue, he put all his cards on the table. If he didn't tell her now, he'd end up doing it the next time they made love. The call was beyond his control.

Kalli's stomach danced with butterflies. She'd never been claimed before but she knew that it would be a sign to the pack that she was his potential mate. Her wolf rolled in submission, baring her neck, awaiting his mark. "Do it. I want to be yours. I know it's taken me a while to trust, but you've shown me how important it is to be myself. But the next moon…I'll need your help."

Tristan's pride swelled at her words. He breathed a sigh of relief; she'd felt it too. Not ready to mention he truly believed she was his mate, he celebrated the fact that she wanted this.

"Baby, you've got no idea how much I'm going to help you. Your first shift with the pack; I promise you that it will be a magical experience," he declared. "You'll carry my mark. But you must know that there is no other for me from here on out." He moved his hand downward, now circling her very pretty, very hard, pink tips.

"Alpha, are you giving up your naughty ways?" she teased.

"No way, chérie. I'm only providing full disclosure. All kinky practices are now officially reserved for you." He pinched her nipple, enjoying hearing her squeak in pleasure. Declaring his intention to mark her ignited her excitement. Her delicious scent filled the room. His little wolf was terribly aroused. Goddess, he loved that she was so responsive. Truth be told, he loved everything about her.

"Ah," she moaned at his touch. "Do tell me all about these kinky practices. Hmm….I don't think I can wait." She found herself involuntarily grinding her hips against his leg.

He shifted, reaching over to slide open a bedroom drawer, retrieving a small black bag. A dark smile broke across his face, aware that he was about to push her limits.

"A mystery?" she queried, nervously biting her lip. *He'd been planning this? What was in the damn bag?*

"What? I know how to shop for more than dresses and earrings. In fact, I think this little store may become one of our favorite spots," he boasted, anticipating playing with her. She'd nearly fallen apart at his dark intrusion the last time they'd made love. He opened the bag, gesturing for her to look inside it.

Kalli gasped as she pulled out the small plug. Her eyes widened at him in disbelief.

"I…I don't know, Tristan," she stammered, trying to conceal her excitement.

"No hiding your real feelings, chérie. I know the truth. The way you flew apart last time I touched you with my fingers, I thought a little toy was in order. As much as I'd love to take you there, and I would," he crooned in a low sexy voice, melting away her concerns, "that's not happening tonight. But I know you'll love this little toy, here. Don't you trust me? Perhaps you need another lesson?" he breathed, sliding his palm down her belly.

"Ah, yes," Kalli moaned in anticipation, his fingers teasing below her belly button.

"The very thought of me taking you there excites you, doesn't it? Your lovely flushed skin and rapid breathing gives you away," He slid his hand down into her slick heat, pressing a finger up into her core. "Ah, yes. You're soaking wet."

"Tristan, yes."

"I've gotta taste you, baby." Tristan flipped Kalli onto her back, settling his face between her legs. His warm breath skated across her mound while he continued gliding his finger in and out of her hot sheath. With his other hand, he ran two fingers down her nether lips, gently separating her to expose her treasured pearl.

"Mon amour, your pussy is so fucking beautiful. So smooth. Now relax, let me taste you," he ordered right before he delved into her aching sex. With a broad sweep of his flat tongue, he brushed over her clit, and she cried out in ecstasy.

"Oh my God." She reached to grab onto the sheets, balling them up in her fists. As his satiny tongue rubbed her sensitive bud, she nearly flew off the bed. She began panting wildly as he relentlessly laved her.

He darted his tongue through her folds, relishing her honeyed cream. Adding another thick finger, he pumped into her while increasing the pressure on her swollen nub. Over and over he flicked, storming her senses.

Kalli thrashed her head back and forth as her orgasm danced within reach. Panting gave way to incoherent screaming as she begged for release. "Tristan, please, I can't…I need…yes."

Her pleading was music to his ears. As her walls began to quiver, he sucked on her clitoris, pressing his tongue against it at the same time.

A slamming release shook Kalli to her very core. "Tristan!" she mouthed, over and over, feeling as if she'd left her body. Thrusting her hips up into his mouth, she sought to milk the shuddering climax which ripped from her head to her toes. By the time he'd released her, she was breathing so hard it was as if she'd run a marathon. Her face flamed as she descended back into reality, cognizant of how she'd lost it.

Giving her no time to think, Tristan roughly flipped her over on her stomach. He adjusted her positioning so that her arms and head comfortably rested on the pillow. Pulling her hips upward, he spread her legs so he fit nicely at her entrance.

Frustrated at the emptiness, she mewled in protest.

"Easy, baby," he cajoled. "I could feast on you all day, but it's time for your toy."

Kalli nodded into the pillow in agreement, eager for him to enter her.

She was on fire with need. His finger ran through her slippery folds yet again, and she released a gasp in relief. As Kalli wriggled toward him, seeking his touch, she felt a cool liquid run down her bottom.

"Relax now, Kalli. Push back," he instructed as he slowly pressed the small plug into her back hole.

"Ahhh…Tristan. It's…it's…I can't," she hissed, while pushing backward.

"You're doing it chérie. That's it. Almost there."

The small burn she'd felt, was quickly replaced with a fullness she'd never experienced. Foreign yet erotic, she loved the feel of it inside her. She moved back to him, enjoying the strange stimulation that roused her hunger for him.

"It's all the way in, baby. Just get used to it for a minute." He pushed the rubber stub in further, twisting it back and forth. The way she was writhing on it, he reckoned she'd come if he kept at it. "There you go. Just feel. Breathe."

"Yes, Tristan. I need you in me now."

His erect manhood throbbed in excitement. Sliding a hand under her belly and holding the plug in place, he edged the head of his erection at her most tender flesh. Inch by glorious inch, he eased himself into her until he was fully seated.

Kalli sucked a breath as he entered her. There were no words to describe the incredibly overwhelming sensation of being entirely filled. As he began to move, she found herself pushing back onto him in cadence. Quickening gasps accompanied by ripples of pleasure flowed deep within her womb, taking her to the edge. As he played with the plug, pulling it out and then pressing it back in, at the same time he thrusted.

She shuddered, no longer able to hold back the tidal wave threatening to crash over her. "Tristan! Fuck me! Harder! Yes! I'm coming. Please," she yelled into the pillow, convulsing into orgasm.

As her tight core fisted his cock, sweat broke across his brow. The feel of the plug through the thin barrier, stroked his manhood, as she pulsed around him. As she began to scream, he sank himself into her again and again, harder and harder. The sound of his flesh meeting hers echoed in the room. Breathing hard, his body seized in the frenzy of the simultaneous explosion. With an unfettered cry of fulfillment, he reached up under her belly with both hands until her back was pressed to his chest. With a final thrust, he roared. Canines extended, he bit down hard onto her shoulder, forever marking her as his.

Kalli reared up to accept his bite, still lost in the crescendo of her climax. As his teeth met her golden skin, she cried out in delight as the power of her Alpha entered her body. As much as she was his in that moment, he was hers in return.

Chapter Twenty

The ride up to the mountains took a little over two hours. Tristan had explained that the burial wouldn't take place until dusk. This time of year the sun set around seven thirty, so they'd have plenty of time to get settled in before the ritual began. Logan had already left for the mountains, as had most of the city wolves. After finishing several business calls, Tristan and Kalli set off around noon in a large SUV that towed a small Harley trailer. The warm September weather was a great time to ride, and Tristan was looking forward to taking Kalli out on his bike.

Since it was early in the month, some of the leaves were beginning to change color, preparing the trees for their winter slumber. By late September, the foliage would be at its peak. From Mountain Maples to Sweetgums, the leaves frolicked in the warm autumn wind. The scenic drive helped to soothe Kalli's racing thoughts. She absentmindedly fingered the spot where Tristan had marked her. While the skin was not broken or scarred, the sweet tingle of his bite remained. Growing up, she'd been told that each pack had its own distinctive markings. Once claimed, the mark would either grow more prominent as the couple forged their way toward mating or conversely, it would fade if the pair separated.

When she'd looked at her shoulder in the mirror that morning, it looked like a tiny rose-colored tattoo in the shape of an infinity symbol, as if two loops were intertwined. She supposed it suited her, reminding her of how she and Tristan fit perfectly together. As soon as he'd bitten her skin, her wolf had awakened. She struggled helplessly to emerge, begging to claim him in return. But since she hadn't turned in so long, it was impossible. She needed to shift again in order to mark him.

She wondered nervously what it would be like to shift into her wolf with Tristan at her side. In the past, it had been an exceedingly lonely experience. But the more time she spent with Tristan, the more she wanted to share everything with him: her body, her mind and her wolf.

"Hey, we're here," Tristan commented, jarring her from her contemplations.

Large pine trees towered over and around an imposing grid-ironed fence, which looked like it could easily impale someone if they tried to climb over it. Tristan pulled the car up to a security panel. Punching in a code, the doors opened, allowing them access to the unmarked compound.

"See there." He pointed to a large A-framed building. "That's the clubhouse. Tennis courts and the pool are behind it. There's a small general store in there that we run. Carries sundries, a small selection of groceries…stuff like that. We kind of run the place like a resort, but some of the people stay year round."

They continued down and around a curvy road, which led into what could best be described as a development of cabins interspersed between the enormous trees.

"These, here, are mostly owned by families. We've got a condo building too, where a lot of the single wolves stay. My place is up here near the top of the mountain. Logan usually stays with me most of the time, even though he's got a condo. It's got plenty of rooms, and I like the company," he explained.

As they passed a flat clearing, Kalli was surprised to see several horses in a rolling field; a barn sat in the distance. "You keep horses?"

"Yeah. Janie's in charge of the stables. She gives lessons to the pups, and some of us pay her to care for our horses."

Making a right turn into a winding driveway, a two-story home sat enclosed in forest. "And this is home," he declared.

"It's beautiful, Tristan, really." Admiring the tan-colored log cabin, Kalli wondered what it would be like to grow up here. A stark contrast to the sleek skyscraper, it was warm and inviting.

"You like?" he asked proudly. It was his escape from the city, and he hoped his urban woman would enjoy the country. He treasured his time in the mountains, and this truly was his sanctuary. It was important to him that she loved it as much as he did.

"What's not to like? Hey, do we have time to go for a hike?" she asked excitedly.

Tristan laughed. Warmth settled in his chest. As his mate, she fit him like a glove. The more time he spent with her, the stronger their bond grew. He loved being with her, talking to her, making love to her. He shook his head silently as it hit him. The mark; it was only the beginning. As much as he wanted to deny the feelings deep within his heart, he was falling in love with her. And it all felt natural, like it was meant to be.

He never thought he'd live to see the day when he considered mating a female. But now, happily, his world had been turned upside down by a raven-haired half-wolf who enjoyed cooking in her underwear. He laughed.

"What?" Kalli smiled as if she read his thoughts.

"Nothing. Just thinking about how I like to see you cook in your underwear."

Kalli began laughing with him. "Well, I guess it is a good thing we found each other, considering your penchant for nudity, Alpha. I can see why you like this isolated house," she teased.

"Wait until you see the hot tub. I've got plans for you," he promised, getting out of the car without waiting for a response. His cock jerked just thinking about her hot little body sitting on top of him while the hot bubbles massaged their skin.

A high vaulted ceiling with a floor to ceiling stone fireplace greeted them as they entered his home. The home's airy feeling was counterbalanced by the glow of the gas-lit fire. A U-shaped, sienna leather sectional sofa facing the hearth sat on oak planked floors. The general décor was clean and classic with exposed woods offset by earthy brown tones. A modern white kitchen, complete with black speckled granite countertops merged seamlessly with the great room.

Considering Kalli had spent her entire adult life living inside matchbook-sized apartments, the spacious house felt extraordinarily cozy and relaxing. Conjuring up thoughts ranging from roasting marshmallows, to making love on the floor in front of the fire, to chasing toddlers, Kalli wrapped her arms around herself. She inwardly questioned her own feelings. It was not like as a girl or even as a young woman she'd ever dreamed of getting married or having a family. But everything about Tristan was changing how she saw the world, how she felt about everything. He was like a missing piece in the puzzle that was her life.

As she explored, Tristan set down the bags and got to work preparing something special. "I've got a surprise for you," he announced from the kitchen.

She looked over to see him mulling about in his kitchen. *Was he preparing a meal?*

"Does the surprise include food? Because if it does, I'm in."

"Did you bring jeans?" he asked. "As much as I love easy access, you really need pants for this surprise. Also, boots or sneakers would be good."

"You're bad! Easy access, huh? Somehow that does not surprise me. You are something else, wolf," she chuckled.

"Hey, I am *the* wolf, to you."

"That you are," she assured him. "Well, I do love a good surprise. But I love food even more." *I really just love you.* The words ran through her head, and she smiled at the thought. God, she was in deep with no means of escape. At this point there was no fighting the tide. Crossing the great room, she reached over the counter, snatched up a piece of cheese and stuffed it in her mouth before she could say anything else that would divulge her true feelings.

"No guessing. And no more food either, until we get to our secret destination," he said mysteriously.

"Meanie," she jested, wondering what was in store for her next. A myriad of emotions stirred. She was already nervous about meeting his pack. How would people react to a hybrid that hadn't shifted in two years? A hybrid who'd created the drug that prevented Toby from shifting? Would they blame her for his death? And then there was the mark, his claim on her body and soul. How would they feel about their Alpha, who'd marked her as his female? Her mind raced trying to figure out what he possibly could have cooked up as a surprise. In the recesses of her mind, she considered the enlightening, very sensual lessons Tristan had given her. *Trust.* She took a deep breath as she attempted to put her education to good use.

"This! Is! Awesome!" Kalli squealed while trying not to frighten the horse or fall off it, both of which seemed like possibilities. "I love it! Really. I can't believe this was my surprise. Thank you so much!"

"Easy, chérie. Snowflake is very relaxed, but you gotta watch where you're going," Tristan warned. He'd made her cover her eyes on the way over to the stables. When she saw the dressed horses, she jumped up and down like a kid at Christmas. Such a basic way to get in touch with nature - a ride through the woods. But for Kalli, he could tell it had been a first. He wished he could create many firsts for her as they built their life together. Struggling not to move too quickly, he'd sworn to himself that he'd patiently let her adjust to being a wolf again, and then tell her that she was his mate.

At this rate, Tristan honestly couldn't understand how she didn't know. Though they'd only known each other for days, his wolf could recognize the soul for whom he'd been waiting for over one hundred years. It was the human part of Tristan who'd resisted. First he'd fought through the cloudy confusion, unsure of how he could possibly want to mark a female. But now his primary concern was ensuring that her shift was pleasurable, and ultimately, that she was accepted by the pack. Acceptance was something she'd have to earn herself. But she was exceedingly strong, despite her hybrid status. If given the chance, he was quite certain she'd attain both their respect and trust.

As they approached the lake on horseback, Tristan eyed one of his favorite spots to rest. Whether in human or wolf form, he loved lying in the soft grass, listening to the sounds of nature, relaxing by the water.

"Whoa. Pull back on your reins, Kal. We'll stop here," he instructed. Dismounting his horse, he gave it an appreciative pet. Pulling off the bridle, he slid on a halter, which he'd kept in his backpack, and then tied the leather lead around a low tree branch. As wolf, he was considerate of the horse's comfort, since he planned a leisurely late lunch that might take several hours. Kalli followed his example and also dismounted. He repeated the procedure with her horse, ensuring that both the mare and stallion were secure and content.

"This is the best surprise anyone has ever given me, you know. Okay, maybe it is the only time anyone has ever done something like this for me.

It's just so…I don't know. It's special. Amazing. The horses. The mountains. The lake. And you," she marveled. It was Tristan who'd changed her perceptions about pack life and what it meant to be Alpha.

Tristan came up behind Kalli, wrapping his arms around her waist. He kissed her ear and for a long while just held her, while they both stared out toward the water.

"Tristan," she whispered.

"Yeah, baby.

"No one's ever done anything like this for me," she croaked, trying not to cry. "Don't say it's no big deal, because it is."

"I want to do this for you. Even if there wasn't this thing…this connection between us. I just want to see you be happy, not locked up in a human's body, denying your wolf her due."

"As usual, you are right," she joked lightly.

"See, I knew you'd start seeing things my way." He smiled broadly. "Come on, let's eat lunch, then we'll talk. I'd say 'I'm so hungry I could eat a horse', but I don't want to offend our rides."

Tristan proceeded to spread a thin blanket onto the soft knoll while Kalli set out the food and drinks. After enjoying a leisurely picnic in the sun, they laid back on the warm fabric, taking in the sun.

"You're too far away," Tristan complained. "I need you next to me."

Kalli complied by rolling from her back onto her stomach, resting her head on his chest. She lazily draped her jean-clad thigh across his legs.

"Much better, mon amour."

"Hmm…yes," she replied.

"We need to talk about tonight. Toby's funeral. It's probably going to last several hours. To be honest, I haven't attended too many wolf burials. You know that whole immortal thing. But it happens from time to time."

"What's going to happen?" Kalli inquired, rubbing her hand on his chest.

"The first part is not all that different than some human rituals. We gather around the gravesite; talk about our experiences with that person, what made them special. It takes a while because there are many of us. Then we run, and mourn. We celebrate Toby's life, comfort each other."

"I can't run," she commented.

"I know, baby. That's why I wanted to talk."

"I'll go to the human part and skip the other. I mean, I can't shift, and to be honest, I'm a little worried about how the pack will react to me being there at all."

"They'll be fine. You're mine. Trust me." He pinned her with his eyes.

"Okay," she sighed, knowing he was probably right but that that wouldn't stop her from worrying.

"We won't be gone long, though. I'll be home right after the run."

Tristan squeezed her tight, wishing she could run with him. "But then tomorrow night…we will run together. It's the full moon."

"Yes it is." She breathed in a deep breath and blew it out.

"That's the other reason we need to talk. You've never shifted with other wolves. It…it can be overwhelming…Things can happen."

"Things? What things?" Kalli sat straight up in worry, looking down into Tristan's warm amber eyes. She tried not to panic but 'things' did not sound good.

"Come back here and relax," he ordered, pulling her back into his arms. "It's not bad. It's just that sometimes when we shift in a pack, all your senses are enhanced. And at the same time, you're in touch with others."

"Yeah." That didn't sound so bad, she thought.

"You know that we are very sexual, chérie. Not that we can't control our urges, because we can. But the temptation is there; wolves can partake or refuse. It's up to each and every wolf how far they want to go. And of course, no means no, even to wolves. Most wolves have great restraint and control. But often on a full moon, they, for lack of a better word, 'indulge' in their impulses."

Kalli tensed in his arms. "Are you saying what I think you're saying?

"Okay, here's the thing. Tomorrow, your hormones, your libido is going to react strongly to the pull of the pack. Before you run, after you run…you're going to want…well, you know, a release."

"Sex?"

"Well, yes, but it can be overwhelming. But, I'll be there for you. In fact, I think that tomorrow, when you change, maybe just you and I should run together. I don't want you getting lost or hurt."

"Or getting screwed?" she blurted out, on the verge of freaking out.

"No, chérie. It won't happen as wolf. But after…"

"What, Tristan? What's going to happen after?" She heard her voice rising as her anxiety worsened.

"After, we're going to go home. You and me. And I'm going to fuck you senseless, baby," he teased. "But remember the other night at the gala?"

"What about it?" she snapped, knowing where this was leading.

"Logan's my beta. I trust him with my life. And as much as it will kill me, I trust him with you, with us…together. After this first shift with the pack, you'll be able to control it. But this first time, I want it to be special for you, Kalli."

"I know. But Tristan, what exactly are you saying? It's not that I'm not open to experiencing different things with you. I won't lie, Logan's nice and he's good-looking, but he's so not….he's not…you. You're the one I want to claim."

Tristan leaned forward, capturing her lips in a soft kiss. "I know, baby. I just want us to be good…for the change to be the most incredible thing you've ever experienced. Logan cares for you. You'll be safe with us. We'll take care of you, I promise."

"Are you sure about this, Tristan? You do know that you're freaking me out. I don't want to turn into some kind of a sex crazed maniac tomorrow night," she insisted.

Tristan laughed. "It's not like that at all, Kal. In fact, I'm doing a pretty shitty job of explaining this whole thing. All I can tell you is that it will be beautiful; your shift, our lovemaking, everything."

"This is so crazy. It's not like I haven't shifted, but it's just been me, though. How pathetic is it that I don't even know something so basic, like what color I am or how to hunt with another wolf?"

"It'll come naturally. All of it. Our bond, Kalli, that's what's new…for both of us. Can you feel it?" he whispered.

"Yes." She skimmed two fingers over her mark. "I've never felt so strongly for anyone else in my entire life, Tristan."

"I feel the same way. My mark," Tristan slid his fingers under hers, tracing the symbol, "I want everyone to see it so they know you're mine. You've changed everything for me."

"Not nearly as much as you've changed things for me. I've been scared for so long, I've forgotten who I was or how to trust. And you're changing that, and it's unbelievable to feel again. But I can't imagine what I've done for you."

"Let's put it this way, I've been alone a long, long time. And I've never once in all those years wanted to be with one female…one woman." God, he wanted to tell her how she was his mate and how much he loved her. But she hadn't even shifted yet. He didn't want to scare her.

"When you say all those years, what do you mean? How old are you?"

Tristan laughed. "Old enough to know I'm robbin' the cradle when it comes to you, my little wolf."

"But you look like you're maybe thirty in human years. And even that is pushing it. Fess up," Kalli pressed with a smile.

"Born in 1862. You do the math." He grinned.

"So that puts you around one hundred and fifty?" She quickly calculated.

"That's what I get for falling for such a smart woman. Pretty quick on the math facts, huh?"

"Did you know that as a half breed I carry the benefit of immortality too? Ironically, both my parents are dead, anyway."

"Ah, but your mum was human. And your dad, well, he fought and lost. Even vampires can die. It's just the way of…"

"Nature?" Kalli finished his sentence, laughing.

"See? My lessons are rubbing off on you, young grasshopper," Tristan teased. "I've got lots of wonderful things I can't wait to teach you."

"I think it's time I teach you a lesson or two, oh great one," she jested, moving her hand over his leg, skating across the juncture of his thighs. "Although being the student definitely has its perks."

Tristan tensed as her hand skimmed over him. The evidence of his growing arousal pressed against the zipper of his jeans. Pulling her closer, he kissed the top of her head.

"Baby, whatever role you want is fine with me. You up for a little 'how to' in the great outdoors kind of lesson?"

Kalli cried his name in delight as he flipped her over onto her back. Straddling her, he ran his hand up under her tank top, caressing her breast.

"Yes please," she moaned, ready to take anything and everything he was willing to give her. Her heart was lost to him.

Chapter Twenty-One

After making love at the lake, Tristan and Kalli rode back to the barn, turned over their horses and hurried back home to get ready for Toby's memorial. Unsure what to wear, Kalli settled on rolled-up jean capris and a black tank top. By six-thirty, it had cooled only slightly after a ninety degree day, and Tristan had warned her that they'd be sitting for a while and to dress comfortably. Sliding on a pair of sandals, she bounded down the stairs to find Tristan and Logan lounging on the sofas but engaged in a serious conversation. Assuming it was about Toby, she quietly sidled up to Tristan.

"Hey there, we were just talking about how we're going to run things tonight. Fortunately, we don't need to have many funerals 'round here."

"Hi Kalli," Logan greeted, looking handsome in jeans and a white t-shirt, his bare feet crossed and rested on the coffee table.

"Hey Logan," she replied, looking to Tristan for guidance. For some reason, she'd become slightly worried about how people would react to Tristan's mark, his claim on her.

"He knows, Kalli. It's okay. We talked about everything," Tristan assured her, giving her thigh a quick squeeze.

Like how I'm going to turn into a sex craved maniac tomorrow night, she thought to herself.

As if Tristan could read her thoughts, he continued with a sexy grin. "He knows about us, and yes, we've talked about tomorrow night."

Logan interrupted, wanting to put Kalli at ease. "It's okay. I understand why you created CLI and hid your wolf. Self-preservation is pretty damn important when you're alone. But now you have us." He looked to Tristan and then back at Kalli. "And we won't let anything happen to you. Not tonight, tomorrow or any other day."

"Thanks," she acknowledged, willing herself to remain composed. "It's…it's not easy growing up in a pack like I did…alone. I just want you to know that I really appreciate you and Tristan looking out for me."

Tristan wrapped an arm around her, pulling her to him. "Soon, the whole pack will be there for you. You'll never be alone again."

Kalli gave him a small smile, giving in to her need to snuggle him, to touch him.

"I can't imagine what it was like for you all those years…shifting alone. It's just not right. You're going to love running with the pack. Tristan said he's running with you tomorrow night. I'll lead the pack then meet up with you guys later." He caught Tristan's eyes and smiled. "I won't lie, Kalli. I'm honored to be a part of your shift and helping you with your…um…needs. You know…should a *need* arise."

"Oh my God. This is so embarrassing," she gasped, putting her hands over her eyes. Her cheeks flamed. "Is there nothing you guys don't discuss?"

Tristan's eyes fixed on him with a glare. "What don't you understand about 'be cool'? As for tomorrow, don't get used to it, wolf. She's mine."

Logan laughed, enjoying riling up his friend. "Yeah, yeah, yeah. As if I was ever not clear on that. Come on…I am the great seer."

"Do share your visions…seems like you've been holdin' back on me, bro," Tristan accused.

"I can't share all my secrets. It's fate, anyway. I mean, look at your mark, it's beautiful."

"That it is. She's mine, and I want the whole pack to know it."

"Thank you, both. I couldn't be happier to wear it. And soon, I will be leaving my own mark on you, my Alpha," she purred openly. She didn't care if Logan was there to hear her. The way she felt, she'd shout it from the mountains. Claiming him would be one of the first things she did once her wolf reemerged.

Tristan gave her a quick hug. "Hey, I'll be right back. I just want to check on something before we go, okay?" He ran up the stairs, leaving Kalli and Logan alone.

"So are you staying here tonight?" Kalli asked Logan. "Tristan said that you usually stay here with him, and I want you to know that just because I'm here I don't ever want that to change. You guys have your thing, and I don't want to intrude or make things weird with me being here."

"Weird, no. Better, oh yeah. I'm really looking forward to watching you make breakfast," he grinned wolfishly, referring to her cooking attire or lack thereof.

Kalli laughed. "Hmm…I guess there really is no denying my wolf. She gets hot when she cooks."

A knock at the door interrupted them. Kalli got up to answer it. As she went to turn the handle, the hair on the back of her neck pricked.

Surprised to see Kalli in Tristan's home, Mira stood frozen in the entranceway. "What are you doing here?" she sniffed. "May I come in?"

"By all means." Regardless of her instinct to say no, Kalli ushered her into the foyer. A rush of anger flooded her body, and she struggled not to lose it. *Who the hell did this she-wolf think she was?*

"Where's Tristan?" Mira barked.

"Mira, come sit," Logan insisted, sensing things could get dicey.

"Why is she here, Logan? This is pack business. I want to talk to Tristan."

Logan stood. "Come on, Mir. Let's have a drink before we go. Don't do this."

Mira turned to Kalli, readying to lay into her, when she noticed Tristan's mark. Furious, she stalked up to her, gesturing to her neck. "Tell me this isn't what I think it is? Tell me now!"

While Kalli was more than accustomed to dealing with irate humans in the ER, Mira's mere presence in Tristan's home infuriated her. It wasn't just Mira's anger toward her. No, this woman threatened her bond with Tristan, and she had no tolerance for the intrusion. Her wolf, recognizing the aggressive alpha female, sought her submission; nothing less would suffice.

When Kalli didn't respond right away, Mira attempted to walk upstairs in search of Tristan. Instantly, Kalli growled and blocked her access to the staircase. With her hands clasping the railings, she refused to let Mira walk another step.

"Let's get something straight, Mira. Tristan will come back down here when he's damn well ready and yes, this is exactly what you think it is." She pulled her strap aside so Mira could get an unobstructed view of Tristan's mark, then she leaned toward Mira, staring her down.

"Tristan has claimed me. And after tomorrow night, he will be claimed as mine. So you have two choices: you can either be respectful in this house or you can get the hell out. I realize you've been friends with Tristan for a long time, but I'm warning you that I won't tolerate this nonsense. I don't want to hear one more word out of those finely painted lips of yours until you make your decision. And if you're thinking of challenging me, bring it."

Silence fell over the house as Kalli stood firmly planted, waiting for a response. Logan bit his lips in a tight smile and looked up to Tristan, who'd come to rescue Kalli after hearing Mira's rant. Tristan grinned back proudly at Logan, raising a knowing eyebrow at his beta. They'd briefly discussed this possibility earlier. While it was natural that Mira would feel threatened, both Tristan and Logan agreed that Kalli wouldn't allow another female to intrude on her relationship, especially now that she'd stopped taking those pills. Her wolf, who he suspected was also very much an Alpha, would seek to protect her mate. Not wanting to interfere, both men waited on the females to resolve their conflict.

Mira, sensing Tristan, lowered her eyes in submission. There was no arguing his mark; he'd selected Kalli as a potential mate. Even though she knew she wasn't Tristan's mate, she was devastated that he would claim a half breed. Worse, it meant she'd be cast aside in favor of his mate.

"I will be respectful in this house," Mira bit out. She turned on her heels and stomped toward the door.

Logan went to stop her. "Mir, wait."

"I'll meet you at the funeral," she spat, not looking back at him. Slamming the door, she set off toward the field.

Tristan descended the steps, and smiled at Kalli. "Okay?"

"Yeah, sorry. I'm not putting up with that 'I'm the alpha female' shit from her. I know she's your friend, but…"

"Hey, I'm proud of you. And I agree she was being disrespectful. I care about Mira, but you're my…." *Mate.* "You're mine. She needs to learn her place. Besides, I love how you want to claim me. I am so looking forward to it, too." He wrapped his hands around her waist and kissed her gently on her lips.

"I'm yours," she whispered in response.

Chapter Twenty-Two

Tristan had assigned Willow to lead the memorial service. In traditional preparation, an unmarked grave had been dug in a field on the property. Toby, wrapped in plain linen cloth, had been carried to the site by Tristan, who with the help of others, had lowered the dead wolf to his final resting place. The open gravesite was canopied by a clear starry sky. Settling around it, several pack members laid towels and blankets on the dewy grass.

Kalli quietly sat, watching the proceedings. While she'd attended several human funerals, she hadn't experienced one within a pack. Silent in her thoughts, she glanced over at Mira who was casting her an icy stare. She ignored her. It wasn't the place for arguments. No, it was a time for mourning and reflection. And Kalli, more than anyone, could appreciate loss.

Tristan stood solemnly before his pack and released a breath in preparation for the eulogy. "Lyceum Wolves, tonight we celebrate our young Toby's life. Whether studying hard or working hard, Toby always had a kind word for everyone and did his best to support our pack. From chasing the pups and teaching them how to hunt, to chasing the ladies, Toby lived life to the fullest. He'd shown many Alpha attributes, and perhaps would have led his own pack one day. Our brother's great spirit now shines within Lupus above, sparkling down on us. Tonight we share our experiences and our love with him and each other."

Many of the pack members smiled recalling his actions, and openly wept in sadness, realizing he was really gone. It was one thing to find out someone had died; it was another to see the empty shell of their body lying in the dirt. The finality of his violent passing could not be denied. Noticing that Kalli sat alone, Logan got up and sat next to her, protectively wrapping an arm around her shoulder.

"But before we begin the reminiscence, I want to take a few minutes to make sure every one of you knows that danger remains. The boy lying in this grave serves as a cold reminder that the immortal are susceptible to the call of death. Pack must remain strong in the throes of battle, as the survival of our species is a never ending war. Enemies shall never cease to exist, my friends. In only a few more days, we will once again go on the offensive to eradicate those who seek to harm us. Until they are contained, we must remain diligent at home in our efforts to protect the pack and our territory," he declared.

Tristan was planning an attack on the Wallace pack, but kept his strategy under wraps, given the circumstances. It was clear to him that Sato could not have been working alone. Perhaps at one time Sato had feigned lone wolf status in order to travel freely within territories. But Tristan's investigation of Gerald indicated that even though their pack was not large, they'd been committing atrocities for well over a century. Tristan could not accept another attack on Lyceum Wolves or Kalli. They needed to be dealt with, swiftly and without mercy.

Bringing his thoughts back to Toby, he gazed upon the grief-stricken faces and continued. "As many of you know, Toby's untimely death was met with vengeance last night. The blood of a wolf responsible for his death was shed in retribution. But the fight is not over. There's another wolf who shares culpability in this heinous act; one who will soon meet the same fate," he growled.

"But tonight, we honor Toby. Then we'll mourn in remembrance, as only wolves do. I'll begin." Tristan gently knelt, looking down into the grave. "Toby. Son. I'm going to miss you so much. Teaching you how to ride a motorcycle was a memory I'll always cherish. Even though you scratched my Harley up good your first try, you made me proud." He laughed softly at the memory. "The look on your face when I got you your own bike for your birthday last year…it was like I was the one who got the gift. Little brother, you were more than an adopted pup to me. As I run tonight, I know that you'll always be there in spirit with us. Be at peace, Toby." Tristan gave a small smile up toward the constellations, as a lone tear ran down his cheek.

Kalli began to quietly cry as she listened to Tristan talk to the boy he loved. She wished she could go back in time and find another way to hide instead of creating CLI. If he hadn't taken it, he might still be alive. Perhaps her mere presence in the Lyceum Wolves territory had brought war by the Wallace Pack. Even after all these years, she should have known they'd never simply let her go. While she may have been lower than an omega, they viewed her as their property. Sato's vile words toward her had confirmed that their hate was alive and well.

One by one, the wolves shared their goodbyes, sharing memories of Toby. The experience reminded her of a Quaker funeral she'd once attended for one of her colleague's parents who'd passed. Beautiful stories were met with both laughter and tears. Sitting with Logan and Tristan, listening to the crickets sing their music, she felt oddly at ease within the pack. By the time everyone who wanted to speak was finished, it was nearly midnight.

Tristan whispered in Kalli's ear, as the last speaker finished. "Chérie, we're gonna run now. I'll meet you at home in a few hours." He kissed her on the cheek, stood and walked over to pick up a shovel.

"And now my wolves, we'll return Toby's body to our great Earth. We're pack in life and in death." Tristan shoved the cold metal into the massive pile of dirt. With a heave, the red and brown particles scattered over the linen-shrouded form below. Several joined in to help, digging and pitching, until the burial site was sealed. Young pups placed wild flowers and seeds onto the loose terra, in an effort to bring forth a new circle of life onto the otherwise barren covering.

Wolves didn't leave headstones, for with scent, they'd always know where their loved one was buried. And in their hearts, they believed that lost souls returned to the Goddess of nature from whence they came. Their land was life. When they played or rode through this field, they'd be reminded of Toby and of his great spirit within their pack.

In preparation for their run, pack members began to strip. Feeling like an interloper, Kalli flicked on her flashlight and began to walk back toward the cabin. Out of curiosity, she briefly stopped and turned back, to catch a glimpse of her Alpha shedding his clothes, right before he turned into his spectacular black wolf. His lean, tanned body glowed under the stars giving way to shiny raven fur. Fascinated, Kalli quietly sat down on a rock, voyeuristically watching the remarkable sight. From afar, she admired her Alpha, and her heart tightened as she yearned to be with him.

Falling in love with a man like Tristan was easy. His physical beauty paled in comparison to his charismatic personality and cunning intellect. It took her breath away how he approached every single thing in his life with passion and vigor, from business to making love. She'd never witnessed such compassion and dominance in one man. Tonight, observing him command his wolves both as human and beast, exhilarated her.

In that reflective moment, Kalli realized she'd fallen in love with him. There was no mistaking the ache in her heart. As her mark tingled upon her shoulder, she was reminded that she was his. Her wolf begged to claim him in return. *Mate.* The word ran through her mind as if it was as natural as swimming on a warm summer day. Kalli released a small gasp as Tristan ran back and forth, playfully corralling the pups who sought to frolic on the outskirts. She indulged in her own fantasy, imagining him playing with their own children. He'd make a wonderful father. Raking her hand through her hair with a sigh, she once again wished she could run with him, to ease his pain. Speaking her thoughts aloud, she whispered, "I love you, Tristan. Run well tonight."

As if he'd heard her, the black wolf stopped to gaze upon her. His penetrating glare told her that he'd known she'd been watching all along. Giving him a small smile, she waved from the distance and slowly began her track back to the house.

Tristan heard the words, a mere whisper upon her lips. His heart beat wildly at her confession. His mate loved him. He wished to go to her, to tell her that he loved her as well, and make love to her all night long until she screamed his name over and over. But it would have to wait a few hours;

his responsibility to the pack came first. He released a celebratory howl, and the pack snapped to attention, readying to follow his orders. Respecting his command, Lyceum Wolves raced into the night.

It had been nearly two days since she'd taken CLI, and her proximity to the pack had left her skin itching to shift. But only the draw of the full moon could initiate her change after suppressing her wolf for so long. Her wolf was clawing to escape, to run with her Alpha. By the time Kalli got back to the cabin, she felt on fire with the need to shift. Like in the past, she could feel the change coming. But instead of resisting the transformation, her body and mind craved it. Even though she was still terrified, Kalli knew that, with Tristan, she'd be safe. And like her wolf, she planned to mark him the first chance she got.

Being with the other wolves pulled at her emotions in ways she'd never thought possible or expected. Seeing their naked skin melting into fur drove her into a muted exhilaration. She rubbed her limbs, which tingled in anticipation. Everything seemed amplified; sound, touch, smell. Safely within the wooden walls of Tristan's home, the cries of the night were still audible to her hypersensitive hearing. All senses on alert, she took a hot shower, hoping it'd subdue the overwhelming sensations racking her body.

Even though the warm water had helped to take the edge off, she felt like she was clinging to a precipice, rocks slipping under her feet. Wrapping her bare skin in Tristan's thin cotton robe, she made a cup of calming chamomile tea. But finding the chocolate truffles in his pantry was like finding gold in a mine. When it came to chocolate, the answer was always 'yes' as far as Kalli was concerned. As she bit into the tasty delicacy, a small gasp of pleasure escaped her lips. *Oh yes. Next to sex, it was the best thing on the planet.* Grabbing her warm mug and a book off one of Tristan's bookshelves, she trudged upstairs on a mission to lose herself within its pages.

After thirty minutes of reading on an overstuffed chair, she gave in to her exhaustion and opted for the mattress. Within seconds of lying down in Tristan's bed, she found she could no longer keep her eyes open. The smell of him on his pillow calmed every nerve in her body. Like an animal, Kalli rubbed her face into it, wishing his strong arms were wrapped around her. Shedding her robe, she slipped into the soft cool linens and embraced sleep, awaiting his return.

"Hmm, Tristan," Kalli purred, breathing in the masculine scent of her

Alpha. Kissing his skin, eyes still closed, she brushed her tongue over his nipple, teasing it with her teeth until it hardened. Feeling his arms pull her closer, she slid her hand down his chest. Finding the growing evidence of his arousal, she wrapped her soft fingers around him.

"Kalli," he groaned. Tristan had thought of nothing else but Kalli for the past three hours. *She loved him.* After running, he quickly showered and slid next to the warmth of her body. He could tell she wasn't quite awake but not asleep either. The touch of her hand sent blood rushing to his cock. Dominance still fresh in his system, he cuffed her wrist, demanding he take the lead.

She protested with a small moan, but was rewarded with a long, drugging kiss, bolting passion throughout her blood. In a fluid motion, he turned her onto her back, nudging her legs apart with his knees until he was comfortably settled on top of her. Supporting his weight with his elbows alongside of her head, his fingers pushed through her hair, fisting large spools of black curls as he continued kissing her deeply and thoroughly.

Kalli breathlessly kissed Tristan back, intoxicated by his essence. She welcomed the pressure of his body restraining her against the bed, allowing him to command their lovemaking. Wanting to be utterly possessed by him, she opened her heart and mind, submitting to their pleasure. The womanly heart of her ached to be taken. Moist and desperate for his touch, she acquiesced to the agonizing anticipation.

Releasing her lips, Tristan lowered his head to suckle a bared rosy tip. Gently, he swirled his tongue around the quivering areola until the throbbing peak stood stiff. Switching to the opposite breast, he continued his arousing assault.

"You are so perfect," he murmured as he licked and sucked her sensitive skin.

"Tristan," she whispered in response, altogether lost in his touch. She pushed her hips upward until she felt the tip of his straining sex.

"Kalli. Open your eyes," Tristan urged.

With heavy-lidded eyes, she peered up into the universe of his soul.

Tristan gazed into her eyes as he trailed his thumb along the seam of her lips. "I love you too. You're mine as I'm yours. You're my mate," he professed as he slid the hard length of him into her slick heat.

Her mouth opened in a soft cry as he buried himself in one swift motion. He gently cupped her cheek, pushing his thumb into her mouth. She wrapped her lips around his finger, allowing him to pull her cheek against the cool pillow, baring her neck to him. She moaned in response to the thrilling sensation of being purely dominated by her loving Alpha. Her mouth, the stretching walls of her tight depths, her swollen breasts and the rest of her soft curving flesh was his to take however he wanted. She offered it up to him on a platter, reveling in the ecstasy streaming through her consciousness.

At her passionate submission, Tristan nearly came. It was if he could sense the exact moment Kalli gifted him with her boundless trust. She gave herself freely, and he sought to take everything she offered.

"Feel me, Kalli," he instructed as he began to move within her. "Feel us."

He began thrusting his thick hardness in and out of her core, teasing every last moan from her body. Kissing her taut neck, he gently bit down on his mark, reminding her of his claim. She dug her fingernails into his back, feeling as if she'd explode any second. Her entire being, ignited in arousal, ached for release.

"That's it baby, feel me inside of you," he encouraged as she set free a cry of pleasure. "We are made for each other."

Tristan ground his pelvis against her clit, and she writhed upward, savoring every second of their joining. Propelling her to the edge of rapture, he plunged into her again.

"Please," she beseeched him. "I need to come. It's so good…so close…please."

Ravishing her mercilessly, he continued to work her into a frenzied state of euphoria. He fought for his own breath as she panted, releasing cries with each deep thrust she received. As his powerful fullness built up her orgasm, she moaned as the clenching spasms racked her body. She screamed his name, embracing the uncontrollable quivering waves of climax, grinding herself into him as he slammed against her.

"Fuck, yes, Kalli, I can feel you around me. So tight. I'm coming," Tristan yelled, as her warm sheath pulsed around him. Abandoning himself to his orgasm, he bit her again, stifling his masculine groans of satisfaction while exploding deep within her core.

"I love you," she whispered, slowly recovering from the erotic release.

Tristan gently slid out of her, yet never let go. As he fell on to his back, he brought her with him so that she rested on his chest. With one hand intertwined with hers on his belly, he caressed her hair with the other.

"Mon amour, what you do to me." His heart bloomed with emotion. Loving her would consume him forever, and he couldn't imagine living his life any other way.

Chapter Twenty-Three

From the minute Kalli woke, her senses were uncontrollably sensitive. While making love throughout the night had brought tears of joy, she now felt unsettled, overwrought with a thousand sensations bombarding her body and mind. She knew immediately that the rudimentary signs of her impending transformation had officially commenced. But this was different. Symptoms exaggerated exponentially; she assumed the influence of the pack drove the intensification of the effects. Every nerve and sense stood alert. The smell of the wildflowers. The sound of the birds. It was all too much. And then there was her hunger.

Tearing through the refrigerator, she cooked a huge feast of eggs, bacon, pancakes, sausage and toast. Ravenous, she ate five eggs, several pieces of bacon and two pancakes. While Tristan normally loved watching his little she-wolf make breakfast, he sought to comfort her. But there was nothing much he could do to ease the evidence of her affliction. Her first shift around pack would be difficult, he was certain. But once she got over the hump, she'd learn control over the way the pack heightened one's already animalistic ways.

Tristan stood behind her while she sat drinking tea, hands shaking as the amber liquid washed over the lips of the cup. Rubbing her shoulders, he worked the knots; she moaned in relief.

"Chérie, how about we take a run? It'll help release some of the tension."

"I'm sorry, Tristan. I don't know what's happening to me. Everything was so special last night…" her words trailed off, as she remembered the intensity of the evening.

"It's okay. Come up here." Tristan took her by the hands, pulling her upward and hugged her. "Tonight will be even more special than last night. I can't wait to see your beautiful wolf. I promise that it's going to be incredible. You'll learn how to trust in the reckless abandon of being wolf. The smell of the trees and animals. The taste of the hunt. We're going to run and then come back, take a hot tub…celebrate. As for the sexual release, it will be what it is…and with you it's always incredible."

"But what if I get lost? Go crazy? And Logan…I could seriously die of embarrassment that I could attack him as if I'm in heat," she huffed.

"Remember who's Alpha, chérie. No matter what happens later, you are mine. Trust me when I tell you that your wolf will not forget, nor will Logan's. I'll control what happens, I promise. Come on, now. Go get your shoes on. We're going for a walk. I want to show you around in the daylight, before tonight. It's beautiful here."

"Tristan," she said quietly, looking up into his golden eyes. "I know we didn't talk about things last night. About mating…I want you to know that I meant what I said. I love you. I want to claim you tonight…after the shift."

"Aw baby, you will. And believe me, I can't wait." He gave her a broad smile. "And after this mess is cleaned up with the Wallace Pack, we'll announce our mating to all of Lyceum Wolves, and hold a formal ritual…just you and me."

"I don't know how…I mean, I haven't been around wolves long enough to know how it works. I can just feel it within me. I want you…to be with you. God, this is so crazy."

"No it's not. But in a way, I know how you feel. Before you, the whole need to mate never made a lick of sense. But now, it's perfectly clear."

She smiled, knowing that everything always came back to nature for Tristan. Kalli wished she could be so confident, knowing what to do and say. But every minute she spent with Tristan, she grew more and more aware of the mating bond. More than a human's love, it bound their wolves eternally. Organic and instinctive, their mating would bond them irrevocably throughout time.

Tristan had taken Kalli for a long and winding walk through the woods, stopping to teach her about the plants and even point out the natural habitats of small game and reptiles. As a veterinarian, she found it fascinating. She was amazed at how much he knew about the environment and conservation. By the time they reached a small spring, she was unusually relaxed. He showed her how they'd fostered the spring. The cool clean water ran from the pipe in the rock into his stainless steel canteen as he filled it. As she drank the nectar, she eyed him thoughtfully, wondering exactly what he couldn't do. Whether it was riding a Harley or identifying a copperhead snake, he did it all with a cool air of confidence and a smile.

By the time they got back, Tristan directed her to eat lunch and take a nap, one that, regretfully, he insisted did not include sex. Instead, he'd stripped her bare, massaging every last muscle until she'd fallen asleep at his hands. He knew that her body was storing energy for the shift. Eating. Drinking. Exercising. And finally sleeping. It was everything she needed to make a smooth transition to lupine.

After a long nap, Tristan woke Kalli. Red streaks painted the dusky sky as the sun fell below the horizon. Wearing only cotton bathrobes, both Kalli and Tristan stood on the last step of the large cedar deck which wrapped around the back of the cabin. The harmonious sounds of the cicadas and crickets blanketed tranquility over Kalli's mind.

In the distance, she heard the yips of wolves, already singing in celebration of the full moon. Tendrils of her Alpha's power danced along her skin as she disrobed. Fully bared to the twilight, she closed her eyes and took a cleansing breath in preparation for her shift. Her wolf rejoiced in appreciation, no longer confined to the deep recesses of her soul. No, tonight the wolf would command her very being and in truth, Kalli delighted at the prospect. The gravitational force of the pack's quintessence reminded her of how this change represented a threshold to a new life. No longer a lone wolf, she'd claim her mate and belong to pack.

Turning to Tristan, she lifted her eyes to meet his. He smiled down at her, enjoying the sheer bliss she'd been experiencing at finally coming to acceptance of her nature. Tonight, he'd watch out for her, making sure she learned the land and was comfortable with him before introducing her to the pack. He expected that certain females such as Mira might try to challenge her. And while he was fully confident of her Alpha tendencies, tonight there'd be no fighting. Tonight was about helping Kalli while she rediscovered her wolf and learned to control the exhilarating, but sometimes distracting, assault to both one's senses and libido when in the presence of other wolves.

"I'm ready, Tristan," she breathed. "My wolf is here and can't wait to run."

"Okay chérie. Remember what we talked about. The tendency to want to go with the others will be strong, so pay attention to me. We'll introduce you to the pack another night. Logan's with them and he'll let them know you're around, but they've been instructed to leave you be." He tossed his robe onto the wooden planks, and took Kalli's hand in his.

His eyes narrowed into a serious expression. "That being said, expect their influence to be significant. This means you might feel unusually aggressive if one of them nears, especially given your need to claim me. You also will be extraordinarily hungry, so we'll hunt. Given that you've only hunted alone, I'll teach you how to hunt as a pair. Then eventually, we'll hunt with the pack, as a team. It's much better that way…power in numbers and all. Plus, we work collectively to teach the pups how to catch prey."

"Anything else I should know?" She smiled, listening to him reiterate what he'd already told her on their walk. She loved the way he cared so much about taking care of his pack, her, and making sure that she was prepared for what would happen. Given her terrifying past experiences, she had high expectations based solely on the facts that Tristan had told her. She laughed to herself, realizing how much she'd grown to trust him. A week ago, she'd considered her life that of a human, revolted by the life of a wolf. It was amazing how her Alpha had changed her thinking, her life.

Tristan wrapped a finger around one of her long curls and gave it a little tug, in an attempt to get her to focus. He could see the wheels spinning, and needed her to remain on task, so she'd be safe and calm within the forest. With a closed smile, he reminded her about the other topic she really wanted to avoid discussing. "The last thing I want to remind you of is one of my favorite topics, sex. I know we talked about this, but your libido will be on fire. Any full moon revs us all up, but this being your first around pack is going to make you one little randy girl," he teased, winking at her.

She rolled her eyes. "Please, let's just not talk about it."

"Don't be embarrassed. It's just our way…to want to be close to those that we love. And in your case, you'll learn to control it, but don't worry about it tonight. We'll just see how it goes after we shift back. I've got a nice set up for us afterwards to help you relax. No matter what happens tonight, I'll be there to protect you…always. Never forget that, Kalli." His voice took on a serious tone. "Ready now?"

Kalli gave a self-assured smile. Thanks to Tristan, she honestly was ready. "Hell yes. Let's do this thing. See if you can catch me, wolf!"

Untwining her hand from Tristan's, she broke free into a full sprint, seamlessly shifting into her wolf.

Tristan gasped in awe at the beautiful sight of her. Splendid white fur touched with grey down her back and legs, she darted across the green grass. She circled round him, running quickly, purely engrossed in her release. As Tristan stood erect, still in human form, she ringed once more, slowing as she came to face him. Falling at his bare feet, she playfully bowed her head toward the ground, looking upward at him with her tail wagging, hindquarters raised high in the air.

Reaching forward, Tristan ran his palm over her small head, in approval, rubbing her ears. "Chérie, you're stunning. Just beautiful, baby," he crooned.

She barked in response, and began chasing the wind in large circles as if to encourage him to shift. Taking off like a missile toward him, she swiftly missed him and ran toward the woods. Coming to a halt, she looked eagerly over her shoulder, waiting for him to change.

He laughed at her exuberance. After all the angst regarding her change, she was the one running circles around him. Or so she thought. Fluently, Tristan metamorphosed into his handsome, magisterial wolf. Stalking toward her, he sought her submission. Expecting pursuit, Kalli took flight toward the woods. Spotting his prey, Tristan flew past her, corralling her to the ground. Gleefully, she rolled to her back, baring her neck in defeat. He licked her muzzle, assuring her of his affections. With a nip, she reminded him that it was time to hunt; her wolf hungered for a kill. Free to run the land, she sought exploration and sport. Tristan nudged her belly, encouraging her to roll to her feet. Following her Alpha, they bounded into the night.

Rounding a clearing, Kalli spotted a rabbit in the field. Tristan sensed her distraction, waiting to see how she'd handle hunting with him near. Wagging her tail, ears up, she instinctively focused on her prey. Tristan watched intently, prepared to rush the rabbit from the other side should she miss. Quietly approaching the rabbit, she struck out in a sprint, snapping its neck, resulting in an instant kill. Sharing her spoils, they ate the small snack then ran to the spring for a drink.

While lapping up the water, Kalli froze; she sensed the pack was approaching. Ears down, the hair on her back bristled as the first wolf came into sight. A smaller white she-wolf followed a silky grey male. Kalli, unused to being in pack, immediate recognized them as Mira and Logan. Subordinates trailed, staying cautiously behind the pair. Tristan stepped forward to block their access. *What the hell were they doing?* He'd told Logan that he didn't want them near Kalli. Growling, he warned them to come no closer. Yet Mira ignored him, and continued to pad toward him. While she lowered herself in submission, she advanced nonetheless. In a sign of dominance, Tristan sent her a hard stare.

Upon seeing Mira close in upon Tristan, Kalli's posture straightened. Threatened, she lifted her tail and edged around Tristan. Emitting a low growl, she locked her eyes on Mira in an angry menacing act of intimidation. When she refused to submit, Kalli maintained her confident stance, and bared her canines. Ready to attack, in the moment she resisted the aggression that begged to escape. Not only did she want a subtle signal of submission, she wanted Mira on her back.

Within seconds, Mira looked away and whined, yielding to Kalli's threats.

Logan, watching the interaction play out, knew that Tristan would be pissed as hell that he'd let the pack come near Kalli. But they'd been running for over an hour and happened to be near the spring. He'd hoped that Tristan would have moved Kalli in time. He could sense the confusion and surprise of the subordinates as Kalli, who hadn't been formally introduced as pack, not only stood marked as Tristan's but had just forced Mira to publicly submit.

Tristan nearly had a heart attack when his little wolf challenged Mira. After witnessing Kalli dressing down Mira in his home the previous day, it was just a matter of time before she confronted her without reserve in front of the pack. Even though he knew it had to be done, he was hoping to delay any confrontation until Kalli had had a chance to be comfortable within her wolf. He also wanted time to announce his intention to mate Kalli so that when Mira submitted it would be a less bitter pill for her to swallow. While Mira was currently the Alpha female, she was not his mate. The pack subordinates would expect his mate to be the strongest, most intelligent female, and after her little display of dominance, she was.

As the pack ran off, Kalli howled in jubilation. There was no way that, after everything she'd been through, she'd allow another female near her male. Mira, without a doubt, was formidable. She reckoned that it would not be her last challenge. Yet confidence raced through her veins. Forcing Mira to physically submit would be a pleasure that her wolf would someday see to fruition, of that she was certain.

Tristan howled along with Kalli, proud of her courage and assertiveness. His woman matched his own authoritative constitution. And while he trusted in fate and nature, he couldn't help but be amazed at how she fit him precisely in every way. Nuzzling his muzzle along her side, she returned his action in kind. The sheer adrenaline of the night brought forth a surge of emotions they both longed to explore. Nudging her forward, he willed her to follow; it was time to celebrate their first successful run together, one of many in their eternal lifetime.

Chapter Twenty-Four

"That was phenomenal!" Kalli exclaimed, letting the hot spray clean her skin. An oversized nozzle delivered the warm water into the open-aired shower which sat next to the outdoor Jacuzzi. Overwrought with both desire and exhilaration, she squealed in delight as Tristan delivered a spank to her bottom. "Hey, what's that for?"

"I couldn't resist with you wagging your tail at me like that all night. A man can only take so much. Seeing your wolf has given me some very naughty ideas…ones that I'm sure you'll like," he promised in a sexy low voice. Slipping out of the shower, he grabbed a clean beach towel off a hook and slung it around his waist, beads of water dripping off his lithe body. "I'm goin' inside to get a few things. Go 'head and get in the hot tub, and I'll be right out."

Kalli sighed in anticipation, washing the last of the dirt off her skin. As usual, he'd been right about everything. She'd been ravenous when she'd attacked her prey, and then, with her aggression toward Mira, protecting her Alpha had been foremost in her wolf's mind. And now desire for him raged like a wildfire. She had no idea what he was getting or planning but he'd damn well better hurry up.

Easing into the hot tub, she hissed as bubbling water caressed her in all the right spots. "Oh. My. God. This feels so good," she declared, sinking in all the way up to her neck. Closing her eyes, she laid her head against the soft padding along the rim. A door opening caused her to lift her lids. Gloriously naked and erect, Tristan exited the house with a tray full of goodies. Food? Champagne? Something else that she couldn't quite identify?

At this point the only sustenance she required was Tristan, as he was, and in her. She lazily smiled, watching him pour three glasses, presumably a third for Logan, who hadn't yet arrived. She wondered if he was okay, given her fight with Mira. She knew the three of them had all been childhood friends, and she wished things could be different, but now that she had Tristan, she wasn't letting some she-wolf try to push her away. There was a new sheriff in town, and she wasn't going to tolerate Mira's nasty interference.

Tristan lowered himself into the tub slowly, reaching for Kalli. The sexual tension between them crackled the air. She needed him, and so much more. And as promised, he was there for her.

"Come here, mon amour," he purred into her shoulder, licking over his mark, sending a bolt of desire to her already pulsing core.

"Tristan, I am so….I can't wait to have you in me, please," she begged. Every nerve screamed for his touch.

"Yes, baby, I know. I know what you need." He pulled her on top of him, so she sat straddling his legs. Reaching down between her legs, he brushed his thumb over her clit. He planned to take her hard and fast the first time.

She screamed at the brief caress of her nub. "Oh God, yes!"

"That better? How 'bout this?" Guiding his engorged head to her entrance, he pulled her downward, impaling her on his rock hard cock. So deep inside her, he filled her completely. "Ah yes, Kalli."

"Yes, that's it. Fuck me!" she screamed loudly into the night.

Knowing how to take the edge off, Tristan passionately captured her lips, sweeping his tongue into her mouth. Wrapping her long hair around his fist, he kissed her, engrossed in her ambrosial essence.

Kalli returned his bruising kiss, sucking and biting. As the animalistic excitation overtook her being, she took all he gave and demanded even more. "Oh yes! Harder! Yes! Tristan! So close!"

"That's it. Yeah, take me all in. Feel how hard you make me." Seeking to give her the release she needed, he slid his hand in between her legs. Circling and pressing against her ripe nub, he felt her convulse around him. "Let it go."

As he applied pressure to her sensitive pearl, she flew apart, screaming his name, grinding herself hard against his pelvis. In the heat of her climax, she extended her canines and bit deep into Tristan's shoulder, effectively claiming him forever. A part of her wished it could have been a gentle process, but her wild territorial wolf insisted she claim him on her terms, deliberately carnal. There could be no mistaking her intentions.

Tristan nearly split in half as she marked him. The pleasure of her bite racked through him and he struggled not to come. "Yes, Kalli. I'm yours," he grunted through the sweet pain.

Kalli laved over her bite, resting her head upon his shoulder, while he remained stiff inside her. Feeling unchained, she could feel the ache start to build once again.

Tristan sucked her neck, kissing behind her ear. "Goddess, I love you, woman. You feel so good around me."

"I love you too," she moaned as she relaxed against him.

"Rest a minute, chérie; we're just getting started." He looked up to find Logan smiling at him from across the hot tub; he'd been watching them make love. Like Kalli and Tristan had done, he was taking a shower.

Kalli caught a glimpse of Logan as he tilted his head back and closed his eyes to rinse the bubbles off his taut skin. Like a sculpted statue in a fountain, water sluiced off his corded muscles. The sight of him rubbing his hands over his hard masculine form caused her sheath to clench even tighter around Tristan.

Intellectually, she knew that whatever sexual feelings she had toward Logan were only driven by the extraordinary experience of learning to shift with the pack. Tristan had warned her that this would happen. She wasn't in love with Logan, in any sense of the imagination, but the overwhelming sexual attraction of the night pulled at her. A pang of guilt stabbed her, aware that her libido was out of control. Mortified at her hidden desires, she buried her face into Tristan's shoulder, looking away. God help her, she wanted to make love to them both tonight.

Tristan felt Kalli vise around him, her eyes darting to Logan. Sensing her interest, he was torn between finishing what they'd started and wanting to wait for Logan to join them. Loving his beta and his mate, he sought to exhaust her heightened sex drive in unison, certain that it would prove to be both a wondrous and provocative adventure. His most visceral animal instincts encouraged the sexual interaction; he loved them both unconditionally and as Alpha, whatever happened, both Kalli and Logan would be under his command.

He smiled down at her, appreciating that she was truly a babe in the woods when it came to living as wolf. It was no longer about secretly shifting once a month to get it over with…no, she was learning how to saturate her mind with the experience, learn the power of the pack and accept the happiness that came with being wolf. Their mating would be both a life affirming and life changing experience, one that would eventually affect every member of Lyceum Wolves. Nothing would ever be the same, and he didn't want it any other way. And while for most of his life, he'd never imagined or wanted a mate, he knew for certain that now he had Kalli in his life, he'd never be able to live without her.

Tristan slid out of her, but still kept her pulled against him in an embrace. "It's okay, Kalli, I want this too," he whispered into her ear. "Remember that nothing will happen that you don't want to happen."

"I am out of control," she confessed, refusing to look at him.

"No you're not. You're just in touch with the pack and your shift. It's all good. Nature, baby, remember? Next time you run with the pack, you'll still feel a little bit like this, but you'll have better control. I promise I'll take care of you. Tonight, just enjoy how you feel, how we make you feel."

"As opposed to feeling like I could crawl out of my own skin just to get off," she joked, finally looking him in the eyes. "God, I really am a wolf in heat."

"Hmm, not yet, but someday. And I won't lie, I am looking forward to that, chérie," he purred. The thought of her pregnant with his children tugged at his heart. She'd make a wonderful mother.

"Don't even tell me what will happen when I go into heat. All I know is that I can't keep my hands to myself as it is. I can't believe the dirty thoughts running through my head," she laughed. "Are you sure this is normal?"

"Perfectly. Now does someone need another lesson in trust?" he asked with a chuckle, aware of all the naughty things he planned to do to her lovely little body in just a few short minutes.

"I suppose I do," she teased back, kissing his cheek softly. "You were planning on teaching me, Alpha?"

"Hey people," Logan interrupted with a smile. "Looks like I'm missing all the fun."

"Hey yourself," Kalli replied as she drank in the view of his glistening body.

"Come on in, bro," Tristan called over to him; a look of mutual understanding passed between them. They'd discussed in detail how the shift would affect Kalli and others in the pack. As leaders, they were ultra-aware of the implications of adding another pack member and the side effects of Kalli's shift. While it was unusual to be a lone wolf as Kalli had been, it wasn't unheard of, so they knew what to expect.

Logan languidly slid into the hot water, groaning in pleasure. "Oh man, that feels good."

"Yes it does. You know what feels even better?" Tristan raised an eyebrow at him. "Hold her for me, will you? I want to rub her feet. My girl ran hard tonight."

Kalli's heart pounded, hearing Tristan offer her up to Logan like a piece of roast beef. *What the hell was he doing? Trust, trust, trust.* Oh God, she knew she should trust Tristan after everything they'd been through, but he wasn't making it easy.

Tristan pulled her toward him once again and gently kissed her. "You're okay, chérie. Now give me your feet." Easily maneuvering Kalli's small frame, he set her so that her back was against Logan's chest. "That's it. Just relax and let us take care of you."

Logan didn't attempt to touch Kalli; he simply let her rest against him as if she was sitting in a chair. They both kind of just relaxed into the hot steam.

But once Tristan went to work on the insoles of her feet, Kalli gave a satisfying moan. "Oh my, that feels amazing. Please, do not ever stop." Letting her head loll back onto Logan's chest, she closed her eyes.

Tristan smiled at Logan, who was waiting for instructions. "Logan, why don't you massage our little wolf? She did so well tonight, don't you think?"

Logan returned the smile, given permission to touch her. "Yes she did. And I must say that I enjoyed watching her go all alpha, standing her ground."

"What a bitch," Kalli snapped. "I know you guys are friends, but I'm not backing down."

"Nor should you," Tristan agreed. "But that shouldn't have happened tonight, because I asked Logan to keep the pack away. You are a ferocious girl, you know that. But really, Mira damn well knows that she shouldn't have approached me out there, especially since I claimed you. I'm sure her submission did not sit well with her, but Mir's ego will survive."

"Yeah, I'm really sorry about that, man, but I thought you guys were on your way out of the spring. But damn, if watching your woman growl didn't turn me on," he chuckled. "Dominance is hot." He wiggled his eyebrows, and they all laughed.

Logan gently took his hands to Kalli's shoulders, moving slowly down her arms. When he finally reached her fingers, he moved to her hips, adjusting her so the firm ridge of him nestled in her bottom. Sliding his palms up her belly, he finally arrived where he wanted. Collecting her tantalizing breasts in both hands, he gently squeezed them.

Kalli's pulse raced in arousal. Her eyes flew open to Tristan, who watched her intently.

"Breathe, Kalli," he reminded her. "Goddess, you are so radiant tonight. Seeing you in Logan's hands…it really turns me on, baby."

At his words, arousal took flight within her once again. The predatory look in Tristan's eyes made her pussy tighten. She wanted him in her again. Having Logan touch her while he watched, only served to ramp up her desire even more.

"She's so soft," Logan commented to Tristan as he placed a kiss to her ear. The evidence of his growing arousal pressed up against her backside and Kalli squirmed in excitement.

Running his palms from the tips of her toes to the inside of her thighs, Tristan brushed over her mound then pulled away again, edging her up with desire. Hearing her breath catch as he nearly touched the heart of her sent a surge of blood to his groin. "Logan, sit up on the edge. I need to taste her…that's it," he encouraged.

Using his muscular thighs, Logan pushed up so that he and Kalli sat along the wide border of the hot tub. Bared to the night, Kalli sucked a breath as the cool air hit her skin; her exposed ripe peaks hardened.

Like a lion stalking his prey, Tristan's eyes locked on hers, advancing until he pushed both Kalli's and Logan's knees wide open, his face mere inches from the apex of her thighs.

"Hmm…such a pretty pussy, look, Logan. She's so wet for us, aren't you Kalli?" Tracing his forefinger through her slick folds he stroked up and down, avoiding her swollen center.

In the past, Kalli would have been offended at such dirty talk, but Tristan's words sent her into overdrive. No longer a scared and timid human wannabe, she sought to experience all and everything Tristan offered. Logan's hands continued to massage her, now paying special attention to her nipples, rolling them between his forefingers and thumbs. Kalli pushed her hips upward seeking his mouth, unable to wait. She strained as Tristan's breath brushed over her lips.

"Tristan, please, don't tease me," she begged.

As much as Tristan wanted to draw out her pleasure, he knew that tonight of all nights, she desperately craved release. Her body would be on fire with arousal and he planned to drench her in his love. Darting his tongue forward, he licked open her seam and pushed two firm fingers up into her at the same time.

"Yes!" Kalli screamed.

"You taste so sweet," he mumbled into her wetness. Circling her with his tongue, he dragged a flat broad stroke against her golden flesh. He lapped at her honeyed cream, gently taking her into his lips. Turning his fingers upward, he petted along the long strip of nerves that ran deep inside her.

"There, oh yes, there," she confirmed. Writhing, she raked both hands through his hair, clasping him to her. As he wrapped his lips around her clit and sucked, her orgasm slammed into her hard. She fought for air, shaking in Logan's arms as Tristan continued to pull on her little peak, draining every last wave from her.

"Tristan," she gasped, unable to string together a coherent thought. The things this man did to her sent her over the edge and then some. Just as she was starting to recoup, he spun her around so she was on her hands and knees on the step of the tub.

"Kalli, take Logan, while I take you." She heard Tristan say. Opening her eyes, her gaze flew to Logan's. Nestled between his legs, Logan's hard shaft begged to be touched. He reached down to stroke himself, but she stopped him.

"Logan, come to me," she commanded. God help her, she wanted him too. He'd given her nothing but assurance since she'd met the man. And here he was before her, gorgeous and hot with need.

Obeying his Alpha's mate, he leaned forward, his hardness so close to her warm mouth. In the heat of the moment, no longer embarrassed, Kalli craved him. Tristan wanted this as much as she did, so when he pressed at her core, she parted her lips and dragged her tongue over Logan's straining sex. He tasted of maleness, spicy and delicious. She took him all the way into her mouth. She mewled softly, and Logan threw back his head, willing himself to let her suckle him at her own pace.

The sight of his woman pleasuring Logan sent a hedonistic pulse to Tristan's already throbbing hardness. Slowly, he pushed into Kalli's tightness, stretching the walls of her body. "Aw, Kalli," he groaned. "So amazing."

She moaned in excitement, reveling in the feel of Tristan inside her while she sucked Logan harder and harder, bringing him pleasure.

Tristan surged into the warmth between her legs. "Ah yeah. Feel how good we all are together." Settling his hands on her bottom, he slowly rocked in and out, all the while watching Kalli attend to Logan. The quickening energy flowed between all three of them, building the sexual tension to a new high.

Massaging her smooth cheeks, Tristan ran his finger along the crease of Kalli's ass and brushed over her rosebud. She moaned in response, wriggling back toward his touch. Remembering how she'd so enjoyed the anal play the other night and the way she came apart with the toy, he'd been dying to expand their repertoire.

"Mon amour, I want to take you here tonight," he breathed, pressing a finger into her puckered flesh while continuing his sensual rhythm. "It will be so good." He swore he'd make it the most amazing, pleasurable experience she'd ever known.

Her senses flooded, her pulse quickened at the thought. Momentarily releasing Logan from her mouth, she hesitated to admit what she secretly wanted. "I…I don't know," she breathed.

"Trust," he reminded her with a soft smack to her ass. The sting sent a jolt to her already aching pussy, elevating her desire. She swore she could feel the wetness flow in response to his demand.

"Ah yes. Yes, do it," she responded with urgency. Part of her wondered what was wrong with her that she liked the feel of him slapping her bottom. But then again, everything he did felt so good. Her body thrummed in excitement, awaiting his next move.

"I think she likes being spanked," Logan remarked as she took him once again into her mouth. "Oh yeah, definitely. Kalli, that feels so good."

Kalli hissed as a cool liquid ran down her backside, realizing what Tristan was doing to her. As his generously lubricated finger probed her, she pushed back into him. "Tristan, yes. Please."

He added another finger and a small burning sensation hit her. "I…I can't…."

"Breathe, baby. Just give your body a minute. We've got to slow down."

Relaxing into his touch, the burn gave way to fullness as he pushed in and out, his fingers now scissoring her, preparing her for him. An erotic pleasure that she'd never known coursed through her body, every part of her full with the men she trusted.

Logan removed himself from her mouth, resting her forehead on his legs, so she could relax as Tristan entered her. Lying back onto the wide rim, perpendicular to them, he looked up to their faces. The position also freed him so that he could stroke his rigid sex and have one hand to touch Kalli.

"Okay, chérie, I'm going to go slowly. I'm right here. Now push back a little as I push into you," he instructed. Kalli gasped into Logan's thigh as Tristan pushed the first inch of his rock hard cock into her tight ring.

The slight pain soon gave way to a blissful wholeness. She took ragged breaths as he slowly entered her, anticipating his entire sinewy length. "Oh my God, Tristan. Please, don't stop," she screamed at the feel of his dark intrusion.

"You feel so good, Kal. So tight. You okay?" he asked, his hand gripped to her hips.

"Yes, please…make love to me," she cried, nodding her head. Filled with a hunger she'd never known, she couldn't take any more. So out of control, yet so filled with ecstasy, she needed all of him, every last bit he was willing to give.

Carefully, he moved in and out of her, taking care to make sure she was enjoying every stroke. Sliding his hands around her belly, he pulled her upward until they were both up on their knees. His chest against her back, he held her breasts, pinching her nipples into firm nubs.

She released a groan, overwhelmed with the feel of his hands on her, the fullness. "Tristan, I love you," she moaned.

"Love you too, baby. Feel us."

Logan was about to burst at the sight of them together, so beautiful. Tristan eyed him, willing him to remain in contact. With his free hand, Logan pushed a long, thick finger into the slick wetness of her arousal, thumbing her clitoris.

"Oh my God, I…I…" She ecstatically shuddered at yet another touch to her body. Tristan pushed in and out of her rosebud as Logan pressed inside her core. Sinfully delighted, she hurtled toward her orgasm. Screaming Tristan's name over and over again, a frenzy of convulsing waves rippled throughout her whole body. Tristan held her tightly, as she thrashed back and forth, crying out in reckless fervor.

As she spasmed, Tristan groaned low and hard, stiffening in release. "Ah, I'm coming!" He held tight to her body as the fiery culmination of their explosions continued to rack their bodies. Logan grunted, a hard climax rocking him, his seed jetting upon his rock hard abs.

For a long minute, the trio rested in their respective positions, unable to move. Slowly, Tristan pulled himself from Kalli, scooping her up into his arms. Taking her over to the shower, he turned on the warm spray, carefully washing her body as she laid her face against his chest.

The night could not have been more perfect, Kalli thought as she clung to Tristan. As if she'd been born again, she'd breached the curtain of apprehension and fear that had plagued her life. She was wolf and woman, inside and out. Her Alpha. Her pack. Grateful for her awakening, she whispered, 'I love you', before finally submitting to the gratifying exhaustion that took over her body and mind.

Chapter Twenty-Five

The birds serenaded them from the tree branches as the streaks of sun burst through the skylights. Kalli could have sworn she'd died and gone to heaven after the magical night she'd spent running with Tristan, and then making love to him under the stars. Not even Logan's participation felt awkward in retrospect. It all was as Tristan had said it would be; natural and loving.

She felt like the luckiest woman in the world. After the years of abuse and hiding, she could finally embrace her wolf and everything she was. True, she was still a well-respected veterinarian, who would continue her work at the university and shelter. But it was as if a huge piece of her being had been discovered: lover, mate and pack member. For the first time in her entire life, she felt complete.

"Hey, what are you thinking about?" Tristan asked sleepily.

"How do you do that?"

"What?"

"Know what I'm thinking?" she laughed.

Tristan kissed the top of her head. "It's not that I know exactly what you're thinking. I can't really explain it except to say that I bond with every single pack member. I feel them and they, to some extent feel me. I can push forth feelings, power, for lack of a better word. It can cause excitement or calming; things like that. Intimidation, if challenged. It's hard to explain; it's just part of me."

"And with me? What do you feel?" She trailed her fingers along the contours of his chest.

"Ah, with you I feel every emotion tenfold, as if it's magnified somehow. I sense how you are feeling, what you're thinking. It's all part of me claiming you and you claiming me. Our bodies and minds work in preparation for our mating, so that we get used to working as one, leading as one. As my mate, you'll have status within the pack. But the dominance you demonstrated over Mira yesterday, as wolf, well. Let's just say, tongues will be wagging instead of tails this morning."

"And how does the pack feel today?"

"They feel good about the stability of me taking on a mate, something they've wanted for a long time but never thought they'd get. And frankly neither did I. But now that I have you, I'm not letting go."

"About that…our mating. I don't know…I mean I never had a female to explain it to me. I've met mated wolves but never really understood how…the details."

He smiled, remembering her naivety. "Not that complicated really. I mean technically we're halfway there, having claimed each other and all." He traced her mark with his forefinger. "We just have to declare our commitment to each other while making love and then exchange, you know, bites. But a little harder this time, so that we have a blood exchange. Of course, afterward, we'll formally announce our mating in front of the pack. We can hold a more traditional reception if you want. It'll be beautiful, like you. And from then on, we'll be mated, be able to have children. So, how do you feel about that?"

"It sounds wonderful," she responded, mentally paused on the thought of children.

"How do you feel about children?"

"Honestly? I never gave it a thought before I met you. But watching you the other day at the funeral, playing with the pups… I really would love to have your children someday. You'd make a great Dad."

"And you'd make a great mother. Seeing you with your puppies…makes me want to have a whole litter," he halfheartedly joked, hoping not to scare her too much.

Tristan's heart had constricted on hearing her words. She wanted *his* children. He'd never thought he'd mate, let alone have kids until he saw her that day in the shelter, caring for all the animals. He laughed to himself, taking note of the one-eighty he'd made over the past week. He had always subscribed to the idea that one should not mess with Mother Nature. And boy was she ever teaching him a lesson.

Changing the subject, he inquired how she felt about last night. "So how do you feel today? About your run? About our mad lovemaking session in the hot tub?" He laughed.

"You get right to it, don't you?" she giggled. "I feel amazing. A bit sore in all the right places, but I am just feeling so whole. So complete. Shifting with you last night, was the single most phenomenal thing that has ever happened to me. Well, aside from what we did afterward. That was pretty awesome too."

She quieted in a serious manner, cupping his face and gazing directly into his piercing amber eyes. Unprecedented emotions rose in her chest; tears threatened to fall. "I just…I want you to know how grateful I am to you. And no, don't even say it's nothing. Everything you've done for me, I've never had this before…you've made me…you've made me whole. I can't even say 'whole again' because I've never felt like I belonged or even felt comfortable in my own skin. Then all those years, being terrified. Because of you, I'm safe, true to my nature and most importantly, loved."

Tristan leaned in, kissing her tears, and just held her. He loved her so much. He knew she didn't want his pity. She just wanted to say thank you, and he welcomed her appreciation with love.

The sound of the phone ringing broke the moment, and he reached over to pick it up. "Tristan," he answered.

Holding the phone to his hand, he addressed Kalli. "Janie wants to know if you can look at one of our mares. She's sick. Doc Evans checked her a few days ago but Janie would feel better if you came by to check on her again today…since you're here and all."

Kalli nodded, smiling in agreement. Secretly, she was thrilled that someone from the pack would think to ask her for help. Even though she and Tristan would only be up the mountains on weekends, she'd be happy to help care for the horses in the future.

"She can make it. I'll drop her off in about a half hour on my way to the clubhouse. Later." Hanging up the phone, Tristan stretched slowly, wrapping his hands back around her. "Well baby, as much as I'd love to stay in bed all day, you've got a date with a horse and I've got an early meeting. We're running through the plan for when we go to South Carolina tomorrow."

Nearly jumping out of the bed, Kalli sat straight up and shot him a questioning look. "South Carolina? When are we going? Did they find him?"

Tristan returned her look with a serious expression. "You, my lovely little wolf, are not going anywhere. And yes, we've found Gerald. I expect the wolf who killed Toby will be with him, or he'll know his location. Logan's got all the intel, and we're flying in tomorrow night on the jet."

As much as Kalli wanted to see Tristan rip Gerald's throat out, she still held a healthy fear of the man who'd wanted to hurt her. All things considered, she should be happy that Tristan didn't want to take her with him. But her protective streak couldn't let him go alone.

"Tristan, here's the thing, I know that place. I know how to get around in the woods, where they hide, the wolves. I can help," she suggested, trying to convince him to let her go.

"Not an option, baby." Swinging his legs off the bed, he strode across the room. There was no way in hell he was putting her in danger.

"Please. Just think about it. Gerald, he's ruthless. He doesn't play by the rules."

Tristan turned before going into the bathroom. His eyes narrowed into the predatory scowl she'd seen at the Summit. "There won't be anyone left when this is done, Kalli. I'll spare the women and pups, but subordinates who support him will die. I've got this. As for you, you're staying here. End of discussion."

Kalli's stomach lurched as she thought about Tristan, Logan and the others going after the Wallace pack. Merciless, they'd go for the kill every time. While she was confident that Tristan could best Gerald one to one, they played dirty, often employing human weapons that could injure wolves, weakening their prey. Maybe Tristan thought her going wasn't an option, but losing him wasn't an option either. Quietly, she resolved to try and talk him into taking her after she checked the horses.

"Stop worrying," Tristan ordered as he pulled the car in front of the barn. "Seriously, you've got to let it go and trust that I will handle this. I've got news for you; it's not my first time to the rodeo. I won't be able to do my job if you're there with me. It's literally impossible to concentrate when I'm within five feet of you." He gave her a small smile. "Now go take care of my baby…my big four-legged baby, that is."

"Baby, huh?"

"Jellybean's the one who's sick. She's a sweet girl, picked her out myself. And yes, she's my baby. So go give her a look, would you? Janie can give you a ride back if you want."

"Nah, I think a walk back to the house would do me good. I'll take the path you showed me yesterday. Should only take me about ten minutes, right?"

"Yep, the cabin's open. I should be done in a few hours, okay?"

Kalli leaned over, giving him a brief kiss on the lips. As she contemplated kissing him more deeply, she ran her tongue across the seam of his lips. He reluctantly resisted, softly laughing.

"If you keep this up, I swear I'll have you up in that hay loft within five seconds. I don't think Janie would appreciate us going like rabbits in her stables."

She smiled against his lips. "Later. You owe me," she teased seductively.

With a peck to his cheek, she opened the car door, shut it and walked into the barn. Janie, a pixie-sized woman with red cropped hair, waved her over. Looking around, Kalli considered maybe taking a ride, but regretfully, she hadn't thought about it when dressing in a pair of shorts. She admired the neatly kept facilities. The stable already housed around twelve horses, and it appeared as if it could easily hold twelve more.

"Janie?" Kalli asked, extending her hand.

"Kalli?" They shook hands and she quickly ushered Kalli toward Jellybean's stall. She was a beautiful palomino American Quarter Horse, standing fourteen hands high with a small refined head and strong muscular body.

Slowly approaching her, Kalli flattened her palm, letting the horse sniff her before gently stroking her neck. "That's a girl. Now what seems to be wrong? You a sick baby?" she crooned.

Janie shot her a broad smile. "You really are Tristan's mate, aren't you?"

Kalli nodded, smiling in kind. "Yes, I am. Or, I should say that I will be.

Why?"

"They're his babies too, you know. I'm glad to have you in the pack. He needs a good woman," she offered. "And I couldn't be happier now that we've got ourselves a pack veterinarian."

"I'd love to help with them when we're here, but I'm more of a generalist. Not a lot of expertise with these big babies, I'm afraid. But I'd be happy to check her vitals. What did Dr. Evans say?"

"He said she was doing better. She had been diagnosed with influenza. She seems all right, but I get worried, ya know. She's been on stall rest, isolated. I figured since you were here, you could give her a looksee."

"I'd love to. Got a stethoscope handy?" Kalli happily opened the stall and began her exam.

After checking all of Jellybean's vitals, she was happy to report that the big girl was making a speedy recovery. Janie and Kalli talked horses for over an hour before she decided to get home. Promising to return later in the day for a ride, she took off toward the path.

Enjoying the warm afternoon, Kalli took her time on the trails, thrilled that she actually remembered her way through the forest after their run. Approaching the spring, she sat on a rock, trying to decide the best way to convince Tristan to take her with him to South Carolina. She was sure she could help him, even if she agreed to stay in the car. Perhaps if she remotely assisted via a wire, she could feed them information about location.

Deep in thought, she heard a branch snap. Her lupine senses, having returned to normal, didn't detect any kind of animal or wolf. She sniffed into the air again, wondering if perhaps she was mistaken. The altogether familiar scent of a human wafted into her nostrils. She knew that sometimes humans came onto the compound to bring in supplies to the clubhouse or help with the horses, but was also certain that none should be in the forest.

Like a deer on alert, she stilled, scanning the trees. Seeing nothing, she decided to shift. At the very least, she'd get home more quickly. At worst, she'd outrun any human predator. Crouching down into a defensive stance, she readied to shift, calling her wolf to the surface. But as she went to lift her shirt in an effort to strip, a dark covering fell over her. Struggling to remove it, she hissed in pain. Laced in silver, she'd been effectively blinded and trapped. Strong arms wrapped around her as she fought to escape. The silver restrained her from shifting, weakening her entire body. Screaming for help and writhing, she jerked as a sharp needle pierced her thigh. *Tranquilizer.* Mouthing Tristan's name in silence, she hit the forest floor, enveloped in darkness

They'd spent hours reviewing intel, including maps and names, in preparation for their attack. Logan, in charge of weapons, had worked with Declan to load the plane and procure the necessary bulletproof equipment. While Tristan normally didn't do weapons, he was aware that Gerald liked guns. And he planned on taking him out by any means possible.

'Do you know where Kalli is?' buzzed across his cell phone screen as he finished up with the wolves. The text from Janie didn't automatically send him into a panic, until he realized it was nearly five o'clock in the afternoon and he'd been gone for four hours.

Tapping Janie's mobile number, he waited. "Where is she?" he barked when Janie picked up the line.

"I don't know, Tris. We were supposed to go for a ride hours ago. I tried calling the house, but no answer. I was hoping she was with you."

"Lock up the barn, Janie. Lock all the doors until Simeon comes for you."

"What's wrong?"

"Just do it. Don't let anyone in. Grab the shotgun in the office and wait for Simeon now."

Ending the call, he yelled over to the group. "Logan! Kalli's missing. Simeon, over to the barn, now! Take Declan. Go wolf when you get there, start running the property. Something's wrong. I feel it. Logan, car! Let's get over to the cabin now. Call Mira; tell her we're on lockdown. All wolves need to be inside and ready to shift."

Running out of the building, Tristan and Logan jumped into his car and sped up to the cabin. By the time they got there, Tristan was furious. They tore through the cabin, but he could tell by the scents that she hadn't been home since the morning. She was gone.

Tristan began pacing like a caged tiger, working through where she could be, who'd taken her. "Goddammit, Logan. How'd they breach our property? There's no way in hell any foreign pack could make one step on our land without someone scenting them. The only way anyone could have gotten in is as human. What deliveries did we have today?"

"There was a scheduled food delivery early this morning, but if anything had been wrong, the food service manager would have called us. But you're right; a human has to have done this. The wolves would know if another wolf breached our property. And if someone did go after her, why wouldn't Kalli shift? She should be able to shift on demand by now…after last night," Logan reasoned.

"A human. A fucking human. Or…" He stilled as the horrifying possibility ran through his mind. "A wolf pretending to be a human. The CLI. No one would have scented them. They could have taken her over the fence just about anywhere. We've gotta run the perimeter. Fuck!" He pounded his fist into the wall in frustration.

"And if they silvered her, maybe drugged her, they could stop her shift," Logan added.

Tristan felt as if someone had reached into his chest and pulled out his heart by its bloody roots. They'd come into Lyceum Wolves and taken her. His blood pumped in rage. Stripping off his clothes, he instantly transformed, sprinting off across the yard and into the field. Logan followed in pursuit. By the time they reached the furthest boundary, they'd almost given up hope, but soon Tristan screeched to a dead stop and shifted back to human. Running over to the fence, he peeled off a small scrap of red flannel. Holding it to his nose, he breathed deeply, memorizing every last molecule of its odor.

"Wolf. Not ours," he barked out, raking his fingers through his hair. Handing it off to Logan, he peered over the fence that led into a thin patch of woods next to a small road. No car. No trash. No clues. It didn't matter, because he knew where they'd taken her. And he knew for certain who exactly took her. When he found Gerald, he swore he'd rip his throat out vein by vein. If he weren't a dead man before, he'd just signed his own death warrant.

"Back to the clubhouse. I want every wolf there. I want to make sure no one else is missing and if anyone saw anything," Tristan ordered.

Silently, Logan nodded. His Alpha was about to go on a tear, and he prayed they'd find Kalli. Cursing his damn visions, he couldn't believe he hadn't seen this coming.

Pack members filled the large all-purpose room in the clubhouse. A hum of nervous conversation echoed off the cedar walls. After a quick change of clothes in the locker room, an agitated Tristan entered the open area, parting the sea of people. Instantly it became so quiet you could hear a pin drop. Everyone sat, cautiously watching their Alpha.

Looking to Logan, who'd dressed quickly as well, Tristan assessed the situation. "All wolves accounted for?"

"Yeah, everyone's here except for Simeon. I sent him to the airstrip to make sure the jet was ready tonight, and to change flight plans. We're set to go."

"Listen up everyone," Tristan began in a deadly serious tone. "We've suffered a security breach this afternoon. We believe that at least two persons, possibly wolves taking CLI, came onto Lyceum Wolves' property via the north gate. Somewhere between the barn and my cabin, they abducted Kalli."

The crowd released a small roar of murmurs at the news.

"Settle down," he ordered. "Now I know that most of you noticed her on last night's run…at the spring. I was planning on a formal introduction to the pack later this week, but now it seems there's no other way for me to do this. So for those who haven't been listening to gossip, she's mine; I've claimed her."

A few gasps could be heard. Tristan nodded in response. While most wolves knew he'd claimed Kalli, it seemed as if a few hadn't heard the news. Most of the pack was still happily surprised that he'd found someone after leading Lyceum Wolves for over fifty years as a single wolf.

"And she's my mate," he added, as the room fell silent once again. They all registered the seriousness of the situation. An Alpha's mate kidnapped. Tristan and the pack would suffer enormously if anything happened to her. He would simply not recover from such a loss. While he would assuredly go on without her, he'd probably have to step down as Alpha due to the excruciating grief. There'd be infighting and challenges for his position, despite Logan's status.

"Like I said, I planned to formally introduce her to you after we took down the Wallace pack. We were going to complete our mating afterward. But now…" His words temporarily trailed off as the thought of Kalli dead raced through his mind. It killed him, but he refused to show weakness in front of his pack. As always, they needed him to be a rock, and he never disappointed them. "Tonight we go in to take out Wallace. But before that happens, I want to know who was on the property today. Ellie said the clubhouse was locked up tight. No humans were there after the morning food delivery. Janie told me Doc Evans was out of town; that's why she called on Kalli to check the horses. Somebody here must have seen something, scented something. If you've got anything to say, now's the time. I want the truth," he demanded.

A barely audible cough came from the back of the room as Julie stood. "Alpha." She lowered her eyes. "Coming back from town in my car, I passed the stables. I noticed the mares were in the south field. The boys were in the northern field. I saw two men near them, but I just assumed they were Doc Evan's workers. The interns, you know. They come with him sometimes. I didn't stop. I should have stopped. I…I'm so sorry." A tear escaped at the realization she could have seen the intruders.

"Were they going toward the barn or the field?"

"Toward the fields, into the woods."

"Julie, this is really important." Tristan fixed her with his stare. "What else do you remember? What were they doing?"

"Just walking. They had on backpacks, but again, sometimes Doc has a pack too. I had the windows down, and smelled the humans. Nothing appeared strange…so I kept driving," she muttered.

"Did you see or scent anyone else besides Janie, Kalli or the horses? Humans? Wolves? Animals?"

Recognition flashed across her face. Her eyes darted across the room and then to the floor.

Tristan rushed to her, taking her by the arms. "Look at me, Julie," he insisted forcefully. "Who else was at the barn?"

Julie raised her gaze to his, then her eyes settled on Mira, who'd been sitting up toward the front of the room. Inspecting her perfectly manicured nails, she pretended to ignore Julie.

"Are you sure?" Tristan spat out; his voice rose.

"Yes, as wolf. I didn't see her, but I scented her at the barn. I'm certain," Julie confessed, shaking her head.

The atmosphere in the room crackled with a surge of fear as if they were waiting for a volcano to erupt.

Tristan closed his eyes, taking a deep breath as he contemplated the scenarios of Mira's involvement. It couldn't be possible. She'd been mad about Kalli from the very beginning, jealous even. The public submission at the springs had only served to stoke her anger. But they'd been friends for so long. She knew he'd claimed her. It would crush him, but by Goddess, he needed to know if she was involved in the abduction.

"Mira!" Tristan yelled as the others cowered slightly. Every wolf could sense the powerful waves of anger emanating off of their Alpha.

Mira's head snapped to attention upon hearing her name. With a confident stance, she stood up and faced him, placing a hand to her hip. Inwardly she shook in fright, but she couldn't let them know. She'd done the right thing in sending her away. Kalli was a half breed whore who'd pollute the pack. She didn't belong in Lyceum Wolves. He'd thank her eventually.

"Yes," Mira responded flatly.

"Mira, you've been my friend for a very long time, but I'm only going to ask you this question once. I expect truth. Do you understand?" Tristan growled.

Lowering her gaze slightly but still maintaining eye contact, she nodded. "Yes, Tristan. As always."

Logan started to approach the pair, but Tristan held up a hand, halting him. He shot him a warning look and then narrowed his eyes on Mira once again.

"Were you involved in Kalli's abduction?" Tristan asked in a low menacing voice.

"I…I was just out running. I didn't do anything," she protested.

Sensing deception, Tristan did something he normally didn't do. Opening himself, he let his mind touch Mira's. He wanted her to feel a mere sliver of the sheer wrath that pulsed throughout his being.

As it hit her, Mira gasped in pain. "Tristan, don't," she pleaded.

Logan ran forward. As beta, Tristan's emotions ran through him as if he were experiencing them himself. Tristan held up his palm again, stopping him from moving, all the while never taking his eyes off Mira.

"Stand down, Logan. Do not challenge me," he ordered. "Mira, what did you do?"

Looking to the floor, she shook her head back and forth in denial, yet she felt compelled to tell him. He'd know. There was no way to lie to him. Surely he'd understand that she'd done this for the pack. Steeling her nerves, she looked directly into his eyes. "No, I did not take her personally. But yes, I called them to take her. She's not pack."

As the words hit him, the slicing agony of betrayal cut at his heart.

On your knees!" he commanded, enraged by what she'd done to him. When she refused to listen, his power discharged, spilling over, forcing her to the floor. Standing back, he held his fisted hands at his sides. "Why Mira? We've been friends for over a century. How could you do this to me? To the pack?"

Mira stumbled to the ground, submitting. Tristan's surge of anger held her at the carpet.

"I did this for the pack! She doesn't belong here," she cried in defiance. "I am Lyceum Wolves. Daughter of Alpha. I know how things should be. You wouldn't listen. Something had to be done. She has her own pack! And now she's there! You'll never get her back!"

"Correction, Mira. You were the daughter of Alpha. You were Lyceum Wolves. I can't believe you'd let others come onto our territory…take my mate. But you betrayed me. The pack. You put everyone at risk. I can't understand this." Tristan shook his head, still unable to believe that his best friend had done this to him. Petty jealously was one thing; questioning his leadership was a direct challenge. None of it could go unpunished.

"Mira, if you were a male, I'd kill you on the spot for treason. But in deference to our friendship, I hereby strip you of your lineage."

Mira screamed as she realized what he was about to do to her. "No Tristan! You can't!"

"Silence!" he bellowed, delivering another wave of his power, muting her defiance. "Not only have you engaged in treason by inviting dangerous enemies onto our land, you've challenged your Alpha. In a physical challenge, it'd be unlikely you'd survive. Therefore, I must consider a suitable alternative. You will start a new life in another pack. I will notify other possible Alphas this evening. In the meantime, you will be confined to your cabin and are not allowed to leave this compound. Tomorrow, I'll inform you of your new location."

Mira beat the floor with her fists, "No, no, no…this is my pack. You can't do this!"

"That's where you're wrong, Mir. It's already done. Do not challenge me further, or I'll take drastic action. Now get up off your knees and get out of my sight. Declan, assign guards to Mira. She's no longer Lyceum Wolves. As such, she's not allowed to leave her cabin or interact with the others."

"Yes sir," Declan nodded.

"Logan, find out who Mira spoke to from the Wallace pack. See what she knows and then meet me over at the jet. I'd do it, but I swear I might kill her. Honestly, my wolf is demanding no less than her death, but she's been with us forever. Goddess help me, I've got to show her mercy."

A frozen glare glossed over Mira's face as Declan led her out of the room. Pack members looked away, incredulous that she'd deliberately bring strangers into their sanctuary. It was a miracle no one else had been taken or killed. Tristan, aware of how his anger had affected them, concentrated on sending an air of repose into the otherwise distressed crowd.

"My wolves," he addressed them calmly. "Keep diligent watch until I return. Willow's in charge while I'm gone. I'm asking that you stay indoors, no running until we're sure the situation in South Carolina's been contained. Understood?"

With a nod toward Willow, Tristan pounded out to his car. He'd expected that Mira would have been hurt by him taking a mate, but never had he anticipated such treachery. She'd put the entire pack at risk out of some misguided sense of loyalty. Unforgivable, yet he couldn't bring himself to mete out the deserved retribution; death. Hoping she'd find peace in a new pack, he fired up the car and let his thoughts drift back to Kalli.

Instinctively, he assumed Gerald would keep her alive, perhaps torture her, rather than kill her. Reports indicated that there were only two females left in the pack after he'd killed them off, one by one. No pups had been listed, although Tristan suspected that they could have somehow gone undetected in the flyover. Eleven remaining males kept court at all times of day.

Now that Kalli could shift, she'd have a fighting chance of staying alive. She was strong and intelligent. If an opportunity for escape presented itself, he was confident she'd take it. Rubbing a hand over his face in frustration, he considered how they would have transported her. Drug or silver would be the easiest way to ensure she couldn't shift. Surely they would have flown Kalli out of Pennsylvania, realizing he'd tear the state apart looking for her? Glancing over to the clock, he saw it read seven o'clock. If they managed to leave within the hour, they'd arrive by ten. Every muscle in his body tensed. Blood boiling, he was ready to embrace the retributive justice that would come at his hands tonight.

Chapter Twenty-Six

Kalli vomited onto the floor, unable to control the nausea. Unsure of what drug they used, she thought it had to be some kind of an animal tranquilizer. Wiping the spittle from her lips, she cracked her eyes open, trying to assess her surroundings. The irrefutable smell of human urine and feces permeated the small cemented room in which they'd placed her. Her wrist burned as the silver handcuff, attached to an old metal cot, cut into her skin. The threadbare mattress chafed at her legs, but at least they hadn't entirely restrained her. She struggled to sit up, but managed with a sigh, as she leaned against the cold concrete.

Although it was dark, her eyes quickly adjusted to the light. Taking in the barren accommodations, she noticed a small square window in the wall half way toward the ceiling. More of a hole really, it left no room to escape. The one foot by one foot portal was missing its glass, allowing a cool mountain breeze to seep into the room. Sniffing into the air, a stir of painful memories told her exactly where she was. *Wallace pack*. Heart of the Blue Ridge Mountains; spectacular waterfalls, scenic vistas, wild flowers. Yet the only thing this place held for Kalli was a lifetime of abuse and torture.

Heart racing, she struggled to remain calm as the door to the room flew open. And although the ray of bright light blinded her, she'd never forget the horrific scent of Gerald or the smell of whiskey on his breath. Telling herself she was stronger this time, she fortified her mind, readying for his attack.

"Look who the cat dragged in. Our little hybrid slut thought she'd hide from us. We always find what's ours," he cackled as he approached her, shining a spotlight into her face. "Old Morris lucked out, didn't he? Thought he'd find something up in the big city. We was lookin' for some bitches to bring back here. We're low, ya see. But we knew there'd be plenty of girls we could take. Big city won't miss 'em. Little did he know he'd find you."

"I'm not who you think I am," she protested.

"Oh, yeah, I know who ya are. Fancy degrees, I hear ya made a drug to hide your wolf," he laughed. "Worked real well too. Dumb ole Lyceums didn't know we was even there. Well, now that we got ya, you're gonna make more of those pills. We can sell 'em on the streets. Got big plans for ya, you know?"

Overwhelmed by the odor, Kalli cringed in his presence. As if she were in a swamp at night with gators, she could see the red flecks of light reflecting off his cold black eyes. She wanted so badly to shift, but as long as she was silvered, she couldn't. If somehow she could get the cuff off, she could summon her wolf. In her mind, she'd made the decision to die fighting. Dying seemed a preferable option compared to a lifetime in Wallace. No matter what happened to her, she wouldn't let him manufacture the CLI. He'd never be able to do it without her.

"I don't belong to you anymore," she spat at him. "My mate. He'll come for me."

He ran a finger down her neck. Linking a claw into the rim of her t-shirt, he tore it open, revealing Tristan's mark. "Claimed, I see. But mated, not yet. I can tell a mated bitch, and you're not one. Close but no cigar."

Refusing to give quarter, Kalli defiantly sat with her bra exposed, refusing to let him see how terrified she was.

"My mate will come for you. You'll be dead by morning."

"Maybe you'll be the one who'll be dead after I let a few of my men go at ya. Not many bitches around here. Now here you are, fallin' into our laps."

He ran his hand down her chest, but when he attempted to paw her breast, Kalli struck him between the eyes with the palm of her hand, ramming his nose.

"Fucking bitch," he screamed as blood spurted from his nostrils. In response, he struck Kalli across the face with the back of his hand. Her head smashed into the cinderblock with a resounding crack.

She saw stars as the pain radiated throughout her face and then through the back of her head. Feigning unconsciousness, she kept her eyes closed. It wasn't hard to fake given the injury to her head. She sighed in relief as she heard the door slam as he left, leaving a string of curse words in his wake.

Racking her brain for a way to escape, she needed to get out of the cuff. She was no Houdini, but she'd watched plenty of television shows where people unlocked their own handcuffs. *What did they use? A credit card? No, that was for doors. Come on Kalli, think. A paperclip? A pin?* Where the hell would she get a pin? Her hair, still in a ponytail, only had a rubber band in it. She still had on her shoes but they only held laces. Then it occurred to her that she was wearing a wired bra. She wasn't crazy about the idea of stripping inside of her hellhole prison but if she could get the cuff off, she'd open the door, shift and wouldn't need her clothes.

After managing to unhook her bra, she bit at the fabric with her teeth until a small hole emerged. Threading the wire out, she bent it back and forth until it broke into two pieces. She proceeded to shim the lock by inserting the small wire between the notches and the ratchet. Within a minute, the lock clicked open. Smiling to herself, she had her own plan for Gerald, and it involved him and a dirt bed.

Challenging the Alpha while silvered may not have been the brightest idea she'd had, but damn if she'd deny her mate. Tristan was coming for her. Released from the poison shackle, she could feel it in her blood. Her wolf called to the surface, and she swore she could sense him on the land, in the air. She was certain, in that moment, that Gerald would, indeed, end up a cadaverous, lifeless piece of flesh by sunrise.

Locked and loaded, Lyceum Wolves hit the ground. In a smooth landing, the plane taxied onto the private airstrip nestled on a small strip of land within the mountains. As soon as they came to a grinding halt, Tristan, Logan, Declan, Gavin and Shayne poured out of the plane into two waiting SUVs. Tristan could feel her as soon as they hit the rocky soil. The smell of blood hung in the air, and he swore he'd have vengeance.

The Wallace compound was set against a mountain face, with a myriad of trails leading into the dense brush. They'd parked about a mile outside of the perimeter. Nearly midnight, the waning moon lit the forest floor as they stealthily navigated the terrain. As they neared the housing complex, Tristan signaled to Simeon to take the highest point. Simeon, a former Navy SEAL, was a precision shooter. Aware that the Wallace wolves had a proclivity toward weapons, Tristan had instructed Simeon to pick off any wolf brandishing a gun. But not Gerald. No, Gerald was Tristan's only.

Holding a hand up, Tristan pointed to the right, around the large dilapidated structure. Scenting Kalli, he could tell she was close, within a hundred yards at the very most. Logan, also catching her scent, had been assigned to take Kalli to safety. As beta, he was the only wolf Tristan trusted to ensure her rescue. No words were needed to convey his meaning as they exchanged glances. Furtively, Logan took off with Gavin around the building, as loud music whipped a cadence into the night.

Tristan's primary mission was to annihilate Gerald. The man was a menace who needed taming. In a deliberate manner, with his usual confidence, Tristan strode up to the front door. Armed with silver bullets, Declan and Shayne flanked him. Like a homing missile, Tristan kicked in the door and strode into the melee. The sounds of bullets breaking the windows resounded, while Tristan shrewdly assessed the wolves around him, searching for Gerald. Shayne and Declan started fighting as soon as they entered. Shifting into wolf, the fur literally started to fly. Five wolves fell to the ground in a pool of blood as Simeon carried out his orders.

Tristan's eyes locked onto the stocky wolf crouched in the corner, growling as each of his wolves hit the ground. Intrepidly approaching the wolf, his feet never stopped moving. Images of Toby lying dead in the ground ran through his mind followed by his mate, abused and nearly broken, at the hands of the monster before him. Tristan didn't want to kill

Gerald quickly; he planned on making him suffer the way he'd done to the others.

"What you want wolf? Can't you see here that we're just enjoying a drink?" The words had barely left Gerald's mouth before Tristan had him by the throat.

"Gerald? Alpha of Wallace pack?" Tristan asked with a snarl.

"Yeah, what's it to ya? This is my land, here. Ya need to get off."

"Where are the women and pups?"

"I got a bitch downstairs if ya want her, but we don't got any others right now. We've been pickin' them off up north," Gerald freely admitted, not recognizing Tristan as Alpha of Lyceum Wolves.

"Declan! Downstairs, now! Make sure Logan's got Kalli out of here," Tristan shouted.

Furiously shaking Gerald by the scruff of his shirt, he jammed him up against the wall. A tiny red dot appeared above Gerald's brow as Simeon's laser locked on the broad prominence of his forehead.

"Stand down, Si," Tristan instructed, holding two fingers into the air. A bullet to the brain was too good for Gerald; too easy. After all the pain and suffering he'd inflicted on men, women and children over the years, he'd go down old school. Tristan, not one to be accused of going outside of pack protocol, sought to have him submit as wolf, and die as wolf. There was no other way that would make amends for the bloody atrocities the man had caused to so many.

With a grunt, Tristan threw him clear across the room where he slammed into a pile of aluminum chairs. Aside from the sound of scraping metal, Gerald's heavy panting was the only audible sound. Dead Wallace wolves, well departed from life, provided a macabre background to Gerald's impending demise. Tristan smiled coldly as he noted that Morris, the wolf who had helped to kill Toby, lay among the dead, a silver bullet to his head. Simeon had picked him off; still dressed, the wolf gripped a small handgun. Giving the lifeless body a nudge with his boot, a small bottle of pills spilled out of his front shirt pocket. *CLI.* Never taking his eyes off Gerald, Tristan effortlessly scooped up the bottle and tossed it over to Shayne, who'd shifted back to human.

Disgusted by Toby's needless death and Kalli's abduction, Tristan stalked toward Gerald, who was eyeing a Glock that had fallen into the debris. Kicking the grey metal out of reach, Tristan stood towering above the seething brawny wolf. With an ominous delivery, Tristan informed him of his death sentence as if he were a judge in a courtroom. His menacing stare bored into the malevolent creature who'd taken his mate.

"Gerald, wolf of Wallace. Consider yourself informed of my challenge to your pack. From this minute forward, any females or pups you've hidden will be placed under my protection. I command you to shift. In front of my wolves, we will do this challenge," Tristan demanded, with a cool demeanor. It had to be done this way. The respect of his own wolves was as important as eradicating Gerald. Wolf versus wolf, it was how he was raised, and how he would die.

Tearing off his shirt and pants, Tristan transformed to wolf within seconds. Gerald's husky brown wolf charged at him, jaws snapping, but Tristan sidestepped the attack, snarling in response. Standing proud, the black Alpha wolf circled around the brown, eyes locked on his. With his ears forward and tail lifted, Tristan bared his fangs. His wolf demanded the death of the one who'd dared to challenge him for his mate. Eyes wild, threatening and locked onto Gerald, Tristan's wolf kept low to the ground, readying for attack. Taking flight, he rushed Gerald, and in a submissive move Gerald took off out of the building. With his prey on the move, Tristan gave chase; a rush of adrenaline flooded his system, anticipating the kill.

Gerald only made it a few hundred yards before Tristan pawed him downward, dragging him to the leaf-covered ground. Engaged in a ritualistic combat as old as time, Tristan pinned the brown wolf with his forepaws, exposing his vital areas. Unwilling to submit, Gerald continued to fight, biting a small gash into the black wolf's back leg. With an arched neck and bared fangs, Tristan seized Gerald's vulnerable soft throat, tearing out a huge chunk of fur and flesh. The smell of fresh blood spattered the woods. Furious and violent, Tristan tore apart the brown wolf's neck until the head dangled by a single vertebra.

Tristan. Kalli felt him the instant he landed on the mountain ridge. His unique scent, carried to her on the wind, provided a renewed energy. She hoisted herself to her feet, but wavered. Overwhelmed with dizziness, she fell back to the dirty cot. She thought she should shift, but her head pounded in protest. Reaching her hand into her hair, she felt the large knot of swelling on her skull. *I need to shift.* But then a rustling outside her window called her to the night. Feeling as if she'd faint, she grunted, pushing onto her knees until her fingertips felt the rim of the small window.

"Tristan!" she screamed over and over, praying someone would hear her.

Her breath hitched as a hand found hers. Unable to see, she desperately grabbed onto it.

"Kalli!" Logan yelled into the small dark cavity. He could barely make out Kalli's face through the mask of blood; tendrils of black curls adhered to her skin. As he peered in further, he swore. Tristan was going to kill

Gerald a thousand times over for attacking his mate.

"Logan. Please," Kalli coughed. Between vomiting and screaming, her throat was raw. "Door's locked. There's no way out. I need to shift. My head."

Logan looked to Gavin. "Kalli, this here's Gavin. He's ours."

Gavin knelt down next to Logan, and allowed Logan to put his hand into Kalli's.

"Take his hand. It's okay. He's gonna stay with you. I'll come round to get you. I'll be right there. You're going to be okay."

"Tristan? Where is he? Please, nothing can happen to him," she cried.

"Trust me, Kal, Gerald's the one who's got to worry. Tris will be fine. Just hold tight. I'm coming." He heard her give a small sob at his words. She might have been strong, but he could tell she was on the verge of breaking.

Without a doubt, Tristan was going to go ballistic when he saw Kalli's face. His Alpha, a well-oiled killing machine, didn't need yet another reason to rip into Gerald. Fearing the sight of her could distract him in his quest, Logan took off in a full sprint. Once he found the back entrance, Logan heard growling followed by an eerie silence emanating from another room. Staying focused, he made his way to a staircase that was tucked into an alcove in the kitchen. Making his way down the steps, he found himself in a complicated series of tunnels.

Taking a minute to sniff the dank musty air, he caught her scent. In the dark recesses, he heard crying, voices of children and women. Exploring the cavernous passages, Logan swore, realizing this was some kind of underground prison. He'd need to work on freeing these wolves, but Kalli's injuries warranted his immediate attention. Finally arriving where he believed she was being held, he pulled on a rusty doorknob. *Locked.* A noise alerted him that someone was close behind. Relieved, he found Declan's wolf padding toward him.

"Hey Dec. I need you to shift. Help me break open this door."

Declan shifted back and prepared to help Logan. Heaving their shoulders into the heavy wood, it splintered open. Logan rushed into the room, finding Kalli stretched upward still holding tight to Gavin. Gently uncurling her fingers from Gavin's, he took her into his arms. She was shaking, presumably from shock. Logan wrapped his shirt around her. He needed her to shift so she could heal.

"Come on Kalli, girl. You're okay," he cajoled, more trying to convince himself than her. He felt the significant goose egg on the back of her head. Blood still trickled out of the gash on her face; her eye was swollen shut. Tristan was going to freak the hell out knowing they'd done this to her.

"You need to shift, baby," he insisted.

Kalli shook her head, shivering in his arms. "I know…I just need a minute. I'm tired. My head…"

"You've got to shift, Kalli." Feeling as if he was losing her, he made a split decision to take her to Tristan.

Caught up in the kill, Tristan froze at the scent of Kalli's blood. He quickly turned his head and caught sight of his beta, carrying a broken and bloodied Kalli in his arms. Trudging into the forest, Logan fell to his knees.

"Tristan, please. She needs to shift. I'm guessing she's got a concussion, but I don't know how bad it is. She's in and out. Please," he pleaded softly, aware that Tristan was still very much wild; his feral beast on edge. Seeing his mate hurt would only inflame his animalistic fervor, but Logan knew that she needed her Alpha. He was the only one who could reach her, force her wolf to resurface.

Releasing a growl, Tristan eyed Logan, holding his injured mate. The animal in him, already agitated, possessively snarled at Logan. *His mate. Blood.* He stalked toward him, baring his fangs.

Logan lowered his eyes and gently laid Kalli onto the cool earth. "Tristan," he whispered. "Your mate. Gerald, he hurt her. She needs you to tell her to shift. I think she knows she's gotta shift but she's too weak. But she'll listen to you, her Alpha."

Logan slowly backed away from Kalli's body, careful not to look at Tristan directly. The other wolves lowered their heads and flattened their ears, closing their eyes to slits, demonstrating submission. Satisfied that no challenges would come and all wolves were reverent, Tristan crept over to Kalli and licked her face. His wolf whined loudly as it continued to nuzzle her.

As consciousness of Kalli's predicament took hold, Tristan shifted to his human form. Pulling her gently into his arms, against his naked skin, he brushed the hair from her face.

"Mon amour." He stifled a cry. What had they done to his mate? "I need you baby, come on now. I need you to shift for me."

Kalli's eyes fluttered open. "Tristan," she whispered. *Her Alpha.* He was near.

"Chérie, listen to me now, you've got a bad head injury there. I'm going to help you, okay? Close your eyes, that's it," he coaxed in a gentle tone as she obeyed. Willing himself to remain calm was extraordinarily difficult, but he needed his aura to remain placid. Taking a deep cleansing breath, he concentrated on sending her his power; tendrils of love flowed from his mind to hers.

"Remember our trust, Kalli. Picture your wolf. She's right there on the surface. Now shift," he commanded.

Kalli felt a wave of emotion rush through her psyche. The sound of Tristan's voice spoke to her inner wolf. Listening to the command of her Alpha, she emerged. Cuddling into his arms, she ran her muzzle along his chest, licking, tasting.

Tristan blew out a breath, thanking the Goddess she'd listened. His little wolf was perfectly nestled in his arms. Safe. He caught a glimpse of Logan, who'd watched in awe. Nodding in thanks to his beta, Tristan returned his attention to Kalli.

"You're beautiful, baby. Look at you." He kissed her head, rubbing her pelt until her head fell back in pleasure.

"Logan, we've got to get out of here," he told him, not letting Kalli move away from him.

Logan shuffled up to his feet. "Tris, there's women and pups below. Maybe seven or eight souls from what I could scent. I don't know for sure, but we've gotta get them."

Wiping his face with the back of his hand, Tristan groaned. "Christ, I knew he couldn't have done away with all the pack. Take Dec and the others with you. Get em' out. We're taking them home. When we get back, we'll figure it all out." Tristan looked around, spotting Simeon in a tree.

"Simeon, get the plane ready. Any chance we can get a charter set up for the others?"

"Yeah, sure boss. I'm on it," he replied, climbing down.

"Right, thanks." Tristan acknowledged. He looked back to Logan and extended his hand upward to his beta. "Logan, I can't thank you enough for getting her out. I'm going to take Kalli back now. I'll meet you back at the cabin."

Logan took his Alpha's hand, with great respect. What they'd done hadn't been easy, but it had had to be done. No longer under threat, they'd return to their territory.

As Logan turned to retrieve the imprisoned pack subordinates, Tristan transformed back into his black wolf. Waiting patiently for Kalli to get her bearings, he contemplated loose ends. What still remained a mystery was who had staged the attack on Marcel's wolves. Neither Gerald nor Jax had claimed responsibility. Yet, clearly the wolves who'd attacked his sister belonged to an Alpha, he was sure. Lone wolves rarely engaged in territorial war tactics. He reasoned that Marcel still had cause to remain cautious.

Kalli approached, jarring his mind back to his first priority. Watching her pad toward him, his heart swelled. *His mate.* As soon as they returned, they'd make it official. Soon he'd rule Lyceum Wolves, no longer alone.

Chapter Twenty-Seven

It'd been exactly twenty-four hours since they'd left South Carolina, and for the first time in her life, she felt free. Like an eagle soaring in the sky, she rejoiced in the majestic landscape that was her new life. Fully healed from her shift, they'd agreed that tonight they'd officially mate.

With no reservations, she'd laid perfectly bare on his bed, waiting for Tristan to come to her. As he opened the bathroom door, he gave her a sultry smile, his own nude body attuned to her need. Never one to be dominated, Tristan promptly flipped her onto her stomach, straddling her legs.

Not quite sitting on her bottom, he supported his weight with his well-toned legs. As he leaned forward to massage her back, his hard arousal bulged against her skin. She wriggled against the bed in anticipation, thoroughly enjoying the feel of his velvety hardness against her own skin.

"Yes," Kalli mewled as Tristan ran his magical fingers down the base of her spine.

"Did I tell you today how beautiful you are?"

"Hmm…maybe only five times," she smiled.

"Ah, then I'll have to tell you again and again until you forget the exact number." He kissed her shoulder lightly. "But first, tonight, we're going to mate. And rumor has it that we'll be in for quite the ride once I taste your sweet blood."

"Is that right?" she murmured into her pillow, enthralled by his touch.

"So I've been told. But the only way to know for sure is for us to," he paused to kiss slowly up and down her back, giving her the chills, "experiment. Put things to task as they say. You ready, my little wolf?"

"More than you'll ever know." Stretching her neck to view him, her eyes caught his. "My Alpha, take me."

Tristan reached his arms around her small body. Capturing a warm breast with one hand, he dipped his other down into her wet heat, circling her center of nerves. Continuing to lick and kiss her back, he smiled as Kalli moaned in delight.

Grinding against his hand, Kalli felt the rush of desire. Her orgasm edged her psyche, the painful ache in her core, needing relief. As his erection pressed against the crease of her bottom, she shuddered in arousal. "Tristan, oh, God."

"That's it, baby. So close aren't you?"

"Yes!" she screamed as he inserted a finger into her hot sheath. Unrelenting, he applied pressure to her clit, pushing her over into climax.

She shook against the bed, his hard hot body pressed to hers, his chest to her back.

Before she had a chance to recover, he rolled her to her side and gently kneed open her legs, slowly intertwining their limbs. Nestled together, he took hold of his swollen manhood and slid the hard shaft up and down her glistening folds, coating himself in her juices.

Cupping the cheek of her face, he let his gaze fall upon her eyes, as if seeing deep into her soul. Locked on each other with intent, he slowly rocked up into her warm tight channel. Kalli's breath caught as he entered her, but they never lost eye contact. Reaching for him, she wrapped a hand around his neck, threading the fingers of her other hand in his hand.

Face to face, chest to chest, they made love. One singular moment in time, they wordlessly connected, the emotional intensity vised around their hearts like a steel band. Thrusting in unison, slowly and deliberately, their desire mounted. Breathless, their pulses raced in hunger for each other. Tristan began to lose control as they reached a pinnacle of pleasure.

"Kalli," he panted. "I love you with all that I am. You are mine. My soul. My mate."

"Tristan. You're my everything. My mate."

Before she had a chance to say anything else, Tristan kissed her. A passionate, loving kiss representing their eternal love and connection pushed them into simultaneous orgasm. Spilling himself deep within her, Tristan extended his canines. Piercing into his mark, her honeyed blood solidified the mating bond.

Kalli shuddered around him, clamping down on him, her release finding its way through every cell in her body. As she bit into Tristan, his powerful essence assuaged her heart and soul. Everything that was Alpha and man, merged into her psyche. Like a solar flare, flames of love ignited, dancing into their universe.

Coming down from the climax, they held tightly to each other. Both Kalli and Tristan relaxed into the sweet embrace, not willing to relinquish the intimacy that had passed between them. A bond forged in love and trust that neither had ever dreamed could exist. A new world of leading Lyceum Wolves awaited them.

Epilogue

As the private plane landed in New Orleans, Logan's mind raced. It had been a long time since he'd been home, and he was looking forward to helping Marcel figure out who may have killed Paul. He glanced over to the women and children he'd rescued, who were huddled closely in their seats. He and Tristan had made the decision to relocate the remaining Wallace pack wolves to his old pack instead of keeping them in Philadelphia.

Three women and four children, all dirty and battered, were going to get a new lease on life. After talking with them, he gleaned they'd been kept down in Gerald's makeshift prison for well over a year. Apparently, the former Wallace pack Alpha didn't want to have to even see their faces, let alone hear from them. So he'd condemned them to living in the subterranean hell.

Logan was disgusted that anyone would treat another soul in such an inhumane manner. Sure, he'd grown up hearing the rumors of violence within the old packs, but never in all his years had he witnessed such a horrific sight. It was no wonder Kalli had been so afraid of wolves and created the CLI in order to remain hidden. As he reflected on the women's fate, he reasoned that they too could begin new lives for themselves. But like Kalli, they'd probably be emotionally traumatized by the violence. Even with a new home and pack, life wouldn't be easy for them, regardless of everyone's good intentions.

Julie had accompanied him on his long flight. He observed how she'd taken the initiative and was helping them exit the jet. Goddess, he hoped a good dose of her healing would go a long way to help them assimilate. He waved over to Katrina, Tristan's sister, who'd come to the airport to help. She was taking them to Marcel's bayou compound. She gave him a sad smile and a nod as she helped the women and their pups get settled into a large limo that was waiting on the tarmac. While reluctant to let them go, he was assured they were in good hands. Waving goodbye, he entered into a separate limo that waited for his arrival.

Instead of going toward the country, Logan headed toward the city. Marcel was held up in his Garden District mansion, working on business, and Logan sought to debrief him as to what had occurred in South Carolina. Most importantly, he needed to make it clear that there was still someone out there, who he feared planned another attack on the wolves. Neither Jax Chandler, the Wallace pack nor any other packs had claimed responsibility for Paul's death. And his visions told him there was more death to come….another dead wolf. So when Tristan suggested that he accompany the South Carolina wolves to their new Louisiana home, he eagerly agreed to go. He felt that if he could talk to Marcel in person, he could get a better handle on what was happening, clarify his dreams and help catch the killer.

Strip malls, churches and infamous above-ground cemeteries flashed by his line of vision on the short drive into the city. As they entered the Warehouse District, he was reminded of memories from long ago. During the late eighteen hundreds, Marcel, Tristan, Mira and he would take weekend trips to the French Quarter, attending masked Carnival balls, socializing into the wee hours of the morning. Then later, at the turn of the century, they'd witnessed the beginnings of Jazz played in the Storyville cabarets. And to this day, he never tired of walking the streets, appreciating the historic architecture. No matter how long he'd lived in Philadelphia, New Orleans was home.

As he reflected on happier times with Mira, the thought of her betrayal cut deep. When Tristan had sent her off to live with his eldest brother, Blake, in his Wyoming pack, he'd wholeheartedly agreed with the decision. Even though he loved her, he'd never be able to trust her again after she'd put the entire pack in danger. She was lucky Tristan hadn't killed her. Perhaps in time, wounds would heal, he thought, but not anytime soon.

As he opened the car door, he took a deep breath, reminded of his intentions. Cicadas sung in the night as he drew in the warm southern air. He loved everything about New Orleans, from pralines to eating creole shrimp to sitting in his boat in the swamp, listening to music while watching the gators sun themselves. There wasn't much he didn't like about the Big Easy. He sighed, wishing this trip was for pleasure, but alas, it wasn't.

The sound of a low growl emanating from the house first alerted him that something wasn't right. He quickly ran up the steps and burst through the large front door. As he darted into a large moonlit parlor, he heard the sound of gunfire as Marcel fell to the floor. A burly, masked man dressed in black stuffed the gun into his pants and ran toward the back door.

"Go," Marcel gurgled, holding the side of his neck as bright red blood spurted onto the cream-colored Italian marbled floor.

Logan fell to his knees and ripped off his shirt, holding it against the gaping wound. "You've gotta shift, Marcel," he pleaded.

"Let me go. Don't let him get away with this. Go get him," Marcel ordered. A sobbing woman raced to his side, bringing a towel to help stop the bleeding.

"Call 911," Logan yelled before sprinting after the man, determined to follow Marcel's wishes. He pursued the attacker, wondering where Marcel's beta was. *Where was everyone? Who was the young woman?* Unable to reason through what was happening, he focused on his task. Within seconds, Logan caught up with the perpetrator as he was trying to escape from the rear exit. Unsuccessfully but furiously, he yanked at the lock that prevented him from leaving. Logan scented that he was wolf and reached forward to subdue him.

"What the hell?" Logan yelled as the man spun around and punched him across the mouth. Logan staggered, but managed to wrestle him to the ground, grabbing onto his waist. They both hit the ground with a thud, struggling for control. The man extended his claws, scratching at Logan's face as he attempted to shift while still clothed. But Logan managed to hook a strong arm around the assassin's neck, squeezing until a loud snap resounded throughout the room. The dead wolf collapsed immediately upon Logan. Without hesitation, he cursed, removing the hood. *Calvin. Marcel's beta.* He'd challenged Marcel?

Logan threw Calvin's body aside and ran back to Marcel's side; sirens wailed in the distance. Logan stilled as he came upon the sight of him sprawled on the floor. Oh Goddess no. He fell to his knees, grasping his old friend, pulling him up into his lap.

"Marcel, please man. You've gotta shift," he begged.

"Too late…it's silver," Marcel whispered. "Not gonna make it."

"Goddammit, Marcel. We need you. You can't leave me. Tristan. Katrina. Hell, your whole pack. Your family. We need you. Now come on and shift," he demanded.

Marcel coughed up blood and shook his head.

"Where the hell is 911?" Logan screamed, glancing over to the unidentified sobbing woman crumpled in the corner.

"Calvin. It was Calvin," Marcel grunted.

"Yes. He's dead. I killed him." Logan couldn't think. He'd killed Marcel's beta. Calvin was the second strongest wolf in the pack. And Marcel, the Alpha, was dying in his arms. This couldn't be happening.

"Logan, you're Alpha now."

"No…listen Marcel, you're going to make it. I'm not…"

"Yes, you are. Tristan will understand. This is how this works. You know it. You're my brother too…you've got to do this. You have no choice."

Logan was crying, shaking his head, pulling Marcel's head to his breast. *Goddess no. Please Goddess no.*

"Say it," Marcel choked out, commanding him.

"No, I can't. Please don't leave, Marcel."

"Say it!"

Resigned, Logan took a deep breath. He could hear Marcel's heartbeat flutter. Tristan was right about nature and fucking goddamn fate. No one could fight her. Logan held his friend silently, listening as his pulse slowed. He swore revenge for his friend…for his pack. As the life faded from Marcel's eyes, Logan held his gaze and assured his friend.

"I am Alpha."

LOGAN'S ACADIAN WOLVES

Immortals of New Orleans, Book 4

Kym Grosso

*Acknowledgments*

I am very thankful to everyone who helped me create this book:

~My husband, for being my biggest supporter. I love talking with you about the hot love scenes I write. You give me great feedback and ideas. You are my inspiration.

~My children, for being so patient with me, while I spend time working on the book. You are the best kids ever!

~Julie Roberts, editor, who spent hours reading, editing and proofreading Logan's Acadian Wolves. I really could not have done this without you!

~PickyMe Artist, who helped me to create Logan's sexy cover.

~My beta readers, Cat, Denise, Elizabeth, Gayle, Julia, Julie, Leah, Liz, Nadine, Sharon, Stephanie, Sunny, for volunteering to beta read the novel and provide me with valuable feedback. You are incredible!

~My street team, for all your kind words and for helping spread the word about the Immortals of New Orleans series.

Chapter One

Logan clamped his canines deep into the gritty fur until his opponent whimpered in defeat. The iron-tinged blood only served to further spur his anger. For months, he'd fought challenges to his claim as Alpha. Like the increasing winds of a hurricane, his power grew with every battle. Yet he'd been merciful, never killing another wolf. But tonight, he'd had enough. It was time to put an end to the challenges and force acceptance. As the sanguine droplets coated his tongue, Logan growled. The cowering brown wolf held still, cognizant that a struggle would surely bring his demise.

Sufficiently satisfied with the submission, the Alpha seamlessly transformed. His naked muscular body stood statuesque, rippled in unadulterated strength. Dripping in sweat and blood, Logan's dark eyes narrowed on the shaking form at his feet then rose to scan the sea of eyes watching him, waiting for his next word.

"This ends tonight," he growled, addressing the pack. "The next challenge set forth to me will end in death. There'll be no mercy. I am Alpha. Who here challenges me next?"

Power surged through his veins. Logan sent a small threatening tendril toward his wolves, both a warning and an ultimatum. A faint murmur from the crowd ended as quickly as it started. The tension was palpable, yet the hum of acquiescence danced in the silence of the night. A binding calm blanketed the pack as one by one each wolf crouched down in submission, tails wagging, acknowledging their new leader.

Logan felt it as sure as he knew he was wolf; *he was Alpha*. He closed his eyes, allowing the energy to flow through him, amplifying throughout every molecule in his body. Every wolf accepting, loving, giving all of themselves over to his reign. The seed of dominance had finally germinated into a fully grown tree of command, providing the protection and guidance the pack needed for survival. Thrumming in control, Logan's muscles tensed as he threw back his head, sucking in the chilled evening breeze. A victorious howl emanated from deep within his chest as he claimed his pack, his rule, his dominion. Rising to the call of their Alpha, the wolves joined in his song, celebrating their leader.

Logan stopped his call for only a second to nod in affirmation at his chosen beta, Dimitri. The confident but subservient brown wolf padded toward Logan, eyes darting to his pack mates in recognition of his status.

"Tonight, we celebrate," Logan ordered, shifting back into his large silky gray wolf. He gazed upon his wolves, raising his snout in a cool display of affection.

As they ran through the night, Logan contemplated how he'd gotten to this point. Long ago, he'd been born a pup in the Acadian wolf pack, chasing to keep up with Marcel and his friend, Tristan. It had been mere months since he'd helped Tristan save his mate, taking out the destructive Wallace pack in South Carolina. Then, he'd come to New Orleans to help relocate the abused women and pups they'd found. That fateful night when he'd gone to Marcel, he'd found him shot and dying. Given no choice, Logan had killed the perpetrator, who'd been Marcel's beta. Crying out into the darkness was of no use to stop the inevitable. As Marcel lay dying in his arms, bleeding out onto the floor, Logan had agreed to become Alpha of Acadian Wolves. Marcel was like a brother; he'd do whatever he asked. And Tristan, Marcel's true brother, was Logan's Alpha and best friend in Pennsylvania. But no more. He'd wanted to deny Marcel his dying wish. At first, he'd refused to say it. But as the life faded from Marcel's eyes, Logan accepted his fate, speaking the words that would forever change his life; "I am Alpha".

If it was only that easy. After one hundred and forty-two years of being wolf, he knew full well that his pack wouldn't simply accept the situation, relinquishing the role of Alpha to him, especially since he hadn't been home for so long. Rather than reneging on his promise, he'd fought week after week, sealing his commitment to Marcel. And tonight, threatening death to all who opposed him had been the final chapter in his ascension.

Logan had not truly believed he was Alpha until tonight. He'd been a second away from killing the wolf beneath him. Feral. Savage. Unyielding. This was who he was, who he was meant to be. He ran hard through the bayou refuge, leading the others. Acadian Wolves, his new pack, was his to rule.

As the hot spray sluiced over Logan's tanned corded muscles, a million thoughts raced through his mind. Jacked up from the fight and final acceptance from his pack, he willed the adrenaline rush to subside. But even the high of the night hadn't diminished the pain of losing Marcel. Nor did it ease the sense of loss that remained over being separated from Tristan. When Logan had agreed to take over Acadian Wolves, Tristan had encouraged him to take his rightful place, unwilling to hear any arguments to the contrary. At first, he felt betrayed that his friend would so easily capitulate to losing his beta. But as he'd heard Tristan say many a time, Alphas needed to make difficult decisions, put their own feelings aside for the greater good of the pack.

So in this vein, he'd made a conscious decision to do the same. Regardless of how he felt, his position and responsibility for each and every wolf superseded his own needs. He silently conceded that perhaps he hadn't fully understood what that meant until tonight. Bloodied and bruised, he stood firm, claiming his earned position.

Logan reflected on his former life as Tristan's beta. Nearly a half century ago, he'd followed him to Philadelphia. As the years passed, he remained close to Marcel and their sister, Katrina, who also relocated. His years with Tristan had been prosperous and for the most part, peaceful. He'd been happy. Content. Life was good. No, life was great. Then a single bullet had turned his entire world upside down.

As Logan floated into a quiet contemplation, the blinding, recurring vision launched uncontrollably into his thoughts. Instead of fighting the inevitable, he allowed the colors and movement to appear clearly, hoping he'd see her again. He'd been dreaming of her for weeks, yet with every vision, all he could see was her face. Angelic, sad hazel eyes begged him to help. Paralyzed, he could only watch her, wondering who she was and why she was in danger. Her full, pink lips called into the night, but he couldn't hear her plea.

The panoramic scene continued to materialize before him, but he was unable to direct the movie. The loss of control didn't deter him from watching, however. Goddess, she was beautiful. Her long curly blonde hair whipped across her heart-shaped face. Shaking the locks aside, she screamed uncontrollably until her words turned into rolling sobs. Immobilized, he watched as the monster's clawed hand reached around her neck.

In an instant, the jagged talon transformed her cries into soft gurgling. A bubbling line of blood spewed from her pink skin as he sliced open her throat. Logan's heart pounded against his chest; he thrashed against invisible bindings. A mixture of shock and acceptance flashed across her eyes right before she sagged to the ground. Gasping, Logan struggled, trying to reach her. But nothing came. No movement. No sound. The familiar black tunnel closed inward, ending the terrifying nightmare.

Logan's eyes flew open, and he realized he was still in the shower. He shuddered, wondering when the scene would play out in reality. The visions had plagued him his entire life, but he'd normally taken them in stride, knowing they didn't personally affect his own future. Even though he couldn't identify the alluring woman, he couldn't shake the feeling that her life intertwined with his. Was she a wolf who'd join his pack? An enemy? The emotion that had been deeply woven into the vision told him that he knew her. He cared for her. She was dying and he'd been restrained, unable to save her life.

Logan sighed in disgust. Dismissing the ominous premonition didn't seem feasible. The lingering apprehension wrapped around him like a lead vest. Goddammit. Who was she? And why the hell couldn't he save her?

He didn't need this shit right now. No, it wasn't exactly the optimal time in his life to solve a disturbing, enigmatic vision. But like every other damning event that had slapped him lately, he'd compartmentalize the issue and deal with it.

The jarring of the door handle and a rush of cool air cued him to the fact that he was no longer alone. *Fuck, he hated this house.* Even though he'd moved into Marcel's country home out of necessity, it still felt uncomfortable. To his dismay, too many people lived with him. Granted, he'd brought it on himself by inviting them. Dimitri, his beta and longtime friend, had moved in at his request. And then there was Luci, Marcel's girlfriend, who also shared their home. Both Logan and Luci had witnessed Marcel's last dying breath. She'd collapsed into his arms immediately afterward, and since that moment in time, he'd felt responsible for her. So when he moved into Marcel's bayou mansion, he'd allowed her to stay.

But it was Katrina who shared his bed. She wasn't his mate but he'd felt oddly comforted by her warm body on cool winter nights. Out of grief, they'd clung to each other like a life raft in a storm. As if a kindred spirit, she'd been both sexually adventurous and giving, sharing herself with both Dimitri and him. He'd always been abundantly clear, however, that they couldn't continue on forever. Even if it had felt right at the time, she wasn't his mate. And it no longer was comfortable.

"Logan," Katrina called into the shower.

"In here," Logan responded.

He'd have to tell her tonight that it was over. It wouldn't be easy, but she needed to go back to her life in Philadelphia, and he needed to pay attention to business. It was time to go back to the city.

As warm silky skin slid against his own wetness, he fought the arousal that loomed to distract him from his task. Allowing her to wrap her body around his, he kissed her damp hair.

"Hey, Kat. We need to talk."

"Hmm…talk, huh?" She reached around to caress his ass with both hands, slithering against his semi-erect cock.

Logan pulled away slightly, not disconnecting his touch but enough to cup her face. Taking a deep breath, he narrowed his eyes on hers.

"You know I love you. But it's time for you to go home. We can't keep doing this."

"Doing what? This?" She smiled, reaching down between his legs to wrap her fingers around his shaft.

In a flash, he grabbed her wrists, bringing them against his chest.

"Yeah, that. Seriously, it's time. Now that I've established dominance, it's time for me to go into the city. I've got work to do. And you, my lovely vixen, have a business to run."

She sighed, leaning her forehead against him. It wasn't as if she didn't know what he was saying to be true. Reality was a bitch. A hard sigh escaped her lips at the realization that he was sending her home.

"Kat, we both miss Marcel. It's been hard on both of us. But you've got to go spend time with Tristan. Tend to your shop. And when things settle down, if you still want to come back here, you know you're always welcome. But for now, we're just using each other. It's not healthy…for either of us."

She shook her head in denial. "It's not like I don't know you're right. It's just…I miss him so damn much."

"I do too, baby, but this isn't the answer." Logan pressed his lips to her wet cheek. "It'll be okay. Go home. Comfort Tris. He needs you as much as you need him."

"When are you leaving for the city?" She lifted her head as he gently released her arms.

"Tonight. Dimitri and I are leaving in a few hours," he told her with a small smile.

"I'll miss you. And Dimitri," she contemplated, accepting that her time in New Orleans was coming to an end.

The past months since her brother's death had been awful. The only thing that had made anything slightly tolerable was the hot nights she'd spent with Logan and his beta. Instead of openly grieving, she'd buried her feelings deeply. As sister to the slain Alpha, she chose to be strong for the pack, for Logan.

"I'll miss you too, but it's time. I didn't choose this, but it's my path. I've got to move on for the sake of my wolves," he explained. "And you need to let go of him. Marcel's gone. You need to be able to grieve. As long as you are here, you'll never move on."

The steel band that wrapped her heart in grief tightened. Wolves didn't die, especially not her strong Alpha brother. It was as if Logan's words made it real. She knew he was dead, saw them lower his body into the grave, smelled his scent in the earth every time she went for a run. He was truly gone.

Sensing her retreat within her own mind, Logan pulled her into his arms, cradling her head to his breast. "It's okay to let go," he whispered.

A gasp of devastation gushed from her chest before she had a chance to swallow it. The wave of depression washed over the walls of sanity she'd tried so hard to build. Digging her fingers into his shoulders, she sobbed, the anguish of losing her sibling no longer held at bay. Goddess, she missed her big brother. She knew in that moment that as much as she loved Logan, it was Tristan she needed. He was the only one who'd comprehend the heartache that tore her apart.

Logan held tight to his longtime friend, comforting her as best he could. He'd call Tristan tonight and have her home by morning. They both needed closure, and getting her to face her loss was the only way to commence healing.

"That's it, Kat. It's all right. Let it out."

Realizing how she'd lost it, she tried to pull away from him, but he held her tighter still. "Don't hide."

"But I can't…" she cried, desperately wanting to curl into a ball.

"You don't need to be the strong Alpha's sister. It's just me. And I'm the Alpha who comforts you now. Tomorrow, you'll be with Tris, and it'll all be okay. I promise." Purposefully, he let his power flow; calming waves emanated from his body to hers, wrapping her in a loving cocoon of peace. Refusing to let her retreat, he embraced her until she finally quieted. As her last tears fell, she looked up at him with awe, with the understanding that her friend was no longer her brother's beta. No, he was their equal.

Logan wore the veil of responsibility as if he'd led the pack his entire life. He'd fought over a dozen wolves to earn the title, and it had been respectfully earned. A double-edged sword, loving or lethal, depending on the situation, there was no doubt about the male who held her in his arms. Capable of ameliorating pain or inciting it, he'd provide guidance and discipline to the wolves. As if she'd woken from a long sleep, Katrina looked into Logan's deep blue eyes, shivering with the realization that he'd changed. Altogether deliberate and dominant, a new wolf had been born. He was Alpha.

Chapter Two

Logan sat on the cracked leather barstool watching his wolves celebrate. As he drank his beer, he smiled to himself, amused at the curveball life had thrown him. He felt exhilarated to be back in the French Quarter. After Marcel had died, he'd sold the Alpha's Garden District pack house, per Tristan's request. He was thrilled to be rid of the monstrosity, considering the death he'd caused and witnessed that disastrous night. There was no way he'd step one foot back into that house, let alone hold any pack activities there.

In contrast, his new home soothed his soul, reminding him of his Creole roots. Newly reconditioned, it mirrored his life. Long before Marcel's demise, he'd started restoring the early nineteenth century three-story corner mansion. But his newfound position had accelerated the renovations, so he'd be able to live in the city. As much as he loved running wolf, the urbane food and culture were every bit a part of who he was. He'd made sure that his wolves were close by in adjoining townhouses on his street.

The only wolf he allowed to live with him was Dimitri. The quaint guest cottage on the property gave them both the closeness and privacy they needed. While he'd grown up with Dimitri, the connection between him and his beta had grown stronger over the past month. Their relationship had deepened in both respect and trust. And while Logan had initially felt awkward about his need for a beta, he soon embraced the bond. They'd shared more than a house. Pack challenges. Business. Women. Their intimacy had grown exponentially each day, but Logan no longer questioned why. Instinctively, he knew it was as natural as the sun rising.

After returning to the city and pulling into the carport, Logan insisted that he and Dimitri go to Courettes for drinks and celebration. He felt the wave of contentment that had washed through the pack. They had needed a leader, one determined to withstand multiple challenges, and he'd shown he was worthy. And in return, he needed to be with them and around them.

Courettes was an open-air, casual French Quarter establishment. What made the bar unique was that, thanks to a witch's spell, only paranormals could see into the bar or enter. To humans, it simply looked like a quiet home with closed wooden shutters. Because tonight was an Acadian wolf celebration, few vampires and witches attended. As the zydeco band played, wolves danced sensually to the indigenous beats.

Sitting at the bar, Dimitri shot Logan a questioning look, realizing his mind was far from the party that was going on around him.

"Alpha, what's up?"

"Nothin'. Just feels good to be back home in the city. Life is good," Logan responded, gazing intently at the many she-wolves who'd begun to peel off some of their clothing as the atmosphere became more heated.

"You were amazing tonight." Dimitri clapped his hand on Logan's shoulder. "The pack, they're calm. It's finally over."

"Yeah. And I meant it too. I'm done. Next challenge ends in death," he stated coldly. Logan was so finished with this shit. Acadian Wolves were his and the next wolf who started a fight was as good as dead.

"Oh, I know. You made that perfectly clear. It was awesome, though, bro," Dimitri laughed. "When's Kat leaving?"

"Tomorrow." Logan pinched the bridge of his nose and plowed his hand through his hair. "She's still broken up about Marcel. Then again, it's not every day you lose your brother. Tristan is the only one who can really help her heal. It's not easy letting her go, but it's time for us all to move on. And today, my friend, is that day." He took a swig of his beer.

"Speaking of moving on…" Dimitri nodded nonchalantly over to a gorgeous redhead whose eyes flirtatiously flashed over to his and then back to the band. Her fiery curly hair fell to the middle of her back, accentuating her slim waist and full hips.

"Ah, yes, Fiona. She's been after me for the past two months," Logan confessed.

"No surprise there, I guess." The women had been circling around his new Alpha ever since the first challenge. But after tonight's edict, Dimitri expected them to become more aggressive, actively vying for Logan's attention. "Honestly, between Luci and Kat, you've had your hands full. I cannot begin to tell you how happy I am that we moved back here and out of that mansion."

"Yeah well, soon that mansion is going to be a clubhouse. It's Marcel's, not mine. And since he's not here, it belongs to the pack. Thank Goddess we're back in the city, though, 'cause I need my space. No offense, man." Logan laughed.

"None taken," Dimitri concurred and held up his glass. "I'll be good to go in the cottage house. Close enough but not on top of you."

Logan turned to him, smiling and nodding. They clinked glasses in cheers and drank.

"Alpha." Logan turned his attention toward the submissive voice that sang his name.

"Fiona, how are you? You look beautiful tonight." Logan acknowledged as he and Dimitri stood to greet the alluring wolf.

"Thank you, sir. Hello, Dimitri." She smiled and nodded at him.

"I must agree with our Alpha, cher. You look lovely."

She blushed in response, but didn't move away. "It's because of the challenge. Everyone can feel it. It's been so long since we've felt any peace…with Marcel gone and all."

"How about a dance to celebrate?" Dimitri suggested, glancing over to Logan.

"With you both?" She questioned seductively, batting her eyelashes.

Logan smiled in response, quickly weighing his answer. He supposed one dance with the attractive little she-wolf couldn't hurt. Gently taking her hand in his, he led her out to the dance floor, Dimitri following.

Fiona laughed quietly as Logan swept her into his arms. The music slowed, and Dimitri came up behind her, wrapping his arms around her waist. The threesome began to move as one on the dance floor and a palpable sexual energy snapped in the air. Sandwiched between the tall, sexy men, Fiona rejoiced at her successful seduction. She had wanted these men for such a long time, yet it had been the first time she'd touched them intimately. She immediately bared her throat, offering both the Alpha and his beta everything she was.

Logan, surprised by Fiona's gesture, tried to ignore her invitation. But as she rubbed her pelvis against his, it became difficult not to respond. He wasn't interested in bringing her home with him, but neither did he want to insult her. His beta, on the other hand, clearly felt differently. Logan watched as Dimitri bent his knees, brushing his hard arousal against her bottom.

"Hmm," she cooed, simply swaying back and forth, letting the men dictate the pace and direction of their hot encounter.

"Fi, look what you are doing to my beta," Logan whispered in her ear.

"Alpha," she moaned, digging her nails into his shoulders.

"I do think she's enjoying our dance," Dimitri commented, sliding his hands up her waist, his fingertips nearly touching the swell of her breasts. "Perhaps we could take this somewhere more private?"

"Yes," she gasped.

Logan's eyes met Dimitri's in an effort to silently communicate that he was about to bow out, when he realized something was happening outside the bar. He wasn't sure if it was the smell of her blood or the flash of her long blonde hair that first caught his attention. A bloodied woman tore down the street, vampires following her in pursuit. The woman from his vision. *What the fuck?*

"What is it?" Dimitri tensed, snapping his head around to the street.

"Sorry, Fi. Gonna have to do this another time." Logan kissed her forehead and took off toward the exit. "D. Outside. Now. Something's going down."

Wynter's lungs burned. She bent over trying to catch her breath as she hid behind the rotted wooden door. Her heart beat like a hummingbird as she considered her next move. It had been exactly two months and thirteen days, since she'd been taken hostage. Escaping had been no small feat. With nothing but time, she'd planned for days and had finally done it. Wearing only a dirty white lab coat over her bra and panties, she sprinted down the street. Disoriented, she was uncertain where they'd moved the operation. A quick glance up to the wrought iron balconies lined with cascading ferns told her she was in New Orleans. She shook her head in disbelief. *Fucking assholes.* Wynter had lost track of how many times they relocated her. When she'd first started working for them, she'd been in New York City. But after they'd discovered her intentions, she'd been treated like cargo; blindfolded, handcuffed and gagged as they traveled from state to state.

Endless days in the lab led into nightly bleedings by the vampires. They soon learned, however, that their virologist couldn't think straight if her brain lacked blood. But even after they stopped draining her, their threat remained clear and present. Screw up or argue too much, and they'd drag her to the floor, sinking their fangs into her flesh as punishment. As much as she'd kept her nose buried in the work, managing to mentally catalog their protocols, she'd lost chunks of time. She'd nearly given up hope of living, fearing no one would come for her.

Desperate, her plan had been flimsy at best but she'd rather die trying to escape than be imprisoned. Staking the vampire had been the easy part. Finding her way through the locked corridors had been quite another story. But she'd done it. She was nothing if not resourceful. As the fresh air hit her face, her heart raced, knowing they'd be hot on her heels. She stole a glance over her shoulder; the dark figure was quickly approaching. Her breath quickened in fright as she thought through what she'd do next. If she could disappear through one of the myriad courtyard entranceways along the street, she might have a chance. She could open a gate and lock it behind her, she thought. Or perhaps if she ran further, she could find safety within a shop or bar that catered to humans.

Heaving for breath, she wrapped her bloody fingers around the iron bars that led down a dark alley and shook them. Locked? No, she just needed to open the rusted latch. She fumbled with it as she heard the footsteps growing closer. Her eyes darted down the street and she caught a glimpse of an approaching vampire. Swiftly, she turned her attention back to the door. She grunted, pushing at the bar with her thumb. *Open, dammit, open.* Finally, the latch slid aside. It was at that very second she realized she'd run out of time. A bloodcurdling scream tore from her lips as familiar claws dug into her neck, spinning her around.

"Where do you think you're going?" The vampire sneered, holding her by the throat against the wall.

She choked for air, but didn't waste time answering him. In one hand, she held onto the stake and with the other, she continued to flick open the latch.

"I've got her," he called over to the second thug whose fangs openly wept with saliva.

Wynter's eyes teared. This couldn't be the end. Even though she started to feel the tunnel of unconsciousness closing in, she kicked and gasped in defiance. *Never give up.* They could take her but not without a fight.

"No," she croaked softly. He slammed her wrist against the plastered wall. The stake she'd been carrying slipped from her fingers.

Logan sprinted out of the club after the two vampires just in time to see the larger one holding the human against the wall by her neck. *Why the hell are vampires attacking a human? In the wide open where anyone could see? Where the hell is Kade?* Kade Issacson, the head of the vampires in New Orleans, would kill these idiots for merely chasing after a human, let alone harming one. With no time to call him, Logan came up behind the vampire, reached around his neck and snapped his spine. He took in the sight of the wide-eyed girl, dressed in a lab coat, who coughed for air. Protectively, he pulled her into his arms, while glancing over to Dimitri, who'd slit open the throat of the other vamp.

"It's okay, you're safe," Logan assured her.

Wynter began to struggle, kicking and beating the stranger with her fists. Lost in panic, she didn't hear his words. Fear surged as she immediately sensed he was wolf. *Trust no one.*

"No, let me go! Please don't hurt me…I can't…" she began. She didn't feel good, her mind and body were beginning to shut down. If she lost consciousness, they'd take her again.

"Easy, sweetheart. Now listen," Logan said softly, refusing to release her. "I'm not goin' to hurt you." *What the hell was it with humans? Didn't she get he was helping her?*

Now that Logan had the woman from his vision in his arms, he wasn't going to let her simply walk away. He couldn't believe that she was actually here in New Orleans. Curiosity got the best of him as he let his eyes wander over her. She wore a dirty white coat that was missing buttons. Shoeless, her bare feet were blackened and bloodied. *What had happened to her?* Logan could feel the heat rising from her skin. She felt warm, too warm for a human. Notwithstanding her panicked state, she appeared physically ill.

"Please, just let me go. I swear I won't tell anyone. Please," she cried, fighting back the sobs that threatened to overwhelm her.

Wynter looked up at the attractive wolf who offered her help. Over six-four, with shoulder length dark brown hair, he towered over her small stature. Dressed in worn jeans and a black t-shirt, his well-defined biceps gave her an idea of the incredible body that was under his clothes. A distinctive power rolled off of him as he gently ran a finger down her cheek. *Alpha.*

She thought she'd hyperventilate at the thought. Oh my God, she needed to get away from him. She couldn't be certain if he was an enemy of hers or not. And if he was, she knew he'd kill her. Wynter knew that packs had rules. And some packs killed intruders and asked questions later. Seeing no other way to escape, perhaps she could convince him she was simply a wayward tourist being chased by vampires.

"I'm a tourist," she stammered. "I just got lost. If you let me go, I'll just get back to the hotel."

A tourist? Is she crazy? Logan could smell her lie and her fear. *Perhaps she's not crazy but frightened out of her right mind,* he thought.

"Okay, well, let's try this again, because I don't see many tourists on the run from vamps, dressed like you are. Seriously, you're safe with me. You need to calm down, though," he suggested, with a low, reassuring voice. "Things will be fine. We'll get you cleaned up and then we're going to have a little chat."

He didn't want to stress her further but if she thought she was going to up and leave without telling him what was going on, she had another think coming. He glanced over to the ashes of the two vampires they'd killed. He was going to have to have a serious conversation with Kade.

"Please, sir," she continued to beg.

Logan grew irritated. Why was he trying to talk sense into the human in the middle of a dirty alley? It would be much easier if he could just command her like he could do with the wolves. He let a small bit of his power flow out toward her until she stilled in acknowledgement. He cocked an eyebrow at her in surprise that it appeared to work. Not all humans could sense the supernatural force he wielded. *Intriguing.*

"Listen to me, Miss. I'm going to say it one last time; you are safe. I'm sorry but you do realize that I can't just let you go? I've got some questions about what the hell just happened here, and you're in shock. We're going to go home now. Let's get out of this alley."

"No, no, no. Please just let me go. I'll go home. I'll…" She was about to tell him she'd go to the police, when she saw the vampires coming for her. Her heart caught in her throat. It wasn't just any vampire stalking toward them. It was him. The one who had repeatedly fed on her; he'd enjoyed it. Endorphins flooded her weakened system.

Logan shook his head. Much to his chagrin, she obviously didn't understand that she had no choice in the matter.

"More…more vampires," she whispered, unable to look away. Pointing down the street, she grabbed the wall in an effort to remain upright.

"Stay here," Logan commanded.

Wynter silently nodded, fully intending to run.

"Hey D, looks like a few more partygoers want to dance." Logan spun on his heels, taking off down the street to head off their attackers.

"What can I say, Alpha? You're a good-lookin' guy. Real popular tonight," Dimitri joked as he followed.

Logan grabbed the vampire, smashing him up against the wooden shutters of a townhome. Splinters flew as the wood cracked into several pieces. Tearing a shard off the structure, Logan staked him in his back. "Sorry, pal. Dance card's full."

As the second vampire attempted to bite Dimitri, he flipped him onto his back, driving the wood straight through the bloodsucker until he hit the pavement. He shoved up onto his feet and brushed the debris from his jeans.

"Fuck me. What the hell is happening tonight?" Dimitri huffed. "This is some kind of crazy shit."

"Goddamn vampires." Logan stood, scanning the street and was met with silence. "They're out of control."

"Kade must be going soft if he's letting his skeeters buzz the humans. Not good for tourism, ya know." Dimitri laughed.

"Yeah, I get the feeling that our girl's not a random human either. Shit. Where is she?" Logan asked, realizing she must've taken off down into one of the courtyards. Logan sniffed into the air. Humans were so naïve. It was just a matter of time before he found her. "Did you see which direction she ran?"

"No. But I'm guessing from her little tantrum that she doesn't want our help," Dimitri surmised.

"Well, she doesn't have a choice. I want to know exactly what went down before we saved her pretty little ass. Something's not right, and I'm going to find out what it is." Logan continued, deep in thought. "And she's not getting away from me either. Listen, I'm goin' wolf."

"You need me to go with?"

"No, go back to the party. Fi's waiting." Now that Logan had held the woman from his visions in his arms, he needed to know who she was more than ever. What was she doing in New Orleans? Why did the vampires want her?

"You sure?"

"Yeah, I'm sure. But do me a favor, will ya? Put a call into Kade's office and report our little scuffle. They can call me tomorrow. I've got a bad feeling this isn't over."

"You got it."

"Uh…one more thing…my clothes?" Logan grinned.

"Yeah, okay. You sure you want to do this, man?"

Logan laughed without answering. He ducked into an alleyway, away from prying eyes and threw his clothes and boots over to Dimitri. Not that he had a problem with nudity. Quite the contrary; he enjoyed being naked whenever he got the chance. But it was unusual for Logan to go wolf in the city, preferring to run wild in the country. Tonight, however, the woman gave him little choice.

Remembering her lack of clothing and shoes, he reasoned she couldn't have gone far. Where would a human run to in the middle of the night in the French Quarter? Bourbon Street would be the logical place for her to go. Since they were on the other side of the French Quarter, nearly at the river, she'd have quite a ways to walk in order to get there. At two in the morning, most shops would be closed. Even though she didn't seem to be of a criminal nature, she could try to break into a business or home. But that didn't seem likely given her frightened state, not to mention that she'd soon crash from exhaustion. Against the gate, she'd struggled to remain on her own feet. She'd shown signs of illness, trauma and malnutrition. She wouldn't get far.

Letting go of his human thoughts, Logan let the beast take over and do what it did best: hunt. The sweet smell of her remained strong in his memory. Running hard, he zipped down streets and walkways. As her scent grew stronger, the wolf grew excited. Having the capacity to run for miles if necessary, he was unyielding in his search. Soon, the prey would be his.

Chapter Three

Wynter sank into the shadows, contemplating her next move. Exhaustion racked her body. The lack of food and sleep combined with ongoing stress had taken its toll. She wished she could convince herself otherwise, but her mind was unclear; confusion blanketed her thoughts.

A creaking gate alerted her to a maid leaving one of the homes via a courtyard alley. She watched as the older woman looked around, as if to make sure no one was watching, then typed a code into a security pad. As the worker walked down the street, she swiveled her head, still checking for strangers, while the gate slowly closed behind her. Wynter's heart pounded. *A human? Help?* She closed her eyes for what seemed only a second, but by the time she looked again, the woman had strangely disappeared. The gate, however, was slightly ajar as if it was broken. The motorized hinges roared in protest, finally puttering into silence. Wynter leapt at the opportunity to get off the streets, within the safety of a gated house. Decision made, she stealthily slipped through the iron bars.

Wynter pressed her back against the arched stone wall, praying no one had seen her enter. Panting for breath, she reflected on what had happened near the bar and cursed her indecisiveness. For a minute, she'd actually considered giving herself over to the warm, strong Alpha who'd held her. With her cheek at his chest, she'd allowed herself the small indulgence of smelling his clean, spicy scented cologne. As his strong arms and low voice enveloped her, she wanted nothing more than to give herself to him. He was a stranger, yet the familiar strength of an Alpha reminded her of home.

But there was nothing about him that was like her Alpha. No, something about his presence incited an awareness that she'd thought was long gone; perhaps something she was not capable of experiencing. Raised by an Alpha, dates weren't exactly breaking down her door. Her guardian had seen to that. In high school, no one had had the guts to even ask her out, let alone try to kiss her. It wasn't until college that she'd dated humans, had sex. But once she graduated, she was too focused on work to make men a priority. An occasional fling was all she allowed herself, given the high stakes of her research.

In truth, she'd never been intimate with a wolf. She knew all too well that mating with one didn't always turn out well; her guardian had warned her off that idea. But the Alpha who'd just saved her jolted something within her libido; that brief encounter left her wondering if she'd made the right decision by running. His warmth, coupled with his caring words, aroused her. Maybe if she got out alive and her guardian approved, she could contact him later, she thought.

Wynter blew out a breath, realizing how ridiculous it was that she was even thinking of the stranger. Given her dire situation, she'd be lucky if she made it out of the city alive. *Focus, Wynter.* Silently, she inched her body into the archway until she reached a large courtyard. She stilled, listening for signs of people. Moments passed and she heard nothing but the trickling water bubbling out of the three-layered fountain that had greeted her arrival. Intrepidly, she padded out onto the red herringboned brick patio. Dim ground lighting illuminated a large rectangular swimming pool. Despite the old woman's temporary presence, no lights were on in the adjoining mansion or its rear cottage.

Wynter wondered if anyone even lived there. Obviously if the owners kept on late night help, the house was being used by someone. Or perhaps the property was a vacation home? Either way, she had to try to get help. But after knocking on both the main home and cottage's door, she quickly came to the conclusion that it was vacant. She sighed in disappointment, deciding to wait until daylight to keep searching for help. Even if no one was home, she was grateful to be off the street, inside the safety of a quiet yard. In the morning, she could search around the exterior for a hidden key or see if she could get in the garage. If not, she'd try another house. She could more easily travel during the day as it was a much safer time for humans. All she needed was a phone, so she could make contact. Then she'd be home within hours.

Another wave of fatigue rolled through her body. So tired, she thought if she could catch a few hours of sleep, she'd be well enough to keep going. Spotting a few chaise lounges, she tore off the padding. She would have loved to have simply fallen into the chair, but there was no way she could risk being seen out in the open. Dragging the cushions, she squeezed into a secluded nook in between the fountain and a few large potted ferns. She pushed the foam onto the concrete and prayed that she'd be lucky enough to avoid bugs, knowing full well that was wishful thinking.

Curling onto her side, she released a small sob. *How did I ever get into this mess?* The night was dry at least, but she could feel the temperature dropping. She knew she should look for better shelter, but she felt drained, achy. Physically, she just couldn't go on. The wave of lethargy weighed down her limbs, and she realized that she really didn't feel well. As her adrenaline levels dropped, the burn from within grew, alerting her to the fever. *Oh God no. This can't happen now.*

A spike of panic rose as a flash of possibilities ran through her mind. She knew that there'd been one too many occasions where she'd resisted. And in response they'd held her down; fed until she lost consciousness. She tried hard to remember what had happened during her blackouts. At first she'd been worried about sexual assault but that wasn't their thing. No, they clearly preferred pure pain and intimidation. The vampires they'd entrusted to guard her had only been interested in one thing, her blood.

But why was she feeling so weak? She prayed it was merely the stress, a cold. She'd take a simple rhinopharyngitis any day over the lethal viruses she'd handled in the labs. No upper respiratory symptoms presented. Perhaps she'd caught a cytomegalovirus. Even though the virus she worked on targeted shifters, she'd suspected for months that the others were working on other viruses and genetic modifications targeted at vampires, humans and other supernaturals that she wasn't even sure existed.

Another tear ran down her face. Wynter wished she'd never left New York. She felt indebted to her guardian, determined to help his race survive. He'd saved her all those years ago when her parents died. She'd been so alone. He'd been her loving caretaker, the one who brought her back from the devastation she'd felt when her home had been torn apart. She'd done the one thing she could do to help him, to help the pack. But now that she'd escaped, she wondered if she'd done the right thing. Shivering, feeling like a failure, she softly cried herself to sleep.

Glistening with sweat, Logan stared down in disbelief at where his wolf had led him. Like a baby lamb, his lovely dream girl was curled into a deep slumber. After taking note of the busted gate, he knew how she got into his courtyard. Questions swirled in his head. Did she know who he was? Is that why she came to his home? But if she knew him, why run? And why would she lay on the ground like a common dog, sleeping in the shadows? None of what had happened tonight was making any sense.

Black patches of dried blood mottled her face. The tattered coat did little to cover her bare legs. Goosebumps covered her pale skin as the temperature had dropped into the fifties. Seeing little choice, Logan shoved the plants aside, and bent down to her. Reaching for her face, he cupped her cheek. Damn, she was hot; not just warm, but burning up. He'd been right in the alley; she was sick.

"Aw, sweetheart, you're on fire. Now, why did you run? And more importantly, who are you?" he asked himself out loud.

Her unconscious response was to cuddle further into her makeshift mattress. Swiftly but gently, he slid his hands under her tiny body, lifting her into his arms. Logan cursed silently, angry that he'd let her slip away earlier. Even in the heat of the moment, the aroma of her intoxicating scent had caught him off guard. He stilled, taking a minute to lean into her neck; she smelled so good. Despite the sweat and blood, her underlying essence connected with his wolf.

Shocked and aroused by his reaction, he shook his head. What was he doing? His damn wolf needed to get his act together. The woman was sick for fuck's sake. Now wasn't exactly the greatest time to get a hard on. He huffed and took off toward his back door. It was turning out to be one hell of a day.

With one hand, he typed in the security code and awkwardly leaned into the retina scan, careful not to press her against the exterior wall. As the lock clicked open, he pushed the door inward and entered his home. He raced up the steps and headed toward his bedroom. It felt foreign, bringing a strange woman into his inner sanctuary, but there was something about her that told him she wasn't a threat. His visions. She needed him, but her origin and motives remained a mystery.

Logan strode over to his bed and sat on the edge, still cradling the girl. He'd hoped that with his inadvertent jostling she might wake up and answer his questions. But true to his luck that evening, she remained unconscious. Picking up his phone, he called Dimitri.

"Hey," he addressed his beta. "Listen up, I've got our runner. I need you to get Dana down here." Logan looked to her innocent face, wondering what kind of mess this human was wrapped up in.

"Dana? What's wrong with her?" Dimitri asked. If Logan needed Dana, he knew the woman had been injured. Dana was Fiona's half-sister, a doctor. Since she was hybrid, she'd decided on a career of human medicine.

"Yeah, Dana. The girl's sick. And tell them to get here as soon as possible. Listen, I've gotta go. Just get here, 'K?" Logan told him tersely, hanging up the phone. His patience was stretched thin. It had been one goddamned long day. And at this point, things looked to be getting worse, not better.

Unsure of how to proceed, Logan decided a cool bath would help bring down her fever. He knew she'd panic if she woke up with a strange, nude man in the shower, but he didn't have many options. Unbuttoning the few buttons on her coat, he tugged it off of her arms. His stomach tightened in anger as bite marks on her otherwise beautiful skin were revealed. Shit, he hated vampires. Tristan may have been best friends with a couple of them, but not him.

They could be animals. Bloodsucking, vicious monsters who'd turn on you just to get their next drink. He trailed his fingertips over the half dozen bite marks that littered her body, all in various stages of healing. Whoever had done this hadn't done it while lovemaking, ensuring the holes were sealed clean. Rather, it looked as if they'd bitten and retreated, as if they'd been inflicted to purposefully cause pain, debilitation.

He knew that feeding clubs existed. Some humans and shifters got off on pain. Others enjoyed the intoxicating rush of a vampire-induced orgasm. But even in those kinds of places, there were rules about sealing up wounds and they most certainly kept strict dress codes. No, something about this whole situation was off. Logan wasn't sure what the hell was going on but he planned on meeting with Kade as soon as possible. This shit needed to stop but now. If there were more like her out there, they'd all be fucked.

Logan laid Wynter on the bed so he could prepare the bath. He needed to get her cleaned up and most importantly bring her fever down. It didn't seem right that she wasn't waking up with all the commotion he was making. Even though it had been a while since he'd tended to a sick human, he knew that her lack of consciousness could be a serious issue. But his acute hearing told him that her breathing and heartbeat were both normal. For a brief second, he thought that he should throw her in the car and take her to the ER. Under normal circumstances he may have given it further merit, but this situation reeked of supernatural. She had the answers to his questions, and he was determined to get them. As soon as Dana got there, he'd seek her advice about taking her to a hospital.

He glanced over to her threadbare underwear and bra and considered the best way to go about giving a frightened human woman a bath. He laughed in irritation. *What could possibly go wrong?* As much as Logan loved being naked, and with a woman even more so, he decided that he'd better don a pair of boxer briefs. The last thing he needed was her freaking out, waking up slippery and barely dressed with a naked man she'd only just met. He planned to get her in the tub with him and hold her up so she didn't slip under the water. He figured ten minutes would be enough time to bring down her fever, at least until Dana got there. He'd let her decide what to do next. Being wolf, he didn't keep even an Advil in his house.

Logan picked her up and moved into the bathroom. He stepped into the lukewarm water and lowered them both in so that she laid on him. Her back against his chest, he took the bar of soap in his hands and twisted it into a washcloth.

"Okay, baby. Here we go." He spoke softly to her as if she heard him. She shuddered but never woke, so he kept going. "Just goin' to clean you up a bit. Look at what they did to you. Don't worry; you'll be healed in a few days. What I'd like to know is how you got mixed up with vampires?"

Logan found that he was unable to stop talking to her as he carefully cleaned her arms and face. Even if she didn't hear him, it was possible she'd wake at any second. He wanted her to know that someone cared, that she was safe with him. Logan gently washed her, avoiding touching her breasts. But he couldn't resist slipping his hands around her waist, feeling the smoothness of her belly. Fully submerged, he threw the washcloth aside and simply held her. Pressing his cheek to hers, he could feel her body temperature was lowering.

"That's a girl. You're going to feel better soon. Then, we're going to get to know each other," he whispered.

In the quiet of the night, he focused on listening to her heartbeat. His own heart squeezed in response, hoping that the woman he held would heal soon. He thought about the fucking vision. It was possible that he'd averted her death. He'd saved her from a clawed vampire. Maybe that was the end of it. But a nagging suspicion lingered; something told him that this was just the beginning of trouble.

Logan pushed out of the tub, reaching for a towel and gently dried the woman. Her skin puckered in response to the cool air, yet she still made no show of awaking. As Logan rounded toward his bed, Dimitri, Fiona and Dana ran into his room. He caught the smirk on Dimitri's face as his eyes dropped to his Alpha's dripping briefs.

"What?" Logan asked.

"And they say chivalry is dead? Nice briefs, sexy beast," Dimitri teased with a raised eyebrow.

"Fuck you, D," Logan shot over at Dimitri. Without missing a beat, he addressed Dana. "Hey, can you come check her out? I had her in a cool bath but she's still not conscious."

Dana came around the bed and set her medical bag on the night stand. "A human, huh? How long has she been like this?"

"Yeah. I can't be sure but I'd say she's been out for at least forty-five minutes. A few hours ago she seemed fine. Well, awake anyway. When I touched her earlier, I could tell she was sick, warm." Logan stripped and proceeded to towel off in front of everyone. Comfortable with nudity, the others barely noticed.

Dana continued the brief exam and checked her vitals. "This isn't good," she commented, fingering over the feeding holes riddling Wynter's body. "Who did this?"

"Don't know. But when I find out I'm going to kill them…if I didn't already. Dimitri told you 'bout the vamps at the bar?"

"Seems viral. Fever. Sleep deprivation. Stress." Dana pointed to the dark circles under Wynter's eyes and her short bitten nails. She lifted a hand to her nose and sniffed. A look of confusion washed over her. "You said she was human?"

"Yeah, why?"

"Well, this is very unusual. Tell me Alpha, what do you smell?"

Logan strode across the room and held his nose to the soft inner wrist presented to him. "She smells…smells." He stopped and shook his head. His mouth gaped open as he tried to process what was happening. "No. No, that's not possible. I'm telling you Dana, it's not fucking possible."

Unable to stop himself, he ran the tip of his tongue along her skin.

"No." Logan still refused to believe it.

"Yes, Alpha. She's wolf."

"But I'm telling you that when I saw her in the alley earlier there was no possible way she was wolf. I think I know a human when I smell one. And even if by some miniscule chance the scent of the vampire blood masked her true nature, why didn't she shift? I mean, look at all those bite marks. Some are at least a few days old. She could have shifted to heal them. And here's the biggest problem I see with her being supposedly wolf; wolves don't get sick. This woman is very sick. She's got a fever, for Christ's sake; the kind of thing you only see in humans. That just doesn't happen to wolves. What the hell is going on here, Dana?" Logan had switched over to his low, dominant Alpha voice. All the wolves lowered their eyes.

Dana took a deep breath and carefully chose her words. "Alpha, I don't know what's going on here. You're right on all counts. I mean, she scents wolf. But she's sick and that never happens. Look here, at these marks on her neck." She pointed to a series of marks the size of pinpricks that had scabbed over; under her hairline, they were barely visible.

"I don't know what this is. It almost looks like a taser. Or maybe…no," she stopped herself before saying something ludicrous.

"What, Dana?"

"It's just that it kind of looks like an old polio scar. You know, from the seventies. Or maybe it could be caused by some kind of a multi-needle injection device," she guessed with a shrug. "Whatever made it could be causing this fever. But then if that's true, I've never seen anything like it. Wolves don't get sick."

Logan grew quiet with concern. He'd remembered the Canine Lupis Inhibitor drug that Tristan's mate, Kalli had created. Until he'd heard of that, he would have never believed someone could take a pill to disguise their wolf. And while this was completely different, a wolf getting ill was unheard of unless there was some kind of magic affecting her that could explain the illness.

"Could this be some kind of a spell? A hex?" Logan asked.

"Maybe. It's hard to tell. But you said her fever was really high when you found her, right? I just took her temp again and it isn't going up, so that's good news. Whatever is affecting her could be wearing off. If it's a spell or herbs, it seems short-lived. Tell you what. I'm goin' to take a few blood samples. I'll take them to the lab and personally run them, okay?"

Fiona approached Wynter and brushed a long strand of blonde hair from her face. Logan's jaw tightened in response to having yet another wolf touch his human. Noticing the subtle sign, she backed away from the bed and turned to him.

"Logan, if this is magic, I haven't seen it before either. That's not to say the witches aren't always trying to cook up things to thwart shifters and vamps," she said coyly. "I mean, you know there're always a few bad apples in the bunch. I'll ask around. I can also bring some healing herbs for her…if she still feels sick when she wakes up."

"Thanks, Fi." Logan paced, working through his plan of action.

"Dimitri, call Jake and Zeke. I want them to set up a perimeter guard on my place. Have them fix the damn gate. No one gets in or out. I don't know how long she's going to be down, but my guess is this little bird is going to try to fly the coop when she realizes where she is."

"You got it." Dimitri nodded.

"Dana, I hate to ask the obvious question but is whatever's going on with her a threat to others?"

"Do you mean is what she has contagious? I'd go with no. I can't be sure but if it was brought on quickly and she's already rebounding, it could even be a poison of some kind. I didn't think of it until now, but considering the marks on her neck, it's obvious she was exposed to something. Sorry I can't tell you more," Dana said in defeat. She finished drawing blood, snapped the test tubes neatly into a carrying case and arranged everything back into her medical bag.

"Listen up everyone," Logan snapped. All eyes landed on his hard glare. "No one else in the pack is to know what's going on here with mystery girl, got it? I don't know who this woman is…this wolf is. But something's not right here. And until we figure out what's happening, I want to keep it under wraps. This is a direct order. Do not speak of this to anyone. The story for now is that she's a victim of a vampire attack and she's under my protection, nothing more."

The group nodded in agreement and began filing out the door. Logan stopped Dana, privately asking her if she could change Wynter into one of his t-shirts and boxers. As good as she'd felt in his arms, it felt wrong for him to touch her any further. It was obvious she'd been violated by vampires; he wasn't about to add himself to the list.

Logan had doubts about having the girl sleep in his bed, but his protective instincts told him to keep her close. She was vulnerable, and for at least the night, his responsibility. He wasn't sure whether it was his wolf or his heart driving his actions, but he felt compelled to watch over her, to protect her. In the morning, there'd be plenty of time for questions and rational approaches to solving perplexing conundrums. For now it was just him and her, resting, healing.

Clothed, Logan laid next to Wynter. He pushed over to his side and propped his head with the heel of his hand. He studied her face as if memorizing every curve of her chin, the swell of her lips. Something about her drew his interest. He'd like to have blamed it on his vision, but his visceral reaction to her scent concerned him. Alone and happily content for so many years, he couldn't fathom such an instantaneous and intense attraction toward a woman. Regardless, she smelled incredibly delectable to his wolf. Logan sighed. It would wait until tomorrow. He looked forward to her awakening, to forthcoming answers and mostly to getting to know the little wolf in his bed.

Chapter Four

"Hey sweetheart, can you hear me?" Logan awoke to a cry. Even though her eyelids fluttered, she didn't appear to be moving.

As if an elephant sat on her chest, Wynter felt immobilized, both tired and heavy. The soft bedding was her first clue that she was no longer outside. *Where am I? Please God, don't let them have captured me.* She took a deep breath, forcing her mind to focus. Her hazy vision presented the blurry image of a man. *No, no, no.*

"I've gotta go," she coughed, attempting to push upward. Feeling as if she weighed a million pounds, she got an inch off the mattress before falling backward. She licked her dry lips; tears brimmed in her eyes.

"Hold on there now. You're safe. How do you feel?" Logan asked, brushing the back of his hand across her cheek. She felt much cooler; her fever had subsided.

Wynter heard the sound of his familiar low voice wrapping around her like a warm blanket. The man from the alleyway. Thoughts spilled like droplets of rain as she remembered their brief encounter. He'd protected her. Sexy, dominant and altogether male. But, no, he wasn't a man. He was a wolf. *Alpha.*

"I'm Wyn. Wynter Ryan. I think I'm…" She closed her eyes, trying to piece together what had happened. She hadn't felt well.

"Sick. You gave us a good scare, but your fever's down." Logan finished her sentence. "Here, let me get you some water. You've been out of it for a few hours."

He reached over and grabbed a bottle of water that he'd kept near his bedside. Unscrewing the cap, he slid an arm underneath her neck so he could support her head. Bringing the rim to her lips, he watched as she swallowed a few sips. Almost feeling as if he was feeding an infant, he was careful not to choke her with too much liquid.

"Thank you," she whispered, aware that he was holding her. She gazed into his mesmerizing blue eyes. The handsome planes of his face were only outdone by the small smile he gave her. She'd been scared he'd hurt her. Jax had warned her about male wolves. But instead of being aggressive, her savior spoke to her gently, tending to her like an injured child.

"Do you need anything else? You really should get some sleep," he suggested, even though he wanted to ask her a million questions. Reluctantly, he laid her back onto her pillow and backed away.

Immediately, Wynter felt the loss of his warmth as he removed his arm from the crook of her neck. She barely knew him, so why did the brief embrace feel so good? She diverted her gaze, embarrassed by her situation.

"I'm sorry. I shouldn't have run," she began. "I need to tell you…"

"Shhh…you need to rest now. Tomorrow, Wynter. Tomorrow, we'll talk, okay?" Logan assured her. He could hear her heartbeat race; he assumed from anxiety. He sought to soothe her worries. "Just lay back and close your eyes, little wolf."

"But I'm not," Wynter protested.

"Hey now, no more words, okay? You need to get well." Logan moved away from Wynter. Logical thoughts pressed forward; he should let her sleep alone, go work in his office. He eased off the bed and turned off the lights. "You'll be safe here. Just rest."

As the room fell into darkness, Wynter grabbed the sheet out of fear. She hated the dark. Two long months of no sun had done that to her. The claustrophobia threatened to smother her. In the pitch black of the night, she let out a small sob.

"Please, please not the dark. Don't leave," she cried.

Logan flicked one of the soft hallway lights back on and returned to her side. Goddess, he knew he'd regret this in the morning. This was exactly how he'd ended up with a menagerie of animals as a kid. As if he'd found a stray puppy, he was already becoming attached. But he knew there was something special about this woman, something that would keep him from simply letting her go in the morning. He'd learned long ago that one could not fight nature. He sighed, aware of what he was about to do. Against his better judgment, he slid into the bed next to her.

"Come here, Wynter," he ordered, wrapping an arm around her shoulders.

Goddess almighty, her small body fit his perfectly, and he was pissed at himself. Not only had he let Wynter into his home, his bed, he now had her conveniently and warmly against his chest. The dreams hadn't prepared him for the intense arousal and possessiveness that appeared to be rearing its ugly head. No, he couldn't let this happen. Establishing his dominance within the pack and securing his position as Alpha had been his number one priority. And now that that was accomplished, he needed to focus on continuing to nurture his already successful real estate venture, not become emotionally involved with a stranger.

As he allowed himself the indulgence of pressing his nose to her hair, he mentally shook his head. He didn't know anything about this woman. She seemed human, but now he distinctively scented wolf. And if she was wolf that meant she came from a pack. She belonged somewhere else, possibly to someone else. He cringed slightly at the thought she could be mated. No, that couldn't be possible. She felt so right in his arms. So terribly, wonderfully perfect. And it was all wrong.

Wynter had never been needy or scared. But in that moment, her vulnerability overtook her sense of reason. A small voice in her head told her that it wasn't right to let a stranger hold her, comfort her. Yet the attraction was too hard to resist. Certain that he was Alpha, she wasn't sure if it was his powers she felt humming through her veins or her own arousal, but his protective embrace spoke to her soul, calmed her mind. Acquiescing to his wishes, she cuddled her head on his shoulder and her hand on his chest. *Safe.*

The last thought that ran through her mind was that she needed to call home. God, she missed him. Surely, he'd be ripe with panic. Tomorrow, she thought. Tomorrow, I'll call him.

"Jax," she murmured right before she was lost to sleep.

Logan sucked a breath. *What the fuck did she just say?* He glanced downward. She was completely asleep, but there was no mistaking what she just said. No, it could not be possible. Jax. Jax fucking Chandler; the Alpha of New York City. He'd met him a handful of times. When it came to business, the man was fair, albeit having a flair for the dramatic.

The last time he'd seen the guy in Jersey, he'd presented Tristan with a 'present' of sorts. Of course the 'gift' turned out to be a wolf who'd been involved in killing one of Tristan's wolves. *It's the thought that counts.* In reality, Tristan couldn't have been happier with the present. During the event, Logan had observed Jax, who seemed to take perverse pleasure in watching Tristan attack and kill the wolf. He distinctively remembered Jax comforting Tristan after he'd taken a life, assuring him that he'd done the right thing as Alpha.

At the time he couldn't quite understand the interaction. But now that he was Alpha, he could easily relate to what transpired that day. Jax was merely supporting Tristan, giving him a peace offering after he'd aggressively pursued Tristan's sister. Like leaders of countries, Alphas chose other Alphas as allies, all the while protecting their own packs. Logan had never thought it would be possible to have more respect for Tristan or Jax, but now that he was Alpha, their relationship was even more important.

Did Wynter belong to Jax? Was she his mate? He blew out a breath, knowing that it shouldn't matter. All that really mattered was finding out what the hell happened with the vampires in the alleyway and how a wolf could get sick. Both spelled serious trouble for not just wolves but all supernaturals in the area. The shit was about to hit the fan.

Chapter Five

Wynter woke refreshed, although alone. The bright sun streamed into her room, causing her to yawn. Months of sleeping on the floor, and she was finally home in her warm bed; it felt incredible. She pressed her eyes shut, willing her dream to continue. A sexy mysterious stranger beckoned to her in the distance. She could make out the definition of his abs, but couldn't quite see his face. She strained to listen, to run to him, so she could see who he was.

"Hey sunshine," a male voice called to her.

Startled, she jolted upward, eyes wide open. Scanning the room, she instantly realized her erotic dream of being held in a strong Alpha's arms must have been just that: a dream. *Where am I?* Panic set in once again as an imposing man with tattoos on his forearms approached her. Not the man from her dreams.

"Don't come any closer," she warned him. "I don't know how I got here but I'm leaving." She jumped out of bed, then quickly realized she was naked underneath a man's t-shirt and boxer shorts. *Oh God.*

"Listen, cher. No one here's goin' to hurt you. Just settle down," he suggested and gestured toward a bureau. Yogurt, granola, fruit and juice sat on a tray. "Now that you're feelin' better, maybe you can eat some breakfast."

She wanted to deny it, but her stomach ached in hunger. How long had it been since she'd eaten like a normal human being? Months? But how could she trust this stranger looming across the room? She glanced up at him. Definitely wolf. She could tell by his piercing green eyes. But who was he? Alpha? No, he wasn't Alpha. She'd been with pack long enough to tell this wasn't him. But the man from last night…was he real? She grasped the collar of her shirt, drew it up to her nose and took a deep breath. Clean, male with a touch of cologne. She nearly fell back into the bed taking in his scent. She sighed, closing her eyes. The male from last night. It was him. And it smelled so…good. Memories of their conversation played in her mind. She'd asked him to stay with her. And he did. He'd held her. The arousal she'd felt. Oh God. That couldn't be right. She was in so much trouble. No, no, no. Jax was going to freak out when he finally found her.

Dimitri smiled. *Yep, that's right, baby. Smell your shirt.* Little did she know that Logan was waiting for Dimitri to bring her to him downtown. Whatever had transpired last night between the two of them seemed to have rattled his Alpha. He'd watched as Logan tore out of the mansion at the crack of dawn. Even though he'd mumbled something about meeting preparations, Dimitri knew damn well that his Alpha rarely needed time to prepare for anything. He was the sharpest tool in the shed, both mentally and physically. On the way out, he'd ordered Dimitri to watch over the little wolf, see if he could get her to eat and bring her to the office.

Aside from the entertainment factor, Dimitri liked the idea of his Alpha concentrating on something other than challenges. And this lovely little lady was turning out to be a damn fine distraction, at least for the short term. But they still didn't really know who she was, and that was a wrench in the cog. If she belonged to another wolf or pack, they'd soon claim her. And as it was looking, she was a runner by nature and didn't plan to stick around very long. And then there was her mystery illness, unheard of among wolves. Maybe that's why Logan was all about business? He probably thought a passing attraction to the little wolf would be futile by nature.

Dimitri glanced at Wynter and decided they'd better get moving; he coughed to get her attention. He needed her to accept what was about to happen. He contemplated the best approach for getting her to comply. Deciding on going soft, rather than using force, he crouched down so he could speak to her on eye level, trying to seem less intimidating than he knew he was.

"It's okay, Wynter."

"You know who I am?" she asked timidly.

"Yes, you talked to my Alpha last night. You're remembering, right? His scent?"

"I..." She sniffed the ambrosial-scented fabric once again. What the hell was wrong with her? "I...I guess...yes. But I was sick, right?"

"Sure were. How're you feelin'?" He was genuinely concerned.

"I feel fine," she lied. Physically, she felt fine. But mentally, she was broken. Wynter stared out toward the window, helplessly shaking her head. Tears brimmed in her eyes, and she looked away.

Dimitri sat on the bed at her side and put a comforting hand on her shoulder. Surprisingly, she didn't shrug him off; she just let the tears run down her cheeks.

"I may be old-fashioned but the girls I know who actually feel fine don't cry, cher."

"I'll be fine. I'm just overwhelmed."

This was not going so well, Dimitri thought. He stood up and walked over to the dresser and poured her a glass of orange juice.

"Have something to drink," he told her.

With no energy to argue, she complied, reaching for the glass. The sweet acidy pulp tasted so good. She hadn't had juice for so long, and it made her feel as if she was doing something wonderfully normal. She wiped her tears away with the back of her hand and gave him a small smile.

"That's a girl. Are you sure you don't want to lie down? I was supposed to take you to see the Alpha, but he won't want you to go if you're not well."

"No, really, I'm okay." *I'd be better if I were home.* She looked up at Dimitri in silent defeat, wishing she could just get on the next flight out of New Orleans. But she knew better than to try to outrun a wolf. Well, she used to know better. She figured that last night didn't count; she hadn't exactly been thinking clearly. And now that she was in another pack's home, possibly the Alpha's, there was no way she'd get out on her own. She had to call Jax.

"I need to call someone. Can I use your phone?" she asked quietly.

"Sorry, but you've got to talk with the Alpha first. I don't want to point out the obvious, but we need to know why you were being chased by those vamps last night. And your fever. Alpha's got a lot of questions."

"But I have to call Jax," she protested. "I have to get out of here."

Dimitri stopped dead in his tracks, almost dropping the glass. *Jax.* There was only one Jax that he knew: Jax Chandler. Holy fuck. No wonder Logan was pissed this morning. Seems like the rules of the game just changed. Attempting to hide his reaction, he continued and handed her a yogurt.

"I'm sure my Alpha will be in touch with yours." He could only assume she belonged to the New York pack. And she'd slept with his Alpha. Yeah, this was going to be fun.

"He's not my Alpha. Well, yes he is but…" her words trailed off when she realized she was going to be interrogated ad nauseum about what had happened by the New Orleans' Alpha. Even if he'd acted caring last night, he'd want details about why she was in that alley. But she needed to talk to Jax first. Her eyes darted defiantly up at Dimitri and she said nothing more.

"Okay, little wolf, whatever you say."

"I'm not a wolf," she stated firmly, confused as to why he'd call her that. Any supernatural worth their salt could tell she was very much human.

Dimitri laughed. "Well, that fever must have affected you a little more than I thought." He shook his head, irritated that she'd lie to him. The whole situation was turning into one shitload of crazy that he was ready to dump somewhere else. If that was how she was going to play it, he was ready to take a stricter approach with her.

"Wynter, this's what's goin' happen. You need to eat something and then we're going to see my Alpha. I called over to one of the shops this morning, and they delivered some clothes that should fit you." He pointed to several shopping bags lying near the closet door. "You're welcome to take a shower before we leave but I'd like to leave in an hour. Am I clear?"

"Crystal," she grumbled, conceding she wasn't going to get to call Jax. She knew that condescending, 'do what I say' tone all too well. When decisions needed to be made in a pack, it wasn't exactly the epitome of democracy. Pretty much the exact opposite. And given that she was neither a pack member nor a wolf, she had exactly zero say about her future at the moment.

Logan knew the second she'd entered his building. Occupying the top five floors of a renovated skyscraper on Poydras Street in the Central Business District, he ran pack operations as well as his own personal business. State of the art security had been installed throughout the building and a private, high speed elevator exited directly onto his floor. Logan watched on his plasma security screen as Wynter crammed herself into the corner of the lift, attempting to get away from Dimitri. Logan frowned, wondering what caused her to cower in such a fashion. He'd asked Dimitri to offer her breakfast and bring her to him if she was well. But clearly the morning had not gone how he'd planned.

Even though he'd told Dimitri not to touch her in any way or intimidate her, Logan was aware that his beta's presence didn't exactly put people at ease. A mere look from him would have most males shaking in their boots. Given Dimitri's massive presence, he could understand how the little wolf would be wary. The man looked like a badass enforcer, but in truth, Dimitri was quite the peacemaker within the pack. Sure, he was almost as deadly as Logan given the right circumstances, but in general, he approached life with calm and humor.

Logan swore, remembering the way he'd left her. Oh, he'd wanted to stay all right. But encouraging the uncanny attraction wouldn't help either of them. Holding her, smelling her, it had been too great a temptation. So instead of prolonging the torture, he'd made a judicious decision; he'd left the bedroom before he did something he regretted. Hearing Jax's name should have been enough to douse the flame that heated his burgeoning erection. But as her soft breasts pressed against his chest and her hand wandered up to the ridges of his bare abs, he'd nearly lost it. Erotic thoughts painted over any worries he'd had about the New York Alpha. As she'd unconsciously draped her leg over his in her sleep, brushing her thigh over his hard shaft, he truly imagined he'd come in his boxers. So after three hours of barely sleeping, her intoxicating scent fully ensconced in his consciousness, he'd bailed.

He'd almost thought better of washing her scent away but doing so admittedly cleared his head. Not only did the she-wolf come with major baggage, she didn't belong to him and had called for another man. What was he thinking? He knew the best thing for all of them would be to have a nice sit down in his office where he could wear his professional veneer like a mask. He'd treat their interaction like he should, all business. He'd find out who she was, what pack she belonged to, why the vampires were after her and how the hell she'd gotten sick. The most logical solution was magic, he'd decided. As for the rest, she probably got in a fight with her boyfriend and decided a little fun in the Big Easy was in order. Somehow she got mixed up with some rough vamps who decided they'd take it a little too far. By the time he'd arrived at the office, he'd had the most logical possibility wrapped up with a tidy bow. And his sexual attraction to her was sealed up nice and tight into that same package…until now.

Glued to the screen, he observed her aversion posturing; her eyes darted to Dimitri and then back down to the floor. He could practically smell her fear through the fiber optics. Perhaps she should be nervous, but fear was not an emotion he planned on eliciting…yet. Logan wasn't into pain, but as Alpha, he'd do what he needed to do to protect the pack. As Tristan had pointed out to him on many occasions, an Alpha's decisions weren't based on popularity; rather, they needed to be calculated and implemented in the best interest of the pack. No matter how much his dick longed for her, the small, but real, possibility of her being a threat existed. Even a pocket knife could kill a large man if used correctly. He needed to get his shit together and focus on getting answers instead of getting laid.

He'd already called Jax, letting him know that one of his wolves had gone astray in New Orleans. The brief but necessary conversation caused his gut to twist. *She does not belong to you.* He just needed to keep telling himself those words. It should be easy to remember, considering it was true. Oddly, Jax didn't claim her outright, but instead indicated he or one of his associates would be on a plane as soon as possible to assess the situation. Logan found that interesting in itself. What was there to assess? An Alpha knows all his wolves. But then again, after meeting Jax a few times, his penchant for drama tended to weave itself into everything he did.

The ding of the elevator caused him to suck a breath. This was it; time for answers. *Showtime.* Like clockwork, Jeanette, his secretary, buzzed his speaker, alerting him to their arrival. Jeanette, a human, had been working for Marcel for over forty years. She'd been crushed by his passing but agreed to Logan's offer to stay on, working for him. She was the consummate professional, and he suspected her loyalties ran nearly as deep as those of the wolves in his pack.

Dimitri knocked once on the door and strode into Logan's office, shutting it behind him.

"What did you do to her?" Logan accused, giving him a sardonic stare.

"Nothin', she's perfectly fine. You saw her. She's fed and dressed; just like you asked." Dimitri smiled and dropped into one of the tan leather seats facing Logan's desk.

"Really? Then tell me why she looks like she's scared shitless?" His mouth tightened into a fine line.

Dimitri diverted his gaze looking out the window and back to his Alpha. "It was nothing."

"What was nothing?"

"I swear I was gentle with her," Dimitri assured him. "She wanted to call Jax. I said no. I can't help that she's a little wisp of a thing. And well, I'm…I'm me." He gave Logan a lopsided grin.

"You think this is funny?"

"Well, boss, I must admit it's a little funny. I mean, come on. When was the last time a little she-wolf had the Alpha tearing out of his own home at the crack of dawn? And at the risk of pointing out the obvious, you still seem a little on edge."

Logan rolled his eyes, swiveled in his chair and glanced out the window to look over the cityscape. He took a breath and blew it out, frustrated. "Fuck, yeah, I'm on edge. You try sleeping with a girl like her for a few hours while she calls out Jax Chandler's name. Hearing his name should've been enough to make me treat her like a nun, but man, I was so not saying my prayers. It's so wrong."

Dimitri laughed out loud. "Well, she is fine, but she's not ours. And she very well may be going home tonight. You get ahold of Jax?"

"Yeah, I called him. Cagey bastard's playing his damn games. Says he's coming here to 'assess' the situation. Didn't claim her outright but didn't deny it either. As for little Miss Wynter out there…there's part of me that would like to keep her." Logan smiled over at him like he'd discovered treasure.

"She's not a lost dog, Alpha. You can't just 'keep her'."

"You'd be surprised at what I can do when I put my mind to things," he pondered. *Was he really considering keeping her?* Yes, yes he was. And why not? Jax didn't exactly claim her. Then again, aside from a few hours of cuddling like a horny, blue-balled teen, he didn't even know her. For all he knew, she had the personality of a honey badger.

"That you do. But as your beta, my advice is to go easy." Dimitri shook his head and laughed. Damn if his Alpha wasn't considering the unthinkable.

"I don't do easy," Logan remarked. "I do what I need to do. And right now, I plan to get the truth." He stood, walked over to the bar and pulled a bottle of water out of the mini-fridge. "Speaking of which, we have a meeting with Kade later tonight at Mordez."

"Mordez, huh? Love me a vamp club," Dimitri said sarcastically.

"Yeah, you and me both. You know the vamps. They can't meet in offices like normal people." He shrugged. "Bring Zeke and Jake in case there's trouble. Have them keep eyes on us…discreetly. You know the drill."

Logan detested meeting at a blood club as much as the next wolf, but he'd do it to meet Kade. If there was one vampire he remotely trusted, it was him. Logan would mete out justice when necessary, but it was Kade's job to get his people in line, not his.

"Done," Dimitri responded, making his way over to the door.

"Let's get this show on the road, shall we?" Logan said with a wry smile.

Within seconds of Dimitri's exit, Logan's blonde angel stood in the archway.

Heart racing, Wynter passed through the doorway and looked up at the magnificent stranger who'd saved her. As his eyes locked on hers, her breath caught in her lungs. *Alpha.* The word resounded through her mind like an echo in a valley as she looked over to Logan, who sat carefully watching her every move from behind his desk. Memories of his arms around her body in the heart of the night swirled in her mind. Her face flushed at the confounding arousal she'd felt. Although she tried so hard not to stare, it became impossible to stop. The Alpha was both incredibly sexy and handsome yet he looked dangerous as his lips formed a knowing smile. Dressed in a dark blue suit, his confident posture exuded power. And sex. She tensed as her desire flared again. No, no, no. How could she be attracted to an Alpha? That could not happen. Jax would not be pleased, not one damn bit.

What was wrong with her? She'd been gone from society for months, and she was ready to throw herself at the first man to cross her path? Wynter reasoned that perhaps it was the drugs they gave her. Yes, that had to be it. Maybe she was still feeling the effects of her illness? But as she gazed into his eyes, she couldn't deny the lure of his powerful presence. She tried to shake it off; her brain told her to be cautious. She knew better than to assume a handsome man equated to nice. In her experience, she'd learned that Alphas were charming, often good-looking and exceedingly deadly.

She took a deep breath, trying to tamp down her reaction. *Do not think about how it felt to lie against him in bed. You don't even know him.* No matter how much her libido just got thrown into overdrive, she needed to get it the hell together. Concentrate, she told herself. She needed to call Jax, transfer the intelligence to him and initiate a new plan of action. Pulling over a façade of indifference, she exhaled.

With her misplaced emotions tucked away, she opened her eyes. The Alpha gave her a broad smile as if he knew exactly what she'd been thinking….every dirty, lustful thought. *This cannot be happening.* His voice jarred her back into reality.

"Have a seat." Logan gestured to one of the seats across from his desk.

It was not lost on him how Wynter averted her gaze submissively at his words. *Definitely wolf.* How could he have been so wrong when he first met her in the alley, thinking she'd been human? Sensing both fear and arousal from Wynter, he struggled to remain objective. His wolf sought to pounce on the prey that tempted him so. Logan reminded himself that he really didn't know this woman, no matter how delicious she looked.

He cursed silently as his eyes roamed over her jeans and the pale pink oxford shirt that was unbuttoned just low enough for him to see a hint of cleavage. He imagined that Dimitri had Melinda, one of his wolves who owned several shops, deliver her clothing. Even conservatively dressed, Wynter looked delightfully edible. Free from makeup, she was a natural beauty. While her skin looked pallid, as if she'd been out of the sun, her complexion was bright and clear.

Her long blonde hair was pulled into a tight ponytail. The spiraling curls sprang in all directions, and for a brief second, Logan wished he could snip the rubber band binding her hair, freeing it like the wind. How he'd love to wrap his hand around it while taking her from behind. Yes, indeed, that would be a sinful pleasure. Ah, but it was time for business. Perhaps if he convinced her to stay, he could play with her. But for now, he needed answers; answers that only she could give him.

"You're safe, Wynter." Logan watched her with interest as she sat, nervously playing with her fingers.

Startled to hear her name roll off his lips, she jerked in her chair. Apprehensively, she looked around his large office, checking out the space for an escape route.

"I…I'm sorry, Alpha," she stated, finally raising her eyes to his.

"Do you know who I am?"

She shook her head. "No. I mean, yes, I remember last night. Thank you for taking care of me," she managed.

"Yet you know what I am. You address me as Alpha. You can sense it, no?"

"Yes," she quietly agreed.

"My name is Logan Reynaud, and I'm Alpha of Acadian Wolves here in New Orleans," he informed her. Keeping his voice calm and low, he continued. "Listen Wynter, I'm not going to hurt you. But I need answers about what happened last night, okay? Let's start with what you were doing down in the alley. Why were the vamps after you?" He leaned far back into his chair, resting his hands on the armrests. He cocked his head, waiting for an answer.

"I…they…I was being held." Wynter forced her hands onto her thighs, attempting to relax. "I was working for someone. I had a disagreement with my employer. The vampires. They didn't want me leaving." Okay, that was the truth. Maybe not the whole truth but he couldn't possibly know that.

"So you were working in the middle of the night, tried to leave and they chased you?" The lilt at the end of his sentence indicated that he clearly didn't believe her.

"Well, yes. Please sir, it's complicated."

Sir, huh? While the mere mention of the word shot a rush of blood to his cock, he knew she was trying to conceal information. Sly little she-wolf, she was.

"So tell me, what kind of work do you do?"

She could tell he wasn't buying her story. Oh God, she wished Jax was here to help her. Wynter knew that telling lies to an Alpha generally ended in disaster. She needed to be very careful. Do not lie, but don't tell the whole truth.

"I'm a researcher. I've been working for a long time on some very important projects," she sighed. "I knew things. They didn't want me to leave. I escaped." There, she said it. Again, all truth…but not everything. The memories of being held against her will elicited a fresh sense of fear. As if she was still in the lab, her blood pulsed in panic, and she struggled to remain composed. Pushing down her sleeves, she attempted to hide the scars of her internment that remained on her arms.

"You were working for a company that kept its workers nearly naked and locked up? Is this correct?" Infuriated at her admission, he attempted to stay calm. What kind of monster would keep her imprisoned? And what were they doing in his city?

"Yes," she whispered. A small sob lodged in her throat. Why did she ever think she could work for that company? Although she'd done it to help the pack, it had been so foolish. Her lips tensed together, and she pretended to admire the New Orleans vista through the glass. *Do not cry in front of an Alpha.*

"And tortured? The bites. I saw them," he pushed.

Instead of answering him, she simply nodded, refusing to look at him. Wynter's face whitened at the mention of the bite marks that littered her body. Embarrassment washed over her even though she didn't deserve it. She tugged at her sleeves once again in an attempt to hide. Anger surged. It was none of his business what happened to her. Where the hell was Jax?

"Little wolf, don't be ashamed. These vampires…I know them. They can be vicious," he told her.

Her eyes flashed in confusion. Wolf? Why was he calling her that? Tears threatened to spill from her already reddened eyes. She just needed to go home. Jax would help fix things, including the mess that her life had become.

Logan hated that they'd done this to her. He could tell she was on the edge of losing it, but he had to know what happened. Fighting the urge to wrap his arms around her and offer comfort, he purposefully grounded himself behind his desk.

"Okay, why don't you tell me about the magic? Were you hexed? Do you remember what happened?"

"What magic?" she countered, perplexed by his questions. What was he talking about?

"You were sick last night. Wolves don't get sick," he reminded her.

"Yes, I know," she agreed, meeting his gaze. In truth, she wasn't sure what happened to her. "Wolves don't get sick. But humans do. I must have had the flu." Feeling claustrophobic, Wynter suddenly got up and walked over to the edge of the floor-to-ceiling window. At one time, she'd marveled at the view of New York City from this height. But this wasn't New York. At that moment, she simply wished to escape, as if hoping she could parachute out of the building.

"This is true, Wynter. But you're not human, are you? Last night you were burning up. Something happened. You need to tell me what you remember. Were you around witches? Tell me, little wolf," he asked tersely, growing impatient with her avoidance.

"Stop calling me that!" she snapped. This was it. She truly was losing it. Yelling at an Alpha was not her smartest move but she felt out of control. Why not go for broke? She turned around to face Logan, her back against the cool glass. "I was not around witches. I told you that vampires were holding me. I don't know why I was sick. End of story. Now, I need to call Jax. And I am not a wolf! Can't you see I'm human? You're an Alpha, for God's sake."

Wynter barely saw him coming. Logan leapt across the room, and as his body touched hers, she gasped. His hands pressed hard against the glass on either side of her head. The masculine scent of him wafted into her nose and she fought the instinct to rub her face against his chest. *Oh God, what had she done? How could she be so stupid as to challenge an Alpha? She really must be sick*. Unable to speak, she held still. Initially charged with fear, she realized very quickly that he wasn't hurting her. The tension between them escalated with every minute of silence that passed. And then she felt him, his nose grazing along the side of her neck. A small moan escaped her lips.

At the challenge, Logan strode across the room, pinning her against the wall. *He had to smell her, taste her. Why would she deny her wolf? Why play games?* Logan didn't want to hurt her. Oh no. If anything, he'd like to give her pleasure like she'd never known. But she kept insisting she was human. If she wanted to play, play he would. She was wolf, and he'd prove it to her. But as her sweet scent engulfed his senses, he began to lose control. His wolf clawed at his psyche, begging to take the woman. Like freshly cut roses, the heavenly aroma was familiar yet altogether unique and desirable, although her wolf lingered on the edge; she was there, he could scent her.

In an effort to prevent himself from ravishing her right there in his office, Logan plastered his hands so hard against the window, he thought it'd crack. At the sound of her moan, he darted his tongue out against her silky skin. He had to taste her. Just once. Ah fuck, no; his wolf wanted more. Eyes feral, he locked them with hers, taking her arm. He placed a small kiss to her palm before dragging his tongue along her wrist all the way to the crook of her elbow, releasing a growl of satisfaction.

Wynter's heart pounded as he gently took her arm into his hands. She shivered as he pushed up her sleeve and brought her delicate wrist to his lips. Wet with arousal, she couldn't break their connection as she stared deep into his mesmerizing eyes. *Oh my God. Wolf. Human. I'll be whatever you want me to be…just please, just take me.* Wynter thought her knees would give out, except he had her pressed up against the window. Lost in his spell, she responded by nudging her own hips against his hard arousal as he tasted her skin.

Logan groaned as the territorial need to take her consumed him. He needed to get things under control. *Jax. Fucking, goddamned Jax.* His name alone should have killed his raging hard on, but it wasn't helping one damn bit. No, he needed to separate himself from her before he tore her clothes off. He closed his eyes and blew out a breath, but didn't release her.

"Wolf," he breathed into her hair.

"What?"

"Wolf, sweetheart. You're very much a wolf," he confirmed.

"No, I know I was sick but that just can't be." Wynter tried to move, but he wrapped his arms around her protectively. "I need to see a doctor. Please, Alpha."

Confused, Logan pulled away enough so he could look at her. He wasn't sure why she was denying her wolf. Considering her illness, he tried to be gentle, to calm her. "Wynter," he said softly, noticing that she'd rested her forehead against his chest. "Look at me."

Wynter complied, slowly raising her head. She was overwhelmed. One minute she'd felt a healthy dose of fear, then instantly she was overcome with lust for the Alpha before her. She didn't know him, but something deep down told her that she could trust him. He had nothing to gain from telling her she was a wolf. She suspected she'd been compromised somehow by ViroSun. How, she didn't know.

"Hey, I don't know what's goin' on with you, but we'll deal with this. And given that we've technically slept together, I think you can call me Logan." He winked in an effort to put her at ease. "Last night when you were unconscious, I had my doctor examine you. And before you ask, she's a hybrid so she knows about wolves and humans. But I need you to be honest with me. Why do you keep denying your wolf?"

She sighed, resigned to the fact that she needed his help. While it was true she had to talk to Jax, the man before her was offering her a lifeline and she desperately needed to grab onto it if she had a shot in hell of keeping her sanity. She had to explain to him, tell him more about what happened to her.

"I deny my wolf as you put it, because I'm not a wolf. I'm human," she explained, placing her palms against his chest. "Please listen to me. I swear I'm human. I've never in my life shifted. And I don't know why I scent like wolf to you. But you have to understand, the place I worked; they…they could do things. I was forced to help them do these things."

"Things? What kinds of things?" Logan didn't like where this was headed, but he tried to sound encouraging and not angry. He didn't want to scare her any more than she'd already been.

"I was working on many different things….mostly viruses. When I'd refuse or give them a hard time…let's just say there are parts of my employment that I don't remember. These people…they're evil. And capable of horrible things…things I never knew could be possible," she croaked.

Logan pulled her into an embrace and stroked her hair. "Whatever happened we'll figure it out," he assured her. He couldn't understand how a human could smell like a wolf, but a few months ago he'd been around wolves, who through pharmaceutical means, could hide their wolf, scenting as humans. Perhaps she'd been injected with something similar? "I need to know what exactly you were working on. Sounds pretty important if these vampires were willing to risk going after you out in the open like they did."

Wynter wrenched herself out of his arms and wrapped her arms around herself. She knew he wouldn't like what she was about to tell him. As much as she wanted to tell him everything, her loyalty was to Jax. Her Alpha had first rights to access the intelligence she'd gleaned in her captivity.

"I want to tell you. But…I can't," she said softly. "Jax. I have to talk to him first."

Logan's stomach clenched at the mention of the New York Alpha. He had to know. "Do you belong to him?"

Wynter slowly turned around and gave him a sorrowful frown. "Yes."

As the word left her lips, she wished in that moment it wasn't true. There was something about Logan. She wanted so badly to tell him everything. Her attraction to the gentle wolf couldn't be denied. But she owed Jax her life and her allegiance. Maybe after she talked to Jax, she could explore the budding feelings she had for the New Orleans' Alpha. But now was not the time. No, out of respect for Jax, she needed to speak with him first.

Logan blew out a breath. Needing to put distance between them, he returned to his desk and sat down. He leaned back and stared up at the ceiling, trying to concentrate. If she thought she could tell him that there was something nefarious going on in his city and simply walk away from him, she was surely delusional. The next question he was about to ask was critical to how he'd proceed with regards to her and his investigation.

"Are you his mate?" He held his breath, awaiting her response.

She froze. Jax's mate? She lived with Jax, wore his scent even. But she'd never revealed the true nature of her relationship with Jax to anyone. She and Jax agreed that it would be best if she lived with him, kept others in the dark. He assured her that that would be the only way she'd be protected under his care. Despite the fact that they'd agreed upon it in the past, she couldn't lie to Logan.

"I'm not his mate," she responded, not quite meeting his eyes. *Please, no more questions.* "Logan, I know you don't know me, but I'm begging you. You know how this works. He's my Alpha. What I worked on…it was with Jax's knowledge and approval. I knew what I was getting into or at least I thought I did," she huffed. *Yeah, I knew exactly what I was doing right up until I couldn't leave the compound and became dinner for the guards.* "I need to talk with Jax first. That's how it has to be. You know protocol."

Fuck protocol. He wanted the goddamned truth. But he knew she was right. If she'd been one of his wolves, working for him, she wouldn't be allowed to discuss business with another Alpha. That being said, New Orleans was his city and if Jax wanted answers, wanted her, he had to go through him.

Steepling his fingers, he pinned her with a hard stare. He suspected by the way she carefully responded that she was concealing the true nature of their relationship. Now why was that? If she was his girlfriend, why not just tell him? Maybe because he could have easily fucked her on his desk two minutes ago and she wasn't at all resisting. The scent of her arousal was overwhelming. But if she wasn't his mate, her attraction to another male shouldn't have mattered to her or Jax. No, it actually would have been expected. All wolves played the field, quite unfaithfully, until they found their mate.

So why all the secrecy? Deliberately, he'd let her think she'd won this round of questioning. Logan was determined to influence her into spilling every last secret including her darkest fantasies. But first, he needed to lay down some ground rules. Ah yes, rules were great fun especially when you got to make them.

"Sit down, Wynter," he ordered. She obeyed without question. It was evident to him she'd been around wolves long enough to understand it was in her best interest to listen to an Alpha. "Until Jax gets here, you are under my protection. And I assure you, you will be safe with me. But I've got a few rules."

Wynter should have known this was coming; Alphas and their rules. It was as if she was home. Oddly, she felt relief knowing that for at least now, she'd be safe from ViroSun. She was certain that they'd be looking for her.

They'd want their research finished.

As she looked up to Logan, she was surprised to see him smiling. She couldn't help but give him a small smile in return. What was he thinking? The rules, of course.

"What? Is something funny?" she asked.

"The rules," he continued, ignoring her question. If she was going to stay with him, he might as well have fun with her until she submitted to him fully. As soon as Jax landed, he planned to have a very long conversation with him about his lovely little wolf. "I don't have many, but these two you must follow without question. First, you will not leave my home or office alone. Ever. If for some reason I'm not available, my beta, Dimitri will be. In spite of whatever happened with you two this morning, he'll protect you with his life."

"Yes, don't leave alone…got it," she repeated, uneasy with how happy the thought of spending more time with Logan made her. This first rule would not be hard to follow, because she was scared to death that they'd come after her again.

"Whoever was keeping you captive may decide to kidnap you back. And I'm going to need your help finding the place where they kept you last. I'm guessing they've already made themselves scarce, but after we talk to Kade, we'll check it out."

She nodded in agreement.

"Second rule. I expect honesty. By taking you into my home, I'm assuming responsibility for your safety based upon the little information I have. But I will not put my pack at risk, you understand?"

"But I already told you there are some things I can't tell you," she interrupted.

"Yes. Protocol. I'm well aware about why you prefer to talk to your Alpha first. But other than that, no lies. I'm not playing games."

Wynter bristled at his tone. "I'm hardly playing games. You do realize that it was me who just spent two months imprisoned?"

"Sweetheart, I get it, but remember you're the one withholding info, not me. But I'm not worried. Very soon, I'm confident you'll trust me with all your clandestine secrets and desires," Logan predicted, giving her a sexy smile.

"Um, we'll see," she commented, returning his smile.

Wynter flushed, embarrassed by his insinuation. *Desires.* It had been forever since she'd had sex. Until last night, she'd nearly forgotten she was a woman. Being around Logan was like going from drought to flood. She stared at his lips, remembering the soft way he kissed her wrist and squeezed her legs together. A familiar ache between her thighs overwhelmed her. Taking a deep breath, she shifted in her seat and crossed her legs, attempting unsuccessfully to relieve her arousal.

Those sensual lips of his…on her skin. What would he taste like? As soon as the thought popped into her head, she tensed. If she didn't get it together, she'd be in his lap in two seconds, taking her fill of him. No, she needed to concentrate on something else. *Virus.* Ah yes, that thought dulled her desire. *They'd come for her…slice into her skin, stealing her blood.* That single thought was like having a bucket of ice cold water dumped over her head.

Logan sat quietly watching a wide range of emotions play across her face. His little wolf was terribly aroused but then within seconds he could tell she was thinking of something else, something scary perhaps. Best keep her on her toes. Perhaps he'd learn the entire truth before Jax got here. If he could get her to trust him, she'd break. It wouldn't take much, he reasoned.

"Well, now that that is settled, here. Call him." He took the phone on his desk and turned it toward her. It would matter little if she spoke to Jax. She had to know that with his exceptional hearing, he'd be able to hear what she was telling him.

"I can call Jax?" she asked, surprised he was allowing her to call home.

"Be quick though because I'm hungry," he instructed. He swiveled his chair, focusing his attention to his laptop screen.

"Hungry?"

"Yes. Time for lunch. And while I'd be quite satisfied eating in…just you and me, alone here in my office, I suspect things would be safer if we went out for lunch, if you know what I mean," he quipped.

"Uh, yeah. Lunch. Out would be best." She gave him a small smile, understanding his meaning. She shook her head, trying to ignore his comment and began to dial. *Eat in…or eat her?* Had he pushed further, she suspected she'd let him eat wherever or whatever he wanted. It frightened and excited her. She was finding it hard to think clearly around him as the thought of her spread out on his desk, Logan feasting on her, popped into her mind. Before she could fantasize any further, Jax answered. The voice of her Alpha startled and calmed her all at once. Her eyes darted over to Logan as she made contact.

As suspected, Wynter had revealed few clues during her brief phone call with Jax. Logan suspected the New York Alpha knew he was listening and had kept the call short on purpose. From the brief conversation, Logan had failed to learn the extent of her relationship with him. He'd heard Jax call her the term of endearment 'princess'. *Close friends perhaps? Lovers?* It bothered him that he cared so much about even knowing the status. It shouldn't matter…yet it did.

Logan had been single for well over a hundred years, and he wasn't about to jeopardize his pack over a woman. It wasn't as if he didn't plan on making love to her; no, it was quite the opposite. As long as she wasn't Jax's mate, she was available. But considering her secretive nature, he wasn't about to start a sexual relationship without her full submission and disclosure.

Regardless of the lack of information exchanged during the call, Logan noticed that Wynter was visibly more relaxed as she hung up the receiver. He supposed the voice of her Alpha had assuaged any apprehensions she'd had about him coming for her. It was a shame that she'd leave him so soon, possibly even tomorrow if Jax managed a flight. Deciding to make the most of the afternoon, Logan stood and silently ushered her out of his office. Nodding to his secretary and Dimitri, he smiled as the elevator doors opened.

As they descended, Logan glanced at Wynter, wondering if whatever little nugget she was keeping to herself had the potential to destroy the peaceful coexistence they'd cultivated between vampires and wolves. His gut told him there was far more complexity to the situation than met the eye. With or without her help, he intended to scratch the surface, carving it wide open, exposing the organization that had held her captive. He was deeply troubled that even a few vampires were caught torturing, running down a human or wolf. Like with roaches, when you found just a few, you could be certain that you had an infestation. And Logan planned on carrying out a thorough extermination.

Chapter Six

The Directeur watched the Alpha lead his beloved *feminine scientifique* into the crowd. As he suspected, the beta followed as did a few other wolves. What little they knew. Try as they might, they couldn't keep her from him forever. No, she was his to command as he wished. The little fool thought she could escape him by running? Perhaps she was able to weasel her way out of the physical structure, but the city itself had walls. She'd go nowhere without him.

The Directeur was amused that they thought they could avoid his touch. The dimwitted wolves would never see his great Stratégie coming. And the vampires were far too arrogant to see their weaknesses, let alone acknowledge them. He considered the witches. Surely they thought they were above it all with their potions and spells. But they, too, would have their due. There needed to be limits. Discipline. Too long he'd waited on the sidelines.

When the Mistress had approached him, he'd sworn his allegiance. Beautiful, brilliant and deadly, she was far superior a being than anyone he'd ever met. And now he served at her side, creating the Stratégie. He had to admit she was correct about choosing his historic city as the premier location for the attack. There were far more supernaturals centrally located in New Orleans than any other city on the East Coast.

In truth, the Directeur thoroughly enjoyed creating. He fancied himself an artiste. For too long, Kade, Marcel and Ilsbeth, the witch, had enjoyed their shared ownership of his city. His patience wore thin as he cultivated a picture of an avant-garde New Orleans. Under his direction, he'd transform the city into the vanguard of supernatural supremacy. Soon he'd drag his wide brush of destruction across the city, until whitewash covered every surface. Then he'd paint his masterpiece.

His dick grew hard as he imagined his coronation. Sucking a breath, he ducked into an alley to adjust himself. He wished there was time to relieve the pressure, but he needed to focus on the task at hand. The little bitch. Yes, that is why he was here. To keep watch. Soon, he'd seize the opportunity to take her.

Noticing how they surrounded her, it became obvious to him that the Alpha was aware of the precious nature of his commodity. Indeed, they thought they could protect her, even in the open streets? Interesting, he thought. Why, indeed, would the Alpha take such a liking to the scientifique? Perhaps she'd told him what she'd been working on? And by now, her illness would have set in, taking root in her DNA. A wolf claiming to be a human? Unheard of; he'd think she was insane. And the stories of viruses? Well, she could have been working for anyone in the country. They'd never find the lab, and she knew it. Of course, it'd been moved. She knew their methods and processes. Any breach in security warranted relocation. They frequently moved locations, never staying in one home or city for very long. They couldn't risk discovery.

She laughed at something the Alpha said, and he seethed. She knew her blood was his. Her pleasure and pain were his as well. Breathing deeply, he smiled at the old man playing the trumpet and tossed a twenty into his plastic jar. He stood a mere fifty feet from the Alpha and as usual, went unsuspected. So perfect was his place within New Orleans society, they'd never suspect him. Delightfully ignored, he sat at the French Market bar and flirted shamelessly with the lovely barkeep. He stole a glance as the scientifique blushed. How dare the little slut wantonly bat her eyelashes at the Alpha?

The Directeur laughed out loud, watching as his feminine scientifique stood to leave with the Alpha. Silently, he vowed to inflict the harshest of punishments on her. The betrayal stung his cold dark heart. Not only had she lied when she began her employment, now she appeared to be taken with Reynaud, throwing herself at him. Perhaps he'd whip her mercilessly, drain and fuck her before setting her pretty feet back in the lab where she belonged. Ah, he wished he could do all that and more, but the Mistress would never allow it. No, the Mistress was so much more disciplined than anyone he'd ever known. Work came first over earthly desires without a doubt.

No bother, he'd wait. Soon, she'd finish her project, perfectly as expected. Then he'd have her all to himself as the reward he deserved. The Mistress would allow it then. As long as he didn't kill his scientifique, the Mistress would let him play with his toy. With the Alpha finally out of sight, the Directeur made the decision to remain in the quaint café. Invigorated by his reconnaissance, he slipped through the back entrance to the kitchen in search of his barmaid. As usual, the meek human never sensed his approach. With his hand over her mouth, no one heard the stifled scream as his fangs stabbed into her neck.

Chapter Seven

"She's lying," Logan commented, watching Wynter through the sliding glass door. Her lithe smooth legs bounced in the azure pool water. He wished he could see more of her but she insisted on wearing that damn cover-up. The sheer pink fabric strained tightly against her breasts; her erect nipples pressed through the small black triangles of her bikini top.

"Yep." Dimitri popped a potato chip into his mouth, admiring the new womanly fauna that had recently been added to their courtyard.

"She won't tell me everything I need to know."

"No surprise there." He bit another chip, unable to look away.

"I should send her to stay with Fiona."

"Most definitely."

"But look at those legs," Logan growled.

"Yes, indeed."

"And her breasts. Just so, so…perfect."

"Hell yeah," Dimitri concurred, watching her sun herself.

Logan shot him a glare. "My breasts."

"Whatever you say, Alpha." He smiled and raised an eyebrow. He didn't want to burst Logan's bubble, but they both knew she belonged to Jax. "So why are you in here and she's out there?"

"D, don't get me wrong. I know I shouldn't want her. But there's just something about her. I can't put my finger on it." Logan ignored the question and took a drink of his sweet tea. He really wished that she didn't fascinate him so much; things would be much easier. He sighed. "She's just. Well, I don't know. I just want her."

"And the problem is?"

"Technically, she belongs to Jax," he explained, adjusting his growing arousal. He watched with great anticipation as she slowly pushed up the sheer fabric, revealing her belly button. She was killing him.

"Mated?"

"No."

"Again…the problem is?" Damn, his Alpha was in big trouble if this creature had him tied up so badly. Amused with the situation, he grinned.

"It's complicated…ugh, will you look at her? Just take that pink thing off already," Logan groaned as she fingered the edges.

"Can't stop lookin' at her. And what's complicated? She's, um, a wolf; I think. Anyway it doesn't matter, bro. She's definitely *all* female."

"I told you. Jax didn't claim her but she told me that she belongs to him. She's loyal to him," he bit out.

"In what way does she belong to him exactly? You know that doesn't really matter…except for the protocol. If they're not mates, then it's lady's choice when it comes to sex," Dimitri reminded him. "What else?"

"Secrets. I don't like it."

"But you like her?"

"I said it was complicated." Logan shrugged.

"Nothin' complicated about those legs," Dimitri laughed. "Nothin' at all. I bet they're quite flexible even."

Logan growled in response.

"Just sayin'."

"Being Alpha isn't always easy, you know. It can be very hard as a matter of fact," Logan commented.

"Sometimes when things are hard, it can feel really good." He wagged his eyebrows at Logan.

"Nice mouth, D." The frustrated Alpha began to undress in front of him. "I've gotta check on her."

"And you're in here with me because?" He left his question open ended waiting on Logan's response.

"Because my beta, we're letting her relax. Building trust," he explained. "And then, my friend, after that, it's time to ease the truth out of our new guest."

"I see. And how do you plan to do that?" Dimitri glanced out once again to admire the lovely she-wolf lounging on their patio.

"Watch and learn," Logan told him, tossing his shirt and pants onto the sofa.

"Yeah, okay, Alpha," Dimitri laughed. He surmised that if anyone could get control of the situation, it would be Logan, even if that entailed getting up close and personal.

Dimitri admired how his Alpha wielded his confidence and charm like a sword. Even during the tensest of interactions, the wolf never lost his cool. Damn if his Alpha didn't have some moves, and he reckoned he probably could learn a few tricks from the master. Dimitri laughed as he watched Logan stroll out the door buck naked. Whether this went well or not, it would be entertaining.

Wynter nervously tugged at the suit she'd borrowed from the pool house. What man kept a stock of women's bikinis in his pool house anyhow? A playboy. A hotter than hell, sexy Alpha playboy. One with the bluest eyes she'd ever seen and an easygoing personality that made her want to cuddle into his lap like a purring kitten. She sighed, supposing she shouldn't let herself go there. This was only temporary. As soon as Jax arrived, she knew she'd be whisked back to New York City and reality would commence. She loved the urban scene of the Big Apple but she couldn't help but notice how the quaint French Quarter seemed to speak to her soul. When they'd returned from lunch, she was surprised to see how lovely the courtyard was in the daylight. Complete with ferns, flowers, fountain, pool and hot tub, the entire back yard screamed relaxation.

Captivity had made her both claustrophobic and pale, so the sunshine bred a sense of vitality back into her heart. Logan must have sensed her craving as he suggested she go for a swim. She wished she was stronger to refuse the gift but she just wasn't. Nearly jumping with excitement, she happily took him up on his offer and was even more delighted when he offered her a suit. She supposed that he skinny-dipped, being the wolf that he was. But being the very human she was, or at least thought she was, a suit was a welcome addition.

Wynter swore she could literally feel the cells in her body healing as she basked in the afternoon sun. The cool pool water splashing her feet offered the perfect complement to the stones beneath her towel which emanated heat onto her back. Maybe not heaven but it was damn close to it, she thought. As she soaked up the sun, her thoughts wandered to the conversation she'd had with Logan at lunch. Admittedly, she'd been scared being out in the open where they could find her, but Logan had assured her she was safe with him. Every time she nervously looked around, he'd placed a calming hand to her shoulder, reminding her that she was no longer alone, protected. Not once did he ever raise his voice or make her feel like she'd done something wrong. Even though he knew she hadn't told him everything, he didn't press. Rather, he'd kept the conversation light, asking her where she went to school, her favorite colors, foods and movies. Breakfast at Tiffany's, she told him. And he didn't laugh but instead asked if maybe she'd like to watch it with him sometime after the drama was over.

If she hadn't known any better, she'd have thought she was on a first date. She laughed to herself, realizing how crazy it seemed. But she couldn't deny her gravitation toward the wolf. Logan was undoubtedly the most charismatic man she'd ever met. Both witty and assured, he appeared to approach life with a cool confidence. Yet he wasn't arrogant or demanding. She was finding it difficult to shake off her body's reaction to how he'd tasted her in his office. She'd wanted him to go further but he hadn't. He kept her on the edge of sexual tension all afternoon, and she found herself hoping he'd touch her again, kiss her.

Wynter groaned at the thought. Jax would kill her. While she'd on occasion found a wolf attractive, Jax would have gone ballistic if she'd asked to date within his pack. If he only knew the lustful thoughts that bantered about in her mind, he'd have a fit. She loved him so much, but as

Logan pointedly asked, she was not his mate. Jax had to know she couldn't go on forever living with him. Yet she owed him her loyalty and respect. She'd given him her commitment to see her mission through to the end. And while she was no longer working in the lab, she also wasn't finished.

Her thoughts wandered back to Logan and she smiled. He'd been incredibly dominant and sexy in his business suit earlier. And the night before when he'd held her so tenderly, she'd wondered what it would feel like for him to run his hands all over her skin. The possibility that she could maybe have a relationship with him thrilled her; even if it was just a fantasy. Maybe after the mess with ViroSun was cleared up, she could come back down to New Orleans. She admonished herself for even getting her hopes up; the chances were slim that Jax would simply accept her desire to see Logan again. With her being human, Jax wouldn't hear of it. She'd have to convince him somehow that she could make this decision on her own, but she knew it wouldn't be easy.

Logan quietly padded out of the house. While he prided himself on knowing how to move stealthily in the most dangerous of situations, he hoped she'd scent him right away. Yet Wynter seemed oblivious to his movement. It seemed strange that she didn't even notice him. Most wolves would have immediately reacted. He slowly waded into the water, never taking his eyes off of her. He could hear from her heartbeat that she wasn't quite sleeping; day dreaming perhaps? Time to wake his little wolf.

Wynter startled at the sound of a splash. She quickly pushed up onto her elbows and scanned the area but didn't see anyone. Just as she was about to recline, she caught sight of the most glorious vision she'd ever seen. *Oh. My. God. Logan.* Before her eyes, his six foot five, tanned, muscular body rose from the water like a dripping hot Greek God. Stunned and captivated, she watched as the beads of water rolled off his smooth skin. Unable to control the impulse, her eyes roamed over his wet body from his broad muscular shoulders to the hard ridges of his abdomen. The very smallest dusting of hair trailed down into the water, where she was quite certain she'd find him naked.

Logan laughed out loud at her reaction, snapping her attention back to his face. He shook his shaggy hair and water sprayed all over her legs. She flinched slightly but didn't look away. He was simply the most magnificent male she'd ever seen. Immediately, she pulled her legs together, as desire rushed to her belly. She didn't need an expert to tell her the shark in the water was hungry. She knew he was dangerous, ravenous for his next meal. And oh how she wanted to be bitten. At a loss for words, she returned his smile, waiting for him to speak.

Logan watched her take in the sight of him and tried so very hard to ignore the signs of her arousal. He found it amusing the way she tightened her thighs together in an effort to remain composed. *Ah yes, little wolf, the*

Alpha knows what you want, but will you give it to me? Let's see where this takes us. Smiling, he approached slowly and smoothly, making her wonder what he'd do next.

He enjoyed keeping her on her toes. And now that she'd had time to relax, to be lulled into a false sense of security, he intended to take advantage. As his cock jerked, he wondered, though, who was going to take advantage of who. The closer he got to her, the harder he had to deliberately keep himself from ripping off her clothes and sinking into her sweet heat. Needing to touch her, he placed his hands on her knees. She did nothing to stop him. He could almost feel the electricity sizzle as his cold hands touched her hot skin.

"Ah," she moaned, not exactly protesting.

"Enjoying the sun?" Logan asked softly. His hands held tight to her knees, not moving.

"Yes. It feels so good. The sun…I needed this."

"I see you found the suits Fi brought you," he acknowledged. He'd arranged for clothing to be sent while they'd been at lunch.

"Thank you. I really appreciate everything you've done. I don't know how I can repay you for helping me." *Ah, so that's where all the new suits came from.* Wynter knew it was silly but she felt relieved to know that he'd brought bikinis to his pool house just for her.

"Just showing you a little southern hospitality is all. I've got lots of things to show you as a matter of fact," he laughed.

"I just bet you do," she flirted. "And something tells me that I'd like to see them."

"Well, I'm sure that can be arranged after we're done with our business."

"Yes, that." The reference to business dulled the ache between her legs considerably. How could she forget?

"I got a text from Jax," he mentioned nonchalantly. "He can't get down here tonight. Looks like he'll be here tomorrow at the earliest."

"Why not?" she asked, concerned he wasn't going to come for her. She was about to get up but Logan held her still, placing his palms on the tops of her thighs.

"Snow. Airport's closed. No flights in, no flights out," he explained in a calm voice. "But don't worry; I told him that I'll take good care of you."

"I'm sure you will," Wynter replied sarcastically. And wouldn't she just love it, she thought.

He smiled broadly. Truth was that he wasn't a damn bit upset that Jax was delayed. It gave him more time to get to know Wynter and hopefully, find out what secrets she held.

"In the meantime, we're meeting with some vamps tonight."

Her face went white with fear. Too soon. They'd take her. As much as she wanted to trust Logan, there was no way she could be around another vampire.

"Hey there. It's okay," he coaxed, caressing her skin. "Come on, look at me, Wynter."

She complied, meeting his eyes. Once again tears threatened to fall. "You don't know…what they did. I can't go back."

"I told you that you're safe with me. No one will get to you while you are in my protection. Do you understand?" he asked calmly. *What did they do to her?* He'd seen the bite marks, but hadn't delved any deeper. A serious expression washed over his face. "I would never put you in danger. Ever."

A tear ran down her face as she struggled to maintain contact with the powerful Alpha. She wanted to trust him, but it was so very difficult after everything that had happened.

"Listen sweetheart, I don't know what happened to you…what they did to you, but I promise to stop whatever's happening. Do you remember?" He had to ask. In a low, soft voice he proceeded, trying to be as nonthreatening as possible. "You can tell me…what they did to you. The bite marks…I saw them. They're mostly on your arms, but there were a few on your legs…your thighs."

Wynter closed her eyes and then opened them slowly. She'd thought long and hard about her periods of unconsciousness. "I wasn't raped," she stated definitively. "That is something I'd know. But everything else…"

She'd been violated. Bled. Infected. She looked away from him, embarrassed that she even had to discuss it.

Logan waited for her to finish. He wanted to hold and hide her so that no one could ever hurt her again, but he needed her to open up to him.

"There were times in the beginning…the guards…they fed on me. I was conscious. But then they stopped because the blood loss made it hard for me to work…I couldn't think straight. They eventually figured out it was slowing my progress," she recalled with disgust. "So they stopped…for the most part. If I refused to work, they'd attack me…shove me against my cot…their fangs." She rubbed her arms, reliving the pain.

Logan deliberately calmed himself. He detested the bloodsucking demons he'd met over the years. Yes, most vampires were mainly well integrated within society. But some vampires skated the edge of morality, often justifying the torture they inflicted on their victims. He refocused on Wynter, absorbing every detail she shared.

"The bottom line is that there are missing time periods. I don't remember. Did they bleed me? Yes. Did they infect me with something…change me? I was human. Now look at me," she pleaded. "I don't know what they did…I don't know what I am…I don't know…" Her words trailed off as she shook her head in frustration.

"I'm sorry," Logan told her sincerely. "I don't know what they did to you either, but I promise you that we'll find out."

"I don't know, Logan. This was my responsibility. It's so messed up," she confessed.

"Right now, you're safe. And we're going to work things out. Now, of course, it would be a whole lot easier if you'd tell me everything, but I get that you need time with Jax. I may be new to this Alpha gig, but I assure you that I've been a wolf a very long time. I know protocol. Been livin' and breathin' it for over a hundred years. The last thing I want to do is get you in trouble with your Alpha. In the meantime, we're meeting with Kade Issacson tonight. Yes, he's a vampire. And as hard as it is to believe, he is one of the good guys. I hate to have to drag you there with me, but I can't leave you alone, and this can't wait."

Wynter pursed her lips, unsure that any vampires could be anything less than vicious. But she wanted to trust him. "You're sure? You're sure the vampires won't attack me?"

Logan laughed, "Questioning the Alpha, huh? Seems we're going to have to work on those pack skills of yours."

Wynter gave him a small smile in return. "Ha, ha. Funny wolf."

"And you, too, are a wolf."

"So you say."

"And that is what counts. Hey, I want to tell you a story."

"A story, huh?"

"Yes. A story," he confirmed. "A few months ago in Philadelphia, my Alpha met his mate, Kalli. The interesting thing about Kalli is that she's a lovely little hybrid, but at one time, she denied her wolf. And in the process, she just happened to invent this nasty little drug that essentially masked her scent and stopped her from shifting."

"So if she took the drug you would think she was a human?"

"Exactly." Logan let his hands wander down to her calves as he spoke. Goddess, she felt so good.

"And do you think that is happening to me? Maybe they drugged me?"

"Well, if you were human and now you are wolf, they did something. A drug? Maybe. The drug she created? No. But my point is that there're always things in this world that we don't understand. People will always push the frontier of what we think is possible. Biology. Nature. It's always changing. Slowly but changing. And like what Kalli did, supernaturals and humans are finding ways to accelerate the process regardless of whether it's the right thing to do."

If you only knew, she thought guiltily.

"I'm Alpha for a reason, Wynter. Like Jax, I've been around a long time. I'm not going to sugarcoat what I sense, what I know. You may have been human when you started but I can tell you with certainty that you're wolf now. I don't know how they did it or why they did it, but it's who you are."

Wynter stared off, refusing to verbally acknowledge what he was saying. Deep inside, she knew he was right. Her recovery, even since this morning, had been accelerated, deviating far from what would be considered normal for a human. She was feeling good. No, not just good but excellent. As a scientist, she knew there was no logical reason to explain it. After being bitten and chased, it should take her days to recuperate.

"Look at your skin," he urged, rubbing his hands up her shins until he reached her thighs. Gently placing his hands on her knees, he parted her legs and moved toward her until the insides of her thighs straddled his sides. His fingertips teased the small strings that barely held her bikini bottoms together. *Ah, finally got her attention,* he thought with amusement.

Wynter had barely been listening to his words when she felt him open her legs. At his intrusion, she snapped her focus back on his eyes, not moving but simply watching him as he grazed his palms up over the tops of her thighs until he reached her hips. She didn't try to stop him; she wanted his hands on her skin. Her eyes locked on his as his big strong hands skimmed over her body, flaring her arousal. *What was he saying? Something about her skin?*

"That's it," she heard him say. "Look at your skin. It's healed."

The bite marks were healed. Small pink spots were the only evidence that anything had happened to her.

"I know. I feel it," she admitted.

"Yes, I'm sure you do. I know you're scared. But it's going to be okay. Tell me, what do you know about being wolf?" His hands roamed upward. Goddess, her legs were smooth and silky, begging to be touched. He kept going, pushing the pink fabric upward.

Lifting her arms, Wynter let him remove the sheer barrier that covered her skin. Part of her wanted this, him. Moreover, she yearned to reveal her body and soul to this man, hating to keep secrets from the Alpha who sought to help her. He tossed the fabric aside, and she gasped as he tugged her into the water against him. Her smooth belly met his rock hard abs, and she really thought she might pass out from the rush.

"I…I grew up around a pack," she confessed.

Logan brushed his lips to her hair, resisting the urge to kiss her. Gently, he cradled her in his arms, letting her float along the surface. She held his gaze, never looking anywhere but to him.

"Let go, Wynter. Trust me?" he smiled down on her.

She was helpless to resist. Having no idea what he was doing, she gave in to her desires. "Yes."

"Relax. Let yourself go. I promise to keep you safe."

Wynter willed herself to go limp within his incredibly strong arms. And even though she knew better than to let a wolf touch her, she reveled in the experience of trusting him. As she closed her eyes and the cool water washed over her, every nerve lit on fire with need. In spite of the heat, she opened her hands, her thighs, until she was completely relaxed. And all the while, he never let her go. He adjusted his hold, carefully supporting her upper back and bottom with his hands.

"That's it. You're so beautiful. So calm and at peace," he crooned softly. "Like this, we'll talk about wolves. Tell me about your pack, what do you know?"

"I grew up around wolves. My parents worked with the pack…for Jax. I…I wasn't allowed around the pack that much when I got older. They were afraid I'd get hurt but I knew it'd never happen. My friend, Mika. She's a wolf," she said proudly.

"Okay, so our behavior. Our habits. You must have seen something." Logan watched her soft pink lips break out in a broad smile at his words.

"Ah yes. Wolves. Well, you like to run on a full moon. I never got to see them but I knew."

"That is true. What else?"

"Wolves are competitive. Mika's an alpha. Hates when she loses to me at tennis." She laughed, remembering their last match. "She breaks quite a few racquets. It's actually kind of funny. Good thing she makes a lot of money working at that law firm."

Logan shook his head at the thought. "Sounds delightful."

"She's okay, just a little short tempered is all. Never with me, though. She gets mad at herself. Which brings me to my next observation," she continued. "Loyal. Wolves are very loyal to their friends, their pack."

"That's correct. See, this wolf thing is going to be easy for you." He noticed she frowned at his comment. He kept pushing to distract her from her thoughts. "What else?"

Wynter tried to keep her face impassive as the next idea popped into her head. Considering an incredibly hot wolf was holding her against his bare skin, she reasoned it should have been the first thing she told him.

"Come on then. It can't be that bad," Logan commented as she hesitated to answer him.

"Naked." Her eyes flew open and met his. She giggled. "They love being naked."

"Yes we do. Clothes are very restrictive. Highly overrated."

"I can see that you practice what you preach."

"And how do you feel about that? Does it embarrass you?" He queried as his fingers wandered to the knotted strings tightened against her back.

"I'm not sure how I feel. I mean, it's not like I was allowed to run around naked. I just knew they did. Jax wouldn't be crazy about me doing it though. Not fair really. A double standard I suppose. Believe me; I think the whole pack would freak out if I decided to join them."

"I understand how you are worried about what your pack would think but how do you feel?" He pulled on the strings, releasing the knot. The cords floated freely in the water, no longer tied.

Wynter felt his fingers move along her back. It was if she could actually feel the coolness wash over the skin that had been covered by the small strap. With the tension loosened, her top drifted easily across her breasts but didn't fall away.

"I think…I think it'd be freeing," she whispered, aware of the message she was conveying. Oh God, she wanted him.

"Are you sure?" he asked, seeking her approval. His fingers traveled up to her neck, pinching the remaining knot that held tight around her neck.

"Yes," she breathed. "Yes, I'm sure. Please." She released a small gasp as he tugged the cord free and the flimsy material floated away. Her nipples hardened at the thought of Logan seeing her this way.

Logan didn't think his cock could get any harder but he was wrong. The sight of her gorgeous, perfect breasts nearly made him drop her. He ran his fingers through her wet hair then slowly trailed them across her throat. Skimming his fingertips down the valley of her chest, he stopped to rest his palm upon her belly.

"You're incredible. So, so beautiful, Wynter." He couldn't take his eyes off her face. She was struggling with her own arousal. And selfishly, he considered whether he should make love to her right there in the pool. But she needed to learn from him, not just pleasure but what it would mean for her to be wolf.

"Logan, please," she moaned, closing her eyes.

"Breathe, baby. You're doing so well. Relaxing. Almost naked," he joked.

"Almost," she agreed. She opened her eyes and gave him a sensual smile.

"You sure? Once you go wolf, you never go back."

"Yes, stop teasing me," she cried. She wanted his fingers on her, in her. What was he doing?

With great restraint, Logan slipped his fingers into the side of her bikini bottoms, ever so gently gliding his fingers across her hip. Effortlessly, he tugged the strings on one side then the other. As the panties floated away, no barrier existed between them. *Goddess almighty, she was exquisite.* He wanted so badly to take her. From her reaction, he knew it'd be easy. He watched her chest heave up and down in anticipation of his touch. But in the moment, he was certain he'd never be satisfied with having just part of her. He needed the truth. Craved it.

Overwhelmed with arousal, Wynter moaned loudly in protest when he removed his hands. Why wasn't he touching her? Didn't he find her desirable? *Oh God, she was naked in a pool with the New Orleans Alpha. Jax was going to freak out if he found out.* Her heart began to race with worry.

"Little wolf, you need to stop thinking so much. Lay back and relax into the water. I've got you, now. Just listen to my voice," Logan told her. His patience was of far greater strength than his libido. He wanted to fuck her, but it would be on his terms not hers. "That's it, just breathe….in and out. Hear the sounds around you. Smell the scents in the air. Soon, little wolf, you'll be born into your new life."

Obeying him came naturally as she forced herself to listen to his calm voice. Despite her water-filled ears, the sounds became louder. The more she concentrated, the more she heard. Music played in the distance. A car horn honked. Footsteps echoed on the pavement, coming closer and closer. Wynter's eyes flashed open to Logan's and then she rapidly turned her head, seeking the source. Dimitri. Her cheeks heated in embarrassment.

"Please," she croaked, trying to sit up and cover herself. Logan brushed a calming hand over her hair and her eyes caught his.

"It's okay. I'm here with you, baby. Holding you. Protecting you. It's just Dimitri. He's wolf. And by the way he's looking at you, I'd say that he agrees that you're every bit as amazing as I think you are."

"But I…I…don't know," she protested.

Logan nodded to Dimitri who continued walking and eventually entered his home.

"Whatever you feel, it's natural. Even arousal, it's what we are."

Wynter didn't want to talk about what she felt; it was wrong, dirty. She was so horny; that had to be why she'd felt so aroused when Dimitri looked upon her bareness. She wasn't really attracted to him, yet she'd reacted. And Logan, he simply drove her mad with need. Skin to skin, her proximity to him overloaded her senses. Her pussy ached for him, yet he made no attempt to kiss or touch her. She struggled to find the words to tell him how she felt.

"Please Logan," she groaned. "This is…I'm so…I feel…"

Logan knew exactly how she felt, and he felt the same. He reached across her body and caressed her slippery breast, finally giving in to the temptation. His cock throbbed, begging to be inside her as he watched her wriggle within his grasp. She moaned in response, and he slid his hand up her chest, settling it on her cheek. Running his thumb along the seam of her lips, her mouth parted at his touch, allowing his thumb to enter. She wrapped her lips around his finger as if she was sucking his cock. *Fuck, she was pushing him to the brink*. Logan sucked a breath at the feel of her simulating oral sex on his hand. He pulled his thumb out and spread the moisture on her lower lip. .

"What do you need, Wynter?" He knew he shouldn't touch her but Goddess; she was so responsive.

Wynter's eyes opened, meeting his. "I need you," she whispered.

Barely audible to human ears, her soft words were all he needed to act.

Sliding his hand to cradle the nape of her neck, he brought her to him and kissed her. Water sluiced downward as he pulled her tightly against him, hungrily taking his lips to hers.

Jolted upward, Wynter readily met Logan's lips, wrapping her legs around his waist. As his tongue pushed into hers, she thought she would melt away. Like a tight coil that had just been sprung, all her energy released into their embrace. Her hands raked into his damp hair. Clutching at him, she never wanted him to let her go. She writhed her slick mound against his abdomen, unable to reach the friction she sought. But the taste of him would have to sate her for now, because he didn't touch her there yet. So she simply let herself go, accepting whatever he'd give her.

At the first taste of her, Logan pressed Wynter up against the side of the pool. She tasted like the sweetest peach, so entirely ripe for him. She'd met his kiss with hunger, not fear, taking and giving. He couldn't remember the last time he'd felt an instinctive connection with a woman. It was as if her energy was pouring into his veins, heightening all his senses. Logan deepened the kiss, barely able to restrain himself from grabbing his shaft and thrusting it deep into her. He could feel her swollen folds below wriggling against the small nest of hair above his rigid flesh. It would be so easy to slip into her heat. But he swore that he wouldn't take her like this in the pool. No, when he took her for the first time, there'd be no secrets between them. She'd have to be as emotionally bare as she was physically.

A buzzer sounded faintly as he felt her wrap her small fingers around his cock. "Fuck," he grunted at the feel of her touch. She was a fast little wolf, he thought. It felt so good, but this wasn't happening now. He grabbed her wrist, bringing it quickly to his chest and placed her palm flat against him.

The rush of desire flowed throughout Wynter's body. She was done waiting. Her whole life she'd been waiting for something, for someone to make her feel this way. It was as if she was coming alive for the very first time in her life. Animalistic. Wanton. Free. She couldn't get enough of Logan. As he kissed her, she gave into her instinct to take; reaching down between her own legs, she found his hard arousal. It felt enormous in her fingers. Desperately wanting to bring him pleasure, she stroked it up and down until he breathed a groan into her mouth. She felt his firm grip manacle around her own, denying her. *Why? Why was he stopping?* No, this couldn't be happening.

And as his lips pulled away from hers, she slumped forward, desperately trying to catch her breath, her sanity. Oh God, she'd done something wrong, she just knew it. But she didn't even care. She just wanted, yearned. Logan made her feel and she didn't want to go back to who she was.

Their foreheads pressed together, hearts beating frantically from their encounter. Slowly, they both opened their eyes, panting. Sensing his visitors, Logan retreated.

"Wynter," he breathed. How he'd managed to have enough control to remove her hand from his dick was beyond him. He seriously thought he'd have to go stick his cock in an ice bucket after this tryst. Painful as it was, this wasn't the time or place for their first time. But after that one kiss, he was quite certain that without a doubt, he planned on making love to her long and hard as soon as she revealed what she'd been really doing in New Orleans.

"Logan, I…I'm sorry…I shouldn't have." *I'm sorry? No I'm not.*

"No, don't lie, baby. Remember the rules," he reminded her with a brief kiss.

She laughed, still clutched onto him, their eyes mere inches from one another. "Okay, not sorry," she admitted.

Before she knew what was happening, Logan's hands were on her waist, hoisting her onto the edge of the pool into a sitting position. His eyes never leaving hers, he pulled a sun-warmed towel from behind her and covered her with it.

"Thank you," Wynter responded softly, somewhat shaken by their kiss.

"You're very welcome." Logan smiled then looked over his shoulder. *Company.*

Female voices jarred her connection with Logan, drawing her attention to two women who'd obviously been watching their interaction. Dimitri took the redheaded woman into his arms, kissing her on the lips. Obviously, they were more than friends. The other woman, dressed in a tight black pencil skirt and red bustier, with long black hair and bangs, stared at Wynter. Very Goth, Wynter noted, wondering if the women were also wolves. A hand to her knee brought her focus back to Logan.

"Why don't you go upstairs and relax for a while? Fiona," Logan gestured over to the redhead, who appeared as a love child with her peasant skirt and wild curly hair. "She's going to help you get settled in."

Wynter's brow wrinkled at his suggestion.

"Hey, trust me, Fi's okay. She was here last night. She won't hurt you. You'll see. It'll all work out….now go. I'll see you in a few hours," he promised, and swam over to greet his guests.

Jealousy flared in her stomach as she watched Logan emerge from the water, exiting the pool, his sheer masculinity on display for all to see. To her dismay, both women turned their attention to his amazing body, letting their eyes roam all over him. *Who wouldn't look?* The man was utterly confident, good-looking and oh so very Alpha. Of course, he'd have women chasing him left and right.

That very second, reality came crashing down upon her. She wasn't in some fairytale where the girl got the prince. She was in serious fucking trouble with a major corporation who planned on dragging her sorry ass back to the lab to finish the abomination she'd started. And the gorgeous Alpha she'd been throwing herself at five minutes ago only wanted the information she held so he could protect his pack, not to mention that he probably had a different bitch warming his bed every night.

As she stood, she caught a glimpse of him wrapping a towel around his waist. The fabric tented, barely holding in place. Like a crushing blow to her gut, she watched as he took the Goth Chick into his arms and hugged her. The erection she gave him was touching another woman, and it sickened her to the core. Turning her head, she gathered her cover-up, and stood. Her bathing suit appeared to have sunk to the very bottom of the pool, and she had no intention of going in after it. Inaudibly to others, she swore that she heard something growl. *Was it her?*

This wolf thing was starting to get on her nerves. *Did she really have an animal inside of her?* Instead of letting fear rule her, she took a deep breath, closed her eyes and tried to picture a wolf, her wolf. *Where are you?* Wynter saw nothing and huffed in frustration. If she was a wolf, it was only a matter of time before she shifted. She knew from her friend how it worked. Somewhere inside her lurked the beast that would claw to the surface, and there wasn't a damn thing she'd be able to do about it. The wolf was part of the human and vice versa.

Either way, she was disgusted with herself and Logan. Disoriented and confused, she didn't understand what had just happened. Wynter could have sworn she'd felt something emotional between them in the pool, something other than just lust. But now? Now, he seemed quite content to rub the evidence of his arousal against a strange woman right in front of her. She steeled her nerves, feigning indifference, and casually walked toward the group. *Let the fun begin.*

Pulling the towel tightly around her, every muscle in her body tensed as she approached. Determined not to shatter, she tried to ignore her feelings. Her eyes darted over to Logan once again. No longer hugging, Goth Chick cupped his face, running her blood red fingernails down his cheek. They seemed to be having an intense conversation, and she wondered if they were lovers.

"Hi there. Feeling better?" Wynter heard the redhead ask.

Tearing her eyes away from the sight of Logan and the other woman, she gave Red a tight smile. "Yes, much better. Fiona?"

"Yes," Fiona grabbed one of Wynter's hands, giving it a quick squeeze. She was holding a few large shopping bags. "Nice to see you looking better. We were worried about you last night. You were so sick but now I can see everything's just fine."

Fine? Really? So not fine. Not even close, Wynter thought.

Before Wynter had a chance to respond to Fiona, she glanced up to Dimitri who gave her a warm but knowing smile. "Looks like you got some sun. Enjoy your swim?"

She tried very hard not to roll her eyes at his smart assed question and settled on giving him a cool smile.

"Swim. Yeah. It was a great *swim. Swimming* is awesome," she said, shaking her head. Is that what wolves called it now? Did swimming equate to writhing naked against the hottest Alpha male she'd ever seen? These wolves seemed to know their way around euphemisms.

Dimitri laughed heartily at the feisty little wolf's response. She certainly looked to be getting hot and heavy with his Alpha. And now, her behavior was bordering on aggressive. Almost as if she was territorial. Interesting.

"Leave her alone, Dimitri," Fiona told him with a light swat to his shoulder. "Come on now, I'm sure your swim was quite lovely before we arrived. Are you ready to go get settled in your room?"

"Certainly," Wynter responded in an almost professional tone. As if she was compelled, she could not keep her eyes off Logan as Goth Chick proceeded to trail her talons down his bare shoulder, settling her palm on his chest. A hot anger surged from within and before she knew what she was doing, Wynter found herself walking. Easily squeezing her small but strong body between Logan and Goth Chick, she wrapped her arms around his waist and kissed him.

Logan had been arguing with Luci yet again. He'd meant to introduce the women but the disagreement became a priority as she insisted she had rights to stay with an Alpha, to stay with him in his French Quarter home. He'd explained that there was no way she was living with him. She had to stay in one of the pack apartments. Yet he'd cordially hugged her as always, aware that Wynter had been watching. Sure, he felt strongly about Wynter and planned to explore their relationship further. But he still didn't trust her, and it was best that he conduct business as usual. And Luci was business.

A split second passed before he registered what was happening. One minute Wynter was talking with Fiona and Dimitri and the next, she stalked toward him like a lioness on the prowl. As his eyes locked on hers, he soon found that in a role reversal, he was now prey. Wynter pushed Luci aside and pressed up against him, possessively taking his lips. He welcomed the warm feel of her tongue darting into his mouth. He'd almost forgotten they had an audience, putting on quite the show for his pack members. Never in his life had a female demonstrated this kind of alpha, dominant behavior toward him. And damn if it didn't turn him on even more. He knew he should break it off, tell her no, especially given that she'd done it in front of pack, but her sweet taste enthralled his senses. Vacillating between taking her to the bedroom and pushing her away, became unnecessary when without warning, she released him. She'd been the one to back away, yet still remained between him and Luci, looking directly into his eyes.

"Thanks for the *swim*, sweetheart," she purred, with a glare that conveyed both lust and anger. "See you tonight."

That would teach him, Wynter thought as she proceeded to walk around Logan. Remembering exactly the kind of determined woman she was, there was no man on this green Earth that was going to strip, feel and kiss her senseless and then rub himself onto another woman two minutes later. No damn way. For as long as she remained in this pack of his, she could either be a doormat or establish her role as an alpha female. She'd spent a lifetime of listening to what other people thought was best for her, and it was damn time she stood up for herself.

If Logan wanted Goth Chick, he could have her, but she'd be damned if she let him fawn all over her with her 'hard on'. No, that was her erection; she'd done that to him. She supposed she should be embarrassed, but as she opened the sliding glass door, she could have cared less. Let him think about that kiss, because it might be the last one he'd get from her if he thought he could use her like that. So not happening.

As Logan watched Fiona chase off after Wynter into the house, he looked over to his beta in disbelief over what had just happened. Dimitri gave him a big shit-eating grin, fully enjoying the performance. Luci, on the other hand, seethed, crossing her arms; clearly annoyed that another woman, not her, was living with the Alpha.

Logan shook his head. "D, get Luci settled, would ya? I've got some business to attend to."

"Yeah, I bet you do, Alpha," Dimitri laughed, pointing Luci toward the gate.

"Not funny."

"Good luck with that," he added, unable to resist teasing his Alpha. It was going to be fun to watch Logan handle the new female.

"Yeah, right." Logan turned his back to Dimitri and walked into the house. As he entered, he cocked his hand upward, giving him a wave. His beta was freakin' hilarious. And correct. Something in the back of his mind told him that he was going to need a hell of a lot more than luck to handle his little wolf. Oh yes, her territorial display had been very intriguing, indeed. Considering her behavior, he couldn't wait to see her wolf, and ultimately her submission would be the greatest prize he'd ever earned.

Chapter Eight

As Wynter flew into Logan's home like a bat out of hell, it occurred to her that she had no idea where she was going. She'd been so angry, jealous if she admitted it, she had to get away from Logan and his touchy feely woman. With his kiss still seared on her lips and adrenaline pumping, she finally came to a halt when she reached the foyer. She placed her fingers to her forehead and took a deep breath, trying to understand what had just happened. *Why did she feel that after one kiss with Logan she now wanted to rip the face off of that strange woman as if she were a rabid animal? Where was she even going?*

Glancing at her surroundings, she was stunned at the understated elegance of Logan's home. Wynter noted that someone had taken great care to restore the meticulously kept rooms. Ornate crown molding covered every facet of the ceilings. The cream-colored paint complemented the taupe walls and cherry hardwood floors. A round marble table held a large vase of Asiatic lilies mixed with large pussy willow branches. The enticing scent of the flowers permeated the air. As she caught a glimpse of the living room, she admired the intricately patterned oriental carpets and period piece antique seating. It was a far contrast to the contemporary great room into which she'd first entered the house.

Her eyes swept up the magnificent curved mahogany staircase, and it occurred to her that Logan's bedroom was upstairs. Even though she'd never forget the way Logan had held her that night, and of course the awkward exchange she'd had with Dimitri, she'd hardly taken the time to look at where she'd been. Unable to recollect the décor, she wondered if she'd ever see his room again. After her aggressive exhibition in the courtyard, she wasn't sure what he'd do next.

Wynter's face heated, recollecting their intimate tryst in the pool. She'd felt animalistic, unable to get enough of him. As he walked away and touched that strange woman, she was angry. But it had felt more than that. It felt as if she needed to stake her claim, let the others know he was hers. She'd never been the jealous type but then again, she'd never met a man like Logan. It was silly, she knew. In no universe was he hers nor did she belong to him. She reasoned it must be the changes to her body's chemistry. If the change to her cellular structure could intensify her senses, it was entirely reasonable that her emotions were heightened as well.

Fiona's voice pulled her from her deep contemplation, bringing her back to the fact that she'd been standing immobile, like a statue, in the vestibule.

"Wynter, hold on," Fiona told her, somewhat amused at her behavior.

She placed a comforting hand on Wynter's shoulder. "You okay?"

"Yes, I'm fine," she assured the young woman.

"Well, I've got to say that I've never seen anything so hot. I mean, damn, girl. Possessive much?" she laughed.

"I don't know what you mean. I just…I guess I'm not exactly myself yet," Wynter admitted sheepishly, embarrassed about her behavior in the courtyard.

"Well, Luci won't be crossing your path anytime soon, I can tell you that. Come on, now." Fiona started up the staircase. "Nice place, huh?"

Yes it was. She wondered how Fiona knew Logan's mansion so well. Another one of his women, she supposed. Resigned that she still needed Logan's protection, Wynter obediently followed Fiona.

"Yes, it's beautiful. I've never seen anything like it," Wynter replied. She could literally feel the history oozing from the walls and wondered who'd lived in the home over the years and how old it was.

"He's been renovating it for a long time. But since he became Alpha, he sped up the work."

Fiona opened a heavy wooden door. "Here we go. You're here in the 'Rose Room'. Logan's down the hall just in case you get lonely." She winked. "This is his favorite guest room, you know. I think it says, 'feminine but rich'."

Wynter marveled at the rose-colored walls trimmed in metallic gold crown molding. A day bed with curled gold framing topped with cream-colored pillows took center stage. A lovely cream coverlet adorned with pink and red roses brought life to the piece. A dainty crystal chandelier dangled above.

"It's something, isn't it?" Fiona asked, opening large closet doors. "So, here we go. While you guys were out, I stocked the dresser and closet here with a few clothes. Dimitri said the clothes this morning fit so I bought more things…shoes, all that good stuff."

"You shouldn't have gone to so much trouble. I won't be here long," Wynter insisted, fully anticipating that she'd be leaving soon.

"Logan wants you to be comfortable, and besides, you are going out tonight," she reminded her.

Wynter bit her lip, now mortified by what she'd said at the pool. Hoping she'd spend the remainder of her time alone, waiting for Jax, she'd forgotten that Logan said they were going to meet someone later.

"Yes, I suppose I am." Wynter turned toward Fiona who was getting ready to leave.

"Don't worry, it'll be fine," Fiona stated confidently.

"Hey, I just want to thank you for everything. I know I was really sick last night. You guys helped me, and I know you didn't have to. Thank you."

Wynter didn't even know these people and they were helping her. True, she'd been trying desperately to help their race, but they had no idea what she'd done or who she was. Still, they'd been treating her with respect and kindness despite the fact she'd been less than candid. But instead of throwing her back on the street, they'd fed her, clothed her, saw to her medical needs.

Fiona smiled. "Really, it's no problem. We all need help now and then." She turned to walk away and then hesitated. "By the way, not sure if Logan got a chance to tell you, but my sister Dana, the doc who saw you last night, she got stuck at the hospital today. I know she ran some tests, but before you ask, I don't know anything. She'll probably be over in the morning or call later tonight."

"Thanks, I really appreciate it. People…they just don't…they just don't do these things," she said as if she were deep in thought.

As Fiona waved goodbye, Wynter considered what Jax had done for her. Saved her from a life of foster care. He could have turned his back on her at any time, but never did. Maybe it was wolves and their undying loyalty? Her parents had been loyal to him, and he'd, in turn, been loyal to them by taking her in, protecting her.

She wanted so badly to tell Logan everything she knew, but it was Jax who deserved her allegiance. When she talked to him on the phone, Jax had barely made mention of her work. He only wanted to know if she'd been all right and that Logan was treating her well. If he'd asked about what had happened over the past two months, she'd have told him everything, despite the fact Logan was listening. She supposed doing so would have been fair game. But to tell Logan, to disclose everything she and Jax had worked for without his permission, she just couldn't bring herself to do it. Lust or not, Logan was most likely a temporary distraction in her otherwise boring life.

Despite all of her exceedingly rational thoughts, she couldn't stop thinking about him. After watching the way he'd touched Goth Chick, hugging her, allowing her to continue to touch him, right after he'd been so incredibly intimate with her, it cut her in two. She couldn't make sense out of her feelings, because never in her life had she felt such an intense attraction to a man. Even if she were able to comprehend the biological ramifications of her changes, she couldn't deny a loss of control when it came to how she felt about the Alpha. It appeared as though the tendrils of their incipient connection were evolving in tandem, weaving and strengthening with each second they spent together. And for Wynter, the experience threw her solely into unchartered waters.

After a long shower, Wynter steadied her emotions, committed to getting through the evening with Logan without incident. But as she descended the staircase, butterflies began to dance in her belly, as she nervously anticipated Logan's reaction to her earlier behavior. Alphas could be unpredictable, and she wasn't certain how he'd address her interruption of his conversation with Goth Chick. It was bad enough that she'd been aggressive, obstructing his view of a pack member. But it was the kiss she'd planted on him that had her really worried. It had been a possessive, 'get your hands the fuck away from my man' kiss. She knew her intention wouldn't be lost on Logan and fully expected he'd call her out on what she'd done.

Her emerging wolf clawed at her mind, and she wasn't sure she wanted the message to be lost on him. No, clearly her wolf was staking some kind of a claim. Unfortunately, the human, and logical part of her, seemed to be taking a vacation. Torn between holding on to the threads of her humanity or letting go altogether, giving into her untamed cravings, she couldn't decide if what she'd done was wrong or just a natural part of who she was becoming.

So when Wynter reached the landing of the stairs, she deliberately kept her eyes low in submission. She stole a fleeting glance at Logan, who looked fabulously handsome and with his usual air of danger. His wet hair was neatly combed, and he smelled deliciously spicy and masculine. He was casually dressed in a crisp white dress shirt with rolled up sleeves, and dark dress slacks. She swore her panties grew wet within seconds of being in his presence. It was ridiculous, she knew. Like a teenage girl with a crush on the quarterback, she tried desperately to hide her arousal. But no matter how hard she attempted to shove the carnal thoughts into the deep recesses of her brain, she couldn't seem to control the visceral reaction to the man.

Logan watched intently as Wynter carefully but gracefully navigated the steps. Altogether stunning, Wynter wore a little black dress that tightly hugged her curves. Off-shoulder sleeves accentuated her newly tanned arms, and formed a perfect v into the valley between her breasts, revealing the swell of her cleavage. Resplendent and sexy, she blushed upon his gaze. Her pack experience became apparent as his submissive little wolf looked away. Logan smiled; she simply had no idea how beautiful she really was.

Logan had thought about Wynter's kiss all evening. Even though he intended to play it off, refusing to bring it up at dinner, he had so not forgotten. In a display of dominance, Wynter had shown her alpha tendencies. The way she'd pushed Luci out of the way, then given him that branding kiss; it had amazed him and frightened him all at once. On the one hand, he'd enjoyed the hell out of her choosing him, and he desired her intensely. On the other, he wasn't looking for a mate and didn't want to hurt her. But hell, the way she'd responded to his touch in the pool was positively remarkable.

During dinner, Logan soon found himself enchanted by Wynter's witty humor and intelligence. It was clear to him that she'd been well schooled even though she avoided talking about her career. He knew it was all directly connected to her secrets, the reason why she'd been in New Orleans. But the light conversation allowed him to get to know Wynter better, without her worrying about his expectations.

A look here and there, flirting and blushing, stirred his attraction to her. Although the sexual tension between them hung like a tight electrical wire in a storm just waiting to explode, he'd decided not to snap it during their meal. A glance every now and then to Dimitri told him that his beta was fully aware of their growing connection. The easy banter between him, her and Dimitri flowed naturally, feeling comfortable and easy. He wondered if he'd ever be able to share her like they'd done with other women, seriously doubting it.

Surprised by the easiness of their discussion and the non-mention of the incident by the pool, Wynter relaxed, getting to better know both Logan and Dimitri. Like Logan, his beta radiated a lethal sexiness that appeared to attract women like bees to honey. From the hostess to the waitress, women shamelessly flirted with both men. Controlling her jealousy wasn't as easy as she hoped but Wynter managed to keep it together. While "Kitty", the server, fawned over Logan, Wynter silently recited the periodic table. *Gotta love science.* It did help a little to take her mind off the very uncharacteristic need to throttle the waitress.

After the spectacular dinner with Logan and Dimitri, Wynter relaxed, forgetting where they were headed. However, upon their arrival at the vampire club, her heart raced as she exited the car. Even though both Logan and Dimitri reassured her that she'd be safe with them, seeds of doubt floated. What if one of her former guards frequented this place? What if Kade didn't believe her? What if it was a trap? *Trust me,* he'd told her. She wanted so badly to listen to the cocksure Alpha's words of assurance. Aware that she had no choice in the matter, Wynter wrapped her hand tightly around Logan's arm, holding her breath as the doors opened.

By the time they got to Mordez, Logan's cock was once again painfully hard. He silently cursed as he thought of a half dozen ways he'd like to pleasure the devilishly sweet woman whose bare legs brushed against his own the whole damn way from the restaurant to the club. As she reached for his arm and gave a nervous laugh, he reasoned she had no idea what she was even doing to him.

Collecting his thoughts, he focused on the task at hand. By the end of the evening, he hoped to have the situation with the vampires sewn up neatly, although he knew from experience, things rarely went that easy. Putting on his game face, he swung a protective arm around Wynter and nodded to Dimitri. Time to roll.

The door to Mordez swung open, and Logan guided Wynter into the dark haven. An older gentleman dressed in a tuxedo immediately rushed over to them.

"Mister Reynaud, please come in. We're so honored to have you visit us tonight," he gushed.

Logan acknowledged him with a curt nod, keeping Wynter safely tucked against his side. Dimitri rounded up to her other side so she was effectively surrounded by the two large wolves.

"Will you be taking a seat in the theater, this evening? Charlotte is just about to take the stage. Or if you'd rather, the Cleretti room has recently imported the most wonderful, very rare Italian Barolo. You must try it. As for the other rooms," he coughed and glanced to Wynter, sniffing the air. He gave Logan a knowing look before continuing, "Our private room. Their shows start much later. While I'd be happy to reserve your seating, considering your company, may I suggest that it may not be appropriate….for your guest."

Wynter shivered; a chill settled over her skin as the man spoke to Logan as if she weren't there. The way he looked at her, albeit for only a second, made her queasy. Vampires. Wynter remembered all too well the hungry look in their eyes and the flare of their nostrils right before the pain came. She cringed. He looked as though he was sizing her up like a glass of the wine he'd just mentioned.

"The theater is fine for now. We are meeting Kade Issacson later this evening. We're a bit early, though," Logan explained with not so much as a blink of an eye. "Please ensure our privacy."

"Yes sir. Your needs are our utmost priority," he assured the Alpha. Stealing a glance at Wynter, he licked his lips but quickly turned away. "Please, this way."

Wynter noted the darkened lobby and thought that if they were looking to scare people from entering, keeping it exclusive, they certainly did a good job with that. The flare of candles provided little illumination onto the stone encased foyer. A soft lull of Dixieland jazz poured into the small space and she detected the faint smell of mold. She supposed the club owners were going for a quaint antique décor, congruent with the city's history. However, in her opinion, the vibe was nothing short of creepy. She looked to the older maître d' who'd been speaking to Logan, and caught a glimpse of his pointed canines. He winked at her right before he pushed a black curtain aside. Clutching at Logan a bit tighter, she bravely stood her ground.

Both Logan and Dimitri appeared taller to her, their attitude cold and deadly. Their lips were drawn tight in serious expressions that projected dominance. Far removed from her easygoing dinner date, a dangerous creature had replaced Logan. As a wolf, this was his true nature. Wynter took note of Logan's demeanor, promising never to forget exactly what and who he was.

Emerging from the claustrophobic passageway, Wynter was amazed at the luxurious room in which they'd arrived. Reminiscent of a nineteen-forties tiered dinner theater, the area looked capable of holding at least fifty patrons, all comfortably seated in rows of clam-shelled, semicircular booths classically upholstered in red crushed velvet. The light from the small votive candles on the tables reflected off the blackened plaster walls. The darkened stage eerily sat empty awaiting its starlet.

As Wynter slid onto the seat, she breathed in relief as Logan and Dimitri flanked her. They towered over her small frame, and she felt safe nestled between them. Utterly fascinated that a place like this existed, her eyes roamed overhead to the massive crystal chandelier that precariously hung from the oval ceiling. The booths were arranged on a curve so that every person had a good view of the stage. Wynter glanced over to the patrons seated nearest to them who were laughing and drinking. In their element, they looked almost human until she caught a glint of a fang.

Logan must have discerned her discomfort, because he placed his hand on her thigh and gently squeezed. She looked up to him, noticing that his face had softened. God, this man was killing her inside. Protective and deadly to loving in sixty seconds, every facet of him intrigued her, making her want him even more.

"You okay, Wynter?" Logan asked softly.

"Um, yeah, thanks," she uttered not realizing she'd been holding her breath. As she spoke, her gaze traveled to a pair of lovers. While she couldn't see faces, she could clearly see the tracks of blood running down the woman's backless dress.

"You're shaking. Look at me," Logan instructed, watching how she naturally complied. "You're safe. You are not in a lab. I promise you, nothing will happen to you here that you don't want to happen."

"What's that supposed to mean?" she replied indignantly. Was he implying she wanted to be bitten?

"Look around you, sweetheart. This place is a dark playground where people live out their fantasies. This one just happens to be run by the vamps. But wolves have them too. We come to watch and be seen, to play and be played with. The vamps, they come for the blood. And the shifters, witches and humans all come for different reasons. Some want a walk on the wild side, some want to be bitten, some want sex. Places like this serve a need," Logan told her matter-of-factly. "In Philadelphia, Tristan runs an upscale club. Similar to this one. I'd say his is more urban in nature, but its function is nearly the same."

"You come to these places often?" *Please say no. Please say no.* She couldn't believe what he was telling her. Why would he purposely hang out with vampires?

"I used to help run one in Philadelphia, but here, this is too dark for my tastes." Logan briefly stopped talking when a waitress came to their table. Without saying a word, she efficiently poured glasses of champagne. Setting the bottle in an ice bucket, she quickly scampered away. Logan handed Wynter her glass and continued. "As I was saying, this club can be quite dangerous if you don't know what you are getting into. Of course like Tristan's club, I expect there's tight security. That being said, it doesn't mean that people don't get hurt."

Logan didn't want to scare his little wolf. He simply wished to provide her with knowledge of what existed in his world. Neither evil nor good, the city could be utilized for both, depending on one's intentions. The veil separating the planes of supernaturals and humans was extraordinarily thin in the Big Easy. It was easy to get in trouble if one didn't know what they were doing. Deciding to shift the focus, he changed topics. He knew of one subject that would definitely take her mind off vampires.

"So, Wynter, care to explain what happened at the pool today?" He glanced over to Dimitri who gave a small grin, and then back at her.

Wynter nearly choked on her champagne. What the hell? Where did that come from? Had he been waiting all night to take her off guard? Logan was entirely too confident. Two could play at that game, she thought. Forgetting the 'no game' rule he'd insisted on, she dived right into her answer, which answered his question with a question.

"Whatever do you mean, Alpha?" She batted her eyelashes at him then smiled at Dimitri.

"Come now, you seemed quite bothered with me, running hot and well, hotter. And that kiss…by the side of the pool…in front of everyone. Hmm?"

"Oh, do you mean the kiss you gave me in the pool? That one? I do believe everyone saw that one. Or was it the kiss you gave the other woman who came to the pool? You know, the one you gave her while still exhibiting the," she paused, pretending to give it great thought and then pinned him with a stare. "How should I say it? The one you gave her, wearing the tented towel that I gave you?"

More champagne please…now. Wynter swore her blood pressure rose twenty points just thinking of the incident. A few hours ago she'd told herself to play it cool, but her plan didn't seem to be working out the way she'd imagined it.

Dimitri laughed out loud at her response. His Alpha was going to have his hands full, all right.

Logan smiled. He supposed he should have thought better of kissing Luci with an erection the size of Mount Everest. But in truth, it'd just been a peck hello on the cheek.

"Is my little wolf jealous? You seemed quite, how should I say it? Angry with me," he mused, taking a sip of his drink.

"Nothing to be jealous of. This…this thing between us," she flushed with embarrassment, "it's just…it's just a chemical reaction brought on by whatever they gave me….what they've turned me into."

"A wolf. You can say it."

"Fine. Yes, it's that wolf thing. I'm sure it'll pass. Besides, I have no claims to you." She looked away and stared into her bubbling glass.

"Agreed. You don't have a claim on me. We've just met, after all. Besides, you haven't even shifted yet," he goaded in an effort to test her reaction to his agreement that he wasn't hers. A surge of delight touched his heart as her eyes flashed in anger. Perhaps she didn't believe her own words? She really didn't like it when he repeated them.

"And you have no claims to me either," she quipped, quickly recovering. "I don't belong to you."

Why that hurt, he couldn't say. It was the irrefutable truth. And that was the crux of his problem. Part of him wanted her, not just in bed, but wanted her to belong to him and with his pack.

"So you honestly believe everything that happened today at the pool was just a side effect of your transition to wolf? Hormones? Is that what you're saying?" he pressed.

"Who was she anyway?" Wynter completely ignored his question. She had to know if there was someone else in his life. "The girl at the pool? Is she your girlfriend?"

"Luci?"

"Yes. You know, the woman rubbing all over you, drooling like a St. Bernard in heat." Oh great, she'd just reduced herself to name calling. Whatever. She had one foot in; she might as well jump in all the way.

Logan laughed. Boy, she really was jealous. And why did he seem to enjoy that so much?

"Luci. She was Marcel's girlfriend," he explained, trying to choose his words carefully. He was pretty sure she wouldn't like the rest of the explanation. "I allowed her to live with me in Marcel's bayou mansion. You know, while I was busy establishing my role."

Wynter deliberately closed and opened her eyes, taking time to process what he'd just said. *He did not just say what I think he said.*

"So you are living with her?" *Just perfect. I really am an idiot.*

"No, I said she *was* living with me…as in past tense. And it was only because she already lived in the mansion, and I didn't want to kick her to the curb."

"A humanitarian? Bet it was difficult," she drawled.

"Well with Kat there, I…"

"Who is Kat?" This just kept getting better.

"She's Tristan's sister. But it wasn't like…" He wanted to say that it wasn't anything close to what he'd felt for her, but bit his tongue. "It wasn't like you think, Wynter." Logan's eyes saddened and his voice wavered slightly as the emotions of Marcel's death unexpectedly rushed over him. It had only been a couple of months and it was still hard to comprehend that he was dead.

"Marcel. He was my friend, my mentor. And my Alpha at one time. A few months ago, he was killed. It was difficult for everyone, but Katrina and I…we were just trying to get by. I promised him."

"Promised him what?"

"I'd take over for him." Logan emptied what was left in his glass and set it down. This was not at all what he planned on discussing with Wynter tonight. This conversation was finished.

Wynter saw the sadness in Logan's eyes and recognized his pain all too well. The loss of someone you loved could never be erased or undone. True, the pain would lessen as time went on, but when you lost someone so close to you, a part of your heart and mind would never be the same. She gleaned that he hadn't been Alpha for very long and wondered how he was coping. As a human spending much of her time observing Jax, she would never have known that Logan had just taken over his pack. He seemed such a natural leader. Yet, whatever he'd been doing over the past couple of months must've taken a great emotional and physical toll on him.

Even though there was a part of her that hated that he'd slept with other women, the rational part of her brain finally won out the battle. She swore it was that damn wolf making her so jealous. Of course, he had other women and in the moment, she didn't care. She only wanted to take away his hurt, ease his suffering. Wynter reached to him, lovingly placing her hand on his cheek and looked deep into his eyes.

"I'm sorry," she whispered. "I'm sorry for your loss. I know…I know how it feels. I promise it'll get better someday."

With her words, she wanted to break down and cry, opening up to him about her own parents, everything that had happened with Jax. She'd been so scared and lonely, lost to the world. But she couldn't tell him. It would lead to other questions; ones she wasn't ready to answer.

Logan wrapped his hands around her wrist, holding her hand to his face. His eyes locked on hers in a heated stare. Whatever anger she'd held about Luci and Kat had melted away. This woman, a virtual stranger, genuinely cared that he was hurting over Marcel's death. Kindred souls, they both had experienced great loss at death's hand. His heart constricted. He wished they could forget this Kade business and just go home and be alone. Logan's eyes fell; he glanced at her soft, inviting lips. *Why did he want this woman so badly?*

Their connection was broken as a spotlight flooded the stage and a lilt of music filled the room. Wynter glanced up to the stage, and tried to pull her hand away, but he guided her palm onto his thigh. Logan didn't want what they'd just shared to end. As if she grounded him, the physical touch of her palm, however slight, stoked the fire within his heart.

Wynter considered how precariously close to danger she was. While she'd initially been worried about the vampires, Logan changed the subject and now all she could think about was him and her own feelings that were spiraling out of control. She prayed that it really was just chemistry. Deep down, though, she suspected her feelings were real, and it scared the living daylights out of her.

Wynter's thoughts were interrupted as the big band music boomed from surround sound speakers. A high-heeled burlesque dancer seductively pranced onto the stage. Quite beautiful, with voluptuous curves, the brunette slowly slipped one leg to the side then rolled her wrists; her graceful hands flowed like ribbons into the limelight. Flicking open her red ostrich feather fan, she concealed her body, with a wink. Sweeping it up and around, she continued to tease the audience by caressing the plumage up and over her body.

Playing and tantalizing, she flirted while skillfully removing her gloves, one by one. A man whistled as she threw them to patrons in the front row. Turning her back to the audience, she deftly removed her bra, never revealing her breasts. She swung the garment round and round, then flung it across the room. Though the feathers artfully brushed over her creamy pale skin, revealing little, her erotic display captivated the crowd. The dancer bent over, shaking her behind, and encouraged the audience's catcalls.

Her mesmerizing hips rocked side to side, sexy and slow. As anticipation grew in expectation of the big reveal, Wynter glanced up to both Logan and Dimitri, who, astonishingly, weren't watching the show. Rather, both men were intently watching her, and she blushed. Giving them both a small smile, she drew her attention back to the stage just in time to see the woman raise the fan clear over her head. Striking a pose, she proudly displayed her red sparkling pasties and perfectly matching panties for everyone to admire. The audience clapped wildly in appreciation, while she curtsied.

Wynter had never seen a woman strip before but found the experience both arousing and erotic. The artistic dancing seemed to have the same effect on the crowd as she noticed several couples begin to intimately touch and kiss in response. As the dancer pranced off stage, Wynter felt a tug on her wrist.

"Did you enjoy the show?" Logan inquired with a grin. Judging by her heartbeat, he knew she did.

"Yes. I've never been to a burlesque show before. She was amazing."

Wynter caught both Dimitri and Logan raising their eyebrows at each other. "What? Can't I admire art?"

"I just find it interesting that you spent all that time around a pack and weren't exposed to any nudity," Logan commented. He couldn't understand why Jax would keep her so secluded from his wolves.

"She didn't seem to have a problem with it this afternoon," Dimitri joked.

Wynter's cheeks heated and Logan laughed.

"No, my friend, she didn't. And I must say that I very much like her that way."

Wynter was about to protest and tell them both that it hadn't been her idea to strip in the pool, when the maître d' from earlier rushed over to Logan. He efficiently ushered their party out of the theater and into a different area of the club. Within minutes, they were seated. Their small circular table barely held enough room for their glasses but provided them with an excellent view of the room, including the bar and adjoining dance floor.

Scattered tables filled the lounge, leaving only a small area around the bar stools for standing room. Checkered stone floors and blackened walls adorned with gas lit lanterns reminded her yet again of the club's dark nature. A long copper bar ran the length of a wall where men and woman waited for drinks. Several glass tubes filled with a dark red substance ran from the ceiling down into taps. *Wine? Blood?* She couldn't tell without getting closer and there was no way in hell that was happening.

Sitting between Logan and Dimitri, she felt secure, but curious. "What's with the tubes?" she whispered. "Please tell me it's wine."

Logan lowered his voice. "Blood. They serve it many ways. Live donors are usually preferred by the vamps, but this room is more of a waiting room so to speak. When donors are ready, they can go to private rooms. The disco also has semi-private areas. Feeding occurs everywhere here…even in public."

Wynter's eyes widened and her mouth tightened in surprise, and Dimitri jumped in to explain further.

"The people who come to these clubs…they enjoy it," he told her.

"Enjoy being bitten? Here?" She'd heard it was true but had never really discussed it with anyone who could verify the rumors.

"It's not like I'm into it, but hey, I don't judge. Everybody's looking for something. Humans, wolves, witches, vampires, they're all here for a little kink. Public feeding. Public sex even. You've got voyeurs and exhibitionists and everyone in between," Logan added. "I'm surprised you didn't ever go to a club like this in New York. I mean, there's no doubt this place is a little heavier than most clubs, but that's only because the vampires run it."

"Yeah, they don't mind pushing the envelope of what's unacceptable, which isn't much. It's kind of a free-for-all," Dimitri pointed out. "I'm actually surprised Kade would come here. I didn't think he was into all this, but what do I know?"

"I guess I was sheltered. But Jax, he'd never go somewhere like this." Sure, she'd been sequestered from the nudity but never did she imagine that these clubs could be commonplace in Jax's life or anyone else in his pack for that matter.

"Trust me, Wyn. Even the almighty Jax Chandler has been in a club like this. He's the New York Alpha. He may not like to be bitten, but then again, you never know," Logan sniffed. "But the sex? To see and be seen. Oh, he goes. And if you think he doesn't…well then maybe you don't know him as well as you think you do."

Logan considered her reactions and comments about the club, and it occurred to him that even though she was an adult, she hadn't been exposed to the supernatural culture at all. A whisper of innocence laced her words, and he couldn't help but want to be the one to help her learn.

"Just because I live with Jax, that doesn't mean he tells me everything." Wynter played with her hands, reflecting on her ignorance. She knew she'd been kept in the dark. Her parents had insisted on it, and when they died, Jax continued the ruse. She felt like an idiot, living with an Alpha, yet inexperienced with the way of wolves. "He's a wolf. I'm just a human. We're both busy."

"What do you mean, just a human?" Logan asked. It was going to be interesting when his little wolf shifted. It would finally be real to her.

Wynter was about to attempt to come up with a witty comeback to his question, but noticed both Logan and Dimitri go on alert, both putting their hands possessively on her thighs. As much as she wanted to reflect on how she felt about having two men touch her at once, and oddly, she really did, she was more curious about the spectacle across the room that had captivated the men's interest. She squinted, attempting to see in the dimly lit room and wished whatever supernatural wolf powers she might be getting would apply to her eyes. It wasn't too long before she saw a sight that very much held her attention.

A woman with long flowing black hair writhed on top of a man's lap. His face was altogether buried in the woman's neck and as she moved up and down, it became apparent that they were having sex. Her long flowing skirt covered any evidence of their coupling, but the telltale movement of her hips on his provided little question as to what they were doing. Surprisingly aroused by the sight, Wynter watched intently as the man and woman grunted in ecstasy. Blood ran down the woman's neck, and the man slowly lifted his head. Wynter gasped as the vampire's eyes snapped open and locked on hers.

Chapter Nine

The vampire had licked his bloodied lips and then smiled at her. And that was the exact moment she'd recognized him. Monsieur Devereoux, from New York City. *One of the university's most influential benefactors was a vampire? What was he doing here in this club? Oh my God.*

Her mind raced, as she struggled to compose herself. How was she supposed to talk to Monsieur Devereoux right after she'd watched him have sex? Wynter had found it difficult to tear her eyes away. And oh dear Lord, he knew she'd been watching. Not only did he know, he liked it and smiled at her. Wynter's heart beat frantically as Léopold confidently strode across the room. She tried to look away and could hardly believe this was happening. Logan would know and she'd be forced to tell him everything.

Dressed in a stylish all black suit and tie, Léopold Devereoux looked as debonair as she'd remembered. His perfectly coiffed hair accentuated his model good looks and lithe muscular body. As if he'd stepped out of an issue of GQ, the man was exceptionally handsome. Yet tonight, there was something different about him, an otherworldly, dangerous edge to his presence. All heads turned to watch him as he made his way toward their table, and she'd almost forgotten where she was until he stood before them offering his hand to her. Wynter heard him address her and swallowed the lump that had lodged in her throat. As she did so, she gave a brief nod to both Logan and Dimitri who stood protectively at her sides. Clearly angry at this development, their faces were set into hardened frowns, staring at him.

"How lovely to see you again, Dr. Ryan." Léopold bowed his head slightly, never taking his eyes off hers. Wynter struggled to respond as the shock of hearing his familiar French accent brought forth the reality that he was who she'd thought he was. Time stopped as she gaped in disbelief. She'd just voyeuristically watched as he covertly yet openly, made love to that woman in his lap.

"Monsieur Devereoux. Why, hello. Very good to see you again," she managed with a cough. *What was she supposed to say? Thanks for letting me watch you have sex. And oh by the way, you're a vampire?* She dug deep to find appropriate diplomatic words that seemed to elude her. "I'm surprised to see you here. Are you wintering in New Orleans?"

Léopold took her hand gently into his before pressing his cool lips to her skin. Logan growled in response, and he quickly released her hand. He gave Wynter a puzzled look, sensing she'd changed. *Wolf? Now how did that happen when she'd clearly been human? And where was the ever possessive Jax, letting his little human out to play with strange wolves? Very interesting indeed.* Amused, he smiled at the trio and addressed Wynter.

"I could say the same of you. New York winters can be cold, no? And I see you've taken up with a new Alpha. Hmm," Léopold observed and nodded to Logan. "Monsieur Reynaud. We meet again."

"Monsieur Devereoux," Logan acknowledged without emotion. "This is my beta, Dimitri. Please call me Logan." He reluctantly gestured for him to sit.

"Logan it is." Léopold grabbed a chair from a nearby table and sat. He crossed his legs and picked a piece of lint from his trouser.

From the minute Logan spotted Devereoux, he knew that this evening was fucked. The last time he'd seen the powerful vampire, he'd been in Philadelphia. And while Léopold had been helpful in locating his Alpha's mate, it was no secret the vampire was extraordinarily dangerous. Where the hell was Kade? Why had he sent his maker to meet them? And what exactly was Wynter's connection to the most lethal vampire on the east coast?

When Léopold had kissed her hand, he'd nearly lost it. Logan decided right then and there that he'd be having a sit down with Miss Ryan or Dr. Ryan or whoever the hell she was as soon as they got out of there, because he was sick of the damn lies. Protocol or not, he was done with all the secrets. If he had to call Jax himself tonight, he'd have the truth. In the meantime, he had to deal with Devereoux.

"Where's Kade?" Logan inquired but then was interrupted by Wynter.

"He's not my Alpha, Monsieur Devereoux," she corrected Léopold. "And please call me Wynter."

Logan gave her a stern look. *What the fuck was she doing? Did she have a death wish?* A she-wolf didn't go announcing in the middle of a vampire bar that she wasn't with her Alpha, especially in his city. A lone wolf was a vulnerable wolf. Every protective instinct in him told him to throw her over his shoulder and drag her back to his home.

"Please forgive her ignorance. Wynter is under my protection," Logan explained to Léopold and then turned a hard stare on Wynter. "So until Jax gets here, you're mine." *Mine.* He knew how he was using the term, and it wasn't as if she was a mate. But in the back of his head, the idea bounced around briefly, and it bothered him to think he'd even go there.

Dimitri shot him a look of surprise. Hearing his Alpha go all territorial and call a woman his was unusual, given the conversation they'd all just had in the theater. So far, this evening wasn't going how he expected. He readied himself for more surprises, sizing up the vampire at their table.

Wynter held her breath for a minute, stifling her anger. *Why was Logan saying that she was his*? Jax always made it known that she belonged to him, with his pack. No matter what feelings she was developing for Logan, it could be no other way.

"No, Logan," she argued. She needed to explain the situation to Léopold. She couldn't have him running off to Jax, spreading the misconception that she now belonged to Logan. No, that could not happen. Jax would be pissed, for sure. "While it is true that I'm under his protection, I don't belong to him."

"Ah, seems mademoiselle can't decide where she belongs, Alpha. Perhaps she needs to be schooled in wolf rules, no?" Léopold laughed, well aware of the implications of their conversation.

"Wynter, on this, Léopold is correct. Look around you. This club. Anything goes. By entering, your consent has been granted. If you didn't belong to me, you'd be free to be taken. This is my city, and at least for tonight, you're mine. No one will touch you without my permission. And that's not happening. Now tell me how you know each other," he ordered.

Wynter quieted at his words. Was that true? If he didn't claim her as his wolf, anyone in this place could go after her? God, she hated this club. Great, now Logan was angry at her, and it made her stomach twist. She hadn't intended to make him mad. In fact, she found herself wanting to please him. He'd been so kind to her, and this wasn't how she dreamed of repaying him. In truth, part of her wanted to belong to him. But after their conversation, he agreed that she had no claim to him. She sighed in defeat. Looking around, she realized he was right. What good would it do to declare she belonged to Jax or worse, pretend that she was a single female? It was too dangerous.

"Wynter. Explain. Now," she heard Logan say. Maybe this wasn't how she'd pictured telling Logan, but at this point, she had no choice but to tell him the truth…at least more of it anyway. Uncertain about what Léopold would tell him, she realized it would be best if he heard it from her.

"We…we met last year at a charity gala," she stuttered. "You see, I used to teach, well mostly did research. Virology. There was a fundraiser at the Guggenheim."

"Dr. Ryan, here, gave an excellent speech about the implications of trans-species viral infections. Quite interesting. And how is Jane Doe doing? Your case study?"

"Well, I haven't seen her in a few months," Wynter said sadly. Emma, her best friend Mika's sister. She was the entire reason she'd gone into virology and decided to work at ViroSun.

"Pity, no? You see, Alpha, Jane Doe was a hybrid. Although if I remember correctly, you didn't specify which type of shifter; only that she was a child."

"Well, yes. She's a teen now."

"Hybrids don't get sick. What's wrong with her?" Logan asked.

"Um, it's complicated. It's a long-term illness and it could be fatal, I'm afraid," Wynter commented, trying to avoid his questions. She neglected to specify that she knew Jane Doe and that she had a viral infection. "So anyhow, that's how we know each other. Monsieur Devereoux's made very generous donations to the school, helping to fund our research."

Emma's illness had been the catalyst for Wynter going into virology. Early on, Wynter had suspected leukemia. But unlike human leukemia, which could be treated, sometimes even pushed into remission, this leukemia was lupine in nature. And like feline leukemia, she suspected that it would eventually be fatal. The quagmire rested in the fact that shifters, even hybrids, were supposedly immune to viruses.

She hated lying to Logan. It was wrong and she knew it. But she'd promised Jax that she'd keep everything confidential. As far as she knew, only Jax and his beta knew about the virus. But Logan deserved to know as well. This was his city and he was putting himself out there, killing the vampires who'd attacked her. This was far from over and she knew it. They'd come for her. And she suspected his pack could be in danger because he'd taken her in and protected her. Her heart ached. She couldn't take the guilt. She decided then that if Jax wasn't in New Orleans by the morning, she'd call and ask for permission to tell Logan everything.

Logan tensed as he listened to Wynter explain how she knew Devereoux. The story of how they'd met seemed feasible, but he could tell she was still withholding the truth. When she finished speaking about the sick girl, he noticed she withdrew from the conversation entirely. She wore her sadness like a mask as she stared into her drink. It was as if she held the weight of the world on her shoulders. Whoever the hybrid was, Wynter must have known her. It wasn't just a case; no, it was personal. And like how Wynter had been sick when he'd first met her, it made no sense how a hybrid could contract an illness. Just what exactly had she been working on in New Orleans? He was about to probe further when Devereoux interrupted his train of thought.

"And to answer your other question, Kade is out of the country. And Luca is with him. Business. I do apologize for the surprise. But I'd prefer not to have the whole city on alert that he's gone," Léopold elucidated with an air of arrogance.

Logan simply nodded, not sure about whether he believed his story. He didn't trust the vampire as far as he could throw him. Kade's damn secretary knew their meeting was important, and she'd lied. It seemed like lying was par for the course when it came to vamps, he thought.

Without warning, two large vampires came up behind Léopold. They flashed their exposed fangs at Wynter, and she wondered if they did it on purpose for intimidation. Or maybe they were getting ready to feed? She backed up as far as her chair would let her.

Unfazed by their presence, Léopold blithely introduced the two vampires. "Pardon my manners. These are two of Kade's men. Étienne and Xavier."

Étienne, a young blonde vampire, appeared to be in his mid-twenties, and he gave Wynter a cool smile that didn't reach his eyes. Not wanting to be impolite, she managed to return the smile. She glanced over to the older, exceptionally well-built vampire, Xavier. It appeared to Wynter that perhaps Logan knew the vampire, as he acknowledged him with a handshake.

"Go feed. I still have business here with the Alpha," Léopold ordered with a wave of his hand. The vampires were gone from sight within mere seconds. "Now, where was I? Oui, our meeting. So I understand there was a scuffle of sorts. Something about vampires? I admit, it doesn't sound unusual, but how can I be of service?"

"As much as I'd like to speak with Kade, if he's left you in charge, then I'm afraid I must bring this matter to your attention," Logan began, his low tone emanating anger. "Last night, we were in a local shifter bar off Decatur when four vampires attacked Wynter."

Léopold frowned. He liked the pretty doctor very much and wouldn't want anything to happen to her, not to mention that he and Jax were old friends.

"I'll get to the short of it. Wynter was held captive by her employer and told us that this organization's been using vamps as guards. They did a number on her. Bites, feedings. The usual," Logan told him with a tick in his jaw. His eyebrows furrowed in anger at the thought of what they'd done to her. "She escaped and on her way out, we fought and ended up staking a few of them. Now, I'm sure you know how this works. Under normal circumstances, we'd hold the offenders and turn them over to Kade. But last night, I had no choice."

"Oui, I understand," Léopold replied, skimming his finger over the rim of a glass that was sitting on the table. His voice held an edge of rage, yet his demeanor was controlled. "This is not acceptable…at all."

"So that brings me to you. First of all, it's likely this operation is still here in the city. But my immediate concern is Wynter's safety. She was doing work for them, and they'll probably be back for her. It'd be nice if we knew whether the vampires belong to Kade."

"I can assure you that all in Kade's line are well accounted for. So either these vampires were from outside the city," Léopold paused as if in deep thought, "Or someone in Kade's line is making children without reporting it, which as you know would be a great offense. One that generally ends in death. Now that you've brought this to my attention, I'll certainly look into it."

"You should also be aware that Jax is coming to New Orleans. He was delayed due to the snow, but he'll be here soon. At that time, I expect we'll have more information," Logan hedged. He didn't wish to reveal that

Wynter hadn't told him everything. And frankly, even if she had, he wasn't sure that he'd share it with Devereoux. Yes, he was grateful for his assistance but at the end of the day, he didn't trust him.

"I see. We're finished, no?" Léopold's dark mood seemed to transform back into a playful tone.

"We're finished," Logan confirmed, noticing that Wynter still appeared unresponsive. He wanted to take her home as soon as possible and force her to tell him exactly what she'd been doing in New Orleans. And he wanted every last detail, no more half-truths.

"A dance then, pet? Come, it's been too long," Léopold asked innocently, raising an eyebrow at Wynter. Sensing her hesitation, he glanced over to Logan, requesting permission. "Would you allow it, Alpha?"

Logan's gut churned at the thought of any other man putting his hands on Wynter. But was he going to refuse the bastard whose help he needed? He considered it. After all, Wynter knew Devereoux and didn't seem at all afraid of him. If anything, she was overly friendly with the guy; she hadn't outright said no to the dance. With an air of nonchalance, he glanced at Wynter who looked like a deer in the headlights. He wondered, was she attracted to Léopold? How well did they know each other? A flare of jealousy flamed, but he quickly reined in his feelings.

Fuck, she was driving him crazy. He'd specifically told her earlier that they didn't belong to each other and then when pressed by Léopold, he'd done a one eighty and publicly announced that she was his. Even though he'd said she belonged to him to protect her, his heart was starting to wish she really was. And his cock, well, his cock had already claimed her.

Putting his ego aside, Logan decided he'd allow one dance. One dance. That's all he could handle. And Léopold had better keep his damn hands to himself.

"Wynter, a dance?" Logan asked, stifling the jealousy that tightened in his chest.

Wynter gave Logan a surprised look. Dance with Léopold? A vampire? Her gut told her no, but her mind told her she was being silly. No matter what she'd just seen him do in the club, it had just been sex. He hadn't at all showed a proclivity for violence. Moreover, he was an acquaintance of Jax's.

"You'll be safe. Remember, you belong to me," he stated with confidence, his eyes pinned on Devereoux's.

"I…um…of course…yes," she accepted, not wanting to insult Léopold. Even though she was nervous, he'd been enormously supportive of her department at the university. But as she rose to take Léopold's hand, she wished it was Logan who'd asked her to dance.

Chapter Ten

As soon as she hit the dance floor, Wynter instantly regretted leaving Logan's side. The smell of blood, sweat and sex permeated the room. A sea of undulating bodies, in various states of dress, danced all around her. The separation felt unnatural and panic set in; she should never have accepted this dance.

Wynter gasped as Léopold pulled her tightly against him. She frantically swiveled her neck, in search of Logan. Léopold spun their bodies in a circle, and she caught a glimpse of Logan staring at her. She visibly relaxed at the sight of him. Léopold abruptly slowed his movement. With his lips inches from her ear, he spoke softly to her, all too intimate for Wynter's comfort.

"Quite a mess you've gotten yourself into, I see. Now tell me, my sweet doctor. Why did you lie to the Alpha? Ma chère, tis not wise," he advised.

"I haven't lied. You must understand, Monsieur, I've got to follow protocol. Jax is my Alpha," she explained breathlessly, surprised at herself for revealing that much to Léopold.

"Ah, but you have lied. You may have made your home with Jax at one time, but I can assure you that you now belong to Logan," he lectured, although satisfied with her candor. Léopold pressed his nose to her neck and sniffed. Wynter flinched. He laughed and spun her once again. "And your scent…it didn't seem possible, even to one as old as me, but you are indeed wolf. I must admit that I'm not sure whether to congratulate you or apologize for this unusual development."

"The Alpha, he's very much a bachelor. It may just be a passing fancy. It doesn't matter, though. I can't belong to him….he's just protecting me. As for being wolf, they did something to me. I'm not convinced that it's permanent. I haven't shifted," Wynter found herself confessing to the vampire despite the way he intruded on her sense of privacy.

There was something compelling about Léopold. The first time she'd met him, he'd seemed like a good-hearted man, such a generous donor. He'd taken great interest in her projects. But tonight, he kept her off kilter, she suspected on purpose, wondering what he'd do next. The way he'd smelled her skin and then laughed at her reaction was disturbing, yet he spoke to her as a man who cared about her future. It both intrigued and frightened her.

"Even on the clearest night, we sometimes cannot see the stars that shine most brightly. If you refuse to imagine the possibilities, the constellations will go unnoticed. Release yourself from these bindings. Your Alpha, he yearns for you, but does not know who you are to him," Léopold observed. How ironic it was that two hearts could meet and not know they were mates. He'd seen it many times and always found it tragic how cruel and wonderful fate could be.

"Yearning and loving are two different things. I'm not sure what I am to him. He feels responsibility because he rescued me," she speculated, engaged in the curious banter with Léopold. "Besides, the past few weeks I've lost sight of who I am, I'm afraid."

"Ah oui, nasty bunch, who captured you. Sounds dreadful. I cannot begin to tell you how sorry I am for what happened. But you are due for a rebirth, no? You will listen to me. Your destiny is with the Alpha. You must not fight this, pet. Some things are meant to be."

"You're a romantic?" she stated in surprise.

"Sometimes yes. Sometimes no. I prefer to think of myself as a realist. For as long as I've lived, there are some things that are even beyond my control."

Wynter said nothing as she caught sight of Logan shoving Dimitri's arm away, as if he'd been holding him back. Her breath caught as she saw him approaching with a feral look in his eyes. What the hell?

"Your Alpha comes for you, no? His possessive nature cannot accept another's hands on you as an unmarked wolf. You like experiments, do you not?" Léopold noted, jovially placing a kiss to her shoulder. He was enjoying this all too much, but he'd prove his point, nonetheless.

"Is this a test?" she snapped, trying to retreat. What was he doing kissing her like that? Her heart beat wildly at the sight of Logan coming straight at him.

"You feel it too, don't you? Your wolf. She craves him," he whispered into her ear, pulling her close against his body. He stopped dancing, holding her still, and continued. "And he cannot resist the demands of his beast."

Wynter recoiled at the intimacy Léopold forced upon her. His warm breath on her neck sent chills down her spine. As he turned his head down to look at her, she noticed his fangs had descended. *Vampire.* On the verge of hysteria, her stomach rolled. Shocked and disoriented, she stumbled backwards as he released her from his hold. The music spun in her mind. Léopold stood chuckling, then bowed toward her, bending one arm behind his back and extending his other hand toward her, as if he were some sort of medieval royalty. A scream bubbled in her throat yet she was unable to make a sound.

Before she knew what was happening, Logan embraced her. Wynter eagerly wrapped herself around her Alpha. The realization of what Léopold had been saying slammed into her consciousness. *Logan was her Alpha.* She wasn't sure how she'd known the creature existed, but in her mind's eye, her wolf released a tortured cry. Logan's scent enveloped her being, and both her human and animal psyche accepted the safety of his presence.

"Logan." Wynter reached for the words but they fell from her grasp. She needed to tell him everything about Emma, the contagion and God help her, how she felt about him. Relief and lust swept through her as he pressed her into his chest.

"Never again," he promised. Against his better judgment he'd let her dance with Léopold. But the second Léopold had touched her, his wolf maniacally clawed to emerge. The need to mark Wynter overwhelmed him. It wasn't prudent or logical, he knew. They'd only known each other a day. He hadn't even made love to her yet. None of it made any sense but his wolf needed this woman. Logan had to have her now. Publicly. To claim her.

"Don't let me go," she begged. Dancing with Léopold had driven whatever animal instincts she had to the surface. It felt wrong, terribly wrong. And now that she had Logan in her arms again, she wasn't going to waste another second of her life being afraid. Logan was her Alpha. She would tell him everything and beg for Jax's forgiveness later.

"I'm taking you now, Wynter. Please don't deny me," he growled.

"But we need to talk… I've got to tell you…" The music blared a pounding erotic beat, and she felt his hard length press against her belly. She tried to fight the desire, to be the sensible person she'd always been. The old Wynter would have left the club. Yet, no longer the person she once was, all she wanted was him, more than anyone she'd met in her life. She craved her lips on his skin, wrapped around his cock. Submitting to both her own cravings and his wishes, she'd give it all to him without question.

"Talk later. Let's go in there. Now," he instructed, pulling her toward a sofa that was somewhat concealed behind red, translucent ceiling-to-floor fringe.

Tugging her into the small alcove, Logan couldn't wait any longer. Driven by the flicker of excitement he saw within her eyes, he knew she wanted this every bit as much as he did. Raking his fingers into her hair, he kissed her. A hungry desperate kiss. He pushed his tongue into her warm mouth, sucking and tasting, incited by the wild intensity with which she returned his kiss.

Aroused beyond reason, Wynter greedily ran her hands all over Logan's body, grasping the front of his shirt and yanking it out of his pants. She moaned loudly, running her palms up his bared ripped abdomen. Her pussy ached with need; she wanted him in her now. As if he sensed her thought, Logan cupped her bottom, lifting her up so she could wrap her legs around him. Writhing her pelvis up against his rock hard erection, she gasped in pleasure as tendrils of her release built.

Standing, Logan continued to plunder her mouth while unzipping the back of her dress. Pulling down one sleeve, he exposed her breast which was every bit as spectacular as he'd remembered from the pool. *No bra? She was a little wild after all.* He tore his mouth from hers and captured a nipple with his lips. Like a starved man, he laved it into a firm little point, letting his teeth graze the tip. "Your breasts, oh Goddess, they're so delicious," he groaned.

"Take me," she breathed as he placed her onto her back on the sofa.

Logan fell to his knees before her, never breaking eye contact. Roughly, he pushed up her dress. She heard a rip and realized he'd taken her panties. Wynter felt him push her knees wide open, his lips on her inner thigh. With Logan's head between her legs, she briefly considered her surroundings. The tassels provided a false sense of privacy as she noticed Dimitri across the room. *Was he watching them?* Barely cognizant of where she was, her beast took over, uncaring of who saw them. The animal in her wanted them all to see, to know he was hers. For the first time in her life, she tossed all preconceived ideas about what was right and wrong when it came to sex. Any last doubts disappeared as Logan's tongue swept through the seam of her wet folds. The only thing that mattered was him. Rocking her hips upward, she sought out his mouth on her pussy. She plowed her fingers into his hair, pulling him into her.

Logan slid two fingers down between her labia, surrounding her clit. Squeezing them together gently, her tiny nub protruded, and he lightly flicked his tongue over and around it. Humming into her flesh, he laughed a little when she pushed up at him, tugging his hair. Oh yeah, his little wolf was lovin' this, and he couldn't get enough of her essence. He lifted his head slightly to watch her reaction and he licked over her lips.

"You taste so good, sweetheart."

"Please," she moaned, needing more contact.

"That's it. Tell me, Wyn." His fingers slid through her wetness and teased at her entrance.

"I need…I need. Fuck me. Please."

Logan laughed, slowly pressing two long fingers into her wet tight pussy. Pushing them in and out, gradually increasing the pressure and rhythm, he watched as she ground her hips in tandem.

Wynter opened her heavy-lidded eyes, focusing as he pumped his fingers into her. He smiled at her right before he pulled them out all the way and slid a digit into his mouth, tasting her. Slowly he withdrew it from his lips and plunged his fingers back into her. Her body arched as she cried out in ecstasy. Never in her life had anyone driven her to such delightful insanity.

"That's it baby, fuck my hand," he encouraged. Needing more of her sweet pussy, he crushed his lips against her clit. He made love to her with his mouth, flicking his tongue over her swollen pearl. As he sucked hard, drawing it into his mouth, she began to shudder beneath him.

Between his fingers and his warm lips, Wynter's body was set on fire. Sensations of pleasure and pain rocked her into climax as Logan latched onto her sensitive flesh. She screamed his name over and over, thrashing her head from side to side. Every inch of her skin tingled. But he gave her no reprieve.

Within seconds, he'd withdrawn his mouth, rose up over her and took her mouth to his. Tasting herself on his wet lips drove her further into the erotic madness. His fingers continued to press in and out of her, hurling her into a second orgasm.

"Logan," she cried into his lips.

Pressing his forehead to hers, Logan pulled away. *Fuck, he'd really lost his shit.* Her honeyed cream still lingered on his lips, and he struggled to resist his true desire. He wanted to thrust his cock deep into her hot sheath, expecting it would be the best sex of his life. But goddammit, he had done this to her in the club. It was so not how he envisioned making love to her the first time. He needed to get her home now, in his bed.

The cell phone buzzed in his pocket, but he ignored it. Cupping her cheek, he gently pulled down her dress so that she was no longer exposed.

"Home…let's go home," he suggested in a restrained voice.

Wynter simply nodded, tugging at her dress. *What the fuck did she just do? Oh that's right, she'd just let the Alpha of New Orleans go down on her in a club, while others watched.* Okay, not the brightest idea she ever had but as she straightened her clothes, she realized she didn't care, not even one little bit. The only thing on her mind was getting back to his house as soon as possible so they could make love all night long.

Logan closed his eyes, and adjusted his rock hard dick. Damn, he hurt. But there was no amount of pain that would drive him to have sex with her in this place. He'd temporarily lost control, giving into the temptation. And she'd tasted damn sweet. But what surprised him most was how amazingly open and sensitive she'd been to his touch. He couldn't wait to get her home.

His cell buzzed a second time, and he glanced at the text. From Fiona, it read: *Alpha, need you at Dana's house ASAP. Hurry.* What the hell? His beta shot him a concerned look, and he knew it wasn't good.

Logan opened the curtain and yelled over the noise to Dimitri. "Fi needs us. Let's catch a cab."

They pushed through the crowd moving quickly through the club. Keeping Wynter at his side, he protectively guided her until they were outside. Dimitri opened the door to the car. Wynter jumped in the back seat, confused by their sense of urgency. Logan followed and Dimitri took shotgun.

"What's wrong?" she asked. "Is everything okay?"

Logan held up his hand to silence her, holding his phone to his ear.

"Fi, what's going on?" Logan inquired with a dominant tone that told Wynter that whatever it was, it was deadly serious. His face darkened, and she knew instantly that something very, very bad had happened.

Chapter Eleven

The Directeur scowled as he left the club. Because he was hiding in plain sight, she never saw him. He'd lingered patiently in the shadows, waiting for the opportunity that hadn't come. *'Good things come to those who take'* was his motto. Just a tiny slip and she'd be back in his arms and her essence in his veins. The ruse had worked beautifully for two months. She'd never known that he'd been drinking her blood. He'd even hidden his guilty pleasure from the Mistress. No, she wouldn't be pleased.

As the evening wore on, the watch dogs never left her side. Irritated that he couldn't snatch her, he had been forced to play his role. He'd always told his mother that he should have been an actor. For when the mongrels touched his property, he remained in the distance, calmly stewing. Like magma bubbling and building inside the core of the Earth, his rage burned deep inside. Eventually, he'd let his anger flow like a river of lava, destroying everything in its path.

The Director spat on the sidewalk, forced to leave the club. The urge to steal her was great, yet the Mistress called on his service. The Mistress must be obeyed. She'd reward him greatly, he knew. Still, he barely restrained his shaking hands from strangling the little bitch for touching the Alpha. Retribution was his only solace. Soon, he'd punish her for her indiscretions.

The volcano rumbled. The sides cracked, the seeping evil tunneled toward the surface. It was time to release the vehement steam of wrath on a victim who'd meet his deadly kiss. A willing sacrifice would sate his need to kill, for now.

Dana was dead. Fiona was crying hysterically, explaining how she and Luci had found her, sprawled on the bed. The word 'blood' was tossed around, and Logan expected a grim scene. After he'd finished talking to her, Logan had hung up and handed Dimitri back his phone.

"Maybe Wynter should stay out here," Dimitri suggested.

"No," he responded definitively. "She's going to be pack soon. And she's mine."

"Okay, then," Dimitri commented, getting out of the cab.

He found it interesting to watch Logan's reaction to Wynter. It always amazed him how mated males were usually the last to know. They often alternated between outright denial and beating on their chests like territorial gorillas, before finally accepting and succumbing to the fact they'd found their mate. In the meantime, he imagined it was going to make for some interesting conversations.

As they ran up the steps to Dana's Magazine Street apartment, Wynter glanced around, noticing that the area was well kept and populated. Chic clothing stores, antique shops and restaurants peppered the thoroughfare. Large columned Greek revival styled homes and colorful Victorian cottages were interspersed throughout the neighborhood. A bustling chic café across the street buzzed with late night patrons and served drinks at a sidewalk tiki bar. She wasn't sure what had happened to Dana but if she'd been murdered, her attacker must have blended into the area, and committed the crime silently.

As they entered the apartment, nothing appeared out of sorts. Tastefully decorated in an eclectic mix of antiques and modern pieces, it was neat and clean. As soon as Fiona saw them enter, she rushed over into Dimitri's arms. Luci sat as still as a statue, and scowled at Wynter with abhorrence.

"Where is she?" Logan inquired in an authoritative tone.

"In here," Fiona cried. "She's in the bedroom. I just don't know who would have done this. We were supposed to go clubbing tonight. But then we found her…like this. How could they do something so awful?"

Wynter quietly gasped as they arrived in the small bedroom afraid of what they were about to see. She grabbed onto Logan's arm as she took in the scene, and he briefly touched her hand with his. The white shabby chic décor was splattered with blood. Dana's body had been awkwardly positioned on the bed, so she appeared as a puppet. Wearing nothing more than a purple bra and matching panties, her grayish skin was mottled with bite marks. *Vampire.*

Wynter found herself walking toward the body, both drawn to and horrified by the bites. A wide open slit across Dana's thorax exposed her spine. As a researcher, it wasn't as if she hadn't seen a dead body, but never in her life had she seen one decimated to this extent. Her eyes roamed over the marred pale skin and letters that had been scrawled into the flesh. The monsters had left a message: *SCIENTIFIQUE*. Scientist. No one else called her that; it had to be him. He'd addressed her in that manner in every single message he'd sent during her captivity. She'd never seen his face but had known him only as Director Tartarus. A chill swept over her.

Why would they go after the doctor? Logan had told her that she'd taken blood samples. Was that why they'd gone after Dana? To get the blood? Or hide the results? But why not just take her? Then it occurred to Wynter that she'd been with Logan the entire time. Maybe they were afraid of the Alpha. Her mind whirled and she considered a possibility far worse than the ominous directive. If they'd somehow changed her DNA so that she was wolf, they could have caused Dana's death by giving her a virus.

They had access to any number of highly contagious diseases. And while they hadn't yet perfected a virus for wolves, Emma, a hybrid, was ill. And like Emma, Dana was also a hybrid. Panicked, she attempted to get Logan's attention while he knelt next to the bed with Fiona, who was crying uncontrollably.

"Did anyone touch the body?" she asked, putting a hand on Logan's shoulder.

"She's not a body!" Luci screamed at Wynter. "She's our friend. And she's Fi's sister."

Logan turned his head, and growled a warning at Luci.

Despite Luci's attack, Wynter pressed the issue. "Did anyone touch the body?"

"No, no one touched the body. Okay?" Luci responded curtly. "Can someone tell me what in the hell she is doing here?"

"Logan, we need to get everyone out of the room," she told him quietly.

Logan glanced over his shoulder at Wynter, unsure as to why she was behaving so strangely. "Please, can you just give us a minute? Fi's just lost her sister," he pleaded.

"I know, and I'm so sorry, but Logan, this message. It's for me," she explained with a pleading look.

"Out, everyone out," he commanded. *What the fuck?*

"But Alpha, please," Fiona cried. "I need to stay with her."

Logan hugged Fiona to his chest. Wynter turned her head at the sight, admonishing the small misplaced pang of jealousy that fluttered in her chest.

"It's okay, Fi. I'll be right out. Luci, stay with her. Dimitri, stay. I want you here for this."

Luci shot Wynter a menacing grimace on the way out of the room. As soon as the door closed, Logan turned on her. "What in the hell are you doing, Wynter?"

"They know I'm with you. The people who took me," she said, carefully approaching the body.

"I'm sure whoever took you knows you're with me. It's not exactly like we've been trying to hide that. We've been all over the city today."

"It's the message." She gestured toward Dana's stomach. "Scientifique. It's me. No, I mean, that's what he called me."

"Who called you that?"

"Him. The person who kept me. I never saw him," Wynter recounted with fear in her eyes. Logan never took his eyes off of her as she continued. "Director Tartarus. I only communicated through email with him. And sometimes text messages before they locked me up. But once I was captured, the guard would bring me a flash drive with a single text file on it in the morning. There'd always be one with a letter of sorts…directions from him. At the end of the day, I was instructed to save my results back onto the drive and then I'd give it back to the guard. It was my only communication with him."

"Tartarus. Very funny," Dimitri huffed.

"What?" Wynter asked as she knelt next to the bed, looking carefully at Dana's skin.

"Tartarus. Greek mythology. A place where gods would be sent for punishment," Logan explained.

"A punishment to fit their crime," Dimitri added.

Logan watched Wynter remove the lamp shade from the bedside light, pick it up and shine the light into the soulless stare of Dana's eyes. "What are you doing?"

"Honestly," she sighed. "I just had to be sure that she wasn't sick. I mean, Tartarus. He knows disease. The company I worked for…he'd have access to all kinds of viruses. And even though you told me she was wolf, she was hybrid…" *Like Emma.* "I needed to see for myself. From what I can tell, though, there's no indication of illness. No jaundice, lesions, weight loss. And if you saw her last night and she was healthy…then it's unlikely. But the bite marks. Whoever did this tortured her. She died from exsanguination when they slit her throat."

Just like he'd seen happen to Wynter in his dream, Logan thought. But he knew it wasn't Dana's face in his vision.

"She knew him. Maybe well or not. But she liked him," Logan said with his arms crossed.

"What makes you say that?"

"Make up. Hair's done. The bra and panties."

"I agree about the underwear, but she was going out with Fiona and Luci. Maybe she was hopeful," Wynter said, playing devil's advocate.

"Or maybe she planned on meeting him there? Look around the room. There's no sign of struggle. He targeted her to get to you. But the fact is that he may have known her." The thought that Dana could have known her attacker bothered him. He'd question the girls and see if they knew anything about who Dana had been dating. "Even if he didn't know her, vampires can be very persuasive."

"Logan. I'm not sure if you're planning on calling the police or taking care of this on your own, but in either case, this body…"

"What aren't you telling me, Wyn?"

Wynter shook her head. It was now or never. She'd tell him the truth.

"Emma."

"Huh?" Logan raised an eyebrow at her in confusion.

"Emma. The girl Léopold mentioned. Jane Doe. The one I spoke about at the charity event. She's not just a case study. She's part of Jax's pack. A hybrid. And she's really, really sick." The thought of Emma made Wynter want to crawl into a ball. The girl was going to die, and she still hadn't found a cure.

"Yeah, you said that at dinner, but what's that got to do with Dana?"

"Logan, Emma is going to die soon if I can't find a cure. And it's not just that she's sick, it's *what* made her sick. A virus. You can't tell anyone what I'm about to tell you," she pleaded. Brushing the hair from her eyes, she sucked a breath and blew it out, shaking her head. "You know my friend, Mika, I told you about; Emma's her sister. Her doctors all agreed that her condition was caused by a viral infection but they couldn't explain it. I mean, hybrids don't get sick let alone get terminal diseases. It made no sense. Jax was worried that if word got around about her condition, his wolves would panic. So, her parents brought her to his country home, where she now gets round the clock nursing. I had to do something; something to help her. So I changed my major and started studying virology instead. During my doctoral program, I finally narrowed down the virus, it looked familiar. I should have known." She began to pace.

"It wasn't a natural virus to wolves or humans, but it shared visible traits with other known viruses. But what it most looked like was the feline leukemia virus; and of course that retrovirus has a poor outcome. But it wasn't an exact match. And as we know, wolves are immune to both homosapian and canis lupus diseases as well as most other typical causes of mortality. And while it is true that viruses mutate and adapt to their environment to survive, it's a moot point. I've been investigating, trying to find out if maybe someone gave her this virus. Or created it somehow, manipulated it, perhaps utilizing shifter blood."

As Logan stood listening, it occurred to him that no matter how strong the attraction was that he felt for Wynter, he really didn't know her at all. The way she talked was formal and direct, like a doctor, but he detected the pain she tried to hide. Like he'd suspected, her case was personal. And she'd gotten herself into this mess for her friend's sister? Who does that? *Wolves did that.* They had loyalty that ran as deep as an abyss. But she'd been a human living with an Alpha wolf. Why would she risk her life to save a hybrid wolf? Why was she still living with the Alpha? Who was the woman he almost made love to an hour ago? So many questions and very few answers.

Logan pinched the bridge of his nose, attempting to shake off the distracting thoughts. He needed to focus. Growing impatient, he blew out a breath. An hour ago, he'd been ready to claim this woman in front of everyone. Sure, it may have been a jealous, lust-driven temporary insanity, but still, it didn't negate what happened. As she stood before him now, she was no longer the vulnerable woman he'd held in his arms. No, this person was someone he didn't know at all. A researcher who was up to her eyeballs in some serious shit. And one of his wolves was dead as a result.

"Get to the point, doctor," he warned coldly.

"When I was offered the fellowship at ViroSun, I should have suspected something was off. They're one of the top ten virology companies in the country, typically known for their advanced work with next generation antivirals and vaccines. I'd just earned my doctorate, so why did they pursue me? I thought it was because of my relationship with Jax, but it was Emma. They wanted my knowledge of her and the viruses. I made the mistake of bringing samples of her blood to my lab. I had to know if she was intentionally infected; they had all the latest equipment I needed to find a way to save her," she said quietly. Sadness laced her words and she tried not to cry. She should have never taken that job. She should have listened to her gut and refused the tempting carrot.

"Shortly after I started, they slowly began pumping me for information about Emma…my 'Jane Doe'. I'd done lectures, so they knew of the case. But I could tell they knew exactly who it was. One day someone actually used her name. Later that day, I tried grabbing all the data, to get it to Jax. I was going to leave. And that was the day they locked me in the lab. And I thought, 'how could this happen?' I was working in a large office building. I don't know how they did it. They just locked me in and the next day, they had me moved and on the road. I never knew where I even was. It was always just me in a makeshift lab with the vampires."

Wynter regretted her decision to take the data. She should have just walked out the door that day and gone to Jax. They must have been monitoring her through a camera, known what she was doing with the files. She rubbed her eyes, glanced up at the ceiling and then back to Logan.

"And I have to tell you, Logan; I was close to figuring out what caused it, how it works. But they still don't have what they need yet. It's not finished. The scary part is that I've suspected for some time that they want to make it portable, so it can be actively utilized…on hybrids at first, eventually wolves. You need to know that even though they don't have me, they have the data. I don't understand why they still want me. It doesn't make sense. I already told them most of what I knew about Emma. They could find another scientist to work on it, but this," Wynter gestured to the blood spatter and the words written on the body. "This tells me they aren't going to let me go. I don't know why. I'm so sorry they killed Dana. Sorry I haven't told you everything. I really wanted to tell you but…"

Logan had heard enough. "Yeah, I know protocol. What a bunch of shit, doctor. I take you into my home, and you don't think you owe me the decency to tell me that you've been working on a virus that could have the capability to kill wolves? Fuck," he grunted, shaking his head.

He didn't want to come down so hard on her but he was beyond frustrated. Seriously? A virus that attacks wolves? A corporation looking to exploit the virus? What she was saying didn't seem possible. What was it about the godlike Jax Chandler that drove her to keep this a secret?

"But they can't yet. I told you, that's why they wanted me. I'm sorry," she whispered.

There was nothing else she could say. It was ironic that the past five years she'd done nothing but devote her life to research, all in the name of protecting wolves, and she was no closer to helping Emma. To add to it all, she'd opened her heart and body to an incredible Alpha, one who was very much pissed at her at the moment. She was a fool to have even thought for one minute he'd understand. As her thoughts drifted to Jax, she almost felt relief. If he found out she'd been with Logan, he'd be angry with her too. Her heart broke, because there had been no doubt how she felt about him earlier. She'd been willing to give herself to him in every way, and it couldn't have felt more right. In his arms, she belonged to him. He was her Alpha.

But maybe it had been the wolf who'd claimed him as Alpha? The entirely human part of her now doubted her own feelings. Logan's disappointed expression left no room for misinterpretation. He didn't want her here with him or his wolves. Now that he knew the truth about what was going on with ViroSun and why she was imprisoned, he could align with Jax and deal with the issue on his own. As she watched him, she could see the wheels turning, the ever present leader calculating his next move in the war strategy.

A commotion in the next room jarred her back to focus, and she straightened her back when she heard Léopold's voice. What was he doing here? Was he somehow involved in Dana's death? She quickly sidled up behind Logan, close but not touching. As the door flew open, she held her breath.

Unbeknownst to her, Logan had texted the dark vampire in the car after Fiona had mentioned the state of the body. Logan couldn't be certain if vampires were in charge of this operation or not. True, vampires had tortured Wynter and had a hand in Dana's murder, but in his long life, he'd learned that things weren't always as they appeared. What he hadn't mentioned to Wynter was that it was possible more than one person had killed Dana.

"Thank you for coming," Logan told Devereoux and nodded over to Dana.

Léopold wasted no time, going directly to the body. Picking up the cold arm, he sniffed at the skin and darted his tongue over the small wounds. Unceremoniously, he stood and rubbed his nonexistent five o'clock shadow. Contemplating the situation, his menacing eyes met Logan's.

"Her neck was the fatal blow, no? There's a lot of blood. But someone did drink from her. These bites aren't just for show. No, they took much blood before killing her."

"But there's no signs of struggle," Logan indicated.

"Oui. Pleasure bites, perhaps. It would explain her relaxed positioning, the peaceful look in her eyes. I believe she knew him. Or her." Léopold gently slid his fingers over the woman's eyelids, closing them.

"That I hadn't considered. But your guards were all males, correct?" Logan asked Wynter.

"Yes."

"But still, there's nothing here to indicate the sex of the killer," Logan agreed. "It appears she hasn't been sexually assaulted although an autopsy would be needed to confirm. I don't smell sex."

"The scent is exactly what disturbs me," Léopold pointed out, fisting his finely manicured fingernails.

"We didn't smell anything," Dimitri told him.

"The she-wolves were the ones who found the body," Logan explained. "What do you smell?"

"Ah, it's so very faint, but vampire. And to my great dismay, it is from my line. Perhaps not a direct child," he reasoned. "No, it cannot be. They've all been accounted for. Isn't that interesting? Where did you say you found Wynter last night?"

"Down near Decatur. Courettes. I sent a couple of my guys down there last night afterwards, but they didn't find anything. But if you've got a scent, we should go together," Logan suggested. "Give me an hour and I'll meet you there. First, I've got to get Fiona and Luci home safely."

"They'll be gone," Wynter added softly.

"It's a longshot, but if it gives Devereoux more information about who he's looking for in his ranks, then we're going," Logan said tersely. "Dimitri, take Wynter home."

"I can go with you," she interrupted.

"No, you can't," Logan disagreed. No fucking way was she going anywhere near that place, putting herself in danger again. Logan needed to get away from her for a while anyway. She was clouding his judgment. He should have sent her to Jax the minute he found her. Because of his overactive libido, he'd allowed her to stay and worse, he played with her. The confusing emotions would endanger her and his pack.

"But I could help you find where they kept me," she continued, until Logan turned on her. Wynter's feet moved backward on their own until she'd backed up against a closet door. She'd never understood how the pack and an Alpha communicated, but she swore she could literally feel his anger emanating off of him, snapping across her skin like a whip.

"You. Will. Go. Home. Do not argue with your Alpha, Dr. Ryan. You will learn soon that there are consequences for disobedience within the pack. Do not test me," he growled at her.

"But Logan…" Wynter's eyes brimmed in tears as he admonished her in front of the others. She wanted to scream at him that she wasn't a wolf but thought better of it.

"Not another word. Now go." Logan's face hardened and his eyes fixed on hers before he turned his attention to Dimitri.

"Get her out of here. And keep her safe until I return."

"You got it."

"Hey D, one more thing. Did you call Zeke and Jake? I need them to deal with Dana's body."

"Yes, Alpha."

Dimitri moved over to Wynter and gently put his arm around her. "You okay?" he asked, aware that Logan was watching his every move with her.

Wynter nodded silently. She wanted to leave; she hated this place. She already sensed how Logan had distanced himself from her, well before he yelled at her. No, the embarrassment of being chastised was just the finality she needed to know she had to go home to New York. Confused and alone, she wanted nothing more than a hot shower and to crawl into a bed. She might have to wait to go home to the city, for Jax. But she was good at waiting. Being held captive had taught her that.

If she really was a wolf, she could continue to live with Jax, at least until he found a mate. He'd proved a million times over that he'd protect her, of that she was sure. Jax was everything she'd needed when there was nothing. And by some cruel fate, she once again had nothing. No job. She had a degree in a career that she didn't look forward to jumpstarting. Her health was questionable, infected with an unidentified agent. Her mind would be forever broken by the memories of the torture she'd endured. And the small place she'd begun to open in her heart for Logan was a figment of her imagination. Like a mirage in the desert, the oasis was transforming back into sand.

The last thing she saw when they left the apartment was Fiona curled into Logan's arms. Luci stood next to him, caressing the back of his head. Feeling nauseated at the sight of another touching him, Wynter tried to look away but not before Logan's eyes flashed to hers. His impassive facial expression gave no clues as to what he was thinking, but she recognized the flare in his eyes. *Passion.* Whether filled with hate or love, a storm brewed within him.

Chapter Twelve

The Mistress celebrated the death of the meddling doctor. It couldn't have gone more smoothly, except perhaps for that diabolical vampire. She hadn't counted on him being in New Orleans. Kade would have been much easier to deceive. But Devereoux, he was an entirely different creature. Much too clever for his own good. But now that she knew he was here, she'd be more careful.

She cursed the Directeur. He'd been sloppy, indulging the pretty hybrid in foreplay before killing her. He should have merely slit her throat, leaving no clues as to what kind of creature had taken her life. How unfortunate for him that the ancient one now suspected the Directeur's lineage. Idiocy and arrogance would be his downfall. From the minute they'd met, he'd aspired to a stature well beyond his capabilities. It served him right to be taken down a peg.

If they identified him, she'd eliminate him. Pity, but she couldn't have his mistakes thwart her plans for her Acadian Wolves.

The cab ride back to the mansion was a blur. Wynter didn't want Dimitri to see the tears streaming down her face. She'd looked in the other direction, staring aimlessly into the dark city streets. Long ago, she'd learned that emotions equated to weakness. She may be broken, but she'd never let them see it. A survivor, she'd get through this like every other dreadful experience. Ten years ago, she thought nothing would match the pain and devastation when her loving parents were brutally murdered in a carjacking. It had felt as if a shard of glass had cleaved open her heart. She mourned them for years until life had become tolerable. Up until six months ago, she'd begun to hope that she'd maybe create her own family someday, filling that void in her chest that had never quite mended.

Tonight, Logan might as well have torn her in half when he yelled at her. One minute she'd been ready to make love to him and the next it was over before it started. The final blow had been how he'd allowed Fiona and Luci into the comfort of his arms so quickly. Her cerebral, human self knew that he'd been attending to their grief as Alpha, but her soul felt crushed. Her wolf yelped wildly at the sight, not understanding what she was seeing. The beast was growing stronger. Angry and hurt, her emotions swirled like an out of control tornado uplifting and destroying anything in its path. None of the feelings meshed with her normally levelheaded approach to life.

The wolf within seethed, aware that her Alpha was in the hands of other females. Wynter closed her eyes, trying to push the animal away, but it kept at her, unrelenting. The full moon was only days away, and she suspected there was a chance she would indeed shift. *Oh God. How could this be happening?* She'd been afraid to ask them where Dana had taken her blood or what the results were. She figured that she'd do her own analysis once she got back to New York. Other than the wolf, no physical discomfort or illness remained from her ordeal. No, all the pain she felt was in her own mind. Restless and heartbroken, Wynter didn't know how she was going to get through the night.

Before she knew where she was, she realized she was standing inside the guest room. Had Dimitri walked her all this way? She didn't even remember getting out of the cab. Exhausted, she sat on her bed and put her face into her hands.

Dimitri was worried about the little wolf. She hadn't spoken the entire way home. He couldn't even imagine what it would be like for a human to transform into a wolf. Even if she lived with wolves, it didn't make her one. Adapting to their lifestyle would not be easy. Listening to Logan reprimand her was difficult. But she'd needed to learn that she couldn't openly challenge the Alpha, especially after everything that had transpired; Dana's death, her own confession.

Observing her listless state, his suspicion that she was Logan's mate grew stronger. Her wolf needed her mate, and he'd been with another woman. That alone would have driven her wolf berserk. But it was more than that; Logan had withdrawn after the scene at the club. For a minute, he thought he might have to hold Logan back from tearing Léopold apart limb by limb. Jealousy didn't even begin to describe his Alpha's behavior. He'd watched his Alpha possessively sweep Wynter off her feet. And she, and her wolf, ravenously attacked him in return despite her otherwise modest human nature. It was the hottest thing he'd witnessed in a long time. After seeing her in the pool earlier, Logan wasn't the only one walking around today with an agonizing erection.

Dimitri wished she'd just come clean from the beginning. Protocol was one thing; endangering pack members was an entirely different story. But to be fair to her, he and Logan had taken her into their home knowing someone was still after her. She'd shared as much. The whole situation summed up to a clusterfuck of monstrous proportions. He sure as hell hoped that Logan and Léopold found some kind of clue soon before all-out war broke out in New Orleans, because if they didn't, he was certain his Alpha would tear up the city to find Dana's killer.

Dimitri watched Wynter slump onto her bed. He needed to do

something to help her get through the night; something that did not include touching her too much. His Alpha may not have understood what the female meant to him yet, but Dimitri wasn't fool enough to test his theory. When Logan came home, he'd go in search of her. Similar to Wynter's current reaction from being separated from Logan, the pull to be with her would be too much to resist.

"Hey, Wyn. It's going to be okay," he reassured, sitting down next to her on the bed. "Come here."

The bed depressed and Wynter felt a strong arm around her shoulder. And even though it wasn't the man she wanted, she was oddly calmed by his touch and welcomed his presence. He was warm, and like Logan, his scent was appealing, safe. A sob wrenched from her chest, and she clung to him, seeking comfort.

"That's it, cher." Dimitri wrapped her all the way into his embrace. While he found her attractive, especially after watching her with his Alpha, he only sought to give her peace. There was nothing sexual about the situation for him. Oh no, a cryin' woman was a libido killer, in his book. "It's not your fault."

"I should have told him sooner," she cried. "But it wouldn't have mattered. They want me. I may have to go back to them. They won't stop."

"No, don't think so. You're not going back. Do you think your Alpha would ever let that happen?"

"Jax or Logan. Who is my Alpha?" She pulled away; her eyes were swollen and red. "I don't know who I am, Dimitri. Where I belong. Hell, I don't even know what I am. How could they do this to me? Wasn't it enough to drain me? To chew on me like rodents? And now, I'm just a freak."

"You're wolf, cher. And it's going to be okay. It may not be easy but you'll get through it. As for your Alpha, only you can make that choice."

"I haven't slept with him," Wynter confessed.

"Logan?"

"Jax," she stated.

"Okay, then." Dimitri wasn't sure if he was ready for this conversation but he steadied himself for what came next.

"We live together, making people wonder, leaving it ambiguous to everyone…well, except for his beta."

"Now why would you do that?"

"My parents. They were murdered. I was fifteen," she whispered. She kept her head down. "My Dad worked for him. He was his accountant. They were pretty close friends. Jax trusted Daddy with everything. One day I was in my parents' loving home in Brooklyn and the next thing I knew I'd been moved into Jax's Manhattan penthouse. I had no other family when they died."

"I'm sorry," Dimitri offered, and wrapped his arm around her once again. "It must've been really difficult. You were so young."

"I hated Jax at first. He was overbearing. What else can you expect from an Alpha? But he cared about me….really cared about me. The first year, he never left my side. Seriously, pretty much wherever he went, he made sure I was with him," she reminisced. "He filled my days with school, friends, horseback riding…all kinds of things to keep me busy and growing up right. He loves me."

"Like a father?"

"Like an Alpha," she responded quickly. "No, Jax is quite aware that I'm a woman, but if he's ever wanted me that way, he never told me. We're friends, but he's Alpha. I know that, respect him."

"So why the pretense?"

"He insisted on it. I didn't mind. I mean, the wolves, he kept me from his pack for the most part. I don't think he wanted me around the males. He kept telling me I'd grow up to find a human. It sounded reasonable. It didn't really bother me."

"But why not just tell Logan?" Dimitri persisted.

"I don't know. He asked me if I belonged to Jax, and I do. I did. Or at least that's how it felt before, but now everything is so confusing." She rubbed her face with the back of her hand, trying to dry the tears. "But when I went to dance with Léopold…he frightened me. I saw his fangs, and he kept talking to me about Logan. And I don't know…all I knew is that I wanted Logan and…"

"What?" Dimitri could hear the hesitation in her voice.

"I felt like he really was my Alpha," she said with a shake of her head. "How crazy is that? I mean, I've known the guy for what? A day? Maybe a very long intense day. So to have that thought in my head…him being my Alpha. It's insane, yet it felt so real."

"Sometimes things in life don't make sense, cher. Sometimes our feelings," he put his hand on her chest above her heart, "our gut; that's what you've got to trust. Now I know you're some kind of a scientist and you like data, facts and all that business. But you know since you've been around Jax that that's not how things work in the pack. Fate, she directs the life show. And you've got to trust your heart."

Wynter listened intently. Maybe he was right but she was still ripe with confusion.

"Now look, you've made me all sappy," Dimitri laughed, trying to lighten the mood. "Don't tell Logan. I won't live it down."

"You've gone and spoiled that dangerous mystique of yours," she smiled. "I'll try to take your advice, and I promise I won't tell Logan."

"Oh cher, you don't need to worry about that danger part. Let's hope you don't ever need to see it. Now come on, go get a shower. I'll get you some tea and then you're goin' to bed."

As Wynter emerged from the bathroom, she stared at herself in the long mirror. Dressed in a pink camisole and underwear, she noticed her naturally curly hair had now gone completely haywire, but her skin was smooth and flawless. Too flawless. Unnaturally so. It was physically impossible for a human to heal at this accelerated rate, she knew. Part of her was relieved that she actually looked better than she had prior to taking the job. The other part of her shivered in trepidation. Her molecular structure had changed and was still in flux. Would she shift? Would it hurt? What would it feel like to be an animal?

A blanket of despondency shaded her otherwise optimistic spirit. It was then that she realized why she was so utterly miserable. She missed Logan. More than lust, she wanted to get to know him and talk about things that only lovers would share. Thoughts of what it would be like if they made love danced through her mind. But then that nasty bit of reality cropped up, slamming her back to what was really happening. The reason she was here alone, her lack of transparency.

A sigh drew her attention away from her spiraling misery. She startled at the sight of Dimitri watching her. His one hand was propped on the door jamb, and the other held a steaming cup. At first, she'd found him a little scary with his massive presence, tattoos and sharp goatee. But he'd shown himself to be gentle and caring, and she understood why Logan chose him as a beta.

"Hey, brought you tea." He offered her the warm beverage. "You look beautiful. I mean, tonight you looked great. But look at you; you're all healed."

"Yes. Not very humanlike." She gratefully took the mug, sat on the bed and took a sip.

"No, but it's natural…for a wolf," he countered.

"Can I ask you a question?" She knew she shouldn't ask but she just couldn't take not knowing.

"Ask away. My answer, that'll depend on the question."

"Fair enough. Is he with those women? I'm sorry, I shouldn't have asked." She buried her face into the cup, regretting her question. How embarrassing was it to be so insecure?

He smiled, thinking that they were going to drive each other crazy before admitting what was going on between them.

"Logan's single. As in not attached. That being said, my Alpha's all about business. I'm fairly sure that he's with Léopold right now and not out messin' with girls."

"I feel horrible," she cringed. "I shouldn't have asked. It's none of my business."

"Don't be so hard on yourself. Trust me; there are things at work here that you don't understand." *Like he's your mate.* "Logan'll be home later, cher. Ya'll will work it out. Until then, you need to listen to your beta. I know what'll make you feel better," he predicted, taking her by the hand.

Wynter nervously followed him, unsure of where they were going. But as soon as he opened the large door, she knew. Logan's scent engulfed her, and her wolf rejoiced.

"What are we doing in here?"

"You know where you are, don't you?"

"Yes," she managed. A flick of a light revealed Logan's bedroom. Immaculate, but sparsely decorated, a king sized cherry four-poster bed invited her. A simple white cotton down comforter covered the bed along with a topping of several white pillows. A matching dresser sat across the room in between rectangular windows, and night tables flanked the mattress. Several large potted tropical palm trees added an organic flair to the décor.

She stood frozen watching Dimitri, who walked over to the bed and pulled back the comforter. What was he doing? Wynter tried desperately to quell the nervous flutter in her stomach.

"Come, cher. In you go," he commanded.

She raised an eyebrow at him in confusion. There was no way in hell that she would get into Logan's bed with his beta. No freaking way. Wynter had made enough mistakes for one evening, thank you very much.

"Don't worry, I'm not getting in bed with you," he promised. "Not that I wouldn't want to, but Logan would kill me. Stop stallin' and get on over here."

Wynter smiled at Dimitri. "I don't know. I'm not sure Logan would want me in his bed," she hedged.

"I'm tellin' you. Logan doesn't know what he wants. But this'll be good for you and him. Now get in." He continued to hold the linens up, gesturing in a sweeping motion for her to get in the bed.

She knew she shouldn't do it, but the temptation was too great. The scent in the room was like walking into a chocolate factory and damn if she didn't love chocolate. Just one small bite, a taste, and then she'd leave and go to her guest room. As she pushed her feet into the bed, the smell of Logan grew stronger. Like a cat, she shamelessly rubbed her face into the pillowcase. It felt incredible. Desperately, she kneaded the mattress and pillow, letting the calm of Logan wash over her. She didn't understand why it was happening, and she didn't care. This man, this Alpha, she needed him; he was hers. Oh God, she prayed they'd reconcile. As she drifted off to sleep, all she saw was Logan's face.

Chapter Thirteen

Logan went to the cupboard, pulled out a bottle of scotch and poured himself a generous glass. God damned fucking vampires. Logan cursed them to hell, worried that it was just a matter of time before they attacked another one of his wolves. He and Léopold had gone over every square inch of the blocks surrounding Courettes, and they'd found nothing. Granted, the eccentric vampire had caught a scent off of Dana's body, but it wasn't enough. Despite the failure to find anything, Léopold had assured him that he'd find the lab's location. But Logan didn't trust him, and sure as hell couldn't wait around for Léopold. His pack was in danger, and he needed to take immediate action to protect them. In the morning, he'd planned to call Jax and have it out.

He'd been so angry with Wynter. Still, he felt like shit for yelling at her. But he was sick of the lies. Well, he knew they weren't exactly lies; more like an omission of facts. And even though she may have had her reasons, it still was a bitter pill to swallow. Coupled with her challenge, he'd torn into her, treating her like he'd treat any wolf. And therein lies the rub; she wasn't just any wolf.

The look on her face when she'd left the apartment had ripped his heart out of his chest. Yes, he sought to provide comfort to Fiona and Luci, but he should have never let the women touch him like that. Only an hour earlier, Wynter had opened herself, allowing him to touch her, taste her. He'd been so disrespectful. He wouldn't blame her if she didn't forgive him.

Footsteps alerted him to Dimitri's presence.

"Hey, how'd it go?" Dimitri asked, grabbing a glass, looking to join Logan in a drink.

"Not good," he replied, falling into an overstuffed chair. He propped his feet onto an ottoman.

"I take it you didn't find the lab, huh?"

"Nope. We didn't find a damn thing. Devereoux is certain whoever it is is from his line. But of course, he's as slippery as an eel."

"And Fi?" Dimitri asked all too innocently.

"Fi's Fi. She's upset, of course. But you know, she wasn't exceptionally close to Dana. The two fought like wildcats. Still, they're sisters…half-sisters. Whatever. Luci's staying with her. I didn't really have time. Had to meet Devereoux down at Courettes. How the pack loved seeing him," Logan said acrimoniously, throwing his head backwards into the cushion.

"Yeah, I bet," Dimitri concurred, taking a long swig. He coughed as the caustic liquid burned his throat. "So, uh, what about Wynter?"

"What about her?"

"She's upset."

"Yeah, so am I," he spat out.

"Well it wasn't that way at the club. Y'all seemed in tune then," Dimitri mentioned. "Pretty hot, man."

Logan let that sink in a minute before responding. Goddess, she was amazing. The sweetest he'd ever tasted.

"Yeah, it was," he began. "Didn't go so well after that."

"Yeah, not so much," Dimitri commented, looking into his drink.

"This thing with her…it has me distracted. I've fought hard to be Alpha. The pack needs me." Logan swiped his hand over his eyes, replaying what happened at Dana's. The scene at the apartment was jacked. Guilt dug at him, knowing how he'd treated Wynter. "Fuck, I'm an asshole. How is she doing?"

"I'll be honest. She wasn't lookin' so good earlier. She's torn up about what's happening. I think the whole wolf thing's freaking her out too. But don't worry; I took good care of your girl. She's doing fine now." Dimitri darted his eyes to the side and then finally looked over to Logan and smiled.

"What'd ya do, D?" He blew out a breath.

"Nothin' you wouldn't have done."

Logan stared over at him. "Seriously? Tell me you didn't…"

"Not that. Although, she's sweet, man. I mean, really sweet. Tonight she was wearing these tight little panties, and those breasts…Oh Goddess, save me," he said dramatically, putting his hand to his chest.

"Mine," Logan reminded him with a smile.

"Ah, but are they? You were a little harsh tonight, almighty Alpha," he taunted.

"Still mine, smartass."

"Well, great one, if you want to keep said breasts, you'd better make nice. Your little wolf is getting ready to high tail it back to New York tomorrow," he lied.

"She is?" Logan asked in a panicked voice. *What the hell was wrong with him?*

"Let's just say you shouldn't have let Fi and Luci rub all over you like cats in heat. You know, giving that kind of grief counseling isn't doing you any favors," Dimitri half-heartedly joked.

"Fuck." Letting his anger drive his actions wasn't the smartest thing he'd ever done. He knew full well how jealous Wynter had been when they'd talked earlier in the club. And he couldn't blame her after he'd gone all territorial on her after seeing her dance with the vampire. If he were truthful, he'd admit that he knew the sight of Luci touching him would hurt

Wynter. He shouldn't have let it happen.

"Fuck is right. She didn't like it at all. On the upside," he laughed. "She didn't like it at all."

Logan rolled his eyes.

"Seriously, bro. How would you feel if she didn't care? Think about it. It's not really that bad, all considered." Dimitri shrugged.

"What exactly am I supposed to consider? That my life has been upturned in the past twenty-four hours by a human female? Who's a wolf? That I'm losing it because I'm preoccupied by a woman? And now, one of my own wolves is dead. You and I both know I've got to focus all my priorities on running this pack, D."

"She could be your mate, Logan," he posed quietly. Dimitri's lip curled up on one side, as he waited for a reaction.

"You've got to be joking. No way. I know I've been distracted, but come on," Logan pleaded. "Where is she?"

"Okay, believe what you want, man, but I'm telling you that there's something about that woman…you and her. Today at the pool and then at the club. You've been with lots of females, of all species, but this is different. She's," he took a deep breath, shaking his head, "She's responsive. To you, hell, even to me."

Logan growled at his beta.

"As if I'd touch her without your permission," Dimitri assured him. "It's just that she calmed down with me, and I felt comfortable with her…like I've known her for a long time."

"So what happened?"

"Let's just say that I knew what to do," he said proudly. Dimitri stood up, walked over to the sink and put his empty glass in it.

"And that was?"

"She's in your bed."

"What?" *In his bed?* Even though he acted surprised, there was no place he'd rather have her.

"You heard me. And it worked, by the way. She fell right asleep."

"Have I told you what a great beta you are, D?"

"Yeah, and don't fuck it up." Those were Dimitri's last words as he walked out the door.

Logan laughed. As sure as he was sitting there, he knew without question that Wynter would challenge and reward him in ways he'd never known. But was she his mate? He'd honestly never given it a thought. Whether out of denial or ignorance, he hadn't considered why he'd been nearly obsessed with her since they'd met. She'd gotten under his skin; that was for sure. All he knew was that he had to go to her. Whether she forgave him or not, he needed to say his piece.

On his way up to his bedroom, Logan contemplated what it must be like for her. Her captivity, surviving being bitten and now, her illness or whatever they'd done to her; it was all too much for one wolf, let alone a human to take. Learning to live as a wolf wouldn't be easy, but he was determined to guide her during her transition. And that was the crux of it. He wanted to be the person who stood at her side, not Jax. In spite of everything, it was the fact she lived with another man that irritated him. The New York Alpha would arrive soon and she'd leave.

Cracking open his bedroom door, Wynter's delectable scent hit him, drawing him to her side. Like an angel, she slept peacefully, looking as if she belonged there. *In his bed. In his home.* The temptation to touch her was great, but he needed to shower before lying down. Not only did the stench of death cling to his clothing, he was reminded of how he'd let Fiona and Luci touch him.

After a quick shower, Logan toweled the moisture off his body, letting his thoughts wander. He considered what Dimitri had told him about Wynter. How could the Goddess send him a human as a mate? A human who may or may not be a wolf? Who belonged to another Alpha? Shit, it'd been a long night. But knowing the woman was ten feet away in his bed had him wide awake. They needed to have a real discussion before they made love. Unless she submitted to him, accepted him fully as her Alpha, they had no future.

Steam poured out of the bathroom as he opened the door. The anticipation of touching her again put his system on alert. Even though she was fully covered, he knew the taste of the lovely she-wolf who lay beneath. It would kill him to talk first, play later, but it was the right thing to do. Lifting a corner, he slipped in underneath, his naked skin grazing the sheets. Unable to resist, he slid forward until his chest was against her back and wrapped a hand around her waist. *Damn, she was dressed.* He supposed he didn't want Dimitri taking care of 'everything'. It'd be his pleasure to peel off the flimsy fabric that clung to her body. She stirred and her bottom brushed against his semi-erect shaft. *Sweet mother of nature.* Soon he'd take her like this, he thought; slamming his cock into her tight pussy from behind. He sucked a breath, willing his self -control to kick in. *Better talk quick before I come right here.*

"Wyn, baby." He kissed the back of her hair, inhaling deeply. She smelled so good, like a breath of fresh air.

"Hmm," Wynter responded sleepily. Within seconds, she realized Logan's hard chest was against her. Something about his scent calmed her wolf. But then she remembered how angry he'd been. "Do you want me to leave?" *Please don't make me go.*

Logan gently rolled her toward him so she was facing him. "No, sweetheart. I want to talk about what happened. What's happening with us."

"I'm sorry," she whispered, slowly opening her eyes to meet his. On her side, she reached forward and placed her palms to his chest. She swore she could hear his heartbeat.

He laughed a little. "I'm the one who should be apologizing. I was an ass tonight. I shouldn't have treated you like that."

"I didn't tell you everything. I challenged you in front of everyone," she responded, looking down to his abdomen. Even though she was supposed to be apologetic, and she truly was, the man made her horny as hell. For the love of God, she could lick him all over and never eat another meal.

"The challenging business, well, it's true that's something we can talk about, but honestly, I was just trying to protect you. It could've been dangerous. But the most important thing from now on is that we can't have any more secrets. Seriously, Wynter. And that includes no more withholding the truth. If I don't have all the facts, I can't see the whole picture. It puts all of us at risk."

Wynter nodded.

"Still, I shouldn't have been so harsh…especially since you haven't been wolf for very long," he continued. His eyes roamed over her body; the swell of her cleavage threatened to spill out of her top. "I know you haven't been around wolves, not in a pack anyway. You haven't even shifted yet. After everything that's happened to you…I should've gone easier."

"No more secrets. I promise. But Jax…"

"I know you're worried about Jax, but I'll talk to him and…" *I want you to be mine.*

"I'm not with Jax, not the way you think."

"What?"

"I haven't had sex with him," she interrupted. She lowered her eyes and spoke softly. "He's my guardian. A protector. A friend."

"Why didn't you tell me?" Logan felt as if a thousand pound weight had lifted with the news that she hadn't slept with Jax.

"When my parents died, I was only fifteen. Jax, he took me in that very day, and he's been in my life ever since. He only wants to protect me. That's why he wanted our relationship to remain kind of unclear…to others. He claims me as his, like you did. After all he's done for me…you need to understand. I owe him everything. I didn't want to be disloyal," she explained and then added, "Growing up, and even now as an adult, he doesn't want me around the wolves. Well, he's okay with Mika, but he'd never let me date wolves when I was younger. Believe me, he won't understand."

"I can't blame him. Wolves, we're passionate, but aren't always gentle." He smiled.

"Maybe I don't want gentle," she said seductively. "Maybe I just need the right wolf."

Logan pulled her into an embrace so that her head and body was flush with his. As she molded into him, he wrapped a leg around hers allowing his erection to press into her belly.

"Logan, there's something else. I'm so embarrassed, but I need to tell you. Tonight, when I saw you with Fiona and Luci…my wolf, she…she's so strong…I don't know how to control her…the way I feel…" She couldn't finish. The jealousy had nauseated her.

"Wyn," Logan began, gently raising her chin so she'd look into his eyes. "I'm really sorry. I should have never let Luci touch me after what we had just shared in the club. It was wrong. I shouldn't have let her near me…not like that, anyway. Let's just say that if someone had touched you like she'd done to me, I would have…well, you saw how I reacted to Devereoux earlier. Our wolves, they are an extension of ourselves, and sometimes, they feel and act like what they are, animals. As such, they have a tendency to fiercely protect what they perceive to be theirs."

Relief swept over Wynter. In response, she rubbed her body against his in a slow rhythm. She pressed her mound into the ridge of his hard shaft, seeking to alleviate the throbbing ache between her legs. She cursed that she was dressed when she felt his velvet tip brush against her inner thigh. Her fingertips dug into his back.

Logan's hand slipped from her waist around to her bottom, sliding into her panties. He cupped her ass and traced a finger up and down her cleft, massaging her flesh. His hips pushed into hers, slowly grinding, creating the pressure they both sought.

"I was so angry when I saw you with them. It's like I've lost control of my emotions. I've never been like this before. I can feel it. I'm changing," she admitted. "But it's more than that. I know we've just met, but I want you so much. I've never felt like this…not ever."

"I feel the same way. There's something about you. Us. You have no idea how much I want to make love to you," he breathed, kissing up the side of her neck until he reached her ear. His low sexy voice reverberated between them as he told her what he planned to do next. "Tonight, you're mine, Dr. Ryan. All. Night. Long."

"My Alpha, I'm yours," she whispered, baring her throat. Never in her life had she done this for a man, yet she knew what it meant to wolves. Open and vulnerable. Submitting to him, accepting all that he was. The man. The wolf. The Alpha. And before the night was through, she'd be his.

With a growl, Logan flipped Wynter onto her back. The sight of her submission threw his wolf into a frenzy. Grabbing the hem of her camisole, he ripped it off of her in one smooth motion, exposing her full creamy breasts. Roughly, his lips captured a hardened rosy peak. Taking the tip between his teeth, he tugged then laved it over with his tongue, groaning in male satisfaction.

Wynter gasped as he bit down on her nipple. Pain and pleasure rippled throughout her body, hurling her toward an orgasm. She raked her nails down his back, pushing her hips upward, seeking the pressure she needed. As she heard the sound of her cotton panties tearing away, she moaned.

"Fuck, Wynter. You're so beautiful," he panted as he continued to caress her. He couldn't wait to sink himself into her. "And you smell so good."

"Logan," she cried, in response to his touch.

"We'll make love slower next time," he promised, sitting up on his knees. He splayed her legs open and pulled her to him so that his cock was pressed at her wet entrance. "Look at you, so perfect."

She gazed up at Logan, allowing him access to both her body and mind. With her thighs spread wide, he swiped his thumb down her wet crease, brushing over her taut nub. She shivered in response, so close to coming.

"Your pussy is so, so wet and tight." He pressed two long thick fingers into her tight channel, and she moaned. With his other hand he continued to circle on her clit, increasing the pressure. "Ah yeah, does that feel good, baby?"

"Yes," she responded breathlessly.

As he pumped in and out of her with his hand, he took his rigid flesh and stroked himself. Without entering her, he slid his cock through her swollen lips, coating himself in her juices. Once, twice, three times, its plump head grazed her tender hood.

"Yes, Logan," she screamed. His silky hardness tantalized her clit, driving her over the edge. Exploding in an erotic release, she shuddered uncontrollably, digging her fingers into the sheets.

Logan loved how responsive she was to him. As she came, he drove his straining shaft into her pussy in one full thrust. *Fucking unbelievable,* he thought. The hot walls of her channel clenched around him like a fist, pulsating as she rode the wave of her orgasm. Logan hooked his arms underneath her knees, pulled out and slammed into her again. Like an animal, he took her over and over, encouraged by Wynter's words.

"Yes, harder. Logan. Oh God, yes!" Wynter licked her lips as she saw his thick cock disappear into her. His face was tense with restrained emotion as he pulled out and lost himself inside her once again. No other man had ever taken her so forcefully, possessing her with his passion. His power was altogether addictive and consuming. As Logan filled her completely, she was desperate for more.

Relentlessly he thrust in and out of her, increasing the pace. The harder he fucked her, the more he resisted the instinct to take her from behind. He knew that if he did, he couldn't control the need to mark her. His wolf howled in protest. She was his. But he hadn't discussed it with Wynter. Hell, he hadn't even thought about it himself. Up until now, he'd never had the urge to mark anyone in his life. Sweat beaded on his forehead, as he fought it, pushing his wolf to the side. No, if he marked her, it would be on his own terms, not the beast's. Logan cared too much about Wynter to do that to her without her permission.

Rolling them to their sides, he brought her torso to his and kissed her. A long loving kiss seared their connection. As he drove into her again and again, his fate became clear. Wynter was his. How did this happen? The question flashed and quelled. It didn't really matter. In the moment, she was everything.

Wynter kissed Logan back, feverishly clawing his ass with one hand while holding the back of his head with her other. Nothing in her life would ever be the same. The sinewy length of him stroked inside her, while the nest of his curls brushed against her clitoris. Her climax rose, and she frantically arched up against him, relishing his hard thrusts. She cried Logan's name into the darkness as her passion crested, the climax spilling over her like a waterfall.

Hearing his name on her lips, Logan plunged into her one last time. Her pussy contracted around him, massaging him into release. Groaning in ecstasy, he convulsed in orgasm. His hot seed spilled deep into her womb.

Together, they lay quietly rebounding from the soul-shattering experience they'd just shared. Logan held Wynter tightly, stroking her hair, hardly believing how incredible it had been. An unspoken intimacy bound them and neither wanted to break it.

Logan heard a small sigh against his chest. "Baby, you okay?" He kissed her hair.

"I just…Logan, you don't know," she whispered. "So close…I've never felt so close to someone. It's crazy."

"I know, sweetheart. It's okay. Trust me," he begged. He couldn't lose her now that he had her.

"I just…I can't go back." So relaxed and well loved, Wynter snuggled into his warmth.

"No, you're never leaving me. Not ever." Logan kissed her forehead as she fell asleep.

Everything had changed in his life. He thanked the Goddess he'd been able to restrain his urge to mark her. They'd have to talk tomorrow. He'd always known that someday this could happen to him, but he still wasn't prepared for it. Yet he knew there'd be no controlling destiny. For her will was too great, no matter the efforts of those who tried to resist her wishes. As he drifted off to blackness, there wasn't a cell in his being that wanted anything else than to be with his mate. *Wynter.*

Chapter Fourteen

Logan heard the thunder rumble, but it was the warmth of his mate at his feet that caught his attention. She'd woken him the best way known to a male; her soft lips wrapped around the hard length of him. *What had he ever done to deserve her?* Wynter perched over him, her legs straddling his. Ringlets of her mane scattered over his belly, obscuring his view. He pushed the offending strands aside in time to watch her take him all the way down her throat.

As she rose upward, her lips released his cock with a pop, and she lifted her eyes to meet his with a seductive smile. He hissed in response, but she didn't relent. No, she fisted him with her hand, stroking his wet shaft and lifting it so she could access all of him. Her tongue licked along the soft crinkled skin of his tightened balls right before she took one into her mouth.

Logan threw his head back into the pillow in ecstasy.

"Fuck, you are killin' me," he groaned and pumped his hips up toward her mouth. "Yes, that feels so good."

Wynter merely hummed happily as she continued her assault. Waking to the storm had been the impetus for her pleasure. Wrapped in his arms, she'd let her hands wander all over his sleeping form, hardly believing they'd actually made love. Once her fingers had discovered his hardened dick, the craving to suck him overcame her. Now as she caressed his straining erection and laved his testicles, the juncture of her thighs flooded in excitement.

She glanced at Logan, who wore an expression of strained satisfaction and then shifted her attention back to his cock. Her tongue darted out to lick the drop of seed seeping from his tip, and then plunged him back into her moist mouth, sucking and stroking the base with her hands. She loved his taste and sought to feast on him, inch by delectable inch. She moaned in protest as strong fingers on her arms stilled her actions.

"Baby, stop. Ah shit, I want to come in you," Logan grunted, easily pulling her upward. "Let me see you. Do you know that you're the most beautiful creature I've ever seen?"

Wynter merely licked her lips and hovered her hips above his. She took his throbbing erection into her hands and swiped it over her clit, throwing her head back. Logan wrapped his hand around hers, guiding his pulsing cock to her entrance.

"Fuck me," he demanded with choked desire.

Obliging, Wynter smiled, lifted upward then swiftly impaled herself onto his body. A scream passed her lips as she writhed against his thighs. They both held still but a second, allowing the enormity of him to stretch the contracted walls of her tender flesh. With a breath, Wynter slowly moved against him, her eyes on his. She struggled, unsuccessfully, to hold back the ripples of climax that claimed her.

"That's it Wyn, come for me," he grunted. "You're so goddamn hot."

Logan loved watching her come. Everything about her was unexpected and sensual. As she spasmed above him, he lifted to reach her breast with his mouth and latched onto one of her rose-colored nipples. He moved one of his hands from her waist to caress her other pebbled tip. But it wasn't enough. The need to consume her drove him insane. Releasing her swollen tip, he pressed his mouth to hers. The kiss was wild and frantic. Her hands now caged his head, supporting her weight while she bent into him. Her hips surged down onto his cock, hurling him closer to his own orgasm.

Logan rocked himself up into her, guiding her to his rhythm. His hand wandered to her ass, slowing her movements. Her loud moan against his lips stirred his exploration of her bottom. His forefinger wandered down her ass, brushing over her rosebud. As he circled the puckered flesh, he noticed only a moment's hesitation on her part, and then she encouraged him to continue.

"Logan, ah yes," she cried into his kiss. "Don't stop."

"Oh yeah," was all he could manage before gently inserting his forefinger into her tight hole. Gliding it in and out, he could feel the taut ring of muscle begin to relax.

Logan couldn't believe his little wolf was so open to this experience. *Goddess, did she know what she was doing by giving him such an adventurous mate?* Oh, the things he would do to her. Just the thought of fucking her ass was enough to make him come. Not today, though. No, he'd prepare her, take it slowly. Wynter's ragged breath and increased writhing in response told him that she was enjoying the feel of his touch. He inserted his finger all the way into her, pressing it in and out in accord with his thrusts into her pussy.

Wynter hissed at the dark intrusion that only served to amp her arousal. The pressure filling her threatened to explode. Arching her back, she cried out Logan's name, letting the strong sensation roll through her entire body. As her orgasm crashed into her, her walls spasmed around his shaft and Logan lost it.

Mark her, raced through his mind. *Bite her now,* his wolf told him. His canines elongated in response to the lupine call. He bit his lip, drawing blood, in an attempt to fight the carnal urge. Fiercely thrusting upward, he fought for breath, as he exploded into her hot core. Shuddering from his white hot release, he turned his head and licked the crimson liquid from his lips.

Falling back onto the pillow, he grunted, roughly pulling Wynter into his arms. She easily slid off his sex, immediately shaping herself to his body, like she'd been made for him. Logan's heart slammed against his ribs as he stared up to the ceiling. He'd barely been able to restrain himself. *What if he had bitten her? Was he really ready to be mated?* The woman did amazing things to him in bed, but he hadn't known her for very long at all. Just because his wolf wanted to claim her, that did not mean he had to accept it.

He needed to get his head on straight. If and when he made love to her again, he needed to show her his true nature. Rough and hard, the wolf wouldn't go easy. Maybe he needed to avoid her altogether. The confusing emotions tightened in his chest. Logan silently admonished himself for almost giving in to the temptation to mark her. It was as if he'd temporarily forgotten the bloody battles he'd endured over the past two months. His hard-fought effort to fulfill Marcel's wishes had come to fruition. The distraction that was Wynter Ryan threatened his role as Alpha. *Protect and lead my pack.* That was his destiny.

Taking a mate so soon into his reign could put that into jeopardy if he didn't lead with clarity and objectivity. Loyalty between what he felt for the little wolf and his role as Alpha warred. Fate would not allow him to deny his mate for long; he'd go insane trying to do so. He needed to figure out how to have both. Before he marked her, he'd need to carefully contemplate the ramifications as opposed to allowing a momentary lust-filled roll in the hay to dictate his future.

Wynter's breath slowed and she glanced up to Logan who appeared deep in thought. Her heart constricted. She could fall for this man in a New York minute. Logan would devour her if she let him. Ironically, that was exactly what she wanted. *Her Alpha.* She couldn't remember the last time in her life she'd ever felt so at peace.

"I don't want to leave," she said softly against his chest.

"You're not going anywhere, sweetheart," he assured her, glad she couldn't see the worry reflected in his eyes. Fuck almighty, he'd almost bitten her. He needed some distance before he did something he regretted.

Chapter Fifteen

Logan sat at the kitchen table, drinking his coffee and browsing through work emails. A solid dose of business was exactly what he needed to give him a brief respite from his otherwise chaotic life. The sound of the sliding glass door's security pad beeping alerted him that Dimitri had arrived. He looked up to see his friend, strolling into the family room.

"Hey, D. Coffee's on," he commented, not looking up from his iPad.

"Hey. Beignet?" Dimitri held up a small white bag. He walked into the kitchen, took a clean mug off the counter and poured himself a cup out of the carafe. "Where's Wynter?"

"No thanks. Wyn's upstairs. Showering."

Dimitri put a palm to his chest with a smile and closed his eyes, taking in the thought of her bathing. He lived to tease his Alpha. If Logan had found his mate, it could provide him with hours of material, at least until the novelty of having her around wore off.

"What are you doing?" Logan asked, now distracted by his beta's antics.

"Wait, oh yeah. Just picturing that in my head," he laughed. "You sure she doesn't need any help up there? I'm excellent with a loofah. Yeah, I'll volunteer for that duty any day of the week."

"You're a dick," Logan replied with a smile, shaking his head.

"Speaking of…"

"Don't say it. She could hear you, you know," Logan warned.

"So?" Dimitri sat down, leaned back in his chair and raised an eyebrow at Logan.

"So what?"

"So…how'd it go last night?"

"As if you couldn't hear?" Logan asked sarcastically, refusing to look up from his screen. Dimitri lived across the courtyard but with his preternatural hearing, he probably had heard every last moan.

Dimitri broke out in a hearty laugh. "Got me there," he conceded. He picked up a beignet and pointed it at Logan. "You know, I'm not a total asshole. And for the record, I don't exactly go listening in on your business on purpose. Believe it or not, I do have a life that doesn't include you all the time. And hey, I was very good last night. I do remember someone thanking me for being such a wonderful beta. So let's hear it. Last night she was pretty broken up. I just want to know how she is."

"Yeah, 'cause you're caring like that," Logan said, taking a long drink.

Dimitri took a bite of the pastry and waited patiently for at least thirty seconds before he added, "You know you want to tell me."

"Tell you what? That she's the single most fucking unbelievably passionate little wolf I've ever been with? I am still not over how she woke me up this morning." Dimitri was right. Not only did he want to tell him how he felt about Wynter, he wanted to tell everyone. He wanted to scream it from the rooftops. And that there, was exactly his problem.

"Let's see, D, what else should you know? How about this? She's totally distracting me from my Alpha responsibilities. Oh, you'll like this one; I almost marked her last night." Logan sighed heavily, raked his hand through his hair and clicked open another email.

Dimitri smiled quietly. His Alpha was so far gone. If he'd just give into this, things would go a lot more smoothly. It wasn't as if he didn't feel for him, he really did. It wasn't as if he was itching to be mated. But he'd watched enough wolves over the years go through the process to know that you just had to accept it. You could go easy or you could go hard. But one thing was certain; you were going…and your mate was going with you.

"What, no words? No smooth advice from my beta?" Logan lifted his head, giving him a small grin. He was so fucked.

"I could help you," Dimitri suggested slyly.

"Yeah and how's that?"

"This mating thing. I could give your wolf a little competition. Make him jealous. Kick him into drive. All I'd need to do is hug her a bit, maybe give her a kiss? Call it my beta duty. I'll take one for the team," he teased.

"No." Dimitri was enjoying this a little too much, Logan thought. Just wait until it happened to him. Big man wouldn't think it was so funny then.

"Come on. Just a little kiss. Your wolf, he'd go nuts and overrule any of that logical sludge that's cloggin' your brain. It's better that way. Get it over with fast. Just like jumping into the pool on the first day of spring; sometimes it's best to dive right in. Sure it's cold, but man, does it feel good if you just go for it. Or like a band aid. You know it's better to rip it off quickly."

"No, D. Don't even. Do not touch her," he warned lightly. "No, I just need to ride this out. Concentrate on finding this lab. Dana's killer. When it's over, I can reassess what's going on, claim my little wolf properly. I'm not an animal."

"Yeah, you kind of are, bro. You know, last night she felt pretty good in my arms. I'm excellent at comforting women," he baited.

"Don't go there." Logan flashed his eyes from his tablet over to Dimitri.

"She smelled so good," Dimitri crooned. "So soft too."

"No."

"Just sayin'."

"Leave it be, D. I'll deal with this when the time is right. I know it'll be hard to resist the urge to mark her, but I've got this." *Not really, but I'll try.*

"Does she know?" Dimitri inquired, stroking his goatee.

"No. And honestly, how am I supposed to tell her? She hasn't even shifted yet. I don't even know if she knows about being marked or mated or any of that wolf stuff. In all seriousness, I can't keep my hands off her. And as much control as I have, my friend, and I have shown great restraint, I'm not sure how long it's goin' to last…with or without your help. I fucking bit my lip so hard this morning that it bled."

Dimitri laughed again picturing that scene. Priceless. After all, it was kind of comical. Well, as long as it wasn't happening to him.

"Listen, I know I should tell her but there's a lot of shit going down. Not to mention that I've known her all of two days," he insisted. "And there's Jax, which is a whole other issue."

"I get it. Not sure what to tell you. But if your wolf wants her, you know as well as I do that it's going to be damn near impossible to deny him. It's just a matter of time."

"With Dana dead and some psychopath running around with viruses, my love life should be the least of my problems. We've gotta focus, D." Logan changed the subject. "I just got a text from Devereoux. Looks like he's found the location of what he thinks is the lab. Cagey bastard didn't give me the address. Told him to be here within the hour."

"Sure you want the vamp here? What about the office?"

"No, too many humans around. We'll meet in my conference room here at the house. Don't worry," Logan stated without emotion. "If he crosses me, he'll be leavin' in an urn."

This was exactly why Logan was Alpha, Dimitri thought. The guy could joke around with him and show compassion for his wolves, but at the end of the day, he'd tear the throat out of the enemy without a second thought. A lethal weapon. After what happened to Dana, his Alpha would take swift revenge.

"Can you get the guys over here?" Logan asked. "I'm hoping the vamp is ready with building schematics and details. I'd like to take this place out as soon as possible."

"I'm on it. Anything else?"

Logan blew out a breath and shut the cover on his tablet. "Jax. Looks like the weather up north is clearin' up. He could be here tonight, tomorrow morning at the latest. I was going to call him about Wynter, but this conversation needs to happen in person."

"Is that goin' be a problem?"

"No, just wanted to give you a heads up. Our main focus is tonight, takin' out this lab. I don't know how this thing is going to go down with Devereoux. I don't trust him, but we don't have many options. Also, we're going to have to bury Dana soon; her mom's making the arrangements. The full moon's in a couple of nights too. So I want everyone out of the city right after the funeral."

"Done."

The men stopped as soon as they heard Wynter padding down the stairs. Logan looked over to Dimitri with a knowing look and mouthed, "Not a word."

Dimitri rolled his eyes and sighed. The female really was driving his Alpha mad.

"Hi there," Wynter greeted as she strolled over to Logan. She placed a kiss on his cheek and smiled at Dimitri.

Wynter felt the cloudy skies clear after talking to Logan. No more secrets. She wasn't sure where their relationship was going, but after making love, she hoped they were meant to be. She wasn't a fool, she'd heard about mates and how it worked between wolves. Wolves could mate with wolves and even humans every now and then. But was she destined to be Logan's mate? Of that she couldn't be sure. She wondered if it was something that would just smack her in the head. Maybe after she shifted she would know?

As she looked to Logan and his beta, a rush of happiness broke across her face. She blushed like a schoolgirl. It was so irrational yet she just couldn't help how good it felt to be free: physically, emotionally, and sexually. Logan knew all there was to know of her past. So did Dimitri. Not only that, she'd been made love to thoroughly during the past twelve hours. Being with Logan drove her to new sexual heights. In the past, she'd never been so adventurous. But his touch to her skin ignited her libido; she wanted him in every way and position she could get him.

In the shower, she spent the time fantasizing about Logan, the next time they'd have sex, and actually was hoping that he'd push her further. Not that she'd had a lot of sex with other men, but it'd always been strictly vanilla. With Logan, she imagined she'd let him do anything and everything with her….except for sharing him with another woman. The feel of his fingers in her ass thrilled her, and she couldn't wait to take it further. She laughed silently to herself. She really was changing and damn, if she wasn't enjoying it.

Logan, still seated, wrapped a hand around her waist, pulled her to him and kissed her hip. It felt so good, so natural to have her in his home.

"You want coffee? Something to eat?" he asked lovingly.

"I can get it, thanks," she said with a caress to his cheek. She poured herself some coffee and took a beignet out of the bag on the counter. "So what's up? You guys are awfully quiet all of a sudden."

The men exchanged a look. How much should they tell her? Dimitri averted his gaze, deferring to his Alpha. Logan decided to tell her about tonight. She had every right to know what was about to go down.

"Devereoux thinks he's got a location on the lab. We're goin' in tonight," Logan disclosed.

"We're having a meeting here in a little bit," Dimitri added.

Wynter, determined not to let it get to her, didn't miss a beat. "Okay, I'm in. So when is the meeting? Who's coming?"

Logan coughed. She seriously wasn't thinking of going back to the lab? "Devereoux. He'll probably bring a couple of his vamps."

"I want to go with you…to the lab," she stated, popping a pastry into her mouth.

"No," both men said at once.

She nearly choked. After a chew and a swallow, she propped a hand on her hip. "I could get the data, find the blood samples, help transfer any samples. I know what I'm doing. Listen, I'm not crazy about going back in there, but someone with knowledge of viral transports has to go. That is unless you happen to have another virologist available who's just dying to go into a dangerous situation with a high probability of injury or death." She raised an eyebrow at them.

Dimitri shook his head no. Logan, on the other hand, considered her argument. This was exactly why he should not be involved with Wynter. They needed her. His heart said 'no fucking way', but the objective leader in him told him she was right. He played the scenario through in his mind. They go in guns, teeth and fangs blazing, kick some ass, tear open a vial and end up infecting the neighborhood with some unknown contagion. No, there had to be a way to take her as part of the team and keep her safe.

"Okay, you go," he decided.

"Um, Logan, maybe we should talk about…" Dimitri started.

"She goes," Logan reiterated. "Wynter's right. We'll put someone on her. She stays in the car until we've got an all clear. Then, she'll come in to evaluate the lab."

"Okay, she goes then," he agreed reluctantly. As much as he didn't want her to go, he knew Logan was right. Who else could they bring who had knowledge about viruses?

"So, it's settled. Anything else I should know? God, these things are good," she moaned, closing her eyes. Powdered sugar covered her lips.

For a brief second, Logan considered licking the white powder off her lips, flipping her onto the table and thrusting into her right there. From now on, he was so keeping a supply of beignets in the house. Damn, she was hot. And completely unaware of what she was doing. His little wolf was going to be the death of him.

Logan looked over to Dimitri whose jaw was wide open. Even his beta was not immune to the way she slid her tongue over her pink lips and inserted a finger into her mouth, moaning in ecstasy.

"D?" He snapped his fingers, trying to break him out of her spell.

"Yeah," Dimitri said as if in a daze.

"D," Logan said louder with a smile.

"Sorry." *Yeah, not really sorry.* He grinned back at Logan. "So, what were we talking about?"

Logan laughed at how ridiculous they both were acting. There was no denying that she was captivating. Sensual without being overtly sexual. Maybe the most humorous part of the whole thing was that she was his mate. As she continued licking and sucking her sugary fingers, oblivious to her effect on the males around her, it occurred to him that if Dimitri noticed, so would others. His wolf would not stand for it one bit. Sure, he might eventually share her with his beta but it'd be on his terms. And it would only happen after he'd claimed her, marked her as his own.

Logan sat solemnly at the head of the table in the conference room. When he'd renovated, he'd ensured that his office had an adjoining meeting room. Unlike the other rooms in his home, this room was uber-sleek, modern and secure. Twelve high-backed leather chairs surrounded the boat-shaped mahogany conference table. Trimmed in a black inlay, the well-oiled wooden surface gave off a sheen. A large flat screen monitor hung on the wall behind the captain's chair. Overhead, a retractable projector extended from the ceiling.

Glancing over to Wynter, he almost regretted bringing her to the meeting. Concentrating on something other than how he wanted to tear off her clothes and get her back in bed was going to be a challenge. Beautiful as always, she'd pulled her wild hair back into a ponytail, exposing her sun-kissed neck and shoulders. The spaghetti-strapped royal blue sundress hugged her breasts and fell just above her knees. A hint of lip gloss shone on her soft lips; the same magic lips that'd been wrapped around his cock earlier this morning. She looked up to him with a small smile as she played nervously with the pen in her hands.

Logan quickly refocused his attention to Dimitri who ushered their fanged guests into the room. His face hardened as he nodded to Léopold who'd brought Étienne and Xavier with him. Zeke and Jake followed, cautiously eyeing the vampires. After everyone was seated, Dimitri sat next to Wynter so that she was safely nestled between him and Logan.

Wynter heart raced at the sight of the vampires. With his typical arrogance, Léopold gave her a broad smile as if he'd known she'd slept with Logan. Her face heated as he took his time undressing her with his eyes. A glance to Logan, whose eyes were flared in anger, told her the gesture was not unnoticed. When Léopold finally stopped looking at her breasts and caught her gaze, he nodded as if to say, 'nice rack'. She rolled her eyes in disgust. Léopold may have been gorgeous, but he was trouble, big trouble. After that dance, a cautious smile was all she could manage. *Shit, this was going to be a long meeting. Why was she here again? Yeah, that pesky virus business.*

After reviewing schematics of a small abandoned factory in the Warehouse District, the group agreed on the side entrance. Wynter had tried to tell them that even though she suspected there were other scientists on the premises, the operation was small. It had to be considering the frequent relocation. Regardless, there had to be at least one room for the guards and maybe one for whoever was running the show. But Wynter couldn't be sure because she'd never left the lab.

Every time they'd prepare for a move, it was on short notice. The guard would tell her to pack her equipment. From flasks to pipettes and test tubes to beakers, everything had its container. Similar to the portable labs being used by students in a university, they hadn't relied on a sedentary lab. She wasn't sure how they made quick work of relocating the larger, high priced ticket items like the microscope, incubators and centrifuges. But like clockwork, the next lab would be set up within a day.

After an hour's deliberation, the team decided to let Léopold go in first. He suspected that someone in his line had created children for the sole purpose of protecting their endeavor. Logan was more than happy to let him deal with his own, but when it came to finding the killer, he wanted first dibs on meting out justice. It was the least he could do for Dana and Wynter.

By the end of the meeting, Logan's wolf was strung out, not at all happy with the testosterone filled room. His lips formed a tight line, listening to Léopold pontificate about how he planned to kill his children. Digging his fingers into the chair arms, he observed how Étienne stared at Wynter a little too much. At no point did the vampire take notice that the Alpha watched him like a hawk. He wasn't sure if he sensed a sexual intention or blood lust from him, but he wanted the blonde vampire out of his house.

"Enough," Logan declared. He rose and placed his palms down onto the table's smooth surface. "Devereoux, as much as I appreciate you cooperating with Acadian Wolves, I think we've covered everything. We'll meet you there at nine."

Léopold stood, giving a slight nod to Étienne and Xavier. Dimitri followed suit, intending to accompany them out of the house. As he did, Léopold boldly strode across the room, directly approaching Wynter. Logan growled, pushing in front of her.

The dashing vampire merely chuckled. "Alpha, you've found your wolf, no? I won't harm her."

"It's okay, Logan," Wynter stated calmly, determined to show no fear. She slid around Logan to face Léopold directly. Logan wrapped his arm around her waist, keeping her close to him. "Monsieur Devereoux, I appreciate your help with this. They'll come for me otherwise."

"Brave fille. No matter what you think, I won't let them have you…whoever *they* may be." He reached for her hand, and Wynter found herself allowing him to take it. Logan visibly tensed as Léopold kissed the back of her wrist, letting it go as quickly as he'd taken it.

"This is important. We mustn't fail," she insisted. Wynter brought her palm to her chest, feigning courage.

"A lost battle is a battle one thinks one has lost," Léopold stated.

"Sorry?" Wynter asked.

"Sartre," the vampire quoted. "I'm optimistic, given that they haven't moved."

"We shall see tonight, won't we?" Logan commented.

"That we will…that we will," Léopold repeated, waving a hand in the air as he left the room.

By the time everyone was gone, Logan's confidence regarding the probability of finding the killer had risen.

"Odd vampire, isn't he?" Wynter noted.

"That he is. My gut tells me he abides by some code of honor, but don't ever mistake him for anything but what he is," Logan warned.

"A monster?"

Logan smiled. "Battle not with monsters, lest ye become a monster."

She laughed. "Another quote?"

"Friedrich Nietzsche," Logan confirmed. He took her hands in his. "We have a few hours before it's time to leave. I know I should be encouraging you to go relax, take a nap or something sensible like that."

"Relax, huh? How 'bout a bubble bath? Or a massage?" She winked and dragged her finger down his chest.

"A bath sounds good to me as long as I'm in there with you." Logan pulled her flush to him, burying his head in her neck and growled. "You drive me crazy, do you know that? I can't keep my hands off you."

Wynter giggled, growing aroused, loving the feel of his warm lips on her skin. She looked over to the table and gave him a sexy smile. "My Alpha," she began seductively. "You know, I just noticed that this is a really nice table. Sturdy. Long. Hard."

My Alpha? Logan's cock thickened at her words. *The table isn't the only hard thing in this room, baby.* He glanced to its wooden top then back to her with a smile.

"African mahogany. A friend custom made it for me. You like?"

"Oh I like. I mean, it looks very functional. I bet we could get a lot of *work* done at this table," she mused with a wink. Meeting his eyes, she gave him a suggestive smile and cocked her eyebrow. She slid her hand down between his legs and cupped his hard arousal. "You know, I always wondered what it would be like to be a secretary. I've been looking around here, and it seems you're in need of some assistance."

Logan hissed, closing his eyes. Holy shit, that felt amazing.

"How about *I* fill in for your secretary today?" she asked. "I'm very good at dictation, sir."

Wynter had never in her life been so forward. But after making love to Logan, she craved him more than ever. As though she were addicted to a drug, she needed more. The warmth between her legs grew painful. Feeling flirtatious and horny, she didn't think it would take very long to entice him into her fantasy.

Logan eyed Wynter, hardly believing he could be so lucky. *His naughty little wolf wanted a romp in the office? Seriously?* His brain said 'no way', but his burgeoning erection said, 'hell yes'. He'd have to be careful not to get carried away. His wolf wanted this woman in the worst way, sought to claim her.

"Sweetheart, I don't think you know what you're askin'. My wolf, he's restless." He gently nipped at her collarbone, as if to give her fair warning. If he took her, it was going to be rough and hard.

"But I do…I know exactly what I'm agreeing to." Wynter leaned into Logan and placed a kiss to his chin then dragged her tongue along his bottom lip and kissed him.

"Do you now?" Logan grabbed a fistful of her hair, gently pulling her head backwards. Revealing her neck, he licked at the hollow until she gasped.

"I need it…need you…here…" Wynter breathed.

"Do you submit, little one?" He peppered her with soft kisses. "Is that what you crave?" He pushed up her dress, reached between her legs, sliding his fingers into her slick folds. She tried to move, and he stilled her, holding her by the back of her hair.

"Yes, oh God, yes," she cried.

He drove a thick finger up into her hot pussy, tracing small circles over her clit with his thumb. "Like this? Is this what you want? Oh, yes…yes you do. You're so wet."

Closing her eyes, she nodded and moaned. *Submit? Dominate? It was all good.* She'd do whatever he wanted as long as he made love with her now.

"Turn around," he commanded, pulling his hand out of her panties. "Hands on the table, Miss Ryan."

Wynter complied. No longer able to see, her breath grew rapid in anticipation of what he'd do next.

"That's a girl. Spread your legs," he growled. With his knee, he prodded them open. "Sorry, but these have got to go."

Pushing up her dress, he exposed her bottom. He extended a claw, easily tearing the strings of her thong. She moaned as the cool air hit her skin.

"Please," Wynter begged. Swollen with arousal, she needed him back inside her.

"Patience, baby." Logan bent forward, placing his hands on the front of her thighs and then slid them upward, taking the dress with him. "Arms up. Hands back on the table, now."

Wynter obeyed and caught a glimpse of the dress as it fell to the floor. Fully nude, she leaned over the table.

"Now that is a beautiful sight," he crooned. "I must say that I've never had a secretary like you in my entire life. I suppose you're correct. This table will do nicely. We can get a lot of work done here."

She giggled and went to turn around so she could see him.

"Don't. Move," he said tersely, trying to stifle the urge to slam into her. He was ready to come right there. But she wanted a fantasy. So he'd take his time.

"You still want to play?" he asked, confirming she really wanted this. There was no going back, once they got started.

Play? She was stark naked bent over a conference table with the door to the room open. Dimitri could walk in and see them at any time. A thrill ran through her. Was she really doing this? The old Wynter was conservative and reserved, but the new Wynter; it seemed her wolf wanted to explore and experience everything as long as it was with Logan.

"Yes, Alpha," she assured him, spreading her legs a little wider so he could see into her.

Logan bit his fist, watching her open for him. She was upping the ante, he knew. He'd see her and then some. Logan unbuckled his pants with one hand while running his other down her back. His fingers wandered over her anus until he reached the wetness between her legs. He felt her shiver under his touch.

"You've been a bad, bad secretary, Miss Ryan," he began with a wry smile.

"Yes, yes I have," she agreed. *Oh God, why wouldn't he just fuck her already?*

Logan removed his hand and slowly stood to her side. She looked up at him and smiled.

"You were flirting with my coworker, weren't you?" Her full breasts were heavy with arousal; their rosy tips hardened. Logan loved how turned on she was by their role play.

"Yes. I'm very sorry." She gave him a sexy nod and flashed her eyes at him.

"You need to learn that I do not tolerate that kind of behavior in the office. Perhaps you need a spanking?" he suggested with a raised eyebrow. Logan walked around the table leaving her all alone.

"No, no I don't. I promise I won't do it again."

"I think you might like it," he said playfully, wondering how far he should push her. This was a little kinky, even for him. Dimitri would have a field day if he came back into the house.

"Let's see, Miss Ryan. Should I punish you in private? Or," Logan reached for the doorknob but released it. As if he were deep in thought, he paused, raising an eyebrow. "Maybe you would like me to leave the door open."

She knew she should tell him to shut the damn door, but the words never came. No, she wanted the thrill of knowing anyone could come in and see them. What the hell was wrong with her? She dropped her head in embarrassment, laughing silently to herself.

"You want everyone in the office to see us? You do, don't you? You are a naughty little secretary aren't you?"

"No, I…" she protested.

"You want to do more than flirt with my clients? Two men at once? Is that what you fantasize about, little wolf?" Leaving the door open, Logan quickly rounded behind her.

"No," she lied. Throbbing with need, she began to breathe heavily. The sound of his zipper coming undone rang in her ears.

"Tell me the truth, Miss Ryan. I don't like it when my secretaries lie to me."

She shook her head in denial.

"You are a bad girl," Logan said as his slapped her ass. He could not believe he was doing this with her but at the same time, who was he to deny her fantasy?

She cried out as a sting hit her cheek. "Yes!" she yelled. *What did she just say?*

Logan gave a small laugh, wondering if she was saying yes to two men or to being spanked, and suspected it was both. The scent of her arousal made him hot with need; he knew he couldn't keep this up much longer. He caressed her reddened cheek and then slid two fingers into her hot core. Wynter pushed back on him with a pleasured hiss.

"I can't believe I hired such a naughty secretary. Goddess, this is so hot, Wyn." He broke character and kicked off his pants, letting his hard shaft press into the cleft of her bottom.

"Yes, please don't stop," she pleaded.

"Do you promise to be a good secretary? No more flirting?" He was finding it hard not to laugh. How the hell did this get started? Oh yeah, the conference table.

"Yes sir, I promise. Just keep on…ah," she moaned as he gave her what she needed. His fingers pressed in and out of her wet sheath.

"I'm going to fuck you, Wynter. Now," he growled against her neck.

The sexy whisper in her ear sent chills across her body. She panted in anticipation.

"Hard. And fast. Until you scream for more." Logan withdrew his fingers. Cupping her chin from behind, he slid the creamy digits into her mouth. As she sucked her own juice off his fingers, he placed the head of his cock between her legs.

"Logan, I can't wait. Oh my God," she sighed. Dirty talk had never been her thing, but damn if it didn't make her ache. She needed him now, filling her.

His wolf roared. Her submission and playfulness was more than he could have ever asked for in a mate. Unable to draw out their game, he slammed his cock into her from behind all the way to the hilt. He grunted, holding still for a second. He wanted rough but didn't want to hurt her.

Wynter cried his name as he filled her completely. His long thick flesh stretched her core, and she needed him to move. Gasping for air, she released a whimper, trying to get him to thrust.

"Fuck, Wyn. You make me so hot," he withdrew and plunged into her. "That's it, sweetheart. Take all of me."

"Yes!" she screamed, pressing back onto him. Letting her hands splay forward, she pressed her chest onto the cool table, allowing him to go deeper.

"Oh yeah." Logan slammed into her again and again, fisting her hair so her head lifted off the wood. He reached around, sliding his hand under her chest so that he could hold her breast.

"Fuck me. Harder," she encouraged. God, she loved making love with this man.

Logan's wolf went feral for his mate. Barely aware of his canines extending, he moved his hand from her breast to her belly so he could pull her upright. Bending his knees, he continued to penetrate her with the hardness of his sex. The sound of flesh meeting flesh reverberated throughout the room, driving them into an animalistic fervor. Guiding her head using her ponytail, he sought her mouth, sweeping his tongue into her parted lips.

Wynter craned her neck backwards, kissing him passionately in return. Her body was on fire, the hot pool of her arousal stoked by his movement. As his fingers moved from her belly down to her wet folds, she cried out again. The pressure of her orgasm was so close. Within seconds, the searing climax rocked through her body, throwing her into spasms of pleasure.

Logan hadn't planned on losing control, but in that moment, Wynter was his life. His present and future. No longer would he live his life alone. He'd blame it on his wolf, but in truth, it was the heart of the man who wanted to claim this woman as his own. As she tumbled over into her release, Logan surrendered control to her and to his own nature. With a wild cry of blissful agony and pleasure, he flooded into her, pulsating in orgasm. The walls of sanity came crashing down around him as his fangs bit into her shoulder.

Chapter Sixteen

What did I do? Fuck. Fuck. Fuck. Logan was shocked at what he'd just done, but as he gently took Wynter into his arms, cradling her to his chest, he couldn't summon an ounce of remorse. Instead, his wolf, categorically satisfied, howled in victory, invigorated that he'd marked his mate. Logan knew that it shouldn't have happened like this. But if she'd been a wolf, he wouldn't have needed to explain it to her. It was a natural act after all. Hell, in a perfect world, Wynter would have already marked him back.

Logan carried her up the stairs, quickly finding his bedroom. Before he made it to the mattress, Wynter had curled into his body like a purring kitten and drifted off to sleep. Without disconnecting, he carefully laid on the bed, bringing her with him so her head rested on his chest. Gliding a finger along her shoulder, he smiled. His bite was already transforming into a unique design. Like Wynter, it was small, beautiful and understated. Two intertwining loops had appeared; Logan likened them to linked souls, independent but co-existing as one. It was a sentimental thought, he knew, but a sense of pride clutched at his chest nonetheless.

But what was Wynter going to think when she saw the mark? A nagging twinge of concern spiraled into unanswered questions. What if she rejected him? Denied him as her mate? She hadn't shifted, after all. The concept of claiming and mating was lupine, and she still clung to human expectations and cultural beliefs. Even though she lived with Jax, she'd told Logan that he'd kept her out of pack business, away from wolves. He didn't need to think too hard about how Jax was going to react. Not that he could blame him for being irate, but eventually even Jax would accept it. As Alpha, he'd understand that wolves couldn't deny what nature demanded.

Logan hugged Wynter tightly, placing a kiss on her forehead. He silently grinned at how crazed he'd become when she insisted on role playing. It wasn't as if he hadn't experimented sexually; he'd lived a long time. But he'd never in a million years expected his little scientist to play secretary. When they'd first met, she seemed reserved, afraid of her own nudity, even. Their interaction in the pool was meant to open her to the way of wolves. But he'd had no idea how creative she'd become. The memory of how she'd looked standing naked, bent over that table….Goddess, she was sexy.

She felt so soft and warm in his arms, his heart constricted. Not only was his wolf rolling over in adoration of his mate, Logan could fall for this female. Maybe he was in lust, he reasoned. That would make much more sense. The harder he tried to comprehend the why and how of the situation, the more frustrated he became. This was exactly what he'd been telling Dimitri. No matter his wolf's desire for his new found mate, his inner conflict about it was distracting him from more pressing matters.

The last thought in his mind before he fell asleep was that he needed to get his shit together before they left to find the lab. Logan decided to talk to Wynter about the mark when they got back home. They didn't have time for heavy emotional discussions before going off on a dangerous mission. No, it would wait. Logan cleared his mind of Wynter and focused his thoughts on the killer, on what he'd done to Dana, how he'd tortured his mate. That was all it took to release a fresh river of anger, fueling the revenge he would mete out in just a few short hours.

Wynter dressed in black jeans and a t-shirt that Logan had left for her on the bed. It all seemed very James Bondish to her, but she trusted they knew what they were doing. As she pulled on her socks, she let her mind drift to Logan. When she woke, he was already freshly showered and dressed. With a quick peck to her cheek, he trotted downstairs without saying a word about what had happened in the conference room.

She breathed a sigh of relief, considering what they'd done. At the same time, she felt no regret. As if a magician had revealed the hidden dove, she'd bared her newborn sexuality. She could have blamed it on her wolf, but Wynter knew the truth. Like a caged tigress, she'd been waiting for the right man to unleash her from her prison, unlocking her true nature. Wynter laughed, thinking about how she'd encouraged him to bend her over that table. The way he'd made love to her had been phenomenal. Rough yet gentle, the passion and intimacy embraced both her body and soul. The electricity between them sizzled, threatening to burn down the room.

What surprised her the most was the way he'd tenderly scooped her up in his arms afterwards, petting and caressing her. There wasn't a moment when they'd lost physical contact. As they lay in bed, his soft lips to her forehead sent tendrils of warmth through her body. Wynter wasn't sure if he'd been aware that she'd felt every loving touch and feather-soft kiss. Emotion welled in her chest as she considered her feelings.

Wynter ran her hands through her curls and attempted to lasso her hair into a scrunchie. When she reached back to do so, she felt a small raised area near her neck. *Had he bitten her? Given her a 'love bite'?* Yes he did. And damn, that had been hot. She remembered how the slight pain had pushed her into another orgasm when he'd done it. Was that some kind of kinky wolf trick? Maybe next time, she'd bite him back? She smiled at the thought.

Wynter's focus drifted back to what they were about to do. *I'll be safe...I'll be safe.* She kept saying the mantra over and over. She knew that Logan wouldn't have agreed to let her go if he didn't think he could keep her out of harm's way. If she could just get her hands on the data, she might be able to cure Emma. As she stared at her face in the mirror, she promised to herself that she'd keep her eye on the prize.

"Brought sandwiches," Dimitri commented, taking a big bite out of his po'Boy.

"Thanks, been so busy, I haven't even thought to eat. Are Zeke and Jake ready?" Logan asked.

"Yeah, they're over at my place loading the cars. You ready?"

"Born ready." Logan sat down at the kitchen table, grabbed a muffuletta and started eating.

"Anything you want to get off your chest?" Dimitri noticed his Alpha had been avoiding eye contact with him since he'd come down, which was unusual. Yeah, Logan was definitely trying to dodge talking about something.

"Just eatin' my sandwich. These are good. Where'd you get them?"

"So how's that new table workin' for ya?" Dimitri thought he'd try another tactic. Oh, he'd heard, all right. It almost made him want to go try to find his own mate...almost.

"Fuck off, D."

Laughing, Dimitri almost choked on his food. Bingo. He'd hit the topic.

"You know that I'll never be able to concentrate in there again, don't you? Don't worry, I didn't stay for the show," he assured him, wagging his eyebrows.

"She's my mate," Logan stated nonchalantly, waiting for the ribbing that didn't come.

"Guessed as much. Does she know?"

"No way, man. She hasn't even shifted. I mean, you've talked to her. She hasn't spent a lot of time with wolves. What I mean is that even though she lives with Jax, it sounds like he keeps the pack activities on the down-low."

"Full moon's soon. She's goin' have to learn," Dimitri advised and took another bite.

"Yeah, there's something else." Logan casually placed his sandwich on his plate and proceeded to drop the bomb. "I marked her. And before you ask, she doesn't know."

"What?" Dimitri involuntarily spit his food out in surprise.

"And here's the thing, D, I know I should feel guilty or something rational like that." Logan leaned back and closed his eyes thoughtfully and then stared over to Dimitri. "But I don't. I feel fucking great. I guess I'm an asshole to feel that way. But I'm tellin' ya, it just feels good…really good. She's mine, and I want others to know it. And in that conference room, she was just so…I can't even tell you what it was like. She's beautiful. Playful. Spirited. My wolf…he just wanted her so much."

"Listen, you can't beat yourself up about this. You're a wolf. This is what we do. You know it. And I know it. It feels right because that's how it's meant to be. She'll understand when you tell her." Dimitri stood, slapped Logan on the shoulder and walked over to the sink. "So when are you going to tell her?"

"Tonight. But not until we get back. Right now, I've gotta focus on what we're about to do. Did you bring that item I asked for?"

"Yep, right there on the counter." Dimitri pointed to a holster and gun.

"Okay, thanks. Here she comes," Logan warned, hearing Wynter walking toward the kitchen. "Hey, sweetheart. D brought dinner."

Logan offered her the tray and hoped plying her with food would soften her for what he was about to suggest next.

Wynter joined them, took a sandwich off the plate and bit into it. "Oh. My. God. This is awesome. I could so live down here. Between the beignets and everything else I might weigh five thousand pounds, but who cares?" She laughed.

After a few minutes had passed, Logan stood, took his plate to the sink and then picked up the bag sitting on the counter.

"I've got something for you," he told her. He pulled the Lady Smith out of the holster and checked the safety.

"What the…?" she gaped.

"It's a gun, Wyn."

"Yes, I can see that," she stammered. "But do you really think this is necessary?"

"Yeah, I do. I'm not taking any chances. When we go in, you're staying locked in the car with Jake. But just in case…always need a plan B," he replied, continuing to check to make sure everything that he'd requested was there. Logan took the magazine out of the gun, checked it and set it down.

The reality of what they were about to do made Wynter stop and take a breath. Even though she had to do it, it would be difficult to go back to the same place where she'd been held captive. No longer having an appetite, she wiped her mouth with a napkin and pushed the plate aside.

"Come over here," Logan told her. Wynter got up from the table and stood next to him, watching him work.

"Here you go…just lift your arms," Logan instructed, slipping her arms through the black leather shoulder holster. He adjusted the straps so it fit properly. "There you go. Have you ever used a gun?"

"Well, yes, but…" She straightened her back and moved her arms, trying to get used to the feel of it on her body.

"When was the last time you went shooting?" He looked her over, waiting on her response.

"Well, it's not like I'm a sharpshooter, but Jax insisted that I have one. You know, late night in the city and all that good stuff. Honestly though, I don't carry it with me most days."

"When was the last time you used it?"

"I don't know." She rubbed her hand over her forehead, trying to think. Geez, had it been that long? "Maybe a year ago?"

"Better than nothing. Take it out and let me see you load it."

She did as he asked, and then promptly put the gun back into its sheath.

"That's a girl. Now, let's review what we've got, okay? Silver bullets. Eight in a clip. There's loaded magazines ready to go both here and here." He pointed to the ammunition pouches attached to her holster.

She nodded, but her expression didn't match her assent. Her brow knotted in worry.

"You're going to be safe, Wyn. If something happens, do whatever Jake tells you, okay? Also, there are stakes in the car. Lots of them. Take one with you when you get the go ahead to come into the lab. Just in case."

"Got it," she said with determination. Grabbing a bottle of water, she unscrewed the top and took a long drink, wishing it was whiskey. When she looked up, two large men walked into the kitchen.

"Jake, Zeke, meet Wynter. She's my…uh," he fumbled for the word. *Mate*. No, not the time. "Girlfriend."

Logan glanced over to catch her reaction. Her face flamed, and she failed to hide the smile evident in her eyes. Yep, girlfriend worked just fine.

"Nice to meet you, Wynter. I'm Jake," said the taller man. His blond hair was tightly cropped. He confidently strode around the table and joined them. If she hadn't known any better, she would have thought law enforcement. Maybe military?

The other wolf, standing at the door with his arms crossed, merely gave her a nod. His cool demeanor bristled Wynter. She wondered what his issue was, that he couldn't even offer up a simple 'hello', and determined that maybe her presence wasn't welcome. Wynter made eye contact with him and set her bottle on the counter.

"Don't worry 'bout Zeke over there, cher. He's just the muscle. Lucky for you, you've got the brains lookin' out for you tonight." Jake told her with a smile.

"When will we know if it's safe to go into the lab?" Wynter asked Logan.

"I'll send Dimitri out when it's okay for you to come in. But until he does, you stay in the car with Jake. We've got to be crystal clear on this.

Don't move out of the car until he says you can. Now, the cars…they've been specially outfitted for occasions like this. They've been custom armored. Bulletproofed. Even so, we're going with redundancy in case we run into any problems. You, Jake and I will go in one car. Dimitri and Zeke in the other."

After a long pause, Dimitri rose from the table, as did Jake. Wynter waited until Logan indicated they were leaving and tugged on his sleeve. Without warning, she hugged him tightly. Wynter wanted to tell him how she felt, worried that something bad would happen to him.

"Logan, please be careful. I…I need you," she confessed. It was as much as she could manage.

Logan cupped her cheek and tilted her head up to his. "Nothin's goin' to happen to me, sweetheart. We'll be in and out before you know it. Then we can come home and maybe we'll play 'policeman' without the gun…just handcuffs," he teased, trying to make her smile.

"Well, as long as it involves a thorough strip search, I'm in," she joked lamely.

"Seriously Wyn, we'll all be safe. Now let's go get the bad guys."

"Okay," she reluctantly agreed.

Before she knew what was happening, Logan kissed her. It was a brief loving kiss, confirming what she felt in her heart. And it could not be more simple…or complicated.

Chapter Seventeen

The short drive from the French Quarter to their destination felt as if it took hours. By the time they'd reached their location, Wynter's mind raced, hoping the operation went smoothly. With her nerves working overtime, she played with a stake, envisioning having to use it. Vampires were fast. By the time she had it aimed, they'd be at her throat. Now the gun? That would work. Maybe she hadn't used one in a while, but she reasoned it was like riding a bike. And there was nothing more she'd enjoy than blowing a big hole in one of her former guards.

The Warehouse District had experienced a renaissance of sorts. Many of its abandoned factories had been converted into trendy clubs and condos. Wynter stared at the building where the lab supposedly had been moved. Unlike its chic counterparts, the dilapidated structure looked desolate. The scratched-up tan and black logo depicting leafy sugar cane stalks was plastered on its second story brick exterior. Since it had no yard and edged the sidewalk, she wondered how they'd set up a lab without being seen.

"It's a go," Logan stated and opened the car door. He looked to Wynter then Jake. "Wait here. Don't let anything happen to her."

"I'll protect her with my life," Jake replied. He looked over to the building and back to Logan. "Looks quiet."

"Yeah, a little too quiet. Okay, gotta go. Devereoux's here." Logan watched the dark vampire step out of a black limousine. He shook his head; only a vamp would ride a limo into battle. Both Xavier and Étienne soon exited the car and followed Léopold. With a wink to Wynter, Logan shut the car door. "See ya on the flip side."

As soon as Logan walked away, Wynter crawled over the center console from the back to the front passenger seat. She glanced to Jake who was performing reconnaissance through a pair of high-powered binoculars. They observed Logan approach Devereoux and gesture for him to go first. The men walked down a side alley until they reached a black steel door. All eyes were on Logan. He silently held up his fingers. Three. Two. One.

Wynter couldn't see exactly what was going on in the dark of night, but it seemed like they entered pretty quickly. Did they break down the door? What just happened? They'd entered within seconds. It seemed all too easy.

"Not good," Jake commented quietly.

"What's wrong?" Wynter whispered.

"Door's unlocked. Feels like a set up."

"Oh my God. Can you warn Logan?" she asked, trying to keep her voice low.

"No need. He'll know. We sit tight. Here's another pair of nocs. You can help scope the area," Jake suggested, hoping the task would keep her mind off the fact that Logan was in the building.

The whole vibe felt off. Jake wished Logan would get the hell out of there. Wynter seemed to be holding up well, all things considered. He cracked the window a quarter inch, and concentrated on listening for sounds of a scuffle. The barren silence cloaked the night like an ominous premonition.

"How long will they be in there?" Wynter inquired as she struggled to focus the lenses.

"Something like this shouldn't take long at all. The building isn't that big to begin with and I haven't heard any fighting. It's dead out there."

"But that could be good, right? Maybe they just staked them really quickly," she said hopefully.

"Shhh. Did you hear that?" A tiny click was all he heard, and then silence.

"What?"

"Shhh," he whispered. "Put on your seatbelt. Something's not right."

Trying not to panic, Wynter silently pulled the strap into place.

"I can't hear anything…" she started to say but never finished the thought.

As the blast hit, the car rolled onto its side and Wynter screamed. Mercifully, blackness fell over her the second she jolted against the window.

Bodies. Six dead bodies to be precise. The stench of death hit as soon as the vampire opened the door. With decomposition well under way, flies swarmed around the maggot-covered bodies.

"Jesus Christ," Logan cursed. He held his sleeve to his face and swatted the insects away. "These are humans."

"I'm tellin' ya. This is some sick shit." Dimitri coughed for air. The smell was nearly unbearable.

Logan moved closer so he could get a better look at the corpses. "With the way they're bloating, I'm guessing they've been in here for a few days. They all look pretty young…in their twenties. What the hell is this, Devereoux?"

"Dinner," Léopold commented with disgust. He pulled out a neatly folded handkerchief and put it over his nose. "He's making new vampires. They've little control. Kill easily when feeding."

"Great. Okay, well I don't like this. The unlocked door. It's too quiet," Logan surmised. "We should get outta here."

"I believe you are correct, Alpha," Léopold agreed. No one in his line made vampires without registering them. And his tip about the lab's location was looking more and more like a trap. Never one to lose his cool, he tried to contain his rage, yet could not resist the urge to descend his fangs.

As Logan was getting ready to pull everyone out of the building, a single red flickering light drew his attention. Alerting the group, he raised his hand and pointed silently to an adjoining room. Stealthily he approached, taking care not to fall through the rotted floorboards. The wide open space was empty save for the carcasses of a few dead rats and a portable table. A black laptop sat atop; its power button pulsed a glowing beat in the darkness. As the others gathered round, Logan swiped his finger across the pad, waking it out of slumber. When the screen appeared, a single message in black and white froze on it: *'The scientifique is mine. Nowhere is safe.'* Logan's heart lodged in his throat. *Wynter.*

As fast as his feet would carry him, he ran toward the exit, screaming Wynter's name. By the time he'd reached the sidewalk, he caught a glimpse of her face through the car window as the fiery explosion detonated. Logan and the others were shoved to the ground as the shock waves hit. The roar of the blast sent rubber shrapnel flying into the air, raining down onto the street.

A split second later, Logan sprinted toward the wreckage of the SUV, which had been thrown onto its side. Through smoke and debris, he climbed up to the driver's seat door. The blackened windows obscured his view.

"Wynter!" he screamed into the car. A low moan emanated from inside it.

Logan grunted as he yanked open the door. Gas and dust from the airbag deployment wafted into the air, causing him to cough. He managed to elevate the door fully, exposing the deflated white side curtain bags.

"Hold it open," he ordered, noticing that Léopold had climbed up onto the hood to help. Léopold took hold of the door and effortlessly ripped it off its hinges, tossing it into the street.

Dimitri flipped open his switchblade and passed it forward to Logan, who knifed at the plastic. They tore off the curtain, revealing the inside of the compartment.

"Wyn! Can you hear me, baby? Say something," Logan called into the car. Silence greeted him. As the powder settled, he was finally able to see Jake, whose left arm and face were badly injured.

"Shit," Logan spat out upon seeing the damage inflicted on his friend. "Jake, hey man. Come on, wake up buddy."

With no response, Logan continued talking to him. "We're gonna get you out now. You're going to be all right after you shift."

"Cut 'em down. I'll hold him up so he doesn't crush Wynter," Dimitri suggested. Jake, secured in his seatbelt, hung downward like a marionette on its strings. Thankfully, since he was belted, he hadn't yet fallen onto Wynter.

"Ready, D?" Logan asked as he started slashing at the nylon belt. Dimitri held tightly to Jake. "That's it."

Together, they heaved their friend up and out of the car. Dimitri took Jake in his arms and laid him out on the street.

"Zeke, get him out of his clothes now. He's gotta shift," Dimitri ordered. "I'll be right back. I need to help Logan get Wynter."

Logan's breath caught as Wynter came into view. Still in her seatbelt, her head rested against the sagging airbag. Although she was unconscious, her heart still beat strongly. Logan leaned all the way into the car until most of his body was inside. When he reached the straps, he frantically cut at them.

"Wyn, sweetheart. I'm here. I'm so sorry." Logan pushed the hair out of Wynter's face and kissed her forehead.

Logan cursed; his heart tore in a million pieces seeing her like this. He'd said he'd keep her safe and he'd failed her. Guilt washed over him, and he prayed she'd be okay. He felt the emotion swell up in his chest. Seeing her hurt and vulnerable was more than he could bear. Her heartbeat was steady, but she remained unconscious. He kissed her again, this time on her cheek.

"Please, baby. Wake up now. I need you here with me. You're my…" he choked but couldn't finish.

She moaned and her eyes fluttered. "My Alpha," she whispered.

Thank the Goddess, she'd woken. He wished he could tell her right then about how she was his mate. But sanity won over and he focused on the task at hand; he needed to get her home. They could talk later.

"We're goin' get you out of here, okay? How do you feel? Are you in any pain?"

"Fucking vampires," she coughed. "Do you believe this shit?"

"Fucking vampires," he agreed with a small smile. She was a fighter. His fighter, filled with spirit. An Alpha for an Alpha.

"Hmm," she moaned. "What happened?"

"Someone set off an incendiary device. Not sure how they got it on the car, but it had to be a vampire to get it on without anyone seeing or hearing."

"Jake…he knew. He heard something."

"We'll talk about it later, baby. All right, my tough little wolf. Let's get you out of here." Logan hugged his arms under hers. "D, I'm comin' out."

Dimitri grabbed Logan's hips, helping to hoist him and Wynter out of the car. When they were finally extricated, Logan scooped her up, never letting her feet touch the ground. Logan glanced to Jake who had blacked out on the pavement. Naked, he still hadn't shifted. Second degree burns blistered along his cheek. He began to regain consciousness and groaned in pain.

"Come on, Jake. You gotta shift, man," Logan heard Dimitri say. Zeke was bent down on his knees at his side.

"D, I need you to take Wyn," Logan ordered. He couldn't believe what he was about to do.

Logan had always known that decisions weren't easy for an Alpha. Challenge after challenge, the brutal mauling between wolves had proved that fact early on in his reign. No, easy didn't equate with what was right. Even though he'd just gotten his mate back, he'd have to relinquish her. Trust his beta. Jake was his responsibility and damn if he'd let him die because he couldn't shift on his own.

Dimitri stood, sensing Logan's internal struggle. But as he expected, his Alpha put pack first, above his personal needs. Arms outstretched, he patiently waited to accept Wynter.

"Hey, sweetheart," Logan spoke softly to her. She slowly lifted her lids to look at him. "I need you to go with Dimitri for a minute."

"No," she protested with a small moan. Within the warmth and safety of Logan's embrace, she didn't understand what Logan needed to do or why he'd leave her.

"Just a minute, baby." He kissed her cheek lightly. "Jake needs me. He's burned real bad and is having trouble shifting. I promise you'll be safe with D. This'll just take a few minutes. Then we'll go home. Trust me."

"Okay," she agreed quietly.

"Do not let her go. Not one second, D," Logan instructed, his tone of voice deadly serious. His eyes locked on Dimitri's as he gently placed Wynter's body into his arms.

Dimitri cradled her head into his chest, breathing a sigh of relief. Jake desperately needed his Alpha. At this point, he was too far gone to heal on his own.

"I'll be just a second," Logan promised, running his hand lovingly over Wynter's hair.

Sirens wailed in the distance. Naturally, someone had heard the explosion and had called the authorities. Logan wanted to get out of there before the police came asking questions. New Orleans had a supernatural police force, P-CAP: Paranormal City Alternative Police. But at the moment, Logan couldn't trust anyone, not even P-CAP, to find Dana's killer. He knew they'd come to him eventually when they found the charred car, but he'd deal with that later. It'd be easy enough to tell them it had been stolen. Besides, after they found the dead bodies riddled with bite marks, they'd be busy breathing down Kade's neck for a while.

The Alpha crouched down to the pavement so that his head was level with Jake's, taking his hand. He bent over so that his mouth was inches from his friend's ear. Concentrating, Logan let his power flow, urging Jake to listen, to obey. No longer moaning, Jake could sense his Alpha. His eyes flew open, staring into space as if he was devoid of awareness. Jake's comatose expression didn't worry Logan; the mental connection to the injured wolf strengthened.

"Jake, now listen to me, buddy. It's me, Logan. You've got some pretty bad burns here. I know you're feelin' tired but you've gotta shift. You hear me?"

Jake's eyes closed and in that second, Logan's heart caught in his chest. This would go a whole lot easier if Jake was awake. Jake coughed, his eyes darted to Logan's in acknowledgement. The flesh on Jake's forearm and face had already formed boils, and Logan could feel the pain radiating off his wolf.

"That's it. Okay, we're gonna do this together." Logan began to strip, tearing off his own clothes as fast as he could until he was entirely nude. Calling on his Alpha demeanor, Logan brought forth his dominance. It was time to get his wolf to shift.

"Jake, this is your Alpha. You will shift, do you understand? No matter how tired you are, no matter how much pain you are in, your allegiance is to me and pack. On the count of three, you're going to call on your wolf. Are you ready?" In truth it was a command, not a question.

A tear ran down Jake's cheek as he gave a small jerk of his chin in acceptance. *No matter the pain.*

Logan stared into the young wolf's eyes, until Jake averted his gaze. "Concentrate, Jake. Here we go. One. Two. Three."

Effortlessly, Logan transformed into his wolf. Yet he was unable to supervise the ease of Jake's shift. But at this point, Logan didn't care whether or not his transformation went easily. The only thing that counted was that he shifted. Logan howled, his gray wolf scenting Jake's. A whine alerted Logan that, even though Jake had experienced considerable torment, the shift was complete and effectual. Logan licked Jake's snout affectionately, relieved at the outcome.

Barking at Dimitri, he signaled for the group to move out. Since the one SUV was destroyed, they'd take the other vehicle. Zeke opened the hatch and Dimitri moved to lay down with Wynter. Thinking better of it, he merely sat in the back, holding her, waiting for Logan. Jake, as wolf, jumped into the back seat.

Logan shifted back to his human form so he could address Léopold, who'd been sniffing around the wreckage.

"Vampire," Logan called out to Léopold.

Léopold approached cautiously, recognizing the Alpha was in a fierce state of protection. Between his mate getting injured and the near death of another wolf, Logan would snap if pushed. Léopold held up his palms, lowering his eyes in an attempt to get the human part of Logan to rise to the surface.

"This! This! This cannot happen again, you hear me? Unacceptable, Devereoux. Who'd you get the intel from?" he growled.

"'No worse fate can befall a man than to be surrounded by traitor souls,'" Léopold quoted cryptically. "William S. Burroughs."

"But who is the traitor? You said yourself that someone in your line was at Dana's apartment. I'm tellin' you right now, you'd better deal with this. He almost killed Jake and Wynter tonight," Logan yelled, angered by Devereoux's games. "We can't afford any more mistakes."

"He plays with us," Leo pondered. "But for what purpose?"

Logan raked his fingers through his hair and blew out a breath. As much as he hated to admit it, Léopold was right. Whoever had done this knew exactly what they were doing. They wanted to demonstrate power, drawing out the expectation of kidnapping Wynter. It was a show. And the show was meant to intimidate and instill fear.

"Perhaps, but assuming that's true, then our friend doesn't know me very well. Because now I'm just pissed. And from what I've seen of you, he'd have to be a damn idiot to take on his sire."

"Well, he wouldn't be the first to lose his head. And I mean that quite literally. This person is not a direct child, but in my line. Clearly he's a little power hungry, no? I assure you that this isn't the end. No, merely the beginning. If I have to stake every last one of my children, he'll be found."

Logan turned to leave and paused. "We need to get him before he goes for Wynter. We're moving out of the city tomorrow night. Be in touch, Devereoux."

"That I will, mon ami. That I will," Léopold assured the Alpha, fading into the darkness.

Logan walked to the SUV and sat next to Wynter. He gently took her into his arms and rolled onto his back so she lay atop his torso. With a nod, Dimitri closed the hatch, jumped in the car and they sped off toward his mansion.

Chapter Eighteen

For days, the Directeur had grown dismayed and impatient; it had proved more difficult to kidnap her than he'd originally planned. But all the negativity was now erased by a single blast, replaced by self-gratification. He puffed his chest, exceedingly proud of his plan. It had gone off brilliantly. The Alpha had been delightfully put in his place, unable to protect his scientifique. Like a fool, he'd left her alone with a guard dog. Not entirely alone, as he'd hoped. But this small display of his power would show them how weak and pathetic they all were. The arrogant ancient one would never find out it was he who led him down this path of destruction. He loved watching the vampire squirm, dreaming of the day he'd stake him into ashes.

He silently rejoiced as the Alpha was forced to relinquish his mate. As he predicted, the Alpha would save the burned wolf. The dogs would always choose their pack over her. He restrained himself from laughing at the irony. The mongrels would never accept her, because she'd never truly be wolf.

The ungrateful little bitch would learn soon that it was his hand that had granted her the supernatural gift. The Directeur closed his eyes, reveling in his genius. His great experiment had been spectacularly successful. The full moon would rise soon. And his creation, like a caterpillar turning into a butterfly, would transform. The final test. Ideally he'd have her within her cage in time to witness her shift. They'd celebrate together, making love well into the night. She'd be eternally grateful, begging to live out her life as both his lover and colleague. With their extraordinary minds at work, they'd perfect the viruses in no time at all. His fangs descended, aroused by his musings. As he walked away, he smiled. Very soon, his scientifique would be in his arms, thanking him for his loving gift.

"You can put me down. Really, I swear I'm fine," Wynter insisted. Logan had carried her from the car all the way into his bedroom. She looked down at her arms, which had been scratched by the airbag. "It's amazing. I'm healing already."

"Indulge me." Logan entered the bathroom and sat her on a settee, one he had argued with the decorator to be unnecessary at the time. "See, we're already here and now we're going to take a nice hot bath. Then it's time for bed."

The walls and floor of the enormous bathroom were inlaid with black Spanish marble. It housed a blocked glass shower, modern bamboo vanity with double sinks and separate area for the toilet. An oversized, square-shaped Jacuzzi edged the rear wall of the room. Logan had thought, like the settee, that it had been an unneeded extravagance. Yet the tub he'd finally agreed upon was modern and masculine. Reaching over, he turned the spigot on and returned his attention to Wynter.

"Let's get you undressed first," he suggested, helping pull her shirt off over her head.

"You don't have to tell me twice. I feel so dirty from all the smoke," she told him and started to take off her clothes.

She unsnapped her bra, unzipped her pants and let Logan pull off her jeans and panties in one swift tug. She smiled, realizing that even though Logan had set her down, he'd never once lost physical contact with her.

"Okay, you first. Here we go. Is it too hot?" Logan lifted Wynter up and eased her into the steaming water.

"Feels so good," she breathed. Whatever soreness remained from the accident seemed to melt away.

Logan undressed quickly, taking time to throw their clothes into a laundry chute. Seeing that the tub was nearly filled, he turned off the spigot.

Wynter's eyes roamed over his incredibly well-toned body as he readied to join her. When he turned, she smiled, admiring his broad shoulders that tapered into the smooth muscles of his back and buttocks. His bronzed skin accentuated his exquisite musculature. Logan spun around to face her, and the vision of his washboard abs and hardened chest nearly took her breath away. Like the lithe and powerful animal he was, he advanced toward her. Spellbound, Wynter's eyes fell to his semi-erect cock and then back up to his eyes. Logan shot her a sexy smile, and she knew she'd been thoroughly caught ogling. But she didn't care. This was her man, her Alpha. All hers.

Logan loved that his little wolf enjoyed watching him, but he fought his own arousal. She'd just been in an accident, and he planned on pampering and caring for her, not jumping her bones. But he could tell she had other things on her mind besides bathing. And the way she looked, so beautifully naked and wet, it would be damn difficult to resist her.

He hissed as he stepped into the bath, and slid behind Wynter so that he could feel her in his arms. Spooned perfectly in place, he moved his hips slightly so that the length of him fit nicely against the cleft of her bottom. Logan couldn't seem to get enough of her, and he wondered if the urge would ease once they fully mated. When the car had exploded, he thought he'd die himself. It was then he realized the full extent of his feelings for his mate and the implications of losing her.

Without speaking, he softly rubbed her shoulders. Logan couldn't resist lifting her hair, revealing his beautiful mark. He knew he needed to talk to her about it and hoped she wouldn't be mad. Reaching for the small bottle of shampoo, he began washing her hair. He smiled when she released a small moan as he started to massage her scalp. Logan couldn't remember ever doing this for a woman, and it excited him to know that she appreciated the small gesture, an intimate yet simple task. He lovingly caressed her springy curls and rinsed them in turn.

"Logan," Wynter eventually spoke. "Thanks for getting me out of there tonight."

"You don't have to thank me. The minute we walked in there, we all knew something was off. I should have just left."

"Did you find anything?" she asked.

Corpses. Logan opted to tell her about the computer instead. "The place was empty except for a laptop. Dimitri grabbed it. It's probably wiped. But if they left anything at all, D will find the crumbs. Let's hope they got sloppy."

"Really, nothing else?"

"No, I'm afraid it was all just a ploy to get to you…to us. Devereoux's a pain in my ass, but he's right, they're trying to play with us. Intimidate."

Wynter didn't respond, thinking of how easily they'd gotten to her.

"Hey, let's not talk about this anymore tonight. We've got other things to talk about. Lots of things, actually," he disclosed. *My mark. The fact that you're my mate.*

"Okay."

Logan took the bar of soap and lathered his hands. "We should probably talk about tomorrow." He blew out a breath. "We've got Dana's funeral. It's here in the city. At twilight."

"Don't wolves usually have some kind of special thing they do? I mean when my parents died, I remember going to Jax's country house. Mom and Dad weren't wolves, but Jax, well, he did it his way," she explained. "Buried them on his property. They've got headstones but he told me that wolves don't."

"Well, yeah, that's true. We usually bury the body on our land. 'From the earth we came and back into the earth we go' and all that stuff. We use scent and then later, memory, to know where someone's been buried," Logan described. "But Dana, she's a hybrid. She was pretty much raised by her human mother. Her father died in a challenge when she was younger."

"What happens during a challenge?" Wynter asked.

"Anyone can challenge an Alpha if they want to lead the pack. Honestly, though, it doesn't happen very often." *Except when you become Alpha like I did.* "You fight…as wolf."

"Do challenges always end in death?"

Logan paused, wondering how much he should tell her. Marcel had killed Dana's father during a particularly nasty battle for power. Everyone in the pack knew and accepted the fact without bitterness. It was pack law. He himself had threatened to kill the next wolf who challenged him, to quell dissension.

"Not usually but occasionally it happens. Not all with wolves is dark, nor is it light," he asserted. "The bottom line is that too many challenges to the Alpha disrupt the flow of nature. When it's going on, there's no peace. It's not good for anyone in the pack."

"Yeah, I can see how if people are always peckin' at the Alpha, they wouldn't ever feel like they could rest. I mean, how is the Alpha supposed to be leading if he's always in a sparring match?"

"So like I was sayin', Dana's mother raised her. And her family's plot is in St. Lafayette cemetery. She'll be interred there."

"But why at sundown? Don't the cemeteries close at night?"

"Yes and that's exactly why we prefer it at night. She may have human family, but she's got us too. Wolves may want to shift. We don't need spectators or tourists. No, this'll be private. It may not be what I would want for myself, but the least we can do is support Dana's wishes. Generations of her kin have been put in that plot."

"I'll come with you if you want," Wynter offered quietly.

"Of course you will, sweetheart. I'm not leavin' you alone for a second," Logan told her with a kiss to her shoulder. "After we leave the funeral, we're taking off. Goin' bayou. It'll make it harder for this psycho to find you. Plus the full moon is in two nights."

"It is?"

"Yes, it is. But you know that, don't you?" he chuckled.

"Yes. But that doesn't mean I want it to come. I mean, who knows what's going to happen to me? Could be anything. Or nothing."

"Or something in between. Either way, I'll be there for you, Wyn. No matter what, you can count on me," he said with conviction. "You can trust me."

"Logan," Wynter paused. The thought of shifting was terrifying. "I'm scared. I know I can't control what's happened. But I do…I trust you.'"

Logan's heart warmed at her words. She really did trust him and not just with the shift either. Yet he still hadn't told her that he'd gone and marked her. That wasn't the kind of man he was. To go any longer withholding the truth would not only be disingenuous but could forever fracture their relationship.

"Listen, Wynter, I've got to tell you something…something I should have told you earlier," Logan began.

"Hmm…yes.' Wynter reached out, seeking Logan's wrist. Once found, she wrapped her hands onto his forearms, and brought them around her waist.

"Today, in the conference room." How the hell was he supposed to tell her he'd lost control?

"Ooh, is this dirty story time? Because that one is my favorite," she joked, trying to lighten the mood. All the talk about the funeral and death weighed heavily on her mind. "Once upon a time there was a wolf and his secretary. I love this one."

Logan laughed. "Well yes, something like that." He cleared his throat and dramatically continued. "Once upon a time, there was a smart and sexy princess who was very brave. This princess, she'd been captured by terrible monsters; monsters who wanted to keep her in their tower. But the princess outwitted the monsters and escaped. The monsters were angry and roamed the kingdom looking for her. But a prince found the princess and rescued her. And he slayed the monsters."

"Ah, sounds like a very interesting premise. Seems as though I may have heard this one before," she teased.

"You see when the prince rescued the princess, he thought she was the most beautiful and courageous girl he'd ever met. The prince, he was quite taken with the princess. But it was complicated because there were many others who wanted her." Logan wasn't sure where he was really going with this story but thought he might as well keep at it.

"One day, the princess and the prince decided to make love…in a conference room," he laughed. *How corny could he get?*

Wynter also chuckled. "Here comes the dirty part."

"Don't laugh. The princess had been a naughty girl, and in the prince's defense, he can't stop thinking about her. He cares about her very much."

"Does he now?"

"Yes, you see, even though they like making love," Logan cringed at how he was going about telling her. *Almost there.* "The princess, she's in his heart. He's been alone a very long time. The princess, she makes him feel alive. He wants her, like no other woman. She is his. He just knows."

Wynter's breath caught. She knew full well she was the princess. And he was the prince…the prince who wanted no other. *What was he trying to say?* She prayed he wasn't going to break her fragile heart.

"So what did he do?" she asked innocently.

"Wyn, I've got something to tell you." Logan spun Wynter around until she straddled him. Face to face, he'd tell her what he'd done. "I know this seems a little fast, but my instinct never fails me. We've only been together a few days, but when you're a wolf…sometimes your wolf, it knows things." Goddess, he was fucking this up.

Wynter searched his anguished eyes. What was he trying to say?

"Earlier today…in the conference room. You need to understand, the urge was so strong. I should have talked to you but it just happened."

"What happened?" Wynter asked in surprise.

"When we made love today…it was amazing. I'd been fighting it, but I just couldn't any longer. I know I should be sorry but I'm not. I care about you…a lot. I want you to stay here with me," he told her.

"What, Logan, what did you do?" she whispered, taking his face into her hands. As she leaned into him, her breasts brushed his chest. Her lips were mere inches from his.

Logan held her eyes, distracted by the caress of her soft nipples against his chest. *Concentrate. This is how you got into trouble in the first place.*

"Logan," she repeated, her eyes growing concerned.

"I marked you, Wyn. Goddess help me, I did. I know we should have talked about it, but it just kind of happened. You and I… today… it was so intense, so fucking perfect. And before I knew it, my fangs were at your shoulder."

"So am I really your girlfriend?" she asked. A coy smile broke across her face. A small part of Wynter wished Logan had shared this information prior to biting her, but a bigger part, her heart and wolf, rejoiced.

"Yes you are. But Wyn, it's more than that. You do understand, right?" She thought this was funny? Jesus almighty, he'd been full of angst over telling her and she was joking?

"I know it's important to wolves. But you know I'm not all wolf, at least not yet." She stole a quick kiss, catching him off guard. "Guess that means you're my boyfriend."

"Yes I am," Logan agreed, pulling her toward him. "And so much more."

"My Alpha."

"Yes, that too. But, sweetheart, there's no one but you for me. And me for you," he tried to explain.

"You know, when we made love, I felt it. The princess, she loved that kinky wolf thing." She gave him a sexy smile and winked. "So tell me, prince, does this mean that I get to bite you back?"

The thought of her teeth at his neck caused his cock to jerk to attention. The wolf within paced, craving her mark. He howled at Logan, wanting to declare that he was her mate. But Logan reined in his wolf. Wynter had accepted that he'd marked her, but he could tell from their conversation that she didn't understand all the implications. How could he expect her to really know, given that she'd been human? Perhaps it would be better to just let her adjust to the idea that she was his girlfriend. After all, they'd just met. She hadn't even shifted yet, nor had she met his pack. There were many factors that could affect a successful mating, and he knew it.

"There's nothin' I'd like more, sweetheart, but you're going to have to wait until after you shift."

She frowned.

"Hey, I didn't make the rules. I just follow 'em."

"How about we start making some rules of our own?" She pressed her lips to the side of his neck directly underneath his earlobe and speared her fingers through his hair. Sprinkling kisses downward, she began to writhe her hips over his. "Now that I know you like conference tables, tell me, what do you think of bathtubs?"

"Bathtubs?" Logan grinned. "Bathtubs are great. But are you sure you feel well enough? How's your head?"

"I'm feeling so much pain. It's terrible," she purred, rubbing her breasts up and down against his chest. "But I'm afraid rest isn't the medicine I need."

"Ah, I see. Perhaps we need to play doctor. Sounds like you need one…hell, I think I need one. You're clearly not the only one suffering." If he didn't get inside her soon, he thought he'd explode.

"We can't have that, now, can we?" she teased, biting at his lower lip. God, he tasted good. His hard slippery body was all hers and she intended to explore every square inch of him.

The last string of Logan's restraint snapped as her teeth pulled at his mouth.

"Hold onto me. Wrap your legs around me," he demanded as he hoisted them out of the tepid water. Capturing her lips, he kissed her passionately, sweeping his tongue against hers. Within seconds, Logan was out of the tub. He pressed Wynter's back flush to the wall, clutching her by her bottom. She moaned in appreciation; the roughness sent a lightning bolt of desire to her pussy.

"Fuck yes," she cried as he moved his lips from her mouth to the crook of her neck, peppering her with kisses.

"I can't control myself around you. Bedroom," Logan grunted.

He wasn't sure if he was talking to her or himself at that point. He'd almost taken her against the wall. A shred of sanity reminded him that she'd been hurt earlier no matter her protest that she was fine. The wall could wait for another day. Without watching where he was going with her, he clumsily made his way over to the bed. They fell into it together with Wynter's legs wrapped around his waist.

Logan rolled Wynter onto her back, straddling her hips. Kissing her neck, he began to slowly move downward until his face rested in the valley between her breasts. He sighed in amazement; he'd never get used to how beautiful she was. He cupped each breast, bringing them together so he could easily move from one nipple to the next. Tracing his tongue along the outside of her right areola, he brought the taut peak into his mouth, gently sucking, before repeating the process on her other tip, tenderly making love to them.

Wynter lolled her head backwards, electrified by the sensation of his kisses to her skin. When he took her breast, the aching in her womb threatened orgasm. Not wanting to come so quickly, she raised her head and opened her lids. Logan, lavishing attention on her pink nipples, looked up and caught her eyes. Connected in a gaze, Logan slid downward. Still holding her breasts, he kissed her abdomen, making sure to leave no spot unattended. When he reached her pussy, he gave her a naughty smile.

"Sweetheart," Logan darted his tongue through the seam of her wetness. "I'll never get enough of you. You have the sweetest, most beautiful pussy…and it's mine."

Wynter gasped as Logan pressed two long fingers into her core, stroking the length of her nerves. She contracted against him, the urge to come rushing over her.

"Logan," she panted. She was close, so close. "Oh God."

Parting her labia with his other hand, Logan sought out her sensitive hood. Finding his prize, he lapped at her clit. The second he felt her tighten around his hand, he suckled harder, using his tongue to flick at her nub. Relishing her juices, he moaned, creating a vibration that pushed her over the edge.

Wynter saw stars as her orgasm crashed onto her. Lifting her hips into his mouth, she sought all he had to give. Unrelenting, his rough tongue stroked her until she was thrashing on the bed, splintering into a thousand pieces. Calling out his name was her only relief; the pleasurable assault had left her breathless yet still yearning for him to fill her with his love.

Logan licked his lips, enthralled by the taste of her cream. Slowly ascending his mate, he took in the sight of the pink lips that he'd made so swollen. Divine. Wynter's legs fell open to his body, allowing him to rest between them. Taking his cock in his hands, he stroked himself through her slick folds, drawing out a few more shudders from her.

"Wyn, sweetheart," he uttered. Her eyes flew to his. "Feel me. Feel us."

Logan thrust his rock hard shaft into her hot core. Wynter gasped at the welcome intrusion, bringing her arms around his waist. As he plunged in and out of her, she raked her fingers down his back.

"Ah…" Logan cried. "Fuck yeah."

"You're mine," she whispered into his ear.

The wolf in him roared. Her words ignited his passion to new heights. The controlled rhythm came to a halt when he pulled out.

"Logan," she protested.

He effortlessly flipped her over until she was on her knees. Holding her up by her belly, he guided her into position.

Wynter wanted this, for him to take her, make her his. Blind to him, the waiting drove her insane as she presented herself to him. She felt the cool air at her opening.

"Yes," she screamed as he thrust into her.

"Aw yes, take me, Wyn." Logan sucked a breath, trying not to come. She felt so incredible, fisting him tightly. Seated fully in her, he held still for a minute trying to regain his composure. With one hand wrapped around her waist, he used the other to pet her back, running his fingers down from her shoulders to her ass. As he slowly started to move, he cupped her bottom, letting his thumb brush over her tiny rosebud.

"Please," Wynter heard herself begging. The pad of his finger at her puckered flesh sent sparks flying all over her skin. She wanted to be utterly filled, and sought his touch.

Sensing Wynter's signal, Logan inserted his thumb into her tight hole, slowly but surely penetrating her. He found it incredibly hot to watch his finger disappear into her and sucked a breath at the sensation. It was as if he could feel her walls tighten around his cock in response.

"That's it, sweetheart. Is this what you need?" he crooned, knowing it was.

She moaned in pleasure. "Yes, Logan, don't stop," she pleaded.

"That feels so good to me too, baby. Your ass is so perfect. I'm going to fuck you here soon. Do you want that?" He continued plunging his hard arousal into her in tandem with his hand.

"Hmm," was all she could manage to say. The overwhelming sensation of being filled rocked her world. If she thought she could take his cock in her ass, she'd tell him, but she knew she needed more preparation to do that.

When she didn't respond with words, Logan withdrew his finger. "Tell me, Wyn. Do you want me to stop? Do you want my cock in you…right here?" He traced the pad of his thumb around her puckered skin, waiting on her answer.

"Yes…don't tease me," she cried, pushing backward.

"Oh yeah, someday soon, baby. I think we need to get you a toy," Logan told her. Without missing a beat, his hand found her again, reentering a digit into her anus. Pressing in and out, he added a second finger. Everything constricted as he did so, causing him to shake. Fuck, he was going to come.

The fullness in her bottom and pussy bombarded Wynter. She trembled as the ripples of ecstasy rolled through her body. Screaming Logan's name, she continued to shake as she collapsed into the bed.

Heaving and fighting for air, Logan thrust one last time, acquiescing to his earth-shattering release. Spilling himself into her, he rolled them to their sides so that he could spoon her. His incredible, resplendent mate had taken his heart and soul. He silently celebrated, aware that he was falling for her.

Chapter Nineteen

Wynter woke to the sound of yelling. Immediately recognizing his voice, she jolted out of bed. *Oh my God. Jax is here. Where are my clothes?* She tore across the room, opening Logan's closet doors. He'd neatly placed her bags in the corner and had even hung up a few of her dresses. How long had he been awake? She heard curse words through the shouting. Not good. She yanked a sundress over her head, thankfully managing to put on her bra and panties in her panic. Throwing the bags aside, she slipped her toes into a pair of flip flops. As fast as her feet would carry her, she tore down the hallway and descended the circular stairway.

"She's sleeping. And for the last time, she's fine," Logan shouted at Jax.

"What the hell did you take her for? Goddammit, you should've known this could happen," Jax yelled, pacing Logan's family room. "If you don't go up there and get her right now, I'm doing it myself."

The strikingly handsome New York Alpha's eyes flared in animosity. He ran his hand over his platinum-blonde hair in frustration. Jax was pissed that Wynter had gotten hurt trying to find a cure for Emma. He was even angrier with himself and felt guilty for every last thing that had happened to her, getting kidnapped and now being taken by the New Orleans' Alpha. It was entirely his fault. He should have never allowed her to go work for ViroSun. He should have more thoroughly investigated them. Jax had promised her mom and dad, his longtime friends, that he'd watch over Wynter. Yet, he'd fucked up royally, gone and sent her into a bloodsucking hellhole.

"You'd better stand down, right now, Chandler. For your information, we had to bring her, because she's the only one who knows about this little virus you kept secret. And for the record, you're the asshole who sent her off with vamps. You are the reason this happened to her, not me. So you'd better just calm the hell down," Logan growled and turned his head to the hallway. He sensed immediately when she came into the room. Logan caught a glimpse of her blond curly hair rounding the corner and swore. "Shit."

"Jax!" Wynter screamed in delight. God, she had missed him.

"Princess!" Jax called out, opening his arms to her.

She jumped into his embrace, and he spun her around. Wynter, oblivious to Logan, hugged Jax tightly. Crying in happiness, she pressed her face to his shirt.

Logan growled at the sight; Dimitri caught sight of his Alpha about to attack and held him back. *What the fuck was she doing? Did they not just have the*

'I marked you' discussion? How the hell could she touch him so intimately? Logically, Logan knew that Wynter hadn't slept with Jax, that he was merely her guardian. But as he watched her in the arms of another man, he didn't give a damn. Jax was a single wolf. A male. An Alpha male.

All reason was lost as he watched his mate mold her body to Jax. Like a match to kindling, his anger flared in both jealousy and betrayal. But he refused to be reduced to a dog groveling over a bone. He wasn't about to trash his home over a hug. Logan was nothing if not self-disciplined. The challenges had forced him to become the master of restraint. Logan's jaw tightened as he forced his beast into submission.

"Get off me," Logan spat at Dimitri.

"You okay?" Dimitri asked, unsure whether or not to release his Alpha on Jax. An unmated male wrapped around another man's mate could turn a situation ugly pretty quick.

"I'm fine." He shrugged out of his hold, and stormed toward Jax.

"Get away from her," Logan instructed. Barely restraining the urge to punch Jax in the face, he took a deep breath, fisting his hands at his sides.

"What?" Wynter asked, bewildered. Shocked by Logan's dominant tone of voice, she stilled.

"I said. Get off her, Jax. She's mine," he warned.

The words resonated with Wynter. Realizing the implications, she fell out of her embrace with Jax but still held tight to his hand. Was Logan angry? She didn't understand what was happening, but instantly comprehended the fury in Logan's eyes. Slowly releasing Jax, she wrapped her arms protectively around her waist. Why were they fighting? Jax's fingers on her shoulders alerted her that he, too, was upset. As his hands left her skin, she registered the hurt in his eyes. Or was it guilt?

It took all of two seconds for Jax to understand why the Alpha had gone feral. He grabbed Wynter by her shoulders, brushed her hair away and just as quickly released her.

"You goddamn marked her? Are you fucking kidding me?" Jax exclaimed indignantly. "My Goddess, Wynter, did you agree to this?"

"I…I." Wynter found herself cowering. Digging deep, she mustered the courage to face him. "Yes, I mean, no. But yes, when I found out…Jax, I care about Logan…a lot."

Logan's face visibly relaxed, but she was still too close to Jax. He knew what Jax was going to say next.

"You marked her and didn't talk to her? What the fuck, Alpha?" Jax walked around the sofa, fell back into it and grabbed his head with his hands. "No, don't even tell me anything else. This can be undone. Wyn, you can come back to New York with me. It will take a few months but you'll get through this. It'll fade and you can find a suitable wolf."

Logan looked to Wynter, and they both addressed Jax at the same time.

"No."

"Jax, stop it. I'm not going back to New York. I just told you I care about him. He's claimed me and I'm happy. You just need to accept this," Wynter said softly. She didn't want to challenge him but there was no way in hell she was returning to New York. She needed to be firm on that point. Wynter loved Jax, but she wasn't going to let him steamroll her decision to be with Logan.

"Oh, you'll go back to New York," Jax promised.

"No I won't," she countered.

"You will go. As your Alpha, I order you to go back to New York with me. Do you understand, Wynter Isabelle Ryan? Staying here with him is not an option. You are going to turn into a wolf. You have no choice but to obey me," Jax told her, giving her a hard stare.

Logan watched the interchange, trying his best to let Wynter handle it. Telling Jax she'd made a choice to stay with him warmed his heart. And Jax needed to hear this news from her, not him. But when Jax attempted to give her a direct order, Logan chose to intervene.

"She's my mate," Logan stated confidently. "And as such, you cannot order her to obey you. She's mine. I'm her Alpha."

Wynter's jaw dropped at his words. *Oh my God. What did Logan just say?* She was his mate? Wait, wasn't that something you asked someone first? She couldn't be sure of those nagging wolf rules, but wasn't that like an engagement of sorts? Her mind warred between smacking him or throwing herself at him and tearing off his clothes.

"What?" This was getting better by the minute, Jax thought. He closed his eyes trying to concentrate. How could this have happened? He should have known better. The Alpha wouldn't have marked her otherwise. But still, he had to ask. "Are you sure?"

"I am," Logan insisted, his eyes locked on Wynter's.

This was so not the way he'd imagined himself telling her. Hell, he'd hardly had time to come to terms with it himself. He watched the conflicting emotions play across her face when he'd said the word: mate. Logan swore to himself he'd make this up to her somehow. He shouldn't have done it like this. Even though he'd never been mated before, he damn well knew that it wasn't something you just announced in a room full of people without talking to your mate about it. Granted, mated wolves didn't always come to the realization at the same time, but it was treated with sanctity, with respect. Given the situation, Jax gave him little choice. There'd be no way he'd ever let him take his mate to New York.

"Well, fuck me," he heard Jax say. "I still can't believe I allowed this to happen. You're right about one thing, Logan; I should have never let Wynter go work for that company. I will be forever sorry for that. Wynter should have..."

"I am right here, you two. Oh my God. There's so much testosterone in this building you'd think we were at a bull fight." Wynter was pissed. Not only would she have appreciated the 'will you be my mate?' discussion in private, she was mad at Jax for thinking he could have simply pulled that 'Alpha is ordering you' bullshit. She hadn't seen that side of Jax since she snuck out her bedroom window at sixteen to go to a party with her friends.

"Listen up, both of you." She didn't care at this point whether she challenged them or not. This was her life they were discussing as if she were a child. Having enough, she glared at them and held up her fingers, ticking them off as she spoke. "Number one. This is my life. Not yours, oh great Alpha, Jax. And not yours either, oh great mate of mine. Number two. I am not going to New York. Do you remember why I am even here, Jax? For Emma. Was it the best plan in the world for me to go in there alone? Obviously not. But I'm a scientist, not a cop. And we've still got work to do. And whether you like it or not, I care about Logan a lot. And not like friends. We're lovers. And despite his apparent lack of ability to inform me of these important wolf thingies, like 'hey I want to mark you' or 'hey, I think you are my mate', I want him…He's an incredible person and from what I've seen, a great Alpha. Saved my ass more than once. I think you owe him a little respect."

Wynter blew out a frustrated breath, waiting for the other shoe to drop. She'd been so mad; she hadn't given too much thought as to how the Alphas would react to her heated lecture. Both men glanced away in embarrassment, from time to time, as she pointed out what they'd done. Logan's eyes fixed on her as soon as she'd told Jax they were lovers. Her heart warmed, seeing him smile. She wished she could stay mad at him for at least an hour, but his sexy expression melted away her resolve like sun on ice. She looked away to collect her thoughts, and caught Dimitri sitting on a kitchen stool grinning at her. *Glad he's finding this so amusing.* Unfortunately she wasn't finished giving the two Alphas a piece of her mind.

"And third…third, we all need to work together for Emma's sake. I don't know what they've done, but I was close. So close to finding a treatment. Not a cure, but something that would give her quality of life. Buy me time to work further on it. I need you both to do this. Please. This isn't about me anymore. We've got to get the person who killed Dana. The person that wants to turn my knowledge into a weapon."

Logan bit at his lip. Goddess, she was magnificent. And right. She definitely had a point about Jax. If Logan took Wynter to the country, he could entrust Jax to help cover the city. Aside from Léopold, he needed an ally, someone who understood the enemy and wasn't a vampire. Before he and Jax had gotten into a shouting match, they'd actually had a civilized discussion about Wynter turning wolf and had strategized for an hour about what to do next. But when he told him about what had happened with the explosion, Jax demanded to take Wynter back to New York. Before he knew it, they were arguing over Wynter like two kids fighting over a piece of candy. He rubbed his hand over the back of his neck and sighed.

"I'm sorry. You know I care about you. I'll respect your choices." Jax paused and glanced to Logan. "And your mate. But I still want to talk with you. Alone."

Logan shook his head and rolled his eyes. The guy really didn't give up. He supposed that after everything he'd done for Wynter over the years, he was entitled to have alone time with her. *But take his mate away from the safety of his home? From him?* No fucking way. Logan raised an eyebrow at Wynter in hopes she'd feel his emotion. Since he'd marked her, he'd started to sense her state of mind; confusion, anger and sadness swirled through her consciousness.

"Logan, I want to talk with Jax for a little bit. We need time," she pleaded.

"Fine, you can talk here. I'll go to my office," he countered.

"Alpha, don't take this the wrong way, but I want time alone with her in private. You and I both know there is no such thing as private as long as we're here," Jax argued.

"I'll go," Wynter decided. The truth was that she needed to have a heart to heart with Jax. As loath as she was to leave Logan, she wasn't sure she could do that knowing he was listening to their every word. She wanted privacy.

"Wynter, do you really know what you're asking?" Logan responded angrily. His mate was leaving with another unmated male, one not from his pack. His wolf snarled, wanting him to refuse her.

"Yes I do. You need to remember that I'm not all wolf yet, *mate*." She didn't mean to sound bitter but she couldn't quite forgive him that quickly. "I won't be long, but I am going."

Logan approached her like a stalking panther, his eyes wild and his mouth tight with anger. Placing his hands around her waist, he pulled her against his chest. Ever so softly, he pressed his lips to hers but never deepened the kiss. It was a goodbye kiss, one he hoped she'd regret. But he wasn't going to keep her against her will. She'd come to him willingly or not at all. When he released her from his embrace, Logan's demeanor seethed in dominance.

Wynter, still reeling from the kiss, brought her fingers to her lips. She hated that Logan was so angry, but he needed to understand that she owed Jax. The least she could do was grant him a few hours of her time.

"Funeral's this evening. If you aren't back, I'm coming for you, sweetheart," Logan vowed fiercely, his gaze fixed on hers. He watched her quietly nod and turned to address Jax. "Take care of her, Chandler. I'll be in touch."

Affronted, Logan supposed that perhaps Wynter did need to talk with Jax, but that didn't mean he had to like it or agree with her. He'd decided to let her go as a penance of sorts, given the way he'd fucked up telling her about how they were mates. But when she returned, they'd have a long discussion about loyalty, because she wasn't showing a whole lot of it by going off with Jax.

"D, make sure they get to Jax's hotel safely. Wait for her," he ordered. Logan shot Wynter an icy glare before he turned to walk away.

Wynter's eyes brimmed in tears as Logan took off down the hallway toward his office. None of this made sense. Torn, she questioned her feelings for both Jax and Logan. Deep in her belly, the connection with Logan grew stronger every minute of the day. She'd called him Alpha and meant it. But with Jax here, a conflicting sense of what was right confused her. Since she'd told Logan she planned to go talk with Jax, she supposed she needed to go and get it over with so she could return on time.

The way Logan had spoken to her left her wolf trembling. It was as if she could literally picture her rolling in submission, exposing her underside. Despite her desire to acquiesce to the commanding Alpha, she wasn't entirely wolf. Her human psyche continued to pay credence to her reasoning by telling her that Jax was her guardian, not Logan.

Dimitri slid the door open with a loud banging sound, and gestured for her and Jax to leave. As quickly as she caught his eyes, she averted them. Damn, Dimitri was angry with her as well. Well wasn't that just great? She swore she'd fix things when she returned. But for now, she'd made her bed and had to lay in it. Exhaling loudly, she walked through the door and out of Logan's home.

They rode in silence back to the hotel. Wynter ignored Jax, staring aimlessly out the window. Ten hours ago, Logan had made love to her. Within the strength of his arms, she'd belonged. As her feelings grew stronger, she could feel herself falling for him. But now, his words played in her mind. *Mate. She was his mate?* It wasn't as if she didn't desire Logan, but the revelation, in front of Dimitri and Jax, no less, had shocked her. She wondered if by going with Jax, Logan had interpreted her actions as disrespectful, as if she'd chosen him over her mate.

Even the ever-jovial Dimitri had been cool, refusing to look at her when she'd entered the car. The minute she'd stepped away from Logan, it'd felt uncomfortable. Her wolf clawed and whined, giving her a raging headache. It was all she could do to keep from crying. As if sensing her anguish, Jax slowly put a comforting arm around her shoulder. No matter what had happened in her life, he'd supported her. This was why she needed to go talk to him. So why did it feel so awful?

"Come on, Princess," Jax coaxed. "It's not all that bad, is it?"

"Then why do I feel like shit?" Wynter laid her head on his chest and glanced up to catch Dimitri's frosty glare. She quickly closed her eyes, trying to ignore him.

"Because my dear, he's your mate. Your wolf, she won't like being away from him, especially since he's not marked," he explained casually. "Sorry, I reacted poorly. It's just you and I; we've been together for a long time. I'm not ready to let you go."

She smiled.

"And I'm not used to you being a wolf…not at all."

"I don't know what they did to me," she confided. She felt like a little girl again, hoping he'd chase her nightmares away.

"Logan told me all about it. We'll find out, Wyn. I don't understand it either. But what's done is done. I promise you'll make it through this…your shift."

"But you were so angry back there."

"More like surprised. I consider you mine, but you aren't really…well, not at all now. You were almost like a daughter at one time. But over the years, we've grown into a comfortable friendship. I'll miss you. I suppose I always knew this would happen. But it won't change my being protective of you. That's in *my* nature. Can't be helped," he reflected.

"Logan's so angry with me. I feel bad."

"Don't worry, we'll have you back in no time, your wolf will calm down."

"And what about his wolf? I feel like I did something wrong. Not just wrong, but like I hurt him," she told Jax.

"No, Princess, you didn't do anything wrong. But it does rub against the way of wolves. You agreeing to come with me is a very rational, human thing to do. A very Wynter thing to do. Can't fault you there. And me asking you to go…well, I knew Logan wouldn't be happy, but you're my family. I haven't seen you in months. Goddess, Wynter, I'll never forgive myself for letting you go," he confessed. "This is my fault."

"No…" she began to cry.

"Shhh, I won't hear it. You were my charge. My responsibility. Logan was right. When we get back, we can have lunch and talk about how I can help you both with this colossal fail we've created. The one thing that drives me is that Emma's still hangin' on. And if there's something we can do without putting you into harm's way, then I want to do it."

Wynter wanted to argue with him and tell him that she already was in danger, but she assumed he knew that. It was why he'd been freaking out at Logan. Meanwhile, Logan had done nothing to deserve the death they'd brought to New Orleans. Guilt racked her, but still, after everything that had happened, she wasn't sure she would have done anything differently.

By the time they got up to Jax's suite, Wynter was famished. Opening the door, a warm, familiar face greeted her.

"Hey missy, welcome back. Come on now, give me some sugar," Jax's beta, Nick, told her, giving her a big hug. "Why the sad face? What's wrong?"

"Long story," Jax sighed, taking a seat at the large dining table. Thank Goddess Nick had had lunch delivered. "Sit, let's eat."

"Talk and eat. What gives?"

Jax looked to Wynter. "Do you want to tell him?"

"Abridged version? The vampires who kidnapped me made me work on the virus, but I escaped. Logan Reynaud, the New Orleans' Alpha, rescued me then took me into his home. Apparently the vamps infected me with something during one of their lovely feeding sessions. So, by the way, I'm turning into a wolf." Wynter paused to grab a diet soda. She twisted the cap off, took a drink and snatched a wrap off the tray. "Let's see, what else? Oh yeah, the vamps are still trying to kill me, Logan marked me and I just found out I'm his mate. Yeah, I think that pretty much sums it up."

Both Jax and Nick exchanged a look of surprise. Although she'd been shaken in the car, she appeared to be recovering nicely. She had always been a fighter, Jax knew. But every time she rebounded, it still amazed him that a human so fragile could have the bravery of a lion.

"So, wait, have you mated, have you bonded with Logan?" Nick practically shouted.

"No," she shook her head and pulled her hair aside to show him. "Marked. As in he marked me. Apparently I have to wait until after I shift. So looking forward to shifting…not."

"It'll be okay, Wyn. The way your Alpha tore into me today, I have every confidence he'll protect you. He's an honorable wolf," Jax assured her.

"You say that as if you like him. Just a while ago, you guys almost ripped each other's heads off. It was a real love fest, Nick," she noted with sarcasm.

"That's what Alphas do. We jostle for territory, establish dominance. What you saw today, that was child's play, nothing more."

She rolled her eyes. Men. Wolves. "Well, Logan was good and pissed at me when I left. Some mate I am."

"Yeah, I bet that went over well. Jesus, Jax. What were you thinking taking her away from him?"

"I'm a selfish prick, okay? What do you expect? I haven't seen her for months. Besides, she'll go back after lunch."

"I'm the one who decided, Jax. He's my mate." She nearly choked on the word, tears threatened. The longer she was away, the worse she felt. A change of subject was in order. "Tell me about Emma. How's Mika?"

"Mika's good, really good," Nick winked.

"No way!" Wynter exclaimed, slapping his arm.

"Way," Jax replied. "Bad wolf, Nick."

"No, Alpha, I'm a very good wolf. Why do you think she likes me so much?" Nick teased.

Wynter couldn't believe her friend had hooked up with Jax's beta. How could she have missed that one? She fought the urge to call Mika right then and there. God, how she missed her.

"As for little Emma, well, she's hanging in there," Nick commented. "Good days, bad days. I don't know, Wyn. She's about the same. But damn, I wish we knew what was wrong."

"I'm close. Although I haven't done anything since I escaped the lab. But we've got a laptop. They got it before the car exploded." She tried not to react to Nick's pained expression as she mentioned what had happened. "Jax can fill you in on what all happened…fun times. Anyway, that laptop could have my data on it. Or not. We'll see. The vamps scrubbed it but Dimitri's going to try to recover it. I would have asked this morning how he was making out with it but well, you know…with all the yelling and whatnot, that didn't happen."

"A cure?" Nick posed the question.

"No. 'Fraid not. But it'd give her quality of life. She could lead a normal life again with medication," Wynter speculated. It wasn't a panacea but it would be a far cry from spending her days bedridden.

"Logan told me he's taking you out of the city. Said he's setting up a lab at his house," Jax mentioned.

Wynter stilled. Seemed her sneaky mate was always two steps ahead of her. No wonder the man was Alpha, she thought. "A lab, really, he said that?"

"Yes, he's very committed to helping you, us. Of course, he doesn't want whoever is doing this to proliferate a virus. But he mentioned Emma. He wants to help her…for you." Jax smiled. "It didn't make sense why he was going to such a great extent to help us when I first spoke to him. But that was before I knew you were his. And just like that, all the pieces came together."

Wynter's face flushed like a schoolgirl, thinking of Logan. She really could fall in love with him. No matter what had happened this morning, they'd work through it.

"Ah, love is a wonderful thing," Nick declared with a broad smile.

As if caught with her hand in the cookie jar, Wynter looked down and shoved the wrap into her mouth.

"Wyn, in all seriousness, if you aren't in agreement with this mating, you don't have to stay here. I mean, I'd have to be an idiot not to feel the chemistry between you and Logan. But if you're having second thoughts, you, as a wolf, aren't required to mate with him. This isn't the dark ages," Jax explained.

"What?" Wynter looked up and found both of them staring at her.

"Do you love him, Princess?"

"Maybe," Wynter blurted out before she had a chance to take it back. She decided to backpedal but as she considered how she felt, it was hard to deny her feelings. "I mean I think I could fall in love with him. He's just so caring and loving and larger than life. It's unbelievable. I don't know how this happened."

Nick and Jax both laughed.

"What?"

"Nature, baby," Nick remarked.

"You can't control it," Jax said. He leaned back into his chair and sighed. "Love, she will come for all of us, and there isn't a damn thing we can do."

"I wish we'd talked about this before…this wolf stuff." She smiled, at a loss for the correct terminology. "It's just that even though I can feel something in me, what I think is my wolf…but I feel human too. I know why you wanted to protect me from wolves, from the pack, but now, I'm so alone."

"No, never alone. Your Alpha, he's there for you, to guide you, to love you," he corrected her in a serious tone.

"But how do you know? How do you know I'll be fine?"

"Logan may be a new Alpha, but he's been a beta. And he's been a wolf for a very long time. You must trust him." Jax fell short of telling his lovely human friend that she'd need to submit.

All wolves in a pack must submit for order to exist. She'd learn in time, but he suspected she might have a rough go at it. He'd love to help her, but it was something she needed to do on her own. No lecture could teach that life experience.

Wynter continued eating, considering Jax's advice. The more she thought of Logan the more she missed him and sought to smooth over their disagreement. The look in his eyes when she'd gone with Jax tore at her heart. After another thirty minutes of catching up, Wynter told Jax that she needed to go. He assured her that he wasn't leaving New Orleans and was on call should they locate the lab again. Jax walked her down to the lobby where Dimitri was waiting to take her home. Giving Jax a hug and kiss to the cheek, she quickly departed, walking over to the awaiting car.

Dimitri held open the back door as if he was a chauffeur. Ignoring his gesture, she slipped around him and into the front passenger seat, waiting for him to join her. Apparently, Logan wasn't the only one who needed to talk. His cold disposition had not warmed since she was gone. If anything, he'd spent some time in the freezer. Dimitri slammed the back door and strode around to his side. He sat down, buckled up and started the car without looking at her.

"What? Just say it already," she ordered, like the alpha female which she was becoming.

"Why'd you go with him?"

"I told you already, he's like family. And just because I'm Logan's mate, he's still my friend. I haven't seen him in months. Why do you care anyway? It's not like I'm your mate," she snapped.

"Because darlin', when my Alpha's unhappy, and he's very unhappy at the minute, we all feel it. I know Jax is your family, but you've gotta see what this does to Logan," he pleaded.

"I'm sorry, Dimitri. I am. I didn't mean to upset Logan, and I certainly had no idea you'd be affected. You have to remember that I'm new to this," she said softly. Wynter placed a caring hand on Dimitri's shoulder. "And to be fair, Logan has his own explaining to do. This is not all my fault."

"Yeah, sorry about that mating business."

"Sure you are. You looked real broken up about it earlier. That smile of yours…geez. It really wasn't funny." She gave him a small grin.

He smiled in return, recalling the conversation and laughed out loud.

"I love Logan but man, watching him fall for his mate is kind of funny…very funny actually. You have to give him credit, though. He'd rather risk you being mad at him by telling everyone you were his mate than let another wolf take you away. And he's a new Alpha…going up against Jax like that. Logan is one tough motherfu….well you get the idea."

"I'm glad you were entertained. Because me…I was pretty surprised that he kind of just blurted that out. I mean, it's not like I don't really like Logan. He's incredible. Loving and sexy and…" she said, dreamily, until Dimitri cut her off.

"But the commitment, Wyn. With wolves, it's more, so much more."

"You've marked someone? Mated?"

"Hold on there, cher. No way. Let's just say that like Logan, I've been 'round a long time. Watched my fellow wolves fall deep into their mated bond. Sometimes it goes smoothly. And sometimes," Dimitri paused, concentrating on his driving as it had begun to rain, "well, not so much. But I'll tell ya, it always goes. Because Mother Nature, she gets her way. No use fightin'"

"How mad is he?"

"Logan? Scale of one to ten?" He contemplated. "Ten when you left. Maybe a seven or eight now. And here we are…home."

Wynter cringed. *Would he forgive her? Would he punish her?* Like vampires, wolves had their own interpretation of life's rules. As the gate slid open and they drove into the carport, her stomach flip-flopped. Was he waiting for her? What should she say to him? The car stopped, jolting her back to the present. Dimitri opened the door for her and they both ran into the house, in an effort to escape the downpour. The sliding glass door opened. She hoped Logan would be expecting her, yet she was greeted with silence.

"Upstairs," Dimitri told her, his hand still on the door. He wasn't planning on staying for whatever was about to go down between Logan and Wynter. Even though he loved Logan like a brother, there were things he had to do on his own, and this truly fell in that category.

"Thanks," Wynter whispered. Brushing a kiss to Dimitri's cheek, she fled to her Alpha, disappearing around the corner and up the staircase.

Chapter Twenty

Logan felt her the second they drove onto the property. Silently he breathed a sigh of relief she'd returned, but struggled to understand how she could have left him in the first place. While he fully comprehended her familial relationship with Jax, he'd claimed her. Any true she-wolf would have never gone off with an unmated male wolf under similar circumstances. But Wynter wasn't really a wolf yet. Even if she was about to transform, she hadn't been raised wolf, wasn't even a hybrid. She couldn't possibly appreciate the ramifications of her actions. Logan wanted to forget, forgive, but he simply didn't have that luxury.

Already, he'd spent too much time with Wynter. After nearly killing himself to secure his position as Alpha, he should be leading his pack, not worrying about a human. If she were only a human, it'd be an easy decision. But no, she was his mate. A mate who knew essentially nothing about wolves. What kind of sick joke was the Goddess playing? Logan wondered what would happen if he rejected fate. Maybe he was wrong about her being his? He wished. Whenever she was within five feet of him, his wolf clawed to mate her. There would be no denying him once Wynter shifted.

In the meantime, he resolved to focus on the pack. Convulsing in rage over Wynter's departure had hurt them. Every wolf would have felt his anger, wondering what had caused his virulent excitation. They'd stress, which was the very last thing the pack needed. After the long months of mourning Marcel and enduring the uncertainty of who'd lead them, he'd finally established peace. Today, though, his temper threatened the sanctity he'd worked so hard to create.

The hot spray of the shower had allowed him time to meditate, bringing a sense of balance and stoicism to his thoughts. The solace of his newfound impassivity clarified his strategy. He and Wynter simply could not continue down a path of misunderstandings. There was no other choice. When they got to the bayou, Wynter would learn to submit, learn the way of the wolves. He'd teach her lessons, not just in acquiescence but the importance of her role within the pack. Whether she liked it or not, he fully anticipated her wolf would emerge at the full moon. He'd prepare her for their new life together. As the Alpha's mate, the pack would look to her for guidance, direction. But in order for her to fulfill her role, she must accept him as Alpha and her own transformation.

Her footsteps at the door excited his wolf, but he refused him access. Now was not the time. Dana's funeral started within the hour, and his calming presence was required. Logan planned to do nothing less for his pack, even if that meant isolating Wynter. The rumination over the quandary would wait. For at least a few hours, he planned to ignore her, focus all of his attention on Fiona and the pack. It was the least he could do.

Wynter's heart caught in her throat, seeing her magnificent Alpha at the mirror. Incredibly handsome didn't begin to describe how she saw him. Black pinstripes ran the length of his long legs. His trousers hung easily on his tapered waist, hugging over his bottom, a crisp white dress shirt tucked into them. She watched as he knotted his tie, never losing focus from his task.

"Logan," Wynter called tenderly.

"The funeral's at six. Dimitri and Jake will take you. Once you get there, stay with Jake," he explained coldly. He turned, took his suit jacket off a hanger and dressed.

"We need to talk," she pleaded, walking toward him. The need to touch him overwhelmed her.

Logan adjusted his collar, giving himself one last look in the mirror, never seeking eye contact. He ignored her request and sought to leave the room.

"You'll need to pack your things. You can use the bag I left you in the closet. We're leaving immediately after the burial."

As Logan passed by, Wynter grabbed onto his sleeve, pressing her forehead into his chest. God, he smelled so good. She wanted to apologize, ask for forgiveness, but also talk to him about being his mate. There were too many questions. She needed him to quell her fears, confirm he still cared.

"Please, Logan. Don't do this," she whispered.

Logan tugged his arm from her grasp, calmly backing away. Indifference washed over his face. No longer was the lover present, but the leader; the Alpha commanded the room.

"Get dressed. You have forty-five minutes," he said, looking at his watch.

"Jesus, Logan. Come on," she felt her voice escalate. "I need to talk to you."

"Right now, Wynter, this is not about you. Or me. There is a woman, a wolf. My wolf," he stressed in his dominant tone that told her he was all business. "She's dead. My pack needs me. They need me strong, whole and calm. I can't do that when I'm with you. Not now."

Wynter hung her head and closed her eyes. She wished she could hide her face from him entirely. His withdrawal was too much to bear. She bit her lip; the pain was a welcome distraction from the suffocation blanketing her crushed heart.

Logan could sense her pain as clear as if it were his own. He wanted to take her into his arms, tell her they'd work it out, and then make love to her all night long. Gathering every ounce of willpower he had, Logan turned and walked out the door. After the funeral, she'd be his, he promised himself. Until then, the pack held his full attention.

As Logan walked out the door, Wynter allowed the tears to flow. As if swept into a storm, she no longer knew which direction she was traveling. Having lost her only life preserver, she struggled to keep her head above the swelling waves, yet it wasn't enough. She stumbled into the bathroom and turned on the shower, allowing the cold water to pelt her skin. She slid down the wall, until her bottom hit the floor and she crawled into a ball, sobbing, wishing she had never heard of wolves.

"What's up?" Dimitri nodded to Logan, handing him an umbrella.

"Good, here comes Jake," Logan responded, not answering Dimitri directly.

Jake slid open the door and shook the rain off his head.

"Hey," he greeted. "Nothing like a rainy funeral in the dark. Good stuff."

"Yeah, I don't expect many of us to shift if this rain keeps up," Dimitri added.

"Alpha, you okay?" Jake asked with genuine concern. The anger rolling through the pack earlier had rocked them hard.

"Yeah, I'm good," Logan lied. "I should be asking how you're doing. You took a hard one out there last night."

"Good to go. Thanks to you," he nodded. "Hurt like a motherfucker. Stayed wolf all last night, though, just to be sure I was okay."

"I'm gonna walk over to Fiona's and meet the girls there," Logan told them.

Dimitri cocked an eyebrow at Logan. "Hey man, let me preface this by 'I'm not tellin' you what to do'."

"But you're going to anyway? Let's hear it."

"That's what your beta is for." Dimitri clapped his hand on his shoulder. "First, it's raining cats and dogs. You could just take the car with us. Second, you think it's a good idea to be around the girls without Wynter? I mean, this mating thing doesn't seem to be going so smoothly for either one of you and I'd hate to…"

"I'm not going over there to fuck them, D. Fiona's sister died. I'll be careful not to touch them a lot, but let's be clear, okay, tonight is about Dana. Not me. Not Wynter. And it's sure as hell not about my mating," he huffed. "And yeah, this whole mating thing is not exactly what I thought was going to happen, but then again, I never thought in a million years that my mate was going to walk into my life as soon as I became Alpha. I certainly didn't expect her to be human."

"Yeah, not optimal," Dimitri concurred.

"I'll deal with this…with Wynter, when we get out of the city. I'm not looking to hurt her, but I've got to be with the pack. You know this. Fiona. Luci. They are pack and need me too…especially tonight."

Logan slid open the door and righted the umbrella.

"As for a little rain, it never hurt anyone. Might actually do me some good to breathe in the petrichor. Love it."

"Petrichor?" Dimitri asked, shaking his head. Someone had been doing crossword puzzles again. A strange stress reliever for his Alpha, but whatever it took.

"The smell that comes with the rain, my friend, the smell. Nothin' better." Logan laughed and pressed open the black canopy.

Dimitri laughed but then his thoughts turned dark. He hoped his Alpha worked out things with Wynter sooner than later. He'd caught the wince on Logan's face upon hearing the faint sound of crying coming from his little wolf upstairs. They'd both tried to ignore it as if it wasn't happening. He knew Logan was giving his full attention to the pack, trying to concentrate on maintaining a sense of tranquility for them. And it wasn't the time to get involved between him and Wynter. Sometimes it was better just to let the dust settle.

He looked into a mirror that hung in the kitchen and adjusted the knot in his tie. He hated funerals. Luckily he hadn't attended many for wolves, but still, many of his human friends had passed over the years. As he glanced down at his black shoes, ones that seemed uncomfortably tight, he sighed, knowing what the night had in store for them all. The funeral was going to be as much fun as…well, a funeral.

Within minutes, the clicking of heels let him know Wynter was ready. She rounded the corner, dressed in black with a small tote in her hands. Wet ringlets surrounded her reddened face. Wearing no makeup, she still looked beautiful and determined. She made low maintenance look chic, Dimitri thought. Unsure of what to say, Dimitri gave Jake a knowing smile and went to the closet. Logan had bought Wynter some things she'd need for the trip, and he'd asked him to give them to her.

Wynter had pulled it together after a five minute crying jaunt. Angry and confused, she refused to let life or her lack of control over it hold her down. Ever since her parents died, she'd been fighting. She wasn't sure if or when she'd work things out with Logan, but she still had a purpose: get the data, work on a treatment for Emma. Her other goal was to get through the shift. If Logan rejected her because of a human mistake, then she'd leave and go back to New York. As Jax had explained it, she didn't have to mate him if she didn't want to do it or if he decided a human wasn't suitable for an Alpha's mate. She'd be devastated but she'd get through it. Like the loss of her parents, like being held captive and tortured, she'd dig deep and continue with her life. Self-preservation was a strong motivator.

As she glanced down to her black oxford shirt and matching pencil skirt, she wondered if Logan had selected the outfit himself. And what if he didn't? What if he'd asked those women to do it for him? She shoved the nasty green monster to the back of her mind. No, she would not go there. Still, it hadn't been with the clothing Dimitri had originally brought her to wear, nor were the black leather pumps.

She sighed. None of this really belonged to her. It was merely an illusion of reality. Her life had been stolen. Everything she'd had in her purse was gone, taken by her captors. Smoothing down the soft fabric of her sleeves, she made a mental note to contact Jax's secretary to have her forward her mail. She also needed her home laptop in order to report her credit cards stolen. Every last shred of her personal information was digitalized. His secretary could just download the info and send it to her. She could purchase a new laptop online, but she still needed a cell phone. Maybe tomorrow, she'd arrange to go to a local cell phone carrier where she could purchase a new one.

Dimitri's hand on her shoulder startled her out of her daydream.

"Here, Wyn." Dimitri held up a royal blue trench coat. "Go ahead, put it on. It's nasty out there."

Gratefully, she shrugged into the garment, noticing it was from Burberry. As she buttoned it up and buckled the thin black leather belt around her waist, she considered how she'd never splurge on something so extravagant. She looked up to Dimitri who attempted to give her a black patent leather clutch. Was he giving her someone else's purse?

"But this isn't mine…I mean I lost my bag…" she started.

"He knows. Here take it. I'm guessing it's got all the basic lady stuff in it," he surmised, turning off the kitchen light. "A gentleman doesn't go through a lady's purse."

"Since when are you a gentleman?" Jake joked.

"Hey now, go easy, bro. I am so a gentleman." Dimitri laughed and turned back to Wynter. "And before you ask, Logan got these things for you. I swear, that wolf shops more than a woman does. But then again, you can't walk two feet around here without running into a store of some kind."

"Thank you," she replied thoughtfully.

Logan shopped for her? She wasn't sure why the thought of him doing so made her feel a little better, but it did. The man surprised her at every turn. It made her feel that even if he'd been mad, he'd still cared enough to think of her. A flicker of hope sparked. As she headed out, safely between Jake and Dimitri, the sound of thunder clapped in the distance. She'd have to wait until after the funeral, but later tonight, she hoped they'd talk about what had happened.

A police officer ushered the crowd into the cemetery as the sheets of rain sliced through the lights of his emergency vehicle. The crowd of nearly a hundred people carefully shuffled through the narrow stone walkways. Battery operated lanterns illuminated the pathway toward the crypt. Between the cracked pavement and pebbles, Wynter feared she'd take a nosedive into a marbled tomb. She wrapped her hand around Jake's arm in an effort to steady her feet. Unable to see ahead, she wondered how the jazz band managed to continue playing in the deluge. Yet the funeral dirge pounded a sad beat into the night.

By the time they neared the tomb, the music ended. The small space was thick with people and Wynter struggled to find a spot to stand, settling against the cold stone of another's resting place. Creepy, she reasoned, but there was literally no room for all the living who had come to mourn. Through the bodies, she spotted Logan, who stood next to Luci. Her hateful eyes bore into Wynter. Surmising that Luci was engaging her in some kind of sick wolf intimidation, Wynter stared back as if to dare her to touch Logan. Thankfully, their gaze was broken as all heads turned to watch Fiona and an elderly woman, Dana's mother, make their way toward the casket. Logan had explained to her that Fiona was Dana's half-sister; they shared the same father. Yet Fiona appeared close with Dana's human mother as well.

The smell of incense permeated the air as the priest blessed the tomb. The stone tablet had been removed and the rectangular opening had been draped for the service. The older woman sobbed openly, clutching on to Fiona as the final prayers were said. Wynter leaned her head forward, trying to hear the sermon. Upon a final 'Amen', a word passed between Logan and the priest, silencing the crowd. Her heart caught as she realized Logan was about to speak.

"My wolves," Logan began somberly. "Dana. She was our doctor. Our friend. Our sister. She will be missed by our pack. But always remembered. We knew her as hybrid, but she was as much wolf as any of us."

"And that is what got her killed!" Dana's mother screamed, lunging at Logan. Fiona scrambled to hold onto the old woman, but she slipped from her grasp. "Wolves! You killed my husband! My daughter! I hate you!"

Logan easily caught the woman's wrist as she attempted to slap him in the face. "Marguerite, please. I know this pain. I know," Logan cried. "Don't ever think for a moment I don't. Marcel. Dana. We all miss them."

"My baby, Logan, my baby," the woman wailed as she fell into his embrace. "Oh God help me."

Wynter watched intently as Logan cried along with the old woman. It was evident that he knew her well. It was as if Logan's heart had been splayed open for all to see, but he didn't deny the woman's grief. No, he mourned with her, held her until she calmed. Others wept alongside them as the torrent fell from the skies.

Wynter's feet began to move before her brain had a chance to process what she was doing. A sharp tug on her arm reminded her of where she was. Tears stung her cheeks as Jake pulled her toward him. Her wolf sought to comfort her mate, to care for him. But it wasn't just her wolf, it was Wynter. Every part of her being needed to soothe him. As if Logan sensed what was happening, his eyes pierced the crowd and locked on hers. Both unable to speak or move, it seemed as if centuries passed while they locked in a gaze. The roar of a thunderbolt caused her to look up to the heavens, losing eye contact.

Logan felt Wynter's concern, but it was the touch of an unmated male that caught his attention. But soon, he realized Jake was holding her back. She was coming for him. The caring expression on her face told him how much she needed him. The unspoken encouragement from his mate drove him to continue. Releasing the woman back to Fiona, he touched a loving hand to Dana's coffin.

"Dana, my friend. You will never, ever be forgotten. Your death will not go unpunished. I promise you, as I stand here today," Logan's voice cracked as he fought his emotion, "you will be avenged."

As he spoke his last words, Dana's mother nodded in approval. The funeral director gestured for his workers to remove the draping. Logan gave a silent signal to Dimitri that it was time to place Dana into her final resting place. Six men held the casket by its handles, lifting it gently into the tomb's upper vault. As it disappeared into the dark chamber, Fiona, and Dana's mother led the procession of people to the exit while the sounding trumpets played, 'When the Saints Go Marching In'.

Surreal as it was, Wynter watched as the people poured back into the narrow paths, silently thanking God no one had been struck by lightning. As if all the air had left her lungs, she struggled to make her way out of the cemetery. She concentrated, putting one frozen wet foot in front of the other. Small fingers grasped her wrist, and she peered under the umbrella to see Fiona standing in front of her.

"I am so sorry for your loss," Wynter managed genuinely. If anyone knew loss, it was her.

"Thank you for coming. I know it mustn't have been easy," Fiona related with understanding. "I'll see you in a few days."

Unsure of what to say, Wynter dipped her head in acknowledgement and gave her a sympathetic smile. A gust of wind pushed both women onward toward the exit. Wynter gasped for breath and held tight to Jake, stumbling through the icy puddles. Jake pointed to a waiting limo, and she blindly followed. Relief filled her as a car door opened, and she fell, shivering, into its warm confines. Jake quickly pressed his hip to hers, forcing Wynter to move over into the next seat. As the heat hit her feet, she glanced up to find Logan staring at her.

Chapter Twenty-One

Wynter's stomach dropped as the elevator lurched toward the sky. She didn't understand why they were in Logan's high-rise, but kept quiet on their ascent. Fighting the claustrophobia, she closed her eyes after it passed the floor where she'd first met Logan in his office. A resounding jolt forced her to focus on the opening doors. Rain blew into the small chamber, causing her to gasp. What the hell? Instinctively, she covered her ears upon hearing the deafening whirl of the helicopter blades. Wind hit her face, and she stopped, frozen in disbelief. A small push between her shoulder blades put her feet back in motion, propelling her toward the blinking lights.

The pressure from the spinning rotors sprayed air and water onto them as they crossed the helipad. Wynter felt Logan wrap an arm around her waist, guiding her into the dimly lit cabin. Shocked as she was, she was relieved to be out of the weather. The soft tan leather seats felt smooth on her palms. She took in her surroundings, noticing that the luxury helicopter had four seats, complete with plasma TV screen and bar. Peering forward, she spotted a pilot through the small privacy glass.

Logan sat down next to Wynter, closing the door after Dimitri. Having never been in a helicopter, panic rose in Wynter's throat. She looked to Logan and Dimitri who both appeared solemn but altogether calm as if they'd done this a million times. But of course they have, she thought to herself. Meanwhile, all she could think about was crashing in the middle of the night inside the little tin can. A very lush, expensive tin can, but still it was night and it was raining. Both of those factors could not be good, she reasoned.

"Why are we..?" she began to yell over at Logan, her face white with fright.

He reached behind her seat and grabbed a pair of headphones. Ever so gently, he placed them onto her ears, gliding his thumb down the side of her cheek. Wynter gazed into his eyes, wanting desperately to talk with him about what had happened, but as she went to open her mouth, he looked away and put a set on his own ears.

"Why are we taking a helicopter? Are you sure this is safe?" Wynter asked, her voice laced with alarm. "It's raining."

"Not optimal but it's let up some. Besides, the wind has died down and there's no fog. We don't want to take any chances getting ambushed on the roads. Don't worry, it's safe."

"'Bout forty-five minutes to an hour, if the weather cooperates. You've never flown in a whirlybird, cher?" Dimitri inquired with a relaxed smile.

"No I haven't," she replied, gasping as they vaulted up into the night sky. Her fingernails dug into the leather, and she hoped they wouldn't leave scratches. She watched in wonder as tiny lights below flickered in the distance as they buzzed toward their destination.

Logan, unable to take another minute of his self-imposed isolation, reached for Wynter's hand. Slowly peeling her fingers from the seat, he placed her palm on his leg, and caressed her fingers. Goddess, he missed touching her. The small gesture sent loving tendrils throughout his body, reminding him that she really was his mate. When they got home, they'd have to have a long discussion about their relationship, her future as a wolf.

"It's okay, sweetheart," he assured her in a tender voice that he hadn't used since before she'd left to go with Jax. He continued to massage her hand, sliding a thumb into her palm. "Just rest. We'll be there soon."

Wynter relaxed into the small but poignant contact. Her hand burned with warmth radiating from his thigh, and she fought the urge to lean into him, to touch him, to kiss him. As if her body obeyed his directive, she let her forehead rest against the cool window. Within seconds, she'd fallen fast asleep to the soft lullaby of the humming blades.

Creaking metal woke Wynter. The silence that followed told her they had landed. Logan, who'd already begun exiting, extended his hand.

"We're home," he told her.

Home? No, his home, not hers, she thought. But still, that small spark of hope told her to embrace her future with optimistic curiosity. Her heart fluttered in response. With a cautious smile, she clasped her palm in his, accepting his assistance down the steps.

It was only a short ride from the helipad to Logan's house. When they'd exited the car, Wynter eyed the blue tarp which covered the exterior of the huge contemporary house. It appeared unfinished yet lights glimmered through the undraped casement windows. Floodlights illuminated the fresh landscaping, and the smell of newly laid mulch and fragrant roses permeated the night air.

The rain had subsided, and they quickly made their way up the walkway towards the entrance. Logan flipped open a security pad and typed in a code. The lock clicked open and he turned the handle. As they entered, she followed Logan's lead and kicked off her sodden shoes, thankful she'd gone without stockings. In a few minutes, her feet would dry nicely and the smooth hardwood floor felt soothing to her sore toes.

"Adèle," Logan called.

Wynter looked around the foyer that led into a spacious great room. A modern rectangular shaped gas lit fire blazed atop its round white stones.

The black pit, outlined in stainless steel, stood out against the cream-colored Kasota stone hearth. Three tall vases filled with ornamental grass sat atop a thin dark wooden mantel.

A soft purring creature rubbed against her legs, startling Wynter. She knelt down, petting the sweet cat who meowed and pressed its head into her hands.

"Well, hello, kitty," she said softly, touching its ears.

"I see you've met Mojo," Logan acknowledged.

"Hmm? You have a cat?" Wynter replied in surprise, trying to hide her amusement.

"Here kitty, kitty. Come to Daddy," Logan sang in his best baby voice. The small black ball of fur ran toward him, purring voraciously, and he scooped the kitten into his arms, placing kisses on her head. He continued to talk in a soft voice, pretending to talk to the cat while really answering Wynter. "Yes, I have a kitty. And she's such a good girl, aren't you? Who's a good kitty?"

"Mojo," she repeated, smiling.

Wynter watched in amazement as the Alpha tenderly caressed the sweet little creature. Of all things she thought might happen tonight, this certainly was not one of them. As this terrifyingly attractive side of Logan was revealed to her, she fought the urge to run up and kiss him. The wanting, the temptation was so great; she forced herself into the floor, remaining rooted in place.

"She's not very much into Voodoo, but she's lucky," he explained, petting her and rubbing his face into her soft fur. He caught Wynter examining him as if he had four heads. "What?"

"I'm just…I don't know, surprised. I love cats, but a wolf with a cat? Seems counterintuitive." *And sexy.*

"Yeah, that's what Tristan thought too. His mate runs an animal shelter. One day, I spent quite a bit of time in her cat room. And what can I say?" He shrugged, fixing her with his eyes as if he was talking about her and not the cat. "I fell in love. You know, sometimes, Dr. Ryan, we can't control who we fall in love with. Sometimes even when things don't make sense, they actually make the most sense in the world."

Wynter blushed and looked away. Oh God, she wanted to touch him so badly. Heat filled her body. Desire pulsed through her veins. She tried to think of anything but sex. What was wrong with her? Just as she'd mustered enough bravery to respond coherently, a portly woman with a gray bun wandered into the foyer. Logan let the cat jump to the floor, approached and gave her a hug.

"Ah, Adèle. Meet Wynter. Wyn, this is Adèle. She's kept me in one piece since I've moved home."

"Nice to meet you." Wynter noticed how at ease Logan was with his housekeeper.

"Wynter va rester avec moi," he told the woman. Adèle ran her eyes over Wynter before conceding that she was welcome.

"Oui, oui. Bonjour, Wynter," Adèle greeted. She briskly turned on her heels, speaking rapidly in French. She waved an arm, gesturing for them to follow. "Allons, le dîner est prêt."

"Merci, I'm starving," Logan picked up a piece of fluffy white bread out of a bowl and quickly stuffed it into his mouth before she had a chance to protest. "Merci beaucoup pour obtenir la maison prête. Everything looks great."

Adèle pointed to the large glass dining table, and promptly set out another place setting for his guest. Logan sat at the head of the table and gestured for Wynter to sit at his side. Wynter, famished, obeyed, not sure what she should do next. The enticing aroma of a basket of warmed New Orleans-style French bread teased at her nose. Adèle set out two large bowls of what Wynter thought was gumbo, and plates of salad.

"Salade. Gumbo. Pain," Adèle ticked off her creations and then took off her apron. "See you tomorrow, no?"

"Oui, and thanks again, Adèle. The place is really coming together," Logan noted.

She smiled and nodded, but appeared to be in a hurry to leave. "Oui, Monsieur. Soyez le bienvenu." With a wave, she took off toward the back of the home. A door shutting let them know they were alone.

Following Logan's lead, Wynter dug into the delightful gooey mixture with her spoon. They ate in silence. She noticed that like the great room, the kitchen was sparsely decorated. Dark cherry cabinets and hardwood floors were offset by the white granite countertops. The only item on the counter alongside the wall was a coffeemaker. No dishes or glasses sat atop the oversized rectangular island. In fact, there wasn't much décor at all. No pictures on the walls. Not even a clock. Taking a deep breath, she could smell the new drywall and paint and wondered how long Logan had lived here.

As if he read her thoughts, he was the first to speak. "I just built it," he commented without explanation.

"It's beautiful," she replied.

"It's empty," he countered. "But someday soon, it'll be more of a home than a house."

"How long have you lived here?"

"I haven't."

"Hmm?"

"This is the first meal I've eaten here…with you," he stated, meeting her eyes. Had she no idea how important she was to him? How important she had yet to become? It was killing him. The silence. The lack of understanding. And most of all the lack of intimacy. Intimacy which had shattered into a million bits when she left him to go with Jax. It was time to talk, to not just mend their relationship, but set it on a course that would solidify their future.

Wynter stilled at the realization that he'd brought her here, to his home. He'd told her that he'd lived in Marcel's home, but this was a new beginning. It had been something special he'd built on his own and now shared with her. Her chest tightened, and she struggled to come up with the right words.

"Logan, I…I'm sorry," she began. "Today…it's just that everything has moved so quickly. And not just this…this thing between us. It's everything."

"This thing," he said tersely. "This thing is not a thing. It's a bond, Wynter. I've marked you. We're mates. It's not simply a choice we make. It either is or it isn't."

"Yes, but I…" she placed her spoon on the table and wiped her mouth.

"Do you have any idea what I've been through over the past two months?" Logan asked rhetorically, well aware she couldn't possibly comprehend the struggle he'd endured. The low calm of his voice was edged in a controlled indignation. "My friend, Marcel. We grew up together, spent a lifetime as friends. He was Tristan's brother, but they both are my family in every sense of the word. Two months ago, I sat with his blood on my hands. I watched as the life drained from his eyes."

Logan coughed, sucking back his emotions. Enough tears had been shed. "And minutes before that, do you know what I did, Wyn?"

She quietly shook her head.

"I killed a man…with my own hands. Not as wolf. As a man. That death is on my hands." He held his palms upward, staring at them as if they were dripping in blood.

"That night, I vowed to Marcel that I'd lead his pack, to take care of his wolves. Marcel begged me…I didn't want this, to be Alpha. My role as beta was comfortable, respected. I loved Tristan. It isn't something I did lightly," he reflected, placing his palms down on the table. "But it is done. For the last two months, I've fought challenges. Bloody, ripped up fur and bruises, week after week."

"Logan," Wynter gasped quietly. *What had he been through?*

"I may've vowed to be Alpha. But I also earned it. I paid in blood. I paid in sleepless nights. And only this week as I completed my last challenge, I threatened the next wolf who challenges me with death. Do you know what that means, Wyn?"

Wynter could guess but dared not speak it aloud. She remembered the conversation she'd had with Logan about how Fiona's father had died…in a challenge.

"The next wolf who challenges me is dead," he stated emotionlessly. "I cannot tolerate any more instability. For the sake of the pack, the acceptance of my reign must continue. Every time there is a challenge, the pack becomes unsettled. Volatile. It isn't good for them. Or me."

"I'm sorry. Logan, I didn't understand. I don't know what that has to do with us, though."

"It has everything to do with you. Me. Us. Our mating. Today, when you left," he growled, shaking his head in disapproval. "I was so angry. Angry you'd left me to go with Jax. He's unmated. And whoever else you were with was too."

"But how did you know? I didn't…"

"I could smell them on you when you got home. Goddess, Wyn."

"So because you marked me and you've decided we're mates, I can't even go with my family? Are you kidding me?"

"It isn't just that, Wyn. Aside from the fact that you are very much in danger, I had specifically asked you to stay. Granted, I didn't order you as your Alpha. But I came damn close. And you…how could you not see that I needed you to stay so we could talk? I get that you're not wolf, but any she-wolf would have never left her mate…not until she'd claimed him for her own. Not only did you disrespect me by telling me no and going off with Jax, it was as if your wolf rejected mine by leaving."

"I'm sorry, but you've got to understand that I'm…"

"Human," he finished her words. "Yes, yes you are. But not for long, Wyn. The full moon beckons and even if you choose to deny our mating, you'll have to learn to live within your nature."

Frustrated, Logan loosened his tie, took off his jacket and rolled up his sleeves. He stood at the head of the table; his fingers grasped the back of the chair. The animal in him wanted to throw the damn thing, smash it into kindling. But it was not all who he was. He closed his eyes, willing his wolf to calm.

He took a deep breath and blew it out. "I can't do this. Either you need to accept your wolf or I…I don't know. I just know that I've worked too damn hard to become Alpha. Wolves depend on me. And it isn't just the fact that when I get angry or hurt, the pack feels it. If anyone besides Dimitri had seen what you did today, disrespecting me, blatantly denying my request to stay…it'll lead to a challenge. I can't have that happen. Not over us, anyway."

"But I'd never do that on purpose. It's not like I set out to hurt you or the pack today." She ran her fingers through her hair, nervously twisting at it. "God, Logan can't you see what this is doing to me?"

"The bottom line is this. If there's another challenge, I will kill someone. And while I won't hesitate to do it, that wolf is someone's brother, husband, son," he said softly, contemplating what it'd be like to kill again.

Wynter stood and crossed the kitchen, resting her hands onto the countertop. "Please just hear me out. No matter how hard I try, I don't know what it's like. I'm not a wolf." She rubbed her hand over her reddening eyes. "I don't want to cause anyone's death. I don't want to hurt you. I'm so afraid and confused. But there is one thing I know…I want you…like I've never wanted anyone."

Logan approached Wynter, placing his hand on either side of her waist, gripping the cold stone. "And I want you too, sweetheart. But we cannot go on like this. I'm damn sorry someone did this to you, changed you to wolf. You've barely had time to recover from your captivity, let alone adjust to your new…situation. But I can't put my pack in danger. Lots of lives depend on me. I cannot fail them. I get that it is not fair, but you need to decide."

"Decide what, Logan?" She clasped onto the sides of his shirt in desperation. "I'm scared out of my mind. I don't want to hurt anyone but I don't know how to be wolf. I don't know the rules. I can't do this. I don't know how. I'm sorry, I can't…"

Wynter fell to her knees crying, still clawing at his clothing. She'd let her head fall against his shins. Logan wrapped his hands around her arms and brought her up into his embrace, supporting her.

"Wynter, this is not who you are, sweetheart. You can do this. You are strong, not broken. You will learn how to submit within the pack while remaining fiercely independent. You will run as wolf, but maintain your humanity. I promise you to help you shift; support you in everything you do for the rest of your life. But this decision must be yours, not mine." Logan held her tightly. His own tears brimmed; he needed his mate. Please Goddess, do not let her give up.

Struggling to catch her breath, Wynter swore Logan was doing something to calm her. His scent, his touch, his aura, everything that was of his essence protectively encased her body and heart. Her wolf howled, begging her to run free with her mate. On the verge of collapse, Wynter steeled her resolve. A fighter. Yes, that's who she was. Tonight, however, she was a lover, Logan's mate. Trembling in his arms, she raised her chin to meet his eyes.

"I choose you. Us. This makes no sense to the part of my mind that demands data, evidence and all the other things that I've learned in my years as a scientist," she breathed, placing her hand to his heart. "But my heart. My wolf. I need you."

Logan sighed in relief, pressing a kiss to her head. "You sure, baby? Because I'm ready to start this right now…to teach you what it means to be wolf."

"I'm sure." All her senses on alert, she'd fully committed to doing whatever it took to learn how to be wolf, to be Logan's mate.

Logan leaned in and gently kissed her. His wolf celebrated in anticipation of their union. He tenderly sucked at her lips, licking at her until she opened fully to him. Her sweet taste tempted him, beckoning the urge to make love to her right then. But he knew better of it. He'd patiently demonstrate what it meant for her to submit, to be nothing more than the wild animal that lurked beneath the surface of her skin.

Wynter gave in to his will, tasting, indulging in the warmth of her Alpha. She felt his hands leave her sides, and she pressed up further against the counter's edge. As he ground the hard evidence of his arousal against her belly, she registered his fingertips on her skin. She went to help him, and he grabbed her wrists.

"Hands to your sides, Wynter. Don't move," he growled.

She gasped, complying with his demand. Fingers grazed her belly once again. A tear of the fabric sent her shirt buttons flying. The loud sound of the plastic studs hitting the floor sounded like hail pelting a roof. Cool air brushed her chest as he ripped off her shirt, yanking hard at the sleeves and throwing it across the room. A hand around her back deftly released her bra, leaving her bare to him. Panting with need, she struggled to catch her breath. She never lost eye contact as he tore his lips from hers.

"An Alpha," he began in a tense, sexy tone that wrapped around her soul. Logan trailed his lips down her throat and between her breasts. But he didn't kiss or lick her, he merely hovered, letting her feel the heat of his body, "he's patient. He doesn't act impulsively. Despite the temptation, he waits until the optimal moment to strike."

Wynter resisted the excruciating desire to move. She closed her eyes, relishing the effect of his nearness to her tight nipples. Strong hands on her hips rapidly spun her so she was facing the counter, holding her upright so she wouldn't fall.

"Do you feel it, Wyn? Our bond, it's growing. I'm your Alpha. Your wolf knows. I feel her," he told her seductively. He slid a large strong hand around to her belly. Without touching his lips to her skin, he drifted them close to her shoulder. "And she…she feels me." He pressed his burgeoning erection into her bottom.

Wynter sighed at the welcome feel of him against her. She wished he'd just take her. No, instead, he was teasing her, teaching her. She'd promised to learn. Taking a breath, she tried to relax into his hold. But as she felt his hands at her waist, her heart raced once again.

Logan deftly unzipped her skirt and jerked it down, exposing the creamy skin underneath. He smiled at her hot pink lace thong, the one he'd selected earlier. Slowly, he glided his hands over her hips and hooked his thumbs into the flimsy fabric. He bent at his knees, teasing it off of her legs and feet until she was bare. With a flick, he sent it flying across the floor. *Much better.*

"Do you see how a wolf restrains his own needs, all in an effort to take care of his wolves?"

His hands grazed over the globes of her bottom, barely touching her. The heat between his skin and hers threatened to combust, but he never gave in to the need. Denying her his touch, he reached upward into her hair, wrapping the long strands around his fist. Gently tugging, he pulled her head to the side, revealing her neck. He growled at the sight but still only brought his lips within an inch of the skin and spoke to her.

"I will teach you what it's like to be wolf, to submit. Are you ready for that, sweetheart?"

Wynter moaned, breathing hard. Was she ready? Naked, she felt both emotionally and physically exposed, while he stood fully clothed.

Logan gently tugged again at her hair, until her eyes met his.

"Answer me," he demanded softly.

"Yes," she cried. The torment of him not touching her was nearly unbearable. But before she had time to think about it, he turned her once again so that she was facing him. She watched nervously as he removed his tie.

"Your senses. They are all that a wolf has. As humans, we rely too much on our sight to tell us what we know. We ignore what our heart tells us because our eyes can't see it. Up," he directed, lifting her up onto the large granite island. "Lay back, Wyn."

Wynter struggled to understand what he was doing. He wanted her on this cold countertop? What the hell?

"Don't question. Just do it. Go on now. You're okay, now. I promise you'll enjoy it." He winked, helping her to scoot backwards. He took her head into his hands, tenderly placing it on the hard surface. "You okay?"

She nodded, unsure of where this was going. Despite her apprehension, the ache between her legs throbbed in anticipation. The heat of her skin cooled against the sleek stone. Logan held up his tie, and she almost choked. *What did he plan to do with that?*

"It's all right, sweetheart. Just removing one of your senses. Educational purposes, I assure you," he laughed.

"Yeah right," she giggled in response. Why was she so aroused? At least he wasn't tying her up, but still she'd been laid out naked on a platter for him to do what he wished, and she grew wetter and wetter by the second.

"Seriously, this is not just about trusting me, which you very much need to learn how to do. Nor is it about submission, which you seem to be doing nicely right now," he encouraged.

His dick was so hard he thought his balls would be blue for the rest of his natural life. The sight of his mate splayed out was more than he could take. He wanted so badly to plunge into her, but he reminded himself that there was more at stake besides him getting his rocks off.

Logan wrapped the tie around her eyes until he was certain she couldn't see. "No peeking. You okay?"

"Yes," she breathed. The anticipation of what he'd do to her was maddening. "Please Logan, hold my hand."

"You look beautiful, baby. So gorgeous." Logan briefly kissed her lips and took her hand in his, sending calming waves to her body. The self-control of a saint was all that kept him from taking her right then. "Breathe in and out, Wyn. That's it. I can't hold your hand the whole time but we'll start with something easy. Smell. Wolves, we rely on scent to give us all kinds of information. To hunt prey. To track enemies. To seek out our lovers," He kissed her shoulder. "Scent, it is essential. Tell me what you smell."

Wynter inhaled deeply. Food. Well that made sense, they were in the kitchen. A faint odor of bleach. Maybe another scent, a comforting scent. Logan. "I smell you." She smiled. "Not cologne. It's something else. It smells so good. It's woodsy and fresh and…my wolf, she likes it."

Logan smiled. It was a start. Releasing her hand, he moved to her head and kissed her again. Then he turned and cracked open the window above the sink.

"And now?"

Unable to see, she knew immediately he'd introduced another variable. "Grass? And roses. That could be cheating because I did see them when I came in as well as the mulch. But there's something else…it's musky. Earthy."

"The bayou," he confirmed. "Anything else?"

Wynter's face registered surprise. "It's crazy," she said in disbelief. "We're alone?"

"Are we? You tell me?"

"I think I smell…do I smell Dimitri? Oh God," Wynter exclaimed in embarrassment, wondering how she knew that.

"It's okay, he's not here." Logan smoothed her hair back with his hand. "But he told me that he planned on a run tonight. See how amazing you are?"

"But how do I know..?"

"Instincts. Forget your human self for the moment. Just close your eyes, and look for your wolf. Let her help you. Okay, let's move on," he suggested, brushing his fingertips over her belly. "Hearing. It's the single most acute sense we've got. Rustling of prey. Danger approaching. What do you hear?"

A hot coil built within the pool of her womb as Logan grazed over her stomach. If he'd just move his hand down further. The minute his petting edged her closer to orgasm, he stopped. She squeezed her thighs tightly but no relief came.

"Wyn?" Logan's voice jarred her back to her erotic lesson.

"Yes, um, hearing," she stammered. "Crickets. No, it's louder than that. Cicadas maybe? Frogs…yes, a bullfrog. A splash. Something in the water."

"When you shift, you'll be able to identify all of nature's sounds. To be able to discriminate so discretely you can tell whether a fox is matin' or fightin' a mile away," Logan whispered in her ear.

Wynter sucked air as his warm breath touched her neck. "Please," she begged. Her full heavy breasts tingled in hopes they'd be touched.

"Patience, little wolf. Perhaps the next two should be combined. Touch and taste. No longer having hands, your paws and claws will grip at the dirt, protected by your toughened pads. But as wolf, touch is mostly felt with the tongue." Logan traced the tip of his tongue around one of her areola, until she moaned. Resisting, he retreated and opened a cabinet, extracting his next surprise.

"Open your mouth, Wynter," he ordered, cupping her chin.

"What?" she gasped. Her pulse quickened.

Logan drew his finger across her lower lip, and then dipped it inside. *Fuck yeah, it felt too good.* He'd meant to open her mouth, but she'd latched onto his finger sucking it as if she was giving him a blow job. Her warm tongue swirled around the pad of his finger, and for a few glorious seconds, he indulged. Carefully taking back control, he pulled his digit out enough to skim along her bottom teeth. Her natural reaction was to open. He smiled in response to hers; she'd clearly known what she'd been doing to him.

"You taste so good, Logan. Like you belong to me," she sighed.

"Our taste, our smell…as mates, we're attracted to one another like magnets to iron," Logan said as he positioned the small plastic bear at her lips. "Mouth open. That's it, baby. Now taste."

He squeezed the honey onto her lips, watching as her tongue darted forward to lap up the nectar.

"Honey," she moaned with a smile.

Logan leaned forward and brushed his lips against hers, pressing his tongue into her mouth. They gently sucked and licked at each other until the sticky sweetness was gone. Logan pulled away, leaving Wynter breathless and moaning. With great speed, he walked to her feet. He parted her legs revealing her wet center.

"As wolf, we eat meat and even small berries now and then. But it is the taste of your arousal that drives me mad, sweetheart." Logan paused. He leaned forward and dragged his tongue along the inside of her thigh, but stopped short of her core. He stroked her pussy softly then drove two fingers deep within her. Plunging in and out, he watched as her juices coated his hands, then pulled out of her and brought his fingers to her lips, painting them. With ease, he slipped them into her mouth. "You taste delicious. Better than any meal I've ever had. Better than any wine I've ever known."

Wynter shook with excitement. At his hand she almost came, but he'd withdrawn leaving her empty. She sucked and lapped at his fingers, tasting the evidence of her own arousal on them. Moaning and undulating her hips upward, she sought the friction that never came.

"Please," she managed to say. "I can't take it. Please, Logan."

The sight of Wynter so open and the feel of her sucking him broke his restraint. Logan unbuckled his belt and freed his cock. He retrieved his fingers from her mouth and once again sunk them back into her pussy; his thumb gently applied pressure to her clit. As he continued to bring her toward orgasm, he walked around the island so his hips were near her face.

Wynter cried Logan's name. His fingers stroked the tender strip inside her channel, and she almost flew off the countertop. Writhing her mound up into his hand, she struggled to hold back her climax. Unable to see, she felt the heat of his body radiate close to her, a kiss to her neck.

"Suck me," Logan told her, guiding his pulsing shaft toward her mouth. The silken head of him brushed her lips.

In the darkness, Wynter rolled onto her side, blindly searching for the hardness of his sex. With Logan's assistance, she wrapped her small hand around him. Bringing his swollen flesh to her lips, she licked at his seam, taking in his salty essence. Trembling, Wynter took the length of him all the way into her mouth, allowing the tip of her tongue to play along the underside of his swollen flesh. She rocked her head back and forth, relishing the taste of her mate. Using her hands and lips, she gripped him tightly as she sucked.

Logan dragged in a breath. Her hot mouth suctioned him, pistoning up and down. Drenched in her wetness, he felt her core tighten around his fingers. Unrelenting, he swept the pad of his thumb across her swollen hood once again. As she began to lose the thread of control that held her together, he withdrew his cock, allowing her to fall over the cliff of ecstasy.

Wynter moaned at the loss of him. She wasn't sure of the exact moment she'd embraced the submission, nor did she understand why her body responded to his touch with terrific exuberance. All thought went, lost with the last graze of his fingers. A wall of energy slammed her, driving her into climax, and leaving her shuddering in release. Wynter's chest heaved, trying to recover from the high.

Logan leaned forward to remove his tie from her eyes. Like Wynter's presuppositions about what she thought was wolf, the silk blindfold fell to the floor. Logan smiled as she moaned and gazed up at him. He cupped her face, admiring his spectacular mate. Captivated by her honesty and reckless abandon, his chest tightened with an overwhelming yet unfamiliar passion. Had he fallen in love? Rationally, he'd always known that he could find his mate, but after a hundred years, he'd happily remained single. Now everything was changed forever. A single chance meeting in an alley had resulted in a life-altering experience he could have never anticipated or understood. Only in this moment was he cognizant of the ramifications. Life would never be the same and he didn't want it to be.

With the ache building again, Wynter wiggled her hips in an effort to reach him. She opened her eyes, drinking in the sight of him. His hair was wild; the look in his eyes wild with desire.

"Logan, please," she cried.

"I'll give you everything you need, baby. Every day, every minute, every second."

Tugging her by her hips, he lifted her bottom until it reached the edge of the counter. Logan lifted her legs up over his shoulders, wrapping his hands around her thighs. He pressed against her entrance, thrusting into her pussy in one smooth stroke. As he penetrated her tight heat, his cock slid back and forth into his mate. Groaning, Logan built a slow rhythm, resisting the urge to pound into her relentlessly.

"More, harder," Logan heard her cry.

The demand sent his wolf into a wicked state. With a low growl, Logan cupped her bottom with one hand and wrapped his other arm around her waist. As he lifted her into the air, Wynter wrapped her legs around his waist. Logan spun, crashing his back into the refrigerator. He bent his knees so that he could lower his hips and pump up into her, all the while capturing her breast with his lips.

Like a raging animal, Wynter raked her hands into his hair, and licked the side of his neck. Entirely filled with all that was Logan, she abandoned her humanity and let her wolf run free. In truth, this was who she was with Logan. Passionate. Unrestrained. And totally, utterly in love.

"Please, Oh God," she screamed against his skin. "Take me, Logan."

"Sofa," he grunted.

Logan struggled to kick off his pants while managing to stay pressed inside Wynter. Forced to release her rosy peak, he looked ahead, stumbling forth until he reached the large soft couch. Roughly, they fell into the cushions, Logan thrusted between her legs.

As her head hit the pillows, Wynter nipped at Logan's chest. He was untamed, and she loved it. Logan smothered her body, penetrating deep into her hot core. In response, she scratched her nails down his back nearly drawing blood, encouraging him to go deeper. Licking and sucking, she tasted and smelled and immersed her senses in him like he'd taught her. Her mate, masculine and muscular, drove into her over and over. She raised her pelvis in response, rocking her clitoris against his hips. Each torturous exquisite brush to her tiny nub sent her body singing. As if he was directing the orchestra, he edged her toward the finale. Her heart thumped against her ribs; she struggled to breathe.

"You are wolf, Wyn. Do you hear me? And you're mine," Logan told her. "Fuck, you're fisting me so tight; I'm goin' to come soon. I feel you baby, come with me."

"Yes!" Wynter screamed and then bit down hard on his shoulder. The hot explosion of her release caused her to shatter underneath him. From head to toe, rippling ecstasy flowed through her body.

Logan saw stars as her pussy tightened around his throbbing cock. Growling in his need to possess her, he pumped into her fiercely. As her teeth met his skin, he soared over the edge in unknown pleasure, pulsing his seed deep into her womb. All the air rushed from his lungs in a loud grunt as the last wave rolled through him.

"This is crazy." He laughed into her neck, aware of how wildly they'd just made love. "You have no idea what you do to me."

Wynter giggled, still trying to catch her breath.

"You bit me." He laughed harder.

"You fucked me on a kitchen counter," she answered. "I'll never look at food the same."

"Nor will I." Logan pressed up onto his forearms. "Are you okay? I'm crushing you."

"I'm fine. Please don't go yet. Just stay like this," she breathed, nuzzling her face into his chest.

"There's no place I'd rather be," he assured her.

Letting his body go limp against hers, reveling, he smiled, realizing that he'd set out to teach her a lesson, but by Goddess, she'd schooled him long and hard in her love. Never again would he be alone.

Chapter Twenty-Two

Wynter felt as if she was floating in heaven. After they'd made love, Logan had arranged a soft bed of lambskin and pillows on the great room's floor, creating a temporary Eden. Nestled against Logan's chest, she stared into the dancing flames of the gas lit fire which flickered behind the glass. She shivered, thankful for the heat that radiated onto their skin.

"You cold?" Logan asked, pulling the cashmere blanket over her shoulders.

"Just a little, thanks."

"You're a million miles away. What are you thinking about?" he asked softly and brushed a hair out of her eyes.

"You. Me. Us. It's unbelievable. I mean we barely know each other, really. But this feeling," she tapped her fingers over his heart. "It's intense. And romantic. And wild."

"Regrets?" Logan wondered if she was having second thoughts.

"No way," she replied decidedly. "It feels like I've been asleep my whole life, and now? It's an awakening of sorts. I've never in my life known anyone like you, Logan. Tonight…it was incredible."

"And I've never met anyone like you, either." Logan pressed his lips to her hair. "I've never taught a human to be wolf. Even tonight, Wyn, it won't be a sliver of what you'll feel tomorrow."

"Lying there exposed like that…having my eyes covered helped me to concentrate. The only thing missing was how I will see when I'm a wolf. I'm super-excited about getting badass night vision," she laughed.

"You're something, you know that?"

"How so?"

"You're like this little livewire. The secretary thing…I'm still not over that. And waking up to what you did to me the other morning….those things just don't happen to guys every day."

"Not even to Alphas?" she asked coyly.

"Not even to Alphas," he stated truthfully, "even ones as old as me."

"How old are you?"

"Old enough."

"Old enough that you remember the turn of the nineteenth century?" she guessed, knowing both wolves and vampires lived a long time.

"Old enough," he repeated, smiling at her insistence. Another reason why he was falling in love with her. She was tenacious.

"Come on, you have to tell me. I'm going to be your mate. Let's see…old enough to remember President Lincoln?"

"You really want to know? I don't want my young hot mate running for the hills when she finds out," he joked.

"Yes, I do. I love that you've experienced the world. Well, maybe not the women part but I don't mind, really."

"Born 1871. President Ulysses S. Grant was in office. So I missed President Lincoln by a few years."

Wynter silently computed the years in her head. "One hundred and forty-two."

"You got it." He gave her a tight hug. "Yeah, things were different then. Simpler but harder. I wouldn't exactly say, 'good ole days'. I love the technology we've got now."

"Are your parents still alive?" Wynter drew lazy circles on his stomach.

"Yes ma'am. Papá and Maman took to traveling a few years ago."

"Are they from New Orleans too?"

"Yes and no. Maman came over from France in the early 1700s. Papá, he arrived as part of the Spanish rule a few years later. Nowadays, they travel around the world but still stop home from time to time. I traveled a lot as a pup too," he reminisced. "They're going to love you, sweetheart."

"I wish you could have met my Mom and Dad. God, I miss them. When they died, I was so angry."

"How did they pass?"

"I was told it was a carjacking…they'd been downtown. It all happened so suddenly. When you're a kid like that…well, I never got closure. Maybe that's what bothered me most." Wynter really didn't want to talk about it. She'd worked so hard to learn how to accept the loss. She watched the firelight frolic across the cathedral ceiling and stark walls.

"I like your house." She changed the subject.

"Thanks. It still needs work, but I couldn't spend another night in Marcel's place. It's a reminder of his death and my tumultuous birth as Alpha. The good memories outweigh the bad, but I figure it's time I make a few new memories of my own." Logan smiled. "You could help me, you know. I mean, we haven't talked about it, but I want you here with me…in my home. Wait until you see the wildlife. It's beautiful."

He didn't want to freak her out but he'd be lying if he said that he'd accept her living anywhere else but with him. He knew it might not be easy for either of them. But the strength of the mating bond drove their attraction, the need to be physically close. They could fight it and try to live apart, but he knew it would be excruciating. Still, empathizing with her human mores, he trod lightly around the subject. They had time to get to know each other while she stayed with him, at least until they caught the killer.

Did Logan just ask her to live with him? Wynter wasn't sure what exactly he was saying. If they mated, did that mean they were married? She felt as if she'd gone to Las Vegas and got involved in some quickie wedding. And even though once upon a time, her conservative nature wouldn't have entertained the idea, she was too far gone. She'd fallen in love with Logan, the man and the wolf. She couldn't understand how she could feel so intensely so quickly. As much as she wanted to tell him, she couldn't. She hadn't even considered what would happen to their relationship once they mated or even after they were finally out of danger.

"When we mate, does that mean we are married?" It popped out of her mouth before she could take it back or at least ask in a more diplomatic way.

"You're funny," Logan laughed. He'd been worried about sharing his feelings and asking her to stay with him, and now she was asking if they were married, a very human thought.

"Hilarious, I'm sure. Seriously, if we mate does that mean we are…you are my…you know?" She playfully tapped her hand to his chest.

"No, sweetheart. Getting married, it's a human thing. But mating," he traced a finger down her cheek and across her lips, "it's deeper…visceral."

"What do you mean?"

"It's private, a ritual between you and me. Afterwards, we'd announce it to the pack. And only mated wolves can get pregnant, have pups," he explained. "Now marriages, well, they come and go. I know it's a commitment, but it's a human tradition. Is that something you wanted, Wynter?"

She quieted at his question. Did she want to get married? After everything that had happened to her in her short life, she really never considered it. Sure, as a little girl she dressed up and played bride, but once she was an adult, it never seemed that she'd find someone she loved enough to commit to fully, let alone marry…until now.

"Well, I'm not sure of that," she hedged. "I suppose I've never really loved anyone enough to consider it. When I tell you that there has been no one in my life like you, it's true."

"Hmm." Logan couldn't help but kiss her again. His ego did love to hear that.

"So I guess I'll take a rain check on that question, Alpha," she grinned.

"Tomorrow's a big day." Logan wanted to talk to her about her shift but it wasn't until now that he'd felt she trusted him enough to broach the topic. "Full moon."

"Do you really think I'm going to shift? I know I'm changing but without the blood work, how can I be sure?" Wynter tried to feign courage but it wasn't working. She was scared to death about what would happen to her tomorrow night.

"Yeah, I do think you're going to shift. I don't know what they did to you sweetheart, but I meant it, I can sense your wolf." Logan brushed her hair out of her eyes. "It's part of the reason we needed to have that little lesson tonight. I needed to know where you stood. Would you be able to embrace your senses? Would you trust me without argument? Submit? Could you learn how your actions impact the pack? It's important to know going into this."

"All wolves submit to you?"

"Yeah, it's how it has to be. We need order. With order, there's peace. With peace, the pack is happy, healthy. Everyone can focus on livin' their life and not fightin'."

"Sexually? Like you did to me tonight? Will you take others? Because if you do, I don't think I can…" Her words trailed off.

"Look at me," he told her. Logan waited until their eyes met. "There is no one else for me but you…ever. Do you understand?"

"Yes." Relief flooded over her.

"Now that doesn't mean other she-wolves won't try to undermine you or test you. Don't get me wrong, as a human, you're tough. You survived two long months in that hellhole. That says a lot about a person's will to survive. But even among the females, they fight for rank…to be alpha."

Wynter didn't even want to think about that. The thought of fighting just so she could establish herself within an animal ranking system disgusted her.

"Sorry, I didn't mean to scare you." Logan could tell by the pale look on Wynter's face that he'd said too much. He should have known better than to think she could even conceive of such things happening to her. Logan was certain that his little she-wolf was indeed alpha. But that was something she'd have to learn on her own.

"It's okay, I need to know," she replied. *Not really okay, but what the hell am I supposed to do about it?* "Tell me about tomorrow. The shift."

"You know all those senses we played with?"

"Uh huh."

"You'll feel them heightened as if everything is turned on to overdrive. At first, it's hard to control, but you'll learn quickly how to dial it up or down, depending on the situation. You've already been learning to control it whether you've been conscious of it or not. A human wouldn't have scented D tonight. You did that, because you allowed your wolf to do it. She's there."

"It was incredible," she recalled. "I still have no idea how I knew it was him."

"You've spent time with him, right?"

"Yeah, but still, humans don't do that kind of stuff."

"And there you go. You're wolf. She knows him."

"He's been kind to me," Wynter admitted. "It's strange. That first day, we kind of got off on the wrong foot, but then something changed. It sounds stupid to say this, but it's like he knows what to say to help me when things aren't going so well."

"It's not stupid at all, Wyn. He's my beta. He has a pulse on the pack and helps me lead them when necessary. He can calm wolves. It's hard to explain. I know you can't see it yet, but we're linked, the three of us." Until she actually shifted, there was no way she could possibly understand the extent of the bond he and Dimitri had. "Speaking of D. He's going to stay with us tomorrow, as you shift, run and then afterwards. Jake's going to take the pack for me. We may run with them too, but I want to see how you feel."

"What do you mean?"

"Well, it's kind of like when our young wolves first change. We don't just let them around the older wolves right away. They stay with their mammas and papas for an hour or so, then are told to stay in a certain area with just each other. We can't just have them challenging the older males right away. There'd be trouble."

"Well don't expect that out of me," she said indignantly.

"That's the thing, Wyn. You don't know how you really are going to feel until after you shift. You may feel territorial, hungry, playful. Probably, very, very horny afterwards."

"Are you kidding me? Stop it." Wynter pushed at his arm.

"No, no I'm not. I mean, I just went through something like this with my Alpha and his mate. It's not a joke."

Wynter pushed out of his arms and sat up, legs crossed. "What do you mean exactly?" *Please don't mean what I think it means.*

"Sex, it's something we've become very good at doing." He winked and pulled her toward him. "You and I are excellent at it actually. I can't imagine what it'll be like after you shift."

"You had sex with Tristan's mate?" She pulled away from him. *How could he think this was funny?*

"Come on back down here, baby," he coaxed.

"Don't baby me." She tried to act angry but was really just astonished at what she was learning. With a flick of her hair, she gave him her best eye roll and then smiled.

"Not all sex means that you are 'in love' with someone. Take Tristan. Do I love him? Yeah, I do. He was my Alpha and still is one of my best friends. And his mate, Kalli, she's wonderful, but I wasn't in love with her. But we are friends, and she needed me. *They* needed me. So yeah, I helped with her shift back into the pack. Not really the same situation though. She'd been wolf already, just not around a whole pack."

"So how do you feel about Dimitri?"

"I love him too. He's been a friend ever since we got caught bootleggin' in the twenties."

"What?"

"The gulf coast was a crazy place then, rumrunners and such. But I digress. That's a story for another day. Your shift…where were we?"

"Dimitri, I think."

"It's the shift. It doesn't just affect your basic senses. Your libido will be flying high like a kite. I want him to be there in case…in case we need him."

"Okay," she said, contemplating what he was telling her. She couldn't comprehend wanting to make love to him more than she already did. Was he implying that he wanted Dimitri to be with them? "So I'll want to be with you. I'll just be more enthusiastic?"

"Yeah, kind of like that." He could tell she was having a hard time wrapping her head around what he was trying to tell her. "But you may need…more."

"Don't take this the wrong way. It's not that I don't find Dimitri attractive. I mean, I'd have to be dead not to, but Logan, I don't think that I'd want to do…well, what you're suggesting."

Logan simply smiled and shrugged. "It's up to you, Wyn. But I think that for at least your first shift, you may want this. I won't lie; it won't be easy for me to share you with him."

"You didn't want me near Jax."

"No, I didn't. My wolf, he doesn't really want you near any unmated male. But he knows Dimitri. And for this shift…I want it to be special for you. If this is what your body needs, we'll do it."

"But I don't think I'll need that." Wynter laid back down into his arms, wishing she could stay human. "I don't get it."

"The best I can explain it is that when the full moon hits, us wolves, we're already sexual creatures. We crave the touch of others. Someone who is a friend by day may be a lover during the full moon. Consensual, of course," he added.

"Have you ever watched someone make love?" she asked with great interest. "Well, besides in that vampire club the other night."

"Yes." He smiled broadly. His little wolf never ceased to amaze him. Was she a voyeur? "Like humans, certain wolves like to watch or be watched. It can be a turn on, without a doubt. Is that something you'd like to do?"

Wynter felt his eyes burn over her body at the question. What was she thinking? Threesomes to voyeurism in the course of two minutes was a little bit too much information to process.

"Maybe yes, maybe no," she replied, satisfied with her noncommittal answer.

He raised an eyebrow at her.

"What? Okay, maybe. I can't say I'm not curious. But not tomorrow, okay? I don't think I could do that."

Logan laughed.

"I'm not a prude you know," she protested. A giggle escaped her lips remembering what they'd just done in the kitchen. "Not sure what could have given you that impression. The conference room should have dispelled that notion…not to mention that I just made a nice dessert for you."

Logan's cock jerked as a vision of her lying naked on the countertop flashed in his head. He slid his hand from her belly to cup her breast. Watching her with his beta would be sexually exhilarating. But it would have to be her decision and hers alone.

"Tomorrow, if we do this, it isn't permanent. It's something we could do to make your shift the most amazing experience of your life. But it's still your choice. As mates, the only bond we have will be to each other. I love D. He's my beta and will always be part of our lives, but he won't fall in love with you."

Wynter closed her eyes trying to picture herself sandwiched between the two incredibly sexy and dominant men. She wanted to hate it, she really did. But the thought of them filling her, consuming her made her pussy throb; wetness teased her thighs. Lost in her dream, she startled as Logan brushed his knuckles lovingly across her cheek.

"Sweetheart, what ya thinkin' about?"

"Everything," she admitted softly without saying the word. *Ménage*. She decided right then to wait and see what happened after her shift. If she trusted her wolf, like Logan had been telling her to do, she'd make the right decision tomorrow night. "I want you to know that whatever happens tomorrow, the only person I want is you…just you."

Logan gently kissed her and spoke softly, his lips still touching hers. "You are the only one for me, too. Only." Kiss. "You." Kiss. "Ever." Kiss.

Wynter sighed. She almost told him that she loved him but thought better of it. What would he say? Yes, he was committed to her, that much he'd said.

"I got you a gift," he said with a devious grin.

She kissed his chest. "Hmm, Dimitri said you like shopping."

"He does know me well."

"I'm kind of surprised you got me anything, considering how mad you were."

"Just because I was upset, don't think that for one minute I wasn't thinking of making love to you. In fact, at this point, I might not think of anything else for the rest of my life," he teased. "Okay, let me up. I'll go get it."

"It?"

"You'll see."

The devilish smile on his face made Wynter wonder exactly what he'd gotten her. She fell onto her back, closed her eyes and relaxed. Like he'd taught her to do, she listened intently to see if she could catch a clue to where he'd gone. She heard a door opening and shutting then the patter of his feet coming toward her. She glanced upward to find her gloriously naked mate standing over her, his erect cock jutting outward. Oh yes.

Logan dangled a red and black bag in front of her, blocking her view of his arousal. The fancy packaging sprouted tissue paper and ribbons, making it appear as if it had come from an expensive store. He wagged his eyebrows with a big grin, and she knew she was either in big trouble or in for the best time of her life. Maybe both.

"What's in the bag, darlin'?" she drawled in her best southern accent.

"Well, you know, sweetheart. I've got plans for that sweet lil' ass of yours." Logan knelt down, straddling her legs, hovering an inch over her pelvis so as not to crush her with his weight. He set the bag aside so that he could get comfortable. His aroused flesh pressed into her belly as he leaned in to quickly suck an exposed nipple.

"Well, sir, I do think I might enjoy that," she teased. Why bother with coyness when all she wanted was to be filled with Logan morning, noon and night. She continued in her role as a belle. "It's all the rage, I hear."

"You're a naughty girl, you know that?" Logan laughed. She wanted to play again?

She nodded and licked her lips. After the talk about a threesome, she was more than ready to make love again. Her eyes darted back and forth between his purchase and the mischievous expression on his face.

Logan grabbed the blanket and tossed it aside so he could get a full view of her luscious body. Sliding his palm down her belly, he reached for the bag and pulled a small glass object out. He held it up so she could see it. The bulbous end caught the light; it curved slightly tapering into a ringed handle.

"Toys?" This is what he'd been shopping for? She laughed, excited at the prospect of trying something new with Logan.

"Why yes, Dr. Ryan. I've got a couple of fun toys, in fact. But I thought maybe we'd start with this one. Then, move up to something larger."

"Something larger, like this?" Wynter captured his cock in her hand and gave it a smooth stroke. Logan hissed in delight.

"Oh, don't you worry, baby. You'll have plenty of that tonight, but first let's start small," he suggested. He retrieved a small bottle of lube and flipped it open. "But first, my little tease, open those legs and let me taste how hot you are."

Wynter released Logan as he rose above her. She let her knees fall aside, like he'd asked, allowing him to see all of her. Giving him a playful smile, she licked her fingers and then slowly glided her hand down onto her mound. Captivated by what she was doing, Logan watched intently as she slid a moist digit into her slick crease, parting herself for him. She moaned in response, all the while taking in his reaction.

"Goddammit, Wyn, that is so fucking hot." Logan lay on his stomach, his head between her legs, gaining better access to the heart of her.

His hands clutched her inner thighs as he speared the tip of his tongue into her channel. He felt her startle and then push down onto him in rhythm as he fucked her with his mouth. Once, twice, three times. Withdrawing, he licked over her fingers, groaning in delight.

"Ah baby, no more. Rest your hands on your belly," he instructed. She'd come if they kept going and he wanted her first orgasm to coincide with their new toy.

"Please," she begged. His tongue inside of her nearly sent her into release. The emptiness was killing her.

"Here we go," he told her, spreading the cool gel onto the smooth crystal. Letting his fingers tease her anus, he circled it and slowly pressed one, then two thick digits inside.

"Oh my God, yeah," she moaned. With ease, she began to writhe her hips as he pumped in and out of her. She cried as she felt Logan swipe his tongue through her folds, teasing her further.

"Ah, don't stop," she whined when he withdrew both his mouth and hand. "Logan."

"We're just getting started," he grinned. Smoothing the cool object through her folds, he let it graze over her nub until it found its destination. The tapered tip prodded her puckered skin. Logan pushed and twisted slowly.

"Ah, yes. It feels so…good." Wynter sighed as she relaxed into the sweet pressure. Similar to Logan's fingers, the glass knob wasn't too large yet created a sense of delectable fullness.

"Look at that…all the way in. How does it feel?"

"Full, but not too full. No pain…just pressure. But I need…"

Logan knew exactly what she needed. Plunging his finger into her hot sheath he began to explore her nether lips with his thumb. She'd want him to bring her all the way to orgasm by touching her clit, but he'd save that pleasure for later.

"So wet and pink, sweetheart. I love your pussy," he told her and licked at her inner thigh. As he did so, he pulled out the glass instrument and pushed it back in, causing her to gasp.

"Ah, Logan, I'm so close…"

"Touch your breasts, Wyn. Oh yeah, just like that." His cock was so hard, he could barely move. He watched her take her perfectly shaped mounds and knead them. "Now, play with your nipples."

Through heavy-lidded eyes, Wynter caught his gaze and did what he told her. The sensations were overwhelming. His hands on her labia, the fullness in her bottom and now the pleasurable ache in her tight peaks…it was too much, but not enough.

"You are so hot, baby. My dick is like fucking steel. You are gonna make me come just watching you," Logan groaned. He took his hand away from her heat so that he could take out the next toy. "We need to speed this up because I can't take much more of just watching."

The pressure eased as Logan slid out the glass plug. Wynter looked up to see him preparing a much larger, pink silicone object. Before she had a chance to ask, the cold lubrication pressed at her back hole.

"This one's a little larger, okay? I'll go slowly." Logan inserted it an inch and noticed a grimace on her face. "You're okay, sweetheart. Push into it. That's it. Almost in."

As the plug breached the first ring of muscle, pain flared and then quickly subsided as she bore down. Within seconds, a wonderful pleasure filled her completely. Logan's tongue lapped at her clit, while his fingers added voluminous bonus. Wynter cried Logan's name, bucking her hips into his face. Relentlessly his tongue grazed at her nub. She dug her fingernails into his scalp.

Logan wrapped his lips around her clitoris and suckled her. Wynter screamed so loud she thought she'd wake the dead. Her ass and pussy rippled in orgasm while Logan continued to drink of her essence. Granted little reprieve, she heard Logan growl right before he flipped her over on her stomach.

"Ah yeah, that's it, Wyn. Goddess, you're so beautiful," Logan praised as she knelt on her hands and knees. Holding the plug in place, he waited until she was in position. Scrambling with one hand, he scooped up a control, a surprise he'd kept for Wynter. He positioned the head of his straining cock at her entrance. With a grunt, he plunged into her, sheathing himself completely. Her quivering walls pulsated around him, nearly making him explode.

"Don't move," Logan bit out, digging his fingers into her hips. Fuck, he really was going to come. He breathed in and out, slowly gaining control. Withdrawing, he pumped into her slowly. Logan could feel the probe caressing his shaft through the thin barrier.

Resting her weight on her forearms, Wynter's head fell forward. She'd never been so satiated in her life. Even though she'd just come, she could feel the ache building once again as if someone was turning a crank, winding her up….soon she would spring loose.

"Oh God. I can't even describe. Logan, I never knew." So many thoughts raced through her mind while she endured the marvelous penetration. Again and again, his velvety steel sex stroked her channel of nerves. At the precipice, she moved in his rhythm as her release threatened.

"I'm going to come again. Please."

Logan felt the contractions around his cock and prayed what he was about to do wouldn't make him come before she did. Depressing the button, he clicked on the remote, causing it to vibrate. Logan tugged at the vibrating plug, withdrew it and pressed it in again. At the same time, he imbedded himself into her tight pussy. He'd decidedly gone from the frying pan into the fire. Between the vibrations and her walls milking him, Logan fought the urge to climax.

"Yes, please. Oh God, what is that? It feels…it feels amazing. Don't stop," she encouraged. So full, she gasped as the vibrations spread from her bottom to her pussy. Welcoming the dark intrusion, she pushed back on him, allowing him to guide it in and out of her. Wynter knew she was going to come again but wanted to fly at the same time as Logan. Pleading for more, she lost the ability to speak coherently. "Fuck me, fuck me now. I'm…going to…again."

Breathing heavily, he looked down to see his rigid flesh disappearing into his sweet mate. She gripped him like a vise, the plug tantalizing the length of his shaft. At her words, Logan began to surge in and out of her and with a final thrust, he slammed into her, stiffening in release.

As Logan took her one last time, Wynter came with him. The deep shuddering orgasm reached every cell in her body. Shaking with ecstasy, she fell to the floor, bringing him on top of her. He quickly brought them safely onto their sides and removed himself and the toy. She moaned as Logan stood, covering her tingling skin with a blanket.

A warm cloth between her legs silenced her calls for him. Logan tenderly cleaned both Wynter and himself, discarding the towel and the toys into the bag. Cradling his mate into his strong arms, he lifted her. Euphoria rushed over Logan as he trod up the steps to his room. He'd never experienced such contentment. His heart felt as if it would burst; he loved Wynter with all of his being.

Wynter cuddled against Logan, kissing at his chest as he took her upstairs. He smelled of sex and masculinity, and she resolutely immersed herself in his scent. Within minutes, Logan had snuggled them into his feather-soft bed, and she lay wrapped in his arms. Abounding with happiness, Wynter reveled in the drugging sensation. As she drifted off to sleep, the words she'd been holding back slipped from her lips, *I love you.*

Chapter Twenty-Three

With the room bathed in sunlight, Wynter nuzzled against the pillow. The fog of sleep hung thick in her mind. Reaching blindly for Logan, she stretched a long arm across the bed and found it empty. A groan escaped her lips. Sweeping her arm back to her body, she caught the thin edge of a paper. A note? She squinted as the beams of light accosted her vision. Adjusting to the brightness, she read it: *Good Morning Sweetheart, Breakfast is downstairs. Had an appointment I couldn't miss. Love you, Logan.* Love? Oh God…she'd told him she loved him. Maybe he didn't hear it. Or maybe he did? She wasn't sure how she imagined telling him she loved him, but she had hoped she wouldn't fall asleep afterward.

After she'd used the bathroom, she showered and got dressed. Deciding on simplicity, she'd thrown on a sports bra, pink tank top and black yoga pants. She finger combed her wild mane, pulling it into a messy bun. Taking a glance at herself in the mirror, she looked and felt relaxed despite the fact that someone was out to kidnap her. She shoved the negative thoughts away, but reminded herself to ask Logan about getting the lab equipment. Unsure of what had happened to her blood samples, she wanted to test herself as soon as possible.

Giving her wolf senses a tryout, Wynter closed her eyes. From what she could tell, coffee was on but she couldn't smell anything else. Some wolf she was. Laughing inwardly, she went in search of Logan.

As promised, bagels and croissants sat in a linen-covered tray on the kitchen table. She bit into a crescent-shaped flaky goodness, releasing a sigh. Worth every calorie, she thought. As she looked for the coffee, she caught a glimpse of the granite-covered island, and her cheeks blushed. Never again would she look at that counter the same way or forget the most incredible sensual experience of her life.

Spotting a carafe, she poured herself a large mug. The chicory tasted every bit as good as it smelled. A blur of movement outside caught her attention. She crept over to the window cautiously, unsure of her safety. Upon a closer look, she saw Logan, Dimitri and a child. Logan was pitching to the young boy, who looked as if he was hanging on the Alpha's every word. Dimitri crouched behind him pounding his glove into a catcher's mitt.

This was Logan's appointment? Wynter smiled. She opened the slider, waved at him and then shut the door behind her. Logan winked and then quickly focused back on their game. The patio stones warmed her bare feet but she managed to make it over to a comfortably worn Adirondack chair.

Sitting under a large southern oak tree, she admired the trailing sprigs of resurrection fern that carpeted its trunk and sprawling branches. Nearly two hundred feet from the house, the slow moving bayou teemed with wildlife.

A crack of the bat drew her focus. The boy hit a far one that went sailing over Logan's head. Logan took off in a sprint to get the ball while the hitter ran invisible bases. Dimitri waited at home base ready with a high five. Logan gave the kid a thumbs up in response.

Captivated, Wynter watched the Alpha and his beta instruct the boy. Fluctuating between serious discussion and excitement, the trio played baseball. She watched in both curiosity and admiration. A warmth settled in her chest as she witnessed yet another side of Logan. She'd seen him as a fighter, the first night she'd met him. Later as rescuer. Then at his office, the commanding businessman. She'd seen the Alpha, the leader giving the eulogy. The lover, who was adventurous, dominant and caring. And before she could stop the thought, she pictured him as a father. Father to her own children.

Wynter's words resounded in Logan's mind. *I love you.* Maybe she hadn't meant to say it…but she had. All he knew was that he loved her too and couldn't wait for her to shift. Because once she shifted, she'd be able to mark him. Then after they caught the killer, they'd formally mate. It would be fucking torture waiting; his wolf would protest.

He hated leaving her in the morning, wanting nothing more than to sink himself back into her sweetness. But he'd promised René a game of ball. Practice really. Little league was coming up in the spring. Soon all the pups would be over at his house, wanting to play with him. Logan prided himself on his pitching skills, but always made sure he let the boys get a hit off the Alpha. He taught skills and tried to boost their confidence.

Before René came over, he'd talked with Dimitri about helping with Wynter's shift. Logan wanted Wynter's first transformation to be peaceful and erotic, not traumatic. Not only could Wynter's libido go off the charts, he worried that the she-wolves would attempt a challenge. Two months had gone by and he'd already watched them fighting for their place in his life. And there was no denying the fact that Luci had shared his home. He thanked the Goddess he'd never given in and had sex with her. Regardless, she'd aggressively defend what she perceived as hers. Logan told Dimitri how he planned on letting Jake take the pack while they kept pace with Wynter. Slowly they'd merge, when she was ready, not a second before that. He'd keep her safely tucked between them until the time was right. Fiercely protective, he swore no one would harm a hair on her head.

Logan watched as Dimitri approached Wynter. He'd asked him to talk with her before tonight. Even though it wouldn't be the first time he'd ever shared a woman with Dimitri, he made it clear to him; Wynter was his and his alone. As such, his beta would have to pay close attention to his directions. While his beast possessively insisted on keeping her to himself, he suspected her shift would be rough. They'd let Wynter decide how much or how little sexual relief she needed afterwards. He expected that by the afternoon, her senses would flip into high alert, causing her to become extraordinarily aroused. Hunger. Thirst. Smell. Lust. Her body would prepare for the metamorphosis.

Anticipating a spectacular experience, Logan struggled to contain his excitement. He could not wait to see her as wolf. Keyed up, he needed an outlet. Challenging René to a race, he took off in a sprint across the property.

"Hey cher," Dimitri said with a smile. He pulled off his shirt revealing the prominent ridges of his stomach. "Damn, it's hot."

"Yes it is." Wynter smiled. She couldn't stop her eyes from roaming over his expansive chest. As tall as Logan, he looked as if he was a body builder, not too bulky, but broad and hard. *Shit, what the hell was wrong with her?* "Game over?"

"Yeah, René's a great kid. Logan's runnin' him back to his mamma's."

"Looks like fun."

"So, uh, made up with the Alpha, I see," he commented.

"Yes." Her cheeks turned pink. Just what had Logan told him? *Bad wolf.*

"How're you feelin' today?"

"Um, okay."

"Logan and I talked this morning. About your shift."

"Did Logan tell you everything?" she asked with a small smile, trying not to look at his chest.

"Let's just say that we have few secrets. Kinda comes with the territory." Dimitri took the seat next to hers, laying his head back on the wooden surface. "We trust each other. He knows that no matter what, I have his back. And yours."

"Like tonight?" Damn straight she was going to bring it up. Embarrassed or not, this was her life.

"Like tonight," Dimitri concurred, trying to discuss the topic without making her uncomfortable. "But don't worry. Logan will do whatever he has to do to make everything go smoothly."

"And you?" She noticed Logan walking toward them. He, too, had taken off his shirt. Holy hell, the man was hot. She coughed, trying to focus on what she'd been saying.

"Yeah, me too." Dimitri smiled at Logan, guessing he could hear at least part of their conversation. "Won't lie, cher, I'm looking forward to watching you shift, to helping you."

"I'm scared. But I guess this is going to happen whether I like it or not." Wynter glanced over to the bayou and then bowed her head. "I want you to know that I really appreciate everything you've done for me…your talks, the encouragement the past couple of days. I know this hasn't been easy on you either. Whatever happens tonight…I trust you both."

"Logan and I won't let anything happen to you. It's going to be one of the greatest days of your life." Dimitri smiled at Wynter, reached over and took her hand in his. He wanted so badly to be able to explain the rush she'd feel, but he reasoned it was of no use. Tonight, she'd run with them and learn the way of the wolves. He was confident she'd do well once she shifted.

Wynter squeezed his hand. She'd meant what she'd said. She trusted them, both Logan and Dimitri. Together they'd get through the night.

"Well hello, Logan, have I told you what a beautiful mate you have?" Dimitri said as Logan approached.

"Yes, you have. *My* mate is beautiful, isn't she?" Logan gave him a sardonic smile. He'd told him to talk, not drool.

"Very." Dimitri laughed, enjoying their easy banter.

Logan leaned down and gave Wynter a kiss. *His mate.* So perfect for him.

She reached up to him, pushing her hands into his sweaty hair. Her tongue swept into his mouth. A long drugging kiss ensued and before she knew it, she'd jumped into his arms, her legs wrapped around his waist.

Logan could tell she was starting to feel her increased arousal already. He shuddered to think what would happen later. Thank the Goddess he and his beta had a plan to get through the shift. But until then, he'd have to get her to rest. He smiled into her kiss, breaking away with a sigh. His forehead to hers, they both struggled to catch their breath.

"Hey Wyn, baby, you okay?" he asked gently.

"I…I'm sorry. I'm just so…so…" Oh God, what was happening? She'd woken feeling so happy, so refreshed. Now, she was hot and hungry, for both food and sex.

"I know. Come on, let's get you inside. Your wolf, she's rising. How about we go get something to eat? It'll help." Logan continued to hold Wynter and walked over to the back door.

"But I ate already," she protested, but her stomach rumbled.

"Your wolf's preparing. Eating'll help take the edge off. Being around D probably isn't helping either."

"What?"

"She knows my beta's scent. She'll want to be around him, to touch him."

"But Logan, this makes no sense. I only want you." Humiliation doused her arousal. She buried her head in his shoulder.

"It's okay, Wyn. This is just your body doing this," he reassured her, hugging her to his chest.

Logan yearned to tell her that he loved her, but the timing was off. With her impending change, he only sought to soothe her symptoms. Soon, he'd tell her, but with Dimitri watching and her on the edge, now was not that time.

Wynter retreated into herself. Her emotions, lusting after Dimitri upset her sense of what she knew was right. The night before she'd confessed her love. Unexpectedly, but still, those words fell through her lips. And today? Today, she nearly creamed her shorts over a hot, shirtless beta. What kind of a horrible human being did that? She shook her head, realizing she was no longer human. Yet she wasn't convinced she was one hundred percent wolf. She was made unnaturally, not born a shifter. Sanity would elude her until she ran her own blood tests; she needed to know who and what she really was

The day wore on and Wynter became increasingly restless. Her skin crawled. Her ears rang. Her stomach growled in hunger, despite eating as Logan had told her to do. Wringing her hands up into her hair, she pulled at the blonde springy tendrils, causing a twinge of pain. Sickening as it was, it salved the unending need to scratch and bite. Holed up in the bedroom, she tried to sleep it off, but had only managed a small nap. Logan advised her not to wear constricting clothing, so she'd thrown on a sundress sans underwear. It was far too suffocating; her skin felt raw and chafed against the soft cotton.

She hated that she was changing. None of what had happened had been in her control. Unfair and hurtful. Her parents dying. Being forced to live with Jax. Held captive for months. And now forced against her will to shift into an animal. She despised it. She'd have to make the only choice she had which was to carry on and endure it. Headstrong and determined, she pounded down the stairs, ready to face her Alpha.

Logan had planned a surprise, but things weren't going well. By late afternoon, Wynter had grown more and more uncomfortable and cranky. Unsure what they'd done to her to turn her wolf, he couldn't be certain how smoothly she'd shift. In only a few short hours, they'd know. He hated seeing her in such pain and abhorred the fact that he couldn't control it. That was what he did well: control, dominate. Yet hour after hour, it became more apparent that they'd have to let nature take her course.

By the time Wynter came downstairs, Logan noticed that she looked wild with agitation. Sexy as ever, her unruly curls sprang in all directions. Despite her discomposure, he knew her wolf would be amazing, but he thought better of telling her. For now, he'd orchestrate a diversion of sorts, a lesson on the bayou. He smiled as he led her outside to the waiting airboat. Nothing was more fun, and he suspected it would give her a rush, interrupting the cycle of negative thoughts playing in her mind.

"What is this?" she asked, not sure what they were doing on the docks.

"It's a boat," Logan answered with a wink.

"Yeah, I see that. Is it safe? I don't want to get eaten by alligators. Really, I've had enough fanged creatures sinking their teeth into me lately."

"Nothin' safer. This is our home, chérie and we're goin' to show it to you," he drawled, doing his best imitation of his beta. "We promise to keep you away from the snakes…even though we might eat them later. Maybe go crawfishin'."

"Don't let him fool you, cher. Logan may be a city boy, but he knows his way 'round the swamp…almost as well as I do. Wait 'til you see him pet the gators. He likes to kiss those pretty lips," Dimitri joked.

"Hey now, I may have been up north for the past fifty years, but it's like ridin' a bike. And hell, I've well made up for it these past couple of months," Logan told them. "And he's wrong about the lips…it's their nice white teeth that I like to see."

Wynter rolled her eyes. "As long as those pearly whites stay far away from me, we'll be good to go. Remember, I'm a city girl."

"Ah well, we'll see about that after you shift, baby." Logan gave her shoulder a comforting squeeze. "First, we're gonna go out into the lake a bit, and then we'll take you back in the swamp so you can see it in the daylight. And then, we'll boat on over to our running grounds."

Wynter eyed them both suspiciously. *See it in the daylight?* What was that supposed to mean? He did not think she'd be going into a swamp at night? Not happening.

"Here ya go." Logan handed her a pair of yellow earmuffs as Dimitri fired up the engine. With a small smile, she promptly put them on, cautiously looking forward to her boating adventure.

By the time they'd sped through the lake and hit the swamp, Wynter's body thrummed in exhilaration. The rush of the wind and intermittent spray of water combined with the speed sent her heart racing. She was having fun. It had been so long, she barely recognized the sensation. Smiling from ear to ear, she glanced over to Logan who was pointing to blooming bushes of swamp-rose mallow. The hibiscus petals, in white and pink, brought a splash of color to the otherwise green and brown landscape.

Dimitri cut the engine, and they all took off their earmuffs. Wynter scanned the horizon, astonished at the beauty all around her. Insects sang in the twilight. Blue sky and clouds reflected in the water as the sun went down. Ancient cypress trees stood proud, their knees poking up toward the heavens. Logan tapped her shoulder and held his fingers to his lips to quiet any potential conversation. He pointed to a great white egret poised immobile, hunting for his next meal. The majestic bird took notice of them drifting toward the bank, and took off in flight toward another fishing ground.

"It's unbelievable," she said, swiveling her head.

"Hey Ace," Dimitri called. He dug out a small bucket. A prehistoric swish of a tail followed and eyes rose above the water. "Come on over here."

Wynter reached for Logan's hand and turned so she could watch.

"D likes to feed his boy," Logan commented.

"Ace? How does he know that's the same one?"

"They're territorial. And live a long time too. This is his spot. There's a few of his girls…see there on the bank." Logan called attention to a couple of alligators who were basking in the final rays of the sun.

Wynter watched in great delight as Dimitri held up the raw chicken. The reptile lurched out of the water and snapped it up.

"Amazing," Wynter gasped, grinning at the same time.

"They're just a small part of the ecosystem. This place…it's special."

"Do you all come here a lot?"

"Not enough. As much as I love this place, I'm in the city a lot of the time. Even when I lived in Philly, we split our time between the city and mountains. It's the same here. Poor D is goin' to have to get used to livin' in the French Quarter. But you can't really run wolf in town, so if we want to go for a run, this is the place."

"You run in the swamp?"

"Yes and no, cher. We've got lots of open land that's easier to run on but if need be, we know how to walk in the swamp," Dimitri explained.

"But we'll save that lesson for another day," Logan finished.

"We'd better head out. It's just about time to hit the preserve. Who's up for a sunset?" Dimitri asked. He wiped his hands on a towel and readied to start up the engine.

"Thanks for bringing me here. I love it…it's breathtaking." Wynter tried to hide the emotion rushing up into her throat but a traitorous tear fell. She swiped her finger at her eye, capturing it. With a small smile, she sighed.

"It's going to be okay. Just stick with your wolves, baby." Logan kissed her cheek.

A subtle sense of relief showered his conscience, knowing she liked the swamp. Even though he'd grown up in the French Quarter, his parents had made sure he'd spent plenty of time running in what at that time was considered the 'far country'. Good thing, too, because over the centuries, the city had grown, sprawled over its open spaces and now this land belonged to his wolves. It represented his culture. The bayou. The swamp. Home to his wolf.

Her words of admiration soothed his need for her acceptance. He supposed he hadn't realized just how important it was that she'd approved of his home, the way he lived. A house he could change, but everything else? No, she'd either welcome or reject his world. A final test, the pack, awaited not just her, but him as well.

As the motor roared, Logan wrapped his hand over hers. His gut told him that she could do it. It might not be easy, but fuck easy. Nothing lately in their lives had been easy but that didn't equate to impossible. Like his challenges, he'd won them all right but not without difficulty. Nonetheless, victory had been all the more sweet. He'd kill to make this work, but knew she'd have to fight on her own. And then she'd face the pack. No, not easy. But sometimes the best things in life were hard and well worth the fight.

Chapter Twenty-Four

Dimitri stayed back to tie off the boat. He watched his Alpha and mate through the trees, sensing the struggle. In all his years, he'd never known a human to shift. They were born wolves, not made. Yet defying nature, this was going down. He hadn't told Logan, but he was seriously worried about the pack's reaction to Wynter. Not only was she from New York, she was human. Sure, the pack would welcome a mate for their Alpha, but they'd expected her to be one of their own, and without a doubt, wholly wolf.

The she-wolves had been chasing around Logan since he'd replaced Marcel. Luci, especially, had staked her unofficial claim by continuing to live with Logan. Up until several days ago, she'd made it her daily ritual to knock on Logan's bedroom door. And while he knew Logan had only comforted her, Luci wasn't going to take his impending mating well.

Cognizant that Logan had been busy with Wynter and also Dana's death, Dimitri had hesitated to broach the subject with him. But tonight, he was prepared to step in and assist. And that didn't just include helping Wynter sexually. Yes, he'd grown fond of the little wolf. But at the moment, he was more concerned about her safety. Dimitri had already decided that he'd step in and stop a fight, if necessary. Sure, he'd take a hard hit for intervening but so be it. A direct challenge to Wynter wouldn't negate her status as Logan's mate, but still, it was within a she-wolf's right to attack and kill if necessary. If someone challenged Wynter and she lost, it would further distract Logan from leading the pack. Within days if not hours, another challenge for Alpha might be issued. Logan had promised to kill the next wolf who challenged him, and Dimitri was confident he'd make good on his word

No matter how sexually adventurous she'd felt, Wynter's human notions clashed with her emerging wolf. She watched as Logan stood naked before her, cajoling her to shuck the dress. Wynter reluctantly undressed and immediately covered her breasts with her hands. Realizing that the rest of her body was already exposed, she forced her arms to her sides.

"Come here, Wyn," he told her. Magnanimously nude, she was a spectacular sight, Logan thought. "You trust me?"

"Yes," she responded quietly, looking at her feet. She could feel Logan and Dimitri's eyes on her skin. She was frightened out of her wits. No matter how much she'd told herself this was going to happen, she still wasn't prepared.

A surge of nausea rolled her stomach. Reacting, she bent over, her hands on her knees, willing her stomach to hold the food. She coughed and gagged, managing to push the bile back down her esophagus. *Please God. I will not throw up…no throwing up…especially in front of Logan. Be brave. I can do this. No, I will do this.* She closed her eyes and took a deep cleansing breath. With a whoosh, she blew it out through her mouth. *Logan is with me.* Logan. Oh shit. She'd almost forgotten he was watching her ridiculous panic attack. She stood up and gave him an apologetic smile.

"Are you okay? As gross as it is, if you need to throw up, go ahead. Believe me, you wouldn't be the first."

"You're being nice."

Logan smiled. "Well, it's the pups who usually hurl their first time, but you're kind of like a pup."

She shot him an annoyed look, her hands on her hips.

"Okay, more like a super-hot, naked human lady wolf," he laughed. "Seriously, baby. Nothing and I mean nothing bad is going to happen tonight. We'll shift. We'll run. We'll make love." His voice was low and dominant, guiding her wolf.

She simply nodded, allowing him to take her hand in his.

"Look at me, sweetheart," Logan instructed. When her eyes met his, he continued. "I'm sorry this happened to you…I really am. No matter how much I want you as my mate, I'd never force a shift on you. It sucks. It's not fair, even. But there's no stopping nature. This is like skiing, baby. Sure, it's a little dangerous. You will most definitely fall. Probably will be sore afterwards. And a little dirty. But most certainly, you will have fun. And before you go hatin' my analogy, you've never been skiing with me…and you will love it."

"I like skiing," she disclosed with a small smile. "I'm from New York."

"And someday, we'll do that together too. But today, you'll shift. So let's do this thing, okay?"

"Okay." As soon as she'd agreed, her skin tingled as if she'd stuck her finger in an electrical socket. She looked up at the full moon. As if it reached out with a firm hand striking into her heart, she seized, unable to speak.

Logan saw Wynter freeze and knew immediately it had begun. Damn, this was not how a pup or anyone was supposed to shift. It shouldn't be done under duress. Transformation was a celebratory milestone. Logan focused within, drawing on his inherent Alpha power, attempting to soothe her mind. But her immobility continued and within seconds, she began to shake uncontrollably, saliva dripping from her mouth as if she'd gone into a full grand mal seizure.

Logan put his hands onto her cheeks, forcing her to look at him, but her vacant stare told him she was lost within her own mind. Dimitri sensed trouble and ran to his assistance, but Logan waved him off with a hand. He and he alone would coax her out of the paralysis that had taken over her body.

"Wynter, concentrate on my voice. Listen to me. No matter what's going on inside of you, I know you can hear me. I'm your Alpha. And as such, you will do as I say. Your wolf. She knows this. And you do too. You need to let go. Let me in." Goddess, it shouldn't be this way. He hated to be harsh with her but he needed to force her wolf to the surface. "Close your eyes."

Unresponsive, Wynter continued to quiver.

"Close. Your. Eyes. This is an order from your Alpha. Do it now," he growled.

Recognition registered in her pupils. Her lids flickered but still didn't shut. Her wolf rolled submissively onto her back, yelping in response. At his voice, she struggled, clawing to get out, to run with her mate.

Small though it was, Logan knew she'd heard him. He'd have to be more forceful. A dominant, almost foreign voice emerged. "Wynter, I'm commanding you to shift. Now close. Your. Eyes."

Logan's authoritative directive speared through the palpable numbness that had arrested Wynter's muscles. As if someone had smashed a rock through a pane of glass, her humanity shattered into pieces. Her eyes snapped shut, and the wolf emerged. Utter agony ensued as the metamorphosis completed. Gagged by the shift, her scream pinged within her own consciousness, and she thought she'd died. Mouth opened, no tortured cry would save her. But within seconds, she heard a howl pierce the night air. Blinking her eyes, she realized the animalistic noise had come from her. For it was she, the wolf, acknowledging her shift, calling to her mate. As Logan came into focus, she caught sight of his proud smile.

Logan held his breath as she changed before his eyes. Her silent screams tore open his gut. With great restraint, he held back, allowing her to transform independently. There could be no other way. And within seconds, the red-haired, blue-eyed, she-wolf lay on the dirt.

"Look at you, sweetheart," he whispered and crouched down to the ground.

Goddess, she was every bit as resplendent in her wolf as in her person. His heart constricted seeing that she'd gone into submission. With her ears backward and tail curved under her backside, she whimpered and quivered in fear. Slowly reaching forward, he held his hand out to her.

Distressed and disoriented, Wynter sniffed and licked Logan's hand. She knew her mate. His scent, his taste. Thank God, he was still here with her. He didn't leave. She focused on his voice and touch. Everything about him seemed to calm her and felt peaceful.

"That's right, it's me. I won't hurt you, baby," he assured her, rubbing her ears. He nodded to Dimitri, who'd stripped in preparation for his own shift. But as his friend drew closer, Wynter growled and bared her teeth.

"Come on now, it's okay. It's just D. You know he won't hurt you either."

Wynter saw movement, a human. Defensively, she snarled at the incoming danger. An innate desire to protect surfaced.

Logan eyed Dimitri. "Slowly, D. She looks like she wants to bite. And considering you're nekkid….well, go easy. You've got a low hanging target there," he joked.

"Ya got that right. Geez, she may have just shifted but she's a feisty one." Dimitri carefully sidled up to Logan. He slid his hand down Logan's arm, picking up some of his scent, and then presented a palm to Wynter. He knew that she'd eventually know it was him. But at the moment, the overload on her senses made it difficult for her to process.

Another hand came toward her. Cautiously, she nosed his skin. Logan. Dimitri. Yes, she knew Dimitri, cared for him. A lick of his skin cemented her acceptance. While she'd not tasted Dimitri, both his scent and touch happily appeased her wolf.

"That's it, baby. See, told ya, it's just D," Logan coaxed, continuing to caress her fur.

He smiled over to Dimitri, who also had begun to pet her neck. A pivotal moment for them all, he supposed. His mate, a human, had shifted. And he and his beta had just borne witness to the extraordinary phenomenon. Both men, without jealousy or expectation, nurtured the new little wolf. As she relaxed into their calming strokes, Logan smiled at Dimitri before addressing her.

"Okay little wolf, we've gotta shift too. I'm gonna go first, then D. Don't be afraid now. We won't be able to talk to you like this when we're shifted. But you'll know what to do, I promise. The only thing I ask is that you stay close. Even though the ground here is firm, there's plenty of trouble to get into, so stick with us," he told her as he broke contact. He stood up while Dimitri continued to rub her. "This'll just take a second."

Logan's tall form morphed into a large gray wolf. Towering over Wynter, he pressed his muzzle into her neck, licking her snout.

Wynter snuggled into Logan's long and soft tongue. She relished his wolf, desiring his scent on her fur. In return, she licked up under his chin. In a blink, a second dark gray wolf nudged her alongside of her mate. *Dimitri.* Surreal as it was, she licked both wolves, her Alpha, his beta. Caring and loving, as beasts and men, they'd protected her.

Logan and Dimitri backed away from Wynter, waiting for her to stand. They both knew she'd be unsteady at first. It was expected of all new pups. Standing on four legs, instead of two, naturally would throw her for a loop. But like riding a bike, she'd never forget how to do it once she learned. It was almost painful to watch. Logan thanked the Goddess he was in wolf form so he didn't need to hide a smile. She pushed up onto all fours only to wobble and fall. But never being one to give up, she immediately rebounded. A few steps, then within seconds, she ran joyous circles around him and his beta.

Wynter couldn't believe how easy it was to run around like this. Sure, she'd stumbled a bit, but now she took off like the wind. It was freeing. And fun. She wondered if she'd wake up any minute to find this had all been a dream. But as she followed Logan and Dimitri and the night wore on, she became more comfortable in her newfound reality and a vigorous wave of curiosity overtook her. In a surge of confidence, she raced ahead of her boys, weaving in and out of the trees. A sound caught her attention; she stilled. Both Logan and Dimitri froze, having heard it too, a grunt echoing throughout the woods.

Instinctively Wynter crept toward the noise, but Logan quickly blocked her, contemplating whether or not they should try to attack it. A wild boar would make an excellent meal, but they weren't the easiest prey to catch. With few natural predators, the razorbacks had become an invasive species, disrupting the natural balance of the environment. Nasty, they'd been known to attack animals and humans alike. Despite the known difficulties and dangers associated with hunting one, Dimitri and Logan loved a challenge and had eaten them many a time. A harmless bunny rabbit would have been a better choice to teach Wynter how to hunt. But on the other hand, showing her how the pack worked together to kill big prey was an important lesson that she had to learn eventually. And who better to teach her than him?

Without warning, the feral pig charged at Logan and Wynter, trying to ram them with its head and tusks. Dispersing, the trio confused the prey. Logan growled at the animal while Dimitri rounded from behind. Wynter, having never hunted, hungered for it but also innately sensed the danger. She watched as the dominant males circled the beast. In synchronicity, the Alpha and his beta assaulted the animal. Logan took it on head first, biting into its snout. Dimitri bit into the flank. Even though the boar wasn't fast, its tough skin made it exceptionally difficult to kill. The coordinated attack continued for several minutes, until the squealing pig faltered. As it did so, Wynter cautiously approached. Logan tore off fresh meat, and made room for Wynter to participate in the hunt.

After killing and eating a good portion of the boar, the threesome padded under a tree and lay down. His little wolf had done well, Logan thought. She'd known not to interrupt when he and Dimitri made their first lunge at the wild game. Smart and cunning, she'd waited until it was on the ground to assist. Some wolves weren't always so clever, ending up with a gouging, courtesy of the pig.

A rustle of leaves alerted Logan that the pack was approaching. His ears perked and he barked to Dimitri. In anticipation, they stood protectively flanking her. The integration into the pack was another critical task in her transformation. And for Logan, it'd been the first time he'd run with pack since he'd issued his ultimatum. If anyone challenged him, death lingered as the outcome.

Hunting had sated Wynter's wolf. Alongside her men, she awaited the pack members. She shoved any nervous emotions aside, and assumed a dominant positioning. She may not have had much pack experience, but she knew enough that she planned on being an alpha female. And now especially, with Logan as her mate, she wouldn't let another female, wolf or woman, touch him. Keeping her head held up and tail outward, she dared another to approach.

A black wolf padded forward. *Jake.* Strange, somehow she knew it was him. She sniffed. Yes, his familiar scent pleased her wolf. He'd been her protector. An ally. A gray wolf trailed behind him. *Zeke.* Yes, she was getting good at this. An angry presence invaded her peaceful thought. Smaller white and brown wolves padded toward them. Fiona, the brown. Luci, the white. Around them, others filtered toward them through the trees.

Wynter attempted to read them. Instinctively, she became aware of her given ability to assess the state of the pack. Concentrating, she allowed the lines of communication to spring to life. Logan was feeling protective. Dimitri felt guarded. The pack? The pack resonated with a mixture of both inquisitiveness and jubilation. They loved their Alpha. His contentment reflected their own emotions. The need to please him was paramount in their lives.

She allowed each wolf to approach her, but Logan bared his teeth preventing anyone from getting too close. Dimitri, too, remained next to her, unwilling to leave her side. Optimism rode high within her spirit until a rush of fur crashed into her, sending her flying onto her side. Searing pain shot through her flank, but stumbling, she managed to right herself.

Confusion racked her senses, and as she looked around, she quickly surmised that Luci had blindsided her. The white wolf rushed and snarled at her, and Wynter growled in response. Only seconds passed before Wynter's wolf interpreted Luci's action for what it was: a challenge. Grateful that her human mind didn't have time to contemplate the complexities of the situation, her wolf raised her head, and snapped. Luci charged her and they both rolled on the ground. Wynter yipped as a white hot streak tore at her ear. Panting and staggering, the pair of fighting wolves briefly separated at the sound of their Alpha's bark.

Wynter, surprised at her own voracity and aggression, snarled at Logan when he attempted to intervene. Rage and possessiveness drove her to continue the fight. From the very first time she'd seen Luci, she'd known that she was a threat. *Threat to me. Threat to my mate.* Wynter snapped; her lips pulled high, exposing her canines. Despite her position, Luci continued to approach, staring at Wynter, snarling. Exploding from a crouched position, Wynter rushed Luci and tore at her fur. The first drop of blood to her tongue incited her to continue her offensive strike. By the time her assault ceased, Luci laid belly up. Her wolf insisted on nothing less than death, but Logan's voice stopped her from tearing out the white wolf's throat. With her teeth buried deep into the flesh of Luci's neck, she heard human words, Logan screaming, commanding her to stop.

Stunned, Logan watched as Wynter launched herself at Luci. He knew all too well the need to establish dominance. After Luci initiated the challenge and Wynter successfully managed to avert the attack, he'd grown confident that she truly was alpha. He wanted nothing more than to protect her from the darkness. But being in pack meant establishing rank, something she had to do on her own. And since she'd snarled at him, indicating her wish to proceed, he wouldn't deny her what she sought. But what he had not expected was that she'd attack Luci until she'd pinned her to the ground, intending to slaughter her. While he held no sympathy for Luci, he couldn't allow Wynter to kill the she-wolf. Unfortunately Wynter was too far engrossed in her beast to listen to his wolf's warnings. Shifting to human, he yelled at her to release.

"Wynter, let her go! Do not kill her!" He watched as she disengaged her jaw from the fur, but still held a firm paw to the other wolf's belly. Logan blew out a breath. *Holy fuck, she'd almost killed Luci.*

A slow burn racked the side of Wynter's head, but she shook it off, refusing to show weakness. With a snort, she accepted Luci's submission, removing her paw. Raising her hackles and tail, she padded over to Logan's human form, awaiting his order. His hand on her head, his approval warmed her heart. She scanned the pack once again, registering their state. Anger? No, respect. More so, every single one of them understood her position and who Logan was to her. It was crystal clear. *Mine. He's mine.*

Chapter Twenty-Five

Logan, still unclothed, held Wynter in his arms, wrapped in a blanket. By the time they'd run back to the boat and shifted back, she'd collapsed in exhaustion. Goddess almighty, he hadn't witnessed a fight like that between two she-wolves in a long time. And never had the challenge been about him. While he hated that she'd been injured, she'd done what she needed to do, securing her place as alpha female. No one would mess with her.

Dimitri pulled the boat alongside the swamp cabin, and Logan disembarked. While the modest structure didn't have running water, Dimitri had set up a portable shower. Tossing the soiled blanket to the floor, Logan turned on the solar-powered contraption and stepped under the spray. He scrubbed the dirt and blood off of Wynter first and then handed her over to Dimitri who waited with an oversized towel. Allowing his beta to take her still sleeping form inside, Logan quickly finished his own shower. By the time he entered the cabin, Dimitri had already tucked Wynter into the king-sized futon and was lighting the oil lamps.

"Thanks, man." Logan strode across the room to his mate and sat down next to her. He smoothed his hand over her hair. "She's incredible."

"Can you fucking believe she almost killed Luci?" Dimitri asked, still shocked at how they'd fought. He made his way back over to the door.

"No I can't. But I have to tell you, there's part of me that feels a little better knowing that she can protect herself. I hate to even think about it, but we both know it's not over," Logan affirmed thoughtfully. A day in the country wasn't nearly enough to make him forget that Dana lay bricked into her tomb. Nor did he forget the car bomb that had almost killed Jake and Wynter.

"I made some progress with the laptop. Got some data for your girl. Let's hope she can work her magic until this asshole pops up again or Devereoux finds his demon seed."

"I had a lab set up in the garage today. She doesn't know yet. I'm going to show it to her tomorrow. It's important she can test herself, her blood. She's worried."

"She may be worried but she looked all wolf to me. Tonight, she didn't seem any different than the rest of us."

Logan cocked an eyebrow at Dimitri. "Yeah, except that she almost killed another wolf on her first run with the pack. You ever seen a pup do that? No fucking way. She's strong…unusually so for a new wolf."

"Can't say I've ever seen it but damn glad she took down Luci. Don't get me wrong, Luci can be a great girl, but she's been eyeing you ever since

Marcel died. You knew that wouldn't sit right with Wyn."

"She doesn't want to share her mate," Logan reasoned.

"And you do?"

"I love you, D, but not really." Logan shook his head; his face grew tense with concern. "Listen, I don't know how she's going to feel when she wakes up. I mean her shift didn't go so well. I've never seen a wolf shake like that. And then she wouldn't shift. You saw what happened…I had to command her to do it. And what just went down with Luci? I guess we'll just have to see what happens next. But I need you here."

"Whatever you want. I won't lie; I'm looking forward to being with both of you. Must be the moon…or it could be that I remember how sweet she felt in my arms the other night…yeah, that's it," he teased.

"Yeah, I'm pretty sure this'll be a one-time gig for you, so don't get too attached."

"Got it." Dimitri smiled and grabbed a towel.

"Hey D."

"Yeah." He stopped before going out the door and turned to his Alpha.

"Thanks." Logan's eyes met his beta's. His voice took on a gentle but serious tone. "I mean it. Thanks for being there. Not just tonight…but the past couple of months. I know Marcel wanted this for me, but if you hadn't been there…things might have been way different."

"No problem, man. We all loved him. But he was right about you." He glanced to Wynter and back to Logan. "And about her shift…you're right, it was rough. But she'll be okay. Sometimes things don't turn out how we think they should be. Just how they're supposed to be. However the hell it happened, she's wolf now."

Logan silently regarded his beta. Words couldn't be truer. He hadn't set out to be Alpha nor did he choose a human for a mate. Life, destiny; it chose him, not the other way around. This new chapter in his life may not have been a walk in the park, but he'd come to terms with it.

"Hey, tonight's a celebration," Dimitri offered.

Logan gave him a small smile. "Ah, yes. Well, it seems my mate has taken to sleeping. Unusual reaction to shifting but nothing about her is mundane, that's for sure. Go get a shower and then come join us, okay?"

"I'm gonna check the boat one more time and clean up." Dimitri gave a final wave and left.

Logan threw back the covers, got in bed and pulled Wynter against his torso. He pillowed her head on his chest and ran his hand over her arm, taking her hand in his. His ferocious little mate had torn up out there tonight. The sight of her forcing Luci into submission was fucking unreal. And a huge turn on to his wolf.

Wynter snuggled into Logan's warmth. As her senses awakened, so too, did her desire for him. Her eyes fluttered open and she pushed her leg over his so that the length of him rested on her thigh.

"Logan," she purred.

"Hey baby, how do you feel?"

"Hmm....horny," she laughed. Too tired to sit up, she took in her surroundings from the safety of Logan's arms. Bare wooden walls and a tin roof gave no clue to where they'd taken her. "Where are we?"

"Our cabin."

"You have a cabin?"

"D and I always had one...even before I moved to Philly. So when I got back, we ripped the old one down and put this up. Can you smell that cedar-like scent?"

"Hmm." She nodded.

"That's the cypress."

"Cypress?" Wynter's voice took on a higher octave as she realized exactly where she was. "Are we in the middle of the swamp? At night? With alligators? Bugs?"

Logan laughed. After hunting a wild boar and nearly killing Luci, his delicate little human was back.

"Yes, sweetheart and you're safe. Nothin's going to get you out here besides D and me. This place is sealed up tight. We've got everything we need to survive the night...food, water, a bed. It's peaceful." He kissed her again. "Secluded."

"Secluded, huh? I like the sound of that," she replied huskily. She ran her hand over the ridges of his abs and then traced her fingertip around his flat nipple.

Logan reached for her wrist. "You were gorgeous tonight. A red wolf." He circled the pad of his thumb into her palm. "So wild. And fierce."

"It felt freeing. It was like my wolf...she knew what to do. Some part of her, she knows already how to act." Wynter blushed then shook her head. It still seemed unbelievable that she'd shifted. "It's crazy, right?"

"No, not crazy. That's what it's like. And we're going to be doing a lot of it while we're here."

A memory flashed in her mind, her teeth in a wolf's fur. She looked up at Logan for assurance. "Oh God, is Luci okay? I remember...I bit..."

"She'll be fine. You listened to me, that's the important thing," Logan confirmed.

"I just remember feeling so mad. Did you see how she freakin' rammed into me?"

"Yeah and I'm thinking the fight kind of needed to happen, but I wasn't expecting it tonight, that's for damn sure. But after you growled at me...well, I let the fur fly."

"Sorry." Wynter cringed at the thought.

"Don't be." Logan shrugged.

"What are you saying?" Wynter pushed up on her elbow so she could better see his face.

"Luci, she wants to be the alpha female. If you hadn't made her submit, she wouldn't have stopped coming after me."

"But she's not your mate."

"No, but that wouldn't stop her. I wouldn't ever choose her but as you can imagine, it wouldn't be good for us if every time you weren't around she tried to touch me. Just imagine me coming home with her scent. How do you think that would make you feel?"

"I'd fucking kill her," Wynter stated emotionlessly.

"Yeah. You almost did," Logan replied. "But now, rank's been established. It'll all fall in place. And it happened in front of the pack which is good."

"When did I get so bloodthirsty?" Wynter laid her head back down on his chest. She'd meant the words, 'I'd fucking kill her.' *Was this who she was now?*

"Just stop the train, Dr. Ryan. I know what you're thinking. And you're not a monster. You are, however, wolf. You put her in her place and for that, I'm thankful. Now speaking of being hurt; how's that ear?"

"I'm fine."

"Let me see." Logan pulled her up, so that she was facing him. Pushing her hair to the side, he inspected her ear closely and sucked on her lobe. "Good as new."

As his warm breath caressed her neck, the ache between her legs thrummed with need. When she'd told him she'd felt horny, that didn't begin to describe what was happening to her. Heat rushed to her face, and she pushed the covers aside, trying to cool her body.

"Logan, I…I…" Embarrassed by her state, she tried to hide her face in her hands.

"It's okay, baby. I'll take care of you. I promise by morning, things will be better." He trailed kisses down her neck.

"Touch me," she begged.

Logan caressed her breast, pinching a diamond tip. She moaned, wriggling into him.

"Logan, I think there's something wrong. I'm so…so…" Wynter gasped, pressing her forehead to his chest. She struggled to find the words to describe the sensations afflicting her body. The aching, painful desire was unbearable.

Logan slid his hand around the nape of her neck and brought his lips to hers. Deepening the kiss, he reveled in her taste as their tongues intertwined. They both fought for breath as passion overtook them. His cock thickened in response. Wrapping his hand into her hair, he lost himself in her. He found her sex, and he plunged a finger deep into her tight heat. Straining to hold her, his pecs bulged as she bucked against his tantalizing assault.

Wynter's whimpers were silenced by his mouth. She fervidly kissed him, biting at his lips and sweeping her tongue with his. The delightful suffering plagued every cell of her body from the inside out. Wynter released an animalistic cry as her claws extended from her fingertips and she quickly withdrew them. As the pressure built inside her, she arched her back like a cat. Logan's fingers stroked her bundle of nerves, but it wasn't nearly enough to assuage the tension. The pulse of her orgasm teetered at the brink, eluding her until the pad of his thumb massaged her clit. Screaming Logan's name, her release shattered. She wished it had been enough, but within seconds, her body reignited.

"Logan, please make love to me. I need more," she cried, climbing on top of him, savage with arousal.

"Come here, baby." Logan wished her transition hadn't been so difficult. As much as he loved her adventurous sexuality, he knew she'd be in pain if they didn't appease her wolf. The sound of the door shutting, alerted him to Dimitri's presence.

Wynter looked up to see Dimitri standing at the bottom of the bed. His tanned muscles flexed underneath the beads of water that still clung to his chest. *No, it was wrong.* Her conscience warred, struggling to rationalize her desire for him. Although not her mate, Dimitri represented safety and protection, Logan's friend and confidant.

"Logan, I'll be fine. I just need..." *How could she want to be with two men? Someone other than her mate?*

"Wyn, it's okay. We're here for you." Logan pressed a quick kiss to her lips. Holding her face in his palms, he gazed into her eyes. "What you feel...us...this isn't wrong or dirty. It's what you need. It's a part of your change. And you're beautiful. You're the most beautiful woman I've ever known. This...tonight, the three of us, even if it never happens again, it's special."

"But..." *What if he hated her afterwards? Rejected her?*

"You're mine, baby. D knows that. He's the only person on this Earth who I'd ever trust with you...with us. No matter what we do, you belong to me. Always." Logan growled and then kissed her passionately.

"Yours," she breathed into his mouth. Oh God, she was going to do this. *Her men*...at least for tonight. She trusted Logan on this journey. Most of all, she loved him.

Logan briefly pulled his lips away from hers. Looking into Wynter's eyes, he spoke to her slowly and lovingly. "Listen to me Wynter, you're in control tonight. Now let us take care of you."

Wynter's eyes teared and she nodded. She felt too much. *Too much emotion. Too much desire.* But she'd made her decision.

Dimitri approached slowly. Naked, he sprawled onto the bed. His Alpha's mate's scent enticed him, but he patiently waited. Logan was right. This was special. Over a hundred years on the Earth, and never had he experienced the shift of a human. The enormous respect he held for Logan only heightened the importance of the evening.

Logan wanted to give Wynter the world and then some. Gently, he picked her up by her waist and laid her onto Dimitri so that she was cradled between his legs, her back to his stomach. He looked over to Wynter, who smiled, then above to Dimitri. Reaching for his beta's wrist, Logan placed his hand onto her breast. Dimitri responded, caressing her soft peaks.

"That's it, D. Feel our little wolf," Logan instructed. "Isn't she amazing?"

"Oh Goddess, yes," Dimitri bit out as he touched her, his cock swelled against her ass. He pushed her hair aside and licked at her neck behind her ear. "Cher, you smell so good."

"Dimitri," she breathed.

Logan settled between their legs, his belly pressed to Wynter's. He rested on his forearms so that he could feast on her breasts. Wynter threw her head back, baring her neck to both Logan and Dimitri. Submitting to them both, she allowed the erotic experience to envelop her.

"That's a girl. Feel us," Logan coaxed before taking her nipple into his mouth. He swirled his tongue around its tip. A small bite elicited a gasp from his mate. Logan pressed his hand down between her legs, startling her as he swiped his fingers through her glistening folds. He withdrew his hand and extended it to Dimitri, who met his eyes.

"Taste," he ordered.

Dimitri complied, opening his lips as Logan's finger pressed into his mouth. He moaned, savoring the unique sweetness. So intimate, Dimitri had never tasted from another man but couldn't refuse. And shit, if it didn't make his cock throb.

Wynter watched in fascination as Logan fed Dimitri. *So fucking hot.* It surprised her that he'd touch him so gently. Their closeness had always existed but this was more. Her body flared in response. She rocked her bottom against Dimitri's growing arousal.

"Delicious," Dimitri groaned.

"Relax, sweetheart." Logan slid his body downward until he reached the apex of her legs and held her thighs apart. "Open, that's it."

Wynter caught his eyes, aware that she was fully exposed to them. She shivered as Logan softly grazed his finger through her labia and over her clit.

"Logan, please," she pleaded.

"She's so beautiful, isn't she, D?" Logan kissed the top of her mound, teasing her.

"Oh yeah," Dimitri agreed, taking Wynter's breasts back into his hands while kissing her shoulders.

Logan smiled up at Dimitri and then to Wynter a split second before he swiped his tongue through her swollen lips. His balls tightened as he drank in her creamy essence. She grunted in pleasure as he speared his tongue into her core, and he could tell that she was going to come within seconds.

Dimitri, wanting to taste more of Wynter, slipped out from underneath her, kissing along her collarbone until he reached her breasts. He took a nipple into his mouth, sucking and teasing it with his teeth. She stabbed her fingers into Logan's hair and then Dimitri's, holding them to her skin. She was so close to release. Logan at her pussy. Dimitri's lips on her breasts. And as she felt a tongue trail down her stomach, the energy of her arousal slammed into her.

"Logan, I'm going to…" She tried holding it back, but it was of no use. As the orgasm rolled through her, she was vaguely cognizant of them switching positions.

Unspoken signals passed between Logan and Dimitri as they moved seamlessly so that Dimitri took over for Logan; his mouth suckling Wynter's clit. Logan pressed up onto his knees, positioning himself at her entrance. He watched Wynter's head loll back into the pillow as he plunged his cock into her wet pussy. Unrelenting, Dimitri continued to suck her swollen nub while Logan pumped in and out of her hotness.

Wynter fought for breath as a second climax claimed her. Her eyes flew open and she saw Logan holding her legs, pressing into her, Dimitri's head now in between her legs.

"Yes, fuck, Wyn. So goddamned tight." Logan almost forgot where he was, lost in the heat of his mate. He saw her blindly reaching, grabbing Dimitri's hair. "D, Wynter needs you."

Dimitri licked his lips and knelt up so he could go to her. He hissed as Wynter's hand quickly wrapped around his stiff shaft.

"Take him, Wyn. That's it," Logan directed, still thrusting in and out of her.

"Dimitri, come. Come to me," she ordered, never letting go of him. She moaned in protest. He was too far away for what she had in mind.

Dimitri made his way up to Wynter and leaned up against the headboard next to her. Whatever she wanted, he'd do, but he wouldn't initiate. Dimitri sucked a deep breath as she drew him to her, lapping her tongue at his plump head. He closed his eyes tight, bracing himself as she began to lick his cock.

As Wynter took Dimitri's hardness into her mouth, her eyes locked on Logan's. A hard thrust forced her to gasp.

"That's so fucking hot, sweetheart. Suck him," Logan told her.

He couldn't freaking believe how erotic it was to see her like this with his beta. He watched as Dimitri fought the pleasure, his eyes locked on Logan's. Unexpectedly, no possessiveness or jealousy registered. Love for both of them pulled at his heart. He allowed the rise of his own release to build, knowing they both were so close to coming.

Wynter moved in rhythm with Logan, meeting his thrusts with her own. No longer able to keep her eyes open, she sucked Dimitri hard. Relaxing into the taste of him, she allowed him to fuck her mouth while Logan fucked her pussy. The rush of it all drove her further into her untamed passion. She moaned and released Dimitri, realizing she was going to come again.

"So close, Logan. Please," she begged.

Logan circled his fingers over her clitoris. In response, her quivering channel fisted more tightly around him. He breathed deeply, fighting his own need to come.

Wynter cried out loud as another climax smashed into her, leaving her shaking and rebounding to meet Logan's pelvis. She fought to breathe as the tremors continued to roll throughout her body.

Logan rocked in and out of her slowly, his forehead pressed to hers and he kissed her deeply. He knew Wynter's hand was still on Dimitri's cock, gently stroking him. It felt surreal, joined like this with them. It was one night. It might never happen again. But for tonight, he'd have his mate and beta the way he'd envisioned, sharing them both and they with each other.

"Logan, it feels so good," she panted. "Oh God."

"Do you want us, Wyn?" Logan asked, his eyes pinned on her. "Both of us?"

"Yes," she whispered, nodding. Even though they shared this moment with Dimitri, she felt closer than ever to Logan.

Logan's heated breaths morphed into a shallow sigh as he slowed his pace. With his mate at his chest, he noticed that Dimitri had closed his eyes, presumably trying not to come. Reaching for his beta, Logan pulled at his arm, rolling him onto his side so that his stomach was flush against their sides.

"Come, D. We need you," Logan told him.

Dimitri acceded. He allowed Logan to rest his hand on her belly between both Logan and Wynter. The contact sizzled, solidifying their relationship. His erection pressed against her hip. Kissing along the side of her breast, Dimitri's gaze settled on Logan.

"You sure about this? Logan? Wynter?" Dimitri needed to be certain this was what they both wanted.

Logan nodded. "Sweetheart, there's no going back."

"Please, it's so…so…I need this," she cried into Logan's shoulder.

Every square inch of her body tingled with desire. Unhinged, she nipped at Logan's chest. Her pussy ached, her body craved more. She moaned, aware that her canines were extending. Her wolf wanted to mark her mate, she wouldn't be denied.

"Now," she demanded.

Logan smiled at a wide-eyed Dimitri. It struck him as funny that he, the Alpha, and his beta were being commanded by his feisty little mate in bed. Damn, she'd gone wild.

"You heard her," Logan managed right before he kissed Wynter so she'd stop biting so hard at his chest.

She needed to claim him, he knew. Her wolf demanded it. And his wolf, traitor that he was, rolled in submission, awaiting her bite. The furry beast could have cared less if his beta was here or not. Logan sat up and flipped Wynter onto her stomach. Dimitri helped, taking her into his arms so that her head rested on his chest. With her stomach pressed against his beta's, Logan shoved up her lush mane, laving his mark with his tongue. *Mine.* Gliding his hands down her back and sides, Logan reached for a tiny bottle next to the bed.

Wynter felt the cool gel on her bottom and wiggled up into Logan's caress. As he pushed a slippery finger and then another, into her anus, her breath caught. She moaned into Dimitri's chest, relishing the pleasurable fullness. Undulating her hips, she encouraged him to pump in and out, stretching her.

"Yes, don't stop. More, I need more. Please, I can't wait." She rubbed her mound against Dimitri's belly, seeking pressure. She sighed as Dimitri met her need, slipping his fingers through her folds, easing her ache.

Dimitri thought he'd come just from having her atop him. He couldn't wait to be inside her, but Logan had to go first.

"That's it, just relax into D. Feel his fingers on your pussy." Logan heard her sigh as he saw Dimitri's fingers flicker down through her pink lips.

Withdrawing his own hand from her, Logan lubricated his cock, making sure it was well covered. Gently, he spread her cheeks and guided the head of him into her tight hole. Slowly, he pressed an inch into her ass. Like a vise, she squeezed him. He heard her moan in response.

"You okay, baby?" So goddamn tight, she was, Logan wasn't sure if he could keep going.

Wynter sucked a breath as he pushed into the first tight ring of muscle. Without warning, air rushed out of her lungs as Dimitri simultaneously plunged a finger up into her core. As the burn set in, she dug her fingernails into his shoulders. She swore she'd pass out from the incredible feeling of being taken by both men.

"Don't stop. It's so good."

Holding her waist, Logan slowly eased inward until he was completely sheathed. Dimitri's fingers inadvertently glided along Logan's shaft through the thin membrane, causing him to pause. *For the love of the Goddess.* It took all of his restraint to keep from coming. He bit his lip, hoping a little pain would distract him.

"Now D," Logan directed. He could barely speak, afraid he'd orgasm before they got started. Holding his hips still, he waited for Dimitri to slip into Wynter.

Wynter groaned as she felt Dimitri press into her. Holy shit, it felt incredible. Altogether full and sated, she'd never forget this experience for the rest of her natural life, immortal as it was. In tandem, the men began to move within her, igniting a magical pandemonium held only in check by the power of her Alpha. Tendrils of excitement traveled clear from the top of her head to her toes.

Soaring through the motions, she craned her neck to look up into Logan's eyes. Her ragged gasps broke the silence of the room as she held his gaze. Logan bent his head forward, offering what her wolf sought. The pulse in his neck called to her and before she knew what she was doing, she'd sunk her teeth deep into his skin. As she did so, Wynter flew apart, hurled off the edge of reason. Shuddering, she exploded, her orgasm flowing through her veins with uncontrollable abandon.

"I'm coming…Ah yeah," Logan groaned. Wynter pulsated around his shaft at the same instant Dimitri's cock slid against him through the thin tissue that separated them. Fuck, she wouldn't release him, Logan thought. Sweet agony claimed him as she marked his skin. Stiffening, he spilled himself deep within his mate.

In a haze, Wynter heard Dimitri tell her he was about to come. As he tried to pull out of her, she fought him. No, she wouldn't leave him to skulk off on his own. They'd consensually decided to make love. And that meant, they'd come together. "No, Dimitri."

Dimitri relented to his Alpha's mate. Sweet Jesus, the she-wolf was persistent. And with his cock so far in her pussy, he found it hard to argue with her. With a labored breath, he gave in to her, to them both. Riding the wild wave, he came long and hard, pressing his head into both Logan's and Wynter's shoulders.

Wynter let go of Dimitri, allowing Logan to bring her back with him into bed. She snuggled into his embrace. Her mind had a hard time believing what she'd just experienced yet not a shred of regret shadowed her thoughts.

"That was amazing," Wynter declared happily into Logan's chest. *I love you.* She wanted to tell Logan how she felt about him but with Dimitri there, it didn't seem right.

"Yeah it was. Goddess, baby, you're going to kill me." Logan laughed, still trying to catch his breath.

"And me too," Dimitri concurred, panting. "It's a good thing this is a one-off. I don't think my mere immortal self could handle you two on a regular basis. Wynter has a lot of energy."

"Me?" Wynter giggled.

"Yeah, you." Both Logan and Dimitri responded, laughing along with her.

"Well, this isn't my fault. I blame that little red wolf you all said you were so fond of. She's a bit excited to be out and about. How am I supposed to contain her?"

"Ah, Logan. I fear your mate's learning already."

"Oldest trick in the book, baby. Blame it on the wolf," he joked.

Wynter felt light and tired, but sated. "Thank you, both of you. I can't imagine doing any of this on my own."

Dimitri pulled away and went to get a towel.

"Where do you think you're going, beta?" Logan didn't want him to leave just yet.

"Be back in a minute," he called, going outside.

"Why don't I feel strange about this?" Wynter asked Logan. "And why don't you feel jealous?"

"I love him, Wyn. He's been there for me when no one was. And you?" *I love you…more than words can say.* "You're my mate."

"It really was special. But it's you…you changed my life." Tears brimmed in her eyes. "You saved me. If you hadn't been there…I just don't know…"

"Sweetheart, come on now. No tears. You were spectacular." He stroked her hair.

The tears that followed broke his heart. It wasn't that he didn't understand why. She'd just shifted. Her life was forever revolutionized. Gone was her human self that she'd always known. There was no going back.

Dimitri unerringly let the door slam and looked over to see Wynter sniffling. Considering the situation, he went with humor. "I leave for five minutes. Five freakin' minutes and this's what happens? No, no, no. Not having it."

He handed Logan warm washcloths and was relieved to hear a small laugh spill out of Wynter.

"Sorry, I'm just feeling….a little overwhelmed." She wiped the tears away with her fingers, and gave them a small smile. "See, all better, really."

"You okay now?" Logan asked with a brush of his lips to the back of her hand.

"I'm good. Promise," she replied softly.

It had been a long day for all of them and he knew exactly why Wynter had cried. He loved her so much, and like a dam bursting, the emotions of the night had escalated them all to a new high. As he proceeded to gently clean her, he wondered if his tiny mate had any idea that she held his heart in her hands.

Wynter cuddled into Logan's embrace, wishing the night would never end. She couldn't stop thinking about how much she loved Logan. As if she had been crashed over by the waves of a tsunami, her heart had been swept up by the Alpha.

Chapter Twenty-Six

Interesting, the Mistress thought. She watched through the tall grass as the red wolf pinned the white one. Absurdly strong and alpha, Wynter might be more difficult to kill than she'd anticipated. The Mistress knew her intellectual acuity far exceeded her physical capabilities. This was exactly why she needed the virus to bring the Acadian Wolves to their knees.

She snickered, amused by their show of dominance. It was a farce. The Mistress, through her loving command, would teach them all what true domination looked like. No more challenges would exist under her sovereignty. Her fanged beasts would cower as would the bloodsucking paranormals who sought dominion over wolves. The Directeur had met her needs nicely, doing her bidding as she saw fit. But even he would become obsolete once the Mistress snared control of the pack. For now though, she'd indulge his fantasies.

Fascinated by Wynter's shift, the Mistress drooled in anticipation of the day she'd kill the abomination they'd created. Wynter's blood was ready, thoroughly metamorphosed by her transformation. It belonged to the Mistress. Like a ripened grape, it was time to pluck it off its vine, crush its flesh and strain the juice. Yes, it was time to reap what she'd sown. She smiled in delight. *Enjoy your victory, little Red Riding Hood, the cold embrace of death will be coming for you soon.*

Logan swore out loud when he read the tattered note: *I'm coming for her soon. Enjoy your last days. The Scientifique is mine.* Who the hell could have walked onto his land and shoved it under his front door? He snapped a picture with his phone and messaged it to both Chandler and Devereoux. Afterward, he immediately called Dimitri and insisted they run a background check on the owner of the known lab locations. Frustrated, he couldn't sit back and wait for Devereoux to figure out who had taken Wynter. They'd find the killer on their own, without the vampire.

He asked Dimitri to scrub the laptop again before turning it over to Wynter. They'd analyze every last email, every last byte of data to see if there was a pattern to the flow of information. The hardest decision Logan had to make was not telling Wynter about the ominous message that'd been left for them. She'd been through so much distress over the past few months; he didn't have the heart to worry her. There wasn't a thing she could do about it anyway.

As expected, Wynter had been exhilarated when he'd shown her the newly created lab. It was the least he could do, considering the circumstances. Immediately, she started taking blood samples, not only from herself but from both him and Dimitri. At his request, Chandler donated his blood as well, and Emma's samples had been sent by FedEx from New York. Obsessed and determined, Wynter worked day and night.

Selfishly, Logan wanted more time with her, but the lab provided her with a welcome distraction, keeping her safely in his home. Even though the killer had found out where she was staying, Logan had increased security, ensuring no one could get into the house without his permission. The place had been sealed tight, preventing further attacks. It'd be a cold day in hell before they took her from here, he thought.

The most difficult task for Logan had become resisting his growing need to mate. Each time they made love, he fumbled to tell her how he felt. Goddess, he loved her. But he wanted the memories of their love to be untainted, and right now, they both were obsessed with the killer. Their mating should be extraordinary and peaceful, not laced with the flashbacks of hatred and death.

For the past two days, Wynter had done nothing but work and make love. As wonderful as it was, she still hadn't told Logan she loved him again. Always on the tip of her tongue, she felt as if she was waiting for the right moment. She kept thinking it would be when they mated but he'd delayed it. She wasn't sure of the technicalities of mating, but her wolf was not at all happy. Logan told her that he wanted to wait until they caught the killer. But a small part of her questioned his decision. Why didn't he want to mate with her now? Her wolf didn't understand and neither did she. Why hadn't he told her he loved her? Admittedly, she felt his love every time he smiled at her or caressed her hair, but something about those three little words…she needed to hear it, to tell him. Hell, she needed to tell the whole damn world.

As she looked at the data, she held her excitement with bated breath. While her own blood had showed abnormalities compared to typical wolf samples, unusual gene markers indicated significant anti-viral capabilities. She'd extracted the genes, inserting them into Emma's samples. As impossible as it seemed, her blood had irrevocably irradiated the virus. Given that random mutations could occur within human populations, she considered that perhaps somehow Emma's immune system had been weakened. As she'd known, Emma's blood, as hybrid, didn't register as pure wolf. Her human genes adulterated the wolf genes which provided immunity. A miniscule variation existed within the genetic code. Her initial assumption that Emma had been deliberately infected appeared to be a less plausible theory than random mutation.

But who had genetically modified her own blood? How did they do it? All the time she'd lived in captivity, had they been working on the genetic alteration suspecting it would cure Emma's affliction? If that was true, Wynter's blood had been cultivating for weeks as if she were a human petri dish. No wonder they wanted her so badly. But how would they know if their experiment had worked? They couldn't have known she'd shifted for sure, could they? If they knew she'd successfully shifted, they'd want her back…her blood. Like a possession to be owned, they'd seek out their experiment and wouldn't stop until they had her back. With the virus and the antidote, they'd be able to blackmail, extort and torture others at will.

Startled by her discovery, Wynter inserted the needle into her vein. As she collected the vials, Logan knocked on the door. It was time to tell him. She wanted Jax to personally take her blood to Emma. She'd send the instructions for delivering her plasma in the right dose.

"Hey sweetheart…whoa, what ya doin' there?" Logan asked.

"It's my blood. I'm doing my final tests. I was right," she confirmed with a tight smile.

Logan kissed her cheek and quickly backed away, giving her space to finish. He took a seat at her desk next to where she was standing, grabbing a container of bandages off of a tray.

"I need to get this blood to Emma."

"Okay." Logan's brow creased with worry. Her heartbeat raced, and he could tell she'd come to some kind of conclusion he wasn't going to want to hear.

"They won't stop looking for me, Logan. They'll need my blood. They created me…my wolf," she began.

"I won't let them have you. They can't get you here," Logan interrupted. "Listen to me; that bastard may have done something to you, but that doesn't change who you are inside."

"Don't you see? My genetic structure's been altered. I'm not like you. I'm not human. I'm a monster."

"No, you're not. Stop with this. You're perfect the way you are. Don't ever think otherwise."

Wynter shook her head. Her small smile never reached her eyes, because she knew the truth about what they'd done to her. She loved him so much. She loved that he didn't care what she was or that her genetics weren't quite wolf or human. But she knew her next suggestion wasn't going to go over well. With a small tug, she withdrew the needle from her arm, applying pressure with cotton to the pinhole in her flesh. Later, she planned on extracting more blood, increasing the quantity to pints. If something happened to her, she wanted to make sure there was enough of her blood for future research…for a cure. She steeled her resolve and wiped the bead of sweat from her forehead.

Without asking, Logan readied a Band-Aid. He gently took her arm and applied the dressing.

Wynter blew out a breath, and looked up into his concerned eyes.

"I think we need to use me as bait." There, she'd said it.

"No," Logan told her firmly, without missing a beat. What the hell had she been thinking? So not happening, he thought.

"Please, Logan, just hear me out. He's coming for me. *They're* coming for me. It could be more than one person. Léopold said he made other vampires. Anyway, it doesn't matter. I don't want to just wait here like a sitting duck. We could use me to draw him out, then you and Léopold could catch him. It's the only way..."

"No," Logan repeated. He released her arm and took note of at least fifty vials of blood, Wynter's blood.

"But why won't you listen? I'm telling you that I'm what they want. I'm their antidote. They won't give up. I don't know how they figured out that my blood would cure Emma. They could already have samples of my pre-shift blood. I didn't test it, but it's possible that even then my cells could have cured the virus. If we set up a trap...you could be there. I wouldn't be in any real danger."

"I said no." Logan slammed his palm onto the desk a little harder than he intended. He wasn't so much angry with Wynter as he was with the entire situation. But she needed to understand how serious he was. He didn't want her wandering off and doing something foolish that could put her and the whole pack in danger.

"And for the record, I am listening. But as Alpha, I've made the decision. You will not be used as 'bait' as you so casually put it. I've asked Dimitri to track down the IP address locations of every incoming and outgoing email on that laptop. Within the day, we should have the information we need to look at patterns, possibly identifying where they went next. We cannot risk having something happen to you. No, let me rephrase that, I will not risk having something happen to you."

He glanced again at all the blood-filled tubes. "I'm already concerned something's happening to you. What the hell is with all the blood, Wyn?"

"I'm fine," she dismissed him. Standing too quickly caused her to wobble. He rushed to her side and placed her back in the chair.

"Sweetheart, what are you doing?" Logan knelt before her and exposed her inner arm sporting the bandage.

"I said I'm fine." She pushed at his hand and looked away. Admittedly, she'd taken too much blood, but with her preternatural healing, her sense of balance would quickly return.

"Talk to me, Wyn. What's going on?" Logan shook his head. Damn stubborn little wolf.

A tear threatened to fall from her left eye and she deftly captured it with a finger.

"I just…I know that they aren't going to give up. I don't know about Emma's illness. If it's a random genetic abnormality, then it could happen to another hybrid. The chances are small but I just thought if I stored enough of my blood…I didn't have any bags here or an IV, so I started with the vials…" Stupid, stupid idea, she thought. A cloud of desperation rained overhead.

"Baby, look at me." Logan waited until her red-rimmed eyes met his. "This virus, we only know of one wolf, one hybrid who's been affected. You told me yourself that you don't believe it's mutated yet. Jax will get your blood to Emma. He can be there within the day. As for all this blood…" Logan paused and glanced to the vials.

"It's admirable that you want to store it for future use in case we need it. I get that. But you can't beat yourself up about this. Nor should you turn yourself into a pincushion. If you want to store some bags, we'll order the IV supplies and make it happen and do it later. Right now, though, you need to take care of yourself. You've been working nonstop, barely eating or sleeping. I need you," he told her lovingly.

"I'm just so worried. Something's going to happen. Something bad. I can feel it. I need to make sure there're enough samples of my blood in case…" She knew Logan only wanted to protect her, but the overwhelming sense of foreboding shadowed her thoughts.

Logan refused to admit his visions. It was a dark part of him that he'd openly share with her once she was safe. Last night, the nightmare had surfaced once again. This time, it was clearer; Wynter's face, her neck splayed open. He screamed while the life drained from her body. Refocusing, Logan rubbed her knee and placed his forehead on her thigh.

"I know you're worried. But you have to trust me." He raised his head and took her hands into his. "I'm not going to use you as a lure. I love you too goddamn much. You're not just my mate, you're everything to me."

Wynter's heart caught in her chest. *He loved her.* As the words fell from his lips, she took his face into her hands, and he kissed her palm. "I love you too. My Alpha, I love you so much."

Logan pulled her down into his embrace, kissing her forehead, her cheeks and finally claimed her soft trembling lips. Gently, he coaxed her mouth open, his tongue found hers and they lost themselves in their love, reaffirming their future. Hearts bursting with passion, they took their time exploring and tasting each other.

Logan tore his lips away, pressing his forehead to hers. Chest to chest, their lips were mere inches away from one another.

"I want you to know how badly I want to mate with you. I love you more than life itself. But when we complete the ritual, it'll be without fear, without death. Our day, Wyn; it will belong to no one else but us, do you understand?"

"Logan, I've never felt like this in my life. I wondered why…why we hadn't. I don't understand it all but my wolf…she's there. I want to be your mate in every sense of the word."

"And you will be…forever." Logan captured her lips again, pouring reassurance and love into their kiss. Visions be damned, no one would take her from him…not ever.

The next day Fiona called the house asking if Wynter could go into town to shop. As much as Wynter wanted to get out, she and Logan decided that it wasn't safe for her to leave. At Fiona's suggestion, Logan reluctantly agreed to a short boat ride, allowing the girls to do some crabbing. He figured they all could use an hour or two relaxing. After being cooped up in the house, their wolves were going stir crazy. He hadn't told Wynter yet, but he and Dimitri had narrowed down a few locations where they suspected the killers might have been. Tonight, they planned, along with Devereoux, to do reconnaissance.

When Fiona contacted Wynter, she felt relieved that a member of the pack showed interest in getting to know her. Before they left, she and Fiona ate a light brunch, discussing Dana's passing and also Luci's challenge. Wynter had been worried that other females would read her aggression as being unfriendly, but Fiona showed no animosity. Rather, she explained that even though she and Luci were friends, it was the way of wolves. She did, however, thank her for showing mercy and not killing the she-wolf.

By the time she'd made it down to the dock, Wynter's optimism had returned. The winter sun beat down, warming her exposed skin. Logan brushed a kiss to her cheek, helping Wynter onto the boat. She spied the red and white race vessel, wondering how fast it would go. As she made her way onto its deck, she settled into a comfortable leather seat. Fiona followed her, bringing a bushel of branches she'd secured into a tarp. Wynter knew it had something to do with the crabs but wasn't sure for what. Drinking in the sight of Logan preparing for launch, she couldn't help but notice his well-defined pecs that strained against his white t-shirt. As he pushed on his sunglasses and went to work, Wynter smiled at how totally unaware he was of his uber-sexy presence.

The sleek Cigarette purred as Logan fired up the engine. Guarding Wynter was his priority. There was no way he'd let her go out on the lake by herself with Fi. She'd been right about them coming for her. Despite not seeing the threatening letter they'd delivered to his home, she knew. If he didn't discover the lab's location with the new intel, it'd just be a matter of time before they attacked. A strike in broad daylight was unlikely, but the hum of the six hundred horsepower engine put his mind at ease. Another boat would be hard pressed to outrun his speedboat if they tried.

Unbeknownst to Wynter, Logan had assigned Jake to take up the north shore where Fiona planned on laying her crab trap. A trained sniper, he'd scan the area for trouble. Zeke took his post, fishing at the old Hanover dock, a mile off from where they'd set out to make their stop. It seemed like a lot of work for one run out to the lake. But Wynter was wound tight, and he felt his wolf pacing in response. Their self-imposed seclusion was taking its toll on both of them. He wasn't built to stay indoors for days at a time. Even in the city, he'd get out, running as a human. His dream home felt like it had turned into a prison. The fresh air would do them all some good, and later in the evening, he and Dimitri would resume the search for the killer.

By the time they reached the open lake, Wynter felt as if a weight had lifted. The high speed boat ride had been exhilarating. It was as if the wind against her face had blown away her cobwebs of worry. It wasn't lost on Wynter how much trouble Logan had gone to so they could get out of the house. Part of her knew he just wanted to get her out of the lab so she'd stop obsessing about the virus. Her work would never be done, she thought. Regardless, it warmed her heart that he'd protect her and go to such great lengths so they could all have a few fun hours in the sun.

Soon, they'd reached their destination, and Logan cut the engine. The long, thin dance boat bobbed in the open water. Logan gave the go ahead to the girls. He took Wynter's hand and helped her up the steps so she could lay out on the bow. She shook off her shoes, preferring to go barefoot. Even though it was February, the weather was expected to go into the eighties, so she'd thrown on a bathing suit underneath her clothes. Carefully, she trod onto the smooth fiberglass, laid out an oversized beach towel and sat down. Fiona trailed behind her, carrying the large bound bundle of sprigs.

"Hey, girl, can you hold this rope for me?" Fiona asked, letting the blue tarp fall open onto the bow.

"What are you doing?"

"Oh this? It's Wax Myrtle. I'm goin' bunch it up and throw it into the lake."

Wynter gave her a confused look and glanced back to Dimitri and Logan who didn't look at all surprised. She thought it funny that with such an expensive shiny toy, he could have cared less that Fiona had just laid out a huge canvas on it. She loved that no matter his means, at the end of the day, Logan was down to earth. No pretenses, what you saw was what you got.

Fiona began to tie up the branches and continued. "Yeah, the pre-molt crabs love this stuff. They crawl in and then we'll come back later, pull it out and shake 'em out. Normally, I'd haul this mess in my little skiff, but since that's not an option today, Logan said I could bring it here. Anyway, about the crabs, we catch 'em before their shells return, then we'll eat soft shell crabs."

"Oh," Wynter said, amazed. "So…uh…how did you learn to do this?'

"My daddy. Some folks sell 'em. I just eat 'em. Tasty little critters," she commented as she worked to bale up the plants. Plucking off a leaf, she crushed it and handed it over to Wynter. "Smell."

Wynter took the gooey green mixture and sniffed. She thought better of commenting about Fiona's father, remembering what Logan had told her. "Mmm…nice."

"Yeah, isn't it? They've been using it for hundreds of years. It's our way." Fiona eyed Wynter as she continued to handle the aromatic plant. "You really are a city girl, aren't ya?"

"Born and bred. I may not know how to catch crabs but I can get you from Midtown to Soho faster than anyone else…even at rush hour," she joked. "Have you ever been to the Big Apple?"

Fiona tightened the knots. "Um, yeah. Was there a few years ago. Art show…a charity event. I'm very interested in new artists. I have a little gallery in the quarter. Well, it's more of a natural herb and art gallery combo. I'm technically the pack healer, but that doesn't pay the bills," she quipped.

"I'd love to see it sometime, the art. I haven't spent much time in New Orleans, but it really is very unique. You can feel the history speaking to you, if you know what I mean."

"So Wyn, how are you doing? What I mean is, how do you like being a wolf?" Fiona changed the subject, hurling the bundle overboard. A red bullet-shaped crab float tugged at the surface. She folded up the tarp.

"I've only shifted once, but yes. Logan, he's…" She gave him a backwards glance. She couldn't see his eyes behind the sunglasses but suspected he was watching her. Wynter searched for the right words to describe her situation, unsure how much to share with the young she-wolf. Fiona seemed friendly but she also was friends with Luci. "He's been very supportive."

"Ah, is that what you humans call it? Supportive? I bet he's been very supportive…all day and all night long, huh? Just look at that mark on your neck." Fiona rolled her eyes and relaxed against the side of the boat.

Wynter laughed and absentmindedly traced her fingers over her shoulder. She looked over again at Logan who smiled at her. Deciding on honesty, she turned back to Fiona.

"He's my mate." There, she'd said it. She'd told one person, a friend, about Logan. And it felt freeing and girly. She wished Mika was the first friend she'd told. But Fiona had been kind enough to bring her out on the water, care about how she was doing.

"And?" Fiona drawled with a wicked smile.

"And what?" Wynter asked coyly.

"Do you love him?" Fiona whispered as if she was getting ready to hear a national secret.

Wynter knew Logan could hear every word of their conversation but still, Fiona insisted on whispering. It struck Wynter as funny and she began to giggle, as did Fiona. Just as she was going to respond, something caught her attention. To the east, a medium-sized, black sailboat drifted toward them.

"Hey, that boat over there. He's coming toward us," Wynter observed with a growing panic. As far as she was concerned, any stranger was a potential threat.

Logan pulled out the binoculars. A man in white shorts and a pink polo shirt struggled with the sail control lines while a woman lay on the blood-tinged deck. He suspected she was down with a boom injury. Even experienced sailors were susceptible to accidents, but by the look of things, the man on deck appeared confused, lines strewn every which direction. *Damn fools.* Too many times an overconfident wannabe rented too much of a boat and ended up needing rescue.

"A tourist," Dimitri offered, after taking a look for himself.

"Yeah, probably," Logan hedged. He opened a storage hatch and pulled out his Beretta. The Alpha and his beta exchanged an unspoken conversation at the sight of the weapon. "Just in case."

"Here she comes. About fifty feet off. She's gonna hit starboard," Dimitri warned. He pulled open the back storage compartment and pulled out a couple of boat fenders. He handed one off to Logan and they tied them to the cleats to prevent damage.

"Hold on there. Girls, sit tight," Logan told them as the boat approached. He fired up the engine and then unlocked the safety on the gun. The sailboat slowed as it approached, lightly bumping their speedboat.

The stranger looked to be in his early twenties. His preppy shirt was dotted in crimson stains. The woman on deck laid still, her face away from them.

"Oh my God, I'm so sorry, mister. The boom, it just snapped. Now my girlfriend's hurt. I swear I've had a few lessons, but I can't seem to figure out this radio," he blabbered.

It was a good show, Logan thought. Still, something seemed off. He could hear the hum of the other boat's engine. He sniffed. More than two scents filtered through the air, both vampire and human. Logan knew that although vampires could be extraordinarily dangerous at night, they were rendered virtually human during the daytime.

"We'd be happy to call it in. Anyone else on board?" Logan inquired.

"No sir, just me and my girl. Listen, she took a bad hit to the head. You wouldn't happen to have a first aid kit? This boat's a rental. I can't find anything," he said, rubbing his eyes.

Liar. Logan tightened his grip on the gun.

"D, get on the radio and call it in," he directed.

Never taking his eyes off the man, Logan looked at the woman splayed on the deck, using his peripheral vision. Dammit, she lay unmoving. He hated to leave someone in peril, especially in the middle of the lake, but he'd send another boat to investigate. His immediate concern was getting Wynter away from the stranger. The sailboats glided side by side so that the bows were even, and Logan wrapped his hand around the throttle. But before he had a chance to gun the boat, Fiona quickly stood up and jumped over to the other boat.

"Fiona," Wynter cried, grasping into the air as she tried to pull her back. Wynter rushed to the side of the boat nearest to Fiona, extending her hand to her, hoping she'd jump back. "What are you doing? Get back here."

Too late, Fiona had already gone to the woman. "What does it look like I'm doing? I'm going to help her."

Logan had been so focused on the man, he hadn't had a chance to stop Fiona. What the hell did she think she was doing? Pack healer or not, she'd better get back on the damn boat. Both he and Dimitri tensed at the sight.

"Fi, back on the boat now," Logan demanded, never taking his eyes off the stranger.

"But I can help her. She's still breathing. It may just be a concussion."

"Not a question. It's an order. Get your ass back here now," Logan growled.

Wynter observed the interaction, scrutinizing the slain woman. She swore that she wasn't breathing. Her hands looked too pale…gray. What kind of healing did Fiona think she was doing? That woman was dead.

"Logan," Wynter croaked into a gust of wind. Could he, too, see the woman was not alive? Confusion swept over her.

Logan could not understand why Fiona, a naturally submissive she-wolf, was defying his direct order. There was no time to contemplate her punishment. No, the only decision was to leave Fiona on the sailboat. He knew Dimitri wouldn't be happy, but he needed to get Wynter to safety. Something wasn't right.

Fiona busily fussed with the woman, flipping her over onto her back, blocking their view. It appeared she was attempting some kind of resuscitation.

"I need help," Fiona said, ignoring Logan.

The stranger knelt next to Fiona as if to provide assistance, then yanked her upward toward him. He pulled a gun, aiming it at her head. Using her as a human shield, he kept her in between him and Logan.

"Let her go," Logan demanded. He pointed his gun at him, but couldn't get a clear shot off.

"No, I don't think I will," he laughed. "Do you know what a silver bullet can do to a wolf's brain? Messy, messy. She may survive. Maybe not though."

"It's two against one, asshole, put the gun down," Logan insisted. He sensed Dimitri behind him, who'd also aimed a gun.

The stranger continued to laugh. "You kill me, I kill the girl." He pulled Fiona's hair, making her scream. "Tell you what; I'll make a trade. This girl for that one." His eyes fell onto Wynter.

"Not happening," Logan snarled.

Wynter began to crouch backwards. She'd gone too close to the other boat when she'd gone to retrieve Fiona.

"Don't move, Wynter," the stranger called out to her.

Wynter froze. *How did he know her name? Oh God no, they really are here for me.*

"I have sharpshooters on land," Logan explained coolly. "You'll never get away."

As if Logan and Dimitri weren't in the boat, the man continued to speak to Wynter. "You want to save your friend, doctor?"

"What?" Wynter gasped.

"I said; do you want to save your friend here? You know these wolves aren't as tough as you'd think. Not so hard to kill them, really. With silver in her brain, it'll take her months to recover. No, a shift won't fix this so easily, I'm afraid."

"Don't listen to him, Wyn," Logan yelled.

Wynter looked up at Fiona, whose cheeks and neck were streaked with tears. She couldn't quite see her eyes because her head had been wrenched backward.

"What do you want from me?" Wynter screamed at him. It felt as if a black tunnel was closing in, she couldn't escape. She couldn't live with the blood of another wolf on her hands. It was her fault they'd come to Logan's pack. Her responsibility. She should be the one to die, not Fiona.

"But you already know the answer to that, don't you, Dr. Ryan? Shame to kill this she-wolf, but we will. In fact, we'll take out this whole damn pack if we have to, but I guarantee you this, it will not end. You belong to him. He will not stop. I know he'll take special pleasure in killing your Alpha. Don't think we can't get to him. We left him a note the other day…right at his door."

Shocked, Wynter looked over to Logan. No, it couldn't be true. Logan would have told her.

"Wynter, don't listen to him," Logan cautioned. Wynter's face had gone white. "Get away from the side of the boat."

The stranger laughed maniacally. "I see the great Alpha is keeping secrets from his mate. It's true. The very night you shifted, we were at his house."

"Logan?" Wynter questioned. When he didn't answer right away, she knew it was true. They'd been at his home? Dear God, if they could get to her there, there'd be nowhere they couldn't find her.

"Wynter, listen to me, now. It was just a note. No one was in the house. Fiona, she'll be fine. She's a strong wolf."

"You lie, Alpha. Do you really think I'd bring a knife to a gunfight? These hollow-cavity bullets will mushroom her brain apart with one shot. She's not going to make it back, not like she used to be anyway. And that's if she manages to shift afterwards. No, this little girl's goin' to pop like fireworks."

Wynter tried to drown out his words but it was no use. Her own guilt tore at her heart. Was she really going to sit and do nothing while this monster put a bullet in Fiona's head? God, she loved Logan…so much. Reverting to her training, she considered the known facts, the data. True, Logan would be angry if she sacrificed herself for Fiona. But his boat was powerful, much more so than the small sailboat. Logan would follow, save her and Fiona, too, would be safe. The most important fact was that if she didn't go, another Acadian wolf would die…at her hands.

"Your choice. What's it going to be? You or the wolf?" He dug the muzzle into Fiona's temple and she screamed.

Logan could see that Wynter was lost in her thoughts. Goddammit all, she was considering it. As much as he cared for Fiona, he couldn't lose his mate. His breath caught and he lunged to restrain Wynter to keep her from going. Dimitri broke for the throttle.

"I'm sorry," Wynter cried softly as she leapt over to the sailboat. She skidded onto the deck and fell to her knees.

"No!" Logan screamed. "No, he's going to kill you. Get back here now."

Wynter's body collapsed into the rough landing. She scrambled to stand upright but the man kicked her in the stomach. Her face hit the side of the boom, tearing her lip open.

"Let her go," Wynter pleaded. Her face throbbed but she breathed through it. "You don't need Fiona…just take my blood. No more…no more…I'll do whatever you want. Let her go now."

The stranger cackled wildly and threw Fiona to the floor. With a jerk, the engine roared to life and the boat sped forward. Wynter attempted to push Fiona into the water. If they could get off the boat they'd have a chance.

"Jump," she told her, but Fiona held tight to a cleat.

Logan tore to the helm and jammed the throttle forward. They hadn't gotten far. In his speedboat, they could easily catch up and he'd jump over to get Wynter. But his boat lurched only a few feet before the motor died.

"What the fuck? This is a brand new boat," Logan cursed, banging the dashboard. "Take the wheel." He jumped in the back to check the inboard. Within seconds, he'd located the source of the issue. "Shit. There's a nick in the fuel tank fill hose."

Logan spun and aimed his gun at the tall dark figure that had Wynter by the arm. He knew he could hit him but the man slyly pulled Wynter against him as a shield. Targeting the engine, Logan fired off six shots to the stern. The bullets ricocheted off the screeching motor. As the man instinctively moved to the right to look at the damage, Logan pulled the trigger again, clipping him in the shoulder. He watched the pink-shirted form hit the deck but no longer could he see Wynter, as she too, had fallen.

Pain shot through Wynter's body as fingers grabbed her hair, pulling her to her feet. The man slammed her up against him, holding the gun to her head. With her back to his chest, she faced Logan whose boat grew smaller as the distance between them widened. A loud gunshot jolted Wynter, and she tried to wretch her body out of his grip. Blood sprayed as more shots rang out. As she felt his grip loosen, Wynter tumbled onto the deck. She clawed at the slippery surface, intending to jump, when the chill of a second voice blanketed her consciousness. As she caught a glimpse of the familiar face, her heart stopped. *The Directeur?*

A blur of revolting confusion and hopelessness overtook her body. No, this couldn't be happening. Wynter glanced at Fiona who now sat comfortably, almost peacefully staring toward the horizon. Deception. Betrayal. The Directeur grabbed Wynter, pulling her off her feet into his deadly embrace. She prayed for strength as she let the anger roll through her mind. Anger was good, she thought. It might be the only thing that would save them all.

The sailboat careened away while Dimitri and Logan helplessly watched in disbelief. One fucking hour on the lake. Four men on guard, and within seconds, they'd taken her and Fiona. As they sped off into the distance, the miles-wide freshwater sanctuary hid their path of escape. Logan screamed out to the heavens in agony. His mate was gone.

"Search every goddamned house," Logan growled.

"I'm sorry," Dimitri offered.

"No, D. No words. Action. You," Logan pointed to Zeke and Jake, "every boat. Every pack member needs to be accounted for. I want every wolf up at Marcel's old place now. I don't give a shit who's in the city. Every damn wolf is to get their ass back here immediately," he ordered.

"Someone came into the marina today and cut that hose. I want to see the video now."

Enraged, Logan paced as he barked out orders. Someone had betrayed him, he was certain of it. First the car bomb. Now this. No, it wasn't happenstance that the hose was cut. It had been deliberately done in such a way to allow them enough gas to go out to the lake, but not enough to get back. Whoever had done it knew exactly where they were going and how long they'd be on the lake. It may have been a vampire who'd killed Dana, but it was a wolf who had helped coordinate Wynter's abduction. No one but one of his own wolves would have had access to his boat.

"The pack will be at Marcel's soon. You want to ride with?" Dimitri asked, trying to block the emotion he felt emanating from Logan. His Alpha's caustic rage seethed through his own brain as if they were his own thoughts.

Logan shook him off. As much as he loved D, he couldn't bear to be near him. He was scarcely containing his beast as his unbridled wrath escalated. It wouldn't be good for Dimitri to be so close to him.

"I'm taking my bike. You take the SUV." Logan stopped and rubbed his eyes. "Seriously, D. This ends tonight. I'm going to tear up this entire swamp looking for her. She's got to be here. Every single marina's been secured. No one could land a chopper except at the helipad. Jake's sent men to check the outposts along the lake. No, whoever's done this is still here."

"Hey, I'm with ya, but we're talking about literally thousands of square acres of swamp. In the dark. They could pull off anywhere, skip into a car and be gone."

"No," Logan growled. "Wynter's here. I can feel her."

"But why would they stay here…it doesn't make sense. Logan, I think…"

"Because they're goin' to kill her. They don't need her anymore. My guess is now that she's turned, all they want is her blood." Logan took a deep breath and blew it out, trying to think clearly. "Text Devereoux. I want him here now. And before you ask, I don't care how he gets here. Send the bird if you need to. His line is responsible for this fucking mess. I'll kill him myself if he doesn't comply and you can quote me on that."

Dimitri pulled out his phone and started making calls. Logan went to his gun safe that was located in the laundry room. He extracted several guns, ammo, and strapped on a harness. He preferred to go wolf, but he wasn't taking any chances. In the bayou, his wolf may not be able to get to shore fast enough. A bullet, however, would.

By the time they'd reached Marcel's home, Logan was convinced he knew who had sabotaged his boat. Ferocious, his wolf sought revenge. Nothing but having his mate back safely in his arms would assuage his rage.

He killed the engine and jumped off his motorcycle.

"Hold up, Alpha," Jake called over to him.

"What'd you find out?"

"I don't know…it doesn't make sense," Jake hedged, incredulous as to what he'd seen on the video.

Luci rushed over to Logan, eyes down. "Alpha," she greeted.

At the sight of her, Logan lost it. If anyone had reason to attack him and Wynter, it had been Luci. He should have recognized her aggressive behavior. How she'd connected with the vampires, he didn't know, but he was about to damn well find out why.

"Just where the hell do you think you're going?" As Luci turned to walk away, Logan grabbed her arm.

Jake stepped between them.

"Jake, get out of my way. This is between Luci and me," he snarled.

"But Alpha," Jake began.

"I told you, Luci and I have business." Logan turned his gaze back to her. "I should have known better than to let you stay in the pack. You've been so hot to get in my bed ever since he died. Seriously, did you even care about Marcel? Now listen good, I'm only going to ask you this once. What did you do with Wynter?"

"I didn't…I swear. It wasn't me," she cried.

"Where. Is. She?"

"I didn't…"

Jake put his hand over Logan's, risking a fight. He couldn't let Logan continue after Luci, even though she deserved at least a little bit of his ire.

"Alpha, please. You need to see this," he pleaded.

"What?" Logan asked. His eyes flared.

"The video. Your boat. Luci didn't do it. But someone else from the pack is on there…I'm sorry," Jake said, shaking his head.

"Who? Who did this?" Logan demanded.

"See for yourself." Jake pulled out his mini iPad, and pressed the play button.

Logan couldn't believe it. Of all the people in his pack, it made no sense. The person hadn't even tried to hide from the camera. Instead after they'd cut the line, the perpetrator purposefully stared into the lens and smiled.

Chapter Twenty-Seven

Wynter's wolf whined in agonizing pain, begging to shift. Instinctively, she knew a transformation could heal her injuries, but as she called on her wolf, nothing happened. Her head lolled back against a rough surface and she licked her cracked lips. An iron-tinged crust stuck to her tongue. She felt heavy, drained. Wynter slid her fingertips down her sides and felt metal on her midsection. She shook her head, willing her eyes to open. As she looked to her torso, she was shocked to see the silver chainmail corset that had been fastened to her body. Tugging at the seams, she couldn't get it to budge.

The lethargy didn't stop her from scanning the room for a clue to where they'd taken her. *A dilapidated cabin? Was it the cabin they'd been in the night she shifted?* The lack of screened windows and rotted wood told her no. Listening as Logan had taught her, she could hear the cicadas but other than that, she was met with silence. She knew, though, that she had to be somewhere in the swamp.

Her plan had failed miserably. She wondered what had happened to Logan. There was no way that boat could have outrun him. Why hadn't he come for her? Did they shoot him like they'd threatened to do to Fiona? Wynter stifled the small sob bubbling in her chest. She needed to conserve her energy. She needed to escape.

"You okay?" Wynter heard the question and glanced over to see Fiona sitting in a chair.

It appeared her hands had been fastened behind her back. But there was something odd about her demeanor and posture. On the boat, after Wynter had tried to get her to jump, she'd held on. Then within minutes, she'd rested on the boat, almost as if she were relaxed, content. But now, Fiona had been bound. Had Wynter imagined what she'd seen? No, there had definitely been something strange about Fiona's behavior and even now, her face was bright. Unlike Wynter, whose face was bruised and puffy from crying, Fiona's complexion was clear. But why would Fiona help the vampire? And why was she playing a victim unless she weren't one?

"I'm fine. I can't shift. What is this thing?" Wynter asked, trying to act unsuspecting.

"Silver," Fiona responded without even looking.

"Our kryptonite."

"What?"

"A human throwback. Superman."

"It won't kill you," Fiona told her with an icy stare. "The vampire. He wants to know what you know about the virus."

Wynter gave her a sardonic smile and laughed bitterly. "I just bet he fucking does. Well I wish him good luck with that."

"You have to tell him. He promised to let you go."

"No, he promised to let *you* go. And he didn't. You're still here, Fiona. He's a liar."

Fiona rolled her eyes. "The man on the boat? He's not in charge. No, I speak of the Directeur."

"What? How do you know that name?" Wynter demanded, attempting to stand. She bent her knees and pushed upward, bracing herself against the rickety wall.

"The Directeur told me himself. He wants to know if you managed to cure Emma's virus," Fiona said emotionlessly.

"How do you know about Emma?" Wynter found herself yelling.

"He told me. He said she's sick but that your blood, it'll cure her."

Wynter closed her eyes and took a deep breath. He knew about her blood as she'd suspected. A rush of nausea poured over her and she struggled not to vomit.

"He saw the New York Alpha in New Orleans. He knows that you sent blood to Emma…your blood. He watches you…always. So tell me, did it work?"

"Yes…yes it worked. Why do you care, Fiona? He's got you tied up. Why are you asking me these questions?"

"So it's true then. Have you figured a way to modify the virus? To make it portable?"

A chill crept up Wynter's spine. Fiona was privy to details…details no one but she and Logan knew. And she hadn't jumped from the boat. Was this all for show? Even if Wynter had been close at one time to isolating the virus, allowing others to inject it, she'd never tell a soul. She'd die first.

"No," she lied. "I haven't been working on it. Emma is cured; that's all that matters."

"He knows how to do it. He found a way while you were gone. Did you know he also is a scientist? Perhaps that is why he reveres you so?"

"What?" Wynter couldn't believe Fiona's words.

"It's been him all along. His company. His research."

"Why are you telling me this? How do you know so much about him? They were going to kill you out there on the lake. Why didn't you just jump when I told you to?" Wynter's voice strained. She eyed the door. So weak, but if she could make it outside maybe she could find something to remove the silver.

"I think it's time," Fiona said. She pushed out of the chair, placing her hands on her hips. Uninjured and altogether healthy, she gave Wynter an evil smile before clapping her hands. "Come."

The door flew open and a tall, good-looking vampire entered the room. She knew him…Yes, the man from the boat. Her mind swam with possibilities. No, she'd met him before…at the club…with Léopold. Shocked, Wynter tried to run but Fiona easily stepped in front of her and shoved her to the ground.

"You…you…how could you? And Fiona…Logan's going to kill you." Wynter heaved in a deep breath. On all fours, she looked up to the vampire.

"She really is naïve, isn't she?" Fiona merely laughed.

"You and Phillip shouldn't have hurt her. Just look at what you've done, Mistress. You cannot treat her this way if she's going to work for me." The vampire shot Fiona a nasty look, clearly not pleased.

"Work for you? Are you kidding me? Why would ViroSun be involved with something like this? Who are you?" Wynter laughed and cried at the same time. She rolled onto her bottom, unable to stand.

"Dear scientifique, one question at a time. May I?" He retrieved a crisp handkerchief from his suit pocket and attempted to give it to Wynter. She brushed him away.

"Very well then," he sniffed. "Let's start at the beginning, shall we? My name's Étienne. Étienne St. Claire, son of Kade Issacson sired by Léopold Devereoux. And as my Mistress has introduced, I am the Directeur."

He paced, letting his hands speak flamboyantly into the air.

"However, there is one small discrepancy you should know…you see, we are not ViroSun nor have we ever been. True, though they exist, we forged the necessary documentation to make you believe you were working for them."

"No, I went to the interview. The building, the stationery…I interviewed with them. I met with people. This isn't possible." Wynter shook her head in confusion.

"Ah well, all fake I'm afraid. A necessary expense to make you believe you were going to work for them. You were so eager to find a cure for your friend."

"But how did you know?"

"I travel to New York quite often. And lucky for me, I'd attended one of your speaking engagements. I found it quite captivating…the notion that someone, a supernatural, could be infected with a feline virus. She's a lovely speaker," he told Fiona, who rolled her eyes and pretended to look at her nails. "It didn't take long to find your 'Jane Doe'. Emma's medical records and her blood were easy enough to get at the hospital. I can be very convincing."

"But I'd been working…the lab. There were others with me," Wynter countered.

"Were there? We kept you isolated. Do you recall ever meeting anyone after you insisted on leaving?"

Speechless, Wynter closed her eyes. Like a great illusion, the curtain was revealed and she, the fool, was left the victim of a great hoax. How could this happen? She'd researched the company. The high pressure interview had been held in one of the most conspicuous midtown skyscrapers. They'd done intensive background checks, interviewed her friends, Jax.

"My scientifique, are you listening?"

"Stop calling me that!" Wynter cried.

"But you are so special," he insisted, trailing a long finger over her hair. "Really, darling, did you think you'd stay away from me so long? The Mistress, she's powerful, but I admit, I've crushed on you like a school boy."

"True," Fiona spat out in disgust. Her forehead furrowed. "He's quite obsessed. Too much so."

"But I digress. You see, Fiona and I, we knew each other from New Orleans. She's quite the devious little witch, but not so strong. Power doesn't come easily in the wolf pack…brawn over brains and such. And for me, let's say it's tedious being at Kade's beck and call. But this virus, if it could be used on wolves, well, one can easily extrapolate…vampires could be next."

Wynter shook uncontrollably and rubbed at her eyes. She felt her limbs grow cold. Was he insane? There was no way an animal virus could be transferred to vampires.

"I know what you're thinking. Little Emma's illness is a random mutation…it couldn't possible affect vampires. But the mutation is just a spark we need to turn our discovery into a blazing success. We need to think big…research new ways of modifying the genetic structure of those who are invincible. And as we've proven, even a human can be changed."

"What did you do…my cells? I have to know," Wynter pleaded, her voice barely audible. She stared into his cold black orbs. "You're sick, you know that?"

"Now, now. No need to be nasty. You should be grateful for what I've done to you. I've given you a gift." He smiled proudly.

"Grateful, are you fucking kidding?" Wynter coughed, nervously pulling at her own hair. She felt as if she was the one going insane. How could this be happening?

"I told you, darling. I'm a scientist. I've been playing with genetic material for many years. It's not exactly new technology. The humans have been tampering with their food supply for a while now, developing genetically modified crops and such. They're resistant to weeds, insects and so forth. They've even successfully developed animal organs for potential transplants. What I did to you was slightly more complicated, but in the same vein. The micro-injection of the recombinant DNA was quite easy once my vampires had you subdued. Really, no pain involved. Of course, unlike humans, ethics don't impede my experiments. No, my dear, this…your genetic transformation was my creation and mine alone…although I must thank Fiona for her genetic contribution. She's quite the sport. In the end, you've turned into a fabulously strong transgenic being, don't you agree?"

Unable to keep the bile down, Wynter turned her head to the side. The contents of her stomach spewed onto the floor and she coughed, wiping her mouth. Hearing the horrific details of what he'd done confirmed her suspicions. Forever altered, her genetic structure had been modified to wolf. She'd been an experiment, nothing more, nothing less.

"And I must say that my theory proved correct. Your blood cures the very virus that afflicts the hybrid. But I still do have one small problem. I've been working on it, of course, and am so very close, but I need to be able to transfer the virus to a pure wolf. For whatever reason, the random mutation isn't strong enough to transfer. And that my darling is why I need you."

"Me? My blood?" Wynter whispered.

"Well, of course we need your blood. And lots of it. But I need your mind, darling. With you at my side, doing research, we can make history together," he explained, taking a seat.

"Are you crazy? I told you I don't know anything. And even if I did, I wouldn't tell you," she snapped.

Étienne growled. Snagging Wynter by the arms, he hoisted her so far off the floor her toes scraped the boards. He held her at eye level, mere inches from his face. "You will do this. Or have you forgotten what used to happen when you refused? Perhaps you need a refresher," he sneered, baring his fangs. "I can't tell you how long I've waited. I won't be denied."

Without another word, Étienne pulled Wynter against his body and sliced his teeth into her neck.

Blinding, searing white hot pain speared down into Wynter's body. Not only had he taken her blood, it felt as if he'd stolen the very essence of her vitality. Optimism. Hope. Love. It had all been siphoned away by the monster draining her life force. Her pale lips parted in a silent scream yet the sound was lost in her chest. Wynter squeezed her eyes tight, her fingers digging into his arms in a futile effort to dislodge him. Like a rag doll hung on a hook, she could not shake free. The noose tightened around her neck, and she fought for air. Cloaked in evil, she prayed to God to take her soul.

Fiona whacked a chair over Étienne's back, causing him to release Wynter. As he raised a hand to strike Fiona, she held a sharp shard of wood to his back.

"You fool," she accused. "We need her blood for testing, for the antidote, and you can't control yourself for five fucking minutes. This is why you need me. You've got no discipline."

As if scolded by his mother, Étienne stepped away from them both and lowered his head. "But of course, Mistress. My apologies. She tempts me so."

"Touch her again and I'll stake you and that monstrosity you've created. Do you think I need you? This…all of this," she continued, looking around the room as if talking about a magical place, "is my doing. I found you, not the other way around. I came up with this plan, not you. And you are not going to fuck it up, do you hear me? Now stop screwing around with her, get her to the computer. We've got maybe three hours before Logan tracks us down, and I want to get out of here."

"Your blood, Dr. Ryan. So wild and pungent." Étienne glanced to Wynter who lay sobbing on the floor. "I do think that genetic modification upped your platelet count, because I feel energized."

"Would you stop pontificating and get her working?" Fiona implored.

"Get up," Étienne coerced, yanking Wynter by her arm. He dragged her across the floor to a small table, picked her up and righted her in the chair. Noticing her neck was still bleeding, he stole a glance at Fiona before dragging his tongue over the wound. He licked his lips. "See, I'm quite in control now."

"If you drink from her while I'm gone, you're dead," Fiona warned. "Keep it up and I'll leave you out here by yourself. Logan and the pack will tear you apart, do you understand? I'm the only one who knows how to get out of here. Get the data and then we're leaving."

"Yes, Mistress." Étienne capitulated. He gave Wynter a slap to her face and flipped open a laptop. "Wake up, scientifique. Time to work. Whatever you've worked on this past week, I want the information recorded now. Blood to virus ratios for the cure, viral portability, everything. The Mistress won't allow me another taste of your delectable blood but she didn't say anything about torture."

"That's better. You're a good boy," Fiona praised. She reached up to smooth over Étienne's hair. "Now, I have to go outside to check the boat. And Phillip too. I'll untie him now."

Satisfied with his obedience, Fiona smiled to herself. As the door to the cabin slammed behind her, she eyed Phillip, Étienne's child, who sat tied to a cypress tree, the silver cord bound around his neck so tightly that he could no longer speak. The acrid odor of burnt flesh lingered in the air. She smiled, picking a few splinters from the fragmented stake she'd created from the broken chair. Phillip's wide-eyed stare bled red streaks down his face. Fiona knelt before him, careful not to soil her skirt.

Phillip had served his purpose on the boat. Pity that he had to die, considering his spectacular performance. As Fiona had suspected, Wynter had bought their orchestrated farce hook, line and sinker. Of course the woman on the deck had been dead. Thankfully, Phillip had left enough blood dripping to make it look believable. Like a well-honed speaker, he'd given his oration and convinced Wynter to give herself up to save Fiona. Bleeding-hearted humans. Fiona had seen the look of guilt plastered across Wynter's face at the funeral. Logan, on the other hand, was about to leave her. As suspected, he'd choose his mate over her, a purebred wolf; all the more reason why he shouldn't be Alpha.

But she'd never be Alpha of Acadian Wolves as long as the ancient ways ruled pack law. She wasn't strong enough to challenge most females, let alone a male. Even her father, a virile male, hadn't been able to subjugate Marcel. Death had been his sentence for the challenge. Her plan had merely started out as revenge for her father's death. Convincing Calvin, Marcel's beta, that he was deserving of Alpha took little effort. Stroking his ego, planting the seed of his dream to rule the Acadian pack was ridiculously easy. She could have easily played alpha female to Calvin. But no, no, no. Unexpectedly, Logan had intervened, killing Calvin, and her only chance of ruling the pack.

Despite the mishap, her alternate plan, dominating the vampire, turned out to be quite ingenious. She'd met Étienne years before, allowing him to fuck and feed from her. When he'd told her of the story of the sick wolf, her idea struck like lightning. If she could control the virus and the antidote, she'd control the pack. Étienne, tired of being Kade's lackey, sought the same goal: power. He fancied himself a scientist of great aptitude and aspired to be known throughout history. She played up his fantasy, all the while directing his actions.

Her only mistake had been relying on Étienne to isolate the virus, to turn it into a weapon. Even Wynter had failed to produce the virus in a way it could be injected, swallowed or otherwise used to infect another wolf. But this minor setback didn't deter Fiona. As she'd pored through the volumes of genetic and viral research, she believed it was just a matter of time before a researcher made the discovery. No longer convinced that person was Wynter, she planned to kill her after they got the information she'd gleaned about the antidote. They'd drain Wynter, taking her blood for future research.

Étienne's fascination with the girl had grown dangerous. There was no way Fiona could leave the wolf alive. Logan would never stop searching for his mate. Even if he didn't go after them, dragging Wynter through the swamp wasn't an option. A timely escape was paramount. Afterwards, they'd bide their time, review the data, acquire a new scientist and weaponize the virus. Once she had it ready, she'd attack Logan. Then she'd return to take over the pack.

Lost in her thoughts, she eyed Phillip with faux sympathy. Deep in her chest, she tried to conjure empathy but it didn't come. She knew she should care about his fate, but she simply didn't. Apathy had been the beauty of her strategic plan. All of the killing, and she felt no regret. She supposed the closest she'd felt to guilt was when she'd ordered Dana's death. At the funeral, she'd been a terrific actress, all the while unable to feel anything at all. It had been necessary to kill her. She couldn't have allowed her hybrid half-sister to reveal the results from Wynter's blood tests.

Over the past week, she'd made Étienne kill every single one of the vampires he'd created. She scoffed as the bound bloodsucker whimpered at her feet. Poor Étienne, the fool that he was, believed that he could bring the pink-shirted vampire with them. Of all the children he'd recklessly created, she supposed Phillip had been the most useful one of the bunch. Thankfully, Étienne had believed her lie that he could keep his treasured creature. He would have fought her on the decision to kill him. But they needed to move like the wind. It would be hard enough to escape with the two of them. Fiona thought that she almost felt a tiny shred of compassion as she drove the stake deep into Phillip's black heart. But as he turned to ash, she shrugged. She clapped the dust off her hands and smiled, glad to have felt nothing at all.

"Fiona. What the hell?" Logan couldn't believe what he saw on the video.

"Today on the lake," Dimitri began.

"She jumped to the other boat. I thought she was crazy. But she did it deliberately, luring Wynter. She knew Wynter felt guilty about Dana dying. She used it. I just can't fucking believe this. Why?"

"Your guess is as good as mine, but she's got to be working with a vamp. Dana was bitten up good."

"She may be working with a vampire, but look at her. She's smiling. Baiting us. And the letter. She must have planted it. She's been watching us this whole time," Logan spat out furiously.

"Shit," Dimitri began. "You know with the pack, there's not too many secrets. The guys who worked to build the lab, they may have told her."

"Fiona's here," Logan breathed.

"Fi knows this place just as well as we do. She knows we'll find her."

"She's going to kill Wynter for her blood, then take off."

"We'll have to break the search into sections. The whole pack will help," Jake suggested.

"No, let me think. If she's got Wynter, she's going to want to drain her blood. It's what she's after. But she won't use a vamp, though. She's going to need privacy, supplies…to collect it properly. The swamp's too messy. And she wouldn't keep a boat out in the open. She's going to need shelter.

A cabin maybe."

"Ours?"

"I think…I think she may have built one," Luci interjected quietly.

"What exactly do you know, Luci?" Logan snarled.

"Nothing, I swear. Fiona's been the same person she's always been. Sweet, gentle Fi. This isn't her…she wouldn't hurt anyone. I know she's on that video," she shook her head and gestured to the tablet, "but I'm telling you we've been friends for a long time. I just don't see how she could be capable."

"How long have you known her really? Marcel, he brought you here. You haven't been with the pack that long, Luci. Sometimes, we don't know people," Dimitri told her. "I've known her for the past fifty years and there she is…right there. She did this."

"Where's her cabin? We know every single blade of grass out here. I've never seen it. Where's it at?" Logan demanded.

"We do know what's out there, but maybe she's been busy over the past couple of months. We've been preoccupied with the challenges." Even to Dimitri, it didn't make sense, but there was no denying that he and Logan and the entire pack had been distracted by Marcel's death and the fights that followed.

"She took me there once," Luci said solemnly. "Made me promise not to tell anyone. But last month when I asked, she told me that a storm took it out. I believed her. I had no reason to doubt her. It happens all the time, you know. I guess she could have rebuilt something."

"Let's go." Logan glanced at Dimitri and Jake. "Fiona is not leaving this swamp. And bring stakes. She isn't alone out there."

"But what if Wynter isn't…" *Alive.* Dimitri hesitated to suggest it but the reality of the situation was bleak.

"She's alive." The vision of Wynter dying before him played in his mind like a horror movie. He'd be damned if he let it happen. "She will not die, do you hear me? The next person who suggests it can find another pack. She's mine and I can feel her. Now, let's stop wasting time and go."

Wynter pretended to type out information about the virus. She made up data, dates, measurements and ratios. She'd never help to create a viral weapon. They could kill her; drain her of all her blood, but she'd never ever give them what they needed. Wynter had spent the time gathering her strength, deciding she'd try to escape. But first, she had to shift. If she pretended to comply, she might be able to get him to take off the silver. Then, she'd fight with her last dying breath to get away.

"There's nothing more." Wynter pushed the save button as if she were truly cooperating. A reiteration of what they already knew would help to confirm her story, play to his arrogance. "You were right. My wolf blood, it'll cure Emma. Her immunity will show in her viral titers but the symptoms will disappear. It isn't contagious either."

"See how nice it is when we collaborate, Dr. Ryan? Professionals discussing our research," he lectured as if he was a professor.

"Your genetic modification was spot on. My shift was difficult, but it was enough to manipulate the blood. I need to continue the research to learn more about why my blood is counteracting the virus," she continued.

"That's the spirit. We'll set up a new lab in Wyoming. I've grown quite tired of this heat. And the Mistress, well she'll want to return here eventually. Perhaps the mountain air will entice her to stay."

"Out West? Really? I've always wanted to see Yellowstone." As a camper, not a captive. "When do we leave? I'm a mess."

"Always beautiful in my eyes, darling. Your intellect is captivating," he purred into her ear.

"I'm still weak though. I don't think I'd be able to keep up with you. If I could just shift, I think I'd be okay to go," she suggested innocently.

"We'd need to discuss that with the Mistress. I can't allow…"

"You don't have the power to do it? What I meant to say is that it was your brilliance that researched the genetics, created a wolf from a human. It's the first time it's been done in history. Your name should be published in the New England Journal of Medicine. This is a historic medical breakthrough. It'll have far-reaching implications across the world. I imagine all the Ivy League schools will be clamoring to have you teach," she boasted. She knew she was laying it on thick but she watched in pleasure as his eyes glossed over in dreams of grandeur.

"Sir," Wynter pleaded demurely. Batting her eyelashes, she seductively glided her fingers from her mouth down to the valley between her breasts. "I really am a mess. My lips…my neck. Of course, I'd need to take my clothes off in order to shift."

Étienne's cock jerked in response. How he'd missed watching her in her underwear while he held her in his lab. Viewing her nude was a gift he'd earned, deserved. The Mistress would not approve but she wasn't here, was she? Just a small peek wouldn't hurt. She'd be well enough to travel and he'd fuck her later.

"I suppose it wouldn't hurt, but you must promise to be a good girl." He leaned forward and pressed a kiss to her forehead.

Wynter breathed calmly as his cool lips touched her skin, resisting the urge to flinch. She just needed to shift and then she'd have a chance to escape. In her current condition, she couldn't stand, let alone run or fight. For a second, she thought he'd changed his mind as he stood to retrieve a pair of gloves from his pocket.

"Gloves, darling. The silver," he noted. He knelt before her like Logan had done to her in the lab. "This'll take just a minute."

She squeezed her eyes shut, hoping he'd hurry. Luckily he couldn't get too close to the silver as he wrapped his arms around her, unfastening the corset. Her lungs wheezed as the poisonous metal fell to the floor. A fresh rush of energy circulated throughout her body.

"I think I'm okay," she told him. He'd braced her sides with his hands, his thumbs resting under her breasts. "I need to do this alone. You can watch, of course."

"Of course," he hissed. She was so lovely. And his. With the Mistress gone, he could take her quickly but then thought better of it. He stood and backed away but not before adjusting his erection that strained against his zipper.

Wynter slowly opened her lids and took a cleansing breath. Finally, he'd stopped smothering her. Freed, she could shift. She licked her lips nervously, considering how it would be the first time she'd attempted to do it by herself.

"Go on then," he urged.

"Sorry, I just need a minute to make this work. I'm not as good at it as the others," she told him truthfully.

"Aren't you going to disrobe? I thought you said…"

"I will," she cut him off. The pervert just wanted to see her naked. "I need to concentrate a minute first. The silver, my energy is low."

Wynter closed her eyes again. Breathing in and out, she meditated, searching for her wolf. *Come on, girl, let's go.* In her mind's eye, she saw her wolf crouching, yelping in distress. Another wolf flashed as if she'd seen a vision: *Logan.* She could sense him and was certain he was coming for her.

As Étienne watched, she quickly tore off her shirt, shorts and bikini. The vampire's eyes on her skin repulsed her, but she had no choice. Calling her wolf to the surface, the metamorphosis claimed her. But as quickly as it came her wolf disappeared, leaving her in a naked heap on the floor. She tried to shove off the silver corset that lay across her legs but once again she'd been impaired by the insidious metal. Unable to stand, she scrambled to pull on her shirt and shorts.

"What are you doing?" Fiona screamed at Étienne.

"She needs to shift if she's going to go with us. Also, as you know, the shift enabled her blood count to rise," he explained dryly.

Wynter gave him a look of confusion. Allowing her to shift had been a ruse to get her blood to regenerate? They were going to drain her.

"Idiot," Fiona countered. "You do realize they're coming? Get her blood now. We'll take it with us." She threw a bag at him.

"Sorry darling, this'll only take a minute." Étienne, still gloved, pushed Wynter to the floor, dragging the corset over her torso. He sorted out the needles, tubes, plastic bags now strewn about the wooden planks. "You are a quick dresser, aren't you? Pity."

"No, please," Wynter begged, struggling under the weight of him. She needed to stall. "I promise I'll help."

"Certainly, now just a small prick," he told her, jabbing the hypodermic needle into the crook of her arm. Smiling, he laughed as he did so. "I'm quite good at finding a vein."

Like a quick-moving stream, her blood gushed through the thin plastic tubing, slowly filling the first bag. Wynter turned her face away from him, praying Logan was close. She knew from experience it would take at least ten minutes for him to collect the first pint. A woman of her size probably had only eight pints of blood in her whole body. Even though she hadn't fully recovered her blood volume after his bite, she figured that with her preternatural wolf healing, she might survive after losing four or five pints, which equated to fifty minutes, tops.

"Hurry up with her," Fiona yelled. She took the first bag and then a second from Étienne. "The boat's ready to go. We'll kill her, leave her body. Logan will stay here with his mate for at least a while. We'll have plenty of time to get to shore. It's only a short drive to Mississippi."

"I hate to disappoint you Mistress, but we need to take care in collecting the samples. I don't want to damage the red blood cells. Careful," he instructed. "Put equal bags in the cryo-storage unit and the cooler. Some of these need to be frozen for long-term usage."

"Whatever, just hurry," Fiona said dismissively. "I can feel the pack. They're getting closer."

"I thought you said no one knew where this hellhole was?" he said accusingly.

"No one does," she lied. "Just come on."

She took the third bag and sealed it into the freezer and snapped it shut.

"Just one more bag and then we'll go. She's almost done," he insisted.

"Fine, I'm taking this out to the boat. I'll be right back." *No I won't,* she thought to herself.

Fiona opened and shut the door, careful not to make any noise. With the pack on her heels, time was up. She scurried over to the small skiff, got in and settled the cooling box between her legs. Frozen samples were better than fresh ones, she reasoned. She still had samples of Emma's blood stored safely in another state. All she needed to do was get to dry land. She'd fly under the radar for a month or so and find a new scientist.

As the small outboard purred into the night, she caught the sight of lights in the distance. She smiled coldly knowing her Alpha would find his mate dead. And Étienne would fight to the death, wondering where she'd gone.

"So sorry, I'm afraid this is going to be the last bag, darling. Feeling weak, are you?" Étienne asked, placing it into the cooler.

Wynter's eyelashes fluttered. Unable to speak or move, she lay face up, staring up at the rusted metal ceiling. So this was how she was going to die? A tear ran down her face as she thought of how her life might have been with Logan. They would have mated. Wynter realized she wanted a wedding, with Jax giving her away. She wanted Logan's children. Together forever. But, sadly, it was all a dream. She was dying. Peacefully accepting the inevitable, she closed her eyes and prayed that Logan would survive without her.

Logan's clothes were off as the airboat hit the bank. Man to wolf, he'd morphed to his beast. Wynter. He smelled her blood and couldn't contain the rage. Tearing through the brush, he rammed into the flimsy door. Vampire. His mate. He growled, saliva dripping from his lips, and lunged.

At first, Étienne thought he'd heard Fiona returning, but quickly surmised it was an animal. As the menacing wolf crashed through the door, he clutched Wynter's shoulders and wrapped a muscular arm around her neck. He glared at Logan, daring him to come closer. Grateful that Fiona had taken the frozen blood, he'd have to abandon the rest of the bags. His bargaining chip for his escape was thankfully still breathing, albeit on her way to death. Still, he dangled her in front of the Alpha.

"Good dog," he jeered. "That's right. Look what I've got here."

Logan hit the floor frozen as he watched the vampire lift Wynter into the air by her throat. *His vision. Oh Goddess, no.* He heard and smelled Dimitri and Jake approaching and barked, warning them not to proceed.

"Amazing how responsive animals are when given the proper motivation? Look at your mate. Like a docile puppy," he whispered in Wynter's ear.

Wynter's eyes flew open. She recognized the three wolves before her but was unable to speak. As the life drained from her body, she wished she could tell Logan one more time that she loved him, but she couldn't utter even a hushed word. Struggling, she mouthed, 'I love you'. Tears fell from her eyes. She hoped he'd find another mate someday, be happy. There was nothing he could do. Even if the vampire released her, she was dying.

Logan transformed to man. His eyes bored into the demon that held his mate.

"Give her to me now," he demanded. Logan recognized the vampire as the one from the club with Devereoux, yet he let no hint of recollection show on his face. A shadow of doubt crept into his head. Just how far was Devereoux involved in this mess?

"What makes you think that's going to happen, wolf? I've got Dr. Ryan. I plan to walk out of here, get on that boat…"

"And what boat might that be? My boat?"

"Fiona…she's waiting," he stammered.

"She's gone." The chinks in the vampire's arrogant armor became apparent. Fiona must have betrayed him as well.

"Liar!" Étienne screamed.

"Jake, take Zeke, go after her. She can't have gone far," Logan commanded.

The walls closed in around the vampire. Choices dwindling, he'd have to fight his way out of the cabin and take the Alpha's boat to shore. How hard could it be to get out of this godforsaken swamp, anyway? Fiona would surely be waiting for him. Without his brilliant mind, she'd never get what she wanted from the virus.

"My mate. Give her to me now, and I'll grant you mercy." Logan's cold voice resonated throughout the cabin. Dimitri lowered his head.

"I'll give her to you," he smiled. The lilt of his voice wavered in preparation for what he was about to do.

Étienne was a great fighter, he thought. A mere wolf could not challenge him. Wynter's blood had charged his system. He'd created her, and her special blood now ran through him, making him stronger than any supernatural. As soon as he tasted the Alpha's blood, the lupine vitality would flow into his veins making him nearly invincible.

Logan tensed in preparation, waiting on the vampire to drop Wynter. He'd show mercy all right. He'd stake him quickly as opposed to tearing him apart limb by limb and then decapitating him.

"Mine," he growled.

"Not anymore." Before Logan could charge, Étienne extended a large claw. As if slitting the throat of a farm animal, he slashed it across Wynter's throat. Her eyes bulged right before he tossed her to the floor.

"No!" Logan screamed. As he leapt into the air, he transformed into wolf. Flying directly at the vampire, he lodged his teeth into the vampire's neck.

Étienne flailed at the wolf, digging his claws up into Logan's gut. Eviscerating the Alpha, he tore open the fur. Blood sprayed onto the floor. An enormous burn flared inside Logan yet he refused to release the vampire. He'd killed his mate. No death or torture would appease the revenge he sought. No matter what pain he felt, he'd kill him.

Dimitri transformed to human, scooping Wynter into his arms.

"Wynter, please, oh Goddess," he cried at the sight.

Her pale skin was split open laterally, exposing her trachea's cartilage. He frantically pinched the skin together. Tearing a swathe of cloth from her shirt, he applied pressure to the wound. A sob escaped his lips as he realized it was too late. Logan would never recover from her death, nor would he. Helplessly, he continued to try to stop the bleeding as her heartbeat slowed.

Logan saw Dimitri out of the corner of his eye with his mate. The vision of Wynter dying played out before him. As the vampire shoved his hand up further into his abdomen, he summoned every power he'd been given as Alpha. Strength. Perseverance. Domination. Logan concentrated, focusing his powerful jaw muscles and forced them downward. The crushing pressure sliced through the tendons and muscled tissue, tearing at the vampire's carotid. Wrenching backward, his beast broke away taking the dark flesh with him.

Blood spewed wildly as the vampire stumbled forward, still attempting to leave the cabin. Logan, gravely injured, shifted back to human. Enraged beyond reason, Logan lunged onto Étienne's back wrapping his arm around his already wounded neck. With every ounce of energy he had left, he pressed his knee into Étienne's back, forcing him onto the floor. With a final twist of his arms, he snapped the vampire's neck. Fighting for breath, Logan's beast was unsatisfied. He'd show no mercy. As the vampire's remains twitched on the ground, his eyes searched the room. Stretching to reach the broken chair, he tore off a shard and drove it into Étienne's heart.

Logan roared in agony, turning to Dimitri. While the shift had healed the gaping hole in his abdomen, his heart felt as if it had been decimated. The grief on Dimitri's face confirmed what he'd already known. Wynter was dead. He dropped to the floor on his hands and knees, sobbing. Taking her into his arms, Logan gently cradled his mate.

Fiona leapt from the boat. A few more feet and she'd drive to safety. She knew they were hot on her trail, but she also knew that she was still a few steps ahead of them, as always. Stupid wolves. They always assumed that mere muscle would allow them to lead. Maybe she'd never win a physical challenge, but it was just a matter of time before she had every last wolf begging at her feet. Revenge would be sweet. She'd infect them all with the virus. Then she'd be their savior, whether they liked it or not.

Fiona grabbed the laptop bag and hoisted the small cryo-freezer onto the dirt. Heavy as it was, she only had about a hundred feet to travel through the brush before she reached the small clearing. Shoving the boat adrift with her foot, she set out on her journey. Her eyes darted from side to side. It was quiet. Too quiet, she noted. Not even a cricket could be heard. But she kept on her path, only fifty more feet and she'd be at the car.

With a whoosh, branches split before her eyes. It was dark but she could make out a figure in the moonlight. She sniffed. Vampire. Adrenaline rushed as her mind raced. Had Étienne created more vampires and not told her? He'd been privy to the car's location. She fought to calm her nerves. Why should she fear a vampire? She'd killed many of them while Étienne watched. This was just one more. She crouched in the brush, tore off a stiff branch and began to whittle it into a sharp stake with her claws.

The tall masculine shadow deliberately and confidently tramped toward her until the light of his eyes became apparent. She gasped at the sight of the ancient one. Léopold Devereoux. No, not him. How could he have found her? Like a frightened rabbit, she froze in the darkness, awaiting his approach, hoping he wouldn't see her.

"Ah, I found you," his smooth voice called into the crisp night air. Nearly at her feet, the dark angel loomed. His beautiful but deadly presence resounded in the forest like a drum roll before an execution.

"Petite louve, I smell it. The putrid stink of your evil permeates the air. So familiar am I with the scent," he told her. "You like a chase, no? I assure you this is one you'll not win."

With preternatural speed, he flew to Fiona, snatching her up by her throat. He allowed her feet to remain on the ground as he shook her like a dog with its toy.

"You like to play with vampires? My vampires," he growled. With a flick, he threw her onto the damp earth.

Fiona rebounded, crab-walking backwards, dragging her bottom along the dirt.

"No, Étienne, he came to me freely," she claimed.

"He cannot come to you freely, because he belongs to me," Léopold explained coldly, brushing a weed from his coat sleeve. "And for this you shall die. The only decision to be made is if I should kill you myself? Or perhaps I should let your own tear you to shreds? Such choices."

Léopold smiled casually as the two large male wolves, Jake and Zeke, padded forward. He carefully considered his decision as Fiona sat before him awaiting her fate. His lovely little Dr. Ryan had been tortured by her and Étienne. That alone would have been enough to warrant her death. But the little bitch had gone and killed a wolf using his vampires to do it.

With a glance to the mud, he'd chosen. Oh how he hated to get his new leather shoes soiled.

"The research, the samples. You'll never get them," she stalled, pushing onto her feet.

"You are a devilish schemer aren't you?" he laughed. "A shame you have no discipline. But don't worry your pretty little head. I plan to rectify that right now."

Léopold rushed forward, yanking her upward. He tore open her collar, exposing her long neck. The moonlight glinted off his white fangs right before they pierced her flesh. Her legs flailed, kicking into the night. Neither Jake nor Zeke moved one inch to intervene. Throwing his head backwards, he spat her blood into the grass and tossed her to the wolves.

Her body flinched as she stole looks between the wolves right before they attacked. Barely a scream could be heard as they ripped her flesh until she was no more.

Léopold retrieved a crisp white handkerchief and dabbed at his chin. How he hated messy killings. But responsibility and duty drove his actions. Meting out punishment was never easy, but he watched in pleasure as the wolves executed their own. She'd been a blight who'd caused quite enough trouble. Like the virus she sought to propagate, she'd been eradicated.

As Jake transformed in front of him, he gave Léopold a nod in acknowledgement. Not sure what to make of the vampire, he and Zeke got to work, disposing of Fiona's remains. After they'd fed the alligators, Jake snatched up the laptop so he could give it to Logan.

Léopold strode over to the cooler and flipping it open, saw bags of blood. He tore them open and quickly surmised that it belonged to the Alpha's mate. As he emptied the last of the crimson fluid into the swamp, a hint of dread registered. He sniffed out into the bayou. So much fresher than the samples, it permeated his olfactory senses, exciting unadulterated rage. Wynter's blood. The call of death sang into the night.

Chapter Twenty-Eight

"I can save her," Léopold uttered softly. He watched as the grieving Alpha rocked his mate. Like an animal that had lost one of his own, the wolf refused to release the body.

Dimitri leaned against the wall, his head in his hands. Unlike the Alpha, who was utterly despondent, he peered over to the imposing vampire.

"Devereoux, you need to get outta here. Wyn, she's..." Dimitri couldn't bring himself to say the words.

Although wolves were generally immortal, lethal wounds to the neck effectively killed them. While Wynter's heartbeat was faint, she'd be dead within minutes and shifting was no longer an option. Nothing could be done. As the minutes ticked by, Dimitri had watched his Alpha care for his mate, tell her he loved her. Last words. Last caresses.

"But I can save her, wolf," Léopold persisted.

Logan slowly lifted his head and caught sight of the vampire standing in the doorway. "What?" he choked.

"Alpha, you know my blood can heal wolves." Léopold proceeded cautiously. The Alpha, immersed in his bereavement, could attack.

"She's too far gone; you and I both know that. I can barely hear her heartbeat. The rattle in her lungs has stopped. Please," Logan begged, tears streaming from his eyes. His voice broke into a cry. "I need to say goodbye. She's going to leave me. My mate...he killed her."

"Please listen," Léopold pleaded. "Think about how vampires are created. In the final moments of our deaths, when the soul teeters between the planes of both the living and the dead, one can be snatched from death's grip, born anew. Wynter, she rests in the thin veil that separates us from the other side. You must let me try."

Logan considered Devereoux's explanation. He'd never in his long life heard of a vampire giving their gift to a wolf. He knew that when they created their own, the child belonged to the sire. Wynter would never want to belong to any other man but him. After the scene in the club, Léopold was far from her favorite person. How would she feel about accepting his blood into her body, taking him on as her sire? Yet, selfishly, Logan carefully weighed the offer. He loved Wynter so much; needed his mate alive. How far would he go to save her?

"Will she be vampire?" Logan asked.

"I cannot say. I won't lie to you, this is generally the outcome, but like I said, I'm not certain. Is she truly wolf? Is she still at all human? Complicated questions, no?"

"She belongs to me."

"As her potential sire, I fully and altogether release her to your care, Alpha. I do not wish to command her mind. I swear it."

Unable to resist the possibility of her salvation, Logan conceded. "Do it," he whispered.

What choice did he have? If she returned as vampire, he'd love her as much as when she'd been wolf. It was her soul that he loved, no matter her being.

Léopold breathed a sigh of relief as the Alpha capitulated to his suggestion. In truth, in all his years, he'd never converted a wolf. He was unsure about how his blood would affect her, but they had to try. He stripped off his jacket and rolled his sleeve. Positioning himself next to Logan, he bit into his wrist, and offered it to the Alpha. Logan took Léopold's wrist and pressed it to Wynter's mouth.

The blood trickled over Wynter's face. Listless, she wasn't swallowing.

"Command her," Léopold told him urgently.

"I can't feel her…she's gone," Logan insisted.

"It's the only way. I cannot do it."

Logan meditated, searching his mind for his mate. The tendrils of his power discharged, seeking Wynter. He laughed as a jolt of recognition hit him. She was there, here or on the other side, he couldn't tell. Her spirit danced in the wind.

"Wyn, sweetheart," he spoke lovingly. "I need you to listen to me. Please, please come back to me. Hear me and drink."

In her mind, Wynter floated somewhere lovely and peaceful. But she was alone. The familiar voice sang to her heart, willing her like a lure. *Logan? Where was he?* The mist caressed her skin as she glided along her journey. But the voice called to her again. *Drink? Drink what?* No, this place was warm and comforting. Like a mother's womb, she contentedly existed. *Now, Wynter.* Logan. Logan, her mate. Memories of his scent and love flooded her mind. Back to Logan, she needed to find him. *Drink.*

The taste of power slid down her throat, setting off a firing of synapses. Life. Love. Her mate. So far but so close, just within reach. A wisp of hope flickered and she extended her hand to capture it. A little more and she'd awake to him. A river of sanguine vitality permeated her cells, arousing her soul back to Earth.

Astonished, Logan felt his heart squeeze in relief as he watched his mate flare to life, her pale lips suctioning at the wrist he held. The strained look on Devereoux's face told him that he suffered silently. But Logan wondered if the vampire struggled to conceal pain or lust. Léopold Devereoux, her dark savior, was lethal yet benevolent. As their eyes met, a respectful understanding passed between the two men. He'd forever owe the vampire; a debt he'd gladly repay.

"Enough," Léopold grunted.

Logan slid a finger in between her mouth and Léopold's wrist, breaking the seal. Wynter gasped for air, and then choked, blood spilling from her lips. Her eyes flew open; she was shaking as if she were a newborn babe. She cried, a mixture of fear and happiness spinning through her mind as she glanced from Léopold to Logan. The realization that she'd almost died slammed into her.

"Logan," she whispered.

"Sweetheart." Logan cradled her into his arms so that her head rested against his shoulder. "I love you. I love you so much."

"I love you too. I'm not dead?" she asked with a small smile.

"No, you're not. You're very much alive, thanks to Devereoux."

"Léopold," the vampire corrected. "I do believe we all should be on a first name basis, no?"

"Léopold," Logan agreed with a smile. He'd never been so grateful to another person in his life, vampire or not.

Wynter tried to process what Logan had just told her. Léopold had saved her life. She struggled to comprehend it. She had died. His blood. *Drink*. Logan had told her to drink. She drank Léopold's blood? Connecting the proverbial dots, Wynter sat up, pushing out of Logan's arms.

"Am I a…? No, I couldn't be a…?" She glanced from Logan to Léopold then to Dimitri.

Logan cupped her cheek bringing her gaze to his again. He sniffed. "You still scent wolf, so that's a good sign. We don't know how it could affect you, but you're alive and that's all that matters to me."

"Oh God, Logan. I love you so much." Wynter gently pressed her lips to his. Her forehead fell against his as she spoke to him. "I was so scared. I'm sorry for going on that boat."

Logan stopped her from going any further. "No, Wyn, don't blame yourself. We knew they'd come for you. I should never have agreed to take you out there."

"I can't believe Fiona betrayed the pack like that. Oh God, where is she?" Wynter asked in a panic.

"Dead," Léopold confirmed.

"You're sure?" Logan asked. If she wasn't dead, she would be.

"These swamps are quite messy, wolf. All that mud. Just look at my shoes." Léopold rocked back, brushed his slacks and attempted to right his sleeves. "Good thing your wolves showed up to assist me or I may have ruined my suit. Those gators, they do enjoy an impromptu meal."

Logan shook his head with a small laugh. He'd never mistake the vampire's humor for weakness. Léopold was deadly, but he appeared to do the right thing every now and then. Logan couldn't say he fully trusted him, but he'd gained an ally without a doubt.

"Léopold, thank you." Wynter shifted from Logan's arms and extended her hand to him. She could have sworn she saw him blush.

Léopold took Wynter's wrist, gently holding her fingers. He caught Logan's gaze as if to ask for approval. Logan nodded and with a brush of a kiss, he pressed his lips to the back of her hand.

"Anytime, my fine doctor. That lecture. You made quite the impression on me," he winked. "The world needs your beautiful mind. I'm honored to have helped. And should you spring fangs, please call on me anytime for assistance. But as I've assured your Alpha, you are released from any bond with me, as you and Logan are mates."

Léopold released her hand and stood. He adjusted his pants and scanned the room for his jacket. The black suit looked nearly impeccable as he smoothed out the small wrinkles.

"Dimitri," Wynter said solemnly.

"Wyn." Dimitri scooted next to Wynter and carefully gave her a hug. She'd almost died. The whole pack had come so close to destruction. His eyes rimmed in moisture, the emotion he'd held back burst forth. Logan clamped a hand on his shoulder in an effort to comfort him.

"It's okay, D. She's alive." *Maybe a vampire, though?*

"Look at me. I'm cryin' like a baby over here. How sad is that?" Dimitri laughed in embarrassment and pushed up onto his feet. "I gotta get out of here and relax. Do something manly like go sit in the hot tub with a beer and a cigar."

"As much as I usually love the swamp, I'm with you. It's time to get the hell out of here." In one smooth motion, Logan stood, carrying Wynter.

Jake and Zeke approached the cabin and together ripped away what remained of the door. Logan strode through the doorway, carrying Wynter toward the boat. Dimitri, Léopold and the others followed him.

Léopold glanced at the naked wolves surrounding him and shook his head. *Wolves and their nudity.*

"Seriously, do you wolves ever wear clothes?" he quipped with a raised eyebrow.

"You should try it, vamp. You might like it," Logan replied. He stepped into the boat and cuddled Wynter. "Free like the wind."

"A cold day in hell, mon ami." Léopold shrugged his nose in disgust.

"You gotta loosen up," Dimitri told him.

"Ah, says the man who weeps," Léopold teased with a smile.

"Tears of joy, man. And for the record, I've got plenty of game," Dimitri jibed in return.

"Léopold, maybe you need to start small. A skinny dip, perhaps?" Logan suggested blithely.

"I highly recommend it," Wynter added. Naughty thoughts played in her mind, remembering her time in the pool with Logan.

"A recommendation from the lady? Well, that may be advice I'll take." Léopold appeared lost in a sensual thought. "A beach, no? Oui, that I could do."

"Just add a hot woman into the mix, and he's all in," Dimitri laughed.

"I knew we could convert him." Logan kissed Wynter's hair and reflected on the night's events.

Ironic how one day he'd been single and fighting to be Alpha and today he'd fought for his mate's life, assuring his pack still had a leader. With Wynter back in the safety of his arms, he looked forward to solidifying the bond they'd started. Even if she did turn vampire, he didn't care. As long as Wynter stood at his side, nothing would come between them.

He stole a glance at the debonair vampire who'd saved his mate. On the surface, Léopold wore his years like his designer clothes; tightly reined without a blemish to be found. But Logan's intuition told him that the centuries had taken a toll on Devereoux. He had recognized the familiar loneliness which danced in Léopold's eyes. Had he been a romantic at some point in his life? A courageous fighter, waging war for the greater good? Logan reasoned that he might never truly know Léopold's motives. One thing was certain; the vampire had revealed a side of him rarely seen by others; one that even Logan hadn't known to exist. Léopold, even if just for a moment in time, had cared, not just about Wynter but about the good of the Acadian pack.

Chapter Twenty-Nine

Wynter artfully tied the bows on her pink negligee as if she were wrapping a gift. As she played with the ribbons, she thought about the past few days and how Logan had sweetly cared for her. It hadn't taken long for her blood volume to regenerate after her near death experience. And so far, she hadn't felt any vampiric tendencies. She'd even successfully shifted a few times in the house just to test it out. She laughed to herself thinking about how Logan had enjoyed waking up to find his red little wolf jumping on the bed.

Her brush with death forced her to contemplate the next steps in her derailed career. The choice to go into virology had been born out of her desire to help Emma. And now that she'd done that, she needed to figure out a new future, one that included Logan, pack and hopefully children. But since she'd been injured, they hadn't made love. Logan worried like a mother hen. She knew it was killing him not to press forward with their mating, but since it involved a blood exchange, he'd been reluctant, not wanting to accidentally hurt her.

But her wolf paced impatiently, in anticipation of completing the bond. Wynter looked in the mirror and glossed her lips. She was determined to tempt Logan into their mating. He needn't worry, she was no porcelain doll. She was a red-blooded wolf who couldn't wait to mate with her Alpha. As she brushed out her tight curls, she hoped he would enjoy her plan and be unable to resist her. She laughed to herself, knowing he'd loved to play. Smoothing the see-through fabric, Wynter took a cleansing breath. Yes, this would be fun.

Logan's cock was harder than a cement post. While he'd been more than grateful that Wynter had rebounded, his self-imposed celibacy wasn't going so well. It wasn't that he didn't want to bend her over and sink into her hotness every single time he saw her. At dinner, she'd teased him mercilessly with the grilled kielbasa, and he'd nearly lost his mind. His wolf growled and bit, encouraging him to mate. But he wasn't going to do anything to put her recovery in jeopardy. Unwavering, he'd put her health first and stifled every animalistic thought that had crossed his mind.

As he lay in bed reading, he glanced up, noticing the sound of the bathroom door opening. Logan watched intently as a glimmer of pink teased his eyes. Holy Fuck. What was she wearing? He dropped his iPad, fascinated by the scene. Wynter bent over the dresser, wiggling her bottom. Her creamy globes peeked out at him from underneath the nightie. He swore; damn, his cock could get harder. When she turned around, a broad smile broke across his face. The large map blocked his view and he knew right then and there, she was up to something, a tad more than the average seduction.

Wynter unfolded the New Orleans brochure, smiling coyly. Her horn-rimmed glasses and camera on her wrist added to the character.

"Sir, I've been walking around the city all the day, and I can't seem to find my destination," she told him. She held the paper so that it hid her entire body except for her eyes.

Logan laughed. Was she seriously role playing again? If she didn't show him what was behind that map, he'd leap off the bed. Okay, he was game.

"I know New Orleans well. I'd be happy to show you around. Just where exactly are you going?"

She lowered the map slightly, giving him a view of her ample cleavage. "I'm supposed to meet my friends. I don't know if I should go off with a stranger."

"No stranger here, cher," he said, falling into his best Cajun accent. "I promise to keep you safe."

"Oh dear, now how did I get so lost? Maybe you could help me find my way. I have this map here but I can't seem to make heads or tails of it."

"I'd love to help you out, show you around. Perhaps you'd like to hear music?"

She shook her head. "No, I don't think so."

"A ride on a riverboat, then? Very relaxing," he suggested.

"No." She lowered the map so he could see her dusky nipples. They strained to escape their sexy sheer confines. "I'm looking for something." She pretended to glance at the map.

Logan pushed the blanket off his fully nude form, allowing her a view of his enormous erection. He lazily put his hand behind his head.

Her eyes met his and then took a long peruse of his muscular body. Her pussy clenched at the sight of him. She knew she couldn't keep the dialogue going for much longer. Incredibly hot, he was laid out for her like a delicious dessert; one she'd like to lick from head to toe.

"There's much to see in our fine city," he drawled with a smile, smelling her arousal. His little vixen was getting herself as hot and bothered as she intended to do to him.

"Yes, yes there is. Like the art for example." She smiled and looked down to watch him stroke his shaft. "It's spectacular. I especially enjoy viewing the marbled statue."

Wynter dropped the map further so he could see the crisscrossed pattern of ribbons that begged to be untied. She licked her lips and approached the bed.

"This map, it doesn't seem to help me at all. I'm so glad I found you. I mean, what would I do without such a knowledgeable guide?" She opened her fingers and let the paper drop to the floor.

"I'm looking forward to showing you all the sights and sounds…" Logan began.

"And tastes? I'm so hungry." Wynter's eyes devoured him. She placed her palms on the edge of the bed, bending so that he could get a good view of her breasts.

"Sweetheart, we've got some of the best culinary delights in the country. I'd be more than happy to feed you…all night long." Logan pushed up onto his knees and made short work of meeting her. He wrapped his hands around her waist and pressed his lips to the hollow of her neck.

"I'm starving," she breathed, pushing her fingers into his hair.

"I'll always be here for you Wynter," Logan promised, kissing up her neck. "Always and forever. I missed you so much."

Wynter let herself go limp against him. Back in his arms was exactly what she needed. She tore off her glasses and let the camera slip from her wrist.

"I missed you too, so, so much." She licked and bit at his shoulder.

Logan rolled her onto the bed and slid down her body. Wynter rested her head against the pillows, wiggling against him. Logan smiled and crouched at her feet. Taking one foot, he touched his lips to the inside of her calf. She hissed in delight, pressing her hips upward.

"Logan."

"Yes, mate. Just helping you find your way," he teased, resuming his role. He dragged his tongue up her leg until he reached her inner thigh.

Wynter thought she'd explode in need. It felt incredible.

"You're wicked," she laughed.

"Just helping a tourist in need. I told you; I'm a very good guide. I know all the best spots." He pushed her knees open wider, his face settled into the center of her legs. Pleasantly surprised, he was happy to find she'd worn no panties.

"But I need…" she panted as his warm breath brushed over her mound. If he'd just touch her, she could breathe.

Logan darted his tongue through her moist nether lips and smiled. "We are about to reach one of my favorite destinations. My sweet little tourist, are you ready?"

Without waiting for an answer, he lapped at her clit.

"Oh God yes," she cried. His rough tongue sent shivers through her body. Her sex ached for him. He was everything she'd ever need.

Logan pulled away for just a second to press two long fingers inside of her. "I do believe we are arriving nicely." He curled them upward into her sensitive channel.

"Yes, right there," she screamed.

Logan brought his lips to her clitoris, sucking and flicking it with his tongue. Her sweet cream coated his face, and he couldn't get enough of her.

"I'm coming, I'm coming," Wynter screamed over and over.

Her pelvis rocked into his mouth and hand. She flailed as her orgasm burst, leaving her shaking and gasping for breath. The tendrils of energy rode through her skin.

Logan gave her a final lick before he crawled up to meet her face to face. The hard tip of him rested at the entrance. Goddess, he loved her spontaneity and how receptive she was.

"Wynter Ryan."

Wynter slowly opened her eyes, still lost in the haze of passion. She smiled at the way he'd addressed her and gazed into his eyes.

"Yes, my Alpha."

"Tonight, I take you as my mate." Logan tugged at the satiny ribbons. Her bodice fell open exposing both her neck and breasts.

His expression denoted a seriousness that told Wynter that this was the time. Their mating. Their bond, forged in love and trust; they'd be together till the end of time.

"You, Wynter. You are mine. Our wolves, our souls, we're mates."

"I love you, Logan. I'm yours." She licked along his collarbone. Slight pain alerted her that her canines had descended.

He smiled with a slight shake of his head.

"What?"

"Ah baby, they're sexy." Now was not the time to tell her, but her normally sharp canines looked slightly sharper. Fangs.

"What is it?"

"Nothing, you're perfect. Now where were we?" He captured her lips with his. Their tongues swept along each other's. Reluctantly, he stopped the kiss and spoke into her mouth.

"Tonight, we mate. Forever you are mine, Wynter."

He rocked his straining cock into her slick channel. She gasped, nodding. As he filled her to the hilt, he reared back and bit into her shoulder. Blood trickled into his throat.

The pleasured pain drove Wynter's need to claim him in return. Her fangs sliced into his skin like a knife through hot butter. Thirsting for more, she took a long draw of her Alpha's blood. Powerful and spicy, her mate's spirit danced within her body. The wave of pleasure hurled her into release, and she convulsed against Logan.

The taste of Wynter's blood caused his wolf to howl in pride. With his beast satisfied, he'd laved at her shoulder. But it was Wynter's erotic bite that sent him into orgasm. Claiming him as her mate, she'd sent him into the hardest, hottest climax he'd ever had in his life. As he erupted inside her, he shuddered as he felt her lick over the wound.

Loving filaments weaved through their hearts and minds. Their bond complete, their wolves nuzzled together celebrating. Logan rolled backwards, bringing Wynter with him. Arms and legs intertwined, her cheek rested on his chest.

"I love you," Wynter smiled.

"Love you too, baby," Logan replied, still trying to catch his breath.

"Everything that's happened," she began thoughtfully.

"Shhh, it's over now." He tangled his fingers into her ringlets.

"I would have never met you."

"True."

"Does the pack know?"

"Yes, but I want a formal introduction. You deserve nothing less. We deserve this. And someday, I hope you'll agree to a human mating of sorts…if that's what you want. Marry me?"

"I'd love that." she kissed his chest. "I hear spring in New Orleans is lovely. As is New York."

"A honeymoon. That's what I'm looking forward to," he teased. "Somewhere on a beach. A private beach."

"A beach, huh? Sounds good to me. Make sure you bring your whistle," she told him with a naughty grin.

"A whistle?"

"Well, I may need a lifeguard to save me," she suggested.

"I'm all for a little slippery wet play in the ocean," Logan encouraged. "Or maybe we can go as an Alpha and his mate."

"Yes, that sounds perfect," she agreed.

As they fell asleep for the first time as bonded mates, Wynter and Logan embraced the new chapter in their lives. Dark memories would be washed over by love-filled days and sensual nights. The Acadian Wolves found strength in their Alpha. Peace and contentment rippled throughout the pack. A new chapter in their history had begun.

Epilogue

Léopold cursed as he dug into the frozen tundra. Damn bitch really had thought she was clever. Yet it had been fairly easy for the investigator to locate the safety deposit box where Fiona had left the instructions and thumb drive. Léopold suspected that someone local had helped her stash the blood. Samples from Emma, Wynter and others, had been buried deep within the snow in the heart of Yellowstone.

He and Dimitri had traveled together to retrieve the contents of the box. The wolf, with his humor, continued to insist that Léopold needed to loosen up, clearly not having a clue how difficult a task that would be. Regardless, he had succumbed to Dimitri's unrelenting insistence that he take a hot tub. After several cognacs, he'd given in to the persistent wolf's request. Naked in the woods hadn't been half bad, he supposed. However he was certain that it would have been much more tolerable with a suitable female.

As Léopold recovered the vials, wind and ice blew at his face. Dammit all to hell, he should have made Dimitri come with him to dig out the blood. Even with his extraordinary strength, Yellowstone was exceedingly brutal in the winter. But Léopold had encouraged his newfound friend to visit with Hunter Livingston. Brother to Tristan and friend of Logan and Dimitri, Hunter led the Wyoming wolf pack. While it was customary for an outside wolf to announce his presence within another's territory, Dimitri and Hunter were friends. They were aware of his arrival. It was Léopold who wished to be alone, insisting he could dispose of the vials on his own.

With the temperature at nearly fifteen below zero, Léopold snorted in displeasure. Breathtaking as it was, this weather was not conducive to a vampire's metabolism. The deafening silence was indeed thought provoking but he could not wait to be back in the city. Whether it be New York or New Orleans, the crowds made it easy for him to feed whenever he wished. Anything he wanted was a mere phone call away. Luxury beckoned on his arrival. He had a standing reservation at private clubs from jazz to blood. In an instant, his needs were met.

True, it had been a lonely existence. But the darkness of his past wouldn't allow him to feel. Yet he couldn't deny his reaction to watching the interaction between the Alpha and his mate. It had warmed a layer of ice that he'd allowed to thicken around his heart. That kind of love didn't exist very often. Long ago, as a foolish boy, he'd thought himself worthy of love. But it didn't take long for the harsh realities of life to decimate the naïve, human ideals of love and family. It was through intellect and dominance that he'd survived and ruled. Power and prosperity had been rightly earned via battles and business.

As much as he enjoyed the freedom, he wasn't without compassion. In truth, he'd been strangely bothered since leaving New Orleans. He could not shake the touch of Logan's hand on his wrist and Wynter's lips on his skin. Like a lightning bolt, their bond had penetrated deep into his own energy. Their thoughts, pain and passion funneled through his mind. It was as if the brief connection had jarred his memory, the lingering desire for love.

Léopold cursed his weakness and shoved the thought as far away as he could. Like a well-worn shoe, his cool demeanor had been comfortable. As such, he refused to give up his bachelor ways. A stop at Tristan's club in Philadelphia and a quick romp with the twins would refresh his attitude, he thought. Imprudent, sophomoric thoughts of romance and companionship were for others, not him.

Another gust lashed at Léopold. He shoved the vials into the small backpack, zipped it up and threw it over his shoulder. A wail in the distance caught his attention. Damn humans. Damn wolves. They expected another foot of snow tonight, and he couldn't imagine anything but animals traipsing through the forest. Who the hell would be caught dead in the middle of the night in Yellowstone?

Merde. Léopold grunted and pushed himself up onto the tamped down path. West Thumb Geyser Basin, visited often by tourists in winter, should have been desolate at night. With bubbling hot springs and gurgling mud on either side of the trail, he trod carefully toward the noise, and sniffed. Aside from the sulphuric odor, he could make out the faint smell of a human.

"I should have sent the wolf," he grumbled. Unsure of what lay ahead, he knew it wasn't going to be good.

As he approached a small clearing, he caught a glimpse of the outline of a person in the snow. He took a deep breath, vacillating between materializing and actually helping. It was none of his business. He could disappear like he hadn't seen a thing. The scene between the Alpha and his mate played like a movie through his head and he sighed. It must've made him soft because he was leaning toward helping. Damn, fucking wolves. He growled, realizing that his conscience and curiosity would not let him leave. Resigned, he'd check on the situation and then get the hell out of there.

Léopold's feet crunched through the snow, approaching the noise. He caught sight of the body which wasn't moving except for an isolated twitch. The familiar scents of both humans and wolf hit his nostrils…and blood.

"Identify yourself," he demanded. A strange gurgle responded. The small body was wrapped in a blanket, and he grew concerned as he barely heard a heartbeat. There was no way he was siring another human or wolf.

Perhaps he'd take them to safety, but no more would he do.

"Do you hear me? Are you hybrid? What are you doing out here?" Léopold really didn't want to touch the blanket. He stared up into the constellations and blew out a breath, contemplating his next move. Whatever was underneath the blanket was barely breathing. It was dying. Perhaps he should just leave?

Another gurgle caught his attention. In all his centuries, he'd nearly forgotten the sound. Unsuccessfully, he tried to shake off the painful memories that flared to life. *Gurgle.* No, it didn't make sense. He fell to his knees and feverishly began pulling at the fabric, revealing the head. The cold dead eyes of a woman bored into him. Why would she bring a…? *Gurgle.* He continued to unwrap the blanket until he saw the source of the sound. A small face peered up at him. Horrified, his suspicion was correct. A baby.

"What the hell?" Léopold heard the sound of barking wolves in the distance and hurried to collect the small child in his arms. "Mon bébé. Who would do this to you?"

He made the sign of the cross over the dead body, tugging the blanket out from under it. Quickly, he swaddled the infant. As the danger grew closer, Léopold cursed. Decision made, he cradled the baby into his jacket, and disappeared into the night.

The Immortals of New Orleans

Kade's Dark Embrace
(Immortals of New Orleans, Book 1)

Luca's Magic Embrace
(Immortals of New Orleans, Book 2)

Tristan's Lyceum Wolves
(Immortals of New Orleans, Book 3)

Logan's Acadian Wolves
(Immortals of New Orleans, Book 4)

Léopold's Wicked Embrace
(Immortals of New Orleans, Book 5)

Dimitri
(Immortals of New Orleans, Book 6)

Jax's Story
(Immortals of New Orleans, Book 7) Coming 2015

About the Author

Kym Grosso is the award winning and bestselling author of the erotic paranormal romance series, The Immortals of New Orleans. The series currently includes *Kade's Dark Embrace* (Immortals of New Orleans, Book 1), *Luca's Magic Embrace* (Immortals of New Orleans, Book 2), *Tristan's Lyceum Wolves* (Immortals of New Orleans, Book 3), *Logan's Acadian Wolves* (Immortals of New Orleans, Book 4), *Léopold's Wicked Embrace* (Immortals of New Orleans, Book 5) and *Dimitri* (Immortals of New Orleans, Book 6).

In addition to romance, Kym has written and published several articles about autism, and is passionate about autism advocacy. She also is a contributing essay author in *Chicken Soup for the Soul: Raising Kids on the Spectrum.*

Kym lives with her husband, two children, dog and cat. Her hobbies include autism advocacy, reading, tennis, zumba, traveling and spending time with her husband and children. New Orleans, with its rich culture, history and unique cuisine, is one of her favorite places to visit. Also, she loves traveling just about anywhere that has a beach or snow-covered mountains. On any given night, when not writing her own books, Kym can be found reading her Kindle, which is filled with hundreds of romances.

• • • •

Social Media Links:
Website: http://www.KymGrosso.com
Facebook: http://www.facebook.com/KymGrossoBooks
Twitter: https://twitter.com/KymGrosso
Pinterest: http://www.pinterest.com/kymgrosso/

Want to get the latest release information?
Sign up for Kym's newsletter!
http://www.kymgrosso.com/members-only

Made in the USA
Middletown, DE
23 December 2020

30068066R10442